My Treasury of Spooky Stories

My Treasury of Spooky Stories

Written by
Caroline Repchuk, Claire Keene,
Geoff Cowan, Kat Wootton, and Candy Wallace

Illustrated by
Diana Catchpole, Robin Edmonds,
Chris Forsey, and Claire Mumford

Cover Illustrated by
Steve Boulter

Bath · New York · Singapore · Hong Kong · Cologne · Delhi · Melbourne

Contents

Welcome to the Haunted House!

Step in through the rusty gates—
Be quiet as a mouse.
We're going to sneak, and take
A peek, inside the Haunted House!

Ghosts are hooting in the hallway.
Ghastly ghouls lurk on the stairs.
Imps and sprites have pillow fights
To catch you unawares!

In the kitchen there's a wizard,
Making slug and spider pies.
They're for a very special meal—
A Halloween surprise!

Upstairs in the dusty bedrooms
Skeletons are getting dressed.
Vampires brush their hair and teeth.
All the spooks must look their best!

An empty suit of shiny armor
Is clanking loudly down the hall,
To a party in the ballroom—
It's the Monster's Secret Ball!

So while the party's in full swing,
Be quiet as a mouse.
Tiptoe out while you still can—
Escape the Haunted House!

Hoots 'n' Owls

"OWWW!" A horrible howl rang out through the darkness. Beneath the moon, Hairy the Horrible Hound sat staring at his paws. After a minute the ghostly dog raised his head and howled again.

Hairy had been howling away all evening. He wanted someone to talk to, someone to play with. But because he was a ghost hound no one would come near, let alone throw him a stick to chase. So he lay with his head on his shadowy paws and howled even more loudly.

The moon shone between the clouds and lit up the ruined mansion on top of the hill. The people who once lived there had fled years ago. Now it was just the haunt of three old ghosts...

Shiver, a nervous spook, was resting upstairs on a broken four-poster bed. At the first sound of Hairy's howls, he slid under the tattered sheets and pulled them tightly over his head.

Downstairs, another ghost named Grumblegroan awoke with a start. As usual, he had been dozing on a crumpled old sofa.

"What the...? Doesn't Hairy the Horrible Hound ever stop howling?!" muttered Grumblegroan, miserably.

Meanwhile, Bone Idle, a skeleton, came clattering out of his favorite hiding place, a secret chamber behind the bookcase in the library.

"Pah!" he cried. "That dreadful noise goes right through my skull!"

When the howling finally stopped, all three spooks met in the hall.

"It's too much for a soul to bear!" hissed Shiver.

"How can a ghost rest in peace around here?!" yawned Grumblegroan.

"Something must be done about Hairy!" wailed Bone Idle.

But what? After all, Hairy certainly sounded like a very fierce phantom. And the three ghosts were a lazy bunch. They weren't very good at doing anything—especially because there was never anything to do! So, with much muttering, sighing, and moaning, the spooks sulkily decided to do nothing at all. They certainly weren't about to move house! After all, Hairy's howls were the only thing that ever disturbed them. Apart from that the house was as silent as a grave. But suddenly, on the landing, Shiver heard another call.

"HOO-HOOOOOOO!"

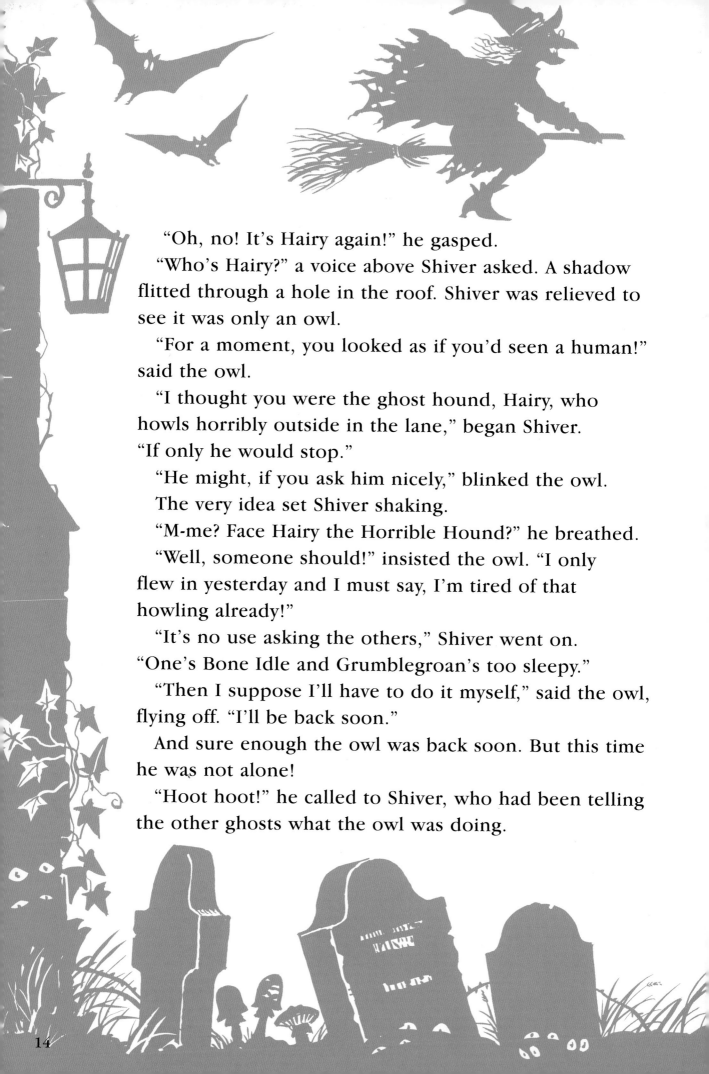

"Oh, no! It's Hairy again!" he gasped.

"Who's Hairy?" a voice above Shiver asked. A shadow flitted through a hole in the roof. Shiver was relieved to see it was only an owl.

"For a moment, you looked as if you'd seen a human!" said the owl.

"I thought you were the ghost hound, Hairy, who howls horribly outside in the lane," began Shiver. "If only he would stop."

"He might, if you ask him nicely," blinked the owl.

The very idea set Shiver shaking.

"M-me? Face Hairy the Horrible Hound?" he breathed.

"Well, someone should!" insisted the owl. "I only flew in yesterday and I must say, I'm tired of that howling already!"

"It's no use asking the others," Shiver went on. "One's Bone Idle and Grumblegroan's too sleepy."

"Then I suppose I'll have to do it myself," said the owl, flying off. "I'll be back soon."

And sure enough the owl was back soon. But this time he was not alone!

"Hoot hoot!" he called to Shiver, who had been telling the other ghosts what the owl was doing.

15

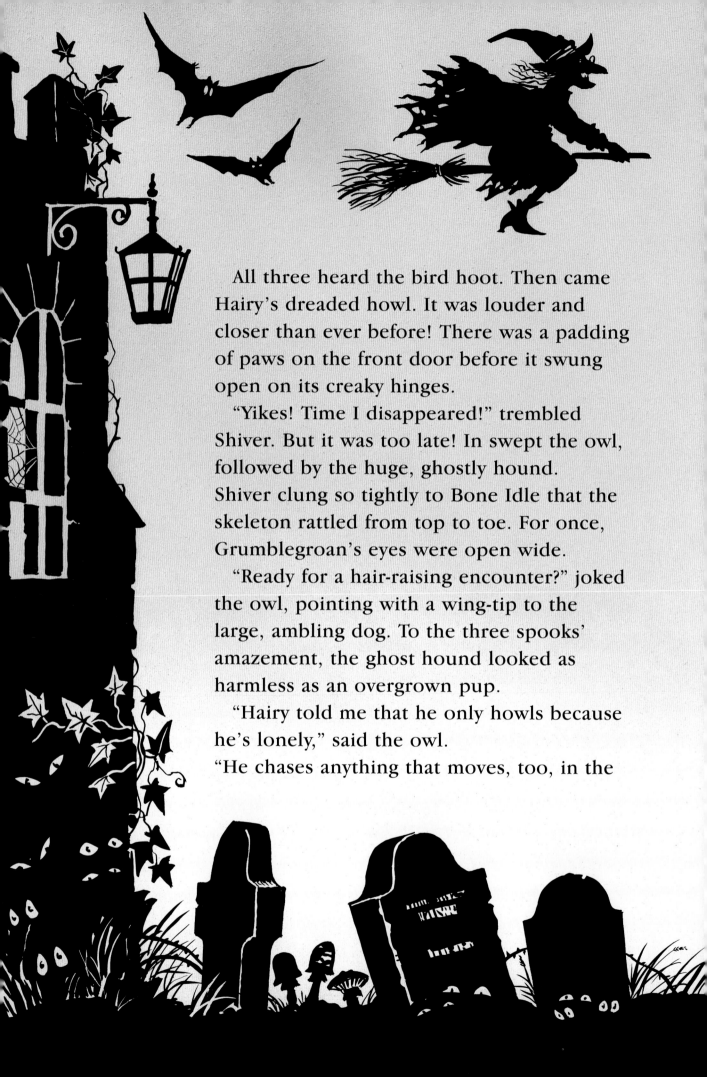

All three heard the bird hoot. Then came Hairy's dreaded howl. It was louder and closer than ever before! There was a padding of paws on the front door before it swung open on its creaky hinges.

"Yikes! Time I disappeared!" trembled Shiver. But it was too late! In swept the owl, followed by the huge, ghostly hound. Shiver clung so tightly to Bone Idle that the skeleton rattled from top to toe. For once, Grumblegroan's eyes were open wide.

"Ready for a hair-raising encounter?" joked the owl, pointing with a wing-tip to the large, ambling dog. To the three spooks' amazement, the ghost hound looked as harmless as an overgrown pup.

"Hairy told me that he only howls because he's lonely," said the owl. "He chases anything that moves, too, in the

hope of finding a phantom friend!"

Bone Idle took a step back because Hairy seemed to eye him hungrily. But it was only the skeleton's imagination.

"Hairy says he hates being left all alone in that cold, drafty lane," the owl went on, pacing up and down with his wings behind his back. "If you want my advice, which you should, because I am a wise owl after all, you should let him come and live with you. I mean, what better than a ghostly guard dog?"

"Humph!" said Grumblegroan. "You've got a point there, I suppose."

"I promise I'd never howl again," pleaded Hairy, hopefully.

He raised a paw to shake Bone Idle's hand. Then he bounded up to Grumblegroan and gave him a huge, slobbery lick. "Please say I can!"

"Oh, very well. Anything! Just stop making that horrid noise!" moaned Grumblegroan.

"You can lie beside my old bed, Hairy," smiled Shiver, who wasn't the least bit nervous now.

"Great!" barked the ghost hound. "I'm so happy I could howwww...."

"No, please don't!" begged Bone Idle. "You did promise. Remember?"

And so Hairy the Horrible Hound had found a home at last. As for the owl, he soon took flight again. But if the three ghosts had hoped for some peace and quiet, they were to be sadly disappointed. For Hairy never left them alone. If he wasn't playfully pulling the sheets off Shiver, he would leap onto Grumblegroan's lap for company.

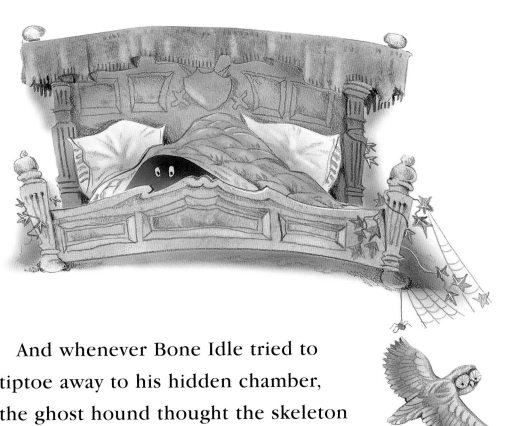

And whenever Bone Idle tried to
tiptoe away to his hidden chamber,
the ghost hound thought the skeleton
wanted him to play haunt and seek!

Slowly, though, the lazy spooks grew
to like things being more lively. Which was
just as well, or Hairy may have had to start
howling again!

Things that go Bump

While you are tucked up,
Fast asleep,
Out from dark corners,
Strange things creep.

But steady your nerves, don't take fright,
When things go bump in the night!

Ghosts glide down the hallway,
Sneak under your bed,
And pull at the pillows
Where you rest your head.

But steady your nerves, don't take fright,
When things go bump in the night!

Spooks pull off your blankets.
They tweak at your toes.
They use small white feathers
To tickle your nose.
But steady your nerves, don't take fright,
When things go bump in the night!

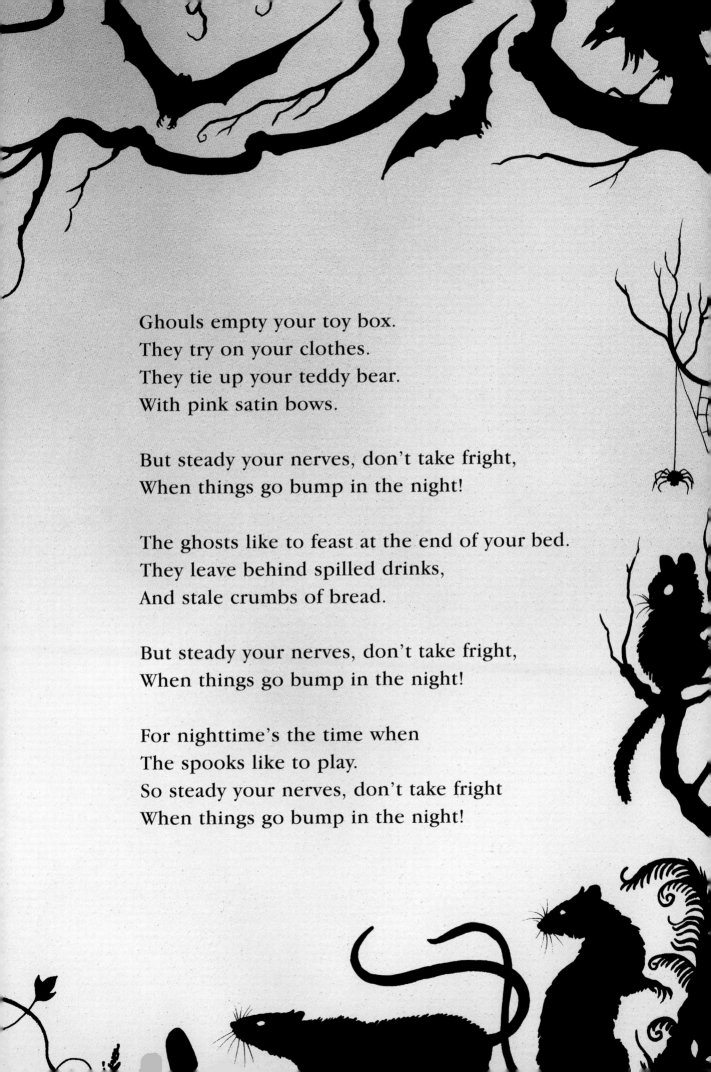

Ghouls empty your toy box.
They try on your clothes.
They tie up your teddy bear.
With pink satin bows.

But steady your nerves, don't take fright,
When things go bump in the night!

The ghosts like to feast at the end of your bed.
They leave behind spilled drinks,
And stale crumbs of bread.

But steady your nerves, don't take fright,
When things go bump in the night!

For nighttime's the time when
The spooks like to play.
So steady your nerves, don't take fright
When things go bump in the night!

Fiddlefingers

Captain Brassbuttons hummed happily and tapped his feet to a lively tune onboard his pirate ship, *The Jolly Jig*. Every now and then, he would stop to stroke his bushy beard and laugh loudly while he watched some of his cut-throat crew dance a hornpipe. Around him other pirates played pipes, tambourines, and accordions. The sound drifted up from below deck to a sinister skull-and-crossbones flag waving high above on the mast.

"Look lively, lads! Ha! Ha!" bellowed Captain Brassbuttons, who was really enjoying himself.

So were his loyal band of buccaneers. Although they were armed to the teeth with pistols and cutlasses, the weapons were now next to useless and rusting badly. You see, the pirates preferred to make music and have a merry time. After all, raiding ships and carrying off their treasure was hard and dangerous work, which was one of the reasons why they had not done it in a very long time.

But there was another reason, too. These days, *The Jolly Jig* and her crew spent most of their time at the bottom of the sea—for *The Jolly Jig* was a ghost ship and Captain Brassbuttons and his colorful crew were ghost pirates!

"'Tis a pity we don't have a fiddle player

among us, cap'n," said Patch one day, as he rested a moment against the ship's big, wooden wheel.

"To be sure!" sighed Brassbuttons. "That would be more of a treasure than all the booty we've ever bagged!"

"But that's enough fun for now, me hearties," continued Brassbuttons, "for 'tis high time we made ready to set sail again!"

"Aye, aye, cap'n!" said Patch and in no time the crew were cheerfully busying themselves. They hauled on ropes, unfurled the ghostly white sails and made ready to raise their phantom ship above the waves. Meanwhile, Captain Brassbuttons hurried to his cabin to put on his best boots, waistcoat, and hat.

A short while later, *The Jolly Jig* rose majestically from beneath the waves to haunt the high seas, which it did whenever the moon was full.

Passengers on passing ships would stare in amazement at the sight of the fantastic phantom ship. From its glowing decks came the sound of music and merry voices, as the creepy crew sang and played. What's more, the ghostly ship was thought to bring good luck to all who saw it.

But all that was about to change. That night, as the moon faded, *The Jolly Jig* sank again toward its watery grave. But, as it was about to touch the bottom, a strong undersea current picked the ghost ship up and swept it along. Brassbuttons and his men were horrified. All they could do was hang on grimly while *The Jolly Jig* did its own wild dance along the ocean floor. At last, the ship settled and its shaken crew floated out from their hiding places.

"Shiver me timbers!" uttered Bones. "That was enough to set any ghost a-quakin' and a-shaking'"

Captain Brassbuttons drifted up on to the deck to check *The Jolly Jig* was still in one piece. To his surprise, the wreck of another old vessel lay in the soft sand nearby.

"Ahoy, me hearties!" Brassbuttons called his men and pointed eagerly. "'Tis time to go a-pirating again!"

And before long the pirate raiding party set off in their longboat, rowing just above the seabed toward the wreck.

The battered ship lay on its side with
a huge hole in the hull. An octopus came
scuttling out. Some sharks swam past too,
eyeing the pirates coldly.

"We'd all be sharks' bait if we were flesh
and bones!" whispered Pigtail.

"Stand by to board," growled
Brassbuttons, leading his sea spooks onto
the ship.

He was first to enter the crew's quarters.
There was a terrible noise coming from a
dark corner, which made his knees knock
and his shoulders tremble.

"Who goes there?" he called, trying to
sound brave and fearless. Then he saw that
the noise was coming from a phantom
figure lying fast asleep in a hammock, and
snoring loudly.

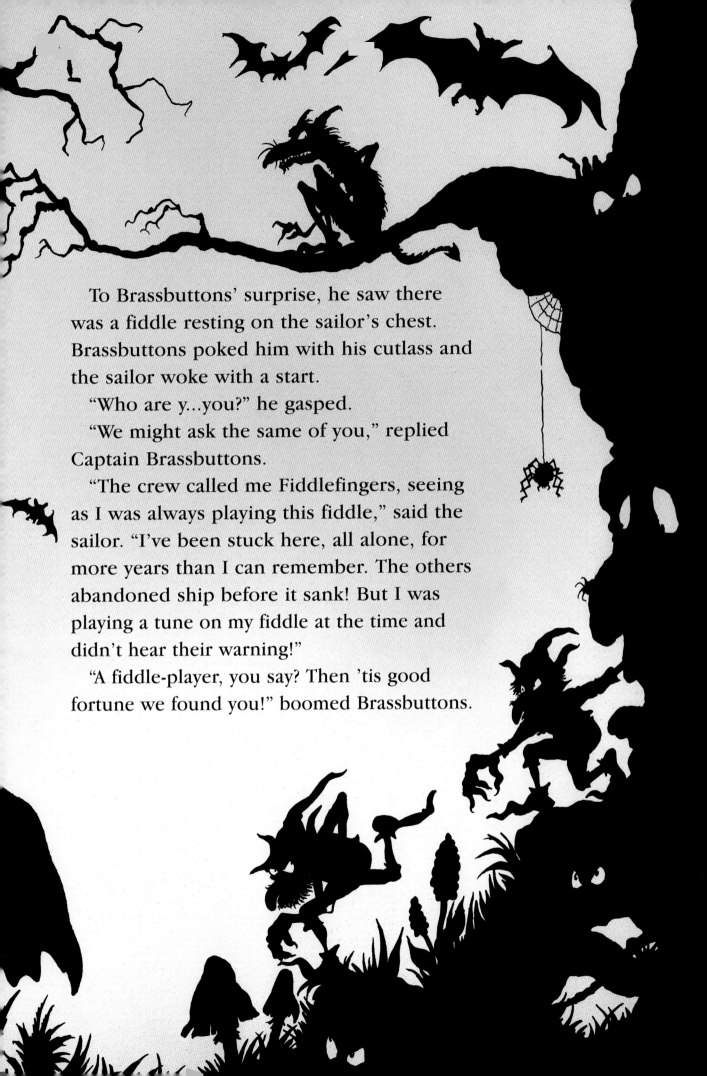

To Brassbuttons' surprise, he saw there was a fiddle resting on the sailor's chest. Brassbuttons poked him with his cutlass and the sailor woke with a start.

"Who are y...you?" he gasped.

"We might ask the same of you," replied Captain Brassbuttons.

"The crew called me Fiddlefingers, seeing as I was always playing this fiddle," said the sailor. "I've been stuck here, all alone, for more years than I can remember. The others abandoned ship before it sank! But I was playing a tune on my fiddle at the time and didn't hear their warning!"

"A fiddle-player, you say? Then 'tis good fortune we found you!" boomed Brassbuttons.

However, the captain and his crew soon changed their minds. No sooner had they welcomed Fiddlefingers aboard *The Jolly Jig* than he began to play his fiddle. But what a shock for the other merrymakers Instead of the tuneful harmony they had so been looking forward to hearing, he made a fearful, scratching screech. It was the most terrible sound the phantom pirates had ever heard. Yet, strangely, Fiddlefingers didn't seem to notice. He just went on playing happily as the other pirates winced.

"No wonder the rest of his crew fled!" grumbled Bones, his bony fingers in his ears.

But rough and ready as he seemed, Captain Brassbuttons was really a kindly soul. He felt sorry for Fiddlefingers left for so long without any ship's company and he didn't have the heart to send him on his watery way again.

So that gloomy day spelled doom for the sorry spooks aboard *The Jolly Jig*. There was no more laughter, dancing, or merry music. Instead, all that could be heard when the ghost ship next appeared beneath the full moon were the woeful wails, horrified howls, and ghastly groans of her poor suffering crew, as they tried to drown out the sound of the awful fiddling. As for Fiddlefingers, he just smiled happily and played on, and on, and on...

A Spelling Lesson!

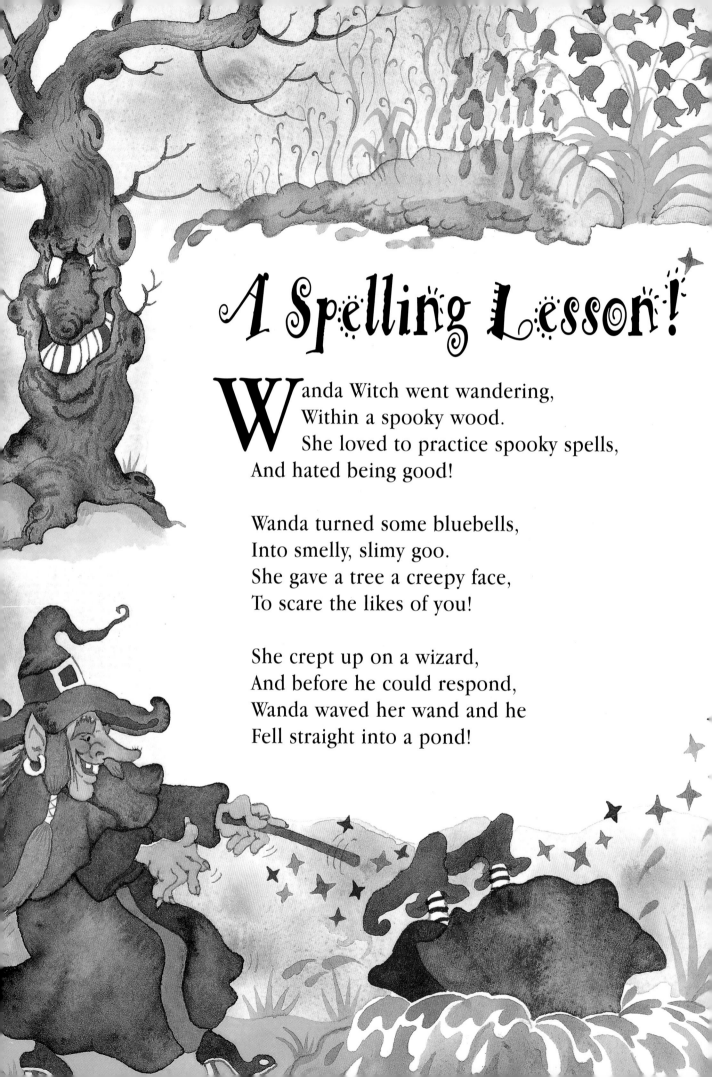

Wanda Witch went wandering,
Within a spooky wood.
She loved to practice spooky spells,
And hated being good!

Wanda turned some bluebells,
Into smelly, slimy goo.
She gave a tree a creepy face,
To scare the likes of you!

She crept up on a wizard,
And before he could respond,
Wanda waved her wand and he
Fell straight into a pond!

Although it was not very deep,
The wizard soon saw red.
He cast a spell that made his cloak,
Flap right around Wanda's head.

It wrapped around her body,
And squeezed her really tight.
"Say sorry," roared the wizard,
"Or stay like that all night!"

The witch agreed and told him,
"Your magic is so fast.
No more naughty spells from me,
I've really cast my last!"

Freaky Friends

Having an old witch as her next-door neighbor was the last thing that Victoria Vampire wanted. No sooner had Winnie moved in, complete with her broomstick, cauldron, pointed hat, and all kinds of pots and potions, than weird things began to happen.

Whenever Winnie stirred up a magical brew indoors, a mass of stars and sparks would fly out of the chimney of her tumbledown old cottage like a fantastic fireworks show.

They whizzed safely beyond her own little yard—and landed in the grounds of Victoria's dark and spooky house instead! Victoria's clean washing was soon spotted with sooty marks and two big holes were burned in her best black cloak.

Then there was the smell, or more precisely, the stinky pong! Whatever was bubbling away in Winnie's cauldron, it was definitely *not* chicken noodle soup. The aroma wafted across into the dark turrets of Victoria's home. In no time it had disturbed Victoria's precious colony of bats that lived in the attic. They poured like dark molasses out of a small skylight and fluttered away to hide in a dark, distant cave. And as if losing her pets wasn't bad enough, Victoria had to keep every door and window tightly closed against the stink. It was enough to make her flash her fangs in anger!

But there was worse to come. Winnie's two cats, Scratch and Sniff, were mouse-mad; they chased them nonstop. So one day, when they spotted some by Victoria's woodshed, the mean-eyed cats set off in hot pursuit. The trouble was that Victoria had just entered the shed to fetch some logs for her fire. Now, being a vampire, she didn't like going out in daylight and, as usual, was wearing her dark sunglasses. So she didn't see Scratch and Sniff slink into the shed—she just felt the sting of their claws as she tripped on them and they lashed out at her legs. Victoria let out a blood-curdling scream, the startled cats screeched "YEOWWL!," wood went flying, and so did Victoria! She crashed into the door, bumping her head and breaking an arm off her precious sunglasses.

Meanwhile, the cats sulkily slipped away, having lost the mice who had taken advantage of all the commotion and disappeared.

Victoria tried to balance her broken sunglasses back on her nose. Then she felt inside her mouth and winced—she had broken one of her fine fangs when she fell. That was the last straw!

"That does it!" she hissed. "I'm going to have a not-so-neighborly word with that pesky witch!"

Victoria marched straight out of her own gate, up the front path to Winnie's cottage and thumped on the door. But Winnie was in the backyard, practicing some spells. She was concentrating so hard she did not hear the visiting vampire. Winnie waved her wand at a carpet beater lying on the lawn. Nearby, a large, dusty rug hung on the laundry line.

"Eye of newt and lizard's spleen, carpet beater start to *clean!*" she chanted.

"There you are!" cried Victoria, stomping around the side of the cottage. "I've got a bone to pick with you."

"Oh, good. Come inside, then. I'm hungry, too," said Winnie, smiling innocently at her.

Victoria was about to set Winnie straight and give her a piece of her mind, when she suddenly stopped dead in her tracks. Something was floating toward her.

It was the carpet beater. Instead of giving
the rug a good beating, it swished and
swiped at Victoria.

"Ooh! Aagh! Help!" she wailed as the
carpet beater chased her out of Winnie's
backyard and all the way home. There she
sat and sulked until the moon rose.

"Enough's enough!" she thought. "It's
time I taught that tiresome witch a lesson!"
She stomped out into the darkness, and was
soon hard at work in Winnie's backyard,
pulling up all the magic plants and
trampling on the special herb patch. Then
she spied Scratch and Sniff curled up fast
asleep in a basket by an open window.
Reaching in with both hands she caught
hold of their long whiskers and pulled with
all her might—Ping! Ping! Ping! The furious
cats howled in pain and leaped into the air.
But, using some special vampire magic of

her own, Victoria turned herself into a bat
and took off into the night. She hadn't
flown far though when, suddenly, something
whizzed past her like a rocket. It was
Winnie on her broomstick.

Caught in its slipstream, Victoria was
tossed about like a leaf in a storm. She had
just made a bumpy landing on Winnie's
lawn when the witch swooped down and
landed right on top of her! As Scratch
prepared to pounce, thinking bat might make
a tasty alternative to mouse, Victoria
changed back with a flash. But she was
bruised and breathless.

"Ohh! My back!" Victoria groaned.

"Deary me!" wailed the witch. "It's all my
fault! I had no idea it was you! Here, please
let me help!"

Victoria was too weary to argue. And help
Winnie certainly did.

Over the next few days, nothing was too much trouble for her. She insisted that Victoria rest at home in bed while she cooked a surprisingly tasty beet soup. It was such a deliciously deep red color that Victoria simply had to have some.

"It would have been better if those pesky cats hadn't dug up my herbs, mind you," said Winnie. While Victoria guiltily enjoyed another bowlful, Winnie searched her spell book.

"Aha! I knew it was here somewhere!" she said. Winnie waved her wand and chanted something about taking care of canines. Then, in a flash, Victoria's two beautiful, long sharp teeth were perfect again.

"*Fangs* very much," she joked.

Further spells repaired the holes in Victoria's cloak, cleaned up her laundry, and brought her bats back to the attic. Another spell made Winnie's broom sweep up the woodshed. Scratch and Sniff eagerly caught every mouse in Victoria's house, which made up a bit for losing their whiskers! Victoria felt ashamed for trying to teach the kind witch a lesson.

"I feel so much better," smiled Victoria, getting up at last. "You're a wonder, Winnie!"

"Nonsense! Nothing like a *spell* in bed," the witch replied, modestly, as she gave her new-found friend a hug.

The Wrong Cat

"I need three dead mice for this spell, Grazelgritch. Go and catch them," said Witch Yukspell, shoving her black cat out of the door.

Poor Grazelgritch—it was freezing cold outside and a nasty sleety rain had started. He headed for the woods and sat under a holly bush waiting for a mouse to pass by.

"Hello," said a voice behind him. "Is this a good place to catch mice?" He turned to see another black cat crouching under the holly. Grazelgritch thought she was beautiful.

"Who are you?" he asked. "I've never seen you in the woods before."

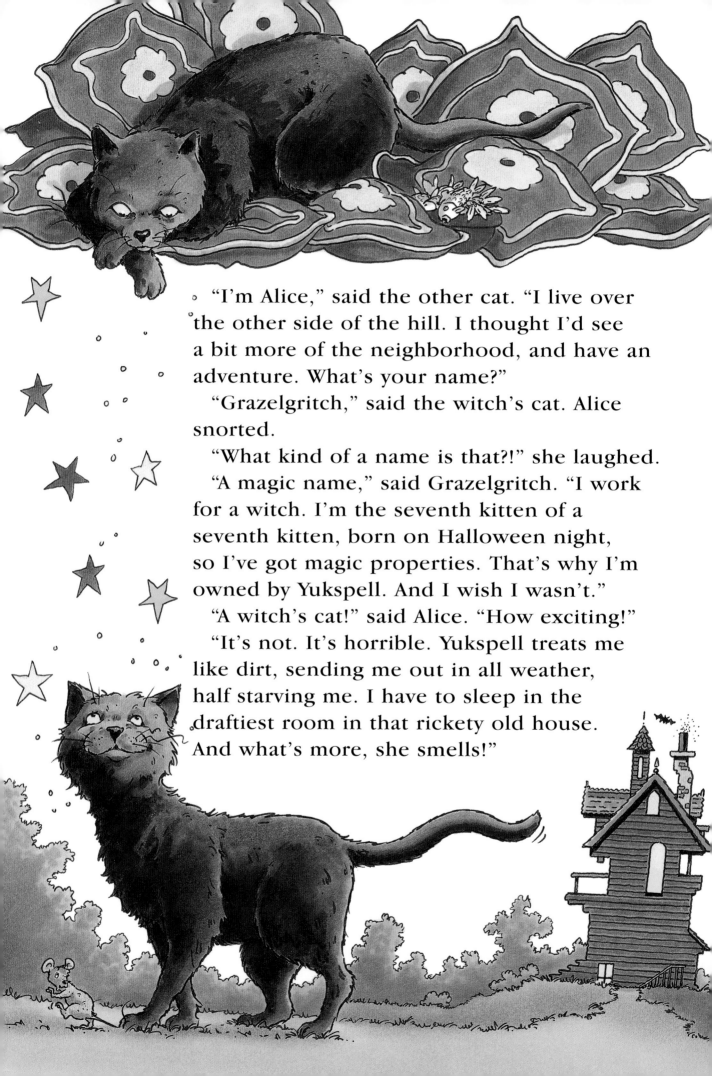

"I'm Alice," said the other cat. "I live over the other side of the hill. I thought I'd see a bit more of the neighborhood, and have an adventure. What's your name?"

"Grazelgritch," said the witch's cat. Alice snorted.

"What kind of a name is that?!" she laughed.

"A magic name," said Grazelgritch. "I work for a witch. I'm the seventh kitten of a seventh kitten, born on Halloween night, so I've got magic properties. That's why I'm owned by Yukspell. And I wish I wasn't."

"A witch's cat!" said Alice. "How exciting!"

"It's not. It's horrible. Yukspell treats me like dirt, sending me out in all weather, half starving me. I have to sleep in the draftiest room in that rickety old house. And what's more, she smells!"

"You poor thing," said Alice. "I lead a very boring life—sleeping most of the day, eating canned food, leftovers if I'm lucky. I have to go to the vet sometimes."

"Sounds like heaven," sighed Grazelgritch, nibbling at a flea between his toes.

"Well, why don't we trade places for a while?" suggested Alice. "Go on—have a vacation.
And I can have my adventure!"

Grazelgritch thought she must be crazy but he agreed at once, and Alice took the dead mice they caught to the witch's house on the hill.

"About time too!" snapped Yukspell, grabbing the mice and flinging them into the cauldron.

She added the ingredients to her wicked witches' brew. It was a spell to make all the local schoolchildren sick.

"Just one more thing," said Yukspell. She grabbed Alice by the scruff of her neck and wrenched out a whisker—ping! Alice yowled in pain and jumped onto the windowsill, whipping her tail back and forth. Yukspell ignored the angry cat and dropped the whisker into the cauldron. At that point the whole mixture was meant to turn green and froth violently. But it didn't.

"Funny," said the witch, checking her spell book. Of course the problem was that Alice was an ordinary cat—the fourth kitten in a litter of six, born at Easter—not a magic cat at all. Yukspell was furious. Four hours of work wasted.

"Grazelgritch!" she screeched. "Were those mice or voles?!" She turned and stared at the black cat. Then slowly the truth dawned on Yukspell.

"An imposter!" she screamed. "You're not Grazelgritch!" She grabbed Alice and threw her out of the window.

SPELLS

"You're lucky I didn't put you in the cauldron!" she shouted after the poor cat, as Alice raced away down the hill.

When Alice got home, she found Grazelgritch purring contentedly on her owner's lap.

"Oh no! That was quick!" he said. "Do I have to go back so soon? I haven't had dinner yet."

"I don't think I'd make a good adventurer," said Alice. "But it's all right, don't go. My owners said just the other day that they'd like to give a home to another cat to keep me company. Well, I choose you!"

Yukspell was furious that Grazelgritch had deserted her. Without a magic cat none of her spells worked anymore, which made life a lot more pleasant for everyone else who lived around her. She had to content herself with scaring people on her broomstick.

Alice's owners were happy to give a home to her new friend. And wouldn't you know it? The following fall, Alice had seven sooty black kittens. But Grazelgritch chose the new home for the youngest kitten very carefully—it went to live with a very nice family in the town. They never knew that they owned a magical cat, and that's exactly how Grazelgritch wanted it.

The Hobgoblin Ball

Late at night when the moon is bright,
  And the air is soft and still,
  Pixies peep and fairies creep,
And goblins roam at will.

Through the trees, a gentle breeze
Stirs brownies from their dreams.
Imps awake, they stretch and shake,
Then slide along moonbeams.

Elves sneak out, and slink about,
Leprechauns come leaping.
Little sprites wave magic lights,
While the world is sleeping.

Singing songs, they skip along,
Toward the forest glade.
Hung with lights, all twinkling bright,
While gentle music's played.

They appear, from far and near,
A host of fairy folk.
This happy band dance hand in hand,
Beneath the magic oak.

Every night, enchanting sights
Await for one and all.
So when day's done, come join the fun,
At the great Hobgoblin Ball!

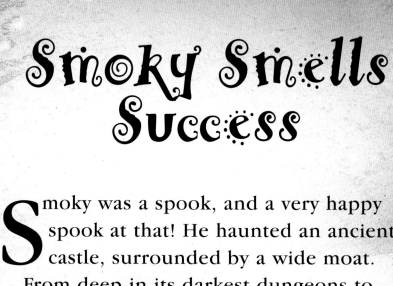

Smoky Smells Success

Smoky was a spook, and a very happy spook at that! He haunted an ancient castle, surrounded by a wide moat. From deep in its darkest dungeons to high on the heights of its battlements, Smoky would appear, mischievously and mysteriously, whenever he wanted. Sometimes, he appeared just as himself— a swirling puff of supernatural smoke. However, being a ghost, Smoky could change shape at will.

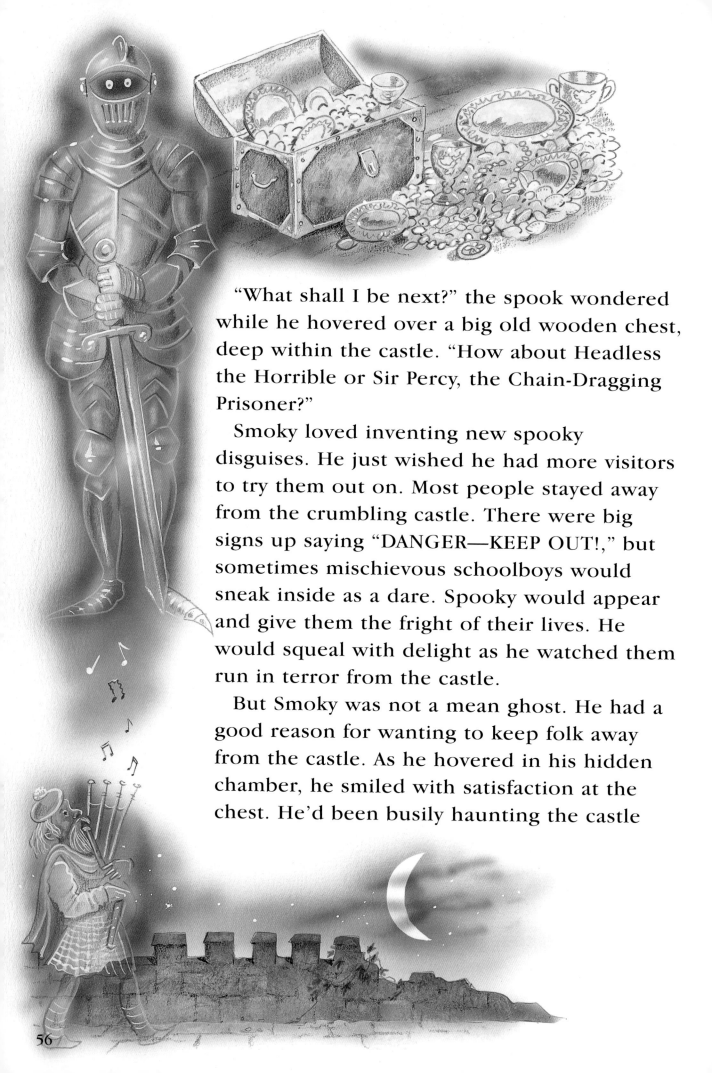

"What shall I be next?" the spook wondered while he hovered over a big old wooden chest, deep within the castle. "How about Headless the Horrible or Sir Percy, the Chain-Dragging Prisoner?"

Smoky loved inventing new spooky disguises. He just wished he had more visitors to try them out on. Most people stayed away from the crumbling castle. There were big signs up saying "DANGER—KEEP OUT!," but sometimes mischievous schoolboys would sneak inside as a dare. Spooky would appear and give them the fright of their lives. He would squeal with delight as he watched them run in terror from the castle.

But Smoky was not a mean ghost. He had a good reason for wanting to keep folk away from the castle. As he hovered in his hidden chamber, he smiled with satisfaction at the chest. He'd been busily haunting the castle

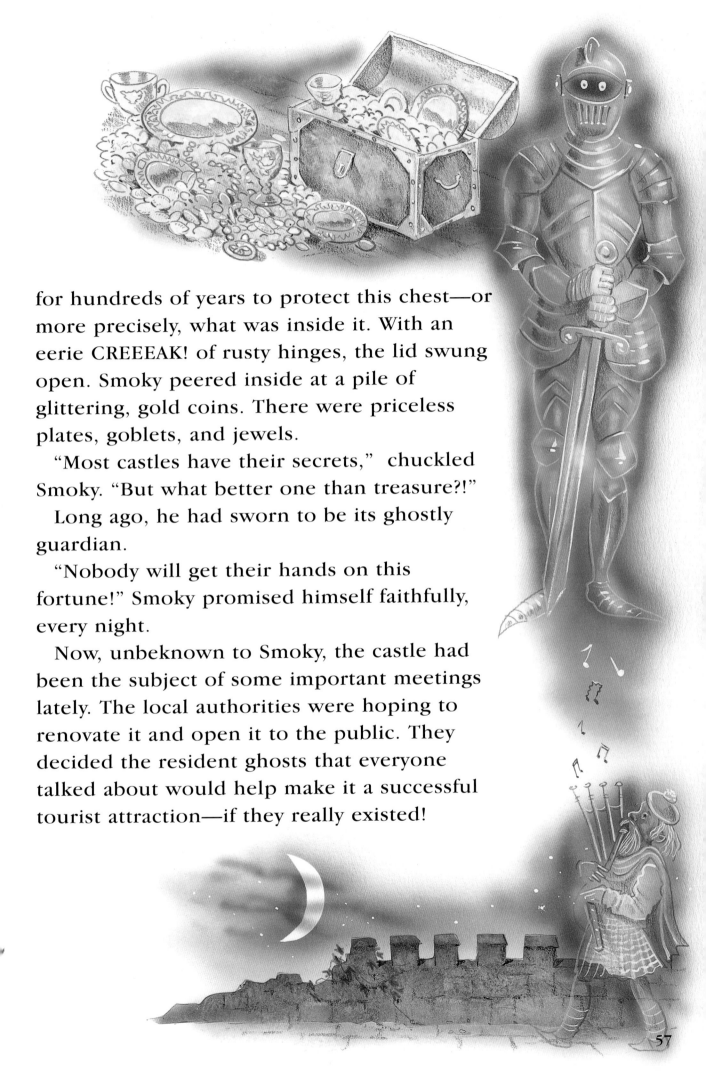

for hundreds of years to protect this chest—or more precisely, what was inside it. With an eerie CREEEAK! of rusty hinges, the lid swung open. Smoky peered inside at a pile of glittering, gold coins. There were priceless plates, goblets, and jewels.

"Most castles have their secrets," chuckled Smoky. "But what better one than treasure?!"

Long ago, he had sworn to be its ghostly guardian.

"Nobody will get their hands on this fortune!" Smoky promised himself faithfully, every night.

Now, unbeknown to Smoky, the castle had been the subject of some important meetings lately. The local authorities were hoping to renovate it and open it to the public. They decided the resident ghosts that everyone talked about would help make it a successful tourist attraction—if they really existed!

So it was that one morning, Smoky heard a car pull up. A man and woman climbed out. They walked slowly around the castle walls, making notes, and looking very serious indeed.

"It's no use," said the man. "This castle's crumbling. If we don't pull it down, it will fall all on its own. We're going to have to forget about opening it to the public."

"Pity," replied the woman. "It's such a grand, historical building. If only we could raise enough money to have it repaired. But that would cost a fortune!"

Smoky froze. For the first time, he understood what it was like to be scared! If his precious castle was pulled down, what would happen to him? He wouldn't want to haunt anywhere else. Something had to be done—and fast!

As the visitors were returning to their car, they suddenly stopped and sniffed the air. There was a wonderful smell coming from the castle. The man pointed to what looked like a thin trail of steam floating by the entrance. It was Smoky, who had conjured up a delicious smell to tempt the visitors in.

"Let's take a look inside," said the man.

"But it's dangerous—and apparently haunted!" said the woman, nervously.

"We'll be careful," said the man. "I have to find out where that incredible smell is coming from."

They followed the lovely smell into the castle. Smoky led the way, disguised as a thin trail of smoke. For once, he didn't want to frighten his visitors away! They crept quietly along the corridors, glancing nervously over their shoulders, but there were no spooks to be seen. Smoky made a secret door in one of the walls swing wide open. A narrow, cobweb-filled passage led the visitors to his hidden chamber and...the treasure chest!

When the officials saw its glittering, golden contents, they shrieked so loudly it made Smoky jump.

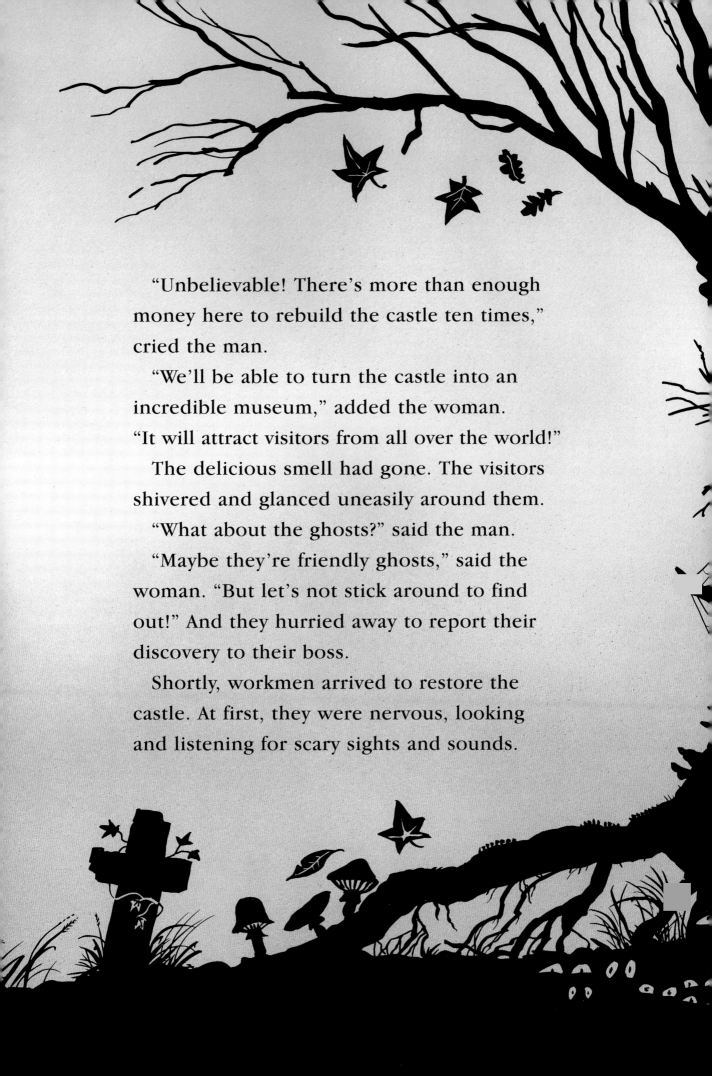

"Unbelievable! There's more than enough money here to rebuild the castle ten times," cried the man.

"We'll be able to turn the castle into an incredible museum," added the woman. "It will attract visitors from all over the world!"

The delicious smell had gone. The visitors shivered and glanced uneasily around them.

"What about the ghosts?" said the man.

"Maybe they're friendly ghosts," said the woman. "But let's not stick around to find out!" And they hurried away to report their discovery to their boss.

Shortly, workmen arrived to restore the castle. At first, they were nervous, looking and listening for scary sights and sounds.

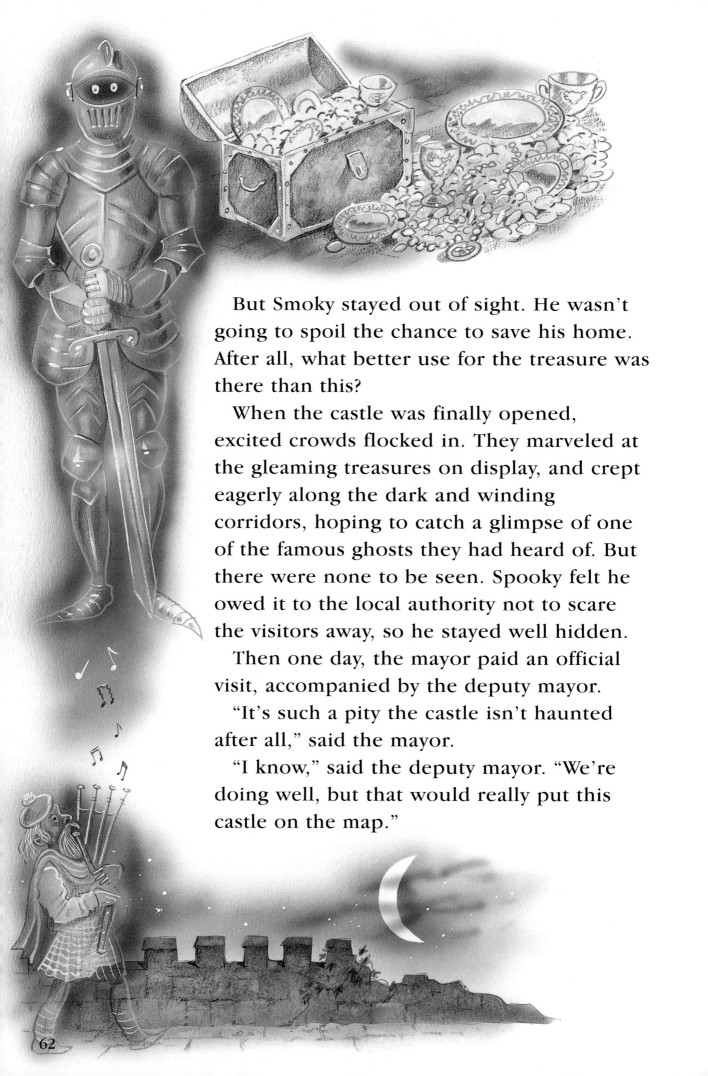

But Smoky stayed out of sight. He wasn't going to spoil the chance to save his home. After all, what better use for the treasure was there than this?

When the castle was finally opened, excited crowds flocked in. They marveled at the gleaming treasures on display, and crept eagerly along the dark and winding corridors, hoping to catch a glimpse of one of the famous ghosts they had heard of. But there were none to be seen. Spooky felt he owed it to the local authority not to scare the visitors away, so he stayed well hidden.

Then one day, the mayor paid an official visit, accompanied by the deputy mayor.

"It's such a pity the castle isn't haunted after all," said the mayor.

"I know," said the deputy mayor. "We're doing well, but that would really put this castle on the map."

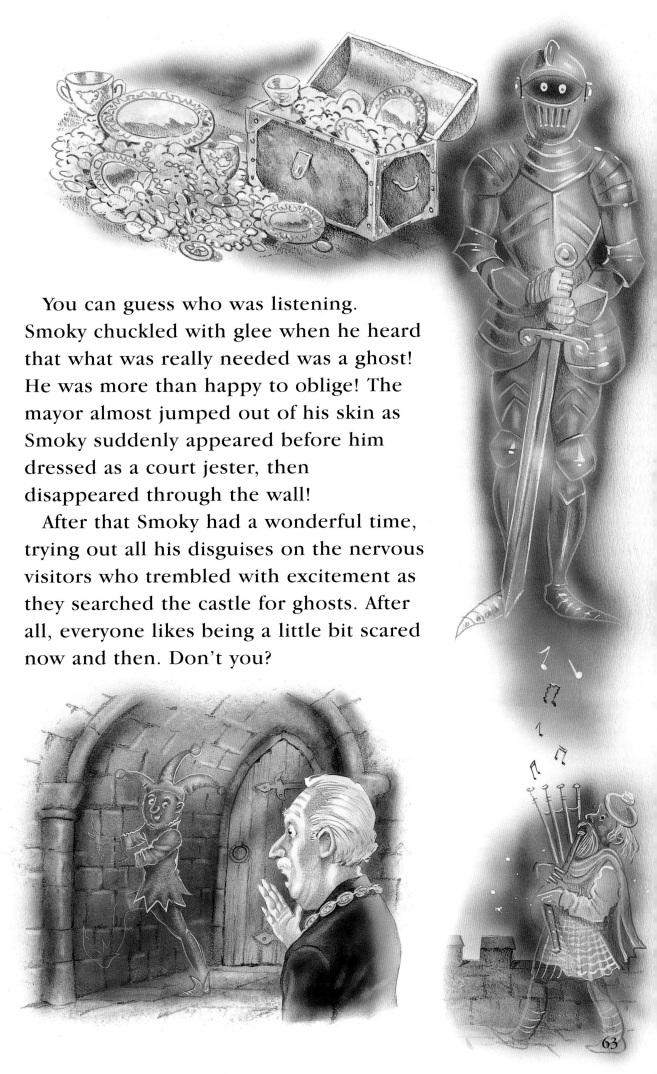

You can guess who was listening. Smoky chuckled with glee when he heard that what was really needed was a ghost! He was more than happy to oblige! The mayor almost jumped out of his skin as Smoky suddenly appeared before him dressed as a court jester, then disappeared through the wall!

After that Smoky had a wonderful time, trying out all his disguises on the nervous visitors who trembled with excitement as they searched the castle for ghosts. After all, everyone likes being a little bit scared now and then. Don't you?

Witch's Brew

Eye of lizard, toe of frog,
Tail of rat, and bark of dog.
Sneeze of chicken, cough of bat,
Lick of weasel, smell of cat.

Stir it up and mix it well,
To make a magic monster spell.

Leech's liver, finely chopped,
Pus of pimple, freshly popped.
Web of spider, slime of toad,
Squish of porcupine, scraped from road.

Stir it up and mix it well,
To make a magic monster spell.

Spell for
Magic
Monster

· will help with
household chores
· will be gentle
and polite
· will definitely
not eat you

Ingredients

Eye of lizard
Toe of frog
Tail of rat
Bark of dog
Sneeze of
chicken
Cough of bat
Lick of weasel
Smell of cat

Now it's done, the spell is ready,
The monster's rising, slow and steady.
"Pleased to meet you," Witchy sighs.
"Pleased to *eat* you," he replies.

What's gone wrong, she cannot tell,
To spoil the magic monster spell.

The witch goes pale, she must act fast,
Or else this day may be her last!
She grabs her wand. She has a notion
Of how to get rid of this potion.

She shakes her wand, which breaks the spell,
And waves the monster fond farewell!

A Night in the Haunted House

High up on a lonely hill, surrounded by a great dark forest, stood an ancient, crumbling mansion, known as the *Haunted House*. It belonged to a greedy old man, who everyone said was a wizard. He lived in a little cottage in the grounds of the mansion, with just his black cat for company. He had no friends to speak of, but he was very happy, because he had a true love. Now, his true love was gold, and he had plenty of it, because he had found a way to make the *Haunted House* serve him well, even though he dare not set one foot inside it himself.

He had pinned a notice to the tall rusting gates of the mansion, promising a reward of five hundred gold coins to anyone who could spend a whole night inside it, and charging them five gold coins for the privilege of trying.

Desperate men and brave adventurers came from far and wide, each certain they could withstand the horrors of the *Haunted House*. Some did well, and lasted many hours before fleeing in terror. Back in the safety of the local tavern, they would mutter and gibber and stutter out tales of ghosts so ghoulish, and monsters so terrifying, that their wide-eyed listeners would gasp with horror and congratulate them for staying in the house so long. Others lasted mere minutes before fleeing into the night in shame.

Now one day, there came a man called Titan, whose bravery was legendary. He was known far and wide as the most fearless adventurer, with towering strength and nerves of steel. He paid his five gold coins to the wizard, who reluctantly gave him the key to the house. This fellow looked a bit too fearless for the wizard's liking.

That night, Titan stepped through the rusty gates, and strode toward the *Haunted House*. Without hesitating, he unlocked the door and went in. A butler appeared from nowhere, carrying his head under his arm. "Jeeves at your service, sir," he said, creepily. "Follow me."

"Thank you, my good man," said Titan, handing him his coat and following him up the creaking staircase without blinking an eye.

Ancient portraits followed him with their eyes. Titan winked at them as he passed. An empty suit of armor waved. Titan waved back. "Good evening," he said.

Jeeves led him on down a murky passage. A heavy door creaked open and they entered a dark bedroom, with a tattered four-poster bed. Cobwebs hung from the ceiling, and a thick layer of dust covered the furniture. Titan opened the closet and a skeleton came leering out. "Oops. Sorry to disturb you," Titan said, brushing the cobwebs from a chair.

The startled butler looked at Titan in amazement. Was this man scared of nothing? "Tea, sir?" Jeeves asked. "Herman will bring it up right away."

Moments later Herman, a drooling two-headed ogre, appeared with Titan's tea. "Thank you," said Titan, pouring the tea without flinching. "That will be all."

And so it continued through the night. The inhabitants of the *Haunted House* did their worst. Ghouls wailed and werewolves howled. Mummies rose up from their tombs and staggered through the room. A ghostly prisoner appeared dragging clanking chains and vanished through the wall. Vampires leered and phantoms jeered.

"This is quite a show!" said Titan, settling back on his pillows, and watching the ghostly goings-on with a cheerful grin.

Meanwhile, down in the little cottage, the wizard kept glancing nervously at the clock, as he shone and polished his precious gold. Slowly the hours passed, and still there was no sign of Titan. Could this be the man who would finally claim the reward?

Back at the house, a fluffy white ghost was hovering over Titan's head, shouting "Boo!" and trying to sound frightening. It was his first night on the job. The startled spooks had had to call out all reserves. How were they going to frighten this man of steel?

Titan reached up and grabbed the ghost in
one mighty swoop. "Just what I need. You'll
make an excellent extra pillow," and he
stuffed the little ghost behind his head, lay
back, and was soon snoring soundly. Hour
after hour the exasperated spooks kept up
their grim hauntings, but Titan just carried
on sleeping, oblivious to their efforts.

Then, as the village clock chimed four
o'clock faraway in the distance, Titan began
to stir. He twitched and wriggled and shook
his head, then turned over, pulling the
pillows tighter to him. But still he was not
comfortable. He tossed and he turned,
groaning and grumbling, but it was no good.

There was something lumpy underneath his pillow that was keeping him from settling back to sleep. He opened his eyes. The exhausted ghouls surged forward, renewing their efforts to terrify him.

"Oh, are you boys still up?!" said Titan, surprised. "Don't you have beds to go to?" The weary ghosts shook their heads in exasperation. Titan felt about under his pillow. What was it that was lodged under there, keeping him awake? Just then, his hand wrapped around something small and soft and furry. He felt a shiver run down his spine. Slowly he pulled out his hand from under the pillow and there, trembling in fright was a tiny, little white mouse. Titan let out an almighty scream! He leaped from the bed and raced for the door.

Down he fled through dusty passages and darkened stairways, then disappeared, still screaming and hollering, into the night.

Through his window, the wizard cackled in delight as he watched him fleeing. He hugged his bag of gold to him, and rubbed his hands together with glee.

"I knew he'd crack," he chuckled. "Something gets to all of them in the end!"

Take the Ghost Train

There's a tumbledown old station,
Where a ghost train waits to go.
All aboard, ghosts, ghouls, and goblins,
Watch the engine brightly glow!

In its cab, a phantom driver,
Helps the engine get up steam.
Chuff-chuff-chuff, it's moving slowly,
Hear its whistle, like a screeeeam!

Creepy conductors are whistling wildly,
Bony fingers wave good-bye,
As along the rails the ghost train glides,
Beneath the moonlit sky.

Witches shriek along the railcars,
While inside the dining car,
Vampires munch and crunch with monsters,
Sipping cocktails at the bar!

On they speed through misty marshes,
What a chilling sight to see.
Ghostly faces at the windows,
Silent wheels turn eerily!

If there were tickets for the ghost train,
Would you dare to take a ride?
Or would you quickly run away,
And find somewhere to hide?

The Sleeper and the Spindle

Neil Gaiman

Illustrated by
Chris Riddell

HARPER

An Imprint of HarperCollinsPublishers

This story first appeared in *Rag & Bones: New Twists on Timeless Tales*,
published in 2013 by Little, Brown.

The Sleeper and the Spindle
Text copyright © 2013 by Neil Gaiman
Illustrations copyright © 2014 by Chris Riddell
HarperCollins Children's Books, a division of HarperCollins Publishers,
195 Broadway, New York, NY 10007.
www.epicreads.com

ISBN 978-0-06-239824-6 (trade bdg.) — ISBN 978-0-06-243503-3 (special ed.)

15   16   17   18   19   PC   10   9   8   7   6   5   4   3
❖
First U.S. Edition, 2015
Originally published in the U.K. in 2014 by Bloomsbury.

For Holly and Maddy, my daughters who woke me up
N.G.

For my daughter Katy, on the beginning of her quest
C.R.

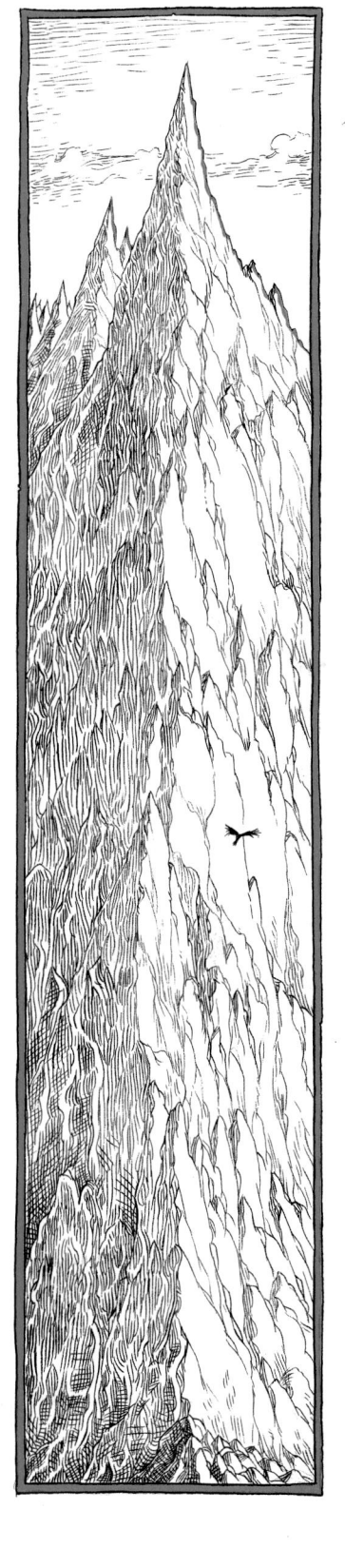

It was the closest kingdom to the queen's, as the crow flies, but not even the crows flew it. The high mountain range that served as the border between the two kingdoms discouraged crows as much as it discouraged people, and it was considered unpassable.

More than one enterprising merchant, on each side of the mountains, had commissioned folk to hunt for the mountain pass that would, if it were there, have made a rich man or woman of anyone who controlled it. The silks of Dorimar could have been in Kanselaire in weeks, in months, not years. But there was no such pass to be found, and so, although the two kingdoms shared a common border, nobody crossed from one kingdom to the next.

Even the dwarfs, who were tough, and hardy, and composed of magic as much as of flesh and blood, could not go over the mountain range.

This was not a problem for the dwarfs. They did not go over the mountain range. They went under it.

Three dwarfs, traveling as swiftly as one through the dark paths beneath the mountains:

"Hurry! Hurry!" said the dwarf at the rear. "We have to buy her the finest silken cloth in Dorimar. If we do not hurry, perhaps it will be sold, and we will be forced to buy her the second finest cloth."

"We know! We know!" said the dwarf at the front. "And we shall buy her a case to carry it back in, so it will remain perfectly clean and untouched by dust."

The dwarf in the middle said nothing. He was holding his stone tightly, not dropping it or losing it, and was concentrating on nothing else but this. The stone was a ruby, roughhewn from the rock and the size of a hen's egg. It was worth a kingdom when cut and set, and would be easily exchanged for the finest silks of Dorimar.

It would not have occurred to the dwarfs to give the young queen anything they had dug themselves from beneath the earth. That would have been too easy, too routine. It's the distance that makes a gift magical, so the dwarfs believed.

The queen woke early that morning.

The queen woke early that morning. "A week from today," she said aloud. "A week from today, I shall be married."

It seemed both unlikely and extremely final. She wondered how she would feel to be a married woman. It would be the end of her life, she decided, if life was a time of choices. In a week from now, she would have no choices. She would reign over her people. She would have children. Perhaps she would die in childbirth, perhaps she would die as an old woman, or in battle. But the path to her death, heartbeat by heartbeat, would be inevitable.

She could hear the carpenters in the meadows beneath the castle, building the seats that would allow her people to watch her marry. Each hammer blow sounded like a heartbeat.

Each hammer blow sounded like a heartbeat.

The three dwarfs scrambled out of a hole in the side of the riverbank, and clambered up into the meadow, one, two, three. They climbed to the top of a granite outcrop, stretched, kicked, jumped, and stretched themselves once more. Then they sprinted north, towards the cluster of low buildings that made the village of Giff, and in particular to the village inn.

The innkeeper was their friend: they had brought him a bottle of Kanselaire wine—deep red, sweet, and rich, and nothing like the sharp, pale wines of those parts—as they always did. He would feed them, and send them on their way, and advise them.

The innkeeper, chest as huge as his barrels, beard as bushy and as orange as a fox's brush, was in the taproom. It was early in the morning, and on the dwarfs' previous visits at that time of day the room had been empty, but now there must have been thirty people in that place, and not one of them looked happy.

The dwarfs, who had expected to sidle into an empty taproom, found all eyes upon them.

"Goodmaster Foxen," said the tallest dwarf to the innkeeper.

"Lads," said the innkeeper, who thought that the dwarfs were boys, for all that they were four, perhaps five times his age, "I know you travel the mountain passes. We need to get out of here."

"What's happening?" said the smallest of the dwarfs.

"Sleep!" said the sot by the window.

"Plague!" said a finely dressed woman.

"Doom!" exclaimed a tinker, his saucepans rattling as he spoke. "Doom is coming!"

"We travel to the capital," said the tallest dwarf, who was no bigger than a child. "Is there plague in the capital?"

"It is not plague," said the sot by the window, whose beard was long and grey, and stained yellow with beer and wine. "It is sleep, I tell you."

"How can sleep be a plague?" asked the smallest dwarf, who was beardless.

"A witch!" said the sot.

"A bad fairy," corrected a fat-faced man.

"She was an enchantress, as I heard it," interposed the pot-girl.

"Whatever she was," said the sot, "she was not invited to a birthing celebration."

"That's all tosh," said the tinker. "She would have cursed the princess whether she'd been invited to the naming-day party or not. She was one of those forest witches, driven to the margins a thousand years ago, and a bad lot. She cursed the babe at birth, such that when the girl was eighteen she would prick her finger and sleep forever."

The fat-faced man wiped his forehead. He was sweating, although it was not warm. "As I heard it, she was going to die, but another fairy, a good one this time, commuted her magical death sentence to one of sleep. Magical sleep," he added.

"So," said the sot. "She pricked her finger on something-or-other. And she fell asleep. And the other people in the castle—the lord and the lady, the butcher, baker, milkmaid, lady-in-waiting—all of them slept, as she slept. None of them has aged a day since they closed their eyes."

"There were roses," said the pot-girl. "Roses that grew up around the castle. And the forest grew thicker, until it became impassible. This was, what, a hundred years ago?"

"Sixty. Perhaps eighty," said a woman who had not spoken until now. "I know, because my Aunt Letitia remembered it happening, when she was a girl, and she was no more than seventy when she died of the bloody flux, and that was only five years ago come Summer's End."

". . . And brave men," continued the pot-girl. "Aye, and brave women too, they say, have attempted to travel to the Forest of Acaire, to the castle at its heart, to wake the princess, and, in waking her, to wake all the sleepers, but each and every one of those heroes ended their lives lost in the forest, murdered by bandits, or impaled upon the thorns of the rosebushes that encircle the castle—"

"Wake her how?" asked the middle-sized dwarf, hand still clutching his rock, for he thought in essentials.

"The usual method," said the pot-girl, and she blushed. "Or so the tales have it."

"Right," said the tallest dwarf. "So, bowl of cold water poured on the face and a cry of 'Wakey! Wakey!'?"

"A kiss," said the sot. "But nobody has ever got that close. They've been trying for sixty years or more. They say the witch—"

"Fairy," said the fat man.

"Enchantress," corrected the pot-girl.

"Whatever she is," said the sot. "She's still there. That's what they say. If you get that close. If you make it through the roses, she'll be waiting for you. She's old as the hills, evil as a snake, all malevolence and magic and death."

16

The smallest dwarf tipped his head to one side. "So, there's a sleeping woman in a castle, and perhaps a witch or fairy there with her. Why is there also a plague?"

"Over the last year," said the fat-faced man. "It started in the north, beyond the capital. I heard about it first from travelers coming from Stede, which is near the Forest of Acaire."

"People fell asleep in the towns," said the pot-girl.

"Lots of people fall asleep," said the tallest dwarf. Dwarfs sleep rarely: twice a year at most, for several weeks at a time, but he had slept enough in his long lifetime that he did not regard sleep as anything special or unusual.

"They fall asleep whatever they are doing, and they do not wake up," said the sot. "Look at us. We fled the towns to come here. We have brothers and sisters, wives and children, sleeping now in their houses or cowsheds, at their workbenches. All of us."

"It is moving faster and faster," said the thin, red-haired woman who had not spoken previously. "Now it covers a mile, perhaps two miles, each day."

"It will be here tomorrow," said the sot, and he drained his flagon, gestured to the innkeeper to fill it once more. "There is nowhere for us to go to escape it. Tomorrow, everything here will be asleep. Some of us have resolved to escape into drunkenness before the sleep takes us."

"What is there to be afraid of in sleep?" asked the smallest dwarf. "It's just sleep. We all do it."

"Go and look," said the sot. He threw back his head, and drank as much as he could from his flagon. Then he looked back at them, with eyes unfocused, as if he were surprised to still see them there. "Well, go on. Go and look for yourselves." He swallowed the remaining drink, then he lay his head upon the table.

They went and looked.

"Asleep?" asked the queen. "Explain yourselves. How so, asleep?"

The dwarf stood upon the table so he could look her in the eye. "Asleep," he repeated. "Sometimes crumpled upon the ground. Sometimes standing. They sleep in their smithies, at their awls, on milking stools. The animals sleep in the fields. Birds, too, slept, and we saw them in trees or dead and broken in fields where they had fallen from the sky."

The queen wore a wedding gown, whiter than the snow. Around her, attendants, maids of honor, dressmakers, and milliners clustered and fussed.

"And why did you three also not fall asleep?"

The dwarf shrugged. He had a russet-brown beard that had always made the queen think of an angry hedgehog attached to the lower portion of his face. "Dwarfs are magical things. This sleep is a magical thing also. I felt sleepy, mind."

"And then?"

She was the queen, and she was questioning him as if they were alone. Her attendants began removing her gown, taking it away, folding and wrapping it, so the final laces and ribbons could be attached to it, so it would be perfect.

Tomorrow was the queen's wedding day. Everything needed to be perfect.

"By the time we returned to Foxen's Inn they were all asleep, every man jack-and-jill of them. It is expanding, the zone of the spell, a few miles every day."

The mountains that separated the two lands were impossibly high, but not wide. The queen could count the miles. She pushed one pale hand through her raven-black hair, and she looked most serious.

"What do you think, then?" she asked the dwarf. "If I went there. Would I sleep, as they did?"

He scratched his arse, unselfconsciously. "You slept for a year," he said. "And then you woke again, none the worse for it. If any of you big people can stay awake there, it's you."

Outside, the townsfolk were hanging bunting in the streets and decorating their doors and windows with white flowers. Silverware had been polished and protesting children had been forced into tubs of lukewarm water (the oldest child got the first dunk and the hottest water) and scrubbed with rough flannels until their faces were raw and red. They were then ducked under the water, and the backs of their ears were washed as well.

"I am afraid," said the queen, "that there will be no wedding tomorrow."

She called for a map of the kingdom, identified the villages closest to the mountains, sent messengers to tell the inhabitants to evacuate to the coast or risk royal displeasure.

She called for her first minister and informed him that he would be responsible for the kingdom in her absence, and that he should do his best neither to lose it nor to break it.

She called for her fiancé and told him not to take on so, and that they would still be married, even if he was but a prince and she a queen, and she chucked him beneath his pretty chin and kissed him until he smiled.

She called for her mail shirt.

She called for her sword.

She called for provisions, and for her horse, and then she rode out of the palace, towards the east.

and then she rode out of the palace, towards the east.

It was a full day's ride before she saw, ghostly and distant, like clouds against the sky, the shape of the mountains that bordered the edge of her kingdom.

The dwarfs were waiting for her, at the last inn in the foothills of the mountains, and they led her down deep into the tunnels, the way that the dwarfs travel. She had lived with them, when she was little more than a child, and she was not afraid.

The dwarfs did not speak as they walked the deep paths, except, on more than one occasion, to say, "Mind your head."

"Have you noticed," asked the shortest of the dwarfs, "something unusual?" They had names, the dwarfs, but human beings were not permitted to know what they were, such things being sacred.

The queen had a name, but nowadays people only ever called her Your Majesty. Names are in short supply in this telling.

Names are in short supply in this telling.

"I have noticed many unusual things," said the tallest of the dwarfs.

They were in Goodmaster Foxen's Inn.

"Have you noticed, that even amongst all the sleepers, there is something that does not sleep?"

"I have not," said the second tallest, scratching his beard. "For each of them is just as we left him or her. Head down, drowsing, scarcely breathing enough to disturb the cobwebs that now festoon them . . ."

"The cobweb spinners do not sleep," said the tallest dwarf.

It was the truth. Industrious spiders had threaded their webs from finger to face, from beard to table. There was a modest web between the deep cleavage of the pot-girl's breasts. There was a thick cobweb that stained the sot's beard grey. The webs shook and swayed in the draft of air from the open door.

"I wonder," said one of the dwarfs, "whether they will starve and die, or whether there is some magical source of energy that gives them the ability to sleep for a long time."

"I would presume the latter," said the queen. "If, as you say, the original spell was cast by a witch, seventy years ago, and those who were there sleep even now, like Red-Beard beneath his hill, then obviously they have not starved or aged or died."

The dwarfs nodded. "You are very wise," said a dwarf. "You always were wise."

The queen made a sound of horror and of surprise.

"That man," she said, pointing. "He looked at me."

It was the fat-faced man. He had moved slowly, tearing the webbing, moved his face so that he was facing her. He had looked at her, yes, but he had not opened his eyes.

"People move in their sleep," said the smallest dwarf.

"Yes," said the queen. "They do. But not like that. That was too slow, too stretched, too *meant*."

"Or perhaps you imagined it," said a dwarf.

The rest of the sleeping heads in that place moved slowly, in a stretched way, as if they meant to move. Now each of them was facing the queen.

"You did not imagine it," said the same dwarf. He was the one with the red-brown beard. "But they are only looking at you with their eyes closed. That is not a bad thing."

The lips of the sleepers moved in unison. No voice, only the whisper of breath through sleeping lips.

"Did they just say what I thought they said?" asked the shortest dwarf.

"They said, 'Mama. It is my birthday,'" said the queen, and she shivered.

They rode no horses. The horses they passed all slept, standing in fields, and could not be woken.

The queen walked fast. The dwarfs walked twice as fast as she did, in order to keep up.

The queen found herself yawning.

"Bend over, towards me," said the tallest dwarf. She did so. The dwarf slapped her around the face. "Best to stay awake," he said, cheerfully.

"I only yawned," said the queen.

"How long, do you think, to the castle?" asked the smallest dwarf.

"If I remember my tales and my maps correctly," said the queen, "the Forest of Acaire is about seventy miles from here. Three days' march." And then she said, "I will need to sleep tonight. I cannot walk for another three days."

"Sleep, then," said the dwarfs. "We will wake you at sunrise."

She went to sleep that night in a hayrick, in a meadow, with the dwarfs around her, wondering if she would ever wake to see another morning.

The castle in the Forest of Acaire was a grey, blocky thing, all grown over with climbing roses. They tumbled down into the moat and grew almost as high as the tallest tower. Each year the roses grew out further: close to the stone of the castle there were only dead, brown stems and creepers, with old thorns sharp as knives. Fifteen feet away, the plants were green and the blossoming roses grew thickly. The climbing roses, living and dead, were a brown skeleton, splashed with color that rendered the grey fastness less precise.

The trees in the Forest of Acaire were pressed thickly together, and the forest floor was dark. A century before, it had been a forest only in name: it had been hunting lands, a royal park, home to deer and wild boar and birds beyond counting. Now, the forest was a dense tangle, and the old paths through it were overgrown and forgotten.

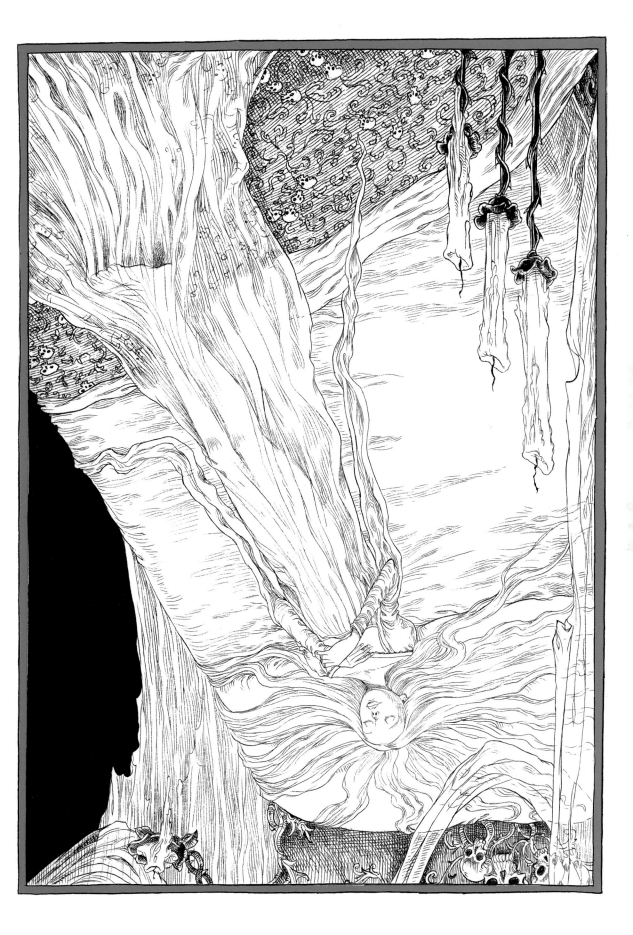

The fair-haired girl in the high tower slept.

All the people in the castle slept. Each of them was fast asleep, excepting only one.

The woman's hair was grey, streaked with white, and so sparse her scalp showed. She hobbled, angrily, through the castle, leaning on her stick, as if she were driven only by hatred, slamming doors, talking to herself as she walked. "Up the blooming stairs and past the blooming cook and what are you cooking now, eh, great lard-arse, nothing in your pots and pans but dust and more dust, and all you ever do is snore."

Into the kitchen garden, neatly tended. The old woman picked rampion and rocket.

Eighty years before, the palace had held five hundred chickens; the pigeon coop had been home to hundreds of fat, white doves; rabbits had run, white-tailed, across the greenery of the grass square inside the castle walls, while fish had swum in the moat and the pond: carp and trout and perch. There remained only three chickens. All the sleeping fish had been netted and carried out of the water. There were no more rabbits, no more doves.

She had killed her first horse sixty years back, and eaten as much of it as she could before the flesh went rainbow colored and the carcass began to stink and crawl with blueflies and maggots. Now she only butchered the larger mammals in midwinter, when nothing rotted and she could hack and sear frozen chunks of the animal's corpse until the spring thaw.

The old woman passed a mother, asleep, with a baby dozing at her breast. She dusted them, absently, as she passed and made certain that the baby's sleepy mouth remained on the nipple.

She ate her meal in silence.

She ate her meal in silence.

It was the first great, grand city they had come to. The city gates were high and impregnable thick, but they were open wide.

The three dwarfs were all for going around it, for they were uncomfortable in cities, distrusted houses and streets as unnatural things, but they followed their queen.

Once in the city, the sheer numbers of people made them uncomfortable. There were sleeping riders on sleeping horses; sleeping cabmen up on still carriages that held sleeping passengers; sleeping children clutching their balls and hoops and the whips for their spinning tops; sleeping flower women at their stalls of brown, rotten, dried flowers; even sleeping fishmongers beside their marble slabs. The slabs were covered with the remains of stinking fish, and they were crawling with maggots. The rustle and movement of the maggots was the only movement and noise the queen and the dwarfs encountered.

"We should not be here," grumbled the dwarf with the angry brown beard.

"This road is more direct than any other road we could follow," said the queen. "Also, it leads to the bridge. The other roads would force us to ford the river."

The queen's temper was equable. She went to sleep at night, and she woke in the morning, and the sleeping sickness had not touched her.

The maggots' rustlings, and, from time to time, the gentle snores and shifts of the sleepers, were all that they heard as they made their way through the city. And then a small child, asleep on a step, said, loudly and clearly, "Are you spinning? Can I see?"

"Did you hear that?" asked the queen.

The tallest dwarf said only, "Look! The sleepers are waking!"

He was wrong. They were not waking.

The sleepers were standing, however. They were pushing themselves slowly to their feet, and taking hesitant, awkward, sleeping steps. They were sleepwalkers, trailing gauze cobwebs behind them. Always, there were cobwebs being spun.

"How many people, human people I mean, live in a city?" asked the smallest dwarf.

34

"It varies," said the queen. "In our kingdom, no more than twenty, perhaps thirty thousand people. This seems bigger than our cities. I would think fifty thousand people. Or more. Why?"

"Because," said the dwarf, "they appear to all be coming after us."

Sleeping people are not fast. They stumble, they stagger; they move like children wading through rivers of treacle, like old people whose feet are weighed down by thick, wet mud.

The sleepers moved towards the dwarfs and the queen. They were easy for the dwarfs to outrun, easy for the queen to outwalk. And yet, and yet, there were so many of them. Each street they came to was filled with sleepers, cobweb-shrouded, eyes tight closed or eyes open and rolled back in their heads showing only the whites, all of them shuffling sleepily forwards.

The queen turned and ran down an alleyway, and the dwarfs ran with her.

"This is not honorable," said a dwarf. "We should stay and fight."

"There is no honor," gasped the queen, "in fighting an opponent who has no idea that you are even there. No honor in fighting someone who is dreaming of fishing or of gardens or of long-dead lovers."

"What would they do if they caught us?" asked the dwarf beside her.

"Do you wish to find out?" asked the queen.

"No," admitted the dwarf.

They ran, and they ran, and they did not stop running until they had left the city by the far gates, and had crossed the bridge that spanned the river.

The old woman had not climbed the tallest tower in a dozen years. It was a laborious climb, and each step took its toll on her knees and on her hips. She walked up the curving stone stairwell; each small, shuffling step she took in agony. There were no railings there, nothing to make the steep steps easier. She leaned on her stick, sometimes, and then she kept climbing.

She used the stick on the webs, too: thick cobwebs hung and covered the stairs, and the old woman shook her stick at them, pulling the webs apart, leaving spiders scurrying for the walls.

The climb was long and arduous, but eventually she reached the tower room.

There was nothing in the room but a spindle and a stool, beside one slitted window, and a bed in the center of the round room. The bed was opulent: crimson and gold cloth was visible beneath the dusty netting that covered it and protected its sleeping occupant from the world.

The spindle sat on the ground, beside the stool, where it had fallen seventy years before.

The old woman pushed at the netting with her stick, and dust filled the air. She stared at the sleeper on the bed.

The girl's hair was the golden yellow of meadow flowers. Her lips were the pink of the roses that climbed the palace walls. She had not seen daylight in a long time, but her skin was creamy, neither pallid nor unhealthy.

Her chest rose and fell, almost imperceptibly, in the semi-darkness.

The old woman reached down, and picked up the spindle. She said, aloud, "If I drove this spindle through your heart, then you'd not be so pretty-pretty, would you? Eh? Would you?"

She walked towards the sleeping girl in the dusty white dress. Then she lowered her hand. "No. I cannot. I wish to all the gods I could."

All of her senses were fading with age, but she thought she heard voices from the forest. Long ago she had seen them come, the princes and the heroes, watched them perish, impaled upon the thorns of the roses, but it had been a long time since anyone, hero or otherwise, had reached as far as the castle.

"Eh," she said aloud, as she said so much aloud, for who was to hear her? "Even if they come, they'll die screaming on the thorns. There's nothing they can do. That anyone can do. Nothing at all."

woodcutter, asleep by the bole of a tree half-felled half a century before, and now grown into an arch, opened his mouth as the queen and the dwarfs passed and said, "My! What an unusual naming-day present that must have been!"

Three bandits, asleep in the middle of what remained of the trail, their limbs crooked as if they had fallen asleep while hiding in a tree above and had tumbled, without waking, to the ground below, said, in unison, without waking, "Will you bring me roses?"

One of them, a huge man, fat as a bear in autumn, seized the queen's ankle as she came close to him. The smallest dwarf did not even hesitate: he lopped the hand off with his hand-axe, and the queen pulled the man's fingers away, one by one, until the hand fell on the leaf mold.

"Bring me roses," said the three bandits as they slept, with one voice, while the blood oozed indolently onto the ground from the stump of the fat man's arm. "I would be so happy if only you would bring me roses."

hey felt the castle long before they saw it, felt it as a wave of sleep that pushed them away. If they walked towards it their heads fogged, their minds frayed, their spirits fell, their thoughts clouded. The moment they turned away they woke up into the world, felt brighter, saner, wiser.

The queen and the dwarfs pushed deeper into the mental fog.

Sometimes a dwarf would yawn and stumble. Each time the other dwarfs would take him by the arms and march him forwards, struggling and muttering, until his mind returned.

The queen stayed awake, although the forest was filled with people she knew could not be there. They walked beside her on the path. Sometimes they spoke to her.

"Let us now discuss how diplomacy is affected by matters of natural philosophy," said her father.

"My sisters ruled the world," said her stepmother, dragging her iron shoes along the forest path. They glowed a dull orange, yet none of the dry leaves burned where the shoes touched them. "The mortal folk rose up against us, they cast us down. And so we waited, in crevices, in places they do not see us. And now, they adore me. Even you, my stepdaughter. Even you adore me."

"You are so beautiful," said her mother, who had died so very long ago. "Like a crimson rose in the fallen snow."

41

ometimes wolves ran beside them, pounding dust and leaves up from the forest floor, although the passage of the wolves did not disturb the huge cobwebs that hung like veils across the path. Also, sometimes the wolves ran through the trunks of trees and off into the darkness.

The queen liked the wolves, and was sad when one of the dwarfs began shouting, saying that the spiders were bigger than pigs, and the wolves vanished from her head and from the world. (It was not so. They were only spiders, of a regular size, used to spinning their webs undisturbed by time and by travelers.)

The drawbridge across the moat was down, and they crossed it, although everything seemed to be pushing them away. They could not enter the castle, however: thick thorns filled the gateway, and fresh growth was covered with roses.

The queen saw the remains of men in the thorns: skeletons in armor and skeletons unarmored. Some of the skeletons were high on the sides of the castle, and the queen wondered if they had climbed up, seeking an entry, and died there, or if they had died on the ground, and been carried upwards as the roses grew.

She came to no conclusions. Either way was possible.

And then her world was warm and comfortable, and she became certain that closing her eyes for only a handful of moments would not be harmful. Who would mind?

"Help me," croaked the queen.

The dwarf with the brown beard pulled a thorn from the rosebush nearest to him, and jabbed it hard into the queen's thumb, and pulled it out again. A drop of deep blood dripped onto the flagstones of the gateway.

"Ow!" said the queen. And then, "Thank you!"

45

hey stared at the thick barrier of thorns, the dwarfs and the queen. She reached out and picked a rose from the thorn-creeper nearest her, and bound it into her hair.

"We could tunnel our way in," said the dwarfs. "Go under the moat and into the foundations and up. Only take us a couple of days."

The queen pondered. Her thumb hurt, and she was pleased her thumb hurt. She said, "This began here eighty or so years ago. It began slowly. It only spread recently. It is spreading faster and faster. We do not know if the sleepers can ever wake. We do not know anything, save that we may not actually have another two days."

She eyed the dense tangle of thorns, living and dead, decades of dried, dead plants, their thorns as sharp in death as ever they were when alive. She walked along the wall until she reached a skeleton, and she pulled the rotted cloth from its shoulders, and felt it as she did so. It was dry, yes. It would make good kindling.

"Who has the tinderbox?" she asked.

The old thorns burned so hot and so fast. In fifteen minutes orange flames snaked upwards: they seemed, for a moment, to engulf the building, and then they were gone, leaving just blackened stone. The remaining thorns, those strong enough to have withstood the heat, were easily cut through by the queen's sword, and were hauled away and tossed into the moat.

The four travelers went into the castle.

The old woman peered out of the slitted window at the flames below her. Smoke drifted in through the window, but neither the flames nor the roses reached the highest tower. She knew that the castle was being attacked, and she would have hidden in the tower room, had there been anywhere to hide, had the sleeper not been on the bed.

She swore, and began, laboriously, to walk down the steps, one at a time. She intended to make it down as far as the castle's battlements, from where she could reach the far side of the building, the cellars. She could hide there. She knew the building better than anybody. She was slow, but she was cunning, and she could wait. Oh, she could wait.

She heard their calls rising up the stairwell.

"This way!"

"Up here!"

"It feels worse this way. Come on! Quickly!"

She turned around, then, did her best to hurry upwards, but her legs moved no faster than they had when she was climbing earlier that day. They caught her just as she reached the top of the steps: three men, no higher than her hips, closely followed by a young woman in travel-stained clothes, with the blackest hair the old woman had ever seen.

47

The young woman said, "Seize her," in a tone of casual command.

The little men took her stick. "She's stronger than she looks," said one of them, his head still ringing from the blow she had got in with the stick, before he had taken it. They walked her back into the round tower room.

"The fire?" said the old woman, who had not talked to anyone who could answer her for six decades. "Was anyone killed in the fire? Did you see the king or the queen?"

The young woman shrugged. "I don't think so. The sleepers we passed were all inside, and the walls are thick. Who are you?"

Names. Names. The old woman squinted, then she shook her head. She was herself, and the name she had been born with had been eaten by time and lack of use.

"Where is the princess?"

The old woman just stared at her.

"And why are you awake?"

She said nothing. They spoke urgently to one another then, the little men and the queen. "Is she a witch? There's a magic about her, but I do not think it's of her making."

"Guard her," said the queen. "If she is a witch, that stick might be important. Keep it from her."

"It's my stick," said the old woman. "I think it was my father's. But he had no more use for it."

The queen ignored her. She walked to the bed, pulled down the silk netting. The sleeper's face stared blindly up at them.

"So this is where it began," said one of the little men.

"On her birthday," said another.

"Well," said the third. "Somebody's got to do the honors."

"I shall," said the queen, gently. She lowered her face to the sleeping woman's. She touched the pink lips to her own carmine lips and she kissed the sleeping girl long and hard.

id it work?" asked a dwarf.

"I do not know," said the queen. "But I feel for her, poor thing. Sleeping her life away."

"You slept for a year in the same witch-sleep," said the dwarf. "You did not starve. You did not rot."

The figure on the bed stirred, as if she were having a bad dream from which she was fighting to wake herself.

The queen ignored her. She had noticed something on the floor beside the bed. She reached down and picked it up. "Now this," she said. "This smells of magic."

"There's magic all through this," said the smallest dwarf.

"No, *this*," said the queen. She showed him the wooden spindle, the base half wound around with yarn. "*This* smells of magic."

"It was here, in this room," said the old woman, suddenly. "And I was little more than a girl. I had never gone so far before, but I climbed all the steps, and I went up and up and round and round until I came to the topmost room. I saw that bed, the one you see, although there was nobody in it. There was only an old woman, sitting on the stool, spinning wool into yarn with her spindle. I had never seen a spindle before. She asked if I would like a go. She took the wool in her hand and gave me the spindle to hold. She held my thumb and pressed it against the point of the spindle until blood flowed, and she touched the blood to the thread. And then she said—"

Another voice interrupted her. A young voice it was, a girl's voice, but still sleep-thickened. "I," said, "now I take your sleep from you, girl, just as I take from you your ability to harm me in my sleep, for someone needs to be awake while I sleep. Your family, your friends, your world will sleep too. And then I lay down on the bed, and I slept, and they slept, and as each of them slept I stole a little of their life, a little of their dreams, and as I slept I took back my youth and my beauty and my power. I slept and I grew strong. I undid the ravages of time and I built myself a world of sleeping slaves."

She was sitting up in the bed. She looked so beautiful, and so very young.

The queen looked at the girl, and saw what she was searching for: the same look that she had seen in her stepmother's eyes, and she knew what manner of creature this girl was.

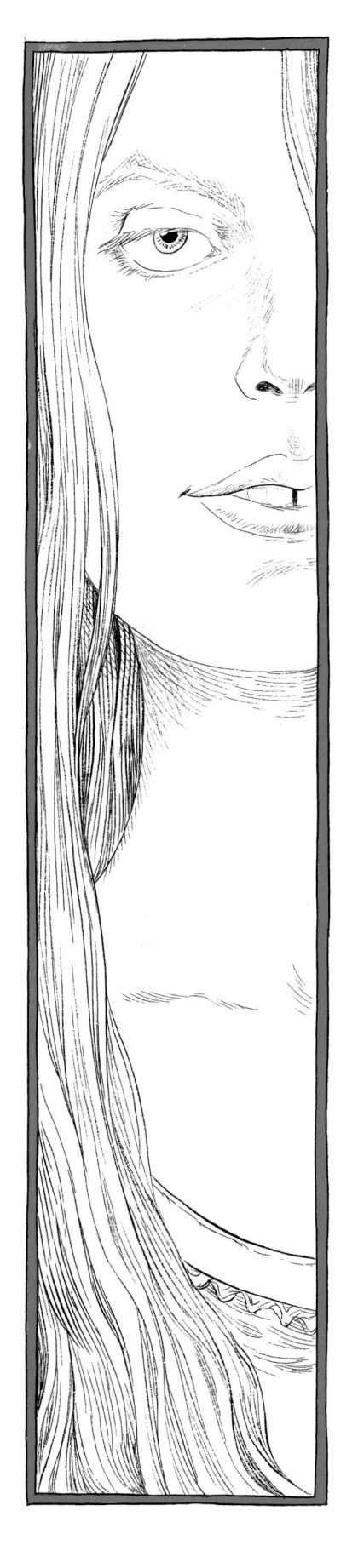

"We had been led to believe," said the tallest dwarf, "that when you woke, the rest of the world would wake with you."

"Why ever would you think that?" asked the golden-haired girl, all childlike and innocent (ah, but her eyes! Her eyes were so old). "I like them asleep. They are more . . . *biddable*." She stopped for a moment. Then she grinned. "Even now they come for you. I have called them here."

"It's a high tower," said the queen. "And sleeping people do not move fast. We still have a little time to talk, Your Darkness."

"Who are you? Why would we talk? Why do you know to address me that way?" The girl climbed off the bed and stretched deliciously, pushing each fingertip out before running her fingertips through her golden hair. She smiled, and it was as if the sun shone into that dim room. "The little people will stop where they are, now. I do not like them. And you, girl. You will sleep too."

"No," said the queen.

She hefted the spindle. The yarn wrapped around it was black with age and with time.

The dwarfs stopped where they stood, and they swayed, and closed their eyes.

The queen said, "It's always the same with your kind. You need youth and you need beauty. You used your own up so long ago, and now you find ever more complex ways of obtaining them. And you always want power."

They were almost nose to nose, now, and the fair-haired girl seemed so much younger than the queen.

"Why don't you just go to sleep?" asked the girl, and she smiled guilelessly, just as the queen's stepmother had smiled when she wanted something. There was a noise on the stairs, far below them.

"I slept for a year in a glass coffin," said the queen. "And the woman who put me there was much more powerful and dangerous than you will ever be."

"More powerful than I am?" The girl seemed amused. "I have a million sleepers under my control. With every

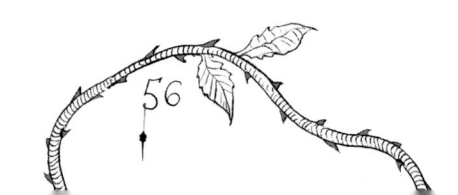

moment that I slept I grew in power, and the circle of dreams grows faster and faster with every passing day. I have my youth—so much youth! I have my beauty. No weapon can harm me. Nobody alive is more powerful than I am."

She stopped and stared at the queen.

"You are not of our blood," she said. "But you have some of the skill." She smiled, the smile of an innocent girl who has woken on a spring morning. "Ruling the world will not be easy. Nor will maintaining order among those of the Sisterhood who have survived into this degenerate age. I will need someone to be my eyes and ears, to administer justice, to attend to things when I am otherwise engaged. I will stay at the center of the web. You will not rule with me, but beneath me, but you will still rule, and rule continents, not just a tiny kingdom." She reached out a hand and stroked the queen's pale skin, which, in the dim light of that room, seemed almost as white as snow.

The queen said nothing.

"Love me," said the girl. "All will love me, and you, who woke me, you must love me most of all."

The queen felt something stirring in her heart. She remembered her stepmother, then. Her stepmother had liked to be adored. Learning how to be strong, to feel her own emotions and not another's, had been hard; but once you learned the trick of it, you did not forget. And she did not wish to rule continents.

The girl smiled at her with eyes the color of the morning sky.

The queen did not smile. She reached out her hand. "Here," she said. "This is not mine."

She passed the spindle to the old woman beside her. The old woman hefted it, thoughtfully. She began to unwrap the yarn from the spindle with arthritic fingers. "This was my life," she said. "This thread was my life. . . ."

"It *was* your life. You gave it to me," said the sleeper, irritably. "And it has gone on much too long."

The tip of the spindle was still sharp after so many decades.

The old woman, who had once been a princess, held the yarn tightly in her hand, and she thrust the point of the spindle into the golden-haired girl's breast.

59

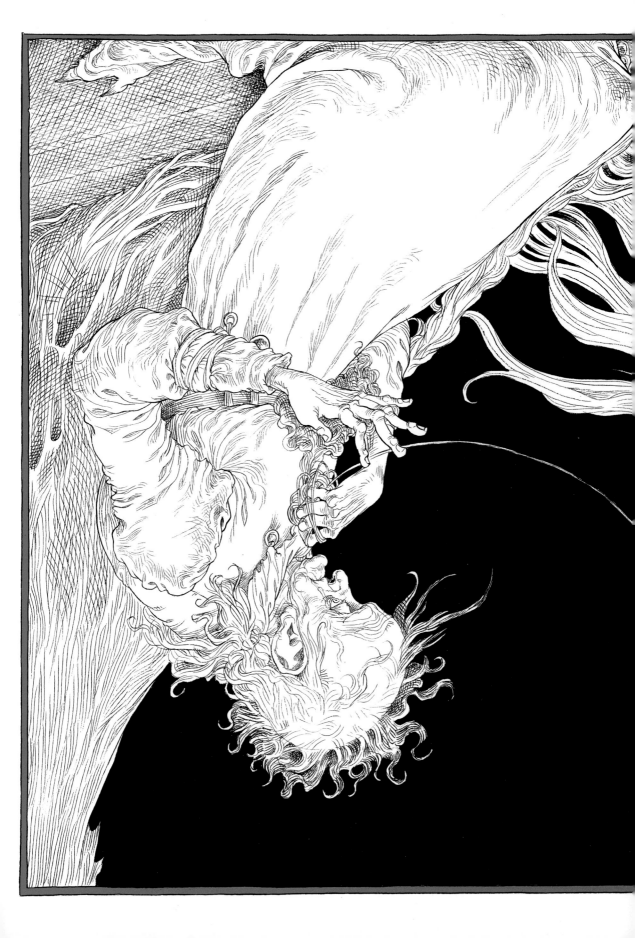

The girl watched as a trickle of red blood ran down her breast and stained her white dress crimson.

"No weapon can harm me," she said, and her girlish voice was petulant. "Not anymore. Look. It's only a scratch."

"It's not a weapon," said the queen. "It's your own magic. And a scratch is all that was needed."

The girl's blood soaked into the thread that had once been wrapped about the spindle, the thread that ran from the spindle to the raw wool in the old woman's hand.

The girl looked down at the blood staining her dress, and at the blood on the thread, and she said only, "It was just a prick of the skin, nothing more." She seemed confused.

The noise on the stairs was getting louder. A slow, irregular shuffling, as if a hundred sleepwalkers were coming up a stone spiral staircase with their eyes closed.

The room was small, and there was nowhere to hide, and the room's windows were two narrow slits in the stones.

The old woman, who had not slept in so many decades, said, "You took my dreams. You took my sleep. Now, that's enough of all that." She was a very old woman. Her fingers were gnarled, like the roots of a hawthorn bush. Her nose was long, and her eyelids drooped, but there was a look in her eyes in that moment that was the look of someone young.

She swayed, and then she staggered, and she would have fallen to the floor if the queen had not caught her first.

The queen carried the old woman to the bed, marveling at how little she weighed, and

placed her on the crimson counterpane. The old woman's chest rose and fell.

The noise on the stairs was louder now. Then a silence, followed suddenly by a hubbub, as if a hundred people were talking at once, surprised and angry and confused.

The beautiful girl said, "But—" and now there was nothing girlish or beautiful about her. Her face fell and became less shapely. She reached down to the smallest dwarf, pulled his hand-axe from his belt. She fumbled with the axe, held it up threateningly, with hands all wrinkled and worn.

The queen drew her sword (the blade's edge was notched and damaged from the thorns), but instead of striking, she took a step backwards.

"Listen! They are waking up," she said. "They are all waking up. Tell me again about the youth you stole from them. Tell me again about your beauty and your power. Tell me again how clever you were, Your Darkness."

When the people reached the tower room, they saw an old woman asleep on a bed, and they saw the queen, standing tall, and beside her, the dwarfs, who were shaking their heads, or scratching them.

They saw something else on the floor also: a tumble of bones, a hank of hair as fine and as white as fresh-spun cobwebs, a tracery of grey rags across it, and over all of it, an oily dust.

"Take care of her," said the queen, pointing with the dark wooden spindle at the old woman on the bed. "She saved your lives."

She left, then, with the dwarfs. None of the people in that room or on the steps dared to stop them or would ever understand what had happened.

A mile or so from the castle, in a clearing in the Forest of Acaire, the queen and the dwarfs lit a fire of dry twigs, and in it they burned the thread and the fiber. The smallest dwarf chopped the spindle into fragments of black wood with his axe, and they burned them too. The wood chips gave off a noxious smoke as they burned, which made the queen cough, and the smell of old magic was heavy in the air.

Afterwards, they buried the charred wooden fragments beneath a rowan tree.

By evening they were on the outskirts of the forest, and had reached a cleared track. They could see a village across the hill, and smoke rising from the village chimneys.

"So," said the dwarf with the brown beard. "If we head due west, we can be at the mountains by the end of the week, and we'll have you back in your palace in Kanselaire within ten days."

"Yes," said the queen.

"And your wedding will be late, but it will happen soon after your return, and the people will celebrate, and there will be joy unbounded through the kingdom."

"Yes," said the queen. She said nothing, but sat on the moss beneath an oak tree and tasted the stillness, heartbeat by heartbeat.

There are choices, she thought, when she had sat long enough. *There are always choices.*

She made one.

The queen began to walk, and the dwarfs followed her.

"You *do* know we're heading east, don't you?" said one of the dwarfs.

"Oh yes," said the queen.

"Well, *that's* all right then," said the dwarf.

They walked to the east, all four of them, away from the sunset and the lands they knew, and into the night.

They walked to the
east,
all four of them, away
from the sunset and
the lands they knew,
and
into
the
Night.

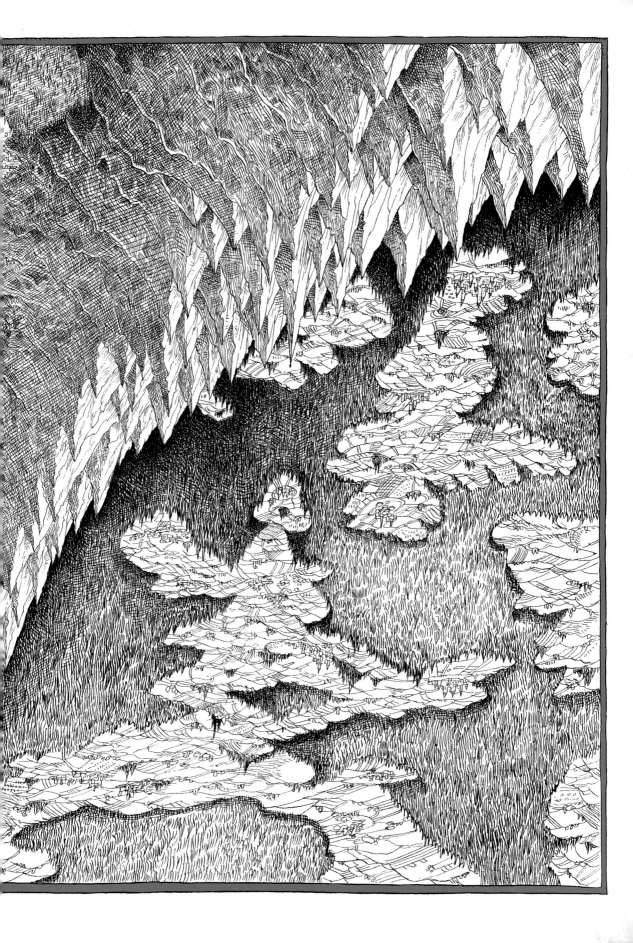

The Sleeper and the Spindle

OTHER BOOKS BY NEIL GAIMAN

Coraline

The Graveyard Book

Fortunately, the Milk

M Is for Magic

Odd and the Frost Giants

Stardust

Unnatural Creatures

Blueberry Girl

Crazy Hair

The Dangerous Alphabet

The Day I Swapped My Dad for Two Goldfish

Instructions

MirrorMask

The Wolves in the Walls

CHU BOOKS

Chu's Day

Chu's First Day of School

Chu's Day at the Beach

to bring suit against the law firm of Lyon & Lyon, American Honda's former general counsel, and two of its partners, Roland Smoot and James Short, who, Batchelder claims, assisted in "covering up" the fraudulent scheme. Batchelder has asserted "shareholder" derivative claims for breach of duty, waste of corporate assets, abuse of control, constructive fraud, mismanagement, and dissemination of false and misleading proxy statements in violation of *United States Code*, title 15, § 78n(a).

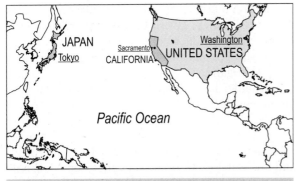

MAP 5-6   California and Japan (1998)

Following the Director Defendants' motion to dismiss, the district court entered a scheduling order staying all discovery in the case pending its resolution. Thereafter, American Honda and Lyon & Lyon also filed motions to dismiss on numerous grounds. Following a hearing, the district court dismissed Batchelder's complaint with prejudice. The district court ruled that Batchelder's complaint failed as a matter of law because, *inter alia:* (1) based on the Deposit Agreement, Batchelder's standing to bring a derivative action must be determined under Japanese law; [and] (2) under Japanese law, Batchelder is not a shareholder and therefore lacks standing to bring a derivative action on behalf of Honda Japan. . . .

Batchelder timely appealed.

II

Batchelder maintains that the district court erred in holding that he lacks standing to bring a shareholder derivative action on behalf of Honda Japan and American Honda. According to Batchelder, the district court erroneously held that his "standing and his right to bring a derivative action . . . must be determined under Japanese law," and wrongly concluded that, as an owner of Honda Japan ADRs, he "is not a shareholder and lacks standing to bring a derivative action on behalf of Honda . . . under governing Japanese law." Batchelder contends that whereas Japanese law provides the substantive law to adjudicate his claims against the Director Defendants, it

does not control his standing to bring California and federal claims on behalf of Honda Japan and American Honda. According to Batchelder, the district court must perform "the requisite conflicts of law analysis" to determine what law governs his right to bring a derivative suit. Batchelder contends that either the *Federal Rules of Civil Procedure*, Rule 23.1 ("Derivative Actions by Shareholders") or the California *Corporation Code* § 800 ("Shareholder Derivative Actions") provides the standing requirements for his claim, not Japanese law.

A

Batchelder's right to bring derivative claims on behalf of Honda Japan and American Honda is indeed governed by Japanese law. Batchelder purchased his ADRs pursuant to the Deposit Agreement, which expressly provides that the law of Japan governs shareholder rights. Section 7.07 of the Deposit Agreement, entitled "Governing Law," states:

> This Deposit Agreement and the [American Depository] Receipts and all rights hereunder and thereunder and provisions hereof and thereof shall be governed by and construed in accordance with the laws of the state of New York, United States of America. It is understood that notwithstanding any present or future provision of the laws of the state of New York, *the rights of holders of Stock and other Deposited Securities, and the duties and obligations of the Company in respect of such holders, as such, shall be governed by the laws of Japan.* (Emphasis added).

The first sentence of § 7.07 provides that contract rights contained in the Deposit Agreement itself or in the ADR certificates, as well as the construction of the Deposit Agreement, are to be governed by the laws of New York. The second sentence of § 7.07, however, explicitly provides that Japanese law governs shareholder rights and the rights of holders of other Deposited Securities, including ADRs. Thus, if an ADR holder seeks to assert a right belonging to shareholders or a right not specifically granted to ADR holders in the Deposit Agreement, the laws of Japan apply. Section 7.07 is simply a choice-of-law clause.

1. We analyze the validity of choice-of-law clauses under *The Bremen v. Zapata Off-Shore Co.*,[183] in which the Supreme Court stated that courts should enforce choice-of-law and choice-of-forum clauses in cases of "freely negotiated private international agreements." There is every reason to believe that the Depository Agreement was such an agreement. . . .

Batchelder has never contended that the Deposit Agreement itself grants ADR holders the right to bring shareholder derivative claims. He argues instead that he is

---

[183]*United States Reports*, vol. 407, p. 1 (Supreme Ct., 1972).

entitled to bring derivative claims because he "is a Honda shareholder" through his ownership of ADRs. Because Batchelder is attempting to assert a right not expressly granted to him by the Deposit Agreement—the right to bring a derivative suit—the plain language of the second sentence of § 7.07 directs this court to apply Japanese law to determine the existence and scope of Batchelder's right. No conflicts-of-law analysis is required.

***

III

Batchelder next argues that, even under Japanese law, he is a Honda Japan shareholder who is entitled to bring suit on behalf of the parent company *and* assert a double derivative claim on behalf of its subsidiary, American Honda. According to Batchelder, the district court "ignored the fact that ADRs are the equivalent of shares of a foreign corporation and ADR holders are equivalent to a shareholder [sic] of that corporation, whether under Japanese law or U.S. law." Batchelder further maintains that the district court erred in finding that he failed properly to assert "double derivative" claims on behalf of Honda Japan and American Honda. He contends that the district court also "ignored the fact that California substantive law applies to derivative claims asserted by Batchelder on behalf of American Honda" as well as "numerous precedents recognizing the validity of 'double derivative' claims under these circumstances."

Article 267 of the Japanese *Commercial Code*, which establishes the derivative remedy, states:

1. Any shareholder who has held a share continuously for the last six months may demand, in writing, that the stock company institute an action to enforce the liability of directors.

2. If the stock company has failed to institute such action within thirty days from the date on which the demand referred to in the preceding paragraph was made, the shareholder referred to in the preceding paragraph may institute such action on behalf of the company.

Notwithstanding his concessions that he holds ADRs, not shares, in Honda Japan, and that Article 267 confers derivative standing only on "any shareholder," Batchelder claims, that as an ADR holder, he is "equivalent to a shareholder" and should have been permitted to proceed with his derivative suit. The weight of authority, however, is against him.

Honda's Japanese law experts testified that only shareholders appearing on Honda Japan's shareholders' register may institute a derivative action under Article 267(1). "ADR holders are not shareholders of record" under Japanese law and therefore "are not allowed to make the demand and then institute a derivative action." According to one of Honda's experts, Professor Kitazawa, "the law on this point is undisputed; I know of no case or scholarly opinion that argues otherwise." Another of Honda's experts stated unequivocally that "Under Japanese law, a holder of [ADRs] would not be considered under Japanese law to be a registered shareholder and, therefore, would have no right or power to make the requisite pre-suit demand or to initiate the instant derivative litigation."

Batchelder has submitted no authority to compel a different conclusion.

***

In light of the foregoing, the district court correctly found that Batchelder lacked standing as an ADR holder under Japanese law to bring his shareholder derivative action on behalf of Honda Japan.

***

For the foregoing reasons, we conclude that the district court did not err in holding that Batchelder, as an ADR holder, lacks standing to bring a shareholder derivative suit on behalf of Honda Japan. . . . The district court's dismissal of Batchelder's action is therefore AFFIRMED.

CASEPOINT: A U.S. citizen holding an ADR receipt for shares of a Japanese company has rights defined by the deposit agreement. In this case, the agreement specified that shareholders' rights are defined by Japanese law. Thus, there is no conflicts-of-law"analysis to perform here; under Japanese law, an owner of an ADR is not a shareholder of record and cannot bring a shareholder's derivative suit.

Many depository agreements include a disclaimer that there is no guarantee that ADR holders will receive proxy materials in sufficient time to vote. It is a standard term of depositary agreements that ADR holders will have the right to vote only if the issuer formally requests the depositary to ask ADR holders for their votes. Some agreements even provide that if ADR holders do not vote, these shares will be assigned to the issuer's management to vote at its discretion.[184]

---

[184]See generally Vincent Duhamel, "Shareholder Rights and the Equitable Treatment of Shareholders, Fourth Asian Roundtable on Corporate Governance," available at http://www.oecd.org/dataoecd/49/12/2484854.pdf, p. 6 (2002).

INSIDER TRADING REGULATIONS

Insider trading: The use of material nonpublic information about a company or the securities market to buy or sell securities for personal gain.

Insider trading occurs when someone takes advantage of material nonpublic information about a corporation or the securities market to buy or sell securities for personal benefit. Some countries (notably the United States, Canada, the United Kingdom, and Germany)[185] regard insider trading as unjust and dishonest. For example, during the U.S. congressional hearings leading up to the adoption of the 1934 Securities Exchange Act that criminalized insider trading, a Senate committee observed:

> Among the most vicious practices unearthed at the hearings before the subcommittee was the flagrant betrayal of their fiduciary duties by directors and officers of corporations who used their positions of trust and the confidential information which came to them in such positions, to aid them in their market activities.[186]

This is not the uniform view, however. Many other countries look upon insider trading as a normal business practice.[187]

The U.S. prohibitions against insider trading are found in Section 10(b) of the Securities Exchange Act of 1934 and in the Securities and Exchange Commission's Rule 10b-5, which implements Section 10(b) of the 1934 act.[188] These forbid an **insider** (e.g., a corporate officer, director, or majority shareholder) who has access to material nonpublic information from buying or selling shares for his or her own account when the person knows that the information is unavailable to the person or persons with whom he or she is dealing. In addition, a **tipper** who has inside information that he or she discloses to a tippee and a **tippee** who acts on that information, knowing that it is not available to the public, are both liable for the profits made by the tippee.[189]

insider: A person, such as a corporate officer, director, or majority shareholder, who has access to material nonpublic information about a company or the securities market.

tipper: A person who has access to material nonpublic information about a company or the securities market and who discloses it to a tippee.

tippee: A person who acts for his or her personal account on information received from a tipper knowing that the information is not available to the public.

material: According to U.S. law, when something is of significance to a reasonable person (i.e., an investor).

Courts interpreting these provisions have held that information is **material** when it is such that a reasonable investor would act upon it, and information becomes *public* once it becomes available to the general public (although an insider must refrain from trading for a "reasonable waiting period" to allow news to be translated into investment action).

The United Kingdom's prohibitions on insider trading are found in the 1985 Company Securities (Insider Dealing) Act, in particular Chapter 8, Section 1. Insiders are defined as persons who are knowingly connected with a company (or were knowingly connected with a company in the past six months). They are forbidden from trading in the shares of the company if they have information that they know to be generally unavailable and that is likely to materially affect the price of the company's shares.[190] Insiders are also forbidden from trading in the shares of another company when they acquire information about that company as a result of its negotiations with their own firm. Additionally, tippees are forbidden from using the information they obtain from these insiders.

---

[185] The German Securities Trading Act defining and criminalizing insider trading came into effect on August 1, 1994. *Bundesgesetzblatt*, vol. I, p. 1749. India adopted similar legislation that came into effect in February 1992. See http://www.itcportal.com/careers_with_itc/code_intrade.html.

[186] Report of the Committee on Banking and Currency, "Stock Exchange Practices," Senate Report No. 1455, 73rd Congress, Second Session, p. 55 (1934).

[187] Countries with small exchanges generally pay little attention to insider trading because few companies are publicly owned and those that are publicly traded are generally owned by only a limited number of individuals. For a recent comparative study of insider trading, see "Do Insider Trading Laws Matter? Some Preliminary Comparative Evidence" by Laura Nyantung Beny in the *American Law and Economics Review*, vol 7, pp. 144–183, (Spring 2005).

[188] See http://www.sec.gov/answers/insider.htm.

[189] Usually insider traders are persons with an employment or other relationship of trust with the corporation, but they do not have to be. Thus, in United States v. Carpenter, *United States Reports*, vol. 484, p. 19 (1987), the U.S. Supreme Court held that a columnist for the *Wall Street Journal* who tipped information about what would be in his investment advice column to tippees before the column appeared in print was liable, as an insider and a tipper, for the profits made by the tippees.

[190] In the United Kingdom, the relevant laws are the Financial Services Act of 1986 and the Financial Services and Markets Act of 2000, which defines an offense of market abuse. It is not illegal to fail to trade based on inside information (whereas without the inside information the trade would have taken place, since from a practical point of view this is too difficult to enforce). It is often legal to deal ahead of a takeover bid, where a party deliberately buys shares in a company in the knowledge that it will be launching a takeover bid.

material: According to British law, when the price of something (i.e., a security) would be significantly affected.

Whereas the British law has some similarities to the American law, it is also very different. Individual victims have no civil remedy in Britain (as they do in the United States). Also, the **materiality** of inside information is ascertained by a different standard. Rather than looking to whether "a reasonable man would attach importance [to the particular information] in determining his choice of action in the transaction in question,"[191] as is done in the United States, the British law asks whether the information would affect the price of a security[192] Finally, violation of the law does not, of itself, make a transaction void.

Japan's insider trading provisions are found in Article 58 of its Securities and Exchange Law. This article parallels Section 10(b) of the United States Securities Exchange Act, making insider transactions voidable if they are based on deceit and making directors liable for damages if their conduct amounts to bad faith or gross negligence. However, like the British act, Article 58 does not provide for civil remedies.

Despite the existence of this legislation, traditionally Japanese law did not view insider trading as improper, and its insider trading provisions were seldom enforced. In the late 1980s, however, several scandals—including one that involved the passing of insider information to politicians—brought about calls for reform; and in 1988 the Securities Exchange Law was amended to give it more teeth. The Ministry of Finance, the agency responsible for enforcing the law, can now require "the issuer of a security listed on the stock exchange, as well as the stock exchange itself, to submit reports concerning the operation of the exchange. . . ."[193] In 2006, Japan's Upper House of Parliament passed legislation bringing stiffer penalties for insider trading, market manipulation, and accounting fraud as a direct result of the scandals involving Yoshiaki Murakami, former head of MAC Asset Management, and Livedoor's ex-CEO, Takafumi Horie. The revised penalties include a maximum five-year prison sentence for insider trading or a ¥5 million (US $43,900) fine, increased from three years and ¥3 million previously.[194]

France, like Japan, also had a tradition of ignoring insider trading violations that was brought to an end by scandals implicating some of its senior politicians.[195] In 1989, it amended its insider trading laws to give the Commission des Opérations de Bourse (the Stock Exchange Oversight Commission) authority "to require the production of documents and testimony from any person" and to impose civil sanctions, in addition to its existing authority to bring criminal charges.[196]

TAKEOVER REGULATIONS

Financiers became actively involved in foreign acquisitions, mergers, and takeovers in the 1980s. British, Canadian, and Japanese corporate raiders made headlines for bidding on or taking over American entertainment, liquor, and publishing businesses. At the same time, efforts by American raiders to reciprocate were usually rebuffed. T. Boone Pickens' failure to gain a seat on the board of directors of the Japanese firm of Koito Manufacturing in 1988 is one such example.

The reason foreign raiders were generally successful in the United States but unsuccessful elsewhere is that securities regulations outside the United States are biased against takeovers. Common barriers to takeover attempts are (1) restrictions on share transferability, (2) cross-ownership of shares, and (3) restrictions on the voting rights of publicly held shares.

---

[191]List v. Fashion Park, Inc., *Federal Reporter, Second Series*, vol. 340, p. 457 at p. 462 (2nd Circuit Ct. of Appeals, 1965), *certiorari* denied, *United States Reports*, vol. 382, p. 811 (Supreme Court, 1965).

[192]Company Securities Act, 1985, chap. 8, § 1(1)(c).

[193]Tomoko Akashi, "Regulation of Insider Trading in Japan," *Columbia Law Review*, vol. 89, p. 1296 at p. 1304 (1989).

[194]See http://www.asialaw.com/default.asp?Page=20&PUB=68&ISS0=22451&SID=649605.

[195]James A. Kehoe, "Exporting Insider Trading Laws: The Enforcement of U.S. Insider Trading Laws Internationally," *Emory International Law Review*, vol. 9, p. 345 at pp. 356–357 (1995).

[196]Michael D. Mann and Lise A. Lustgarten, "Internationalization of Insider Trading Enforcement—A Guide to Regulation and Cooperation," in American Bar Association National Institute on White Collar Crime, *White Collar Crime*, p. 511 at p. 555 (1990).

In the United States and the United Kingdom, stock exchange listing requirements prohibit restrictions on the transferability of shares of publicly held companies.[197] This is not the case in other countries. In Canada, for example, publicly offered shares may contain restrictions prohibiting their sale to non-Canadians.[198] French law allows a *société anonyme* (SA) to forbid the transfer of its shares without the company's consent.[199] And in Switzerland, a corporation can go so far as to prohibit any transfer of registered shares.[200]

Cross-ownership of shares is the placing of large blocks of stock in friendly hands to protect against a hostile takeover. In Japan, cross-ownership of shares is a prevalent practice, although its use now is much less common than it was before World War II.[201]

Voting restrictions on publicly held shares also inhibit takeovers. Continental European corporation statutes impose caps on the total percentage of shares any one owner may vote. For example, in Belgium, no single shareholder may cast more than one-fifth of the total votes.[202] A similar restriction applies in Germany.[203]

In contrast to the countries with takeover barriers, the countries with an active acquisition marketplace—notably the United Kingdom and the United States—have legislation or exchange rules that directly regulate the takeover process.[204] The goal of such regulations is neutrality: to put the raider and the management of the target company on a roughly equal footing.

Without takeover barriers or takeover regulations, the takeover process is weighted heavily in favor of the raider. For example, in the United States, prior to the enactment of the Williams Act of 1968,[205] a tender offer (i.e., a raider's offer to buy publicly held shares) was governed by the principle of *caveat venditor*.[206] The offeror was free to define the terms and conditions of his offer and to hold offerees (shareholders) to a binding contract from the moment they accepted. Commonly, the offer was held open for only a short period of time to exclude the possibility that a competing offer might appear or that the target firm's management could take some defensive action. It was also subject to a variety of conditions that allowed the offeror to back out if he was unable to complete the takeover to his satisfaction. In essence, the offerees were faced with a take-it-or-leave-it proposition, and the target firm's management had little ability to protect itself, while the raider's risks were minimal.

Williams Act: Law enacted by the United States in 1968 that authorizes the Securities and Exchange Commission to issue rules regulating takeover bids.

In the United States, the **Williams Act** attempts to put the contestants on a level playing field by authorizing the Securities and Exchange Commission (SEC) to issue rules governing tender offers for securities of companies registered under the Securities Exchange Act of 1934. The Williams Act and the SEC's rules require an offeror to disclose information about his finances and his reasons for attempting a takeover either before or at the time he announces his offer, and the target's management must be given time to circulate its views on the proposal. The offer must be kept open for a minimum period, and if the offer is for less than all of a target's shares, it may not be accepted on a "first-come, first-served" basis. An

---

[197]Deborah A. Demott, "Comparative Dimensions of Takeover Regulation," *Washington University Law Quarterly*, vol. 65, p. 69 at p. 76 (1987). In the United States, the New York Stock Exchange and the Pacific Exchange prohibit the listing of stock with limitations on transferability. Other exchanges permit such restrictions. *Id.*, p. 74.

[198]See, e.g., Ontario Business Corporations Act, § 42(2) available at http://www.elaws.gov.on.ca/DBLaws/StatEnglish/90b16_e.htm.

[199]French *Code des Sociètés*, Article 274. For more details,see http://www.formacompany.com/france-company-incorporations/france-transfer-of-shares.html.

[200]See "Doing Business in Europe," *Common Market Reporter*, para. 29,215 (summarizing the Swiss Code of Obligations).

[201]For more details about cross-ownership of shares in Japan, read "Networking in Japan: The Case of Keiretsu," by Richard W. Wright, posted at http://www.cic.sfu.ca/forum/wright.html.

[202]See "Doing Business in Europe," *Common Market Reporter*, para. 21,256 (summarizing the Belgian *Commercial Companies Code*). See http://www.nasdaq.com/about/GP2005Europe_Chapter_9.pdf.

[203]*Id.*, at para. 23,213. See http://www.nasdaq.com/about/GP2005Europe_Chapter_11.pdf.

[204]An excellent summary and comparison of the takeover regulations of Australia, Canada, the United Kingdom, and the United States can be found in Deborah A. Demott, "Comparative Dimensions of Takeover Regulation," *Washington University Law Quarterly*, vol. 65, p. 69 (1987) and posted at http://eprints.law.duke.edu/archive/00000049/01/ 65_Wash._U._L._Q._69_(1987).pdf.

[205]See http://law.jrank.org/pages/11330/Williams-Act.html.

[206]Latin: "let the seller beware."

oversubscribed offer must be allocated among tendering subscribers on a pro rata basis. Also, subscribers may withdraw the shares they have tendered within specified time limits. Finally, anyone who acquires more than 5 percent of a publicly traded company's equity securities must disclose his holdings within ten days after the acquisition.[207]

One important aspect of the Williams Act is that it does not restrict the ability of offerors to set conditions that allow them to withdraw their offer. As a consequence, American offerors commonly include in their offers terms that permit them to revoke their offers if financing is unavailable, or too expensive, or their offers are challenged in court.

On the other hand, the Williams Act does not restrict the defensive actions that a target's management may take.[208] The restrictions that do exist are imposed by the states and principally by the state courts. In Delaware and New York, the two states whose courts have addressed the issue most extensively, management is allowed to take any defensive measure that complies with the business judgment rule. That rule allows management to exercise reasonable business discretion, so long as it does so in the best interest of the corporation as a whole.[209]

Takeovers in the United Kingdom are regulated by the London Stock Exchange's **City Code on Takeovers and Mergers** that is issued by the Exchange's Panel on Takeovers and Mergers. The City Code is similar to the Williams Act in that it (1) requires extensive disclosure by offerors, (2) sets a minimum duration for offers, (3) requires prorated acceptance for oversubscribed partial offers, and (4) grants tendering shareholders limited withdrawal rights. Unlike the Williams Act, it regulates conditions set by the offeror, and it forbids conditions "depending solely on subjective judgments by the directors of the offeror." Also, partial offers may be made only with the consent of the panel, and an offeror who acquires more than 30 percent of the shares of a target must offer to buy out the remaining shareholders at the highest price paid during the previous year for comparable shares. Finally, the responses that a target's board of directors may take are more structured. The board, to which the offeror must initially make his offer, has to obtain "competent independent advice" on the offer and share that advice both with its own shareholders and, if requested, any other legitimate offeror. The target board must also obtain shareholder approval of any defensive action it takes that is intended to frustrate a takeover bid.

City Code on Takeovers and Mergers: Rules of the London Stock Exchange issued by the Exchange's Panel on Takeovers and Mergers that regulate takeover bids.

> The text of the London Stock Exchange's City Code on Takeovers and Mergers is posted at http://www.cityandfinancial.com/assets/documents/20060421161725City_Code_WEB.pdf.

[207] *United States Code*, Title 15, § 78m(d) available at http://frwebgate.acc.ess.gpo.gov/cgi-bin/getdoc.cgi?dbname=browse _usc&docid=Cite:+15USC78m.

[208] Examples of immediate defenses to a takeover bid are (a) the *self tender* (an offer by a target to buy its own stock from its shareholders to maintain control); (b) the *white knight* defense (the target arranges a favorable merger with another company); (c) the *Pac Man* defense (the target offers to purchase the raiding corporation); (d) greenmail (the target offers to buy the stock bought by the raider at a premium); and (e) a suit for an injunction (the target claims that the resulting merger or consolidation would violate some state or federal statute, such as the federal antitrust laws).

Long-term tactics that make a corporation more generally unattractive to takeover bids are (a) the *scorched earth* ploy (the target arranges to sell off its principal assets or it has loans that become due immediately after a takeover occurs); (b) the *shark repellent* scheme (the target changes its charter or bylaws to require a higher than normal shareholder vote to approve a merger or consolidation); (c) the *poison pill* (the target's shares are redeemable for cash in the event of a takeover); and (d) *golden parachutes* (which provide for high payments to officers and directors in the event that they are discharged or demoted).

[209] See Unocal Corp. v. Mesa Petroleum Co., *Atlantic Reporter, Second Series,* vol. 493, p. 946 (Delaware Supreme Ct., 1985); and Norlin Corp. v. Rooney, Pace, Inc., *Federal Reporter, Second Series*, vol. 744, p. 255 (2nd Circuit Ct. of Appeals, 1984) (applying New York law).

D. ENFORCEMENT OF SECURITIES REGULATIONS INTERNATIONALLY

International cooperation in the enforcement of securities regulations is a relatively recent development. In 1961, the Organization for Economic Cooperation and Development (OECD) adopted a Code of Liberalization of Capital Movements,[210] which it hoped would abolish stock exchange restrictions among its member states. Many members, however, filed reservations to the code, demonstrating that attitudes about securities regulations were then too diverse for the international community to agree upon a single regulatory mechanism. Also, the code had no effective enforcement provisions, and the OECD member states, in practice, ignored it.[211]

Until the 1980s, no other attempts were made to establish any formal mechanism of international cooperation. Then the United States began pushing its major trading partners to enter into cooperative agreements, and the Council of Europe began work on an insider trading convention.

MEMORANDUMS OF UNDERSTANDING

The U.S. efforts have centered on securing *memorandums of understanding* (*MOUs*), which it regards as the most feasible tool for preventing international securities fraud and enforcing compliance with its own domestic disclosure rules. During the 1980s, it entered into MOUs with Switzerland, the United Kingdom, and Japan.

The U.S.-Swiss MOU is a unilateral agreement designed to overcome Switzerland's banking secrecy laws. Under the MOU, the American SEC can ask the Swiss Bankers Association to provide information and to freeze insider trading profits deposited in a Swiss bank account. In making its request, the SEC must (1) show that it has reasonable grounds for suspecting insider trading that would violate both American and Swiss law, (2) place all of its evidence before the Swiss Bankers Association, and (3) promise not to disclose any information provided by the association except in connection with the enforcement of its insider trading laws. It is up to the Swiss Bankers Association, however, to decide if the SEC has an adequate case; and, if it decides that the SEC does not, it can refuse to honor the request.[212]

Unlike the Swiss agreement, the U.S.-U.K. MOU is a bilateral agreement designed to help both countries enforce their securities (and futures) laws through information sharing. The U.S.-U.K. MOU defines securities transactions broadly: (1) it does not require a violation of both U.S. and U.K. laws; (2) local authorities are to honor a request for information unless they can show "substantial grounds" in writing why it should be denied; and (3) both countries have an affirmative duty to turn over any information they discover that points to a violation of the other country's laws even without a request.

The U.S.-Japanese MOU is both brief and informal. Both sides promise to "facilitate . . . requests for surveillance and investigatory information on a case-by-case basis," but no mechanism for making or honoring requests is established. The MOU only requires that the parties use "good faith" in working out their procedural differences, as that becomes "necessary or appropriate."

THE CONVENTION ON INSIDER TRADING

In 1983, the Council of Europe sponsored a colloquy in Milan, Italy, to review national regulations and to examine the deficiencies in international law with respect to insider trading. The colloquy led to the appointment of a Committee of Experts (drawn from the council's

---

[210]See http://www.oecd.org/dataoecd/10/62/4844455.pdf.
[211]*International Capital Markets and Securities Regulations*, vol. 10, §2. 02 (Harold S. Blumenthal and Samuel Wolff, eds., 1982).
[212]Memorandum of Understanding to Establish Mutually Acceptable Means for Improving International Law Enforcement Cooperation in the Field of Insider Trading, August 31, 1982, United States-Switzerland, reprinted in *International Legal Materials*, vol. 22, p. 1 (1983)

member states, Finland, the United States, and the Commission of the European Community) to draft a convention on insider trading. On April 20, 1989, the council formally adopted the Convention on Insider Trading[213] and opened it for signature.

The convention's purpose is to assist the regulatory agencies of its signatory states by establishing a mechanism for the exchange of information so that those agencies can better supervise their securities markets. In particular, "because of the internationalization of markets and the ease of present-day communications," it focuses on uncovering the insider trading activities "on the market of a state by persons not resident in that state or acting through persons not resident there."[214] The convention does not attempt to establish uniform enforcement provisions or sanctions.

In essence, the convention allows one state to request the assistance of another in uncovering conduct by an individual or individuals in the latter's territory that constitutes insider trading in the requesting state. The requesting state must make a full disclosure of the facts that lead it to believe that insider trading has taken place, and it must state what it will do with the information it receives.[215] The state receiving the request then follows the procedures set up by its own laws in responding to the request, subject to an overall obligation to keep both the request and the assistance it provides secret. The requested state can refuse to honor a request if it is too broad or if the conduct described does not constitute a violation of both states' insider trading rules.[216]

EXTRATERRITORIAL APPLICATION OF U.S. SECURITIES LAWS

One important example of the many attempts to apply securities regulations internationally has been the enforcement of U.S. securities laws extraterritorially. Consideration of this is especially important because American laws apply to a much wider range of activities than those of any other country. The U.S. Securities Act of 1933 requires companies to disclose their financial standing before issuing new shares. The Securities and Exchange Act of 1934 requires managers and owners of large percentages of stock to disclose their ownership interests, and it forbids insider trading and other fraudulent securities transactions. The Williams Act requires corporate raiders to disclose their finances and their reasons for making a takeover bid.

To ensure that persons operating outside the United States do not avoid these laws, the SEC and the U.S. Department of Justice (which are responsible for their enforcement) have regularly instituted suits involving nonresident aliens. This has forced courts to determine if the U.S. securities laws give them the necessary jurisdiction to hear these cases.

---

[213]See Council of Europe, Convention on Insider Trading (1989), available at http://conventions.coe.int/Treaty/en/ Treaties/Html/130.htm.
[214]Council of Europe, Convention on Insider Trading, Preamble.
[215]*Id.*, Exchange of Information, Article 5.
[216]By a special declaration, a signatory state can—subject to reciprocity—agree to provide information on all types of securities regulations, not just insider trading.

Chapter Questions

Approval of Foreign Investment Applications

1. Overseas Investment Co. (OIC), a multinational enterprise with its headquarters in State W, entered into a joint venture with Investment Promotions Facility, Ltd. (IPF), a state-owned company whose board of directors and principal officers had been appointed by the minister of finance of State X. The joint venture agreement provided that, in the event of any dispute, the dispute would be resolved by arbitration. Additionally, because the law of State X says that all foreign investment agreements must be approved by the minister of finance, the minister was present at the signing of the agreement; and after representatives of the two parties put their signatures on the document, the foreign minister added the words "approved and ratified" and his own signature.

Unfortunately, a dispute did arise, and OIC initiated an arbitration proceeding according to the procedures set out in the joint venture agreement, naming both IPF and State X as parties. State X responded by arguing that the arbitration tribunal has no jurisdiction over it. Should State X be excused from participating in the suit? Discuss.

Import Duties in Free Trade Zones

2. The Video Assembly Co. (VAC), a company organized in State Z, entered into an agreement with the U.S. government to assemble video cassette recorders from foreign manufactured parts inside a U.S. FTZ. Before this could be done, however, VAC had to set up an assembly plant. Rather than using an American facility, it imported a completely prefabricated plant. The plant consisted of the building, all of the assembly and packaging equipment, and all of the ancillary tools. The U.S. Customs Service claims that the plant itself did not qualify for exemption from customs duties at the time it came into the FTZ because it was not "merchandise" for assembly, as required by U.S. law, and the Customs Service levied duties on the plant. VAC has appealed to the U.S. Court of International Trade, asking for an order compelling the Customs Service to return the duties it collected. How should the court rule? Discuss.

Modification of Foreign Investment Agreements

3. The Modern Exploration Co. (MEC), a firm organized in State P, entered into an investment contract with State Q to explore for and harvest magnesium nodules from the seabed of State Q's continental shelf. MEC agreed to pay State Q U.S. $100 million in advance for this privilege. State Q, however, did not inform MEC that it would be promulgating certain environmental protection laws within days after signing this contract that would make the endeavor so expensive that it would be effectively impossible for MEC to perform. When MEC discovered this, it asked State Q to either modify the environmental laws or give MEC back its money. State Q refused. MEC then initiated an arbitration proceeding under the auspices of the ICSID in accordance with the terms of the investment agreement and State Q law. How should the tribunal rule? Discuss.

Obligation of Parent for Subsidiary's Debts

4. Turnip Company, a multinational enterprise headquartered in State T, ordered its subsidiary in State R, the Radish Company, to close and to declare itself bankrupt. The Radish Company did so. However, it did not give its employees adequate notice of its closing, and its assets were inadequate for funding the termination payments due the employees under State R law. In the bankruptcy proceeding, the employees asked the bankruptcy tribunal to order Turnip to fund the termination payments that Radish owed them. In support of this, the employees introduced evidence establishing that Turnip had known for some time that Radish was an unprofitable subsidiary and would have to be closed; and that, in anticipation of this, it had taken assets belonging to Radish out of the state so that they would be unavailable at the time of the bankruptcy liquidation. How should the tribunal rule? Discuss.

Takeover Defenses

5. Little, Ltd., is a small publicly traded stock company that owns a valuable patent. Little has approximately 1,000 shareholders and about 100,000 shares authorized and outstanding. Big Company would like to use the patent, but Little has refused to grant it a license. Big offered to buy out all of Little's assets, but Little's board of directors refused. Big has now tendered an offer to all of Little's shareholders to pay them U.S. $10 a share for their stock, a price that is slightly above the current fair-market price. What can Little do to prevent Big from succeeding? Discuss.

Insider Trading

6. Miscellaneous, Ltd., was a company set up as a joint venture in Country M. Its foreign investor was Mammoth Enterprises, Ltd., a company organized in Country N. Mammoth owned 51 percent of Miscellaneous's shares, and it therefore was able to elect all of the directors of Miscellaneous. The other 49 percent of Miscellaneous's shares had been sold through a stock exchange in Country M to the local public. For several years, Miscellaneous had been unprofitable; then, when it was just about to become profitable, its board of directors bought up all of the company's public shares without revealing its current economic status. The Country M agency that supervises securities transactions has learned of this, and it seeks to force Miscellaneous to rescind these purchases. Will it be successful? Discuss.

CHAPTER 6
MONEY AND BANKING

⌐∞∞⌐

CHAPTER OUTLINE

The world's money and banking system is neither coherent nor well organized. In the absence of a convenient set of laws or regulations, custom and practice regulate much of it. The system is highly informal. On the international plane, its players include national institutions governed by national laws, as well as international agencies, such as the International Monetary Fund (IMF) and the Bank for International Settlements, whose operations are governed as often by informal agreements, plans, and accords as they are by treaties or conventions. On the domestic level, each country (or small group of countries) has its own national monetary system and its own specialized and often unique institutions.

A. MONEY

money: Anything customarily used as a medium of exchange and a measure of value.

According to one dictionary, **money** is "anything customarily used as a medium of exchange and measure of value." Economists generally attribute three characteristics to money: it acts (1) as a means of exchange, (2) as a unit of measure or value, and (3) as a medium for storing value over time.[1]

Money can be both private and official. Private money commonly consists of a basket of official currencies, but it can also be a stock of rare metal or any other commodity that is easily transferable and reasonably nonspoilable. Official money is a unit of exchange issued by a government agency (such as a treasury department) or government-controlled financial institution (such as a central bank).[2]

Private money can be used only for making payments between private parties who agree in advance to its use. Most official money (i.e., coins and currency) can be used to pay debts of any kind, whether private or public. However, some types of official money, known as *reserve currencies* (such as the IMF's Special Drawing Right—the SDR), may be used only by governments to pay other governments.

THE VALUE OF MONEY

nominalism: The principle that an obligation to pay a particular sum of money is fixed and does not change even if the purchasing power or foreign exchange rate of the money does change.

While the value of property and services is measured by money, the value of money (i.e., official money) is *nominally* constant. That is, if one agrees to purchase something for 100 units of a specified currency (such as dollars, marks, pounds, or yen), the obligation can be discharged only by paying those particular 100 units. The obligation does not change because the purchasing power or conversion value of the currency has fluctuated. This principle is known as **nominalism**.[3]

If the parties to a contract have not taken care to anticipate changes in the value of the currency they use, the principle of nominalism "puts the risk of depreciation on the creditor and the risk of appreciation (or revaluation) on the debtor and neither part[y] can be heard to complain about unexpected losses."[4] National law in a few countries has mediated the harshness of this rule in extreme circumstances. In Germany, for example, the courts are allowed to revalue money if a currency has totally or almost totally collapsed.[5] In Argentina, Belgium, Germany, and Uruguay, claims are allowed where one party suffers because another fails to pay in a timely fashion and the value of the currency depreciates in the meantime. In England, Italy, and the United States, on the other hand, revaluation is not allowed.[6]

Application of the principle of nominalism can be avoided in the special case where currency is to be delivered not as money, but as a commodity. For example, the seller of a rare

---

[1]J. Carter Murphy, "International Moneys: Official and Private," *International Lawyer*, vol. 23, p. 921 at p. 923 (1989).

[2]The U.S. Uniform Commercial Code's definition is typical of most countries. Section 1–201(24) states: "'Money' means a medium of exchange authorized or adopted by a domestic or foreign government and includes a monetary unit of account established by an intergovernmental organization or by agreement between two or more nations."

[3]F. A. Mann, *The Legal Aspect of Money*, pp. 80–114 (4th ed., 1982). For more information on the nominalism theory, see http://www.socsci.auc.dk/∼cbruun/phd/chap1.pdf.

[4]*Id.*, p. 272.

[5]*Id.*, p. 285.

[6]*Id.*, pp. 286–287. Keith S. Rosenn, "The Effects of Inflation on the Law of Obligations in Argentina, Brazil, Chile and Uruguay," *British Columbia International and Comparative Law Review*, vol. 2, p. 274 (1979). In France the case law is inconsistent, and no settled rule has evolved. Mann, *The Legal Aspect of Money*, p. 287.

coin might be able to set aside the sale if he learns the coin is much more valuable than the agreed-upon price. In the case of *Richard v. American Union Bank*,[7] a dealer in foreign currency successfully argued that the currency he had agreed to buy was a commodity that had become worthless and therefore he was not obliged to accept delivery.

THE CHOICE OF MONEY

money of account: The money used to define the amount of an obligation.

money of payment: The money used to pay off an obligation.

In domestic transactions, obligations are paid in local currency. In international transactions, the parties must designate the money that the buyer has to deliver. Actually, two monies have to be selected. First is the **money of account**. This is the money that expresses the amount of obligation owed. Second is the **money of payment**. This is the money that the buyer must use to pay for the items purchased. In most situations, the money chosen for both will be the same, but it does not have to be. For example, a seller may agree to deliver a product worth 1 million Australian dollars, and a buyer may agree to pay for it in Swiss francs.

In addition to selecting the money of account and the money of payment, contracting parties need to select the place of payment. This is important because virtually all countries allow a foreign money obligation to be satisfied by payment in the local currency at the exchange rate effective on the date payment is due.[8] Absent a selection by the parties, the courts will determine the place of payment, and that determination can vary from country to country.[9] For example, if the United Nations Convention on Contracts for the International Sale of Goods[10] applies, the place of payment will be the place of delivery (if such a place was designated); otherwise, it will be the seller's place of business (Article 57(1)).

By choosing a money of account, a money of payment, and a place for payment, the parties to a contract are also authorizing the courts in the states that issue those monies or the court in the state wherein payment is to take place to resolve disputes related to the interpretation or performance of the contract. This point is considered in Case 6-1.

---

[7]*New York Reports*, vol. 253, p. 166 (1930).
[8]F. A. Mann, *The Legal Aspect of Money*, p. 308 (4th ed. 1982). The conversion rate for foreign currency is specified in the U.S. Uniform Commercial Code as "the current bank-offered spot rate at the place of payment for the purchase of dollars on the day on which the instrument is paid" § 3-107. A similar formula is applied in most other countries.
[9]In some countries, payment is due at the seller's place of business; in others, at the buyer's place of business. F. A. Mann, *The Legal Aspect of Money*, pp. 214–219 (4th ed., 1982).
[10]The text of the convention is posted at http://www.uncitral.org/pdf/english/texts/sales/cisg/CISG.pdf.

━━━━━━━━━━ ⟨ℓℓℓ⟩ ━━━━━━━━━━

Case 6-1   REPUBLIC OF ARGENTINA ET AL. v. WELTOVER, INC. ET AL.

United States Supreme Court
United States Reports, vol. 504, p. 607 (1992).

JUSTICE SCALIA DELIVERED THE OPINION OF THE COURT

This case requires us to decide whether the Republic of Argentina's default on certain bonds issued as part of a plan to stabilize its currency ... had a "direct effect in the United States" so as to subject Argentina to suit in an American court under the Foreign Sovereign Immunities Act of 1976.[11] ...

Since Argentina's currency is not one of the mediums of exchange accepted on the international market, Argentine businesses engaging in foreign transactions must pay in U.S. dollars or some other internationally accepted currency. In the recent past, it was difficult for Argentine borrowers to obtain such funds, principally because of the instability of the Argentine currency. To

---

[11]*United States Code*, Title 28, § 1602 et seq. posted at http://www.law.cornell.edu/uscode/28/usc_sec_28_00001602----000-.html.

address these problems, petitioners, the Republic of Argentina, and its central bank, Banco Central (collectively Argentina), in 1981 instituted a foreign exchange insurance contract program (FEIC), under which Argentina effectively agreed to assume the risk of currency depreciation in cross-border transactions involving Argentine borrowers. This was accomplished by Argentina's agreeing to sell to domestic borrowers, in exchange for a contractually predetermined amount of local currency, the necessary U.S. dollars to repay their foreign debts when they matured, irrespective of intervening devaluations.

Unfortunately, Argentina did not possess sufficient reserves of U.S. dollars to cover the FEIC contracts as they became due in 1982. The Argentine government thereupon adopted certain emergency measures, including refinancing of the FEIC-backed debts by issuing to the creditors government bonds. These bonds, called "Bonods," provide for payment of interest and principal in U.S. dollars; payment may be made through transfer on the London, Frankfurt, Zurich, or New York market, at the election of the creditor. Under this refinancing program, the foreign creditor had the option of either accepting the Bonods in satisfaction of the initial debt, thereby substituting the Argentine government for the private debtor, or maintaining the debtor/creditor relationship with the private borrower and accepting the Argentine government as guarantor.

When the Bonods began to mature in May 1986, Argentina concluded that it lacked sufficient foreign exchange to retire them. Pursuant to a Presidential Decree, Argentina unilaterally extended the time for payment, and offered bondholders substitute instruments as a means of rescheduling the debts. Respondents, two Panamanian corporations and a Swiss bank who hold, collectively, $1.3 million of Bonods, refused to accept the rescheduling, and insisted on full payment, specifying New York as the place where payment should be made. Argentina did not pay, and respondents then brought this breach of contract action in the United States District Court for the Southern District of New York, relying on the Foreign Sovereign Immunities Act of 1976 as the basis for jurisdiction. Petitioners moved to dismiss for lack of subject matter jurisdiction, lack of personal jurisdiction, and *forum non conveniens*.[12] The District Court denied these motions, and the Court of Appeals

affirmed. We granted Argentina's petition for *certiorari*,[13] which challenged the Court of Appeals' determination that, under the Act, Argentina was not immune from the jurisdiction of the federal courts in this case.

... The ... question is whether Argentina's unilateral rescheduling of the Bonods had a "direct effect" in the United States.[14] ... As the Court of Appeals recognized, an effect is "direct" if it follows "as an immediate consequence of the defendant's ... activity."[15]

The Court of Appeals concluded that the rescheduling of the maturity dates obviously had a "direct effect" on respondents. It further concluded that the effect was sufficiently "in the United States" for purposes of the FSIA, in part because "Congress would have wanted an American court to entertain this action" in order to preserve New York City's status as "a preeminent commercial center."[16] The question, however, is not what Congress "would have wanted" but what Congress enacted in the FSIA. Although we are happy to endorse the Second Circuit's recognition of "New York's status as a world financial leader," the effect of Argentina's rescheduling in diminishing that status (assuming it is not too speculative to be considered an effect at all) is too remote and attenuated to satisfy the "direct effect" requirement of the FSIA.[17]

We nonetheless have little difficulty concluding that Argentina's unilateral rescheduling of the maturity dates on the Bonods had a "direct effect" in the United States. Respondents had designated their accounts in New York as the place of payment, and Argentina made some interest payments into those accounts before announcing that it was rescheduling the payments. Because New York was thus the place of performance for Argentina's ultimate contractual obligations, the rescheduling of those obligations necessarily had a "direct effect" in the United States: Money that was supposed to have been delivered to a New York bank for deposit was not forthcoming. We reject Argentina's suggestion that the "direct effect" requirement cannot be satisfied where the plaintiffs are all foreign corporations with no other connections to the United States. We expressly stated in *Verlinden* [*B.V. v. Central Bank of Nigeria*] that the FSIA permits "a foreign plaintiff to sue a foreign sovereign in the courts of the United States, provided the substantive requirements of the Act are satisfied."[18]

---

[12]Latin: "inconvenient forum." Doctrine that a municipal court will decline to hear a dispute when it can be better or more conveniently heard in a foreign court.

[13]Latin: "to be made certain" or "to be certified." It is an order from a superior to an inferior court requiring the latter to produce a certified record of a particular case tried therein.

[14]*United States Code*, Title 28, § 1602(a)(2)

[15]*Federal Reporter, Second Series*, vol. 941, p. 145 at p. 152 (Second Circuit Court of Appeals, 1991).

[16]*Id.*, at p. 153.

[17]*Id.*

[18]*United States Reports*, vol. 461, p. 480 at 489 (Supreme Court, 1983).

Finally, Argentina argues that a finding of jurisdiction in this case would violate the Due Process Clause of the Fifth Amendment [of the United States Constitution], and that, in order to avoid this difficulty, we must construe the "direct effect" requirement as embodying the "minimum contacts" test of *International Shoe Co. v. [State of] Washington.*[19] Assuming, without deciding, that a foreign state is a "person" for purposes of the Due Process Clause,[20] we find that Argentina possessed "minimum contacts" that would satisfy the constitutional test. By issuing negotiable debt instruments denominated in U.S. dollars and payable in New York and by appointing a financial agent in that city, Argen-tina "purposefully avail[ed] itself of the privilege of conducting activities within the [United States]."[21]

We conclude that Argentina's issuance of the Bonds . . . [and] its rescheduling of the maturity dates on those instruments . . . had a "direct effect: in the United States; and that the District Court therefore properly asserted jurisdiction, under the FSIA, over the breach of contract claim based on that rescheduling. Accordingly, the judgment of the Court of Appeals is affirmed.

CASEPOINT: (1) If the place of performance of a contractual obligation is in the United States, there are direct effects in the United States and courts there will have personal jurisdiction; by designating the United States as the place of performance for a contractual obligation, a foreign entity (sovereign or otherwise) "purposely avails itself of the privilege of conducting activities within the US." (2) As a sovereign, Argentina is

MAP 6-1 Argentina (1992)

not entitled to immunity under the FSIA because its change in the maturity dates of the bonds was "commercial activity" that had a direct effect in the United States.

---

[19]*Id.,* vol. 326, p. 310 at p. 316 (Supreme Court, 1945). Argentina concedes that this issue "is before the Court only as an aid in interpreting the direct effect requirement of the Act" and that "[w]hether there is a constitutional basis for personal jurisdiction over [Argentina] is not before the Court as an independent question." Brief for Petitioners, p. 36, n. 33.

[20]Confirm South Carolina v. Katzenbach, *id.,* vol. 383, p. 301 at pp. 323–324 (Supreme Court, 1966) (states of the Union are not "persons" for purposes of the Due Process Clause).

[21]Burger King Corp. v. Rudzewicz, *id.,* vol. 471, p. 462 at p. 475 (Supreme Court, 1985), quoting Hanson v. Denckla, *id.,* vol. 357, p. 235 at p. 253 (Supreme Court, 1958).

MAINTAINING MONETARY VALUE

maintenance of value clause: A contractual provision that says that the price will be adjusted according to the inflation rate.

A seller agrees to deliver 10,000 barrels of crude oil within three months to a buyer in Country X, with payment to be made in Country X's currency at the time of delivery. Country X's currency is inflating at 1,000 percent a year. How does the seller ensure that he will receive a fair price for the oil? Commonly, this is done by including a **maintenance of value** clause in the sales contract. Such a clause stipulates that the price is to be adjusted according to the inflation rate.[22]

---

[22]The inflation rate is typically ascertained by reference to a published index. Until the value of gold began to fluctuate dramatically in the 1970s, gold was commonly used as a standard for ascertaining inflation. F. A. Mann, *The Legal Aspect of Money,* pp. 138–156, 161–172 (4th ed., 1982). For more information on inflation, consult http://www.ofm.wa.gov/economy/econtopics/inflation/default.asp.

A seller of commodities can also avoid the problem of inflation (and the buyer the problem of deflation) by designating a money of account that traditionally maintains its value. The currency most commonly used for this purpose is the American dollar, but the EU euro, the Japanese yen, and the British pound are also widely used.

currency basket: A selected group of currencies whose weighted average is used to define the amount of an obligation.

A third mechanism for avoiding currency fluctuations is the use of a **currency basket**. That is, the money of account in a contract is defined by a weighted average of a selected group of currencies. The basket (or group of currencies) may be created *ad hoc* for a particular agreement. For example, the parties may agree that the money of account for their contract will be a currency basket made up of American dollars, British pounds, and Japanese yen, with the dollar making up 50 percent of the value, the pound 30 percent, and the yen 20 percent. More commonly, however, parties will use an official basket currency established by intergovernmental organizations, such as the IMF's SDR. The SDR is an international reserve asset that member countries can add to their foreign currency and gold reserves and use for payments requiring foreign exchange. Its value is set daily using a basket of four major currencies: the euro, Japanese yen, pound sterling, and U.S. dollar. The IMF introduced the SDR in 1969 because of concern that the stock and prospective growth of international reserves might not be sufficient to support the expansion of world trade. (The main reserve assets at the time were gold and U.S. dollars.) The SDR was introduced as a supplementary reserve asset, which the IMF could "allocate" periodically to members when the need arose and cancel as necessary. The SDR is also the IMF's unit of account.

Originally, the SDR was created to permit governments to discharge their international obligations. However, because the IMF publishes daily quotations on the exchange value of the SDR, the SDR has become widely accepted as a private currency basket. Today, private banks commonly accept deposits denominated in SDRs; and loans, especially those made by governments dealing with the IMF, are denominated in SDRs. (The current SDR basket, past changes in the makeup of the basket, a current valuation of the SDR in U.S. dollars, and change in the valuation of the SDR over the past thirty years are shown in Exhibit 6-1.)

B. THE INTERNATIONAL MONETARY FUND (IMF)

ORIGIN OF THE IMF

Because there is no single international currency that can be spent around the world, foreign currencies have to be converted into local currencies. The set of rules and procedures by which different national currencies are exchanged for each other in world trade is known as the **international monetary system**.

international monetary system: The world's informal money and banking system.

gold standard: A monetary system that provided for the free circulation between states of gold coins of standard specification.

The first modern international monetary system was the **gold standard**. In operation during the late nineteenth and early twentieth centuries, it provided for the free circulation between nations of gold coins of standard specification. The advantage of the gold standard was its stabilizing influence. If a state exported more than it imported, it would receive gold in payment for the difference. This influx of gold would raise domestic prices. These higher prices would then decrease demand for the state's exports and increase the state's internal demand for relatively cheap foreign imports. The result was an eventual return to the original price level. The principal disadvantage of the gold standard was its inherent lack of liquidity: The world's supply of money was necessarily limited by the world's supply of gold. Additionally, any sizable increase in the supply of gold, such as the discovery of a rich new mine, would cause prices to rise abruptly.

gold bullion standard: A monetary system that required states to buy and sell gold bullion with paper currency at a fixed price.

Because of its disadvantages, the gold standard broke down in 1914. It was replaced in the 1920s by the **gold bullion standard**. Under this system, states no longer minted gold coins; instead, they backed their paper currencies with gold bullion and agreed to buy and sell the bullion at a fixed price.[23]

---

[23]*The Columbia Encyclopedia*, p. 1349 (5th ed., 1993).

SDR Basket (For the 5-year period from January 1, 2002, to December 31, 2005)

Currency	Weight (%)
British pound	11
European Union euro	29
Japanese yen	15
U.S. dollar	45

Changes in SDR Basket

Date	Basket
January 1,1970	0.088867088 grams (1/35 of an ounce) of gold.
July 1, 1974	Australian dollar, Austrian schilling, Belgian franc, British pound, Canadian dollar, Danish krone, Dutch guilder, French franc, German mark, Italian lira, Japanese yen, Norwegian krone, South African rand, Spanish peseta, Swedish krona, U.S. dollar.
July 1, 1978	Australian dollar, Austrian schilling, Belgian franc, British pound, Canadian dollar, Dutch guilder, French franc, German mark, Iranian rial, Italian lira, Japanese yen, Norwegian krone, Saudi Arabian riyal, Spanish peseta, Swedish krona, U.S. dollar.
January 1, 1981	British pound, French franc, German mark, Japanese yen, U.S. dollar.
January 1, 2001	British pound, European Euro, Japanese yen, U.S. dollar.

SDR Valuation on July 10, 2002

Currency	Currency Amount[a]	Exchange Rate on July10[b]	U.S. Dollar Equivalent[c]
European Union euro	0.4260	0.99450	0.423657
Japanese yen	21.0000	117.72000	0.178389
British pound	0.0984	1.55210	0.152727
U.S. dollar	0.5770	1.00000	0.577000
		Total	1.331773

[a]The currency components of the SDR basket.
[b]Exchange rates in terms of currency units per U.S. dollar, except for the pound sterling, which is expressed in U.S. dollars per pound.
[c]The U.S. dollar equivalents of the currency amounts divided by the exchange rates.

Changes in SDR Valuation

Date	Valuation Basis	U.S. Dollar Equivalent
January 1, 1970	Gold	SDR 1.00 5 U.S. $1.0000
July 1, 1974	Currency basket	SDR 1.00 5 U.S. $1.2063
July 1, 1978	Currency basket	SDR 1.00 5 U.S. $1.2395
January 1, 1981	Currency basket	SDR 1.00 5 U.S. $1.2717
February 4, 1987	Currency basket	SDR 1.00 5 U.S. $1.2677
August 26, 1991	Currency basket	SDR 1.00 5 U.S. $1.3346
August 15, 1994	Currency basket	SDR 1.00 5 U.S. $1.4561
August 28, 1998	Currency basket	SDR 1.00 5 U.S. $1.3422
July 10, 2002	Currency basket	SDR 1.00 5 U.S. $1.3318

EXHIBIT 6-1 The IMF's Special Drawing Right (SDR)

Sources: IMF Survey (January 1981), *IMF Survey* (September 1991), *IMF Survey* (Supplement, August 1994), Special Drawing Rights: A Factsheet (April 15, 2002) posted on the Internet at www.imf.org/external/np/exr/facts/sdr.htm, and SDR Valuation (July 10, 2002) posted at www.imf.org/external/np/tre/sdr/basket.htm.

Harry Dexter White (1892–1948) and **John Maynard Keynes** (pronounced "canes," 1883–1946) were the two great intellectual founders of the IMF. Keynes, who served at the British Treasury before and during World War II, had revolutionized twentieth-century economics with his classic book *The General Theory of Employment, Interest and Money* (1936), in which he advocated government deficit spending during depressions. White was the chief international economist for the U.S. Treasury from 1942 to 1944 and assistant secretary of the treasury from 1944 to 1946. Both worked on developing a post–World War II economic system, and both agreed on the need for international cooperation and for a mechanism for controlling currency exchanges. Keynes advocated the creation of a world central bank that could regulate the flow and distribution of credit. White proposed the creation of an international equalization "fund" that would promote the growth of international trade and preserve the role of the U.S. dollar in international trade. White's proposal prevailed at the 1944 Bretton Woods Conference, where the

The Intellectual Founders of the International Monetary Fund: Harry Dexter White and John Maynard Keynes (Photo: IMF.)

IMF Charter was drafted, because the United States was the dominant economic power at that time. Ultimately, the link to the dollar proved untenable and the charter was amended in 1968 to provide for IMF's own reserve currency: the SDR.

EXHIBIT 6-2

With the onset of the worldwide Great Depression of the 1930s, the exchange of currencies became both unreliable and expensive. Deteriorating domestic economies[24] led to a widespread lack of confidence in paper money and a demand for gold that national treasuries could not meet. Nations with limited gold reserves, including the United Kingdom, were forced to abandon the gold standard, and because their money no longer bore a fixed relation to gold, its exchange became difficult.

Coupled with the difficulties of currency exchange were other detrimental Depression-era economic policies, including protectionist tariffs and truculent international trade policies. In July 1944, the United Nations convened a meeting in the small town of Bretton Woods, New Hampshire, for the purpose of creating a new international monetary system and an international organization to oversee that system. Representatives of 44 nations attended the UN Monetary and Financial Conference (known as the **Bretton Woods Conference**)[25] to draft the charter for the **International Monetary Fund (IMF)**. The IMF came into being on December 29, 1945, when its charter, formally known as the Articles of Agreement of the IMF, was signed by 29 states. The organization itself began operations in

Bretton Woods Conference: UN-sponsored monetary and financial conference held in Bretton Woods, New Hampshire, in July 1944. It led to the creation of the International Monetary Fund and the World Bank.

International Monetary Fund (IMF): Intergovernmental organization headquartered in Washington, DC. Using funds contributed by its members, it will purchase a currency on the application of a member to help the member discharge its international indebtedness and stabilize its currency exchange rates.

---

[24]Between 1929 and 1932, prices of goods fell 48 percent worldwide and the value of international trade fell 63 percent. David D. Driscoll, *What Is the International Monetary Fund?* p. 3 (1989).
[25]This conference also created the International Bank for Reconstruction and Development (popularly known as the World Bank). The World Bank is discussed in Chapter 12. For more information, see http://www.ibiblio.org/pha/policy/ 1944/440722a.html.

May 1946 at headquarters in the city of Washington, DC.[26] Today, virtually every country in the world is a member of the IMF.

The IMF's home page is the http://www.imf.org

The IMF was created to combat the international monetary and trade conditions that had helped to produce and prolong the Great Depression of the 1930s. The intellectual fathers of the IMF, British economist John Maynard Keynes and U.S. Treasury official Harry Dexter White, identified two such conditions: (1) currency inconvertibility and (2) the lack of a standard for determining the value of national currencies (because of the collapse of the gold bullion standard). To correct these conditions, the IMF was made the overseer of its member states' monetary and exchange rate policies and the guardian of a code of conduct. In particular, the Articles of Agreement[27] establish a system of currency exchange (originally related to the value of gold but later, following an amendment to the Articles, based on exchange agreements) and a system for currency support (that allows the IMF to provide short-term financial resources to member states to help them correct payment imbalances).[28]

The Articles (as they are now amended) also establish a system of surveillance to ensure that member states abide by a code of conduct in their external monetary relations—specifically, that they do not borrow or lend at unsustainable levels, engage in protracted one-way interventions in the exchange market, or follow unwarranted monetary or fiscal policies for balance-of-payments purposes. Surveillance is the regular dialogue and policy advice that the IMF offers to each of its members. On a regular basis, usually once each year, the Fund conducts in-depth appraisals of each member country's economic situation. It discusses with the country's authorities the policies that are most conducive to stable exchange rates and a growing and prosperous economy. Members have the option to publish the Fund's assessment, and the overwhelming majority of countries opt for transparency, making extensive information on bilateral surveillance available to the public. The IMF also combines information from individual consultations to form assessments of global and regional developments and prospects. These views on the IMF's multilateral surveillance are published twice each year in the *World Economic Outlook* and *the Global Financial Stability Report.*[29]

In addition to currency exchange, currency support, and surveillance, the IMF maintains an extensive program of technical assistance through staff missions to member states. These staff missions help member states to reform their fiscal systems and budgetary controls and to establish or adapt institutional machinery, such as central banking and exchange systems.[30]

IMF QUOTAS

IMF quota: The amount of funds that a member of the IMF is required to contribute. It determines the voting rights of a member and the sum of IMF funds that a member may draw upon to stabilize its currency and to meet balance-of-payments obligations.

To become a member of the IMF, a state must contribute a certain sum of money (expressed in SDRs) called a **quota** subscription.[31] The quota is based on the relative size of a member state's economy, and it serves various purposes. First, members' quotas make up a pool of funds on which the IMF can draw to lend to a particular member having financial difficulties.

[26]Driscoll, *What Is the International Monetary Fund?* p. 5 (1989); Margaret Garritsen de Vries, "Bretton Woods and the IMF's First 35 Years," *IMF Survey*, vol. 23, p. 217 (July 11, 1994).
[27]The text of the Articles of Agreement of the IMF is posted at http://www.imf.org/external/pubs/ft/aa/index.htm.
[28]Union of International Associations, *Yearbook of International Organizations 1994/1995*, pp. 968–969 (1994).
[29]For links to the *World Economic Outlook Reports,* see http://www.imf.org/external/ns/cs.aspx?id=29.
[30]Technical assistance is one of the benefits of IMF membership. It is normally provided free of charge to any requesting member country, within IMF resource constraints. More details are available at http://www.imf.org/external/np/exr/facts/tech.htm.
[31]Seventy-five percent of a member's quota may be paid in its own currency; the other 25 percent has to be in a major convertible currency (such as British pounds, French francs, German marks, Japanese yen, or U.S. dollars). Articles of Agreement of the International Monetary Fund, Article III, § 3(a).

Second, quotas determine how much a contributing member can borrow from the IMF and how much it will receive in periodic allocations of SDRs. Third, quotas determine the members' voting power in the IMF.[32] Those who contribute the most to the IMF are given the greatest say in setting its policies. For example, the United States currently has about 370,000 371,743 votes, or about 16.83 percent of the total, while Palau has only about 281 votes.[33] Currently, the IMF has a membership of 185 nations, the total number of quotas is SDR 2,208,981, and the total number of votes is 2,166,749.

Quotas for a state seeking to join the IMF are determined initially by the IMF staff based on formulas that take into consideration the state's gross domestic product, its current account transactions, the variability of its current receipts, and its official reserves. The results of the staff's initial calculations are adjusted both in light of data from existing members of comparable economic size and characteristics and through negotiations with the applicant state. Then the IMF Executive Board and finally the IMF Board of Governors must approve the quota.[34]

The Board of Governors is required to make a general review of quotas at intervals of not more than five years and propose any adjustments that it considers appropriate, taking into consideration the growth of the world economy and changes in the relative economic positions of the members. Any quota changes must then be approved by member states having at least 85 percent of the IMF's total votes. In addition, the change is not effective for a particular state until the state itself both approves of the change and pays for it.[35]

Reading 6-1 takes issue with the quota system as it stood in 2006.

---

[32]Every member is given 250 basic votes plus one vote for each SDR 100,000 of its quota. *Id.*, Article XII, § 5(a).
[33]"IMF Members' Quotas and Voting Power, and IMF Governors" (April 02, 2007), posted at http://www.imf.org/external/np/sec/memdir/members.htm.
[34]"Where Does the IMF Get Its Money? A Factsheet" (April 2002) posted at http:www.imf.org/external/np/exr/facts/finfac.htm.
[35]Articles of Agreement of the International Monetary Fund, Article III, §§ 2(a), 2(c), and 2(d); "Member Countries' Quotas Guide Their Access to IMF Resources," *IMF Survey*, pp. 6–7 (Supplement, August 1994).

Reading 6-1   IMF QUOTA REFORM IS INADEQUATE; REACTION TO IMFC COMMUNIQUÉ

Press release of the Bretton Woods Project
September 18, 2006 www.brettonwoodsproject.org

The Bretton Woods Project—a UK-based network of NGOs including Oxfam, ActionAid, Christian Aid, One World Trust and new economics foundation (nef)—called the IMF proposal to reform its voting structure completely inadequate to address the institution's problems. In reacting to the IMFC communiqué that hailed the reform proposal as a significant step forward, Peter Chowla, policy and advocacy officer at the Bretton Woods Project, stated: "It is a real shame that this proposal has succeeded despite the reservations of more than 50 developing countries. Anything short of fundamental reform of the IMF's governance structure will not restore its credibility."

The IMF proposal initially granted voting rights increases to just four countries—China, South Korea, Turkey, and Mexico—and called for a small increase to basic votes and a revamping of the way quotas are calculated. But the proposal does nothing to alter the imbalance of power in decision-making at the IMF or to give more "voice" to developing countries.[36] The balance of power at the IMF will not appreciably change

---

[36]The *ad hoc* vote increases for four countries and a doubling of basic votes (which would not be implemented for years), will decrease the voting weight of advanced economies from 62 percent of the total to just about 60.5 percent of the total. African countries will see their vote shares increase 0.5 percent to a total of about 6 percent.

with this measure, and developed countries will still maintain control over IMF decisions. Furthermore the revision of the quota formula may negatively impact the voting rights of many low- and middle-income countries.[37]

Mr. Chowla continued, "Developed countries seem determined to waste this opportunity for reform by pushing cosmetic changes that do nothing more than tinker at the edges. The increase in basic votes is just symbolic and will have no substantial affect on the inequality in decision-making making at the IMF."

British NGOs—including Oxfam, ActionAid, Christian Aid and others—have thrown their support behind a proposal for comprehensive reform[38] and demand that the UK government step forward to propose wholesale changes at the IMF, rather than tinkering with quota adjustments within the two-stage process that has been proposed. Their request goes further than the Treasury Select Committee's conclusion that the UK needs to

propose innovative solutions to the problem of voting weights because the current proposals do not address the underlying problems facing the IMF.

Jeff Powell, coordinator of the Bretton Woods Project, explained: "The governance of the IMF needs a fundamental rethink to bring it in line with democratic principles considered acceptable at the national level. This should have been part of a comprehensive package that also addressed the composition of the board and the lack of transparency at the institution."

"One of the most elegant ways to immediately patch up the problems in representation at the IMF would be a system of double-majority voting, so that no decision could be rammed through by rich countries holding most of the votes, nor by an unrepresentative group of small, poor countries," continued Mr. Powell. "This would also be much easier than trying to devise a quota formula that would satisfy all the different countries interested in IMF reform."

---

[37]The third element of the proposal—a redesign of the formula that determines voting power—is hotly contested, and the last time the members of the IMF tried to reach consensus on a change, the issue became deadlocked. If the U.S. preference for a quota formula based almost entirely on GDP at market exchange rates is accepted, then countries like Nigeria, Indonesia, Venezuela, Malaysia, South Africa and nearly every other African country would have diminished voting rights in the organisation.
[38]The full statement from the Bretton Woods Project NGO can be found at http://www.brettonwoodsproject.org/ukimfreform.

ORGANIZATION OF THE IMF

The Board of Governors is the highest authority of the IMF. It comprises a governor and an alternate governor representing each IMF member state. The individuals who serve as governors and alternate governors are usually the ministers of finance or the heads of the central banks of their states.[39] They convene at an annual meeting and may participate in votes by mail or by other means during the remainder of the year. Many of the powers of the Board of Governors have been delegated to an Executive Board made up of 24 directors and a managing director, who serves as its chairman. The election of directors, the conditions for the admission of new members, the adjustment of quotas, and certain other important matters remain the responsibility of the Board of Governors.

The executive directors meet at least three times a week in formal sessions to oversee the implementation of the policies set by the Board of Governors. The other directors represent groupings of the remaining states. The Executive Board seldom makes decisions on the basis of a formal vote; instead, it acts only when its members reach a consensus, a practice that minimizes confrontations on sensitive issues and that ensures full cooperation on the decisions that are taken.

The Executive Board appoints a managing director to both chair the Executive Board and act as the IMF's head of staff. By tradition, the managing director is European. The international staff of some 2,716 from 165 countries is made up mainly of economists but also includes statisticians, researchers, experts in public finance and taxation, linguists, writers, and support personnel. Most of the staff are employed at the IMF's headquarters in Washington, but a few are assigned to small offices in Paris, Geneva, and New York. Unlike the executive directors, who represent particular states or groups of states, the managing

---

[39]"The IMF at a Glance: A Factsheet" (August 2006) posted at http://www.imf.org/external/np/exr/facts/glance.htm.

director and the staff are responsible to the member states as a whole in carrying out the policies of the IMF.

IMF OPERATIONS

A member state obligates itself upon joining the IMF to observe a code of conduct. This code requires the state to (1) keep other members informed of its arrangements for determining the value of its money relative to the money of other states, (2) refrain from placing restrictions on the exchange of its money, and (3) pursue economic policies that will increase in a constructive and orderly way both its own national wealth and that of all the IMF member states. It is important to note that observation of this code is essentially voluntary. The IMF has no mechanism for compelling member states to conform, although it can and does exert moral pressure to encourage its members to comply. Should a state persistently ignore the code of conduct, the Board of Governors may declare that it is ineligible to borrow money from the IMF; or, as a last resort, an offending member can be expelled from the IMF by a vote of "a majority of the Governors having 85 percent of the total voting power."[40]

Since the IMF's creation in 1945, its member states have given it a variety of responsibilities that have changed with the times. Today, the Fund is responsible for (1) supervising a cooperative system of currency exchange, (2) lending money to members in order to support their currencies and their economies, and (3) providing auxiliary services to assist members in establishing and carrying out their external debt and other financial policies.[41]

C. CURRENCY EXCHANGE

CURRENCY EXCHANGE OBLIGATIONS OF IMF MEMBER STATES

IMF par value system: The currency exchange mechanism specified by the IMF prior to 1971, which required all members to declare a value (the par value) at which their currencies could be converted into gold.

The currency exchange mechanism established in 1945 by the Articles of Agreement of the IMF was called the **par value system**. That is, every member of the IMF, on joining the Fund, had to declare a value at which its currency could be converted into gold. The U.S. dollar, for example, was pegged at 1/35th of an ounce of gold. Members were obliged to keep the value of their currency within 1 percent of this par value, and only upon consultation with the IMF and the other members of the Fund could a member make a change.[42]

The par value system worked well so long as inflation rates remained stable and unemployment was low in the major developed countries. It fell apart in the early 1970s, however, when inflation rates and unemployment grew sharply in the United States while remaining low in Europe and Japan. Foreign claims on American gold reserves increased[43] as the U.S. balance-of-payments deficit soared. The system effectively came to an end on August 15, 1971, when President Richard Nixon terminated the convertibility of the dollar into gold. Its final breakdown occurred in 1973, when the United States announced a 10 percent devaluation of the dollar.

IMF Second Amendment system: The currency exchange mechanism established by the IMF in 1978 that allows members to define the value of their currency by any means other than by reference to the value of gold.

Three years lapsed before the IMF system could be reformed. The member states adopted the **Second Amendment** to the Articles of Agreement in 1976, effective in 1978. This new accord, which remains in effect today, allows members to define the value of their currency by any criteria except gold. Many member countries peg their currencies to the currencies of other countries, or to the IMF's SDR, or to a currency basket. Others simply

---

[40]Articles of Agreement of the International Monetary Fund, Article XXVI, § 2(b).

[41]"The IMF at a Glance: A Factsheet" (August 2006) posted at http://www.imf.org/external/np/exr/facts/glance.htm.

[42]For the history of the IMF and the par value system, see David D. Driscoll, "What Is the International Monetary System?" (1989), posted at http://www.imfsite.org/operations/driscoll998.html and http://www.imf.org/external/pubs/ft/history/2001/index.htm and "What Is the International Monetary Fund?" (September 2006) posted at http://www.imf.org/external/pubs/ft/exrp/what.htm.

[43]The exchange rate of $35 for an ounce made gold an irresistible bargain—so much so that U.S. gold reserves were inadequate to meet the demand.

allow the value of their currencies to *float*, that is, to be determined by international supply and demand.[44]

Although a member is free to adopt its own exchange arrangements, it is forbidden to "manipulat[e] exchange rates or the international monetary system in order to prevent effective balance-of-payments adjustment or to gain an unfair competitive advantage over other members."[45] A member is also required "to collaborate with the Fund to promote exchange stability, to maintain orderly exchange arrangements with other members, and to avoid competitive exchange alterations."[46] In addition, members with floating exchange rates are required to "intervene on the foreign exchange market as necessary to prevent or moderate sharp and disruptive fluctuations from day to day and from week to week in the exchange value of its currency."[47]

ENFORCEMENT OF EXCHANGE CONTROL REGULATIONS OF IMF MEMBER STATES

Article VIII, Section 2(b), of the Articles of Agreement of the IMF provides: "Exchange contracts which involve the currency of any member and which are contrary to the exchange control regulations of that member maintained or imposed consistently with this Agreement shall be unenforceable in the territories of any member...."

The purpose of this provision is twofold: (1) to prevent one IMF member from frustrating the legitimate exchange controls of another member and (2) to deter private persons from violating exchange control regulations. It can be invoked in three situations: (1) as a defense to a suit for the breach of an executory contract, (2) as a cause of action for a foreign government to compel rescission or to obtain damages after the execution of a contract that violated its exchange provisions, and (3) as a cause of action for a private person to compel rescission or to obtain damages after the execution of a contract that violates a foreign exchange provision.

The IMF Agreement grants to the Executive Board of the Fund the authority to interpret the provisions of the Agreement.[48] Pursuant to this authority, the directors have interpreted Article VIII, Section 2(b), to mean that the principle of unenforceability is "effectively part [of every member country's] national law."[49] Courts in France, Luxembourg, and the United States have held that they are bound by the directors' interpretation, and most commentators agree that the directors' interpretation is binding on all member states' courts and agencies.

The IMF directors have not interpreted the meaning of the term *exchange contracts*, although these words have been the focus of most of the litigation over Article VIII, Section 2(b). Courts on the European continent have generally given the term a broad meaning. In essence, they define **exchange contracts** as contracts that "in any way affect a country's exchange resources."[50]

American and British courts define the term **exchange contract** restrictively.[51] They hold that an exchange contract is one having as its immediate object the exchange of international

---

Continental European definition of *exchange contract*: Any contract that in any way affects the currency exchange resources of a country.

Anglo-American definition of *exchange contract*: A contract having as its immediate object the international exchange of mediums of payment.

---

[44]Articles of Agreement of the International Monetary Fund, Article IV, § 2(b): "...[E]xchange arrangements may include (i) the maintenance by a member of a value for its currency in terms of the Special Drawing Right or another denominator, other than gold, selected by the member, or (ii) cooperative arrangements by which members maintain the value of their currencies in relation to the value of the currency or currencies of other members, or (iii) other exchange arrangements of a member's choice."

[45]*Id.*, Article IV, § 1(iii).

[46]The *1974 International Monetary Fund Annual Report*, p. 112 (1974).

[47]*Id.*, p. 113.

[48]Article XXIX(a).

[49]*International Monetary Fund Annual Report*, app. XIV, p. 82 (1949).

[50]F. A. Mann, "The Private International Law of Exchange Contracts under the International Monetary Fund Agreement," *International & Comparative Law Quarterly*, vol. 2, p. 102 (1953).

[51]In Mansouri v. Singh, *All England Law Reports*, vol. 2, p. 619 (1986), Lord Justice Neill stated for the English Court of Appeal: "The term 'exchange contract' in § 2(b) of article VIII is to be interpreted narrowly. The term is confined to contracts to exchange the currency of one country for the currency of another; it does not include contracts entered into in connection with sales of goods which require the conversion by the buyer of one currency into another in order to enable him to pay the purchase price...."

mediums of payment, which is usually the exchange of one currency for another.[52] This interpretation excludes (1) securities contracts, (2) sales contracts (including sales of precious metals), and (3) loans (including letters of credits).[53] Case 6-2 illustrates the reasoning used by courts for adopting the narrow interpretation of Article VIII, Section 2(b).

---

[52]This definition originated with Arthur Nussbaum in his article "Exchange Control and the International Monetary Fund," *Yale Law Journal*, vol. 59, p. 426 (1949). See John S. Williams, "Extraterritorial Enforcement of Exchange Controls under the International Monetary Fund Agreement," *Virginia Journal of International Law*, vol. 15, p. 333 (1975); and George B. Schwab, "The Unenforceability of International Contracts Violating Foreign Exchange Regulations: Article VIII, Section 2(b) of the International Monetary Fund Agreement," *Virginia Journal of International Law*, vol. 25, p. 982 (1985).

[53]See Arthur Nussbaum, "Exchange Control and the International Monetary Fund," *Yale Law Journal*, vol. 59, p. 426 (1949) (securities contracts); Wilson, Smithett & Cope, Ltd. v. Terruzzi, *All England Law Reports*, vol. 1976, pt. 1, p. 817 (1976) (sales of metals); and Libra Bank Ltd. v. Banco Nacional de Costa Rica, *Federal Supplement*, vol. 570, p. 899–900 (U.S. District Court for the Southern District of New York, 1983) (loans). But compare United City Merchants (Investment) Ltd. v. Royal Bank of Canada, *All England Law Reports*, vol. 1982, pt. 2, p. 720 at p. 729 (1982), which held that a letter-of-credit transaction was a "monetary contract in disguise."

Case 6-2   WILSON, SMITHETT & COPE, LTD v. TERRUZZI

England, Court of Appeal, 1976.
All England Law Reports, vol. 1976, pt. 1, p. 817 (1976).

LORD DENNING, MASTER OF THE ROLLS

Signor Terruzzi lives in Milan. He is a dealer in metals, trading under the name Terruzzi Metalli. But he is also, it seems, a gambler in differences. He speculates on the rise or fall in the price of zinc, copper and so forth. He speculated in 1973 on the London Metal Exchange. He did so in plain breach of the Italian laws of exchange control. These provide that residents in Italy are not to come under obligations to non-residents save with ministerial authority. Signor Terruzzi never obtained permission.

In making his speculations, Signor Terruzzi established an account with London dealers, Wilson, Smithett & Cope, Ltd. He was introduced to them by their Milan agent, Signor Giuliani, and made his deals through him. All the transactions were in sterling and reduced into writing on the standard contract forms of the London Metal Exchange. Sometimes Signor Terruzzi was a "bull." That is, he thought that the price was likely to rise in the near future. So he bought metal from the London dealers at a low price for delivery three months ahead, not meaning ever to take delivery of it, but intending to sell

it back to the London dealers at a higher price before the delivery date, thus showing him a profit in his account with the London dealers. At other times he was a "bear." That is, he thought that the price was likely to fall in the near future. So he sold metal "short" (which he had not got) to the London dealers at a high price for delivery three months ahead, not meaning ever to deliver it, but intending to buy back from the London dealers a like quantity at a lower price before the delivery date, thus showing him a profit in his account with the London dealers. Such transactions would have been gaming contracts if both parties had never intended to make or accept delivery, and they would not have been enforced by the English courts. But the London dealers were not parties to any such intention. They always intended to make or accept delivery according to the contracts they made. So far as the London dealers were concerned, they were genuine commercial transactions. They were enforceable accordingly by the English courts.[54] But they were not enforceable in the Italian courts because they infringed the exchange control.

The critical months here were October and November 1973. The price of zinc was very high. The price for "forward" delivery (that is for delivery three months ahead) had been steadily rising from £465 on 18th October 1973

---

[54]See Bassett v. Sanker, *Times Law Reports*, vol. 41, p. 660 (1925) (London Metal Exchange); Weddle, Beck & Co. v. Hackett, *All England Law Reports*, vol. 1928, p. 539 (1928) (London Stock Exchange); Woodward v. Wolfe, *All England Law Reports*, vol. 1936, pt. 3, p. 529 (1936) (Liverpool Cotton Exchange); Garnac Grain Co., Inc. v. HMF Faure & Fairclough, Ltd., and Bunge Corp., *All England Law Reports*, vol. 1965, pt. 3, p. 273 (1965) (contracts for lard).

to £520 on 7th November. Signor Terruzzi thought that the price was much too high and that it was likely to fall soon. So he made a series of contracts with the London dealers whereby he sold to them 1,200 tons of zinc for delivery in the next three months. He sold "short," that is he had then no zinc to meet his obligations. Unfortunately for Signor Terruzzi, his forecast was wrong. Even after 7th November the price did not fall. It rose steeply. So much so that within a week it had risen to £650 a ton. By 12th November 1973 the London dealers were anxious as to the ability of Signor Terruzzi to meet his commitments. They asked him to provide a deposit or "margin" of £50,000, as they were entitled to do under the contracts. On the evening of Tuesday, 13th November, Signor Giuliani, on behalf of the London dealers, met Signor Terruzzi at the Café Ricci in Milan. He told him the state of the account. Signor Terruzzi flamed with anger. He said that he was not going to pay anything to the London dealers by way of margin, or otherwise, and they could take him to court. Signor Giuliani telephoned the London dealers. They were fearful that the price might go still higher. There were frantic telexes. In the result the London dealers "closed" the contracts with him, as they were entitled to do under the written terms thereof. They sold back to him 1,200 tons of zinc at the ruling price. They telexed him with details. The result showed a balance due to the London dealers amounting to £220,440.38; and credit was due to him on previous profits of £25,418.37. So on balance the sum of £195,022.01 was due from him to them. On 10th January 1974 they issued a writ against him for that amount in the High Court in England. He got leave to defend by swearing, quite untruly, that the transactions had been carried out without his knowledge or authority. Afterwards he took a different line. He said that the London dealers had failed to advise him properly about the transactions. The trial opened on 9th October 1974. He came to London for the first day. He went back to Italy for the weekend. He had a heart attack there. He never returned to the trial. All his defenses crumbled. So did his counterclaim. The only point which remained was that the contracts were "exchange contracts" and were unenforceable against him by reason of the Bretton Woods Agreements. Judge Kerr decided against him. Signor Terruzzi appeals to this court.

Now for the Bretton Woods Agreements. Bretton Woods is a small town in New Hampshire, U.S.A, but it has a place in history. During the Second World War, even in the midst of raging hostilities, there was a conference there attended by the members of the United Nations. The object was to organize their monetary systems so as to meet the post-war problems. At this conference the United Kingdom was represented by the distinguished economist, Lord Keynes, and by the legal adviser to the Foreign Office, Sir Eric Beckett. In July 1944, Articles of Agreement were drawn up and signed. By the Agreement the International Monetary Fund was established and provisions were made (amongst other things) "to promote international monetary cooperation" and "to promote exchange stability." In 1945, Parliament passed an Act to give effect to the Agreement. In January 1946, an order in council, the Bretton Woods Agreements Order in Council 1946, was made giving the force of law to this provision, among others:

> Article VIII, Section 2(b). Exchange contracts which involve the currency of any member and which are contrary to the exchange control regulations of that member maintained or imposed consistently with this Agreement shall be unenforceable in the territories of any member....

That provision is part of the law of England, but it has given rise to much controversy, particularly as to the meaning of the words "exchange contracts." There are two rival views. First, the view of Professor Nussbaum set out in 1949 in the *Yale Law Journal*.[55] He said that "an exchange contract" is exclusively concerned with the handling of international media of payment as such. Therefore, contracts involving securities or merchandise cannot be considered as exchange contracts except when they are monetary transactions in disguise. This view is in accord with the meaning given by Lord Radcliffe in *Re United Railways of the Havana and Regla Warehouses, Ltd.*[56]:

> ... a true exchange contract ... is a contract to exchange the currency of one country for the currency of another....

Second, the view of Dr. F. A. Mann set out in 1949 in the *British Year Book of International Law* and in his book, *The Legal Aspect of Money*. He said that "exchange contracts" are contracts which in any way affect a country's exchange resources—a phrase which I accepted without question in *Sharif v. Azad*,[57] in the belief that, coming from such a source, it must be right. Dr. Mann recognizes that his view makes the word "exchange" redundant and thus seems counter to established methods of interpretation. But he contends that it is in better harmony with the purpose of the Agreements.

---

[55] *Yale Law Journal*, vol. 59, p. 421 at pp. 426, 427 (1949).
[56] *All England Law Reports*, vol. 1960, pt. 2, p. 332 at p. 350 (1960).
[57] *Id.*, vol. 1966, pt. 3, p. 785 at p. 787 (1966).

Dr. Mann suggests that the lawyers did not take much part in drafting the Bretton Woods Agreements. In this he is mistaken. I trust that I may be forgiven a digression if I borrow from the argument of counsel for the plaintiffs and recite part of the speech which Lord Keynes made at the Final Act of the Conference (as recorded by Sir Roy Harrod in his biography of Keynes):

And, for my own part, I should like to pay a particular tribute to our lawyers. All the more so because I have to confess that, generally speaking, I do not like from results in this lawyer-ridden land, the *Mayflower,* when she sailed from Plymouth, must have been entirely filled with lawyers. When I first visited Mr. Morgenthau in Washington some three years ago accompanied only by my secretary, the boys in your Treasury curiously enquired of him—where is your lawyer? When it was explained that I had none— "Who then does your thinking for you?" was the rejoinder.... [O]nly too often [our lawyers] have had to do our thinking for us. We owe a great deal of gratitude to Dean Acheson, Oscar Cox, Luxford, Brenner, Collado, Arnold, Chang, Broches and our own Beckett of the British Delegation.[58]

So the lawyers did play a large part. I have no doubt that they had in mind an evil which was very much in evidence in the years after the First World War. It is strikingly illustrated by the notorious case of *Ironmonger & Co. v. Dyne*[59] in which a lady, Mrs. Bradley Dyne, speculated in foreign currency. She did it at the instance of prominent officials in the Foreign Office. She dealt with bankers in Throgmorton Street. She used to buy from the bankers French francs and Italian lire for delivery three months in the future; but, before the time for delivery arrived, she sold them again. If the price went up, she took the difference as a "profit." If the price went down, she was liable to pay the difference as a "loss." In no single case was any currency delivered. She operated on an enormous scale. In three years the turnover amounted to 421 million francs and 17 million lira, and large sums in other currencies as well. At the end she was much in debt to the bankers for her "losses." They sued her for it. She pleaded the Gaming Act. Her plea failed because, so far as the bankers were concerned, they were genuine transactions which created obligations to fulfill the contracts according to their tenor if circumstances required it. She was held liable. The British government declared that the transactions were a disgrace to the Civil Service and punished the Foreign Office officials who had engaged in them. But the case is important for present purposes because it shows the great mischief which can be done by such speculations. Lord Justice Scrutton described it in these words:

The transactions in question were not of a pleasant nature. After the War, while Europe was recovering from the various upheavals which were the result of it, the value of currency fluctuated extremely. Contracts for the purchase or sale of currency, which, before the War had been a comparatively sober business, became very speculative in their making and their result. It was possible to make very large profits and equally possible to make very great losses, and, as was to be expected when great profits might be made, the birds of prey gathered together. Reckless speculators, absolutely indifferent to the damage that they were doing to the country in the currency of which they were dealing, began operations. People bought and sold currency to a very large extent, with the most disastrous results to the countries concerned. That was particularly the case with regard to the sales and purchases of French currency, which went near to bringing that country to ruin. People who indulged in those speculations were beneath contempt and ought to be condemned. They were utterly selfish, and had no regard at all to the enormous injury which they were inflicting on the legitimate trade of the country in whose exchange they were speculating.[60]

The mischief being thus exposed, it seems to me that the participants at Bretton Woods inserted Article VIII, § 2(b), in the Agreement so as to stop it. They determined to make exchange contracts of that kind—for the exchange of currencies—unenforceable in the territories of any member. I do not know of any similar mischief in regard to other contracts, that is contracts for the sale or purchase of merchandise or commodities. Businessmen have to encounter fluctuations in the price of goods, but this is altogether different from the fluctuations in exchange rates. So far from there being any mischief, it seems to me that it is in the interest of international trade that there should be no restriction on contracts for the sale and purchase of merchandise and commodities; and that they should be enforceable in the territories of the members.

The Bretton Woods Agreements made provision to that end. Thus Article 1(ii) says that one of the purposes of the International Monetary Fund is to "facilitate the expansion and balanced growth of international trade...." Article VI, § 3, and Article VIII, § 2(a), coupled with Article XIX(i), say that no member is to impose restrictions on payments due "in connection with foreign trade, other current business, including services, and normal short-term banking and credit facilities."

[58]R. F. Harrod, *Life of John Maynard Keynes*, p. 583 (1951).
[59]*Times Law Reports*, vol. 44, p. 497 (1928).
[60]*Id.*, at p. 498.

In conformity with those provisions, I would hold that the Bretton Woods Agreements should not do anything to hinder legitimate contracts for the sale or purchase of merchandise or commodities. The words "exchange contracts" in Article VIII, § 2(b), refer only to contracts to exchange the currency of one country for the currency of another. The words "which involve the currency of any member" fit in well with this meaning, but it is difficult to give them any sensible meaning in regard to other contracts. They show that the section is only dealing with the currencies of members of the fund, and not with the currencies of nonmembers. The reference to regulations "maintained or enforced consistently with this Agreement" covers such regulations as those of Italy here.

It is no doubt possible for men of business to seek to avoid Article VIII, § 2(b), by various artifices. But I hope that the courts will be able to look at the substance of the contracts and not at the form. If the contracts are not legitimate contracts for the sale or purchase of merchandise or commodities, but are instead what Professor Nussbaum calls "monetary transactions in disguise," [61] as a means of manipulating currencies, they would be caught by § 2(b).

I will not say more save to express my appreciation of the judgment of Justice Kerr. He has covered the whole subject most satisfactorily. In my opinion the contracts here were legitimate contracts for the sale and purchase of metals. They were not "exchange contracts." The London dealers are entitled to enforce them in this country. I would dismiss the appeal accordingly.

The appeal was dismissed and leave to appeal to the House of Lords was refused.

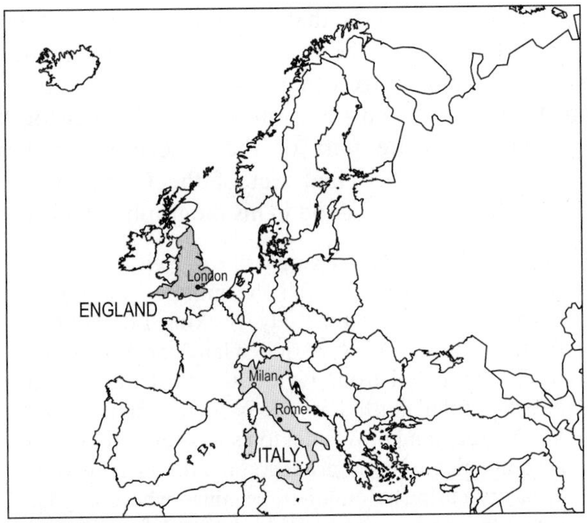

[61]*Yale Law Journal*, vol. 59, p. 421 at p. 427 (1949).

MAP 6-2 Italy and England (1976)

CASEPOINT: The IMF's Article VIII (2)(b) is to be narrowly interpreted. The English international lawyer Dr. F. A. Mann's assumption that since lawyers did not take much part in the drafting of the IMF Article of Agreement the term *currency exchange contract* should be broadly interpreted is wrong. Lawyers did play a large part. As such, it seems that the lawyers had in mind a specific legal problem: currency speculation. It is this that IMF Article VIII(2)(b) addresses and nothing more. The words *exchange contracts* in Article VIII2 (b) refer only to contracts to "exchange the currency of one country for the currency of another."

Finally, the IMF's Articles of Agreement do not describe what constitutes currency exchange regulations, other than to note that they must be "maintained or imposed consistently" with the Articles of Agreement.[62] As with other regulations, however, it seems evident that they need to be adopted in accordance with a member state's constitution and laws and properly promulgated.

ENFORCEMENT OF EXCHANGE CONTROL LAWS IN THE ABSENCE OF IMF MEMBERSHIP

The provision in Article VIII, Section 2(b), of the IMF's Articles of Agreement requiring member states to give effect to the currency exchange regulations of other members is at odds with a long-standing choice of law rule that holds that states do not enforce the revenue laws of other states. The civil code in civil law countries often expressly prohibits the enforcement of foreign revenue laws, including currency exchange regulations. The common

[62]Article VIII, § 2(b).

law countries apply a court-made rule to the same effect, which they trace to a now famous dictum by Lord Mansfield in an international smuggling case that "no country ever takes notice of the revenue laws of another."[63]

The rationale for this rule (both in civil law and common law countries) is that the enforcement of foreign revenue laws infringes on the sovereign rights of the forum state. The rule and the rationalization have been criticized, however, as legally and economically unsound in light of the contemporary interdependence of nations. Nevertheless, the rule continues to be universally observed.

However, because most nations of the world are members of the IMF, the provision in Article VIII, Section 2(b), of the IMF Articles of Agreement effectively overrides the traditional nonenforcement rule in most cases. Of course, not all countries are members of the IMF. When their currency exchange regulations are at issue, those regulations will not, as Case 6-3 illustrates, be enforced abroad.

---

[63]Holman v. Johnson, *English Reports*, vol. 98, p. 1120 at p. 1121 (1775).

Case 6-3   MENENDEZ v. SAKS AND COMPANY

United States, Court of Appeals, Second Circuit, 1973. *Federal Reporter, Second Series*, vol. 485, p. 1355 (1973).

On September 15, 1960, the Cuban government "intervened"[64] in the operation of (i.e., it nationalized) the five leading manufacturers of Cuban cigars (F. Palacio y Compañia, SA; Tabacaler José L. Piedra, SA; Por Larranga, SA; Cifuentes y Compañia; and Menendez, Garcia y Compañia, Limitada). These manufacturers for many years had produced cigars of the highest quality and reputation and had sold them to importers in the United States, principally the parties being sued in this case, Faber, Coe & Gregg (Faber), Alfred Dunhill of London (Dunhill), and Saks & Company (Saks). The importers paid for the cigars in U.S. dollars by checks drawn on New York banks and made payable either (1) to the Cuban exporter, (2) to a New York bank acting as the exporter's collecting agent, or (3) to the order of the Cuban exporter and/or the New York collecting bank. Payments made to the New York collecting banks were transmitted by those banks to the Banco Nacional de Cuba, which in turn credited the exporters with pesos in their own Cuban banks.[65]

Upon the Cuban government's intervention, the owners were immediately ousted and the government designated persons called interventors as its agents to manage the businesses. The interventors continued to operate the

businesses and to export cigars under the same company names to the same importers in the United States. The importers continued to make some payments through their usual channels, but most of these payments were intended to cover only the amounts still owing for the preintervention shipments. Although the importers accepted the cigars shipped after the intervention, they did not pay for most of them. Shipments from Cuba to the U.S. importers continued until February 1961, when relations between the interventors and the importers deteriorated for various reasons. In February 1962, the U.S. government declared an embargo on future trade with Cuba.

Immediately after the Cuban government seized the cigar manufacturing companies, the owners of those businesses fled to the United States and brought actions in New York against the importers to collect the sums due for cigars shipped from their factories in Cuba. Shortly thereafter, the interventors sought to intervene in these actions to replace the owners in prosecuting claims against the importers. The government of Cuba also intervened to support the claims of the interventors.

The trial court held that the importers had to pay the original owners for the cigars exported to the United States before their companies were nationalized and the interventors for the cigars sold after that time. The importers were also allowed to offset monies they had previously paid the interventors. All of the parties appealed.

---

[64]*Intervention* was the euphemistic term used for seizure of a business by the Cuban government in 1960.
[65]This method of making payment through a New York collecting bank was imposed on the exporters by the Castro government soon after it came to power to ensure that the dollars would be available to the Cuban government rather than be kept or used abroad by the exporters.

CIRCUIT JUDGE MANSFIELD

* * *

... The interventors insist that they, rather than the owners, are entitled to the proceeds paid or payable by the importers for the preintervention shipments. They claim that the owners' accounts receivable were included in the property effectively seized by the intervention. They further argue that even if the owners' accounts receivable were not effectively seized, the owners are entitled at most to Cuban pesos, which is all that they would have been permitted to retain had they collected on these accounts while still in Cuba, since Cuban currency regulations require a Cuban exporter who receives payment in a foreign currency to deliver the foreign currency to the "Cuban Stabilization Fund" for exchange into pesos.

* * *

[As for interventors' claim that they are entitled to the proceeds from the preintervention shipments of cigars, we are compelled to deny their request because of] our decision in *Republic of Iraq v. First National City Bank.*[66] Application of the principles of that case here satisfies us that since the owners' accounts receivable had their *situs*[67] in the United States rather than in Cuba at the time of intervention and since the Cuban government's purported seizure of them without compensation is contrary to our own domestic policy, the act of state doctrine does not apply, the confiscation was ineffective, and the interventors' claim must be rejected. The owners rather than the interventors remain entitled to collect these accounts.

* * *

... Cuba and the interventors argue that even if the intervention did not deprive the owners of their right to collect on their accounts receivable from the importers, the district court erred in failing to apply Cuban currency regulations, which would limit the owners to ultimate receipt of pesos rather than dollars for these accounts....

Relying on *Auten v. Auten,*[68] Cuba and the interventors insist that Cuban law was applicable because the contracts were made and were to be performed in Cuba. A Cuban currency regulation in effect since 1959 required all exporters who received payment in a foreign currency to deliver the currency within three days to the Cuban Currency Stabilization Fund for exchange into pesos. The interventors argue that by ignoring these and other regulations[69] the district court has given the owners an unwarranted windfall at the ultimate expense of the interventors and the Republic of Cuba.[70]

Neither the invoices nor other documents evidencing the agreement between the parties specify that payment was to be made in Cuba or in pesos. On the contrary, the business practice of the parties was that the importers for the most part would pay in dollars by checks drawn and delivered to collecting banks located in New York, which acted as the sellers' agents. In those instances where checks were sent directly to the exporters in Cuba, the checks were drawn on New York banks so that final payment was made in New York. Ordinarily, where a contract or agreement authorizes performance in any of several places, the law governing the agreement is that of the place of performance actually chosen.[71]

... Nor are we persuaded that Cuba's currency control regulations should here be given effect on the ground that not to do so would give the owners the benefit of a dollar windfall in lieu of the pesos which the Cuban government would have required them to accept in exchange for their dollars if they had remained in Cuba. The broad question of whether extraterritorial effect should be given to a foreign government's currency controls is not to be resolved on the basis of what the effect will be in a particular case but upon basic policy grounds. Currency controls are but a species of revenue law.[72] As a general rule one nation will not enforce the revenue laws of another,[73] at least in the absence of an agreement between the nations involved to do so.[74] While Article VIII of the Bretton Woods [IMF] Agreement

---

[66]*Federal Reporter, Second Series*, vol. 353, p. 47 (Second Circuit Ct. of Appeals, 1965), *certirorari* denied, *United States Reports*, vol. 382, p. 1027 (Supreme Ct., 1966).

[67]Latin: "situation" or "location." The location of a place of business.

[68]*New York Reports*, vol. 308, p. 155 (New York Ct. of Appeals, 1954), which holds that the law of the state with the most significant contacts governs contractual obligations.

[69]Other regulations or "instructions" established the method of payment through New York collecting banks whereby the exporters would receive only pesos.

[70]The theory of the interventors and Cuba is that if the owners had been awarded pesos rather than dollars, in effect they would have recovered nothing since presently there is no exchange between pesos and dollars. A nominal recovery by the owners, according to the theory, would have reduced the importers' setoff against the interventors.

[71]See, e.g., Anglo-Continentale Treuhand, AG v. St. Louis Southwest Railway, *Federal Reporter, Second Series,* vol. 81, p. 11 (Second Circuit Ct. of Appeals, 1936), *certirorari* denied, *United States Reports*, vol. 298, p. 655 (Supreme Ct., 1936).

[72]Confirm Banco do Brasil, SA v. A. C. Israel Commodity Co., *New York Reports, Second Series*, vol. 12, p. 371 (New York Ct. of Appeals, 1963), *certirorari* denied, *United States Reports*, vol. 376, p. 906 (Supreme Ct., 1963).

[73]See Colorado v. Harbeck, *New York Reports*, vol. 232, p. 71 (New York Ct. of Appeals, 1921).

[74]See, e.g., Bretton Woods *International Monetary Fund Agreement.*

evidenced a commitment on the part of signatory nations to enforce each other's exchange controls as a matter of international cooperation[75] Cuba has long since withdrawn from the Fund Agreement. Cuba cannot, therefore, predicate its attempted enforcement of its currency regulations upon any treaty or international agreement with the United States.

. . . Here the agreement bound the importers to pay dollars, not pesos. . . . Although the effect of our judgment is to award to the owners dollars, which are worth more on the market than the pesos which the owners would be required by Cuban law to accept if they were in Cuba, this does not constitute a valid ground for enforcement here of Cuba's revenue laws. . . .

The judgment of the trial court was affirmed.

CASEPOINT: The accounts receivable have their *situs* in the United States, as payment was due in New York with U.S. dollars. Therefore, the intervention (expropriation) in Cuba by the Cuban government does not trigger the act of state doctrine, because the accounts receivable were effectively "in" the United States at the time of the Cuban government's purported seizure of them.

Where a contract or agreement authorizes performance in any of several places, the law governing the

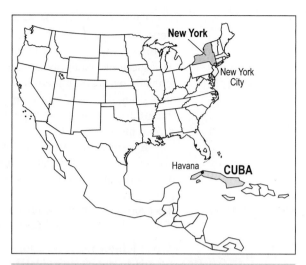

MAP 6-3 Cuba and the United States (1973)

agreement is that of the place of performance actually chosen. Here the contracts were actually paid in New York, so the governing law is New York law. Thus, Cuban currency regulations would not apply.

Even if Cuban currency regulations did apply, as a general rule one nation will not enforce the revenue laws of another, at least in the absence of an agreement between the nations involved to do so.

---

[75]See, e.g., Meyer, "Recognition of Exchange Controls After the International Monetary Fund Agreement," *Yale Law Journal*, vol. 62, p. 867 (1953).

ENFORCEMENT OF OTHER IMF MEMBER STATE CURRENCY EXCHANGE OBLIGATIONS

The "General Obligations of Members" of the Fund are contained in Article VIII of the IMF Articles of Agreement. Section 2(b), as we have seen, makes exchange contracts that violate a member's currency regulations unenforceable in other member states. Section 2(a) forbids member states from imposing restrictions on the payments or transfers involving current international transactions. A **current international transaction** is any transaction other than the transfer of capital.[76] Restrictions on the transfer of currency between member countries are therefore forbidden on transactions that involve any of the following:

> **current international transaction:** Any currency transaction other than the transfer of capital.

1. All payments due in connection with foreign trade, other current business, including services, and normal short-term banking and credit facilities.
2. Payments due as interest on loans and as net income from other investments.
3. Payments of moderate amount for amortization of loans or for depreciation of direct investments.
4. Moderate remittances for family living expenses.

---

[76]Article XXX(d).

Section 3 of Article VIII forbids a member from engaging in any "discriminatory currency arrangements" or "multiple currency practices,"[77] and Section 4 requires a member to buy its own currency from other members who have acquired it as the result of "current transactions." Sections 5, 6, and 7 require members to furnish information to the IMF, to consult with other members when adopting special or temporary currency exchange restrictions, to collaborate in promoting international liquidity, and to work with other members to make the "special drawing right the principal reserve asset in the international monetary system."

Except for Section 2(b) of Article VIII, the member states' obligations do not give rise to any private rights. As a consequence, the other provisions of the IMF Articles of Agreement are seldom the subject of court disputes.[78]

EXEMPTIONS FOR NEW MEMBERS FROM IMF MEMBER STATE CURRENCY EXCHANGE OBLIGATIONS

Upon joining the IMF, a state does not have to accede to all of the currency exchange obligations set out in Article VIII (Sections 2, 3, and 4) of the IMF's Articles. Article XIV sets out transitional provisions that give a new member the option of maintaining the restrictions on payments and transfers for current international transactions in effect on the date it becomes a member. Only those restrictions may be maintained, however. Any later restrictions will automatically fall under Article VIII and will require IMF approval.

At the time the IMF Agreement was first signed in 1945, only the United States and nine other countries (all from Latin America) did not claim this exemption. As of 2007, more than 166 states (more than three-quarters of all IMF members) had agreed to comply with the obligations imposed by Article VIII, including many of the more advanced developing states. This is a significant development, as it indicates that most IMF members are committed to pursuing sound economic policies and will forgo any future reimposition of exchange restrictions.

D. CURRENCY SUPPORT

In addition to its principal function as the regulatory body for the international currency exchange system, the IMF serves as a short-term source of funds for member states having difficulty meeting their balance-of-payments obligations. These funds are drawn principally from the quota subscriptions paid by members, although the IMF also borrows from commercial banks. As of June 2007, the total quota subscriptions amounted to 216.7 billion SDRs or U.S. $327.7 billion.[79]

IMF FACILITIES

IMF facilities: The financial assistance programs available to IMF members.

The IMF's financial resources are made available to its members through a variety of **facilities.** These facilities are funded from (1) the General Resources Account (consisting of funds from the members' subscriptions and funds borrowed from banks by the IMF), (2) the Special Disbursement Account (made up of funds derived originally from the sale of the IMF's gold holdings between 1976 and 1980, and later from interest paid by borrowers), and

---

[77] *Multiple currency practices* is the maintenance of several different rates of exchange for a currency, such as one rate for nationals, another for foreign individuals, and a third for government agencies.

[78] Article IX, which establishes the fund's status, immunities, and privileges, was the focus of a dispute before the U.S. Federal Communications Commission (FCC) in International Bank for Reconstruction and Development & International Monetary Fund v. All America Cables and Radio, Inc., *Federal Communications Commission Reports*, vol. 17, p. 450 (1966). In that decision, the FCC held that the IMF was entitled to the same privileges for transmitting its international cables as those given to foreign governments.

[79] "IMF Members' Quotas and Voting Power, and IMF Governors," posted at http://www.imf.org/external/np/sec/memdir/members.htm.

(3) the Enhanced Structural Adjustment Facility Trust Fund (which has resources from loans and donations from members). As of April 2007, the IMF had credits and loans outstanding of $78 billion to 74 countries.[80]

The IMF provides regular, concessional, and special facilities for its member states.

Regular IMF Facilities

Facilities available to all IMF member states include the following:

Reserve *Tranche* Each member has an IMF *tranche* that it may withdraw at any time and that technically does not constitute the use of an IMF credit. This *tranche* consists of that share of a member state's quota that it did not contribute in its own currency (i.e., 25 percent of its quota).[81]

tranche: (French: "installment" or "block of shares.") A percentage of an IMF member's quota that it may withdraw to stabilize its currency or to meet balance-of-payments obligations.

Credit *Tranche* A member is entitled to four credit *tranches,* each equivalent to 25 percent of its quota. The first one is generally made available when a member faces relatively minor balance-of-payments difficulties and is subject to few conditions. Subsequent *tranches* (collectively known as *upper credit tranches*) are subject to progressively more stringent conditions.[82]

Extended Fund Facility These facilities help member states overcome balance-of-payments problems for longer periods (i.e., financing is available for up to three years) and for amounts larger (i.e., up to 140 percent of the member's quota) than those available under the credit *tranche.*[83]

Standby Arrangements These are designed to help countries address short-term balance-of-payments problems. Standbys have provided the greatest amount of IMF resources. These facilities are in essence *bridging loans* provided to member states while the IMF deliberates about whether to provide other funds to the particular member state. Typically, they are granted for 12–24 months and repayment is normally expected within 2¼–4 years. Surcharges apply to high access levels.[84]

Concessional IMF Facility

The IMF has one facility, established in 1987, enlarged and extended in 1994, and renamed and revised in 1999, that is designed for low-income member countries with protracted balance-of-payment problems. The Poverty Reduction and Growth Facility provides loans at concessional interest rates of 0.5 percent per annum to such countries. During 2006, some 78 low-income countries were eligible for PRGF assistance.[85]

Special IMF Facilities

Compensatory Financing Facility Created in 1963, this facility helps a country deal with a temporary depletion of its foreign exchange reserves when this comes about as the consequence of economic developments beyond its control (such as a crop failure or natural disaster).[86]

Supplemental Reserve Facility This facility provides short-term financial assistance for exceptional balance-of-payments difficulties due to a large short-term financing need that is the result of a sudden and disruptive loss of market confidence.[87]

---

[80]"The IMF at a Glance: A Factsheet" (April 2007) posted at http://www.imf.org/external/np/exr/facts/glance.htm.
[81]"Financial Organization and Operations of the IMF," p. 22 (IMF Pamphlet Series No. 45, 6th ed. 2001) posted at http://www.imf.org/external/pubs/ft/pam/pam45/contents.htm.
[82]*Id.*, p. 20.
[83]*Id.*, p. 42.
[84]"How Does the IMF Lend? A Factsheet" (September 2006) posted at http://www.imf.org/external/np/exr/facts/howlend.htm.
[85]"The IMF's Poverty Reduction and Growth Facility (PRGF): A Factsheet" (August 2006) posted at http://www.imf.org/external/np/exr/facts/prgf.htm.
[86]"Organization and Operations of the IMF," pp. 44–45 (IMF Pamphlet Series No. 45, 6th ed. 2001) posted at http://www.imf.org/external/pubs/ft/pam/pam45/contents.htm.
[87]*Id.*, p. 42.

Contingent Credit Lines Established in 1999 in response to the spread of turmoil through global financial markets during the Asian crisis, this is a precautionary facility designed to help members with strong economic policies and sound financial systems that find themselves threatened by a crisis elsewhere in the world economy—a phenomenon known as *financial contagion*.[88]

IMF CONDITIONALITY

IMF conditionality: Principle that a member's right to the use of credit *tranches* and credit facilities will depend on its progress in regularizing its balance-of-payments obligations and developing sustained economic growth.

Use of the IMF's resources is limited by the policies set out in the Articles of Agreement and the policies adopted under them. This requirement is known as **conditionality**.

The essence of conditionality is that access to the IMF's credit *tranches* and other credit facilities is linked to a member's progress in implementing policies to restore balance-of-payments viability and sustainable economic growth. It is based not on a rigid set of operational rules but on a general set of guidelines. The current guidelines, which the Executive Board adopted in 1979, encourage members to adopt corrective measures at an early stage, stress the importance of respecting the member state's domestic social and political objectives, limit the number and content of performance criteria, and emphasize that IMF arrangements are not contractual agreements but rather decisions of the IMF that set out the conditions for continued financial assistance.[89]

E. DEVELOPMENT BANKS

World Bank: Informal name for the International Bank for Reconstruction and Development. An intergovernmental organization, headquartered in Washington, DC, that provides development financing for its members.

International Development Association (IDA): A subsidiary of the World Bank that provides concessional development financing to less developed countries.

International Finance Corporation (IFC): A subsidiary of the World Bank that provides development financing to private enterprises.

Global Environment Facility (GEF): A World Bank source of grant and concessional funding for protecting and improving the global environment.

There exist on the international, regional, and national levels specialized financial organizations that promote economic development. The International Bank for Reconstruction and Development (IBRD)—known informally as the **World Bank**—was established, along with the IMF, at the United Nations meeting at Bretton Woods in 1944. Membership in the bank is restricted to the members of the IMF, and in essence, the bank operates as the development arm of the IMF.

Complementing the World Bank are two subsidiaries: the **International Development Agency (IDA)**, and the **International Finance Corporation (IFC)**. The World Bank provides development financing to the national governments and political subdivisions of its member states. The IDA provides less restrictive financing for less developed countries, and the IFC provides loans to private enterprises.[90] Together, the World Bank, the IDA, and the IFC are the world's largest providers of development assistance to developing countries and countries in transition, providing some $20 billion in new loans each year.

The World Bank is also responsible for managing the Trust Fund of the **Global Environment Facility (GEF)**. The GEF, which became a permanent international facility in 1994, provides grant and concessional monies to developing countries to fund projects dealing with four global environmental problems: climate change, biological diversity, international waters, and ozone layer depletion.[91] Only countries that are parties to the Climate Change Convention[92] or the Convention on Biological Diversity[93] are eligible to receive funds from

[88]"The IMF's Contingent Credit Lines: A Factsheet" (March 2004) posted at http://www.imf.org/external/np/exr/facts/ccl.htm.
[89]IMF Policy Development and Review Department, "Conditionality in Fund-Supported Programs—Overview" (February 20, 2001), posted at http://www.imf.org/external/np/pdr/cond/2001/eng/overview/index.htm.
[90]As of April 2007, the World Bank had 185 members; the IDA had 166; and the IFC had 179. The World Bank's Web site is at http://www.worldbank.org.
[91]Instrument for the Establishment of the Restructured Global Environment Facility, Article I, § 2, posted at http://www.gefweb.org/GEF_Instrument3.pdf.
[92]The Climate Change Secretariat's home page at http://www.unfccc.de contains the full text of the United Nations Framework Convention on Climate Change. As of April 2007, there were 189 states parties.
[93]The Biological Diversity Secretariat's home page at http://www.biodiv.org/ has the full text of the convention. As of April 2007, there were 190 states parties.

International Fund for Agricultural Development (IFAD): An intergovernmental organization, headquartered in Rome, that provides financing to its developing member states to promote food production.

the GEF. Unlike in other World Bank facilities, an independent Council made up of 32 states participating in the GEF determines which projects will be funded.[94]

Another international development organization, the **International Fund for Agricultural Development (IFAD)**, was created by a special UN conference held in Rome in 1976. Membership is open to any UN member.[95] The IFAD's primary objective is to provide financing for projects that introduce, expand, and improve food production systems in its developing member states.

Regional development organizations exist to promote the economic and social development of regional groups. The names and purposes of the major regional organizations are listed in Exhibit 6-3.

National development agencies exist in virtually every developed country. The most important ones are discussed in Chapter 12.

CURRENT CONTROVERSIES AT THE WORLD BANK

The oft-noted corruption at the World Bank was revealed by the World Bank itself in a 2005 study by its Department of Institutional Integrity. Fraud seems to be endemic in World Bank projects. As a *U.S. News and World Report* article outlined in 2007, the World Bank is a deeply troubled institution where corruption may have meant the loss of $100 billion or more over the years. It is also not clear to many what the $20 billion in loans and grants the bank makes each year are accomplishing. Middle-income nations can "tap global financial markets if they need a loan, and the aid money seems to be making little difference in the world's poorest countries."[96] From 1980 to 2002, 23 of 45 sub-Saharan

EXHIBIT 6-3 Regional Development Organizations

Name	Objectives
African Development Bank	Complementary regional economic development
Asian Development Bank	Complementary regional economic development
Arab Bank for Economic Development in Africa	African economic independence through Arab-African cooperation
Arab Fund for Economic and Social Development	Joint Arab development projects
Caribbean Development Bank	Economic cooperation and integration
Central African States Development Bank	Multinational development projects leading to economic integration
Central American Bank for Economic Integration	Economic integration and balanced economic development
East African Development Bank	Regional economic development
Inter-American Development Bank	Economic growth and development
Islamic Development Bank	Economic development in accordance with Islamic law
Nordic Investment Bank	Nordic economic development and Nordic exports
OPEC Fund for International Development	Economic cooperation and development
Southern African Development Coordination	Regional economic integration Conference
West African Development Bank	Economic integration and development

Source: Based on Robert Fraser, *The World Financial System*, pp. 398–454 (Phoenix, AZ: Oryx Press, 1987).

[94]Instrument for the Establishment of the Restructured Global Environment Facility, Article I, §16. Any UN member may become a participant in the GEF by depositing an instrument of participation with the GEF Secretariat or by making a deposit in the Trust Fund. *Id.*, Article I, § 7. As of April 2007, there were 177 member countries. See http://www.gefweb.org/participants/Members_Countries/members_countries.html.
[95]The IFAD has 161 member countries. See the IFAD home page at http://www.ifad.org.
[96]James Pethokoukis, "The Post-Wolfowitz World Bank," *U.S. News & World Report*, May 17, 2007.

African countries experienced negative compounded economic growth, when adjusted for inflation.[97]

While many may bid for a contract to build a road or to provide tractors, the bank provides the cash while the borrowing government chooses the winning bid. A 2005 article by Dr. Nathaniel Hobbs indicated that in 90 bank contracts (worth $90 million in total) in over 20 countries, a kickback was sought by local officials in every case. The kickbacks averaged 10 to 15 percent.

Some estimates indicate that the bank will finance 45,000 contracts a year. Rooting out corruption is a difficult process, and watching every cent is not possible, so the bank looks first at cases where the bank's staff may be involved or the reputation of the bank is at risk. If a scandal tainted a bank project with the U.S. Agency for International Development (US AID),[98] the bank would be quick to act and has made examples of some. A seven-year ban on Lahmeyer International (a German firm found to have bribed an official in Lesotho) has sent a definite signal to some potential bribers.

The themes of corruption and ethics brought the World Bank into greater public view in the spring of 2007 when Paul Wolfowitz, the president of the bank, was questioned for arranging a sweetheart deal for his companion, Shaha Ali Riza, who had worked at the bank for seven years before his arrival. Because of their relationship, bank rules required that she leave the bank's employ. In arranging for her salary as a liaison to the State Department, he may or may not have violated bank procedures.[99] His resignation followed many weeks of controversy, some of it opaque, as to whether his own ethics were lacking. Ultimately, the board of the bank accepted his resignation with a statement issued May 17, 2007.

The board wrote that they had "considered carefully the report of the ad hoc group, the associated documents, and the submissions and presentations of Mr. Wolfowitz," and went on to note that Mr. Wolfowitz "assured us that he acted ethically and in good faith in what he believed were the best interests of the institution, and we accept that," while acknowledging that "a number of mistakes were made by a number of individuals in handling the matter under consideration, and that the Bank's systems did not prove robust to the strain under which they were placed. " The board expressed gratitude for his service at the bank and noted achievements over a two-year period that included "the Multilateral Debt Relief Initiative, the Clean Energy Investment Framework, the Africa Action Plan, and the Avian Flu Initiative." The board also noted the value of emergency action programs in Liberia, the Democratic Republic of the Congo, and the Central African Republic, as well as the new strategy for the bank's efforts to improve governance and combat corruption.[100]

At the time of the Wolfowitz resignation, many critics of the bank were contending that it no longer had a useful role to play in global development. After World War II, the World Bank was often the lender of first resort. But the bank itself must raise funds from sometimes skeptical governments, and also faces stiffer competition for aid dollars than ever before. There are over 150 multilateral bodies—from the African Development Bank to the United Nations Children's Fund—and a host of funds, facilities, and initiatives dedicated to specific causes, such as the President's Malaria Initiative launched by George W. Bush. Also, as noted above, middle-income nations can go to global financial markets if they need a loan.

Yet, certain kinds of development loans seem unlikely to be made by the private sector. For example, in 2007 the bank approved a $45.65 million concessionary credit to Pakistan for a Land Record Management and Information System Project (LRMIS). LRMIS is aimed at improving a system of land titles that dates back to the nineteenth century. The inefficiencies and costs of the current system make it very difficult for Pakistanis in the Punjab region to

---

[97]*Id.*
[98]http://www.usaid.gov.
[99]Steven R. Weisman, "Bank's Report Says Wolfowitz Violated Ethics," *New York Times*, May 15, 2007.
[100]Statement of Executive Directors, available at http://web.worldbank.org/WBSITE/EXTERNAL/NEWS/ 0, contentMDK:21339650∼menuPK:34463∼pagePK:34370∼piPK:34424∼theSitePK:4607,00.html.

get and maintain clear titles to real property. Having clear title to land is a formative and essential part of creating an entrepreneurial class.[101]

The credit comes from the bank's International Development Association (IDA) with thirty-five years' maturity and a ten-year grace period. Under the project, "service centres would be established where land records would be maintained and made available to the public in digital form and pilot linkages between the land records system and the system for registration of deeds."[102] Under the project, land records will be provided within 30 minutes of application at the service centres; currently, it can take weeks for this process to be completed. Transaction costs are expected to be reduced significantly, as well.

What the future role of the World Bank is for global development remains to be seen. It is less likely to put its financial muscle behind privatization or trade liberalization in countries that do not want either. It may find more efficient ways of dealing with corruption, both inside the bank and without. It is likely to find a way to persist, if only because it has considerable institutional momentum. Still, the bank must find a way not only to accommodate the changing needs of a developing world, but also to achieve a closer understanding of its role *vis-a-vis* the IMF. The differences between the two are discussed in Reading 6-2.

---

[101]See Hernando DeSoto, *The Mystery of Capital* (2000).
[102]Misrar Khan, "World Bank to Give $45.65 Million for Punjab Land Record Management," *Business Recorder,* Jan. 27, 2007, p. 83.

Reading 6-2   THE IMF AND THE WORLD BANK

How Do They Differ?[103]

David D. Driscoll http://www.imf.org/external/pubs/ft/exrp/differ/differ.htm

If you have difficulty distinguishing the World Bank from the International Monetary Fund, you are not alone. Most people have only the vaguest idea of what these institutions do, and very few people indeed could, if pressed on the point, say why and how they differ. Even John Maynard Keynes, a founding father of the two institutions and considered by many the most brilliant economist of the twentieth century, admitted at the inaugural meeting of the International Monetary Fund that he was confused by the names: he thought the Fund should be called a bank, and the Bank should be called a fund. Confusion has reigned ever since.

Known collectively as the Bretton Woods Institutions after the remote village in New Hampshire, U.S.A., where they were founded by the delegates of 44 nations in July 1944, the Bank and the IMF are twin intergovernmental pillars supporting the structure of the world's economic and financial order. That there are two pillars rather than one is no accident. The international community was consciously trying to establish a division of labor in setting up the two agencies. Those who deal professionally with the IMF and Bank find them categorically distinct. To the rest of the world, the niceties of the division of labor are even more mysterious than are the activities of the two institutions.

Similarities between them do little to resolve the confusion. Superficially the Bank and IMF exhibit many common characteristics. Both are in a sense owned and directed by the governments of member nations. The People's Republic of China, by far the most populous state on earth, is a member, as is the world's largest industrial power (the United States). In fact, virtually every country on earth is a member of both institutions. Both institutions concern themselves with economic issues and concentrate their efforts on broadening and strengthening the economies of their member nations. Staff members of both the Bank and IMF often appear at international conferences, speaking the same recondite language of the economics and development professions, or are reported in the media to be negotiating involved and somewhat mystifying programs of economic adjustment with ministers of finance or other

---

[103]This article can be found on the IMF Web site at http://www.imf.org/external/pubs/ft/exrp/differ/differ.htm.

government officials. The two institutions hold joint annual meetings, which the news media cover extensively. Both have headquarters in Washington, D.C., where popular confusion over what they do and how they differ is about as pronounced as everywhere else. For many years both occupied the same building and even now, though located on opposite sides of a street very near the White House, they share a common library and other facilities, regularly exchange economic data, sometimes present joint seminars, daily hold informal meetings, and occasionally send out joint missions to member countries.

Despite these and other similarities, however, the Bank and the IMF remain distinct. The fundamental difference is this: the Bank is primarily a development institution; the IMF is a cooperative institution that seeks to maintain an orderly system of payments and receipts between nations. Each has a different purpose, a distinct structure, receives its funding from different sources, assists different categories of members, and strives to achieve distinct goals through methods peculiar to itself.

PURPOSES

At Bretton Woods the international community assigned to the World Bank the aims implied in its formal name, the International Bank for Reconstruction and Development (IBRD), giving it primary responsibility for financing economic development. The Bank's first loans were extended during the late 1940s to finance the reconstruction of the war-ravaged economies of Western Europe. When these nations recovered some measure of economic self-sufficiency, the Bank turned its attention to assisting the world's poorer nations, known as developing countries, to which it has since the 1940s loaned more than $330 billion. The World Bank has one central purpose: to promote economic and social progress in developing countries by helping to raise productivity so that their people may live a better and fuller life.

The international community assigned to the IMF a different purpose. In establishing the IMF, the world community was reacting to the unresolved financial problems instrumental in initiating and protracting the Great Depression of the 1930s: sudden, unpredictable variations in the exchange values of national currencies and a widespread disinclination among governments to allow their national currency to be exchanged for foreign currency. Set up as a voluntary and cooperative institution, the IMF attracts to its membership nations that are prepared, in a spirit of enlightened self-interest, to relinquish some measure of national sovereignty by abjuring practices injurious to the economic well-being of their fellow member nations. The rules of the institution, contained in the IMF's Articles of Agreement signed by all members, constitute a code of conduct. The code is simple: it requires members to allow their currency to be exchanged for foreign currencies freely and without restriction, to keep the IMF informed of changes they contemplate in financial and monetary policies that will affect fellow members' economies, and, to the extent possible, to modify these policies on the advice of the IMF to accommodate the needs of the entire membership. To help nations abide by the code of conduct, the IMF administers a pool of money from which members can borrow when they are in trouble. The IMF is not, however, primarily a lending institution, as is the Bank. It is first and foremost an overseer of its members' monetary and exchange rate policies and a guardian of the code of conduct. Philosophically committed to the orderly and stable growth of the world economy, the IMF is an enemy of surprise. It receives frequent reports on members' economic policies and prospects, which it debates, comments on, and communicates to the entire membership so that other members may respond in full knowledge of the facts and a clear understanding of how their own domestic policies may affect other countries. The IMF is convinced that a fundamental condition for international prosperity is an orderly monetary system that will encourage trade, create jobs, expand economic activity, and raise living standards throughout the world. By its constitution the IMF is required to oversee and maintain this system, no more and no less.

SIZE AND STRUCTURE

The IMF is small (about 2,300 staff members) and, unlike the World Bank, has no affiliates or subsidiaries. Most of its staff members work at headquarters in Washington, D.C., although three small offices are maintained in Paris, [in] Geneva, and at the United Nations in New York. Its professional staff members are for the most part economists and financial experts.

The structure of the Bank is somewhat more complex. The World Bank itself comprises two major organizations: the International Bank for Reconstruction and Development and the International Development Association (IDA). Moreover, associated with but legally and financially separate from the World Bank are the International Finance Corporation, which mobilizes funding for private enterprises in developing countries, the International Center for Settlement of Investment Disputes, and the Multilateral Guarantee Agency. With over 7,000 staff members, the World Bank Group is about three times as large as the IMF and maintains about 40 offices throughout the world, although 95 percent of its staff work at its Washington, D.C., headquarters. The Bank employs a staff with an astonishing range of expertise: economists, engineers, urban planners, agronomists, statisticians, lawyers, portfolio managers, loan officers, and project appraisers, as well as experts in telecommunications, water supply and sewerage, transportation, education, energy, rural development, population and health care, and other disciplines.

SOURCE OF FUNDING

The World Bank is an investment bank, intermediating between investors and recipients, borrowing from the one and lending to the other. Its owners are the governments of its 180 member nations with equity shares in the Bank, which were valued at about $176 billion in June 1995. The IBRD obtains most of the funds it lends to finance development by market borrowing through the issue of bonds (which carry an AAA rating because repayment is guaranteed by member governments) to individuals and private institutions in more than 100 countries. Its concessional loan associate, IDA, is largely financed by grants from donor nations. The Bank is a major borrower in the world's capital markets and the largest nonresident borrower in virtually all countries where its issues are sold. It also borrows money by selling bonds and notes directly to governments, their agencies, and central banks. The proceeds of these bond sales are lent in turn to developing countries at affordable rates of interest to help finance projects and policy reform programs that give promise of success.

Despite Lord Keynes's profession of confusion, the IMF is not a bank and does not intermediate between investors and recipients. Nevertheless, it has at its disposal significant resources, presently valued at over $215 billion. These resources come from quota subscriptions, or membership fees, paid in by the IMF's 182 member countries. Each member contributes to this pool of resources a certain amount of money proportionate to its economic size and strength (richer countries pay more, poorer less). While the Bank borrows and lends, the IMF is more like a credit union whose members have access to a common pool of resources (the sum total of their individual contributions) to assist them in times of need. Although under special and highly restrictive circumstances the IMF borrows from official entities (but not from private markets), it relies principally on its quota subscriptions to finance its operations. The adequacy of these resources is reviewed every five years.

RECIPIENTS OF FUNDING

Neither wealthy countries nor private individuals borrow from the World Bank, which lends only to creditworthy governments of developing nations. The poorer the country, the more favorable the conditions under which it can borrow from the Bank. Developing countries whose per capita gross national product (GNP) exceeds $1,305 may borrow from the IBRD. (Per capita GNP, a less formidable term than it sounds, is a measure of wealth, obtained by dividing the value of goods and services produced in a country during one year by the

number of people in that country.) These loans carry an interest rate slightly above the market rate at which the Bank itself borrows and must generally be repaid within 12–15 years. The IDA, on the other hand, lends only to governments of very poor developing nations whose per capita GNP is below $1,305, and in practice IDA loans go to countries with annual per capita incomes below $865. IDA loans are interest free and have a maturity of 35 or 40 years.

In contrast, all member nations, both wealthy and poor, have the right to financial assistance from the IMF. Maintaining an orderly and stable international monetary system requires all participants in that system to fulfill their financial obligations to other participants. Membership in the IMF gives to each country that experiences a shortage of foreign exchange—preventing it from fulfilling these obligations—temporary access to the IMF's pool of currencies to resolve this difficulty, usually referred to as a balance of payments problem. These problems are no respecter of economic size or level of per capita GNP, with the result that over the years almost all members of the IMF, from the smallest developing country to the largest industrial country, have at one time or other had recourse to the IMF and received from it financial assistance to tide them over difficult periods. Money received from the IMF must normally be repaid within three to five years, and in no case later than ten years. Interest rates are slightly below market rates, but are not so concessional as those assigned to the World Bank's IDA loans. Through the use of IMF resources, countries have been able to buy time to rectify economic policies and to restore growth without having to resort to actions damaging to other members' economies.

WORLD BANK OPERATIONS

The World Bank exists to encourage poor countries to develop by providing them with technical assistance and funding for projects and policies that will realize the countries' economic potential. The Bank views development as a long-term, integrated endeavor.

During the first two decades of its existence, two thirds of the assistance provided by the Bank went to electric power and transportation projects. Although these so-called infrastructure projects remain important, the Bank has diversified its activities in recent years as it has gained experience with and acquired new insights into the development process.

The Bank gives particular attention to projects that can directly benefit the poorest people in developing countries. The direct involvement of the poorest in economic activity is being promoted through lending for agriculture and rural development, small-scale enterprises, and urban development. The Bank is helping the poor to be more productive and to gain access to such necessities as safe water and waste-disposal facilities, health care, family-planning assistance, nutrition, education, and housing. Within infrastructure projects there have also been changes. In transportation projects, greater attention is given to constructing farm-to-market roads. Rather than concentrating exclusively on cities, power projects increasingly provide lighting and power for villages and small farms. Industrial projects place greater emphasis on creating jobs in small enterprises. Labor-intensive construction is used where practical. In addition to electric power, the Bank is supporting development of oil, gas, coal, fuelwood, and biomass as alternative sources of energy.

The Bank provides most of its financial and technical assistance to developing countries by supporting specific projects. Although IBRD loans and IDA credits are made on different financial terms, the two institutions use the same standards in assessing the soundness of projects. The decision [on] whether a project will receive IBRD or IDA financing depends on the economic condition of the country and not on the characteristics of the project.

Its borrowing member countries also look to the Bank as a source of technical assistance. By far the largest element of Bank-financed technical assistance–running over $1 billion a year recently–is that financed as a component of Bank loans or credits extended for other purposes. But the amount of Bank-financed technical assistance for free-standing loans and to prepare projects has also increased. The Bank serves as executing agency for technical assistance projects financed by the United Nations Development Program in agriculture and rural development, energy, and economic planning. In response to the economic climate in many of its member countries, the Bank is now emphasizing technical assistance for institutional development and macroeconomic policy formulation.

Every project supported by the Bank is designed in close collaboration with national governments and local agencies, and often in cooperation with other multilateral assistance organizations. Indeed, about half of all Bank-assisted projects also receive co-financing from official sources, that is, governments, multilateral financial institutions, and export-credit agencies that directly finance the procurement of goods and services, and from private sources, such as commercial banks.

In making loans to developing countries, the Bank does not compete with other sources of finance. It assists only those projects for which the required capital is not available from other sources on reasonable terms. Through its work, the Bank seeks to strengthen the economies of borrowing nations so that they can graduate from reliance on Bank resources and meet their financial needs, on terms they can afford directly from conventional sources of capital.

The range of the Bank's activities is far broader than its lending operations. Since the Bank's lending decisions depend heavily on the economic condition of the borrowing country, the Bank carefully studies its economy and the needs of the sectors for which lending is contemplated. These analyses help in formulating an appropriate long-term development assistance strategy for the economy.

Graduation from the IBRD and IDA has occurred for many years. Of the 34 very poor countries that borrowed money from IDA during the earliest years, more than two dozen have made enough progress for them no longer to need IDA money, leaving that money available to other countries that joined the Bank more recently. Similarly, about 20 countries that formerly borrowed money from the IBRD no longer have to do so. An outstanding example is Japan. For a period of 14 years, it borrowed from the IBRD. Now, the IBRD borrows large sums in Japan.

IMF OPERATIONS

The IMF has gone through two distinct phases in its 50-year history. During the first phase, ending in 1973, the IMF oversaw the adoption of general convertibility among the major currencies, supervised a system of fixed exchange rates tied to the value of gold, and provided short-term financing to countries in need of a quick infusion of foreign exchange to keep their currencies at par value or to adjust to changing economic circumstances. Difficulties encountered in maintaining a system of fixed exchange rates gave rise to unstable monetary and financial conditions throughout the world and led the international community to reconsider how the IMF could most effectively function in a regime of flexible exchange rates. After five years of analysis and negotiation (1973–78), the IMF's second phase began with the amendment of its constitution in 1978, broadening its functions to enable it to grapple with the challenges that have arisen since the collapse of the par value system. These functions are three.

First, the IMF continues to urge its members to allow their national currencies to be exchanged without restriction for the currencies of other member countries. As of June 2007, 166 members had agreed to full convertibility of their national currencies. Second, in place of monitoring members' compliance with their obligations in a fixed exchange system, the IMF supervises economic policies that influence their balance of payments in the presently legalized flexible exchange rate environment. This supervision provides opportunities for an early warning of any exchange rate or balance of payments problem. In this, the IMF's role is principally advisory. It confers at regular intervals (usually once a year) with its members, analyzing their economic positions and apprising them of actual or potential problems arising from their policies, and keeps the entire membership informed of these developments. Third, the IMF continues to provide short- and medium-term financial assistance to member nations that run into temporary balance of payments difficulties. The financial assistance usually involves the provision by the IMF of convertible currencies to augment the afflicted member's dwindling foreign exchange reserves, but only in return for the government's promise to reform the economic policies that caused the balance of payments problem in the first place. The IMF sees its financial role in these cases not as subsidizing further deficits but as easing a country's painful transition to living within its means.

How in practice does the IMF assist its members? The key opening the door to IMF assistance is the member's balance of payments, the tally of its payments and receipts with other nations. Foreign payments should be in rough balance: a country ideally should take in just about what it pays out. When financial problems cause the price of a member's currency and the price of its goods to fall out of line, balance of payments difficulties are sure to follow. If this happens, the member country may, by virtue of the Articles of Agreement, apply to the IMF for assistance.

To illustrate, let us take the example of a small country whose economy is based on agriculture. For convenience in trade, the government of such a country generally pegs the domestic currency to a convertible currency: so many units of domestic money to a U.S. dollar or French franc. Unless the exchange rate is adjusted from time to time to take account of changes in relative prices, the domestic currency will tend to become overvalued, with an exchange rate, say, of one unit of domestic currency to one U.S. dollar, when relative prices might suggest that two units to one dollar is more realistic. Governments, however, often succumb to the temptation to tolerate overvaluation, because an overvalued currency makes imports cheaper than they would be if the currency were correctly priced.

The other side of the coin, unfortunately, is that overvaluation makes the country's exports more expensive and hence less attractive to foreign buyers. If the currency is thus overvalued, the country will eventually experience a fall-off in export earnings (exports are too expensive) and a rise in import expenditures (imports are apparently cheap and are bought on credit). In effect, the country is earning less, spending more, and going into debt, a predicament as unsustainable for a country as it is for any of us. Moreover, this situation is usually attended by a host of other economic ills for the country. Finding a diminished market for their export crops and receiving low prices from the government marketing board for produce consumed domestically,

farmers either resort to illegal black market exports or lose the incentive to produce. Many of them abandon the farm to seek employment in overcrowded cities, where they become part of larger social and economic problems. Declining domestic agricultural productivity forces the government to use scarce foreign exchange reserves (scarce because export earnings are down) to buy food from abroad. The balance of payments becomes dangerously distorted.

As an IMF member, a country finding itself in this bind can turn to the IMF for consultative and financial assistance. In a collaborative effort, the country and the IMF can attempt to root out the causes of the payments imbalance by working out a comprehensive program that, depending on the particulars of the case, might include raising producer prices paid to farmers so as to encourage agricultural production and reverse migration to the cities, lowering interest rates to expand the supply of credit, and adjusting the currency to reflect the level of world prices, thereby discouraging imports and raising the competitiveness of exports.

Because reorganizing the economy to implement these reforms is disruptive and not without cost, the IMF will lend money to subsidize policy reforms during the period of transition. To ensure that this money is put to the most productive uses, the IMF closely monitors the country's economic progress during this time, providing technical assistance and further consultative services as needed.

In addition to assisting its members in this way, the IMF also helps by providing technical assistance in organizing central banks, establishing and reforming tax systems, and setting up agencies to gather and publish economic statistics. The IMF is also authorized to issue a special type of money, called the SDR, to provide its members with additional liquidity. Known technically as a fiduciary asset, the SDR can be retained by members as part of their monetary reserves or be used in place of national currencies in transactions with other members. To date the IMF has issued slightly over 21.4 billion SDRs, presently valued at about U.S. $30 billion.

Over the past few years, in response to an emerging interest by the world community to return to a more stable system of exchange rates that would reduce the present fluctuations in the values of currencies, the IMF has been strengthening its supervision of members' economic policies. Provisions exist in its Articles of Agreement that would allow the IMF to adopt a more active role, should the world community decide on stricter management of flexible exchange rates or even on a return to some system of stable exchange rates.

Measuring the success of the IMF's operations over the years is not easy, for much of the IMF's work consists in averting financial crises or in preventing their becoming worse. Most observers feel that merely to have contained the debt crisis of the 1980s, which posed the risk of collapse in the world's financial system, must be counted a success for the IMF. The Fund has also gained some recognition for assisting in setting up market-based economies in the countries of the former Soviet Union and for responding swiftly to the Mexican peso crisis in 1994, but its main contribution lies in its unobtrusive, day-to-day encouragement of confidence in the international system. Nowhere will you find a bridge or a hospital built by the IMF, but the next time you buy a Japanese camera or drive a foreign car, or without difficulty exchange dollars or pounds for another currency while on holiday, you will be benefiting from the vast increase in foreign trade over the past 50 years and the widespread currency convertibility that would have been unimaginable without the world monetary system that the IMF was created to maintain.

COOPERATION BETWEEN BANK AND IMF

Although the Bank and IMF are distinct entities, they work together in close cooperation. This cooperation, present since their founding, has become more pronounced since the 1970s. Since then the Bank's activities have increasingly reflected the realization that the pace of economic and social development accelerates only when sound underlying financial and economic policies are in place. The IMF has also recognized that unsound financial and economic policies are often deeply rooted in long-term inefficient use of resources that resists eradication through short-term adaptations of financial policies. It does little good for the Bank to develop a long-term irrigation project to assist, say, the export of cotton if the country's balance of payments position is so chaotic that no foreign buyers will deal with the country. On the other hand, it does little good for the IMF to help establish a sound exchange rate for a country's currency, unless the production of cotton for export will suffice to sustain that exchange rate over the medium to long term. The key to solving these problems is seen in restructuring economic sectors so that the economic potential of projects might be realized throughout the economy and the stability of the economy might enhance the effectiveness of the individual project.

Around 75 percent of the Bank's lending is applied to specific projects dealing with roads, dams, power stations, agriculture, and industry. As the global economy became mired in recession in the early 1980s, the Bank expanded the scope of its lending operations to include structural- and sector-adjustment loans. These help developing countries adjust their economic policies and structures in the face of serious balance of payments problems that threaten continued development. The main objective of structural-adjustment lending is to re-structure a developing country's economy as the best basis for sustained economic growth. Loans support programs that are intended to anticipate and avert economic crises through economic reforms and changes in investment priorities. By using so-called policy-based lending, the Bank stimulates economic growth in heavily indebted countries—particularly in Latin America and in sub-Saharan Africa—that are undertaking, often at much social pain, far-reaching programs of economic adjustment.

In addition to its traditional function as provider of short-term balance of payments assistance, the advent of the oil crisis in the mid-1970s and the debt crisis in the early 1980s induced the IMF, too, to rethink its policy of restricting its financial assistance to short-term lending. As balance of payments shortfalls grew larger and longer-term structural reforms in members' economies were called for to eliminate these shortfalls, the IMF enlarged the amount of financial assistance it provides and lengthened the period within which its financial assistance would be available. In doing so, the IMF implicitly recognizes that balance of payments problems arise not only from a temporary lack of liquidity and inadequate financial and budgetary policies but also from long-standing contradictions in the structure of members' economies, requiring reforms stretching over a number of years and suggesting closer collaboration with the World Bank, which commands both the expertise and experience to deal with protracted structural impediments to growth.

Focusing on structural reform in recent years has resulted in considerable convergence in the efforts of the Bank and IMF and has led them to greater reliance on each other's special expertise. This convergence has been hastened by the debt crisis, brought on by the inability of developing countries to repay the enormous loans they contracted during the late 1970s and early 1980s. The debt crisis has emphasized that economic growth can be sustained only when resources are being used efficiently and that resources can be used efficiently only in a stable monetary and financial environment.

The bedrock of cooperation between the Bank and IMF is the regular and frequent interaction of economists and loan officers who work on the same country. The Bank staff brings to this interchange a longer-term view of the slow process of development and a profound knowledge of the structural requirements and economic potential of a country. The IMF staff contributes its own perspective on the day-to-day capability of a country to sustain its flow of payments to creditors and to attract from them investment finance, as well as on how the country is integrated within the world economy. This interchange of information is backed up by a coordination of financial assistance to members. For instance, the

Bank has been approving structural- or sector-adjustment loans for most of the countries that are taking advantage of financial assistance from the IMF. In addition, both institutions encourage other lenders, both private and official, to join with them in co-financing projects and in mobilizing credits to countries that are in need. Cooperation between the Bretton Woods institutions has two results: the identification of programs that will encourage growth in a stable economic environment and the coordination of financing that will ensure the success of these programs. Other lenders, particularly commercial banks, frequently make credits available only after seeing satisfactory performance by the borrowing country of its program of structural adjustment.

Cooperation between the Bank and the IMF has over the past decade been formalized with the establishment in the IMF of procedures to provide financing at below-market rates to its poorest member countries. These procedures enable the IMF to make available up to $12 billion to those 70 or so poor member countries that adjust the structure of their economies to improve their balance of payment position and to foster growth. The Bank joins with the IMF in providing additional money for these countries from IDA. But what IDA can provide in financial resources is only a fraction of the world's minimum needs for concessional external finance. Happily, various governments and international agencies have responded positively to the Bank's special action program for low-income, debt-distressed countries of the region by pledging an extra $7 billion for co-financing programs arranged by the Bank.

The Bank and the IMF have distinct mandates that allow them to contribute, each in its own way, to the stability of the international monetary and financial system and to the fostering of balanced economic growth throughout the entire membership. Since their founding 50 years ago, both institutions have been challenged by changing economic circumstances to develop new ways of assisting their membership. The Bank has expanded its assistance from an orientation toward projects to the broader aspects of economic reform. Simultaneously the IMF has gone beyond concern with simple balance of payment adjustment to interest itself in the structural reform of its members' economies. Some overlapping by both institutions has inevitably occurred, making cooperation between the Bank and the IMF crucial. Devising programs that will integrate members' economies more fully into the international monetary and financial system and at the same time encourage economic expansion continues to challenge the expertise of both Bretton Woods institutions.

F. THE BANK FOR INTERNATIONAL SETTLEMENTS

Bank for International Settlements (BIS): Intergovernmental organization, headquartered in Basel, that functions as a bank for the world's central banks.

The oldest international organization involved in monetary cooperation is the **Bank for International Settlements (BIS)**, headquartered in Basel, Switzerland.[104] Founded in 1930, it has three main purposes: (1) to act as a bank for the world's central banks, (2) to promote

EXHIBIT 6-4 Compared: The IMF and the World Bank

World Bank	International Monetary Fund
• Principal aim of assisting the world's less developed nations through long-term financing of projects and programs.	• Oversees the international monetary system.
• Provides to the poorest developing countries special financial assistance through the International Development Association (IDA).	• Promotes exchange stability and orderly exchange relations among its member countries.
• Encourages private enterprises in developing countries through its affiliate, the International Finance Corporation (IFC).	• Assists all members experiencing temporary balance-of-payments problems with short- to medium-term lending.
• Acquires most of its financial resources by borrowing on the international bond market	• Uses SDRs to supplement the currency reserves of members as needed, in proportion to their quotas.
• Has a staff of 7,000 drawn from 180 member countries	• Has a staff of 2,300 drawn from 182 member countries.

---

[104]The BIS's home page is at http://www.bis.org.

international monetary cooperation, and (3) to act as an agent for international settlements. It currently holds and invests between 10 and 15 percent of all of the world's monetary reserves. The legal structure of the BIS is somewhat unique. While it is clearly endowed with an international personality and the privileges and immunities of an international organization, it is also a limited company incorporated under Swiss law.[105] This structure is partly the result of historical accident and partly intentional. In 1930, most of the central banks that helped found the BIS were private corporations rather than public institutions.[106] More important, however, the bank's founders were concerned that the BIS should be insulated, as much as possible, from direct governmental influence. The BIS is structured, therefore, as a banking company limited by shares. Originally, when the BIS's initial capital was issued, part of the Belgian and French issues and all of the American issue were sold to the public. After an Extraordinary General Meeting held in January 2001, the BIS Statutes were amended to restrict ownership of shares exclusively to central banks, and the 14 percent of the shares that then remained in private hands shares were bought back. Now, all of the shares are owned solely by central banks.[107]

Today, the central banks of 55 countries are represented at the BIS.[108] General meetings of shareholders are held at least once a year, and voting rights are exercised in proportion to the number of shares subscribed (including those held privately) in the state that a central bank represents. A board of directors is dominated by the largest European central banks. Its membership is made up of (1) the governors of the central banks of Belgium, France, Germany, Italy, and the United Kingdom and the chairman of the Board of Governors of the U.S. Federal Reserve; (2) for each of these governors, a second director of the same nationality appointed by that governor; and (3) up to nine additional directors elected by the board from among the governors of the central banks of other members states.[109] The board meets at least 10 times a year and makes decisions by majority vote from among those present or represented by proxy. The board selects the president of the bank from among its own members. The president serves both as the titular head of the bank and the chairman of the board. In turn, the president nominates a general manager, who is appointed by the board. The general manager is responsible for appointing the staff and carrying out the day-to-day operations of the bank.[110]

THE CENTRAL BANKS' BANK

One of the BIS's main functions is to serve as a bank for the world's central banks. It does so by helping some 140 central banks manage and invest their monetary reserves (now amounting to some SDR 133.2 billion).[111] Most of these funds are placed in the world's money market in the form of commercial bank deposits and short-term negotiable instruments (such as certificates of deposit).

BIS facilities: The financial assistance programs available to central banks from the BIS.

Beyond placing surplus funds in the international marketplace, the BIS occasionally makes liquid resources available to central banks. Such transactions (called **facilities**) include swaps of currency for gold, credits advanced against a pledge of gold or marketable short-term securities, and, less frequently, unsecured credits and standby credits. The bank also carries on exchange transactions in foreign currency and gold both with the central banks and with the markets.

---

[105]The current international status of the BIS is defined in the Swiss Headquarters Agreement of 1987 posted on the Internet at http://www.bis.org/about/hq-ex.htm.

[106]The National Bank of Belgium and the Bank of Switzerland remain limited companies that have legal status, bodies, and operating rules that discriminate them from other limited companies.. The central banks of most countries have now been nationalized or, upon the establishment of their governments, were created as public institutions.

[107]BIS, *Profilae 2004*, p. 2 (June 2004) at http://www.bis.org/about/profil2004.pdf.

[108]*Id.*

[109]Traditionally, the presidents of the Netherlands Bank and the Swiss National Bank, along with the governor of the Bank of Sweden, have been among these nine.

[110]*Id.*

[111]*Id.*, p. 2. (SDR 133.32 billion is approximately 202.27 billion U.S. dollars.)

bridging loan: Short-term loan that allows a debtor to meet its current obligations until a permanent loan can be obtained.

Recently, the bank has undertaken a new role as a source of large-scale, short-term **bridging loans** to help the central banks of developing countries with their balance-of-payments difficulties. These loans have helped the central banks of Latin American and Eastern European countries cope with cash flow problems pending the receipt of credits from the IMF.

PROMOTER OF INTERNATIONAL MONETARY COOPERATION

The BIS undertakes a variety of functions to encourage cooperation among the world's bankers. The bank's offices in Basel regularly host meetings of the world's finance ministers, central bank governors, and banking experts. The BIS also staffs the permanent secretariats of the Committee of Governors of the EU's central banks, the Board of Governors of the European Monetary Cooperation Fund, and the Committee on Banking Regulations and Supervisory Practices of the so-called Group of Ten (G-10) countries.[112] These secretariats collect data on national banking regulations and national surveillance systems, identify problem areas, and suggest measures for safeguarding bank solvency and liquidity. In addition, the bank itself collects and publishes banking statistics on a quarterly basis.

AGENT FOR INTERNATIONAL SETTLEMENTS

Much of the impetus for the creation of the BIS came from the need to settle the problem of German reparations to the victorious allies in the aftermath of World War I. The solution the founders agreed to was the reduction and commercialization of the German payments under the supervision of the bank. The BIS was put in charge of the loans floated by Germany and Austria, and it managed them until the onset of World War II.[113]

From time to time since then, the bank has entered into settlement arrangements with vari-ous countries and international organizations. It managed the currency exchange settlements system set up by the European Payments Union and its successor, the European Monetary Agreement, during the 1950s and 1960s. During the 1970s, the bank managed the Organization for Economic Cooperation and Development's Exchange Guarantee Agreement, which again involved a multilateral system for settling currency exchanges. From 1973 to 1993, the BIS managed the European Monetary Cooperation Fund for the European Community [114] And in 1994, the BIS assumed responsibility for rescheduling Brazil's external debt. It assumed similar responsibilities for Peru beginning in 1997 and for the Ivory Coast in 1998.[115]

G. REGIONAL MONETARY SYSTEMS

Several groups of countries have set up regional monetary organizations. These vary in their structure and evolution, from those that emulate the IMF in promoting currency exchange and financial support for balance-of-payments obligations to those that have established a complete monetary union.

Regional organizations that carry on many of the same functions as the IMF include the Central American Monetary Union (*Unión monetaria centroamericana*, or UMCA)[116] and

---

[112]The Group of Ten is made up of eleven industrial countries (Belgium, Canada, France, Germany, Italy, Japan, the Netherlands, Sweden, Switzerland, the United Kingdom, and the United States) that consult and cooperate on economic, monetary, and financial matters. For more information see http://www.bis.org/publ/g10.htm.

[113]The old obligations were revived under new terms in 1953, and they were again managed by the BIS.

[114]Beginning January 1, 1994, the functions of the European Monetary Cooperation Fund were taken over by the European Monetary Institute. See "The Bank for International Settlements: Profile of an International Organization" at http://www.bis. org/about/prof-gh.htm.

[115]*Id.*

[116]Established in 1964 by Costa Rica, El Salvador, Guatemala, Honduras, and Nicaragua.

the Arab Monetary Fund (AMF).[117] Both work to maintain the values of their members' currencies, stabilize their exchange ratios, jointly manage foreign exchange reserves, and promote eventual monetary union.

The most developed monetary unions are the West African Economic and Monetary Union (*Union economique et monétaire ouest-africaine*, or UEMOA), the Eastern Caribbean Currency Authority (ECCA), and the Economic and Monetary Community of Central Africa (or CEMAC) from its name in French, *Communauté Économique et Monétaire de l'Afrique Centrale*). Each has established a central bank, a common currency, and a single pool of exchange reserves.[118]

The EU is currently in the process of establishing a fully integrated economic and monetary union (known as the European Monetary Union or EMU). The criteria for setting up the EMU were agreed to in 1992 with the adoption of the Maastricht Treaty.[119] At that time the members elected the president, vice president, and four other executive board members of a new European Central Bank (ECB).[120] The ECB came into being on June 1, 1998.[121]

Because the Maastricht Treaty envisioned that some EU member states would not be participating in the EMU, it established a rather complex structure to oversee the EU's monetary policies. This is known as the European System of Central Banks (ESCB) and is made up of the European Central Bank and the 27 EU national central banks (NCBs). See Exhibit 6-5.

The main responsibilities of the ESCB are (1) defining and implementing the monetary policy of the EU, (2) conducting foreign exchange operations, (3) holding and managing the official foreign reserves of the EU member states, and (4) promoting the smooth operation of payment systems. In addition, the ESCB advises the EU organs—the Commission, Council, Parliament, and so on—about the banking matters it is responsible for.

The ESCB is governed by the decision-making bodies of the ECB: the Governing Council, the Executive Board, and the General Council. The Governing Council is made up of the six members of the Executive Board and the governors of the national banks of the 13 EMU states. It sets the monetary policy—including interest rates—for the EMU independent of the EU Commission, Council, and Parliament, much like the German central bank (the Bundesbank) on which it was modeled.[122] The Executive Board is then responsible for carrying out this policy.

The General Council of the ECB is made up of the president and vice president of the Executive Board and the governors of the 27 EU national central banks. It is responsible for

---

[117]Established in 1976, its current members are Algeria, Bahrain, Comoros, Djibouti, Egypt, Iraq, Jordan, Kuwait, Lebanon, Libya, Mauritania, Morocco, Oman, Palestine, Qatar, Saudi Arabia, Somalia, Sudan, Syria, Tunisia, the United Arab Emirates, and Yemen. Goals of the AMF include "correcting disequilibria in the balances of payments of the member states," stabilizing currency exchange ratios, promoting economic integration, and "paving the way for the creation of a unified Arab currency." See http://www.amf.org.ae.

[118]Current members of UEMOA are Benin, Burkina Faso, Guinea-Bissau, Ivory Coast, Mali, Niger, Senegal, and Togo. Its bank is the Central Bank of West African States, and its currency is the franc. Current members of the ECCA are Antigua and Barbuda, Dominica, Grenada, Montserrat, Anguilla, Saint Kitts and Nevis, Saint Lucia, and Saint Vincent and the Grenadines. Its bank is the Eastern Caribbean Central Bank, and its currency is the dollar. See Frits van Beek et al., "The Eastern Caribbean Currency Union: Institutions, Performance, and Policy Issues," International Monetary Fund Occasional Papers No. 195 (August 11, 2000) at http://www.imf.org/external/pubs/nft/op/195. The CEMAC is an organization of states of Central Africa established to promote economic integration among countries that share a common currency, the CFA franc. CEMAC is the successor of the Customs and Economic Union of Central Africa (UDEAC), which it completely superseded in June 1999 (through an agreement from 1994).

[119]The Treaty on European Union sets out the monetary policy of the EU in Articles 105–109. See http://europa.eu.int/en/record/mt/top.html.

[120]The European Central Bank's Web site is at http://www.ecb.int.

[121]Between June 1, 1998, and January 1, 1999, the ECB took over the functions of the European Monetary Institute (established in 1993), which it replaced. These were (1) to strengthen central bank cooperation and monetary policy coordination and (2) to make the preparations required for the establishment of the European System of Central Banks (ESCB). See "Constitution of the ESCB: History—Three Stages towards EMU" at http://www.ecb.int/ecb/history/emu/ html/index.en.html.

[122]The Governing Council, which uses English as its common language, meets every other Thursday, just as the German Bundesbank used to do. See http://www.ecb.int/ecb/orga/decisions/govc/html/index.en.html.

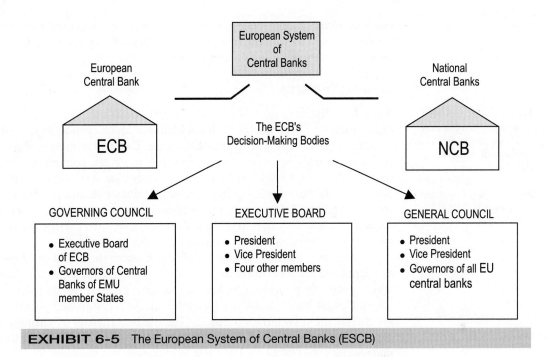

EXHIBIT 6-5 The European System of Central Banks (ESCB)

establishing common accounting and reporting provisions for the EU, collecting and disseminating statistical information, and setting the capital contribution requirements for the ECB.

On January 1, 1999, the ESCB began functioning as the central banking authority for the EU. On that same date, the euro became the new currency for the EMU. Euro coins and notes, however, did not begin circulating until January 1, 2002. During the intervening three years, national currencies continued to be legal tender at permanent exchange rates that were based on the exchange rates that existed on December 31, 1998.

H. NATIONAL MONETARY SYSTEMS

NATIONAL MONETARY ORGANIZATIONS

There are three types of organizations that operate on the national plane to implement national monetary policies. At the highest level is a political agency of the national government that sets national fiscal policy and carries on the financial functions of the government. In most countries, this is a cabinet-level agency, such as a Ministry of Finance or a Treasury Department.

At the next level is a **central bank**, such as the Bank of England, the Bank of Japan, or the U.S. Federal Reserve System.[123] In most countries, it is owned by the national government, but through a variety of mechanisms (such as lengthy fixed terms for directors), the bank is given some degree of independence from the government and from the day-to-day pressures of politics. Its most important functions are (1) to issue bank notes and coins, (2) to regulate the quantity of money in circulation, (3) to maintain and invest currency reserves, and (4) to act as a lender of last resort.

At the third level are the **commercial banks** that accept and manage deposits, make loans, and offer trust services.[124] In the domestic arena one finds a variety of financial institutions

central bank: A state's bank that is responsible for issuing the state's currency, regulating the quantity of its money in circulation, maintaining currency reserves, and acting as a lender of last resort.

commercial bank: A business firm that maintains custody of money deposited by its customers and pays on drafts written by its customers. It earns its profits by investing the money it has on deposit.

---

[123]A current listing of national central banks can be found at dir.yahoo.com/Business_and_Economy/Finance_and_ Investment/Banking/Central_Banking.
[124]See Yahoo!'s listing of commercial banks at dir.yahoo.com/Business_and_Economy/Shopping_and_ Services/ Financial_Services/Banking/Banks.

(such as savings banks, savings and loan associations, and credit unions), but internationally, the commercial bank is the institution most likely to be involved. Commercial banks may be owned privately or by the government.[125]

BANK DEPOSITS

bank deposit: Money held by a bank. The bank may freely use this money as it best sees fit. A depositor only has a claim against the bank as a general creditor and not as a bailor of specific property deposited with the bank.

Bank deposits are monies placed with a bank for its use. The term *deposit* suggests the notion of a bailment,[126] which implies that a bank has an obligation to keep the funds it receives in a vault for safekeeping. This is not the case. Except for monies delivered for a designated purpose, deposits become a bank's funds. A bank can commingle them and use them as it sees fit. Most commonly, banks use these funds to make short- and medium-term loans. The depositor, in return for his or her deposit, receives a claim against the bank as a general, unsecured creditor. Additionally, for some accounts, a depositor acquires the authority to write checks, payment orders, or drafts for the benefit of third parties, with the value of the checks, orders, or drafts being deducted from his or her claim.[127]

Commonly, banks pay interest on the monies they hold on deposit. When large sums are deposited for short-term investment, banks typically issue certificates of deposit (CDs), which generally provide a higher rate of interest than funds left in a general deposit account. Not all banks, however, pay interest. As Reading 6-3 points out, interest payments are forbidden in countries following Islamic law. Instead of earning interest, depositors in Islamic banks become the equivalent of joint venturers in the investments that their banks underwrite.

---

[125] A commercial bank's particular structural organization and its authority to participate in international banking depend upon the laws of its home country. In the United States, a commercial bank's ability to operate abroad through branches is regulated by the Federal Reserve Act and Federal Reserve Board Regulations. *United States Code*, Title 12, §§ 601 and 604(a) and *Code of Federal Regulations*, Title 12, § 211 et seq. The Edge Act of 1919 authorizes federally chartered corporations to engage in international banking and permits U.S. national banks to invest in them. *United States Code*, Title 12, § 611. The International Banking Act of 1978 eliminates those provisions of the Edge Act (such as restrictions on liabilities and reserve requirements) that put American banks at a competitive disadvantage with foreign banks. *United States Code*, Title 12, § 611a. Finally, since 1981, American banks are authorized to establish International Banking Facilities; that is, they can set up segregated asset and liability accounts for foreign customers that otherwise would be subject to the liability and reserve restrictions of domestic accounts. *Code of Federal Regulations*, Title 12, §§ 204 and 217.

[126] A bailment is an arrangement by which property is delivered in trust to another for a special purpose and for a limited time.

[127] The statutory provisions governing bank deposits in countries with major financial centers are reasonably consistent around the world. Most provide for charter supervision, liquidation, the regulation of business practices, and the status of depositors. However, with few exceptions, these statutes do not contemplate deposits made by foreign persons, deposits made at foreign branch banks, or the problem of conflicts with regulations issued by a foreign sovereign. Peter S. Smedresman and Andreas F. Lowenfeld, "Eurodollars, Multinational Banks, and National Laws," *New York University Law Review,* vol. 64, p. 733 at pp. 737–738 (1989).

━━∽◌∽◌∽━━

Reading 6-3   ISLAMIC BANKING

UNDERLYING CONCEPTS OF ISLAMIC ECONOMICS AND BANKING

Across the Muslim world there is a move to create Islamic financial institutions. This is but one manifestation of a much broader phenomenon, the revival of Islam and its values. The contribution of the Muslim world to a new international economic order could be based upon the application of the Shari'a to modern economic and financial transactions.

An Islamic economic order represents for the world's Muslims an alternative to capitalistic and socialist systems. Islamic concepts are different from capitalism by their opposition to excessive accumulation of wealth and, in contradiction to socialism, by their protection of the rights to property, including ownership of the means of production.

As defined by the "Egyptian Study," the Islamic economic system is based upon a number of principles that regulate human life. They constitute a sum of wisdom accumulated over the centuries by Islamic thinkers, who addressed themselves to broad political and economic issues and the history of human societies. For them, a true Islamic society must not be an arena where opposing interests clash, but rather a place where harmonious relations can be achieved through a sense of shared responsibilities. The individual's rights must be equitably balanced against those of society at large.

Islamic economics are regulated by [the] Shari'a, the laws derived from the Koran and Sunna. Unlike the Christian world, Islam makes no distinction between secular and religious law. It follows that the economic and financial practices of Islamic banks must abide by these guiding principles, although they do have a certain flexibility to adapt to new economic situations.

The traits that distinguish Islamic economy and finance from their Western counterparts reflect a different understanding of the value of capital and labor. In lieu of a lender–borrower relationship, Islamic finance relies on equitable risk-sharing between the person who provides the capital and the entrepreneur. This practice derives from the central tenet of Islamic banking based on the Koran, which forbids *riba*, that is, interest charges or payments.

Contrary to what Westerners often think, interest-free banking should not be considered as merely a concessionary or subsidized financial practice. Viewed in its historic context, Islamic law on interest was above all practical. The economy of the Arabian peninsula in the seventh century was that of trading city-states living in a hostile environment. In economic terms, the constraints were illiquidity and scarcity and the results were usury and hoarding. Islamic precepts aimed to control such undesirable social phenomena. If interest rates imposed on long-distance traders were too high, this either discouraged trade or substantially increased the cost of commodities for investors as well as consumers, resulting in a net loss to the community.

The original ban on interest charges stemmed from the fact that moneylenders were exploiting the poor by charging usurious rates. Even if this may no longer apply to modern, monetized economies, a different rationale has evolved to justify the principle of banning interest. There is no need for loan financing, it is claimed, because an active involvement in a company through profit sharing is a superior way to direct capital into productive outlets without putting an additional financial burden on the community.

For Islamic economists, the economic rationale for profit sharing is not only distributive justice but efficiency, economic stability and growth. M. N. Siddiqui, for example, argues that interest financing can be very unfair when entrepreneurs alone incur the losses or, on the contrary, reap disproportionately high benefits. As far as public debts are concerned, interest financing is felt to be inequitable in the case of national emergencies, such as crop failures or floods, and inefficient for development aid purposes. The role of interest in international debt comes in for heavy criticism, as the following statement aptly sums up: "Three decades of debt financing did not help the debtor countries to become self-sufficient, or less dependent, or capable of generating a surplus to pay back."

As far as allocative efficiency is concerned, it is contended that debt financing usually goes to the most creditworthy borrower and not necessarily to the most productive and potentially profitable projects. As for stability, the argument is advanced that an interest-based economy has a built-in tendency towards inflation because the creation of money is not linked to productive investment at the level either of central banks or of commercial banks. Lastly, interest charges decrease the supply of risk capital and therefore hamper economic growth.

Some Islamic economists hold different views on the interdiction of interest in today's economies. Islamic "modernists" find a literal reading of the Koran too restrictive and favor an interpretation of the spirit of the law. They thus contend that the Koran has prohibited usury but not legitimate interest. Nevertheless, the vast majority of Islamic economists maintain—and Islamic banks concur—that interest should be prohibited.

Today no Islamic bank charges or pays interest, although certain fiduciary business operations allow partners to circumvent this difficulty. Charging interest is permissible for financial transactions with "Dar Al Harb," that is, non-Muslim countries, or for Muslims living beyond the rule of Islam, known as "Dar Al Islam."

A second tenet governing money matters is that it is forbidden to hoard. Men have a moral obligation to put money to productive use, for themselves and for the good of the community, by investing in profitable opportunities. Though Islamic banks are trying to promote such schemes, this is still an ideal. Until a complete Islamic system is instituted, hoarding continues to be widespread. It has been estimated that some $80 billion are sitting idle in Muslim countries. If Islamic banks could attract broader segments of the population, which have till now considered Western-style banking with distrust, it could mobilize this capital into productive outlets.

Another important aspect of Islamic finance is a tax called *Zakat*, in some ways similar to the Christian tithe.

Paying *Zakat* is one of the five imperative religious obliga-tions for a Muslim. It is levied on traded goods and revenues from business and real estate, but not on personal property like houses, furniture or jewelry. Computation is complex: as a rule, peasants pay anywhere from 5 to 10 percent on their produce, while the rest of the population contributes 2.5 percent of their revenues....

Individuals may give their *Zakat* contribution directly to a beneficiary or else to a special institution set up to distribute funds. Most Islamic banks administer *Zakat* funds in a separate account and can use them, if necessary, to help out depositors in temporary difficulty. Contributions are over and above secular taxes.

RECENT DEVELOPMENTS IN DOCTRINE AT THE INTERGOVERNMENTAL LEVEL

During the Seventies, several Muslim countries undertook various efforts at the international level to define basic concepts and applications of Islamic banking in today's world. These endeavors included conceptual studies, the establishment of an inter-governmental Islamic development bank, the creation of international training and research institutions as well as control by monetary authorities over Islamic institutions.

A study presented by the Arab Republic of Egypt on the "Institution of an Islamic Bank, Economics and Islamic Doctrine" was discussed and adopted on the occasion of the Third Islamic Conference of Foreign Ministers in Jeddah [in] 1972. Experts from 18 Muslim countries prepared this document under the leadership of the Egyptian Ministry of Economics. The basic issues addressed were the functioning and operations of Islamic banks. It was clearly postulated that loan finance based on interest should be replaced by profit-and-loss sharing participation schemes. Three phases were suggested to implement this novel financial concept.

As a first step, it was proposed that an Islamic advisory agency be established to deal with problems of Islamic economics and banking. Its mandate would be to help establish new Islamic financial institutions and advise them how to operate.

The second proposed step was to set up an international Islamic bank which would manage the income from interest received from non-Muslim countries, as well as from *Zakat* funds. Furthermore, it would serve as a clearinghouse for international payments between Muslim countries and finance reciprocal trade. At the national level, central agencies would be created to prepare for the subsequent establishment of local Islamic banks.

In a third step, Islamic savings, investment and development banks would be created to complement the umbrella institutions at the national and international levels.

What actually developed was somewhat different. The advisory agency, the International Association of Islamic Banks (IAIB), was established only in 1977, after the Islamic Development Bank (IsDB) in 1975 and then commercial Islamic banks had been set up in several countries. A central agency to help establish Islamic banks at the local level has yet to be founded in the various Muslim countries. Nevertheless, the "Egyptian Study" was instrumental in furthering the development and implementation of Islamic banks, and many of its conceptual proposals have been adopted along the lines laid down.

***

TRADITIONAL AND NEW ISLAMIC FINANCIAL INSTRUMENTS

Since Islamic law does not recognize corporations in the Western sense, companies are based on partnerships, originally only between two individuals but later extended to more. Two legal forms are basically utilized to provide funds on the basis of profit-and-loss sharing: *Musharaka* and *Modaraba*. Both are old Arab/pre-Islamic constructions which were originally developed for the requirements of trading city-states in a hostile environment to cope with socially undesirable phenomena, like scarcity of goods and usury for credit.

The *Musharaka* contract is formally a limited partnership, whereby both the bank and the customer provide capital for a specific project. Another possibility is the participation of the bank in an existing enterprise by means of a capital contribution. The pro-rata distribution of profits between bank and customer is subject to a contract between the parties. Losses are shared according to capital contribution. The bank may participate in the management, but it may also waive this right.

There exist *Musharaka* contracts with either constant or decreasing participation. The latter form is offered by the Jordan Islamic Bank, for example where the participation of the bank decreases over time. The bank keeps the profit share of the customer to pay back the capital contribution.

The *Modaraba* contract is formally a silent partnership with a clear distinction between the capital provider and the entrepreneur who controls the management of the project. Remuneration is again based upon a predetermined percentage of profits; losses have to be borne by capital providers alone. The entrepreneur then foregoes remuneration for his work.

Literature on Islamic banking has extensively commented on *Modaraba* contracts. Originally, the bank was the capital provider (*Raab Al-Mal*); it financed a project proposed by an entrepreneur (*Modareb*). Today,

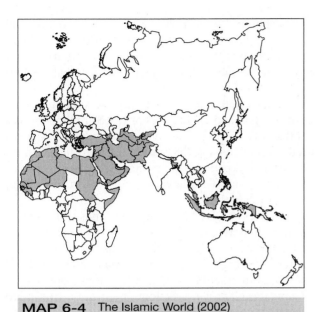

MAP 6-4 The Islamic World (2002)

vestment accounts, etc.) and shares with the bank the risk of the operations. He is guaranteed neither a profit nor the full return of his principal. In the case of current accounts, the bank assumes all risks alone, but does not share profits with the depositor (often Islamic banks specify a minimum balance above which no handling charges on current accounts are levied).

In investment, the bank issues nominal or bearer certificates (often negotiable) which entitle the holder to share in the profits of the activities being undertaken by the investment company. This can be specific to a single project or a general share in all activities. The duration can be for a fixed date, at fixed intervals, on call, etc.

For the supply of goods and equipment, Islamic banks use the *Murabaha* contract. The financial institution purchases raw materials, goods or equipment at cost and sells them to the client on a cost-plus-negotiated-margin basis. Other transactions are rental financing (*Ijara*), whereby the bank acquires equipment or buildings and makes them available to the client on a straightforward rental basis. In the case of hire-purchase financing (*Ijara Wa Iktina*), a similar construction is applied. The client, however, has the possibility of acquiring ownership of the rental equipment or buildings by paying installments into a savings account. The reinvestment of this accumulated capital works in favor of the client, allowing him to offset rental cost.

Modarabas can be applied to various economic activities, the most important of which are described below.

In banking, the institution offers its services as a manager of capital (*Mudareb*) and invites deposits from the public (*Raab Al-Mal*). The customer is offered a variety of fixed term instruments (e.g. security accounts, in-

EUROCURRENCY DEPOSITS

Eurocurrency deposits:
Foreign currency on deposit in a bank, on which the bank pays interest in the same foreign currency.

Accounts in domestic banks that are maintained and paid in a foreign currency are generally known as **Eurocurrency deposits**.[128] Such deposits are commonly free of the monetary control restrictions imposed by their issuing country. American dollars (or *Eurodollars*[129]) are the most common Eurocurrency; however, British pounds, Canadian dollars, EU euros, Japanese yen, and Swiss francs are also used.

THE INTERBANK DEPOSIT MARKET

The worldwide economic expansion that began in the 1950s put such enormous financial demands on commercial banks that they were unable to service their *core* or customer-placed deposits. Because banks operating in the United States were (and are) generally forbidden to open branches and solicit deposits from outside the geographical area of their parent bank, they had to turn to other sources for raising funds.[130] Thus, they began to borrow from

---

[128]The *Euro* prefix stems from its origins in London's currency market and is, of course, no longer accurate. For a short history of the Eurocurrency market see F. A. Mann, *The Legal Aspect of Money*, pp. 61–62 (4th ed., 1982).

[129]Eurodollars are financial assets denominated as U.S. dollars and having at any given time the same value as a U.S. dollar in the United States, but are not subject to the control exercised by the U.S. central bank (the Federal Reserve System) over either interest rates or money supply. Peter S. Smedresman and Andreas F. Lowenfeld, "Eurodollars, Multinational Banks, and National Laws," *New York University Law Review*, vol. 64, p. 733 at p. 744 (1989).

[130]*United States Code*, Title 12, § 36(c) (1998), requires national banks to comply with the branch banking rules of the state in which they operate. Section 1831(u) allows banks to maintain branches in different states following a merger (occurring after June 1, 1997), but not if this would violate an express state prohibition.

banks and corporations with short-term surpluses. By the 1970s, this interbank market had become international, with banks in New York, London, Tokyo, and the world's other financial centers operating as active international traders.[131] Trades are made throughout the day and night, every day of every year, by telephone and over the Internet in a global marketplace that is virtually unregulated.

A variety of short-term liquid instruments are traded in this interbank market, but the most common is the **certificate of deposit (CD)**, issued in multiples of U.S. $1 million for maturity periods of one, three, and six months. A CD is a form of commercial paper, defined as "an instrument containing an acknowledgment by a bank that a sum of money has been received by the bank and a promise by the bank to repay the sum of money."[132] As such, it is a negotiable instrument. However, because interbank CDs have relatively short maturities, they are seldom transferred from one holder to another.

certificate of deposit (CD): A promissory note issued by a bank in which the bank promises to repay money it has received, plus interest, at a certain time.

Banks are no longer the principal purchasers of CDs. Money market funds and corporations with excess cash have supplanted them, in part, because CDs held by American banks are not regarded (under the U.S. Federal Reserve System's regulations) as the equivalent of cash and, therefore, cannot be used to reduce a bank's obligation to maintain reserves.[133] Even so, banks do deposit huge sums of money in other banks as a means of rate positioning based on their differing perceptions about the market's direction. Often these trades are made in rapid-fire order and commonly without the use of certificates. In the fastest-moving sector of the interbank market, both the issuance and the safekeeping of certificates would be burdensome. Trades are made over the telephone, confirmed in brief messages sent by telex or fax, and then followed up with a written *ticket* that is mailed by the depositary to the depositor.

THE FOREIGN EXCHANGE MARKET

A buyer in Lusaka, Zambia, wants to buy 100,000 gallons of maple syrup from a seller in Toronto, Canada. The buyer is able to pay with Zambian kwachas, but the seller requires Canadian dollars. To carry out the purchase (which is called a **foreign exchange**), the buyer will contact his bank in Lusaka to buy the needed dollars. If the Lusaka bank does not have Canadian dollars on hand (which is likely the case), it will undertake to buy them on the world's **foreign exchange market**. Despite its name, the foreign exchange market does not exist in any place. It is, rather, an informal network of banks, foreign exchange brokers, and foreign exchange dealers. The Lusaka bank's foreign currency trader will contact them in the hopes of making an exchange. This may be difficult, however, because the international market for kwachas is limited, and the bank may only have a limited supply of other currencies (called *hard currencies*) that it can readily convert into Canadian dollars. *Hard currencies* (i.e., the currencies of the major free-market nations) are freely exchangeable. The currencies of developing countries, like Zambia's kwacha, are commonly called *soft currencies* because they are not freely exchangeable.

foreign exchange: The conversion of the money of one state into that of another state.

foreign exchange market: An informal network of banks, foreign exchange brokers, and foreign exchange dealers who facilitate the exchange of currencies.

If the Lusaka bank is unable to purchase sufficient Canadian dollars to carry out the trans-action for the buyer, it will have to turn to Zambia's central bank for assistance. The Bank of Zambia may or may not have enough Canadian dollars or other hard currencies to sell to the Lusaka bank. If it does not, it may contact the Bank for International Settlements to exchange gold or whatever currencies it does have for dollars. Should this be impossible, the central bank will ask the Zambian government to exchange the SDRs that it holds in the IMF for Canadian dollars. If the central government does not have SDRs, it may arrange for a short-term loan from the IMF or the World Bank to acquire the needed dollars.

---

[131]The top 10 banks in the interbank foreign exchange market as of May 2006 were (1) Deutsche Bank, (2) UBS, (3) Citigroup, (4) Barclays Capital, (5) Royal Bank of Scotland, (6) Goldman Sachs, (7) HSBC, (8) Bank of America, (9) JPMorgan Chase, and (10) Merrill Lynch.
[132]United States, *Uniform Commercial Code*, § 3–104.
[133]United States, *Code of Federal Regulations*, Title 12, § 204.3(f)(1) (1998).

Once the dollars have been acquired, they will be deposited in a major bank in one of the major financial centers, such as New York, London, or Tokyo, for the account of the Lusaka bank. The major bank in this instance is known as a **correspondent bank**. When the buyer confirms that the seller has delivered the maple syrup, the Lusaka bank will instruct its correspondent bank to transfer the dollars to the seller's bank or to that bank's correspondent bank.

This somewhat simplified example of a foreign currency exchange highlights the principal participants involved in the transaction. Normally, the two major actors are commercial and central banks. In addition, arbitrageurs, importers, exporters, multinational firms, tourists, governments, and intergovernmental organizations may become involved. The transaction itself is generally unregulated, although governments in developing countries sometimes impose licensing requirements on banks and traders and often require that all exchanges be made through their central banks.

Commercial banks participate in the foreign exchange market both as intermediaries for importers, exporters, multinational corporations, and the like, and as correspondent banks in the interbank marketplace. In combination, they play three important roles: (1) they operate the payment mechanism, (2) they extend credit, and (3) they help to reduce the risk of international transactions.

Central banks participate as lenders of last resort and as regulators of currency exchange rates. In addition to providing funds for local transactions when no other funds are readily available, central banks may independently intervene in the foreign currency market to maintain orderly trading conditions. This sometimes involves the purchase of weaker currencies. For example, in the 1980s, Germany and Japan helped support the U.S. dollar by purchasing the American currency at a time when its value was falling. In 1992, the Bank of France spent billions of deutsche marks to help support the weaker pound, lira, and French franc, and in 2000 the U.S. Federal Reserve and the European Central Bank intervened successfully to stem the decline of the euro, which had fallen to 82 cents against the dollar.

In making currency exchanges, traders typically use a widely traded intermediary currency. For instance, in the previous example, the buyer's bank in Lusaka might purchase U.S. dollars, which in turn would be converted by the seller's bank in Toronto to Canadian dollars. The most commonly used *intermediary*, or international exchange currency, is the American dollar. Exchange rates for converting the dollar into the world's other hard currencies are published daily in major newspapers around the world. Exchange rates for other currencies are published weekly in major financial newspapers (such as the *Financial Times* and the *Wall Street Journal*) and can be obtained from major banks on a more frequent basis.

FOREIGN EXCHANGE CONTRACTS

Foreign exchange contracts may be made as spot, future, forward, or option contracts. A **spot contract** is simply a transaction involving the immediate sale and delivery of a commodity, such as a currency.[134] A **future contract** (or *future*) is simply a promise to buy or sell a commodity (e.g., a currency) for a specified price, with both delivery and payment to be made at a specified future date. Because there is a market in futures (they are sold on commodity exchanges), such contracts are both standardized and transferable.[135] Trading in futures, however, seldom results in the physical delivery of the commodity. More often, the obligations of the parties are extinguished by offsetting transactions that produce a net profit or loss. Futures are used primarily as a way to transfer price risks from suppliers, processors, and distributors (called *hedgers* when they become parties to these *hedging* contracts) to those who are more willing to take the risk (called *speculators*).

correspondent bank: A bank that acts as an agent of another bank, especially in carrying a deposit balance for the latter.

spot contract: A contract for the immediate sale and delivery of a commodity, such as a currency.

future contract: A promise to buy or sell a commodity (e.g., a currency) for a specified price, with both delivery and payment to be made at a specified future date.

[134]The Federal Reserve Bank of New York posts spot foreign exchange rates for the New York interbank market at http://www.newyorkfed.org/markets/fxrates/noon.cfm.
[135]Futures contracts are characterized as being fungible, that is, being readily transferable or exchangeable. Salomon Forex, Inc. v. Tauber, *Federal Reporter, Third Series*, vol. 8, p. 966 at p. 967 (Fourth Circuit Ct. of Appeals, 1993).

The uses of hedging as well as the risks involved in such contracts are explored in Case 6-4.

IN BRIEF: **Case 6-4**   HUNT ET AL. v. ALLIANCE NORTH AMERICAN GOVERNMENT INCOME TRUST, INC. ET AL.

United States Court of Appeals, District of Columbia Circuit, 1987.

FACTS

Plaintiffs are shareholders in Alliance North American Government Income Trust, Inc., an open-ended mutual fund formed to make investments in government securities in Canada, Mexico, and the United States. The fund sold shares pursuant to registration statements and prospectuses that stated that the fund managers would use hedging techniques to avoid the adverse consequences of currency fluctuations. In particular, the prospectuses said that the fund "may" enter into futures contracts and options on futures contracts, and that the fund intended to write covered put and call options on the government securities it was trading in.

Following Mexico's devaluation of the peso in December 1995, the net asset value of the fund decreased dramatically. The plaintiffs brought suit alleging (among other things) in a revised pleading that the fund had misrepresented that hedging techniques to reduce currency risk were available, when in fact the fund knew that they were not available (because they were too expensive). The trial court dismissed the complaint, stating that investors could not have been misled by the prospectuses and that the prospectuses gave "no assurances" that the

hedging techniques they described could be effectively used. The plaintiffs appealed.

ISSUE

Did the prospectuses mislead investors into believing that hedging techniques were available to the fund when in fact they were not?

HOLDING

Yes.

LAW

Cautionary language in a prospectus will not foreclose liability if it warns investors of liability from contingencies different than the contingencies described in the prospectus.

EXPLANATION

Plaintiffs claim that the prospectuses promised that the fund would attempt to use hedging devices when in fact it could not. Because the prospectuses could have misled a reasonable investor, the plaintiffs have stated a cause of action for which relief can be granted. Their complaint, therefore, should not have been dismissed.

ORDER

District court's order is reversed.

---

forward contract: A contract in which a commodity is presently sold and the price presently paid but delivery is, by agreement, delayed to a later date.

option contract: A contract that creates the right—but not the obligation—to buy or sell a specific amount of a commodity (e.g., currency) at a fixed price within an agreed-upon period of time.

A **forward contract** (or, in the case of currency, a *cash forward contract*) is simply a transaction in which a commodity is presently sold and the price presently paid but the delivery is, by agreement, delayed to a later date. In comparison with a future contract, which is readily transferable, a forward contract is generally negotiated individually by the parties who will actually make and receive physical delivery of the goods involved.

An **option contract** (or *option*) creates the right—but not the obligation—to buy or sell a specific amount of a commodity (e.g., currency) at a fixed price within an agreed-upon period of time. If the right is to buy a commodity, the option is known as a *call*; if the right is to make a sale, the option is known as a *put*. If the right involves a combination of these—to either buy or sell—the option is known as a *straddle* or *spread eagle*. Unlike spot, futures, or forwards contracts, the holder of an option is not required to go through with the transaction. The holder must pay a fee or some other consideration to acquire the option, but the total risk assumed in purchasing it is the loss of that fee.

ARBITRAGE

arbitrage: (From French *arbitrer*: "to arbitrate" or "to regulate.") The nearly simultaneous purchase of currencies (or other commodities) in one market and their resale in another in order to profit from the price differential.

Arbitrage is the nearly simultaneous purchase of a commodity (such as a currency) in one market and its sale in another to profit from the price differential. Because there are differences in the prices of the world's currencies, both over time and between locations, arbitrageurs are active participants in the international foreign exchange market. For example, suppose that the EU euro is trading among traders in London for U.S. $0.9725 and among traders in Tokyo for U.S. $0.9735. An arbitrageur would buy euros in London and sell them in Japan. For example, assuming that the arbitrageur purchases 1,028,278 euros (i.e., U.S. $1 million) in London and sells them in Tokyo, he will receive $1,010,286, for a net profit of $10,286 or 1.3 percent. Of course, the purchase of euros in London will drive up their price there, and their sale in Tokyo will drive down their price in Japan. The process will continue until the exchange rate becomes the same in both places.[136]

Today, arbitrageurs and other currency traders carry on their transactions at lightning speed using telephones and the Internet. The minimum contract is normally U.S. $25,000, but contracts of $1 million are more common. Offers have to be accepted immediately, and then performed regardless of a later dispute. If there is a dispute, traders commonly split the difference.

THE TRANSFER OF MONEY

instruction: Order to a bank to disburse funds to a particular person.

bill of exchange (also known as a *draft*): A three-party instrument on which the drawer makes an unconditional order to a drawee to pay a named payee.

A bank transfers money internationally by setting up a correspondent bank relationship with a foreign bank and depositing funds to its own account in that bank. When a customer goes to his or her own bank and asks to transfer money overseas, the bank accepts the customer's money at its domestic office, then arranges for the correspondent bank to disburse funds in the foreign country to whomever the customer has designated. This may be done by **instruction**, in which case the domestic bank directs its correspondent to pay funds directly to a particular payee, or by the use of a **bill of exchange** that is drawn on the domestic bank's account at the foreign correspondent bank. In the latter case, the bill of exchange is given to the customer, who in turn sends it to the payee. The payee then cashes it at the correspondent bank.

The actual physical delivery of currency internationally is seldom done. When required, it is arranged for by central banks and is commonly managed by the BIS.

BRANCH BANKING

International **banks**, unlike most other multinational companies, prefer to operate in host countries through branches rather than subsidiaries. And in most major host countries, including France, Germany, Japan, Switzerland, the United Kingdom, and the United States, branch operations (without separate incorporation) are not only allowed, they are encouraged.[137] On the one hand, host countries impose few regulations limiting the operations of foreign banks. On the other hand, they assume few supervisory responsibilities. Thus, unlike domestic banks, foreign banks do not have to maintain reserves to cover potential losses. Foreign banks, however, cannot turn to the host country's central bank as a lender of last

---

[136]Arbitrageurs, by taking advantage of momentary discrepancies in prices between markets, perform the economic function of making these markets more efficient.

[137]See, for example, U.S. Treasury Department, *Report to Congress on Foreign Government Treatment of U.S. Commercial Banking Organizations*, p. 19 (1979).

Prior to becoming a party to the North American Free Trade Agreement, Canada required local incorporation of banks. Canada Bank Act, *Revised Statutes of Canada*, vol. 1, chap. B-1, § 302(1)(b) (1985). Now foreign banks may establish branches so long as the bank's home state provides like treatment for foreign banks. *Id.*, vol.1, chap. B-1.01, § 24 (1991). Canada's statutes are posted on the Internet at http://www.canada.justice.gc.ca/Loireg/index_en.html.

resort. From the perspective of the host country, a foreign bank is required to stand behind the local obligations of its branches with its entire worldwide assets.

Although host states generally impose minimal regulations on foreign branches, the presence of a foreign branch has sometimes been used as a means to obtain information from a foreign parent bank. In particular, the U.S. government, in an effort to curtail the use of foreign banks as conduits for laundering illegal profits from narcotics smuggling, income tax evasion, securities fraud, and other business crimes, has attempted to extend its regulatory jurisdiction over foreign banks by asking courts to issue subpoenas[138] exercisable against their U.S. branches.[139] Such subpoenas require the U.S. branch to obtain information from the parent and then turn it over to the American government. Needless to say, many countries regard the American actions as an invasion of their sovereign rights, and legislation to counter the U.S. efforts is not uncommon.[140]

Not only foreign countries but the U.S. courts as well have taken a dim view of this attempt by the political arms of the U.S. government to exercise extraterritorial jurisdiction over foreign banks. Case 6-5 illustrates the reaction of one appellate court to the U.S. government's use of a grand jury subpoena to compel one branch of a foreign bank to produce records held by its parent.[141]

---

[138]A subpoena is a command to appear at a certain time and place to give testimony upon a certain matter.

[139]A report issued by the U.S. House of Representatives Committee on Banking and Currency in 1970 stated that secret foreign bank accounts encourage "white collar" crimes. *House of Representatives Report No. 975*, 91st Congress, 2nd Session, p. 12 (1970).

[140]See, e.g., Foreign Proceedings (Prohibition of Certain Evidence) Act, 1976, *Acts of the Parliament of the Commonwealth of Australia*, No. 121; amended by Foreign Proceedings (Prohibition of Certain Evidence) Amendment Act, 1976, *id.*, No. 202; repealed and replaced by Foreign Proceedings (Excess of Jurisdiction) Act, 1984, *id.*, No. 3. Foreign Extraterritorial Measures Act, *Statutes of Canada*, chap. 49 (1984). Confidential Relationships (Preservation) Law, Cayman Islands Law 16 of 1976 and the Confidential Relationships (Preservation) (Amendment) Law, Cayman Islands Law 26 of 1979.

Sometimes, however, states other than the United States seek to obtain information from banks located abroad. See In re Request for Assistance from Ministry of Legal Affairs of Trinidad and Tobago, *Federal Reporter, Second Series*, vol. 848, p. 1151 (Eleventh Circuit Court of Appeals, 1988).

[141]An excellent discussion of the conflict-of-laws implications that arise from the use of subpoenas to compel foreign banks to produce evidence can be found in Silvia B. Piñera-Vàzquez, "Extraterritorial Jurisdiction and International Banking: A Conflict of Interest," *University of Miami Law Review*, vol. 43, p. 449 (1988).

Case 6-5   IN RE SEALED CASE

United States, Court of Appeals, District of Columbia Circuit, 1987.
Federal Reporter, Second Series, vol. 825, p. 494 (1987).

PER CURIAM[142]

These consolidated appeals are taken from orders in a miscellaneous proceeding below collateral to a grand jury investigation. The government sought and obtained orders in the district court compelling appellants, a bank and an individual, to respond to a grand jury subpoena by producing documents and giving testimony. When appellants continued to refuse to respond to the grand jury's demands, the court found appellants in contempt.

The grand jury investigation has not been completed, and the records in the district court and this court have been sealed. In order to maintain this secrecy, we do not identify the parties in this opinion.

***

I.

From the beginning, the manager and the bank have cooperated to a certain extent with the investigation. The manager has come to Washington several times to meet with the prosecutors and testify before the grand jury about his knowledge of the targets and their activities that he learned in his personal capacity (not through bank

---

[142]Latin: "by the court." A phrase used to indicate that the whole court rather than any one judge wrote the opinion.

operations). Except for information concerning three customers from whom they obtained releases, however, the manager and the bank refused to testify before the grand jury about the targets' banking activities or produce documents on the ground that to do so would violate Country Y's banking secrecy laws and subject the manager and the bank to criminal prosecution in Country Y.

The bank has taken the position that the government should use other means to attempt to obtain the documents from Country Y, a course that the government believes is inappropriate and would be ineffective. The manager based his refusal to testify on Fifth Amendment grounds, claiming that the act of testifying would subject him to criminal sanctions in Country Y. The government secured use immunity for the manager but he continues to decline to answer on the ground that a United States court could not immunize him from criminal prosecution in Country Y. Since the act of testifying would violate the laws of Country Y, he contends that to require him to testify would violate his Fifth Amendment protection against self-incrimination.

***

II.

The manager's Fifth Amendment claim is based on his assertion that Country Y could convict him of a crime solely for revealing information protected by Country Y's banking secrecy law. He does not claim that the substance of his testimony would incriminate him for any crime that he has committed, under either the laws of the United States, of Country X, or of Country Y. The manager argues that, despite the district court's grant of immunity, his real and substantial fear of prosecution in Country Y cloaks his refusal to testify with Fifth Amendment protection. We disagree.

***

The district court concluded that even if the Fifth Amendment does apply to a situation in which the witness asserts the threat of foreign prosecution, it "[was] not convinced that the fear of prosecution in this case is 'real' as required by *Zicarelli v. New Jersey Comm'n of Investigation*."[143] ... It based this finding on the strict secrecy provisions of Rule 6(e) of the Federal Rules of Criminal Procedure.[144]

We agree that the manager's fear of prosecution is not real, but for a different reason. The manager could only be prosecuted by Country Y as a result of his own voluntary act—returning to Country Y. We recognize his substantial connections to Country Y, but he no longer lives or works there. He is not himself a citizen of that country and his immediate family is with him in this country. As the manager concedes, the offense with which he could be charged by Country Y for his testimony here is not an offense for which he could be extradited. He could only be punished for this offense if he were to return voluntarily. "It is well established that the [Fifth Amendment] privilege protects against real dangers, not remote and speculative possibilities."[145] We only add that it does not protect against dangers voluntarily assumed. We, therefore, affirm the order of the district court holding the manager in contempt for refusing to testify before the grand jury.

III.

The bank argues that the district court erred in entering a civil contempt order[146] that compels it to act in violation of the laws of Country Y. The federal courts have disagreed about whether a court may order a person to take specific actions on the soil of a foreign sovereign in violation of its laws and about what sanctions the court may levy against a person who refuses to comply with such an order....

... Be that as it may, here we simply conclude that even if a court has the power to issue such contempt orders under certain circumstances, on the peculiar facts of this case the order should not have issued. Most important to our decision is the fact that these sanctions represent an attempt by an American court to compel a foreign person to violate the laws of a different foreign

---

[143]*United States Reports*, vol. 406, p. 472 at pp. 478–81 (Supreme Ct., 1972).
[144]The secrecy provision of Rule 6(e) of the Federal Rules of Criminal Procedure is as follows—
(A) No obligation of secrecy may be imposed on any person except in accordance with Rule 6(e)(2)
(B) Unless these rules provide otherwise, the following persons must not disclose a matter occurring before the grand jury:
(i) a grand juror;
(ii) an interpreter;
(iii) a court reporter;
(iv) an operator of a recording device;
(v) a person who transcribes recorded testimony;
(vi) an attorney for the government; or
(vii) a person to whom disclosure is made under Rule 6(e)(3)(A)(ii) or (iii).
The text of the Federal Rules of Criminal Procedure is posted at http://judiciary.house.gov/ media/pdfs/printers/ 108th/crim2004.pdf.
[145]*Id.*, at p. 478.
[146]Contempt of court is a court ruling that, in the context of a court trial or hearing, deems an individual as holding contempt for the court, its process, and its invested powers. In civil proceedings there are two main ways to be "in contempt" of court.
1. Failing to attend court despite a subpoena requiring attendance.
2. Failing to comply with a court order.

sovereign on that sovereign's own territory. In addition, the bank, against whom the order is directed, is not itself the focus of the criminal investigation in this case but is a third party that has not been accused of any wrongdoing. Moreover, the bank is not merely a private foreign entity, but is an entity owned by the government of Country Y. We recognize that one who relies on foreign law assumes the burden of showing that such law prevents compliance with the court's order, . . . but here the government concedes that it would be impossible for the bank to comply with the contempt order without violating the laws of Country Y on Country Y's soil. The district court specifically found that the bank had acted in good faith throughout these proceedings. The executive branch may be able to devise alternative means of addressing this problem, but the bank cannot.

***

A decision whether to enter a contempt order in cases like this one raises grave difficulties for courts. We have little doubt, for example, that our government and our people would be affronted if a foreign court tried to compel someone to violate our laws within our borders. The legal expression of this widespread sentiment is found in basic principles of international comity. But unless we are willing simply to enter contempt orders in all such cases, no matter how extreme, in utter disregard of comity principles, we are obliged to undertake the unseemly task of picking and choosing when to order parties to violate foreign laws. It is conceivable that we might even be forced to base our determination in part on a subjective evaluation of the content of those laws; an American court might well find it wholly inappropriate to defer to a foreign sovereign where the laws in question promote, for example, torture or slavery or terrorism. . . . We have no doubt that Congress could empower courts to issue contempt orders in any of these cases, or

that the executive branch could negotiate positive agreements with other nations to the same end. If we were asked to act in accord with such a distinct and express grant of power, it would be our duty to do so. Indeed, any such measures would be a welcome improvement over the difficulties and uncertainties that now pervade this area of law.

In sum, we emphasize again the limited nature of our holding on this issue. If any of the facts we rest on here were different, our holding could well be different. And though we reserve the district court's order holding the bank in civil contempt on the facts of this case, we of course intend no challenge to proposition that the vital role of grand jury investigations on our criminal system endows the grand jury with wide discretion in seeking evidence. It is therefore also relevant to our conclusion that the grand jury is not left empty-handed by today's decision. The manager will be available and able to testify as to many of the facts that the grand jury may wish to ascertain. The government may find alternative means to obtain additional information from or through the bank. Though we recognize that the grand jury's investigation may nonetheless be hampered, perhaps significantly, we are unable to uphold the contempt order against the bank.

Affirmed in part and reversed in part.

CASEPOINT: (1) With respect to prosecution in a foreign jurisdiction, a person wishing to claim the right not to be compelled to incriminate himself in a U.S. court has to be in "real and substantial fear" of being prosecuted in the foreign state. No real fear can exist where the person must voluntarily return to the foreign state to be prosecuted. The contempt order against the bank manager is therefore affirmed. (2) However, U.S. courts cannot compel the bank—an entity owned by the foreign state—to violate the laws of the foreign state; the contempt order against the bank is reversed.

From the perspective of the parent bank, the foreign branch is often treated as a separate business unit, with its own profit-and-loss statement, its own foreign tax liabilities, and its own separate account with the parent bank.[147] In terms of home state law, however, the treatment of foreign branches is not so easily described. Inconsistency is the common rule, both between and within states. Sometimes foreign branches are treated as peculiar separate entities. For example, statutes commonly require a parent bank to get permission from its home state banking authority before it may establish a foreign branch.[148] Similarly, some courts have refused to issue subpoenas directed against foreign branches,[149] and others have

---

[147]Peter S. Smedresman and Andreas F. Lowenfeld, "Eurodollars, Multinational Banks, and National Laws," *New York University Law Review*, vol. 64, p. 733 at p. 742 (1989).
[148]*United States Code*, Title 12, § 601 (1998), requires a federally chartered bank to obtain authorization from the Board of Governors of the Federal Reserve System before opening a foreign branch.
[149]In McCloskey v. Chase Manhattan Bank, *New York Reports, Second Series*, vol. 11, p. 936 (1962), the New York Court of Appeals held that an attachment served on a New York bank does not reach deposits made at its foreign branch.

treated letter-of-credit transactions between a parent and a branch bank as if the two were unrelated entities.[150]

Sometimes, however, home country statutes and courts treat foreign branches as mere extensions of their parents. For example, in 1979, in response to the Iranian hostage crisis, the United States froze Iranian government assets held in U.S. banks and their foreign branches.[151] Courts, similarly, have held that a parent bank can be ordered to freeze the account of a foreign corporation held in the bank's foreign branches.[152] And courts commonly hold that a parent bank is liable for the debts incurred by its foreign branches, because the branch is subject to the supervision and control of the parent.[153]

In Case 6-6, the U.S. Second Circuit Court of Appeals considered the responsibilities of a parent bank for funds deposited in a foreign branch when the foreign branch and its assets are seized by the host country.

[150]Pan-American Bank & Trust Co. v. National City Bank of New York, Federal Reporter, Second Series, vol. 6, p. 762 (Second Circuit Ct. of Appeals, 1925).
[151]See *Weekly Compilation of Presidential Documents*, vol. 15, p. 2117 (November 14, 1979), and *United States Code*, Title 50, §§ 1701–1706 (1982 and Supp. V, 1987).
[152]In United States v. First National City Bank, *United States Reports*, vol. 379, p. 378 (Supreme Ct., 1964), the U.S. Supreme Court reasoned that a foreign bank branch is not a separate entity and, therefore, its parent has both actual and practical control of its operations.
[153]Sokoloff v. National City Bank of New York, *New York Miscellaneous Reports*, vol. 130, p. 66 (New York Supreme Court, 1927). A different rationale was used in Wells Fargo Asia, Ltd., v. Citibank, N.A., *Federal Supplement,* vol. 695, p. 1450 at p. 1456 (1988). There the U.S. District Court for the Southern District of New York concluded that "under New York law, which governs this question, Citibank is liable for the debt of its Manila branch and plaintiff is entitled to look to Citibank's worldwide assets for satisfaction of its deposits." For additional similar cases, see Patrick Heininger, "Liability of U.S. Banks for Deposits Placed in Their Foreign Branches," *Law and Policy in International Business*, vol. 11, p. 903 (1979).

Case 6-6 VISHIPCO LINE ET AL. v. CHASE MANHATTAN BANK, N.A.

United States, Court of Appeals, Second Circuit, 1981. *Federal Reporter, Second Series,* vol. 660, p. 854 (1981).

CIRCUIT JUDGE MANSFIELD

***

From 1966 until April 24, 1975, Chase operated a branch office in Saigon. Among its depositors were the ten corporate plaintiffs, which were principally engaged at that time in providing shipping services to the U.S. Government in Southeast Asia, and the individual plaintiff, who owned a 200 million piastre CD issued by Chase's Saigon branch. Chase's operations in Saigon came to an end at noon on April 24, 1975, after Chase officials in New York determined that Saigon would soon fall to the Communists. After closing the branch without prior notice to depositors, local Chase officials balanced the day's books, shut the vaults and the building itself, and delivered keys and financial records needed to operate the branch to personnel at the French Embassy in Saigon. Saigon fell

on April 30th, and on May 1st the new government issued a communiqué which read as follows:

All public offices, public organs, barracks, industrial, agriculture and commercial establishments, banks, communication and transport, cultural, educational and health establishments, warehouses, and so forth—together with documents, files, property and technical means of U.S. imperialism and the Saigon administration—will be confiscated and, from now on, managed by the revolutionary administration.

Shortly thereafter, the French embassy turned over records from the Chase branch to the new government.

Tran Dinh Truong, who is a major shareholder of most, if not all, of the ten corporate plaintiffs and who represents them here, fled South Vietnam just prior to the Communist takeover, as did Nguyen Thi Cham, the individual plaintiff. After arriving in the United States, Truong and Cham demanded that Chase repay the piastre deposits made in Saigon, but Chase refused to do so. . . . Truong, acting under his powers of attorney, subsequently caused the plaintiffs to bring this action against Chase for breach of contract, seeking recovery of the dollar value of the piastre deposits held by its Saigon branch for them at the time it was closed, as well as the value of the certificate of deposit owned by Cham.

The evidence was undisputed that on April 24, 1975, the ten corporate plaintiffs held demand piastre deposits (or overdrafts) with Chase in the following sums:

Name of Account	Balance
Vishipco Line VN	$22,995,328
Ha Nam Cong Ty	9,053,016
Dai Nam Hang Hai C.T.	9,397,598
Rang Dong Hang Hai C.T.	8,974,556
Mekong Ship Co. SARL	7,239,661
Vishipco SARL	(12,498,573)
Thai Binh C.T.	68,218
VN Tau Bien C.T.	5,925,249
Van An Hang Hai C.T.	87,439,199
Cong Ty U Tau Sao Mai	380,419

Chase also concedes that on November 27, 1974, it issued to Ms. Cham a CD in the sum of 200,000,000 Vietnamese piastres, payable on May 27, 1975, and that the CD bore interest at the rate of 23.5 percent per annum, payable at maturity.

***

DISCUSSION

***

Chase ... argues that the Vietnamese decree confiscating the assets which maritime corporations such as the corporate plaintiffs had left behind had the effect of seizing the piastre deposits at issue in this case. As a result, according to Chase, the corporate plaintiffs may not sue to recover the deposits because they no longer own them, and the act of state doctrine bars any challenge to the validity of the governmental seizure. We disagree. There is no evidence that plaintiffs' existence as corporate entities was terminated. Moreover, it is only by way of a strained reading of the Vietnamese confiscation announcement that one can even argue that choses[154] in action were meant to be included. The plain meaning of the statement that

the Saigon-Gia Dinh Management Committee quickly took over the management of all maritime transportation *facilities* abandoned by their owners [emphasis supplied].

is that the seizures involved physical assets only and did not reach whatever claim the corporate plaintiffs might have on their departure for payment of the amounts owed to them by Chase.

More importantly, however, upon Chase's departure from Vietnam the deposits no longer had their *situs*[155] in Vietnam at the time of the confiscation decree. As we have said in the past, "[f]or purposes of the act of state doctrine, a debt is not 'located' within a foreign state unless that state has the power to enforce or collect it."[156] The rule announced in *Harris v. Balk*[157] continues to be valid on this point: the power to enforce payment of a debt depends on jurisdiction over the debtor. Since Chase had abandoned its Saigon branch at the time of the Vietnamese decree, and since it had no separate corporate identity in Vietnam which would remain in existence after its departure, the Vietnamese decree could not have had any effect on its debt to the corporate plaintiffs. As one qualified commentator has observed:

> The *situs* of a bank's debt on a deposit is considered to be at the branch where the deposit is carried, but if the branch is closed, . . . the depositor has a claim against the home office; thus, the *situs* of the debt represented by the deposit would spring back and cling to the home office. . . . [U]nder the act of state doctrine, the courts of the United States are not bound to give effect to foreign acts of state as to property outside the acting state's territorial jurisdiction.[158]

. . . Since in our case Chase's branch in Saigon was neither open nor operating at the time of the confiscation and had in fact been abandoned prior to that time, the Vietnamese decree was ineffective as against Chase's debt to the plaintiffs.

***

Chase next argues that under Vietnamese law its failure to repay plaintiffs' deposits in the period prior to May 1, 1975, was not a breach of its deposit contract, because the conditions prevailing in Saigon at the time rendered payment impossible. In support of this argument, Chase cites various sections of the South Vietnamese Civil Code which excuse performance under various extenuating circumstances, as well as the provisions in-

---

[154]French: "a thing." A "chose in action" is a right to bring a suit or to recover a debt or money.
[155]Latin: "location."
[156]Menendez v. Saks and Co., *Federal Reporter, Second Series*, vol. 485, p. 1355 at p. 1364 (Second Circuit Ct. of Appeals, 1973), reversed on other grounds in the case of Alfred Dunhill of London, Inc. v. Republic of Cuba, *United States Reports*, vol. 425, p. 682 (Supreme Ct., 1976).
[157]*United States Reports*, vol. 198, p. 215 (Supreme Ct., 1905).
[158]Patrick Heininger, "Liability of U.S. Banks for Deposits Placed in Their Foreign Branches," *Law and Policy in International Business*, vol. 11, p. 903 at p. 975 (1979).

cluded in the deposit contracts used by the Saigon branch which purported to discharge the bank's responsibility for losses to depositors resulting from a variety of unexpected and uncontrollable sources.

This argument must be rejected for the reasons that impossibility of performance in Vietnam did not relieve Chase of its obligation to perform elsewhere. By operating in Saigon through a branch rather than through a separate corporate entity, Chase accepted the risk that it would be liable elsewhere for obligations incurred by its branch. As the official referee in the *Sokoloff* [v. *National City Bank of New York*] case ... summarized the law:

> [W]hen considered with relation to the parent bank, [foreign branches] are not independent agencies; they are, what their name imports, merely branches, and are subject to the supervision and control of the parent bank, and are instrumentalities whereby the parent bank carried on its business. ... Ultimate liability for a debt of a branch would rest upon the parent bank.[159]

U.S. banks, by operating abroad through branches rather than through subsidiaries, reassure foreign depositors that their deposits will be safer with them than they would be in a locally incorporated bank. ... Indeed, the national policy in South Vietnam, where foreign banks were permitted to operate only through branches, was to enable those depositing in foreign branches to gain more protection than they would have received had their money been deposited in locally incorporated subsidiaries of foreign banks. Chase's defenses of impossibility and *force majeure*[160] might have succeeded if the Saigon branch had been locally incorporated or (more problematically) if the deposit contract had included an explicit waiver on the part of the depositor of any right to proceed against the home office. But absent such circumstances the Saigon branch's admitted inability to perform did not relieve Chase of liability on its debts in Saigon, since the conditions in Saigon were no bar to performance in New York or at other points outside of Vietnam. ...

A bank which accepts deposits at a foreign branch becomes a debtor, not a bailee,[161] with respect to its depositors. In the event that unsettled local conditions require it to cease operations, it should inform its depositors of the date when its branch will close and give them the opportunity to withdraw their deposits or, if conditions prevent such steps, enable them to obtain payment at an alternative location. ... In the rare event that such measures are either impossible or only partially successful,

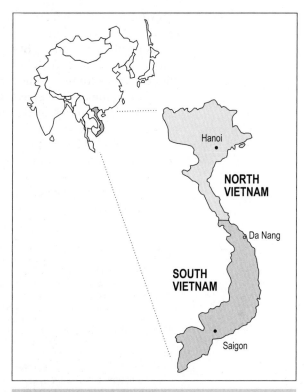

MAP 6-5 Vietnam (1975)

fairness dictates that the parent bank be liable for those deposits which it was unable to return abroad. To hold otherwise would be to undermine the seriousness of its obligations to its depositors and under some circumstances (not necessarily present here) to gain a windfall.

Reversed and remanded for further proceedings consistent with the foregoing.

CASEPOINT: (1) When a bank opens a branch in a foreign country, as opposed to incorporating a local subsidiary in that foreign country, the bank remains liable for obligations incurred by its branch. (2) The power to enforce a debt depends on jurisdiction over the debtor; the *situs* of a a debt incurred by the branch in that foreign country which closes prior to a seizure order by the government will be where the parent resides. In this case, the court has jurisdiction over the parent bank in the United States. (3) The act of state doctrine does not apply here, because the *situs* of the debt is in the United States, and the Vietnam government decree cannot affect a right to recover a debt whose *situs* is no longer Vietnam.

---

[159]Sokoloff v. National City Bank of New York, *New York Miscellaneous Reports*, vol. 130, p. 66 at p. 73 (New York Supreme Court, 1927).
[160]French: "superior force." An event or effect that cannot be anticipated or controlled.
[161]A bailee is a person to whom personal property is delivered that is to be returned to the person who delivered it, the bailor, after it has been held for some purpose.

Conflicts between Host and Home State Regulations

State X enacts legislation requiring foreign branches of its domestic banks to comply with its rules regulating deposits. State Y enacts legislation requiring local branches of foreign parent banks to comply with State Y's rules regulating deposits. Bank P, with its headquarters in State X, has a foreign branch in State Y. Which law does the branch obey?

Two commentators have suggested that a branch bank should be subject only to the rules and regulations of the host country, regardless of the directives given by the home country to the parent bank. They argue that such a rule "would most accurately reflect the expectations" of banks and depositors, and would be perceived by governments as the "most reasonable allocation" of their powers to regulate banks and bank deposits.[162] Their rule, however, is only a proposal. No case law has clearly emerged to cover this circumstance, although cases involving conflicting regulations have become more and more common in recent years.[163] Case 6-7 describes one British judge's solution to this enigma.

---

[162]Peter S. Smedresman and Andreas F. Lowenfeld, "Eurodollars, Multinational Banks, and National Laws," *New York University Law Review*, vol. 64, p. 733 at p. 800 (1989).

[163]In the United States, the court in Wells Fargo Asia, Ltd. v. Citibank, N.A., *Federal Supplement*, vol. 695, p. 1450 (District Ct. for S. District of New York, 1988), reached a conclusion at odds with Smedresman and Lowenfeld's proposed rule. However, in the companion cases of Braka v. Bancomer, SA, *Federal Supplement*, vol. 589, p. 1465 (District Ct. for S. District of New York, 1984), affirmed in *Federal Reporter, Second Series*, vol. 762, p. 222 (Second Circuit Court of Appeals, 1985), and Callejo v. Bancomer, SA, *id.,* vol. 764, p. 1101 (Fifth Circuit Court of Appeals, 1985), the decisions support the rule.

Some developments in reaching international accords for the joint supervision of branch banks, especially in the area of capital adequacy, have begun to take shape. The Committee of Banking Regulations and Supervisory Practices, established by the central banks of the member countries of the Group of Ten, has issued several reports suggesting how supervisory responsibility should be allocated. Several of the member countries, including the United States and the United Kingdom, have started the process of enacting the recommendations into law. See Joseph J. Norton and Sherry C. Whitley, *Banking Law Manual*, § 15.09 (1990).

=⟪⟫=

Case 6-7 LIBYAN ARAB FOREIGN BANK v. BANKERS TRUST COMPANY

England, High Court of Justice, Queen's Bench Division, Commercial Court, 1987. *Lloyd's Reports,* vol. 1988, pt. 1, p. 259 (1988); *International Legal Materials*, vol. 26, p. 1600 (1987).

On January 8, 1986, the Libyan Arab Foreign Bank (Libyan Bank)[164] *had over $131.5 million deposited in a call account with the London branch of Bankers Trust Company (Bankers Trust), a New York corporation (and $161.4 million in a demand account in New York). On that day, effective 4:10 P.M., the president of the United States froze all Libyan assets in the United States. According to New York law, but not according to English law, that included the Libyan Bank's London deposit. The Libyan Bank sued Bankers Trust in the United Kingdom for, among other claims, recovery of its deposit. Bankers*

Trust argued that it was not liable because (1) New York law governed the deposit arrangement and (2) New York law prohibited it from making transfers out of the London account. In particular, Bankers Trust points to an agreement between the parties made in December 1980 (the managed account arrangement) that provided for the New York office of Bankers Trust to oversee the Libyan bank's accounts in both New York and London as support for its argument that New York law applied.

MR. JUSTICE STAUGHTON

***

As a general rule the contract between a bank and its customer is governed by the law of the place where the account is kept, in the absence of agreement to the

---

[164]The Libyan Arab Foreign Bank was a Libyan corporation wholly owned by the Central Bank of Libya. It carried on an offshore banking business and did not engage in domestic banking in Libya.

contrary.... [T]here was no challenge to that as a general rule....

That rule accords with the principle, to be found in the judgment of Lord Justice Atkin in *N. Joachimson v. Swiss Bank Corporation,*[165] and other authorities, that a bank's promise to repay is to repay at the branch of the bank where the account is kept.

In the age of the computer it may not be strictly accurate to speak of the branch where the account is kept. Banks no longer have books in which they write entries; they have terminals by which they give instructions; and the computer itself with its magnetic tape, floppy disc or some other device may be physically located elsewhere. Nevertheless it should not be difficult to decide where an account is kept for this purpose; and is not in the present case. The actual entries on the London account were, as I understand it, made in London, albeit on instructions from New York after December 1980. At all events I have no doubt that the London account was at all material times "kept" in London.

Mr. Sumption [the attorney representing Bankers Trust] was prepared to accept that the proper law governing the London account was English law from 1973 to December 1980. But he submitted that a fundamental change then took place, when the managed account arrangement was made. I agree that this was an important change, and demands reconsideration of the proper law from that date. That the proper law of a contract may be altered appears from *James Mill & Partners, Ltd. v. Whitworth Street Estates, Ltd.*[166]

Mr. Cresswell, for the Libyan Bank, submits that there then arose two separate contracts, of which one related to the London account and remained governed by English law; alternatively he says that there was one contract, again governed by English law; or that it had two proper laws, one English law and the other the law of New York. Mr. Sumption submits that there was from December 1980 one contract only, governed by New York law.

Each side has relied on a number of points in support of its contentions. I do not set them out, for they are fairly evenly balanced, and in my view do little or nothing to diminish the importance of the general rule, that the proper law of a bank's contract is the law of the place where the account is kept. Political risk must commonly be an important factor to those who deposit large sums of money with banks; the popularity of Swiss bank accounts with some people is due to the banking laws of the Cantons of Switzerland. And I have already found on the evidence of Bankers Trust, that the Iranian crisis

was at the back of everyone's mind in 1980. Whatever considerations did or did not influence the parties to this case, I believe that banks generally and their customers normally intend the local law to apply. So I would require solid grounds for holding that the general rule does not apply, and there do not appear to me to be such grounds in this case.

I have, then, to choose between the first and third of Mr. Cresswell's arguments—two separate contracts or one contract with two proper laws. It would be unfortunate if the result of this case depended on the seemingly unimportant point whether there was one contract or two. But if it matters, I find the notion of two separate contracts artificial and unattractive....

Mr. Sumption argues that difficulty and uncertainty would arise if one part of the contract was governed by English law and another by New York law. I do not see that this would be so, or that any difficulty which arose would be insuperable.

There is high authority that branches of banks should be treated as separate from the head office. See for example *R. v. Grossman,*[167] where Lord Denning, Master of the Rolls, said:

> The branch of Barclays Bank in Douglas, Isle of Man, should be considered as a different entity separate from the head office in London.

That notion, of course, has its limits. A judgment lawfully obtained in respect of the obligation of a branch would be enforceable in England against the assets of the head office. (That may not always be the case in America.) As with the theory that the premises of a diplomatic mission do not form part of the territory of the receiving state, I would say that it is *true for some purposes* that a branch office of a bank is treated as a separate entity from the head office.

This reasoning would support Mr. Cresswell's argument that there were two separate contracts, in respect of the London account and the New York account. It also lends some support to the conclusion that if, as is my preferred solution, there was only one contract, it was governed in part by English law and in part by New York law. I hold that the rights and obligations of the parties in respect of the London account were governed by English law.

The High Court allowed the Libyan Bank to recover the $131.5 million on deposit in the London branch of Bankers Trust as well as $161.4 million of the funds in the New York office because, according to the managed account arrangement, Bankers Trust was supposed to have transferred that sum from its New York office to its

---

[165]*Law Reports, King's Bench,* vol. 1921, pt. 3, p. 110 at p. 127 (1921).
[166]*Law Reports, Appeal Cases,* vol. 1970, p. 583 (1970), per Lord Reid at p. 603, Lord Wilberforce at p. 615.
[167]{195} *Law Reports, Criminal Appeal Reports,* vol. 73, p. 302 at p. 307 (1981).

London branch on the morning prior to the presidential freeze, and it had no excuse for not having done so. ■

CASEPOINT: (1) The general rule is that a bank contract is governed by the law of the place where the account is kept. (2) For some purposes, a branch is treated as a separate entity from its home office. This rule has its limits—a home office is liable for the obligations of its branch.

Chapter Questions

Dealing with Currency Fluctuation

1. X and Y are foreign exchange traders in Germany. X agreed to sell 100 million Mexican pesos to Y for delivery within one week at an agreed-upon price in German marks. X was three days late in making delivery. During those three days, the Mexican government acted to devalue the Mexican peso by 20 percent. Y now sues in a German court to have the contract set aside. Will Y be successful? Explain.

2. X in State A and Y in State B plan to enter into a contract. What can they do to avoid the impact of a fluctuation in the value of their money of account?

Exchange Contracts and Exchange Control Regulations

3. The State of Q forbids its citizens to take more than 1,000 units of its currency out of the country in any one-month period. To avoid this limitation, Ms. Ecks, a State Q citizen who lives abroad in State X, engages in the following scheme with a friend, Mr. Zed, a travel agent in Tokyo, Japan. Ms. Ecks buys yen from Mr. Zed at a sizable premium. She pays for the yen with checks, made out to Mr. Zed, that she draws on her account with QueBank, located in the capital city of State Q. Mr. Zed regularly accompanies tour groups to State Q, and when he is there, he cashes Ms. Ecks's check at QueBank. Mr. Zed, accordingly, makes a nice profit from selling yen to Ms. Ecks, and Ms. Ecks is able to get as much money as she wants out of State Q. Somehow the government of Q State learned of this transaction, and it ordered QueBank to freeze Ms. Ecks's account so long as she is abroad. Mr. Zed, unable to cash Ms. Ecks's latest checks, sues Ms. Ecks in State X to get back the money he had already advanced her. Both State Q and State X, as well as Japan, are members of the IMF. Will Mr. Zed succeed? Explain. (Consider the *Wilson, Smithett & Cope, Ltd. v. Terruzi*, case.)

Branch Banking

4. MultiBank is a large London bank with a branch office in Boston. The American government believes that a prominent American underworld figure, Mr. Z, has been depositing stolen money in MultiBank's Boston branch as well as with the bank's home office in London. The government's prosecutor has asked an American court to issue a subpoena ordering the manager of the Boston branch to turn over all records relating to Mr. Z from both the Boston branch and the London home office. Should the court issue the subpoena? Explain.

5. Q Bank, located in State A, has a branch in State B. X has State A currency on deposit in that branch. X directs the branch to transfer the funds to a branch of P Bank that is located in State B. P Bank itself is, like Q Bank, located in Country A. The customary method for making such a transfer is for Q Bank's branch to request its parent to make a transfer through State A's central bank, debiting its own account with its parent and crediting P Bank's account at the central bank. In turn, P Bank will credit its branch's account with the transfer. State A, however, has imposed an embargo on all transfers relating to monies belonging to X, and neither Q Bank nor P Bank will make the transfer. X files suit in State B and seeks an order for the two branches to make the transfer locally without going through their parent banks or State A's central bank. Will X be successful?

Arbitrage

6. You are an arbitrageur in London. Swiss francs are presently selling in London for U.S. $0.67. You anticipate that they will increase in value and be selling for U.S. $0.70 in thirty days. You purchase $1 million worth of francs on the spot market. Is there anything that you can do to hedge your bet? That is, is there some way to ensure that you won't lose all of your money in case the value of the franc plummets?

CHAPTER 7
TRADE IN GOODS

A. HISTORY OF CONTEMPORARY INTERNATIONAL TRADE LAW

International trade has grown dramatically in the past sixty years. In great measure, this is because the world's nations have cooperated in eliminating protectionist domestic legislation and in promoting the free exchange of goods.[1] Indeed, one of the most remarkable trends in international law during the past six decades has been the steady movement away from tariffs and quotas and toward free trade among the nations of the world. As the next several paragraphs will explain, where once most nations maintained laws to promote and protect their own businesses and producers, since the 1940s there has been a continual shift toward multilateral efforts to reduce tariffs and other barriers. As is described below, the several GATT treaties, the EU, the WTO, and many other international agreements and organizations have resulted in a dramatic lowering of tariffs—each nation giving up a little in order to get reciprocal reductions—and a tremendous increase in international trade. Business now operates in a truly global economy.

However, we may have reached a point where future trade liberalization will be more difficult to achieve. Within the past few years, many voices have been raised in protest of globalization. It is now clear that there are both winners and losers as trade becomes more free and more global. It appears that large multinational firms and large, powerful nations have received more benefits from the removal of trade barriers than smaller businesses, farmers, and nations. "The rich get richer" has become a battle cry for antiglobalization protesters at most large international economic and trade meetings.

Other groups have complained that free trade ignores important environmental and labor issues, with dire consequences for the environment and workers in developing countries. In addition, employee organizations in developed nations—Europe and the United States in particular—argue that free trade and globalization have led to the loss of thousands of good jobs, as manufacturing plants are moved and work is outsourced to lower-wage nations. Corporate profits in developed nations have sharply increased in recent years, while wages have stagnated. And as globalization moves forward, the trade deficit of the United States has jumped, to a record $763 billion in 2006 as Americans purchased more and more goods manufactured abroad, particularly from China and other low-cost nations.

As the *Wall Street Journal* noted in one article describing the topics and agenda of the World Economic Forum meetings in Davos, Switzerland, in early 2007:

> Globalization isn't working for everyone. Stagnating wages and rising job insecurity in developed countries are creating popular disenchantment with the free movement of goods, capital and people across borders. If unchecked, popular fears could turn into a political backlash that could lead to protectionism—or at least make broad free-trade agreements harder to achieve in the future.[2]

Nevertheless, despite the protests, it is clear that globalization is here to stay. The clock cannot be turned back. The technical, social, and political developments of the past sixty years cannot be reversed—we now live and do business in a global marketplace. So, now let us turn our attention to the long, steady series of events, treaties, agreements, and organizations that have created—and set the rules governing—the free trade world.

PROTECTIONISM

The Great Depression of the 1930s in many ways was a direct consequence of protectionism. When the United States raised tariffs on more than 900 items with the Hawley-Smoot Tariff Act of 1930, the other major trading nations of the world reciprocated with similar increases. The United Kingdom, for one, enacted its first major protective trade legislation of the

---

[1]For a brief history of developments leading up to the establishment of the World Trade Organization, see "Understanding the WTO" at http://www.wto.org/english/thewto_e/whatis_e/tif_e/tif_e.htm.
[2]Marcus Walker, "Just How Good Is Globalization?" *Wall Street Journal*, January 25, 2007, p. A10.

twentieth century in 1931. That same year, the League of Nations tried to cool what had become a tariff war by convening a Tariff Truce Conference, but the effort failed. By 1932, world trade had fallen 25 percent from its 1929 level, and the world's industrial production had fallen 30 percent. In 1933, the last major prewar multilateral conference on trade, the World Monetary and Economic Conference, adjourned without results because the participants refused to relax their trade restrictions. Not until 1936 did industrial production return to its 1929 level, and not until 1940 did international trade return to its pre-Depression level.

Recovery from the Great Depression was U.S. President Franklin Roosevelt's main goal upon his election in 1932, and liberalization of international trade was at the heart of his program for achieving that end. Beginning in 1934, the United States entered into bilateral trade negotiations with its major trading partners to reduce tariffs on a reciprocal (instead of a unilateral) basis. The United States kept up this program until, during, and after World War II.

The idea that tariffs should be reduced through bilateral and multilateral negotiations became part of the Atlantic Charter, the declaration issued by President Roosevelt and British Prime Minister Winston Churchill in 1941 as a rallying cry for nations opposing the military and economic aggression of fascist Germany, Italy, and Japan. In addition to calling for the permanent renunciation of territorial aggrandizement and the disarmament of all aggressor states, the charter set out goals for the postwar era, many of which were based on international economic cooperation. Among these was the assertion that every nation has the right to expect that its legitimate trade will not be diverted or diminished by excessive tariffs, quotas, or restrictive unilateral or bilateral practices.

During World War II, the protectionist sentiments of the 1930s were rejected as destructive, and they were swept aside in a rush to arrange a comprehensive network of multilateral agreements to settle the world's political and economic problems. The nations fighting Germany, Italy, and Japan allied themselves as the United Nations, and in 1943 they called for the creation of a permanent international organization to replace the League of Nations and an integrated international system to encourage trade liberalization and multilateral economic cooperation. Both efforts began the following year. A first draft of a United Nations Charter was agreed to at a conference at Dumbarton Oaks (a mansion in Georgetown, Washington, D.C.) and an international conference on economic relations convened at Bretton Woods, New Hampshire. A final draft of the United Nations Charter was approved and adopted at San Francisco in 1945.

U.S. President Frankling Roosevelt (center) and British Prime Minister Winston Churchill (left) aboard a ship off Newfoundland from which they issued the Atlantic Charter on August 14, 1941. (Photo: 24469 UN/DPI.)

THE BRETTON WOODS SYSTEM

The negotiators who met for the United Nations Monetary and Financial Conference in Bretton Woods in July 1944 were determined to create a system that would promote trade liberalization and multilateral economic cooperation. The Bretton Woods System was meant to be an integrated undertaking by the international community to establish a multilateral institutional framework of rules and obligations.

As originally planned, the Bretton Woods System was to have had at its core three major international organizations: the International Monetary Fund (IMF), the International Bank for Reconstruction and Development (IBRD or World Bank), and the ill-fated International Trade Organization (ITO). Together they were to collectively administer and harmonize world trade. The IMF was to ensure monetary stability and facilitate currency exchange. The World Bank was to assist war-ravaged and developing countries reconstruct or upgrade their economies. The ITO was to administer a comprehensive code governing the conduct of world trade. This code was to be broad and encompassing, dealing with a wide range of issues, including trade and trade barriers, labor and employment, economic development, restrictive business practices, and intergovernmental commodity agreements.

The Articles of Agreement of the IMF were adopted at Bretton Woods and ratified in 1945. See Exhibit 7-1. The World Bank was organized and its Agreement ratified in 1945 as well. Not until 1946 did the United Nations Economic and Social Council (ECOSOC) appoint a Preparatory Committee to draft an agenda and set up a conference to create the ITO.

EXHIBIT 7-1   The Bretton Woods Conference

Representatives from 44 countries participated in the United Nations Monetary and Financial Conference in Bretton Woods, New Hampshire, July 1–22, 1944. The conference drafted the Articles of Agreement of the International Monetary Fund (IMF) and proposed the creation of the International Bank for Reconstruction and Development (IBRD) and an International Trade Organization (ITO). The IMF came into being in 1945 and the IBRD in 1946, but the ITO was not established (as the World Trade Organization) until 1994. (Photo: Gamma Liaison.)

The strongest advocate of an ITO was the U.S. government, which produced a "Suggested Charter" for consideration by the committee that met in London in October 1946. After a second session in Geneva in 1947, the ITO Charter was adopted in a "Final Act" and its contents were agreed to by the 53 countries participating in a UN-sponsored Conference on Trade and Employment in Havana in 1948. But the American government, which had worked hard to create the ITO in 1946, withheld support in 1948. President Harry Truman, fearing that the ITO Charter (or Havana Charter) would be rejected by an opposition Congress that had become conservative and protectionist and that American foreign policy would be adversely affected, did not submit the ITO Charter to the Senate for ratification. All but two of the other participants at the Havana conference had waited to see if the United States would ratify the charter, and when it did not, no further effort was made to establish the organization. It would be nearly fifty years before the idea would come to fruition with the establishment of the World Trade Organization (WTO).

THE 1947 GENERAL AGREEMENT ON TARIFFS AND TRADE

General Agreement on Tariffs and Trade (GATT) 1947: Multilateral agreement that set out the rules under which the contracting states parties were committed to negotiate reductions in customs tariffs and other impediments to international trade in goods.

Instead of creating an ITO, the developed market-economy countries entered into an accord in 1947 called the **General Agreement on Tariffs and Trade** (GATT 1947).[3] The original contracting parties were the same states that had formed the Preparatory Committee that had drafted the ITO Charter, and they borrowed liberally from that document in drafting GATT 1947.[4]

---

[3]The Final Act Embodying the Results of the Uruguay Round of Multilateral Trade Negotiations (1994) refers to the original GATT as *GATT 1947* to distinguish it from the GATT annexed to the Agreement Establishing the World Trade Organization, which it calls *GATT 1994*. The same nomenclature will be used here.
[4]For a history of GATT through the completion of the Tokyo Round (1973–1979), see Frank Stone, *Canada, the GATT and the International Trade System* (1984) and "Understanding the WTO" at http://www.wto.org. See also Jeffrey J. Schott and Johanna W. Buurman, "The Uruguay Round: An Assessment" (1994) and "What Is the WTO?" at http://www.wto.org/english/thewto_e/whatis_e/whatis_e.htm#intro.

GATT 1947 was a multilateral treaty that set out the principles under which its contracting states,[5] on the basis of "reciprocity and mutual advantage," were to negotiate "a substantial reduction in customs tariffs and other impediments to trade." With the addition of other states in subsequent years, GATT 1947 came to govern almost all of the world's trade.

The main principles of GATT 1947 were as follows: (1) Trade discrimination was forbidden. Each contracting state had to accord the same trading privileges and benefits (or **most-favored-nation status**) to all other contracting states equally; and, once foreign trade goods were imported into one contracting state from another, the foreign goods had to be treated (according to the **national treatment** principle) the same way as domestic goods. (2) With some exceptions, the only barriers that one contracting state could use to limit the importation of goods from another contracting state were customs tariffs. (3) The trade regulations of contracting states had to be **transparent**, that is, published and available to other contracting states and their nationals. (4) Customs unions and free trade agreements between contracting states were regarded as legitimate means for liberalizing trade so long as they did not, on the whole, discriminate against third-party states that were also parties to GATT. (5) GATT-contracting states were allowed to levy only certain charges on imported goods: (a) an import tax equal in amount to internal taxes, (b) anti-dumping duties to offset advantages obtained by imported goods that were sold below the price charged in their home market or below their actual cost, (c) countervailing duties to counteract foreign export subsidies, and (d) fees and other proper charges for services rendered.[6]

The legal framework established at Geneva in 1947 remained essentially unchanged until the creation of the World Trade Organization (WTO) in 1994. Even under that agreement, the substantive provisions of GATT 1947 live on, becoming one of the annexes to the Agreement Establishing the WTO (under the name GATT 1994).[7]

MULTILATERAL TRADE NEGOTIATIONS

To keep GATT 1947 up-to-date, the contracting parties regularly participated in *multilateral trade negotiations* (informally called **rounds**). Including the Geneva Round in 1947, when GATT was originally adopted, eight rounds of MTNs were held. Most were held at Geneva, the location of the GATT headquarters.[8] The current "round," begun at Doha, Qatar (the "Doha Round") has dissolved into a number of long-standing disputes, primarily over U.S. and EU subsidies for their own agricultural industries.

Since one of the main purposes of the GATT agreement was to reduce tariffs, the first five rounds were devoted almost exclusively to tariff reductions, while the last three completed rounds (the Kennedy, Tokyo, and Uruguay Rounds) expanded their agendas to nontariff matters. Negotiations in the early rounds were generally carried on bilaterally, on a product-by-product basis. That is, the two states most interested in a particular product would negotiate a bargain through the time-honored process of offer, counteroffer, and agreement. Agreed-upon concessions in the form of bound tariff rates were then extended to all other GATT contracting parties as a consequence of the most-favored-nation principle.

More comprehensive negotiating techniques were proposed and used for the first time in the **Kennedy Round** (1964–1967). At a plenary session of the contracting parties held immediately prior to this MTN, the contracting states issued a declaration defining the

most-favored-nation status: When a GATT member nation sets a favorable tariff rate on a particular type of goods imported from one GATT member, that member nation may not assess a higher tariff on the particular type of goods being imported from any GATT nation.

national treatment: Once goods are legally imported, they must be treated the same way as domestic goods (no additional requirements).

transparent: Trade regulations of GATT members must be published and available to all other GATT nations and their nationals.

round: A meeting of the contracting parties of GATT to participate in MTNs.

Kennedy Round: GATT MTNs held from 1964 to 1967 that established the practice of setting an agenda for and defining the techniques to be used during GATT negotiations.

[5]There were 23 original contracting states parties to GATT 1947. At that time they accounted for 80 percent of the world's trade. There are now 150 members, who account for 97 percent of world trade.
[6]GATT 1947, in addition to these basic principles, contained various exceptions that could be invoked in special situations. These included balance-of-payments disequilibriums, serious and unexpected damage to domestic production, the need to promote economic development, the need to protect the production of domestic raw materials, and the need to protect domestic national security interests.
[7]The provisions of GATT 1947 are carried forward to GATT 1994 with few changes. Essentially, only the Protocol of Provisional Application was not readopted.
[8]The eight rounds were Geneva (parallel with the negotiation of GATT 1947); Annecy, France (1949); Torquay, England (1950–1951); Geneva (1955–1956); the Dillon Round in Geneva (1961–1962); the Kennedy Round in Geneva (1964–1967); the Tokyo Round in Geneva (1973–1979); and the Uruguay Round in Montevideo, Geneva, Montreal, and Marrakesh (1986–1994).

agenda and the negotiation techniques to be used. The declaration also called for two kinds of across-the-board tariff reductions. One was a uniform percentage reduction in tariffs among all contracting parties. The other was the use of various mathematical formulas to make the various tariff schedules more consistent; that is, higher tariffs were reduced more and lower tariffs less. Fifty-four states participated in the negotiations and 400,000 tariff headings that were covered. The result was an average 35 percent reduction in duties levied on industrial products that was phased in over a five-year period.

In addition to the negotiations on tariffs, the Kennedy Round dealt with the problems of nonreciprocity for developing states and with nontariff obstacles. The developing states parties successfully added a new part to the General Agreement entitled "Trade and Development," which called for stabilization, as far as possible, of raw material prices; reduction or elimination of customs duties and other restrictions that unreasonably differentiate between products in the primary (or raw) state and the same products in their finished form; and renunciation by the developed states of the principle of reciprocity in their relations with developing states. In the area of nontariff barriers to trade, the Kennedy Round produced an agreement on anti-dumping (popularly called the Anti-dumping Code).

Tokyo Round: GATT MTNs held from 1973 to 1979 that produced six nontariff codes.

The next multilateral trade negotiations, known as the **Tokyo Round** (1973–1979), were characterized by an ambitious agenda and the participation of non-GATT states. In all, 102 states participated. As with the Kennedy Round, formulas for negotiating tariffs were again applied, but with less success. For a variety of political reasons, tariff rates for some items (e.g., agricultural products and exempt industrial products) were not cut at all, and the cuts on other items were larger or smaller than they would have been if the formulas had been applied. Nevertheless, the tariffs on industrial products were cut, again, an average of 35 percent, to an overall range of 5 to 8 percent among the developed states parties.

Also, following the example of the Kennedy Round, the Tokyo Round produced several special agreements (popularly known as *codes*) to regulate nontariff matters as well as several sectoral agreements to promote trade in particular commodities. These codes, which were sponsored but not administered by GATT, were multilateral treaties open to ratification by any state. Six codes were completed: (1) customs valuation, (2) subsidies and countervailing measures, (3) anti-dumping, (4) standards, (5) import licensing, and (6) government procurement. In addition, three sectoral agreements were concluded on trade in civil aircraft, dairy products, and bovine meat.

THE URUGUAY ROUND

Uruguay Round: GATT MTNs held from 1986 to 1994 that resulted in the establishment of the World Trade Organization.

The **Uruguay Round** (1986–1994)[9] brought about a major change in the institutional structure of the GATT, replacing the informal GATT institution with a new institution: the *World Trade Organization*.[10] The round concluded on April 15, 1994, when representatives of 108 states signed its *Final Act*[11] at a ceremony in Marrakesh, Morocco, and committed their governments to ratify the results of the round.[12] Again, as it had with the ITO Charter, the world waited to see if the U.S. Congress would approve of the new institution. This time, after much delay, including time out for an election, Congress convened in an extraordinary session and ratified the Final Act on December 8, 1994. Moments after the vote was announced in

---

[9]Calls for a new round of MTNs were made soon after the Tokyo Round was completed. GATT set up a preparatory committee in 1982 to create an agenda for a new round, but it was not until 1986, after much debate, that the GATT members formally began negotiations.

[10]For a historical overview of the Uruguay Round, see "Understanding the WTO. The Uruguay Round" at http://www.wto.org/english/thewto_e/whatis_e/tif_e/fact5_e.htm. The introduction to this WTO Web page discussing the Uruguay Round begins, "It took seven and a half years, almost twice the original schedule. By the end, 123 countries were taking part. It covered almost all trade, from toothbrushes to pleasure boats, from banking to telecommunications, from the genes of wild rice to AIDS treatments. It was quite simply the largest trade negotiation ever, and most probably the largest negotiation of any kind in history."

[11]Its full title is the Final Act Embodying the Results of the Uruguay Round of Multilateral Trade Negotiations.

[12]The European Community (now the European Union) and 108 states signed the Final Act at Marrakesh. Bureau of National Affairs, International Trade Reporter, vol. 11, p. 610 (April 20, 1994). At the conclusion of the Uruguay Round, 125 states were participating in the negotiations. John Kraus, *The GATT Negotiations: A Business Guide to the Results of the Uruguay Round*, p. 6 (1994).

Washington, the representatives of the old GATT convened an Implementation Conference in Geneva and agreed that its successor institution, the World Trade Organization, would officially come into existence on January 1, 1995.[13]

The Uruguay Round Final Act is made up of three parts that together form a single whole. The first part, the formal Final Act itself, is a one-page "umbrella" that introduces the other two parts. Most importantly, this first part provides that its signatories agree to (1) submit the Agreement Establishing the World Trade Organization (WTO Agreement) and its annexes (with the exception of four Plurilateral Trade Agreements) to their appropriate authorities for ratification and (2) adopt the Ministerial Declarations, Decisions, and Understandings agreed to during the course of the negotiations.

The second part of the Final Act is made up of the WTO Agreement and its annexes, of which there are two kinds: multilateral trade agreements and plurilateral trade agreements. *Multilateral Trade Agreements* are "integral parts" of the WTO Agreement and are "binding on all members" of the WTO.[14] They consist of (1) 14 Agreements on Trade in Goods (including GATT 1994), (2) the General Agreement on Trade in Services (GATS), (3) the Agreement on Trade-Related Aspects of Intellectual Property Rights (TRIPS), (4) the Understanding on Rules and Procedures Governing the Settlement of Disputes (DSU), and (5) the Trade Policy Review Mechanism (TPRM). The four *Plurilateral Trade Agreements* are also part of the WTO Agreement, but they are only binding on those member states that have accepted them. They "do not create either obligations or rights for members that have not accepted them."[15]

The third and final part comprises the ministerial declarations, decisions, and understandings just mentioned.[16] See Exhibit 7-2.

B. THE WORLD TRADE ORGANIZATION

World Trade Organization (WTO): Intergovernmental organization responsible for (1) implementing, administering, and carrying out the WTO Agreement and its annexes, (2) acting as a forum for ongoing MTNs, (3) serving as a tribunal for resolving disputes, and (4) reviewing the trade policies and practices of WTO member states.

The **World Trade Organization (WTO)** is best described as an umbrella organization under which the agreements that came out of the Uruguay Round of MTNs are gathered.[17] As the WTO Agreement states, the WTO is meant to provide the "common institutional framework" for the implementation of those agreements.[18] The WTO thus serves four basic functions:

1. To implement, administer, and carry out the WTO Agreement and its annexes,[19]
2. To act as a forum for ongoing multilateral trade negotiations,[20]
3. to serve as a tribunal for resolving disputes,[21] and
4. to review the trade policies and practices of member states.[22]

---

[13]GATT 1947 was itself to continue to function "in tandem" with the WTO until the end of 1995 so that the business then being carried on by GATT could gradually be turned over to the WTO. GATT state parties became free to withdraw from GATT 1947 at the end of 1995. Bureau of National Affairs, *International Trade Reporter*, vol. 11, p. 1925 (December 14, 1994).

[14]Agreement Establishing the World Trade Organization, Article II, para. 2 (1994).
The requirement that the member states of the WTO have to participate in the Multilateral Trade Agreements (which include updated versions of many of the Tokyo Round codes) "ends the free ride of many GATT members that benefited from, but refused to join, new agreements negotiated in the GATT since the 1970s." Many states, especially developing states, must now adopt trade rules to bring themselves into compliance. In this respect, the WTO Agreement requires a higher degree of commitment from its members than the old GATT, which had allowed its contracting states to decline participation in its ancillary agreements. Jeffrey J. Schott and Johanna W. Buurman, *The Uruguay Round: An Assessment*, p. 133 (1994), quoting John H. Jackson.

[15]Agreement Establishing the World Trade Organization, Article II, para. 3 (1994).

[16]The Final Act, the WTO Agreement, and a selection of the annexes and ministerial decisions and declarations are reproduced in *International Legal Materials*, vol. 33, pp. 1–152 (1994). They are also available on the Internet at http://www.wto.org/english/docs_e/legal_e/legal_e.htm#wtoagreement.

[17]The WTO home page is at http://www.wto.org. For the WTO's own description of what it does, see "What Is the World Trade Organization?" at http://www.wto.org/english/thewto_e/whatis_e/whatis_e.htm#intro.

[18]Agreement Establishing the World Trade Organization, Article II, para. 1 (1994).

[19]*Id.*, Article III, para. 1.

[20]*Id.*, para. 2.

[21]*Id.*, para. 3.

[22]*Id.*, para. 4.

I. FINAL ACT

II. AGREEMENT ESTABLISHING THE WORLD TRADE ORGANIZATION (WTO AGREEMENT)

    Annex 1A: Agreements on Trade in Goods
1. General Agreement on Tariffs and Trade 1994
2. Uruguay Round Protocol to the General Agreement on Tariffs and Trade 1994
3. Agreement on Agriculture
4. Agreement on Sanitary and Phytosanitary Measures
5. Agreement on Textiles and Clothing
6. Agreement on Technical Barriers to Trade
7. Agreement on Trade-Related Investment Measures
8. Agreement on Implementation of Article VI [concerning anti-dumping]
9. Agreement on Implementation of Article VII [concerning customs valuation]
10. Agreement on Preshipment Inspection
11. Agreement on Rules of Origin
12. Agreement on Import Licensing Procedures
13. Agreement on Subsidies and Countervailing Measures
14. Agreement on Safeguards

    Annex 1B: General Agreement on Trade in Services
    Annex 1C: Agreement on Trade-Related Aspects of Intellectual Property Rights
    Annex 2: Understanding on Rules and Procedures Governing the Settlement of Disputes
    Annex 3: Trade Policy Review Mechanism
    Annex 4: Plurilateral Trade Agreements
        Annex 4(a): Agreement on Trade in Civil Aviation
        Annex 4(b): Agreement on Government Procurement
        Annex 4(c): International Dairy Agreementa
        Annex 4(d): International Bovine Meat Agreementb

III. MINISTERIAL DECISIONS AND DECLARATIONS

EXHIBIT 7-2 Outline of the Final Act Embodying the Results of the Uruguay Round of MTNs

aThe International Dairy Agreement was terminated at the end of 1997. See "Understanding the WTO. The Agreements," posted at http://www.wto.org.
bThe International Bovine Meat Agreement was also terminated at the end of 1997. See *id.*

Additionally, the WTO is to cooperate with the IMF and the World Bank in order to achieve greater coherence in global economic policy making.[23]

The WTO's Web site is at

http://www.wto.org.

THE WTO AGREEMENT

The Agreement Establishing the World Trade Organization (WTO Agreement) has been described as a "mini-charter"[24] because it is much less complex than the ITO's Havana Charter. The Havana Charter, of course, was never ratified—GATT 1947 was adopted instead.

---

[23]*Id.*, para. 5.
[24]Jeffrey J. Schott and Johanna W. Buurman, *The Uruguay Round: An Assessment*, p. 133 (1994), quoting John H. Jackson.

What the WTO Agreement does is to transform GATT 1947, which was a trade accord serviced by a professional secretariat, into a membership organization.[25]

The WTO Agreement, to reiterate, is not a reenactment of the stillborn Havana Charter. Its provisions are exclusively institutional and procedural, unlike those of the Havana Charter, which contained substantive provisions of its own.[26] The WTO Agreement in essence establishes a legal framework to bring together the various trade pacts that were negotiated under GATT 1947. Thus, the WTO was created as a unified administrative organ to oversee all of the Uruguay Round Agreements. This unification solves two problems that hampered the old GATT. First, because GATT 1947 dealt with trade in goods, there was no obvious mechanism for handling agreements relating to trade in services and the protection of intellectual property rights. The WTO Agreement, which "separates the institutional concepts from the substantive rules,"[27] eliminates this difficulty. Second, because the ITO never came into existence, the old GATT had no formal institutional structure. The establishment of the WTO rectifies this.

The WTO Agreement, however, is not substantially different either in scope or function from the old GATT. It does not create a new supranational organization with the power to usurp the sovereignty of its members.[28] In fact, the WTO is to be guided by the procedures, customary practices, and decisions of the old GATT.[29] As Professor John Jackson, the author of an early draft of what was to become the WTO Agreement, told the U.S. Senate Finance Committee about the WTO, it "has no more real power than that which existed for the GATT under the previous agreements."[30]

Later in this chapter, GATT 1994 and the other multilateral agreements relating to trade in goods are examined in some detail. The General Agreement on Trade in Services (GATS) is discussed in Chapter 8 and the Agreement on Trade-Related Aspects of Intellectual Property Rights (TRIPS) is explored in Chapter 9.

MEMBERSHIP OF THE WTO

Tonga joined the WTO in July 2007, bringing its total membership to 151. The members of the WTO[31] comprise both states and customs territories that conduct their own trade policies.[32] States that were members of GATT 1947 on January 1, 1995,[33] along with the EU,

---

[25]*Id.*

[26]Thomas J. Dillon, Jr., "The World Trade Organization: A New Legal Order for World Trade," *Michigan Journal of International Law*, vol. 16, p. 349 at p. 355 (1995).

[27]Uruguay Round Legislation, March 23, 1994, Hearings before the Senate Finance Committee, 103rd Congress, Second Session, p. 195 at p. 197 (testimony of John H. Jackson).

[28]Thomas J. Dillon, Jr., "The World Trade Organization: A New Legal Order for World Trade," *Michigan Journal of International Law*, vol. 16, p. 349 at pp. 355–356 (1995).

[29]Agreement Establishing the World Trade Organization, Article XVI, para. 1 (1994).

[30]Uruguay Round Legislation, March 23, 1994, Hearings Before the Senate Finance Committee, 103rd Congress, Second Session, p. 195 at p. 197 (testimony of John H. Jackson).

[31]For a current list of WTO members, see http://www.wto.org. As of July 31, 2007, there were 150 members, plus 32 countries or territories that had applied for admission and that had observer status, and one other country (the Vatican) with observer status. The members were Albania, Angola, Antigua and Barbuda, Argentina, Armenia, Australia, Austria, Bahrain, Bangladesh, Barbados, Belgium, Belize, Benin, Bolivia, Botswana, Brazil, Brunei Darussalam, Bulgaria, Burkina Faso, Burundi, Cameroon, Canada, the Central African Republic, Chad, Chile, China, Colombia, Congo, Costa Rica, Côte d'Ivoire, Croatia, Cuba, Cyprus, the Czech Republic, the Democratic Republic of the Congo, Denmark, Djibouti, Dominica, the Dominican Republic, Ecuador, Egypt, El Salvador, Estonia, the European Community, Fiji, Finland, the Former Yugoslav Republic of Macedonia, France, Gabon, Gambia, Georgia, Germany, Ghana, Greece, Grenada, Guatemala, Guinea Bissau, Guinea, Guyana, Haiti, Honduras, Hong Kong, Hungary, Iceland, India, Indonesia, Ireland, Israel, Italy, Jamaica, Japan, Jordan, Kenya, Kuwait, the Kyrgyz Republic, Latvia, Lesotho, Liechtenstein, Lithuania, Luxembourg, Macao, Madagascar, Malawi, Malaysia, the Maldives, Mali, Malta, Mauritania, Mauritius, Mexico, Moldova, Mongolia, Morocco, Mozambique, Myanmar, Namibia, Nepal, the Netherlands, New Zealand, Nicaragua, Niger, Nigeria, Norway, Oman, Pakistan, Panama, Papua New Guinea, Paraguay, Peru, the Philippines, Poland, Portugal, Qatar, Romania, Rwanda, Saint Kitts and Nevis, Saint Lucia, Saint Vincent and the Grenadines, Saudi Arabia, Senegal, Taiwan, Sierra Leone, Singapore, Slovakia, Slovenia, the Solomon Islands, South Africa, South Korea, Spain, Sri Lanka, Suriname, Swaziland, Sweden, Switzerland, Chinese Taipei, Tanzania, Thailand, Togo, Tonga, Trinidad and Tobago, Tunisia, Turkey, Uganda, the United Arab Emirates, the United Kingdom, the United States of America, Vietnam, Uruguay, Venezuela, Zambia, and Zimbabwe.

[32]Agreement Establishing the World Trade Organization, Article XII, para. 1 (1994).

[33]On December 8, 1994, Guinea became the 125th member of GATT 1947 and the last state to qualify for becoming an original member of the WTO. Bureau of National Affairs, *International Trade Reporter*, vol. 12, p. 36 (January 4, 1995).

were eligible to become "original members" of the WTO.[34] These members agreed to adhere to all of the Uruguay Round multilateral agreements and to submit their Schedules of Concessions and Commitments concerning industrial and agricultural goods and their Schedules of Specific Commitments concerning services within a year after joining.[35] Original members, however, that are recognized by the United Nations as being among the least developed states, were required to undertake only commitments and concessions consistent with their individual development, financial, and trade needs and within their administrative and institutional capabilities.[36] They also were given an additional year in which to submit their schedules.[37]

A state that did not qualify for admission as an original member must negotiate entry into the WTO on terms to be agreed on between it and the WTO and approved by the WTO Ministerial Conference by a two-thirds majority of the member states of the WTO.[38]

At the time a state becomes a member of the WTO, but only then, it may take advantage of Article XIII of the WTO Agreement, entitled "Nonapplication of Multilateral Trade Agreements between Particular Members." This provision (which is analogous to GATT Article XXXV) allows one member state to ignore another member state's participation in the WTO Agreement or in the Multilateral Trade Agreements.

Finally, a member may withdraw from the WTO six months after notifying the director-general of its intention to do so.[39]

STRUCTURE OF THE WTO

The WTO has five main organs: (1) a Ministerial Conference, (2) a General Council that also functions as the WTO's Dispute Settlement Body and Trade Policy Review Body, (3) a Council for Trade in Goods, (4) a Council for Trade in Services, and (5) a Council for Trade-Related Aspects of Intellectual Property Rights. In the tradition of GATT, the Ministerial Conference and the General Council are made up of representatives from all the member states.[40] In essence, they are each "committees of the whole." The General Council names the members of the other main organs.[41] See Exhibit 7-3.

The composition of the Ministerial Conference and especially the General Council has been criticized on the grounds that "[m]ass management does not lend itself to operational efficiency or serious policy discussion."[42] However, attempts at the Uruguay Round to establish a small executive body, similar to the executive boards of the IMF and the World Bank, were not successful. The smaller states oppose this type of structure, as it would undoubtedly be dominated by the larger trading states, as is the case for the IMF and the World Bank. In the absence of some such arrangement, however, it is likely that the major trading states will continue to resort, as they did under GATT 1947, to extralegal mechanisms like the Quad (an informal group made up of the United States, the EU, Canada, and Japan). Or, as was the case for the Uruguay Round negotiations on agriculture, the United States and the EU may simply "cut their own deal" and then insist that the other states accept it.[43] However, since the Doha Ministerial Conference in 2001, the developing and less developed countries have formed their own subgroups and have tried to assert themselves .

---

[34]Agreement Establishing the World Trade Organization, Article XI, para. 1 (1994).
[35]*Id.,* Article XIV, para. 1.
    A state eligible for original membership that became or becomes a member after January 1, 1995 (when the WTO Agreement came into force), must "implement those concessions and obligations in the Multilateral Trade Agreements that are to be implemented over a period of time starting with the entry into force of this Agreement as it if had accepted this Agreement on the date of its entry into force." *Id.,* Article XIV, para. 2.
[36]*Id.,* Article XI, para. 2.
[37]Ministerial Decision on Measures in Favor of Least-Developed Countries, para. 1 (1994).
[38]Agreement Establishing the World Trade Organization, Article XII, paras. 1–2 (1994).
[39]*Id.,* Article XV, para. 1.
[40]*Id.,* Article IV, paras. 1–4.
[41]*Id.,* Article IV, para. 5.
[42]Jeffrey J. Schott and Johanna W. Buurman, *The Uruguay Round: An Assessment,* p. 139 (1994).
[43]*Id.*

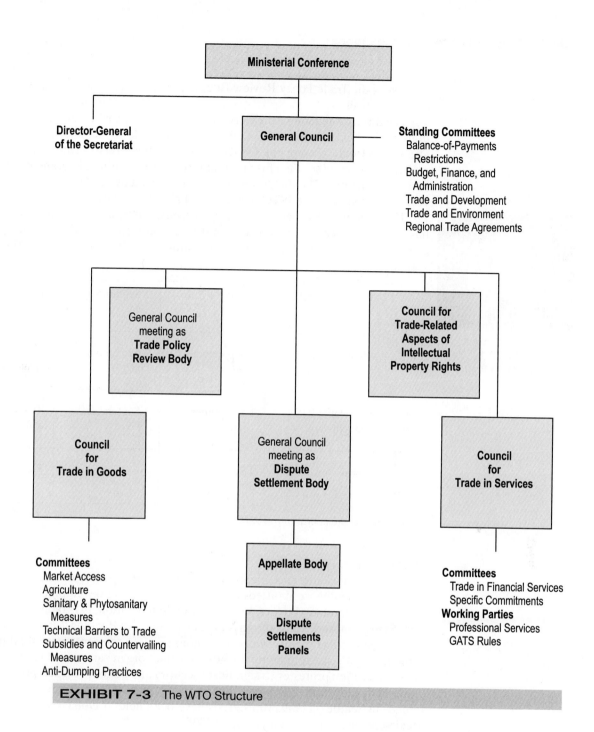

EXHIBIT 7-3 The WTO Structure

In addition to the main organs of the WTO, there is also a secretariat headed by a director-general,[44] who is appointed by the Ministerial Conference.[45] The staff of the GATT 1947 secretariat became the staff of the WTO secretariat on the latter's inauguration. Traditionally, the role of the GATT secretariat was limited, and its small budget put tight restraints on its staff's ability to initiate studies or carry on programs on its own. The responsibility of the secretariat has grown because of its new role in assessing member state trade policies in

---

[44]Renato Ruggiero of Italy became the first WTO director-general on May 1, 1995, succeeding Peter Sutherland, the GATT 1947 director-general, who had served as acting director-general since the WTO's inauguration on January 1, 1995. "WTO Formally Accepts Ruggiero as Its First Director-General," Bureau of National Affairs, *International Trade Reporter*, vol. 12, p. 567 (March 29, 1995).
[45]Agreement Establishing the World Trade Organization, Article VI, para 2 (1994).

support of the Trade Policy Review Body; nevertheless, it is likely that the staff will remain relatively small.

The director-general of the WTO is responsible for supervising the administrative functions of the WTO. Because WTO decisions are made by member states (through either a Ministerial Conference or the General Council), the director-general has little power over matters of policy, other than his or her ability to negotiate, mediate, and persuade. The role is largely managerial. The director-general is appointed by WTO members for a term of four years and supervises the WTO secretariat of about 700 staff.

The current director-general (since September 2005) is Pascal Lamy of France. Mr. Lamy has had a long career in international trade and political affairs, and served as trade commissioner for the EU prior to his appointment as director-general of the WTO.

Pascal Lamy, Director General of the WTO, 2007 (Photo: WTO Web site)

1. Renato Ruggiero	1 May 1995	1 September 1999	Italy
2. Mike Moore	1 September 1999	1 September 2002	New Zealand
3. Supachai Panitchpakdi	1 September	1 September 1999	Thailand 2002
4. Pascal Lamy	1 September 2005	—	France

Directors-General of the WTO

Ministerial Conference

The Ministerial Conference meets at least every other year to oversee the operation of the WTO. Five standing committees deal with (1) trade and development; (2) balance-of-payments restrictions; (3) budget, finance, and administration; (4) trade and the environment; and (5) regional agreements.[46] As is further explored in Reading 7–1, the Ministerial Conferences have become major events, with thousands of representatives of all member nations (now 150), activists from many nongovernmental organizations (NGOs) around the world, antiglobalization protesters, a significant security and police presence, press from around the globe, and many more attendees of various interests. Since the tumultuous Ministerial Conference in Seattle in 1999, Ministerials have been held in Doha, Qatar, in 2001, in Cancun, Mexico, in 2003, and in Hong Kong in 2005.

General Council

The General Council carries on the functions of the Ministerial Conference in the intervals between the meetings of the Conference. It also "convene[s] as appropriate" to function as the WTO Dispute Settlement Body and the WTO Trade Policy Review Body. Each of these bodies has its own chairman. In addition, the three subordinate councils—the Council for Trade in Goods, the Council for Trade in Services, and the Council for Trade-Related Aspects of Intellectual Property Rights—function under the guidance of the General Council

---

[46]The first three committees are specified in *id.,* Article IV, para. 7. The committee on trade and environment was added by the Ministerial Conference meeting at Marrakesh in April 1994—see http://www.wto.org/english/tratop_e/envir_e/envir_e.htm – and the committee on regional agreements by the Ministerial Conference meeting at Singapore in December 1996: see http://www.wto.org/english/tratop_e/region_e/region_e.htm. See also Jeffrey J. Schott and Johanna W. Buurman, *The Uruguay Round: An Assessment*, p. 137 (1994).

to oversee the implementation and administration of the three main WTO agreements (GATT 94, GATS, and TRIPS).[47]

The General Council is also responsible for making arrangements for "effective cooperation" with other intergovernmental organizations (IGOs) whose responsibilities are related to the WTO and for "consultation and cooperation" with NGOs involved in matters of interest to the WTO.[48]

DECISION MAKING WITHIN THE WTO

consensus: The making of a decision by general agreement and in the absence of any voiced objection.

The WTO Agreement says that the WTO will "continue the practice of decision making by consensus followed under the GATT 1947."[49] **Consensus** is the making of a decision by general agreement and in the absence of any voiced objection.[50] The WTO, however, can make a decision by a vote if a consensus cannot be reached. At meetings of the Ministerial Conference and the General Council, each WTO member state has one vote, with the EU having a number of votes equal to (but not more than) the number of its member states that are members of the WTO. Should a vote be required, the decision will be made by a simple majority in most cases.[51]

The role of the WTO and the controversies surrounding it are analyzed from differing perspectives in Reading 7-1.

---

[47]Agreement Establishing the World Trade Organization, Article IV, paras. 2–5 (1994).
[48]*Id.*, Article V.
[49]*Id.*, Article IX, para. 1.
[50]See Understanding on Rules and Procedures Governing the Settlement of Disputes, para. 2.4, n. 1 (1994).
[51]Agreement Establishing the World Trade Organization, Article IX, para. 1 (1994).
Decisions that require a larger than simple majority vote include decisions to adopt interpretations of the WTO Agreement and the multilateral trade agreements (*id.*, Article IX, para. 2); waivers of obligations imposed on members by the WTO Agreement and the multilateral trade agreements (*id.,* Article IX, para. 3); amendments to the WTO Agreement or the multilateral trade agreements (*id.*, Article X); and decisions of the General Council when convened as the Dispute Settlement Body (Understanding on Rules and Procedures Governing the Settlement of Disputes, para. 2.4 [1994]).

Reading 7-1   THE WTO FROM SEATTLE TO DOHA TO HONG KONG (AND BEYOND)

When the WTO was established, the powers and duties of this new international organization based in Geneva, Switzerland were known mainly to politicians and individuals and businesses involved with international trade. The general public knew little about the WTO. How things have changed in a few years! Today the WTO and the issues surrounding "globalization" are controversial topics, sparking heated discussions on the street, in national legislatures, and in all types of media. The WTO really became a major topic of public interest during the Ministerial Conference held in Seattle in December 1999.

The Ministerial Conference, the WTO's main decision making body, meets at least every two years. All the members of the world-wide organization, more than 140 nations at that time, send officials to the meeting. In ad-

dition, thousands of other members of non-governmental organizations (NGOs) and environmental and labor groups attend some WTO meetings and/or organize demonstrations outside the meetings. At the Seattle Conference, protesters campaigning for causes ranging from the environment to animal rights to various labor and employment issues took to the streets and, despite the tear gas and rubber bullets of the police, eventually brought the Conference to a standstill.

THE PROTESTORS' ARGUMENTS.

Over 70,000 people and 500 global civil society organizations brought the attention of the world to the streets of Seattle where people of all ages, from many countries and all walks of life demonstrated their concerns about the World Trade Organization. The demonstrators claimed that the WTO would lead to the "corporatization" of all areas of the global commons including food security, health care, public education, cultural integrity, water, air, forest conservation, labor standards, human rights, local development, intellectual property rights and patents on plant, animal, and even human genetic material. The protestors claimed the Seattle events showed that the world was awakening to the realization that the scope of the WTO reached far beyond the closeted world of Geneva (WTO headquarters) and into the very roots of democratic values and the lives of individuals

The voices of 35,000 trade union representatives and the emerging inter-national global citizens movement challenged the WTO's credo that: globalization was natural and irreversible, that it benefited the developing countries and that free trade is really free, despite the volumes of rules governing its form of highly regulated, corporate managed trade.

At the same time as serious activists were trying to achieve mass education about the WTO and its agenda to the global media, unknown provocateurs began smashing windows downtown. Word was passed that a group of extremely violent individuals was roaming the streets. As the marchers—including those dressed as sea turtles—and other environmental representatives neared downtown, they were split and diverted away from the main demonstration already jamming the streets and were sidelined to a sit-down protest some blocks away.

By nightfall the curfew had been announced and first scenes of excessive and indiscriminate use of force were starting to be reported and broadcast on television. Viewers saw protestors, largely engaged in peaceful acts of civil disobedience, being met by forces in fully equipped riot gear; true life violence, capturing the attention of the world. While media coverage riveted viewers on the street action, the "Battle of Seattle" was also taking place within the Trade and Convention Center itself, and in a myriad of venues throughout the downtown core where discussions and debates flourished.

Rumors were rife, action lines and curfew boundaries kept moving, buses to events were cancelled in largely unsuccessful attempts to thwart public mobility and access; ministers and delegates from developing nations within the WTO scrambled to find meetings scheduled in unknown locations (infamous "green rooms" only announced to select participants) and called the WTO's own internal process "the ultimate in nontransparency."

Many activists claimed that the chaos being reported from the streets was mirrored in much more subtle forms within the Convention Center itself. The much-touted NGO Symposium (a WTO first) was postponed by three hours to become an hour and a half

lecture to the NGO's by the presiding table chaired by Charlene Barshevsky (U.S. Trade Representative) and Michael Moore (WTO Director General) on the benefits of trade. Finally, only a small number of NGO representatives were allowed to address the table and "in the interest of time for all," not permitted to ask questions.

THE WTO RESPONSE.

Mike Moore, then the Director General of the WTO argued that the WTO was getting a bad rap. "First let's be clear about what the WTO does not do," he said. "The WTO is not a world government, a global policeman, or an agent for corporate interests. It has no authority to tell countries what trade policies—or any otaher policies—they should adopt. It does not overrule national laws. It does not force countries to kill turtles or lower wages or employ children in factories. The WTO is not a supranational government, and no one has any intention of making it one.

Mr. Moore pointed out that WTO decisions must be made by the Member States, agreements ratified by Parliaments and every two years Ministers meet to supervise their work. "There's a bit of a contradiction with people outside saying we are not democratic, when inside over 120 Ministers all elected by the people or appointed by elected presidents, decide what we will do."

"The WTO is an international organization that mediates trade disputes, seeks to reduce barriers between countries, and embodies the agreements. Globalization is a fact today and is being driven above all by the power of technology—by faster and cheaper transportation, by new communications, by the increasing weightlessness of our economies—the financial services, telecommunications, entertainment, and e-commerce that make up a growing share of global trade. It's also driven by common values of freedom, democracy and the desire to share what the world has to offer."

Mr. Moore stated, "the real question we should ask ourselves is whether globalization is best left unfettered—dominated by the strongest and most powerful, the rule of the jungle—or managed by an agreed system of international rules, ratified by sovereign governments. How will the global economy be made more stable by undermining its foundation of rules and cooperation? By returning to the same system of regional blocs and trade anarchy that helped plunge us into world war in the 1930's?"

Mr. Moore posed several questions regarding the role of the WTO. "How are developing countries helped by shutting our markets, restricting their exports, and worsening their marginalization? How is the global environment improved by retarding growth, distorting prices, or subsidizing the consumption of scarce resources? How will we find jobs for the unemployed—or homes for the dispossessed—by making our economies and societies poorer? Consider this: exports have accounted for more than a quarter of U.S. economic growth in the United States in the past six years. And almost 20 million new jobs...."

"What are we fighting for in Seattle? We are fighting for a multilateral trading system that is an essential component of the architecture for international cooperation— a firm foothold in an uncertain world. The world would not be a safer place without the UN, IMF, World Bank, or WTO despite their imperfections. The GATT/ WTO system is a force for international peace and order. A fortification against disorder. This is reason enough to insist on the rightness of what we are doing."

"We are also fighting to reduce poverty and to create a more inclusive world. We all want a fairer world, a world of opportunity accessible to all. Just ask the mother with a sick child who wants the best medical advice the world has to offer—whether its from Boston or Oxford or Johannesburg. There is a strong argument that economic, social and political freedom is a basic pre-requisite for development."

"I began by asking what the world would be like without the multilateral trading system? Let me answer my own question. It would be a poorer world of competing blocs and power politics—a world of more conflict, uncertainty, and marginalization. Too much of this century was marked by force and coercion. Our dream must be a world managed by persuasion, the rule of law, the settlement of differences peacefully by the law and in cooperation. Seattle ought to be remembered then with confidence, in our case that economic and political freedom means higher living standards and a better lifestyle. Let's hope our vision of the new century matches that of our parents who lived through depression and war, then created us and our institutions. Let's honor them."

WHAT HAS HAPPENED SINCE THE SEATTLE MINISTERIAL?

In the years since the Seattle conference, there have been WTO Ministerial Conferences in Doha, Qatar in 2001, in Cancun, Mexico in 2003 and in Hong Kong in 2005. At each conference (and at many other international economic and financial meetings) there have been protests against "globalization." More than 1,000 activists and protesters were arrested at the Hong Kong Conference. At the Doha conference, the members signed an agreement called the "Doha Development Agenda" by which they promised to negotiate over the next several years to improve conditions for developing countries, to reduce government subsidies for agriculture, to reduce barriers to trade on agricultural products, reduce tariffs on many other goods, to reconsider some anti-dumping provisions, and much more.

The original agreement reached at Doha contemplated that negotiations on these matters would be completed in a few years, but agreement on these complex issues has been elusive, deadlines established at Doha have been extended several times, and talks are still going on, as we move into 2008. In July 2006, frustrated by the lack of progress toward agreement, DG Pascal Lamy suspended negotiations on the Doha Agenda. Mr. Lamy reached the conclusion to suspend the negotiations after talks among six major members broke down on July 23. Ministers from Australia, Brazil, the European Union, India, Japan and the United States had met in Geneva to try to follow up on instructions from a meeting in St Petersburg on July 17. The main blockage was in the two agriculture legs of the triangle of issues, market access and domestic support, Mr. Lamy said. The six did not even move on to the third leg, non-agricultural market access, he observed.

But in early 2007, citing an "increasing level of political engagement and clear signals of renewed commitment" to a successful conclusion of the Round, Mr. Lamy announced the resumption of full negotiations on the Doha Agenda. He stated that he had received messages from the highest political levels around the world, stressing both the importance and the urgency of concluding the negotiations.

Some of the more important Doha Development issues which were discussed (but not resolved) at the Hong Kong Ministerial meeting and are now the subject of intense negotiation as set forth below. This information is from the WTO website, under "Briefing: Hong Kong Ministerial."

- **Agriculture**
  Comprehensive negotiations, incorporating special and differential treatment for developing countries and aimed at substantial improvements in market access; elimination of all forms of export subsidies, as well as establishing disciplines on all export measures with equivalent effect, by a credible end date; and substantial reductions in trade-distorting domestic support. Special priority is given to cotton.

- **Services**
  Negotiations aimed at achieving progressively higher levels of liberalization through market-access commitments and rule-making, particularly in areas of export interest to developing countries.

- **Nonagricultural products**
  Negotiations aimed at reducing or, as appropriate, eliminating tariffs, including the reduction or elimination of tariff peaks, high tariffs, and tariff escalation, as well as non-tariff barriers, in particular on products of export interest to developing countries.

- **Rules**
  Negotiations aimed at clarifying and improving disciplines dealing with anti-dumping, subsidies, countervailing,

regional trade agreements, and fisheries subsidies, taking into account the importance of this sector to developing countries.

• **Trade facilitation**
Negotiations aimed at clarifying and improving disciplines for expediting the movement, release and clearance of goods, and at enhancing technical assistance and support for capacity-building, taking into account special and differential treatment for developing and least-developed countries.

• **Intellectual property**
Negotiations aimed at creating a multilateral register for geographical indications for wines and spirits; negotiations aimed at amending the TRIPS Agreement by incorporating the temporary waiver which enables countries to export drugs made under compulsory license to countries that cannot manufacture them; discussions on whether to negotiate extending to other products the higher level of protection currently given to wines and spirits; review of the provisions dealing with patentability or non-patentability of plant and animal inventions and the

protection of plant varieties; examination of the relationship between the TRIPS Agreement and biodiversity, the protection of traditional knowledge and folklore.

• **Dispute settlement procedures**
Negotiations aimed at improving and clarifying the procedures for settling disputes.

• **Trade and environment**
Negotiations aimed at clarifying the relationship between WTO rules and trade obligations set out in multilateral environmental agreements; and at reducing or, as appropriate, eliminating tariff and non-tariff barriers to environmental goods and services.

Sources: WTO Web site, "Briefing, Hong Kong Ministerial"; Global Exchange Website (see information below); Joseph Kahn and David Sanger, "Trade Obstacles Unmoved, Seattle Talks End in Failure," New York Times, Dec. 4, 1999; Keith Bradsher, "Trade Officials Agree to End Subsidies for Agricultural Exports," Dec. 19, 2005; Judith Maltz, The Watertalk Forum (Dec. 5, 1999) at http://www.watertalk.org/forum/WTO-Seattle.html.

http://www.globalexchange.org/campaigns/wto/3688.html is the Web site for Global Exchange, a group that is critical of the WTO, arguing that it represents primarily the interests of powerful nations and corporations. This site also contains much detailed information about the issues presented in this chapter, although from an environmentalist and developing-nation perspective.

WAIVERS

waiver: The relinquishment of an obligation owed by another.

GATT 1947 was sometimes characterized as a system of loopholes held together by **waivers**.[52] The WTO agreements dramatically changed this. First, with one exception,[53] the waivers of obligations in existence under GATT 1947 terminated no later than two years after the inauguration of the WTO.[54] Second, the procedures for obtaining new or continuing waivers are more rigorous. Thus, an applying member state must (1) describe the measures that it proposes to take, (2) specify the policy objectives it seeks to obtain, and (3) explain why it cannot achieve those objectives without violating its obligations under GATT 1994.[55] Third, waivers must be approved by the Ministerial Conference, which has up to ninety days to do so by consensus. If a consensus cannot be reached in that period, waivers must then be approved by a three-quarters majority of the members.[56] Waivers are reviewed

[52]John Kraus, *The GATT Negotiations: A Business Guide to the Results of the Uruguay Round*, p. 78 (1994).
[53]The exception allows the waiver that applies to the U.S. Jones Act (which restricts the use, sale, or lease of non-U.S. ships in the movement of goods between points in national waters or the waters of an exclusive economic zone) to continue in force, subject to a first review after five years, and then subsequent reviews every two years by the WTO Ministerial Conference. General Interpretive Note to Annex IA (GATT 1994), para. 1:e.
[54]Understanding in Respect of Waivers of Obligations under GATT 1994, para. 2.
 A list of these waivers can be found in footnote 7 to the General Interpretive Note to Annex 1A (GATT 1994). Among these are waivers relating to German unification, the United Kingdom's dependent overseas territories, the U.S.–Canada Auto Pact, the U.S. Caribbean Basin Economic Recovery Act, and the U.S. Andean Trade Preference Act.
[55]Understanding in Respect of Waivers of Obligations under GATT 1994, para. 1.
[56]Agreement Establishing the World Trade Organization, Article IX, para. 3 (1994).

annually thereafter.[57] Fourth, any dispute that arises in connection with a waiver, whether or not the waiver is being carried out in conformity with its terms and conditions, can be referred for settlement under the Dispute Settlement Understanding.[58]

DISPUTE SETTLEMENT

The Understanding on Rules and Procedures Governing the Settlement of Disputes (the *Dispute Settlement Understanding* or *DSU*) carries forward and improves on the dispute settlement procedures of GATT 1947.[59] Most importantly, the DSU establishes a unified system for settling disputes that arise under the WTO Agreement and its annexes (other than the annex establishing the Trade Policy Review Mechanism).[60] See Chapter 3 for a discussion of the WTO's dispute settlement procedures.

TRADE POLICY REVIEW

Annex 3 of the WTO Agreement establishes a Trade Policy Review Mechanism. This mechanism is built around a *Trade Policy Review Board* (*TPRB*) that is meant to be the WTO's auditor or watchdog. It is responsible for promoting "improved adherence" by all WTO member states to the WTO Multilateral Trade Agreements and, for the member states that are signatories, the Plurilateral Trade Agreements. The TPRB, however, is meant neither to enforce the agreements nor to settle disputes between members.[61] To accomplish its goal, the TPRB (1) carries out periodic reviews of the trade policies and practices of all member states and (2) prepares an annual overview of the international trading environment.

C. THE 1994 GENERAL AGREEMENT ON TARIFFS AND TRADE

General Agreement on Tariffs and Trade (GATT 1994): Annex to the Agreement Establishing the World Trade Organization that sets out the rules under which the member states of that organization are committed to negotiate reductions in customs tariffs and other impediments to international trade in goods.

The current **General Agreement on Tariffs and Trade (GATT 1994)** (see Exhibit 7-4) is made up essentially of the same set of rules as GATT 1947. The changes in the text of GATT 1994 amount mainly to changes in terminology (e.g., *member* replaces *contracting party* and references to the "contracting parties acting jointly" are taken to mean to the WTO or its Ministerial Conference).[62] Even so, despite the similarity between GATT 1994 and GATT 1947, they are described by the WTO Agreement as "legally distinct" instruments.[63]

The significance of the two instruments being legally distinct is that (1) the WTO is not the "legal successor"[64] to the old GATT organization and (2) the members states of GATT 1994 owe no legal obligations to the contracting parties of GATT 1947. Thus, the WTO is not bound to service GATT 1947, nor is it bound by any obligations made by the previous GATT organization except to the extent that it expressly assumes those responsibilities.

In addition, states that become member states of GATT 1994 without withdrawing from GATT 1947 will be bound by two different sets of commitments involving two different lists of states. Similarly, states that withdraw from GATT 1947 after becoming members of GATT

---

[57]*Id.*, para. 4.

[58]Understanding in Respect of Waivers of Obligations under GATT 1994, para. 3.

[59]At the Uruguay Round, negotiators identified and worked to remedy three basic flaws in the old dispute settlement procedures: (1) the long times taken by panels in concluding their proceedings, (2) the ability of participating states to deny the consensus needed to approve the panel findings and to authorize retaliation, and (3) the difficulty of obtaining compliance with panel decisions.

[60]The Trade Policy Review Mechanism (1994) is meant to be a political rather than a legal process, and its exclusion from the DSU is therefore quite logical.

[61]Trade Policy Review Mechanism, para. A(i) (1994).

[62]See General Interpretive Note to Annex 1A, para. 1(d) (1994).

[63]Agreement Establishing the World Trade Organization, Article II, para. 4 (1994).

[64]Statement of GATT Director-General Peter Sutherland quoted in Amelia Porges, "Introductory Note, General Agreement on Tariffs and Trade—Multilateral Trade Negotiations (the Uruguay Round): Final Act Embodying the Results of the Uruguay Round if Trade Negotiations," *International Legal Materials*, vol. 33, p. 1 at p. 4 (1994).

Article I: General Most-Favored-Nation Treatment
- To be applied by each member to the imports and exports of all other members.

Article II: Schedules of Concessions
- Individual country tariff concessions, as annexed to the Agreement, to be applied to all other members.

Article III: National Treatment on Internal Taxation and Regulation
- Products of one member imported into the territory of another must be accorded treatment no less favorable than that given like products of national origin in respect to their internal sale or distribution.

Article VI: Anti-dumping and Countervailing Duties
- Antidumping duties to be imposed only if goods are sold for export at a price below that which they are sold for domestic consumption.
- Antidumping duties may not be greater than the amount by which the domestic price exceeds the export.
- Countervailing duties may not be greater than the amount of the estimated "bounty" or subsidy.
- Antidumping and countervailing duties may be imposed only if there is a threat of material injury to an established industry in the importing country or if it materially retards the establishment of such an industry.

Article XI: General Elimination of Quantitative Restrictions
- Import and export quotas and licenses are prohibited, with certain exceptions for critical shortages, grading or marketing standards, and domestic marketing or production programs.

Article XII: Restrictions to Safeguard the Balance of Payments
- Permits nondiscriminatory quotas as necessary to forestall a serious decline in monetary reserves to increase such reserves from too low a level.
- Requires annual consultation procedures and progressive relaxation of the restrictions.
- Developing countries operate under the separate but similar provisions of Article XVIII, which requires consultations at two year intervals.

Article XIII: Nondiscriminatory Administration of Quantitative Restrictions
- Requires that export and import quotas be administered on a nondiscriminatory basis.
- Requires that import quotas be fairly allocated among suppliers.

Article XVI: Subsidies
- Seeks to avoid use of subsidies generally and prohibits use of export subsidies (other than on primary products).
- Requires reporting of subsidies, consultations with parties affected, and equitable sharing of markets for primary products.

Article XVIII: Government Assistance to Economic Development
- Permits developing countries to modify or withdraw tariff concessions by agreement with parties affected and after efforts to provide compensatory concessions.
- Recognizes persistent balance-of-payment pressures on developing countries and permits quantitative restrictions to deal with them.
- Specifies procedures whereby developing countries may use protective import quotas to promote infant industries.

Article XIX: Emergency Action on Imports of Particular Products
- The "escape clause" of the General Agreement.
- Authorizes importing country to suspend, withdraw, or modify tariff concessions if increased imports threaten serious injury to domestic producers.
- Requires notice and consultation with parties affected and permits exporting country to restore previous balance of concessions.

Article XXII: Consultation
- Provides for bilateral consultation and settlement of disputes.

EXHIBIT 7-4 Selected Descriptive Contents of the General Agreement of Tariffs and Trade 1994

Article XXIII: Nullification or Impairment
* Establishes procedures for bilateral consultation and for referral of disputes to a plenary session of the members for a recommendation and a ruling, whether or not the issue in dispute constitutes a violation of the Agreement.

Article XXIV: Territorial Application; Frontier Traffic; Customs Unions and Free Trade Areas
* Deals with the application of the General Agreement to colonial territories.
* States exceptions to the rule of nondiscrimination for customs unions and free trade areas.

Article XXVIII: Modification of Schedules
* Permits a member, at the beginning of each three-year period, or under "special circumstances," to modify or withdraw a concession after renegotiation with the members affected.

Article XXXV: Nonapplication of the Agreement between Particular Members
* Permits a member to withhold the application of its tariff concessions from another member with which it has not entered into tariff negotiations.

Article XXXVI: Trade and Development: Principles and Objectives
* Expresses the need and desire of the members to give special preferences to developing countries.

EXHIBIT 7-4 *Continued*

1994 (which they may do any time after December 31, 1995) will only continue to have GATT obligations under GATT 1994.[65]

Although GATT 1994 is not the legal successor of GATT 1947, most of the past decisions of the GATT Council, the GATT contracting parties acting jointly, and the GATT Dispute Settlement Panels relating to the text of the General Agreement continue to have force.[66] Some decisions, however, were modified at the time GATT 1994 came into force by a series of "Understandings" annexed to the new General Agreement.

direct effect: The principle whereby a treaty may be invoked by a private person to challenge the actions of a state that is a party to the treaty.

DIRECT EFFECT

Some of the provisions of GATT 1994 are directly effective. That is, they may be relied upon by private persons (including both natural and juridical persons) to challenge the actions of a member state. In particular, those provisions that prohibit a state from taking action contrary to the General Agreement are directly effective. Those that require a contracting state to take some positive action may only be challenged by individuals if the state adopts implementing legislation authorizing such a challenge. This rule is set out in Case 7-1.

---

[65]*Id.*

[66]Agreement Establishing the World Trade Organization, Article XVI, para. 1 (1994), provides: "Except as otherwise provided for under this Agreement or the Multilateral Trade Agreements, the WTO shall be guided by the decisions, procedures, and customary practices followed by the CONTRACTING PARTIES [Au: full caps correct here?] of the GATT 1947 and the bodies established in the framework of the GATT 1947."

Case 7-1   FINANCE MINISTRY v. MANIFATTURA LANE MARZOTTO, SPA

Italy, Court of Cassation (Joint Session), 1973.
Foro Italiano, vol. 1, p. 2443 (1973); *Italian Yearbook of International Law*, vol. 1976, p. 383 (1976); *International Law Reports*, vol. 77, p. 551 (1988).

Manifattura Lane Marzotto, SpA, an Italian manufacturer of woolen goods, sued the Italian Finance Ministry after being charged an "administrative services duty" (dirrito per servizi amministrativi) on wool it imported from Australia, claiming that this duty violated GATT. GATT 1947, Article III(1)(b), prohibits member states from charging duties in excess of those set out in the Agreement's annexes and schedules, or from increasing its duties after the time the member state accedes to the General Agreement. Because the law that first imposed the administrative services duty was enacted after Italy acceded to the General Agreement, Marzotto claimed that it was illegal. The Finance Ministry asked the court to dismiss the case, contending that Article III(1)(b) was not directly effective because parliament had not adopted implementing legislation. The trial court in Milan dismissed the suit, but the Court of Appeal reversed, ruling that the duty was illegal. The Finance Ministry appealed to the Court of Cassation.

JUDGMENT OF THE COURT:

***

Article III . . . of the General Agreement deals first with ordinary customs duties and provides that they are applicable to the products included in the schedules at a rate not higher than that indicated in those same lists. It then establishes that duties other than ordinary customs duties may not be higher than those in force on the date of the General Agreement. . . .

Law No. 295 of 5 April 1950, which implemented the GATT Agreement, provides in Article 2:

> The aforementioned Agreements, Annexes and Protocols are fully and entirely implemented as from the time limits established by the Protocol of Annecy. . . .

As Italy has fully integrated into its legal system the first part of the General Agreement—including the provision concerning customs duties—it remains to be seen whether this provision is merely a simple declaration of principle, deprived of any direct legal effect within the country. If that is so, the member states would only be obliged to each other to harmonize their laws, and there would be no immediate right for individuals to bring actionable claims. According to the Finance Ministry, parliament is the only entity that can properly determine when and to what extent the existing customs laws should be modified, and no other person or entity should be allowed to do so.

This Court cannot agree. It seems clear to us that the provision of the General Agreement that we are examining is directly effective, giving rights both to the member states of the GATT and to individuals within those states, without any need for additional legislative

MAP 7-1   Italy (1973)

implementation. The provision—which is essentially a prohibition against increasing duties above those in effect on the date a member state accedes to the General Agreement—is clearly one which imposes on the acceding state an obligation not to act. There is, therefore, no need for the state to act. Accordingly, this prohibition is complete and directly effective not only between the member states but also between the member states and their nationals. . . .

Thus, in compliance with the law implementing the General Agreement, we hold that goods imported from one GATT member state to another are not subject to internal duties and charges of any kind which are higher than those that were in force on the date the General Agreement became effective. . . .

The judgment of the Court of Appeal was affirmed. ■

CASEPOINT: The court decided that the GATT provision that prohibits a GATT member from increasing duties on imported products above the level established when the member nation acceded to the agreement was directly effective. Thus, it was part of Italian law and an individual citizen or company could bring a lawsuit to enforce this provision.

NONDISCRIMINATION

The most fundamental principle of GATT is that international trade should be conducted without discrimination. This principle is given concrete form in the *most-favored-nation* (MFN) and *national treatment* rules.

The MFN Rule

Article I of GATT requires each member to apply its tariff rules equally to all other members. Paragraph 1 of that article provides:

> . . . [A]ny advantage, favor, privilege, or immunity granted by any member to any product originating in or destined for any other country shall be accorded immediately and unconditionally to the like product originating in or destined for the territories of all other members.

The MFN rule is not without exceptions, however. The rule does not apply to

1. The use of measures to counter dumping and subsidization.[67]
2. The creation of customs unions and free trade areas.[68]
3. Restrictions that protect public health, safety, welfare, and national security.[69]

In addition to these three exceptions[70] to the MFN rule and the principle of nondiscrimination, GATT provides for a special exception in the case of developing states. In order both to promote and protect the economies of developing states, GATT encourages the developed states not to demand reciprocity from them in trade negotiation, and it authorizes developed member states to adopt measures that give preferences to developing member states.[71]

The contracting parties to GATT 1947 approved two preferential treatment schemes that are carried forward into GATT 1994. One, the **Generalized System of Preferences (GSP)**, allows developing countries to export all (or nearly all) of their products to a participating developed country on a nonreciprocal basis. The hope is that the GSP will make developing countries more competitive in world markets and less dependent on the production of raw or primary goods.[72] The other, the **South-South Preferences** (so called because most developing nations are located in the Southern Hemisphere), lets developing countries exchange tariff preferences among themselves without extending the same preferences to developed states.[73]

The National Treatment Rule

The national treatment rule is the second manifestation of the principle of nondiscrimination that appears in GATT. In contrast to the MFN rule, which requires nondiscrimination at a country's border, the national treatment rule requires a country to treat products equally with its own domestic products once they are inside its borders.[74] Article III, paragraph 4, of GATT provides:

> The products of the territory of any member state imported into the territory of any other member state shall be accorded treatment no less favorable than that accorded to like products of national origin in respect of all laws, regulations and requirements affecting their internal sale, offering for sale, purchase, transportation, distribution, or use. . . .

Generalized System of Preferences (GSP): A GATT scheme that allows a developing state to obtain tariff concessions from a developed state on a nonreciprocal basis.

South-South Preferences: A GATT scheme that allows developing states to grant tariff preferences to each other without having to grant them to developed states.

national treatment rule: Once imported goods are within the territory of a state, that state must treat those goods no less favorably than it treats its own domestic goods.

---

[67]General Agreement on Tariffs and Trade 1994, Article VI.

[68]*Id.*, Article XXIV, para. 8.

[69]*Id.*, Articles XX and XXI.

[70]These three exceptions are discussed later in this chapter.

[71]*Id.*, Article XXXVI, para. 8, provides: "The developed members do not expect reciprocity for commitments made by them in trade negotiations to reduce or remove tariffs and other barriers to the trade of less-developed members."

[72]GATT, *Analytical Index: Guide to GATT Law and Practice*, pp. 49–50, 53–54 (6th ed., 1994).

Eight developed states, plus the EU (now 27 member nations), presently participate in the GSP. The states are Australia, Canada, Finland, Japan, New Zealand, Norway, Switzerland, and the United States. *Id.*, p. 50.

[73]*Id.*, pp. 50–51, 53–54.

[74]Section 801(a)(2) of the Restatement of Foreign Relations Law of the United States, Tentative Draft No. 4 (1983), states that " 'national treatment' by a state means according to the nationals of another state treatment equivalent to that which the state accords to its own nationals."

To ensure that member states comply with the national treatment standards, GATT requires them to promptly notify other members of any new trade regulations they may enact. See General Agreement on Tariffs and Trade 1994, Article X, para. 1.

Article III, paragraph 2, sets out the same nondiscriminatory requirement with respect to internal taxes. In Case 7-2, a WTO Panel was asked to determine if Japan was taxing imported alcoholic beverages differently than a domestically produced beverage known as *shochu.*

━━━◦◦◦━━━

Case 7-2   JAPAN—TAXES ON ALCOHOLIC BEVERAGES

World Trade Organization, Dispute Settlement Panel, 1998.
Panel Reports WT/DS8/R, WT/DS10/R, WT/DS11/R.[75]

Canada, the EU, and the United States complained that Japan imposed lower taxes on shochu, a locally produced alcoholic beverage, than it did on imported alcoholic beverages, including vodka, in violation of Article III, paragraph 2, of GATT 1994.

REPORT OF THE PANEL

***

The Panel noted that the complainants are essentially claiming that the Japanese Liquor Tax Law is inconsistent with GATT Article III:2 (hereinafter "Article III:2"). Article III:2 reads:

> The products of the territory of any contracting party imported into the territory of any other contracting party shall not be subject, directly or indirectly, to internal taxes or other internal charges of any kind in excess of those applied, directly or indirectly, to like domestic products. Moreover, no contracting party shall otherwise apply internal taxes or other internal charges to imported or domestic products in a manner contrary to the principles set forth in paragraph 1.

GATT Article III:1 (hereinafter "Article III:1"), which is referred to in Article III:2, reads:

> The contracting parties recognize that internal taxes and other internal charges, and laws, regulations, and requirements affecting the internal sale, offering for sale, purchase, transportation, distribution, or use of products, and internal quantitative regulations requiring the mixture, processing, or use of products in specified amounts or proportions, should not be

applied to imported or domestic products so as to afford protection to domestic production.

***

ARTICLE III:2, FIRST SENTENCE

a) Definition of "Like Products"

The Panel noted that the term "like product" appears in various GATT provisions. The Panel further noted that it did not necessarily follow that the term had to be interpreted in a uniform way. In this respect, the Panel noted the discrepancy between Article III:2, on the one hand, and Article III:4 on the other: while the former referred to Article III:1 and to like, as well as to directly competitive or substitutable products (see also Article XIX of GATT), the latter referred only to like products. This is precisely why, in the Panel's view, its conclusions reached in this dispute are relevant only for the interpretation of the term "like product" as it appears in Article III:2.

The Panel noted that previous panels had agreed that the term "like product" should be interpreted on a case-by-case basis, but had not established any particular test to be followed in defining likeness. Previous panels had used different criteria in order to establish likeness, such as the product's properties, nature and quality, and its end-uses; consumers' tastes and habits, which change from country to country; and the product's classification in tariff nomenclatures.

In the Panel's view, "like products" need not be identical in all respects. However, in the Panel's view, the term "like product" should be construed narrowly in the case of Article III:2, first sentence. This approach is dictated, in the Panel's view, by two independent reasons: (i) because Article III:2 distinguishes between like and directly competitive or substitutable products, the

---

[75]This Dispute Settlement Panel Report is posted on the WTO's Internet Web site at http://www.wto.org/english/tratop_e/dispu_e/cases_e/ds8_e.htm.

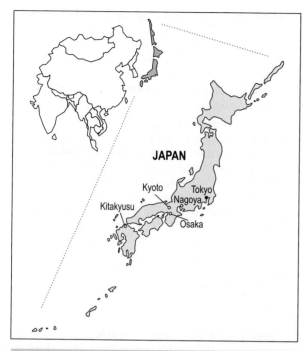

MAP 7-2   Japan (1998)

latter obviously being a much larger category of products than the former; and (ii) because of the Panel's conclusions reached with respect to the relationship between Articles III and II.

As to the first point, the distinction between "like" and "directly competitive or substitutable products" has already been discussed. As to the second point, as previous panels had noted, one of the main objectives of Article III:2 is to ensure that WTO Members do not frustrate the effect of tariff concessions granted under Article II through internal taxes and other internal charges, it follows that there should be a similar interpretation of the definition of products for purposes of Article II tariff concessions and the term "like product" as it appears in Article III:2. This is so in the Panel's view, because with respect to two products subject to the same tariff binding and therefore to the same maximum border tax, there is no justification, outside of those mentioned in GATT rules, to tax them in a differentiated way through internal taxation. . . .

***

. . . In the view of the Panel, the term "like products" suggests that for two products to fall under this category they must share essentially the same physical characteristics. Flexibility is required in order to conclude whether two products are directly competitive or substitutable. In the Panel's view, the suggested approach can guarantee

the flexibility required, since it permits one to take into account specific characteristics in any single market; consequently, two products could be considered to be directly competitive or substitutable in market A, but the same two products would not necessarily be considered to be directly competitive or substitutable in market B. The Panel next turned to an examination of whether the products at issue in this case were "like products," starting first with vodka and shochu. The Panel noted that vodka and shochu shared most physical characteristics. In the Panel's view, except for filtration, there is virtual identity in the definition of the two products. The Panel noted that a difference in the physical characteristic of alcoholic strength of two products did not preclude a finding of likeness especially since alcoholic beverages are often drunk in diluted form. The Panel then noted that essentially the same conclusion had been reached in the 1987 Panel Report, which

> . . . agreed with the arguments submitted to it by the European Communities, Finland, and the United States that Japanese shochu (Group A) and vodka could be considered as "like" products in terms of Article III:2 because they were both white/clean spirits, made of similar raw materials, and the end-uses were virtually identical.

Following its independent consideration of the factors mentioned in the 1987 Panel Report, the Panel agreed with this statement. The Panel then recalled its conclusions concerning the relationship between Articles II and III. In this context, it noted that (i) vodka and shochu were currently classified in the same heading in the Japanese tariffs. . . and (ii) vodka and shochu were covered by the same Japanese tariff binding at the time of its negotiation. Of the products at issue in this case, only shochu and vodka have the same tariff applied to them in the Japanese tariff schedule.

Consequently, in light of the conclusion of the 1987 Panel Report and of its independent consideration of the issue, the Panel concluded that vodka and shochu are like products. In the Panel's view, only vodka could be considered as [a] like product to shochu since, apart from commonality of end-uses, it shared with shochu most physical characteristics. Definitionally, the only difference is in the media used for filtration. Substantial noticeable differences in physical characteristics exist between the rest of the alcoholic beverages at dispute and shochu that would disqualify them from being regarded as like products. More specifically, the use of additives would disqualify liqueurs, gin and genever; the use of ingredients would disqualify rum; lastly, appearance (arising from manufacturing processes) would disqualify whisky and brandy. . . .

b) Taxation in Excess of That Imposed on Like Domestic Products

The Panel then proceeded to examine whether vodka is taxed in excess of the tax imposed on shochu under the Japanese *Liquor Tax Law*. The Panel noted that what was contested in the Japanese legislation was a system of specific taxes imposed on various alcoholic drinks. In this respect, it noted that vodka was taxed at 377230 Yen per kiloliter—for an alcoholic strength below 38°—that is 9927 Yen per degree of alcohol, whereas shochu A was taxed at 155700 Yen per kiloliter—for an alcoholic strength between 25° and 26°—that is 6228 Yen per degree of alcohol. The Japanese taxes on vodka and shochu are calculated on the basis of and vary according to the alcoholic content of the products and, on this basis, it is obvious that the taxes imposed on vodka are higher than those imposed on shochu. Accordingly, the Panel concluded that the tax imposed on vodka is in excess of the tax imposed on shochu.

The Panel then addressed the argument put forward by Japan that its legislation, by keeping the tax/price ratio "roughly constant," is trade neutral and consequently no protective aim and effect of the legislation can be detected. In this connection, the Panel recalled Japan's argument that its aim was to achieve neutrality and horizontal tax equity. To the extent that Japan's argument is that its *Liquor Tax Law* does not impose on foreign products (i.e., vodka) a tax in excess of the tax imposed on domestic like products (i.e., shochu), the Panel rejected the argument for the following reasons:

(i) The benchmark in Article III:2, first sentence, is that internal taxes on foreign products shall not be imposed in excess of those imposed on like domestic products. Consequently, in the context of Article III:2, first sentence, it is irrelevant whether "roughly" the same treatment through, for example, a "roughly constant" tax/price ratio is afforded to domestic and foreign like products or whether neutrality and horizontal tax equity is achieved.

(ii) Japan had argued that the comparison of tax/price ratios should be done on a category-by-category basis, but its statistics on which the tax/price ratios were based excluded domestically produced spirits from the calculation of tax/price ratios for spirits and whisky/brandy. Since the prices of the domestic spirits and whisky/brandy are much lower than the prices of the imported goods, this exclusion has the impact of reducing considerably the tax/price ratios cited by Japan for those products. In this connection, the Panel noted that one consequence of the Japanese tax system was to make it more difficult for cheaper imported brands of spirits

and whisky/brandy to enter the Japanese market. Moreover, the Panel further noted that the Japanese statistics were based on suggested retail prices and there was evidence in the record that these products were often sold at a discount, at least in Tokyo. To the extent that the prices were unreliable, the resultant tax/price ratios would be unreliable as well.

(iii) Nowhere in the contested legislation was it mentioned that its purpose was to maintain a "roughly constant" tax/price ratio. This was rather an *ex post facto*[76] rationalization by Japan and at any rate, there are no guarantees in the legislation that the tax/price ratio will always be maintained "roughly constant." Prices change over time and unless an adjustment process is incorporated in the legislation, the tax/price ratio will be affected. Japan admitted that no adjustment process exists in the legislation and that only *ex post facto* adjustments can occur. The Panel lastly noted that since the modification in 1989 of Japan's *Liquor Tax Law* there has been only one instance of adjustment.

***

Consequently, the Panel concluded that, by taxing vodka in excess of shochu, Japan is in violation of its obligation under Article III:2, first sentence.

***

[The Panel also found that "shochu, whisky, brandy, rum, gin, genever, and liqueurs are 'directly competitive or substitutable products' and Japan, by not taxing them similarly, is in violation of its obligation under Article III:2, second sentence, of the General Agreement on Tariffs and Trade 1994."]

***

The Panel recommends that the Dispute Settlement Body request Japan to bring the *Liquor Tax Law* into conformity with its obligations under the General Agreement on Tariffs and Trade 1994. ■

CASEPOINT: The WTO panel considered whether Japan's policy of taxing imported vodka (and whiskey, brandy, and other imported alcoholic beverages) at a higher rate than Japanese shochu was a violation of GATT Article III. This section of GATT requires that imported goods be accorded "national treatment"—that is, not subjected to higher internal taxes than similar domestic products. After comparing vodka and shochu, the panel decided that they were indeed like products. Since imported vodka was taxed at a higher rate, this practice constituted a violation of Japan's obligations under GATT-WTO rules.

---

[76][Latin : "After the fact."]

As with the most-favored-nation rule, exceptions apply to the application of the national treatment rule. These include:

1. The maintenance of preferences existing at the time GATT 1947 came into effect.[77]
2. Discrimination in the procurement of goods by government agencies for governmental purposes only.[78]
3. Discrimination in the payment of subsidies to domestic producers.[79]
4. Discrimination in the screening of domestically produced cinematographic films.[80]

PROTECTION ONLY THROUGH TARIFFS

tariffs: Governmental charges imposed on goods at the time they are imported into a state.

The second major principle of the GATT is that each member state may protect its domestic industries only through the use of **tariffs**. Quotas and other quantitative restrictions that block the function of the price mechanism are forbidden by Article XI of GATT.[81] Additionally, to ensure that internal taxes are not disguised as tariffs, Article II requires that tariffs be collected "at the time or point of importation."

As with the other GATT principles, exceptions apply to the principle of protection through tariffs. The main exceptions include:

1. The imposition of temporary export prohibitions or restrictions to prevent or relieve critical shortages of foodstuffs or other essential products.[82]
2. The use of import and export restrictions related to the application of standards or regulations for classifying, grading, or marking commodities.[83]
3. The use of quantitative restrictions on imports of agricultural and fisheries products to stabilize national agricultural markets.[84]
4. The use of quantitative restrictions to safeguard a state's balance of payments.[85]
5. The use of quantitative restrictions by a developing state to further its economic development.[86]

bound tariff rates: The highest tariff rates a WTO member state may set on imports from another member state.

GATT requires member states not only to use customs tariffs as the primary device for protecting their domestic trade, but also to work toward their "substantial reduction." Tariff reductions are negotiated among the member states and then recorded as Schedules of Concessions annexed to GATT. A **bound tariff rate** represents the highest rate that a member state may set on an item under the terms of GATT (tariffs are "bound" to this rate). Once such a rate is negotiated, the member state is required to extend it to all other GATT members by the MFN rule.[87]

[77]General Agreement on Tariffs and Trade, 1994, Article III, para. 6.
[78]*Id.*, para. 8(a).
[79]*Id.*, para. 8(b).
[80]*Id.*, para. 10, and Article IV.
[81]*Id.*, Article XI, para. 1, states: "No prohibitions or restrictions other than duties, taxes or other charges, whether made effective through quotas, import or export licenses, or other measures, shall be instituted or maintained by any member on the importation of any product of the territory of any other member or on the exportation or sale for export of any product destined for the territory of any other member."
The rationale underlying Article XI was provided in a statement by the U.S. delegate at the First Preparatory Session of GATT: "In the case of a tariff the total volume of imports can expand with the expansion of trade. There is flexibility in the volume of trade. Under a quota system the volume of trade is rigidly restricted, and no matter how much more people may wish to buy or consume, not one single more unit will be admitted than the controlling authority thinks fit.
"In the case of tariffs, the direction of trade and the source of import can shift with changes in quality and cost and price. Under a quota system the direction of trade and the sources of imports are rigidly fixed by public authority without regard to quality, cost or price. Under a tariff, equality of treatment of all other states can be assured. Under a quota system, no matter how detailed our rules, no matter how carefully we police them, there must almost inevitably be discrimination as amongst other states." UN Document EPCT/A/PV. 221 at pp. 16–17 (1947).
[82]General Agreement on Tariffs and Trade 1994, Article XI, para. 2(a).
[83]*Id.*, para. 2(b).
[84]*Id.*, para. 2(c).
[85]*Id.*, Article XII, para. 1, provides: ". . . [A]ny member, in order to safeguard its external financial position and its balance of payments, may restrict the quantity or value of merchandise permitted to be imported. . . ."
[86]*Id.*, Article XVIII, para. 4(a).
[87]*Id.*, Article XXVIII(bis).

TRANSPARENCY

transparency: Principle that governments must make their rules, regulations, and practices open and accessible to the public and other governments.

Essential to the operation of GATT is the principle of transparency. *Transparency*, as defined in Article X, is the requirement that governments disclose to the public and other governments the rules, regulations, and practices they follow in their domestic trade systems. Complementing this principle is the requirement, found in Article VIII, that member states must strive to simplify their import and export formalities. The operation of both of these principles can be seen in the way countries classify imports for the purpose of imposing duties.

While negotiations were underway in Geneva in 1947 to set up the original GATT, discussions were also being held in Western Europe to establish a customs union. For political reasons this early attempt failed, but the participants agreed to take advantage of the accords that had been reached to establish a standardized system (or *nomenclature*) for classifying goods for the purpose of imposing customs duties. In 1950, the Convention on Nomenclature for the Classification of Goods in Customs Tariffs was signed, and the Customs Cooperation Council (CCC), an international organization based in Brussels, was established to administer it.

Harmonized System (HS): A system of classifying goods for customs purposes established by the Convention on Nomenclature for the Classification of Goods in Customs Tariffs.

Most countries have ratified this convention. On January 1, 1989, the United States—the last major holdout—brought its tariff schedules into line with the CCC or "Harmonized" system. The Harmonized System (HS) is made up of a schedule of about 900 tariff headings, which are interpreted through explanatory notes and classification opinions published and regularly updated by the CCC. Both the notes and opinions are commonly incorporated into the tariff interpretation rules used by states that have adopted the HS.

REGIONAL INTEGRATION

GATT seeks to promote international trade through regional economic integration. It accordingly encourages WTO member states to participate in free trade areas and customs unions. A **free trade area** consists of a group of states that have reduced or eliminated tariffs among themselves but that maintain their own individual tariffs in dealing with other states.[88] A **customs union** involves a group of states that have reduced or eliminated tariffs among themselves and have also established a common tariff for all other states.[89]

free trade area: A group of states that have reduced or eliminated tariffs among themselves but that maintain their own individual tariffs in dealing with other states.

customs union: A group of states that have reduced or eliminated tariffs among themselves and have also established a common external tariff.

WTO member states may participate in these regional groups, however, only if the groups do not establish higher duties or more restrictive commercial regulations with respect to other WTO countries. The same prohibition also applies to interim agreements leading to the establishment of these groups.[90]

Any member state seeking to participate in a free trade area or customs union is required to "promptly notify" the WTO of its intentions. The proposed agreement and a transition schedule are then reviewed by WTO working parties to ensure that they comply with GATT Article XXIV. The results of this review are reported to the WTO Ministerial Conference, which in turn approves the proposal or makes recommendations for modification. *Recommendations* are actually demands to make changes. GATT Article XXIV, paragraph 7(b), says that "members shall not maintain or put into force. . . such [an] agreement if they are not prepared to modify it in accordance with these recommendations."

Once a free trade area or customs union is established, GATT rules apply to the area or union as a whole and not to its constituent states.

In many respects, a customs union or free trade area operates as a regional GATT, with its own tariff and nontariff codes. The North American Free Trade Agreement (see Exhibit 7-5) illustrates this.

---

[88]General Agreement on Tariffs and Trade 1994, Article XXIV, para. 8(b).
[89]*Id.*, Article XXIV, para. 8(a). Free trade areas and customs unions can exist between *customs territories* (areas within states that are treated as separate territories for customs purposes) as well as between states. *Id.*, para. 8.
[90]*Id.*, Article XXIV, paras. 5(a) and 5(b).

Tariffs. The North American Free Trade Agreement (NAFTA) was scheduled to eliminate all tariffs on products traded between Canada, Mexico, and the United States by 2007. Almost all tariffs have been removed, with just a few difficult issues yet to be resolved. Tariffs between Canada and the United States were eliminated at the end of 1998 under a free trade agreement between those two states that was agreed to prior to the establishment of NAFTA.

Rules of Origin. Only those Canadian, Mexican, and U.S. products that meet NAFTA's rules of origin qualify for preferential tariff treatment. In other words, only products that are principally produced or manufactured in Canada, Mexico, or the United States will qualify for the special tariff rates.

Safeguards. Should imports from a NAFTA member state seriously injure or threaten to seriously injure another member state's businesses or workers, the affected state may temporarily impose quotas or tariffs on the goods causing the injury.

Investment. NAFTA removes investment barriers (in particular, government approval is no longer required for member state nationals to invest in a wide range of business activities); it removes investment distortions (by eliminating requirements concerning domestic content, the transfer of technology to local competitors, and minimum levels of exports and maximum levels of imports); and it protects investors (by guaranteeing the right to repatriate capital and profits, the right to obtain fair compensation in the event of expropriation, and the right to use international arbitration in the event of a dispute between an investor and a government).

Services. Virtually all service areas (except for air and maritime transport and basic telecommunications) are opened to service providers from the three member states. That is, firms in one member state do not have to relocate to another member state in order to provide services. The licensing of professionals, including accountants, doctors, and lawyers, will be based on competency rather than nationality or residency.

Border-Crossing Procedures. NAFTA streamlines border-crossing procedures for business visitors, professionals, traders and investors, and intracompany transferees and ensures that qualified persons will be permitted entry. The right of blue-collar workers to move across borders to take jobs, however, is not provided for.

Government Procurement. NAFTA authorizes firms in its member states to compete on an equal basis for a wide range of government contracts as well as contracts with government-controlled enterprises. Government procurement procedures are to be transparent and subject to independent review.

Standards. Standards (including both voluntary and mandatory technical specifications concerning the characteristics of a product, such as quality, performance, or labeling) have to be applied on a nondiscriminatory basis. The process of developing new standards has to be open and transparent, and nationals of the other member states are allowed to participate in this process.

Dispute Resolution. NAFTA creates a Trilateral Trade Commission to oversee trade relations and to appoint bilateral or trilateral panels to resolve disputes. Disputes must be resolved in no more than eight months. Member states must comply with panel recommendations or offer acceptable compensation. If they do not, then the affected state can retaliate by withdrawing *equivalent trade concessions.* Special provisions apply in certain areas, including investment and commercial disputes. These allow investors and merchants to go directly to international arbitration.

EXHIBIT 7-5   Principal Features of the North American Free Trade Agreement

commodity arrangements: Intergovernmental agreements regulating the production and supply of primary commodities.

primary commodities: Products obtained by extraction or harvest that require minimal processing before being used.

COMMODITY ARRANGEMENTS

Commodity arrangements are trade regulations meant to stabilize the production and supply of basic or *primary* commodities through the intergovernmental regulation of supply and demand. **Primary commodities** are, generally speaking, those derived by extraction (fuels and ores) or harvest (foodstuffs and fish) and that require minimal industrial processing before being used or consumed. The list commonly includes bananas, bauxite, cocoa, coffee, copper, cotton and cotton yarns, hard fibers and their products, iron ore, jute and its products, manganese, meat, phosphates, rubber, sugar, tea, tropical timber, tin, and vegetable oils including olive oil and oil seeds.

GATT allows member states to participate in commodity agreements, provided that they involve both exporting and importing countries and are submitted to the WTO for approval.[91] In developing and overseeing commodity agreements in the past, the GATT 1947 organization cooperated with both the UN Economic and Social Council (ECOSOC) and the UN Conference on Trade and Development (UNCTAD). The most active of the three in promoting commodity agreements was UNCTAD. At a meeting in Nairobi in 1976, UNCTAD adopted (under pressure from its developing member states) an **Integrated Program for Commodities (IPC)**. The IPC called for the early conclusion of commodity agreements covering 10 *core* commodities—cocoa, coffee, copper, cotton, hard fibers, jute, rubber, sugar, tea, and tin—and for the establishment of a $6 billion internationally financed Common Fund to underwrite the costs of maintaining the buffer stocks commonly used in stabilizing the supply of the core commodities. To date, commodity arrangements have been set up for cocoa, coffee, rubber, sugar, and tin, but the money needed to establish the Common Fund has yet to be found.[92]

Once established, the organizations created by commodity agreements operate independently of the WTO, ECOSOC, or UNCTAD. They typically come under the supervision of a council made up of representatives of all participating states and a permanent secretariat appointed by the council. To support both supplies and prices, the agreements set up one or more stabilization programs. Typically, these include contractual arrangements to buy and sell the goods at agreed-upon prices; export quotas to limit the quantities available to the world market during stressful times; and internationally financed buffer stocks, operated by a central body, which buys and sells from those stocks to stabilize market prices.[93]

ESCAPE CLAUSE

Article XIX of GATT 1994—entitled "Emergency Action on Imports of Particular Products"—is an **escape clause** or safety valve that allows a member state to avoid, temporarily, its GATT obligations when there is a surge in the number of imports coming from other member states. The injured state can impose emergency restrictive trade measures—known as **safeguards**—if it can demonstrate that there is an actual or seriously threatened injury to one of its domestic industries.[94]

A state making use of the escape clause must notify the WTO and consult with the affected exporting state to arrange for compensation.[95] If a notifying country fails to negotiate, the injured exporting countries are authorized to *retaliate*—that is, withhold "substantially equivalent concessions" in order to restore the previous balance of trade between the two states.[96] The procedures for engaging in consultations and for withholding concessions are incorporated in a new Safeguards Agreement, discussed later in this chapter.

EXCEPTIONS

The drafters of GATT realized that states sometimes need to take certain measures as a matter of public policy that conflict with GATT's general goal of liberalizing trade. Article XX sets out "General Exceptions" and Article XXI "Security Exceptions."

Integrated Program for Commodities (IPC): Proposal of developing countries that would establish a Common Fund to underwrite the costs of maintaining a buffer stock of primary commodities as a way to stabilize supplies.

escape clause: Allows a WTO member state to escape temporarily from its GATT obligations when there is a surge in the number of imports coming from other member states.

safeguards: Emergency trade measures imposed to protect domestic industry from a surge of imports.

---

[91]*Id.*, Article XX(h), authorizes members to enforce measures "undertaken in pursuance of obligations under any intergovernmental commodity agreement which conforms to criteria submitted to the World Trade Organization and not disapproved by the WTO or which is itself so submitted and not so disapproved."

[92]Frank Stone, *Canada, the GATT, and the International Trade System,* pp. 120–124, 139–154 (1984).
    Note that no commodity agreements were ever submitted to the GATT 1947 organization for its approval under Article XX(b). GATT, *Analytical Index: Guide to GATT Law and Practice*, p. 547 (6th ed., 1994).

[93]*Id.* at 144–145.

[94]General Agreement on Tariffs and Trade 1994, Article XIX, para. 1(a).

[95]*Id.*, Article XIX, para. 2.

[96]*Id.*, Article XIX, para. 3. See GATT, *Analytical Index: Guide to GATT Law and Practice*, pp. 488–489 (6th ed., 1994).

general exceptions: Situations that excuse a WTO member state from complying with its GATT obligations in order for the state to protect certain essential public policy objectives.

The **general exceptions** excuse a member state from complying with its GATT obligations so long as this is not done as "a means of arbitrary or unjustifiable discrimination" or as "a disguised restriction on international trade." They allow a state to take measures contrary to GATT that

1. are necessary to protect public morals;
2. are necessary to protect human, animal, or plant life or health;
3. relate to the importation or exportation of gold or silver;
4. are necessary to secure compliance with laws or regulations that are not inconsistent with GATT;
5. relate to the products of prison labor;
6. protect national treasures of artistic, historic, or archaeological value;
7. relate to the conservation of exhaustible natural resources;
8. are undertaken in accordance with an intergovernmental commodity agreement;
9. involve restrictions on exports of domestic materials needed by a domestic processing industry during periods when the domestic price of those materials is held below world prices as part of a governmental stabilization plan; or
10. are essential to acquiring products in short supply.

In Case 7-3, the Appellate Body explains how these general exceptions are interpreted and applied.

Case 7-3   UNITED STATES—IMPORT PROHIBITION OF CERTAIN SHRIMP AND SHRIMP PRODUCTS

World Trade Organization, Appellate Body, 1998. Appellate Body Report WT/DS58/AB/R.[97]

I. INTRODUCTION: STATEMENT OF THE APPEAL

This is an appeal by the United States from certain issues of law and legal interpretations in the Panel Report, *United States—Import Prohibition of Certain Shrimp and Shrimp Products.* . . .

***

The United States issued regulations in 1987 pursuant to the Endangered Species Act of 1973[98] requiring all United States shrimp trawl vessels to use approved Turtle Excluder Devices ("TEDs") or tow-time restrictions in specified areas where there was a significant mortality of sea turtles in shrimp harvesting.[99] These

regulations, which became fully effective in 1990, were modified so as to require the use of approved TEDs at all times and in all areas where there is a likelihood that shrimp trawling will interact with sea turtles, with certain limited exceptions.

. . . Section 609(b)(1) imposed. . . an import ban on shrimp harvested with commercial fishing technology which may adversely affect sea turtles. Section 609(b)(2) provides that the import ban on shrimp will not apply to harvesting nations that are certified by the U.S. Department of State. To be certified a nation must either (a) not have any of the relevant species of turtles in its waters; (b) harvest shrimp exclusively by means that do not pose a threat to sea turtles, e.g., harvest shrimp exclusively by artisanal means; or (c) conduct its commercial shrimp trawling operations exclusively in waters subject to its jurisdiction in which sea turtles do not occur.

---

[97]This report is posted at the WTO's Web site at http://www.wto.org/english/tratop_e/dispu_e/ cases_e/ds58_e.htm.
[98]Public Law 93–205, *United States Code*, title 16, § 1531 et seq.
[99]United States Federal Regulation, title 52, para. 24244, June 29, 1987 (the "1987 Regulations"). Five species of sea turtles fell under the regulations: loggerhead (*Caretta caretta*), Kemp's ridley (*Lepidochelys kempi*), green (*Chelonia mydas*), leatherback (*Dermochelys coriacea*) and hawksbill (*Eretmochelys imbricata*).

MAP 7-3 United States (1998)

Second, certification shall be granted to harvesting nations that provide documentary evidence of the adoption of a regulatory program governing the incidental taking of sea turtles in the course of shrimp trawling that is comparable to the United States program and where the average rate of incidental taking of sea turtles by their vessels is comparable to that of United States vessels.[100] According to the 1996 [*Administrative*] *Guidelines* [*for Implementing the Endangered Species Act*] the Department of State assesses the regulatory program of the harvesting nation and certification shall be made if the program includes: (i) the required use of TEDs that are "comparable in effectiveness to those used in the United States. Any exceptions to this requirement must be comparable to those of the United States program..."; and (ii) "a credible enforcement effort that includes monitoring for compliance and appropriate sanctions."...

***

In the Panel Report, the Panel reached the following conclusions:

> ...[W]e conclude that the import ban on shrimp and shrimp products as applied by the United States on the basis of Section 609 of Public Law 101–162 is not consistent with article XI: 1 of GATT 1994, and cannot be justified under article XX of GATT 1994.

***

IV. ISSUES RAISED IN THIS APPEAL

The issues raised in this appeal by the appellant, the United States, are the following:

***

(b) whether the Panel erred in finding that the measure at issue constitutes unjustifiable discrimination between countries where the same conditions prevail and thus is not within the scope of measures permitted under article XX of the GATT 1994.

VI. APPRAISING SECTION 609 UNDER ARTICLE XX OF THE GATT 1994

***

A. [Introduction]

***

Article XX of the GATT 1994 reads, in its relevant parts:

> **ARTICLE XX**
> **GENERAL EXCEPTIONS**
> Subject to the requirement that such measures are not applied in a manner which would constitute a means of arbitrary or unjustifiable discrimination between countries where the same conditions prevail, or a disguised restriction on international trade, nothing in this agreement shall be construed to prevent the adoption or enforcement by any Member of measures:
>
> ***
>
> (g) relating to the conservation of exhaustible natural resources if such measures are made effective in conjunction with restrictions on domestic production or consumption;
>
> ***

In *United States—[Standards for Reformulated and Conventional] Gasoline*,[101] we enunciated the appropriate method for applying article XX of the GATT 1994:

> In order that the justifying protection of article XX may be extended to it, the measure at issue must not only come under one or another of the particular exceptions—paragraphs (a) to (j)—listed under article XX; it must also satisfy the requirements imposed by the opening clauses of article XX. *The analysis is, in other words, two-tiered: first, provisional justification by reason of characterization of the measure under XX(g); second, further appraisal of the same measure under the introductory clauses of article XX.* (emphasis added)

The sequence of steps indicated above in the analysis of a claim of justification under article XX reflects,

---

not inadvertence or random choice, but rather the fundamental structure and logic of article XX. The Panel [in its Report] appears to suggest, albeit indirectly, that following the indicated sequence of steps, or the inverse thereof, does not make any difference. To the Panel, reversing the sequence set out in *United States—Gasoline* "seems equally appropriate." We do not agree.

***

We hold that the findings of the Panel. . . and the interpretative analysis embodied therein, constitute error in legal interpretation and accordingly reverse them.

***

B. Article XX(g): Provisional Justification of Section 609

In claiming justification for its measure, the United States primarily invokes article XX(g). . . .

1. "Exhaustible Natural Resources"   We begin with the threshold question of whether Section 609 is a measure concerned with the conservation of "exhaustible natural resources" within the meaning of article XX(g). . . . India, Pakistan, and Thailand contended that a "reasonable interpretation" of the term "exhaustible" is that the term refers to "finite resources such as minerals, rather than biological or renewable resources." We are not convinced by these arguments. Textually, article XX(g) is not limited to the conservation of "mineral" or "non-living" natural resources. The complainants' principal argument is rooted in the notion that "living" natural resources are "renewable" and therefore cannot be "exhaustible" natural resources. We do not believe that "exhaustible" natural resources and "renewable" natural resources are mutually exclusive. One lesson that modern biological sciences teach us is that living species, though in principle, capable of reproduction and, in that sense, "renewable," are in certain circumstances indeed susceptible of depletion, exhaustion and extinction, frequently because of human activities. Living resources are just as "finite" as petroleum, iron ore and other non-living resources.

***

We believe it is too late in the day to suppose that article XX(g) of the GATT 1994 may be read as referring only to the conservation of exhaustible mineral or other non-living natural resources. Moreover, two adopted GATT 1947 panel reports previously found fish to be an "exhaustible natural resource" within the meaning of

article XX(g).[102] We hold that, in line with the principle of effectiveness in treaty interpretation, measures to conserve exhaustible natural resources, whether living or non-living, may fall within article XX(g). Further, since all seven recognized species of sea turtle are today listed in the Convention on International Trade as "endangered species" we conclude that the sea turtles involved here do constitute "exhaustible natural resources" for the purpose of article XX(g) of the GATT 1993.

***

C. The Introductory Clauses of Article XX: Characterizing Section 609 Under the Chapeau's Standards

***

Although provisionally justified under article XX(g), Section 609, if it is ultimately to be justified as an exception under article XX, must also satisfy the requirements of the introductory clauses—the "chapeau" [hat][103]—of article XX, that is,

> **ARTICLE XX**
> **GENERAL EXCEPTIONS**
> Subject to the requirement that such measures are *not applied in a manner which would constitute a means of arbitrary or unjustifiable discrimination between countries where the same conditions prevail, or a disguised restriction on international trade,* nothing in this agreement shall be construed to prevent the adoption or enforcement by any Member of measures: (emphasis added)

We turn, hence, to the task of appraising Section 609, and specifically the manner in which it is applied under the chapeau of article XX; that is, to the second part of the two-tier analysis required under article XX.

***

In the previous case, *United States—Gasoline,* we stated that "the purpose and object of the introductory clauses of article XX is generally the prevention of 'abuse of the exceptions of [article XX].'" We went on to say that:

> . . . The chapeau is animated by the principle that while the exceptions of article XX may be invoked as a matter of legal right, they should not be so applied as to frustrate or defeat the legal obligations of the holder of the right under the substantive rules of the General Agreement. In other words, the exceptions must be applied reasonably, with due regard both to the legal duties of the party claiming the exception and the legal rights of the other parties concerned.

---

[102]United States—Prohibition of Imports of Tuna and Tuna Products from Canada, adopted 22 February 1982, BISD 29S/91, para. 4.9; Canada—Measures Affecting Exports of Unprocessed Herring and Salmon, adopted 22 March 1988, BISD 35S/98, para. 4.4.
[103][French: "hat."]

At the end of the Uruguay Round, negotiators fashioned an appropriate preamble for the new WTO Agreement, which strengthened the multilateral trading system by establishing an international organization, *inter alia*,[104] to facilitate the implementation, administration and operation, and to further the objectives, of that agreement and the other agreements resulting from that Round. The drafters followed much of the language of the former GATT preamble but specifically did not include as one objective the phrase "full use of the resources of the world," apparently believing that this was no longer appropriate to the world trading system of the 1990's. Instead, they decided to qualify the original objectives of the GATT 1947 with the following words:

> . . . while allowing for the optimal use of the world's resources in accordance with the objective of sustainable development, seeking both to protect and preserve the environment and to enhance the means for doing so in a manner consistent with their respective needs and concerns at different levels of economic development. . . .

[T]his language demonstrates a recognition by WTO negotiators that optimal use of the world's resources should be made in accordance with the objective of sustainable development. As this preambular language reflects the intentions of negotiators of the WTO Agreement, we believe it must add color, texture and shading to our interpretation of the agreements annexed to the WTO Agreement, in this case, the GATT 1994. . . .

***

Turning then to the chapeau of article XX, we consider that it recognizes the need to maintain a balance of rights and obligations between the right of a Member to invoke one or another of the exceptions of article XX, and the substantive rights of the other Members under the GATT 1994, on the other hand. In our view, the language of the chapeau makes clear that each of the exceptions in paragraphs (a) to (j) of article XX is a limited and conditional exception from the substantive obligations contained in the other provisions of the GATT 1994, that is to say, the ultimate availability of the exception is subject to the compliance by the invoking Member with the requirements of the chapeau. . . .

***

2. "Unjustifiable Discrimination"   We scrutinize first whether the U.S. regulations have been applied in a manner constituting "unjustifiable discrimination between countries where the same conditions prevail." Perhaps the

most conspicuous flaw in this measure's application relates to its intended and actual coercive effect on the specific policy decisions made by foreign governments, Members of the WTO. Section 609, in its application, is, in effect, an economic embargo which requires *all other exporting Members*, if they wish to exercise their GATT rights, to adopt *essentially the same* policy (together with an approved enforcement program) as that applied to, and enforced on, United States domestic shrimp trawlers. As enacted by the Congress of the United States, the *statutory* provisions of Section 609(b)(2)(A) and (B) do not, in themselves, *require* that other WTO Members adopt *essentially the same* policies and enforcement practices as the United States. Viewed alone, the statute appears to permit a degree of discretion or flexibility in how the standards for determining comparability might be applied, in practice, to other countries. However, any flexibility that may have been intended by Congress when it enacted the statutory provision has been effectively eliminated in the implementation of that policy through the 1996 *Guidelines* promulgated by the Department of State and through the practice of the administrators in making certification determinations.

According to the 1996 *Guidelines*. . . any exceptions to the requirement of the use of TEDs must be comparable to those of the United States program. . . . [And] in practice, the competent government officials only look to see whether there is a regulatory program requiring the use of TEDs or one that comes within one of the extremely limited exceptions available to United States shrimp trawl vessels.

The actual *application* of the measure. . . *requires* other WTO Members to adopt a regulatory program that is not merely *comparable*, but rather essentially the same, as that applied to the United States shrimp trawl vessels. Thus, the effect of the application of Section 609 is to establish a rigid and unbending standard by which United States officials determine whether or not countries will be certified, thus granting or refusing other countries the right to export shrimp to the United States. Other specific policies and measures that an exporting country may have adopted for the protection and conservation of sea turtles are not taken into account, in practice, by the administrators making the comparability determination.

. . . It may be quite acceptable for a government, in adopting and implementing a domestic policy, to adopt a single standard applicable to all its citizens throughout that country. However, it is not acceptable, in international trade relations, for one WTO Member to use an economic embargo to *require* other Members to adopt essentially the same comprehensive regulatory program, to achieve a certain policy goal, as that in force within that Member's territory, *without* taking into consideration different conditions which may occur in the territories of those other Members.

[Furthermore, the record shows that] *shrimp caught using methods identical to those employed in the United States* have been excluded from the United States market solely because they have been caught in waters of *countries that have not been certified by the United States*. The resulting situation is difficult to reconcile with the declared policy objective of protecting and conserving sea turtles. This suggests to us that this measure, in its application, is more concerned with effectively influencing WTO Members to adopt essentially the same comprehensive regulatory regime as that applied by the United States to its domestic shrimp trawlers, even though many of those Members may be differently situated. We believe that discrimination results not only when countries in which the same conditions prevail are differently treated, but also when the application of the measure at issue does not allow for any inquiry into the appropriateness of the regulatory program for the conditions prevailing in those exporting countries.

***

3. "Arbitrary Discrimination"   We next consider whether Section 609 has been applied in a manner constituting "arbitrary discrimination between countries where the same conditions prevail." We have already observed that Section 609, in its application, imposes a single, rigid and unbending requirement that countries applying for certification under Section 609(b)(2)(A) and (B) adopt a comprehensive regulatory program that is essentially the same as the U.S. program, without inquiring into the appropriateness of that program for the conditions prevailing in the exporting countries. Furthermore, there is little or no flexibility in how officials make the determination for certification pursuant to these provisions.[105] In our view, this rigidity and inflexibility also constitute "arbitrary discrimination" within the meaning of the chapeau.

***

. . . The certification processes under Section 609 consist principally of administrative *ex parte*[106] inquiry or verification by staff of the Office of Marine Conservation in the Department of State with staff of the United States National Marine Fisheries Service. With respect to both types of certification, there is no formal opportunity for an applicant country to be heard, or to respond to any arguments that may be made against it, in the course of the certification process before a decision to grant or to deny certification is made. There is no formal written, reasoned decision, whether of acceptance or rejection, rendered on applications and countries are not even notified of denial of their applications, but must await the publication of a list of approvals in the Federal Register. No procedure for review of, or appeal from, a denial of an application is provided.

***

We find, accordingly, that the United States measure is applied in a manner which amounts to a means not just of "unjustifiable discrimination," but also of "arbitrary discrimination" between countries where the same conditions prevail, contrary to the requirements of the chapeau of article XX. The measure, therefore, is not entitled to the justifying protection of article XX of the GATT 1994. . . .

In reaching these conclusions, we wish to underscore what we have *not* decided in this appeal. We have not decided that the protection and preservation of the environment is of no significance to the Members of the WTO. Clearly, it is. We have not decided that the sovereign nations that are Members of the WTO cannot adopt effective measures to protect endangered species, such as sea turtles. Clearly, they can and should. And we have not decided that sovereign states should not act together bilaterally, plurilaterally or multilaterally, either within the WTO or in other international fora,[107] to protect endangered species or to otherwise protect the environment. Clearly, they should and do.

What we have decided in this appeal is simply this: although the measure of the United States in dispute in this appeal serves an environmental objective that is recognized as legitimate under paragraph (g) of article XX of the GATT 1994, this measure has been applied by the United States in a manner which constitutes arbitrary and unjustifiable discrimination between Members of the WTO, contrary to the requirements of the chapeau of article XX. . . .

***

---

[105]In the oral hearing, the United States stated that "as a policy matter, the United States government believes that all governments should require the use of turtle excluder devices on all shrimp trawler boats that operate in areas where there is a likelihood of intercepting sea turtles" and that "when it comes to shrimp trawling, we know of only one way of effectively protecting sea turtles, and that is throughTEDs."

[106]Latin: "from one party or side." An *ex parte* inquiry is one conducted without notice to the other party or parties adversely interested and without the latter being present or having the opportunity to contest the decision made there.

[107]Plural of "forum." A meeting place, such as a court or tribunal.

The Appellate Body *recommends* that the DSB request the United States to bring its measure found in the Panel Report to be inconsistent with article XI of the GATT 1994, and found in this Report to be not justified under article XX of the GATT 1994, into conformity with the obligations of the United States under that agreement. ■

CASEPOINT: The WTO Appellate Body considered whether the U.S. ban on imported shrimp that were harvested in a manner not meeting U.S. environmental requirements violated GATT rules. Generally, WTO members must treat imported goods the same way as domestic goods and not subject them to additional requirements. There are some exceptions to these rules, including one that allows a nation to take action to protect "exhaustible natural resources." The United States had imposed strict rules on shrimp harvesting, in an effort to protect endangered sea turtles, and then required all other nations to essentially adopt the same rules in order for shrimp to be imported into the United States.

The panel first concluded that the sea turtles involved here did constitute "exhaustible natural resources" under Article XX(g) of the GATT, and thus the exception might apply. However, the WTO panel held that the U.S. rules were discriminatory under the chapeau (heading) of Article XX of the treaty in that they were applied in a rigid manner, without regard to any measures taken to protect turtles by other nations. In addition, the panel found that the U.S. procedure for determining whether other nations met the U.S standards constituted arbitrary discrimination, in that the decision was made without any opportunity for other nations to present evidence, or to have a hearing or consultation, and no review or appeal was allowed.

security exceptions: Situations that excuse a WTO member state from complying with its GATT obligations when those are in conflict with its essential security interests or its duties under the United Nations Charter.

The **security exceptions** set out in Article XXI allow member states to avoid any obligations they may have under GATT that are contrary to their "essential security interests" or that conflict with their duties "under the United Nations Charter for the maintenance of international peace and security."

EXPORT CONTROLS

Member states commonly employ GATT exceptions to limit certain kinds of exports. Noteworthy examples of export controls that fit under the general exceptions found in Article XX are several multilateral treaties that limit the removal of cultural artifacts from their countries of origin. Examples of export controls that relate to the security exceptions set out in Article XXI include export restrictions for national security reasons or in support of actions taken by the United Nations in maintaining the peace.

Protection of Cultural Property

The United Nations Education, Scientific, and Cultural Organization (UNESCO), the Organization of American States (OAS), and the International Institute for the Unification of Private Law (Unidroit) have each sponsored conventions to control the international transfer of cultural artifacts.[108] The UNESCO-sponsored Convention for the Protection of Cultural Property in the Event of Armed Conflict, signed at The Hague in 1954, is the oldest of these agreements.[109] It is important in defining cultural property (i.e., "movable or immovable property of great importance to the cultural heritage of every people"); in prohibiting the theft, pillage, misappropriation, or exportation of cultural property during an armed conflict; and in establishing the principle that obligations under cultural property

---

[108]UNESCO's Convention Concerning the Protection of the World Cultural and Natural Heritage (1972) is concerned principally with the identification and protection of cultural sites within the borders of member states. The Council of Europe's European Convention on the Protection of the Archaeological Heritage (Revised 1992) primarily regulates the exploration of archaeological sites; it only peripherally restricts the exportation of cultural property. The text of the Convention is posted on the Council of Europe's Web site at www.coe.fr/eng/legaltxt/143e.htm.

[109]The text is in *The Protection of Cultural Property I: Compendium of Legislative Texts*, pp. 335–356 (UNESCO, 1984). It is also posted on UNESCO's Web site at http://www.unesco.org/ general/eng/legal/cltheritage/hague/index.html. Currently, 116 states are parties to this convention. See http://www.unesco.org/general/eng/legal/cltheritage/hague/rat.html. Accessed Feb. 3, 2007.

conventions are not retroactive.[110] The UNESCO-sponsored Convention on the Means of Prohibiting and Preventing the Illicit Import, Export, and Transfer of Ownership of Cultural Property, signed at Paris in 1970, establishes that the import, export, and transfer of ownership of cultural property are illegal if they are done contrary to laws adopted by states to protect their national heritage. The convention also requires member states to take all steps necessary to return stolen cultural properties to their state of origin.[111]

The OAS's 1976 Convention on the Protection of the Archaeological, Historical, and Artistic Heritage of the American Nations copies most of the provisions of the 1970 UNESCO Convention, adding articles that make enforcement easier.[112]

The 1995 Unidroit Convention on Stolen or Illegally Exported Cultural Objects requires member states to return stolen cultural objects. Claims must be made within three years after the owner learns of the location of such property and within fifty years of the time of the theft.[113]

Maintenance of National Security

States have long imposed restrictions on strategically important exports as a matter of national security. Following World War II, export restrictions became a prominent feature of the West's Cold War with the East, and by 1949, the United States and its Western European allies had enacted legislation limiting exports to the Soviet Union and its Eastern European allies. The U.S. Export Control Act of 1949, for example, restricted American exports of strategic commodities to Communist countries for three reasons: (1) national security, (2) foreign policy, and (3) to preserve materials in short supply. In 1949, the United States and its allies formed the Coordinating Committee on Multilateral Export Controls (COCOM). COCOM maintained a list of commodities and technological information that each country agreed not to export to Communist and certain other states. In 1993, with the Cold War at an end, the COCOM member states agreed that its East-West focus was no longer an appropriate basis for establishing export controls, and they agreed to bring the committee to an end. The following year, at a meeting in Wassenaar, the Netherlands, the member states formally terminated COCOM and agreed to establish a new multilateral arrangement.

Wassenaar Arrangement: Intergovernmental arrangement and organization to coordinate national policies so that transfers of conventional arms and dual-use goods and technologies do not contribute to the development or enhancement of military capabilities that undermine international and regional security and are not diverted to support such capabilities.

The Wassenaar Arrangement   In July 1996, 33 countries[114]—including Canada, France, Great Britain, Japan, Russia, and the United States—approved the Wassenaar Arrangement on Export Controls for Conventional Arms and Dual-Use Goods and Technologies.[115] As of April 2007 there were 40 members of the Wassenaar Arrangement. Its goals are to promote transparency, the exchange of views and information, and greater responsibility in transfers of conventional arms and dual-use goods and technologies. Member countries, through their own national policies, seek to ensure that such transfers do

---

[110]See Autocephalous Greek-Orthodox Church of Cyprus v. Goldberg & Feldman Fine Arts, Inc., *Federal Supplement*, vol. 717, p. 1374 (1989), for an example of a case where the recipient of artifacts expropriated by an occupying military force was required to return them to their country of origin.

[111]The text is in *The Protection of Cultural Property I: Compendium of Legislative Texts*, pp. 357–364 (UNESCO, 1984). It is also posted on UNESCO's Web site at http://www.unesco.org/general/eng/legal/cltheritage/bh572.html. Currently, 110 states are parties to this convention. See http://www.unesco.org/general/eng/legal/cltheritage/bh572-rat.html. Accessed Feb. 3, 2007.

[112]The text is in *id.*, at pp. 370–374. It is also posted on the OAS's Web site at http://www.oas.org/En/prog/ juridico/english/Treaties/c-16.html. The current member states are Argentina, Bolivia, Costa Rica, Ecuador, El Salvador, Guatemala, Haiti, Honduras, Nicaragua, Panama, Paraguay, and Peru. See http://www.oas.org/En/ prog/ juridico/english/Sigs/c-165.html. Accessed Feb. 3, 2007.

[113]The convention is posted on the Unidroit Web site at http://www.unidroit.org/english/conventions/c-cult.htm. The convention entered into force on July 1, 1998. Currently, there are 28 member parties. See http://www.unidroit.org/english/implement/i-95.htm.

[114]Current members are Argentina, Australia, Austria, Belgium, Bulgaria, Canada, Croatia, the Czech Republic, Denmark, Estonia, Finland, France, Germany, Greece, Hungary, Ireland, Italy, Japan, Latvia, Lithuania, Malta, Luxembourg, the Netherlands, New Zealand, Norway, Poland, Portugal, the Republic of Korea, Romania, Russia, Slovakia, Slovenia, South Africa, Spain, Sweden, Switzerland, Turkey, Ukraine, the United Kingdom, and the United States. Wassenaar Secretariat at http://www.wassenaar.org/. Accessed Feb. 10, 2007.

[115]The "Initial Elements" of the Wassenaar Arrangement are posted at http://www.wassenaar.org/docs/IE96.html. Accessed Feb. 3, 2007.

not contribute to the development or enhancement of military capabilities that undermine international and regional security and are not diverted to support such capabilities. The Wassenaar Arrangement, however, is not meant to impede bona fide transactions and, unlike COCOM, is not directed against any state or group of states.[116]

Member countries are required to maintain export controls on a list of agreed-upon items.[117] They meet regularly in Vienna, where a small secretariat is located,[118] to update the list and to exchange information. Additionally, they make semiannual reports on the transfer of arms and controlled dual -use items.

Membership is open to all countries on a nondiscriminatory basis. A member must be a producer of arms or an exporter of industrial equipment; maintain nonproliferation policies and appropriate national policies, including adherence to relevant nonproliferation regimes and treaties; and maintain fully effective export controls.[119]

OTHER MULTILATERAL EXPORT-CONTROL PROGRAMS

Australia Group: Multilateral group of states concerned with curbing the proliferation of chemical and biological weapons.

In addition to the Wassenaar Arrangement, there are four other multilateral export-control programs. The **Australia Group** is an informal multilateral group of states established in 1984 to address concerns about the proliferation of chemical and biological warfare capabilities.[120] Members[121] meet annually to share information about proliferation dangers and to harmonize their national export controls in an effort to curb the transfer of materials or equipment that could be used in the creation of chemical or biological weapons. The group maintains lists of items that should be controlled, as well as warning lists of items whose purchase may indicate proliferation activities.[122]

Zangger Committee: Exporting states parties to the Treaty on Non-Proliferation of Nuclear Weapons that seek to harmonize their interpretations of the treaty's export-control provision.

The **Zangger Committee** was set up the year after the Treaty on Non-Proliferation of Nuclear Weapons[123] came into force in 1970.[124] Also known as the Non-Proliferation Treaty Exporters' Committee,[125] it works to harmonize the member states' interpretations of the export-control provision of the treaty.[126] This provision calls for exporters to require International Atomic Energy Agency safeguards as a condition for the supply of nuclear material or items "especially designed or prepared for the processing, use, or production of special fissionable material." The safeguards include peaceful end-use assurances and assurances that an item will not be reexported to a nontreaty nonnuclear weapon state unless the receiving state accepts safeguards on the item.[127]

---

[116]See "What Is the Wassenaar Arrangement?" at http://www.wassenaar.org/docs/talkpts.html.

[117]The lists are posted at http://www.wassenaar.org/List/Table%20of%20Contents%20-%2098web.html.

[118]The secretariat maintains a Web site at http://www.wassenaar.org.

[119]Links to Web sites describing the export-control programs of all the Wassenaar Agreement member states are located on the secretariat's home page at http://www.wassenaar.org.

[120]The Australia Group Secretariat maintains a Web site at http://www.australiagroup.net.

[121]Currently there are 39 members: Argentina, Australia, Austria, Belgium, Bulgaria, Canada, Cyprus, the Czech Republic, Denmark, Estonia, the European Commission, Finland, France, Germany, Greece, Hungary, Iceland, Ireland, Italy, Japan, Latvia, Lithuania, Luxembourg, Malta, the Netherlands, New Zealand, Norway, Poland, Portugal, Romania, Slovakia, Slovenia, South Korea, Spain, Sweden, Switzerland, Turkey, the United Kingdom, and the United States. Australia Group Secretariat at http://www.australiagroup.net/agpart.htm. Accessed Feb. 3, 2007.

[122]The lists are posted at http://www.australiagroup.net/agcomcon.htm.

[123]The text of the treaty is posted on the U.S. Arms Control and Disarmament Agency's Web site at http://www.acda.gov/treaties/npt1.htm.

[124]See U.S. Department of Statement, Bureau of Nonproliferation, "Factsheet" (January 20, 2001) at http://www.state.gov/t/np/rls/fs/2001/3054.htm.

[125]The Zangger Committee was named in honor of Professor Claude Zangger of Switzerland, who chaired the committee from its inception in 1971 until 1989. U.S. Arms Control and Disarmament Agency, *Annual Report*, Chap. 6 (1997), posted at http://www.acda.gov/reports/annual/chpt6.htm.

[126]There are 36 member states of the Zangger Committee: Argentina, Australia, Austria, Belgium, Bulgaria, Canada, China, Croatia, the Czech Republic, Denmark, Finland, France, Germany, Greece, Hungary, Ireland, Italy, Japan, Luxembourg, the Netherlands, Norway, Poland, Portugal, the Republic of Korea, Romania, Russia, Slovakia, Slovenia, South Africa, Spain, Sweden, Switzerland, Turkey, Ukraine, the United Kingdom, and the United States. The committee's Web site is http://www.zanggercommittee.org. Accessed Feb. 3, 2007.

[127]U.S. Arms Control and Disarmament Agency, Annual Report, chap. 6 (1997), posted at http://www.acda.gov/reports/annual/chpt6.htm.

The **Nuclear Suppliers Group (NSG)** is a group of nuclear supplier countries—including members and nonmembers of the Treaty on Non-Proliferation of Nuclear Weapons—that seeks to contribute to the nonproliferation of nuclear weapons by maintaining control lists for nuclear exports and nuclear-related exports.[128] The NSG's lists aim to ensure that nuclear trade for peaceful purposes does not contribute to the proliferation of nuclear weapons or other nuclear explosive devices without hindering international trade and cooperation in the nuclear field.[129]

The **Missile Technology Control Regime** was established in 1987 to limit the proliferation of missiles "capable of delivering nuclear weapons." This is an informal group with no permanent organization; each member administers its missile-related export controls independently. The members convene at regular meetings to exchange information and to agree on the goods and technologies that need to be controlled.[130]

United Nations Action to Maintain International Peace

The United Nations Charter authorizes the UN Security Council to impose sanctions, including the adoption of bans on trade, on states whose actions threaten international peace,[131] and on several occasions it has imposed such sanctions. For example, in 1966, when Rhodesia's minority white government unilaterally declared independence from the United Kingdom in the hope of preserving white domination of the country, the Security Council ordered members of the United Nations to suspend trade in certain commodities with Rhodesia.[132] In 1977, in reaction to the use of apartheid laws, the Security Council imposed a mandatory ban on the sale of arms to South Africa.[133] And most recently, following Iraq's invasion of Kuwait, the Security Council imposed an economic embargo on Iraq that is still in place.[134] And of course, there have been many other UN resolutions dealing with Iraq in recent years. Perhaps the best known is Resolution 1441, adopted by the Security Council in Novermber 2002, finding that Iraq had violated a number of previous UN resolutions regarding weapons inspection and other matters and ordering compliance.[135]

D. MULTILATERAL TRADE AGREEMENTS

In addition to GATT 1994, there are 13 other Agreements on Trade in Goods annexed to the WTO Agreement: Nine of these deal with regulatory matters; two are *sectoral agreements* that extend GATT to certain types of goods not covered under GATT 1947; one is a program to devise a new agreement; and one is a protocol. The regulatory agreements deal with

---

[128]The 45 current members are Argentina, Australia, Austria, Belarus, Belgium, Brazil, Bulgaria, Canada, China, Croatia, Cyprus, the Czech Republic, Denmark, Estonia, Finland, France, Germany, Greece, Hungary, Ireland, Italy, Japan, Kazakhstan, South Korea, Latvia, Lithuania, Luxembourg, Malta, the Netherlands, New Zealand, Norway, Poland, Portugal, Romania, Russia, Slovakia, Slovenia, South Africa, Spain, Sweden, Switzerland, Turkey, Ukraine, the United Kingdom, and the United States. The Web site of the Nuclear Suppliers Group Secretariat is at http://www.nuclearsuppliersgroup.org/member.htm. Accessed Feb. 3, 2007.

[129]See the Nuclear Suppliers Group Secretariat Web site at http://www.nuclearsuppliersgroup.org.

[130]Arms Control Association, "Fact Sheet: Missile Technology Control Regime," at http://www.armscontrol.org/factsheets/mtcr.asp. The 34 current members are Argentina, Australia, Austria, Belgium, Brazil, Bulgaria, Canada, the Czech Republic, Denmark, Finland, France, Germany, Greece, Hungary, Iceland, Ireland, Italy, Japan, Luxembourg, the Netherlands, New Zealand, Norway, Poland, Portugal, Russia, South Africa, South Korea, Spain, Sweden, Switzerland, Turkey, Ukraine, the United Kingdom, and the United States.

[131]Article 41 of the United Nations Charter provides: "The Security Council may decide what measures not involving the use of armed force are to be employed to give effect to its decisions, and it may call upon members of the United Nations to apply such measures. These may include complete or partial interruption of economic relations and of rail, sea, air, postal, telegraphic, radio, and other means of communication, and the severance of diplomatic relations." The Charter is posted on the UN's Web site at http://www.un.org/aboutun/charter.

[132]The text of the UN Declaration is in *International Legal Materials*, vol. 5, p. 141 (1967).

[133]Security Council Resolution 418 (November 4, 1977), in *UN Monthly Chronicle*, p. 10 (December 1977) and posted on the UN Web site at gopher://gopher.undp.org:70/00/undocs/scd/scouncil/s77/16.

[134]Security Council Resolution 661 (August 6, 1990), posted on the UN Web site at gopher://gopher.undp.org:70/00/undocs/scd/scouncil/s90/15.

[135]http://daccessdds.un.org/doc/UNDOC/GEN/N02/682/26/PDF/N0268226.pdf?OpenElement.

(1) customs valuation, (2) preshipment inspection, (3) technical barriers to trade, (4) sanitary and phytosanitary measures, (5) trade-related investment measures, (6) import-licensing procedures, (7) subsidies and countervailing measures, (8) anti-dumping, and (9) safe-guards.[136] The sectoral agreements cover (1) agriculture and (2) textiles and clothing. The program to devise a new agreement relates to rules of origin. The protocol describes how the Schedules of Commitments and Concessions of the member states were phased in following the adoption of the WTO Agreement.

The most significant aspect of these agreements is that they have to be acceded to by all WTO member states. Under GATT 1947, member states were not required to participate in its nontariff codes and many did not.[137] This change is intended to produce much greater international harmony in the way trade is conducted.

Another important harmonizing factor found in all of the new nontariff agreements is that disputes between member states over their application are now uniformly governed by the WTO Dispute Settlement Understanding. Previously, each agreement had its own dispute settlement provisions. Procedures to settle disputes between individuals and governments over the latter's compliance with the provisions of a particular agreement continue, however, to be specified in each agreement.

CUSTOMS VALUATION

Agreement on Implementation of Article VII of GATT 1994 (Customs Valuation Code): Harmonizes the methods used by WTO member states for determining the value of goods for customs purposes.

transaction value: Customs value of imported goods that is based on the price actually paid or payable for goods at the time they were sold for export.

When goods cross an international frontier, they are charged a tariff that is based on a percentage of their value. The **Agreement on Implementation of Article VII of GATT 1994 (Customs Valuation Code)** is designed to harmonize the methods used by WTO member states to determine the value of those goods.[138] Its detailed rules are meant to provide for a fair, neutral, and uniform system of customs valuation. A primary method and fallback methods are established.

The primary method of customs valuation is to figure the **transaction value** of the imported item. This is based on "the price actually paid or payable for the goods when sold for export to the country of importation"[139] plus certain amounts reflecting packing costs, commissions paid by the buyer, any royalties or license fees paid by the buyer, and any resale, disposal, or use proceeds that accrue to the seller.[140]

deductive value: Customs value of imported goods that is based on the price actually paid for similar goods by unrelated persons in the importing country at about the same time.

computed value: Customs value of goods that is based on their price calculated from the cost of manufacture, overhead, and handling.

If the transaction value of imported items cannot be fairly determined (which is the case, for example, when the seller and buyer are related), then fallback methods are used. The first such method involves determining the transaction value of identical goods sold for export to the same importing country at about the same time.[141] If this value cannot be established, then the second method is to determine the transaction value of similar items sold for export to the importing country at about the same time.[142] Third, if neither of these values can be ascertained, the **deductive value** method is used. In this case, the customs value is based on the price actually paid for the greatest number of units sold to unrelated persons in the importing country at about the same time.[143] Under the fourth method, the **computed value** is derived from the sum of (a) the cost or value of the materials, including the cost of fabrication or

---

[136]The Agreement on Government Procurement, adopted at the Tokyo Round, was carried forward as a Plurilateral Trade Agreement under the WTO rather than as a Multilateral Trade Agreement.
[137]See the table setting out acceptances of the Tokyo Round agreements in GATT, *Analytical Index: Guide to GATT Law and Practice*, pp. 1056–1059 (6th ed., 1994).
[138]The Agreement on Implementation of Article VII of GATT 1994 reproduces the text of the 1979 Tokyo Round agreement. This is supplemented in Part III of the Final Act by a "Decision Regarding Cases Where Customs Administrations Have Reasons to Doubt the Truth or Accuracy of the Declared Value" and by "Texts Relating to Minimum Values and Imports by Sole Agents, Sole Distributors, and Sole Concessionaires." These supplements address concerns of developing countries relating to difficulties they commonly encounter in determining the value of goods for customs purposes.
[139]Agreement on Implementation of Article VII of GATT 1994, Article 1, para. 1.
[140]*Id.*, Article 8, para. 1.
[141]*Id.*, Article 2, para. 1(a).
[142]*Id.*, Article 3, para. 1(a).
[143]*Id.*, Article 5, para. 1(a).

processing, (b) the profit and overhead that customarily apply to the particular goods in the exporting country, and (c) charges for handling, transportation, and insurance.[144] Finally, if none of these methods can be applied, a **derived value** is used. This is determined by applying whichever of the other methods best fits and adjusting it to the particular circumstances.[145]

derived value: Customs value of goods that is determined by using whichever of the other methods best fit and adjusting it to the particular circumstances.

PRESHIPMENT INSPECTION

Developing states frequently engage private companies to verify price, quantity, quality, customs classifications, and other characteristics of goods before the goods are shipped from other states. This *preshipment inspection* (PSI) is meant to prevent over- and underinvoicing and fraud, and thus prevent the flight of capital and the evasion of customs duties.

The **Agreement on Preshipment Inspection** authorizes developing states (other states are not mentioned) to make use of PSI, but it also tries to limit its harmful trade effects. Accordingly, WTO member states that use PSI must ensure that

Agreement on Preshipment Inspection: Allows WTO developing member states to use preshipment inspections, subject to certain criteria, to prevent over- and underinvoicing and fraud.

a.   PSI activities are carried out in a nondiscriminatory manner;[146]

b.   products subject to PSI activities and imported from other member states are accorded no less favorable treatment than national products;[147]

c.   inspections are carried out either in the state of export or the state of manufacture;[148]

d.   quantity and quality inspections are performed in accordance with the standards defined by the buyer and seller in their purchase agreement or, in the absence of those standards, according to relevant international standards;[149]

e.   PSI activities are conducted in a transparent manner;

f.   information, guidelines, and regulations relating to PSI must be readily available to exporters;

g.   information received as part of the PSI is treated as business confidential;

h.   conflicts of interest between entities engaged to carry out PSI activities and entities subject to those activities are avoided; and

i.   unreasonable delays are avoided in carrying out PSI activities.

Central to the PSI process is the verification of prices. The PSI Agreement allows an entity engaged to carry out PSI activities to reject a contract price it believes wrong only if the entity follows certain guidelines. Most importantly, it may only compare the contract price of the goods being exported to "the price(s) of identical or similar goods offered for export from the same country of exportation at or about the same time, under competitive and comparable conditions of sale, in conformity with customary commercial practices and net of any applicable standards discounts."

In addition to the states making use of PSI, the states in which PSI activities are carried out also have certain obligations. These states must ensure that their laws and regulations relating to PSI activities are applied nondiscriminatorily and transparently. If requested, they also must offer to provide technical assistance to the states engaging in PSI activities within their territories.

Disputes between an exporter and an entity engaged to carry out PSI activities are to be resolved by mutual accord.[150] If not, either party may refer the matter for review to an independent review body[151] that will appoint a panel of three trade experts to decide the matter

---

[144]*Id.*, Article 6, para. 1(a).

At the request of the importer, the order of application of the deductive value and the computed value methods will be reversed. *Id.*, Article 4.

[145]*Id.*, Article 7, para. 1

[146]Agreement on Preshipment Inspection, Article 2, para. 1 (1994).

[147]*Id.*, para. 2.

[148]*Id.*, para. 3.

[149]*Id.*, para. 4.

[150]The entity carrying out the PSI activities must designate officials to receive, consider, and promptly render decisions on grievances. *Id.*, Article 2, para. 21(a).

[151]This body will be constituted jointly by an organization representing PSI entities and an organization representing exporters. *Id.*, Article 4, para. (a).

within eight working days. The decision of the panel will be binding on both the PSI entity and the exporter.

TECHNICAL BARRIERS TO TRADE

Agreement on Technical Barriers to Trade (TBT Agreement): Establishes rules governing the way WTO member states draft, adopt, and apply technical regulations and standards.

technical regulations: Mandatory laws and provisions that specify the characteristics of products; the processes and production methods for creating products; and the terminology, symbols, packaging, marking, or labeling requirements for products, processes, or production methods.

standards: Voluntary guidelines that specify the same things that technical regulations mandatorily specify.

conformity assessment procedures: Any procedure used, directly or indirectly, to determine that relevant requirements in technical regulations or standards are fulfilled.

The **Agreement on Technical Barriers to Trade (TBT Agreement)** establishes rules governing the way WTO member states draft, adopt, and apply technical regulations and standards to ensure that they (1) provide an appropriate level of protection for the life and health of humans, animals, and plants, as well as for the environment; (2) prevent deceptive practices; and (3) do not create unnecessary obstacles to trade.[152] **Technical regulations** are mandatory laws and provisions specifying (1) the characteristics of products; (2) the processes and production methods for creating products; and (3) the terminology, symbols, packaging, marking, or labeling requirements for products, processes, or production methods.[153]

Standards are voluntary guidelines that specify the same kind of requirements. **Conformity assessment procedures** include the sampling, testing, and inspecting of products; their evaluation, verification, and assurance of conformity; and their registration, accreditation, and approval.

All products, including agricultural and industrial products, are covered by the TBT Agreement, but purchasing specifications related to the production or consumption requirements of governmental bodies (which are covered by the Agreement on Government Procurement) and sanitary and phytosanitary measures (which are covered by the Agreement on Sanitary and Phytosanitary Measures) are not. The TBT Agreement applies to local governments and NGOs, and central governments are required to take "reasonable measures" (in other words, to try their best) to see that these bodies do so. Ultimately, however, only the central governments are responsible for the observance of this agreement.

The main provisions of the TBT Agreement are as follows:

1. WTO member states must establish one or more offices where information and assistance about technical regulations, standards, and conformity assessment procedures can be obtained by other member states and any interested parties.[154]
2. Accepted international systems should be used in devising technical regulations, standards, and conformity assessment procedures wherever possible.[155]
3. With respect to the application of technical regulations, standards, and conformity assessment procedures, WTO member states shall ensure that products imported from other member states shall be accorded no less favorable treatment than like national products or like products originating in any other state.
4. Technical regulations, standards, and conformity assessment procedures are not to be prepared, adopted, or applied so as to create unnecessary obstacles to international trade.
5. Technical regulations, standards, and conformity assessment procedures are to be adopted or amended openly, unless international standards are used.
6. If requested, WTO member states are to provide technical assistance to other member states and especially to developing member states.

---

[152]The 1994 TBT Agreement replaces the 1979 Tokyo Round Agreement on Technical Barriers to Trade (popularly known as the Standards Code).

[153]Agreement on Technical Barriers to Trade, Annex I, para. 1 (1994).

[154]In the United States, the National Institute of Standards and Technology (NIST), part of the Department of Commerce, maintains a National Center for Standards and Certification Information. The NIST Web site describes its mission as follows. "Founded in 1901, NIST is a non-regulatory federal agency within the U.S. Commerce Department's Technology Administration. NIST's mission is to promote U.S. innovation and industrial competitiveness by advancing measurement science, standards, and technology in ways that enhance economic security and improve our quality of life." See http://www.nist.gov. The United States also monitors and provides information about the standards programs of other countries. See the Global Standards Program page on the NIST Web site at http://www.nist.gov.

[155]Agreement on Technical Barriers to Trade, Article 9 (1994). The International Organization for Standardization (ISO) is the principal IGO responsible for establishing international standards. It is a worldwide federation of national standards bodies from 130 countries. Its Web site is http://www.iso.org/iso/en/aboutiso/introduction/index.html.

SANITARY AND PHYTOSANITARY MEASURES

Agreement on the Application of Sanitary and Phytosanitary Measures (SPS Agreement): Defines the measures that WTO member states may take to protect the life and health of humans, animals, and plants.

The **Agreement on the Application of Sanitary and Phytosanitary[156] Measures (SPS Agreement)** is meant to complement the Agreement on Technical Barriers to Trade by defining the measures that may be taken by WTO member states to *protect human, animal, and plant life and health*. Member states may protect the life and health of living things, but they may not do so as a disguised means for restricting international trade,[157] nor may they act arbitrarily to unjustifiably discriminate between states where identical or similar conditions exist. In addition, the measures taken must generally be justified by scientific evidence.

For much of the past ten years the United States and several other countries have been at odds with the EU over the EU's ban on biotech foods and other genetically modified food products. This is a highly sensitive issue, with European governments such as those of France and Germany and several environmental groups claiming that genetically modified foods are unsafe for humans and the environment. In late 2006, the WTO officially adopted a panel decision finding that the 1998 EU ban on such foods lacked the necessary scientific proof to be justified under the SPS Agreement. The WTO ruling was 1,148 pages long—the longest ever issued by the WTO—and followed a three-year process of investigating the EU justification for banning biotech food.

The prevailing parties—Canada, Argentina and the United States—hailed the decision as a win "for the principle of science-based policymaking over unjustified, anti-biotech policies." The U.S. Trade Representative called the ruling a rejection of "an unjustified trade barrier that has impeded both U.S. exports and the global use of technology that promises great benefit to farmers and consumers around the world." Surprisingly, the EU decided not to appeal the ruling. The top EU trade negotiator said that it had already removed the moratorium on modified sweet corn, and it had come into compliance on the other issues in the case, calling the WTO ruling "theoretical." Thus, the EU took the position that no new action was needed on its part, while the United States, Argentina and Canada all called for the EU to immediately "remove its WTO-inconsistent measures."[158]

Case 7-4 illustrates how the SPS Agreement is applied.

---

[156]From Greek *phyto*, meaning "plant," and *sanitary*, meaning "of or pertaining to health or the conditions affecting health." Phytosanitary measures are measures taken to ensure the health of plants.
[157]Agreement on the Application of Sanitary and Phytosanitary Measures, Preamble and para. 20 (1994).
[158]"WTO Adopts Ruling That EU Illegally Blocked Biotech Food From U.S. and Others," *FindLaw.com*, Nov. 21, 2006.

≈≈≈

Case 7-4   AUSTRALIA—MEASURES AFFECTING IMPORTATION OF SALMON
Canada v. Australia

World Trade Organization, Appellate Body.
Case AB-1998–5 (1998).

REPORT OF THE APPELLATE BODY
I. INTRODUCTION

Australia and Canada appeal from certain issues of law and legal interpretations in the Panel Report, *Australia—Measures Affecting Importation of Salmon*.[159] The Panel

was established to consider a complaint by Canada regarding Australia's prohibition on the importation of fresh, chilled, or frozen salmon from Canada under Quarantine Proclamation 86A ("QP86A"), dated 19 February 1975 and any amendments or modifications thereto.

Before the promulgation of QP86A on 30 June 1975, Australia imposed no restrictions on the importation of salmonid products. QP86A "prohibit[s] the importation

---

[159]WT/DS18/R, 12 June 1998.

into Australia of dead fish of the sub-order Salmonidae, or any parts (other than semen or ova) of fish of that sub-order, in any form unless . . . prior to importation into Australia the fish or parts of fish have been subject to such treatment as in the opinion of the Director of Quarantine is likely to prevent the introduction of any infectious or contagious disease, or disease or pest affecting persons, animals, or plants." Pursuant to QP86A and in accordance with the authority delegated therein, the Director of Quarantine has permitted the entry of commercial imports of heat-treated salmon products for human consumption as well as non-commercial quantities of other salmon (primarily for scientific purposes) subject to prescribed conditions. Canada requested access to the Australian market for fresh, chilled or frozen, i.e., uncooked, salmon. Australia conducted an import risk analysis for uncooked, wild, adult, ocean-caught Pacific salmonid product ("ocean-caught Pacific salmon"). This category of salmon is to be distinguished from the other categories of salmon for which Canada seeks access to the Australian market ("other Canadian salmon"). The risk analysis on ocean-caught Pacific salmon was first set forth in the 1995 Draft Report, revised in May 1996 and finalized in December of 1996 (the "1996 Final Report").[160] The 1996 Final Report concluded that:

> . . . it is recommended that the present quarantine policies for uncooked salmon products remain in place.

The Director of Quarantine, on the basis of the 1996 Final Report, decided on 13 December 1996 that:

> . . . having regard to Australian Government policy on quarantine and after taking account of Australia's international obligations, importation of uncooked, wild, adult, ocean-caught Pacific salmonid product from the Pacific rim of North America should not be permitted on quarantine grounds.

***

. . . The Panel found that Australia has acted inconsistently with Articles 5.1, 5.5 and 5.6 and, by implication, Articles 2.2 and 2.3 of the *Agreement on the Application of Sanitary and Phytosanitary Measures* (the "*SPS Agreement*"). In paragraph 9.1 of its Report, the Panel reached the following [conclusion, among others]:

***

(i) Australia, by adopting arbitrary or unjustifiable distinctions in the levels of sanitary protection it considers to be appropriate in different situations (on

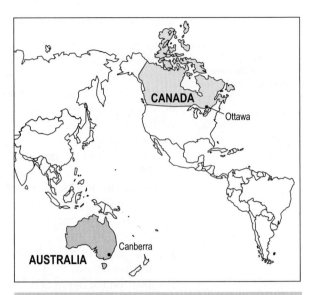

MAP 7-4 Australia and Canada (1998)

the one hand, the salmon products at issue from adult, wild, ocean-caught Pacific salmon and, on the other hand, whole, frozen herring for use as bait and live ornamental finfish), which result in discrimination or a disguised restriction on international trade, has acted inconsistently with the requirements contained in Article 5.5 of the Agreement on the Application of Sanitary and Phytosanitary Measures and, on that ground, has also acted inconsistently with the requirements contained in Article 2.3 of that Agreement. . . .

***

ARTICLE 5.5 OF THE SPS AGREEMENT

The next issue we address is whether the Panel erred in law in finding that Australia has acted inconsistently with Article 5.5 of the *SPS Agreement*.

Following our Report in *European Communities— Hormones*,[161] the Panel considered:

> . . . that three elements are required in order for a Member to act inconsistently with Article 5.5:

1. the Member concerned adopts different appropriate levels of sanitary protection in several "different situations";

2. those levels of protection exhibit differences which are "arbitrary or unjustifiable"; and

3. the measure embodying those differences results in "discrimination or a disguised restriction on international trade."

---

[160]Department of Primary Industries and Energy, Salmon Import Risk Analysis: An assessment by the Australian Government of quarantine controls on uncooked, wild, adult, ocean-caught Pacific salmonid product sourced from the United States of America and Canada, Final Report, December 1996.
[161]Adopted 13 February 1998, WT/DS26/AB/R, WT/DS48/AB/R para. 214.

The Panel found that all three conditions are fulfilled. . . .

***

Australia appeals from this finding of inconsistency with Article 5.5 and, by implication, Article 2.3 of the *SPS Agreement*. Without challenging the Panel's three-step legal test for inconsistency with Article 5.5 as such, Australia contends that the Panel has made a series of errors of law in the interpretation and application of the test. . . .

FIRST ELEMENT OF ARTICLE 5.5

With regard to the first element of Article 5.5, namely, the existence of distinctions in appropriate levels of protection in different situations, the Panel cited our Report in *European Communities—Hormones*, where we stated that "situations . . . cannot, of course, be compared, unless they are comparable, that is, unless they present some common element or elements sufficient to render them comparable."[162] The Panel found that:

> . . . in the circumstances of this dispute, we can compare situations under Article 5.5 if these situations involve either a risk of "entry, establishment or spread" of the same or a similar disease *or* of the same or similar "associated biological and economic consequences" and this irrespective of whether they arise from the same product or other products. (emphasis added)

On this basis, the Panel determined that the import prohibition on fresh, chilled or frozen salmon for human consumption *and* the admission of imports of (i) uncooked Pacific herring, cod, haddock, Japanese eel and plaice for human consumption; (ii) uncooked Pacific herring, Atlantic and Pacific cod, haddock, European and Japanese eel and Dover sole for human consumption; (iii) herring in whole, frozen form used as bait ("herring used as bait"); and (iv) live ornamental finfish, are "different" situations which can be compared under Article 5.5 of the *SPS Agreement*.

***

Australia. . . contends that the Panel erred in determining that its examination on the comparability of different situations must be limited solely to those disease agents positively detected. According to Australia, the Panel diminished Australia's right to a cautious approach to determine its own appropriate level of protection. Australia argues that the Panel failed to interpret the provisions of Article 5.5 in their context and in the light of the object and purpose of the *SPS Agreement*. According

to Australia, the terms "likelihood" and "potential" in regard to the definition of "risk assessment" contained in paragraph 4 of Annex A, and the terms "scientific principles" and "sufficient scientific evidence" contained in Article 2.2, make it clear that the basic SPS right set out in Article 2.1 to take SPS measures necessary for the protection of animal life or health, is not contingent on positive scientific evidence of disease detection.

We note that, contrary to what Australia argues, the Panel did not limit its examination under Article 5.5 to diseases positively detected in fresh, chilled or frozen ocean-caught Pacific salmon. On the contrary, it appears clearly from Annex 1 to the Panel Report, entitled "The Four Comparisons under Article 5.5", that the Panel examined diseases of concern which, according to Australia, may be carried by fresh, chilled or frozen ocean-caught Pacific salmon but which have not yet been positively detected in this type of salmon. We also note that the Panel stated explicitly that:

> . . . To the extent that both the other products and the salmon products further examined are known to be hosts to one of these disease agents or—for the salmon products—give rise to an alleged concern for that disease agent, they can be associated with the same kind of risk, namely a risk of entry, establishment or spread of that disease.

In addition, we believe that for situations to be comparable under Article 5.5, it is sufficient for these situations to have in common a risk of entry, establishment or spread of *one* disease of concern. There is no need for these situations to have in common a risk of entry, establishment or spread of *all* diseases of concern. Therefore, even if the Panel had excluded from its examination some diseases of concern not positively detected in fresh, chilled or frozen ocean-caught Pacific salmon, this would not invalidate its finding . . . on comparable situations under Article 5.5.

We, therefore, uphold the Panel's finding . . . that the import prohibition on fresh, chilled or frozen salmon for human consumption and the admission of imports of other fish and fish products are "different" situations which can be compared under Article 5.5 of the *SPS Agreement*.

SECOND ELEMENT OF ARTICLE 5.5

With regard to the second element of Article 5.5, namely, the existence of arbitrary or unjustifiable distinctions in appropriate levels of protection in different situations, the Panel began its analysis by noting that in view of the difference in SPS measures and corresponding levels of protection for salmon products, on the one

---

[162]Adopted 13 February 1998, WT/DS26/AB/R, WT/DS48/AB/R para. 217.

hand, and the four categories of other fish and fish products, on the other, one might expect some justification for this difference, such as a higher risk from imported salmon. However, as the Panel noted:

> . . . the arguments, reports, studies and expert opinions submitted to us in this respect—rather than pointing in the direction of a higher risk related to . . . [ocean-caught Pacific salmon], in order to justify the stricter sanitary measures imposed for these products—all provide evidence that the two categories of non-salmonids [herring used as bait and live ornamental finfish], for which more lenient sanitary measures apply, can be presumed to represent at least as high a risk—if not a higher risk—than the risk associated with . . . [ocean-caught Pacific salmon].

The Panel, therefore, found that, on the basis of the evidence before it, the distinctions in levels of sanitary protection reflected in Australia's treatment of, on the one hand, ocean-caught Pacific salmon and, on the other, herring used as bait and live ornamental finfish, are "arbitrary or unjustifiable" in the sense of the second element of Article 5.5.

Australia argues that the Panel erred in determining that its examination under Article 5.5, second element, must be limited solely to those disease agents positively detected in ocean-caught Pacific salmon. Australia raises the same objections to this limitation as it did in the context of the first element discussed above.

We do not agree with Australia that the Panel excluded diseases of concern which have not been positively detected in ocean-caught Pacific salmon from its examination under Article 5.5. The Panel explicitly took into account diseases which have not been positively detected in ocean-caught Pacific salmon but had been detected in herring used as bait and live ornamental finfish. . . .

THIRD ELEMENT OF ARTICLE 5.5

With regard to the third element of Article 5.5, i.e., that the arbitrary or unjustifiable distinctions in levels of protection result in "discrimination or a disguised restriction on international trade", we note that the Panel identified three "warning signals" as well as three "other factors more substantial in nature". The Panel considered that each of these "warning signals" can be taken into account in its decision on the third element of Article 5.5. In . . . its Report, it concluded:

> On the basis of all "warning signals" and factors outlined above, considered cumulatively, . . . the distinctions in levels of protection imposed by Australia for,

on the one hand, . . . [ocean-caught Pacific salmon] and, on the other hand, herring . . . use[d] as bait and live ornamental finfish, . . . result . . . in "a disguised restriction on international trade", in the sense of the third element of Article 5.5.

Australia contends that the Panel made a number of substantive errors of law in using these "warning signals" to come to its conclusion on the third element of Article 5.5.

The first "warning signal" the Panel considered was the arbitrary or unjustifiable character of the differences in levels of protection. It noted what we stated in *European Communities—Hormones*:

> . . . the arbitrary or unjustifiable character of differences in levels of protection. . . may in practical effect operate as a "warning" signal that the implementing measure in its application might be a discriminatory measure or might be a restriction on international trade disguised as an SPS measure for the protection of human life or health.[163]

The Panel, therefore, considered that:

> . . . In this dispute, . . . the arbitrary character of the differences in levels of protection is a "warning signal" that the measure at issue results in "a disguised restriction on international trade."

According to Australia, the Panel erred in according the first "warning signal", the status of evidence which demonstrates that the measure results in a disguised restriction on international trade. We note however, that it appears clearly from the Panel Report, and in particular, from the reference therein to our Report in *European Communities—Hormones*, that the Panel considered the arbitrary or unjustifiable character of differences in levels of protection as a "warning signal" for, and not as "evidence" of, a disguised restriction on international trade.

The second "warning signal" considered by the Panel was the *rather substantial difference* in levels of protection between an import prohibition on ocean-caught Pacific salmon, as opposed to tolerance for imports of herring used as bait and of live ornamental finfish. The Panel noted our statement in *European Communities—Hormones* that:

> . . . the degree of difference, or the extent of the discrepancy, in the levels of protection, is only one kind of factor which, along with others, may cumulatively lead to the conclusion that discrimination or a disguised restriction on international trade in fact results from the application of a measure.[164]

[163] Adopted 13 February 1998, WT/DS26/AB/R, WT/DS48/AB/R, para. 215.
[164] Adopted 13 February 1998, WT/DS26/AB/R, WT/DS48/AB/R, para. 240.

On that basis, the Panel stated:

> . . . we do consider that the rather substantial difference in levels of protection is one of the factors we should take into account in deciding whether the measure at issue results in "a disguised restriction on international trade", as argued by Canada.

Australia contends that this second "warning signal" is effectively no different in character from the first "warning signal" and should therefore be discounted. We note, however, that in this case the degree of difference in the levels of protection (prohibition *versus* tolerance) is indeed, as the Panel stated, "rather substantial." We, therefore, consider it legitimate to treat this difference as a separate warning signal.

The third "warning signal" the Panel considered was the inconsistency of the SPS measure at issue with Articles 5.1 and 2.2 of the *SPS Agreement*. The Panel considered that its earlier finding of inconsistency with Articles 5.1 and 2.2:

> . . . may, together with other factors, lead to the conclusion that the measure at issue results in a "disguised restriction on international trade." Indeed, considering these violations of Articles 5.1 and 2.2 it would seem that the measure at issue constitutes an import prohibition, i.e., a restriction on international trade, "disguised" as a sanitary measure. We do stress, however, that this additional "warning signal" as such cannot be sufficient to conclude that the measure results in a "disguised restriction on international trade."

Australia objects to the use of this inconsistency as a warning signal in the context of the third element of Article 5.5. It argues that inconsistency with Article 5.1 cannot "presume" or pre-empt a finding under Article 5.5. We note that a finding that an SPS measure is not based on an assessment of the risks to human, animal or plant life or health—either because there was no risk assessment at all or because there is an insufficient risk assessment—is a strong indication that this measure is not really concerned with the protection of human, animal, or plant life or health but is instead a trade-restrictive measure taken in the guise of an SPS measure, i.e., a "disguised restriction on international trade." We, therefore, consider that the finding of inconsistency with Article 5.1 is an appropriate warning signal for a "disguised restriction on international trade.". . .

We, therefore, uphold the Panel's finding that, by maintaining the measure at issue, Australia has acted inconsistently with its obligations under Article 5.5, and, by implication, Article 2.3 of the *SPS Agreement.*

CASEPOINT: Australia had banned the importation of fresh, chilled, or frozen salmon from North America under Quarantine Proclamation 86A, claiming that such protection was allowed by the GATT SPS regulations to protect against disease. Canada brought an action to the WTO challenging the ban and pointing out that Australia had not banned either herring or live ornamental fish. A WTO panel, and now the Appellate Body, ruled that Australia had violated the GATT by adopting arbitrary or unjustifiable distinctions in the levels of sanitary protection it considered to be appropriate in different situations. The Appellate Body found that the Australian action was not based on thorough scientific evidence or risk assessment and was, rather, a "disguised restriction on international trade."

TRADE-RELATED INVESTMENT MEASURES

Agreement on Trade-Related Investment Measures (TRIMs Agreement): Forbids provisions commonly found in foreign investment laws that distort or reduce international trade, including provisions that discriminate against foreigners and that impose quantitative restrictions on the use of foreign products by foreign-owned local enterprises.

The **Agreement on Trade-Related Investment Measures (TRIMs Agreement)** is aimed at facilitating foreign investment and eliminating some of the provisions commonly found in foreign investment laws that distort or reduce international trade. In particular, the agreement forbids provisions in investment laws that discriminate unfavorably against foreigners (i.e., that do not accord them "national treatment")[165] and that impose quantitative restrictions on the use of foreign products by foreign-owned local enterprises.[166] Examples include requirements that a foreign-owned enterprise must purchase or use a certain amount or proportion of domestic products ("local contents requirements") and requirements that restrict

---

[165]Agreement on Trade-Related Investment Measures, Article 2, para. 1 (1994).
[166]*Id.*, para. 2.

Developed member states were given until December 31, 1996, to eliminate any provisions inconsistent with the TRIMs Agreement. Developing states had until December 31, 1999, and " . . . [A] product is to be considered as being dumped, i.e., introduced into the commerce of another country at less than its normal value, if the export price of the product exported from least-developed member states had until December 31, 2001." *Id.*, Article 5, para. 2. Further negotiations on these issues are still taking place in 2008 as one of the many items still on the Doha Agenda.

the volume or value of an enterprise's imports by linking them to the volume or value of its exports ("trade-balancing requirements") or by correlating an enterprise's access to foreign exchange to its foreign exchange earnings ("foreign exchange balancing restrictions").[167]

IMPORT-LICENSING PROCEDURES

Agreement on Import-Licensing Procedures: Requires that the import-licensing procedures of WTO member states be neutral in their application and that they be administered in a fair and equitable manner.

Because licensing requirements may restrict or distort trade, the **Agreement on Import-Licensing Procedures** seeks to ensure that import-licensing procedures are neutral in their application and administered in a fair and equitable manner.[168] Forms and procedures are to be as simple as possible and applicants should have to deal only with a single administrative body.[169] Import licenses are not to be denied because of minor errors in completing the application;[170] nor are imports to be barred because of minor deviations in the value, quantity, or weight designated on the license.[171]

ANTI-DUMPING

Agreement on Implementation of Article VI of GATT 1994 (Anti-dumping Code): Allows WTO member states to counter dumping through the application of anti-dumping duties.

The **Agreement on Implementation of Article VI of GATT 1994**, or the **Anti-dumping Code,** replaces codes negotiated during the Tokyo and Kennedy Rounds. The current code defines **dumping** in the following way:

dumping: Selling exported goods at prices below their normal value.

> A product is to be considered dumped, i.e. introduced into the commerce of another country at less than its normal value, if the export price of the product exported from one country to another is less than the comparable price, in the ordinary course of trade, for the like product when destined for consumption in the exporting country.[172]

> For several years the United States and Canada have been involved in a dispute over the importation of softwood lumber into the U.S. After many hearings before WTO dispute settlement bodies, the WTO Appellate Body issued its final decision in 2006. The U.S. Department of Commerce (DOC) had placed anti-dumping duties on Canadian softwood lumber exporters, which were challenged by Canada, as violative of WTO rules. After a ruling in favor of Canada, the U.S. DOC had calculated new rates, but those were then challenged by Canadian authorities. After several hearings, the WTO Appellate Body found that the DOC calculations, which used a so-called "zeroing" method, violated the WTO anti-dumping rules and must be changed. The "Zeroing" approach takes into account imports which enter the country at prices deemed to be below a "dumping" threshold, but ignores any shipments of the same product which come in at higher prices. [173]

Significantly, the Anti-dumping Code does not prohibit dumping. It recognizes instead that the dumping of imports may be countered through the application of anti-dumping duties, but only if an investigation determines that the dumped imports cause or threaten to cause material injury to, or materially retard the establishment of, a domestic industry within the importing country.[174] A *domestic industry* is defined by the code as the domestic producers as a whole of like products or those domestic producers whose collective output of products makes up a major share of the total output of such products within their state.[175]

---

[167]*Id.*, Annex, paras. 1–2.
[168]Agreement on Import Licensing Procedures, Article 1, para. 3 (1994).
[169]*Id.*, paras. 5–6.
[170]*Id.*, para. 7.
[171]*Id.*, para. 8.
[172]Agreement on Implementation of Article VI of GATT 1994, Article 2, para. 1.
[173]See WTO Appellate Body Issues Compliance Report for US/Canada Lumber Dispute, *International Law Update*, Vol. 12, September 2006, p. 176 and also WTO Rules Outlaw "Zeroing" in Anti-dumping Cases, *Agra Europe* 2204 (April 21, 2006).
[174]*Id.*, Article 3, n. 9.
[175]*Id.*, Article 4, para. 1.

An investigation to determine the existence, degree, and effect of an alleged dumping may be initiated (1) "upon a written application by or on behalf of the [affected] domestic industry";[176] (2) "in special circumstances" by governmental authorities of the affected state;[177] or (3) by an application made by authorities of an affected third country.[178] In any of these cases, the application must disclose evidence showing (1) dumping, (2) material injury or threat of injury to, or material retardation to the establishment of, a domestic industry, and (3) a causal link between the dumped imports and the alleged injury.[179]

The authorities carrying out an investigation must give all interested parties notice of the investigation, an opportunity to present written evidence, and the opportunity to examine and rebut adverse evidence.[180] Even so, the investigation is to be carried out expeditiously, and the procedures that allow interested parties to participate may not be used by the parties as a means of delaying the investigation, reaching a preliminary or final decision, or applying provisional or final anti-dumping measures.[181]

Provisional measures (i.e., the imposition of a provisional anti-dumping duty or the deposit of a security equal to a provisionally estimated anti-dumping duty) may be imposed after an investigation has been initiated, a preliminary determination has been made of dumping and consequential injury to a domestic industry, and the authorities concerned believe that such measures are necessary to prevent injury being caused during the course of the investigation.[182] Final anti-dumping duties may be imposed at the discretion of the authorities concerned upon the completion of an investigation and a final determination that dumping, injury, and a causal link between them exist.[183]

The monetary amount of an anti-dumping duty may not exceed the difference between a product's normal value (i.e., the price charged for the same or similar products exported to third countries, or their cost of production plus a reasonable amount for administrative and other costs and for profits) and the price at which it was actually exported.[184] Such a duty may remain in force as long as necessary to counteract dumping that is causing injury.[185]

Dumping investigations are lengthy, complex procedures that involve many hearings, much fact-finding, and actions by several different administrative agencies and courts. The procedure in the United States is explained in Case 7-5.

---

[176]Id., Article 5, para. 1.

[177]*Id.*, Article 5, para. 6.

[178]*Id.*, Article 14, para. 1.

[179]*Id.*, Article 5, paras. 2 and 6; and Article 14, para. 2.

The investigation will be terminated and no anti-dumping duties will be imposed if "the margin of dumping is *de minimis*, or [if] the volume of dumped imports, actual or potential, or the injury, is negligible. The margin of dumping shall be considered to be *de minimis* if this margin is less than 2 percent, expressed as a percentage of the export price. The volume of dumped imports shall normally be regarded as negligible if the volume of dumped imports from a particular country is found to account for less than 3 percent of imports of the like product in the importing country unless countries which individually account for less than 3 percent of the imports of the like product in the importing country collectively account for more than 7 percent of imports of the like product in the importing country." *Id.*, Article 5, para. 8.

[180]*Id.,* Article 6, paras. 1–2.

Interested parties include "(i) an exporter or foreign producer or the importer of a product subject to investigation, or a trade or business association a majority of the members of which are producers, exporters, or importers of such product; (ii) the government of the exporting country; and (iii) a producer of the like product in the importing country or a trade and business association a majority of the members of which produce the like product in the importing country." *Id.*, para 11.

[181]*Id*, para. 14.

[182]*Id.*, Article 7, paras. 1–3.

[183]*Id.*, Article 9, para. 1.

[184]*Id.*, Article 9, para. 3; and Article 2.

[185]*Id.*, Article 11, para. 1.

Reviews must be held periodically and, if no review is conducted for a five-year period, the duty will automatically terminate. *Id.*, Article 11, paras. 2 and 3.

—⟶⟍⟍⟍⟵—

Case 7-5   NIPPON STEEL CORPORATION v. UNITED STATES

United States Court of Appeals for the Federal Circuit
Decided: August 10, 2006

MICHEL, CHIEF JUDGE

The United States and Mittal Steel USA ISG Inc. ("Mittal") appeal the decision of the United States Court of International Trade ("trade court") instructing the United States International Trade Commission ("Commission") to issue a determination that the domestic industry was not materially injured by less-than-fair-value ("LTFV") imports of tin- and chromium-coated steel sheets ("TCCSS") from Japan. This anti-dumping case has a procedural history spanning six years, which now includes four determinations by the Commission, four opinions from the Court of International Trade, and one prior opinion from this court.

Appellants argue that the Court of International Trade erred in *Nippon IV* by reweighing the facts and substituting its own credibility determinations, in contravention of law and this court's remand instructions in *Nippon Steel Corp. v. Int'l Trade Comm'n*, 345 F.3d 1379, 1380 (Fed. Cir. 2003) ("*Nippon III*"). Appellants further argue that the Court of International Trade erred in holding in *Nippon IV*—that the Commission's affirmative material injury determination in its second remand determination, was supported by less than substantial evidence.

We agree. Accordingly, we reverse the Court of International Trade's decisions in *Nippon IV* and *Nippon V*, and instruct the trade court to vacate the Commission's negative material injury and negative threat of material injury determinations and reinstate the Commission's affirmative material injury determination.

I.

A Brief History of This Case

In 2000, the Commission made a final determination that the domestic industry was materially injured by TCCSS dumping from Japan, which required consideration of import volume, price effects, impact on domestic producers, and causation. Nippon Steel Corporation, NKK Corporation, Kawasaki Steel Corporation, and Toyo Kohan Co., Ltd. (collectively, "Nippon") sought review in the Court of International Trade, which sustained the Commission's finding of a small but significant volume, but remanded for a reevaluation of price effects and causation. *Nippon Steel Corp. v. United States*, 182 F. Supp. 2d 1330, 1340, 1356 (Ct. Int'l Trade 2001) ("*Nippon I*").

On remand, the Commission again made an affirmative material injury determination. Nippon again appealed, and the Court of International Trade found lingering flaws in the Commission's analysis of price effects and causation. ("*Nippon II*"). However, rather than remand for further proceedings, the court vacated the affirmative material injury determination and directed the Commission to enter a negative material injury determination. The court declined to remand because, it stated, the Commission had "demonstrated an unwillingness or inability to address the substantial claims made by the respondents or the concerns expressed by the court in *Nippon I*."

The Commission then appealed to this court. We vacated the decision of the Court of International Trade in *Nippon II* and ordered a remand to the Commission for additional data gathering and analysis. (*Nippon III*), 345 F.3d at 1380. We explained that "to the extent [that] the Court of International Trade engaged in refinding the facts (e.g., by determining witness credibility), or interposing its own determinations on causation and material injury . . . [it] exceeded its authority", and held that the trade court abused its discretion by declining to remand the case to the Commission.

On the second remand, the Commission yet again made an affirmative material injury determination. Nippon sought review once more, and the Court of International Trade remanded for a third time, again instructing the Commission to enter a negative material injury determination. (*Nippon IV*), 350 F. Supp. 2d. at 1189. In addition, the trade court directed the Commission to determine whether the domestic industry was threatened with material injury.

The Commission entered a negative material injury determination on the third remand, stating: "this outcome is dictated by the Court's findings in *Nippon IV*; it is not, however, the determination we would have made in the absence of those findings." In its decision the Commission expressed its concern about the actions of the Court of International Trade, stating that "we believe that the trade court has committed the same mistakes identified by the Federal Circuit in *Nippon III*. For example, the Court has again re-found facts by substituting its view of the record for that of the Commission . . . and has also rejected the Commission's witness credibility

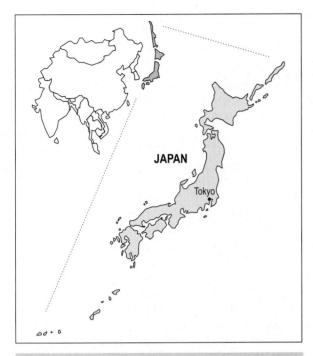

MAP 7-5 Japan (2006)

determinations, substituting the Court's own assessment of the accuracy of testimony."

II

The Role of Administrative Agencies and the Courts

Congress created a highly specialized system for resolving anti-dumping allegations, which recognizes and exploits each participant's area of expertise. An anti-dumping inquiry is divided into two sub-inquiries: (1) a determination of whether the subject imports were, or were likely to be, sold at Less Than Fair Value (LTFV), and (2) a material injury determination. Congress placed responsibility for the LTFV determination with industry experts at the Department of Commerce, and placed responsibility for the material injury determination with trade experts at the Commission.

Members of the International Trade Commission are appointed by the President, and confirmed by the Senate, because of their expertise in recognizing, and distinguishing between, fair and unfair trade practices. They presumably are selected to be Commissioners based on their expertise in, *inter alia*, foreign relations, trade negotiations, and economics. Because of this expertise, Commissioners are the factfinders in the material injury determination: "It is the Commission's task to evaluate the evidence it collects during its investigation. Certain decisions, such as the weight to be assigned a particular piece of evidence, lie at the core of that evaluative process." *U.S. Steel Group v. United States*, 96 F.3d 1352, 1357 (Fed. Cir. 1996).

In contrast, Article III judges have expertise primarily in law. Accordingly, Congress assigned the Court of International Trade, and, through our appellate authority, this court, the responsibility to review the legal sufficiency of a Commission determination. When the Commission has made a final determination of material injury or threat of material injury to a domestic industry, federal law provides that the Court of International Trade should reject any finding or conclusion which is "unsupported by substantial evidence on the record, or otherwise not in accordance with law." Judges of the Court of International Trade are experts in such cases, which form most of their docket.

Congress did not specify a standard of review for this court in reviewing judgments of the Court of International Trade. We have previously adopted the "substantial evidence" judicial review standard for the trade court as our appellate standard of review. Because the substantial evidence standard requires review of the entire administrative record, we consider both the trade court's prior decisions and the Commission determinations, including "the evidence presented to and the analysis by the Commission."

III

WHAT IS "SUBSTANTIAL EVIDENCE?"

A

"Substantial evidence" is difficult to define precisely. However, the Supreme Court, Congress, and prior panels of this court have provided some guidance. In *NLRB v. Columbian Enameling & Stamping Co.*, 306 U.S. 292, 300 (1939), the Court explained that "[s]ubstantial evidence is more than a scintilla, and must do more than create a suspicion of the existence of the fact to be established." A reviewing court must consider the record as a whole, including that which "fairly detracts from its weight", to determine whether there exists "such relevant evidence as a reasonable mind might accept as adequate to support a conclusion." A party challenging the Commission's determination under the substantial evidence standard "has chosen a course with a high barrier to reversal."

Accordingly, the question for the Court of International Trade was, and for this court is, "not whether we agree with the Commission's decision, nor whether we would have reached the same result as the Commission had the matter come before us for decision in the first instance." Rather, "we must affirm a Commission determination if it is reasonable and supported by the record as a whole, even if some evidence detracts from the Commission's conclusion." In short, we do not make the determination; we merely vet the determination.

In a material injury inquiry, the Commission is required by statute to evaluate the volume, price effects, and impact of the subject imports. When the Commission makes an affirmative material injury determination, it must decide *whether the material injury to the domestic industry is "by reason of"* the subject imports. (emphasis added)

The Commission engaged in substantial research and analysis prior to issuing its initial affirmative material injury determination. It created, distributed, and analyzed responses to detailed questionnaires sent to all seven domestic TCCSS producers, as well as the five largest domestic purchasers of TCCSS. From producers, the Commission obtained and analyzed information on production, geographic scope of sales, pricing and discounting practices, capacity utilization, shipments, inventories, and employment. From purchasers, the Commission obtained and analyzed information on final bids of domestic and Japanese suppliers, negotiation tactics, and purchasing volume, and attempted to verify producers' lost sale allegations. Two Commission staff members visited complainant Weirton Steel's premises and interviewed several employees regarding the TCCSS manufacturing process, negotiations, pricing, and contracts. In addition, Commissioners heard a full day of testimony, including that of officers of four domestic purchasers, the CEO of Weirton Steel, and seven members of Congress, including Senator John D. Rockefeller IV.

In earlier proceedings the Commission had found there was a small but significant volume (sustained by the trade court) and that there was a significant impact (not questioned on appeal.) Thus, as of *Nippon IV,* two of the three factors to be considered in a material injury determination has been established. The evidence rejected by the Court of International Trade in *Nippon IV* related to the remaining factor, price effects, and to causation.

We therefore state the issue before us as whether the Commission's findings that Japanese TCCSS *dumping could be linked to price effects* in, and causation of injury to, the domestic market so distorts or detracts from the evidence in favor of injury as to render the evidence supporting the Commission's ultimate affirmative material injury determination *insubstantial* on the record.

1

Price Effects

U.S. law [Section 1677(7)(C)(ii)] provides that in evaluating price effects, the Commission shall consider whether:

   I. there has been significant price underselling by the imported merchandise as compared with the price of domestic like products of the United States, and

   II. the effect of imports of such merchandise otherwise depresses prices to a significant degree or prevents price increases, which otherwise would have occurred, to a significant degree.

The Commission evaluated the producers' financial data, noting that the domestic industry's overall cost of goods sold ("COGS") had increased in relation to net sales, from 96.4 percent of sales in 1997 to 97.8 percent in 1998 and 101.3 percent in 1999. The Commission attributed this change to a corresponding decline in unit prices "at a rate that outstripped the industry's unit costs" and noted that the industry's profitability levels also declined consistently during the relevant period, with operating losses increasing from 0.9 percent in 1997 to 3.0 percent in 1998 to 6.5 percent in 1999. The Commission acknowledged that the operating losses decreased to 1.9 percent in the interim year 2000, but attributed this change to the filing of the anti-dumping petition in October 1999. The Commission found that the subject imports caused the suppression of domestic prices, based on the Commission's underlying finding that the domestic industry was suffering from a cost-price squeeze.

The Court of International Trade agreed that "the domestic industry generally may have been experiencing a cost-price squeeze,"[186] but rejected the Commission's conclusion based on Nippon's assertion that the two domestic producers competing most directly with Japanese TCCSS importers reported positive operating margins during the period of investigation. Implicit in Nippon's assertion, and the Commission's rejection thereof, is the fact that *other* domestic producers showed negative operating margins. Thus, we are faced with a situation where some domestic producers, and the industry as a whole, were in a cost-price squeeze, while two major producers were not. Substantial evidence exists on both sides of the issue. The Commission opted for one inference, and the Court of International Trade for another. In such a situation, however, the statutory substantial evidence standard compels deference to the Commission.

Competition Issues

Likewise, we cannot uphold two of the trade court's rejections of Commission findings regarding conditions of competition in the domestic industry. First, the trade court rejected the Commission's finding that U.S. and Japanese negotiations take place on [an] equal footing. As directed by the Court of International Trade, the Commission looked at the domestic producers' "lead time advantage" and found that it was offset by pur-

---

[186]When the cost of goods sold ("COGS") exceeds the price, the producer is unable to sell the product for more than what it costs to produce the product; if the producer is unable to raise prices, the industry finds itself in what is referred to as a *cost-price squeeze. See Nippon IV*, 350 F. Supp. 2d at 1198

chasers engaging in negotiations far in advance of production needs and by Japanese producers' willingness to carry the cost of consignment inventories at storage facilities in the United States.

We do not agree that the Commission's finding was unreasonable in light of the evidence as a whole. In any purchasing situation, competing producers are not identical. As the Commission explained, "each supplier, regardless of whether it is foreign or domestic, negotiates to maximize premiums based on its unique capabilities." The Commission's finding of equal footing was thus plausible given the evidence in the record.

Second, the trade court substituted its own inference regarding the significance of Weirton's inability to provide contemporaneous documentary evidence of Japanese price competition. The Weirton representative submitted documentation from the period of investigation that only contained pricing data from other domestic firms. He testified that he only discovered "after the fact" that Weirton was competing with Japanese prices, and thus was not informed by customers that a particular quoted price was from a Japanese producer. The Commission accorded the absence of contemporaneous documentation little weight. The Commission stated that "the record reflects that purchasers do not specify the identity of suppliers with which they are negotiating, making it more difficult for a supplier to pinpoint its competition."

The trade court rejected the Commission's inference-drawing, stating that "the fact that Weirton—a party to this action and principal supporter of the petition—is unable to provide evidence supporting its allegations, is important evidence of lack of injury." Again, we do not agree that the Commission's finding was unreasonable in light of the evidence as a whole. The Weirton representative's testimony was consistent and was not impeached, and was corroborated by testimony of its sales manager and by documents from the purchaser involved in the negotiations. *The assessment of the proper weight to accord to testimony is within the role of the Commission, not this court and not the Court of International Trade.*

Here, the record as a whole *contained substantial evidence* supporting Weirton's assertions. Accordingly, the trade court erred in rejecting the Commission's conclusion regarding the conditions of competition in the domestic industry.

2

Causation

Section 1673d(b)(1) provides that, once the Commission has made an affirmative material injury determination, it must determine whether the injury arises "by reason of imports, or sales (or the likelihood of sales) for importa-

tion. . . . If the Commission determines that imports of the subject merchandise are negligible, the investigation shall be terminated." This causation requirement is met so long as the effects of dumping are not merely incidental, tangential, or trivial.

In rejecting the Commission's finding on causation, *we must conclude that the Court of International Trade again improperly substituted its own credibility determinations for those of the Commission.* The Commission's finding of causation was based entirely on its interpretation of purchaser questionnaires, testimony, and purchasing history. Purchaser F's questionnaire response indicating that two domestic suppliers had been dropped because of price, and internal documents indicating that its sourcing decisions were driven primarily by price. Although quality and delivery issues were also mentioned, the Commission concluded that the evidence that import purchases were made because of price was more credible, and found that injury to the domestic industry was not caused solely by problems with domestic producers' quality and delivery. Under the substantial evidence standard, when adequate evidence exists on both sides of an issue, assigning evidentiary weight falls exclusively within the authority of the Commission.

C

The Court of International Trade engaged in an extremely thorough, careful examination of the record—indeed it may well have conducted a better analysis than did the Commission. As explained *supra*, a party challenging the Commission's determination under the substantial evidence standard "has chosen a course with a high barrier to reversal." *Mitsubishi*, 275 F.3d at 1060. "[E]ven if it is possible to draw two inconsistent conclusions from evidence in the record, such a possibility does not prevent [the Commission's] determination from being supported by substantial evidence." Here, it is significant that the trade court already had accepted the Commission's findings on the first two factors supporting its affirmative material injury determination: volume and impact.

Ample evidence existed on both sides of the remaining factor, price effects, and on the question of causation. When the totality of the evidence does not illuminate a black-and-white answer to a disputed issue, it is the role of the expert factfinder—here the majority of the Presidentially-appointed, Senate-approved Commissioners—to decide which side's evidence to believe. So long as there is adequate basis in support of the Commission's choice of evidentiary weight, the Court of International Trade, and this court, reviewing under the substantial evidence standard, must defer to the Commission.

IV

For the reasons articulated above, we hold that the Court of International Trade erred in assessing credibility and in reweighing the evidence before the Commission, and erred in concluding that the Commission's finding of material injury to the domestic injury was not supported by substantial evidence. Accordingly, we reverse the Court of International Trade's decisions in *Nippon IV* and *Nippon V*, set aside the Commission's negative material injury and negative threat of material injury determinations and direct that the trade court reinstate the Commission's affirmative material injury determination.

REVERSED. ■

CASEPOINT: This demonstrates the complex interaction between the various agencies involved in making a determination as to whether illegal dumping has occurred. The federal appellate court finally resolves a long-running dispute between the U.S. International Trade Commission and the Court of International Trade concerning the elements of proof necessary to prove dumping and which agency has the role of making which finding. In this case, the important findings of fact made by the commission were improperly disregarded by the Trade Court, and the federal circuit court therefore reverses the decision and reinstates the findings made by the commission that there was a material injury to a domestic industry.

SUBSIDIES AND COUNTERVAILING MEASURES

subsidy: A financial contribution made by a government or other public body that confers a benefit on an enterprise, a group of enterprises, or an industry.

A **subsidy** is a financial contribution made by a government (or other public body) that confers a benefit on an enterprise, a group of enterprises, or an industry. Examples of subsidies are (1) direct transfers of funds (e.g., grants, loans, and equity infusions), (2) potential direct transfers of funds (e.g., loan guarantees), (3) the foregoing of revenues (e.g., tax credits), (4) the providing of goods or services (other than general infrastructure), and (5) the conferring of any form of income or price support.[187] Subsidies, moreover, may be made directly by a government or indirectly through funding mechanisms or private bodies.[188]

When improperly used by a government to promote its export trade to the detriment of another state, subsidies are forbidden by GATT 1994. If subsidies have an unreasonable impact on another country's internal market, that country can impose countervailing duties to offset their impact, but only if it follows certain conditions to ensure that its reaction is justified, appropriate, and not excessive.

Agreement on Subsidies and Countervailing Measures (SCM Agreement): Classifies subsidies as prohibited, actionable, and nonactionable; forbids the first class and allows affected WTO member states to request consultation, to obtain a remedy from the WTO, or to impose countervailing duties independently.

The **Agreement on Subsidies and Countervailing Measures, or SCM Agreement**, replaces the 1979 Subsidies Code concluded at the Tokyo Round. The 1979 code was criticized because it failed to define a subsidy, to establish criteria for determining if harm had been or was about to be caused by a subsidy, and to calculate a subsidy's impact.[189] These deficiencies are all remedied in the new SCM Agreement.

The SCM Agreement clearly states that its "disciplines" (i.e., member state obligations) apply only to "specific" subsidies—that is, subsidies that target (1) a specific enterprise or industry, (2) specific groups of enterprises or industries, or (3) enterprises in a particular region.[190] The disciplines do not apply to (1) nonspecific subsidies, (2) certain specific subsidies defined in the agreement, and (3) agricultural subsidies (which are governed by the Agreement on Agriculture).

Categories of Specific Subsidies

Specific subsidies (i.e., those regulated by the SCM Agreement) are divided into three categories: (1) prohibited subsidies (informally referred to as *red* subsidies), (2) actionable subsidies (*yellow*), and (3) nonactionable subsidies (*green*).

prohibited subsidy: A subsidy that is presumed to be trade distorting because it requires export performance or is contingent upon the use of domestic instead of imported goods.

Prohibited subsidies (red subsidies) are subsidies that either (1) depend upon export performance (in other words, on a firm's or industry's success in exporting its products)[191] or

---

[187]Agreement on Subsidies and Countervailing Measures, Article 1 (1994).
[188]*Id.*
[189]John Kraus, *The GATT Negotiations: A Business Guide to the Results of the Uruguay Round*, p. 33 (1994).
[190]Agreement on Subsidies and Countervailing Measures, Article 2 (1994).
[191]*Id.*, Article 3, para. 1(a).
An illustrative list of 12 examples is provided in Annex I of the SCM Agreement.

(2) are contingent upon the use of domestic instead of imported goods (e.g., subsidies based on so-called domestic content rules.)[192] Red subsidies are presumed to be trade distorting, and WTO member states are forbidden to grant or maintain them.[193]

actionable subsidy: A subsidy that may be challenged as trade distorting if it injures the domestic industry of another WTO member state, nullifies or impairs the benefits due another member state, or causes or threatens to cause serious prejudice to the interests of another member state.

Actionable subsidies (yellow subsidies) are subsidies that may or may not be trade distorting, depending upon how they are applied (thus the reason for their designation as yellow). They are defined[194] as specific subsidies that, in the way they are used, (1) injure a domestic industry of another member state, (2) nullify or impair benefits due another member state under GATT 1994, or (3) cause or threaten to cause "serious prejudice"[195] to the interests of another member state. WTO member states are discouraged, but not forbidden, from using actionable subsidies.[196]

nonactionable subsidy: A subsidy that is permissible and nonchallengeable, such as government funding to underwrite research activities, to aid disadvantaged regions, or to help existing facilities adapt to new environmental requirements.

Nonactionable subsidies (green subsidies) consist of nonspecific subsidies and certain specific infrastructural subsidies. These infrastructural subsidies involve government funding to (1) assist (but not fully cover) the costs of research activities carried on by or on behalf of business firms, (2) aid disadvantaged regions (i.e., regions with low per capita income or high unemployment), or (3) help existing facilities adapt to new environmental requirements.[197] They are known as green subsidies because, as a general rule, they are permissible and non-challengeable.[198]

Remedies and Countervailing Measures

A WTO member state that believes that its domestic industries have been injured by either prohibited subsidies or actionable subsidies is given four options: (1) do nothing, (2) request consultations, (3) seek a remedy from the WTO, or (4) independently impose countervailing duties. If an injured member state chooses to do nothing, neither the WTO nor any other member state is entitled to intervene.[199]

To obtain a remedy from the WTO, a member state claiming an injury must first consult with the subsidizing member state.[200] If the two states are unable to find a mutually acceptable solution, either one may refer the matter to the WTO's Dispute Settlement Body (DSB)

---

[192]*Id.*, para. 1(b).

[193]*Id.*, para. 2.

[194]*Id.*, Article 5.

[195]Serious prejudice "may arise in any case where one or several of the following apply: (a) the effect of the subsidy is to displace or impede the imports of like product into the market of the subsidizing member; (b) the effect of the subsidy is to displace or impede the exports of like product of another member from a third country market; (c) the effect of the subsidy is a significant price undercutting by the subsidized products as compared with the price of a like product of another member in the same market or significant price suppression, price depression, or lost sales in the same market; (d) the effect of the subsidy is an increase in the world market share of the subsidizing member in a particular subsidized primary product or commodity as compared to the average share it had during the previous period of three years and this increase must follow a consistent trend over a period when subsidies have been granted." *Id.*, Article 6, para. 3.

Serious prejudice is presumed to exist "in the case of: (a) the total *ad valorem* subsidization of a product exceeding 5 percent; (b) subsidies to cover operating losses sustained by an industry; (c) subsidies to cover operating losses sustained by an enterprise, other than one-time measures which are nonrecurrent and cannot be repeated for that enterprise and which are given merely to provide time for the development of long-term solutions and to avoid acute social problems; (d) direct forgiveness of debt, i.e., forgiveness of government-held debt, and grants to cover debt repayment." *Id.*, para. 1.

A subsidizing member state can nevertheless overcome these presumptions by showing that none of the effects first mentioned above (Article 6, para. 3) apply. *Id.*, para. 2.

[196]The SCM Agreement, Article 5, uses the permissive phrase "no member should" in describing the obligations of member states in connection with actionable subsidies.

[197]*Id.*, Article 8, para. 2.

[198]Nonactionable subsidies may be challenged, nonetheless, if a member state believes that they have caused serious adverse effects to one of its domestic industries. Such a challenge begins with consultations between the concerned state members. If they are unable to agree to a solution, either one may refer the matter to the Committee on Subsidies and Countervailing Measures, a body created by the SCM Agreement, which will review the matter. If the committee determines that the adverse effects exist, it may recommend that the subsidizing member state modify its program. If that member state does not comply, the committee may then authorize the complaining state to take appropriate countermeasures. *Id.*, Article 9.

[199]Articles 4 and 7 of the SCM Agreement, which provide for the consultations and WTO remedies, and Articles 10 through 23, which authorize the imposition of countervailing duties, only allow a member state claiming an injury to one of its domestic industries to initiate these proceedings.

[200]Agreement on Subsidies and Countervailing Measures, Article 4, para 1, and Article 7, para. 1 (1994).

for the latter to set up a Panel.[201] If the Panel—which may seek the assistance of a Permanent Group of Experts (a body established by the SCM Agreement)—concludes that there is a prohibited subsidy, it will recommend the subsidy's withdrawal; if it concludes that there is an actionable subsidy, it will recommend that the subsidizing member state either remove the subsidy's adverse effects or withdraw the subsidy.[202] If neither party appeals to the DSB's Appellate Body, the DSB must promptly adopt the report (unless it rejects it by consensus).[203] If there is an appeal, the Appellate Body's decision must be unconditionally observed.[204]

If a member state does not comply with a DSB-adopted report or Appellate Body decision, the DSB will authorize (unless it agrees by consensus not to do so) a complaining member state to adopt countervailing measures.[205] A **countervailing measure** is defined in the SCM Agreement simply as a duty specially levied to offset a subsidy.[206]

countervailing measure: A duty specifically levied to offset a subsidy.

As an alternative to seeking a WTO-authorized remedy, a state may independently impose countervailing duties so long as it follows the procedures specified in the SCM Agreement[207] (which are the same as those used in the Antidumping Code for the adoption of anti-dumping measures). The reason a state may prefer to adopt countervailing duties independently instead of seeking a WTO-authorized remedy is that its administrative agencies will have greater control over the process. On the other hand, a state with limited resources will find the WTO-funded process more economical.

IN THE NEWS: CURRENT INTERNATIONAL DEVELOPMENTS

In February 2007, the United States started legal action at the WTO alleging that China had used various types of government support and tax policies to bolster Chinese firms in competition with U.S. and other foreign companies in a wide range of industries, from steel to paper to computers. "The United States believes that China uses its basic tax laws and other tools to encourage exports and to discriminate against imports of a variety of American manufactured goods," said U.S. Trade Representative Susan Schwab.

A request for consultation is the first step in what could be a lengthy process to determine whether Chinese subsidies violate WTO rules. First, the two countries must try to negotiate a solution, and if that fails, the United States could request a dispute resolution panel to arbitrate its subsidy complaint against China. If the panel finds in favor of the United States, it would clear the way for the imposition of economic sanctions against China, but if China prevails, it could retain the subsidies.

The case follows complaints in the U.S. Congress that the Bush administration had not been tough enough in confronting the Chinese government. The U.S. trade gap with China has been growing at a fast rate in recent years. For the first eleven months of 2006, the trade deficit with China had surged to $213.5 billion, now representing almost 30 percent of the total U.S. shortfall. "China's subsidies can particularly distort trade conditions for small- and medium-sized American enterprises and their workers," said Ms. Schwab.

Sources: New York Times, International Herald Tribune, Wall Street Journal.

---

[201]The referral may be made after thirty days in the case of prohibited subsidies, *id.*, Article 4, para. 4; and after sixty days in the case of actionable subsidies, *id.*, Article 7, para. 4.

[202]The report must be submitted within 90 days for prohibited subsidies, *id.*, Article 4, para. 4; and 120 days for actionable subsidies, *id.*, Article 7, para. 4.

[203]This must be done within thirty days. *Id.*, Article 4, para. 8; Article 7, para. 6.

[204]The Appellate Body must hand down its decision within thirty (in exceptional circumstances sixty) days for prohibited subsidies, *id.*, Article 4, para. 9; and within sixty (in exceptional circumstances ninety) days for actionable subsidies, Article 7, para. 7.

A prohibited subsidy must be withdrawn within a time period specified by the panel, *id.*, Article 4, para. 7; and an actionable subsidy must be withdrawn within 6 months of the DSB or Appellate Body's decision, *id.*, Article 7, para. 9.

[205]*Id.*, Article 4, para. 10; Article 7, para. 9.

[206]*Id.*, Article 10, provides: "The term 'countervailing duty' shall be understood to mean a special duty levied for the purpose of offsetting any subsidy bestowed directly or indirectly upon the manufacture, production, or export of any merchandise, as provided for in Article VI:3 of the GATT 1994."

[207]*Id.*, Articles 10–23.

Case 7-6 illustrates the procedures that must be followed for a state to impose counter-vailing duties.

═══◦◦◦═══

Case 7-6   MUKAND LTD. v. COUNCIL OF THE EUROPEAN UNION

European Union, Court of First Instance.
Case T-58/99 (2001).

JUDGMENT

Facts

The applicants produce and export to the Community stainless steel bright bars (hereinafter "SSBBs").

On 26 September 1997, the Commission received a complaint from Eurofer, the European confederation of iron and steel industries, alleging that imports of SSBBs originating in India were benefiting from subsidies and were thus causing material injury to the Community industry. A notice of initiation of anti-subsidy proceedings concerning the imports was published in the Official Journal of the European Communities of 30 October 1997.

***

On 17 July 1998, the Commission adopted Regulation (EC) No 1556/98 imposing a provisional counter-vailing duty on imports of stainless steel bars originating in India (hereinafter "the Provisional Regulation").

***

On 13 November 1998, the Council adopted Regulation (EC) No 2450/98 imposing a definitive counter-vailing duty on imports of stainless steel bars originating in India and collecting definitively the provisional duty imposed (hereinafter "the Contested Regulation").

***

Substance

The applicants . . . in support of their action . . . allege infringement [by the Council] of Article 1(1), Article 8(1), (6) and (7) and Article 15(1) of [Council Regulation (EC) No 2026/97 of 6 October 1997 on Protection Against Subsidized Imports from Countries Not Members of the European Community (hereinafter "the Basic Regulation")] and Articles 15 and 19 of the Agreement

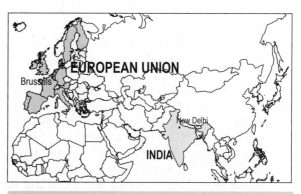

MAP 7-6   European Union and India (2001)

on Subsidies and Countervailing Measures concluded within the World Trade Organization in the context of the Uruguay Round of Negotiations (hereinafter "the ASCM"), and a manifest error of assessment, in that the Contested Regulation imposes a countervailing duty without there being any proper and substantiated finding that imports of the product in question have caused significant damage to Community undertakings producing similar products. . . .

Arguments of the Parties

The applicants argue that, in accordance with Article 1(1), Article 8(1), (6) and (7) and Article 15(1) of the Basic Regulation and Articles 15 and 19 of the ASCM, countervailing duties may be imposed only if it has been concluded, through proper investigation, that the subsidized imports cause material injury to a Community industry. Any harm caused by other factors, in particular by anti-competitive conduct on the part of Community industry itself, must not be attributed to the imports in question.

The applicants refer to paragraph 16 of the judgment of the Court of Justice in *Extramet Industrie v. Council*[208] (hereinafter "Extramet II") and submit that, in the present case, the Community institutions similarly failed in their duty properly to assess what injury might

[208]Case C-358/89, *European Court Reports*, vol. 199, pt. 1, p. 3813.

have been caused. As a result, the institutions made a manifest error of assessment of both the injury caused and the question of causation.

In their pleadings, the applicants argue that Community producers of SSBBs engaged in the same anti-competitive practices as those imputed [by the Commission] in Decision 98/247 to Community producers of flat products. They also argue, in the alternative, that, whether or not Community producers of SSBBs did engage in such practices, the practices of Community producers of flat products necessarily influenced the price of SSBBs. Whichever is the case, the Community institutions neglected to take these factors into account in their assessment of the injury.

The applicants explain, . . . that, throughout the period under consideration in the anti-subsidy investigation, Community producers of SSBBs systematically applied, in respect of their European sales, a surcharge system that was identical, *mutatis mutandis*,[209] to the alloy surcharge system censured in Decision 98/247, the surcharge applied to SSBBs simply being the product of multiplying the surcharge applicable to flat products by a "yield factor" of 1.35. The fact that all Community producers of SSBBs uniformly applied that factor was confirmed by the Commission in . . . [a decision it made on] 21 April 1999.

The applicants conclude that, from February 1994 onwards, SSBBs produced within the Community were also being sold at inflated prices. They emphasize that, according to . . . Decision 98/247, following the imposition of the alloy surcharge, the price of stainless steel increased almost two-fold between January 1994 and March 1995. They also point out that the price of SSBBs changed in much the same way as did the price of flat products over the course of the years in question and maintain that such significant price distortion could not have been overlooked in the anti-subsidy proceedings, particularly in establishing price undercutting, the appropriate level of profitability in the Community industry and loss of market share.

. . . Thus, other than the worsening results of the Community industry, the Commission had no adequate, reliable information from which it could reach a firm view of any injury caused.

As regards causation, the applicants argue, similarly, that the adverse effects allegedly sustained by the Community industry are attributable not to imports of SSBBs from India but to "other factors," namely the conduct of producers of flat products and its effect on the price of SSBBs.

***

In response to the argument advanced by the applicants, the Council contends that the prices charged on the SSBB market could not be regarded as artificially high given that Community SSBB producers had not acted in concert to fix those prices. The application of the yield factor and the fixing of its level, as well as the fixing of the final price of SSBBs, was a matter of free choice for each SSBB producer and was not the inevitable result of decisions taken in concert by producers of flat products. The Council submits that these are distinct products which are not substitutable for SSBBs and that there are therefore no grounds for concluding that anti-competitive conduct of the part of producers of flat products had any effect on the prices charged on the market for SSBBs.

Findings of the Court

According to Article 1(1) of the Basic Regulation, a countervailing duty may be imposed for the purpose of offsetting any subsidy granted, directly or indirectly, for the manufacture, production, export, or transport of any product whose release for free circulation in the Community causes injury.

Article 8 of the Basic Regulation provides:

1. For the purposes of this regulation, the term "injury" shall, unless otherwise specified, be taken to mean material injury to the Community industry. . . .

***

2. It must be demonstrated, from all the relevant evidence . . . , that the subsidised imports are causing injury within the meaning of this regulation. . . .

3. Known factors other than the subsidised imports which are injuring the Community industry at the same time shall also be examined to ensure that injury caused by these other factors is not attributed to the subsidised imports pursuant to paragraph 6. Factors which may be considered in this respect include . . . restrictive trade practices of . . . third country and Community producers. . . .

Under Article 15(1) of the Basic Regulation,

[w]here the facts as finally established show the existence of countervailable subsidies and injury caused thereby, and the Community interest calls for intervention . . ., a definitive countervailing duty shall be imposed by the Council. . . .

Articles 15 and 19 of the ASCM, headed "Determination of Injury" and "Imposition and Collection of Countervailing Duties," respectively, contain substantially the same provisions as those cited in . . . [the] present judgment.

---

[209][Latin: "with the necessary changes having been made."]

As regards the implementation of those provisions by the Community institutions, it must be remembered that the question whether a Community industry has suffered injury and, if so, whether that injury is attributable to dumped or subsidized imports involves the assessment of complex economic matters in respect of which, according to settled case-law, the institutions enjoy a wide discretion. Consequently, judicial review of any such assessment must be confined to ascertaining whether the procedural rules have been complied with, whether the facts on which the contested decision is based have been accurately stated and whether there has been any manifest error of assessment of the facts or any misuse of powers.[210]

As regards, more specifically, review of compliance with the procedural rules, the Court of Justice held, in paragraph 16 of its judgment in Extramet II, a case involving dumping, that, in determining the injury, the Council and the Commission are under an obligation to consider whether the injury on which they intend to base their conclusions actually derives from dumped imports and must disregard any injury deriving from other factors, particularly from the conduct of Community producers themselves. In that case, having found nothing in the preamble to the regulation at issue to show that the institutions had actually considered whether the Community industry might itself have contributed, by its refusal to sell, to the damage sustained or that the institutions had established that the injury found did not derive from the factors mentioned by Extramet, the Court held that the Community institutions had not followed the proper procedure in establishing the injury.

In the present case, however, it is clear from both . . . recital[s] in . . . the Provisional Regulation and . . . the Contested Regulation that the institutions did consider whether the Community industry might not itself have contributed, by its anti-competitive conduct, to the injury suffered, as the applicants alleged during the administrative procedure. So, as regards the procedural requirement laid down by the Court of Justice in Extramet II, the institutions did, formally at least, set about determining the injury in the proper way.

It nevertheless remains to be established whether the institutions made a manifest error of assessment in as much as, when deciding whether or not injury had been caused and whether or not there was any causal link between any such injury and the subsidised imports, they overlooked all factors other than the imports in question, including the matters which the applicants alleged were damaging the Community industry at the same time. It is for the applicants to adduce evidence to enable the Court of First Instance to find that such an error was made.[211]

In this connection, the applicants have argued that SSBB prices had been artificially inflated either by concerted application of the alloy surcharge by SSBB producers themselves, this being the applicants' principal argument, abandoned at the hearing, or by concerted application by producers of flat products of the alloy surcharge in conjunction with uniform application by SSBB producers of the yield factor, this being the applicants' alternative argument, maintained at the hearing. SSBB prices could not, therefore, provide a reliable basis on which to establish price undercutting in respect of Indian products.

In the present proceedings the Council does not dispute the fact that, as a matter of practice in the Community iron and steel industry, SSBB prices are calculated by adding together a base price and an alloy surcharge calculated by multiplying the alloy surcharge applied by producers of flat products by a yield factor of 1.35. Moreover, in its decision of 21 April 1999, the Commission acknowledged that Community producers of SSBBs had been applying this factor of 1.35 for at least 10 years. It also emerged from information provided by the institutions at the hearing that the Commission discovered in the course of its investigations that producers of hot-rolled bars (a product falling . . . constituting the main input in the manufacture of SSBBs to the extent of making up approximately 85 percent of their final sale price) also calculated the alloy surcharge applicable to their own products by multiplying the alloy surcharge for flat products by a factor of 1.2. The Council does not take issue with the transparency for buyers of this mechanism, especially in view of the mandatory publication of the price lists of ECSC producers and dealers.

Nevertheless, the institutions emphasise that they have no evidence that the implementation and application of this formula for calculating the alloy surcharge for SSBBs amounts to a concerted practice by SSBB producers. In its pleadings, the Council argues, more specifically, that each SSBB producer freely exercised its own discretion in fixing the level of, and applying, the yield factor and in fixing the final price of SSBBs, and was not constrained by decisions taken in concert by producers of flat products. Given that these are distinct, non-substitutable products, there are no grounds for concluding that anti-competitive conduct on the part of producers of flat products had any effect on the market prices of SSBBs.

[210]See, *inter alia*. . . Case T-51/96 Miwon v Council, *European Court Reports*, vol. 2000, pt. 1, p. 1841, para. 94.
[211]See Case T-121/95 EFMA v Council, *id*., vol. 1997, pt. 2, p. 2391, para. 106. . . .

This argument of the institutions cannot be accepted and it must be held that their assessment of the injury and of the causal link between the injury and the subsidised imports set out in the Contested Regulation is vitiated by a manifest error.

Indeed, in circumstances such as those of the present case, the simple fact that it could not be proved that the final sale prices of SSBBs were fixed by Community producers acting in concert does not mean that those prices were to be regarded as reliable and consistent with normal market conditions in the determination of the injury sustained by those producers as a result of subsidised Indian imports. On the contrary, given that changes in the price of flat products were closely mirrored by changes in the price of hot-rolled bars and SSBBs, because producers of hot-rolled bars and SSBBs uniformly and consistently applied to the alloy surcharge for flat products a yield factor of 1.2 and 1.35 respectively, the institutions ought to have accepted that the anti-competitive conduct of producers of flat products could have had significant repercussions on SSBB prices, most likely increasing them artificially, even though SSBB prices themselves were not directly the subject of any unlawful concerted practice on the part of producers.

That is all the more true in a context in which the Commission found, in its decision of 21 April 1999, that "flat products represent about 85 pecent of the ECSC finished products, delivered by EU producers" and that, "due to the importance of flat products, price developments in the stainless steel markets are very often driven by pricing decisions of flat products producers."

Thus, by failing to take account of the uniform, consistent industrial practice of Community producers of SSBBs and hot-rolled bars, the objective effect of which was automatically to mirror, in the markets for those products, the artificial price increases achieved through concertation by producers of flat products, the institutions disregarded a known factor, other than the subsidised imports, which might have been a concurrent cause of the injury sustained by the Community industry.

***

Moreover, contrary to the Council's submission, the incontrovertible fact that one component of the final sale price of SSBBs (namely the amount of alloy surcharge applied to flat products, before application of the yield factor of 1.35) was artificially increased as a result of unlawful concerted practices on the part of producers of flat products was bound to affect the final sale prices of SSBBs, rendering them unreliable.

First of all, in a market where it is industry practice to calculate the final sale price of a product by adding together a number of distinct items, it is clear that external factors affecting the amount of one or other of those items will, in the absence of exceptional circumstances, necessarily have an effect on the final sales price. That effect is likely to be even more marked in a market such as the market in SSBBs, where the prices of the principal manufacturing input, which represented approximately 85 percent of their final sale price . . ., will also have been affected by the same external factors and where the mechanism determining the prices of that input is transparent and understood by purchasers and vendors alike, in particular, by virtue of ECSC price lists.

Secondly, the Council's reasoning stands in contradiction to the Commission's own finding in Decision 98/247. There, the Commission found that the concerted amendment of the reference values for the formula for calculating the alloy surcharge applicable to flat products, whilst not being the sole cause of the near doubling of prices of stainless steel flat products between January 1994 and March 1995, had nevertheless "greatly contributed to it through the mechanical price increase that it caused."

***

In view of the foregoing, the Court finds that the argument which the applicants put forward in the alternative is well founded.

***

On those grounds, THE COURT OF FIRST INSTANCE (First Chamber, Extended Composition), hereby. . . Annuls Council Regulation (EC) No 2450/98 of 13 November 1998 imposing a definitive countervailing duty on imports of stainless steel bars originating in India. . . ■

CASEPOINT: The Court of First Instance for the EU found that although the Stainless Steel Bright Bars (SSBBs) imported into Europe might have been subsidized by India, the exporting country, there were other factors that had significant influence on the price of the SSBBs in Europe. EU and WTO rules require that countervailing duties may be imposed only if it has been concluded, through proper investigation, that the subsidized imports cause material injury to a European Community (EC) industry. There was evidence that European producers of SSBBs engaged in certain anti-competitive practices, similar to those those imputed [by an earlier EU decision] to European producers of flat products, and that such practices necessarily influenced the price of SSBBs. The court found that the countervailing duties must be withdrawn in this case, since the EC institutions neglected to take these other factors into account in their assessment of the injury to the local industry.

Developing States and States Transitioning to Market Economies

Developing states are given special treatment in the SCM Agreement. The least developed states and developing states with a per capita income of less than U.S. $1,000 are allowed to use subsidies based on export performance and were given until the year 2003 to phase out subsidies based on domestic content.[212] Other developing states were required to phase out both kinds of subsidies by the end of 1999.[213] Less rigorous procedures were also applied to developing countries with respect to remedies and countervailing duties.[214]

States in the process of transforming themselves from centrally planned to market economies were allowed to adopt programs necessary to facilitate the transformation, and they were given until 2002 to phase out any existing prohibited and actionable subsidies.[215] How these developments are to be phased in is one of the many items under negotiation as part of the Doha round.

SAFEGUARDS

safeguard: An emergency action that a WTO member state may take in order to protect its domestic industry from serious injury due to a sudden increase in the quantity of an imported product.

Agreement on Safeguards: Establishes multilateral controls over the use of safeguards by WTO member states.

Safeguards are emergency actions that a WTO member state may take to protect its domestic industries from serious injury from a sudden increase in the quantity of an imported product. Until the **Agreement on Safeguards** was adopted with the inauguration of WTO, the provisions of Article XIX (entitled "Emergency Actions on Imports of Particular Products") of GATT 1947 governed safeguards. The problem with this was that Article XIX was simply ignored by the GATT 1947 contracting parties.[216] Instead of withdrawing concessions in the manner provided for by Article XIX, states found it easier to resort to alternative protectionist devices that limited exports instead of imports. Examples were *orderly marketing arrangements* (OMAs)[217] and *voluntary export restraints* (VERs).[218]

Even though OMAs, VERs, and other similar arrangements are restraints on exports, they nevertheless violate GATT,[219] and it is the purpose of the Agreement on Safeguards to establish multilateral control over them and over safeguards in general. Thus, safeguard measures in existence at the time the WTO was inaugurated[220] had to be phased out by the end of 1999,[221] and new safeguards can be instituted only in specific limited cases and only for limited time periods.

A WTO member state may apply safeguard measures against a product only after conducting an official investigation to determine that the product is being imported into its territory in such increased quantities and under such conditions as to cause or threaten to cause

---

[212]Agreement on Subsidies and Countervailing Measures, Article 27, paras. 2 and 2 bis (1994).
[213]*Id.*
[214]*Id.*, Article 27, paras. 6–14.
[215]*Id.*, Article 29, paras. 1–2.
[216]John Kraus, *The GATT Negotiations: A Business Guide to the Results of the Uruguay Round*, p. 37 (1994).
[217]OMAs are formal agreements between importing and exporting states as to the quantity of a particular product that the exporting state will export to the importing state. OMAs that include industry participation are known as *voluntary restraint agreements* (VRAs). Organization for Economic Cooperation and Development, *Obstacles to Trade and Competition*, p. 17 (1993).
[218]VERs are government-sponsored arrangements among exporting firms that limit exports to a predetermined ceiling. *Id.*
[219]Although sometimes classed as being within a "gray area" under GATT because they involved exports (*id.*, p. 21), both VERs and OMAs, as well as other forms of export restraint agreements, clearly violate GATT. Article XI, para. 1, of GATT provides: "No prohibitions or restrictions other than duties, taxes, or other charges, whether made effective through quotas, import or *export* licenses, or other measures, shall be instituted or maintained by any member on the importation of any product of the territory of any other member or on the *exportation or sale for export* of any product destined for the territory of any other member." (Emphasis added.)
[220]See Kent A. Jones, *Export Restraint and the New Protectionism: The Political Economy of Discriminatory Trade Restrictions*, pp. 12–17 (1994), for a list of voluntary restraints and similar measures that were in existence as of mid-1990.
[221]Agreement on Safeguards, paras. 21 and 22(b) (1994).
An exception allowed each importing member state to maintain one existing OMA or VER until the end of 1999. *Id.*, para. 23. One example is mentioned in the Annex to the Agreement on Safeguards. It involves an agreement between the EU and Japan on certain types of motor vehicles. According to the WTO, no other member took advantage of this exception. See "Understanding the WTO—Agreements: Anti-dumping, subsidies, safeguards, contingencies, etc." posted on the Internet at http://www.wto.org/english/thewto_e/whatis_e/tif_e/agrm8_e.htm.

serious injury to the domestic industry that produces like or directly competitive products.[222] The measures must then be applied to a product (1) regardless of its origin (i.e., the GATT principle of nondiscrimination applies)[223] and (2) only for the time and to the extent necessary to prevent or remedy serious injury and to facilitate adjustment.[224]

To encourage domestic industries to make adjustments, any safeguard measure that is to last longer than one year must be progressively liberalized at regular intervals over its lifetime. If it is to last for more than three years, a review must be made by its midterm to determine if the measure should be withdrawn or liberalized more quickly.[225]

In late 2006, the WTO published the latest statistics on safeguards actions notified by WTO members pursuant to the Agreement on Safeguards. According to these statistics, from January 1, 1995, until October 23, 2006, a total of 155 safeguard investigations were initiated, and a total of 76 safeguard measures were imposed. These figures were far smaller than antidumping (2938 initiations and 1875 measures for the period January 1, 1995–June 30, 2006) and relatively small compared to countervailing duty measures (183 initiations and 113 measures for the same period.) (http://www.wto.org/english/news_e/news06_e/sfg_29nov06_e.htm)

The number of safeguard investigations newly initiated during the most recent period was 13. The number of new initiations of safeguard investigations peaked in 2002 at 34, and the figure has stayed low since then, with 15 initiations, 14 initiations, and 7 initiations in 2003, 2004, and 2005, respectively. The member notifying the largest number of new initiations since 1995 was India, with 15 initiations. Chile and Jordan followed with 11 initiations each and Turkey and the United States with 10 initiations each. The 13 initiations reported for the most recent period (January 1–October 23, 2006) were by Argentina, Chile, Indonesia, Jordan, Panama, the Philippines, Tunisia (2 initiations) and Turkey (5 initiations).

Concerning application of new final safeguard measures, during the period January 1–October 23, 2006, six new measures (of which Turkey notified four) were imposed. This was basically in line with the recent level — four new measures imposed in 2004 and four in 2005. Since 1995, India has reported the largest number of measures (eight), followed by Chile, Turkey, and the United States (six measures each), followed by Jordan and the Philippines (five measures each)[226]

AGRICULTURE

Agriculture has always been one of the most difficult items on the WTO agenda. All nations want to protect and assist their farmers, and many governments provide them with substantial financial subsidies. This obviously distorts the free market for, and has a substantial effect on the prices of, agricultural goods around the world. The reduction and/or elimination of the subsidies is one of the central and most difficult matters that has prolonged the Doha negotiations. While the EU and the United States have attempted to obtain tariff reductions from other nations for their exports, other countries and regional groups have demanded that the EU and the United States substantially reduce their agricultural subsidies in return. The **Agreement on Agriculture** establishes guidelines for "initiating a process of reform of trade in agriculture." Its ultimate goal is the establishment of a market-oriented system for trade in agricultural products that is free of restrictions and distortions.

To begin the process of reform, the agreement (1) specifies the agricultural products it governs; (2) requires that nontariff barriers to agricultural imports be converted into customs tariffs; (3) defines permissible forms of domestic supports; (4) defines export subsidies; (5) phases in initial reductions in tariffs, impermissible domestic support measures, and export subsidies during a six-year implementation period (developing countries are given a

Agreement on Agriculture: Establishes guidelines for initiating a process of reform to progressively integrate international trade in agricultural products into the GATT system.

---

[222]*Id.*, para. 2.
[223]*Id.*, para. 5.
[224]*Id.*, para. 10.
[225]Id., para. 13
[226]Agreement on Agriculture, Preamble (1994).

ten-year period); and (6) progressively integrates international trade in agricultural products into the GATT system.

The agricultural products governed by the agreement include foodstuffs (except for fish and fish products), hides, skins, animal hairs, raw cotton, raw flax, raw hemp, raw silk, and certain related products.[227]

Upon becoming members of the WTO and parties to the Agreement on Agriculture, states agreed to convert their existing nontariff barriers to agricultural imports (including quotas, levies, and licenses)[228] into equivalent customs tariffs. The process for doing this involved taking the difference in internal and external prices and making appropriate adjustments (for differences in quality or variety, for freight and other charges, and for other elements that provided protection to domestic producers).[229] These tariff rates were then incorporated into a Schedule of Concessions that each member state deposited with the GATT Secretariat to be appended to GATT 1994 along with its commitment to reduce its tariff rates during the implementation period.[230] On average, agricultural tariffs were reduced 36 percent for developed countries and 24 percent for developing countries.[231] With a few exceptions, all of these tariffs are bound (i.e., guaranteed against increase).[232]

As was mentioned, domestic agricultural support measures can sometimes restrict or distort trade. Developed states have agreed to reduce the monetary impact of measures that have this effect by 20 percent and developing countries by 13.3 percent (two-thirds of 20 percent) during the implementation period.[233] Not all support measures restrict or distort trade, however, and the Agreement on Agriculture defines those that are exempt. Exempt measures must satisfy two basic requirements: (1) they must be publicly funded government programs and (2) they must not have the effect of providing price supports to producers. Examples include support for research, pest and disease control, training services, extension and advisory services, inspection services, marketing and promotion services, and infrastructure services; food security and domestic food aid; direct payments to producers (including income support that is not linked to production); participation in social or crop disaster insurance; structural adjustment assistance; environmental protection; and regional assistance programs.[234]

Export subsidies for agricultural products can similarly restrict or distort trade. As with domestic support measures, the developed states have agreed to reduce export subsidies by 36 percent and developing states by 24 percent during the implementation period.[235] These measures are defined in the Agreement on Agriculture as subsidies that are contingent upon export performance.[236] Examples include direct government payments that are contingent upon export performance; the sale for export of governmental noncommercial stocks of agricultural products at less than their fair market value; government payments to exporters even when financed from levies on the exports; subsidies for marketing or transporting exports; and subsidies on farm products contingent on their incorporation in exported products.[237]

The Agreement on Agriculture provides for the gradual phasing in of member state obligations. In addition to the six-year implementation period (ten years for developing states) for

---

[227]*Id.*, Article 2.
[228]*Id.*, Article 4, para. 2, n. 1.
[229]*Id.*, Attachment to Annex 5.
[230]Uruguay Round Protocol to the General Agreement on Tariffs and Trade 1994, para. 1.
[231]See "Understanding the WTO—Agreements: Agriculture," posted on the Internet at http://www.wto.org/ english/thewto_e/whatis_e/tif_e/agrm3_e. htm.
[232]Agreement on Agriculture, Article 4, p
[233]See "Understanding the WTO—Agreements: Agriculture," posted on the Internet at http://www.wto.org/ english/thewto_e/whatis_e/tif_e/agrm3_e.htm.
    The means for determining the value of these support measures is described in Agreement on Agriculture, Article 1(a), (d), and (h) (1994).
[234]*Id.*, Annex 2.
[235]See "Understanding the WTO—Agreements: Agriculture," posted on the Internet at http://www.wto.org/ english/thewto_e/whatis_e/tif_e/agrm3_e.htm.
[236]Agreement on Agriculture, Article 1(e) (1994).
[237]*Id.*, Article 9, para. 1.

reducing tariffs, impermissible domestic support measures, and export subsidies, there was a nine-year transition period during which measures and supports maintained in conformity with the agreement would not be subject to actions otherwise available under the GATT and the SCM Agreement unless they cause or threaten to cause injury.[238] Even then, member states agree to exercise "due restraint" before initiating any countervailing duty investigations.[239]

TEXTILES AND CLOTHING

Agreement on Textiles and Clothing: Establishes a process for the phasing out of existing special arrangements governing international trade in textiles and clothing and the integration of those products into the GATT system.

The **Agreement on Textiles and Clothing** is designed to eliminate the current system of special arrangements governing international trade in these products. Prior to its adoption, a series of collateral arrangements had been entered into by the states principally involved in the clothing and textiles trade that created an exception to the GATT principle of protection through tariffs.

These arrangements came about because of the rapid growth in the 1950s of cotton textile imports into the United States from low-cost suppliers, most notably Japan. Under pressure from its own textile industry, the U.S. government negotiated concessions from Japan and other low-cost exporters to voluntarily limit their textile exports. Then, in 1961, the United States proposed that GATT agree to administer an "arrangement for the orderly development of the trade in such products . . . while at the same time avoiding disruptive conditions in import markets."[240] The European Community (which had a long-standing policy of restricting the importation of nearly all textiles) and other importing states supported the American initiative. The low-cost exporting states reluctantly agreed to the proposal bo in the hopes that it might improve access to the European market and avoid the unilateral imposition of restrictions by the other importing states, especially the United States. A one-year Short-Term Arrangement Regarding Trade in Cotton Textiles, adopted in 1961, evolved into a Long-Term Arrangement Regarding Trade in Cotton Textiles, which was replaced in 1973 by the Arrangement Regarding International Trade in Textiles, commonly known as the Multi-Fiber Arrangement (MFA).[241]

The MFA was important because it applied to about half of the developed world's $100 billion worth of imports from developing countries. It allowed participating states to establish quantitative limits on imports of textiles through bilateral restraint agreements. Unlike the Generalized System of Preferences and the South-South Preferences (discussed earlier), the MFA was not designed to give preferences to developing states. Quite to the contrary, it overtly allowed developed states to discriminate against developing states. Although the MFA itself came to an end with the adoption of the Agreement on Textiles and Clothing, the quotas that it established and that were in existence on December 31, 1994, were carried forward under the new agreement.

The Agreement on Textiles and Clothing provides for the complete elimination of the MFA at the end of a ten-year transition period. Upon the agreement's adoption, WTO member states had to remove at least 16 percent of their textile and clothing imports from quota controls. An additional 17 percent was removed as of 1998, another 18 percent as of 2001, and the remaining quotas were to be removed by 2005. At that time, all the WTO member states' international trade in clothing and textiles was to be fully "integrated" into GATT 1994, and all quantitative restrictions inconsistent with GATT were to be abolished.[242] However, there are still some matters remaining to be resolved as of 2008.

Once textiles and clothing are fully integrated into the GATT system, the Agreement on Textiles and Clothing itself will come to an end. It is the only WTO multilateral agreement that provides for its own termination.[243]

---

[238]*Id.*, Article 13, paras. 1 and 3.
[239]*Id.*, paras. 2(a) and 3(a).
[240]Gardner Paterson, *Discrimination in International Trade: The Policy Issues, 1945–1965*, p. 309 (1966).
[241]See GATT Secretariat Study, *Textiles and Clothing in the World Economy* (1984).
[242]Agreement on Textiles and Clothing, Article 2, paras. 6, 8 (1994).
[243]See "Understanding the WTO—Agreements: Textiles," posted on the Internet at http://www.wto.org/english/ thewto_e/whatis_e/tif_e/agrm5_e.htm.

RULES OF ORIGIN

As the WTO itself says "Determining where a product comes from is no longer easy when raw materials and parts criss-cross the globe to be used as inputs in scattered manufacturing plants. Rules of origin are important in implementing such trade policy instruments as anti-dumping and countervailing duties, origin marking, and safeguard measures."[244] The **Agreement on Rules of Origin** is essentially a program outlining procedures for bringing about an international system of harmonized rules of origin. **Rules of origin** are the laws, regulations, and administrative procedures used by states to determine the country of origin of goods.[245] The program for harmonization was instituted with the inauguration of the WTO and is being carried out in conjunction with the Customs Cooperation Council (CCC).[246] The agreement called for the program to be completed by mid-1998; however, "due to the complexity of [the] issues" involved, the WTO postponed the completion date to November 1999, which was subsequently postponed to 2005, but no agreement was reached by the end of 2007.

According to the guidelines set out in the Agreement on Rules of Origin, the resulting rules of origin are to be (1) coherent;[247] (2) objective, understandable, and predictable; (3) administered in a consistent, uniform, impartial, and reasonable manner; (4) applied equally to each member state's nonpreferential commercial policy instruments (e.g., most-favored-nation treatment, anti-dumping and countervailing duties, safeguard measures, origin marking requirements, quantitative restrictions, and tariff quotas); and (5) based on a positive standard (i.e., one that states what confers, rather than what does not confer, origin). Furthermore, the rules are not to be used as instruments of trade policy, nor should they restrict, distort, or disrupt trade. Finally, the *country of origin* is to be the one where a particular good was obtained or, when more than one country is involved in its production, the one in which the last substantial transformation is carried out.

During the transition period, these same principles are to govern the member states' existing rules. In addition, both during and after the transition, member states are required to observe the basic GATT principles of nondiscrimination[274] and transparency.[248] Finally, the usual GATT 1994 procedures for review, consultation, and dispute settlement apply.[249]

Agreement on Rules of Origin: Establishes a three-year program aimed at bringing about an international system of harmonized rules of origin.

rules of origin: Laws, regulations, and administrative procedures used by states for determining the country of origin of goods.

---

[244]http://www.wto.org/english/tratop_e/roi_e/roi_e.htm.
[245]Agreement on Rules of Origin, Article 1, para. 1 (1994).
[246]*Id.*, Article 9, para. 1.
[247]Agreement on Rules of Origin, para. 1(f) (1994).
[248]*Id.*, Article 3(e).
      A member state's laws, regulations, administrative actions, and court decisions establishing, implementing, or interpreting rules of origin must be promptly published. *Id.* Also, copies must be filed with the WTO Secretariat. *Id.*, Article 5.
[249]*Id.*, Articles 6, 7, and 8.

Chapter Questions

Customs Valuation

1. The Widget Company has just imported 10,000 widgets into State A. Describe how the Customs Service of State A, a signatory of the Customs Valuation Code, will go about determining the value of these goods in the process of collecting an import tariff.

WTO Import Restrictions

2. Several automobile manufacturers from State J are importing large numbers of cars to State K, taking over a large share of K's automobile market and putting K's own automobile manufacturers and workers out of business. State J's manufacturers are not subsidized by State J, nor are they dumping their cars at below-cost prices. Under GATT 1994, what can State K do? Discuss.

3. State D and State V are both members of the WTO. At the time of joining the WTO, State D prohibited the importation of foreign-grown rice. The prohibition has never been lifted. Presently, rice

in State D sells for about four times the world price. State V, a large grower of rice, wants access to State D's market. Under GATT 1994, what can State V do? Discuss.

4. State R, a country with a centrally planned economy, uses prison labor to manufacture export goods at very low cost. When State S learns this, it imposes an import embargo on these goods. Both countries are members of the WTO, and State R complains to the WTO's Dispute Settlement Body. Assuming that a Dispute Settlement Panel is appointed to resolve this matter, how will the panel rule? Explain.

Sanitary and Phytosanitary Restriction Measures

5. Recently, State E, concerned that its nationals are being poisoned by chemical growth stimulants fed to livestock to make them grow faster and heavier, enacted legislation that forbids its livestock producers from using these stimulants and also forbids the sale of any meat from such animals within its territory. The law also forbids the importation of any animal fed a growth stimulant or any product from such an animal. Because it is impossible to detect the growth stimulant either in live animals or in their meat, the legislation requires importers to certify that the animals (or the animals from which an animal product is derived) have never been fed a growth stimulant.

  The livestock producers in State F have been using growth stimulants for many years to grow larger animals at lower cost, and they believe any possible health risk to consumers is insignificant. State F's Ministry of Health also agrees that growth stimulants pose little risk to consumers, and it encourages its livestock producers to use them. Because State F's livestock producers are no longer able to export their animals or the products from those animals to State E, they have asked their government to take action through the WTO on their behalf. Both State E and State F are members of the WTO. Consultation with State E proved unsuccessful, so State F asked the WTO's Dispute Settlement Body to appoint a Dispute Settlement Panel. This has been done. How should the panel rule on State F's request for a finding that State E's legislation violates the latter's obligations under GATT 1994? Discuss.

Countervailing Duties

6. State H provides general subsidies to all of its export manufacturers by means of low-cost loans, foreign currency exchange guarantees, and discounted prices for fuel and electricity purchased from the state's energy monopoly. HowdyDoo Company, a State H manufacturer of shampoos that has taken advantage of all of these subsidies, exports its goods to State I, where its products are in direct competition with those of several local manufacturers. State I's manufacturers have complained to their government, asking it to impose a countervailing duty on HowdyDoo. Both State H and State I are members of the WTO. Should the countervailing duty be imposed? Explain.

7. State C is a major exporter of lumber products (especially plywood) to State U. State C's lumber companies are able to manufacture and sell their products in State U inexpensively because (unlike State U) State C's government charges only a nominal fee for cutting lumber in its national forests. In State U, on the other hand, the cutting fee is substantial, adding 15 to 20 percent to the cost of the finished lumber product. One of State U's plywood lumber companies, Multi-Ply, Inc., has lost much of its market share in State U due to imports from State C. Multi-Ply has complained to State U's government, arguing that State C is unfairly subsidizing its lumber companies by charging such a low forest-cutting fee. Multi-Ply would like State U's government to impose a countervailing duty on imports of plywood from State C. May State U do so? Note that both State C and State U are members of the WTO. Discuss.

Anti-dumping Duties

8. The Snicker Company, the largest manufacturer of Snickerdoodles in State F, decided about two years ago to enter the cookie market in State G. Several small companies in State G manufacture Snickerdoodles, but the market has traditionally been very small. When Snicker entered State G's market, it undertook a widespread advertising campaign to promote Snickerdoodle consumption and to encourage consumers to try its product by publishing coupons in newspapers that allowed purchasers to buy Snicker's Snickerdoodles below their actual cost. As a consequence of this campaign, the sales of Snickerdoodles in State G have skyrocketed. In addition, the sales of Snickerdoodles manufactured by State G firms have more than tripled. State G's Snickerdoodle manufacturers are, nonetheless, displeased, because their market share has gone from 100 percent to 30 percent in two years. Concerned with this loss, they have asked State G to impose anti-dumping duties on Snicker, since its snickerdoodles are being sold below cost. Both State F and State G are members of the WTO. Should State G impose anti-dumping duties on Snicker? Explain.

National Product Standards

9. State Z's automobile manufacturing industry is one of the largest and most highly regarded in the world. The industry is concerned that it may lose some of its domestic market share to inexpensive, low-quality cars manufactured in newly industrialized countries. To avoid this, the industry lobbies the State Z government until it enacts new standards for the sale of cars in the country. The standards are set in such a way that only cars manufactured in State Z can meet them. Assuming that State Z is a member of the WTO, can the governments of those newly industrialized countries (also members of the WTO) do anything to get State Z to rescind its new standards? Explain.

National Security and Public Morals

10. Eve, a national of State A, owns the technology for manufacturing a video game called "Porn-Man" that involves the use of the latest and most advanced computer technology to show lifelike images of Porn-Man doing truly obscene things. State A is a member of the WTO and of the Coordinating Committee on Multilateral Export Controls (COCOM). State A's government has issued an administrative order prohibiting Eve from (1) exporting the computer chips to State O (a country that is listed in State A's export-control legislation as being off limits for all high-technology exports), where the video games are supposed to be assembled and (2) reimporting assembled and operational video games back into State A. Eve has brought suit in a State A court to obtain the appropriate order to lift the government's prohibition. What are the chances of her success? Discuss.

Relevant Internet Sites

http://www.wto.org is a huge site containing detailed information on all aspects of the WTO, including history, news, agreements, dispute settlement procedures and results, and much more information on all the issues discussed in this chapter.

http://globaledge.msu.edu/index.asp is a large site, sponsored by Michigan State University, that contains a great deal of information on legal issues involved in international trade and other topics of international and global interest.

http://library.lawschool.cornell.edu/RESOURCES/International_Resources is part of the extensive Cornell University online library, with resources on all legal topics; this is the URL for the index to available international online resources.

CHAPTER 8
SERVICES AND LABOR

INTRODUCTION

This chapter examines the international rules that govern services and labor. The rules on services are now found principally in the General Agreement on Trade in Services and in the agreements creating certain regional economic organizations such as the EU and the North American Free Trade Area. The rules governing labor—especially the movement of laborers—are to be found in the international labor standards promulgated by the International Labor Organization, in the agreements creating some regional organizations, and in national legislation.

General Agreement on Trade in Services(GATS): Multilateral agreement in force from January 1, 1995, that contains rules and principles governing international trade in services and establishes guidelines for negotiating the future liberalization of such trade.

GENERAL AGREEMENT ON TRADE IN SERVICES

The **General Agreement on Trade in Services (GATS)** came into effect on January 1, 1995, as one of the three main multilateral annexes to the Agreement Establishing the World Trade Organization (the other two being the General Agreement on Tariffs and Trade [GATT] and the Agreement on Trade-Related Aspects of Intellectual Property Rights [TRIPS]). The purpose of GATS is to give international trade in services a set of rules and principles and a basis for liberalization similar to those that GATT has applied to goods for the past five decades.

GATS is made up of three interrelated components: (1) the agreement itself (often called the *Framework Agreement*),[1] which contains the rules applicable to all member states of the World Trade Organization (which are automatically parties to the GATS); (2) the sectoral annexes that deal with issues unique to particular economic sectors (i.e., movement of natural persons, air transport services, financial services, maritime transport services, and telecommunications); and (3) the national Schedules of Specific Commitments each member state has agreed to undertake, which were agreed to mainly through negotiations undertaken as part of the Uruguay Round of Multilateral Trade Negotiations that produced the WTO Agreement (see Chapter 7).

THE FRAMEWORK AGREEMENT

The Framework Agreement lays out the basic parameters of GATS in six parts. These parts deal with (1) the scope and definition of GATS, (2) general obligations and disciplines of member states, (3) obligations and disciplines concerning specific commitments of member states, (4) a schedule for progressively liberalizing the world's trade in services, (5) the institutional structure for implementing GATS, and (6) miscellaneous provisions (including definitions of key terms).

Although much of GATS is based on the provisions in GATT and uses much of the same terminology, the "architecture" of GATS is significantly different. Unlike GATT, which provides for a single set of obligations that apply to all measures affecting trade in goods, GATS contains two sets of obligations: (1) a set of general principles and rules that apply to all measures affecting trade in services and (2) a set of principles and rules that apply only to the specific sectors and subsectors that are listed in a member state's schedule. The consequence of this division of obligations is that the principles and rules in GATS, as we shall see, are less binding than those in GATT.[2]

Scope and Definition

The Framework Agreement covers all trade in services in any sector except those supplied in the exercise of governmental functions; however, the agreement does not define either service or service sector. In common usage, a **service** is an act or an action, such as work rendered or performed for another,[3] and this definition seems to fit with the use of the term in the agreement. The dictionary definition of a sector is a division or a part,[4] and the agreement and the GATS annexes provide several examples of service sectors, including banking, finance, insurance, telecommunications, and transportation. Thus, while not defined, the services referred to in the Framework Agreement seem to mean the work performed by one person for another, while **service sectors** are any parts of the economy related to the

service: An act or action, such as work rendered or performed for another.

service sectors: Any parts of the economy involving the performance of a service.

---

[1]John Kraus, *The GATT Negotiations: A Business Guide to the Results of the Uruguay Round*, p. 40 (1994). The texts of GATS and other WTO agreements are available on the Internet at http://www.wto.org/english/docs_e/legal_e/legal_e.htm.

[2]Bernard Hoekman, "The General Agreement on Trade in Services," a paper presented to an OECD Workshop on The New World Trading System, Paris, April 25–26, 1994, reprinted in John H. Jackson, William J. Davey, and Alan O Sykes, Jr., *Legal Problems of International Economic Relations* (4th ed. 2002).

The reason for the difference in the architecture of GATS and GATT relates to the interests of the states involved in its negotiation. The United States, which saw trade liberalization as a means for enhancing its competitiveness, proposed that rules on most-favored-nation (MFN) treatment and national treatment be applied, as they are in GATT, equally to all member states as a general obligation. The EU and several of the major developing countries, which were reluctant to open their markets to foreign (especially U.S.) service suppliers, opposed this concept of *hard* obligations and offered a proposal of *soft* obligations meant to achieve comparable access to markets on a sector-by-sector basis for all participating states. Ultimately, this second proposal prevailed. Thus, MFN treatment was adopted subject to exemptions and national treatment (discussed *id.* below) and was made to apply only to the sectors the member states included in their Schedules of Commitments.

[3]See Indiana Department of State Revenue, Sales Tax Division v. Cable Brazil, Inc., *North Eastern Reporter, Second Series*, vol. 380, p. 555 at p. 561 (Indiana Ct. of Appeals, 1978).

[4]*The American Heritage Dictionary*, p. 1109 (2nd ed., 1985).

performance of such work. The Annex on Movement of Natural Persons makes it clear, however, that the GATS rules apply neither to laborers, except those temporarily involved in delivering a service, nor to member states' laws governing the permanent employment of natural persons.[5] Also, because GATS is but one of the three main annexes to the agreement creating the WTO, it is clear that GATS governs neither trade in goods (which is covered by GATT) nor the trade-related aspects of intellectual property rights (which are covered by TRIPS).

The Framework Agreement does define trade in services. It does so in terms of *modes of supply*. Four modes are described: (1) the cross-border supply of services that do not require the physical movement of either the supplier or the consumer (such as telecommunications), (2) the supply of services that require the consumer to go to the supplier (such as tourism), (3) services supplied by a service supplier[6] from one member state by means of a commercial presence[7] in another member's territory (such as banking), and (4) services supplied in the territory of a member state by a service supplier from another member state by means of the temporary presence of natural persons of another member state (such as construction or consulting work).[8] This four-sided definition is significant both because it broadly covers all forms of trade in services and because member states are allowed to exclude, for particular service sectors or subsectors, one or more of these modes of supply in their Schedules of Specific Commitments.[9]

In Case 8-1, the issue arose as to whether GATT and GATS could apply to the same factual situation or whether they were mutually exclusive.

---

[5]Annex on Movement of Natural Persons Supplying Services under the Agreement, paras. 1–2.
[6]The Framework Agreement defines the term *service supplier* as "any person that supplies a service" (General Agreement on Trade in Services, Article XXVIII, para. g [1994]). It further defines a *person* as "either a natural person or a juridical person" (*id.*, para. [j]).
[7]A *commercial presence* means any type of business or professional establishment, which may be in the form of a subsidiary, a branch, or a representative office. General Agreement on Trade in Services, Article XXVIII, para. (d).
[8]*Id.*, Article I, § 2.
[9]Although the right of member states to make exclusions as to modes of supply is not specifically stated in GATS, this may be inferred from Article XVI, § 1, n. 9, and Article XVII, § 1.

=◄᷾◎᷾▻=

Case 8-1   EUROPEAN COMMUNITIES—REGIME FOR THE IMPORTATION, SALE, AND DISTRIBUTION OF BANANAS
Ecuador, Guatemala, Honduras, Mexico, United States v. European Communities

Case WT/DS27/AB/R, AB-1997-3.
World Trade Organization, Appellate Body (1997).

The European Communities [the name used by the WTO to refer to the EU] and Ecuador, Guatemala, Honduras, Mexico, and the United States (the "Complaining Parties") appeal from certain issues of law and legal interpretations in the Panel Reports, *European Communities—Regime for the Importation, Sale and Distribution of Bananas* (the "Panel Reports"). The

Panel was established on 8 May 1996 to consider a complaint by the Complaining Parties against the European Communities concerning the regime for the importation, sale and distribution of bananas established by Council Regulation (EEC) No. 404/93 of 13 February 1993 on the common organization of the market in bananas ("Regulation 404/93"), and subsequent EC legislation, regulations and administrative measures, including those reflecting the provisions of the Framework Agreement on Bananas (the "BFA"), which implement, supplement, and amend that regime. [The EC legislation, regulations, and measures provided for preferential tariff treatment for former colonies of EC member states that were importing bananas to the EC. The WTO Panel held that the EC was in violation of the General Agreement on Tariffs and Trade of 1994 (GATT 1994) and the General Agreement on Trade in Services (GATS). The Panel recommended that the EC amend its banana tariff regulations to bring them into compliance with both GATT 1994 and GATS. In most respects, the Appellate Body affirmed the Panel's holding on the applicability of GATT 1994. The Appellate Body then considered the applicability of GATS.]

***

C. GENERAL AGREEMENT ON TRADE IN SERVICES

1. Application of the GATS

There are two issues to consider in this context. The first is whether the GATS applies to the EC import licensing procedures. The second is whether the GATS overlaps with the GATT 1994, or whether the two agreements are mutually exclusive. With respect to the first issue, the Panel found that:

> . . . no measures are excluded *a priori* [beforehand] from the scope of the GATS as defined by its provisions. The scope of the GATS encompasses any measure of a Member to the extent [that] it affects the supply of a service regardless of whether such measure directly governs the supply of a service or whether it regulates other matters but nevertheless affects trade in services.

For these reasons, the Panel concluded:

> We therefore find that there is no legal basis for an *a priori* exclusion of measures within the EC banana import licensing regime from the scope of the GATS.

The European Communities argues that the GATS does not apply to the EC import licensing procedures because they are not measures "affecting trade in services" within the meaning of Article I:1 of the GATS. In the view of the European Communities, Regulation 404/93 and the other related regulations deal with the importation, sale, and distribution of bananas. As such, the European Communities asserts, these measures are subject to the GATT 1994, and not to the GATS.

In contrast, the Complaining Parties argue that the scope of the GATS, by its terms, is sufficiently broad to encompass Regulation 404/93 and the other related regulations as measures affecting the competitive relations

between domestic and foreign services and service suppliers. This conclusion, they argue, is not affected by the fact that the same measures are also subject to scrutiny under the GATT 1994, as the two agreements are not mutually exclusive.

In addressing this issue, we note that Article I:1 of the GATS provides that "[t]his Agreement applies to measures by Members affecting trade in services". In our view, the use of the term "affecting" reflects the intent of the drafters to give a broad reach to the GATS. The ordinary meaning of the word "affecting" implies a measure that has "an effect on", which indicates a broad scope of application. This interpretation is further reinforced by the conclusions of previous panels that the term "affecting" in the context of Article III of the GATT is wider in scope than such terms as "regulating" or "governing".[10] We also note that Article I:3(b) of the GATS provides that "'services' includes *any service* in *any sector* except services supplied in the exercise of governmental authority" (emphasis added), and that Article XXVIII(b) of the GATS provides that the "'supply of a service' includes the production, distribution, marketing, sale, and delivery of a service". There is nothing at all in these provisions to suggest a limited scope of application for the GATS. We also agree [with the Panel] that Article XXVIII(c) of the GATS does not narrow "the meaning of the term 'affecting' to 'in respect of.'" For these reasons, we uphold the Panel's finding that there is no legal basis for an *a priori* exclusion of measures within the EC banana import licensing regime from the scope of the GATS.

The second issue is whether the GATS and the GATT 1994 are mutually exclusive agreements. The GATS was not intended to deal with the same subject matter as the GATT 1994. The GATS was intended to deal with a subject matter not covered by the GATT 1994, that is, with trade in services. Thus, the GATS applies to the supply of services. It provides, *inter alia*,[11] for both MFN treatment and national treatment for services and service suppliers. Given the respective scope of application of the two agreements, they may or may not overlap, depending on the nature of the measures at issue. Certain measures could be found to fall exclusively within the scope of the GATT 1994, when they affect trade in goods as goods. Certain measures could be found to fall exclusively within the scope of the GATS, when they affect the supply of services as services. There is yet a third category of measures that could be found to fall within the scope of both the GATT 1994 and the GATS. These are measures that involve a service relating to a particular good or a service supplied in conjunction

---

[10]See, for example, the panel report in *Italian Agricultural Machinery,* adopted 23 October 1958, BISD 7S/60, para. 12.
[11][Latin: "among other things."]

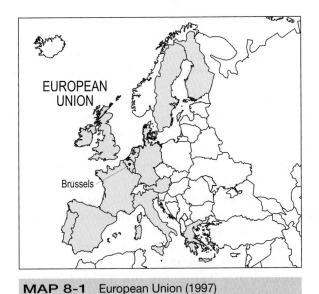

MAP 8-1   European Union (1997)

with a particular good. In all such cases in this third category, the measure in question could be scrutinized under both the GATT 1994 and the GATS. However, while the same measure could be scrutinized under both agreements, the specific aspects of that measure examined under each agreement could be different. Under the GATT 1994, the focus is on how the measure affects the goods involved. Under the GATS, the focus is on how the measure affects the supply of the service or the service suppliers involved. Whether a certain measure affecting the supply of a service related to a particular good is scrutinized under the GATT 1994 or the GATS, or both, is a matter that can only be determined on a case-by-case basis. This was also our conclusion in the Appellate Body Report in *Canada—Periodicals*.[12]

For these reasons, we agree with the Panel that the EC banana import licensing procedures are subject to both the GATT 1994 and the GATS, and that the GATT 1994 and the GATS may overlap in application to a particular measure.

2. Whether Operators Are Service Suppliers Engaged in Wholesale Trade Services

The European Communities raises two issues concerning the definition of wholesale trade services and the application of that definition. Both these issues relate to the Panel's finding that:

> . . . operators in the meaning of Article 19 of Regulation 404/93 and operators performing the activities defined in Article 5 of Regulation 1442/93 are service

suppliers in the meaning of Article I:2(c) of GATS provided that they are owned or controlled by natural persons or juridical persons of other Members and supply wholesale services. When operators provide wholesale services with respect to bananas which they have imported or acquired for marketing, cleared in customs or ripened, they are actual wholesale service suppliers. Where operators form part of vertically integrated companies, they have the capability and opportunity to enter the wholesale service market. They could at any time decide to re-sell bananas which they have imported or acquired from EC producers, or cleared in customs, or ripened instead of further transferring or processing bananas within an integrated company. Since Article XVII of GATS is concerned with conditions of competition, it is appropriate for us to consider these vertically integrated companies as service suppliers for the purposes of analyzing the claims made in this case.

First, the European Communities questions whether the operators within the meaning of the relevant EC regulations are, in fact, service suppliers in the sense of the GATS, in that what they actually do is buy and import bananas. The European Communities argues that "when buying or importing, a wholesale trade services supplier is a buyer or importer and not covered by the GATS at all, because he is not providing any reselling services". The European Communities also challenges the Panel's conclusion that "integrated companies", which may provide some of their services in-house in the production or distribution chain, are service suppliers within the meaning of the GATS.

On the first of these two issues, we agree with the Panel that the operators as defined under the relevant regulations of the European Communities are, indeed, suppliers of "wholesale trade services" within the definition set out in the Headnote to Section 6 of the [Central Product Classification, an international agreement classifying services activities, which is abbreviated as] CPC.[13] We note further that the European Communities has made a full commitment for wholesale trade services (CPC 622), with no conditions or qualifications, in its Schedule of Specific Commitments under the GATS.[14] Although these operators, as defined in the relevant EC regulations, are engaged in some activities that are not strictly within the definition of "distributive trade services" in the Headnote to Section 6 of the CPC, there is no question that they are also engaged in other activities involving the wholesale distribution of bananas that are within that definition.

---

[12]Appellate Body Report, WT/DS31/AB/R, adopted 30 July 1997, p. 19.
[13]Provisional Central Product Classification, United Nations Statistical Papers, Series M, No. 77, 1991, p. 189.
[14]European Communities and their Member States' Schedule of Specific Commitments, GATS/SC/31, 15 April 1994, p. 52.

The Headnote to Section 6 of the CPC defines "distributive trade services" in relevant part as follows:

> ...the principal services rendered by wholesalers and retailers may be characterized as reselling merchandise, accompanied by a variety of related, subordinated services....

We note that the CPC Headnote characterizes the "principal services" rendered by wholesalers as "reselling merchandise". This means that "reselling merchandise" is not necessarily the only service provided by wholesalers. The CPC Headnote also refers to "a variety of related, subordinated services" that may accompany the "principal service" of "reselling merchandise". It is difficult to conceive how a wholesaler could engage in the "principal service" of "reselling" a product if it could not also purchase or, in some cases, import the product. Obviously, a wholesaler must obtain the goods by some means in order to resell them.[15] In this case, for example, it would be difficult to resell bananas in the European Communities if one could not buy them or import them in the first place.

The second issue relates to "integrated companies". In our view, even if a company is vertically-integrated, and even if it performs other functions related to the production, importation, distribution, and processing of a product, to the extent that it is also engaged in providing "wholesale trade services" and is therefore affected in that capacity by a particular measure of a Member in its supply of those "wholesale trade services," that company is a service supplier within the scope of the GATS.

For these reasons, we uphold the Panel's findings on both these issues.

***

The Appellate Body recommends that the Dispute Settlement Body request the European Communities to bring the measures found in this Report and in the Panel Reports, as modified by this Report, to be inconsistent with the GATT 1994 and the GATS into conformity with the obligations of the European Communities under those agreements. ■

CASEPOINT: The Appellate Panel of the WTO considered whether a business operation could be subject to regulation under both GATT (goods) and GATS (services) and decided that this was indeed possible in certain cases. Then the panel held that the actions of banana wholesalers in purchasing, reselling, and conducting "a variety of related services" did constitute the provision of services under GATS.

---

[15]After all, as the European Communities has pointed out, "goods cannot walk" or be resold by themselves (EC's appellant's submission, para. 236).

General Obligations and Disciplines

Two general obligations in the Framework Agreement apply to all WTO member states: (1) most-favored-nation (MFN) treatment and (2) transparency. The **most-favored-nation (MFN) treatment** provision provides that "each member shall accord immediately and unconditionally to services and service suppliers of any other member treatment no less favorable than that it accords to like services and service suppliers of any other country."[16] This means that a privilege a state grants to any country (including non-WTO members), such as allowing a foreign bank to operate within its territory, must be granted immediately and unconditionally to other WTO members.

The MFN treatment rule in the Framework Agreement (unlike the rule in GATT) is not, it is important to note, a binding requirement that must be uniformly observed. During the Uruguay Round negotiations, the representatives of service industries in a number of industrialized nations opposed binding and unconditional MFN treatment on the ground that the level of market openness at that time varied too greatly among countries. They argued that unconditional MFN treatment would allow states with restrictive laws governing services to keep those laws in place while their own service suppliers would get a "free ride" into the markets of states with more open laws. To force states with closed markets to open them, the service industry representatives successfully advocated the use of MFN exemptions.[17] An

most-favored-nation (MFN) treatment: GATS requirement that its member states accord immediately and unconditionally to services and service suppliers of other members treatment that is no less favorable than that it accords to like services and service suppliers of any other state.

---

[16]General Agreement on Trade Services, Article II, § 1 (1994).
[17]Bernard Hoekman, "The General Agreement on Trade in Services," paper presented to an OECD Workshop on the New World Trading System, Paris, April 25–26, 1994, reprinted in John H. Jackson, William J. Davey, and Alan O Sykes Jr., *Legal Problems of International Economic Relations* (4th ed., 2002).

annex was added to GATS that (1) allowed the original WTO member states to submit a list of MFN exemptions that became effective when GATS came into force and (2) provided that any later applications for exemptions will be considered using the ordinary WTO waiver procedures.[18] The MFN exemptions, furthermore, are to be limited in time (lasting no longer than ten years) and subject to periodic review and to negotiation in future trade liberalization rounds.[19] Nevertheless, while this provision for exemptions does put pressure on states with restrictive laws to open up their markets, it clearly diminishes the effectiveness of GATS, making it (like the old GATT 1947) little more than a collection of loopholes held together by waivers.[20]

transparency: GATS requirement that its member states publish their regulations affecting trade in services, that they notify the Council for Trade in Services of any relevant changes, and that they respond promptly to requests for information from other members.

The **transparency provision** in GATS requires member states to publish, prior to their entry into force, all of their national measures and international agreements that affect their obligations under GATS.[21] Additionally, they have to notify the Council for Trade in Services of any relevant changes to those measures and agreements at least annually,[22] and they are obliged to respond promptly to another member state's requests for information and to establish points of inquiry to facilitate this.[23]

In addition to its core obligations of MFN treatment and transparency, the Framework Agreement establishes other general criteria governing trade in services (most of which are analogous to similar provisions in GATT). To encourage the participation of developing countries, the agreement authorizes developed and developing member states to enter into negotiations (similar to those that produced GATT's General System of Preferences and South-South Preferences) targeted at improving the capacity, efficiency, and competitiveness of the developing members.[24]

GATS seeks to encourage regional economic integration both in trade in services and in the movement of labor with provisions comparable to those in GATT that deal with the establishment of common markets and free trade areas for goods. A service integration agreement among member states is required to have substantial sectoral coverage[25] and must provide for the elimination of all or substantially all discrimination among the parties in the sectors it covers.[26] A labor-market integration agreement has to exempt nationals of states parties from residency and work permit requirements.[27] In either case, the participating states parties have to notify the Council for Trade in Services of their proposed agreement for the council's review and approval.[28]

GATS requires its member states to ensure that their domestic regulations affecting trade in services are administered in a reasonable, objective, and impartial manner. It forbids them from applying their existing licensing, qualification requirements,[29] and technical standards in a burdensome, restrictive, or nontransparent manner; and, as soon as the Council on

---

[18]Annex on Article II Exemptions (1994).

[19]*Id.,* para. 6.

[20]See John Kraus, *The GATT Negotiations: A Business Guide to the Results of the Uruguay Round,* p. 78 (1994).

[21]General Agreement on Trade in Services (1994), Article III, § 1.

[22]*Id.,* § 3.

[23]*Id.,* § 4.

[24]*Id.,* Article IV, § 1(a).

[25]"This condition is [to be] understood in terms of number of sectors, volume of trade affected, and modes of supply." *Id.,* Article V, § 1(a), n. 1.

[26]*Id.,* Article V, § 1(b).

[27]*Id.,* Article V bis.

A footnote to Article V b notes that "[t]ypically, such integration provides citizens of the parties concerned with a right to free entry to the employment markets of the parties and includes measures concerning conditions of pay, other conditions of employment, and social benefits."

[28]While the Framework Agreement requires only that the council be notified, one can anticipate that the council will treat this notification process in the same way that the CONTRACTING PARTIES under the old GATT 1947 treated a similar notification requirement—that is, that notification means submission, review, and approval. See Chapter 7.

[29]*Qualification requirements* are the training or experience requirements that a service provider must have before offering a service.

Trade in Services adopts harmonizing guidelines in these areas, it will require them to bring their practices into compliance with those guidelines.[30]

A member state may grant monopoly rights to a service supplier (such as granting an assigned frequency to a radio or television broadcaster), but in doing so, it must not allow the supplier to act inconsistently with the member's MFN treatment obligation or its specific commitments.[31] As for other business practices that restrain competition and therefore restrict international trade in services, GATS requires each member state, at the request of any other, to participate in consultations aimed at the eventual elimination of those practices.[32]

No restrictions may be applied by member states to international transfers and payments for current transactions[33] relating to a member state's specific commitments. Nevertheless, restrictions, including those just mentioned, may be adopted or maintained if a member state suffers serious balance-of-payments difficulties, especially if the member is developing or is in transition to a market economy.[34] When restrictions are imposed, they must not discriminate among member states or unnecessarily damage another member's economic interests; they must conform to the Articles of Agreement of the International Monetary Fund; they may not be excessive; and they must be temporary and progressively phased out as their purpose is achieved.[35]

In addition to the core requirements of MFN treatment and transparency, as well as the other obligations just discussed, other obligations and disciplines were being considered for inclusion in the Framework Agreement during the Uruguay Round but were not included before the round came to an end. The negotiating parties, nevertheless, agreed to continue multilateral negotiations on these items.[36] Negotiations to devise rules on emergency safeguard measures, government procurement of services, and trade-distorting subsidies began in January 1997 and are still ongoing.[37] Negotiations to agree on rules concerning the links between the services trade and the environment began in January 1995, and they are also still ongoing.[38] The Framework Agreement provides for general exceptions[39] and security exceptions[40] that are analogous to those found in GATT. The GATS general exceptions include, additionally, a provision for a departure from the principle of national treatment

---

[30]General Agreement on Trade in Services (1994), Article VI, §§ 1, 4, and 5.

So that service suppliers are able to meet local criteria for operating, GATS encourages mutual recognition of education, experience, licenses, and certifications. Similarly, member states that are parties to existing bilateral or multilateral recognition agreements are encouraged to let other member states join or negotiate comparable new agreements. *Id.*, Article VII, §§ 1 and 2.

[31]*Id.*, Article VIII, § 1.

[32]*Id.*, Article IX, § 2.

[33]*Id.*, Article XI, § 1. For the definition of *current transaction*, see Chapter 4.

[34]*Id.*, Article XII, § 1.

[35]*Id.*, Article XII, § 2.

[36]See *id.*, Articles X, XIII, and XV and the Ministerial Decision on Trade in Services and the Environment (1994).

[37]General Agreement on Trade in Services, Article X (1994), required the WTO to issue rules for emergency safeguard measures no later than January 1, 1998. The member states were unable to do so, and they extended the deadline to June 1999. As of March 2007, however, the rules had not been issued and no notice of a new deadline had been agreed upon. In fact, WTO Director-General Pascal Lamy, in an address to the UNEP Global Ministerial Environment Forum in Nairobi on February 5, 2007, urged ministers to work hard toward completion of the Doha negotiations linking trade reform to environmental sustainability. Mr. Lamy warned that a failure of the Doha negotiations "would strengthen the hand of all those who argue that economic growth should proceed unchecked" without regard for the environment. He stressed that "trade, and indeed the WTO, must be made to deliver sustainable development." Mr. Lamy concluded, "As imperfect as the WTO may be, it continues to offer the only forum worldwide that is exclusively dedicated to discussing the relationship between trade and the environment. Through [the] Doha Round, decisions on that relationship can finally be made, influencing the way that the relationship is shaped. I call upon the environmental community to support the environmental chapter of the Doha Round, and to provide its much needed contribution." *See* http://www.wto.org/english/news_e/ sppl_e/sppl54_e.htm, accessed on May 21, 2007,

[38]See "About Trade and the Environment in the WTO," posted at http://www.wto.org/english/tratop_e/envir_e/envir_e.htm.

[39]General Agreement on Trade in Services, Article XIV (1994).

[40]*Id.*, Article XIV bis.

(discussed later) to ensure that direct taxes may be effectively collected on services or from foreign service suppliers,[41] as well as a provision that authorizes an exception to the MFN treatment rule when the difference in treatment is the result of an agreement for the avoidance of double taxation.[42]

Specific Commitments

GATS is designed to open up specific service sectors of the WTO member states' markets to international access on a sector-by-sector and a state-by-state basis. Following negotiations, or on its own initiative, a member is to submit a *Schedule of Specific Commitments* for annexation to GATS that *lists the sectors (or subsectors) it is opening to market access.*[43] The member may *also list limitations* that apply to these sectors, and it must do so as to six categories of limitations if it wants those six to apply. The categories of limitations that the member must either list or not apply are limitations on (1) the number of service suppliers allowed, (2) the total value of transactions or assets, (3) the total quantity of service output or the number of service operations, (4) the number of natural persons that may be employed in a particular service sector, (5) the type of legal entity or joint venture arrangement that a service supplier may use in supplying a service, and (6) the participation of foreign capital in terms of a maximum percentage limit on foreign shareholding or the total value of individual or aggregate foreign investment.[44]

For the sectors listed in a member state's Schedule of Specific Commitments, and subject to the limitations listed there, the member must observe two specific obligations: market access and national treatment. **Market access** is defined as giving services and service suppliers of other members "treatment no less favorable" than that listed in the member's schedule.[45] **National treatment** is giving services and service suppliers of other members "treatment no less favorable" than what the member grants its own like services and service suppliers.[46]

As mentioned earlier, the arrangement in GATS that separates obligations into two sets, general and specific, and that only requires a member state to observe its specific obligations to the extent that it opens its markets to international access, means that GATS is a much weaker agreement than GATT (since GATT does not correlate the observance of any of its obligations to commitments on market access). Considering, however, that GATT was, at its outset, observed more often in the breach than in its performance, the decision to limit the extent to which members are required to subject themselves to the obligations and disciplines of GATS, at least in its initial version, was undoubtedly prudent.

Progressive Liberalization

The long-term objective of GATS is to encourage its member states to open as many of their service sectors to market access as possible. Article XIX, Section 1, describes how this is to be done:

> In pursuance of the objectives of this Agreement, members shall enter into successive rounds of negotiations, beginning not later than five years from the date of entry into force of the WTO Agreement and periodically thereafter, with a view to achieving a progressively higher level of liberalization. Such negotiations shall be directed to the reduction or elimination of the adverse effects on trade in services of measures as a means of providing effective market access. This process shall take place with a view to promoting the interests of all participants on a mutually advantageous basis and to securing an overall balance of rights and obligations.

market access: GATS requirement that a WTO member state accord to services and service suppliers of other member states treatment no less favorable than that listed in its GATS Schedule of Specific Commitments.

national treatment: GATS requirement that a WTO member state accord to services and service suppliers of other member states treatment no less favorable than what the member grants its own like services and service suppliers.

---

[41]*Id.*, para. (d).
[42]*Id.*, para. (e).
[43]*Id.*, Article XX, § 1.
[44]*Id.*, Article XVI, § 2.
[45]*Id.*, § 1.
[46]*Id.*, Article XVII, § 1.

Although progressive liberalization is the goal of GATS, member states are not permanently bound to the commitments they make in their Schedules of Specific Commitments. After a period of three years from the entry into force of a commitment, a member may modify or withdraw it. Before doing so, however, the member must give the Council for Trade in Services at least three months' notice; and, if a member state affected by the change asks, the notifying member must participate in negotiations to agree on appropriate compensatory adjustments.[47]

Institutional Structure

Council for Trade in Services: A committee of representatives of all WTO member states that oversees the General Agreement on Trade in Services.

The operation of GATS is overseen by a **Council for Trade in Services** made up of representatives of all WTO member states.[48] Subordinate to the council are several bodies, including sectoral committees responsible for the operation of the different sectoral annexes (e.g., the Committee on Trade in Financial Services).[49]

The Council for Trade in Services is meant to function within the WTO structure. Thus, the council is, in essence, the WTO Secretariat that provides technical assistance to developing countries on matters related to trade in services.[50] And both consultations and dispute settlements related to GATS are governed by the WTO's Understanding on Rules and Procedures Governing the Settlement of Disputes.[51]

GATS ANNEXES

As stated earlier, the annexes are the second component of GATS. Together with several supplementary instruments (Ministerial Decisions and Ministerial Understandings), they deal with special aspects of particular service sectors or issues. The provisions of these annexes are summarized in Exhibit 8-1.

GATS SCHEDULES OF SPECIFIC COMMITMENTS

Each WTO member state is required to submit for annexation to GATS a Schedule of Specific Commitments regarding the service sectors that it has opened to international market access. For each such sector, its schedule must specify (as discussed earlier) (1) terms, limitations, and conditions on market access, (2) conditions and qualifications on national treatment, (3) undertakings relating to additional commitments, (4) the time frame for implementing its commitments (if that applies), and (5) the date of entry into force of its commitments.[52]

Of course, members are not required to open all of their service sectors, and one study has indicated that developing countries have opened only about one-fifth of their service sectors and developed countries about two-thirds of theirs.[53] Nevertheless, GATS is but a first step. The Framework Agreement requires, and the member states have agreed, that negotiations continue to liberalize the international trade in services.

---

[47]*Id.*, Article XXI, § 1(b), § 2(a).
[48]*Id.*, Article XXIV.
[49]Decision on Institutional Arrangements for the General Agreement on Trade in Services (1994).
[50]General Agreement on Trade in Services, Article XXV, § 2 (1994).
[51]Panelists for the dispute settlement panels in service matters, however, are taken from a special list of persons with special knowledge of GATS and/or trade in services, and panels for disputes regarding sectoral matters must be made up of persons with the necessary expertise relative to the sector concerned. Decision on Certain Dispute Settlement Procedures for the General Agreement on Trade in Services (1994).
[52]General Agreement on Trade in Services, Article XX, § 1 (1994).
[53]Bernard Hoekman, "The General Agreement on Trade in Services," paper presented to an OECD Workshop on the New World Trading System, Paris, April 25–26, 1994, reprinted in John H. Jackson, William J. Davey, and Alan O Sykes Jr., *Legal Problems of International Economic Relations* (4th ed. 2002).

Annex on Movement of Natural Persons Supplying Services under the Agreement

Provides that the entry into and temporary residence of natural persons within a WTO member state's territory may be regulated by that member state unless it makes a commitment to the contrary. More particularly, this Annex makes clear that GATS does not apply either to measures of WTO member states affecting natural persons seeking employment or to measures regarding citizenship, residence, or employment on a permanent basis.[a]

Annex on Air Transport Services

Makes clear that GATS does not replace the various bilateral and multilateral agreements on air traffic rights (i.e., rights to carry passengers, cargo, or mail for remuneration to, within, or across a country) and related services. In particular, GATS is to apply only to (a) aircraft repair and maintenance services, (b) the selling and marketing of air transport services, and (c) computer reservation system (CRS) services.

Annex on Financial Services

States that a WTO member state may adopt, in regulating financial services (i.e., insurance, banking, and their related services), prudential measures to protect investors, depositors, policyholders, and others, and it may take such other actions as are necessary to protect its financial system as a whole. Additionally, member states are free to maintain or adopt measures that protect the confidentiality of financial service customers.[b]

Annex on Negotiations on Maritime Transport Services

Provides that member states are not obliged to list in their Schedules of Commitments measures applicable to maritime transport services that are inconsistent with most-favored-nation treatment until the negotiations on such services (that began in 1994) are concluded.[c]

Annex on Telecommunications

Requires WTO member states that have granted market access to service suppliers of other members to ensure that those suppliers have access to the use of public telecommunications transport networks and services (other than cable and broadcast radio and television) on reasonable and nondiscriminatory terms within their territories and across their borders. Permits member states to place conditions on access to and use of these networks and services, but only to (a) ensure that they are available to the public generally, (b) protect their technical integrity, or (c) prevent suppliers from providing services that are not listed on the concerned member's Schedule of Specific Commitments. [d]

EXHIBIT 8-1 Annexes to the General Agreement on Trade in Services

[a]This annex is supplemented by the Decision on Negotiations on Movement of Natural Persons (1994). The decision called for negotiations on liberalization of the movement of natural persons to begin in May 1994 and to conclude in June 1995.
[b]A Second Annex on Financial Services (1994) gave member states an extension of up to six months after the entry into force of the WTO Agreement in which to list, modify, or withdraw their specific commitments regarding financial services.
[c]Member states must submit their list of commitments related to maritime transport services not later than (1) the date the Negotiating Group on Maritime Transport Services specifies for implementing the results of its negotiations or (2) if the negotiations fail, the date when the Group issues its final report. A Decision on Negotiations on Maritime Transport Services (1994) called for the negotiations to be completed by June 1996. At the end of June 1996, however, the member states were unable to reach an agreement, and they suspended the negotiations indefinitely. See "GATS: Maritime Transport," posted on the WTO Web site at http://www.wto.org/english/tratop_e/serv_e/transport_maritime_e.htm.
[d]In 1997, the WTO concluded negotiations on market access for basic telecommunications services. Sixty-nine governments agreed to offers that were annexed to the Fourth Protocol of the GATS. The one-page protocol and its annexed schedules and MFN exemption lists entered into force on February 5, 1998. See "GATS: Basic Telecommunications," posted at http://www.wto.org/english/tratop_e/ serv_e/telecom_e/telecom_e.htm.

B. REGIONAL INTERGOVERNMENTAL REGULATIONS ON TRADE IN SERVICES

EU LAW ON TRADE IN SERVICES

The EU is a common market not only for goods but also for services and (as discussed later in the chapter) labor. In comparison with GATS, the Treaty Establishing the European Community (EC Treaty), the principal source of law in the EU, creates a much more open and liberal market for services (and business in general) between and among its member states. The EC Treaty provides that, within the EU, "restrictions on the freedom to provide services"[54] and "restrictions on the freedom of establishment"[55] are to be progressively abolished. In essence, service suppliers and entrepreneurs are acquiring (as the EU integrates and EU law evolves) the right to do business in all EU member states.

EU freedom to provide services: Right of member state nationals and firms to market their services on a temporary or nonpermanent basis throughout the EU.

EU right of establishment: Right of member state nationals and firms to settle permanently and carry on a business throughout the EU.

The **freedom to provide services** relates to economic activities carried out on a temporary or nonpermanent basis. It applies, for example, when a Danish firm of consultants advises businesses in Greece or an Italian construction company erects a building in Spain.

The **right of establishment** authorizes a natural person or a company to settle permanently in a member state and carry on a business.[56] It includes the right to set up and carry on a business both as an individual and as an employer.[57]

Concern has been expressed that some cases fall between the scope of both of these guarantees.[58] An example would be a British camera crew filming scenes in France and Germany. Because the crew is neither establishing itself nor providing or receiving services, neither of the two guarantees fits exactly. However, in several cases, the European Court of Justice has read the two provisions together and hinted that it regards them as part of a general right of a self-employed person to pursue activities throughout the EU regardless of the location of his principal office or the kind of economic endeavor he is involved in.[59]

To ensure that the right of establishment and the freedom to provide services are meaningful guarantees, the EC Treaty declares that the self-employed and the employees of service suppliers are entitled to travel freely within the member states of the EU and to carry on their activities free from discrimination.[60] In order to "create a real internal services market by 2010" the EU enacted the so-called Services Directive in 2006 (Directive 2006/123/EC). This legislation aims to "facilitate freedom of establishment for providers in other Member States and the freedom of provision of services between Member States." The directive (which must be implemented by all members by December 29, 2009) aims to "increase the choice offered to recipients and improve the quality of services both for consumers and businesses using these services."

The 2006 Services Directive, which only applies to most services provided for economic return,[61] requires EU members to examine and simplify the procedures required to access and exercise a service activity, and to provide a single point of contact where a provider can complete all necessary formalities, perhaps using online methods. The directive also requires members to remove legal and administrative barriers to the development of service activities to ensure nondiscrimination.

These are not absolute rights, however. Entry can be limited on the grounds of public policy, public security, and public health,[62] and contracts with the public service can be limited to nationals of the member state.[63] In general these limitations are narrowly construed.

It should be noted that in addition to these limitations, the accession agreements allow the "old" 15 EU member states to apply, for a few years, restrictive measures against workers from the 12 "new" member states that joined the EU in 2004 and 2006. These restrictions can be applied for a transitional period of "two plus three plus two" years (adding up to seven years). In the first two years after enlargement, the old member states can freely decide not to open their labor markets to workers from the new member states. After those

---

[54]Treaty establishing the European Community, Article 59
[55]*Id.,* Article 52
[56]Zoltan Horvath, *Handbook on the European Union*, p. 290 (2nd ed. 2005)
[57]Fearon, Case 182/83, *European Court Reports*, vol. 1984, p. 3677 (1984).
[58]Zoltan Horvath, *Handbook on the European Union*, p.290 (2nd ed. 2005).
[59]See Coenen v. Sociaal-Economische Raad, Case 39/75, *European Court Reports*, vol. 1975, p. 1547 (1975); and Koestler, Case 15/78, *European Court Reports,* vol. 1978, p. 1971 (1978).
[60]Treaty Establishing the European Community, Articles 52 and 59.
[61]Some exceptions are financial services, noneconomic services of general interest, electronic communication services covered by other directives, transport and port services, healthcare services, audiovisual services, gambling, services connected with the exercise of official authority, and private security services. Directive 2006/123/EC. The directive can be viewed at: http://www.europa.eu/scadplus/leg/en/lvb/l33237.htm.
[62]*Id.*, Articles 56 and 66.
[63]*Id.*, Articles 55 and 66.

two years, they can decide to continue their national transition arrangements for an additional three years. At the end of this three-year period, the old members can only prolong these restrictions for another two years if they can demonstrate that workers from the new member states pose a real threat of serious disturbance in the domestic labor market.

PROVISIONS GOVERNING TRADE IN SERVICES IN THE NORTH AMERICAN FREE TRADE AGREEMENT (NAFTA)

The trade-in-services provisions in NAFTA are very similar to those found in GATS. There are, nonetheless, some differences.

As is the case with GATS, each of the NAFTA countries (Canada, Mexico, and the United States) has to observe the basic rules of transparency,[64] MFN treatment,[65] and national treatment.[66] In addition, each NAFTA country is required to accord the better of national or MFN treatment to services and service suppliers of the other two countries.[67]

Also, as in GATS, service providers establishing a commercial presence in NAFTA countries, including providers from non-NAFTA states, are granted several important rights, including the right to be free from performance requirements,[68] the right to make inward and outward transfers,[69] the right to have the international standard of care doctrine applied to expropriations,[70] and the right to have investor–state disputes resolved by binding international arbitration.[71]

One important difference between GATS and NAFTA is that NAFTA does not deal with services generally, but rather by sectors. Its main service provisions, accordingly, are in three core service chapters (cross-border trade in services, telecommunications, and financial services), two associated chapters (investment and temporary entry of businesspeople), and three annexes (land transportation, professional services, and specific reservations and exceptions).[72] Because of this arrangement, rules such as transparency, MFN treatment, and national treatment are repeated (with minor variations) in different chapters.

Another difference is that NAFTA does not specifically define the four basic *modes of supply*, as GATS does, and instead deals with them piecemeal. NAFTA's chapter on cross-border trade in services covers that mode.[73] The chapter on investments generally covers the commercial presence mode of supply. Other chapters cover the movement of consumers and the temporary movement of natural persons.

A third difference between NAFTA and GATS is the manner in which NAFTA deals with sectoral coverage. Unlike GATS, which requires states to list the sectors covered (a *positive list*) and then list the limitations that apply to them (a *negative list*), NAFTA requires its countries to specify the sectors that are not covered by the agreement (a negative list) and the limitations that apply to them (a negative list). Thus, if a NAFTA country does not list a sector or a limitation, NAFTA's rules automatically apply.[74]

---

[64]North American Free Trade Agreement, Articles 1306, 1411, and 1802 (1993).

[65]*Id.*, Articles 1103, 1203, and 1406.

[66]*Id.*, Articles 1102, 1202, and 1405.

[67]*Id.*, Articles 1104, and 1204.

[68]*Id.*, Article 1106.

[69]*Id.*, Article 1109.

[70]*Id.*, Article 1110.

[71]*Id.*, Article 1120.

[72]Harry G. Broadman, "International Trade and Investment in Services: A Comparative Analysis of the NAFTA," *International Lawyer*, vol. 27, p. 623 at pp. 637–644 (1993).

[73]Significantly, the agreement provides that NAFTA countries may not compel a cross-border service provider to establish an office or maintain a local presence. North American Free Trade Agreement, Article 1205 (1993).

[74]*Id.*, Articles 1108, 1206, 1409.

NAFTA itself lists one service sector that is not covered by the agreement: the general civil aviation sector. *Id.*, Article 1201, para. 2(b).

The principal exempted service sectors that the NAFTA countries have listed are (1) government-provided social services (exempted by all three countries), (2) basic telecommunications services (all three countries), (3) cultural industries (Canada), (4) sectors that are constitutionally reserved to nationals (Mexico), (5) legal services (Mexico and the United States), and (6) maritime transport services (all three countries). Harry G. Broadman, "International Trade and Investment in Services: A Comparative Analysis of the NAFTA," *International Lawyer*, vol. 27, p. 623 at p. 919 (1993).

Finally, the NAFTA countries may modify their lists of sectors and limitations. However, they may not, unlike GATS member states, make the lists more restrictive.[75]

C. INTERNATIONAL LABOR LAW

International law has been concerned with the rights of laborers from the beginning of the twentieth century. Following World War I, as part of the Treaty of Versailles, the international community agreed to establish the International Labor Organization (ILO), which has become the principal international advocate of workers. With the creation of the United Nations after World War II, the right of laborers to have reasonable working conditions became part of the basic human rights that were incorporated in the UN's Universal Declaration of Human Rights. In the materials that follow, we discuss both the ILO and those human rights rules that apply to workers.

INTERNATIONAL LABOR ORGANIZATION

International Labor Organization (ILO): A specialized agency of the United Nations responsible for promoting international efforts to improve working conditions, living standards, and the equitable treatment of workers worldwide.

General Conference: The legislative body of the ILO, made up of representatives from government, labor, and management from each member state.

Governing Body: The governing body of the ILO, responsible for setting the ILO's agenda. It is made up of representatives from government, labor, and management from 28 member states.

The **International Labor Organization (ILO)** has as its primary goal the improvement of working conditions, living standards, and the fair and equitable treatment of workers in all countries. Created in 1919 by the Treaty of Versailles, it became a specialized agency of the United Nations in 1946. Headquartered in Geneva, the ILO carries out its objectives by issuing recommended labor standards, organizing conferences to draft international labor conventions,[76] monitoring compliance with its recommendations and conventions, and providing technical assistance to member states.

The ILO's institutional structure is made up of a **General Conference** that acts as a legislative body, approving conventions and adopting recommendations; a **Governing Body** that serves as the executive; and an **International Labor Office** headed by a Director-General that functions as the organization's secretariat. The membership of the General Conference comprises representatives from government, labor, and management. Each national delegation includes four representatives: two from government, one from labor, and one from employers. The same tripartite representation also exists in the Governing Body, which is composed of 56 members, half of whom are appointed by governments, a quarter by workers' groups, and a quarter by employers' organizations. Of the 28 seats reserved for government representatives, 10 are further reserved for delegates from the world's principal industrial powers.

The authors of the ILO's Constitution probably meant for the organization to involve itself primarily with manual, or blue-collar, labor and not with other forms of employment. This reflected the interests of the labor movement at the end of World War I, but it did not represent its concerns only a few years later. In the **Employment of Women at Night Case**, the Permanent Court of International Justice (PCIJ) considered whether the ILO could sponsor conventions that did not involve manual labor, in particular a 1919 Convention Concerning Employment of Women at Night. The PCIJ stated:

> It is certainly true that the amelioration of the lot of the manual laborer was the main preoccupation of the authors of Part XIII of the Treaty of Versailles of 1919; but the Court is not disposed to regard the sphere of activity of the International Labor Organization as circumscribed so closely, in respect of the persons with which it was to concern itself, as to raise any presumption that "Labor convention" must be interpreted as being restricted in its operation to manual workers, unless a contrary intention appears. . . .
>
>   To justify the adoption of a rule for the interpretation of "Labor conventions" to the effect that words describing general categories of human beings such as "persons" or

---

[75]North American Free Trade Agreement, Article 1108, para. 1(c); Article 1206, para. 1(c); Article 1409, para. 1(c) (1993).
[76]The ILO has sponsored more than 180 conventions.

"women" must *prima facie*[77] be regarded as referring only to manual workers, it would be necessary to show that it was only with manual workers that the International Labor Organization was intended to concern itself. . . .

The text . . . of Part XIII does not support the view that it is workers doing manual work—to the exclusion of other categories of workers—with whom the International Labor Organization was to concern itself. . . .[78]

The PCIJ's decision makes it clear that the scope of the ILO's concerns includes all forms of labor, whether it be blue-collar or white-collar, for hire or done gratuitously, and whether employed by the state or the private sector.

> The ILO Web site is at
>
> http://www.ilo.org.

International Labor Standards

To pursue its goal of improving the lot of all working people, the ILO attempts to establish rules or *standards* that have international effect. Three reasons are sometimes given for why these standards need to have international effect. The *first*, and most practical one, is that individual states are not inclined to enact domestic labor laws because this would put them at a competitive disadvantage in the world market by increasing local labor costs. The adoption of an internationally effective agreement would, accordingly, keep multinational companies from practicing what is sometimes called *social dumping*.[79] *Second*, the establishment of fair and equitable labor standards helps promote world peace. *Third*, the establishment of uniform labor standards is a matter of both justice and humanity.[80]

ILO conventions: Labor conventions sponsored by the ILO.

ILO recommendations: International Labor Office opinions as to proper labor practices and as to how ILO conventions should be interpreted.

Two instruments are used to create international standards: ILO conventions and ILO recommendations. **Conventions** are sponsored by the ILO when there is substantial agreement in the international community about a particular labor practice. **Recommendations** are issued by the International Labor Office staff when the situation is more amorphous—for example, when the subject at hand is complex, or when there is no consensus on how a problem should be solved, or sometimes as a supplement to a convention that covers a matter in more general terms.

Over the years, ILO conventions and recommendations have dealt principally with three concerns. First, they have focused on the basic issues of labor protection, such as employment conditions (e.g., hours of work, weekly rest, holidays with pay, etc.) and the protection of women and children. (In general, these were also the issues the ILO addressed during its own earliest years.) Second, they have concentrated on setting up the basic machinery and institutions that are needed to make labor protection effective (e.g., labor inspection, employment service, labor statistics, and minimum wage–fixing machinery). Third (and this has been the focus of much of the ILO's work since the end of World War II), they have worked to promote and protect the human rights and fundamental freedoms of workers (e.g., freedom of association, freedom from forced labor, and freedom from discrimination in employment and occupation).

The ILO, among other things, studies and reports on a wide variety of employment and workplace issues of importance. For example in May 2007, the ILO issued a report on workers with disabilities, from which the following excerpt is taken.

---

[77][Latin: "at first sight." A fact presumed to be true until disproved by some contrary evidence.]
[78]Advisory Opinion, *Permanent Court of International Justice Reports,* Series A/B, No. 50 (1932).
[79]Social dumping is the practice of directing services to the wealthy (e.g., developed countries) and letting the poor (e.g., underdeveloped countries) fend for themselves because of the high cost of providing services to the poor.
[80]See *International Human Rights in Context: Law, Politics, Morals* by Henry Steiner and Philip Alston (2000). Section by Nicholas Valticos begins on p. 327.

═══◦◦◦═══

Reading 8-1:   EQUALITY AT WORK:TACKLING THE CHALLENGES OF DISABILITY

Equality at Work: Tackling the Challenges, **Global Report under the follow-up to the ILO Declaration on Fundamental Principles and Rights at Work, International Labour Conference, 96th Session 2007, International Labour Office, Geneva. ISBN 978-92-2-118130-9, ISSN 0074-6681. Used with the permission of the ILO.**

The challenge for enhancing the employability of people with disabilities is significant. But according to a new ILO global report on discrimination in the world of work, there is growing evidence that people with disabilities are not only more productive, they may actually be more skilled in certain types of jobs than non-disabled people. Proof can be found in the cash management department of one of Sri Lanka's biggest banks, where millions of rupees are counted and sorted every day by people who can neither speak nor hear.

Ms. Jayamali Fernando is a pioneer. The 41 year old woman from Athurugiriya in Sri Lanka is one of the best employees in the cash counting department at the head office of Sampath Bank in Colombo. Ms. Fernando also cannot speak or hear. She is one of seven hearing and speech impaired people hired by Sampath Bank in a unique partnership set up by the bank, the country's employer's organization, and the ILO.

According to the ILO global report *Equality at work: Tackling the challenges*, some 650 million people, one out of every 10 people on the planet, live with a disability, either physical or mental. The new report, published on 10 May 2007, provides a global report card on progress in addressing many forms of discrimination over the past four years.

"In a developing country like Sri Lanka, economic underdevelopment and massive unemployment mean that jobs are scarce, and the risk of discrimination is significant. Although there is a large body of labour laws and legal safeguards in place to prevent abuses in Sri Lanka's private sector, disabled people are particularly vulnerable", says Manuela Tomei, an ILO specialist on discrimination issues.

The Employer Network on Disability was created, with the help of the ILO, to give disabled people a chance to become productive workers. The Network's prime mover is the Employer's Federation of Ceylon (EFC), Sri Lanka's principal employers' organization, which represents 500 employers in sectors ranging from manufacturing to services, from banking to import/export firms to sales and marketing businesses.

Back in 1999, with assistance from the ILO, the EFC started the Network, which connects organizations that help disabled people with the business community, by enhancing employment opportunities as well as helping disabled people get access to vocational training. The EFC's Meghamali Aluvihare says it began with an awareness raising program to help dispel preconceptions about workers with disabilities. The EFC also created a database, matching disabled workers with the businesses that needed them, and later hosted a job fair connecting disabled people with local employers.

"Sampath Bank has a strong commitment to developing its people, and has made a major investment in training and human resources", says the Ms. Aluvihare, making it an ideal company for hiring disabled people. The bank hired seven speech and hearing impaired people who attended the job fair set up by the EFC. The bank's managers thought they had just the right opportunity for the disabled workers.

The Central Cash Department at the bank's head office in Colombo is where all of the bank's cash is collected and categorized. Every day, millions of rupees are sorted, packed, counterfeit notes detected, and transported out. It is a job that involves minimal interaction with the rest of the bank's operations, but requires a high degree of honesty, integrity, and attention to detail.

For every banker, cash handling is a core skill, and the seven speech and hearing impaired people the bank hired had to be trained to do the job. The trainers had to learn sign language to communicate with the new workers, and even the bank officer in charge of the department was given special training to communicate with his new team of disabled workers.

The results have far exceeded expectations, especially of those who thought it could never work. All seven of the hearing and speech impaired workers have so successfully integrated into the department that they are no longer considered disabled.

According to the department's manager, the disabled workers' level of productivity and efficiency has been rated as much as three times as high as that of other people working in the same division, and what's more, the manager says they are not only punctual, but that none of the disabled workers has ever claimed a single day of sick leave . . . and, most importantly for the operation of the cash department, there has never been a single complaint of dishonest or suspicious conduct in all the years of this initiative.

One of the biggest surprises, according to the department's manager, was that the hearing and speech impaired workers showed a special, unexpected talent: because of their highly attuned vision and superior tactile skills, they are particularly good at detecting counterfeit notes.

Over the last years, the EFC has taken further steps to bring more of these special workers into productive jobs. Over the years, the EFC has held five job fairs, at which over 250 people with disabilities have gotten jobs in the private sector. Meanwhile, the EFC is codifying what it has learning, including launching a "Code for Managing Disability Issues in the Workplace" for employers.

Hiring people with disabilities makes good business sense as well. "The Sampath Bank story isn't an isolated case. People with disabilities are not only among the most productive of workers, hiring them makes good business sense as well", says Ms. Tomei.

The new global report cites research that reveals some provocative results. Two thirds of Australian employers surveyed who hired disabled people said the cost of accommodating the workplace for them was neutral, as only 4 per cent of disabled people of working age require additional adjustments in the workplace. Many companies actually reduced costs by hiring disabled workers. The Australian survey found that the average recruitment cost of employee with a disability is 13 per cent below the cost of recruiting an employee without a disability.

The ILO global report also cites long term studies conducted by DuPont, showing that disabled employees perform equally or better compared to their non-disabled colleagues.

For Ms. Fernando, her disability is no longer an issue at work. She is not "deaf and dumb" but simply another valued, productive member of Sampath Bank's cash management team. And just like every other employee, Ms. Fernando benefits from the bank's strong culture of learning, taking advantage of training opportunities and building her skills in the job she loves, and excels at.

─────※─────

ILO Reports

The member states of the ILO are obliged to provide annual reports to verify compliance with the conventions they have ratified,[81] as well as irregular reports (when solicited by the director-general) to provide information on both recommendations and unratified conventions.[82] The report format required for both recommendations and conventions is essentially the same. In general, it consists of four main parts, which require the submitting country to provide the following:

Part I   Copies of the state's statutory legislation and administrative regulations dealing with the particular convention or recommendation and any documentary material (such as forms, booklets, handbooks, and reports) interpreting these.

Part II   An interpretation of the materials provided in Part I, showing how they have given effect to the provisions of the particular convention or recommendation.

Part III   (a) A description of the actions that need to be taken to modify existing legislation or practice to give effect to all or part of the provisions of the particular convention or recommendation; (b) reasons why those actions have not been taken; and (c) a statement as to whether or when those actions will be taken.

Part IV   The names of employers and workers' organizations to which copies of the report were given, and the comments that those organizations made.

A summary of the information contained in the member states' reports is prepared annually by the International Labor Office for use by the General Conference. Since 1927, this has been the job of the **Committee of Experts on the Application of Conventions and Recommendations**. The committee's members are appointed by the Governing Body as

ILO Committee of Experts on the Application of Conventions and Recommendations: A committee of the ILO's Governing Body that analyzes annual reports to determine the extent of member state compliance with ILO recommendations and conventions.

---

[81]The ILO Constitution, Article 22, states: "Each of the members agrees to make an annual report to the International Labor Office on the measures which it has taken to give effect to the provisions of conventions to which it is a party. These reports shall be made in such form and shall contain such particulars as the Governing Body may request."

[82]*Id.*, Article 19.

individuals and not as representatives of particular governments or groups. They must have a reputation for being impartial, independent, and knowledgeable of international labor law. Commonly they are drawn from the judiciary and academia.

The Committee of Experts does more than merely prepare a summary of the aforementioned reports. It analyzes and evaluates the submissions, indicating, in the case of unratified treaties and ILO recommendations, how close international practice is to the standards set by the organization; and, in the case of ILO conventions, the extent to which the parties have complied with their obligations.

ILO Conference Committee on the Application of Conventions and Recommendations: Committee of the ILO General Conference responsible for making a list of member states that have defaulted on their obligations to the ILO.

special list: List of member states that have defaulted on their obligations to the ILO.

A special **Conference Committee on the Application of Conventions and Recommendations** reviews the summary at the General Conference. This Conference Committee, after hearing comments from governments, employers, and workers, compiles a **special list** of the governments that have defaulted on their obligations to the ILO. The list contains seven categories of deficiencies. Six deal with the failure of particular governments to submit reports, to respond to requests for information, or to participate in discussions concerning an alleged failure to comply with an ILO convention obligation. The seventh and most serious category alleges that certain governments have failed to implement fully one or more of the ILO conventions they have ratified.

Each year the Conference Committee's special list is presented to the General Conference for review and adoption. This is often an awkward time for those states named on the list, especially those in Category 7. One especially memorable debate occurred in 1974, when the Soviet Union was named in Category 7. The U.S.S.R. was included for an alleged breach of the 1930 Convention Concerning Forced or Compulsory Labor because, among other things, its laws did not allow a collective farm laborer to quit work without the permission of the farm's management. After a lengthy and heated discussion, the General Conference was unable to obtain a quorum when a vote was called, so the special list was not adopted.[83]

The failure of the General Conference to take action against the U.S.S.R., together with Soviet bloc and Third World nation interference with the independence of employee and employer groups and an increase in political debates at the General Conference, led the United States to withdraw from the ILO in 1977. The withdrawal had a dramatic impact on the ILO, in part because the United States was the major financial supporter of the organization. By 1980, when the United States rejoined, the ILO had adopted resolutions to strengthen the tripartite system of decision making; it also had censured the Soviet Union, adopted the use of secret ballots, defeated an anti-Israeli resolution, begun screening out resolutions that violated ILO procedures, and reduced the number of meetings dealing with political affairs.[84]

Settlement of Disputes between ILO Member States

If an ILO member state violates the ILO Constitution, an ILO convention that it has ratified, or the ILO Convention on the Freedom of Association (whether it is a party to it or not), there are several dispute-resolution procedures that can be invoked to reach a settlement. These include (1) the investigation of complaints of noncompliance with ratified conventions by commissions of inquiry, (2) the investigation of abuses by the Fact-Finding and Conciliation Commission on Freedom of Association, and (3) interpretations of the ILO Constitution and ILO conventions by the International Labor Office.

inquiry: (From Latin *inquirere*: "to seek.") The process by which an impartial third party makes an investigation to determine the facts underlying a dispute without resolving the dispute itself.

The Commission of Inquiry   Article 26(1) of the ILO Constitution authorizes any member state to file a complaint with the ILO "if it is not satisfied that any other member is securing the effective observance of any convention which both have ratified." Upon receiving such a complaint, the "Governing Body may appoint a Commission of Inquiry to consider the complaint and to report thereon."[85]

---

[83]See "Proceedings Regarding Soviet Inclusion in the Special List," International Labor Conference, 59th Session, *Record of Proceedings*, pp. 733–760 (1974).
[84]Linda L. Moy, "The U.S. Legal Role in International Labor Organization Conventions and Recommendations," *International Lawyer*, vol. 22, pp. 768–769 (1988).
[85]International Labor Organization Constitution, Article 26(2).

Although this procedure has been available since the ILO was founded, the first Commission of Inquiry was appointed only in 1961, and only a few other commissions have been appointed since.[86]

ILO Fact-Finding and Conciliation Commission on Freedom of Association:
Special ILO committee of inquiry that considers complaints that a state has violated the ILO's freedom of association conventions. If the state consents, the inquiry can proceed even though the state is not a member of the ILO.

The Fact-Finding and Conciliation Commission on Freedom of Association   The Preamble of the ILO Constitution establishes the "recognition of the principle of freedom of association" as one of the organization's primary purposes. To implement this principle, the General Conference adopted two labor conventions: the Convention Concerning Freedom of Association (ILO Convention No. 87) and the Convention Concerning the Application of the Principles of the Right to Organize and to Bargain Collectively (ILO Convention No. 98). The first grants workers the right to form and join trade unions free from governmental interference; the second protects workers from antiunion discrimination and protects unions from employer domination.

Although both conventions have been widely ratified,[87] it was feared at first that they would not be. Because the Commission of Inquiry procedure allowed by Article 26 of the ILO Constitution can be invoked only if both the complaining and offending states have ratified the convention involved, the expected delay in ratification of the two freedom of association conventions meant that Commissions of Inquiry could not be used. This was unacceptable to the Governing Body, which regarded the two conventions as especially important, so it established a special commission, modeled on the Article 26 Commission of Inquiry but not depending on the ratification of a convention to carry out its tasks.[88]

Together with the UN Economic and Social Council (ECOSOC), the Governing Body established in 1950 a nine-member **Fact-Finding and Conciliation Commission** to consider complaints involving violations of the two freedom of association conventions. Under the guidelines established for the commission, it can hear complaints against a state that has ratified either of the conventions; and, if the state against which a complaint has been made gives its consent, the commission can consider a complaint even though the state has not ratified either.[89]

Few states have consented to investigations by the Fact-Finding and Conciliation Commission; however, as the two conventions have become widely ratified in recent years, the requirement of consent has become of less concern. Most recent investigations have involved states that are parties to one or both of the freedom of association conventions. In these cases the Fact-Finding and Conciliation Commission is, except for its name and the focus of its investigation, nothing more than an Article 26 Commission of Inquiry.

International Labor Office:
The secretariat of the ILO.

The International Labor Office   The ILO Constitution provides that "[a]ny questions or dispute relating to the interpretation . . . of any convention . . . shall be referred for decision to the International Court of Justice." Only one case, however, has ever been considered by the ICJ. As a practical matter, reference to the ICJ is cumbersome and expensive, so governments in doubt about the meaning of an ILO convention have taken to the practice of asking for the International Labor Office to express an opinion. As the office has stated:

---

[86]See Clarence Wilfred Jenks, *Social Justice in the Law of Nations: The ILO Impact after Fifty Years,* p. 48 (1970).
[87]They have not been ratified by the United States.
[88]See James A. Nafziger, "The International Labor Organization and Social Change: The Fact-Finding and Conciliation Commission on Freedom of Association," *New York University Journal of International Law & Politics,* vol. 2, p. 1 at p. 11 (1969).
[89]The requirement that a state that has not ratified a convention must consent to an investigation by the Fact-Finding and Conciliation Commission was thought necessary because there is no provision in the ILO Constitution for setting up commissions other than the one in Article 26. Even with the addition of this requirement, the establishment of this commission was thought to be unconstitutional by Australia and South Africa. For a discussion of the debate on the establishment of the Commission, see Clarence Wilfred Jenks, *The International Protection of Trade Union Freedom,* pp. 190–193 (1957).

The Office has always considered it to be a duty to assist governments in this manner, though it has invariably pointed out that it has no special authority to interpret texts of Conventions; the opinions given by the Office have, when of sufficient general interest, been submitted to the Governing Body and published. Though not authoritative in the same final sense as an interpretation by the Court, these interpretations therefore enjoy such authority as derives from their having been formulated by the International Labor Office in its official capacity at the request of governments of members of the Organization.[90]

Settlement of Disputes between Intergovernmental Organizations and Their Employees

ILO Administrative Tribunal: Special court that hears complaints from employees in the secretariats of the ILO and other IGOs.

The **Administrative Tribunal** of the ILO[91] is a special court that hears complaints from employees in the secretariats of the ILO and 39 other intergovernmental organizations (IGOs) that have recognized the competence of the tribunal.[92] The tribunal's jurisdiction extends to disputes involving the "nonobservance, in substance or in form, of the terms of appointment of officials" and to violations of the Staff Regulations of the ILO or other IGOs.[93]

Currently, more than 2,000 cases have been heard by the three-judge Administrative Tribunal,[94] and almost all of the decisions have been accepted and implemented by the officials and organizations involved.[95] The power of the tribunal to issue judgments, however, is limited. It has the power to "order the rescinding of the decision impugned or the performance of the obligation relied upon." It does not have the power to order an IGO to undertake an action it has not begun on its own, as Case 8–2 demonstrates.

---

[90]International Labor Office, *The International Labor Code*, 1951, vol. 1, Preface, p. cix (1952).

[91]The tribunal maintains a home page at http://www.ilo.org/public/english/tribunal.

[92]As of June 1, 2007, the IGOs that have recognized the competence of the ILO's Administrative Tribunal are the International Labour Organization (ILO), including the International Training Centre, World Health Organization (WHO), including the Pan American Health Organization (PAHO), International Telecommunication Union (ITU), United Nations Educational, Scientific and Cultural Organization (UNESCO), World Meteorological Organization (WMO), Food and Agriculture Organization of the United Nations (FAO), including the World Food Programme (WFP), European Organization for Nuclear Research (CERN), World Trade Organization (WTO), International Atomic Energy Agency (IAEA), World Intellectual Property Organization (WIPO), European Organisation for the Safety of Air Navigation (Eurocontrol), Universal Postal Union (UPU), European Southern Observatory (ESO), Intergovernmental Council of Copper Exporting Countries (CIPEC), European Free Trade Association (EFTA), Inter-Parliamentary Union (IPU), European Molecular Biology Laboratory (EMBL), World Tourism Organization (WTO), European Patent Organisation (EPO), African Training and Research Centre in Administration for Development (CAFRAD), Intergovernmental Organisation for International Carriage by Rail (OTIF), International Center for the Registration of Serials (CIEPS), International Office of Epizootics (OIE), United Nations Industrial Development Organization (UNIDO), International Criminal Police Organization (Interpol), International Fund for Agricultural Development (IFAD), International Union for the Protection of New Varieties of Plants (UPOV), Customs Co-operation Council (CCC), Court of Justice of the European Free Trade Association (EFTA Court), Surveillance Authority of the European Free Trade Association (ESA), International Service for National Agricultural Research (ISNAR) (until July 14, 2004), International Organization for Migration (IOM), International Centre for Genetic Engineering and Biotechnology (ICGEB), Organisation for the Prohibition of Chemical Weapons (OPCW), International Hydrographic Organization (IHO), Energy Charter Conference, International Federation of Red Cross and Red Crescent Societies, Preparatory Commission for the Comprehensive Nuclear-Test-Ban Treaty, Organization (CTBTO PrepCom), European and Mediterranean Plant Protection Organization (EPPO), International Plant Genetic Resources Institute (IPGRI), International Institute for Democracy and Electoral Assistance (International IDEA), International Criminal Court (ICC), International Olive Oil Council (IOOC), Advisory Centre on WTO Law, African, Caribbean and Pacific Group of States (ACP Group), Agency for International Trade Information and Cooperation (AITIC), International Organization of Legal Metrology (OIML), European Telecommunications Satellite Organization (EUTELSAT), and the International Organisation of Vine and Wine (OIV). See http://www.ilo.org/public/english/tribunal.

A UN Administrative Tribunal has a similar responsibility for the United Nations, the International Civil Aviation Organization (ICAO), and the International Maritime Organization.

[93]Statute of the International Labor Organization Administrative Tribunal, Article 2.

[94]All of the tribunal's judgments are available online at http://www.ilo.org/public/english/tribunal.

[95]The judgments of the Administrative Tribunal are "final and without appeal," except that challenges to the court's jurisdiction and claims of a "fundamental fault in the procedure followed" can be appealed to the ICJ. *Id.*, Articles 7 and 12.

〰〰〰

Case 8-2 DUBERG v. UNESCO

International Labor Organization Administrative Tribunal, 1955.
Judgment No. 17, *International Labor Organization Official Bulletin*, vol. 38, no. 7, p. 251 (1955).

In 1949, Peter Duberg, an American citizen, began working for the United Nations Educational, Scientific and Cultural Organization (UNESCO) in Paris, France. In 1953, the U.S. government sent him a loyalty questionnaire that required him to swear that he was loyal to the United States and not sympathetic with any subversive organizations or ideas, including communism. When he did not return the questionnaire, the U.S. government asked him to appear before an International Employees Loyalty Board at its embassy in Paris. He refused as a matter of conscience. In 1954, the Director-General of UNESCO refused to renew his employment contract, citing Duberg's failure to appear before the Loyalty Board as the reason for doing so. The director-general's letter of dismissal stated, "In the light of what I believe to be your duty to the Organization, I have considered very carefully your reasons for not appearing before the International Employees Loyalty Board where you would have had an opportunity of dispelling suspicions and disproving allegations which may exist regarding you." Duberg requested the director-general to reconsider and, while his request was being reviewed, the chairman of the Loyalty Board wrote the director-general that "[it] has been determined on all of the evidence that there is a reasonable doubt as to the loyalty of Norwood Peter Duberg to the government of the United States" and that "this determination, together with the reasons therefore, in as much detail as security considerations permit, are submitted for your use in exercising your rights and duties with respect to the integrity of the personnel employed by the United Nations Educational, Scientific and Cultural Organization." The director-general refused to reconsider Duberg's employment. Duberg appealed to UNESCO's Appeals Board. The board issued an opinion that Duberg should be rehired, but the director-general informed the board that he would not comply with its recommendation. Duberg appealed to the ILO's Administrative Tribunal.

THE ADMINISTRATIVE TRIBUNAL OF THE INTERNATIONAL LABOR ORGANIZATION: . . .

A.

Considering that the defendant Organization holds that the renewal or nonrenewal of a fixed-term appointment depends entirely on the personal and sovereign discretion of the Director-General, who is not even required to give his reasons therefore; . . .

B.

Considering that if the Director-General is granted authority not to renew a fixed-term appointment and so to do without notice or indemnity, this is clearly subject to the implied condition that this authority must be exercised only for the good of the service and in the interest of the Organization; . . .

***

E.

Considering that . . . the ground for complaint of the Director-General is based solely on the refusal of the official to participate in measures of verbal or written inquiry to which his national government considers it necessary to subject him; That the Director-General of an international organization cannot associate himself with the execution of the policy of the government authorities of any state member without disregarding the obligations imposed on all international officials without distinction and, in consequence, without misusing the authority which has been conferred on him solely for the purpose of directing that organization towards the achievement of its own, exclusively international, objectives; That this duty of the Director-General is governed by Article VI, paragraph 5, of the Constitution of the defendant Organization, in the following terms:

> The responsibilities of the Director-General and of the staff shall be exclusively international in character. In the discharge of their duties they shall not seek or receive instructions from any government or from any authority external to the Organization. They shall refrain from any action which might prejudice their position as international officials. Each state member of the Organization undertakes to respect the international character of the responsibilities of the Director-General and the staff, and not to seek to influence them in the discharge of their duties;

> Considering that the fact that in this case the matter involved is an accusation of disloyalty brought by a government which enjoys in all respects the highest prestige must be without any influence upon the consideration of the facts in the case and the determination of the principles whose respect the Tribunal must ensure;

That it will suffice to realize that if any of the 72 states and governments involved in the defendant Organization brought against an official, one of its citizens, an accusation of disloyalty and claimed to subject him to an inquiry in similar or analogous conditions, the attitude adopted by the Director-General would constitute a precedent obliging him to lend his assistance to such inquiry and, moreover, to invoke the same disciplinary or statutory consequences, the same withdrawal of confidence, on the basis of any opposal by the person concerned to the action of his national government; That if this were to be the case there would result for all international officials, in matters touching on conscience, a state of uncertainty and insecurity prejudicial to the performance of their duties and liable to provoke disturbances in the international administration such as cannot be imagined to have been in the intention of those who drew up the Constitution of the defendant Organization; Considering, therefore, that the only ground for complaint adduced by the Director-General to justify the application to the complainant of an exception to the general rule of renewal of appointments, that is to say his opposal to the investigations of his own government, is entirely unjustified;

***

Considering that it results therefrom that the decision taken must be rescinded; but that nevertheless the Tribunal does not have the power to order the renewal of a fixed-term appointment, which requires a positive act of the Director-General over whom the Tribunal has no hierarchical authority;

That in the absence of such a power, and unless the Director-General should consider himself in a position to reconsider his decision in this manner, the Tribunal is nonetheless competent to order equitable reparation of the damage suffered by the complainant by reason of the discriminatory treatment of which he was the object; . . .

That the decision not to renew the appointment is one which should not only be rescinded in the present case, but also constitutes a wrongful exercise of powers and an abuse of rights which consequently involves the obligation to make good the prejudice resulting therefrom; that this prejudice was aggravated by the publicity given to the withdrawal of confidence as being due to lack of integrity, this ground having been given in a press communiqué issued by the defendant Organization, without it being possible seriously to maintain the view that there could have existed the slightest doubt as to the identity of the persons to which the said communiqué referred; . . .

That redress will be ensured *ex aequo et bono* [96] by the granting to the complainant of the sum set forth below;

ON THE GROUNDS AS AFORESAID— THE TRIBUNAL

***

Orders the decision taken to be rescinded and declares in law that it constitutes an abuse of rights causing prejudice to the complainant;

In consequence, should the defendant not reconsider the decision taken and renew the complainant's appointment, orders the said defendant to pay the complainant the sum of 15,500 dollars, plus children's allowance for two years, the whole together with interest at 4 per centum from 1 January 1955;

Orders the defendant Organization to pay to the complainant the sum of 300 dollars by way of participation in the costs of his defense. ■

CASEPOINT: The ILO Administrative Tribunal decided that Mr. Duberg's rights had been violated by the director-general of UNESCO, an agency of the United Nations. The director-general had bent to the pressure of one nation (the United States) rather than preserving the international character and independence of his organization, as its constitution requires. However, the tribunal did not have the power to give Mr. Duberg his job back, so it ordered that he be paid a sum of money by UNESCO if the director-general did not reconsider his decision to terminate Mr. Duberg.

MAP 8-2 France (1995)

[96][Latin: "according to what is just and good." Maxim that disputes shall be resolved amicably and by compromise and conciliation.]

THE HUMAN RIGHTS OF WORKERS

The basic principles underlying contemporary international labor law are found in the Universal Declaration of Human Rights and in the International Covenant on Economic, Social and Cultural Rights. Both the declaration, adopted by the United Nations General Assembly in 1948, and the covenant, adopted by the General Assembly in 1966 and in force from 1976, reflect the international community's aspiration and sensibilities following World War II.

The civilized world was shocked by the Nazis' attempt during the war to annihilate all the Jews of Europe and to enslave and destroy millions of others, including Poles, gypsies, Soviet prisoners of war, homosexuals, and the mentally and physically handicapped. For many, the efforts of the Allied forces to defeat the Nazis and their allies became synonymous with a struggle for human rights.

The impetus for establishing the universal recognition of basic human rights came from U.S. President Franklin D. Roosevelt's "Four Freedoms" speech before the U.S. Congress in 1941. This speech asserted that there were four basic freedoms that could never be legitimately abridged: freedom of speech and expression, freedom of worship, freedom from want, and freedom from fear.[97] U.K. Prime Minister Winston Churchill likewise asserted that an Allied victory would bring about the "enthronement of human rights." In August 1941, Roosevelt and Churchill jointly issued the Atlantic Charter, announcing their goals in the war. The charter reiterated Roosevelt's four freedoms and proclaimed that the Allies sought "the object of securing for all improved labor standards, economic advancement, and social security."[98]

Germany's defeat brought more news of Nazi atrocities, and this led to a determination to secure enduring respect for human rights. The cause was taken up at the Conference on International Organization, held in San Francisco in April 1946, to draft a charter for the United Nations. While many human rights advocates had hoped that the charter would contain a Bill of Rights, they were nevertheless pleased that the charter committed the international community to protect and preserve human rights.

The Preamble to the United Nations Charter declares that human rights are one of the four founding purposes of the United Nations. Article 1 declares that member states agree to work together "in promoting and encouraging respect for human rights." Article 55 states that the United Nations will promote "universal respect for, and observance of, human rights and fundamental freedoms," and Article 56 says that the members "pledge themselves to take joint and separate action" to achieve that respect.

Soon after the United Nations came into existence, its Economic and Social Council accepted the recommendation of a "nuclear commission," chaired by Eleanor Roosevelt (see Exhibit 8-2), and established a Commission on Human Rights. Among the commission's first acts was the creation of a subcommittee to draft an International Bill of Rights. At the suggestion of Eleanor Roosevelt, who was aware of the political difficulties of getting a human rights treaty adopted, the subcommittee began working on a declaration—the Universal Declaration of Human Rights—to be issued by the UN General Assembly, as well as two treaties, one dealing with civil and political rights, the other the International Covenant on Economic, Social, and Cultural Rights.

The Universal Declaration of Human Rights

The Universal Declaration of Human Rights was promulgated by the General Assembly on December 10, 1946. It proclaims civil and political rights as well as economic, social, and cultural rights. The first of these—the civil and political rights—are based on the traditional Western civil liberties and political rights derived from the English Bill of Rights of 1689, the French Declaration of the Rights of Man and Citizen of 1789, the U.S. Bill of Rights of 1790, and similar instruments. The economic, social, and cultural rights were included at the insistence of the Soviet Union, its allies, and other non-Western countries.

---

[97]The Four Freedoms Speech is available at http://www.fdrlibrary.marist.edu/4free.html .
[98]The Atlantic Charter is posted on the U.S. State Department's Web site at usinfo.state.gov/usa/infousa/facts/democrac/53.htm.

The economic, social, and cultural rights listed in the Universal Declaration of Human Rights include provisions dealing with the rights of laborers. These are expressed as follows:

Everyone has the right to:

- "freedom of peaceful assembly and association" (Article 20)

No one shall be

- "held in slavery" (Article 4)
- "subject to torture" (Article 5)
- "compelled to belong to an association" (Article 20)

Everyone has the right to:

- "social security" (Article 22)
- "work" (Article 23)
- "equal pay for equal work" (Article 23)
- "just and favorable remuneration" (Article 23)
- "form and . . . join trade unions" (Article 23)
- "rest and leisure" (Article 24)
- "a standard of living adequate for the health and well-being of himself and of his family" (Article 25)
- "education" (Article 26)

Legal Effect of the Universal Declaration of Human Rights   The Universal Declaration is not a treaty. From its beginnings, however, commentators have argued at length about whether or not it constitutes customary international law.[99] Eleanor Roosevelt campaigned in the United States for the declaration's adoption by arguing that it was not legally binding. Some of the members in the General Assembly, however, were not so sure. South Africa and the Soviet Union, among others, expressed fears that the declaration would impose new legal obligations, and six states joined them in abstaining from the final vote of adoption.[100]

In the years since its adoption, more and more writers have made the case that the Universal Declaration is a statement of customary international law. Several developments can be cited in support of this argument: (1) The United Nations consistently relies on the Universal Declaration when it applies the human rights provisions of the UN Charter,[101] (2) The General Assembly has said that the rights delineated in the Universal Declaration "constitute basic principles of international law,"[102] (3) International conferences attended by large numbers of states have adopted resolutions stating that the Universal Declaration "constitutes an obligation for the members of the international community,"[103] (4) More than 70 states have incorporated the Universal Declaration in their constitutions or main laws,[104] (5) Court decisions have held that the Universal Declaration is customary international law.[105]

---

[99]See Michael J. Dennis, "Human Rights in 2002: The Annual Sessions of the UN Commission on Human Rights and the Economic and Social Council," *The American Journal of International Law*, Vol. 97, No. 2. (Apr., 2003), pp. 364–386.

[100]Howard Tolley, Jr., *The UN Commission on Human Rights*, pp. 23–24 (1987).

[101]See ILO Fundamental Principles and Rights at Work, at http://www.ilo.org/dyn/declaris/DeclarationWeb.Index-Page and Humphrey Waldock, "Human Rights in Contemporary International Law and the Significance of the European Convention," *The European Convention of Human Rights*, p. 1 at p. 14 (*International & Comparative Law, Supplementary Publication No. 11*, 1965).

[102]General Assembly Resolution 2625 (XXV) (October 24, 1970).

[103]United Nations International Conference on Human Rights at Teheran, 1968, *American Journal of International Law*, vol. 62, p. 674 (1969).

[104]The adoption of the Universal Declaration in a state's constitution has sometimes been advised by the UN Commission on Human Rights in the reports it has made following its investigation of human rights violations. Such was the case for Equatorial Guinea. Commission on Human Rights Resolution 32 (XXXVII), 1981; United Nations Doc. E/CN.4/1494 (1981).

[105]See Case 1–9, De Sanchez v. Banco Central de Nicaragua, *Federal Reporter, Second Series*, vol. 770, p. 1385 (5th Circuit Ct. of Appeals 1985) for a list of cases looking to the Universal Declaration as a source of human rights law.

Among the most influential case decisions supporting the idea that the Universal Declaration is a statement of customary international law is the U.S. Second Circuit Court of Appeals case of *Filartiga v. Pena-Irala*.[106] That case, which dealt with issue of whether torture is a violation of international law, held that the prohibition against a state's torturing its citizens "has become part of customary international law, as evidenced by the Universal Declaration of Human Rights . . . which states in the plainest terms, 'no one shall be subject to torture.'"

Case 8–3, which relies on the *Filartiga* decision, deals with the question of whether or not forced labor is prohibited by international law.

Eleanor Roosevelt (1884–1962), the wife of President Franklin Roosevelt (1882–1945), was one of the world's great humanitarians. Born in New York City to a socially prominent family, she married Franklin Roosevelt in 1905 and over the next 11 years gave birth to six children. During World War I she was actively involved with the Red Cross and after the war she was active in the League of Women Voters, the Women's Trade Union League, and the women's division of the Democratic Party. In 1921, her husband was stricken with polio and she became his close adviser and political stand-in in his campaigns for governor of New York in 1928 and the presidency in 1932, 1936, 1940, and 1944. As First Lady she held weekly conferences with women reporters, had her own radio program, wrote her own newspaper column, and lectured widely. Traveling around the country, she was her husband's eyes and ears and a strong advocate for the underprivileged and racial minorities. Following the death of her husband and the end of World War II, President Harry Truman made her a member of the U.S. delegation to the United Nations. As chairman of the Commission on Human Rights she was instrumental in the drafting and adoption of the Universal Declaration of Human

Eleanor Roosevelt with a copy of the Universal Declaration of Human Rights © 2006 European Parliament

Rights. She resigned from the UN in 1952 only to be appointed again in 1961 by President John Kennedy.

EXHIBIT 8-2 Eleanor Roosevelt with a copy of the Universal Declaration of Human Rights

---

[106]*Federal Reporter, Second Series*, vol. 630, p. 876 (1980).

Case 8-3   DOE v. UNOCAL CORP.

United States District Court for the Central District of California
Federal Supplement, Second Series, vol. 110, p. 1294 (2000).

DISTRICT JUDGE RONALD S. W. LEW:

***

I. Introduction

***

Plaintiffs allege that Unocal entered into a joint venture with Total S.A. ("Total"), a French oil company, and the Myanmar government, to extract natural gas from oil fields off the coast of Burma and to transport the gas to the Thai border via a gas pipeline. Plaintiffs further allege that Unocal is liable for international human rights violations perpetrated by the Burmese military in fur-

therance and for the benefit of the pipeline portion of the joint venture project.

***

II. Background

Burma's elected government was overthrown by a military government in 1958. In 1988, Burma's military government suppressed massive pro-democracy demonstrations by jailing and killing thousands of protesters and imposing martial law. At that time, a new military government took control, naming itself the State Law and Order Restoration Council ("SLORC") and renaming the country Myanmar. In May 1990, SLORC held multiparty elections in which the National League for Democracy, the leading opposition party, won 80 percent of the parliamentary seats. After the elections, SLORC refused to relinquish power and jailed many political leaders.

The international community has closely scrutinized the SLORC's human rights record since it seized power in 1988. Foreign governments, international organizations, and human rights groups have criticized SLORC for committing such human rights abuses as torture, abuse of women, summary and arbitrary executions, forced labor, forced relocation, and arbitrary arrests and detentions.

In 1982, large natural gas deposits that were to become known as the Yadana field were discovered in the Andaman Sea off the coast of Burma. Sometime in the late 1980s and early 1990s, Unocal conducted an oil and gas exploration in central Burma, and in or about 1991, several international oil companies, including Unocal, began negotiating with SLORC regarding oil and gas exploration in Burma....

***

In 1992, the Myanmar government established a state-owned company, the Myanma Oil and Gas Enterprise ("MOGE"), to hold the government's interest in its energy products and to produce and sell the nation's oil and gas resources. MOGE then auctioned off a license to produce, transport, and sell the natural gas discovered in the Andaman Sea. Despite Control Risk Group's report, Unocal bid on the contract but lost to the French oil company, Total. Total set up a subsidiary, Total Myanmar Exploration and Production ("TMEP"), to receive Total's interest in the contract, and on July 9, 1992, TMEP and MOGE formed the Moattama Gas Project (the "Project") by entering into two agreements: the Production Sharing Contract (the "PSC") and the Memorandum of Understanding (the "MOU," collectively the "Agreements").

The Agreements set forth the rights and obligations of the parties and established TMEP as the Operator and Contractor of the Project. The Agreements further provided that "MOGE shall assist and expedite Contractor's execution of the Work Program by providing . . . security protection and rights of way and easements as may be requested by Contractor." ...

. . . The Agreements also provided that the Project would consist of two entities. The first entity, referred to as the Joint Venture, was responsible for the production of gas. The second entity, referred to as the Gas Transportation Company, was charged with constructing and operating the gas pipeline.

The pipeline was to run eastbound through Burma's Tenasserim region, a rural area in the southern portion of Burma that is home to "rebels" who disfavor the SLORC. Accordingly, the Myanmar military increased its presence in the pipeline region to provide security for

the Project. In addition, the military prepared for a Commercial Discovery by building army barracks and helipads and clearing roads along the proposed pipeline route. Plaintiffs are Tenasserim villagers who allege that the Burmese military committed human rights violations against them in connection with the Project. According to the deposition testimony of Plaintiffs and witnesses, the military forced Plaintiffs and others, under threat of violence, to work on these projects and to serve as porters for the military for days at a time. Plaintiffs further contend that the military forced entire villages to relocate for the benefit of the pipeline project. The deposition testimony recounted numerous acts of violence perpetrated by Burmese soldiers in connection with the forced labor and forced relocations. Plaintiffs allege international law violations including torture, rape, murder, forced labor, and forced relocation.[107] . . .

In 1992, Unocal and Total negotiated an assignment of a portion of Total's interest in the Project to Unocal. On November 25, 1992, Unocal made an $8.6 million offer for a 47.5 percent participating interest in Total's rights and interests under the Agreements, which Total accepted in December 1992. Unocal then incorporated Unocal Myanmar Offshore Company ("UMOC") to hold Unocal's interest in the Project and on January 22, 1993, UMOC acquired an undivided 47.5 percent interest in TMEP's rights under the Agreements.

During the negotiations, Unocal and Total discussed the potential problems of having the Myanmar military provide security for the Project. Stephen Lipman, Unocal's Vice President of International Affairs, testified that

> in our discussions between Unocal and Total, we said that the option of having the military provide protection for the pipeline construction and operation of it would be . . . they might proceed in the manner that would be out of our control and not be in a manner that we would like to see them proceed, I mean, going to the excess. So we didn't know. It's an unknown, and it's something that we couldn't control. So that was the hazard we were talking about. It was out of our control if that kind of full relinquishment of security was given to the government.

***

In early 1995, representatives from Unocal met with Human Rights Watch ("HRW"). In this meeting, the HRW representatives told Unocal that HRW was not against investment in foreign countries, even those nations without spotless human rights records. Myanmar, though, was an exception. HRW's director informed Unocal that forced labor was "so pervasive" in the country

---

[107]The violence perpetrated against Plaintiffs is well documented in the deposition testimony filed under seal with the Court and need not be recited in detail in this Order.

that HRW cannot condone any investment that would enrich the current regime.

A 1995 letter written by a consultant to Unocal states:

> My conclusion is that egregious human rights violations have occurred, and are occurring now, in southern Burma. The most common are forced relocation without compensation of families from land near/along the pipeline route; forced labor to work on infrastructure projects supporting the pipeline (the SLORC calls this government service in lieu of payment of taxes); and imprisonment and/or execution by the army of those opposing such actions. Unocal, by seeming to have accepted SLORC's version of events, appears at best naive and at worst a willing partner in the situation.

***

In April 1996, Unocal CEO Roger Beach and Unocal President John Imle visited the Project. A report was prepared, apparently for their review, which provides charts representing the amount of money paid by the Project to local "project helpers" by month. One chart documents the numbers of "villagers" hired by Army Battalions. Another chart documents money spent on food rations for the army and villagers.

A U.S. State Department cable summarizes a conversation the U.S. government official had with Unocal's Joel Robinson regarding the Project's relationship to the Myanmar military. The State Department official noted:

> Robinson acknowledged that army units providing security for the pipeline construction do use civilian porters, and Total/Unocal cannot control their recruitment process. Robinson said Total meets the porters at the marshaling camp, where a Total doctor gives them a physical exam. Some are sent home due to their poor physical condition (the companies accept only males between 18–45 years of age). Robinson said Total keeps careful records of the porters to ensure they are paid. He said these records of workers and porters showed that they had not been overly drawn from just one village, in fact, the most that had been drawn from a particular village was three.

Another State Department cable dated May 20, 1996 stated:

> Forced labor is currently being channeled, according to NGO reports, to service roads for the pipeline to Thailand. The mode of operation apparently is to build the service road first, then lay pipe alongside. There are plans for a helicopter pad and airstrip in the area . . . in part for use by oil company executives. When foreigners come on daily helicopter trips to inspect work sites, involuntary laborers are forced into the bush outside camera range.

***

III. Discussion

. . . Plaintiffs allege that Unocal is liable for torts committed against them by the Myanmar military for the benefit of the Project. According to Plaintiffs, Unocal, Total, and the Myanmar government formed a joint venture to produce natural gas and transport it via pipeline from the Andaman Sea to the Thai border. The Agreements executed by and between the parties placed responsibility for the security of the pipeline with the Myanmar government. The Myanmar military did provide security as well as other services for the benefit of the Project such as road clearing and the construction of helipads and army barracks.

Plaintiffs filed these related claims in the United States District Court pursuant to the Alien Tort Claims Act ("ATCA"). . . . Unocal now moves for summary judgment on all of Plaintiffs' claims.

***

B. The Alien Tort Claims Act

1. The Act The Alien Tort Claims Act ("ATCA"), [which is codified in United States Code, title 28, § 1350,] states:

> The district courts shall have original jurisdiction of any civil action by an alien for a tort only, committed in violation of the law of nations or a treaty of the United States.

The ATCA provides both subject matter jurisdiction and a cause of action.[108] To state a claim under the ATCA, a plaintiff must allege (1) a claim by an alien, (2) alleging a tort, and (3) a violation of the law of nations (international law). The parties do not dispute that the first two elements are satisfied. The issue is whether the conduct of the Myanmar military violated international law, and if so, whether Unocal is liable for these violations.

Actionable violations of international law must be of a norm that is specific, universal, and obligatory.[109] When ascertaining the content of the law of nations, the Court must interpret international law not as it was in 1789 (the year the ATCA was enacted), but as it has evolved and exists among the nations of the world today.

---

[108]In re Estate of Ferdinand Marcos, Human Rights Litigation, *Federal Reporter, Third Series*, vol. 25, p. 1467 at pp. 1474–75 (9th Circuit Ct. of Appeals 1994).

[109]*Id.* at p 1475 citing Filartiga v. Pena-Irala, *Federal Reporter, Second Series*, vol. 630, p. 876 at p. 881 (2nd Circuit Ct. of Appeals 1980)); Tel-Oren v. Libyan Arab Republic, *id.*, vol. 726, p. 774 at p. 781 (District of Columbia Circuit Ct. of Appeals 1984).

[110] The norms of the law of nations are found by consulting juridical writings on public law, consider-ing the general practice of nations, and referring to judicial decisions recognizing and enforcing international law.[111]

***

2. State Action Requirement and Individual Liability The Second Circuit's decision in *Filartiga* [*v. Pena-Irala*] marked the beginning of a new era of reliance on section 1350 in international human rights cases and was the first Circuit decision interpreting the ATCA. "Construing this rarely-invoked provision, [the Court held] that deliberate torture perpetrated under color of official authority violates universally accepted norms of international law of human rights."[112]

. . . [T]he Second Circuit's decision in *Kadic* [*v. Karadzic*] in 1995 provides a reasoned analysis of the scope of the private individual's liability for violations of international law. There, the court disagreed with the proposition "that the law of nations, as understood in the modern era, confines its reach to state action. Instead, [the court held] that certain forms of conduct violate the law of nations whether undertaken by those acting under the auspices of a state or only as private individuals."[113] While crimes such as torture and summary execution are proscribed by international law only when committed by state officials or under color of law, the law of nations has historically been applied to private actors for the crimes of piracy and slave trading, and for certain war crimes.[114]

3. Liability as a State Actor "The 'color of law' jurisprudence of *United States Code*, title 42, §1983, is a relevant guide to whether a defendant has engaged in official action for purposes of jurisdiction under the Alien Tort Claims Act."[115] A private individual acts under "color of law" within the meaning of section 1983 when he acts together with state officials or with significant state aid.

***

Plaintiffs argue that Unocal's participation in the Joint Venture constitutes state action under the joint action test. Under the joint action test, state action is present if a private party is a "willful participant in joint action with the State or its agents."[116] "Courts examine whether state officials and private parties have acted in concert in effecting a particular deprivation of constitutional rights."[117]

***

In *Gallagher* [*v. Neil Young Freedom Concert*, a case before the Tenth Circuit Court of Appeals] a group of concert goers sued the concert's promoter and the security guard provider under section 1983 after being subjected to a pat-down search before entering a Neil Young concert at the University of Utah. Two weeks before the concert, University officials met with the promoter and the security team to discuss security for the event. At this meeting, the promoter directed the security company to perform the type of pat-down searches generally performed by the security company at rock concerts. The Tenth Circuit concluded that the joint action test did not apply in this situation because the evidence did not show that University officials jointly participated in the pat-down searches. The Tenth Circuit commented that in applying the joint action test,

> some courts have adopted the requirements for establishing a conspiracy under Section 1983. These courts [require] that both public and private actors share a common, unconstitutional goal. Under this conspiracy approach, state action may be found if a state actor has participated in or influenced the challenged decision or action.[118]

The Tenth Circuit then stated that other courts require a "'substantial degree of cooperative action' between state and private officials." "However, some state involvement is too minimal to establish that a private actor and a state official have jointly participated in a deprivation of constitutional rights." In applying the test to the facts, the Court held that the University's silence as to the kind of security provided or its acquiescence in the practices of the parties does not establish state action under the joint action test. Moreover, the fact that the defendants and the University shared the common goal of producing a profitable music concert does not establish the necessary degree of concerted action. "Under [the joint action] approach, state and private entities must share a specific goal to violate the plaintiff's constitutional rights by engaging in a particular course of action."

Here, Plaintiffs present evidence demonstrating that before joining the Project, Unocal knew that the military had a record of committing human rights abuses; that

---

[110] Kadic v. Karadzic, *Federal Reporter, Third Series*, vol. 70, p. 232 at p. 238 (2nd Circuit Ct. of Appeals 1995).
[111] *Id.* at p. 241.
[112] *Federal Reporter, Second Series,* vol. 630, at p. 878.
[113] *Federal Reporter, Third Series*, vol. 70, at p. 239.
[114] *Id.* at p. 239.
[115] *Id.* at p. 245.
[116] Dennis v. Sparks, *United States Reports*, vol. 449, p. 24 at pp. 27–28 (Supreme Ct. 1980).
[117] Gallagher v. Neil Young Freedom Concert, *Federal Reporter, Third Series*, vol. 49, p. 1442 at p. 1453 (10th Cir. 1995).
[118] *Id.* at p. 1454.

the Project hired the military to provide security for the Project, a military that forced villagers to work and entire villages to relocate for the benefit of the Project; that the military, while forcing villagers to work and relocate, committed numerous acts of violence; and that Unocal knew or should have known that the military did commit, was committing, and would continue to commit these tortious acts. As in *Gallagher,* Unocal and SLORC shared the goal of a profitable project. However, as the *Gallagher* Court stated, this shared goal does not establish joint action. Plaintiffs present no evidence that Unocal "participated in or influenced" the military's unlawful conduct; nor do Plaintiffs present evidence that Unocal "conspired" with the military to commit the challenged conduct.

***

4. Forced Labor   As discussed above, individual liability under the ATCA may be established for acts rising to the level of slavery or slave trading. Plaintiffs contend that forced labor is "modern slavery" and is therefore one of the "handful of crimes" to which individual liability under section 1350 attaches....

The International Labor Organization ("ILO") is the agency within the United Nations that has primary responsibility for all matters related to the rights of workers. The ILO sets international labor standards in binding treaties called Conventions. Burma joined the ILO in 1948 and has ratified 21 ILO Conventions, including Forced Labor Convention No. 29. Convention 29 prohibits the use of forced labor and defines forced labor as "all work or service which is exacted from any person under the menace of any penalty and for which the said person has not offered himself voluntarily." Over the past 40 years, the ILO has repeatedly condemned Burma's record of imposing forced labor on its people contrary to Convention 29. In 1996, for only the tenth time in its almost 80 year history, the ILO established a Commission of Inquiry to investigate allegations concerning Burma's non-compliance with Convention 29. On July 2, 1998, the Commission issued its report. This report acknowledges that the definition of slavery has historically been a narrow one, but then states that the term "slavery" now encompasses forced labor.

> In international law, the prohibition of recourse to forced labor has its origin in the efforts made by the international community to eradicate slavery, its institutions and similar practices, since forced labor is considered to be one of these slavery-like practices.... Although certain instruments, and particularly those

adopted at the beginning of the nineteenth century, define slavery in a restrictive manner, the prohibition of slavery must now be understood as covering all contemporary manifestations of this practice.[119]

[In this case there] is ample evidence in the record linking the Myanmar government's use of forced labor to human rights abuses.... Moreover, there is an issue of fact as to whether the forced labor was used to benefit the Project as opposed to the public's welfare.

5. Unocal's Role in the Forced Labor   To prevail on their ATCA claim against Unocal, Plaintiffs must establish that Unocal is legally responsible for the Myanmar military's forced labor practices. Plaintiffs contend that under international law principles of direct and vicarious liability, Unocal is legally responsible for the Myanmar military's forced labor practices....

Plaintiffs . . . argue that *Iwanowa v. Ford Motor Co.*[120] supports their argument that Unocal is liable for the Myanmar military's forced labor practices. In *Iwanowa,* the plaintiff alleged that after being abducted by Nazi troops and transported from Rostov, Russia to Germany, Ford Werke, a German subsidiary of Ford Motor Co., purchased her and forced her to perform heavy labor from 1942 until Germany surrendered in 1945. The district court denied Ford's motion to dismiss for lack of jurisdiction, finding there to be jurisdiction for the plaintiff's claims of slave labor under the ATCA. The court held that Ford Werke's "use of unpaid, forced labor during World War II violated clearly established norms of customary international law."

In this case, there are no facts suggesting that Unocal sought to employ forced or slave labor. In fact, the Joint Venturers expressed concern that the Myanmar government was utilizing forced labor in connection with the Project. In turn, the military made efforts to conceal its use of forced labor. The evidence does suggest that Unocal knew that forced labor was being utilized and that the Joint Venturers benefited from the practice. However, because such a showing is insufficient to establish liability under international law, Plaintiffs' claim against Unocal for forced labor under the Alien Tort Claims Act fails as a matter of law.

***

IV. Conclusion

For the reasons set forth above, Unocal's motion for summary judgment as to Plaintiffs' federal claims is GRANTED.... ■

[119]"Forced Labor in Myanmar (Burma): Report of the Commission of Inquiry Appointed Under Article 26 of the Constitution of the International Labor Organization to Examine the Observance by Myanmar of the Forced Labor Convention, 1930 (No. 29)," ILO, Part IV.9.A., p.198 (1998).
[120]*Federal Supplement, Second Series*, vol. 67. p. 424 (District Court for the District of New Jersey 1999).

CASEPOINT: The court decided that the Alien Tort Claims Act made the U.S. court system available to a citizen of another country who can prove conduct that violates the law of nations. Torture and forced labor (a type of slavery) are both condemned internationally. The court further noted that private parties (Unocal, in this case), as well as national governments, can be held liable for such violations, but only where the plaintiffs can prove "joint action" between the private and public parties, In this case, mere knowledge of illegal government or military actions were not enough to hold Unocal liable.

UPDATE ON THE UNOCAL CASE AND ANOTHER RECENT ALIEN TORT CLAIMS ACT CASE

This case was appealed to the Ninth Circuit Court, where the lower court's dismissal of Unocal was reversed and the case remanded for a full trial. The appellate court issued a strong decision, finding that if the plaintiff's allegations were proved, Unocal could be held liable under the Alien Tort Claims Act (ACTA) both for its own actions and for "aiding and abetting" violations by the Myanmar military and government. Furthermore, the court held that many of the alleged "torture, rape, forced labor, and murder" actions would violate the ACTA's prohibition of "specific, universal, and obligatory" international norms and the law of nations.

In addition, whereas the lower court found that Unocal had not engaged in "state action," the appellate court held that although "acts of rape, torture, and summary execution," like most crimes, "are proscribed by international law only when committed by state officials or under color of law," to the extent that they were committed *in isolation*, these crimes "are actionable under the Alien Tort [Claims] Act, without regard to state action, to the extent that they were committed *in pursuit of genocide or war crimes.*" Thus, even crimes like rape, torture, and summary execution, which by themselves require state action for ATCA liability to attach, would *not* require state action when committed in furtherance of other crimes like slave trading, genocide, or war crimes, which by themselves do not require state action for ATCA liability to attach.

However, Unocal asked for, and was granted, a rehearing before the Ninth Circuit Court *en banc* (all judges participating). One day before that hearing, the case was settled by the parties and the prior Ninth Circuit opinion was "vacated." Unocal reportedly paid millions of dollars (the settlement terms were not publicly disclosed) as part of the settlement, but the vacating of the prior Ninth Circuit opinion means that this opinion is no longer publicly available, and is no longer available as a legal precedent-establishing opinion.

The ACTA has become controversial, and has now become part of the political arena as well. The Bush administration has opposed an expansive, broad interpretation of the ATCA (allowing many suits against corporations for actions taken abroad), arguing that this view would have a detrimental effect on the war on terror and a chilling effect on international trade. There are some indications (in late 2007) that Congress may hold hearings on the law.

The U.S. Supreme Court finally did accept a case involving the ACTA and issued its long-awaited opinion in *Sosa v. Alvarez Macha* in June 2004.[121] This case arose after Mr. Alvarez Machain (Alvarez) was indicted in California for complicity in the kidnapping and murder of a U.S. Drug Enforcement Administration (DEA) agent. Several U.S. DEA officials organized a plan to hire a group of Mexican men (including Mr. Sosa) to arrest Mr. Alvarez in Mexico. The operation was successful and Mr. Alvarez was captured in April 1990, then transported to Los Angeles, where he remained in custody until his trial in late 1992. However, after the government had presented its case at trial, the district judge granted Mr. Alvarez's motion for acquittal, finding that the evidence was insufficient to support a gulty verdict. The judge stated that the case was based on "suspicion and hunches" but no proof, and the government's theory was "of whole cloth, the wildest speculation."[122]

---

[121]542 U.S. 692 (2004).
[122]*Alvarez-Machain v. United States*, 331 F.3d 604, 610 (9th Cir. 2003)

The next year Mr. Alvarez brought a civil lawsuit against Mr. Sosa, the United States, and several other defendants alleging numerous constitutional and tort claims arising from his abduction, detention, and trial. The lower court entered judgment for Mr. Alvarez for $25,000 on the basis that the ATCA provided the basis for claims of arbitrary abduction and detention and that the state-sponsored transborder detention violated "specific, universal and obligatory" norms of international law. The Ninth Circuit Court of Appeals affirmed Sosa's liability, although using slightly different grounds. The appellate court did not find that the transborder abduction was a violation of customary international law, but did hold that there was a specific, universal, and obligatory norm enforceable under the ATCA concerning arbitrary arrest and detention.[123]

The U.S. Supreme Court unanimously reversed the Ninth Circuit and held that Mr. Alvarez was not entitled to a remedy under the ATCA. The Court's opinion, delivered by Justice Souter, however, did not totally prohibit individual claims for human rights abuse under the statute—the door was left slightly open. The Court's opinion traced the history of the ATCA, and particularly noted the lack of legislative history regarding the passage of the law. The Court took the view that Congress must have intended the act to provide a remedy for torts in violation of the law of nations as it existed when the law was passed (1789). The conclusion was that Congress intended the law to confer jurisdiction on federal courts "for a relatively modest set of actions" including piracy, violations of safe conduct, and infringement of the rights of ambassadors."[124]

The Court noted, however, that Congress had taken no action to curb the developments regarding interpretation of the ATCA in the next 191 years, culminating in the more expansive view taken in the *Filartiga* case (discussed earlier). Still, Justice Souter refused to adopt a broad view of the possible causes of action under the ATCA, and said that such claims must "rest on a norm of international character accepted by the civilized world and defined with specificity comparable" to the causes of action accepted in the eighteenth century. The Court stated that "judicial power should be exercised on the understanding that the door is still ajar subject to vigilant doorkeeping, and thus open to a narrow class of international norms today."[125]

Justice Souter's opinion stated that Congress was in the best position to decide on the creation of new private rights of action, especially since there were many considerations regarding U.S. foreign relations; thus, the courts should proceed with great caution. International law norms would not be recognized unless they had the type of acceptance among civilized nations as those three types of claims accepted when the law was enacted. The Court did note that piracy and torture were two of a "handful of heinous actions" having such acceptance and thus would be actionable under the ATCA.[126]

The Supreme Court concluded that Mr. Alvarez's claims of arbitrary detention were not covered by any obligatory international norms. The Court stated that the Universal Declaration of Human Rights was only a statement of aspirations and did not impose binding obligations upon nations. Furthermore, the International Covenant on Civil and Political Rights was ratified in the United States on the express understanding that it was not self-executing and thus did not establish a binding international norm.[127] Although the *Sosa* case did not directly involve any transnational corporations, the rationale and holding of this case will no doubt be most important in all future cases against such business entities concerning human rights abuses. It would appear that the judiciary should proceed slowly and carefully in recognizing any specific obligatory international norms, which may give rise to private actions under the ACTA. As Justice Souter wrote "the door is still ajar, but subject to diligent doorkeeping."

[123]*Id.* at 620–623.
[124]*Sosa v. Alvarez-Machain*, 542 U.S. 692, 714.
[125]*Id.* at 729.
[126]*Id.* at 732
[127]*Id.* at 735.

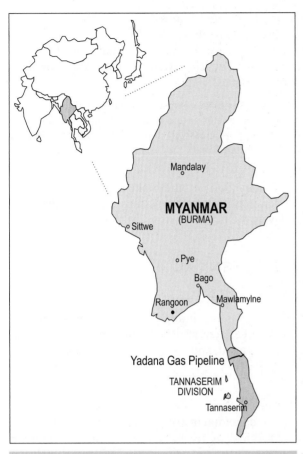

MAP 8-3   Myanmar (2000)

Before the trial in *Doe v. Unocal*, human rights activists failed in their attempt to get Unocal's shareholders to adopt resolutions to withdraw from its operations in Myanmar. While the shareholder's meeting was in progress one Burmese demonstrated outside the company's headquarters. (Photo: Dang Ngo.)

International Covenant on Economic, Social, and Cultural Rights

The International Covenant on Economic, Social, and Cultural Rights was adopted by the UN General Assembly on December 18, 1966. It entered into force on January 3, 1976. As of June 2007, there were 193 parties to the Covenant, [128] including the member countries of the

---

[128] As of June 2, 2007, the parties that had signed the covenant were Afghanistan, Albania, Algeria, Andorra, Angola, Antigua and Barbuda, Argentina, Armenia, Australia, Austria, Azerbaijan, Bahamas, Bahrain, Bangladesh, Barbados, Belarus, Belgium, Belize, Benin, Bhutan, Bolivia, Bosnia and Herzegovina, Botswana, Brazil, Brunei Darussalam, Bulgaria, Burkina Faso, Burundi, Cambodia, Cameroon, Canada, Cape Verde, Central African Republic, Chad, Chile, China, Colombia, Comoros, Congo, Cook Islands, Costa Rica, Croatia, Cuba, Cyprus, Czech Republic, Côte d'Ivoire, Democratic People's Republic of Korea, Democratic Republic of the Congo, Denmark, Djibouti, Dominica, Dominican Republic, Ecuador, Egypt, El Salvador, Equatorial Guinea, Eritrea, Estonia, Ethiopia, Fiji, Finland, France, Gabon, Gambia, Georgia, Germany, Ghana, Greece, Grenada, Guatemala, Guinea, Guinea-Bissau, Guyana, Haiti, Holy See, Honduras, Hungary, Iceland, India, Indonesia, Iran (Islamic Republic of), Iraq, Ireland, Israel, Italy, Jamaica, Japan, Jordan, Kazakhstan, Kenya, Kiribati, Kuwait, Kyrgyzstan, Lao People's Democratic Republic, Latvia, Lebanon, Lesotho, Liberia, Libyan Arab Jamahiriya, Liechtenstein, Lithuania, Luxembourg, Madagascar, Malawi, Malaysia, Maldives, Mali, Malta, Marshall Islands, Mauritania, Mauritius, Mexico, Micronesia, Federated States of), Monaco, Mongolia, Morocco, Mozambique, Myanmar, Namibia, Nauru, Nepal, Netherlands, New Zealand, Nicaragua, Niger, Nigeria, Niue, Norway, Oman, Pakistan, Palau, Panama, Papua New Guinea, Paraguay, Peru, Philippines, Poland, Portugal, Qatar, Republic of Korea, Republic of Moldova, Romania, Russian Federation, Rwanda, Saint Kitts and Nevis, Saint Lucia, Saint Vincent and the Grenadines, Samoa, San Marino, Sao Tome and Principe, Saudi Arabia, Senegal, Serbia and Montenegro, Seychelles, Sierra Leone, Singapore, Slovakia, Slovenia, Solomon Islands, Somalia, South Africa, Spain, Sri Lanka, Sudan, Suriname, Swaziland, Sweden, Switzerland, Syrian Arab Republic, Tajikistan, Thailand, The Former Yugoslav Republic of Macedonia, Timor-Leste, Togo, Trinidad and Tobago, Tunisia, Turkey, Turkmenistan, Tuvalu, Uganda, Ukraine, United Arab Emirates, United Kingdom of Great Britain and Northern Ireland, United Republic of Tanzania, United States of America, Uruguay, Uzbekistan, Vanuatu, Venezuela, Vietnam, Yemen, Zambia, and Zimbabwe; posted at http://www.unhchr.ch/pdf/report.pdf.

EU, Brazil, China, India, Japan, and Russia; the United States (President Jimmy Carter) signed the treaty in 1977, but the Senate has so far failed to ratify it.[129]

The covenant implements the rights set out in the Universal Declaration of Human Rights and gives them the binding force of treaty law. The extent to which the provisions apply, however, varies from country to county. Article 2(1) provides:

> Each State Party to the present Covenant undertakes to take steps, individually and through international assistance and cooperation, especially economic and technical, to the maximum of its available resources, with a view to achieving progressively the full realization of the rights recognized in the present Covenant by all appropriate means, including in particular the adoption of legislative measures.

In other words, countries that ratify the covenant do not undertake to give immediate effect to its provisions. Rather, a country only commits itself to taking steps "to the maximum of its available resources" to achieve "progressively the full realization" of those provisions.

D. REGIONAL INTERGOVERNMENTAL REGULATIONS ON LABOR

Workers' rights are protected by a variety of regional intergovernmental organizations. Among those that are most active in advancing the interests of labor are the EU, the Organization for Economic Cooperation and Development, and the Council of Europe.

EMPLOYMENT LAWS IN THE EU

EU freedom of movement for workers: Right of member state nationals to seek and accept employment throughout the EU.

The **freedom of movement of workers** between the now 27 member states of the EU is a basic tenet in the treaties that constitute the fundamental instruments creating the Union.[130] The European Atomic Energy Community forbids any restrictions based on nationality in the employment of qualified workers in the atomic energy industry.[131] The Treaty Establishing the European Community (EC Treaty), which is meant to promote the comprehensive economic integration of EU member states, provides that "freedom of movement for workers shall be secured" within the EU.[132] Article 39 of the EC Treaty allows workers, no matter what their occupations, to accept offers of employment and to remain in any member state to carry out that employment.[133] Article 40 authorizes the EU Council to remove and harmonize administrative procedures that obstruct the free movement of workers and to set up

---

[129]Conservatives in the U.S. government have opposed the covenant for a variety of reasons. Originally, segregationists saw it as a device for ending segregation. Later, economic conservatives looked upon the covenant as an assault on capitalism. During the administration of Ronald Reagan (1981–1989), Secretary of State Alexander Haig approved a memorandum that denied that economic, social, and cultural rights were "rights." The memorandum stated that U.S. foreign policy regarded human rights as "meaning political rights and civil liberties" only, and it directed members of the administration to "move away from 'human rights' as a term, and [to] begin to speak of 'individual rights,' 'political rights,' and 'civil liberties.'" Memorandum quoted in Hurst Hannum and Dana D. Fischer, eds., *U.S. Ratification of the International Covenants on Human Rights*, p. 15 (1993).

[130]For current information on the status of the movement of workers in the EU, see the European Parliament's Fact Sheet on the Freedom of Movement of Workers on the Parliament's Web site at http://www.europarl.eu.
[131]European Atomic Energy Community Treaty, Article 48.
[132]Treaty Establishing the European Community, Article 39 (formerly Article 48).
[133]*Id.*, Article 39, provides:
1. Freedom of movement for workers shall be secured within the [Union]....
2. Such freedom of movement shall entail the abolition of any discrimination based on nationality between workers of the member states as regards employment, remuneration and other conditions of work and employment.
3. It shall entail the right, subject to limitations justified on grounds of public policy, public security, or public health: (a) to accept offers of employment actually made; (b) to move freely within the territory of member states for this purpose; (c) to stay in a member state for the purposes of employment in accordance with the provisions governing the employment of nationals of that state laid down by law, regulation or administrative action; (d) to remain in the territory of a member state after having been employed in that state, subject to conditions which shall be embodied in implementing regulations to be drawn up by the Commission.
4. The provisions of this Article shall not apply to employment in the public service.

the machinery necessary to match job hunters in one state with job offers in another. Article 42 grants the EU Council the power to "adopt such measures in the field of social security as are necessary to provide freedom of movement for workers."[134]

In 1968, the Council of Ministers enacted Directive 68/360 to implement the EC Treaty provisions on the free movement of workers. The directive guarantees workers (and their families)[135] the right to leave their own country and to enter any other member state both to take up and to search for a job.[136] Workers must produce an identity card or passport, but no exit or entry visa can be required. And workers who secure employment are entitled to an automatically renewable residence permit allowing them to remain within a member state for at least five years, subject only to the requirement that they do not voluntarily quit their job or absent themselves from the country for a prolonged period.[137] Article 39(2) of the EC Treaty states that workers who are citizens of a member state cannot be treated differently because of their nationality.[138] This guarantee is implemented by Regulation 1612/68, which declares that national laws and administrative rules are void to the extent that they explicitly or implicitly limit the right of a worker to take up and pursue employment. Examples of improper requirements that relate to the finding of a job include those that

1. prescribe a special recruitment procedure for foreign nationals;
2. limit or restrict the advertising of vacancies in the press or through any other medium or subject it to conditions other than those applicable in respect of employers pursuing their activities in the territory of that member state; and
3. subject eligibility for employment to conditions of registration with employment offices or impede recruitment of individual workers where persons who do not reside in the territory of that state are concerned.[139]

Once a worker has found employment, discrimination in the amount of "remuneration" is improper. Thus, a foreign worker is entitled to "enjoy the same social and tax advantages as national workers"[140] and to "enjoy all the rights and benefits accorded to national workers in matters of housing, including the ownership of the housing he needs."[141] Finally, foreign workers may not be treated differently in the manner in which they are dismissed or in their "reinstatement or reemployment" if they have become unemployed.[142]

The right of workers to move freely across the borders of EU member states is subject to three broad limitations: Travel can be denied on the grounds of public policy, public security, and public health.[143] However, these limitations apply only to the right to enter or leave a member state, not to the right of equal treatment once a worker has been admitted to a state.[144]

---

[134]Articles 40 and 42 were previously numbered 49 and 51 prior to renumbering of the Treaty Establishing the European Community agreed to by the Treaty of Amsterdam. For further information on the provisions regarding employment that were added by the Treaty of Amsterdam, see http://europa.eu/scadplus/leg/en/lvb/a13000.htm.
[135]A worker's family is defined by Regulation 1612/68 as "(a) his spouse and their descendants who are under the age of 21 years or are dependents; (b) dependent relatives in the ascending line of the worker and his spouse."
[136]The right to search for a job is not expressly contained in either Article 39 of the EC Treaty or in Directive 68/360. However, in construing both the treaty and the directive, the European Court of Justice, in Procurer du Roi v. Royer, Case 48/75, *European Court Reports*, vol. 1976, p. 496 (1976), stated that a worker had the right to enter the territory of any member state to "look for" employment.
[137]Workers looking for employment are allowed three months to find a job.
[138]Treaty Establishing the European Community, Article 39(2).
[139]European Union, Regulation 1612/68, Article 3.
[140]*Id.,* Article 9. Some of the social advantages that foreign workers are entitled to include a guaranteed minimum subsistence allowance (Hoeckx, Case 249/83, *European Court Reports,* vol. 1985, p. 973 [1985]); old-age benefits for individuals without a pension entitlement under the national social security system (Frascogna, Case 157/84, judgment of June 6, 1985); and a guaranteed minimum income for the elderly (Castelli, Case 261/83, *European Court Reports,* vol. 1984, p. 3199 [1984]).
[141]European Union, Regulation 1612/68, Article 9(1).
[142]*Id.,* Article 7.
[143]Treaty Establishing the European Community, Article 39(3).
[144]"On the grounds of public policy or public security a foreigner may not be permitted to enter a country and take up employment there, but those considerations have no bearing on conditions of work once employment has been taken up in an authorized manner." Advocate General Gand in Ugioli, Case 15/69, *European Court Reports,* vol. 1969, p. 369 (1969).

The scope of these limitations was narrowed gradually in the 1970s and 1980s in a series of cases decided by the European Court of Justice. In 1974 in the case of *Van Duyn v. Home Office*, the court recognized that a member state had the right to restrict the entry of a foreign national for public policy reasons.[145] The next year, in *Rutili v. French Minister of the Interior*, the court stated that "restrictions cannot be imposed on the right of a national of any member state to enter the territory of another member state, to stay there [or] to move within it unless his presence or conduct constitutes a *genuine and sufficiently serious threat* to public policy."[146] Then in 1977, the court added that the genuine and serious threat had to affect "one of the fundamental interests of society."[147] Finally, in 1981 in *Adoni,* the court defined the fundamental interests of society as those listed in the European Convention on Human Rights, which, it pointed out, has been ratified by all the member states.[148]

The dramatic expansion of the EU in 2004 and 2006 from 15 to 27 members, including many Eastern European nations, caused considerable concern in the "older" Western European EU members. Politicians worried about the "flood of workers" who might move to these older countries, disrupting the labor markets. Thus, as part of the accession agreements, the 15 EU members as of 2003 were given a period of years when they could restrict the flow of workers moving from the newer EU members, as the following reading from the EU Parliament website discusses.

---

[145]Case 41/74, *European Court Reports*, vol. 1974, p. 1337 (1974).
[146]Case 36/75, id., vol. 1975, p. 1219 (1975). (Emphasis added.)
[147]Regina v. Bouchereau, Case 30/77, id., vol. 1977, p. 1999 (1977).
[148]Cases 115 and 116/81, *id.*, vol. 1982, p. 1665 (1982).

Reading 8-2   FREER MOVEMENT EXISTS IN THE EUROPEAN UNION BUT RESTRICTIONS REMAIN

Source: http://www.europarl.europa.eu/news/public/story_page/048-8008-123-05-18-908-20060510STO08007-2006-03-05-2006/default_en.htm, accessed June 1, 2007.

"Old" and "new" Europe took a step closer in mid-2006 as Spain, Portugal, Finland and Greece opened their labour markets to workers from the 8 Central and Eastern European countries that joined the EU in 2004. They join Britain, Ireland and Sweden who opened their labour markets when the new members joined two years ago. With 2006 being the European year of workers' mobility the news received a cautiously optimistic response from some MEPs closely involved in the issue.

Jan Andersson, the Swedish Social democrat who chairs Parliament's Employment and Social committee, welcomed the move saying, "the EU has a set of rules on how to deal with transitional restrictions and the Member States need to respect it. At the same time I believe that the EU states [that] have not yet abolished the restrictions on access to their labour market for workers . . . should do so as soon as possible."

This was echoed by Hungary's Csaba Ory from the European Peoples Party. As a leading member of the Employment committee he drafted a report on workers mobility that was adopted by the Parliament in April. The report states that "continued denial of opportunities for workers from the new member states . . . has fuelled more illegal work, promotion of the black economy, and worker exploitation". It also calls for an end to restrictions to send a "clear message of solidarity between Western and Eastern Europe".

DEADLINE OF 2011 FOR LAST RESTRICTIONS

The economic migration of workers is a delicate subject, explaining why, after the last enlargement of the European Union in 2004, all but 3 of the 15 old Members maintained "transitional periods" for the access of labour to their markets. The maximum time period allowed for this is seven years—although a "2+3+2 years" formula allows worker mobility to be introduced in stages. The deadline to remove all restrictions is 2011.

France, Italy and Luxembourg have indicated that they may lift certain restrictions for jobs where it is difficult to find recruits. This also applies to Belgium, where in Brussels the local authorities have asked for privileged treatment for nurses, plumbers, electricians and car mechanics. The Parliament of the Netherlands is due to consider the issue before the end of the year.

Germany and Austria will maintain restrictions until 2009, although Germany has already issued 500,000 work permits to migrants from the new EU members.

FROM WARSAW TO LONDON, DUBLIN, STOCKHOLM

Since 1 May 2004 just over 500,000 people have travelled to the UK and Ireland in search of work, 60% of whom are from Poland—the largest of the new members.

The issue is given greater sensitivity as the "free movement of persons" is one of the fundamental freedoms guaranteed under European law. In fact it is enshrined in the 1957 Treaty of Rome. Article 39 lays down the right to look for a job in another member, the right to work, the right to reside and the right to equal access to employment and equal working conditions. Those planning to work abroad will be hoping for this to be applied by all EU members as soon as possible.

The EU Website for information on free movement of workers is

http://ec.europa.eu/employment_social/free_movement/docs/pr_en.pdf.

A final limitation to the free movement of workers is found in a clause in Article 39 of the EC Treaty stating that the "provisions of this Article shall not apply to employment in the public service." This does not mean that foreign nationals are forbidden from working in any job in the public service, nor does it allow discrimination in the terms and conditions of employment once a worker has been hired. The public service limitation applies only to jobs that are related to the activity of governing. In *Commission v. Belgium (No. 1)*, the Court of Justice said: "Such posts in fact presume on the part of those occupying them the existence of a special relationship of allegiance to the state and reciprocity of rights and duties which form the foundation of the bond of nationality."[149] In *Commission v. Belgium (No. 2)*, the court gave examples of public service and nonpublic service jobs. Head technical office supervisor, principal supervisor, works supervisor, and stock controller for the municipalities of Brussels and Auderghem fell within the first group, while railway shunters, drivers, platelayers, signalmen and nightwatchmen, nurses, electricians, joiners, and plumbers employed by the same municipalities fell in the second group.[150]

EMPLOYMENT STANDARDS OF THE ORGANIZATION FOR ECONOMIC COOPERATION AND DEVELOPMENT (OECD)

OECD Guidelines for Multinational Enterprises: Norms suggested by the OECD for the operation of multinational firms both in home and host states.

The OECD[151] has worked to better the working standards of laborers. In order "to encourage the positive contributions" of multinational enterprises, "to minimize and resolve the difficulties" that can arise out of their operations, and "to contribute to improving the foreign investment climate," the **OECD's Guidelines for Multinational Enterprises** establishes norms for the employment of workers in both home and host countries. These norms are as follows:

---

[149]Case 149/79, No. 1, *id.*, vol. 1980, p. 3881 (1980).

[150]Case 149/79, No. 2, *id.*, vol. 1982, p. 1845 (1982).

[151]The OECD's Web site is at http://www.oecd.org.

Employment and Industrial Relations

Enterprises should, within the framework of law, regulations, and prevailing labor relations and employment practices, in each of the countries in which they operate:

1. respect the right of their employees to be represented by trade unions and other bona fide organizations of employees, and engage in constructive negotiations, either individually or through employers' associations, with such employee organizations with a view to reaching agreements on employment conditions, which should include provisions for dealing with disputes and for ensuring mutually respected rights and responsibilities;

2. (a) provide such facilities to representatives of the employees as may be necessary to assist in the development of effective collective agreements; (b) provide to representatives of employees information which is needed for meaningful negotiations on conditions of employment;

3. provide to representatives of employees where this accords with local law and practice, information which enables them to obtain a true and fair view of the performance of the entity or, where appropriate, the enterprise as a whole;

4. observe standards of employment and industrial relations not less favorable than those observed by comparable employers in the host country;

5. in their operations, to the greatest extent practicable, utilize, train and prepare for upgrading members of the local labor force in cooperation with representatives of their employees and, where appropriate, the relevant governmental authorities;

6. in considering changes in their operations which would have major effects upon the livelihood of their employees, in particular in the case of the closure of an entity involving collective layoffs or dismissals, provide reasonable notice of such changes to representatives of their employees, and where appropriate to the relevant governmental authorities, and cooperate with the employee representative and appropriate governmental authorities so as to mitigate to the maximum extent practicable adverse effects;

7. implement their employment policies including hiring, discharge, pay, promotion, and training without discrimination unless selectivity in respect of employee characteristics is in furtherance of established governmental policies which specifically promote greater equality of employment opportunity;

8. in the context of bona fide negotiations with representatives of employees on conditions of employment or while employees are exercising a right to organize, not threaten to utilize a capacity to transfer the whole or part of an operating unit from the country concerned in order to influence unfairly those negotiations or to hinder the exercise of a right to organize;

9. enable authorized representatives of their employees to conduct negotiations on collective bargaining or labor management relations issues with representatives of management who are authorized to make decisions on the matters under negotiation.[152]

Although the guidelines are only voluntary, they have had some influence because they establish, in essence, minimum international standards. Companies that fall below these standards are put in an awkward position when dealing with local governments, local unions, and the local and international media.

PROTECTION OF WORKERS' RIGHTS BY THE COUNCIL OF EUROPE

European Convention on Human Rights of 1950: Establishes and guarantees civil and political rights for the nationals of the member states of the Council of Europe.

The Council of Europe is responsible for enforcing the **European Convention on Human Rights of 1950**[153] and the European Social Charter of 1961.[154] The Human Rights Convention is concerned mainly with civil and political rights, whereas the Social Charter deals

---

[152]"Guidelines for Multinational Enterprises," Declaration on International Investment and Multinational Enterprises by the Governments of the OECD Member Countries (June 21, 1976). The guidelines and information about their application are available on the OECD's Web site at http://www.oecd.org.

[153]*European Treaty Series*, No. 5 (1950). Forty-seven states were parties as of 2007. See Council of Europe, Chart of Signatures and Ratifications, Convention for the Protection of Human Rights and Fundamental Freedoms, posted on the Council of Europe Web site at http://www.coe.int.

[154]*United Nations Treaty Series*, vol. 529, p. 90. There were 22 parties as of 1999. See Council of Europe, Chart of Signatures and Ratifications, European Social Charter, posted at http://www.coe.fr/tablconv35t.htm.

primarily with economic, social, and cultural rights. Despite the division in emphasis, there is some overlap between the two treaties.

In particular, the Human Rights Convention includes, as part of its guarantee of freedom of assembly, the right to join a trade union. Article 11 of the Convention provides as follows:

1. Everyone has the right to freedom of peaceful assembly and to freedom of association with others, including the right to join trade unions for the protection of his interests.
2. No restrictions shall be placed on the exercise of these rights other than such as are prescribed by law and are necessary in a democratic society in the interests of national security or public safety, for the prevention of disorder or crime, for the protection of health or morals, or for the protection of the rights and freedoms of others. This Article shall not prevent the imposition of lawful restrictions on the exercise of these rights by members of the armed forces, of the police or of the administration of the State.

European Social Charter of 1961: Establishes and guarantees economic, social, and cultural rights for the nationals of the member states of the Council of Europe.

Much broader provisions protecting the rights of workers are found in the **European Social Charter**.[155] Part I lays out, in general terms, the "rights and principles" that the charter aims to protect:

1. Everyone shall have the opportunity to earn his living in an occupation freely entered upon.
2. All workers have the right to just conditions of work.
3. All workers have the right to safe and healthy working conditions.
4. All workers have the right to a fair remuneration sufficient for a decent standard of living for themselves and their families.
5. All workers and employees have the right to freedom of association in national or international organizations for the protection of their economic and social interests.
6. All workers and employers have the right to bargain collectively.
7. Children and young persons have the right to a special protection against the physical and moral hazards to which they are exposed.
8. Employed women, in case of maternity, and other employed women as appropriate, have the right to a special protection in their work.
9. Everyone has the right to appropriate facilities for vocational guidance with a view to helping him choose an occupation suited to his personal aptitude and interests.
10. Everyone has the right to appropriate facilities for vocational training.
11. Everyone has the right to benefit from any measures enabling him to enjoy the highest possible standard of health attainable.
12. All workers and their dependents have the right to social security.
13. Anyone without adequate resources has the right to social and medical assistance.
14. Everyone has the right to benefit from social welfare services.
15. Disabled persons have the right to vocational training, rehabilitation, and resettlement, whatever the origin and nature of their disability.
16. The family as a fundamental unit of society has the right to appropriate social, legal, and economic protection to ensure its full development.
17. Mothers and children, irrespective of marital status and family relations, have the right to appropriate social and economic protection.
18. The nationals of any one of the contracting parties have the right to engage in any gainful occupation in the territory of any one of the others on a footing of equality with the nationals of the latter, subject to restrictions based on cogent economic or social reasons.
19. Migrant workers who are nationals of a contracting party and their families have the right to protection and assistance in the territory of any other contracting party.

Part II contains articles describing in detail these rights and principles. For example, Article 4 describes the "Right to a Fair Remuneration" as follows:

---

[155]It is reproduced in *United Nations Treaty Series*, vol. 529, p. 90 (1965). The charter, signed on October 18, 1961, came into force on February 26, 1965.

With a view to ensuring the effective exercise of the right to a fair remuneration the contracting parties undertake:

1. to recognize the right of workers to a remuneration such as will give them and their families a decent standard of living;
2. to recognize the right of workers to an increased rate of remuneration for overtime work, subject to exceptions in particular cases;
3. to recognize the right of men and women workers to equal pay for work of equal value;
4. to recognize the right of all workers to a reasonable period of notice for termination of employment;
5. to permit deductions from wages only under conditions and to the extent prescribed by national laws or regulations or fixed by collective agreements or arbitration awards.

The exercise of these rights shall be achieved by freely concluded collective agreements, by statutory wage-fixing machinery, or by other means appropriate to national conditions.

Part III of the European Social Charter sets out the specific obligations that the contracting parties must undertake after ratifying the charter. They are not required to adhere to all 19 "rights and principles" described in Parts I and II. Rather, they must adhere to "at least" 10 articles or 45 numbered paragraphs. [156] This formulation has created a bizarre maze of adoptions.

For example, paragraph 3 of Article 4 (which establishes the right to equal pay for equal work) has been adopted in about half of the contracting states and ignored in the other half. Articles 1, 3, 5, 6, 13, 14, 15, 16, and 17, on the other hand, have been adopted in their entirety by nearly all the parties.

TRANSNATIONAL ORGANIZED LABOR

Transnational labor unions, with the ability to represent employees across international boundaries, can exist only where IGOs have the power to sanction them. Both the EU and the Council of Europe have such power. Although the EU has yet to authorize the establishment of any transnational labor unions, the Council of Europe's European Social Charter specifically provides for them. Article 5 declares that the "Right to Organize" includes "the freedom of workers and employers to form local, national or international organizations for the protection of their economic and social conditions and to join such organizations." As noted earlier, Article 5 has been adopted by nearly all of the states that have ratified the Social Charter.

Several transnational labor organizations have been set up as coordinating bodies by municipal labor unions. They are designed to encourage cooperative action, to support national organizations, and to advocate the rights of workers before regional IGOs. Two reasonably successful examples are the International Secretariat of the World Auto Council and the European Confederation of Trade Unions. In addition to exchanging information about labor conditions and advocating labor issues, transnational labor organizations have been actively involved in collecting and disbursing *solidarity funds* to support national labor actions.

E. MOVEMENT OF WORKERS

The Universal Declaration of Human Rights, promulgated by the United Nations in 1948, states that "everyone has the right to leave any country, including his own, and to return to

---

[156]European Social Charter, Article 20(1), states: "Each of the contracting parties undertakes: (a) to consider Part I of this Charter as a declaration of aims to which it will pursue by all appropriate means, as stated in the introductory paragraph of that Part; (b) to consider itself bound by at least five of the following Articles of Part II of the Charter: Articles 1, 5, 6, 12, 13, 16, and 19; (c) in addition to the Articles selected by it in accordance with the preceding subparagraph, to consider itself bound by such a number of Articles or numbered paragraphs of Part II of the Charter as it may select, provided that the total number of Articles or numbered paragraphs by which it is bound is not less than 10 Articles or 45 numbered paragraphs."

passport: A warrant of protection and authority to travel between nations.

his country."[157] This is not, however, the generally accepted rule in international law today. Many countries require that their citizens have a **passport** and permission from the government before traveling abroad. The U.S. government, for example, has repeatedly held that American citizens do not have a right to have a passport or a right to leave the country.[158] In the case of *Haig v. Agee*,[159] the U.S. Supreme Court observed:

> A passport is, in a sense, a letter of introduction in which the issuing sovereign vouches for the bearer and requests other sovereigns to aid the bearer....
>
> With the enactment of travel control legislation making a passport generally a requirement for travel abroad, a passport took on certain added characteristics. Most important for present purposes, the only means by which an American can lawfully leave the country or return to it—absent a Presidentially granted exception—is with a passport.... As a travel control document, a passport is both proof of identity and proof of allegiance to the United States. Even under a travel control statute, however, a passport remains in a sense a document by which the government vouches for the bearer and for his conduct....
>
> Revocation of a passport undeniably curtails travel, but the freedom to travel abroad with a "letter of introduction" in the form of a passport issued by the sovereign is subordinate to national security and foreign policy considerations; as such, it is subject to reasonable governmental regulations. The Court has made it plain that the freedom to travel outside the United States must be distinguished from the right to travel within the United States.[160]

A similar rule was applied in the United Kingdom before it joined the European Community (now the EU) on January 1, 1973. Until that time, passports could not be obtained as a matter of right, and a passport, once granted, could be impounded or canceled at any time. The EU requires its member states to issue and renew passports valid for travel throughout the EU, and it forbids member states from requiring exit visas or equivalent documents for travel to other EU member states.[161] To the extent that the EU rules do not apply (i.e., to travel outside the Union), U.K. law still regards the issuance of a passport as a matter of "royal prerogative."[162]

Case 8–4 illustrates how one country justifies its restrictions on issuing passports.

---

[157]Universal Declaration of Human Rights, Article 13(2) (1948). A more detailed provision is contained in the International Covenant on Civil and Political Rights (1966). Article 12 provides:

> 1. Everyone lawfully within the territory of a State shall, within that territory, have the right to liberty of movement and freedom to choose his residence.
> 2. Everyone shall be free to leave any country, including his own.
> 3. The above-mentioned rights shall not be subject to any restrictions except those which are provided by law, are necessary to protect national security, public order, public health or morals, or the rights and freedoms of others, and are consistent with the other rights recognized in the present Covenant.
>
>   No one shall be arbitrarily deprived of the right to enter his own country.

[158]American citizens, however, can hold passports from other countries, as can the nationals of most states.

[159]*United States Reports*, vol. 453, p. 280 (Supreme Ct., 1981).

[160]*Id.*, at pp. 293–306.

[161]EC Directive 68/360 (October 15, 1968), *Official Journal*, p. L257/13 (1968).

[162]See David E. Williams, "British Passports and the Right to Travel," *International Comparative Law Quarterly*, vol. 23, p. 642, at pp. 647–648, 652–653 (1974).

Case 8-4   STATE v. NAGAMI

Japan, Nagasaki District Court, 1968.
Criminal Case 267, *Hanreijiho*, No. 599, p. 8 (1968); *Japanese Annual of International Law*, No. 16, p. 103 (1972).

Akie Nagami, a Japanese national, sought to obtain a Japanese passport that would allow her to visit China with her husband, Earle L. Reynolds, a U.S. national. Nagami and Reynolds were activists in the world peace movement, and they hoped to visit the People's Republic of China to promote understanding between China, Japan, and the United States. Japan did not recognize China at this time, and its Passport Law required nationals who wanted to visit an unrecognized country to obtain and attach to their passport applications an entrance permit from the particular country. Nagami was unable to obtain an entrance permit from China; and Japan, accordingly, refused to grant her a passport endorsed for entrance into China. Undaunted, Nagami and Reynolds sailed for China on Reynolds' yacht anyway. The Nagasaki harbor police, having been notified that this might happen, arrested both Nagami and Reynolds, charging her with leaving the country without a valid passport and him with being an accessory to her crime. At their trial, the accused argued that denying a person a passport is a breach of a fundamental human right as well as a breach of the Japanese constitutional provision establishing the right to travel.

JUDGMENT OF THE COURT:

Article 3 of the Passport Law specifies the papers that an applicant must submit to the Foreign Minister in order to obtain a passport. . . .

The Court will now consider whether this provision [i.e., Article 3] gives too much discretion to the Foreign Minister to restrict the freedom of travel to foreign countries. . . .

Because this provision imposes a substantial restriction on a fundamental human right—the right of an individual to travel freely to foreign countries—it has to be narrowly interpreted. Because a passport serves not only to identify an individual and establish his nationality, but also as a letter from a government asking another government to ensure the care and safety of a traveler, it is appropriate to conclude that procedures established by the Passport Law are meant to ensure that the bearer will be safe and secure in the country being visited. In this respect, Article 19(1)(4) of the Passport Law specifically provides that the Foreign Minister or a consular official may demand that an individual return a passport in circumstances where the Minister or official believes that the individual's life, person, or property are at risk. It seems appropriate, accordingly, that if an individual is subject to these same risks at the time that he applies for a passport, that the passport need not be given him.

The government's evidence establishes that it has long followed the practice of requiring nationals who want to visit a country with which Japan has no diplomatic relations to obtain and attach to their passport applications an entrance permit from that country. Several reasons are given for this practice. First, entrance into a country with which Japan does not have diplomatic relations may prove difficult for an individual who has not

made advance arrangement. Second, after a person enters an unrecognized foreign state, it is not possible for the government to protect them or provide them with any assistance.

Considering that the practice of requiring applicants seeking to enter an unrecognized country to obtain an entrance permit is long standing, that the procedure is consistent with the general purpose of the Passport Law, and that there are good reasons for imposing this requirement, one cannot conclude that the discretionary authority given to the Foreign Minister in Article 3(1)(7) is overly broad or that it has been misused.

The Court will now consider whether the regulations of the Foreign Minister implementing Article 3(1)(7) of the Passport Law violate the guarantee set out in Article 22(2) of the Constitution, which establishes that freedom of travel is a fundamental right, or whether those regulations are an exception to that guarantee permitted by the Constitution's public welfare clause. We must begin by observing that the freedom of movement is not an unlimited or unrestricted right. We also observe that a restriction on a fundamental right in the interest of public welfare is allowed if it is based on substantial and rational reasons, and is not unduly burdensome.

The Foreign Minister's regulations, we note, are clear cut and succinct: they forbid travel to the People's Republic of China by anyone who cannot obtain an entrance permit from that country's government. While it may be difficult to obtain this authorization, it is not impossible. The government's evidence established that more than 3,000 Japanese visited China in 1968, having first received entrance permits. Consequently, it cannot be said that the procedure established by the Foreign Minister's regulations is unduly burdensome. Also, because the purpose of the regulations is to insure that travelers are safe in their person and property, it is obvious that they are based on substantial reasons and reasons rationally related to objectives of the Passport Law.

. . . The accused contend that it is irrational to punish individuals who do not wish to have the protection of their government, especially when that protection is realistically unavailable. In this regard, it has to be noted that Japan, which is a signatory of a Security Treaty with the United States, follows the U.S. lead in international relations, and, as a consequence, is opposed internationally to China. . . . It is also a fact, as established by the government's evidence, that the People's Republic of China has not given adequate protection to the Japanese who reside there. As a consequence, the probability that Japanese visitors will be in danger in China is very high.

The contention that protection should not be forced on persons who do not want it is untenable for the following reasons. First, the government has the responsibility—

which it cannot relinquish—of ensuring the safety and security of Japanese who are abroad, and it was quite proper in this case that it took an interest in the accused and attempted to protect them from the dangers which they were very likely to face in the People's Republic of China.... Second, an important reason why the government is concerned with the safety of persons traveling overseas . . . is that foreign travel has, by its nature, a close connection with international relations and national security. In this regard, we cannot ignore the historical fact that the persecution or injury of nationals in foreign countries has often produced international tension. In sum, the government, in restricting the foreign travel of nationals, is acting both out of concern for the safety of the individual and also for the country's national security.

For these reasons, we hold that the Foreign Minister, acting out of concern for the public welfare, acted properly in restricting the travel of [Akie Nagami]. . . .

Akie Nagami was fined 50,000 yen. Her husband, Earle L. Reynolds, having been an accessory, was fined 30,000 yen. ■

CASEPOINT: The court held that the granting of a passport is not a fundamental human right, and a government can lawfully establish rules and regulations governing the issuance of passports. The court pointed out that there was a strong basis, both for the safety of its

citizens and for international diplomatic and security reasons, for the Japanese government to enact and enforce restrictions on travel to China.

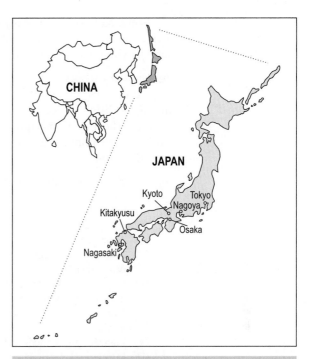

MAP 8-4   Japan (1968)

VISAS

Visa: Formal authorization to enter a country.

Visas are a host state's counterpart of the passport. They grant permission for an alien to enter a country. As with passports, issuance is discretionary with the host state, and both the length of time that an alien may stay in a country and the activities the alien may carry on while there can be limited. With respect to their duration, visas are classified as either temporary or permanent. An alien who receives a temporary visa is expected to leave the country after a stated time period. An alien who receives a permanent visa is allowed to stay indefinitely, and often an alien who seeks a permanent visa is expecting to apply for nationalization.

Commonly, an alien who wishes to obtain a visa must go to a state's overseas embassies or consulates and make an application before traveling to the state. An alien who is already inside a host state and has questions about his or her visa or wants to change from one kind of visa to another needs to contact the state's immigration service. For example, in the United States this was formerly known as the Immigration and Naturalization Service, but it is now called the Citizenship and Immigration Services; in Canada it is called Citizenship and Immigration Canada; and in the United Kingdom it is called the Immigration and Nationality Directorate.[163]

---

[163]For information about U.S. immigration laws and policies, visit the U.S. Citizenship and Immigration Services' home page at http://www.uscis.gov/portal/site/uscis. The United Kingdom's Immigration and Nationality Directorate home page is at http://www.ind.homeoffice.gov.uk. Canada's Citizenship and Immigration Canada bureau's home page is at http://www.cic.gc.ca. Information on other countries' immigration laws and policies can be obtained from their embassies. For a list of embassy home pages, see the Yahoo! listing at http://dir.yahoo.com/Government/Embassies_and_Consulates/?skw=embassies+and+consulates.

Some countries, especially developing countries, allow aliens to obtain a visa upon their arrival in the country. When this is the case, aliens have a duty to contact the immigration service within a reasonable period of time to obtain a visa.

Temporary Visas

Most countries' immigration laws establish many categories of temporary visas, reflecting the many different activities that aliens may carry on while temporarily residing in a host country. The U.S. Immigration and Nationality Act, for instance, establishes the following categories of nonimmigrant aliens who are allowed to enter the United States for limited periods of time:

(a) Foreign government officials
(b) Visitors
(c) Transits
(d) Crewmen
(e) Traders and investors
(f) Students in colleges, universities, seminaries, conservatories, academic high schools, other academic institutions, and language training programs
(g) Representatives of international organizations
(h) Temporary employees
(i) Representatives of information media
(j) Exchange aliens
(k) Fiancées and fiancés of U.S. citizens
(l) Intracompany transferees
(m) Students in established vocational or other recognized nonacademic institutions other than language training programs
(n) Parents and children of certain special immigrants
(o) Aliens of extraordinary ability
(p) Artists, athletes, and entertainers
(q) International cultural exchange visitors
(r) Religious workers
(s) NATO nonimmigrant aliens
(t) Alien witnesses and informants[164]

The most common temporary visas are visitor visas for tourists.[165] Tourists ordinarily have to apply for a visa at an overseas embassy or consulate of the country they intend to visit. Many countries, however, have a Visa Waiver Program (VWP) that allows tourists from designated countries (usually countries with a reciprocal arrangement) to enter without a visa. The United States VWP, for example, does not require visas for tourists to enter the United States, for up to ninety days, from 27 countries, including Andorra, Australia, Austria, Belgium, Brunei, Denmark, Finland, France, Germany, Iceland, Ireland, Italy, Japan, Liechtenstein, Luxembourg, Monaco, the Netherlands, New Zealand, Norway, Portugal, San Marino, Singapore, Slovenia, Spain, Sweden, Switzerland, and the United Kingdom.[166]

In 2007 the Bush administration proposed a "modernization" of the VWP that would require innovations such as electronic registration of VWP travelers, as well as more data sharing and better reporting of lost and stolen passports. These new measures, which have been sent to Congress for consideration, would enhance security at U.S. borders, according to the Bush administration. Some 13 nations have applied to join the U.S. VWP, and if approved, the new requirements would initially apply only to them. But an official for the Department of Homeland Security stated that it was hoped that the new security measures would eventually be applied to all VWP participants. "We have no interest in running two-tiered VWP,"

---

[164]*United States Code*, Title 8, §§ 1101, 1103, 1182, 1184, 1186a, 1187, 1221, 1281, and 1282.
[165]In the United States, these are known as B-1 visas.
[166]*United States Code of Federal Regulations*, Title 8, part 217.2 (January 1, 2002). U.S. immigration laws and regulations are available on the U.S. Citizenship and Immigration Service's Web site at http://www.uscis.gov/portal/site/uscis.

said the official. "The same security standards should apply to all member countries regardless of when they were admitted to the program."[167]

EU member nations whose citizens can now travel to the United States without visas are carefully watching the developments before deciding on reciprocal action. Currently, U.S. citizens can travel to EU countries without a visa. However, because of the EU principle of equal treatment across the EU, all EU citizens might be required to obtain online visas if the U.S. program is fully implemented in the future.[168]

Another common temporary visa is given to business visitors.[169] Most countries allow business visitors to enter for short-term visits (typically for no more than six months) to contact customers, attend trade shows and conventions, show samples, take orders, and engage in other business activities. They must be acting on behalf of a foreign firm, however, and not working for a local employer.[170]

Following the terrorist attacks on the United States on September 11, 2001, the United States reorganized its administrative structure regarding entry into this country. The former Immigration and Naturalization Service has been replaced by the U.S. Citizenship and Immigration Service (USCIS), a division of the Department of Homeland Security. It is more difficult to enter the United States today than it was before September 11. U.S. citizens as well as foreign citizens now need a passport to enter the United States when arriving by plane from outside the United States.

For example, one of the opening pages of the USCIS Web site gives some initial information about visitors to the United States as set forth in Reading 8-3.

---

[167]"Officials Urge Congress to Modernize, Expand Visa Waiver Program," http://usinfo.state.gov/, accessed June 2, 2007.
[168]"U.S. Visa Issue Causes EU Divisions," EUObserver.com, April 26, 2007.
[169]In the United States, these are called B-2 visas.
[170]The United States allows business visitors to "be admitted for not more than one year" and they "may be granted extensions of temporary stay in increments of not more than six months." *United States Code of Federal Regulations*, Title 8, § 214.2(b).

Reading 8-3   UNITED STATES VISA REGULATIONS

USCIS Web site: http://www.uscis.gov.

U.S. VISA LAWS FOR BUSINESS OR PLEASURE VISITORS

Generally, a citizen of a foreign country who wishes to enter the United States must first obtain a visa, either a nonimmigrant visa for temporary stay or an immigrant visa for permanent residence. The visitor visa is a nonimmigrant visa for persons desiring to enter the United States temporarily for business (B-1) or for pleasure or medical treatment (B-2). Persons planning to travel to the U.S. for a different purpose, such as students, temporary workers, crewmen, journalists, etc, must apply for a different visa in the appropriate category. Travelers from certain eligible countries may also be able to visit the U.S. without a visa, through the Visa Waiver Program. Read more about how to participate in the Visa Waiver Program on the U.S. Customs and Border Protection (CBP) website. More helpful information on the Visa Waiver program is found on the State Department Visa Services website.

Also, you may want to find out more about "How Do I Get Legally Admitted to the U.S." (or "How Will I be Inspected When I Come to a U.S. Port of Entry") on the CBP website.

QUALIFYING FOR A VISA

Applicants for visitor visas must show that they qualify under provisions of the Immigration and Nationality Act. The presumption in the law is that every visitor visa applicant is an intending immigrant. Therefore, applicants for visitor visas must overcome this presumption by demonstrating that:

- The purpose of their trip is to enter the U.S. for business, pleasure, or medical treatment;
- They plan to remain for a specific, limited period; and
- They have a residence outside the U.S. as well as other binding ties which will insure their return abroad at the end of the visit.

Alien truck drivers may qualify for admission as B-1 visitors for business to pick up or deliver cargo traveling in the stream of international commerce. Please see "How Do I Enter the United States as a Commercial Truck Driver" for more information.

PASSING THROUGH A U.S. PORT OF ENTRY

Applicants should be aware that a visa does not guarantee entry into the United States. Immigration authorities have the authority to deny admission and determine the period for which the bearer of a visitor visa is authorized to remain in the United States.

The USCIS Web site is

http://www.uscis.gov

Most developed countries have a special category of visa for students.[171] To qualify, students typically must obtain a statement in advance from the educational institution showing that they have been admitted to a course of study.[172] They also need to prove that they have sufficient resources to cover their course of study and to return home upon its completion.[173] Some countries allow students to work on campus,[174] but many do not.[175]

Other important temporary visas are those given to temporary employees[176] and the intracompany transferees of multinational enterprises.[177] Typically, these visas are granted only on the petition of an employer,[178] and an alien who has such a visa and changes jobs must get the new employer to apply for a new visa.[179]

---

[171]In the United States, these are F-1 visas for students in academic institutions and M-1 visas for students in vocational programs.

[172]A student seeking to study in the United States must have the U.S. institution complete form I-20 A-B/I-20 ID, "Certificate of Eligibility for Nonimmigrant (F-1) Student Status," or form I-20M-N, "Certificate of Eligibility for Nonimmigrant (M-1) Student Status." *Id.*, §§ 214.2(f)(1)(I)(A) and 214.2(m)(1)(i)(A).

[173]*Id.*, §§ 214.2(f)(1)(i)(B) and 214.2(m)(1)(i)(A). Students enrolled at academic institutions are allowed to leave and return on the same visa for annual vacations. *Id.*, § 214.2(f)(5)(iii).

[174]*Id.*, § 214.2(f)(9). Students in U.S. vocational programs may only work in practical training programs after completing their course of study. *Id.*, § 214.2(m)(i)(13) and (14).

[175]United Kingdom, *Immigration Rules* (HC 395), para. 57(vii).

[176]In the United States, these are known as H-1 visas.

[177]These are called L-1 visas in the United States.

[178]For example, *United States Code*, Title 8, § 1101(a)(15)(H), provides that an alien may be authorized to come to the United States temporarily to perform services or labor for, or to receive training from, an employer if petitioned for by that employer. The alien must be a registered nurse, a fashion model, a temporary or seasonal agricultural worker, a professional athlete, a trainee, a participant in a special education exchange visitor program, or an individual who will perform services in a specialty occupation, or services relating to a Department of Defense cooperative research and development project or coproduction project, or who is of distinguished merit and ability. See *United States Code of Federal Regulations*, Title 8, § Sec. 214.2(h)(1)(i).

United States Code, Title 8, § 1101(a)(15)(L), provides that an alien who within the preceding three years has been employed abroad for one continuous year by a qualifying organization may be admitted temporarily to the United States to be employed by a parent, branch, affiliate, or subsidiary of that employer in a managerial or executive capacity, or in a position requiring specialized knowledge.

[179]See *United States Code of Federal Regulations*, Title 8, § 214.2(h)(2)(i)(c).

Permanent Visas

All states limit the number of permanent visas that they grant to immigrants. This is because they want to ensure that the persons who are granted permanent visas will contribute to the state's society and will not be a burden on it. States typically establish a scheme that gives certain classes of persons a priority claim to visas with permanent immigrant status and that limits the total number of aliens who may enter from particular foreign countries.

For example, the U.S. Immigration and Nationality Act[180] establishes two categories of aliens with priority claims to permanent visas: (1) aliens who are family members of American citizens or of aliens who are already permanent residents of the United States[181] and (2) aliens with special skills.[182] Among this second category are aliens with extraordinary ability (such as well-known writers and philosophers), outstanding professors and researchers, and highly qualified multinational executives and managers.[183]

Once all of the aliens with priority claims to permanent visas have been granted them, then persons who do not have such a claim are given visas, usually on a first-to-apply basis. There is ordinarily a limit on the number of visas that will be granted to aliens from any particular country and on the number of visas that will be granted in any one year. For example, the total number of visas that the United States grants annually is approximately 675,000.[184]

Most immigration schemes also provide for special cases, especially refugees and aliens seeking political asylum. Ordinarily, these applicants are not considered in determining the total number of visas that are granted on an annual basis.[185]

Compliance with Visa Obligations

Aliens are obliged to comply with the terms of their visas and to leave a country when their visa expires or when it is withdrawn. Moreover, the issuance or denial of a visa, the extension or the refusal to extend an existing visa, and the revocation of a visa are all matters of executive discretion. As a consequence, such decisions are noncontestable in the courts of most countries, as Case 8–5 illustrates.

---

[180]*United States Code*, Title 8, §1101 *et seq.*

[181]These are known as *family-sponsored immigrants*, and they have priority in the following order: first, unmarried sons and daughters of citizens; second, spouses and unmarried sons and daughters of permanent resident aliens; third, married sons and daughters of citizens; and, fourth, brothers and sisters of citizens. *Id.*, § 1153.

[182]*Id.*

[183]Other aliens with priority claims to permanent residency visas based on special skills are (in order of preference) aliens who are members of the professions and who hold advanced degrees or who have exceptional ability; skilled workers whose skill requires two or more years of training or experience; professionals; other workers who have qualifications that are not available in the United States; and persons who have or will establish a business in the United States. *Id.*

[184]*Id.*, §1151.

[185] For example, see *id.*, §1157 (for refugees).

≈〰≈

Case 8-5   ENGLAND AND ANOTHER v. ATTORNEY-GENERAL OF ST. LUCIA

Court of Appeal of the Eastern Caribbean States, Civil Division, 1985.
West Indian Reports, vol. 35, p. 171 (1987).

The appellants, David and Jean England, who were British subjects, moved to St. Lucia with their family in 1968 and became residents (but not citizens). On August 9, 1983, David England was informed by the prime minister of *St. Lucia that the government had information indicating that he was helping political extremists in their efforts to recruit St. Lucians for terrorist training in Libya. The prime minister did not indicate the source of this information. He did, however, tell David England that the government regarded him as a threat to the security of the state and that he was no longer welcome.*

David England, through his solicitor, denied these allegations, and he asked to present his side of the matter before the government took any action. The government did not give him the opportunity. On September 2, two orders concerning David and Jean England were made by the governor-general in council under Section 4(3)(b) of St. Lucia's Immigration Ordinance. The orders declared the Englands to be prohibited immigrants and authorized the chief immigration officer to remove them from the country on or before September 4. On September 5, the solicitor for the Englands filed motions challenging the procedure taken by the government and the validity of its two orders.

ASSOCIATE JUSTICE BISHOP DELIVERED THE JUDGMENT OF THE COURT: . . .

On 1st September 1983 the Immigration Ordinance (Amendment) Act became law in St. Lucia. As a result, the Immigration Ordinance and Deportation (British Subjects) Ordinance were significantly affected. For the purposes of the instant case, in the former Ordinance there was no longer the section that created a class of persons who were "deemed to belong" to St. Lucia and the immigration of persons or of any person specified in an Order made by the Governor-General in Council was prohibited, unless there was some statutory barrier to such prohibition. Put another way, Section 2(2) and that part of Section 5 to which I alluded earlier were both deleted. The whole of the Deportation (British Subjects) Ordinance was repealed. The result was that the England family were without the description or classification of persons who were deemed to belong to St. Lucia for immigration and for deportation purposes. Further, they could be deemed prohibited immigrants under the Immigration Ordinance, as amended.

In my view, from the date when St. Lucia became an independent sovereign country, there were those persons who became citizens without more, there were persons who became citizens upon registration, and there were those persons who were not citizens, some of whom could apply for citizenship. It is clear and undisputed that, on 22nd February 1979 and after, the Englands were not registered as citizens and were not citizens. It does not arise for determination in this appeal whether the Englands could or should be registered as citizens on making application in the proper form. If and when application is made, that decision or a declaration from this court may become necessary. For the moment it is sufficient, in my opinion, to say that there was no application made for registration as citizens. The Englands did not have a right, in law, to reside in St. Lucia. They did not have a right, in law, not to be deported from St. Lucia. They did not have a right in law, not to be declared prohibited immigrants.

On 2nd September 1983, around 3.30 p.m, two Orders (the David England (Prohibited Immigrant) Order and

the Jean England (Prohibited Immigrant) Order) were served on the parties therein named. They were similar in substance and in their terms, the sole difference being the names, and so I shall quote only one of them.

WHEREAS by Paragraph (b) of Subsection (3) of Section 4 of the Immigration Ordinance, Chapter 76, it is provided that where the Governor-General in Council is satisfied on information or advice that any person is undesirable as an inhabitant of, or a visitor to St. Lucia, he may by Order declare such a person to be a prohibited immigrant and direct that such person be removed from St. Lucia forthwith or by such time as shall be stipulated,

AND WHEREAS the Governor-General in Council is satisfied on information received that David England is undesirable as an inhabitant of, or a visitor to St. Lucia,

NOW THEREFORE the Governor-General in Council in pursuance to the power conferred upon him as aforesaid orders and declares and it is hereby ordered and declared as follows:

1. *Short Title.* This Order may be cited as the David England (Prohibited Immigrant) Order 1983.

2. *Declaration of Prohibited Immigrant.* David England is declared to be a prohibited immigrant as an inhabitant of, or a visitor to St. Lucia.

3. *Removal of Prohibited Immigrant.* The Chief Immigration Officer is hereby authorized to remove David England from St. Lucia by Sunday 4th September 1983.

Made by the Cabinet under the authority of Subsection (3) of Section 4 of the Immigration Ordinance, Chapter 76, 2nd September 1983.

On 3rd September 1983, David and Jean England, through their solicitor, prepared and signed notices of motions and supporting affidavits, as a direct consequence of the service of the above Orders. These notices were filed on 5th September 1983 after the Englands had been removed from St. Lucia. Upon completion of the hearing of the motion the trial judge reserved his decision for delivery on 23rd November 1983 and, as I have already indicated, he refused all the relief and prayers sought by the Englands in their motions.

. . . It was submitted by counsel for the Englands that the Governor-General in Council acting under Section 4(3) of the Immigration Ordinance, as amended, was an authority prescribed by law for the determination of the existence or extent of the civil right of persons falling in the category created by Section 102(1)(b) of the Constitution of St. Lucia and that, if that were so, the rules of natural justice ought to have been observed in arriving at the decision to remove the Englands from St. Lucia as the Governor-General in Council was made a *quasi*-judicial body.

Counsel for the Attorney-General submitted that the Governor-General in Council was not a tribunal nor was any exercise of a judicial or *quasi*-judicial function required under Section 4(3) of the Immigration Ordinance. He submitted, further, that it could not be reasonable, when the Governor-General in Council was satisfied that a person should be removed, to expect that that person should then be called and told of the information or advice given, as well as its source, so that that person could be afforded an opportunity to be heard. According to counsel, there were certain areas in government which were reserved for the state (for example, security and deportation) and "the courts could not substitute themselves for the state."...

In my opinion the Governor-General in Council was not acting as judicial tribunal nor was the function required by the Section one of a *quasi*-judicial nature. When it is borne in mind that the Governor-General is Her Majesty the Queen's representative in St. Lucia (Section 19 of the St. Lucia Constitution) and when the Immigration Ordinance (as amended in 1983) is considered, it becomes clear that under Section 4(3)(b) the Governor-General in Council, in September 1983, acted solely under executive powers and in no sense as a court.[186] As I perceive it, the Governor-General in Council was not called upon or empowered by the Section to adjudicate in any matter of contention between parties, nor was any procedure laid down or any provision made for anyone to be heard or for the person who would be affected by an Order to make any representation, oral or written. The Section did not state, either expressly or by implication, that the Governor-General in Council should conduct an inquiry. If Parliament had so intended or wished it would have been simple to state in the Section that the Governor-General in Council should be satisfied "after holding due inquiry," and not "on information or advice." So that there was no statutory requirement that there be evidence or that the source of information or advice on which the Governor-General in Council acted be disclosed or be controlled in accordance with any law. Indeed, it must be obvious that disclosure of the source, or of the information or advice, to the person who may be affected by the Order of the Governor-General in Council, would not only be highly understandable but could involve disclosure of confidential national matters, including defense policy, security and the internal safety of the public. Again, as was indicated by the Chief Justice, the Earl of Reading, in *R. v Leman Street Police Station Inspector, ex parte Venicoff*:[187]

MAP 8-5 Saint Lucia (1987)

It might well be that a person against whom it was proposed to make such an order would take care, if he had notice of such an inquiry, not to present himself, and, as soon as he knew that an inquiry would be held, would take steps to prevent his apprehension.

There was no claim that the Governor-General in Council acted other than in good faith. Of course, had there been any assertion of bad faith, it would have had to be specifically alleged, with particulars, and the burden of proof would have been on the Englands. Nor could it have been asserted that the Governor-General in Council was not satisfied on information received that David England and Jean England were undesirable as inhabitants of, or visitors to St. Lucia.

***

. . . I have found no cause to disturb the decision of the trial judge and would therefore dismiss the appeal.

***

The appeal was dismissed. ∎

CASEPOINT: The court decided that the laws of St. Lucia had recently been amended to allow for the summary deportation procedure that was followed by the government. The governor-general was empowered to act in an executive capacity by the law, and his decision was not reviewable in the court system in the absence of bad faith, which was not alleged.

[186]Eshugbayi Eleko v. Officer Administering the Government of Nigeria, *Law Reports, Appeal Cases*, vol. 1931, p. 662 (1931).
[187]*All England Law Reports*, vol. 1920, p. 157 (1920).

REGULATION OF FOREIGN WORKERS

Aliens who enter a country to work must obtain an appropriate entry visa (i.e., one that allows them to be gainfully employed), and they must comply with the host state's employment laws. Commonly, the same labor laws that apply to nationals govern foreign workers once they are allowed to enter a country. This is often so even when a foreign worker and a foreign employer agree to abide by the labor laws of their home state.

percentile legislation: A law requiring a certain percentage of employees to be local nationals.

Many states impose special rules on foreign workers. Some use **percentile legislation** to ensure that a certain percentage of the local work force is made up of nationals.[188] Others limit the benefits that foreign employees can be given. Singapore, for example, requires that alien employees be paid at the same rate as nationals. Singapore employers, furthermore, are responsible for ensuring that their alien employees get adequate housing and that a physician examines them before they enter the country; the employers additionally must make social security contributions and assume the cost of the employees' repatriation.[189]

Sometimes the rules governing foreign workers seem to grant them special privileges. This seems especially to be the case when the rules are set out in a treaty. For example, treaties of Friendship, Commerce, and Navigation commonly establish a reciprocal right for the national businesses of either signatory state to employ certain categories of their national workers within the territory of the other state. An example is the 1953 Japanese–United States Friendship, Commerce, and Navigation Treaty:[190]

> Nationals and companies of either party shall be permitted to engage, within the territories of the other party, accountants and other technical experts, executive personnel, attorneys, agents, and other specialists of their choice. Moreover, such nationals and companies shall be permitted to engage accountants and other technical experts regardless of the extent to which they may have qualified for the practice of a profession within the territories of such other party, for the particular purpose of making examinations, audits and technical investigations exclusively for, and rendering reports to, such nationals and companies in connection with the planning and operation of their enterprises, and enterprises in which they have a financial interest, within such territories.
>
> Nationals of either party shall not be barred from practicing the professions within the territories of the other party merely by reason of their alienage. . .

On its face, this provision allows a foreign business to discriminate in favor of its national employees by assigning its nationals to senior executive positions and by denying promotions to employees in the host state. This was not, however, the intent of the treaty's drafters. As Case 8–6 points outs, foreign employers and foreign workers are both subject to the employment laws of the host state unless a treaty or domestic law clearly and specifically provides otherwise.

---

[188]Oman's Ministry of Social Affairs and Labor has issued regulations that are a variant of percentile legislation. Ministerial Decision No. 51, effective August 17, 1993, provides that foreign workers may be employed only when Omani labor is inadequate. In addition, no more than 15 non-Omanis may be employed in Oman Chamber of Commerce and Industry category four companies, 30 in category three companies, and 60 in category two companies. Also, some industries, such as fishing, are forbidden to employ non-Omani workers, whereas others, such as tailoring, are not. Adrian Creed, "Oman Issues New Rules for Non-Omani Workers," *Middle East Executive Reports*, vol. 16, no. 12, p. 17 (December 1993).

[189]International Labor Organization, "Protecting the Most Vulnerable of Today's Workers," Chap. 4 (1997), posted at http://www.ilo.org/public/english/protection/migrant/research/others/1997-01/ch4.htm.

[190]Article VIII, paras. 1–2, *United States Treaties and Other International Agreements*, vol. 4, pt. 2, p. 2063 at p. 2070 (1953).

〰〰〰

Case 8-6 SPIESS ET AL. v. C. ITOH & CO. (AMERICA), INC.

United States, District Court, Southern District of Texas, 1979.
Federal Supplement, vol. 469, p. 1 (1979).

DISTRICT JUDGE CARL O. BUE, JR.:

Plaintiffs, non-Japanese employees of the defendant, have filed suit against defendant pursuant to Title VII of the Civil Rights Act of 1964, . . . alleging racially discriminatory employment practices. C. Itoh & Co. (America), hereinafter "Itoh-America," is a domestic corporation incorporated under the laws of New York and a wholly-owned subsidiary of C. Itoh & Co., Ltd., of Japan, hereinafter "Itoh-Japan," a Japanese corporation which is not a party to the instant suit. Presently before the Court for consideration is Itoh-America's . . . motion to dismiss for failure to state a claim upon which relief may be granted. The issue presented is a novel question of first impression: Does the 1953 Treaty of Friendship, Commerce and Navigation between the United States and Japan provide American subsidiaries of Japanese corporations with the absolute right to hire managerial, professional and other specialized personnel of their choice, irrespective of American law proscribing racial discrimination in employment? . . .

. . . Itoh-America asserts that the Treaty gives it three absolute rights, the combined effect of which "is to create an absolute right on the part of United States and Japanese nationals and companies to send their own nationals to the other country to hold managerial and specialized positions within their respective affiliates and subsidiaries." The rights claimed are:

1. The absolute right to establish, maintain, control, and manage a wide variety of commercial enterprises by nationals and companies of one country in the other country (Article VII, paragraph 1).

2. The absolute right of nationals of the two countries to enter the other country for the purpose of carrying on trade and engaging in related commercial activities between the two countries (Article I, paragraph 1).

3. The absolute right of nationals and companies of either country to engage, within the other country, managerial, professional, and other specialized personnel "of their

choice," including their own nationals (Article VIII, paragraph 1).

. . . The crucial section of the Treaty relied upon by Itoh-America is Article VIII(1) which by its terms provides that "nationals and companies of either party shall be permitted to engage within the territories of the other party [personnel] of their choice." Stated otherwise in terms of the instant inquiry, a company of Japan is entitled to engage within the territory of the United States personnel of its choice. Thus, the pivotal issue becomes the nationality of Itoh-America. Plaintiffs urge that the Treaty's own definitional section provides the unequivocal answer to this question: Article XXII(3) provides that "[c]ompanies constituted under the applicable laws and regulations within the territories of either party shall be deemed companies thereof. . . ." Under this definition Itoh-America is a company of the United States because it is incorporated under the laws of the State of New York. Its business operations in the United States are, therefore, those of a United States company in the United States, not the activities of a company of one party within the territory of the other party. Accordingly, plaintiffs argue any immunity from United States discrimination laws conveyed by Article VIII(1) does not apply to Itoh-America.

. . . This analysis is supported by the case of *United States v. R. P. Oldham*,[191] wherein the court used a similar standard for determining corporate nationality for purposes of the 1953 Japanese-American Treaty. Kinoshita & Co., Ltd., U.S.A. ("Kinoshita-America"), an American subsidiary of Kinoshita & Co., Ltd., Tokyo, was indicted along with others for conspiracy in restraint of commerce in Japanese wire nails. Kinoshita-America argued that Article XVIII of the Treaty dealing with antitrust violations provided the exclusive remedy available to the government in dealing with antitrust violations by American corporations which are wholly owned by Japanese corporations. The District Court held that Article XVIII was not intended as an exclusive remedy; rather than replace American antitrust laws, Article XVIII was intended to supplement them. This conclusion was based on the fact that "[t]he tenor of the

---

[191]*Federal Supplement*, vol. 152, p. 818 (District Ct., N. Dist. of Calif., 1957).

entire Treaty is equal treatment to nationals of the other party, not better treatment."[192] . . . The Court further held that even if Article XVIII were held to provide an exclusive remedy for antitrust violations, Kinoshita-America lacked standing to invoke its protection.

The Court engaged in a two-step process to arrive at the conclusion that Kinoshita-America was not shielded from United States antitrust laws by Article XVIII. The first step was the determination of the nationality of Kinoshita-America. In order to resolve this question the Court looked to Article XXII, the only definitional section of the Treaty, and pursuant to paragraph three of that Article determined that:

> [B]y the terms of the Treaty itself, as well as by established principles of law, a corporation organized under the laws of a given jurisdiction is a creature of that jurisdiction, with no greater rights, privileges or immunities than any other corporation of that jurisdiction.[193]

Once the question of the nationality of Kinoshita-America was determined, the Court completed the two-step inquiry by concluding that an American corporation has no standing to invoke Article XVIII as a defense to the United States antitrust laws. Any protection against application of United States law would extend only to Japanese corporations, concluded the Court:

> If . . . conspirator Kinoshita & Co., Ltd., Tokyo had wished to retain its status as a Japanese corporation while doing business in this country, it could easily have operated through a branch. Having chosen instead to gain privileges accorded American corporations by operating through an American subsidiary, it has for the most purposes surrendered its Japanese identity with respect to the activities of this subsidiary.[194]

***

Despite the fact that the Treaty's own definitional section provides that the place of incorporation determines the nationality of a company for purposes of the Treaty and the fact that the Court in *Oldham* determined that an entity identically situated to Itoh-America was an American corporation for purposes of the Treaty, Itoh-America urges this Court to reach a different result.

As support for its argument that it should be considered a Japanese corporation, Itoh-America refers to guidelines promulgated by the Department of State for use by consular officials in determining whether a foreigner seeking admission to the United States qualifies

as a "treaty-trader". Article I, paragraph 1 of the Japanese-American Treaty authorizes Japanese nationals to enter the United States as so-called treaty-traders "for the purpose of carrying on trade between the territories of the two parties and engaging in related commercial activities. . . ." In order to qualify as a treaty-trader an alien must satisfy Department of State regulations which require, among other things, that the alien "be employed by an individual employer having the nationality of the treaty company, or by an organization which is principally owned by a person or persons having the nationality of the treaty country."[195] Department of State guidelines provide further that:

> [t]he nationality of the employing firm is determined by those persons who own more than 50 percent of the stock of the employing corporation "regardless of the place of incorporation."

. . . Since it is wholly owned by Japanese interests, and thus is a Japanese corporation for treaty-trader purposes, Itoh-America urges that it should be considered a Japanese corporation for purposes of Article VIII(3). Any other conclusion, it argues, requires the absurd result that once a Japanese corporation exercises the right given to it by Article VII(1) to incorporate an American subsidiary, that subsidiary loses all other rights under the Treaty.

The Court finds that resort to the treaty-trader guidelines to determine corporate nationality for purposes of interpretation of the Treaty provisions is unwarranted in the face of the clear definitional provisions included in Article XXII(3) of the Treaty itself. Article XXII(3) unequivocally states that for the purpose of the Treaty the nationality of a corporation is determined by the place of incorporation. The fact that nationality is determined by a different standard for other purposes cannot alter the clearly stated test of the Treaty itself.

. . . Given the Treaty's own definitional terms, Itoh-America is a company of the United States for purposes of the interpretation of Articles VIII(1). Thus, it can claim no direct protection under Article VIII(1), which applies only to companies of one party within the territories of the other party. Furthermore, even assuming that Article VIII(1) provides absolute immunity from Title VII to Itoh-Japan and that Itoh-America has standing to assert Itoh-America's Treaty rights in this action, questions the Court need not resolve, the motion to dismiss must be denied. Any absolute rights granted to Itoh-Japan apply only to its own hiring decisions; the

---

[192]*Id.*
[193]*Id.*, at p. 823.
[194]*Id.*
[195]*Code of Federal Regulations*, Title 22, § 41.40 (1977).

practices challenged in the present litigation are those of Itoh-America. Itoh-America is a United States company for purposes of Title VII and, like other United States companies, is subject to suit on the grounds that its employment practices are racially discriminatory. Accordingly, Itoh-America's motion to dismiss for failure to state a claim upon which relief may be granted is hereby denied. ■

CASEPOINT: The court needed to decide whether the employer here was subject to the civil rights laws of the United States, which prohibit employment discrimination. After finding that the employer-defendant in this case, although a wholly owned subsidiary of a Japanese company, was incorporated as a separate company under the laws of New York, the court ruled that the company was subject to U.S. law. The 1953 Treaty of Friendship, Commerce and Navigation between the United States and Japan did not provide American subsidiaries of Japanese corporations with the absolute

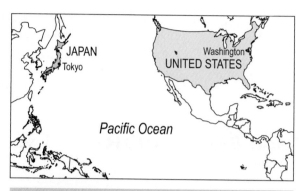

MAP 8-6   Japan and United States (1979)

right to hire managerial or professional personnel of their choice, irrespective of American law prohibiting racial and national origin discrimination in employment, where the subsidiaries are incorporated in the United States.

APPLICATION OF HOME STATE LABOR LAWS EXTRATERRITORIALLY

Traditionally, countries have refused to apply their labor laws extraterritorially. This priciple is based on the concept of *sovereignty*, by which each nation is independent, and not subject to the laws of other nations. For example, as long ago as 1804, the U.S. Supreme Court ruled that the laws of the United States will not be interpreted to violate the laws of other nations unless no other interpretation is possible.[196] In keeping with this, the Supreme Court has denied a Danish seaman's petition to have American tort law apply to an injury he suffered on a Danish ship in Havana harbor;[197] it has refused to give the National Labor Relations Board the authority to regulate collective bargaining among crewmen serving on foreign ships;[198] and it has held that the Equal Pay Act does not apply outside the territorial jurisdiction of the United States.[199]

However, even though the U.S. Supreme Court ordinarily assumes that the U.S. Congress does not intend for its legislation to apply extraterritorially, it does recognize that Congress "has the authority, in certain cases, to enforce its laws beyond the territorial boundaries of the United States."[200] And Congress—contrary to the practice in most other countries—has enacted labor-related laws that expressly apply extraterritorially, including the antidiscrimination provisions of Title VII of the Civil Rights Act of 1964[201] and the Americans with Disabilities Act of 1990, which apply to American citizens working for American employers overseas.[202]

---

[196]The Charming Betsy, *United States Reports*, vol. 6, p. 64 (Supreme Ct., 1804).
[197]Lauritzen v. Larsen, *id.*, vol. 345, p. 571 (Supreme Ct., 1953).
[198]Benz v. Compañia Naviera Hidalgo, SA, *id.*, vol. 353, p. 138 (1957).
[199]Windward Shipping (London), Ltd. v. American Radio Assn., AFL-CIO, *id.*, vol. 415, p. 104 (Supreme Ct., 1974).
[200]Equal Employment Opportunity Commission v. Arabian American Oil Co., *id.*,, vol. 499, p. 244 at p. 248 (1991).
[201]*United States Code*, Title 42, § 2000e(f), as amended by Public Law 102-166 of 1991. This amendment was adopted after the Supreme Court held in Equal Employment Opportunity Commission v. Arabian American Oil Co., *United States Reports*, vol. 499, p. 244 (1991), that the Civil Right Act did not apply to American employees working for American employers overseas.
[202]*Id.*, Title 42, § 12111(4), Public Law 101–336, § 2 of 1990.
   While Congress may adopt regulations that apply extraterritorially, the states of the United States may not do so, as these regulations can conflict with the power of the federal government to regulate international commerce. Crosby, Secretary of Administration and Finance of Massachusetts v. National Foreign Trade Council, *United States Reports*, vol. 530, p. 363 (U.S. Supreme Ct. 2000).

In Case 8–7, a U.S. federal court was asked to determine if Congress intended the Age Discrimination Employment Act of 1967 to apply extraterritorially.

━━◦◐◦━━

Case 8-7 MORELLI v. CEDEL

United States, Second Circuit Court of Appeals.
Federal Reporter, Third Series, vol. 141, p. 39 (1998).

RICHARD D. CUDAHY, CIRCUIT JUDGE:

This appeal requires us to decide whether the domestic employees of certain foreign corporations are protected under the Age Discrimination and Employment Act of 1967 (the ADEA), and, if so, whether a foreign corporation's foreign employees are counted for the purpose of determining whether the corporation has enough employees to be subject to the ADEA. We answer both questions in the affirmative.

BACKGROUND

After the defendant fired the plaintiff, the plaintiff sued the defendant. The plaintiff's amended complaint asserted that the defendant violated the ADEA. . . . The district court dismissed the complaint on the grounds that the defendant was not subject to the ADEA. . . . The plaintiff appeals. . . .

As alleged in the complaint, the facts relevant to this appeal are as follows. The plaintiff, Ida Morelli, was born on April 11, 1939. The defendant is a Luxembourg bank. On or about June 29, 1984, the defendant hired the plaintiff to work in its New York office. On or about February 26, 1993, the plaintiff became an assistant to Dennis Sabourin, a manager in the defendant's New York office. About one year later, Mr. Sabourin summoned the then 54-year-old plaintiff to his office, handed her a separation agreement, and insisted that she sign it.

Under the terms of the separation agreement, a copy of which was attached to the complaint, the plaintiff would resign, effective April 30, 1994. She would continue to receive her salary and benefits until the effective date of her resignation, but she would be relieved of her duties as an employee, effective immediately. Both the defendant and the employee would renounce all claims arising out of "their past working relationship." Mr. Sabourin told the plaintiff that she would receive the three months' severance pay, medical coverage for three months, and her pension only on the condition that she sign the agreement on the spot. The plaintiff had never

seen the separation agreement before and had no warning that she was going to be asked to resign. But in the face of Mr. Sabourin's ultimatum, she did sign the agreement immediately and returned it to him. The defendant, however, never provided her with a pension distribution.

DISCUSSION

1. Age Discrimination

(a) Does the ADEA Cover a U.S.-Based Branch of a Foreign Employer? The ADEA was enacted in 1967 to prevent arbitrary discrimination by employers on the basis of age—it protects workers 40 years of age and older. In order to determine whether the defendant is subject to the ADEA, we must first determine whether the ADEA generally protects the employees of a branch of a foreign employer located in the United States.

It is undisputed that Cedel is a foreign employer with fewer than 20 employees in its sole U.S. branch. . . .

Section 4(h)(2) of the ADEA provides that "the prohibitions of [the ADEA] shall not apply where the employer is a foreign person not controlled by an American employer." At a minimum, this provision means that the ADEA does not apply to the foreign operations of foreign employers—unless there is an American employer behind the scenes. An absolutely literal reading of §4(h)(2) might suggest that the ADEA also does not apply to the domestic operations of foreign employers. But the plain language of §4(h)(2) is not necessarily decisive if it is inconsistent with Congress' clearly expressed legislative purpose.

Section 4(h)(2) was not part of the original ADEA. It was added in 1984. The context in which it was added reveals that Congress' purpose was not to exempt the domestic workplaces of foreign employers from the ADEA's prohibition of age discrimination. Instead, the purpose of adding this exclusion was to limit the reach of an extraterritorial amendment adopted as part of the same legislation.

In 1984, before §4(h)(2) was added, several courts of appeals had concluded that the ADEA did not apply to "Americans employed outside the United States by

American employers."[203] . . . Within a few months of the 1984 court decisions, Congress amended the ADEA in a way that superseded the holding of these cases by "providing for limited extraterritorial application" of the ADEA.

The 1984 amendments amplified the definition of "employee" in §11(f) of the ADEA, which had previously embraced any "individual employed by any employer," except for certain elected public officials and political appointees. One of the 1984 amendments specified that "the term 'employee' includes any individual who is a citizen of the United States employed by an employer in a workplace in a foreign country."

Companion amendments dealt with the cases of foreign persons not controlled by an American employer—now §4(h)(2) of the ADEA—and foreign corporations controlled by American employers—now §4(h)(1). . . .

The 1984 revision to the definition of "employee" in §11(f) was intended "to assure that the provisions of the ADEA would be applicable to any citizen of the United States who is employed by an American employer in a workplace outside the United States."[204] The other 1984 amendments, to §4 of ADEA, conform the ADEA's reach to "the well-established principle of *sovereignty*, that no nation has the right to impose its labor standards on another country."[205] Thus §4(h)(2) of the ADEA merely limits the scope of the amended definition of employee, so that an employee at a workplace in a foreign country is not protected under the ADEA if the employer is a foreign person not controlled by an American employer.[206] There is no evidence in the legislative history that these amendments were intended to restrict the application of the ADEA with respect to the domestic operations of foreign employers.

***

If §4(h)(2) does not exempt the domestic operations of foreign companies from the ADEA, there is no other basis for such an exemption. . . . International comity does not require such an exemption; the 1984 amendments anticipate that American corporations operating abroad will be subject to foreign labor laws, and Congress presumably contemplated that the operations of foreign corporations here will be subject to U.S. labor laws.

We have previously concluded that even when a foreign employer operating in the United States can invoke a Friendship, Commerce and Navigation treaty to justify employing its own nationals, this "does not give [the employer] license to violate American laws prohibiting discrimination in employment."[207] . . .

We therefore agree with the E.E.O.C., the agency charged with the enforcement of the ADEA, that the law generally applies "to foreign firms operating on U.S. soil."[208] For the reasons we have discussed, we are confident that Congress has never clearly expressed a contrary intent.

(b) Are Employees Based Abroad Counted in Determining Whether a U.S.-Based Branch of a Foreign Employer Is Subject to the ADEA? Cedel will still not be subject to the ADEA by virtue of its U.S. operations unless Cedel is an "employer" under the ADEA. A business must have at least twenty "employees" to be an "employer."[209] Cedel maintains that, in the case of foreign employers, only domestic employees should be counted. The district court agreed, and, since Cedel had fewer than 20 employees in its U.S. branch, the court granted Cedel's motion to dismiss for lack of subject matter jurisdiction without considering the number of Cedel's overseas employees.

***

The district court reasoned that the overseas employees of foreign employers should not be counted because they are not protected by the ADEA. But there is no requirement that an employee be protected by the ADEA to be counted; an enumeration, for the purpose of ADEA coverage of an employer, includes employees under age 40, who are also unprotected, see 29 U.S.C. §631(a). The nose count of employees relates to the scale of the employer rather than to the extent of protection.

***

. . . Cedel contends that because it has fewer than 20 employees in the United States, it is the equivalent of a small U.S. employer. This is implausible with respect to compliance and litigation costs; their impact on Cedel is better gauged by its worldwide employment. Cedel would not appear to be any more a boutique operation in the United States than would a business with ten

[203]Cleary v. United States Lines, Inc., *Federal Reporter, Second Series*, vol. 728, p. 610 (3d Circuit Ct. of Appeals, 1984). . . .
[204]Senate Report 98–467, at p. 27 (1984). . .; see EEOC v. Arabian American Oil Co., *United States Reports*, vol. 499, p. 244 at pp. 258–59 (Supreme Ct., 1991).
[205]Senate Report at p. 27.
[206]See *id.* at pp. 27–28 ("The amendment . . . *does not* apply to foreign companies which are not controlled by U.S. firms.") (emphasis added).
[207]Avigliano v. Sumitomo Shoji America, Inc., *Federal Reporter, Second Series*., vol. 638, p. 552 at p. 558 (2d Circuit Ct. of Appeals, 1981), vacated on other grounds, *United States Reports*, vol. 457, p. 176 (Supreme Ct., 1982).
[208]E.E.O.C. Policy Guidance, N-915.039, Empl. Prac. Guide (CCH) paras. 5183, 6531 (March 3, 1989).
[209]*United States Code*, Title 29, § 630(b).

employees each in offices in, say, Alaska and Florida, which would be subject to the ADEA. Further, a U.S. corporation with many foreign employees but fewer than 20 domestic ones would certainly be subject to the ADEA.

Accordingly, in determining whether Cedel satisfies the ADEA's 20-employee threshold, employees cannot be ignored merely because they work overseas. We therefore vacate the judgment on the plaintiff's ADEA count.

***

CONCLUSION

The judgment is vacated . . . and the case is remanded for further proceedings not inconsistent with this opinion. ∎

CASEPOINT: The Second Circuit Court of Appeals (the second highest court level in the United States) held that (1) the federal Age Discrimination in Employment Act (ADEA) did indeed protect U.S. employees of foreign corporations that have operations in the United States and that (2) all employees of the company (within and outside the United States) will be counted in determining whether the company has 20 or more employees and is thus subject to the ADEA.

MAP 8-7 Luxembourg (1998)

Chapter Questions

Allowable WTO Restrictions

1. State A, an Eastern European country, is in the process of transforming its command economy to a market economy. It is also a WTO member state that has granted market access to its financial services sector to foreign banks. Unfortunately, it recently began to have difficulty with its balance-of-payments obligations. After notifying the GATS Council on Trade in Services and the International Monetary Fund, it issued a decree restricting the right of foreign banks to transfer funds abroad. It put no similar limitations, however, on its own banks or on the banks of other Eastern European countries making the transition to market economies. Big Bank, a bank with its place of establishment in State B and a branch in State A, objected to the State A decree and sought the help of State B to get State A to modify or rescind its decree. State A has contacted State B for consultations, and both parties have notified the WTO Dispute Settlement Body of their intent to engage in consultations. How should this dispute be resolved? Explain.

GATS and NAFTA Commitments

2. State C is a WTO member state and a party to NAFTA. It has made no specific agreements under either GATS or NAFTA as to its road transport sector. Now, two freight companies, one from State D (a WTO member state) and one from State E (a party to both the WTO and NAFTA), wish to provide overland freight transportation services in State C using trucks operating out of terminals in their states of establishment. May they do so? If so, to what extent? Explain.

Role and Power of the ILO Fact-Finding and Conciliation Commission

3. State A has not ratified either the ILO Convention Concerning Freedom of Association or the ILO Convention Concerning the Application of the Principles of the Right to Organize and

Bargain Collectively. Several workers within State A have lodged complaints with the ILO about their right to associate and bargain collectively. Can the ILO's Fact-Finding and Conciliation Commission consider their complaints?

Power of the ILO Administrative Tribunal

4. Armstrong worked for a United Nations specialized agency in Geneva for seven years. As part of his job, he tracked the civil rights activities of the agency's member states. One state did not appreciate his listing of certain civil rights abuses that he alleged that country was perpetrating against its nationals. The country refused to pay its dues to the agency unless he was fired. The secretary-general of the agency then fired him. Armstrong appealed this decision to the ILO's Administrative Tribunal, which has jurisdiction over these kinds of disputes. Armstrong asked the tribunal to order the agency to rehire him or, if it could not, then to order the agency to pay him compensation for the loss of his job. How should the tribunal rule? Discuss.

Freedom of Speech and Press in the EU

5. Barton works as a freelance reporter covering stories in State F, a member state of the EU. Her revealing stories, which she sells to a variety of progressive independent newspapers throughout the EU, have caused a great deal of embarrassment to a certain minister in the State F government, and the minister has asked the State F parliament to pass a law forbidding foreign news reporters from working in State F without the permission of that minister's office. Parliament has asked State F's attorney general for an opinion on the legality of the minister's request in light of State F's membership in the EU. What advice should the attorney general give Parliament? Discuss.

Right of an Attorney to Employment in Another EU Country

6. Caruso, a national of State G, is licensed as a lawyer in that state. Caruso, however, wants to work as a courtroom advocate in State H. May Caruso do so, despite the fact that under State H law, only citizens may be courtroom advocates in State H? (Both State G and State H are members of the EU.) Discuss.

U.S. Passport Rules

7. Dickens is a dual national of the United States and Ireland. The United States has a prohibition on travel and employment of U.S. nationals in Cuba. If Dickens goes to work in Cuba using his Irish passport to enter and leave Cuba, may the United States take any action against Dickens? Discuss.

National Government Power Over Visas

8. The faculty of Public University (PU), located in State I, has invited Karl Engels, a "revolutionary Marxist" from State J, and Bishop Biggott, an advocate of apartheid from State K, to participate in a symposium at PU. Both individuals have agreed to attend, but both have been denied visas to enter State I by that state's Foreign Ministry. The ministry acted according to State I law, which grants the ministry authority to deny visas for reasons of public policy, public safety, or public health. The PU faculty petitioned the ministry for a waiver, but the foreign minister refused to grant it. The faculty members have now brought a suit claiming (1) that their rights under State I's Constitution (which guarantees both freedom of speech and freedom of assembly) to hear the viewpoints of Mr. Engels and Bishop Biggott have been denied and (2) that the government has no basis on which to deny either applicant admission to State I. Will the faculty succeed on either of these grounds? Discuss.

Treaties of Friendship, Commerce, and Navigation

9. Americana, Inc., a large multinational corporation with its headquarters in the United States, has a subsidiary in Tokyo. It refuses to appoint any Japanese nationals to the senior executive posts of the subsidiary, claiming that it is specifically allowed to do so by the 1953 Japanese-United States Friendship, Commerce, and Navigation Treaty. Is this true? Explain.

Extraterritorial Application of U.S. Law

10. Edison, an employee of Big Corporation, works for Big at its subsidiary in State Y. Edison is an American citizen and Big is an American corporation. Big fires Edison because he is a member of a racial group that is generally despised in State Y. Edison now brings a suit in the United States claiming that his American civil rights have been violated. Have they? Explain.

CHAPTER 9
INTELLECTUAL PROPERTY

INTRODUCTION

intellectual property: Useful artistic and industrial information and knowledge.

artistic property: Artistic, literary, and musical works.

industrial property: Inventions and trademarks.

Intellectual property is, in essence, useful information or knowledge. It is divided, for the purposes of study (and for establishing legal rights), into two principal branches: artistic property and industrial property. **Artistic property** encompasses artistic, literary, and musical works. These are protected, in most countries, by copyrights and neighboring rights.

   Industrial property is itself divided into two categories: inventions and trademarks. Inventions include both useful products and useful manufacturing processes. They are protected in a variety of ways, the most common protection being in the form of patents, petty patents, and inventors' certificates. Trademarks include "true" trademarks, trade names, service marks, collective marks, and certification marks. All of these are markings that identify the ownership rights of manufacturers, merchants, and service establishments. They are protected by trademark laws.

Regardless of its form, intellectual property is a creature of national law. International law does not create it. International law does, however, set down guidelines for its uniform definition and protection, and it sets up ways that make it easier for owners to acquire rights in different countries.

National law—and sometimes regional law—is also important in establishing the rules for assigning and licensing intellectual property. Recently, the international community has worked to establish international norms for the transfer of intellectual property, but so far the effort has not been fully successful.

These aspects of intellectual property law—its creation, protection, and transfer—form the subject matter of this chapter. Each will be discussed in its turn.

A. THE CREATION OF INTELLECTUAL PROPERTY RIGHTS

The realm of information that can be owned, assigned, and licensed is as broad as human inventiveness and imagination. Such information can involve either statutory or nonstatutory rights. The former include copyrights, patents, and trademarks. The latter include *know-how* (a term of American origin that has now been adopted as a term of art in many languages).[1] Today, many multinational companies have more of their total value tied to intellectual property than to hard assets. The creation, development, and protection of patents, copyrights, trademarks, and trade secrets is obviously a matter of the highest importance for firms in high-tech industries. But these types of intellectual property also have critical implications for businesses engaged in manufacturing, agriculture, and service operations, as we will see in this chapter.

COPYRIGHTS

copyright: An incorporeal statutory right that gives the author of an artistic work, for a limited period, the exclusive privilege of making copies of the work and publishing and selling the copies.

A **copyright** is title to certain *pecuniary rights* and, in most countries, certain *moral rights* for a specified period of time. These rights belong to the authors of any work that can be fixed in a tangible medium for the purpose of communication, such as literary, dramatic, musical, or artistic works; sound recordings; films; radio and television broadcasts; and (at least in some countries) computer programs. Unlike a patent, a copyright does not give its owner the right to prevent others from using the idea or the knowledge contained in the copyrighted work; it only restricts the use of the work itself. That is, anyone can use the information in the work to make, use, or sell a product, but they will be limited in the way they may use a particular copy.

The duke of Milan issued the first known copyright—a grant of the exclusive right to print a work—in 1481 to the printer of a local history. Similar grants were given to other printers in Germany, France, Italy, and Spain at about the same time. The first true copyright act, which protected authors without requiring them to obtain an individual grant from their sovereign, was enacted in England in 1709. Similar statutes appeared in Spain in 1764, in the United States in 1790, in revolutionary France in 1791, and in the German Confederation in 1837. Comprehensive acts, granting both pecuniary and moral rights to authors with minimal formality, appeared on the European Continent in the 1880s—the Belgian Copyright Law of 1886 being the first of several. Also, in 1886, 10 countries, including Belgium, Britain, France, Germany, Italy, Spain, and Switzerland, signed the Berne Convention[2]—by far the most

---
[1]Paul H. Vishny, *Guide to International Commerce Law*, vol. 1, § 3.09 (1994).
[2]Berne Convention for the Protection of Literary and Artistic Works (Paris 1886, revised in Paris 1896, Berlin 1908, Berne 1914, Rome 1928, Brussels 1948, Stockholm 1967, and Paris 1971).

influential international copyright convention—at Berne, Switzerland. This convention followed the Continental European model, requiring signatory states to impose minimal formalities and to protect both pecuniary and moral rights. Today, most of the nations of the world have ratified the Berne Convention, including, finally—in March 1989—the United States, thereby giving substantial (but certainly not complete) uniformity to the world's copyright laws.

Pecuniary Rights

pecuniary right: The right of an author to exploit a copyrighted work for economic gain.

Economic or **pecuniary rights** are legislative or judicial grants of authority that entitle an author to exploit a work for economic gain. Historically, there were only two channels for doing so. One was through the printed medium (i.e., a work was printed and then distributed through book shops, music stores, poster shops, etc.), and the other was through an entertainment establishment (i.e., a work was performed or shown at theaters, music halls, galleries, etc.). Today, as a consequence, most of the nearly 100 countries that grant copyrights protect two kinds of pecuniary rights: the *right of reproduction* (which, in many jurisdictions, also includes the rights to exhibit and disseminate a work) and the *right of public performance*. An example of the pecuniary protection granted in a typical statute is found in Section 15 of the German Copyright Law:

I.   The author shall have the exclusive right to exploit his work in material form; the right shall comprise in particular:

   1. the right of reproduction;
   2. the right of distribution;
   3. the right of exhibition.

II.   The author shall further have the exclusive right to publicly communicate his work in nonmaterial form (right of publicly communicating); the right shall comprise in particular:

   1. the right of recitation, representation and performance;
   2. the right of broadcasting;
   3. the right of communicating the work by means of sound or visual records;
   4. the right of connecting broadcast transmissions.

right of reproduction: The exclusive right of an author to make multiple copies of a copyrighted work.

Reproduction, the oldest and most common of the copyright rights, is consistently defined in the market countries of the West. For example, the German statute defines it as the "right to make copies of a work, irrespective of the method or number"[3]; the British Copyright Act refers to "reproducing the work in any material form"[4]; the French Copyright Law defines a work reproduction as "the material fixation of a work by any method that permits indirect communication to the public"[5]; and the U.S. Copyright Act refers merely to the making of "copies."[6]

In socialist countries, although a copyright does include the right of reproduction, the right can be exercised effectively only by state agencies. As a consequence, copyright holders have to assign their rights to an agency—commonly their employer—and hope that the agency will promote their copyrighted work.[7]

Of course, the development of the Internet and the World Wide Web in the past 15 years has totally changed the ease with which copyrighted works may be reproduced. It is now possible—though not necessarily legal—to instantly send a perfect copy of a work of art,

---

[3]Germany, Copyright Law, § 16 (September 9, 1965, as amended).
[4]United Kingdom, Copyright Act, § 2(5) (1956 as amended).
[5]France, Law No. 57-298, Article 28 (March 11, 1957, as amended). Similar language appears in the Russian Civil Code, Article 479.
[6]United States, Copyright Act, § 106(1) (1976).
[7]For an illustration of one individual's trials and tribulations in the old Soviet Union, see Peter Gumbel, "Tetris Game Wins Big for Nintendo But Not for Soviet Inventors: They're Left Out as Software Falls into Western Hands and Then into Litigation," *Wall Street Journal*, June 8, 1990.

music, literature, or software to millions of people around the world with the click of a mouse. The rapid developments in technology have made enforcement of copyright law much more difficult, and business firms have been struggling to protect their intellectual property in this new age.

right of distribution: The right of an author to place a copy of a copyrighted work into circulation for the first time.

Distribution rights, unlike reproduction rights, are neither consistently defined nor consistently granted by one country to another. To understand distribution rights, one has to consider two questions: (1) What is meant by distribution? and (2) When are distribution rights *exhausted*?

The German Copyright Law defines distribution as "the right to offer to the public,[8] or to place in circulation, the original work or copies of the work."[9] Similar provisions are found in the American, Austrian, British, Scandinavian, and Swiss statutes.[10] Most countries do not directly grant such a right. For example, while the French Copyright Law does not directly grant a right of distribution, it does provide for essentially the same thing in the form of a limitation on a transferee's rights. Thus, a transferee only acquires those rights "specifically mentioned in the transfer agreement,"[11] and any attempt to assume greater rights is considered a crime. A French transferee who attempts "the sale, exportation or importation of unlawful copies of [copyrighted] works" is subject to penal sanctions.[12]

doctrine of exhaustion: Once a copy of a copyrighted work is in circulation, the author has no further right to control its distribution.

In most countries, once a particular copy of a work has been sold to a public transferee, the author's right to control any subsequent transfers of that particular copy ends. This is known as the **doctrine of exhaustion**.[13] Practically, this doctrine is a necessary corollary to the right of distribution; otherwise, the copyright owner would be able to control every transfer of every copyrighted work.

There are three important limitations to the doctrine of exhaustion. The first is that the right only applies to sales. An author who transfers an original or a copy by lending, leasing, or as part of an exhibition retains his or her distribution right as to any subsequent transfer. The second limitation is that the doctrine only applies to the right of distribution. The right to reproduce the original work, as well as other rights (such as performance rights and moral rights), is not affected. For example, making photocopies of a book purchased by a transferee is still an infringement of the copyright holder's right of reproduction. The third limitation has to do with the author's right to limit rentals of distributed original works and copies. By a widely subscribed-to international agreement, authors are entitled (at least with regard to computer programs and motion pictures) to prohibit commercial rentals of their copyrighted works.[14]

---

[8]While the statutory provisions do not define *public*, commentators generally agree that the circulation of one or two copies to members of one's family or to close friends is not a public distribution. See Stig Strömholm, "Copyright—Comparison of Laws," *International Encyclopedia of Comparative Law*, vol. 14, chap. 3, p. 52.
[9]Germany, Copyright Law, §17(1) (September 9, 1965, as amended).
[10]United States, Copyright Act, § 106(1) (1976); Austria, Copyright Law, § 16; United Kingdom, Copyright Act, § 2(5) (1956 as amended); Switzerland, Federal Copyright Law, Article 12(1) (December 7, 1922, as amended). An example of the Scandinavian provisions is Sweden's Law No. 729 on Copyrights, § 2(3) (1960 as amended).
[11]France, Law No. 57–298, Article 31(3) (March 11, 1957, as amended).
[12]France, Penal Code, Article 425(3).
[13]The doctrine of exhaustion was first introduced in the nineteenth century by Josef Kohler, a German law professor, and his ideas are now incorporated in the German Copyright Law, §17(2), and in the other copyright laws that provide for an express grant of the right of distribution.

The U.S. exhaustion-of-rights rule is set out in §27 of the U.S. Copyright Act, which states that "nothing in this title shall be deemed to forbid, prevent, or restrict the transfer of any copy of a copyrighted work the possession of which has been lawfully obtained." The EU's exhaustion-of-rights rule is a court-made rule. It was first applied by the European Court of Justice in a copyright dispute in the case of Deutsche Gramophone v. Metro, Case 78/70, *European Community Reports*, vol. 1971, p. 487 (1971) and then fully set out in Musik-Vetrieb Membran v. GEMA, joined Cases 55/80 and 57/80, *European Community Reports*, vol. 1981, p. 147 (1981).
[14]The Agreement on Trade-Related Aspects of Intellectual Property Rights, Article 11 (1994), provides: "In respect of at least computer programs and cinematographic works, a [World Trade Organization] member shall provide authors and their successors in title the right to authorize or to prohibit the commercial rental to the public of originals or copies of their copyright works. A member shall be excepted from this obligation in respect of cinematographic works unless such rental has led to widespread copying of such works which is materially impairing the exclusive right of reproduction conferred in that member or authors and their successors in title. In respect of computer programs, this obligation does not apply to rentals where the program itself is not the essential object of the rental."

right of performance: The right of an author to communicate a copyrighted work to the public.

In addition to reproduction and distribution rights, copyright owners have a pecuniary **right of performance**. There are basically two approaches to the granting of this right. One, set out in the British, French, and U.S. laws, among others, is to grant a *general* right of performance (*droit de représentation*). The French law, which was extensively amended in 1985, provides a good example of this method. The right of performance is the right "to communicate the work to the public by any means whatsoever, including public recitation, lyrical performance, public presentation, public projection, and telecommunication."[15]

The second approach, followed in various countries but most fully utilized in Germany, is to create several *subsidiary* rights[16]—in particular, the right to recite a literary work, the right to perform a musical work, the right to make a remote presentation over loudspeakers or similar devices, the right to make a projected image, the right to communicate by visual or sound records, and the right to make radio and television broadcasts.[17]

Regardless of the approach, the right of performance applies only to public performances. Private performances—that is, performances limited to a small group of people "inter-connected personally by mutual relations or by a relationship to the organizer"[18]—do not infringe the copyright. Examples of public performances from U.K. case law (all of which will infringe the copyright holder's performance right) include the performance of a play by members of a ladies' club to other members of the same club and playing music in the lobby of a hotel, in a television showroom, in a record shop, over loudspeakers to workers in a factory, and to members of a dance club.[19] A private performance would be a reading of a book to one's family or to a small group of close friends. The difference between public and private performances is examined in Case 9–1.

---

[15]France, Law No. 57-298, Article 27 (March 11, 1957, as amended). Similar provisions are found in the United Kingdom Copyright Act, §§ 2(5) and 3 (1956 as amended), and the United States Copyright Act, §§ 101 and 106(4) (1976).

This same general prohibition was incorporated into the Agreement on Trade-Related Aspects of Intellectual Property Rights Article 14 (1994). This agreement is discussed later in this chapter.

[16]See, as well, Italy's Law No. 633 for the Protection of Copyrights, Article 16 (April 22, 1941, as amended).

[17]Germany, Copyright Law, §§ 15(2), 19 (September 9, 1965, as amended).

[18]*Id.*, § 15(3).

[19]See Stig Strömholm, "Copyright—Comparison of Laws," *International Encyclopedia of Comparative Law*, vol. 14, chap. 3, p. 57.

＝〰〰〰＝

Case 9-1 PERFORMING RIGHT SOCIETY, LIMITED v. HICKEY

Zambia, High Court at Lusaka, 1978.
The Zambia Law Reports, vol. 1979, p. 66 (1979).

JUDGE SAKALA:

The plaintiff's claim is for an injunction to restrain the defendant—whether by himself or by his servants or agents—from authorizing or procuring communication to the public of the musical works "Kung Fu Fighting," "House of Exile," and "Money Won't Save You," or any other musical works the copyright of which vests in the plaintiff. The plaintiff also claims for damages.

In support of the claim, Ronald Clarence Chipumza, an accountant with Lightfoot Advertising, told the Court that he is also the Zambian Agent for the Performing Right Society, Limited, the plaintiff in this case. He testified that the objective of the plaintiff is to protect the copyright of musical writers, artists, and composers. The Society represents them and collects fees on behalf of its members, which in the end [are] distributed to the members. In Zambia, the position of the plaintiff is to represent the copyright of the affiliated societies throughout the world. He testified that in early 1975 a search was conducted at the defendant's premises to determine the extent to which the copyright of the society members was being violated. He told the Court that in September a letter was sent to the defendant advising him that the plaintiff's copyright was being infringed. Another letter was sent in October 1975 reminding the defendant of the consequence of performing copyrighted music without the consent of the copyright owner. The witness further testified that he also wrote the defendant suggesting to him to take out the society's license. But there was no reply to any of these letters. Further, the defendant made no attempt to arrange for a meeting. In the end the matter was referred to the plaintiff's solicitors. The witness further testified that he physically, on several occasions, made searches at the defendant's premises. First of these occasions was on the 4th of April 1975. He discovered that the Society's copyright was being infringed. The inspections were carried out after the defendant failed to reply to the correspondence. At the time of the inspections, the songs that were being performed were "Kung Fu Fighting," "House of Exile," and "Money Won't Save You." These last two songs were composed by Jimmy Cliff, while "Kung Fu Fighting" was by Carl Douglas. He testified that copyright in these works subsists in the plaintiff. The witness also told the Court that after the institution of the present proceedings, he carried out another search at the defendant's premises on the 11th of July 1978. It was again established that the copyright of the Society was still being violated. He said about five searches in all were carried out by him personally. He said that other works of the plaintiff are still being infringed, in addition to those specifically mentioned in the pleadings. . . .

In defense, Francis Anthony Hickey testified that he is one of the proprietors of Bar-B-Que Drive-in Restaurant. He agreed that on the 26th of April, 1976, he caused to be heard in public three records, namely, "Kung Fu Fighting," "House of Exile," and "Money Won't Save You." He said that it is not his intention to carry on breaking the copyright. He said, before then, he received several letters from the plaintiff's solicitors asking him to stop playing copyrighted music, but he did not know what they were asking him. He has never in his life heard that there is a copyright in music. He testified that he has bought records and played them. The letters he received did not mention any specific records and the pamphlet he received did not specify the music. He said he only realized that the letters referred to "Kung Fu Fighting," "House of Exile," and "Money Won't Save You" when he approached his lawyer, who explained [the letters] to him. Otherwise, before then, he had no idea. He said he does not intend to play these records until he obtains a license from the rightful owner. He told the Court that nobody approached him at his restaurant asking him to

stop playing the records. He said he holds about one dance a week depending on the license allocated to him by the police.

In cross-examination, he said [that] on receipt of the various letters from the plaintiff, he asked his various friends who run discos and in their case, they did not know anything of copyright and as he was a beginner himself, he thought that these letters were some sort of a money making racket. He said he does not remember whether he read the pamphlet sent to him. He said he understood the word copyright to mean that you cannot manufacture the item in question.

. . . The contention by the plaintiff is that they have lost royalty fees by reason of the defendant's refusal and/or negligence to take out the plaintiff's license. As a result, they are claiming for an injunction to restrain the defendant by himself, or by his servants or agents, from causing to be heard, in public at the defendant's premises, the said musical works or any other such work the copyright of which vests in the plaintiff or from authorizing performance without a license from the plaintiff. They also ask for damages for infringement of the copyright.

. . . The defense is that the performance was done innocently and under mistake. The submission on behalf of the defendant was that, in matters of copyright infringement it is a good defense that at the time of the infringement that the defendant was not aware and had no reasonable grounds for suspecting that copyright subsisted. A further submission on behalf of the defendant is that if the plaintiff suffered any damages, the damages should only relate to the one day as pleaded. In the circumstances, counsel for the defendant urged that the damages should either be nominal or nil. It is conceded on behalf of the defendant in the submissions that the granting of an injunction cannot be opposed and was never at any stage objected to. The plaintiff's contention is that regard being had to all the correspondence sent to the defendant, the defense of innocence must be rejected. The law governing copyright of musical works and other works in Zambia is contained in the *Copyright Act*, Chapter 701. I must confess that, in my research, I have not come across any Zambian authority based on the *Copyright Act*. Even in the submissions, I was not referred to any local decided cases. Musical works under the Act are eligible for copyright. Infringement of copyright is specifically provided for in § 13 of the Act. Section 13 reads as follows:

> Copyright shall be infringed by any person who does, or causes any other person to do, an act falling within the copyright without the license of the person in whom is vested either the whole of the copyright or, where there has been a partial assignment or partial testamentary disposition, the relevant portion of the copyright.

In the instant case, the defendant admits that on the 26th of April, 1976, he did perform or cause the performance of the three musical works without a license.

***

…Section 13(3) provides a defense to infringements of copyright. The subsection reads as follows:

> Where in an action for infringement of copyright it is proved or admitted—(a) that an infringement was committed; but (b) that at the time of the infringement the defendant was not aware, and had no reasonable grounds for suspecting, that copyright subsisted in the work or other subject matter to which the Section relates; the plaintiff shall not be entitled under this Section to any damages against the defendant in respect of the infringement, but shall be entitled to an account of profits in respect of the infringement whether any other relief is granted under this Section or not.

As already mentioned, the defense raised is one of innocence. Quite clearly, § 13(3) of Chapter 701 provides a good defense of innocence of infringements of copyright. Although there is no decided authority in Zambia, …English decisions based on the English *Copyright Act* of 1956 … have very strong persuasive value … bearing in mind that the wording of §13(3) of Chapter 701 is the same as § 17(2) of the English *Copyright Act* of 1956.… Innocence as a defense under this Section has been considered in a number of English cases, reference to which will be found in *Halsbury's Laws of England*.[20] Part of that paragraph reads as follows:

> In general, any invasion of a right of property gives a cause of action to the owner against the person responsible for the invasion, whether it is intentional or not. Consequently, innocence is no defense to an action for infringement of copyright or for the conversion or detention of any infringing copy or a plate.
>
> Where, however, it is proved or admitted in an action for infringement that an infringement was committed, but that at the time of the infringement the defendant was not aware and had no reasonable grounds for suspecting that copyright subsisted in the work or other subject matter to which the action relates, the plaintiff is not entitled to damages, but is entitled to an account of profits whether any other relief is granted to not.

On the evidence before me, I am satisfied and find as a fact that at the time of the defendant's admitted infringement, he was not aware and had no reasonable grounds for suspecting that copyright subsisted in the

MAP 9-1   Zambia (1978)

plaintiff's three musical works. This being the case, I hold that the plaintiff is not entitled to any damages against the defendant in respect of the infringement. The Section, on the other hand, provides an alternative to damages in that the plaintiff is entitled to an amount of profits in respect of the infringement whether any other relief is granted or not. On the defendant's admission of the infringement of the plaintiff's copyright of the three musical works on April 26th, 1976, I hold that the plaintiff is entitled to the profits made on that day. As to quantum, I grant the parties liberty to apply in chambers. The defendant, at least from the evidence, does not appear to object to the injunction being granted. In the circumstances, I grant the injunction in respect of the three works pleaded. ■

CASEPOINT: The defendant admitted that he played records of copyrighted music during a public disco at his establishment in Zambia. Thus, a *performance* was done, without permission of the copyright owner, which constituted an infringement of the song composer's rights. The judge decided that the defendant did not fully understand copyright at that time, so did not award damages but did hold him liable for the profits made that day at the disco.

[20]4th ed., vol. 9 at paragraph 938, p. 602.

Moral Rights

The personal rights of authors to prohibit others from tampering with their works are called **moral rights.** These rights are independent of the author's pecuniary rights, and in most states that grant moral rights, they continue to exist in the author even after the pecuniary rights have been transferred. In France, for example, they are inalienable.[21]

moral rights: The right of an author to prohibit others from tampering with a copyrighted work.

The concept of moral rights is a product of nineteenth-century German legal philosophy. Starting in the period of the natural law thinkers (such as Locke, Montesquieu, and Pufendorf), a belief gained currency that there existed in nature certain legal rights (called *Persönlichkeitsrecht* or personal rights) that were inherent in the persons of individuals. Later, the Positivists, including Hegel, Jellinek, and Triepel, accepted that such rights ought to exist, even if they did not exist in nature. For example, Immanuel Kant, the eminent eighteenth-century German philosopher, looked upon the *Persönlichkeitsrecht* as a grant of freedom essential to the existence of an ethical society.[22]

The principal nineteenth-century German legal commentators—the Pandectists—were generally opposed to the notion of *Persönlichkeitsrecht;* it did not fit into the patterns of Roman law, which they regarded as conclusive and unimprovable. Nonetheless, a small group of writers, who studied German rather than Roman laws, were adamant defenders of the idea. These *personalists,* led by Otto von Gierke, took the view that a copyright was a single unified privilege that included both economic rights (i.e., reproduction and distribution) and moral rights. For these writers, a copyright was essentially personal; it could not be transferred, seized, or banned.[23]

Although the unitary view of von Gierke and the other personalists may have been philosophically and logically sound, it did not reflect actual practice. Copyright laws in every country allowed authors to transfer, at a minimum, their pecuniary rights. Josef Kohler proposed, about 1880, a *dualist* theory of copyright law. This divided copyrights into economic and moral rights—the latter being those rights that reflected the creative interests and concerns of the author. Kohler's theory was based on extensive studies of British and French case law (German case materials were generally unavailable at that time), and his ideas were especially influential in France.

Judicial decisions in France in the 1870s—under the influence of German scholarship—came to recognize moral rights as separate and distinct from economic rights. The French decisions, and Kohler's dualist theory, were incorporated in statutory form for the first time in the Belgian Copyright Law of 1886.

The 1886 Belgian Copyright Law recognized what today are considered the three basic moral rights: (1) the right to object to distortion, mutilation, or modification (*droit de respect*), (2) the right to be recognized as the author (*droit à la paternité*), and (3) the right to control public access to the work (*droit de divulgation*). These same rights were recognized in French and German copyright laws at the beginning of the twentieth century; and, in 1928, the Berne Convention (which provides for the international recognition of national copyright laws) was amended to specifically recognize these three moral rights. France and Germany have subsequently added a fourth moral right—the right to correct or retract a work (*droit de repentir, Rückrufsrecht*), but it is not as universally recognized as the other three.

---

[21]The Berne Convention for the Protection of Literary and Artistic Works defines an artist's moral rights as "the right to claim authorship of the work and to object to any distortion, mutilation, or other modification of, or other derogatory action in relation to, the said work, which would be prejudicial to his honor or reputation." See Berne Convention for the Protection of Literary and Artistic Works, July 24, 1971, 24 U.S.T. 1749, art. 6 bis, available at http://www.law.cornell.edu/treaties/berne/6bis.html.

[22]In "Von der Unrechtmässihkeit des Büchernachdruckes," *Berlinische Monatsschrift*, at p. 416 (1785), Kant described a copyright as "not a right in the thing . . . but an innate right, inherent in the author's person, which implies the faculty to protest against another making him speak unwillingly to the public."

[23]*Deutsches Privatrecht*, vol. 1, pp. 756–766 (1895).

Moral rights are not recognized in the copyright laws of the United Kingdom, the United States, and most countries that have inherited their law from England. The United Kingdom, which is a signatory of the Berne Convention and therefore obliged to protect the moral rights of authors, complies with its international obligations, at least arguably, by claiming that an author can bring an action for libel to complain of distortion, mutilation, or modification and an action for passing off to protect the author's rights of paternity. It also has argued that the right to control public access is inseparable from the economic right of reproduction and therefore is similarly protected.

American courts and legal writers have often denied the existence of moral rights in the United States.[24] It was long suggested that the principal reason that the United States refused to become a signatory of the Berne Convention was the treaty's requirement that member states recognize moral rights (Article 6bis). With U.S. ratification of the Berne Convention in 1989, however, this explanation was no longer viable.[25] In ratifying the Berne Convention, the U.S. Congress carefully avoided accepting the moral rights portion, arguing that "existing state and federal law in the United States satisfied Article 6bis." This claim, that "there is a composite of laws in this country that provides the kind of protection envisioned by Article 6bis," was always seriously doubted.[26] A few American writers have suggested—in the fashion of British commentators—that moral rights are protected by tort and contract law.[27] These suggestions, however, have been halfhearted at best and, with the recent adoption of the Agreement on Trade-Related Aspects of Intellectual Property Rights, probably no longer necessary.

The Agreement on Trade-Related Aspects of Intellectual Property Rights (TRIPs Agreement), which is an annex to the Agreement Establishing the World Trade Organization, requires WTO member states to comply with provisions of the Berne Convention (whether or not they are parties to that convention) with one significant exception: Member states are not required to grant moral rights to authors.[28] It seems likely as a consequence, at least for now, that authors in the United Kingdom, the United States, and other countries that follow the English tradition will continue to do without moral rights, despite the provisions in the Berne Convention and the practice in most of the rest of the world.[29] However, as the following case demonstrates, moral rights are recognized in India, which generally follows the English legal tradition.

---

[24]See, Kimberly Y. W. Holst, "A Case of Bad Credit?: The United States and the Protection of Moral Rights in Intellectual Property Law," 3 *Buff. Int's Prop. L.J.* 105 (2006).

[25]See Clint A. Carpenter, "Mother May I? Moral Rights, Dastar, and the False Advertising Prong of Lanham Act Section 43(A)," *Washington and Lee Law Review*, vol. 63, 1601 (Fall 2006)

[26]Melville B. Nimmer and David Nimmer, Nimmer on Copyright, § 8D.02[D][1] (2005) (stating that Congress's determination that current U.S. law met the Article 6bis requirements "flies in the face of numerous judicial and scholarly pronouncements on the subject").

[27]See Earl Kinter and Jack Lahr, *An Intellectual Property Law Primer*, p. 335 (1975); see also William Patry, "The United States and International Copyright Law: From Berne to Eldred," *Houston Law Review*, vol 40, 749, 751–52 (2003)

[28]Agreement on Trade-Related Aspects of Intellectual Property Rights, Article 9, para. 1 (1994).
The Agreement specifies that WTO member states are to comply with the Berne Convention as revised in Paris in 1971.

[29]One commentator recently urged that there was a strong need for more uniformity of protection for moral rights. "In light of new technologies that are present and those that will be developed, legislation is not keeping up with the rate at which technological advances are developing, which makes a multilateral agreement strictly enforcing the moral rights of an artist that much more imperative. Moral rights protection must be strictly imposed and enforced under a multilateral treaty with proper guidelines such as the French regime which would prohibit the waiver of these rights. To achieve such a treaty, given the many differences among the nations on the scope of moral rights, compromise will be needed. One possible compromise is to limit the term of moral rights protection to the term of copyright protection. When the copyright term of protection expires, therefore, the moral rights protection will expire as well. This compromise will further the objective of copyright protection which is to encourage artistic creation by economically protecting those creations for a limited period, while respecting the artistic integrity of the work." Patry, *supra* note 27.

Case 9-2   AMAR NATH SEHGAL v. UNION OF INDIA

30 PTC 253 (2005)

In 1959, the Ministry of Works, Housing and Supplies of the Government of India commissioned a talented sculptor, Amar Nath Sehgal, to design a mural. The work was to adorn the walls around a central arch of the Vigyan Bhawan, a venue for important government functions in New Delhi, the capital city. The design was approved by the first Prime Minster of India, Pandit Jawahar Lal Nehru, and the mural was completed in 1962. In its final shape, it measured a mammoth 40 feet high and 140 feet long.

The mural won widespread acclaim, and gave the world a glimpse of the "real" India—its farmers, artisans, women and children, their daily chores and celebrations, frozen in time, and molded from tons of solid bronze. For nearly 20 years the mural attracted dignitaries and art connoisseurs from all over the world. It became a landmark in the cultural life of the capital. Then the Vigyan Bhawan buildings were renovated. In the process, the mural was ripped off the walls and the remnants put into storage.

Distressed by the destruction of his artistic work, and after petitioning the authorities for years without a response, Mr. Sehgal brought a lawsuit against the government for violation of his moral rights. Specifically, he claimed that:

- the dismemberment of the homogeneous blend of the pieces of each tile in the mosaic constituted an act of mutilation;
- the Ministry's action was prejudicial to his honor and reputation as an artist, because, by reducing the mural to junk, it dealt a body blow to the esteem and celebrity bestowed on the work at its inception;
- the obliteration of his name on the work violated his right to claim authorship.

Though too late to rescue the mural by the time his grievance came to court in May 1992, Mr. Sehgal was nonetheless granted an interim injunction restraining the defendants from causing further damage to the work. It turned out, fortunately for Mr. Sehgal, that the presiding Judge was himself an art aficionado with, literally, a flair for poetic justice. The restraining order handed down by Justice Jaspal Singh came across as an acutely empathetic one:

> Sometime in the year 1962, the barren walls of Vigyan Bhawan were blessed with a mural . . . created by the

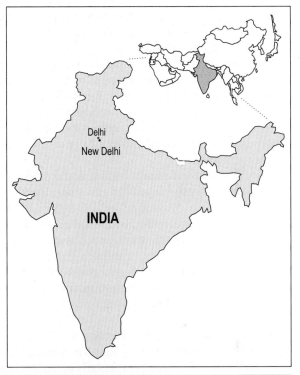

MAP 9-2 India (2005)

magic hands of eminent sculptor Amar Nath Sehgal, approved by connoisseurs of all that is beautiful. . . . For years, it was dance to the discerning eye, and song to the ears who could hear. However, in 1979, it was pulled down and dumped in a storehouse. It is said that improper handling caused immense damage, and that bits and pieces have altogether disappeared, including the name of its creator. . . . In a country rightly proud of its creativity and ingenuity, men who can hardly distinguish the heads of Venus from those of Mars cannot be allowed to decide the fate of artists who create our history and heritage. Section 57 of the Copyright Act provides the light. . . .

The defense objected at the outset to the power of the court to intervene in the matter. Confident that the ministry was within its legal rights, the government argued that:

- the plaintiff (Mr. Sehgal) had assigned his copyright to the defendant (the government) in an agreement dated 31st October 1960;

- the defendant had purchased all rights from the plaintiff, and was consequently free to do as it pleased with the mural;
- the mural had already been damaged in a fire in the Vigyan Bhawan;
- according to the terms of the 1960 agreement, any grievance should be referred to an arbitrator appointed by the defendant.

The case was then set to go to trial, though not before further months were spent in unsuccessful efforts to find a mutually acceptable solution which Mr. Sehgal felt would vindicate his honor and reputation.

At the outset, the odds appeared to be stacked heavily against the artist. Not only had he created the work on commission, but he had also explicitly assigned his copyright—and so all economic rights—to the commissioning ministry. He faced a powerful opponent in the Indian government.

The success of Mr. Sehgal's legal action rested upon the "moral rights" established by the single statutory provision in Section 57 of the Indian Copyright Act (1957) on "author's special rights." Based on the Berne Convention Article 6bis, this section codifies the concept of moral rights, by protecting an author's right, independent of his copyright, to claim to authorship of his work, and to restrain any distortion, mutilation or modification of the work which could be prejudicial to his honor or reputation.

The court noted that if the mural [had] been completely destroyed, it was unlikely that Mr. Sehgal could have obtained the same relief, particularly given the long gap between the removal of the mural and the institution of the legal proceedings. However, since the stored remnants were still redeemable, upon viewing them, the court could visualize the magnitude of the work.

The fact that the defendant was the government was also significant. One of the arguments that the court adopted was that, unlike a private owner of an artwork, the Indian government had an obligation, enshrined in the national 5-year plan, to protect, preserve and respect cultural rights and the country's artistic and cultural heritage. Extracts from UNESCO's non-copyright cultural conventions also helped create a link between the facts of this case and governmental obligations.

When the matter came up for final hearing, Justice Pradeep Nandrajog of the Delhi High Court ruled that: "All rights of the mural shall henceforth vest with Mr. Sehgal." The court ordered the return of the remains of the mural to the sculptor, and also slapped damages of Rs.500,000 (some US $12,000) on the defendant.

But the fight was still not quite over. The decree was not fulfilled, and Mr. Sehgal again took recourse to the court in execution proceedings, while the defendant appealed against the decree to a division bench of the court. Ultimately, the matter was amicably resolved. After the hard fought and emotional battle, Mr. Sehgal, grateful for his victory, waived the claim of damages against the government in exchange for the return of the mural. ∎

CASEPOINT: The case involving Mr. Sehgal's mural shows the importance of the moral rights section of the Berne Convention, as adopted in the Indian Copyright Act, and the weight it has been given by courts in India and Europe. The law is based on the principle that there should be a law to protect the soul and essence of artistic expression as much as the physical or tangible form of that expression, separate and distinct from the economic rights of the artist or author.

Source: Binny Kalra, "Copyright in the Courts: How Moral Rights Won the Battle of the Mural," *WIPO Magazine*, April 2007. This article originally provided by the World Intellectual Property Organization (WIPO), the owner of the copyright. The WIPO Secretariat assumes no liability or responsibility with regard to the transformation of this data.

Works Covered

work: An artistic, literary, musical, or scientific creation.

The object of copyright protection is a **work**, that is, an intellectual creation in the field of art, literature, music, or science. Particular examples of works covered are provided in many copyright laws.[30] For example, the 1976 U.S. Copyright Act lists seven categories of works that are eligible for copyright protection:

1. Literary works
2. Musical works, including any accompanying words
3. Dramatic works, including any accompanying music

---

[30]A similar list of examples can be found in the United Kingdom Copyright Act, § 3 (1956 as amended); the German Copyright Law, § 2 (September 9, 1965 as amended); and French Law No. 57-298, Article 3 (March 11, 1957 as amended).

4. Pantomimes and choreographic works
5. Pictorial, graphic, and sculptural works
6. Motion pictures and other audiovisual works
7. Sound recordings

originality: Creative effort invested by an author in raw materials that gives them a new quality or character.

Not every work that falls within these categories qualifies for copyright protection, however. A work must also be **original**; that is, an author must infuse creativity into it. As Lord Atkinson once stated in a famous Privy Council case: "To secure [a] copyright . . . it is necessary that labor, skill and capital should be expended sufficiently to impart to the product some quality or character which the raw material did not possess, and which differentiates the product from the raw material."[31] Originality, however, should not be confused with the patent law requirements of novelty or merit. Two painters, for example, may paint the same still life. Each painting is an original, since it reflects the creativity of the maker. Accordingly, even though neither is novel, and even if they both lack any artistic merit whatsoever, both painters are entitled to a copyright for their works.

What is protected is not the idea or knowledge contained in the work, but the expression of the work. That is, copyrights do not apply to "ideas, procedures, methods of operations, or mathematical concepts as such."[32] Anyone may use the information or knowledge in the work; they are limited only in the way they may use the original or a particular copy.[33]

Of course, before there can be a copy, there must be an original. The original must be such that it is capable of being "fixed in any tangible medium of expression, now known or later developed."[34] A story written down on paper with pen and ink is the classic example of an original work that has been fixed in a tangible medium. So, too, is a picture painted with oils on a canvas, an image sculpted in marble, and music recorded on a record, tape, or compact disc.

Most copies (other than performances) must also be fixed in a tangible medium. That being so, is a copy made when the data stored on a computer disk are placed in the computer's central memory? The court in *MAI Systems v. Peak Computer*[35] was faced with this question. In that case, MAI Systems, a computer programming company, wrote unique operating system programs for its customers' computers, which were stored on the computers' hard disks. MAI also serviced those computers whenever they needed it. Peak Computer, a rival programming company, contracted to service many of MAI's customers' computers for substantially less money than MAI Systems charged. MAI was not happy about this, and it sought to stop Peak by suing for copyright infringement. MAI, which had licensed only its customers to use the operating system programs installed on their computers, claimed that Peak had made unauthorized copies whenever it turned on the computers. The court agreed. Peak was able to view the error log generated by MAI's operating system program when a computer with the program was turned on. This meant that a perceivable copy of the program was taken from the hard disk and placed in the computer's operating memory. Although the copy was removed when the computer was shut down, it still existed for "more than a transitory period." That is all that is required. The court, therefore, enjoined Peak from infringing MAI's copyrights. (Because this meant that Peak could not turn on the computers with MAI's programs, Peak was effectively stopped from competing against MAI.)

[31]MacMillan & Co., Ltd. v. Cooper, *Times Law Reports*, vol. 40, p. 188 (Privy Council, 1923).
[32]Agreement on Trade-Related Aspects of Intellectual Property Rights, Article 9, para. 2 (1994).
[33]This principle is formally stated in many copyright laws. For example, Colombia, Law No. 23 on Copyright, Article 6(2) (January 28, 1982), provides: "The ideas or conceptual content of literary, artistic and scientific works may not be the subject of appropriation."
[34]United States, Copyright Act, § 102 (1976). Similar provisions are found in Argentina, Law No. 11,723 on Copyright, Article 1 (September 28, 1933, as amended); Colombia, Law No. 23 on Copyright, Article 2 (January 28, 1982); Ghana, Copyright Law, § 2(2) (March 21, 1985); Kenya, Copyright Law, § 3(2) (Act No. 3 of February 24, 1966, as amended); Malaysia, Copyright Act, § 7(3)(b) (April 30, 1987); Nigeria, Law No. 61 on Copyright, § 1(2)(b) (December 30, 1970); and Uganda, Copyright Act, § 2 (1966).
[35]*Federal Reporter, Second Series*, vol. 991, p. 511 (9th Circuit Ct. of Appeals, 1993).

Neighboring Rights

Copyright laws generally apply to most works of an artistic, literary, musical, or scientific nature. Technology, however, has a habit of producing new kinds of works that fall outside of existing definitions. Two recent examples are computer programs and semiconductor chips. Legislatures respond to such changes in different ways. Sometimes they make amendments to existing copyright laws to incorporate these new works. Copyright laws in most developed countries were amended in the mid-1980s to include protection for computer programs.[36] Sometimes, however, new laws, parallel to but separate from the existing copyright statutes, are enacted. The rights created by such laws are often called **neighboring rights** (from the French *droits voison*) because they are neighbors to, but not part of, an author's copyright. For example, in 1989, two new international treaties governing rights similar to, but different from, the traditional copyright were adopted: the Treaty on the International Registration of Audiovisual Works and the Treaty on Intellectual Property in Respect of Integrated Circuits.[37]

neighboring rights: Rights similar to copyrights that are protected by different statutes.

Formalities

The Berne Convention, as amended in Berlin in 1908, established that the title granted by copyright laws is subject to no formalities. When the United States became a member of the Berne Convention in March 1989, this became the rule throughout the world.[38]

Prior to March 1989, the United States was the only country that required authors to observe certain formalities to obtain a copyright. In particular, all publicly distributed copies of a work had to include a copyright notice consisting of the symbol (c) or the word "Copyright" or the abbreviation "Copr."; the year the work was first published; and the name of the copyright owner. In addition, two copies of certain kinds of works (e.g., books and phonographs) had to be deposited with the Copyright Office of the U.S. Library of Congress.[39] This is no longer the case.

Scope

A copyright applies only within the territory of the state granting it. A state will not prevent the making of copies of copyrighted material outside its territory. However, most states will keep unauthorized copies of copyrighted works from being imported into their territory.[40]

Duration

The common rule for the duration of a copyright was established in 1948 in a revision of the Berne Convention. That is, a copyright lasts for 50 years *post mortem auctoris* (i.e., for 50 years following the author's death).[41] The WTO's Agreement on Trade-Related Aspects

---

[36]For example, the German Copyright Law, § 2(1) (September 9, 1965, as amended in 1985), now includes computer programs among the examples it provides of "literary writings"; the U.K. Copyright (Computer Software) Amendments Act (1985), amends the U.K. Copyright Act (1956) to grant protection to computer programs; and the U.S. Computer Software Protection Act (1980) amends § 117 of the U.S. Copyright Act (1976) to make computer programs copyrightable.

This change was also incorporated in the Agreement on Trade-Related Aspects of Intellectual Property Rights, Article 10, para. 1 (1994) (which applies to all WTO member states). It provides: "Computer programs, whether in source or object code, shall be protected as literary works under the Berne Convention ([as amended in Paris in] 1971)."

[37]The substantive provisions of the Treaty on Intellectual Property in Respect of Integrated Circuits have been made applicable to WTO member states by the Agreement on Trade-Related Aspects of Intellectual Property Rights, Article 35 (1994).

[38]Argentina requires copyright holders to deposit copies of certain works (e.g., books and phonographs) with the government, subject to a "suspension of the rights of the author" for failing to comply. Argentina, Law No. 11,723 on Copyright, Articles 47–63 (September 28, 1933 as amended). France also requires registration of films, videograms, and contracts relating to such works, but failure to comply does not affect the author's copyright in the works. See Roland Dumas, *La Propriété littéraire et artistique*, pp. 325–327 (1987).

[39]United States, Copyright Act, §§ 401–407 (1976 as amended). A copyright holder also has a right (but no duty) to register a copyright with the Copyright Office. *Id.*, §§ 408–412.

[40]For example, *United States Code*, Title 17, § 602(a), provides that the unauthorized importation of copyrighted works constitutes infringement even when the copies were lawfully made abroad.

[41]Berne Convention for the Protection of Literary and Artistic Works, Article 7, para. (1) (1886 as revised in Brussels in 1948).

of Intellectual Property Rights follows this precedent, requiring WTO member states to provide copyright protection of at least 50 years, and many nations, including the United States, have extended the duration to 70 years following the author's death[42]

Exceptions to Copyright Protection

Virtually every copyright law describes certain uses of works that do not constitute an infringement of the author's copyright. These exceptions, however, vary widely, and only a few main examples will be listed here.

Copyrighted material can be used lawfully in at least some countries (1) in a court or administrative proceeding or by the police should the material (such as a portrait) be needed to maintain public safety[43]; (2) for instructional purposes in schools[44]; (3) for purely private use (except that computer programs may not be copied, regardless of the use involved)[45]; (4) in brief quotations in scholarly or literary works or in reviews[46]; and (5) in extended quotations of newsworthy speeches or political commentaries.[47]

PATENTS

patent: An incorporeal statutory right that gives an inventor, for a limited period, the exclusive right to use or sell a patented product or to use a patented method or process.

A **patent** is "a statutory privilege granted by the government to inventors, and to others deriving their rights from the inventor, for a fixed period of years, to exclude other persons from manufacturing, using, or selling a patented product or from utilizing a patented method or process."[48] Although a patent is commonly referred to as a monopoly, it is not truly so. The owner of a patent may be prevented from exploiting the grant by other laws (such as national security laws or unfair competition laws) or by contractual agreement. What a patent grants, rather, is the protection of a monopoly. As the U.S. Supreme Court put it in *Zenith Radio Corp. v. Hazeltine Research, Inc.*:

> The heart of [a patentee's] legal monopoly is the right to invoke the state's powers to prevent others from utilizing his discovery without his consent.[49]

Historically, two reasons have been given to justify the granting of patents. Those reasons are (1) that patents are a confirmation of the private property rights of the inventor and (2) that a patent is a grant of a special monopoly to encourage invention and industrial development.

The first of these two justifications—that patents are private property rights—can be found in the wording of the eighteenth- and nineteenth-century patent legislation of several continental European countries. For example, the French Patent Law of 1791 states:

> Every novel idea whose realization or development can become useful to society belongs primarily to the person who conceived it, and it would be a violation to the very essence of the rights of man if an industrial invention were not regarded as the property of its creator.

This private property justification for patents was also incorporated into the Paris Convention for the Protection of Industrial Property in 1878. The Paris Convention—

---

[42]Agreement on Trade-Related Aspects of Intellectual Property Rights, Article 12 (1994).

For example, Germany, Austria, and Switzerland grant protection for 70 years. France grants protection for 70 years for musical compositions. Spain grants protection for 60 years. Brazil follows a 60-year *post mortem auctoris* rule, the United States 70 years *post mortem*, Colombia and Guinea 80 years *post mortem*, and the Ivory Coast 99 years *post mortem*.

All states provide for similar terms when a work is created by a business firm or other juridical entity. Currently, the United States establishes a term of 95 years from the date of first publication or 120 years from the date of creation, whichever expires first, for such works. Sonny Bono Copyright Term Extension Act, Public Law 105–298 (1998) amending United States, Copyright Act, § 102(b) (1976).

[43]E.g., Germany, Copyright Law, § 47 (September 9, 1965, as amended).
[44]E.g., United States, Copyright Act, § 110(01) (1976).
[45]E.g., Germany, Copyright Law, § 53 (September 9, 1965, as amended).
[46]E.g., United Kingdom, Copyright Act, § 6(2) (1956 as amended).
[47]E.g., France, Law No. 57-298, Article 41(3) (March 11, 1957, as amended).
[48]*The Role of Patents in the Transfer of Technology to Developing Countries*, p. 9 (UN Doc. Sales No. 65.II.B.1, 1964).
[49]*United States Reports*, vol. 395, p. 100 (Supreme Ct., 1917).

now the principal international patent and trademark convention—includes the following statement:

> The right of inventors and of industrial creators in their own work, or the right of manufacturers and businessmen over their trademarks, is a property right. The law enacted by each nation does not create these rights, but only regulates them.

The private-property-right approach to patents has, however, some theoretical shortcomings. In particular, it does not take into account the restrictions that governments commonly impose on patents. Among these are a patent's fixed duration, its inapplicability to certain kinds of inventions, and its forfeiture or compulsory licensing when it is not worked. As a consequence, the second explanation for granting patents—to encourage inventors and public development—seems the better explanation.

This second public-interest justification for granting a patent monopoly appears in some of the earliest patent laws. For example, the Preamble to the Patent Law of 1474 of the Republic of Venice states that it was meant to serve as an incentive to inventors. It also is the underlying rationale of the English Patent Law of 1623, the first modern patent law.

In England, in the fourteenth and fifteenth centuries, a patent monopoly was a matter of sovereign prerogative, granted by the king. That power, however, was used almost exclusively as a way of raising revenue. As a consequence, many of the early English patents involved day-to-day necessities completely lacking in novelty or invention. To combat what was clearly an abuse of the royal prerogative, the English Parliament enacted the Statute of Monopolies in 1623. This made illegal all monopolies, grants, and patents that had given individuals the right to buy, sell, or use particular things within the country. Only one category was excepted: patents for inventions.

The English Statute of Monopolies also set down, for the first time, the principle that patents were to be made available on a uniform basis "to the true and first inventor" for the purpose of encouraging inventions and manufacturing. Later, a court decision construed the words *true and first inventor* to include the first person to introduce a new process or procedure from abroad, thereby extending patent protection to imported technologies, as well as to completely new inventions.

The idea that patents should be granted to reward inventors for advancing the public interest was incorporated in the U.S. Constitution of 1789. The Constitution gives the U.S. Congress the power "to promote the progress of science and useful arts by securing for a limited time to authors and inventors the exclusive right to their respective writings and discoveries."

In 1809, the emperor of Brazil promulgated the fourth modern patent law (following the British, U.S., and French statutes), which set out the following policy:

> It being highly convenient that inventors of any new machinery should have an exclusive privilege for a certain time, I hereby order that no matter who should be in such a position to submit the plans of his invention to the Royal Board of Trade which, verifying that such invention is really worthy, should be given the exclusive right for the period of fourteen years after which the invention should be published so that all the nation might have the right to share the benefits of such invention.

Today, both the private rights of inventors and the public's interest in promoting development continue to be the primary justifications given both in patent acts and by legal writers for the granting of inventors' privileges. In some respects, however, a patent is now viewed as a device for reconciling these two competing interests. For example, a 1964 United Nations study that compared the patent laws of the world concluded that a patent is "essentially a process in which account is taken of, and an attempt is made to reconcile and satisfy, the whole scheme of public and private interests pressing for recognition."[50] On the private

---

[50]*The Role of Patents in the Transfer of Technology to Developing Countries*, p. 10 (UN Doc. E/3861, 1964).

side are the inventor's claims for recognition and economic advantage. On the public side, there is not only the interest of the government in promoting economic development but also the social benefit in encouraging invention, as well as the desire of consumers to purchase goods for fair value.

Patents and Other Inventor's Grants

The primary method of protecting and rewarding inventors is the patent. As defined earlier, a patent is an exclusive privilege granted to an inventor, for a fixed term, to manufacture, use, and sell a product or to employ a method or a process. Most countries, accordingly, grant three basic kinds of patents:

design patent: Patent granted to protect new and original designs of an article of manufacture.

plant patent: Patent granted for the creation or discovery of a new and distinct variety of a plant.

utility patent: Patent granted for the invention of a new and useful process, machine, article of manufacture, or composition of matter.

- **Design patents** are granted to protect new and original designs of an article of manufacture.
- **Plant patents** are granted for the creation or discovery of a new and distinct variety of a plant.
- **Utility patents** are granted for the invention of a new and useful process, machine, article of manufacture, or composition of matter.

There are also several variations on these basic patents, including *confirmation patents* (which are issued for inventions already patented in another country),[51] *patents of addition* (which cover improvements on already patented inventions), and *precautionary patents* (which are issued for short periods of time to an inventor who has not completely perfected an invention so that he or she will be notified when any other inventors apply for a patent on the same invention and so that he or she will have the opportunity to object to their applications).

petty patent: A statutory right given to the authors of minor inventions.

In addition, a few countries provide protection for lesser inventions (i.e., technical improvements of a minor nature). Developed in Germany and Japan and adopted in a few other countries (most notably Spain), this form of protection is known as a **petty patent** or an inventor's right in a *utility model*.

The German system of *Gebrauchmuster* (utility or working models) was established in 1891; the Japanese Utility Model Law was enacted in 1905. In Germany, a petty patent will be granted for a period of three years following a determination by the German Patent Office that the invention is novel (i.e., that no other inventor has obtained a patent or petty patent for the same invention). In Japan, a petty patent, which lasts for 15 years, will only be issued after the Patent Office determines both novelty and inventiveness (i.e., that the invention is not something that was obvious to the scientific community at the time of its invention).

Inventions That Qualify for Patent Protection

Patents may be obtained for inventions in every field of technology, whether products or processes, as long as they are "new, involve an inventive step, and are capable of industrial application."[52] An invention is (1) **new** if no other inventor has obtained a patent for the same invention; it (2) involves an **inventive step** if the "subject matter" of the invention was not "obvious at the time the invention was made to a person having ordinary skill in the art to which said subject matter pertains"[53]; and it is (3) **capable of industrial application** if the product or process is one that can be used in industry or commerce.

new: An invention is new if no other inventor has obtained a patent for the same invention.

inventive step: The subject matter of an invention was not obvious at the time of the invention's making to a person having ordinary skill in the art of the subject matter.

Case 9–3 examines more fully what is meant by the term *inventive step*.

capable of industrial application: The product or process of an invention can be used in industry or commerce.

---

[51]Confirmation patents are most commonly recognized in Latin America, where they are seen as a device for promoting the introduction and domestic exploitation of foreign inventions. A similar device called a *patent of importation* is available in Belgium and Spain.

[52]Agreement on Trade-Related Aspects of Intellectual Property Rights, Article 27, para. 1 (1994).

"For the purposes of this Article, the terms 'inventive step' and 'capable of industrial application' may be deemed by a member to be synonymous with the terms 'nonobvious' and 'useful' respectively." *Id.*, n.5.

[53]United States, Patent Act, § 103 (1952).

—⦅✺⦆—

Case 9-3 MONSANTO CO. v. CORAMANDAL INDAG PRODUCTS, (P) LTD.

India, Supreme Court, 1986.
Supreme Court Journal, vol. 1, p. 234 (1986).

JUDGE CHINNAPPA REDDY:

The long and grasping hand of a multinational company, the Monsanto Company of St. Louis, Missouri, United States of America, has reached out to prevent the alleged infringement of two of their patents (Numbers 104120 and 125381) by the defendant, an Indian Private Limited Company. Though the suit, as initially laid, was with reference to two patents, the suit was ultimately confined to one patent only (Number 125381), the period for which the other patent (104120) was valid having expired during the pendency of the suit....

We may first refer to a few preliminary facts. Weeds, as is well known, are a menace to food crops, particularly crops like rice which belong to the grass variety. Research has been going on for years to discover a weed killer which has no toxic effect on rice, that is to say, an herbicide which will destroy the weeds but allow rice to survive without any deleterious effect. For long the research was futile. But in 1966–67 came a breakthrough. A scientist, Dr. John Olin, discovered CP 53619 with the formula 2-Chloro-2, 6-Diethyl-N-(Butoxy-Methyl)-Acetanilide, which satisfied the requirement of a weed killer which had no toxic effect on rice. The annual report of the International Rice Research Institute for 1968 stated: "Weed control in rice was an important part of the agronomy program. The first agronomic evidence of the efficacy of granular-trichloroethyl styrene for the selective control of annual grasses in transplanted rice was obtained at the Institute. *Another accession, CP 53619, gave excellent weed control in transplanted flooded and nonflooded, upland rice.*" It was further stated: "CP 53619 at 2 and 4 kg/ha appeared at least twice among the 20 best treatments," and "the most outstanding new pre-emergence herbicide was 2-Chloro-2, 6-Diethyl-N-(Butoxy-Methyl)-Acetanilide (CP 53619)." The annual report of the International Rice Institute for 1969 shows that the herbicide CP 53619 came to acquire the name of Butachlor.

... The first plaintiff is the Monsanto Company and the second plaintiff is a subsidiary of the first plaintiff registered as a company in India. It was stated in the plaint that the first plaintiff was the patentee of inventions entitled "Phytotoxic Compositions" and "Grass Se-lective Herbicide Compositions," duly patented under patent numbers 104120 dated March 1, 1966, and 125381 dated February 20, 1970. The claims and the particulars relating to the inventions... stated ... and this is very important, "the active ingredient mentioned in the claim is called 'Butachlor.'" It suggested, without expressly saying it, that the plaintiffs' patents covered Butachlor also, which in fact it did not, as we shall presently see. It was next stated that the first plaintiff had permitted the second plaintiff to work the patents from 1971 onwards under an agreement dated September 3, 1980.... It came to the notice of the plaintiffs, it was averred, that the defendant was attempting to market a formulation of Butachlor covered by the said patents. They, therefore, wrote to the defendants drawing their attention to the existence of the patents in their favor. Some correspondence ensued. In the second week of May, 1981, the second plaintiff found that the defendant was marketing a formulation of Butachlor covered by the patents of the first plaintiff. Sample tins of "Butachlor 50" manufactured by the defendant were purchased by the plaintiffs....

According to the plaintiffs, the legends on the tins containing substance manufactured by the defendant showed that what was sold by the defendant was nothing but a reproduction of the first plaintiff's patented formulation. The formulations of the defendant were sent to the Shri Ram Institute for analysis and they were said to contain the chemical "Butachlor, the chemical formula for which is 2 Chloro, 6-Diethyl-N-(Butoxymethyl) Acetanilide." On these averments the plaintiffs alleged that the defendant had infringed their patents, numbers 104120 and 125381, by selling formulations covered by them. The plaintiffs sued for an injunction....

... [T]he defendant claimed, as he was entitled to do under Section 107 of the Patents Act 1970, that the patents were liable to be revoked.... The defendant also made a counterclaim seeking revocation of the patents.

A close scrutiny of the plaint and a reference to the evidence of the witnesses for the plaintiff at once exposes the hollowness of the suit. We must begin with the statement in the plaint that "the active ingredient mentioned in the claim is called 'Butachlor,'" which suggests that Butachlor was covered by the plaintiffs' patents and the circumstance now admitted that no one, neither the plaintiff nor any one else, has a patent for Butachlor. The admission was expressly made by PW-2, the power of attorney holder of the first plaintiff and Director of the second plaintiff company. The learned counsel for the plaintiffs also admitted the same before us. PW-1, Dr. Dixon, a chemist of the first plaintiff company, after explaining the use of an emulsifying agent, in answer to a direct question, whether his company claimed any patent or special knowledge for the use of any particular solvent or particular emulsifying agent, in the formulation in their patent, had to admit that they had no such patent or special knowledge. He further admitted that the use of solvent and emulsifying agent on the active ingredient was one of the well-known methods used in the pesticide industry to prepare a marketable product. He also expressed his inability to say what dilutents or other emulsifying agents the defendant used in their process. PW-2 admitted that Butachlor was a common name and that the Weed Science Society of America had allotted the common name. He stated that "Machete" was the brand name under which their company manufactured Butachlor. He also stated that there could be a number of concerns all over the world manufacturing Butachlor, but he was not aware of them. He admitted that they did not claim a patent for Butachlor. He stated that though his company did not claim a patent for Butachlor, they claimed a patent for the process of making a Butachlor emulsifiable concentrate to be used as an herbicide composition for rice. Pursued further in cross-examination, he was forced to admit that they used kerosene as a solvent for Butachlor and an emulsifier manufactured by a local Indian company was an emulsifying agent. He then proceeded to state that he claimed secrecy with regard to the manufacture of their formulation. When he was asked further whether the secrecy claimed was with regard to the solvent or with regard to the stabilizer, he answered in the negative. He finally admitted that his secret was confined to the active ingredient Butachlor about which, as we know, there is no secret. . . .

We, therefore, see that Butachlor (which was the common name for CP 53619) was discovered prior to 1968 as an herbicide possessing the property of nontoxic effect on rice. The formula for the herbicide was published in the report of the International Rice Research Institute for the year 1968 and its common name Butachlor was also mentioned in the report of the International Rice Research Institute for the year 1969. No one patented the invention Butachlor and it was the property of the population of the world. Before Butachlor, or for that matter any herbicide could be used for killing weeds, it had to be converted into an emulsion by dissolving it in a suitable solvent and by mixing the solution with an emulsifying agent. Emulsification is a well-known process and is no one's discovery. In the face of the now indisputable fact that

there is no patent for or any secrecy attached to Butachlor, the solvent, or the emulsifying agent, and the further fact that the process of emulsification is no new discovery, the present suit based on the secrecy claimed in respect of the active ingredient Butachlor and the claim for the process of emulsification must necessarily fail. Under Section 61(1)(d) [of the Patents Act, 1970], a patent may be revoked on the ground that the subject of any claim of the complete specification is not an invention within the meaning of the Act. Under Section 64(e), a patent may be revoked if invention so far as claimed in any claim of the complete specifications is not new, having regard to what was publicly known or publicly used in India before the date of the claim, etc. Under Section 64(1)(f), a patent may be revoked if the invention so far as claimed in any claim of the complete specification is obvious or does not involve any inventive step having regard to what was publicly known or publicly used in India or was published in India before the priority date of the claim (the words "or elsewhere" are omitted by us as the patents in the present case were granted under the Indian Patents and Designs Act, 1911, i.e., before the Patents Act, 1970). "Inventions" has been defined by Section 2(j) as follows:

> Invention means any new and useful—(i) art, process, method, or manner of manufacture; (ii) machine, apparatus, or other article; (iii) substance produced by manufacture, and includes any new and useful improvement of any of them, and an alleged invention.

It is clear from the facts narrated by us that the herbicide CP 53619 (Butachlor) was publicly known before patent number 125381 was granted. Its formula and use had already been made known to the public by the report of the International Rice Institute for the year 1968. No one claimed any patent or any other exclusive right to Butachlor. To satisfy the requirement of being publicly known as used in clauses (e) and (f) of the Section 64(1), it is not necessary that it should be widely used to the knowledge of the consumer public. It is sufficient if it is known to the persons who are engaged in the pursuit of any knowledge of the patented product or process, either as men of science or men of commerce or consumers. The section of the public who, as men of science or men of commerce, were interested in knowing about herbicides which would destroy weeds but rice, must have been aware of the discovery of Butachlor. There was no secret about the active ingredient Butachlor, as claimed by the plaintiffs, since there was no patent for Butachlor, as admitted by the plaintiffs. Emulsification was a well-known and common process by which any herbicide could be used. Neither Butachlor nor the process of emulsification was capable of being claimed by the plaintiffs as their exclusive property. The solvent and the emulsifier were not secrets and they were admittedly ordinary market products. From the beginning to the end, there was no secret and there was no invention by the plaintiffs. The ingredients, the active ingredient, the solvent, and the emulsifier, were known; the process was known; the product was known; and the use was known. The plaintiffs were merely camouflaging a substance whose discovery was known throughout the world and trying to enfold it in their specification relating to patent number 125381. The patent is, therefore, liable to be revoked.... The appeal is dismissed with costs. ■

CASEPOINT: Monsanto Corporation and an Indian subsidiary brought this action in India for patent infringement against a local Indian company that manufactured and sold an herbicide product that killed weeds growing in rice fields. The court looked into the history of the product, and found that its active ingredient (Butachlor) and its composition were well-known before the patent was granted, and that the emulsification necessary to apply the product was also a common practice in the industry. Thus, the court revoked the patent and found no infringement, since neither the product nor the process claimed by Monsanto were new, nor did they involve any inventive steps not already known.

MAP 9-3 India (1986)

Determining Qualifications

Questions about the existence or nonexistence of newness, inventive steps, and industrial application may arise at various stages in the life of a patent. They may arise during the initial review of an application, during the appeal of a denial, during a revocation or cancellation hearing, or in suits for infringement where the person charged with infringement disputes the validity of the patent, as in the previous case.

With regard to the first of these questions—the review of an application by a patent office—procedures vary from country to country. They range from a simple review of the application form to an extensive search of domestic and foreign materials to determine if the product or process is both novel and inventive. The different procedures (for a select group of countries) are summarized in Exhibit 9-1.

In completing an application form, an inventor is uniformly required to disclose sufficient information about the product or process "in such full, clear, concise, and exact terms as to enable any person skilled in the art to which it pertains, or with which it is most clearly connected, to make and use the same."[54] In addition, in the United States, the application must disclose the "best mode" known to the inventor for carrying out the invention.[55] Most other countries, however, allow an applicant to elect to disclose only one mode, and that does not necessarily have to be the best mode.

In Europe and Japan, and in most of the developing world, the information contained in a patent application has to be published before a patent will be granted. In the developing world, this publication requirement acts as a substitute for an examination of novelty and in-

---

[54]United States, Patent Act, § 112 (1952).
[55]*Id.*

Procedure	Countries Using Procedure
1. Examination of the application form only.	Egypt, Iran, Italy, Lebanon, Liberia, Morocco, Spain, Switzerland,[a] Tunisia, Turkey
2. Examination as to form, then publication followed by a period in which the public may object to the grant of a patent.	Colombia, Peru, Venezuela
3. Examination as to form and novelty. Only domestic patents are searched in ascertaining novelty.	Argentina
4. Examination as to form and novelty. Domestic and foreign patents are searched in ascertaining novelty.	India, Israel
5. Examination as to form and inventiveness. Domestic and foreign developments are searched in ascertaining inventiveness.	France
6. Examination as to form, novelty, and inventiveness. Only domestic patents and developments are searched in ascertaining novelty and inventiveness.	Mexico
7. Examination as to form, novelty, and inventiveness. Domestic and foreign patents and developments are searched in ascertaining novelty and inventiveness.	Brazil, Canada, Czechoslovakia, Germany, Japan, the Netherlands, Pakistan, Russia, Sweden, United Kingdom, United States

[a]Switzerland requires an examination as to form, novelty, and inventiveness for patents involving textiles and textile dyes.

EXHIBIT 9-1   Procedures Used in Reviewing Patent Applications

ventiveness by a patent office. In Colombia, for example, a patent will be issued 30 days after publication in the *Diario Official* (official journal) unless some private party raises an objection.[56] In the developed world, the publication date is the date on which the patent vests, although it will not be enforceable until it is formally granted by a patent office.

Publication during the application process is not required in the United States. Nevertheless, most litigation in the United States concerning the validity of a patent application arises during the application process. In part, this is because of the size and nature of the U.S. Patent Office. In most other countries (despite the requirements for disclosure during the application process), most challenges to the validity of a patent arise after a patent is granted.[57]

Inventions Excluded from Patent Protection

Patents may be denied to inventions that do not meet the basic definition of patentability (i.e., being new, involving an inventive step, and being capable of industrial application). They may also be denied to inventions that violate basic social policies. The Agreement on Trade-Related Aspects of Intellectual Property Rights, for example, allows a WTO member state to deny a patent to an inventor in order "to protect ordre public or morality" so long as the state also forbids the commercial exploitation of the invention.[58] (That is, a state cannot deny an inventor a patent on this basis and still let the invention be exploited freely by others.) In particular, patents may be denied for this reason in order to protect the lives or health of humans, animals, or plants or to protect the environment from serious injury.

---

[56]Colombia, Patent Law (1925 as amended).
[57]Alan Gutterman, "A Legal Due Diligence Framework for Inbound Transfers of Foreign Technology Rights," *The International Lawyer*, vol. 24, p. 982 (1990).
[58]Agreement on Trade-Related Aspects of Intellectual Property Rights, Article 27, para. 2 (1994).

The TRIPs Agreement also allows WTO member states to deny patents for certain inventions without also prohibiting their commercial exploitation. (In other words, the invention may be freely exploited within the territory of the state.) These inventions may include (1) diagnostic, therapeutic, and surgical methods for the treatment of humans and animals; (2) plants and animals other than microorganisms (except that member states must provide patent protection or its equivalent for plant varieties); and (3) essentially biological processes for the production of plants or animals.[59]

Duration of Patents

With the coming into force of the TRIPs Agreement on January 1, 1995, the minimum term of protection for patents has now been set at twenty years for WTO member states.[60] Previously, the terms that countries had established varied widely, ranging from 3 to 26 years (including extensions).[61] The uniformity provided by the new 20-year standard should greatly encourage inventors, who will now be able to exploit their inventions much more widely and for a longer period overall than they were able to do in the past.

Scope of Patents

A patent is valid only within the territory of the state granting it; hence, states cannot prevent the use of patented technology outside their territory. States will, however, stop the importation of goods from countries that infringe a patent. On the other hand, many states will not stop someone inside their territory from using patented technology (without permission from the patent owner) to produce a product for export and sale abroad, although this is no longer allowed in the United States.[62]

TRADEMARKS

Merchants and others use five marks to identify themselves and their products. These are (1) trademarks (or sometimes *true trademarks* to distinguish them from other marks), (2) trade names, (3) service marks, (4) collective marks, and (5) certification marks. In practice, all five are commonly called *trademarks*.

true trademark: A mark or symbol used to identify goods of a particular manufacturer or merchant.

A **true trademark** is "any word, name, symbol, or device or any combination thereof adopted and used by a manufacturer or merchant to identify his goods and distinguish them from those manufactured or sold by others."[63] It is different from a **trade name**, which is the name of the manufacturer rather than the manufacturer's products. *PepsiCo*, for example, is the well-known trade name of PepsiCo, Inc., a company that manufactures and sells products under trademarks such as *Pepsi-Cola, Fritos*, and *Gatorade*.

trade name: A mark or symbol used to identify a manufacturer or merchant.

service mark: A mark or symbol used to identify a person who provides services.

A **service mark** is a "mark used in the sale or advertising of services to identify the services of one person and distinguish them from the services of another."[64] Yum! Brands, Inc., for example, uses the service marks of *KFC, Pizza Hut*, and *Taco Bell* to identify its service establishments.

As the examples indicate, a mark can be used for more than one purpose. Thus, *KFC* is both a trademark and a service mark. Similarly, *Coca-Cola* is used both as a trade name and a trademark.

When trademarks or service marks are used by members of an association, collective, or cooperative organization to identify their products or services to members, they are called

---

[59]*Id.*, para. 3.
[60]*Id.*, Article 33.
[61]See Ray August, *International Business Law: Text, Cases, and Readings*, pp. 610–611 (1st ed., 1993).
[62]For example, in Deepsouth Packing Co. v. Laitram Corp., *United States Reports*, vol. 406, p. 518 at pp. 526–529 (1972), the U.S. Supreme Court held that the shipment overseas of materials that, when assembled in combination, violated a U.S. patent did not result in liability for contributory infringement. The U.S. Congress subsequently reversed this decision by statute. See Patent Law Amendments of 1984, codified as amended at *United States Code*, Title 35, § 271(f) (1992). In the United States, accordingly, the manufacture of a product in the United States using a U.S.-patented process will infringe the patent, even if the product is intended for shipment abroad and requires final assembly overseas.
[63]Lanham Trademark Act (1946), in *United States Code*, Title 15, § 1127.
[64]*Id.*

collective mark: A mark or symbol used by a group to identify itself to its members.
certification mark: A mark or symbol used by a licensee or franchisee to indicate that a particular product meets certain standards.

collective marks. Examples include the identifying names and insignias of the American Greek letter fraternities and sororities or the uniforms or cookies of Boy Scouts and Girl Scouts.

A **certification mark** is a mark used exclusively by a licensee or franchisee to indicate that a product meets certain standards. Examples include "*Champagne*," "*Roquefort*," and "*Grown in Idaho*," which indicate places of origin,[65] and the "*Underwriters' Seal of Approval*," which attests to certain standards of quality. Unlike true trademarks, trade names, and service marks, a licensor or franchisor may not use a certification mark.

Trademarks (using the term broadly) have several functions. From the perspective of an owner, a trademark is the right to put a product protected by the mark into circulation for the first time.[66] From the viewpoint of a consumer, a trademark serves to (1) designate the origin or source of a product or service, (2) indicate a particular standard of quality, (3) represent the goodwill of the manufacturer, and (4) protect the consumer from confusion.[67]

The following reading examines a recent dispute about the use of trademarks in international trade.

---

[65]The Agreement on Trade-Related Aspects of Intellectual Property Rights, Article 22 (1994), requires WTO member states to provide the legal means for interested parties to prevent the use of geographical indications of origin that mislead the public. Geographical indications of origin relating to wine are protected even if they are not misleading (for instance, even if the true geographical origin is accompanied by words such as *kind, type, imitation*, etc., it may not be used). *Id.*, Article 23. Also, the TRIPs Council (established by the agreement) is to undertake negotiations to establish a multilateral system for notifying and registering geographical indications of the origins of wines. *Id.*, para. 4.
[66]Centrafarm v. Winthrop, Case 16/74, *European Court Reports*, vol. 1974, p. 1183 (1974).
[67]J. Gilson, *Trademark Protection and Practice*, § 1.03 (1975). See, as well, Hanover Star Milling Co. v. Metcalf in *United States Reports,* vol. 240, at p. 412 (Supreme Ct., 1916).

=◆◆◆=

Reading 9-1   COFFEE TRADEMARK DISPUTE BETWEEN STARBUCKS AND ETHIOPIA

Sources: "Storm in a Coffee Cup," *The Economist*, Nov. 30, 2006; "Starbucks and Ethiopia Make Bad Blend," ABC News.com, Oct. 26, 2006; J. Adamy and R. Thurow, "Ethiopia Battles Starbucks Over Rights to Coffee Names," *Wall Street Journal*, March 5, 2007; "Starbucks in Ethiopia Coffee Row," BBC News.co.uk, Oct. 26, 2006; "Starbucks vs. Ethiopia," *Fortune Magazine*, Feb. 26, 2007, accessed at CNN.Money.com; "Starbucks Recognizes Ethiopia's Ownership of Premium Coffee Strains," *International Herald Tribune*, June 21, 2007; "Oxfam Celebrates Win-Win Outcome for Ethiopian Coffee Farmers and Starbucks," OxfamAmerica.org, June 20, 2007.

Starbucks, the giant coffee chain, has been involved in a dispute with Ethiopia, one of the world's poorest countries, over the right to use certain place names on coffee. Ethiopia is considered—by Starbucks and others—as the birthplace of coffee, and in March 2005 the government filed an application with the U.S. Patent and Trademark Office (USPTO) seeking to trademark the names of its most famous coffee regions–Sidamo, Harar and Yirgacheffe—which names also appear on the packaging of Starbucks and some other coffee roasters.

The goal of the trademark effort, say Ethiopian leaders, is to gain more control over the distribution and promotion of its coffee, and eventually to secure better prices for its farmers. The goal was to force those who use those particular Ethiopian coffees to sign licensing agreements, thus producing more income for Ethiopian farmers. ABC News reported that securing trademark rights to these names would produce a "spectacular" rise in Ethiopia's coffee revenues—perhaps as much as $88 million. Many of Ethiopia's 15 million coffee growers live on less than a dollar per day. The growers in Fero, in the Sidamo region, receive between 75 cents and $1 per pound for their coffee. Starbucks has sold the processed product for as much as $26 per pound.

However, the Ethiopian government and Oxfam, a British non-governmental organization (NGO), trying to help the coffee farmers have claimed that Starbucks tried to block the trademark registration, which was held up by a protest from the National Coffee Association in the United States. "Starbucks is using its influence on the National Coffee Association to block the application in the U.S." said one Oxfam official, a contention denied by Starbucks. Oxfam urged customers to send postcards to Starbucks complaining about its stance, and posted a video on You.Tube.com regarding the trademark dispute and the low prices paid to Ethiopian farmers.

At least 70,000 customers contacted Starbucks to complain, prompting the firm to post leaflets in its stores defending its behavior and to create and post its own video on You.Tube. Starbucks accused Oxfam of "misleading the public" and stated that the campaign "needs to stop." Starbucks was clearly stung by the criticism, having prided itself on its social responsibility efforts and pointing out that it had spent $2.4 million on social projects in Ethiopia. In past years, Starbucks has made a commitment to buy 6% of its coffee from "fair trade" certified co-ops which guarantee farmers a minimum price. It has also bought 53% of its coffee from sellers who adhered to guidelines the company established to promote economic sustainability for farmers. In this particular case, Starbucks' employees had gone to the Fero region and worked with farmers on a new method of drying the beans. After the first season flopped (and Starbucks bought all the coffee) the second year produced wonderful coffee which became very popular quickly. Starbucks' people consulted with local farmers on a name, and they came up with "Shirkina," which means "partnership." After the coffee was named "Shirkina Sun-Dried Sidamo" Starbucks filed for a trademark on that name with the USPTO. Later when Ethiopia applied for a trademark on "Sidamo" it was denied because of Starbucks' earlier registration. Ethiopians were shocked, feeling "it is rude and selfish of a company to take the name of its partner," while Starbucks said it only wanted to keep competitors from stealing the word "shirkina." After receiving the protests from Ethiopia, Starbucks withdrew its trademark application for Shirkina Sun-Dried Sidamo. Ethiopia did successfully register some of its regional names in Canada, Japan and the European Union, and secured a trademark on Yirgacheffe in the United States. However, the U.S. National Coffee Association later asked the U.S. trademark office to deny Ethiopia trademarks for Sidamo and Harar, arguing they were generic names—the applications are pending. Trademark applications were also made by Ethiopia in Brazil, China, India and South Africa.

Starbucks pointed out that it opposed the Ethiopian trademark idea because it believed that a "geographical certification" was a better plan, arguing that this was the preferred method around the world for guaranteeing to customers that a product comes from a certain region but allows companies to use the term in their branding. Products such as Idaho potatoes, Roquefort cheese and Jamaican Blue Mountain and Hawaiian Kona coffee use geographic certifications. "I can't name one case where there are trademarks for coffee," said Dub Hay, senior vice-president for coffee and global procurement at Starbucks

Mr. Hay traveled to the Fero region of Ethiopia to meet with the farmers, but no agreement was reached. The Fero farmers say the best gift would be higher prices, stating that they only received 75 cents per pound of dried beans. On a return visit to Ethiopia, Mr. Hay promised to double the coffee purchases from East Africa and increase technical support to farmers. He also announced that Starbucks would no longer try to prevent Ethiopia from obtaining trademarks and "respects the right of the Government of Ethiopia to trademark its coffee brands." However, Starbucks still refused to sign a licensing agreement with Ethiopia.

Finally, in June 2007, Starbucks and the Ethiopian intellectual property office announced that they had reached an agreement to work together to promote the three types of African coffee that were the subject of the dispute. The two entities announced that they had reached a licensing, marketing and distribution agreement that acknowledges Ethiopia's ownership of the names Yirgacheffe, Hirar and Sidamo, regardless of whether they are trademarked. Both sides hailed the resolution of the trademark dispute. "This agreement is broader than those proposed in the past," said Sandra Taylor, Starbucks' senior vice-president. "We are very excited about the opportunity to work cooperatively with Ethiopia in support of its coffee farmers." Getachew Mengistie, director of Ethiopia's intellectual property office, said, "This agreement marks an important milestone in our efforts to promote and protect Ethiopia's specialty coffee designations. . . . Having the commitment and support of Starbucks will enhance the quality of Ethiopian fine coffees and improve the income of farmers and traders."

Even the NGO Oxfam praised the resolution of the dispute. "Congratulations to our Ethiopian coffee farming partners and to Starbucks on an agreement that recognizes Ethiopians' right to control the use of their specialty coffee brands. This agreement represents a business approach in step with 21st century standards in its concern for rights rather than charity and for greater equity in supply chains rather than short-term profits," said the president of Oxfam America.

Acquiring Trademarks

Trademarks are acquired in two ways: (1) by use and (2) by registration. In a few countries, registration is not available. In two countries—Canada and the Philippines—a trademark can be registered only if it has already been put into use. In the rest of the world, a mark can be registered even if it has never been used in commerce.[68]

The fact that a trademark cannot be registered does not mean that its owner is without rights. In *McDonald's Corp. v. Hassan Arzouni*, the Civil Court of Sharjah, one of the United Arab Emirates, held that McDonald's could enjoin a local entrepreneur from using its name and golden arches logo on a restaurant, even though Sharjah has no trademark registration law. The court said:

> The fact that such trademark has not been registered in the U.A.E. is irrelevant, because of the fame of this trademark worldwide and the possibility of the simultaneous presence of the two products in the U.A.E. market, considering the ease of transportation, the wide range of commerce, and the fact that the U.A.E. imports most of its consumer products, including foodstuffs.[69]

As the *Hassan Arzouni* case points out, "famous" trademarks (i.e., ones well known throughout the world) may not have to be registered to be protected. In another case involving McDonald's, *Colourprint Ltd. v. McDonald's Corp.*, the American fast-food retailer opposed an application in Kenya by a local company to register the McDonald's name and double arches logo as a trademark. McDonald's had not registered its trademark and did not have it in any restaurants in Kenya. Nevertheless, the Kenyan deputy registrar of trademarks would not allow the local company to register the mark as its own. The deputy stated:

> I have no doubt in my mind that local reputation of the mark is very important, but I am also of the view that reputation outside Kenya cannot be ignored altogether. It is also important to consider whether any section of the Kenyan public were aware of the existence of the opponents' mark at the time when the applicants' mark was filed for registration. This is relevant because the likelihood of confusion or deception must be considered at the time of the application.
>
> A section of the Kenya public has not only seen the opponent's mark in the magazines referred to, but I accept that they have traveled to some countries outside Africa where the opponents' mark is well known. The opponents run the business of hotels [sic] and no doubt some Kenyans are familiar with the products of the opponent.[70]

The same result has been reached in Australia, Canada, Colombia, India, New Zealand, the United Kingdom, and the United States. In other countries (e.g., Panama and Taiwan), a foreign owner of a famous unregistered trademark can oppose registration but cannot sue a local company for infringement. In still other countries (e.g., most of thjose in South America), only a locally registered owner can protest either registration or infringing use.[71]

Of course, in any of the countries that allow an unregistered foreign trademark holder to challenge either a competing registration or an infringing use, the trademark in question must be well known. For example, in *Wienerwald Holding, A.G. v. Kawn, Wong, Tan, and Fong*, the High Court of Hong Kong concluded that the name "Wienerwald Restaurant," which was the service mark of a Swiss restaurant company, was so little known in Hong Kong that the Swiss owner could not object to a competing registration in Hong Kong by a local firm of chartered accountants.[72]

---

[68]Prior to 1988, the United States also stated that a trademark could not be registered until it had been put in use. Now a trademark will be granted based on the applicant's intent to use the mark. The mark must then be used within six months (although extensions can be obtained so that the period can be three years) or the registration will be revoked. The Trademark Law Revision Act, Public Law 100-667, § 134 (1988).
[69]Case No. 823/85, decided January 13, 1986 (unpublished); quoted in *Trademark Reporter*, vol. 76, p. 354 (1986).
[70]Decision by Deputy Registrar of Trademarks in Kenya, TM No. B23964, May 21, 1980, at p. 9 (unreported); quoted in Thomas Hoffmann and Susan Brownstone, "Protection of Trademark Rights Acquired by International Reputation without Use of Registration," *Trademark Reporter*, vol. 71, pp. 21–22 (1981).
[71]*Id.*, pp. 1–37.
[72]*Fleet Street Patent Law Reports*, vol. 1979, p. 381 (January 20, 1979).

In addition to the objections that can be raised by famous trademark holders, most countries allow a local user of a mark to object to its registration by another individual—even if the mark is not famous—so long as the opponent's local use began before that of the applicant. However, a few states will register a trademark to the first person to apply for it, regardless. Thus, prior users are denied the right to challenge the application or to later seek cancellation of the registration.[73]

Registration

One registers a trademark to publicly notify other potential users of one's claim in a mark. The registration process commonly begins with an examination done by an official in the Trademark Office to determine a mark's suitability for registration. In most countries, this consists simply of an examination of the application form for compliance with statutory definitions and an examination of the office's own records to ensure that the mark has not been previously registered. In wealthier countries with the resources to maintain a large library and a large staff, the examination can include the examination of records from other countries, records of the states of a federal or economic union, or private materials, such as newspapers, magazines, or trademark association reports.

Registration Criteria

distinctive: Possessing a unique design that distinguishes a product from other similar products.

The common statutory definitional criterion that appears in all trademark laws is **distinctiveness**. This means that a mark must possess a unique design that functions to distinguish the product on which it is used from other similar products. In sum, to be registered, a trademark must (1) not infringe on another mark and (2) be distinctive.

In Case 9–4, an international arbitration panel had to determine whether an Internet domain name—which is treated very much like a trademark—was confusingly similar to a registered mark.

---

[73]American Bar Association, Section of Patent, Trademark and Copyright Law, *1990 Committee Reports*, p. 96 (1990).

Case 9-4 EXPERIENCE HENDRIX, L.L.C. v. HAMMERTON

World Intellectual Property Organization Arbitration and Mediation Center. Administrative Panel Decision, Case No. D2000-0364, August 2, 2000.

PANELIST MARYLEE JENKINS:

The Parties

Experience Hendrix, L.L.C. ("Complainant"), is a Washington limited liability company with a principal place of business at 14501 Interurban Avenue South, Tukwila, Washington, 98168, U.S.A. The company was formed in 1995 by the family of the late Jimi Hendrix, an internationally known guitarist and musician. Experience Hendrix, L.L.C., is the owner and administrator of substantially all rights relating to Jimi Hendrix, including rights in his music, name, image, and recordings.

The Respondent, Denny Hammerton ("Mr. Hammerton"), an individual, is listed as the administrative contact for the registration of the domain name in issue and lists a mailing address of P.O. Box 1103, Minneola, Florida, 34744, U.S.A. The Respondent, The Jimi Hendrix Fan Club ("Fan Club"), added by amendment to the Complaint, is the registrant of the domain name registration and has the same mailing address as Mr. Hammerton.

***

Factual Background

The Complainant is the owner of all rights in the name "JIMI HENDRIX", including all common law rights therein, and is the owner of several trademarks and service marks registered or pending with the U.S. Patent and Trademark Office. . . .

***

The Complainant is also the registrant of the domain names "jimi-hendrix.com," "jimi-hendrix.org," and "jimihendrix.org" and is the owner and operator of the "Experience Hendrix Interactive—The Official Jimi Hendrix Web site" located at " www.jimi-hendrix.com."

A search result from a query of the Registrar's Whois database shows that the domain name in issue was registered on April 5, 1996, to "The Jimi Hendrix Fan Club" with Mr. Hammerton listed as the administrative contact.

Some time between the domain name registration and April 30, 1997, the Respondent created a Web site at "www.jimihendrix.com" that offered for sale vanity e-mail addresses incorporating the "jimihendrix.com" domain name ("Site").

The Complainant's representatives communicated with the Registrar and asked the Registrar to initiate the Registrar's Domain Name Dispute Policy then in effect with respect to the domain name "jimihendrix.com." On April 30, 1997, the domain name was placed on "Hold" status by the Registrar.

In a letter dated March 21, 2000, the Registrar notified the Complainant's representatives that on May 2, 2000, the Registrar would terminate the dispute, remove the domain name registration from "Hold" status and reactivate the domain name unless the Registrar . . . received a complaint filed pursuant to the Policy and this proceeding was file in response to the Registrar's March 21st letter.

Parties' Contentions

Complainant   The Complainant contends that the domain name "jimihendrix.com" is identical or confusingly similar to the name and marks owned by the Complainant.

The Complainant contends that the Respondent has no rights or legitimate interests in the domain name based upon:

  (i)   the Respondent choosing the domain name in issue not arbitrarily but intending to misappropriate and use the goodwill in the Complainant's marks for his own commercial benefit by advertising vanity e-mail addresses for sale on a Web page located at "http://www.jimihendrix.com."
 (ii)   the Complainant having not at any time, assigned, granted, licensed, sold, or otherwise transferred any of its rights in the name and mark JIMI HENDRIX to the Respondent.
(iii)   the Respondent's use of the domain name being purely commercial in nature with the effect of diluting and harming the Complainant's legitimate rights in the name and mark.

 (iv)   the Respondent, Mr. Hammerton, being a domain name speculator and registering and selling domain names for no legitimate purpose other than to profit from the name relying on a front page article in the *San Francisco Chronicle* quoting Mr. Hammerton as saying "[s]ome people like it, some people don't—that's tough. . . . It's real estate is what it is. If I buy land that somebody wants, then lucky me." The Complainant further quotes the article as stating that Mr. Hammerton claimed to own rights to "some 2,000 Web site names, including, http://www.jimihendrix.com, www.jethrotull.com, and http://www.fleetwoodmac.com."

The Complainant contends that the Respondent has registered and used the domain name in bad faith based upon:

  (i)   the Respondent knowing at all times prior to, during, and following registration of the domain name that he did not own or have any legal rights to the name or mark JIMI HENDRIX.

***

(iii)   a recent search of a domain name reseller site showing Mr. Hammerton advertising to sell the "jimihendrix.com" domain name for $1 million dollars as "the most unique domain/jimi was a 'hit' maker."

***

(v–vi) Mr. Hammerton being a domain name speculator that registers and sells domain names for no legitimate purpose other than to profit from the name. [In the past he has advertised for sale many celebrity domain names including] "elvispresley.net" for $39,000, "jethrotull.com" for $8,000, "lindamccartney.com" for $15,000–$25,000, "mickjagger.com" for $25,000, "paulmccartney.com" for $25,000-$51,000, "ringo.com" for $15,000–$21,000, "rodstewart.com" for $15,000–$21,000, and "twiggy.com" for $10,000 on different domain name reseller sites.

***

(viii)   the Respondent, by using the domain name, having intentionally attempted to attract, for commercial gain, Internet users to his Web site by creating a likelihood of confusion with the Complainant's mark as to source, sponsorship, affiliation, and endorsement of his Web site or the services he offers on the site.

***

(ix) the Respondent, although having registered the domain name "jimihendrix.com" in the name of a fan club, not being a true "fan club" existing at the address "www.jimihendrix.com" or providing any traditional fan club services, but being nothing more than a sales promotion site—selling vanity e-mail addresses.

Based upon the above, the Complainant requests that the Panelist transfer the domain name "jimihendrix.com" to it.

Respondent The Respondent, Mr. Hammerton, contends that he registered the domain "jimihendrix.com" on April 5, 1996. Before registering the domain name, he contends that he conducted a search of the USPTO database for any trademarks on "Jimi Hendrix" and found none.

The Respondent contends that from April of 1996, he ran a Web site for "The Jimi Hendrix Internet Fan Club" on the Internet until a complaint by the Complainant was sent to the Registrar in 1997 resulting in the domain name "jimihendrix.com" being placed on Hold. . . .

The Respondent contends that a word with a .com on the end is not identical to a word without a .com on the end and inferentially asserts that the domain name is not identical or confusingly similar to the Complainant's mark.

The Respondent contends that he has never offered "jimihendrix.com" as a domain name for sale [and] . . . that he has never used the domain name "jimihendrix.com" in bad faith.

The Respondent contends that "it becomes a violation of human rights and free speech that an arbitrary board such as WIPO which contradicts itself [in] case after case should have any rights over any domain which is owned by the original paying domain name owner."

The Respondent contends that "once WIPO takes [sic] that domain name away from the original owner it constitutes theft under the American Constitution in that the Jurisdiction under Human Rights should not allowed."

Discussion and Findings

***

The Proceeding—Three Elements

Paragraph 4(a) of the Policy [of the domain name registrar, Network Solutions, Inc., governing dispute settlements, which the respondent agreed to be bound by,] states that the domain name holder is to submit to a mandatory administrative proceeding in the event that a third party complainant asserts to an ICANN approved dispute provider that:

(i) the domain name holder's domain name is identical or confusingly similar to a trademark or service mark in which the complainant has rights ("Element (i)"); and

(ii) the domain name holder has no rights or legitimate interests in respect of the domain name ("Element (ii)"); and

(iii) the domain name of the domain name holder has been registered and is being used in bad faith ("Element (iii)").

Element (i)—Domain Name Identical or Confusingly Similar to Mark The Complainant is the owner of both the common law trademark rights in the name JIMI HENDRIX as well as the registered trademarks identified above. Although the Respondent contends that a word with a ".com" on the end is not identical to a word without a ".com" on the end, the COM suffix is not relevant in determining whether a domain name is identical or confusingly similar to a mark. Rather, one looks to the second-level domain "jimihendrix" of the domain name for such a determination since the suffix COM is merely descriptive of the registry services and is not an identifier of a source of goods or services. Accordingly, the Panelist concludes that the domain name is identical to the mark JIMI HENDRIX and that Element (i) has been satisfied.

Element (ii)—Rights or Legitimate Interests in the Domain Name Paragraph 4(c) of the Policy sets out circumstances, in particular but without limitation, which, if found by the Panelist to be proved based on its evaluation of all evidence presented, can demonstrate the holder's rights to or legitimate interests in the domain name. These circumstances include:

(i) before any notice to the holder of the dispute, the holder's use of, or demonstrable preparations to use, the domain name or a name corresponding to the domain name in connection with a bona fide offering of goods or services; or

(ii) the holder (as an individual, business, or other organization) has been commonly known by the domain name, even if the holder has acquired no trademark or service mark rights; or

(iii) the domain name holder is making a legitimate noncommercial or fair use of the domain name, without intent for commercial gain to misleadingly divert consumers or to tarnish the trademark or service mark at issue.

The Respondent contends that he registered the domain name prior to the Complainant's registration of the Complainant's marks and was unaware of the Complainant's trademark registrations at the time of registration. However, based upon the evidence presented, the registration and use of the domain name by the Respondent do not predate the Complainant's use and rights in the name and mark but rather appears to be an attempt to usurp the Complainant's rights therein. Indeed, the registration of the domain name by "The Jimi Hendrix Fan Club" is a clear indication of the Respondent's awareness of the wide recognition and fame associated with the name JIMI HENDRIX. The Respondent's alleged lack of knowledge concerning the trademark registrations involved in this proceeding is insufficient.

The Respondent further contends that the domain name was registered to "The Jimi Hendrix Fan Club" and that he was operating a Web site for the Fan Club. A review of the submitted evidence, however, shows that the Respondent was not operating as a fan club site but rather had created a site at "www.jimihendrix.com" advertising vanity e-mail addresses incorporating the domain name "jimihendrix.com" for sale on the Site. No evidence was presented that at any time had the Complainant ever assigned, granted, licensed, sold, transferred, or in any way authorized the Respondent to register or use the name and mark JIMI HENDRIX in any manner. Accordingly, the Panelist finds that the Respondent, prior to any notice of this dispute, had not used the domain name in connection with any type of bona fide offering of goods or services.

Additionally, no evidence has been presented that the Respondent is commonly known by the domain name or has been making any legitimate noncommercial or fair use of the domain name without the intent for commercial gain to misleadingly divert consumers or to tarnish the mark at issue. Indeed, the Respondent's use of the domain name cannot be characterized as non-commercial or fair use based on: (i) the creation and use of the Site located at "www.jimihendrix.com" for selling vanity e-mail addresses incorporating the "jimihendrix.com" domain name; (ii) the offering for sale of the domain name itself for $1,000,000 on a domain name reseller site; and (iii) a news article identifying Mr. Hammerton as a domain name speculator and quoting him as the owner of the rights to some 2,000 domain names for sale including "jimihendrix.com".

The Respondent also contends that this proceeding is a "violation of human rights", "free speech," and "theft

under the American Constitution." The Panelist finds that these contentions lack foundation and that no evidence has been submitted by the Respondent to support these contentions.

Based upon the above, the Panelist concludes that the Respondent has no rights or legitimate interests in the domain name and that Element (ii) has been satisfied.

Element (iii) – Domain Name Registered and Used in Bad Faith Paragraph 4(b) of the Policy states that evidence of registration and use in bad faith by the holder includes, but is not limited to:

(i) circumstances indicating that the holder has registered or has acquired the domain name primarily for the purpose of selling, renting, or otherwise transferring the domain name registration to the complainant who is the owner of the trademark or service mark or to a competitor of that complainant, for valuable consideration in excess of the holder's documented out-of-pocket costs directly related to the domain name; or

(ii) the holder has registered the domain name in order to prevent the owner of the trademark or service mark from reflecting the mark in a corresponding domain name, provided that the holder has engaged in a pattern of such conduct; or

(iii) the holder has registered the domain name primarily for the purpose of disrupting the business of a competitor; or

(iv) by using the domain name, the holder has intentionally attempted to attract, for commercial gain, Internet users to the holder's Web site or other online location, by creating a likelihood of confusion with the complainant's mark as to the source, sponsorship, affiliation, or endorsement of your Web site or location or of a product or service on the holder's Web site or location.

Based upon the Respondent's contention that he registered the domain name prior to the Complainant's registrations of the above-identified marks, the Panelist finds that the Respondent had actual knowledge at the time he registered the domain name of the use and rights of the Complainant in the name JIMI HENDRIX. Indeed, the record demonstrates that at the time of registering the domain name "jimihendrix.com" the Respondent was well aware of the name JIMI HENDRIX and the Respondent has not submitted evidence or argued to the contrary.

... The Respondent has contended that he never offered the domain name "jimihendrix.com" for sale and has never used the domain name in bad faith. The Complainant did submit copies of Web pages from a domain name reseller site located at "www.domainsmart.com" where the domain name "jimihendrix.com" is being offered for sale for $1,000,000. The Respondent has provided no evidence in rebuttal.

To further support its contention of bad faith by the Respondent, the Complainant submitted evidence of other domain names incorporating the names of well-known celebrities that the Respondent registered and which are being advertised for sale on different domain name reseller sites. Additionally, the Complainant submitted news articles that identified Mr. Hammerton as a domain name speculator who had registered and sold several domain names incorporating names of other celebrities.

Based upon these facts, the Panelist finds that the Respondent registered the domain name "jimihendrix. com" in order to prevent the Complainant from reflecting the name and mark in a corresponding domain name and that the Respondent has engaged in "a pattern of such conduct" of registering and offering for sale domain names incorporating well-known names in which the Respondent has no rights or legitimate interests.

The Panelist therefore concludes that the Respondent has registered and used the domain name "jimihendrix. com" in bad faith and that Element (iii) has been satisfied.

Decision

The Panelist concludes: (i) that the domain name in issue is identical to the Complainant's mark; (ii) that the Respondent has no rights or legitimate interests in the domain name; and (iii) that the Respondent registered and used the domain name in bad faith. Accordingly, the Panelist requires that the registration of the domain name "jimihendrix.com" be transferred to the Complainant. ■

MAP 9-4 Washington and Florida (2000)

CASEPOINT: The WIPO panelist heard considerable evidence about the company Experience Hendrix, LLC, which holds most of the legal rights to the Jimi Hendrix name and likeness and operates several Hendrix Web sites, and Denny Hammerton, a man from Florida who created and registered the domain name "jimihenrix.com." The panelist decided that Mr. Hammerton had registered the domain name merely in order to make a profit, as he had done with several other domain names based on famous persons. The panelist found that Hammerton's domain name would be likely to confuse the public as to the identity of the real Jimi Hendrix Fan Club; that he had no legitimate rights to the name; and since he knew that Experience Hendrix LLC claimed all rights in the name "Jimi Hendrix," his actions were in bad faith. Thus, his domain name—jimihendrix.com—was transferred to the Experience Hendrix LLC.

Refusing Registration

The statutory grounds for refusing a trademark vary from country to country. Nevertheless, most criteria are reasonably similar. For example, a mark or name will be denied in the United States if it

1. does not function as a trademark to identify the goods or services as coming from a particular source (for example, the matter applied for is merely ornamentation);
2. is immoral, deceptive, or scandalous;
3. may disparage or falsely suggest a connection with persons, institutions, beliefs, or national symbols, or bring them into contempt or disrepute;

4. consists of or simulates the flag or coat of arms or other insignia of the United States, or a state or municipality, or any foreign nation;

5. is the name, portrait, or signature of a particular living individual, unless he has given written consent; or is the name, signature, or portrait of a deceased President of the United States during the lifetime of his widow, unless she has given her consent;

6. so resembles a mark already registered in the Patent and Trademark Office as to be likely, when applied to the goods of the applicant, to cause confusion, or to cause mistake, or to deceive;

7. is merely deceptive or deceptively misdescriptive of the goods or services;

8. is primarily geographically descriptive or deceptively misdescriptive of the goods or services of the applicant; or

9. is primarily merely a surname.[74]

Registration Review

Once a Trademark Office official determines that a mark is suitable for registration, the mark will be published in the office's official gazette. Opponents to the registration then have a period of time—typically thirty to ninety days—in which to oppose the registration or to ask for an extension to do so. An *opposition* hearing is then held before a review board of the Trademark Office. If no opposition is filed or if the review board rules in favor of the applicant, a registration will issue.[75]

The Term of Registered Trademarks

The Agreement on Trade-Related Aspects of Intellectual Property Rights (TRIPs) requires WTO member states to protect trademarks for a term of at least seven years. Additionally, it provides that trademarks are to be indefinitely renewable.[76]

Usage Requirements

After a trademark is registered, many countries require the holder to present proof, upon the renewal of registration, that the mark was actually used within the country during the prior term.[77]

A few countries require the trademark owner to present interim proof of use before the term expires. Mexico, for example, requires the holder to present evidence of usage at the end of the third year. The United States requires the same thing at the end of the sixth year.

What constitutes proof varies, of course, and many countries do not specify what may be used. Colombia does, and its listing is representative of actual practice in other countries.

---

[74]U.S. Patent and Trademark Office, *Trademark Manual of Examining Procedure*, chap. 1200 (2002), available at http://www.uspto.gov/web/offices/tac/tmep.

[75]In the United States, the average length of time in which a mark will be registered or an application abandoned is 13 months from the date the application was filed. *Id.*

[76]Agreement on Trade-Related Aspects of Intellectual Property Rights, Article 18 (1994).

[77]The requirement is contained in the Trademark Law Treaty adopted in Geneva in 1994, to which the following states were parties as of June 8, 2007: Australia, Austria, Bahrain, Belarus, Belgium, Bosnia and Herzegovina, Burkina Faso, China, Costa Rica, Côte d'Ivoire, Croatia, Cuba, Cyprus, the Czech Republic, Denmark, the Dominican Republic, Egypt, Estonia, the European Community, Finland, France, Gabon, Germany, Greece, Guinea, Hungary, Indonesia, Ireland, Israel, Italy, Japan, Kazakhstan, Kenya, Kyrgyzstan, Latvia, Liechtenstein, Lithuania, Luxembourg, Malta, Mexico, Moldova, Monaco, Montenegro, Morocco, the Netherlands, Poland, Portugal, the Republic of Korea, Romania, Russia, Senegal, Serbia, Slovakia, Slovenia, South Africa, Spain, Sri Lanka, Swaziland, Sweden, Switzerland, Togo, Trinidad and Tobago, Turkey, Ukraine, the United Kingdom, the United States, Uruguay, and Uzbekistan, See http://www.wipo.int/treaties/ip/tlt. The text of the treaty is posted at http://www.wipo.int/treaties/en/ip/tlt/trtdocs_wo027.html.

The 1977 Bangui Agreement creating the African and Malagasy Intellectual Property Organization contains the same requirement. The Bangui Agreement is the law governing industrial property rights in each of the member states of the African Intellectual Property Organisation (OAPI). Established on November 13,1962, in Libreville, this organization had, on June 8, 2007, sixteen member states: Benin, Burkina Faso, Cameroon, Central Africa, Congo, Côte d'Ivoire, Gabon, Guinea, Guinea Bissau, Equatorial Guinea, Mali, Mauritania, Niger, Senegal, Chad, and Togo, and a population of more than 100 million inhabitants. Its headquarter is in Yaounde, Cameroon The text of the agreement, in French, is posted at http://www.eldis.org/ipr.

Colombia permits the trademark holder to use any of the following to establish usage: newspaper and magazine advertisements, catalogs, samples, sales invoices, sales licenses, import licenses, chamber of commerce certificates, health department registrations, advertising agency billings, depositions, and inspections by the reviewing officer.[78]

In addition to requiring the user to prove use at the time of renewal, many countries allow third parties to bring actions to cancel the trademark if it has not been used for some specified period of time. The TRIPS Agreement now sets this period of time at no less than three years.[79]

It must be pointed out that not all countries have a user requirement[80] and that a few, such as Canada and the United States, make it difficult for challengers to establish nonuse by additionally requiring them to prove that the owner intentionally abandoned the use of a trademark.[81] Also, it must be noted that challenges for nonuse are uncommon. Many trademark owners have a policy of never initiating a nonuse action against others for fear of retaliatory actions against their own unused marks. Similarly, challenges against new registrants attempting to file marks that are similar or identical to marks already in use are equally uncommon. What is more likely, in such a case, is a settlement and the establishment of a coexistence agreement.

KNOW-HOW

Know-how: Practical expertise acquired from study, training, and experience.

Know-how is practical expertise acquired from study, training, and experience. It has been defined as factual knowledge, not capable of separate description but that, when used in an accumulated form, after being acquired as a result of trial and error, gives to the one acquiring it an ability to produce something that he or she otherwise would not have known to produce with the same accuracy or precision found necessary for commercial success.[82]

Unlike other forms of intellectual property, know-how is generally not protected by specific statutory enactments. It is protected, rather, by contract, tort, and other basic legal principles. When specific information or know-how is kept secret, it is often called *trade secrets* and protected in some countries by trade secrecy laws.

The TRIPs Agreement requires WTO member states to protect what the agreement calls "undisclosed information." [83] That is, natural and legal persons must be given the legal means to prevent information from being disclosed to, acquired by, or used by others without their consent in a manner contrary to honest commercial practice. The information, however, must (1) be secret, (2) have commercial value because it is a secret, and (3) have been reasonably protected from disclosure by its owner. [84]

Most commonly, the legal protection given know-how comes about in connection with its use by an assignee, licensee, or employee. That is, the owner of know-how may prevent an assignee, licensee, or employee from disclosing secret know-how to third parties and may require these same people to pay for the training or assistance or use of the know-how they acquire from the owner. Because owners' rights in know-how are determined by the contractual relationship they have with assignees, licensees, and employees, the discussion of these rights is included with the materials on transfer and licensing considered later in this chapter.

---

[78] American Bar Association, Section of Patent, Trademark and Copyright Law, *1987 Committee Reports*, p. 98 (1987).

[79] Agreement on Trade-Related Aspects of Intellectual Property Rights, Article 19 (1994). Prior to the adoption of this agreement, there was an extensive debate over what the proper time period of nonuse should be. See Richard Taylor, "Loss of Trademark Rights through Nonuse: A Comparative Worldwide Analysis," *Trademark Reporter*, vol. 80, p. 207–208 (1990).

[80] E.g., Bolivia, Chile, Costa Rica, Denmark, El Salvador, Norway, and Uruguay.

[81] In the United States, nonuse during the initial two-year period following registration gives rise to a presumption of abandonment, thereby shifting the burden of proof to the trademark owner.

[82] Mycalex Corp. of America v. Pemco Corp., *Federal Supplement*, vol. 64, p. 425 (Dist. Ct. for Maryland, 1946).

[83] Agreement on Trade-Related Aspects of Intellectual Property Rights, Article 39 (1994).

[84] *Id.*, para. 2.

B. INTERNATIONAL INTELLECTUAL PROPERTY ORGANIZATIONS

Two main international organizations take an active role in defining and protecting international intellectual property rights: the World Intellectual Property Organization (WIPO) and the Council for Trade-Related Aspects of Intellectual Property Rights (TRIPs Council) of the World Trade Organization.[85]

WORLD INTELLECTUAL PROPERTY ORGANIZATION

World Intellectual Property Organization (WIPO): Intergovernmental organization responsible for administering the principal international intellectual property conventions.

The **World Intellectual Property Organization (WIPO)** was created in 1967 with the adoption of the Stockholm Convention.[86] WIPO succeeded the International Bureau of Paris and the International Bureau of Berne, which had administered the International Convention for the Protection of Industrial Property (Paris Convention) and the Berne Convention for the Protection of Literary and Artistic Works (Berne Convention). These two bureaus had been supervised by the Swiss Federal Council and, functionally, were joined together as the United International Bureaus for the Protection of Intellectual Property (*Bureaux Internationaux Réunis pour la Protection de la Propriéte Intellectuelle*—BIRPI).

In contrast to its predecessors, WIPO has much broader authority. It is responsible for administering the Paris and Berne Conventions (as well as several new conventions established since its creation) and, generally, promoting intellectual property rights. WIPO's governing body, the General Assembly, is made up of representatives of states parties to the Stockholm Convention that are also parties to either the Paris or Berne Convention. WIPO is also a specialized agency of the United Nations.[87] There are now 184 states that are parties to the Stockholm Convention.[88]

> WIPO's Web site is
>
> http://www.wipo.int/portal/index.html.en.

---

[85] With the advent of the WTO and the WTO's TRIPs Council, the international influence of other organizations has diminished. The Intergovernmental Copyright Committee of the United Nations Educational, Scientific and Cultural Organization (UNESCO) no longer plays much of a role in this area following the decision by the United States and several other states to become parties to the Berne Convention and to, in effect, abandon their commitments under the Universal Copyright Convention that UNESCO had sponsored and overseen. The United Nations Conference on Trade and Development (UNCTAD), which was primarily interested in devising a Code of Conduct on Technology Transfer, has seen many of its proposals incorporated into the Agreement Establishing the World Trade Organization and that agreement's annexes. Moreover, the institutional role that UNESCO had played has now been taken over by the WTO.

[86] The convention is formally known as the Convention Establishing the World Intellectual Property Organization. It is posted on the Internet at http://www.wipo.int/treaties/convention/index.html.

[87] For more information about the history and operation of WIPO, see its home page on the Internet at http://www.wipo.int.

[88] The states parties as of June 2007 were Afghanistan, Albania, Algeria, Andorra, Angola, Antigua and Barbuda, Argentina, Armenia, Australia, Austria, Azerbaijan, Bahamas, Bahrain, Bangladesh, Barbados, Belarus, Belgium, Belize, Benin, Bhutan, Bolivia, Bosnia and Herzegovina, Botswana, Brazil, Brunei Darussalam, Bulgaria, Burkina Faso, Burundi, Cambodia, Cameroon, Canada, Cape Verde, the Central African Republic, Chad, Chile, China, Colombia, Comoros, Congo, Costa Rica, Côte d'Ivoire, Croatia, Cuba, Cyprus, the Czech Republic, Democratic Republic of the Congo, Denmark, Djibouti, Dominica, the Dominican Republic, Ecuador, Egypt, El Salvador, Equatorial Guinea, Eritrea, Estonia, Ethiopia, Fiji, Finland, France, Gabon, Gambia, Georgia, Germany, Ghana, Greece, Grenada, Guatemala, Guinea, Guinea-Bissau, Guyana, Haiti, Holy See, Honduras, Hungary, Iceland, India, Indonesia, Iran, Iraq, Ireland, Israel, Italy, Jamaica, Japan, Jordan, Kazakhstan, Kenya, Kuwait, Kyrgyzstan, Laos, Latvia, Lebanon, Lesotho, Liberia, Libya, Liechtenstein, Lithuania, Luxembourg, Macedonia, Madagascar, Malawi, Malaysia, Maldives, Mali, Malta, Mauritania, Mauritius, Mexico, Moldova, Monaco, Mongolia, Montenegro, Morocco, Mozambique, Myanmar, Namibia, Nepal, the Netherlands, New Zealand, Nicaragua, Niger, Nigeria, North Korea, Norway, Oman, Pakistan, Panama, Papua New Guinea, Paraguay, Peru, the Philippines, Poland, Portugal, Qatar, Romania, Russia, Rwanda, Saint Kitts and Nevis, Saint Lucia, Saint Vincent and the Grenadines, Samoa, San Marino, Sao Tome and Principe, Saudi Arabia, Senegal, Seychelles, Sierra Leone, Singapore, Slovakia, Slovenia, Somalia, South Africa, South Korea, Spain, Sri Lanka, Sudan, Suriname, Swaziland, Sweden, Switzerland, Syria, Tajikistan, Thailand, Togo, Tonga, Trinidad and Tobago, Tunisia, Turkey, Turkmenistan, Uganda, Ukraine, the United Arab Emirates, the United Kingdom, the United Republic of Tanzania, the United States, Uruguay, Uzbekistan, Venezuela, Vietnam, Yemen, Yugoslavia, Zambia, and Zimbabwe. See WIPO, "Member States" at http://www.wipo.int/treaties/en.

WIPO's promotional activities include the sponsoring and hosting of conferences for the development of new intellectual property rights agreements. The Patent Cooperation Treaty, for example, was the result of a WIPO initiative. WIPO also studies, through the appointment of expert committees, new legal and technological developments, and it regularly reports the results through both monthly journals and occasional reports.[89]

One of WIPO's more important tasks is to facilitate the transfer of technology, especially to and among developing countries. Two permanent committees—one for Development Cooperation Related to Industrial Property and one for Development Cooperation Related to Copyrights and Neighboring Rights—are responsible for helping countries modernize their national intellectual property laws, for helping them develop administrative agencies for supervising those laws, and for helping them increase, both in quantity and quality, the creation of new intellectual property by their own nationals.

Since 1994, the WIPO Arbitration and Mediation Center based in Geneva, Switzerland, has offered Alternative Dispute Resolution (ADR) options, in particular arbitration and mediation, for the resolution of international commercial disputes between private parties. Developed by leading experts in cross-border dispute settlement, the procedures offered by the center are widely used to resolve disputes involving technology, entertainment, and other intellectual property issues. An increasing number of cases are being filed with the center under the WIPO Arbitration, Expedited Arbitration, Mediation and Expert Determination Rules. The subject matter of these proceedings includes both contractual disputes (e.g., patent and software licenses, trademark coexistence agreements, distribution agreements for pharmaceutical products, and research and development agreements) and non-contractual disputes (e.g., patent infringement).[90]

The WIPO Arbitration and Mediation Center has proved to be an effective way for parties to solve complex international patent, copyright, and trademark issues. Several examples are given on the WIPO Web site, including the following dispute:

WIPO Arbitration of a Biotech/Pharma Dispute
A French biotech company, holder of several process patents for the extraction and purification of a compound with medical uses, entered into a license and development agreement with a large pharmaceutical company. The pharmaceutical company had considerable expertise in the medical application of the substance related to the patents held by the biotech company. The parties included in their contract a clause stating that all disputes arising out of their agreement would be resolved by a sole arbitrator under the WIPO Arbitration Rules.

Several years after the signing of the agreement, the biotech company filed a request for arbitration with the Center alleging that the pharmaceutical company had deliberately delayed the development of the biotech compound and claiming substantial damages.

The Center proposed a number of candidates with considerable expertise of biotech/pharma disputes, one of whom was chosen by the parties. Following the parties' written submissions, the arbitrator held a three-day hearing in Geneva, Switzerland for the examination of witnesses. This not only served for the presentation of evidence but also allowed the parties to re-establish a dialogue. On the last day of the hearing, the disputants accepted the arbitrator's suggestion that they should hold a private meeting. As a result of that meeting, the parties agreed to settle their dispute and continued to cooperate towards the development and commercialization of the biotech compound.[91]

A new responsibility taken on by WIPO is that of resolving Internet domain disputes. In 1999, WIPO's Arbitration and Mediation Center was selected by the Internet Corporation for Assigned Names and Numbers (ICANN), which oversees the Internet, and was given responsibility for implementing ICANN's Uniform Domain Name Dispute Resolution Policy. The policy gives holders of trademarks a procedure for efficiently resolving disputes involving

[89]The *WIPO Magazine* and other WIPO publications are posted on the Internet at http://www.wipo.int/freepublications/en.
[90]See the WIPO Arbitration and Mediation Center Web site: http://www.wipo.int/amc/en.
[91]http://www.wipo.int/amc/en/arbitration/case-example.html, accessed June 3, 2007.

bad-faith cybersquatting of trademarks. The center is authorized to resolve disputes if (1) the domain name registered by the domain name registrant is identical or confusingly similar to the complainant's trademark or service mark; and (2) the domain name registrant has no rights or legitimate interests in the disputed domain name; and (3) the domain name was registered and is being used in bad faith.[92] Earlier in this chapter, Case 9-4 (the Jimi Hendrix Web site case) was an example of a trade name dispute decided by WIPO.

COUNCIL FOR TRADE-RELATED ASPECTS OF INTELLECTUAL PROPERTY RIGHTS

Council for Trade-Related Aspects of Intellectual Property Rights (Council for TRIPs): Organ of the World Trade Organization responsible for administering the Agreement on Trade-Related Aspects of Intellectual Property Rights.

The **Council for Trade-Related Aspects of Intellectual Property Rights (Council for TRIPs)** was created in 1995 with the adoption of the Agreement Establishing the World Trade Organization (WTO Agreement). The council is charged with overseeing the operation of the Agreement on Trade-Related Aspects of Intellectual Property Rights, which is an annex to the WTO Agreement. In particular, the council is responsible for monitoring WTO member state compliance with the Agreement on TRIPS, for helping members consult with each other on trade-related aspects of intellectual property rights, and for assisting members in settling disputes. The council consults with WIPO and cooperates with WIPO's constituent bodies.[93]

The Web side for the TRIP Council is

http://www.wto.org/english/tratop_e/trips_e.htm.

C. INTELLECTUAL PROPERTY TREATIES

Intellectual property rights are protected and regulated internationally by both bilateral treaties and multilateral conventions. Bilateral treaties were the original means of preventing illegal copying, and they were once quite commonplace. With the growing popularity of multilateral conventions in the mid-nineteenth century, their use has diminished. Today, most bilateral intellectual property treaties are used by states that are not parties to the multilateral conventions. This does not mean that parties to multilateral agreements are prevented from entering into bilateral arrangements. For example, the Berne Convention for the Protection of Literary and Artistic Works specifically provides:

> The governments of the countries of the Union reserve their rights to enter into special agreements among themselves, in so far as such agreements grant to authors more extensive rights than those granted by the Convention, or contain other provisions not contrary to the Convention.[94]

Similar provisions can be found in the International Convention for the Protection of Industrial Property.[95]

Nevertheless, multilateral treaties nowadays regulate most matters relating to intellectual property rights. These treaties generally cover industrial property or artistic property, but not both together. Moreover, patents, petty patents, and trademarks are commonly dealt with in a single treaty, while copyrights are dealt with separately. As already mentioned, most of these conventions are administered by WIPO and the TRIPs Council.

---

[92]See WIPO's Domain Name Dispute Resolution Service at http://www.wipo.int/amc/en/domains.
[93]Agreement on Trade-Related Aspects of Intellectual Property Rights, Article 68 (1994).
[94]Berne Convention for the Protection of Literary and Artistic Works, Article 20(1) (1886, as revised in 1971).
[95]International Convention for the Protection of Industrial Property, Article 19 (1883 as revised in 1967).

COMPREHENSIVE AGREEMENTS

The principal comprehensive agreement establishing general intellectual property obligations for most of the world's states is the Agreement on Trade-Related Aspects of Intellectual Property Rights.

Agreement on Trade-Related Aspects of Intellectual Property Rights

Agreement on Trade-Related Aspects of Intellectual Property Rights (TRIPs Agreement): Annex to the Agreement Establishing the World Trade Organization; it creates a multilateral and comprehensive set of rights and obligations governing the international trade in intellectual property.

The **Agreement on Trade-Related Aspects of Intellectual Property Rights (TRIPs Agreement)**, which is an annex to the Agreement Establishing the World Trade Organization, came into effect with the WTO in 1995.[96] As is the case for the WTO Agreement's other multilateral annexes, all of the WTO member states are automatically members of the TRIPs Agreement.

The purpose of the TRIPs Agreement is to create a multilateral and comprehensive set of rights and obligations governing the international trade in intellectual property. As a consequence, the agreement establishes a common minimum of protection for intellectual property rights applicable within all the WTO member states. It does this in five ways. [97] First, it requires WTO members to observe the substantive provisions of the most important existing multilateral intellectual property treaties: the 1883 International Convention for the Protection of Industrial Property (Paris Convention) as revised in 1967; the 1886 Berne Convention for the Protection of Literary and Artistic Works (Berne Convention) as revised in 1971; the 1961 International Convention for the Protection of Performers, Producers of Phonograms, and Broadcasting Organizations (Rome Convention); and the 1989 Treaty on Intellectual Property in Respect of Integrated Circuits (IPIC Treaty). Moreover, the TRIPS Agreement provides that its substantive provisions do not in any way reduce the obligations of WTO member states under the Paris, Berne, and Rome Conventions or the IPIC Treaty.[98]

Second, the substantive provisions of the TRIPs Agreement create obligations that are meant to "fill in the gaps" in the other international intellectual property conventions. Some important provisions are otherwise missing, such as the length of life for a patent.[99]

Third, the TRIPs Agreement establishes criteria for the effective and appropriate enforcement of intellectual property rights[100] and for the prevention and settlement of disputes between the governments of the WTO member states.[101]

Fourth, to encourage the widest possible adoption and application of the common rules and obligations set out in the TRIPs Agreement, the agreement establishes transitional arrangements that give more time to developing member states and to member states in transition from a centrally planned economy to a free market economy to comply, and even more time to those that are the least developed. Developed member states were required to be in full compliance by January 1, 1996; developing member states and states transitioning to a market economy were required to comply by January 1, 2000; and the least developed states have until January 1, 2016.[102]

Finally, and most importantly, the TRIPs Agreement extends the basic principles of the General Agreement on Tariffs and Trade (GATT) to the field of international intellectual property rights. The national treatment principle requires each member state to extend to nationals of other members treatment no less favorable than that which it gives its own nationals regarding protection of intellectual property. [103] The transparency principle requires

---

[96] The TRIPs Agreement is posted on the Internet at http://www.wto.org/english/docs_e/legal_e/27-trips.doc.
[97] Agreement on Trade-Related Aspects of Intellectual Property Rights, Preamble (1994).
[98] *Id.*, Articles 1–2.
[99] *Id.*, Articles 9–40.
[100] *Id.*, Articles 41–62.
[101] *Id.*, Articles 63–64.
[102] *Id.*, Articles 65–66. The date for compliance for least developed states was extended to 2016 at the WTO Doha Ministerial Conference. WTO, See, "Least-Developed Country Members—Obligations Under Article 70.9 of the TRIPS Agreement with Respect to Pharmaceutical Products" at http://www.wto.org/english/tratop_e/trips_e/art70_9_e.htm.
[103] Agreement on Trade-Related Aspects of Intellectual Property Rights, Article 3 (1994).

member states to publish and notify the Council for TRIPs of all relevant laws, regulations, and the like and to respond to requests from other members for information.[104]

National treatment and transparency provisions are found, of course, in other intellectual property agreements. The TRIPs Agreement is unique, however, in including a provision requiring most-favored-nation treatment for such property. Under this provision, "any advantage, favor, privilege, or immunity granted by a member to the nationals of any other country [whether or not it is a WTO member] shall be accorded immediately and unconditionally to the nationals of all other members."[105] Read together with the national treatment provision and the transparency provision, this requires each member state to treat the nationals of other member states as least as well as (and possibly better than) it treats its own nationals.[106]

ARTISTIC PROPERTY AGREEMENTS

The main international agreements dealing with artistic property are the Berne Convention for the Protection of Literary and Artistic Works; the International Convention for the Protection of Performers, Producers of Phonograms, and Broadcasting Organizations; the Patent Cooperation Treaty; the Satellite Transmission Convention; and the WIPO Copyright Treaty.

Berne Convention

Berne Convention for the Protection of Literary and Artistic Works: Requires member states to establish common minimum rules to protect the pecuniary and moral rights of authors without requiring them to comply with particular formalities.

Adopted in Paris in 1886, the **Berne Convention for the Protection of Literary and Artistic Works (Berne Convention)** came into force in 1887.[107] Its nine original member countries[108] have now grown to 163.[109]

The original text of the convention established procedures for its revision, and revisions have been regularly made: in Paris in 1896, Berlin in 1908, Berne in 1914, Rome in 1928, Brussels in 1948, Stockholm in 1967, and Paris in 1971.

nonconditional protection principle: Protection is not to be conditioned on the use of formalities.

The Berne Convention establishes a "union" of states that is responsible for protecting artistic rights. Four basic principles underlie the members' obligations: (1) The principle of *national treatment* requires each member state to extend to nationals of other member states treatment no less favorable than that which it gives its own nationals. (2) **Nonconditional protection** is the requirement that member states must provide protection without any formalities. A country of origin may, however, condition protection on the author's first making an application for registration, or registering the work, or reserving rights in a contract of sale, or a similar condition. (3) The principle of **protection independent of protection in the country of origin** allows authors who are nationals of nonmember states to obtain protection within the Berne Union by publishing their works in a member state. (4) The principle of common rules establishes minimum standards for granting copyrights common to all

protection independent of protection in the country of origin principle: Protection is granted to any person publishing a work in a member state, even if he or she is not a national of a member state.

common rules principle: Common minimum standards for granting copyrights must be observed by all member states.

[104]*Id.*, Article 63.

[105]*Id.*, Article 4.

[106]John Kraus, *The GATT Negotiations: A Business Guide to the Results of the Uruguay Round*, p. 52 (1994).

[107]The text of the convention is posted on the Internet at http://www.wipo.int/treaties/ip.

[108]Belgium, Britain, France, Germany, Haiti, Italy, Spain, Switzerland, and Tunisia. Haiti, however, withdrew in 1941, and it did not rejoin until 1996.

[109]As of June 8, 2007, the member states of the Berne Convention were Albania, Algeria, Andorra, Antigua and Barbuda, Argentina, Armenia, Australia, Austria, Azerbaijan, Bahamas, Bahrain, Bangladesh, Barbados, Belarus, Belgium, Belize, Benin, Bhutan, Bolivia, Bosnia and Herzegovina, Botswana, Brazil, Brunei, Bulgaria, Burkina Faso, Cameroon, Canada, Cape Verde, the Central African Republic, Chad, Chile, China, Colombia, Comoros, Congo, Costa Rica, Côte d'Ivoire, Croatia, Cuba, Cyprus, the Czech Republic, Democratic Republic of the Congo, Denmark, Djibouti, Dominica, the Dominican Republic, Ecuador, Egypt, El Salvador, Equatorial Guinea, Estonia, Fiji, Finland, France, Gabon, Gambia, Georgia, Germany, Ghana, Greece, Grenada, Guatemala, Guinea, Guinea-Bissau, Guyana, Haiti, Holy See, Honduras, Hungary, Iceland, India, Indonesia, Ireland, Israel, Italy, Jamaica, Japan, Jordan, Kazakhstan, Kenya, Kyrgyzstan, Latvia, Lebanon, Lesotho, Liberia, Libya, Liechtenstein, Lithuania, Luxembourg, Macedonia, Madagascar, Malawi, Malaysia, Mali, Malta, Mauritania, Mauritius, Mexico, Micronesia, Moldova, Monaco, Mongolia, Montenegro, Morocco, Namibia, Nepal, the Netherlands, New Zealand, Nicaragua, Niger, Nigeria, North Korea, Norway, Oman, Pakistan, Panama, Paraguay, Peru, the Philippines, Poland, Portugal, Qatar, Romania, Russia, Rwanda, Saint Kitts and Nevis, Saint Lucia, Saint Vincent and the Grenadines, Samoa, Saudi Arabia, Senegal, Serbia, Singapore, Slovakia, Slovenia, South Africa, Spain, Sri Lanka, Sudan, Suriname, Swaziland, Sweden, Switzerland, Syria, Tajikistan, Tanzania, Thailand, Togo, Tonga, Trinidad and Tobago, Tunisia, Turkey, Ukraine, the United Arab Emirates, the United Kingdom, the United States, Uruguay, Uzbekistan, Venezuela, Vietnam, Venezuela, Zambia, and Zimbabwe. *See* http://www.wipo.int/treaties/en/ip/berne.

EXHIBIT 9-2   Principal Provisions of the Berne Convention

Provision	Description
Persons entitled to protection	Nationals and habitual residents of any member state and persons of any state who publish first or simultaneously in a member state
Definition of "publication"	Manifestation in a tangible form (may not include intangible reproduction by performance or telecommunication)
Definition of "simultaneous publication"	Publication within a 30-day period
Protected works	Literary, artistic, scientific, and architectural
Author's rights	Pecuniary and moral rights
Formalities	Member states may not require formalities (except that protection in the country of origin may be conditioned on application, registration, reservation of rights, etc.)
Translations	Author loses right to make a translation if it is not published within 10 years of original publication
Exemptions for developing countries	Developing country may grant a nonexclusive nonassignable compulsory license to make copies for use in teaching, scholarship, and research if the author fails to grant such a license
Term	Author's life plus 50 years

member states. These and the other requirements of the Berne Convention are summarized in Exhibit 9-2.

Rome Convention

The **International Convention for the Protection of Performers, Producers of Phonograms, and Broadcasting Organizations (Rome Convention)** was agreed to in 1961.[110] The draft for the convention was prepared by a joint committee of experts appointed by the Berne Union, UNESCO, and the International Labor Organization. The convention, accordingly, attempts to balance the interests of performers, producers of phonograms, and broadcasting organizations. Currently, there are 86 states parties.[111]

The Rome Convention protects artists from the unauthorized recording of their original performances and from the use of authorized recordings for a purpose other than that to which the artist consented. Producers of phonograms are protected from the direct or indirect reproduction of their works. Broadcasters are protected from the unauthorized recording, rebroadcasting, and use of their broadcasts.

In addition to these rights, the Rome Convention provides that a broadcaster making a public communication or broadcast of an authorized phonogram is required to pay the producer or the artist, or both, a single equitable payment. This caused some consternation

International Convention for the Protection of Performers, Producers of Phonograms, and Broadcasting Organizations (Rome Convention): Prohibits the unauthorized recording of live performances, the unauthorized reproduction of recordings, and the unauthorized recording or rebroadcasting of broadcasts.

[110]The text of the convention is posted on the Internet at http://www.wipo.int/treaties/en/ip/rome.
[111]The states parties as of June 8, 2007, were Albania, Algeria, Andorra, Argentina, Armenia, Australia, Austria, Azerbaijan, Bahrain, Barbados, Belarus, Belgium, Bolivia, Brazil, Bulgaria, Burkina Faso, Cambodia, Canada, Cape Verde, Chile, Colombia, Congo, Costa Rica, Croatia, the Czech Republic, Denmark, Dominica, the Dominican Republic, Ecuador, El Salvador, Estonia, Fiji, Finland, France, Georgia, Germany, Greece, Guatemala, the Holy See, Honduras, Hungary, Iceland, India, Ireland, Israel, Italy, Jamaica, Japan, Kyrgyzstan, Latvia, Lebanon, Lesotho, Liechtenstein, Lithuania, Luxembourg, Macedonia, Mexico, Moldova, Monaco, Montenegro, the Netherlands, Nicaragua, Niger, Nigeria, Norway, Panama, Paraguay, Peru, the Philippines, Poland, Portugal, Romania, Russia, Saint Lucia, Serbia, Slovakia, Slovenia, Spain, Sweden, Switzerland, Syria, Togo, Turkey, Ukraine, the United Arab Emirates, the United Kingdom, Uruguay, Venezuela, and Vietnam. See http://www.wipo.int/treaties/en/ip/rome.

among several countries, which feared that such a system of compensation would diminish the proceeds that their artists were entitled to under their own laws. As a consequence, the convention allows member states to make reservations to this provision.

Phonogram Piracy Convention

Convention for the Protection of Producers of Phonograms Against Unauthorized Duplication of Their Phonograms: Requires member states to protect producers of phonograms from the unauthorized reproduction of their works.

The **Convention for the Protection of Producers of Phonograms Against Unauthorized Duplication of Their Phonograms** was signed in 1971 at Geneva.[112] It provides that member states must protect producers of phonograms from the unauthorized reproduction and importation of their works for a period of not less than 20 years. The means for doing this, however, is left to each individual state. In the common law countries, including the United Kingdom and the United States, protection is provided through copyright legislation. Most of the countries of continental Europe use neighboring rights laws. Japan provides protection with penal sanctions. At present, there are 76 states parties to the Phonogram Piracy Convention.[113]

Satellite Transmission Convention

Convention Relating to the Distribution of Program-Carrying Signals by Satellite: Requires member states to prevent the unauthorized transmission of electronic communications by satellite from their territory.

The **Convention Relating to the Distribution of Program-Carrying Signals Transmitted by Satellite**, sponsored jointly by WIPO and UNESCO, was concluded in Brussels in 1974.[114] It requires member states to take "adequate measures" to prevent the unauthorized distribution in or from their territory of any program-carrying signal transmitted by satellite. As with the Agreement on Phonogram Piracy, the means of implementing this convention is left up to each member state. The number of states parties at present is 30.[115]

WIPO Copyright Treaty

World Intellectual Property Organization Copyright Treaty: Requires member states to extend the provisions of the Berne Convention to computer programs and databases.

The **World Intellectual Property Organization Copyright Treaty** was adopted in 1996 by a conference of member states of the Berne Union for the purpose of extending the provisions of the Berne Convention to computer programs and databases and protecting copyright ownership information embedded in programs and databases.[116] There are currently 64 states parties.[117]

---

[112] The text of the convention is posted on the Internet at http://www.wipo.int/treaties/en/ip/phonograms.

[113] The member-states parties as of May 21, 2007, were Albania, Argentina, Armenia, Australia, Austria, Azerbaijan, Barbados, Belarus, Brazil, Bulgaria, Burkina Faso, Canada, Chile, China, Colombia, Costa Rica, Croatia, Cyprus, the Czech Republic, Democratic Republic of the Congo, Denmark, Ecuador, Egypt, El Salvador, Estonia, Fiji, Finland, France, Germany, Greece, Guatemala, the Holy See, Honduras, Hungary, India, Iran, Israel, Italy, Jamaica, Japan, Kazakhstan, Kenya, Latvia, Liberia, Liechtenstein, Lithuania, Luxembourg, Mexico, Moldova, Monaco, Montenegro, the Netherlands, New Zealand, Nicaragua, Norway, Panama, Paraguay, Peru, the Philippines, South Korea, Romania, Russia, Saint Lucia, Serbia, Slovakia, Slovenia, Spain, Sweden, Switzerland, Macedonia, Togo, Trinidad and Tobago, Ukraine, the United Kingdom, the United States, Uruguay, Venezuela and Vietnam. See http://www.wipo.int/treaties/en/ip/phonograms.

A related convention is the 1996 WIPO Performances and Phonograms Treaty, which establishes both moral and pecuniary rights for performers and creators of phonograms. The text of that treaty is posted on the Internet at http://www.wipo.int/treaties/en.

[114] The text of the convention is posted on the Internet at http://www.wipo.int/treaties/en.

[115] The states parties to the Satellite Transmission (Brussels) Convention as of June 8, 2007, were Argentina, Armenia, Australia, Austria, Bahrain, Belgium, Bosnia and Herzegovina, Brazil, Costa Rica, Côte d'Ivoire, Croatia, Cyprus, France, Germany, Greece, Israel, Italy, Jamaica, Kenya, Lebanon, Mexico, Montenegro, Morocco, Nicaragua, Panama, Peru, Portugal, Russia, Rwanda, Senegal, Serbia, Singapore, Slovenia, Spain, Switzerland, Macedonia, Togo, Trinidad and Tobago, the United States, and Vietnam. See http://www.wipo.int/treaties/ip/brussels.

[116] The text of the convention is posted on the Internet at http://www.wipo.int/treaties/ip.

[117] As of June 2007, the states party to the World Intellectual Property Organization Copyright Treaty included Albania, Argentina, Armenia, Australia, Austria, Azerbaijan, Bahrain, Belarus, Belgium, Benin, Bolivia, Botswana, Bulgaria, Burkina Faso, Canada, Chile, China, Colombia, Costa Rica, Croatia, Cyprus, the Czech Republic, Denmark, the Dominican Republic, Ecuador, El Salvador, Estonia, the European Community, Finland, France, Gabon, Georgia, Germany, Ghana, Greece, Guatemala, Guinea, Honduras, Hungary, Indonesia, Ireland, Israel, Italy, Jamaica, Japan, Jordan, Kazakhstan, Kenya, Kyrgyzstan, Latvia, Liechtenstein, Lithuania, Luxembourg, Mali, Mexico, Moldova, Monaco, Mongolia, Montenegro, Namibia, the Netherlands, Nicaragua, Nigeria, Oman, Panama, Paraguay, Peru, the Philippines, Poland, Portugal, Qatar, the Republic of Korea, Romania, Saint Lucia, Senegal, Serbia, Singapore, Slovakia, Slovenia, South Africa, Spain, Sweden, Switzerland, the former Yugoslav Republic of Macedonia, Togo, Ukraine, the United Arab Emirates, the United Kingdom, the United States, Uruguay, and Venezuela. See http://www.wipo.int/treaties/en/ShowResults.jsp?lang=en&treaty_id=16.

INDUSTRIAL PROPERTY AGREEMENTS

The principal international conventions concerned with industrial property are the International Convention for the Protection of Industrial Property, the Treaty on Intellectual Property in Respect of Integrated Circuits, the Madrid Agreement for the Repression of False or Deceptive Indications of Sources of Goods, the Patent Cooperation Treaty, and the Trademark Law Treaty.

Paris Convention

Drafted in 1880, the **International Convention for the Protection of Industrial Property (Paris Convention)** was ratified by 11 states in 1883 and came into effect in 1884. As of June 2007, the number of participants has grown to 171.[118]

The convention establishes a "union" of states responsible for protecting industrial property rights. Among the members' duties is the obligation to participate in regular revisions. Revision conferences to expand the coverage of the convention have been held regularly: in Rome in 1886, Madrid in 1890 and 1891, Brussels in 1897 and 1900, Washington in 1911, The Hague in 1925, London in 1934, Lisbon 1958, and Stockholm in 1967.

Three basic principles are incorporated in the Paris Convention: (1) national treatment, (2) right of priority, and (3) common rules. National treatment is the requirement that each member state must grant the same protection to the nationals of other states that it grants to its own nationals. The **right of priority** gives an applicant who has filed for protection in one member country a grace period of 12 months in which to file in another member state, which then must treat the application as if it were filed on the same day as the original application. The principle of common rules sets minimum standards for the creation of intellectual property rights. These are as follows: (1) a member state may not deny protection to industrial property because the work incorporating an invention was not manufactured in that state; (2) member states must protect trade names without requiring registration; (3) member states must outlaw false labeling (i.e., any indication that falsely identifies the source of goods, or the trader or manufacturer); and (4) each member state is required to take "effective" measures to prevent unfair competition. Beyond these common rules, the convention leaves to each member the right to make rules governing the application, registration, scope, and duration of patents, trademarks, and other forms of industrial property.

Treaty on Intellectual Property in Respect of Integrated Circuits

The **Treaty on Intellectual Property in Respect of Integrated Circuits (Washington Treaty)**, adopted in 1989, obligates member states to protect the designs used in integrated circuits (such as the designs of computer memory chips).[119] Like the Berne Convention, this treaty

International Convention for the Protection of Industrial Property (Paris Convention): Requires member states to provide national treatment, right of priority, and common minimum rules to protect owners of industrial property rights.

right of priority: For a period of one year, an application for a patent in a second member country will be treated as though it had been filed on the same date as the application made in the first member country.

Treaty on Intellectual Property in Respect of Integrated Circuits (Washington Treaty): Requires member states to provide national treatment and common minimum rules to protect owners of integrated circuits.

[118]As of June 2007, the states party to the International Convention for the Protection of Industrial Property were Albania, Algeria, Andorra, Antigua and Barbuda, Argentina, Armenia, Australia, Austria, Azerbaijan, Bahamas, Bahrain, Bangladesh, Barbados, Belarus, Belgium, Belize, Benin, Bhutan, Bolivia, Bosnia and Herzegovina, Botswana, Brazil, Bulgaria, Burkina Faso, Burundi, Cambodia, Cameroon, Canada, the Central African Republic, Chad, Chile, China, Colombia, Comoros, Congo, Costa Rica, Côte d'Ivoire, Croatia, Cuba, Cyprus, the Czech Republic, Democratic People's Republic of Korea, Democratic Republic of the Congo, Denmark, Djibouti, Dominica, the Dominican Republic, Ecuador, Egypt, El Salvador, Equatorial Guinea, Estonia, Finland, France, Gabon, Gambia, Georgia, Germany, Ghana, Greece, Grenada, Guatemala, Guinea, Guinea-Bissau, Guyana, Haiti, the Holy See, Honduras, Hungary, Iceland, India, Indonesia, Iran (Islamic Republic of), Iraq, Ireland, Israel, Italy, Jamaica, Japan, Jordan, Kazakhstan, Kenya, Kyrgyzstan, Lao People's Democratic Republic, Latvia, Lebanon, Lesotho, Liberia, Libyan Arab Jamahiriya, Liechtenstein, Lithuania, Luxembourg, Madagascar, Malawi, Malaysia, Mali, Malta, Mauritania, Mauritius, Mexico, Moldova, Monaco, Mongolia, Montenegro, Morocco, Mozambique, Namibia, Nepal, the Netherlands, New Zealand, Nicaragua, Niger, Nigeria, Norway, Oman, Pakistan, Panama, Papua New Guinea, Paraguay, Peru, the Philippines, Poland, Portugal, Qatar, the Republic of Korea, Romania, the Russian Federation, Rwanda, Saint Kitts and Nevis, Saint Lucia, Saint Vincent and the Grenadines, San Marino, Sao Tome and Principe, Saudi Arabia, Senegal, Serbia, Seychelles, Sierra Leone, Singapore, Slovakia, Slovenia, South Africa, Spain, Sri Lanka, Sudan, Suriname, Swaziland, Sweden, Switzerland, the Syrian Arab Republic, Tajikistan, the former Yugoslav Republic of Macedonia, Togo, Tonga, Trinidad and Tobago, Tunisia, Turkey, Turkmenistan, Uganda, Ukraine, the United Arab Emirates, the United Kingdom, the United Republic of Tanzania, the United States, Uruguay, Uzbekistan, Venezuela, Vietnam, Yemen, Zambia, and Zimbabwe. See http://www.wipo.int/treaties/en/ShowResults.jsp?lang=en&treaty_id=2.

[119]The text of the Washington Treaty is posted on the Internet at http://www.wipo.int/treaties/en/ip/washington.

incorporates the principles of national treatment and common rules. The common rules include the obligation of member states to protect against the making of unauthorized copies and the importing of contraband copies.[120]

Although the member states of the WTO are obliged to comply with the provisions of the Washington Treaty,[121] the treaty itself is not currently in force.[122]

Patent Cooperation Treaty

Patent Cooperation Treaty: Establishes an international mechanism that allows inventors to make a single application for patent protection that is equivalent to making a filing in all member states.

The **Patent Cooperation Treaty**, agreed to in 1970, establishes a mechanism for making an international application whose effect in each member state is the same as the filing for a national patent.[123] Applications are submitted to a member state's patent office, which forwards them to one of several international searching authorities, where an international search is made to determine novelty. The goal of the treaty is the elimination of unnecessary repetition by both patent offices and applicants. Eventually, the member states plan to establish a single international search authority. As of June 10, 2007, there were 137 states parties to the Patent Cooperation Treaty.[124]

Agreement on Sources of Goods

Madrid Agreement for the Repression of False or Deceptive Indications of Sources of Goods: Requires member states to deny importation to goods bearing false or misleading indications as to their source.

The **Madrid Agreement for the Repression of False or Deceptive Indications of Sources of Goods**, drafted in 1891, requires its members to either deny importation to or confiscate at the time of importation any goods bearing false or deceptive indications about their source.[125] There are 35 states parties to the agreement at present.[126]

---

[120] Article 6.

[121] Agreement on Trade-Related Aspects of Intellectual Property Rights, Articles 1 and 2 (1994).

[122] See World Trade Organization, "Intellectual Property: Protection and Enforcement," posted at http://www.wto.org/english and http://www.wipo.int/treaties/en/ip/washington.

[123] The text of the Patent Cooperation Treaty is posted at http://www.wipo.int/treaties/en.

[124] The 137 members in June 2007 were Albania, Algeria, Antigua and Barbuda, Argentina, Armenia, Australia, Austria, Azerbaijan, Bahrain, Barbados, Belarus, Belgium, Belize, Benin, Bosnia and Herzegovina, Botswana, Brazil, Bulgaria, Burkina Faso, Cameroon, Canada, the Central African Republic, Chad, China, Colombia, Comoros, Congo, Costa Rica, Côte d'Ivoire, Croatia, Cuba, Cyprus, the Czech Republic, Democratic People's Republic of Korea, Denmark, Dominica, the Dominican Republic, Ecuador, Egypt, El Salvador, Equatorial Guinea, Estonia, Finland, France, Gabon, Gambia, Georgia, Germany, Ghana, Greece, Grenada, Guatemala, Guinea, Guinea-Bissau, the Holy See, Honduras, Hungary, Iceland, India, Indonesia, Iran (Islamic Republic of), Ireland, Israel, Italy, Japan, Kazakhstan, Kenya, Kyrgyzstan, the Lao People's Democratic Republic, Latvia, Lesotho, Liberia, Libyan Arab Jamahiriya, Liechtenstein, Lithuania, Luxembourg, Madagascar, Malawi, Malaysia, Mali, Malta, Mauritania, Mexico, Moldova, Monaco, Mongolia, Montenegro, Morocco, Mozambique, Namibia, the Netherlands, New Zealand, Nicaragua, Niger, Nigeria, Norway, Oman, Papua New Guinea, the Philippines, Poland, Portugal, the Republic of Korea, Romania, Russian Federation, Saint Kitts and Nevis, Saint Lucia, Saint Vincent and the Grenadines, San Marino, Senegal, Serbia, Seychelles, Sierra Leone, Singapore, Slovakia, Slovenia, South Africa, Spain, Sri Lanka, Sudan, Swaziland, Sweden, Switzerland, the Syrian Arab Republic, Tajikistan, the former Yugoslav Republic of Macedonia, Togo, Trinidad and Tobago, Tunisia, Turkey, Turkmenistan, Uganda, Ukraine, the United Arab Emirates, the United Kingdom, the United Republic of Tanzania, the United States, Uzbekistan, Vietnam, Zambia, and Zimbabwe. See http://www.wipo.int/treaties/en/ShowResults.jsp?lang=en&treaty_id=6.

Related treaties are the 1925 Hague Agreement Concerning the International Deposit of Industrial Designs (posted on the Internet at http://www.wipo.int/treaties/en/registration/hague), which sets up a mechanism for registering industrial designs with WIPO, which then handles individual filings in member states; the 1968 Locarno Agreement Establishing an International Classification for Industrial Designs (posted on the Internet at http://www.wipo.int/treaties/en/classification/locarno); and the 1971 Strasbourg Agreement Concerning the International Patent Classification (posted at http://www.wipo.int/treaties/en/classification/strasbourg), which classifies technologies in eight main categories and approximately 52,000 subcategories, each of which is assigned a symbol.

Additionally, Articles 25 and 26 of the Agreement on Trade-Related Aspects of Intellectual Property Rights (1994) address industrial designs. This agreement establishes, among other things, that the term of protection is a minimum of 10 years. *Id.*, Article 26, para. 3.

[125] The text of the Madrid treaty is posted at http://www.wipo.int/treaties/en/ip/madrid.

[126] As of June 8, 2007, the states parties to the Madrid Agreement as revised in 1958 were Algeria, Brazil, Bulgaria, Cuba, the Czech Republic, the Dominican Republic, Egypt, France, Germany, Hungary, Iran, Ireland, Israel, Italy, Japan, Lebanon, Liechtenstein, Moldova, Monaco, Montenegro, Morocco, New Zealand, Poland, Portugal, San Marino, Serbia, Slovakia, Spain, Sri Lanka, Sweden, Switzerland, Syria, Tunisia, Turkey, and the United Kingdom. See http://www.wipo.int/treaties/en/ShowResults.jsp?lang=en&treaty_id=3.

Another agreement dealing with the origins of goods is the 1958 Lisbon Agreement for the Protection of Appellations of Origin and Their International Registration (posted on the Internet at http://www.wipo.int/treaties/en/registration/lisbon), which provides protection for geographic names used to designate agricultural products (e.g., wines, spirits, cheeses).

Trademark Law Treaty:
Requires member states to
establish common mini-
mum rules to protect trademarks.

Trademark Law Treaty

The **Trademark Law Treaty**, adopted in 1994, is meant to simplify both national and regional trademark registration systems by establishing common minimum rules.[127] In addition, the term for renewal of a trademark is set at ten years. Currently, 68 states are parties to the treaty.[128]

D. THE INTERNATIONAL TRANSFER OF INTELLECTUAL PROPERTY

There are five ways in which intellectual property rights are transferred from one country to another: (1) the owner may work the property rights abroad, (2) the owner may transfer or assign the rights to another, (3) the owner may license another to work them, (4) the owner may establish a franchise, or (5) a government may grant a compulsory license so that a third party may exploit them.

The procedures and international regulations for setting up a business, a subsidiary, or a joint venture were discussed in Chapters 4 and 5. Those same procedures and regulations apply to firms established to work intellectual property rights.

The rules and procedures for transferring or making a full assignment of an owner's rights in intellectual property are the same as those for any other sale. Those rules and procedures are discussed in Chapter 10.

license: Authority granted
by the owner of an intellectual property to another
allowing the latter the right
to use it in some limited
way.
franchise: Special license
that requires the franchisee
to work the licensed property under the supervision
and control of the
franchisor.

A **license** is a nonexclusive revocable privilege that allows a licensee to use a licensor's property. A license is created by contract, and standard contractual rules are used to interpret it. It is to be distinguished from a **franchise**, which is a specialized license that requires a franchisee to work the property under the supervision and control of a franchisor.

A license allows a licensee to use a property for the licensee's own purposes. Depending on the licensing agreement, the licensee may use the property as a component in its own products, it may sell the property or the products derived from it under the licensor's name, or it may do the same thing under its own name. Sometimes the licensee may even sell the property, or the products derived from it, in direct competition with the licensor.

By contrast, a franchisee has more limited rights. The key difference is that a franchisee is regarded as a unit or element of the franchisor's business. Three types of franchises have evolved since their initial establishment at the beginning of the twentieth century: (1) distributorships, (2) chain-style businesses, and (3) manufacturing or processing plants.

distributorship: A franchise
in which a manufacturer
licenses a dealer to sell its
products.
chain-style business: A
franchise in which a franchisee operates under the
franchisor's trade name
and is identified as part of
the franchisor's business.

A **distributorship** franchise exists when a manufacturer licenses a dealer to sell its products. A common example is the automobile dealership.

A **chain-style business** franchise is an arrangement in which a franchisee operates under a franchisor's trade name and is identified as part of the franchisor's business chain. Examples include McDonald's, KFC, Pizza Haven, and other fast-food restaurants.

---

[127]The text of the treaty is posted at http://www.wipo.int/treaties/ip.

[128]As of June 2007, there were 68 states party to the Trademark Law Treaty. They were Australia, Austria, Bahrain, Belarus, Belgium, Bosnia and Herzegovina, Burkina Faso, China, Costa Rica, Côte d'Ivoire, Croatia, Cuba, Cyprus, the Czech Republic, Denmark, the Dominican Republic, Egypt, Estonia, the European Community, Finland, France, Gabon, Germany, Greece, Guinea, Hungary, Indonesia, Ireland, Israel, Italy, Japan, Kazakhstan, Kenya, Kyrgyzstan, Latvia, Liechtenstein, Lithuania, Luxembourg, Malta, Mexico, Moldova, Monaco, Montenegro, Morocco, the Netherlands, Poland, Portugal, the Republic of Korea, Romania, the Russian Federation, Senegal, Serbia, Slovakia, Slovenia, South Africa, Spain, Sri Lanka, Swaziland, Sweden, Switzerland, Togo, Trinidad and Tobago, Turkey, Ukraine, the United Kingdom, the United States, Uruguay, and Uzbekistan. See http://www.wipo.int/treaties/en/ShowResults.jsp?lang=en&treaty_id=5.

Other agreements dealing with trademarks are the 1881 Madrid Agreement Concerning the International Registration of Marks (posted on the Internet at http://www.wipo.int/treaties/en/registration/madrid), which establishes a mechanism for registering marks with WIPO, which then handles the filing in the individual member states where registration is sought; the 1957 Nice Agreement Concerning the International Classification of Goods and Services for the Purposes of the Registration of Marks (posted at http://www.wipo.int/treaties/en/classification/nice), which sets up a uniform classification system involving 34 classes of goods and eight classes of services; the 1973 Vienna Agreement Establishing an International Classification for the Figurative Elements of Marks (posted at http://www.wipo.int/treaties/en/classification/vienna); and the 1981 Nairobi Treaty for the Protection of the Olympic Symbol (posted at http://www.wipo.int/treaties/en/ip/nairobi).

Manufacturing or processing plant franchise: A franchise in which the franchisee sells products it manufactures from a formula or from ingredients provided by the franchisor.

A **manufacturing or processing plant** franchise comes about when a franchisor provides the franchisee with the formula or the essential ingredients to make a particular product. The franchisee then wholesales or retails the product according to the standards established by the franchisor. Examples of this kind of franchise are Coca-Cola, Pepsi-Cola, and the other soft-drink firms.

Although a franchisee has more limited rights than a licensee, the rules and regulations that govern franchise agreements are the same as those governing licenses.

Compulsory licenses are common in most countries of the world, especially developing countries. In these countries, if the owner of intellectual property (in particular, patents or copyrights) refuses to work the property in the country within a certain period of time, a third party may apply for a compulsory license. The government issues such a license without the consent of the owner, so it is not subject to the same rules that apply to licensing and franchising.

E. LICENSING REGULATIONS

Grants of patents, trademarks, and copyrights create monopolies. In free-market countries, these grants run contrary to unfair competition laws.[129] In centrally planned economies, they run contrary to the notion of state ownership of the means of production. To balance the interests of consumers in free-market countries and the interests of the state in planned- economy countries with the rights of intellectual property owners, most countries treat intellectual property rights as special exceptions to their general laws prohibiting monopolies. As such, the rights held by patent, trademark, and copyright owners are strictly construed and limited to the narrow confines of the grant. The U.S. Supreme Court, for example, has stated that the grant of a patent is

> ... an exception to the general rule against monopolies and to the right to access to a free and open market. The far-reaching social and economic consequences of a patent, therefore, give the public a paramount interest in seeing that patent monopolies spring from backgrounds free from fraud or other inequitable conduct and that such monopolies are kept within their legitimate scope.[130]

Licensing arrangements involving statutory grants must, accordingly, be limited to the rights contained in the grant. Any attempt to go beyond the scope of the grant—such as trying to license an expired patent, trademark, or copyright—is a misuse of the grant and (depending on the country) is either without effect or illegal.

Nonstatutory grants (in particular, know-how) do not qualify for the special exceptions granted to patents, trademarks, and copyrights. As such, any licensing of these rights has to comply with the appropriate unfair competition laws.

The propriety of states adopting rules to regulate the anticompetitive aspects of intellectual property licenses is now specifically recognized in international law. Article 40, paragraph 2, of the Agreement on Trade-Related Aspects of Intellectual Property Rights provides:

> Nothing in this Agreement shall prevent [WTO] members from specifying in their national legislation licensing practices or conditions that may in particular cases constitute an abuse of intellectual property rights having an adverse effect on competition in the relevant market. As provided above, a member may adopt, consistently with the other provisions of this

---

[129] The conflict between intellectual property rights and unfair competition laws is not a new problem. As the U.S. District Court in SCM Corp. v. Xerox Corp., *Federal Supplement*, vol. 463, p. 996 (1978), pointed out: "Ever since the [English Court of] King's Bench considered a patent-antitrust conflict in 1602 in the first reported case on the subject [Darcy v. Allein, *English Reports*, vol. 77, p. 1260 (1602)] the issues arising in this field have yielded few clear or satisfying answers. Economic arguments could be made that these statutes have a common goal of maximizing wealth by facilitating the production of what consumers want at the lowest cost.... Whatever their economic congruency, there can be little doubt that these two sets of laws are juridicially divergent."

[130] Walker Process Equipment, Inc. v. Food Machines & Chemical Corp., *United States Reports*, vol. 382, p. 177 (Supreme Ct., 1965).

Agreement, appropriate measures to prevent or control such practices, which may include for example exclusive grantback conditions, conditions preventing challenges to validity, and coercive package licensing, in the light of the relevant laws and regulations of that member.

In developing countries (including Argentina, Hungary, Mexico, Poland, Russia, and the members of the Andean Common Market), such anticompetition rules are commonly found in transfer-of-technology codes. In the developed free-market countries (e.g., Germany, France, the United Kingdom, and the United States), they are found in long-standing anti-monopoly legislation. The U.S. Sherman Antitrust Act, among the oldest laws prohibiting unfair competition, is a good example of this type of legislation. It provides:

1. Every contract, combination in the form of trust or otherwise, or conspiracy, in restraint of trade or commerce among the several states, or with foreign nations, is hereby declared to be illegal. . . .
2. Every person who shall monopolize, or attempt to monopolize, or combine or conspire with any other person or persons, to monopolize any part of the trade or commerce among the several states, or with foreign nations, shall be deemed guilty of a felony. . . .[131]

rule of reason: Court-adopted rule that allows a reviewing court to consider the overall impact of a particular agreement on competition within its relevant market.

Similar provisions are found in Articles 81 and 82[132] of the EU's European Community Treaty.[133] Unlike the Sherman Antitrust Act, however, the EC Treaty provisions contain an express exemption (Article 81(3)) that allows the European Commission to authorize arrangements that would otherwise violate the general prohibitions, either through block grants (that apply to a particular category of agreements) or on a case-by-case basis. The commission may do so when the overall effect of a challenged activity is one that "contributes to improving the production or distribution of goods, or to promoting technical or economic progress, while allowing consumers a fair share of the resulting benefit." The same result is achieved in the United States with the development of a court-made **rule of reason**. Except for certain agreements, such as horizontal price-fixing, which the courts regard as illegal *per se*,[134] the rule of reason requires courts to consider the overall impact of the particular agreement on competition within the relevant market. Courts, accordingly, must identify the pro-competitive effects of the agreement and then weigh them against its anticompetitive effects. A common example involves the sale of a firm. In order to sell the firm, the seller may have to agree not to compete with the buyer by setting up a new business in the same area for a reasonable period of time. Such an agreement allows the seller to make a sale and the buyer to protect the goodwill it has purchased, and overall, it increases competition.[135]

---

[131] *United States Code*, Title 15, §§ 1 and 2.

[132] Articles 81 and 82 were previously Articles 85 and 86 prior to the renumbering of the Treaty Establishing the European Community agreed to by the Treaty of Amsterdam.

[133] European Union, Treaty Establishing the European Community, Article 81, provides:

1. The following shall be prohibited as incompatible with the common market: all arrangements between undertakings, decisions by associations of undertakings and concerted practices which may affect trade between Member States and which have as their object or effect the prevention, restriction or distortion of competition within the common market. . . .

2. Any agreement or decision prohibited pursuant to this Article shall be automatically void.

3. The provisions of paragraph 1 may, however, be declared inapplicable in the case of: any agreement or category of agreements between undertakings; any decision or category of decisions by associations of undertakings; any concerted practice or category of concerted practices; which contributes to improving the production or distribution of goods, or to promoting technical or economic progress, while allowing consumers a fair share of the resulting benefit, and which does not:

　(a) impose on the undertakings concerned restrictions which are not indispensable to the attainment of these objectives;

　(b) afford such undertakings the possibility of eliminating competition in respect of a substantial part of the products in question.

Article 82 provides: "Any abuse by one or more undertakings of a dominant position within the common market or in a substantial part of it shall be prohibited as incompatible with the common market in so far as it may affect trade between Member States. . . ."

[134] Latin: "by itself" or "in itself"; "intrinsically."

[135] See National Society of Professional Engineers v. United States, *United States Reports*, vol. 435, p. 689 (Supreme Ct., 1978).

Although it can be stated as a general proposition that (1) licenses granting statutory intellectual rights are enforceable exceptions to technology transfer codes and the unfair competition laws and that (2) licenses granting nonstatutory rights must comply with both, this is only a general statement. Countries differ in their application of these general rules. We will look, therefore, at several examples of how particular licensing clauses are regulated in different countries.

In considering the following licensing provisions and their corresponding regulations, one needs to keep in mind that they apply to different kinds of intellectual property in varying degrees. Export restrictions, for example, apply to all kinds of intellectual property (including copyrights, patents, trademarks, and know-how), whereas restrictions on research and development, as another example, apply—obviously—only to patents and know-how.

TERRITORIAL RESTRICTIONS

In almost every country, a restriction on the territorial scope granted in the license of a statutory right (i.e., a patent, trademark, or copyright) is treated as a normal incidence of that right. Article 24 of the 1919 Honduran Law on Patents provides a typical example:

> In the instrument of transfer an indication shall be given of whether . . . the transfer is effective in a certain area only or throughout the Republic.

Such restrictions, however, apply only to the immediate licensee. Attempts to limit the territory in which an article can be traded after it has left the hands of the licensee are universally condemned. The rationale underlying this is a doctrine known as *exhaustion of rights*.

exhaustion-of-rights doctrine: Once a good made or sold under license is in circulation, the licensor has no further right to control its distribution.

Although the **exhaustion-of-rights doctrine** first appeared as a court-made rule in the United States and Germany,[136] the European Court of Justice has given the doctrine its broadest application and its most careful analysis. This is because the EU is confronted with the problem of rationalizing the separate intellectual property laws of its member states with its own express goal of establishing the free movement of goods among those states. As the Court of Justice observed in *Parke, Davis v. Centrafarm*:

> The national rules relating to the protecting of industrial property have not yet been unified within the Community. In the absence of such unification, the national character of the protection of industrial property and the variations between the different legislative systems on this subject are capable of creating obstacles both to the free movement of the patented products and to competition within the common market.[137]

This rationalization problem is, in some respects, made more difficult by the EU's fundamental law—the EC Treaty—which expressly recognizes the rights of the member states to regulate intellectual property rights. Article 30 of the treaty provides:

> The provisions of Articles 28 and 29 [which establish the free movement of goods within the EU] shall not preclude prohibitions or restrictions on imports, exports, or goods in transit justified on grounds of . . . the protection of industrial and commercial property. Such prohibitions or restrictions shall not, however, constitute a means of arbitrary discrimination or disguised restriction on trade between Member States.

To avoid the conflict between the rights of the EU and the rights of the member states, which Article 30 seems to create, the Court of Justice has taken the novel, although somewhat

---

[136]The first statement of the rule by the U.S. Supreme Court was in Adams v. Burks, *United States Reports*, vol. 84, p. 453 (1873). In Continental T.V., Inc. v. GTE Sylvania, Inc., *id.*, vol. 433, p. 36 (1977), the Supreme Court set out the rule this way: "[U]nder the Sherman Act, it is unreasonable without more for a manufacturer to restrict and confine areas or persons with whom an article may be traded after the manufacturer has parted with dominion over it."

For a statement of the German rule, see Federal Cartel Office decision of May 5, 1960, *Wirtschaft und Wettbewerb, Entscheidungssammlung*, p. 251.

[137]Case 24/67, *European Court Reports*, vol. 1968, p. 71 (1968).

obvious, step of narrowly defining the "industrial and commercial property" rights retained by the member states. Thus, in the landmark case of *Terrapin v. Terranova* the court stated:

> ... whilst the Treaty does not affect the existence of rights recognized by the legislation of the Member States in matters of industrial and commercial property, yet the exercise of those rights may nevertheless, depending on the circumstances, be restricted by the prohibitions in the Treaty. Inasmuch as it provides an exception to one of the fundamental principles of the common market, Article 30 in fact admits exceptions to the free movement of goods only to the extent to which such exceptions are justified for the purposes of safeguarding the rights which constitute the specific subject-matter of the property.[138]

In other words, although the court recognizes that the member states can create and grant rights in the "specific subject-matter" of intellectual property, when the "exercise" of those rights impacts on the EU, then EU law will govern. Put yet another way, the rights created by the member states are "exhausted" whenever the protected goods move across the national boundaries of the member states.

The leading EU patent case dealing with the exhaustion-of-rights doctrine is *Centrafarm v. Sterling Drug*.[139] The case involved patents for a drug used in the treatment of urinary infections that were held by Sterling Drug, an American company, in the Netherlands and the United Kingdom. Sterling sued Centrafarm (a company famous in the annals of the Court of Justice as a parallel importer of pharmaceuticals) for infringement of the Dutch patent. Centrafarm's alleged impropriety was the importation into the Netherlands for sale of certain quantities of the patented drug that had been lawfully marketed in the United Kingdom by Sterling licensees. This was commercially attractive to Centrafarm because the goods were marketed in the United Kingdom under government price regulations for about half of what they sold for in the Netherlands.

The Court of Justice defined the rights that member states could grant to the owner of a patent. Thus, a patent is

> ... the guarantee that the patentee, to reward the creative effort of the inventor, has the right to use an invention with the view to manufacturing industrial products and putting them into circulation for the first time, either directly or by the grant of licenses to third parties, as well as the right to oppose infringements.

By this definition, a patent's essential function is to reward and encourage creative effort. The reward comes from the grant of a monopoly, which allows the patent owner to manufacture the protected product and to put it into circulation for the first time. This monopoly may be exercised either directly or through licensees. It is a significant grant, because the patent owner is also given the corollary right of objecting to its infringement.

The patent owner's rights, however, are significantly limited by this definition. The monopoly consists only of manufacturing the protected products and putting them into circulation for the first time. In other words, the patent owner may not restrict any subsequent circulation of the products.

Considering this limitation, the Court of Justice gave two examples of when a patent owner in one member state could restrict imports from another member state. One example is where a product is patentable in State A but not in State B. If it is manufactured in State B by a third party without the consent of the State A patent owner and then imported into State A, the patent owner may object. The other example is where the product is patented in both State A and State B, but the original owners of the two patents are persons who are legally and economically independent.[140] Either may object to the other's product being imported into its state.

In contrast to these two cases, the Court of Justice said that a patent owner would not be justified in opposing importation "where the product has been put onto the market in a legal

---

[138] Case 119/75, *id.,* vol. 1976, p. 1039 (1976).
[139] Case 15/74, *id.,* vol. 1974, p. 1147 (1974); *Common Market Law Reports*, vol. 1974, pt. 2, p. 480 (1974).
[140] The converse of this situation is the *common origin* doctrine, discussed below.

manner, by the patentee himself or with his consent, in the member states from which it has been imported, in particular in the case of a proprietor of parallel patents." To hold otherwise, the court said, would allow a patent owner to cordon off each member state into a separate national market—something that is contrary to the notion of the free movement of goods, which is basic to the EU common market. In conclusion, the court noted:

> [T]he exercise, by a patentee, of the right which he enjoys under the legislation of a Member State to prohibit the sale, in that state, of a product protected by the patent which has been marketed in another Member State by the patentee or with his consent is incompatible with the rules of the EEC Treaty concerning the free movement of goods within the common market.

In *Centrafarm v. Winthrop*,[141] the Court of Justice applied the exhaustion-of-rights doctrine—with the same result—to a trademark infringement case. The court also applied the doctrine to a copyright case in *Deutsche Gramophone v. Metro*[142] and to a neighboring rights case in *Coditel v. Ciné Vog Films* (No. 1).[143] The EU Commission's Block Exemption for Know-how Licensing extends it to know-how licenses.[144]

Case 9-5 is a landmark EU intellectual property case involving a German manufacturer of electronic equipment that had attempted to grant "absolute territorial protection" to its French licensee. The manufacturer did so by allowing the licensee to register in France a unique trademark that the manufacturer affixed to products it produced for sale in France and by promising not to deliver the products, even indirectly, to competitors of its licensee.

---

[141]Case 16/74, *European Court Reports,* vol. 1974, p. 1183 (1974).
[142]Case 78/70, *id.*, vol. 1971, p. 487 (1971).
[143]Case 62/79, *id.*, vol. 1980, p. 881 (1980). The particular case involved the unauthorized rebroadcast over a cable network of a film that had been broadcast over a different network in another member state.
[144]European Union, Block Exemption for Know-How Licensing, Articles 3(6), 3(7), 3(12), and 9(5) (1987).

Case 9-5   CONSTEN AND GRUNDIG v. COMMISSION EUROPEAN COMMUNITY[145]

Court of Justice, 1966.

European Community Reports, Cases 56/64 and 58/64, p. 299 (1966).

Grundig, a German firm, manufactured radios, televisions, tape recorders, and other electronic equipment. Consten, a French firm, was an electronics wholesaler. In 1957 the two entered into an exclusive distributorship contract that granted Consten the sole right to sell Grundig products in France. The contract contained a provision requiring Grundig to include in its other distributorship agreements a clause preventing Grundig products from being shipped to France. In return, Consten agreed to handle Grundig products exclusively and not deliver those products outside of France.

The Grundig products all carried the trademark GINT. Grundig consented to Consten's registering the mark in France in Consten's name. The reason for doing this was so that Consten could use the French trademark law to keep other importers from bringing Grundig goods carrying the same mark into France. Grundig itself owned the GINT trademark in Germany, and other exclusive Grundig distributors owned the mark in other countries.

The European Economic Community came into being in 1958, and in 1962 the EEC Council promulgated Regulation 17 requiring the parties to agreements such as this to notify the EEC Commission about them. Grundig did so.

---

[145]The European Community became the European Union, the European Economic Community Treaty became the European Community Treaty, and the Court of Justice of the European Community became the European Court of Justice in November 1993.

At about the same time, competitors of Consten were buying Grundig products outside of France and importing them into France, where they were selling them at lower prices. Consten brought suit in the French courts against these competitors to enjoin their infringement of its GINT trademark.

The competitors informed the EEC Commission of the suit, and the commission, after studying the agreement between Consten and Grundig, issued a decision addressed to the two firms holding that their agreement violated Article 85 (now Article 81[146]) of the EEC Treaty. Accordingly, the commission forbade the firms from hindering competitors from importing Grundig products into France from other EEC member states. The decision was appealed to the EEC Court of Justice pursuant to Article 173 (now Article 230) of the EEC Treaty.

Article 85 of the EEC Treaty (now Article 81) prohibits, among other things, agreements "which may affect trade between Member States and which have as their object or effect the prevention, restriction, or distortion of competition within the common market." Paragraph (2) declares such agreements "automatically void."

Consten, Grundig, and the Italian government (which had intervened in the case) argued that the restrictive agreements addressed by Article 85 are not "horizontal agreements" (i.e., contracts between competitors at the same level, such as those between two manufacturers or two distributors) but rather "vertical agreements" (i.e., contracts between firms that are not competitors, such as those between a manufacturer and a wholesaler or a wholesaler and a retailer).

The two firms and the German government (which also had intervened) argued that the agreement did not restrict trade but actually improved trade between France and Germany. These parties also argued that the order issued by the EEC Commission was too broad in that it annulled the entire contract, not just those provisions that violated Article 85.

Finally, the firms argued that the commission's decision prohibiting Consten from using its trademark right to stop parallel imports from other EEC member states violated Article 222 of the EEC Treaty. Article 222 (now Article 295) declares that the treaty "shall in no way prejudice the rules in Member States governing the system of property ownership."

GROUNDS OF JUDGMENT

The Complaints Concerning the Applicability of Article 85(1) to Sole Distribution Agreements

The applicants submit that the prohibition in Article 85(1) applies only to so-called horizontal agreements....

Neither the wording of Article 85 nor that of Article 86 gives any ground for holding that distinct areas of application are to be assigned to each of the two articles according to the level of the economy in which all the contracting parties operate. Article 85 refers in a general way to all agreements which distort competition within the common market and does not lay down any distinction between these agreements based on whether they are made between competitors operating on the same level in the economic process or between noncompeting persons operating at different levels. In principle, no distinction can be made where the Treaty does not make any distinction.

Competition may be distorted within the meaning of Article 85(1) not only by agreements which limit it as between the parties, but also by agreements which prevent or restrict the competition which might take place between one of them and third parties. For this purpose, it is irrelevant whether the parties to the agreement are or are not on a footing of equality as regards their position and function in the economy. This applies all the more since, by such an agreement, the parties might seek, by preventing or limiting the competition of third parties in respect of the products, to create or guarantee for their benefit an unjustified advantage at the expense of consumers, contrary to the general aims of Article 85(1).

Finally, an agreement between producer and distributor which might tend to restore the national divisions in trade between Member States might be such as to frustrate the most fundamental objectives of the Community. The Treaty, whose preamble and content aim at abolishing the barriers between states, and which in several provisions gives evidence of a stern attitude to their reappearance, could not allow undertakings to reconstruct such barriers.

The submissions set out above are consequently unfounded.

---

[146]European Community Treaty Articles 85, 86, 173, and 222 were renumbered as 81, 82, 230, and 295 by the Treaty of Amsterdam. For a table of equivalencies see Annex IV of the Treaty of Amsterdam at http://europa.eu.int/eur-lex/en/treaties/selected/livre550.html.

The Complaints Relating to the Concepts of "Agreements . . . Which May Affect Trade Between Member States"

The applicants and the German Government maintain that the Commission has relied on a mistaken interpretation of the concept of an agreement which may affect trade between Member States and has not shown that such trade would have been greater without the agreement in dispute.

The defendant replies that this requirement in Article 85(1) is fulfilled once trade between Member States develops, as a result of the agreement, differently from ways in which it would have done without the restriction resulting from the agreement, and once the influence of the agreement on market conditions reaches a certain degree. Such is the case here, according to the defendant, particularly in view of the impediments resulting within the Common Market from the disputed agreement as regards the exporting and importing of Grundig products to and from France.

The concept of an agreement "which may affect trade between Member States" is intended to define, in the law governing cartels, the boundary between the areas respectively covered by Community law and national law. It is only to the extent to which the agreement may affect trade between Member States that the deterioration in competition falls under the prohibition of Community law contained in Article 85; otherwise, it escapes prohibition.

In this connection, what is particularly important is whether the agreement is capable of constituting a threat, either direct or indirect, actual or potential, to freedom of trade between Member States in a manner which might harm the attainment of the objectives of a single market between states. . . . In the present case, the contract between Grundig and Consten, on the one hand by preventing undertakings other than Consten from importing Grundig products into France, and on the other hand by prohibiting Consten from re-exporting those products to other countries of the Common Market, indisputably affects trade between Member States. These limitations on the freedom of trade, as well as those which might ensue for third parties from the registration by Consten of the GINT trademark which Grundig places on all its products, are enough to satisfy the requirement in question.

Consequently, the complaints raised in this respect must be dismissed.

***

The Complaints Relating to the Extent of the Prohibition

The applicant Grundig and the German Government complain that the Commission did not exclude from the prohibition, in the operative part of the disputed decision, those clauses of the contract in respect of which there was found no effect capable of restricting competition, and that it thereby failed to define the infringement.

It is apparent from the statement of the reasons for the contested decision that the infringement is not to be found in the undertaking by Grundig not to make direct deliveries in France except to Consten. That infringement arises from the clauses which, added to this grant of exclusive rights, are intended to impede, relying upon national law, parallel imports of Grundig products into France by establishing absolute territorial protection in favor of the sole concessionaire.

The provision in Article 85(2) that agreements prohibited pursuant to Article 85(1) shall be automatically void applies only to those parts of the agreement which are subject to the prohibition, or to the agreement as a whole if those parts do not appear to be serviceable. The Commission should, therefore, either have confined itself to declaring that an infringement lay in parts only of the agreement, or else it should have set out the reason why those parts did not appear to be severable.

Article 1 of the contested decision must therefore be annulled, in so far as it renders void, without any valid reason, all the clauses of the agreement.

The Submissions Concerning the Finding of an Infringement in Respect of the Agreement on the GINT Trademark

The applicants complain that the Commission infringed Article 222 of the EEC Treaty and furthermore exceeded the limits of its powers by excluding, in its decision, any possibility of Consten's asserting its rights under national trademark law to oppose parallel imports.

Consten's right under the contract to be the exclusive user of the GINT trademark is intended to make it possible to place an obstacle in the way of parallel imports. Thus the agreement tends to restrict competition.

That agreement therefore is one which may be caught by the prohibition in Article 85(1). The prohibition would be ineffective if Consten could continue to use the trademark to achieve the same object as that pursued by the agreement which has been held to be unlawful.

Article 222 confines itself to stating that the "Treaty shall in no way prejudice the rules in Member States governing the system of property ownership." The injunction contained in the contested decision to refrain from using rights under national trademark law in order to set an obstacle in the way of parallel imports does not affect the grant of those rights but only limits their exercise to the extent necessary to give effect to Article 85(1). . . .

The above-mentioned submissions are therefore unfounded. ∎

CASEPOINT: The European Court of Justice examined the agreement between the German manufacturer (Grundig) and the French retailer, which contained various restrictions on importing and selling Grundig products. The court weighed the contract provisions against the key EU principle of *free movement of goods* and found the restrictions, in large part, to violate this EU treaty obliga-

tion. One of the most critical sections of the Treaty of Rome, establishing the European Community, stated that any agreement that resulted in the "prevention, restriction, or distortion of competition within the common market" was illegal. The court found that the contracts in this case did have an effect on free competition within the EU and thus were invalid for the most part.

MAP 9-5 European Community (1966)

The European Court of Justice has devised another doctrine, related to the doctrine of exhaustion of rights, to promote the free movement of goods at the expense of trademark owners. This is the **common origin doctrine**, which was first announced in the case of *Van Zuylen v. Hag*, then revised and narrowed in *CNL-Sucal v. Hag*.

The *Van Zuylen* case was a trademark infringement action that arose as the result of the importation into Luxembourg of decaffeinated coffee manufactured in Germany by Hag AG and bearing the HAG trademark. In 1927, Hag AG had established a subsidiary in Belgium to which it assigned the rights to the HAG trademark for both Belgium and Luxembourg. After World War II, the Belgian government expropriated the subsidiary as enemy property and ultimately sold it to the Van Oevelen family, who, in 1971, assigned the trademark to Van Zuylen Frères. Van Zuylen Frères was the owner of the mark at the time that Hag AG began its imports to Luxembourg. In sum, the case involved a trademark that had originally been the property of a common owner but that was now owned in one member state by the original owner and in another state by a legally and economically unrelated company. The Court of Justice concluded that the Belgian expropriation of the subsidiary did not break the common origin of the HAG trademark. It therefore held that the parallel importation into Luxembourg had to be allowed. The court stated:

> The exercise of a trademark right tends to contribute to the partitioning off of the markets and thus to affect the free movement of goods between Member States, and all the more so

common origin doctrine: Owners of the same intellectual property right who acquired it from a common predecessor cannot restrict each other from using the right.

since—unlike other rights of industrial and commercial property—it is not subject to limitations in point of time.

Accordingly, one cannot allow the holder of a trademark to rely upon the exclusiveness of a trademark right—which may be the consequence of the territorial limitation of national legislations—with a view to prohibiting the marketing in a Member State of goods legally produced in another Member State under an identical mark having the same origin. Such a prohibition, which would legitimize the isolation of national markets, would collide with one of the essential objects of the Treaty, which is to unite national markets in a single market.

The holding in the *Van Zuylen* case was later summarized by the Court of Justice in *Terrapin v. Terranova*. There the court said that a trademark could not be used to prevent goods from being sold in the state granting the mark when the mark was "the result of the subdivision, either by voluntary act or a result of public constraint, of a trademark right which originally belonged to one and the same proprietor."[147]

In 1990, the Court of Justice overruled its decision in the *Van Zuylen* case. In *CNL-Sucal v. Hag*, the court held that the expropriation of the HAG mark by Belgium after World War II had indeed broken the unity of the trademark and destroyed the common origin. As a consequence, there were now two separate marks, which enjoyed full protection in their respective territories. Each owner was now "able to prevent the importation and marketing in the Member State where the mark belongs to him, of products originating from the other owner."[148]

Although there is some authority for the proposition that the EU's common origin doctrine may apply to other forms of intellectual property, there are several good arguments for believing that it applies only to trademarks. In particular, the primary function of a trademark is to assure consumers of the place of origin of a product, while the primary function of patents and copyrights is to reward creativity. Also, the subdivision of a market through the use of trademarks is a reasonably serious matter because a trademark is essentially permanent, whereas patents and copyrights are temporary monopolies.[149]

It is important to note that both the exhaustion-of-rights doctrine and the common origin doctrine apply only in cases involving the movement of goods between the member states of the EU.[150] When protected products are manufactured outside the EU, they may not be imported into the EU without the express consent of the EU intellectual property owner. This was the circumstance in the *EMI v. CBS* cases.[151] Until 1917, the same company had owned the COLUMBIA trademark in Europe and the United States. In 1931, however, EMI acquired the European mark, and in 1938 CBS acquired the American mark. Because the trademarks were of a common origin, CBS attempted to take advantage of the common origin doctrine announced in *Van Zuylen v. Hag* to be able to sell its products in Europe. The Court of Justice rejected CBS's arguments, holding:

> [T]he exercise of a trademark right in order to prevent the marketing of products coming from a third country under an identical mark, even if this constitutes a measure having an effect equivalent to a quantitative restriction, does not affect the free movement of goods between Member States and thus does not come under the prohibitions set out in Article 30 [now Article 28] *et seq* of the Treaty.

---

[147] Case 119/76, *European Court Reports*, vol. 1976, p. 1039 (1976); *Common Market Law Reports*, vol. 2, p. 482 (1976).

[148] Case 10/89, *Common Market Law Reports*, vol. 3, p. 571 at 609 (1990).

[149] For additional reasons, see Derrick Wyatt and Alan Dashwood, *The Substantive Law of the EEC*, p. 499 (2nd ed., 1987).

[150] The exhaustion-of-rights doctrine and the common origin doctrine also do not apply in the European Free Trade Area, which is a free-trading group made up of the EU, Iceland, Norway, Liechtenstein, and Switzerland. Case E2/97, Mag Instrument Inc. v. California Trading Company (EFTA Court of Justice 1997), posted at http://www.dinesider.no/customer/770660/archive/files/Decided%20Cases/1997/97%2002%20advisory%20opinion.pdf.

[151] Case 51/75, EMI Records v. CBS United Kingdom, *European Court Reports*, vol. 1976, p. 811 (1976); *Common Market Law Reports*, vol. 1976, pt. 2, p. 235 (1976); Case 86/75, EMI Records v. CBS Grammofon, *European Court Reports*, vol. 1976, p. 871 (1976); Case 96/75, EMI Records v. CBS Schallplatten, *id.*, vol. 1976, p. 913 (1976).

gray marketing: The domestic sale of products manufactured under a license that only grants a foreign licensee the right to sell the goods overseas.

Like the European Court of Justice, U.S. courts have faced the problem of parallel imports of protected products that have been lawfully manufactured outside the United States—a problem known in the United States as **gray marketing**—and have come to very similar conclusions.

EXPORT RESTRICTIONS

Export restrictions limit, partially or entirely, the rights of a licensee to export goods from the territory where the licensee or its production facilities are located. Most countries, as a general rule, prohibit export restrictions.[152] This rule, however, is often subject to many exceptions.

In some countries, restrictions will be tolerated if they limit exports to a country where (1) the licensor owns intellectual property rights and (2) the local laws allow the licensor to restrict foreign imports.[153] In other countries, export restrictions will be tolerated if the limitation applies to a territory where (1) the licensor is manufacturing or distributing the restricted goods or (2) the licensor has granted an exclusive license to a third party to manufacture or distribute the goods.[154]

horizontal competition agreements: Agreements between competitors that have the effect of diminishing competition.
vertical competition agreements: Agreements between sellers and buyers.

In the United States, export restriction agreements between competitors (so-called **horizontal competition agreements**) have been held to be *per se* violations of the Sherman Antitrust Act.[155] For example, in *United States v. National Lead Co.*, the U.S. Supreme Court found a worldwide patent pool covering an entire industry and dividing the whole world into exclusive territories to be illegal.[156] On the other hand, agreements between a seller and a buyer (**vertical competition agreements**) are not bad *per se* and will be tested by a *rule of reason*.[157]

In the EU, export restriction agreements that affect the movement of goods between EU member states violate the Union's European Community Treaty's unfair competition article (Article 81), whether they are reasonable or not, as we saw in the *Grundig* case.[158] Restrictions on exports to countries outside the EU,, however, are prohibited only if they can be shown to have a direct effect on the member states. Such a case exists where, because of geographical proximity and the absence of tariff duties, the goods could easily be reimported from a third country into a member state. Otherwise, export restrictions that apply outside the EU are enforceable in the Union.[159]

---

[152] E.g., India, *Guidelines for Industries*, Chap. 3, Article 9(v) (1988), provides: "To the fullest extent possible, there should be no restrictions on free exports to all countries." Similar provisions exist in Nigeria, the Philippines, Portugal, Spain, and Zambia.

[153] E.g., Brazil, Normative Act No. 015 of the National Institute of Industrial Property, Articles 2.5.2(b)(i), 3.5.2(c)(i), 4.5.2(d)(i), and 5.5.2(d)(i) (1975); Japan, Antimonopoly Act Guidelines for International Licensing Agreements, § 1.1(a) (1969); Mexico, Summary of the General Criteria for the Application of the Law Concerning Registration of the Transfer of Technology and the Use and Working of Patents, Trade Names and Trademarks (September 1974).

[154] E.g., Argentina, Law No. 21617 on the Transfer of Technology, Article 10(c) (August 12, 1972); Japan, Antimonopoly Act Guidelines for International Licensing Agreements, § 1.1(b) (1969); Mexico, Summary of the General Criteria for the Application of the Law Concerning Registration of the Transfer of Technology and the Use and Working of Patents, Trade Names and Trademarks (September 1974); Serbia and Montenegro, Law on Long-term Cooperation in Production, Commercial-technical Cooperation and the Awarding and Acquiring of Technology Between Organizations of Associated Labor and Foreign Persons, Article 37(10) (1978).

[155] United States v. Topco Associates, Inc., *United States Reports*, vol. 405, p. 596 (Supreme Ct., 1972); United States v. Sealey, Inc., *id.*, vol. 388, p. 350 (Supreme Ct., 1967).

[156] *Federal Supplement*, vol. 63, p. 513 (Dist. Ct. for S. Dist. of New York, 1945), affirmed *United States Reports*, vol. 332, p. 319 (Supreme Ct., 1947).

[157] For patent licenses, see Continental T.V., Inc. v. GTE Sylvania, Inc., *United States Reports*, vol. 433, p. 36 (1977); for trade secret licenses, see United States v. E.I. Du Pont de Nemours and Co., *Federal Supplement*, vol. 118, p. 41 (Dist. Ct. for Delaware, 1953), affirmed *United States Reports*, vol. 351, p. 377 (Supreme Ct., 1956); for trademarks, see United States v. Topco Associates, Inc., *id.*, vol. 405, p. 596 (Supreme Ct., 1972).

[158] See, for example, Kabelmetal/Luchaire, *Official Journal*, No. L 222, p. 34 (August 22, 1975) (Commission Decision).

[159] See, for example, Junghans, *id.*, No. L 30, p. 10 (February 2, 1977) (Commission Decision). he rule in Germany parallels that of the EU. Restrictions on exports to territories within Germany or to EU member states are unenforceable, but restrictions on exports to countries outside the EU are valid. See Bundeskartellamt, Decision of June 20, 1963, *Wirtschaft und Wettbewerb, Entscheidungssammlung*, p. 254 (1963).

CARTELS

A **cartel** is an agreement between several business enterprises that is designed, among other things, to allocate markets, to fix prices, to promote the exchange of knowledge resulting from technical and scientific research, to exchange patent rights, or to standardize products. Arrangements of this sort are often called *cross-licensing agreements, patent pools*, and *multiple licensing agreements*.

A **cross-licensing agreement** is an arrangement between two parties to exchange licenses; that is, each party is both a licensor and a licensee. A **patent pool** is an agreement among several owners of related technology to "pool" their patents and other related technology. A **multiple licensing agreement** involves the licensing of technology to a number of recipients by a single licensor. In themselves these agreements are not restrictive, but they may contain restrictive clauses. When they do, some countries prohibit them.

The EU, for example, forbids cartel-type arrangements when they have as their purpose or effect the prevention, restriction, or distortion of competition between EU member states. Such arrangements may include agreements to allocate markets between competitors (i.e., *horizontal* market allocation), horizontal price fixing, and patent pools.[160] In its Block Exemption for Know-how Licensing, the EU Commission has indicated that it will not object to information exchanges and cross-licensing agreements between a single licensor and a single licensee that involve know-how, patents, and trademarks so long as they do not have the effect of stifling competition. In particular, agreements to cross-license improvements and new applications are valid for up to seven years so long as licensees are not precluded from using their own improvements or licensing them to third parties.[161] On the other hand, cross-licensing agreements that involve any territorial restraint with respect to the manufacture, use, or marketing of goods are invalid.[162]

In the United States, cross-licensing and patent pooling are not unlawful unless they are used to divide up territories among competitors, exclude others from competing, or otherwise restrain trade.[163] Moreover, a rule known as the **bottleneck principle** may require the participants in an industry-wide patent exchange to grant reasonable access to any firm wishing to compete so that no firm will be disadvantaged and competition will not be impaired.[164] Price-fixing and division of markets between competitors, however, are held illegal *per se* in both the United States and the EU.

Japan provides much broader exemptions to its basic prohibition against cartels than do either the European Community or the United States. Thus, manufacturing cartels, which are designed to avoid economic depression of an industry through restrictions on production facilities, production quantities, or sales volumes, are valid.[165] Likewise, manufacturers' rationalization cartels aimed at improving technology, productivity, product quality, cost reduction, or any similar entrepreneurial rationalization scheme are also legal.[166] Other cartel-type arrangements are reviewed by the Japanese Fair Trade Commission using a rule-of-reason standard to determine if they have the effect of unreasonably restraining trade.[167]

EXCLUSIVE LICENSES

Laws in several countries expressly state that the grant of a patent, trademark, or copyright gives the owner the right to confer either an **exclusive license** or a nonexclusive

---

cartel: A combination of independent business firms organized to regulate the production, pricing, and marketing of goods by its members.

cross-licensing agreement: An agreement to exchange licenses.

patent pool: An agreement to share patents and other technology.

multiple licensing agreement: A contract for the licensing of industrial property rights to two or more licensees.

bottleneck principle: Participants in an industry-wide patent pool must grant reasonable access to the pool to any firm wishing to compete so that no firm will be disadvantaged.

exclusive license: A license that restricts who may compete with the licensee.

---

[160] European Union, Block Exemption for Know-how Licensing, Articles 3(8) and 5.1(1).
[161] Licensees may, however, be restricted from disclosing secret know-how to third parties. *Id.*, Article 2.1(4).
[162] *Id.*, Articles 5.1(3) and 5.2.
[163] See United States v. National Lead Co., *Federal Supplement*, vol. 63, p. 513 (Dist. Ct. S. Dist. of New York, 1945); affirmed *United States Reports*, vol. 332, p. 319 (Supreme Ct., 1947); Zenith Radio Corp. v. Hazeltine Research, Inc., *id.*, vol. 395, p. 100 (Supreme Ct., 1969).
[164] Standard Oil Co. (Indiana) v. United States, *id.*, vol. 283, p. 163 (Supreme Ct., 1931).
[165] Law No. 54 on the Prohibition of Private Monopolies and the Preservation of Fair Trade, Articles 24–3.1, 24–3.2, and 24-3.3 (April 14, 1974).
[166] *Id.*, Article 24–4.1.
[167] *Id.*, Articles 24–3 and 24–4.

license.[168] In most other countries, both the government and the courts have held that such arrangements are implicitly proper.

Parties to agreements granting these rights need to be careful, however, in defining the terms they use. A licensee may receive *sole rights* (to the exclusion of all others, including the licensor), *exclusive rights* (preventing everyone except the licensor from competing), or *nonexclusive rights* (which allow the licensor to grant other licenses). Merely using these terms, however, may cause confusion because the terms are interpreted differently in different countries. For example, in the United States, the term *exclusive rights* is generally held to mean that the licensor may not give a license to another licensee or exploit the licensed property himself unless he specifically reserves the right to do so.[169] In France, on the other hand, an exclusive license does not prevent the licensor from personally competing unless the agreement specifically provides otherwise.[170]

The importance of fully and carefully defining the terms used in a licensing contract is illustrated by Case 9-6.

---

[168]E.g., Austria, Korea, and Zambia.
[169]See Cutter Laboratories, Inc. v. Lyophile-Cryochem Corp., *Federal Reports, Second Series*, vol. 179, p. 80 (Ninth Circuit Ct. of Appeals, 1949).
[170]Philippe Nouel, "Licensing in France," *International Licensing Agreements*, p. 158 (2nd ed., Götz M. Pollizen & Eugen Langen, eds., 1973).

Case 9-6 RANSOME-KUTI v. PHONOGRAM, LTD.

Ghana, High Court at Accra, 1976.
Ghana Law Reports, vol. 1, p. 220 (1976).

JUDGE EDUSEI:

The plaintiff in this application is seeking an order of this court "restraining the defendant by itself, its agents, servants, and privies from publishing or causing to be published for distribution, sale, or use in Ghana, a musical tape entitled 'Everything Scatter' owned and produced by the plaintiff between May and October 1975."

The facts as revealed by the rival affidavits are not seriously in dispute. It is admitted by the defendants that the plaintiff created and composed a musical work entitled "Everything Scatter" in Nigeria, but by an agreement, Exhibit A, made between the plaintiff and Phonogram, Ltd. (Nigeria) dated 14 October 1975, the plaintiff assigned to Phonogram, Ltd. (Nigeria) the sole and exclusive right to produce or reproduce and sell the work on records and tapes as a single album as well as recordings on cassette tapes and cartridges all over the continent of Africa for a period of three years from 14 October 1975, in consideration of sums of money specified in the said agreement.

The plaintiff is contending that Phonogram, Ltd. (Nigeria) (hereinafter referred to as the Nigerian company) has no right whatsoever to delegate its duty of publishing to the defendants, and counsel for the plaintiff referred to the case of *Griffith v. Tower Publishing Co., Ltd.*,[171] where it was decided that a publishing agreement between an author and his publisher or firm of publishers is personal to the parties and cannot be assigned without the author's consent. In that case, the plaintiff agreed with the defendant-company, a firm of publishers, for the printing and selling of his three novels, but the publishers went into liquidation and were arranging for another company to publish the said novels. On application for an injunction to restrain the defendants and the receiver, the court said an injunction should go. It is clear from the judgment that the copyright in the novels remained in the plaintiff, who was entitled to protect his interest in so far as the printing and selling of the novels were concerned. And, in the absence of any power in the defendants to assign their right and interest in the agreement, it is clear that they could not without the consent of the author (the plaintiff) attempt to assign the publication of the novels to another

---

[171]*All England Law Reports*, vol. 1895–99, p. 323.

company. Again, it seems that the right to assign any interest in the agreement was not reserved to either of the parties. There can be no doubt that this decision confirms the principle that such contracts are personal and on the facts of the case the decision in my view was correct.

In the case before me the parties entered into a formal agreement, Exhibit A, in which the parties include their successors-in-title and assigns. The opening words of the agreement, Exhibit A, presuppose that the right to assign the interest in the agreement is reserved to both parties unless there is a term to the contrary further down in Exhibit A. Again, by paragraph (5) of Exhibit A, the copyright in the musical work has passed to the Nigerian company for a period of three years during which the sole and exclusive right to produce or reproduce and sell the work in records and tapes over the continent of Africa is vested in the Nigerian company. The Nigerian company has licensed the defendants, a sister company in Ghana (part of Africa) to reproduce the said musical work in Ghana for them, and Section 10(5) of the *Copyright Act*, 1961 (Act No. 85), which permits the grant of licenses, stipulates as follows: "A license to do an act falling within the copyright may be written or oral, or may be inferred from conduct, and may be revoked at any time." Also, Section 10(2) states:

> An assignment or testamentary disposition may be limited so as to apply to only some of the acts which the owner of the copyright has the exclusive right to control or to a part only of the period of the copyright.

By virtue of Exhibit A, the plaintiff has no copyright in the said musical work to protect—at least for three years in Africa. Indeed, paragraph (6) of Exhibit A makes the position of the plaintiff clearer. It states:

> The author [i.e., the plaintiff] further warrants that any records or works pressed or waxed on any other label . . . shall not be sold . . . in any part of the continent of Africa by the author, his agents, his representatives or any other person to whom the copyright shall be granted by the author outside the continent of Africa.

This quotation from Exhibit A means that the plaintiff is at liberty to grant to any other person outside the continent of Africa [the right] to reproduce the work on records and cassette tapes, but such records and cassette tapes cannot in any way be sold in Africa. In so far as the continent of Africa is concerned, the copyright in the musical work is vested in the Nigerian company. The Nigerian company—that has the copyright for a period of three years in Africa—has, in my opinion, every right to permit anyone in Africa under license to reproduce the work for that company.

. . . Since the copyright in the musical work is vested in the Nigerian company and the said company has given license to the defendant to reproduce the tape in this country which is part of the continent of Africa, I cannot see any infringement of the copyright by the defendants. It seems to me that I should be doing wrong if I decided that there has been an infringement in the face of Exhibit A and the facts in this case. . . .

The plaintiff's application was dismissed. ■

CASEPOINT: In this case the court was faced with the question of whether the license granted to a Nigerian company to reproduce the plaintiff's copyrighted musical work throughout Africa for three years also gave the licensee the right to subcontract the rights to produce records in Ghana to another firm. The plaintiff cited a previous case that had prohibited such secondary assignment regarding a book. However, in that case, the contract had said nothing about reassignment, while in this case, the contract used the phrase "successors and assigns" right at the beginning. Thus, the court found that reassignment of the right to produce records to another company in Ghana was allowed.

SALES AND DISTRIBUTION ARRANGEMENTS

A sales or distribution arrangement limits a licensee's freedom to organize its distribution system independently of the licensor.

There are three basic approaches to the regulation of these agreements. One group of developing countries (e.g., Brazil, Serbia and Montenegro, and Zambia) prohibits any interference by the licensor in the licensee's distribution system.[172] A second group of developing and developed countries (e.g., Japan, Mexico, Nigeria, and Venezuela) prohibits only those

---

[172]For example, Zambia's Industrial Development Act, Article 16 (1977), provides: "A contract for the transfer of technology and expertise shall not contain any condition: . . . (c) Which restricts the manner of sale of products or the export of products to any country. . . ."

provisions that give the licensor exclusive distribution rights.[173] Finally, a third group of generally developed countries (e.g., Germany, Portugal, Spain, the United States, and the European Community) only prohibit those exclusive sales arrangements that tend to allocate or monopolize markets.[174]

PRICE-FIXING

price-fixing clause: Provision requiring a licensee to sell products at a price set by the licensor.

A **price-fixing clause** requires a licensee to sell products at a price specified by the licensor. It may specify either maximum or minimum prices. It may be restricted to the technology or goods being licensed, or it may cover other products as well. It may apply only to the price charged by the licensee, or it may extend to the prices charged by retailers who purchase the goods from a wholesaler-licensee.

Price-fixing also arises in the context of cartels, particularly cross-licensing and patent pools.

Most countries—both developed and developing—prohibit all forms of price-fixing.[175] One exception is India, which allows a licensor to specify the price at which a licensee may sell a product manufactured using the licensor's technology or to which the licensor's trademark has been affixed (i.e., a vertical licensing arrangement).[176]

NONCOMPETITION CLAUSES

noncompetition clause: Provision forbidding a licensee from competing with the licensor.

Noncompetition clauses forbid a licensee from entering into agreements to acquire or distribute technologies or products that compete with ones furnished or designated by the licensor. Direct prohibitions may include an understanding that the licensee is not to manufacture or sell competing technologies, or that the licensee is to terminate the use of particular technologies or terminate the manufacture and distribution of particular products. Indirect prohibitions may require the licensee not to cooperate with a competing business or not to pay higher royalties for competing products.[177]

In general, noncompetition clauses are prohibited in all countries.[178] A few countries allow them under exceptional circumstances. The German Federal Cartel Office, for example,

---

[173] For example, Venezuela's Decree No. 746 on Transfer of Technology Agreements, Article 1(e) (February 11, 1975), forbids any clause in a transfer of technology contract that "requires all or part of the goods produced to be sold to the supplier."

[174] See, for example, Elder-Beerman Stores Corp. v. Federated Dept. Stores, Inc., *Federal Reports, Second Series,* vol. 459, p. 138 (Sixth Circuit Ct. of Appeals, 1972); United States v. Imperial Chemical Industries, Ltd., *Federal Supplement,* vol. 105, p. 215 (Dist. Ct. for S. Dist. of New York, 1952).

[175] E.g., Argentina, Law No. 21617 on the Transfer of Technology, Article 10(i) (August 12, 1972); Brazil, Normative Act No. 015 of the National Institute of Industrial Property, Articles 2.5.2(b)(i) 3.5.2.(c)(i), 4.5.2(d)(i), and 5.5.2.(d)(i) (1975); Japan, Antimonopoly Act Guidelines for International Licensing Agreements, § 1.6 (1969); Mexico, Law on the Registration of the Transfer of Technology and the Use and Working of Patents, Trade Names, and Trade Marks, Article 7(xi) (December 29, 1972); Nigeria, Decree No. 70 Establishing the National Office of Industrial Property, Article 6.2.(j) (September 14, 1979); the Philippines, Regulation to Implement Article 5 of Presidential Decree No.1520 establishing the Technology Board within the Ministry of Industry, Article 5.1 (c) (October 10, 1978); Portugal, Foreign Investment Code (Legislative Decree No. 348/77, August 24, 1977), Article 28.1(f); Spain, Ministry of Industry Order Regulating the Entry of Contracts for the Transfer of Technology in the Register Established by Decree No. 2342 of September 21, 1973, § 3.6 (December 5, 1973); Serbia and Montenegro, Law on Long-Term Cooperation in Production, Commercial-Technical Cooperation and the Awarding and Acquiring of Technology between Organizations of Associated Labor and Foreign Persons, Article 37.9 (1978); European Union, Treaty Establishing the European Community, Article 81.1(a) (1957 as amended). Price-fixing in the United States is *per se* illegal. Northern Pacific R. Co. v. United States, *United States Reports,* vol. 356, p. 1 (Supreme Ct., 1958); United States v. Trenton Potteries Co., *id.,* vol. 273, p. 392 (Supreme Ct., 1927).

[176] Monopolies and Restrictive Trade Practices Act No. 54, Article 39.3 (1969).

[177] A clause requiring a licensee to use its best efforts may sometimes work as an indirect noncompetition clause.

[178] A typical prohibition is Australia's Patents Act 1990 No. 83 of 1990, Article 144(1): "A condition in a contract relating to the sale or lease of, or a license to exploit, a patented invention is void if the effect of the condition would be: (a) to prohibit or restrict the buyer, lessee or licensee from using a product or process (whether patented or not) supplied or owned by a person other than the seller, lessor or licensor, or a nominee of the seller, lessor or licensor. . . ." The Australian Patents Act is posted on the Piper's Patent Attorneys' Web site at http://www.piperpat.co.nz/aulaw/aupatact.html.

Similar statutory prohibitions exist in Argentina, Austria, India, Japan, Mexico, Nigeria, the Philippines, Portugal, Serbia and Montenegro, Spain, the United Kingdom, and Zambia.

has sometimes granted an exemption to the German Act against Restraints on Competition when the restriction is narrowly drawn and when it is meant to prevent disclosure of confidential technical information.[179] In the United States, the courts have held that a clause prohibiting a trademark licensee from dealing in competing goods is not *per se* unlawful. Applying a rule of reason, the U.S. courts will consider the need to protect the mark, the need to avoid public confusion, and the impact of the restriction on competition.[180] Also, in connection with patent licenses, the U.S. courts have sometimes tolerated a noncompetition clause where the licensee has acquired an exclusive license.[181]

CHALLENGES TO VALIDITY

no-challenge clause: Provision forbidding a licensee from challenging the validity of a licensor's claim to a particular statutory right.

No-challenge clauses forbid a licensee from challenging the validity of the statutory right granted by the licensor. The purpose of these clauses is to ensure that a licensee will comply with the agreed-to restrictions and payment obligations.

Only a few countries (e.g., Germany) permit no-challenge clauses generally.[182] Most consider such a clause in a patent or copyright license to be a restrictive trade practice. Many developing countries (e.g., Brazil, the Philippines, and Serbia and Montenegro) expressly condemn them in their transfer-of-technology codes.[183] Most developed countries (including the United States and EU member states) interpret their unfair competition laws as forbidding no-challenge clauses in patent and copyright licenses.[184]

No-challenge clauses in trademark licenses are regarded in the same negative way by developing countries[185] and some developed countries. The EU, accordingly, views such clauses as a violation of the unfair competition article (Article 81(1)) of the European Community Treaty.[186]

The United States, however, does not regard a no-contest clause in a trademark license as violating either its trademark laws or its antitrust laws.[187]

TYING CLAUSES

tying clause: A provision requiring a licensee to acquire or use, apart from the technology wanted, goods or personnel designated by the licensor.

A **tying clause** is a provision that requires a licensee to acquire or use, separately from the technology wanted, additional goods (such as raw materials, intermediate products, machines, or additional technology) or designated personnel either from the licensor or from a

---

[179]E.g., Bundeskartellamt Decision of June 20, 1963, *Wirtschaft und Wettbewerb, Entscheidungssammlung*, p. 254 (1963).

[180]See American Motor Inns, Inc. v. Holiday Inns, Inc., *Federal Reporter, Second Series*, vol. 521, p. 1230 (Third Circuit Ct. of Appeals, 1975); Susser v. Carvel Corp., *id.*, vol. 332, p. 505 (Second Circuit Ct. of Appeals, 1964), *certiorari* denied, *United States Reports*, vol. 381, p. 125 (Supreme Ct., 1965); Denison Mattress Factory v. Spring-Air Co., *Federal Reports, Second Series*, vol. 308, p. 403 (Fifth Circuit Ct. of Appeals, 1962).

[181]See Carbo-Frost, Inc. v. Pure Carbonic, Inc., *Federal Reporter, Second Series*, vol. 103, p. 210 (Eighth Circuit Ct. of Appeals, 1964), *certiorari* denied, *United States Reports*, vol. 308, p. 569 (Supreme Ct., 1939); see also Wood v. Lucy, Lady Duff-Gordon, *North East Reporter*, vol. 118, p. 214 (New York Ct. of Appeals, 1917).

[182]Germany, Act against Restraints on Competition, Article 20.2(4).

[183]Brazil, Normative Act No. 015 of the National Institute of Industrial Property, Article 2.5.2 (1975); the Philippines, Regulation to Implement Article 5 of Presidential Decree No. 1520 establishing the Technology Board within the Ministry of Industry, Article 5.1.c.5 (October 10, 1978); Serbia and Montenegro, Law on Long-Term Cooperation in Production, Commercial-Technical Cooperation, and the Awarding and Acquiring of Technology between Organizations of Associated Labor and Foreign Persons, Article 37(4) (1978).

[184]See Lear, Inc. v. Adkins, *United States Reports*, vol. 395, p. 653 (Supreme Ct., 1969); AOIP/Beyard, *Official Journal*, No. L, p. 31 (January 13, 1976) (Commission Decision).

[185]E.g., Serbia and Montenegro's Law on Long-Term Cooperation in Production, Commercial-Technical Cooperation and the Awarding and Acquiring of Technology between Organizations of Associated Labor and Foreign Persons, Article 37(4) (1978), prohibits all no-contest clauses affecting rights in any form of industrial property.

[186]See Goodyear Italiana/Euram, *Official Journal*, No. L 38, p. 11 (February 12, 1975) (Commission Decision); but compare Penneys, *Official Journal*, No. L 60, p. 19 (March 2, 1978) (Commission Decision), in which the Commission held that a no-contest clause that ran for a period of only 5 years was not an appreciable restriction on competition.

[187]See Beer Nuts, Inc. v. Kings Nut Co., *Federal Reporter, Second Series*, vol. 477, p. 328, *certiorari* denied, *United States Reports*, vol. 414, p. 585 (Supreme Ct., 1973); Seven-Up Bottling Co. v. The Seven-Up Co., *Federal Supplement*, vol. 420, p. 1246 (Dist. Ct. for E. Dist. of Montana, 1976).

source named by the licensor. In other words, the acquisition of these additional goods or services is a prerequisite to obtaining the technology license.

In general, tying clauses are illegal in virtually every country. Most countries, however, provide for exemptions in varying degrees. The most common exemption is granted on the grounds that a tie-in is necessary to protect quality standards or to protect the goodwill of a trademark.[188] Other exemptions (in a few countries) allow tie-ins if the licensee is not charged an excessive price,[189] if the licensee is free to terminate the tie-in arrangements at any time,[190] or if the licensee is allowed to terminate the clause as soon as a dependable local source of supply can be found.[191]

QUANTITY AND FIELD-OF-USE RESTRICTIONS

quantity restriction: Provision in a license limiting the quantity of goods that may or must be produced.
field-of-use restrictions: Provision limiting the fields in which goods acquired or produced under license may be used.

Countries regulate licensing arrangements with **quantity** and **field-of-use restrictions** in three ways. Developing countries (with transfer-of-technology codes) generally regard limitations on the quantity of goods that may or must be produced, or limits on the fields in which goods may be used or sold, as illegal. The prohibition in Article 16 of Zambia's Industrial Production Act of 1977 is a typical example:

A contract for the transfer of technology and expertise shall not contain any condition: . . .

e. Which restricts the volume or structure of production;
f. Which limits the ways in which patents or other know-how may be used. . . .

Similar provisions exist in Brazil,[192] Mexico,[193] and the Philippines.[194]

A second group of countries, including Japan, the European Community, the United States, and most countries in the developed world, regard quantity and field-of-use restrictions as implicit elements in the statutory rights of a licensor. Section III of Japan's Antimonopoly Act Guidelines for International Licensing Agreements of 1969 is a representative example:

In international licensing agreements on patent rights, etc., the following acts shall be regarded as the exercise of rights under the Patent Act or the Utility Model Act: . . .

1. To restrict the manufacture of patented goods to a limited field of technology or to restrict the sale thereof to a limited field of sales;
2. To restrict the use of patented processes to a limited field of technology;
3. To restrict the amount of output or the amount of sales of patented goods or to restrict the frequency of the use of patented processes; . . .

Most of these countries do not, however, allow licensors to impose quantity or field-of-use limitations on nonstatutory rights. When they relate to know-how and other contractually based rights, these provisions are typically held to violate unfair competition rules.[195] When

---

[188] E.g., India, Patents Act, Article 140.4(c) (1970); United Kingdom, Patents Act, Article 44.6 (1977); European Union, Block Exemption for Patent Licensing, Article 2(9).
In the United States, a tying clause was held to be justified to protect the licensor's goodwill in Dehydrating Process Co. v. A. O. Smith Corp., *Federal Reporter, Second Series*, vol. 292, p. 1 (1st Circuit Ct. of Appeals, 1961), *certiorari* denied, *United States Reports*, vol. 368, p. 931 (Supreme Ct., 1961), and when it was used to ensure that the product was manufactured according to the licensor's standards in Electric Pipe Line, Inc. v. Fluid Systems, Inc., *Federal Reporter, Second Series*, vol. 231, p. 370 (2nd Circuit Ct. of Appeals, 1956).
[189] E.g., Australia's Patents Act 1990 No. 83 of 1990, Article 144(2)(a); United Kingdom, Patents Act, Article 44.4(a) (1977).
[190] E.g., Australia's Patents Act 1990 No. 83 of 1990, Article 144(2)(b); United Kingdom, Patents Act, Article 44.4(b) (1977).
[191] E.g., Mexico, Law on the Registration of the Transfer of Technology and the Use and Working of Patents, Trade Names, and Trade Marks, Article 7(x) (December 29, 1972).
[192] Brazil, Normative Act No. 15 of the National Institute of Industrial Property, Article 2.5.2 (September 11, 1975).
[193] Mexico, Law on the Registration of the Transfer of Technology and the Use and Working of Patents, Trade Names and Trade Marks, Article 7 (December 29, 1972).
[194] Philippines, Regulation to Implement Article 5 of Presidential Decree No. 1520 establishing the Technology Board within the Ministry of Industry, Article 28.1 (October 10, 1978).
[195] See Continental T.V., Inc. v. GTE Sylvania, Inc., *United States Reports*, vol. 433, p. 36 (Supreme Ct., 1977).

they attempt to expand a statutory grant beyond its ordinary scope, such a license is treated as a misuse of the grant. For example, in *United States v. Studiengesellschaft Kohle, M.B.H.*, an American court found that a sales limit imposed on unpatented goods produced according to a patented process was a form of patent misuse.[196] One exception to this is the EU's Block Exemption for Know-How Licensing, which expressly allows licensors to confine a licensee's exploitation of know-how to a specific field of application or market. However, restrictions on customers who may be supplied within a particular field of use or market, restrictions on quantities sold, or restrictions on supplying persons who would resell the product within the EU are all illegal.[197]

A third approach to quantity and field-of-use restrictions is found in Germany. There, restrictions on both statutory and nonstatutory rights—including limitations on the use of know-how and trade secrets—are expressly allowed. Article 20.1 of Germany's 1957 Act Against Restraints on Competition expressly states that "restrictions pertaining to the type, extent, quantity, territory, or period of exercise" of statutorily granted industrial property rights are "within the scope" of the statutory grant itself, and therefore valid and enforceable. Article 21.1 states that the same rule applies to agreements limiting the use of "legally unprotected inventions, manufacturing methods, instructions, technique-improving processes and secret plant-breeding methods."

RESTRICTIONS ON RESEARCH AND DEVELOPMENT

Restrictions on research and development may relate to two different kinds of activities: (1) the research, adaptation, and improvement of the transferred technology or (2) the research and development of competing technologies. Both of these are condemned in almost all countries.[198] The one significant exception is the United States, where a restriction on research to adapt transferred technology will be tolerated if it preserves a product's reputation or protects the licensor from liability.[199] Also, if the restriction is comparable to a valid field-of-use restriction, it may also be justified.[200]

QUALITY CONTROLS

Requirements that a licensor meet certain quality standards or comply with certain quality controls imposed by the licensor are almost uniformly accepted in all countries. In particular, **quality control clauses** are justified where the trademark of the licensor is being applied to a product manufactured and/or distributed by the licensee.[201] They are also justified when they are imposed for the purpose of avoiding product liability.[202]

quality control clause: Provision requiring a licensee to meet quality standards or operate under quality controls set by a licensor.

---

[196] *Federal Supplement*, vol. 426, p. 143 (Dist. Court for the District of Columbia, 1976).

[197] European Union, Block Exemption for Know-how Licensing, Articles 2.1(10), 3(6), 3(7), 3(12), and 9.5 (1987).

[198] A typical provision is found in Nigeria's Decree No. 70 Establishing the National Office of Industrial Property, Article 6.2(3) (September 14, 1979), which prohibits any transfer-of-technology provision "where limitations are imposed on technological research or development by the transferee."

[199] See Tripoli Co. v. Wella Corp., *Federal Reporter, Second Series*, vol. 452, p. 932 (Third Circuit Ct. of Appeals, 1970), *certiorari* denied, *United States Reports*, vol. 400, p. 831 (Supreme Ct., 1970).

[200] See Reliance Molded Plastics, Inc. v. Jiffy Products, *Federal Supplement*, vol. 215, p. 402 (Dist. Ct. for Dist. of New Jersey, 1963), affirmed without an opinion, *Federal Reporter, Second Series*, vol. 337, p. 857 (Third Circuit Ct. of Appeals, 1964).

[201] Germany, Act against Restraints on Competition, Article 20.2(1) (1957). United States, Lanham Trademark Act, para. 1127 (1976); European Union, Block Exemption for Patent Licensing, Article 2(9).

A leading U.S. case, Siegel v. Chicken Delight, Inc., *Federal Reporter, Second Series*, vol. 448, p. 51 (Ninth Circuit Ct. of Appeals, 1971), *certiorari* denied, *United States Reports*, vol. 405, p. 955 (Supreme Ct., 1972), observed: "For a licensor, through relaxation of quality control, to permit inferior products to be presented to the public under his licensed mark, might well constitute a misuse of the mark." An often-cited decision of the EU Commission, Campari, *Official Journal*, No. L 70, p. 69 (March 13, 1978), makes a similar observation.

[202] See Tripoli Co. v. Wella Corp., *Federal Reporter, Second Series*, vol. 452, p. 932 (Third Circuit Ct. of Appeals, 1970), *certiorari* denied, *United States Reports*, vol. 400, p. 831 (Supreme Ct., 1970).

Quality control clauses are prohibited, however, where they are used as a means of improperly tying in other products or services,[203] where they seek to make the licensee dependent on the licensor,[204] or where they seek to allocate trade territories.[205]

GRANT-BACK PROVISIONS

grant-back provision:
Agreement that a technology licensee will transfer to the licensor any improvements, inventions, or know-how it acquires while using the technology.

A **grant-back provision** requires a technology recipient (i.e., a patent or know-how recipient) to transfer back to the supplier any improvements, inventions, or special know-how that it acquires while using the technology. Such a provision may be unilateral or reciprocal, exclusive or nonexclusive. A unilateral grant-back provision requires one of the parties—usually the licensee—to transfer back new knowledge, whereas a reciprocal provision requires both to do so. Sometimes a reciprocity agreement will require both parties to exchange their developments (i.e., a true reciprocal exchange), but at other times only one party will be required to transfer new knowledge, while the other will be required merely to pay adequate compensation (i.e., a compensated unilateral exchange).

An exclusive grant-back provision requires one of the parties—usually the licensee—to transfer any rights (i.e., patent or know-how rights) in the new development to the other party. A nonexclusive (or *sharing*) provision allows the parties to share these rights.

Most countries prohibit grant-back provisions that unilaterally require the licensee to transfer exclusive rights to the licensor. One exception is the United States, which permits such a provision so long as it has no anticompetitive effect.[206]

In contrast, most countries do not prohibit (and a few expressly allow) grant-back provisions that are reciprocal and nonexclusive—that is, provisions that require the parties to share the new knowledge. This is so for both *true* reciprocal exchanges (i.e., technology exchanged for technology) and compensated unilateral exchanges (i.e., technology exchanged for money).

Exhibit 9-3 summarizes the different approaches to grant-back provisions in several representative countries.

RESTRICTIONS THAT APPLY AFTER THE EXPIRATION OF INTELLECTUAL PROPERTY RIGHTS

Countries generally hold that payment obligations or restrictions based on statutory intellectual property rights must terminate when the statutory right expires.[207] The reason for this was stated succinctly by the U.S. Supreme Court in *Scott Paper Co. v. Marcalus Mfg. Co.*, a patent case:

---

[203] *Bericht der Bundeskartellamtes über seine Tätigkeit im Jahre 1974 sowie über Lage und Entwicklung auf seinem Ausgabengebeit*, p. 91.

[204] Nigeria, Decree No. 70 Establishing the National Office of Industrial Property, Article 6.2(o) (September 14, 1979); Venezuela, Decree No. 746 on Transfer of Technology Agreements, Article 1(d) (February 11, 1975).

[205] E.g., Standard Oil v. United States, *United States Reports,* vol. 337, p. 293 (Supreme Ct., 1949).

[206] See Transparent Wrap Machine Corp. v. Stokes and Smith Co., *United States Reports*, vol. 329, p. 637 (Supreme Ct., 1947). There the U.S. Supreme Court said that a unilateral grant-back of exclusive rights to a licensor was not a *per se* violation of the antitrust laws and would be permitted so long as it had no anticompetitive effect beyond that inherent in patents or know-how. This decision was followed in Santa Fe Pomeroy, Inc. v. P. and Z. Co., *Federal Reporter, Second Series*, vol. 569, p. 1084 (Ninth Circuit Ct. of Appeals, 1978), where the evidence showed that the grant-back provision did not unduly restrain trade or suppress industry development. A grant-back provision was held illegal in United States v. Aluminum Co. of America, *Federal Supplement*, vol. 333, p. 410 (Dist. Ct. for S. Dist. of New York, 1950) because it tended to enhance the technological superiority of a company with monopoly or near-monopoly power.

[207] As to payment obligations, most countries simply state that the obligations cease when the statutory right expires. Thus, Article 71 of Venezuela's Decree No. 2442 on the Treatment of Foreign Capital, Trademarks, Patents, Licenses and Royalties (1977) provides: "No payments shall be permissible by way of royalties or other charges in respect of the use of trademarks, processes, patents or industrial models for a period exceeding the period of validity of the industrial property rights recognized by the relevant legislative provision."
In the United Kingdom and many of its former colonies, including Australia and India, the obligations that arise under an intellectual property license will terminate at the time that the underlying statutory right expires and upon the licensee giving three months' notice to the licensor. See United Kingdom, Patents Act, Article 45(1) (1977); Australia's Patents Act No. 83 of 1990, Article 144(2)(b); India, Patents Act, Article 141(1) (1970).
As to restrictions on the free use of the protected technology after the expiration of the underlying statutory grant, countries commonly hold that it expires with the grant (e.g., Germany) or within a reasonable time after the grant (e.g., Brazil). See Germany, Act Against Restraints on Competition, Article 20.1 (1957); Brazil, Normative Act No. 015 of the National Institute of Industrial Property, Article 4.5.2(d)(vi) (1975).

EXHIBIT 9-3   Regulation of Grant-Back Provisions

Types of Provisions	Expressly Prohibited	Expressly Permitted
Reciprocal exchange True reciprocal exchange (Technology for technology)		Argentina, Germany, Japan, Mexico
Compensated exchange (Technology for money)		Portugal, Serbia and Montenegro
Unilateral Exchange Exclusive (Transfer of all rights to one party)	Argentina, Japan, Mexico, Nigeria, Philippines, Spain, Venezuela, European Union	United States[a]
Nonexclusive (Sharing of rights with the other party)	Philippines	Brazil

[a]Permitted so long as there is no anticompetitive effect.

> If a manufacturer or user could restrict himself, by express contract . . . from using the invention of an expired patent, he would deprive himself and the consuming public of the advantage to be derived from his free use of the [patent] disclosures. . . . Hence, any attempted reservation or continuation in the patentee or those claiming under him of the patent monopoly, after the patent expires, whatever the legal device employed, runs counter to the policy and purpose of the patent laws.[208]

package licensing: The transfer of multiple statutory rights under a single license.

The principal problem that arises in connection with the expiration of statutory rights involves package licenses. **Package licensing** is the transfer of multiple statutory rights (often including multiple patents and multiple trademarks) under a single license. Generally, if the licensing agreement was entered into voluntarily by both sides and the payment obligations do not extend beyond that of the last-to-expire statutory right, these agreements will be enforceable. On the other hand, if the licensee was at an economic disadvantage and given only the option of taking or leaving the arrangement, it will commonly be found to be illegal as a form of statutory misuse. For example, in the American case of *McCullough Tool Co. v. Well Surveys, Inc.*, the court upheld a licensing arrangement under which the licensee agreed to pay level royalties on a package of patents, some of which were to expire during the period of the agreement. The court did so because the term of the license did not extend beyond the last-to-expire patent and because the licensee was not required to accept the package on a take-it-or-leave-it basis.[209] On the other hand, in *American Securit Co. v. Shatterproof Glass Corp.*, the court found that a package of patents, which the licensee was required to accept on a take-it-or-leave-it basis, was patent misuse.[210]

Concerning restrictions and payment obligations in connection with nonstatutory rights, in particular trade secrets and other secret know-how, there are several different approaches. In Germany, for example, a licensor may not enforce payment obligations or other restrictions once the know-how has lost its secret character or becomes economically worthless or technically outdated.[211] With respect to package licenses, a German licensee may bring suit to obtain an adjustment in the payment obligation or termination of the entire contract if some of the rights become worthless and the amount being paid is not reasonably related to the value of the remaining rights.[212]

---

[208]*United States Reports*, vol. 326, p. 29 (Supreme Ct., 1945).
[209]*Federal Reporter, Second Series*, vol. 343, p. 381 (Tenth Circuit Ct. of Appeals, 1965).
[210]*Id.*, vol. 268, p. 769 (Third Circuit Ct. of Appeals, 1959).
[211]*Bericht der Bundeskartellamtes über seine Tätigkeit im Jahre 1974 sowie über Lage und Entwicklung auf seinem Ausgabengebeit*, p. 90.
[212]*Id.*, p. 104, item 3.

In some developing countries, such as Brazil and Serbia and Montenegro, national legislation prohibits any restriction on the free use of know-how once a reasonable period has lapsed following the transfer of the technology. This is so even if secret know-how has not lost its secret character.[213] In other developing countries, including Zambia, the obligation to pay for the use of secret know-how will cease when it "becomes public knowledge otherwise than through the fault of the licensee."[214]

By contrast, in the United States, a licensee's agreement to pay for the use of secret know-how will remain in effect even after the secret becomes public knowledge, so long as the licensee's contractual obligation was "freely undertaken in arm's length negotiations."[215]

RESTRICTIONS THAT APPLY AFTER THE EXPIRATION OF THE LICENSING AGREEMENT

Licensing agreements may impose obligations on the licensee that continue even after the expiration of the license. Common examples include noncompetition agreements, limitations on the right to carry out research and development activities related to the technology transferred by the licensor, and, in particular, the obligation to keep secret and not make use of confidential information after the licensing arrangement expires.

The national regulations that apply to these kinds of arrangements can be categorized into three groups. One group of countries—including Germany and the United States—allows licensors to impose most types of reasonable restrictions. Continuing restrictions on the use of statutory rights (i.e., patents, trademarks, and copyrights) are valid, but only if the statutory rights have not expired. Restrictions on the use of secret know-how are valid as long as the know-how has not entered the public domain.[216] Noncompetition agreements must be reasonable to avoid conflict with unfair competition laws. In particular, they must (1) be *ancillary* to the license (i.e., they must relate to the use of the subject matter of the license), (2) not be overly broad (i.e., they must relate only to matters in the license), and (3) be limited in duration and geographical scope.

The second group of countries, including India and the European Community, generally takes the same approach as the countries in the first group, except that they hold that a former licensee has a right to continue to use any acquired know-how (despite the expiration of the license) so long as the licensee pays reasonable compensation.[217]

The third group of countries—which includes Brazil, Mexico, the Philippines, Serbia and Montenegro, Venezuela, and Zambia—holds that a former licensee is free to use or dispose of the statutory property rights or secret know-how once the licensing agreement terminates.[218]

---

[213]Brazil, Normative Act No. 015 of the National Institute of Industrial Property, Articles 4.5.2(d)(vi), 5.5.2(d)(vi) (1975); Serbia and Montenegro, Law on Long-Term Cooperation in Production, Commercial-Technical Cooperation and the Awarding and Acquiring of Technology between Organizations of Associated Labor and Foreign Persons, Article 37(5) (1978).

[214]Zambia, Industrial Development Act, Article 15(b) (1977).

[215]See Aronson v. Quick Point Pencil Co., *United States Reports*, vol. 440, p. 266 (Supreme Ct., 1979).

[216]See *Bericht der Bundeskartellamtes über seine Tätigkeit im Jahre 1976 sowie über Lage und Entwicklung auf seinem Ausgabengebeit*, p. 107, for the German rules on statutory property rights and secret know-how. The U.S. rule on statutory property rights can be found in Scott Paper Co. v. Marcalus Mfg. Co., *United States Reports*, vol. 326, p. 249 (Supreme Ct., 1945); and the rule on secret know-how in Kewanee Oil Co. v. Bicron Corp., *id.*, vol. 416, p. 470 (1974).

[217]See India's Guidelines for Industries, Chap. 3, Article 9.ix (1976–1977). For the EU's position, see the decision of the European Commission in Kabelmetal/Luchaire, *Official Journal*, No. L 222, p. 34 (August 22, 1975).

[218]See Brazil, Normative Act No. 015 of the National Institute of Industrial Property, Articles 4.5.2(d)(vi), 5.2.(d)(vi), 6.5.2(b) (1975); Mexico, Law on the Registration of the Transfer of Technology and the Use and Working of Patents, Trade Names, and Trade Marks, Article 7(xi) (December 29, 1972); the Philippines, Regulation to Implement Article 5 of Presidential Decree No. 1520 Establishing the Technology Board within the Ministry of Industry, Article 5.1(c)(1) (October 10, 1978); Venezuela, Decree No. 2442 on the Treatment of Foreign Capital, Trademarks, Patents, Licenses, and Royalties, Article 1 (1977); Serbia and Montenegro, Law on Long-Term Cooperation in Production, Commercial-Technical Cooperation and the Awarding and Acquiring of Technology between Organizations of Associated Labor and Foreign Persons, Article 37(5) (1978); Zambia, Industrial Development Act, Article 15(b) (1977).

F. COMPULSORY LICENSES

compulsory license: The grant, by state decree, of a license to use a statutory right when the owner has failed to work it.

As mentioned earlier, **compulsory licenses** are common in most countries, especially in developing countries. They arise when the owner of intellectual property (in particular, patents or copyrights) refuses or is unable to work the property in a particular country within a certain period of time. In such a case, a third party may apply for a compulsory license, which will be issued by the government without the consent of the owner.[219]

PATENTS

The International Convention for the Protection of Industrial Property (the Paris Convention) recognizes the right of countries to "grant . . . compulsory licenses to prevent abuses of the exclusive rights conferred by the patent."[220] The WTO's Agreement on Trade-Related Aspects of Intellectual Property Rights similarly allows its member countries to grant "use of the subject matter of a patent without the authorization of the right holder,"[221] provided that

- such use may only be permitted if, prior to such use, the proposed user has made efforts to obtain authorization from the right holder on reasonable commercial terms and conditions and that such efforts have not been successful within a reasonable period of time. This requirement may be waived by a Member in the case of a national emergency or other circumstances of extreme urgency or in cases of public non-commercial use. In situations of national emergency or in other circumstances of extreme urgency, the right holder shall, nevertheless, be notified as soon as reasonably practicable. In the case of public noncommercial use, where the government or contractor, without making a patent search, knows or has demonstrable grounds to know that a valid patent is or will be used by or for the government, the right holder shall be informed promptly.[222]

- such use shall be non-exclusive.[223]
- such use shall be non-assignable.[224]
- any such use shall be authorized predominantly for the supply of the domestic market of the Member authorizing such use.[225]
- the right holder shall be paid adequate remuneration in the circumstances of each case, taking into account the economic value of the authorization.[226] Reading 9-2 describes how compulsory licenses are sometimes used by countries to protect vital national interests.

---

[219] See Michael Scott, "Compulsory Licensing of Intellectual Property in International Transactions," *European Intellectual Property Review*, vol. 10, pp. 319–325 (1988).

[220] States with compulsory patent-licensing provisions include the member states of the African Intellectual Property Organization (Benin, Cameroon, the Central African Empire, Chad, Congo, Ivory Coast, Mauritania, Niger, Senegal, Togo, and Upper Volta), Algeria, Australia, Austria, Bangladesh, Barbados, Bermuda, Bolivia, Brazil, Bulgaria, Canada, Chile, China, Columbia, the Czech Republic, Denmark, Ecuador, Egypt, El Salvador, Finland, France, Germany, Greece, Guatemala, Guyana, Honduras, Hungary, Iceland, India, Iraq, Israel, Italy, Japan, Jordan, Libya, Luxembourg, Malawi, Malta, Mexico, Monaco, Namibia, Nauru, the Netherlands, New Zealand, Nigeria, Norway, Pakistan, Paraguay, Peru, the Philippines, Portugal, Romania, Russia, Serbia and Montenegro, Slovakia, South Africa, South Korea, Spain, Sri Lanka, Sweden, Switzerland, Taiwan, Thailand, Turkey, the United Kingdom, Uruguay, Zambia, and Zimbabwe.

[221] For an analysis of the TRIPs Agreement's compulsory license provisions and their application to pharmaceuticals, see James Love, "Compulsory Licensing: Models for State Practice in Developing Countries, Access to Medicine and Compliance with the WTO TRIPS Accord," Consumer Project on Technology (Prepared for the United Nations Development Program, January 21, 2001); see http://www.cptech.org/ip/health/cl/recommendedstatepractice.html.

[222] Agreement on Trade-Related Aspects of Intellectual Property Rights, Article 31(b) (1994).

[223] *Id.,* Article 31(d)

[224] *Id.,* Article 31(e)

[225] *Id.,* Article 31(f)

[226] *Id.,* Article 31(h).

≈ ✺✺✺ ≈

Reading 9-2 **COMPULSORY LICENSING OF PATENTS ON AIDS DRUGS: WTO RULES AND ACTIONS BY CERTAIN NATIONS**

Sources for the following reading include:

S.S. Abdool Karim , Introduction to *HIV/AIDS in South Africa* (eds. S.S. Abdool Karim and Q. Abdool Karim (pp. 405–418) (2006); Ricardo Amaral, "Brazil Bypasses Patent on Merck AIDS Drug," Reuters, May 4, 2007; Celia W. Dugger, "Thailand: Plan to Override Patent for AIDS Drug," *New York Times*, December 1, 2006. ; R.A. Smith and P.D. Siplon, *Drugs into Bodies: Global AIDS Treatment Activism* (2006); Donald G. McNeil, "India Alters Law on Drug Patents," *New York Times*, Mar. 24, 2005; "Pharmaceuticals: A Gathering Storm," *The Economist*, June 9, 2007; "Thai Health Ministry Breaks Patent, Issues Compulsor License for Abbott's Antiretriviral Kaletra," *Medical News Today*, Feb. 1, 2007; World Health Organization, "Significant Growth in Access to HIV Treatment in 2006—More Efforts Needed for Universal Access to Services," (retrieved Apr. 16, 2007). http://www.who.int/mediacentre/news/releases/2007/pr16/en/index.html

THE AIDS CRISIS

AIDS (Acquired Immunodeficiency Syndrome) is the most severe health issue facing the world. One author has described it as the 4th most deadly epidemic in the history of the world, after the Black Death (Bubonic Plague), the Spanish Flu of 1918–19, and malaria. (Abdool Karim, S.S., *HIV/AIDS in South Africa*, Cambridge University Press, London, 2005)

HIV (Human Immunodeficiency Virus) is a blood-borne pathogen that attacks immune cells or white blood cells which protect the body from disease. The first stage of the disease, called Acute Retroviral Syndrome, is characterized by symptoms very similar to [those of] mononucleosis, including fever, fatigue, muscle aches, loss of appetite and more. Many people do not realize they have such a serious disease at this point unless they are tested. During latency, the second stage, most of the symptoms disappear for a time (sometimes several years). Then the disease progresses into the third and terminal stage, called AIDS, where the patient's immune system is severely compromised and infections from fungi, bacteria and other viruses prove deadly due to a suppressed immune system.

There is no cure for AIDS and it can be a swift killer. However, with aggressive treatment, including use of highly active anti-retroviral therapy (HAART), very effective control of the disease can be achieved. Unfortunately, HAART is not widely used in the countries where it is most needed because of its high cost—approximately $10,000–15,000 per year per patient in 2004. In its 2006 report of the Global AIDS Epidemic, the World Health Organization (WHO) stated that there were 38.6 million people living with AIDS (0.6% of the world population) and 2.8 million deaths due to AIDS. The WHO estimated that in many poor countries in Africa, Asia and South America, less than 10% of the infected people who need anti-retroviral medication are receiving it.

The large pharmaceutical companies which make the most effective drugs have spent millions of dollars researching and testing these drugs, and vigorously protect and enforce their patent rights. AIDS activists and health groups believe that the drug companies' desires to earn high profits are keeping the life-saving drugs from people who need them. Many groups have raised ethical issues about the rights of the large drug firms (often called "Big Pharma") as opposed to the millions of poor people who could be saved if the drugs were made available at lower cost.

When the TRIPs agreement was reached in 1995, the developed nations made sure that intellectual property rights were fully protected (as this chapter has discussed). But as the AIDS epidemic spread, governments around the world began to demand that the drugs be sold to them more cheaply, or that compulsory licenses be issued so they could make the drugs locally at much lower cost.

The WTO Compulsory License Rule Modifications

At the request of African governments, and other lesser developed countries, the WTO re-visited the drug patent issue, regarding AIDS and other urgent questions of public health. At the 2001 Doha meeting of the WTO, new agreements were reached regarding the sections of TRIPS which allowed, in some cases, for compulsory licensing of drugs essential to public health. The following information is from the WTO website, in the section entitled "TRIPS and Pharmaceutical Patents." (http://www.WTO.org)

The Doha Declaration on TRIPs and Public Health

Some WTO member governments were unsure of how these TRIPs flexibilities would be interpreted, and how far their right to use them would be respected. A large part of this was settled at the Doha Ministerial Conference in November 2001. WTO member governments stressed that it is important to implement and interpret the TRIPs Agreement in a way that supports public health—by promoting both access to existing medicines and the creation of new medicines.

They therefore adopted a separate declaration on TRIPs and Public Health. They agreed that the TRIPs Agreement does not and should not prevent members from taking measures to protect public health. They underscored countries' ability to use the flexibilities that are built into the TRIPs Agreement, including compulsory licensing and parallel importing. And they agreed to extend exemptions on pharmaceutical patent protection for least-developed countries until 2016.

On one remaining question, they assigned further work to the TRIPs Council—to sort out how to provide extra flexibility, so that countries unable to produce pharmaceuticals domestically can obtain supplies of copies of patented drugs from other countries. (This is sometimes called the "Paragraph 6" issue, because it comes under that paragraph in the separate Doha declaration on TRIPs and public health.)

IMPORTING UNDER COMPULSORY LICENSING ('PAR.6')

Article 31(f) of the TRIPs Agreement says products made under compulsory licensing must be "predominantly for the supply of the domestic market". This applies to countries that can manufacture drugs—it limits the amount they can export when the drug is made under compulsory license. And it has an impact on countries unable to make medicines and therefore wanting to import generics. They would find it difficult to find countries that can supply them with drugs made under compulsory licensing.

The legal problem for exporting countries was resolved on 30 August 2003 when WTO members agreed on legal changes to make it easier for countries to import cheaper generics made under compulsory licensing if they are unable to manufacture the medicines themselves. When members agreed on the decision, the General Council chairperson also read out a statement setting out members' shared understandings on how the decision would be interpreted and implemented. This was designed to assure governments that the decision will not be abused.

"This is a historic agreement for the WTO," said then WTO Director-General Supachai Panitchpakdi. "The final piece of the jigsaw has fallen into place, al-

lowing poorer countries to make full use of the flexibilities in the WTO's intellectual property rules in order to deal with the diseases that ravage their people. It proves once and for all that the organization can handle humanitarian as well as trade concerns."

Carefully negotiated conditions apply to pharmaceutical products imported under the system. These conditions aim to ensure that beneficiary countries can import the generics without undermining patent systems, particularly in rich countries. They include measures to prevent the medicines from being diverted to the wrong markets. And they require governments using the system to keep all other members informed, although WTO approval is not required. At the same time, phrases such as "reasonable measures within their means" and "proportionate to their administrative capacities" are included to prevent the conditions becoming burdensome and impractical for the importing countries.

All WTO member countries are eligible to import under this decision. But 23 developed countries have announced voluntarily that they will not use the system to import. And after they joined the EU in 2004, another 10 Eastern European countries have been added to the list. And 11 more said they would only use the system to import in national emergencies or other circumstances of extreme urgency: Hong Kong, China, Israel, Korea, Kuwait, Macao, China, Mexico, Qatar, Singapore, Chinese Taipei, Turkey, United Arab Emirates.

COMPULSORY LICENSES ISSUED IN BRAZIL AND THAILAND

In February 2007 Thailand's Ministry of Public Health announced that it was "breaking" a patent on Abbott Laboratories' antiretroviral drug Kaletra by issuing a compulsory license to produce a lower-cost version, under the WTO rules allowing such action in a "national emergency." Thailand had, at that time, about 580,000 people living with HIV/AIDS and had launched a national drug program treating more than 82,000 HIV-positive people. However, Kaletra cost $347 per patient monthly, while the lower-cost version was expected to cost about $120 per patient monthly. "We have to do this," said the Thai Health Minister Mongkol Na Songkhla , "because we don't have enough money to buy safe and necessary drugs for the people under the universal health scheme."

The pharmaceutical companies criticized the decision. According to the chair of the Pharmaceutical industry association, "After the company does 10 years of research, then suddenly the Thai government would like to impose the compulsory license, taking away their property, their assets–this is not a good practice." (*Thai Health Ministry Breaks Patent, Issues Compulsory License for Abbott's Antiretroviral Kaletra*, MedicalNewsToday.com, Feb. 1, 2007)

Abbott Labs, the large U.S.-based drug company, was not happy. Abbott pulled its seven drug applications pending before health regulators in Thailand, thus cutting off the country's 65 million residents from new medications developed by the Chicago, Illinois, company. Abbott had issued massive price cuts on Kaletra in dozens of developing countries, and offered to submit a cheaper version of the drug to Thai regulators in exchange for continued patent protection, but so far the country has rebuffed any concessions, although discussions did continue.

Health Minister Mongkol has said, "the excessively high drug prices have obstructed us from achieving real universal access." Meanwhile drug industry officials are worried that other nations may adopt Thailand's practices. "This misguided focus on short-term 'budget fixes' could come at a far greater long-term cost, potentially limiting important incentives for research and development that are necessary to positively impact the lives of millions of patients worldwide," said the head of the American Pharmaceutical Association. (*U.S. Drugmaker Abbott, Thailand, Face Off in AIDS Drug Patent Stalemate*, FindLaw.com, June 7, 2007)

On May 4, 2007, Brazilian President Luiz Inacio Lula da Silva authorized Brazil to break the patent on the AIDS drug Efavirenz made by Merck & Co. and import a generic version from India instead. Efavirenz is the principal component in a 17-drug cocktail to treat AIDS and is used by 38% of AIDS patients. Talks with Merck broke off when the health ministry rejected the New Jersey (U.S.)-based drug company's offer to cut its $1.59 per pill price by 30%. Brazil wanted to pay what Merck charges Thailand, or $0.65 per pill. (*Brazil Bypasses Patent on Merck AIDS Drug*, Reuters, May 4, 2007)

Brazil's government provides free universal access to AIDS drugs and distributes condoms and syringes as part of a prevention program the United Nations has praised. The program has helped slow infection rates and avoid what experts predicted would become an epidemic. But government spending on antiretroviral drugs has doubled in the past 4 years. The health ministry said it plans to import a generic version of the drug from India, at about 45 cents per pill.

The government said the decision respects World Trade Organization rules, which agreed in 2001 that countries with emergency health issues could, within limits, break patent protection because of public health concerns. But the government stated that it is still willing to listen to any proposals from Merck.

AIDS activists hailed the decision. "This is certainly an important advance in terms of widening access. We are very happy that Brazil is moving in the right direction," said Michel Lotrowska, who heads AIDS treatment in Brazil for a humanitarian group, Medecins Sans Frontieres (Doctors Without Borders). Lotrowska said that "This is progress, as it's the only way to cut drug prices since patents don't allow a natural competition in the market." He said that this was the first time that Brazil had by-passed a patent under the WTO rules. (*Brazil to Break Merck AIDS Drug Patent to Lower Price*, Bloomberg.com, May 4, 2007)

Merck said it was "profoundly disappointed," but remained open to further discussions, calling the decision a misappropriation of intellectual property that would stifle research. The government agreed to pay Merck 1.5% of the price of the generic drug as a royalty for three years.

Other developing countries have dropped hints that they, too, might need to employ compulsory licensing. Drug company executives are furious, saying that compulsory licensing was meant to be used only as "a last resort," only in emergencies, and only after lengthy efforts to negotiate prices with firms. "It's easy to see Big Pharma as a source of evil," says Daniel Vasella, Chairman of Novartis, a Swiss drug giant. But he asserts that without patent protection, innovation will suffer and future generations will have fewer life-saving drugs–"which is equally unethical as lack of access" (*Pharmaceuticals: A Gathering Storm*, The Economist, June 9, 2007).

Other complicating issues are the role of middle-income countries and the rising generics industry. One analyst says that middle-income countries have long used the threat of compulsory licensing to win discounts, thus shifting the balance of power away from the drug companies. The result may be that these countries are getting cheaper drugs than poorer but quieter neighbors. "Brazil is not Rwanda, which cannot afford to pay," says Tadataka Yamada of the Gates Foundation, a huge charity.

One sure winner in the trend toward compulsory licensing is the generic drug industry. Under the TRIPS treaty, countries that invoke compulsory licensing but lack domestic manufacturing are allowed to import generic drugs from another country. Canada encourages firms to produce copycat drugs for just such a purpose. Several firms in India are producing large quantities of even cheaper generic drugs for export.

—◦◦◦—

statutory copyright license: Authorizes a third party to use a copyrighted work for a fee stipulated in the statute.

Copyrights

Two types of compulsory licensing apply to copyrights. A **statutory copyright license** authorizes third parties to use a copyrighted work in exchange for a fee, which is fixed either in the legislation itself or by a public or private agency authorized to fix, collect, and distribute

compulsory copyright license: Compels a copyright owner to grant a license but allows the owner to negotiate the fee.

license fees.[227] A **compulsory copyright license** compels a copyright owner to grant a license, but it allows the owner to negotiate the terms of the license (subject to the intervention of a court or an administrative tribunal if the parties cannot agree).

The Berne Convention for the Protection of Literary and Artistic Works recognizes the right of countries to impose compulsory licenses for broadcasting and recording. This right is limited, however, by the proviso that compulsory licenses may "not in any circumstances be prejudicial to the moral rights of the author, nor to his right to obtain equitable remuneration which, in the absence of agreement, shall be fixed by competent authority."[228]

Chapter Questions

Copyright Infringement

1. Alvin, Bob, Calvin, Don, and Edgar are friends who enroll in a university course to study international business law. The textbook required for the course costs $50, which the five friends agree is expensive. They agree to chip in $10 each and buy one copy from a bookstore. They then take the copy to the local Discount Copy Store and make five copies of the complete book for $15 a copy. Then they return the book to the bookstore and get a refund of their original purchase price. Have the five friends done anything wrong? If so, what? Explain.

Moral Rights of Authors and Artists

2. Elvira is an abstract painter with incredible talent but little fame. One of her paintings, entitled *Blue Lady 13*, is a work of intense power and sensuality. In 1990, she sold it to Mega Company for display in the main public entrance of the business's new headquarters building. Several art critics attending the opening of the building mistook the painting for a long-lost work of Pablo Picasso. They wrote about it in their newspaper columns as though they had made a great discovery. When people began flooding into the Mega Building to see *Blue Lady 13,* the directors of Mega were delighted. They even went so far as to put up a sign that said: "This painting, entitled *La Dama Azul*, was probably painted by Pablo Picasso during his blue period, ca. 1913." Is there anything that Elvira can do? Explain.

Can a Similar "Look and Feel" Be Copyright Infringement?

3. The First-to-Market Computer Software Company owns the copyright to a highly successful spreadsheet program—Blossom 3-2-1—which has dominated the worldwide market for several years. Recently, Clone Software Co. devised a look-alike program that does everything that the Blossom 3-2-1 program does, except that the Clone sells for only one-tenth the price of the original. First-to-Market has sued Clone for copyright infringement. Clone defends itself by saying that the coding of its program is entirely different from that of Blossom 3-2-1 and that the only similarity between the programs is that the images that appear on the computer screen and the key sequences used to operate the program are identical. Has Clone infringed First-to-Market's copyright? Explain.

Patents on Previously Known Technology

4. The Whopper Co. is a manufacturer of gumballs. The technology and know-how to do this are well known in the scientific and engineering community in Whopper's home country, where gumballs have been popular with consumers for decades. Whopper decided recently to expand into Country X and to introduce gumballs to a market that has never seen them before. Before doing so, Whopper filed for a patent in Country X. The local patent office examined the application as to form (it was fine), searched the local records to determine if the technology was known locally (it was not), and then published notice of the application in the *Patent Gazette* for public comment.

---

[227]Statutory licenses for the recording of musical works are provided, for example, in the United States, Copyright Act, § 115 (1976), and in the United Kingdom, Copyright Act, Article 12 (1956).

[228]Berne Convention for the Protection of Literary and Artistic Works, Article 11 bis, § 2 (broadcast rights) (1886). A similar provision relating to recording rights is in *id.*, Article 13(1).

There was no public comment, and the patent was issued. Now Bubble Co., a local Country X business, has begun manufacturing and selling gumballs in Country X that are identical to those being manufactured and sold by Whopper. Whopper brings suit for patent infringement. Bubble countersues to have Whopper's patent revoked. Who will win? Explain.

Trademarks and the Shape of Goods

5. Jacques Pierre manufactures and sells a line of perfume—Le Peux—in distinctively shaped containers that are instantly recognizable. May Jacques Pierre register the shape of the containers as a trademark? Explain. If not, how else might Jacques Pierre keep competitors from selling their perfumes in similar containers?

Non-Use of a Trademark

6. Barley Beer Co. owns the trademark "Super Suds" for use on bottled and canned beer in Country X. Barley has not used the mark in Country X for six years. Hops Beer Co. would like to use the mark, and it brings suit in a Country X court to have Barley's trademark revoked. Will Hops succeed? Explain.

Importation of Gray Market Goods

7. A Japanese firm, Omega Company, manufactures cassette tapes with the trademark TXX. Omega licensed Alpha Company to distribute and sell the tapes in Australia and Sigma Company to do the same in South Africa. The license with Sigma expired after three years, and Omega refused to renew the license. Sigma then began buying cassettes from Alpha in Australia in bulk quantities and importing them into South Africa. These tapes had no individual wrappers or labels, and Sigma affixed both wrappers and labels with the TXX trademark on the cassettes, which it then sold throughout South Africa. Omega, which owns the TXX trademark in South Africa, has brought suit to enjoin Sigma from importing the cassettes into South Africa. Will Omega succeed? Would it make any difference if Omega's license with Alpha forbade Alpha from selling tapes for export to South Africa? Explain.

8. "Preventing the importation of gray goods legitimately manufactured outside the country is, in reality, injurious to consumers and contrary to basic principles of unfair competition laws." Comment.

Legality of Patent Pools and Cross-Licensing Agreements

9. The world's seven principal manufacturers of widgets have entered into an agreement to exchange with each other for a period of seven years all of their patents, petty patents, and know-how, and to enter into jointly funded research and development activities to improve widgets. Is this agreement enforceable? Explain. Would it matter if all of the participants were located in the EU? Japan? The United States?

Noncompetition Clauses

10. The Slinky Co. is a manufacturer of revealing bedroom apparel, especially negligees and pajamas, which it sells through franchised retail outlets that operate under its trade name. The franchisees are prohibited from handling any other line of clothing. One franchisee has challenged this particular provision in court, arguing that it is an invalid noncompetition clause. Will the franchisee be successful? Explain.

CHAPTER 10
SALES

CHAPTER OUTLINE

L. Excuses For Nonperformance
Force Majeure
Dirty Hands
Chapter Questions

A. UNITED NATIONS CONVENTION ON CONTRACTS FOR THE INTERNATIONAL SALE OF GOODS

The 1980 United Nations Convention on Contracts for the International Sale of Goods (CISG) came into force January 1, 1988, climaxing more than fifty years of negotiations. CISG supersedes two earlier conventions, the Convention Relating to a Uniform Law on the International Sale of Goods (ULIS) and the Convention Relating to a Uniform Law on the Formation of Contracts for the International Sale of Goods (ULF), which were never widely adopted.

Support for ULIS and ULF was limited because they were drafted without the participation of the Third World or the Eastern bloc. CISG, on the other hand, is the work of more than 62 states and 8 international organizations. Adopted at a conference in Vienna in 1980, it incorporates rules from all the major legal systems. It has, accordingly, received widespread support from developed, developing, and communist countries. See Exhibit 10-1.

Ratifying Country	Became a Party on	Ratifying Country	Became a Party on
Argentina	January 1, 1988	Lesotho	January 1, 1988
Australia	April 1, 1989	Liberia	September 16, 2005
Austria	January 1, 1989	Lithuania	February 1, 1996
Belarus	November 1, 1990	Luxembourg	January 30, 1997
Belgium	November 1, 1997	Mauritania	September 1, 2000
Bosnia and Herzegovina	March 6, 1992	Mexico	January 1, 1989
Bulgaria	August 1, 1991	Moldova	November 1, 1995
Burundi	October 1, 1999	Mongolia	January 1, 1999
Canada	May 1, 1992	Montenegro	June 3, 2006
Chile	March 1, 1991	Netherlands	January 1, 1992
China	January 1, 1988	New Zealand	October 1, 1995
Colombia	August 1, 2002	Norway	August 1, 1989
		Paraguay	February 1, 2007
		Peru	April 1, 2000
Croatia	October 8, 1991	Poland	June 1, 1996
Cuba	December 1, 1995	Republic of Moldova	November 1, 1995
		Republic of Korea	March 1, 2005
Czech Republic	January 1, 1993	Romania	June 1, 1992
Denmark	March 1, 1990	Russia	September 1, 1991
Ecuador	February 1, 1993	Saint Vincent & the Grenadines	October 1, 2001
Egypt	January 1, 1988	Singapore	March 1, 1996
El Salvador	December 1, 2007	Serbia	April 27, 1992
Estonia	October 1, 1994	Slovakia	January 1, 1993
Finland	January 1, 1989	Slovenia	June 25, 1991
France	January 1, 1988	Spain	August 1, 1991
Gabon	January 1, 2006	Sweden	January 1, 1989
		Switzerland	March 1, 1991
Georgia	September 1, 1995	Syrian Arab Republic	January 1, 1988

EXHIBIT 10-1 Parties to the United Nations Convention on Contracts for the International Sale of Goods

Ratifying Country	Became a Party on	Ratifying Country	Became a Party on
Germany	January 1, 1991	The former Yugoslav Republic of Macedonia	
Greece	February 1, 1999		November 17, 1981
Guinea	February 1, 1992	Uganda	March 1, 1993
Honduras	November 1, 2003	Ukraine	February 1, 1991
Hungary	January 1, 1988	United States	January 1, 1988
Iceland	June 1, 2002	Uruguay	February 1, 2000
Iraq	April 1, 1991	Uzbekistan	December 1, 1997
Israel	February 1, 2003	Venezuela	
Italy	January 1, 1988	Zambia	January 1, 1988
Kyrgyzstan	June 1, 2000		
Latvia	August 1, 1998		

Source: Reprinted with permission of the United Nations Commission on International Trade Law (UNCITRAL).

CISG is organized in four parts: Part I (Articles 1 to 13) contains the convention's general provisions, including rules on the scope of its applications and rules of interpretation. Part II (Articles 14 to 24) governs the formation of contracts. Part III (Articles 25 to 88) governs the rights and obligations of buyers and sellers. Part IV (Articles 89 to 101) contains provisions for the ratification and the entry into force of the Convention.

B. TRANSACTIONS COVERED IN CISG

international sale: A sale involving a buyer and seller with places of business in different states.

CISG applies to contracts for the **international sale** of goods—that is, the buyer and seller must have their places of business in different states.[1] In addition, either (1) both of the states must be contracting parties to the convention or (2) the rules of private international law must "lead to the application of the law of a contracting state."[2]

CISG may apply even if the buyer's and seller's places of business are not in a contracting state. For example, assume that Seller has a place of business in State A (a noncontracting state) and Buyer a place of business in State B (also a noncontracting State). They enter into a contract in State C (which is a contracting state) and the Seller breaches performance in State C. Buyer brings an action in State B, whose choice-of-law rules point to the laws of State C as applying to the contract. Because State C is a contracting party and the transaction is international, CISG would apply.

This possibility—that the convention could apply in situations where neither the seller nor the buyer had a place of business in a contracting state—was a cause of concern for some

---

[1]Contracts carried out entirely within one country's borders are governed by that country's laws. In the United States, the principal domestic law governing the sales of goods is the Uniform Commercial Code (UCC); in the United Kingdom, the Sale of Goods Acts (1893 and 1979) apply; in France, sales of goods are regulated by both the law of obligations in the Civil Code (*Code Civil*) of 1804 and the Code of Commerce (*Code de Commerce*) of 1807; in Germany, the law of obligations in the Civil Code (*Bürgerliches Gesetzbuch*) of 1896 applies.
[2]UN Convention on Contracts for the International Sale of Goods, Article 1 (1980), provides: "(1) This Convention applies to contracts of sale of goods between parties whose places of business are in different states: (a) when the states are contracting states; or (b) when the rules of private international law lead to the application of the law of a contracting state. (2) The fact that the parties have their places of business in different states is to be disregarded whenever this fact does not appear either from the contract or from any dealings between, or from information disclosed by, the parties at any time before or at the conclusion of the contract. (3) Neither the nationality of the parties nor the civil or commercial character of the parties or of the contract is to be taken into consideration in determining the application of this Convention."

of the convention's drafters. They feared that the choice-of-law rules might lead to the application of one state's laws for the formation of a contract and to another state's laws for its performance. This could mean that only parts of CISG might apply, when the convention was meant to apply as a unified whole. As a consequence, the final provisions of the convention allow a ratifying state, if it wishes, to declare that it will apply CISG only when the buyer and seller are both from contracting states.[3]

OPTING IN AND OUT

While either the contracting states or the choice-of-law rules may direct that CISG apply, the parties to a contract may exclude (i.e., they may opt out) or modify its application by a **choice-of-law clause**.[4] Whether they can use that same clause to exclude a domestic law and adopt CISG in its place (i.e., opt in) depends on the rules of the state where the case is heard.

Case 10-1 deals with the question of when the CISG applies and what parties to a contract must do to opt out of the convention.

choice-of-law clause:
Contractual provision that identifies the law to be applied in the event of a dispute over the terms or the performance of the contract.

---

[3]*Id.*, Article 95 states: "Any state may declare at the time of the deposit of its instrument of ratification, acceptance, approval or accession that it will not be bound by subparagraph (1)(b) of Article 1 of this Convention." The United States, for one, has so declared.
[4]*Id.*, Article 6: "The parties may exclude the application of this Convention or, subject to Article 12, derogate from or vary the effect of any of its provisions."

Case 10-1 ASANTE TECHNOLOGIES, INC. v. PMC-SIERRA, INC.

United States, District Court for the Northern District of California.
Federal Supplement, Second Series, vol. 164, p. 1142 (2001).

DISTRICT JUDGE WARE:

I. Introduction

This lawsuit arises out of a dispute involving the sale of electronic components. Plaintiff, Asante Technologies Inc., filed the action in the Superior Court for the State of California, Santa Clara County, on February 13, 2001. Defendant, PMC-Sierra, Inc., removed the action to this Court, asserting federal question jurisdiction pursuant to *United States Code*, title 28, section 1331. Specifically, Defendant asserts that Plaintiff's claims for breach of contract and breach of express warranty are governed by the United Nations Convention on Contracts for the International Sale of Goods ("CISG"). Plaintiff disputes jurisdiction and filed [a] Motion to Remand. . . .

II. Background

The Complaint in this action alleges claims based in tort and contract. Plaintiff contends that Defendant failed to provide it with electronic components meeting certain designated technical specifications. Defendant timely removed the action to this Court on March 16, 2001.

Plaintiff is a Delaware corporation having its primary place of business in Santa Clara County, California. Plaintiff produces network switchers, a type of electronic component used to connect multiple computers to one another and to the Internet. Plaintiff purchases component parts from a number of manufacturers. In particular, Plaintiff purchases application-specific integrated circuits ("ASICs"), which are considered the control center of its network switchers, from Defendant.

Defendant is also a Delaware corporation. However, defendant asserts that, at all relevant times, its corporate headquarters, inside sales and marketing office, public relations department, principal warehouse, and most design and engineering functions were located in Burnaby, British Columbia, Canada. Defendant also maintains an office in Portland, Oregon, where many of its engineers are based. Defendant's products are sold in California through Unique Technologies, which is an authorized distributor of Defendant's products in North America. It is undisputed that Defendant directed Plaintiff to purchase Defendant's products through Unique, and that Defendant honored purchase orders solicited by Unique. Unique is located in California. Determining Defendant's "place of business" with respect to its contract with Plaintiff is critical to the question of whether the Court has jurisdiction in this case.

Plaintiff's Complaint focuses on five purchase orders. Four of the five purchase orders were submitted to Defendant through Unique as directed by Defendant. However, Plaintiff does not dispute that one of the purchase orders, dated January 28, 2000, was sent by fax directly to Defendant in British Columbia, and that Defendant processed the order in British Columbia. Defendant shipped all orders to Plaintiff's headquarters in California. Upon delivery of the goods, Unique sent invoices to Plaintiff, at which time Plaintiff tendered payment to Unique either in California or in Nevada.

***

Plaintiff now requests this Court to remand this action back to the Superior Court of the County of Santa Clara pursuant to *United States Code*, title 28, section 1447(c), asserting lack of subject matter jurisdiction. . . .

III. Standards

A defendant may remove to federal court any civil action brought in a state court that originally could have been filed in federal court.[5] When a case originally filed in state court contains separate and independent federal and state law claims, the entire case may be removed to federal court.[6]

The determination of whether an action arises under federal law is guided by the "well-pleaded complaint" rule.[7] The rule provides that removal is proper when a federal question is presented on the face of the Complaint.[8] However, in areas where federal law completely preempts state law, even if the claims are purportedly based on state law, the claims are considered to have arisen under federal law. Defendant has the burden of establishing that removal is proper. . . .

The Convention on Contracts for the International Sale of Goods ("CISG") is an international treaty which has been signed and ratified by the United States and Canada, among other countries. The CISG was adopted for the purpose of establishing "substantive provisions of law to govern the formation of international sales contracts and the rights and obligations of the buyer and the seller."[9] The CISG applies "to contracts of sale of goods between parties whose places of business are in different States . . . when the States are Contracting States."[10] Article 10 of the CISG provides that "if a party has more than one place of business, the place of business is that which has the closest relationship to the contract and its performance."

IV. Discussion

Defendant asserts that this Court has jurisdiction to hear this case pursuant to *United States Code*, title 28, section 1331, which dictates that the "district courts shall have original jurisdiction of all civil actions arising under the Constitution, laws, or treaties of the United States." Specifically, Defendant contends that the contract claims at issue necessarily implicate the CISG, because the contract is between parties having their places of business in two nations which have adopted the CISG treaty. . . .

A. Federal Jurisdiction Attaches to Claims Governed by the CISG Although the general federal question statute, *United States Code*, title 28, § 1331(a), gives district courts original jurisdiction over every civil action that "arises under the . . . treaties of the United States," an individual may only enforce a treaty's provisions when the treaty is self-executing, that is, when it expressly or impliedly creates a private right of action.[11] The parties do not dispute that the CISG properly creates a private right of action.[12] Therefore, if the CISG properly applies to this action, federal jurisdiction exists.

B. The Contract in Question Is Between Parties from Two Different Contracting States The CISG only applies when a contract is "between parties whose places of business are in different States."[13] If this requirement is not satisfied, Defendant cannot claim jurisdiction under the CISG. It is undisputed that Plaintiff's place of

[5]*United States Code*, title 28, § 1441(a). . . .

[6]*Id.*, § 1441(c).

[7]Franchise Tax Board v. Construction Laborers Vacation Trust, *United States Reports*, vol. 463, p. 1 (Supreme Ct. 1983).

[8]*Id.* at p. 9.

[9]U.S. Ratification of 1980 United Nations Convention on Contracts for the International Sale of Goods: Official English Text, *United States Code*, title 15, App. at p. 52 (1997).

[10]*United States Code*, title 15, App. Article 1 (1)(a).

[11]See Tel-Oren v. Libyan Arab Republic, *Federal Reporter, Second Series*, vol. 726, p. 774 at p. 808 (District of Columbia Circuit Ct. of Appeals 1984) (Judge Bork concurring). . . .

[12]See Delchi Carrier v. Rotorex Corp., *Federal Reporter, Third Series*, vol. 71, p. 1024 at p. 1027–28 (2nd Circuit Ct. of Appeals 1995). . . .

[13]*United States Code*, title 15, App. Article 1(1)(a).

business is Santa Clara County, California, U.S.A. It is further undisputed that during the relevant time period, Defendant's corporate headquarters, inside sales and marketing office, public relations department, principal warehouse, and most of its design and engineering functions were located in Burnaby, British Columbia, Canada. However, Plaintiff contends that, pursuant to Article 10 of the CISG, Defendant's "place of business" having the closest relationship to the contract at issue is the United States. [The court looked at Plaintiff's claim that Unique Technologies was an agent for PMC-Sierra and found no evidence of consent or authorization as an agent, and thus ruled that PMC'c place of business was in Canada.]

***

C. The Effect of the Choice of Law Clauses   Plaintiff next argues that, even if the Parties are from two nations that have adopted the CISG, the choice of law provisions in the "Terms and Conditions" set forth by both Parties reflect the Parties' intent to "opt out" of application of the treaty.[14] Article 6 of the CISG provides that "the parties may exclude the application of the Convention or, subject to Article 12, derogate from or vary the effect of any of its provisions."[15] Defendant asserts that merely choosing the law of a jurisdiction is insufficient to opt out of the CISG, absent express exclusion of the CISG. The Court finds that the particular choice of law provisions in the "Terms and Conditions" of both parties are inadequate to effectuate an opt out of the CISG.

Although selection of a particular choice of law, such as "the California Commercial Code" or the "Uniform Commercial Code" could amount to implied exclusion of the CISG, the choice of law clauses at issue here do not evince a clear intent to opt out of the CISG. For example, Defendant's choice of applicable law adopts the law of British Columbia, and it is undisputed that the CISG is the law of British Columbia.[16] Furthermore, even Plaintiff's choice of applicable law generally adopts the "laws of" the State of California, and California is bound by the Supremacy Clause to the treaties of the United States.[17] Thus, under general California law, the

CISG is applicable to contracts where the contracting parties are from different countries that have adopted the CISG. In the absence of clear language indicating that both contracting parties intended to opt out of the CISG, and in view of Defendant's Terms and Conditions which would apply the CISG, the Court rejects Plaintiff's contention that the choice of law provisions preclude the applicability of the CISG.

D. Federal Jurisdiction Based upon the CISG Does Not Violate the Well-Pleaded Complaint Rule   The Court rejects Plaintiff's argument that removal is improper because of the well-pleaded complaint rule. The rule states that a cause of action arises under federal law only when the plaintiff's well-pleaded complaint raises issues of federal law.[18]

It is undisputed that the Complaint on its face does not refer to the CISG. However, Defendants argue that the preemptive force of the CISG converts the state breach of contract claim into a federal claim. Indeed, Congress may establish a federal law that so completely preempts a particular area of law that any civil complaint raising that select group of claims is necessarily federal in character.[19]

It appears that the issue of whether or not the CISG preempts state law is a matter of first impression. In the case of federal statutes, "the question of whether a certain action is preempted by federal law is one of congressional intent. The purpose of Congress is the ultimate touchstone."[20] Transferring this analysis to the question of preemption by a treaty, the Court focuses on the intent of the treaty's contracting parties.[21]

In the case of the CISG treaty, this intent can be discerned from the introductory text, which states that "the adoption of uniform rules which govern contracts for the international sale of goods and take into account the different social, economic and legal systems would contribute to the removal of legal barriers in international trade and promote the development of international trade."[22] The CISG further recognizes the importance of "the development of international trade

---

[14]Plaintiff's Terms and Conditions provides "APPLICABLE LAW. The validity [and] performance of this [purchase] order shall be governed by the laws of the state shown on Buyer's address on this order." The buyer's address as shown on each of the Purchase Orders is San Jose, California.
    Defendant's Terms and Conditions provides "APPLICABLE LAW: The contract between the parties is made, governed by, and shall be construed in accordance with the laws of the Province of British Columbia and the laws of Canada applicable therein, which shall be deemed to be the proper law hereof. . . ." It is undisputed that British Columbia has adopted the CISG.
[15]*United States Code*, title 15, App. Article 6.
[16]International Sale of Goods Act, chap. 236, *Statutes of British Columbia*, vol. 1996, § 1 *et seq.*
[17]U.S. Constitution, Article 6, clause 2: "This Constitution, and the laws of the United States which shall be made in pursuance thereof; and all treaties made, or which shall be made, under the authority of the United States, shall be the supreme law of the land."
[18]Gully v. First National Bank, *United States Reports*, vol. 299, p. 109 (Supreme Ct.1936). . . .
[19]Metropolitan Life Ins. Co. v. Taylor, *id.*, vol. 481, p. 58 at p. 62 (Supreme Ct.1987). . . .
[20]Pilot Life Ins. Co. v. Dedeaux, *id.*, vol. 481, p. 41 at p. 45 (Supreme Ct.1987).
[21]See Husmann v. Trans World Airlines, Inc., *Federal Reporter, Third Series*, vol. 169, p. 1151 at p. 1153 (8th Circuit Ct. of Appeals 1999). . . .
[22]*United States Code*, title 15, App. 15 at p. 53.

on the basis of equality and mutual benefit."[23] These objectives are reiterated in the President's Letter of Transmittal of the CISG to the Senate as well as the Secretary of State's Letter of Submittal of the CISG to the President.[24] The Secretary of State, George P. Shultz, noted:

> Sales transactions that cross international boundaries are subject to legal uncertainty—doubt as to which legal system will apply and the difficulty of coping with unfamiliar foreign law. The sales contract may specify which law will apply, but our sellers and buyers cannot expect that foreign trading partners will always agree on the applicability of United States law. ... The Convention's approach provides an effective solution for this difficult problem. When a contract for an international sale of goods does not make clear what rule of law applies, the Convention provides uniform rules to govern the questions that arise in making and performance of the contract.[25]

The Court concludes that the expressly stated goal of developing uniform international contract law to promote international trade indicates the intent of the parties to the treaty to have the treaty preempt state law causes of action.

***

V. Conclusion

For the foregoing reasons, Plaintiff's Motion to Remand is DENIED.... ■

CASEPOINT: In this case, the real legal issue before the U.S. federal court was whether it had jurisdiction of this case. In order to possess jurisdiction to hear the case, it was necessary that federal law was involved. The court considered whether the parties were from different states (nations), decided that they were, and thus the CISG applied to this contract dispute. Then the court analyzed the plaintiff's claim that the parties had opted

MAP 10-1   British Columbia and California (2001)

out of the CISG (as they are entitled to do) but found little factual evidence to support that argument. Finally, the court ruled that when Congress ratified the CISG, it intended to preempt conflicting state laws; thus, although the CISG was not specifically mentioned in the complaint, it was the law that applied here.

---

[23]*Id.*
[24]*Id.*, at pp. 70–72.
[25]*Id.*, at p. 71.

━━⟨⟩⟨⟩⟨⟩━━

SALES DEFINED

sale: The exchange of goods for an amount of money or its equivalent.

CISG does not directly define **sales**. Instead, it speaks of the seller's and buyer's obligations. The seller is to "deliver the goods, hand over any documents relating to them and transfer the property in the goods, as required by the contract and this Convention"[26]; the buyer, in exchange, is to "pay the price."[27] Although not stated in a single article, this is the same definition found in many domestic laws, including the U.S. Uniform Commercial Code, which describes a sale as the "passing of title from the seller to the buyer for a price."[28]

---

[26]UN Convention on Contracts for the International Sale of Goods, Article 30.
[27]*Id.*, Article 54.
[28]Uniform Commercial Code, § 2-106.

GOODS DEFINED

good: A movable, tangible object. For the purposes of CISG, goods do not include things bought for personal use or at an auction or foreclosure sale, nor may they be oceangoing vessels or aircraft.

CISG also does not directly define **goods**. Instead, it defines those kinds of sales that are not governed by the convention. Six specific categories are excluded. Three are based on the nature of the transaction, three on the kinds of goods. The excluded transactions are (1) "goods bought for personal, family, or household use"; (2) auction sales; and (3) sales "on execution or otherwise by authority of law." The excluded goods are (1) stocks, shares, investment securities, negotiable instruments, or money; (2) ships, vessels, hovercraft, or aircraft; and (3) electricity.[29]

The drafters adopted this list of exclusions on the assumption that the convention applies only to goods that are movable and tangible. The nature of goods was made clearer in the French-language version of the 1964 *Convention Relating to a Uniform Law on the International Sale of Goods*, which used the phrase *objets mobiliers corporels*.[30] In CISG, however, the French version uses the term *marchandises*.[31] Regardless, legal usage internationally is consistent in its interpretation of the word *goods* (*marchandises*). In addition, many transactions, such as the sale of real property, are by their very nature domestic rather than international. The list of exclusions, therefore, only includes goods that the drafters felt were not already obviously excluded.[32]

Goods bought for personal, family, or household use are excluded for two reasons. First, a double standard could arise if different rules governed sales by local shopkeepers to foreigners. Second, many local laws protect consumers, and that protection would be lost if CISG applied. This exclusion does not apply, however, "unless" the seller "knew or ought to have known" that the goods were bought for personal use or consumption.

This "unless" clause is best illustrated by an example. Seller, a computer retailer, receives an order for a computer from Buyer, a resident of State B. The order is for a powerful, expensive computer of the sort commonly bought for use in business firms. When a dispute about the sale arises, Seller relies on CISG. Buyer then offers evidence that he bought the computer for his personal use as a hobbyist. In this example, Seller should be able to show that he neither knew nor ought to have known that the computer was bought for personal use. The convention would then apply.

Auction sales, sales on execution, and sales "otherwise by authority of law" are excluded because of the uniqueness of the transactions involved. Auction sales present problems in determining when the contract was formed. Executions and other kinds of forced sales do not involve the negotiation of terms by the parties. Special local laws govern these sales, and CISG does not disturb that arrangement.

Transactions in stocks, shares, investment securities, negotiable instruments, and money are excluded because a wide variety of local rules govern them, and the drafters could not agree on how to harmonize the rules in this convention. However, the drafters did not exclude a long list of other similar assets, such as patent rights, copyrights, and trademarks, whose international sale is now governed by CISG.

Sales of ships, vessels, hovercraft, aircraft, and electricity were also excluded from CISG because most domestic legal systems have special rules that apply to them.

MIXED SALES

A seller of goods often furnishes services when delivering a product to a buyer. For example, restaurants provide both food and service. Manufacturers that contract to produce goods similarly provide both goods and services. Are these sales of goods or sales of services?

CISG looks upon mixed sales and services contracts—the restaurant example—as sales of goods, unless "the preponderant part of the obligations" of the seller "consists in the supply

---

[29]UN Convention on Contracts for the International Sale of Goods, Article 2 (1980).
[30]French: "tangible movable objects."
[31]French: "goods," "wares," or "commodities."
[32]See John Honnold, *Uniform Law for International Sales under the 1980 United Nations Convention*, pp. 85–87 (1982), for a discussion of the drafters' intent on the meaning of goods.

of labor or other services." One may assume that *preponderant* has its normal meaning of "more than half," but whether this is measured by the cost, the sale price, or some other basis is something the convention does not make clear.

Contracts for goods to be manufactured are treated by CISG as sales of goods unless the buyer "undertakes to supply a substantial part of the materials." Although *substantial* probably means less than half, how much less is unclear. The French-language version of the convention suggests a possible test, as it uses the term *une part essentielle*.[33] Thus, if the buyer provides the components essential to the manufacture of a product—regardless of their size or value—the convention would not apply.

C. CONTRACTUAL ISSUES EXCLUDED FROM THE COVERAGE OF CISG

Courts face a variety of issues in determining if a contract should be enforced or if a remedy should be granted when a contract is breached. CISG only deals with (1) the formation of the contract and (2) the remedies available to the buyer and seller. It specifically excludes questions about (1) the legality of the contract, (2) the competency of the parties, (3) the rights of third parties, and (4) liability for death or personal injury.[34]

ILLEGALITY AND INCOMPETENCY

Domestic laws vary greatly in determining when a contract is illegal and when it is void or voidable because one or both of the parties are incompetent. Contraband, for example, cannot be legally sold. However, what constitutes contraband in one country may not in another; for example, alcohol, drugs, pornography, religious tracts, political tracts, and so on, may be treated differently from one country to the next. Similarly, the extent to which a contract can be avoided because it was fraudulently obtained varies greatly. Domestic rules on insanity, infancy, and other contractual disabilities are equally diverse.

The drafters of the convention recognized that legality and competency are sensitive issues that reflect the mores and social values of particular cultures. To avoid a disagreement that might have jeopardized the adoption of CISG, these questions were left for settlement by domestic law.

THIRD-PARTY CLAIMS AND PERSONAL INJURIES

Equally diverse domestic laws apply to the matters of third-party claims and the liability of a seller for death or personal injury. Again, to avoid the possibility of a deadlock in the drafting of the convention, the drafters left them out.

PREEMPTION

preempt: To take precedence over.

To determine if CISG applies to a particular contractual issue, one must look to the convention itself, not to domestic law. If the convention does apply, domestic law is **preempted**. That is, the remedies provided in CISG are the only remedies available. This result is the consequence of the convention's basic function: to establish uniform rules for international sales contracts.[35]

---

[33]French: "an essential part."
[34]UN Convention on Contracts for the International Sale of Goods, Article 4 (1980), provides: "This Convention governs only the formation of the contract of sale and the rights and obligations of the seller and the buyer arising from such a contract. In particular, except as otherwise expressly provided in this Convention, it is not concerned with: (a) the validity of the contract or any of its provisions or of any usage; (b) the effect which the contract may haveon the property in the goods sold."

Article 5 states: "This Convention does not apply to the liability of the seller for death or personal injury caused by the goods to any person."
[35]*Id.*, Article 7(1).

Preemption applies both in cases where domestic law calls the matter contractual and where it gives it some other name. Consider the following example. A seller delivers to a buyer chemicals that are defective. The chemicals spontaneously burst into flames, burning down the buyer's warehouse. In such a circumstance, some domestic law systems would impose a sanction in tort that is commonly called *product liability*. To prove product liability, the injured buyer must typically show (1) that the goods failed to conform to the contract, (2) that the damage resulted from the defect, and (3) that the seller failed to exercise due care. Under CISG, however, a remedy is available if the goods failed to conform to the contract (Article 35) and damage resulted from the defect (Article 74). Despite the fact that local law requires a third proof element to establish product liability, this does not mean that a tort or delict remedy is available. The only permissible remedy is the one provided by CISG.

For reference, a summary comparison of CISG rules and the sale-of-goods rules in France and the United States is set out in Exhibit 10-2

D. INTERPRETING CISG

The underlying goal of CISG is the creation of a uniform body of international commercial sales law. In deciding questions governed by the convention, Article 7(2) directs a court to look to the following sources, in the following order: (1) the convention, (2) the general principles on which the convention is based, and (3) the rules of private international law.

THE CONVENTION

When the words of CISG itself require interpretation, Article 7(1) directs a court to consider (1) the international character of the convention, (2) the need to promote uniformity in the convention's application, and (3) the observance of good faith. Article 7(1), however, does not describe the sources the court may—or must—use in making its interpretation.

plain meaning rule: A statute or treaty is to be interpreted only from the words contained within the statute or treaty.

travaux préparatoires: (French: "preparatory work.") The legislative history of a statute or treaty, that is, the negotiations leading up to its final drafting and adoption.

On its face, CISG implies that a court may use only the **plain meaning** of the language in the convention. The plain meaning rule is common to countries whose judicial practices follow those of England. In England, at least until very recently, courts may deduce the meaning of legislation only from the words contained in a statute.[36] In most other countries, however, including the United States and the civil law countries, the courts also look to a statute's legislative history—the *travaux préparatoires*—to determine its intent. Additionally, when an international tribunal interprets a treaty, its legislative history is commonly used both to confirm the meaning derived from the treaty's terms and to determine the treaty's meaning when the terms are ambiguous or obscure.[37] Considering the widespread general use of *travaux préparatoires*, it seems likely that most courts will turn to it in interpreting CISG's provisions, especially as the record of the convention's preparation is now widely available.[38]

---

[36]In 1980, the English House of Lords used legislative history in interpreting the Warsaw Convention's provisions on the liability of air carriers. In the landmark decision of Fothergill v. Monarch Airlines, *All England Law Reports,* vol. 1980, pt. 2, p. 696 (1980), a majority of opinions relied on the rules of interpretation in the Vienna Convention on the Law of Treaties (1969). Article 32 of that treaty expressly provides for the use of "the preparatory work of the treaty and the circumstances of its conclusion" in interpreting international conventions.

[37]Article 31(1) of the Vienna Convention on the Law of Treaties (1969) provides: "A treaty shall be interpreted in good faith in accordance with the ordinary meaning to be given to the terms of the treaty in their context and in the light of its object and purpose." Article 32 adds: "Recourse may be had to supplementary means of interpretation including the preparatory work of the treaty and the circumstances of its conclusion, in order to confirm the meaning resulting from the application of Article 31, or to determine the meaning when the interpretation according to Article 31 (a) leaves the meaning ambiguous or obscure; or (b) leads to a result which is manifestly absurd or unreasonable."

[38]See John Honnold, *Uniform Law for International Sales under the 1980 United Nations Convention* (1982), and John Honnold, *Documentary History of the Uniform Law for International Sales* (1989).

Contract Provision	French Civil Code and Code of Commerce	United States Uniform Commercial Code	United Nations Convention on Contracts for the International Sale of Goods
Sale is a passage of title for a price.	Yes	Yes	Yes
Goods are movable and tangible things.	Yes	Yes	Yes
Mixed sales and service transactions that predominantly involve the delivery of goods are governed by sales law provisions.	Yes	Yes	Yes
Sales law applies only to merchants.	No	No	Yes
A merchant is	A person who engages in a defined list of commercial acts.	A person who deals in goods of the kind involved in a particular transaction, or who by his occupation holds himself out as having special knowledge or skill related to the sale, or who is represented by a merchant.	A person who has a place of business.
Parties must act in good faith.	Yes	Yes	Yes
Unconscionable contracts are unenforceable.	Yes	Yes	Yes
A sales contract must be memorialized in a writing signed by the party against whom it is being asserted.	Yes, if the party against whom the contract is being asserted is a nonmerchant and the price is €800 or more; no, if the party against whom the contract is being asserted is a merchant.	Yes, if the price is $500 or more; no, if both parties are merchants and one of the parties sends a written confirmation that is not promptly objected to.	No
Subjective intent of parties may be used to interpret contracts.	Yes	No	Yes
Parol evidence is admissible to interpret written contracts the parties intended to be a final expression of their agreement.	Yes, if the party objecting is a merchant; no, if the party is a nonmerchant unless the parol evidence is supported by a written memorandum originating with the objecting party.	No	Yes

EXHIBIT 10-2   Comparative Summary of French, United States, and United Nations Convention Sale of Goods Provisions

Contract Provision	French Civil Code and Code of Commerce	United States Uniform Commercial Code	United Nations Convention on Contracts for the International Sale of Goods
A contract may be explained or interpreted by a course of performance, a course of dealing, and a usage of trade.	Yes	Yes	Yes
Terms that should not be left open are	Price	Quantity	Price and quantity.
Firm offers can be made by	Anyone	Merchants in a signed writing.	Merchants
If offeror does not specify a medium for acceptance, any reasonable medium may be used.	Yes	Yes	Yes
An offer may be revoked prior to an acceptance's	Receipt	Dispatch	Dispatch
Acceptance is effective upon	Receipt	Dispatch	Receipt
Acceptance is valid even if it contains additional terms.	No	Yes	No
Additional terms in an acceptance become proposals for addition that offeror may accept or reject.	No	Yes, when either party is a nonmerchant.	No
Additional terms become part of a contract unless promptly objected to by offeror.	No	Yes, if both parties are merchants.	No
Offeree who accepts by performance must notify the offeror within a reasonable time after beginning performance.	No	Yes	No
The scope of a specific performance decree is to	Carry out any terms of the contract.	Deliver the goods.	Same as local law.
Place for delivery	(1) As specified in contract; (2) Location of goods at time of sale; (3) Seller's residence.	(1) As specified in contract; (2) Seller's business place; (3) Seller's residence; (4) Known location of goods.	(1) As specified in contract; (2) Carrier's business place; (3) Known location of goods.
Time for delivery	(1) As specified in contract.	(1) As specified in contract; (2) Reasonable time after contracting.	(1) As specified in contract; (2) Reasonable time after contracting.
			(*continued*)

EXHIBIT 10-2 *(continued)*

Contract Provision	French Civil Code and Code of Commerce	United States Uniform Commercial Code	United Nations Convention on Contracts for the International Sale of Goods
Conformity of goods (guarantees and warranties)	(1) Fit for ordinary purpose; (2) Fit for a particular purpose.	(1) Warranty of merchantability; (2) Warranty of fitness for a particular purpose.	(1) Fit for ordinary purpose; (2) Fit for a particular purpose.
Waiver of guarantees conformity requires use of specific words.	No	Yes	No
Waiver of guarantee of conformity must be made expressly.	Yes	Yes	No
Buyer must promptly notify seller of any nonconformity.	Yes	Yes	Yes
Seller may cure defects before delivery time.	Yes	Yes	Yes
Seller may cure defects after delivery time.	No	No	No
Time and place when buyer must pay is	Delivery	Delivery	Delivery
Seller must make formal demand for payment.	Yes	No	No
Buyer must pay price once risk passes.	Yes	Yes	Yes
Risk passes when goods are delivered.	Yes	Yes	Yes
Risk passes for goods sent by carrier when the goods are identified to contract and delivered to carrier.	Yes	Yes	Yes
Remedies and damages are cumulative.	Yes	Yes	Yes
A period of grace is available to delay the granting of remedies.	Yes	No	No
Nonconforming party is entitled to Nachfrist notice.	Yes	No	Yes
Buyers' remedies include price reduction.	Yes	No	Yes
General remedies include suspension of performance and anticipatory avoidance.	Yes	Yes	Yes
Injured party has duty to mitigate damages.	Yes	Yes	Yes
Excuse of force majeure is available.	Yes	Yes	Yes

EXHIBIT 10-2 *(continued)*

In addition to *travaux préparatoires*, courts in most countries use case law to interpret statutes and treaties.[39] At present, the number of cases that have interpreted CISG are few. Undoubtedly, this situation will change quickly. As it does, the courts will have to keep in mind the convention's admonitions: that CISG is an international treaty, that its purpose is to establish uniform international rules, and that the courts are bound by the principle of good faith in interpreting the convention. Because CISG is an international treaty, the courts of many countries will interpret it. The directive that it be interpreted to promote uniformity in its application compels courts to examine and follow the decisions of the courts in other contracting states. The requirement to use good faith means that courts must accept foreign decisions as precedents and depart from them only when they are clearly distinguishable, clearly erroneous, or no longer applicable to changed international circumstances.[40]

GENERAL PRINCIPLES

general principles: Those principles underlying and common to a statutory scheme or treaty.

CISG calls for courts to look to the **general principles** on which the convention is based when interpreting its provisions, but it gives no list of general principles. It is for the courts to divine those principles. The following two have been suggested: (1) A party to a contract has the duty to communicate information needed by the other party, and (2) parties have the obligation to mitigate damages resulting from a breach.[41] Both concepts appear, in varying forms, throughout the convention.[42]

Although CISG does not give a list of general principles, it does set out the mechanism for determining them. They must be derived (as is the case for the suggestions listed above) from particular sections of the convention and then extended, by analogy, to the case at hand.[43] In choosing this particular mechanism, the drafters rejected the adoption of general principles derived from public or private international law, as well as from domestic law codes. This limitation on the sources that the courts may turn to in creating general principles was consciously made, and it reflects the drafters' concern for uniformity and consistency, both in the drafting and in the evolution of the convention.

RULES OF PRIVATE INTERNATIONAL LAW

The rules of private international law are the third and final source for interpreting the convention. They may be used, however, only when CISG itself does not directly settle a matter or when the matter cannot be resolved by the application of a general principle derived from the convention itself.

Private international law rules vary from country to country. Some states—notably those in Central and Eastern Europe—have enacted private international law codes,

[39]Scholarly writings (doctrine) are also widely relied on in civil law and the United States to interpret legislative materials. In England, and in the countries that derive their judicial practice from England, scholarly writing is generally given little weight. Because the convention does not name the sources that courts are to use in its interpretation, this disparity will undoubtedly continue.
[40]The use of case law will present difficulties when different courts come to different conclusions based on similar facts. Absent the existence of a single appellate court to harmonize differing opinions, the principle of good faith imposes on every court that is hearing a dispute the obligation to harmonize its decision with those of other courts and, where there are conflicting precedents, to harmonize the precedents. The principle of good faith that appears in CISG is apparently limited. The drafters meant that it be used only in interpreting the provisions of the convention, and not as a loose or general obligation imposed on the parties. This is in contrast to its much broader application in the German Civil Code, § 242; the United States Uniform Commercial Code, § 1–203; and other code systems. However, one might note that the drafters of the German Civil Code also originally meant for good faith to be used in a similar limited way. Nevertheless, German judges ignored the drafters' intention because the principle proved to be a convenient tool for adding flexibility. One can also anticipate that courts accustomed to a more liberal use of the concept will apply it in a similar liberal way when interpreting CISG.
[41]John Honnold, *Uniform Law for International Sales under the 1980 United Nations Convention*, pp. 131–132 (1982).
[42]The general duty to communicate is in the UN Convention on Contracts for the International Sale of Goods, Articles 19(2), 21(2), 26, 39(1), 48(2), 65, 71(3), 72(2), 79(4), and 88(1) (1980). The duty to mitigate is in *id.*, Articles 77, 85, and 86.
[43]*Id.*, Article 7(2), states: "Questions concerning matters governed by this Convention which are not expressly settled in it are to be settled in conformity with the general principles on which it is based. . . ." The mechanism is described in more detail in John Honnold, *Uniform Law for International Sales under the 1980 United Nations Convention*, p. 132 (1982).

whereas others—such as the English common law countries—rely on case law. This will undoubtedly produce inconsistent holdings. Nevertheless, these rules are much more harmonious internationally than other rules of domestic law, and adoption of their use represents a pragmatic decision by the authors of the convention. By allowing courts to turn to the rules of private international law, the convention avoids the possibility that courts will adopt interpretive aids on an entirely *ad hoc*[44] basis.

E. INTERPRETING SALES CONTRACTS

In determining if a contract has been made, in interpreting its terms, and in ascertaining if it has been performed as agreed, courts throughout the world look at the statements, the conduct, and the usages and practices of the parties, as well as the practices of the trade to which the contract relates. Article 8 of CISG establishes rules for interpreting the statements and conduct of the parties; Article 9 deals with usages and practices.

STATEMENTS AND CONDUCT OF THE PARTIES

subjective intent approach: Rule that contracts should be interpreted according to the actual intent and understanding of the parties at the time they made their agreement.

A contract is sometimes said to be formed only when the parties have a "meeting of the minds" or a "common intent." This comes from the idea, commonly accepted in many civil law countries, that parties are only bound by a contract when they subject their "will" to its terms. Such a **subjective approach**, however, has its problems. If a dispute arises about the meaning of the contract, the parties are hardly impartial witnesses about what was in their minds at the time they made the contract. This shortcoming has led some courts, notably those in the common law countries, to reject completely the use of subjective intent in the interpretation of a contract. As Oliver Wendell Holmes, a noted American judge, once wrote: "The law has nothing to do with the actual state of the parties' minds. In contract, as elsewhere, it must go by the externals, and judge parties by their conduct."[45]

objective intent approach: Rule that contracts should be interpreted according to the understanding that a reasonable person would have had at the time the agreement was made.

Of course, the subjective intent of the parties is the best evidence for interpreting a contract—if it can be fairly ascertained—and CISG allows courts to turn to it first. Thus, courts are to use the subjective intent of a speaker, but only if "the other party knew or could not have been unaware" of the speaker's intent. When a speaker's intent is not clear, CISG directs the court to look at **objective intent**. In that case, a party's statements and other conduct "are to be interpreted according to the understanding that a reasonable person of the same kind as the other party would have had in the same circumstances."

NEGOTIATIONS

negotiations: The preliminary discussions leading up to the adoption of an agreement.

When a court is to determine intent—be it the party's subjective intent or a reasonable person's objective understanding—Article 8(3) of CISG directs that "due consideration" be given "to all relevant circumstances," including (1) the **negotiations** leading up to the contract, (2) the practices that the parties have established between themselves, and (3) the parties' conduct after they agree to the contract.

common law parol evidence rule: When a contract describes itself as being complete and final, preliminary or informal agreements made prior to or at the same time the contract was made will be ignored when interpreting it.

The purpose of Article 8(3) is to do away with the technical rules that domestic courts sometimes use to interpret contracts. One notable example is the common law's **parol evidence rule**.[46] This rule forbids a court from considering any "prior" or any "contemporaneous oral understanding" when it is interpreting a writing that the parties intended as a "final expression of their agreement."[47] Article 8(3) specifically allows courts to consider the parties' preliminary negotiations when they interpret a contract.

---

[44]Latin: "for this." Something done for a specific purpose, circumstance, or case.
[45]Oliver W. Holmes, *The Common Law*, p. 242 (M. A. DeWolfe Howe, ed., 1963).
[46]CISG does not directly mention the parol evidence rule. To have done so, one commentator has suggested, "would have mystified jurists from legal systems that have no such rule." John Honnold, *Uniform Law for International Sales under the 1980 United Nations Convention*, p. 142 (1982).
[47]United States, Uniform Commercial Code, § 2-202.

Nevertheless, while Article 8(3) gives a court the flexibility to consider all relevant evidence, Article 6 allows the parties to "derogate from or vary the effect of" any of the provisions of the convention. Thus, if the parties include a contract term (often called an *integration clause*) that directs a court to ignore all prior or contemporaneous agreements, the court will have to give effect to that term. In other words, if the parties choose to adopt the parol evidence rule, they can do so. However, unless they specifically do so, the court will look at all the relevant circumstances of the case.

In addition to considering prior and contemporaneous conduct, CISG lets a court consider the parties' subsequent conduct. Again, this is contrary to the practice in some domestic tribunals.[48] CISG, however, does reflect the most widely followed practice, and, as is the case for parol evidence, the parties are free to insert a provision in their contract excluding its consideration.

PRACTICES AND USAGES

practice: The method of performance established between parties by their actions or conduct.
usage: The customary method of performing or acting that is followed by a particular group of people, such as people within a particular trade.

Both Article 8(3) and Article 9(1) of CISG state that parties are bound by "any **practices** which they have established between themselves." Article 9(1) also allows a court to consider any **usages** that the parties agreed to,[49] and Article 9(2) lets it consider "a usage of which the parties knew or ought to have known and which in international trade is widely known to, and regularly observed by parties to contracts of the type involved in the particular trade concerned."

Article 9(2) was a compromise between the capitalist and communist delegates who participated in the drafting of CISG. In the former Soviet bloc, certainty was more important than flexibility. Trade usages are not considered unless a contract specifically adopted them and they did not violate statutory rules. In the Western world, on the other hand, flexibility and freedom of contract are more important than certainty. In some circumstances, trade usages apply in the West even when they contradict a statutory provision or the contract is silent.[50] The delegates ultimately agreed to let a court consider international trade usages, but only if they are "widely known" and "regularly observed."

Case 10-2 concerns a contract dispute in which the primary legal issue is whether a term's *customary usage in trade* should take precedence over the parties' understanding of that term based upon their course of dealings.

---

[48]Lord Denning's criticism of the English practice is in Port Soudan Cotton Co. v. Chettiar and Sons, *Lloyd's Law Reports*, vol. 2, p. 5 at p. 11 (Ct. of Appeal, 1977).
[49]An example would be a provision that trade terms, such as *FOB, CIF*, and the like, must comply with the International Chamber of Commerce's Incoterms.
[50]See United States, Uniform Commercial Code, §§ 1-205 and 2-208.

=༼ↄ∫Ɔ༽=

Case 10-2 TREIBACHER INDUSTRIE, A.G. v. ALLEGHENY TECHNOLOGIES, INC.

United States Court of Appeals, Eleventh Circuit
464 F.3d 1235, (11th Cir. 2006)

OPINION BY CIRCUIT JUDGE TJOFLAT

I. (A) This lawsuit arises out of two contracts, executed in November and December of 2000, respectively, whereby Treibacher Industrie, AG ("Treibacher"), an Austrian vendor of hard metal powders, agreed to sell specified quantities of tantalum carbide ("TaC"), a hard metal powder, to TDY Industries, Inc. ("TDY") for delivery to "consignment." TDY planned to use the TaC in manufacturing tungsten-graded carbide powders at its plant in Gurney, Alabama. After it had received some of the amount of TaC specified in the November 2000 contract, TDY refused to take delivery of the balance of the TaC specified in both contracts, and, in a letter to

MAP 10-2 Austria (2006)

Treibacher dated August 23, 2001, denied that it had a binding obligation to take delivery of or pay for any TaC that it did not wish to use.

Unbeknownst to Treibacher, TDY had purchased the TaC it needed from another vendor at lower prices than those specified in its contracts with Treibacher. Treibacher eventually sold the quantities of TaC of which TDY refused to take delivery, but at lower prices than those specified in its contracts with TDY. Treibacher then filed suit against TDY, seeking to recover the balance of the amount Treibacher would have received had TDY paid for all of the TaC specified in the November and December 2000 contracts.

The case proceeded to a bench trial, where TDY and Treibacher disputed the meaning of the term "consignment"—the delivery term contained in both contracts. TDY introduced experts in the metal industry who testified that the term "consignment," according to its common usage in the trade, meant that no sale occurred unless and until TDY actually used the TaC. Treibacher introduced evidence of the parties' prior dealings to show that the parties, in their course of dealings (extending over a seven-year period), understood the term "consignment" to mean that TDY had a binding obligation to pay for all of the TaC specified in each contract but that Treibacher would delay billing TDY for the materials until TDY had actually used them.

The district court ruled that, under the United Nations Convention on Contracts for the International Sale of Goods ("CISG"), evidence of the parties' interpretation of the term in their course of dealings trumped evidence of the term's customary usage in the industry, and found that Treibacher and TDY, in their course of dealings, understood the term to mean "that a sale had occurred, but that invoices would be delayed until the materials were withdrawn." The court therefore entered judgment against TDY, awarding Treibacher $5,327,042.85 in compensatory damages (including interest).

(B) TDY now appeals, contending that, under the CISG, a contract term should be construed according to its customary usage in the industry unless the parties have expressly agreed to another usage. TDY argues, in the alternative, that the district court erred in finding that, in their course of dealings, Treibacher and TDY understood the term "consignment" to require TDY to use and pay for all of the TaC specified in each contract.

Reviewing the district court's legal conclusions *de novo* and factual findings for clear error, we hold that the district court properly construed the contract under the CISG—according to the parties' course of dealings – and did not commit clear error in finding that the parties understood the contracts to require TDY to use all of the TaC specified in the contracts. We therefore affirm the judgment of the district court.

II. (A) We begin our analysis by discussing the CISG, which governs the formation of and rights and obligations under contracts for the international sale of goods. (CISG, arts. 1, 4). The parties do not dispute that the CISG governs their dispute. Article 1 of the CISG provides, in relevant part, that it "applies to contracts of sale of goods between parties whose places of business are in different States . . . when the States are Contracting States." The United States and Austria are contracting states. Article 4 of the CISG provides, in relevant part, that it "governs . . . the formation of the contract and the rights and obligations of the seller and buyer arising from such a contract." The parties dispute their respective "rights and obligations" under the contracts at issue in this case.

Article 9 of the CISG provides the rules for interpreting the terms of contracts. Article 9(1) states that, "parties are bound by any usage to which they have agreed and by any practices which they have established between themselves." Article 9(2) then states that, "parties are considered, unless otherwise agreed, to have impliedly made applicable to their contract . . . a usage of which the parties knew or ought to have known and which in international trade is widely known to . . . parties to contracts of the type involved in the particular trade concerned."

Article 8 of the CISG governs the interpretation of the parties' statements and conduct. A party's statements and conduct are interpreted according to that party's actual intent "where the other party knew ... what that intent was," [CISG, art. 8(1)], but, if the other party was unaware of that party's actual intent, then "according to the understanding that a reasonable person ... would have had in the same circumstances" [CISG, art. 8(2)]. To determine a party's actual intent, or a reasonable interpretation thereof, "due consideration is to be given to all relevant circumstances of the case including the negotiations, any practices which the parties have established between themselves, usages and any subsequent conduct of the parties" [CISG, art. 8(3)].

In arguing that a term's customary usage takes precedence over the parties' understanding of that term in their course of dealings, TDY seizes upon the language of article 9(2), which states that "parties are considered, unless otherwise agreed, to have made applicable to their contract" customary trade usages. TDY contends that article 9(2) should be read to mean that, unless parties to a contract expressly agree to the meaning of a term, the customary trade usage applies.

In support of its argument, TDY points to the language of article (9)(1), which binds parties to "any usage to which they have agreed and by any practices which they have established between themselves." According to TDY, the drafters of the CISG, by separating the phrase "usages to which they have agreed" from the phrase "practices which they have established between themselves," intended the word "agreed," in article 9, to mean express agreement, as opposed to tacit agreement by course of conduct. Applying this definition to the language of article 9(2), TDY contends that contract terms should, in the absence of express agreement to their usage, be interpreted according to customary usage, instead of the usage established between the parties through their course of conduct.

TDY's construction of article 9 would, however, render article 8(3) superfluous and the latter portion of article 9(1) a nullity. The inclusion in article 8(3) of "any practices which the parties have established between themselves," as a factor in interpreting the parties' statements and conduct, would be meaningless if a term's customary usage controlled that term's meaning in the face of a conflicting usage in the parties' course of dealings. The latter portion of article 9(1) would be void because the parties would no longer be "bound by any practices which they have established between themselves."

Instead, in the absence of an express agreement as to a term's meaning, the parties would be bound by that term's customary usage, even if they had established a contrary usage in their course of dealings. We therefore reject TDY's interpretation of article 9(2), and, like the district court, adopt a reading that gives force to articles 8(3) and 9(1), namely, that the parties' usage of a term in their course of dealings controls that term's meaning in the face of a conflicting customary usage of the term. A previous case decided by this court held that "A statute should be construed so that effect is given to all its provisions, so that no part of it will be inoperative or superfluous, void or insignificant."

(B) The district court did not commit clear error in finding that, in their course of dealings, TDY and Treibacher defined the term "consignment" to require TDY to accept and pay for all of the TaC specified in each contract. The parties do not dispute that they executed, between 1993 and 2000, a series of contracts in which Treibacher agreed to sell certain hard metal powders, such as TaC, to TDY. In each instance, TDY discussed its needs with Treibacher, after which Treibacher and TDY executed a contract whereby Treibacher agreed to sell a fixed quantity of materials at a fixed price for delivery to "consignment." Treibacher then delivered to TDY the specified quantity of materials—sometimes in installments, depending upon TDY's needs.

TDY kept the materials it received from Treibacher in a "consignment store," where the materials were labeled as being from Treibacher and segregated from other vendors' materials. As it withdrew the materials from the consignment store for use, TDY published "usage reports," which documented the amounts of materials withdrawn. TDY sent the usage reports to Treibacher, and Treibacher, in turn, sent TDY invoices for the amounts of materials withdrawn at the price specified in the relevant contract. TDY then paid the invoices when they came due. In each instance, TDY ultimately withdrew and paid for the full quantity of materials specified in each contract.

A particularly telling interaction, the existence of which the parties do not dispute, occurred in February 2000, when a TDY employee, Conrad Atchley, sent an e-mail to his counterpart at Treibacher, Peter Hinterhofer, expressing TDY's desire to return unused portions of a hard metal powder, titanium carbonitride ("TiCN"), which Treibacher had delivered. Hinterhofer telephoned Atchley in response and explained that TDY could not return the TiCN because TDY was contractually obligated to purchase the materials; Treibacher had delivered the TiCN as part of a quantity of TiCN that it was obligated to provide TDY under a contract executed in December 1999.

Atchley told Hinterhofer that TDY would keep the TiCN. TDY subsequently used the TiCN and sent a usage report to Treibacher, for which Treibacher sent TDY an invoice, which TDY paid. This interaction—evidencing TDY's acquiescence in Treibacher's interpretation of the contract—along with TDY's practice, between 1993 and 2000, of using and paying for all of the TaC specified in each contract amply support the district court's finding that the parties, in their course of dealings, construed their contracts to require TDY to use and pay for all of the TaC specified in each contract.

III. In sum, the district court properly determined that, under the CISG, the meaning the parties ascribe to a contractual term in their course of dealings establishes the meaning of that term in the face of a conflicting customary usage of the term. The district court was not

clearly erroneous in finding that Treibacher and TDY understood their contracts to require TDY to purchase all of the TaC specified in each contract and that Treibacher took reasonable measures to mitigate its losses (selling the unused TaC whenever possible) after TDY breached. Accordingly, the judgment of the district court is **AFFIRMED.** ■

CASEPOINT: In this case, the court had to decide how to interpret, under the CISG, the word *consignment* in a contract between two business firms—one in Austria and one in the United States. The result of the case turned on whether that word should be interpreted according to its meaning based on the "course of dealings" between the parties or on its "customary usage in trade." After reviewing the relevant sections of the CISG, the court found that, in the course of their dealings, TDY and Treibacher had defined the term *consignment* to require TDY to accept and pay for all of the TaC specified in each contract, and that this is how the term should be interpreted.

FORM

Traditionally, many countries have required that a contract be in writing. The English Statute of Frauds of 1677 required a signed writing to enforce a wide variety of contracts, including contracts for the sale of goods.[51] This same requirement reappears in the U.K. Sale of Goods Act of 1893, the U.S. Uniform Sales Act of 1896, and, more recently, the U.S. Uniform Commercial Code.[52] In 1954, however, the United Kingdom repealed the writing requirement when it revised its Sale of Goods Act,[53] and this revision was adopted by many former colonies that had inherited the British act.[54]

In the civil law countries, the requirement that a contract be in writing generally does not apply to commercial transactions.[55] In socialist countries, on the other hand, the need for certainty both in interpreting and enforcing foreign trade contracts is of paramount concern. The laws of the former Soviet Union, for example, imposed strict writing and registration requirements on foreign trade contracts.[56]

Most of the delegates involved in the drafting of CISG were of the opinion that a writing requirement is inconsistent with modern commercial practice, especially in market economies where speed and informality characterize so many transactions. The Soviet delegates, however, insisted that a writing requirement is important for protecting their country's longtime pattern of making foreign trade contracts. The result of this disagreement was a compromise. First, Article 11 of the convention states:

> A contract of sale need not be concluded in or evidenced by writing and is not subject to any other requirements as to form. It may be proved by any means, including witnesses.

---

[51]*Charles II*, Year 29, chap. 3, § 17.
[52]United States, Uniform Commercial Code, § 2-201.
[53]United Kingdom, Law Reform (Enforcement of Contracts) Act (1954).
[54]Including Australia and Canada. See Kenneth C. Sutton, "Formation of Contract: Unity in International Sales of Goods," *University of Western Ontario Law Review,* vol. 16, pp. 148–150 (1977).
[55]E.g., France, Civil Code, Article 1341; and see Stojan Cigoj, "International Sales, Formation of Contracts," *Netherlands International Law Review*, vol. 23, pp. 270–272 (1976), which surveys the rules of many countries.
[56]John Honnold, Uniform Law for International Sales under the 1980 United Nations Convention, p. 155 (1982).

Article 96, however, authorizes a contracting state "whose legislation requires contracts of sale to be concluded in or evidenced by writing" to make a declaration at the time of ratification that Article 11 (and some other provisions of the convention involving requirements of form) "does not apply where any party has his place of business in that state."[57]

F. FORMATION OF THE CONTRACT

A contract is formed, and the parties are bound by its provisions, when an offer to buy or sell a good is accepted.[58]

THE OFFER

offer: A proposal by one person to another indicating an intention to enter into a contract under specified terms.

An **offer** is a proposal addressed to specific persons indicating an intention by the offeror to be bound to the sale or purchase of particular goods for a price.[59] The pro forma invoice shown in Exhibit 10-3 (page 539) is an example of an offer commonly used in international trade. Should there be some doubt whether a communication is an offer or not, CISG directs a court to ascertain if the offeror communicated an intention to be bound. This can be determined from the general rules of interpretation in Article 8 of the convention—that is, by looking at the offeror's proposal within its full context, including any negotiations, any practices between the parties, any usages, and any subsequent conduct. It can also be determined from the subsidiary rules contained in Article 14.

Definiteness

According to Article 14, a "proposal is sufficiently definite if it indicates the goods and expressly or implicitly fixes or makes provision for determining the quantity and price." In other words, an offer must describe the goods with sufficient clarity that the parties know what is being offered for sale, and it must also state the quantity and price.

The price provision in Article 14 has to be read together with Article 55, which was added to the convention at the last minute, during the Diplomatic Conference that adopted CISG. The delegates to the conference were concerned that Article 14, standing alone, could be confusing. For example, if a buyer needs a particular part for a machine to keep a production line operational, he may ask the seller to rush it to him without first agreeing to the price, assuming that the seller will charge the customary price. In such a circumstance, the seller would probably treat the buyer's request as an offer. However, if the seller was unaware of the urgency of the buyer's request, the seller might well disregard it, since the proposal does not fix a price. If the seller did so, would the buyer be entitled to a remedy under CISG? Probably not, since Article 14 suggests that it is the duty of the offeror (the buyer in this example) to communicate the means for fixing a price. On the other hand, if the seller shipped the part anyway and the buyer changed his mind, would the seller have a remedy? Possibly, because the buyer originally subjectively intended to be bound, even though he did

---

[57]UN Convention on Contracts for the International Sale of Goods, Article 12 (1980), further describes the effect of a state making a declaration under Article 96: "Any provision of Article 11, Article 29 or Part II of this Convention that allows a contract of sale or its modification or termination by agreement or any offer, acceptance or other indication of intention to be made in any form other than in writing does not apply where any party has his place of business in a contracting state which has made a declaration under Article 96 of this Convention. The parties may not derogate from or vary the effect of this Article."

A few provisions of the convention refer to the use of a writing. Article 21(2) refers to a "letter or other writing containing a late acceptance," and Article 29(2) states that a "contract in writing which contains a provision requiring any modification or termination by agreement to be in writing may not be otherwise modified or terminated by agreement." Neither of these requires that a writing be signed. Article 13 states that "for the purposes of this Convention 'writing' includes telegram and telex."

[58]*Id.*, Article 23.

[59]*Id.*, Article 14(1): "A proposal for concluding a contract addressed to one or more specific persons constitutes an offer if it is sufficiently definite and indicates the intention of the offeror to be bound in case of acceptance. A proposal is sufficiently definite if it indicates the goods and expressly or implicitly fixes or makes provision for determining the quantity and price."

International Sales Company 1234 Main Street Pullman, Washington 99163 U.S.A.	**Pro Forma** **I N V O I C E**	
Date: **July 1, 2008**	Invoice No.	**030701**

To: **Compañía Mundial, S.A.**
     567 Avenida de Mayo
     Buenos Aires
     1103 Argentina
	Order No.	

	Shipped:	
	Payment:	

Identifying Marks & Nos.	Qty	Description	Unit Price	Amt.
		<u>Widgets</u> As per specification and samples forwarded by air parcel on **June 7, 2003.**	<u>FOB</u> port of Seattle	
	Each Each Each	Type "A" Type "B" Type "C″	US$ 1.23 4.56 7.89	
		Packing: Each in inner box; 144 per double export carton weighing 14 kg and measuring 25 x 25 x 10 cm. Shipment within 30 days after receipt of your firm order and payment. Payment: Irrevocable Letter of Credit for 100% of invoice value payable at sight through Washington National Bank of Pullman. Minimum Order: 144 each per type. Offer Duration: Effective until **August 15, 2008.**		

International Sales Company

Jane Doe

Jane Doe, Pres.

EXHIBIT 10-3   An Offer—Pro Forma Invoice

not objectively indicate this. Remember that Article 8 allows courts to rely on subjective intent in interpreting the terms of a contract.

To avoid any possible confusion, Article 55 was added to CISG. It provides:

Where a contract has been validly concluded but does not expressly or implicitly fix or make provision for determining the price, the parties are considered in the absence of any indication to the contrary, to have implied made reference to the price generally charged at the time of the conclusion of the contract for such goods sold under comparable circumstances in the trade concerned.

Thus, even though an offer does not "expressly or implicitly" fix a price, it is still a valid offer. The offeror is assumed to have "impliedly made reference to the price generally charged."[60]

Specific Offerees

For a proposal to be an offer, it must be addressed to "one or more specific persons." Proposals made to the public are ordinarily intended to be nothing more than invitations to negotiate. For example, an advertisement in a newspaper for the sale of goods at a particular price might put the advertiser in the awkward position of having to deliver more goods than he has on hand because of heavier than expected demand, or of absorbing a substantial loss because of an increase in the cost of the goods between the time the advertisement was placed and the time it appeared. CISG, accordingly, adopts the rule that public offers are only invitations to negotiate "unless the contrary is clearly indicated."[61]

EFFECTIVENESS OF AN OFFER

An offer becomes effective only after it reaches the offeree.[62] Thus, offers—including offers that promise that they are irrevocable—can be withdrawn before they reach the offeree.[63]

Revocation

revocation: Cancellation by the offeror of an offer.

Offers that do not state that they are irrevocable can be **revoked** any time before the offeree dispatches an acceptance.[64] This rule is based on the famous English common law *mailbox rule*,[65] which limits the ability of the offeror to cancel an offer where the offeree has reasonably relied on it. Under the common law, the acceptance had to be returned using the same medium in which the offer was originally sent (e.g., a mailed offer had to be accepted by mail). Under CISG, the acceptance can be sent by any means.

Firm Offers

firm offer: An offer that the offeror promises to keep open for a fixed period of time.

Under traditional Anglo-American common law rules, the doctrine of consideration prevents an offeror from making an offer irrevocable. An option contract (i.e., one in which the offeree pays the offeror for the promise to keep the offer open) has to be used. The doctrine of consideration does not apply to CISG, however, and **firm offers** (i.e., ones where the offeror promises to keep the offer open for a fixed period) are enforceable. Most common law countries have modified the traditional rule, allowing offerees to enforce firm offers made by merchants if they are made in writing, are signed by the offeror, and are effective for only a limited time period.[66] CISG goes further than this. The promise of irrevocability does not have to be signed, does not have to be in writing, and there is no time limitation. A firm offer is enforceable if the offeror makes the offer irrevocable or if the offeree can reasonably rely on conduct that implies that the offer is firm.[67]

ACCEPTANCE

acceptance: Agreement to enter into a contract proposed by an offeror.

A contract comes into existence at the point in time an offer is accepted. **Acceptance** is a statement or conduct by the offeree indicating assent that is communicated to the offeror.

---

[60]*Id.*, Article 55. If a contract fixes a price based on weight but does not specify the gross or net weight, Article 56 says that "in case of doubt it is to be determined by the net weight."
[61]*Id.*, Article 14(2).
[62]*Id.*, Article 24, defines when a communication reaches an addressee as follows: "For the purposes of this Part of the Convention, an offer, declaration of acceptance or any other indication of intention 'reaches' the addressee when it is made orally to him or delivered by any other means to him personally, to his place of business or mailing address or, if he does not have a place of business or mailing address, to his habitual residence."
[63]*Id.*, Article 15.
[64]*Id.*, Article 16(1).
[65]The mailbox rule applies in most Anglo-American common law countries, including England, Australia, Canada, New Zealand, and the United States. The original cases developing the rule are Adams v. Lindsell, *English Reports*, vol. 106, p. 250 (1818), and Dunlop v. Higgins, *English Reports*, vol. 9, p. 805 (House of Lords, 1848).
[66]See United States, Uniform Commercial Code, § 2–205.
[67]UN Convention on Contracts for the International Sale of Goods, Article 16(2) (1980).

The form or mode in which an offeree expresses assent is unlimited; however, the offeree must communicate his assent to the offeror.[68] The purchase order shown in Exhibit 10-4 is an example of an acceptance commonly used in international trade.

Compañia Mundial, S.A. 567 Avenida de Mayo Buenos Aires 1103 Argentina	**PURCHASE ORDER**

Date: **August 2, 2008**	No.	080203

To: **International Sales Company** **1234 Main Street** **Pullman, Washington 99163** **U.S.A.**	Date Required:	**Sept. 15, 2008**
	Deliver to:	**Address above**
	Packing:	**Standard Export**
	Payment:	**Irrevocable Letter**

Identifying Marks & Nos.	Qty.	Description	Unit Price	Amt.
		FOB Port of Seattle	**US $**	**US $**
	Each	**Type "A"**	1.23	531.36
	Each	**Type "B"**	4.56	1313.28
	Each	**Type "C"**	7.89	<u>1136.16</u>
				2980.80

Packing: As per your offer sheet, each in cardboard inner box, 144 per double export carton weighing 14 kg and measuring 25 x 25 x 10 cm.
Shipment via M/V El Mar from port of Seattle to Buenos Aires
Payment: Irrevocable Letter of Credit for 100% of invoice value payable at sight through Banco del Sur, Buenos Aires, to Washington National Bank of Pullman.
Notify party: Agencia Rosas, 989 Calle de los Marineros, Buenos Aires, 1117 Argentina

Case Mark: Cia Mundial
Buenos Aires
Made in USA
C/No. _____

Accepted	**Confirmed**
_____	*Juan Valdez* J. Valdez, Gte.

EXHIBIT 10-4 An Acceptance—Purchase Order

---

[68]*Id.*, Article 18(1).

Silence

Silence or inactivity does not, in and of itself, constitute acceptance. For example, if a seller sends a buyer an offer that says, "I know that this is such a good deal that I will assume that you have accepted unless I hear otherwise," the fact that the buyer does not respond will not create a contract. A different result will occur, however, if the seller sends the buyer an invitation to negotiate that says, "Unless you hear otherwise from me within three days after I receive your order, I will deliver the widgets you need at $100 each." In such a case, the seller's silence constitutes acceptance. In the first instance, the seller attempted to force acceptance on the buyer. In the second, the seller voluntarily assumed the duty to respond.

Time of Acceptance

Acceptance must be received by the offeror within the time period specified in the offer. If no time period is given, acceptance must be received within a reasonable time. If the offer is oral, the acceptance must be made immediately, unless the circumstances indicate otherwise.[69]

In devising the acceptance rule for CISG, the drafters opted for the receipt theory used in civil law countries. In common law countries, the dispatch or mailbox theory is used. The difference between the two relates to the allocation of risk when an acceptance is lost or delayed. For example, a buyer sends a seller an acceptance through the mail and the acceptance is lost. If the dispatch theory were applied, a contract would have come into existence at the time the acceptance was mailed, and the seller would be required to perform. Under the receipt rule adopted by CISG, however, no contract would exist, and the buyer would be left empty-handed. The reason the drafters chose the receipt rule was a perception that it more fairly allocates responsibility for loss or delay. Because it is the offeree who chooses the medium through which to send a response, it is the offeree who is better able to avoid the risk of loss or delay, and therefore CISG imposes responsibility for avoiding that risk on the offeree.[70]

In Case 10-3, the court was asked to determine if an offer had been made and if a contract came into effect at the time the offeror received the offeree's acceptance.

---

[69]*Id.*, Article 18(2).

[70]*Id.*, Article 21(1), allows an offeror to treat a late acceptance as valid "if without delay the offeror orally so informs the offeree or dispatches a notice to that effect." Article 21(2) says that an offeror who receives a late acceptance under such circumstances that he can see that it was delayed in transmission must give the acceptance effect "unless, without delay, the offeror orally informs the offeree that he considers his offer as having lapsed or dispatches a notice to that effect."

=⟪ʊⁿʊ⟫=

Case 10-3 UNITED TECHNOLOGIES INTERNATIONAL, INC. v. MAGYAR LÉGI KÖZLEKEDÉSI VÁLLALAT

Hungary, Metropolitan Court of Budapest, 1992. Case No. 3.G.50.289/1991/32.[71]

Magyar Légi Közlekedési Vállalat (Málev Hungarian Airlines) planned to buy wide-bodied jet aircraft either from Boeing Aircraft Co. of the United States or Airbus Industries of Europe. It planned to buy the engines for these aircraft separately. After completing negotiations for *engines with the Pratt & Whitney division of United Technologies International, Málev Hungarian Airlines reneged on going forward with the purchase. United Technologies International thereupon sued in the Metropolitan Court of Budapest to obtain a declaratory judgment holding that a valid contract existed between Pratt & Whitney and Málev.*

---

[71]Another English translation of this case is posted on the Internet at http://cisgw3.law.pace.edu/cases/920110h1.html.

JUDGE PISKOLTI

***

The Offer

The plaintiff [Pratt & Whitney] delivered an offer to the defendant's [Málev Hungarian Airlines'] General Manager on December 14, 1990. This offer described Pratt & Whitney's financial assistance plans, product warranties, as well as the support services that it would provide for its PW4056 engine. The offer updated and amended an earlier offer made on November 9, 1990. It said that plaintiff was "pleased to submit this revised support services proposal in connection with Málev Hungarian Airlines' purchase of two 767-200ER aircraft, powered by Pratt & Whitney PW4056 engines (with an option to purchase a third such aircraft), and the purchase of one PW4056 spare engine (with an option to buy a second spare), all of which are scheduled to be delivered as stated in Attachment 1.". . . The plaintiff's offer also set out a complete technical description of the PW4000 series engines. . . .

Paragraph Y of the plaintiff's offer is entitled "Purchase Agreement." This states that the buyer agrees to buy, and the seller agrees to sell, four new PW4056 engines to be mounted on two 767-200ER aircraft according to the attached schedule. The buyer also is given an option to buy two more new PW4056 engines in the event that it exercises its option to buy an additional 767-200ER aircraft. Additionally, the buyer agrees to buy one PW4056 engine as a spare. . . . The plaintiff's Purchase Agreement also establishes a deadline of December 21, 1990, for the buyer to accept the offer. If the buyer needs additional information or assistance, it is encouraged to contact the plaintiff's legal and accounting staff. In this regard, the plaintiff's offer notes that the buyer's acceptance is conditional on the agreement being approved by the governments of both Hungary and the United States.

***

Extension of the Offer

In a separate document, also delivered to the defendant on December 14, 1990, the plaintiff offered to sell to the defendant its PW4152 or PW4156/A engines. Again, this offer updated and amended an earlier offer made on November 9, 1990. It also described the assistance the plaintiff would provide the defendant with respect to defendant's purchase of two A310-300 aircraft (with an option to buy a third) that were to be equipped [with] either the two PW4152 or two PW4156/A engines (with the option to [buy] a third engine) according to the attached schedule. . . . Additionally, paragraph W of this

offer, which is entitled "Spare Engine Price," states that the base price of a new PW4152 is $5,552,675 and the base price of a new PW4156/A engine is $5,847,675. Finally, once again, December 21, 1990, is set as the date by which the buyer must accept the plaintiff's offer.

***

The parties have stipulated that their relationship is governed by the United Nations Convention on Contracts for the International Sale of Goods (CISG).[72] According to CISG, Article 14(1), "a contract addressed to one or more specific persons constitutes an offer if it is sufficiently definite and indicates the intention of the offeror to be bound in case of acceptance." Additionally, "[a] proposal is sufficiently definite if it indicates the goods and expressly or implicitly fixes or makes provision for determining the quantity and the price."

It is clear from the circumstances that the plaintiff's proposal was addressed to the defendant. What needs to be ascertained, first, is whether the offer sufficiently describes the goods involved. The first of the offers described above clearly states that the goods offered for sale are PW4056 and PW4060 engines and the second offer clearly states that goods offered are the PW4152 and PW4156/A engines. . . . The fact that the defendant has the right to choose between the listed engines, depending on whether it elects to buy the Boeing 767-200ER aircraft (which requires either the PW4056 or the PW4060 engine) or the Airbus A310-300 (which requires the PW4152 or the PW4156/A engine) does not affect the description of the goods. The offer gives the buyer the right to choose between offered engines. Such a unilateral right is common in . . . commercial practice and it does not make the description of the goods uncertain, as the defendant has argued. Contrary to the defendant's argument, the plaintiff's proposals unambiguously describe the goods offered to the defendant.

Defendant also argues that the plaintiff's proposals could not be construed to be offers because they do not establish the quantity of the goods involved [because the defendant is allowed to choose between taking two or three engines]. This argument is also untenable. Again, the offer gives the unilateral right to the defendant to determine the quantity.

That is, the defendant is able to determine the quantity involved based on its choice as to the number of aircraft. . . . As the plaintiff has pointed out in oral argument, the plaintiff's proposal clearly indicates that the defendant intended to purchase at least two aircraft, whether they were made by Boeing or Airbus, and that the defendant had an option to purchase a third aircraft. If the defendant does not choose to exercise its option to

---

[72]The convention is in force in Hungary. See Law Decree No. 20 of 1987. [The convention was also in force in the United States at the time of this dispute.]

buy a third aircraft, the quantity specified in the plaintiff's proposal is for four engines and one spare engine. If the defendant does choose to exercise its option, then quantity would be six engines and one spare.

The defendant's argument that the plaintiff's offers fails to state a price is also unfounded. The plaintiff's written offers (described above) state that the price of a PW4056 engine is $5,552,675 and the price of the PW4152 and PW4156/A engine is $5,847,675. . . .

Finally, the plaintiff's proposals include a schedule setting out the time for the delivery of the engines, so the defendant could not be uncertain as to this either.

In light of the above, it is clear that the plaintiff's proposal of December 14, 1990, is an offer. It clearly describes the goods, states the price and quantity, and sets out the time for delivery. Thus, the plaintiff's offer satisfies all of requirements of Article 14(1) of CISG.

The Acceptance

On December 21, 1990, the defendant sent a letter of acceptance to the plaintiff. This was within the deadline set by the plaintiff. In its letter of acceptance the defendant informed the plaintiff that it had chosen the PW4000 series engine for its fleet of wide-bodied aircraft. Moreover, it gave its reasons for doing so (namely, that its decision was based on a thorough technical and economic evaluation). . . .

The letter unambiguously states it accepts all of the terms and conditions set out in the plaintiff's proposal of December 14, 1990. It only asks that the letter be kept confidential until the parties can make a joint public announcement. . . .

. . . According to Article 18(1) of CISG, an acceptance is "[a] statement made by, or other conduct of, the offeree indicating assent to an offer is an acceptance." It is clear that the defendant's letter of acceptance is just that.

Article 19(1) of CISG adds that "[a] reply to an offer which purports to be an acceptance but contains additions, limitations, or other modifications is a rejection of the offer and constitutes a counter-offer." The request made by the defendant at the end of its letter of acceptance [to keep the letter confidential until a joint announcement could be made] cannot be construed as an addition, limitation, or other modification. It is not a counter-offer. This being so, the defendant's letter of acceptance is an acceptance. That being so, it had the effect of creating a contract between the plaintiff and defendant.

***

CISG, Article 23, provides that "[a] contract is concluded at the moment when an acceptance of an offer becomes effective in accordance with the provisions of this Convention." Accordingly, the present contract came into effect when the plaintiff received the defendant's letter of acceptance. In other words, the effect of the defendant's letter of acceptance agreeing to all of the terms of the plaintiff's offer was to create a contract between them.

***

[The Condition Requiring Government Approval]

. . . Section 215(1) of the Hungarian *Civil Code* states, that, if the conclusion of a contract requires the approval of a third person, or official approval, the contract will not come into force until the approval is obtained. . . . Section 228(1) of the *Civil Code* states that, if the parties agree to terms that makes a contract's entry into force dependent on an the occurrence of an uncertain future event (a condition precedent), the agreement will not come into force until the event occurs. And Section 228(2) provides that, if the parties provide for the termination of a contract upon the occurrence an uncertain future event (a condition subsequent), the contract will terminate upon the occurrence of that event.

Notably, there are no provisions of this sort to be found in the CISG. Accordingly, these provisions cannot be used in ascertaining the validity of the contract under consideration. . . .

While there are no provisions in CISG describing the effect of a condition, there is also nothing in the CISG that forbids the parties from agreeing to a condition. Thus, the provision in the plaintiff's offer that "Málev Hungarian Airlines' acceptance of this offer is conditional on the agreement being approved by the governments of both Hungary and the United States" is not ineffective. However, the exact nature of the provision's effect has to be determined in light of the CISG's directive that a contract comes into existence at the time that an acceptance is received by the offeror. The parties may not ignore this mandate, even though they are otherwise free to set the terms and conditions of their contract.

During the course of the oral hearings in this case, it became evident to the court that the plaintiff viewed the condition that it had included in the contract as a device for avoiding governmental interference . . . and not as a condition precedent to the creation of a contract. . . .

***

[Only after the plaintiff received the defendant's acceptance] did it become clear to the plaintiff that the defendant, although owned by the State, was an independent company that did not require the State's approval to make decisions. The Hungarian Ministry of Transportation, Communication, and Construction eventually did make a declaration in connection with the contract at hand, but this was to assure the plaintiff that the defendant had the right to act on its own.

As for the approval required from the U.S. government, the plaintiff was only thinking in terms of obtaining the appropriate export license. . . .

In sum, the plaintiff intended, and the defendant agreed to, a condition subsequent. That is, to a condition that would terminate the contract. They did not agree to a condition precedent; a condition that must be fulfilled before a contract can come into effect.

Considering all of the above, it is the opinion of this court that the parties entered into a valid and enforceable contract. ■

CASEPOINT: The legal issue before the court in this case was whether an offer had been made and accepted under the CISG and international rules. After reviewing the correspondence and actions of the parties, the court found that it was clear that an offer and acceptance had been made, and a binding contract had come into existence. The term requiring *government approval* was not a condition precedent to a valid contract, but was only a condition subsequent, which, if it occurred, might suspend

MAP 10-3 Hungary (1992)

the parties' obligations. Thus, there was an enforceable contract between the parties.

Assent by Performance of an Act

If the offeror asks for performance of an act rather than the indication of acceptance, the acceptance is effective at the moment the act is performed. However, the offer, a trade usage, or the practice of the parties must make it clear that the offeree is not required to notify the offeror.[73] Consider the following example. A buyer sends a seller the following offer: "Ship me 100 widgets at your customary price for delivery on or before May 31." The seller responds by shipping the goods for delivery on May 30. The day after the goods are shipped, however, the buyer calls the seller and withdraws his offer. Can the buyer withdraw the offer? The buyer might argue that Article 18(2) says that a contract only becomes effective when "the indication of assent reaches the offeror." Here, of course, the buyer would not have been aware of the acceptance until the goods arrived. The seller would, however, be able to rely on Article 18(3), which says that an offeree "may indicate assent by performing an act . . . without [giving] notice to the offeror." The seller shipped the goods precisely in the manner requested by the buyer, and the buyer's offer did not ask for notice of acceptance or even confirmation of shipment.

Withdrawal

withdrawal: Cancellation by the offeree of an acceptance.

Because an acceptance is normally not effective until the offeror receives it, an offeree may **withdraw** his acceptance any time before or simultaneous with its receipt.[74]

Rejection

rejection: Refusal by an offeree to become a party to a proposed contract.

A **rejection** becomes effective when it reaches the offeror.[75] If an offeree were to dispatch both a rejection and an acceptance at the same time, the one that reached the offeror first would be the one given effect.

---

[73]UN Convention on Contracts for the International Sale of Goods, Article 18(3) (1980).
[74]*Id.*, Article 22.
[75]*Id.*, Article 17

ACCEPTANCE WITH MODIFICATIONS

A seller sends an offer to a buyer. The buyer responds with an acceptance that modifies some of the terms in the offer. Is there a contract?

This scenario—commonly called the *Battle of the Forms*—occurs when merchants use preprinted forms both to make offers and to send back acceptances. The typed-in descriptions commonly match up; it is the "fine print" on the back of the forms, however, that contains differences.[76] Under CISG, if the inconsistencies are "material" the would-be acceptance is a counteroffer.[77] Article 19(3) states:

> Additional or different terms relating, among other things, to the price, payment, quality of the goods, place and time of delivery, extent of one party's liability to the other, or the settlement of disputes are considered to alter the terms of the offer materially.

Terms that are not material are considered to be proposals for addition that will become part of the contract unless the offeror promptly objects.[78]

Case 10-4 compares the way that CISG and the U.S. Uniform Commercial Code treat acceptances with additional terms.

---

[76]One businessperson wryly observed when responding to a survey on the use of forms that business would come to a halt if buyers and sellers "read the backsides of the other's forms." Quoted in John Honnold, *Uniform Law for International Sales under the 1980 United Nations Convention*, p. 166 (1982).

[77]UN Convention on Contracts for the International Sale of Goods, Article 19(1) (1980).

[78]*Id.*, Article 19(2). This CISG rule is based on legislation originally drafted in the Scandinavian countries. Article 19 is based on Article 6 of the Swedish Conclusion of Contracts Act (1915). The same act was adopted in Denmark in 1917, Norway in 1918, Finland in 1929, and Iceland in 1936. John Honnold, *Uniform Law for International Sales under the 1980 United Nations Convention*, p. 191 (1982).

=⟪⟫=

Case 10-4 FILANTO, SPA v. CHILEWICH INTERNATIONAL CORP.

United States, District Court, Southern District of New York.
Federal Supplement, vol. 789, p. 1229 (1992).

Filanto, SpA, the plaintiff, was an Italian corporation engaged in the manufacture and sale of foot-wear. Chilewich International Corp. (Chilewich), the defendant, was an export-import firm incorporated in New York.

On February 28, 1989, Chilewich's agent in the United Kingdom, Byerly Johnson, Ltd., signed a contract with the Soviet Union's Foreign Economic Association (known as Raznoexport) that obligated Byerly Johnson and Chilewich to deliver footwear to Raznoexport in what is now Russia. This contract (the Russian Contract) contained an arbitration clause that read, in part, as follows:

> All disputes or differences which may arise out of or in connection with the present Contract are to be settled, jurisdiction of ordinary courts being excluded, by the Arbitration at the USSR Chamber of Commerce and

Industry, Moscow, in accordance with the Regulations of the said Arbitration. [sic]

In order to fulfill the Russian Contract, Chilewich and Byerly Johnson met with Filanto, which was then supplying them with footwear under various ongoing contracts. On July 27, 1989, Mr. Melvin Chilewich sent a letter to Mr. Antonio Filograna, chief executive officer of Filanto, which summarized the negotiations at this meeting and then stated:

> Attached please find our contract to cover our purchase from you. Same is governed by the conditions which are enumerated in the standard contract with the Soviet buyers [the Russian Contract], copy of which is also enclosed.

Filanto claims that it sent a reply on September 2, 1989, that excluded the arbitration provision of the Russian Contract and that requested Chilewich to accept

Filanto's counteroffer. Chilewich claimed not to have received this correspondence.

On March 13, 1990, Chilewich sent Filanto a Memorandum Agreement to confirm that Filanto was to deliver a total of 250,000 pairs of boots to Chilewich. This memo again referred to the arbitration provision in the Russian Contract. Filanto did not immediately respond, and Chilewich proceeded to obtain a letter of credit in Filanto's favor in the sum of $2,595,600 on May 11, 1990.

On August 7, 1990, Filanto signed and returned the Memorandum Agreement. Filanto's cover letter, however, stated that it would not be bound by several provisions of the Russian Contract, including the arbitration provision and the provision governing procedures for making claims.

Chilewich accepted delivery and paid Filanto for 100,000 boots on September 15, 1990. Then in January 1991, Chilewich accepted and paid for another 60,000 boots. However, because Chilewich claimed that some of these boots were defective, it never purchased the 90,000 boots that made up the balance of its original order. Filanto, as a consequence, filed a complaint in a U.S. federal trial court in New York on May 14, 1991, alleging breach of contract. Chilewich answered the complaint by asking the court to stop the proceedings while the matter was arbitrated in the Soviet Union.

CHIEF JUDGE BRIEANT: . . .

. . . [The law] to be applied in this case is found in the United Nations Convention on Contracts for the International Sale of Goods (the "Sale of Goods Convention"). This Convention, ratified by the Senate in 1986, is a self-executing agreement which entered into force between the United States and other signatories, including Italy, on January 1, 1988. Although there is as yet virtually no U.S. case law interpreting the Sale of Goods Convention, it may safely be predicted that this will change: absent a choice-of-law provision, and with certain exclusions not here relevant, the Convention governs all contracts between parties with places of business in different nations, so long as both nations are signatories to the Convention. Since the contract alleged in this case most certainly was formed, if at all, after January 1, 1988, and since both the United States and Italy are signatories to the Convention, the Court will [apply] . . . the substantive international law of contracts embodied in the Sale of Goods Convention.[79]

Not surprisingly, the parties offer varying interpretations of the numerous letters and documents exchanged between them. The Court will briefly summarize their respective contentions.

Defendant Chilewich contends that the Memorandum Agreement dated March 13, which it signed and sent to Filanto, was an offer. It then argues that Filanto's retention of the letter, along with its subsequent acceptance of Chilewich's performance under the Agreement—the furnishing of the May 11 letter of credit—estops it from denying its acceptance of the contract. Although phrased as an estoppel argument, this contention is better viewed as an acceptance by conduct argument, e.g., that in light of the parties' course of dealing, Filanto had a duty timely to inform Chilewich that it objected to the incorporation by reference of all the terms of the Russian Contract. Under this view, the return of the Memorandum Agreement, signed by Filanto, on August 7, 1990, along with the covering letter purporting to exclude parts of the Russian Contract, was ineffective as a matter of law as a rejection of the March 13 offer, because this occurred some five months after Filanto received the Memorandum Agreement and two months after Chilewich furnished the Letter of Credit. Instead, in Chilewich's view, this action was a proposal for modification of the March 13 Agreement. Chilewich rejected this proposal, by its letter of August 7 to Byerly Johnson, and the August 29 fax by Johnson to Italian Trading SRL, which communication Filanto acknowledges receiving. Accordingly, Filanto under this interpretation is bound by the written terms of the March 13 Memorandum Agreement; since that agreement incorporates by reference the Russian Contract containing the arbitration provision, Filanto is bound to arbitrate.

Plaintiff Filanto's interpretation of the evidence is rather different. While Filanto apparently agrees that the March 13 Memorandum Agreement was indeed an offer, it characterizes its August 7 return of the signed Memorandum Agreement with the covering letter as a counteroffer. While defendant contends that under *Uniform Commercial Code* § 2-207 this action would be viewed as an acceptance with a proposal for a material modification, the *Uniform Commercial Code*, as previously noted, does not apply to this case, because the State Department undertook to fix something that was not broken by helping to create the Sale of Goods Convention, which varies from the *Uniform Commercial Code* in many significant ways. Instead, under this analysis, Article 19(1) of the Sale of Goods Convention would apply. That section, as the Commentary to the Sale of Goods Convention notes, reverses the rule of *Uniform Commercial Code* § 2-207, and reverts to the common law rule that "A reply to an offer which purports to be an acceptance but contains additions, limitations or other

---

[79]United Nations Convention on Contracts for the International Sale of Goods (1980), Article 1 (1)(a).

modifications is a rejection of the offer and constitutes a counteroffer."[80] Although the Convention, like the *Uniform Commercial Code*, does state that nonmaterial terms do become part of the contract unless objected to,[81] the Convention treats inclusion (or deletion) of an arbitration provision as "material."[82] The August 7 letter, therefore, was a counteroffer which, according to Filanto, Chilewich accepted by its letter dated September 27, 1990. Though that letter refers to and acknowledges the "contractual obligations" between the parties, it is doubtful whether it can be characterized as an acceptance.

Since the issue of whether and how a contract between these parties was formed is obviously related to the issue of whether Chilewich breached any contractual obligations, the Court will direct its analysis to whether there was objective conduct evidencing an intent to be bound with respect to the arbitration provision.

The Court is satisfied on this record that there was indeed an agreement to arbitrate between these parties.

There is simply no satisfactory explanation as to why Filanto failed to object to the incorporation by reference of the Russian Contract in a timely fashion. As noted above, Chilewich had in the meantime commenced its performance under the Agreement, and the Letter of Credit it furnished Filanto on May 11 itself mentioned the Russian Contract. An offeree who, knowing that the offeror has commenced performance, fails to notify the offeror of its objection to the terms of the contract within a reasonable time will, under certain circumstances, be deemed to have assented to those terms.[83] The Sale of Goods Convention itself recognizes this rule.

Article 18(1), provides that "A statement made by or other conduct of the offeree indicating assent to an offer is an acceptance". Although mere "silence or inactivity" does not constitute acceptance,[84] the Court may consider previous relations between the parties in assessing whether a party's conduct constituted acceptance.[85] In this case, in light of the extensive course of prior dealing between these parties, Filanto was certainly under a duty to alert Chilewich in timely fashion to its objections to the terms of the March 13 Memorandum Agreement—particularly since Chilewich had repeatedly referred it to the Russian Contract and Filanto had had a copy of that document for some time.

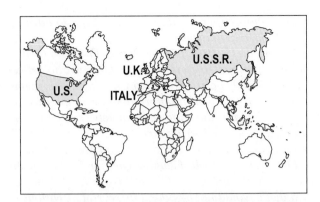

MAP 10-4 United States, United Kingdom, Union of Soviet Socialist Republic, and Italy (1991)

. . . [Filanto's letter of June 21, 1991, to Byerly Johnson], which responds to claims by Johnson that some of the boots that were supplied were defective, expressly relies on Section 9 of the Russian Contract—another section which Filanto had in its earlier correspondence purported to exclude. The Sale of Goods Convention specifically directs that "[i]n determining the intent of a party . . . due consideration is to be given to . . . any subsequent conduct of the parties."[86] In this case, as the letter postdates the partial performance of the contract, it is particularly strong evidence that Filanto recognized itself to be bound by all the terms of the Russian Contract.

In light of these factors . . . the Court holds that Filanto is bound by the terms of the March 13 Memorandum Agreement, and so must arbitrate its dispute in Moscow. ■

CASEPOINT: This case involves a contract between two parties in different countries concerning the sale of a large quantity of shoes. The buyer later claimed that the shoes furnished did not meet the contract specifications and never completed the purchase of all the shoes under the contract, leading to this lawsuit. The key legal issue is whether, under the CISG, the parties were bound to a contract provision requiring arbitration of any contractual disputes in Russia. After reviewing all the correspondence and the conduct of each party, the court concluded that the arbitration clause was indeed part of the contract.

---

[80]*Id.*, Article 19(1).
[81]*Id.*, Article 19(2).
[82]*Id.*, Article 19(3).
[83]Restatement (Second) of Contracts, § 69 (1981).
[84]United Nations Convention on Contracts for the International Sale of Goods (1980), Article 18(1).
[85]*Id.*, Article 8(3).
[86]*Id.*

G. GENERAL STANDARDS OF PERFORMANCE

CISG imposes general standards of performance on both the buyer and seller. In general, both parties are entitled to get from their contract what they expect.[87] A party that fails to perform accordingly is in breach of contract. When one party breaches, the other party may avoid the contract or make a demand for specific performance.

FUNDAMENTAL BREACH

When one party substantially fails to deliver what the other reasonably anticipated receiving, there is a fundamental breach. Article 25 defines a fundamental breach this way:

> A breach of contract committed by one of the parties is fundamental if it results in such detriment to the other party as substantially to deprive him of what he is entitled to expect under the contract, unless the party in breach did not foresee and a reasonable person of the same kind in the same circumstances would not have foreseen such a result.

AVOIDANCE

avoidance: Notification by a party that he is canceling a contract and returning everything already received.

If there has been a fundamental breach, one remedy available to the injured party is **avoidance** (i.e., notification by the party that he is canceling the contract). To be entitled to avoid a contract, however, the injured party must—in all cases—notify the other party[88] and be able to return any goods he has already received.[89]

When a party avoids, only the obligation to perform is affected. Avoidance does not cancel (1) any provision in the contract concerning the settlement of disputes (such as arbitration, choice-of-law, or choice-of-forum clauses) or (2) any other provisions governing the rights and duties of the parties "consequent upon the avoidance of the contract."[90]

REQUESTS FOR SPECIFIC PERFORMANCE

CISG authorizes an injured party to ask a court "to require performance" if the other party fails to carry out his obligations.[91] A court is not obliged to grant this request, however, unless the court can do so under its own domestic rules.[92]

specific performance: A court order directing a party to carry out the obligations he had contractually promised to do.

What constitutes **specific performance** varies from country to country, and the rule in CISG reflects the difficulties the drafters had in defining the concept. In common law countries, the concept is fairly narrow, referring to a court decree that compels a defendant to do a specific act, such as delivering goods. Disobeying the decree can be serious. It is treated as a *contempt of court* punishable by fine or imprisonment. In the civil law countries, the idea of *requiring performance* is much broader and includes such things as the buying of a substitute at the defaulting party's expense; however, the sanctions are not as burdensome—a court may not impose a fine or throw a disobedient party into jail.[93]

The prerequisites that must be shown before a party can obtain specific performance also vary. The United Kingdom's Sale of Goods Act of 1893, which is widely followed in the common law world, states that a court, "if it thinks fit," may enter a decree requiring a party in breach of contract to deliver "specific or ascertained goods."[94] The difficulty of determining when goods are "specific or ascertained," however, is a problem that limits the

---

[87]UN Convention on Contracts for the International Sale of Goods, Articles 53 and 54 (1980).
[88]*Id.,* Article 26.
[89]*Id.,* Article 82.
[90]*Id.,* Article 81(1).
[91]*Id.,* Article 46, provides that "[t]he buyer may require performance by the seller of his obligations," and Article 62 states that "[t]he seller may require the buyer to pay the price, take delivery or perform his other obligations."
[92]*Id.,* Article 28.
[93]Harry M. Flechtner, "Buyers' Remedies in General and Buyers' Performance-Oriented Remedies," *Journal of Law and Commerce,* vol. 25, pp. 339–347 (2005–2006).
[94]United Kingdom, Sale of Goods Act, § 52 (1893).

application of this section. In the United States, the Uniform Commercial Code allows for decrees of specific performance that "a court may deem just," so long as "the goods are unique" or "in other proper circumstances."[95] In the civil law countries, a party is "entitled" to require performance. Civil judges do not have the discretion to deny a decree, as their common law brethren do, nor is the remedy limited by the nature of the goods involved.[96]

H. SELLER'S OBLIGATIONS

A seller is required to (1) deliver the goods, (2) hand over any documents relating to them, and (3) ensure that the goods conform with the contract.[97] If a contract fails to specify how this is done, CISG provides rules to fill in the gaps.

PLACE FOR DELIVERY

The place for delivery is the place agreed to in the contract; otherwise, it is (1) the first carrier's place of business if the contract involves the carriage of goods or (2) the place where the parties knew the goods were located or were to be manufactured or produced.[98]

If the contract requires the seller to arrange for shipping but does not specify the carrier or the terms, the transportation selected must be "appropriate in the circumstances" and made "according to the usual terms for such transportation."[99] Also, if the seller is not required to arrange for insurance, "he must, at the buyer's request, provide him with all available information necessary to enable him to effect such insurance."[100]

In addition to providing insurance information when requested, the seller must, at the time he delivers the goods to a carrier, either (1) identify to the carrier both the goods and the buyer "by markings on the goods, by shipping documents or otherwise," or (2) "give the buyer notice of the consignment of the specifying goods."[101] Failure to comply with this requirement is a breach of the contract, and the seller will be liable for any damages that may result.[102]

TIME FOR DELIVERY

The seller is to deliver the goods on the date fixed in the contract or, if no date is fixed, within a reasonable time after the conclusion of the contract.[103] If a time period is provided, the seller may deliver at any time within that period, unless the contract expressly says that the buyer is to choose the time.[104]

THE TURNING OVER OF DOCUMENTS

At the time and place for delivery, the seller must turn over any documents relating to the goods that the contract requires. If he does so early, he has the right to "cure any lack of conformity in the documents," so long as this does not cause the buyer "unreasonable inconvenience or unreasonable expense."[105]

---

[95]United States, Uniform Commercial Code, § 2-716(1).
[96]See Shael Herman, "Specific Performance: A Comparative Analysis," *Edinburgh Law Review*, vol. 7, issue 1, pp. 5–26 (January 2003) and issue 2, pp. 194–217 (May 2003) (article comparing specific performance in Spain and the United States under common law and civil law principles).
[97]UN Convention on Contracts for the International Sale of Goods, Article 30 (1980).
[98]*Id.*, Article 31.
[99]*Id.*, Article 32(2).
[100]*Id.*, Article 32(3).
[101]*Id.*, Article 32(1).
[102]*Id.*, Articles 45, 49, and 74.
[103]*Id.*, Article 33.
[104]*Id.*, Article 33(b).
[105]*Id.*, Article 34.

CONFORMITY OF GOODS

Article 35(1) of CISG states that the seller "must deliver goods which are of the quantity, quality, and description required by the contract and which are contained or packaged in the manner required by the contract." This provision is similar to many warranty provisions found in common law countries, with the notable exception that it does not use the terms *warranty* or *guarantee*.[106] This is important, because the seller's obligation (and the buyer's right) arises—and can be waived—without the use of these terms.[107]

Determining Conformity The rules for determining whether the goods conform are set out in Article 35(2).

> Except where the parties have agreed otherwise, the goods do not conform with the contract unless they:
> (a) are fit for the purposes for which goods of the same description would ordinarily be used;
> (b) are fit for any particular purpose expressly or impliedly made known to the seller at the time of the conclusion of the contract, except where the circumstances show that the buyer did not rely, or that it was unreasonable for him to rely, on the seller's skill and judgment;
> (c) possess the qualities of goods which the seller has held out to the buyer as a sample or model;
> (d) are contained or packaged in the same manner usual for such goods or, where there is no such manner, in a manner adequate to preserve and protect the goods.

Third-Party Claims Goods also do not conform if they are subject to third-party claims. Third-party claims include assertions of ownership[108] and rights in intellectual property such as patents, copyrights, and trademarks.[109]

Waiver Although the seller is obliged to produce goods that conform to the contract, the parties may (1) expressly excuse him from complying[110] or (2) impliedly excuse him if the buyer knew or "could not have been unaware" that the goods were nonconforming.[111] These rules are similar to the waiver provisions found in most common law countries, except—as mentioned earlier—there is no requirement to use any particular terms to make the waiver.[112] Moreover, unlike the practice in many civil law countries, a waiver can be implied from the buyer's conduct.[113]

The basic philosophy of the convention—that the parties should determine the terms of their contract—compelled the drafters of CISG to adopt these waiver provisions. As noted earlier, the parties under Article 6 may "derogate from or vary the effect of any" provision; and under Article 35(2), the convention-defined obligation of the seller to produce conforming goods does not apply "where the parties have agreed otherwise."

Time for Examining Goods The buyer has an obligation to examine the goods for defects "within as short a period as is practicable" after delivery. If the goods are shipped, the examination "may be deferred until after the goods have arrived at their destination"; and, if the buyer has to redirect or redispatch the goods while they are in transit, the examination

[106]United States, Uniform Commercial Code, § 2-313 (express warranties) and § 2-314 (implied warranties). United Kingdom, Sale of Goods Act, § 14 (warranties) (1979).
[107]See Peter Schlechtriem, "Subsequent Performance and Delivery Deadlines—Avoidance of CISG Sales Contracts Due to Non-conformity of the Goods," *Pace International Law Review*, vol. 18, issue 1 (Spring 2006).
[108]UN Convention on Contracts for the International Sale of Goods, Article 41 (1980).
[109]*Id.*, Article 42. Third-party claims to intellectual property will make goods nonconforming, but only if the claims exist in (a) the state where the goods are sold or (b) the state where the buyer has his or her place of business.
[110]*Id.*, Articles 35(3), 41, and 42.
[111]*Id.*, Articles 35(2) and 42.
[112]*Id.*, Articles 35(3), 41, and 42.
[113]*Id.*, Articles 35(2) and 42.

"may be deferred until after the goods have arrived at the new destination," so long as the seller "knew or ought to have known of the possibility of such redirection or redispatch."[114]

Notice of Defect   In order for the buyer to avoid waiving his rights to require performance, he is obligated to inform the seller of any defects he discovers within a reasonable time after delivery. If the buyer discovers a defect at some later time, he must also promptly notify the seller in order to preserve his rights.[115] In any event, the seller will not be responsible for a defect that arises more than two years after delivery unless (1) the seller knew or ought to have known of a nonconformity and did not disclose it to the buyer or (2) the contract establishes a longer "period of guarantee."[116]

CISG does not describe specifically what the buyer has to do in notifying the seller of a defect, but the notice undoubtedly must be sufficient to inform the seller of the problem.

Curing Defects   If the seller delivers his goods early, he may correct or cure any defect up to the agreed-upon date for delivery, so long as this does not cause the buyer any unreasonable inconvenience or expense. Nevertheless, even if the seller does make a cure, the buyer retains the right to claim any damages that are provided for in CISG.

I. BUYER'S OBLIGATIONS

A buyer is required to (1) pay the price and (2) take delivery of the goods.[117] Again, as is the case for the seller's obligations, CISG's rules apply only when a contract fails to describe how this is done.

PAYMENT OF THE PRICE

The buyer is obliged to take whatever preliminary steps are necessary "under the contract or any laws or regulations to enable payment to be made."[118] He is then to pay the price at the time and place designated in the contract. If no time is specified, the buyer is to pay when "the goods or the documents controlling their disposition" are delivered.[119]

Contrary to the practice in some civil law countries (of requiring the seller to make a formal demand for payment), the buyer has to pay "without the need for any request or compliance with any formality on the part of the seller."[120] However, unless the parties agree otherwise, the buyer does not have to pay until after he has had a chance to examine the goods.[121]

If the parties have not agreed to a place for payment but have agreed to a place for the delivery of either the goods or their controlling documents, then payment will be made at that place.[122] If they did not specify a place for delivery, then the buyer must pay at the seller's place of business.[123]

In Case 10-5, the court was asked to determine if the buyer had breached its obligation to make payment to the seller.

[114]*Id.*, Article 38(3).
[115]*Id.*, Article 39(1).
[116]*Id.*, Articles 39(2) and 40.
[117]*Id.*, Article 53.
[118]*Id.*, Article 54.
[119]*Id.*, Articles 58(1) and 58(2).
[120]*Id.*, Article 59. In France the request is called a *mise en demeure*, in Germany a *Mahnung*. See Konrad Zweigert and Hein Kötz, *An Introduction to Comparative Law*, vol. 2, pp. 164, 171 (Tony Weir, trans., 1977).
[121]UN Convention on Contracts for the International Sale of Goods, Article 58(3) (1980).
[122]*Id.*, Article 57(1)(b).
[123]*Id.*, Article 57(1)(a).

Case 10-5 THE NATURAL GAS CASE

Austria, Supreme Court, 1996.
Case No. 518/95.
Österreichische Zeitschrift für Rechtsvergleichung, vol. 1996, p. 248 (1996).

In the fall of 1990, the plaintiff, a German company, negotiated to buy natural gas from the defendant, an Austrian partnership. After a series of proposals and counterproposals, the plaintiff faxed the defendant on December 18, 1990, offering to buy 700 to 800 metric tons of propane gas from the defendant. The defendant responded the next morning that it could ship the propane from the United States for delivery to the plaintiff in Belgium for $376 per ton, and the plaintiff agreed. Because the parties had not dealt with each other before, the plaintiff agreed to secure its purchase with a letter of credit. In the December 19 fax, the plaintiff asked the defendant to identify the place in the United States where the gas would be loaded aboard a tanker, because the plaintiff's bank needed this information before it would issue a letter of credit. The defendant responded by fax, stating that it was waiting to get the information from the United States as to the place of loading.

While this exchange of faxes was taking place, the parties were talking to each other on the telephone. The defendant wanted the plaintiff to order a larger quantity of propane to make the transaction more worth its time. The plaintiff, in response to this request, contacted a Dutch natural gas reseller that agreed to buy 3,000 tons of propane at $381 per ton. The plaintiff then increased its order by 3,000 tons.

On January 2 and 3, 1991, [not having heard if the propane had been loaded for shipment as the parties had agreed,] the plaintiff sent two faxes to the defendant asking to be notified of the place where the propane would be loaded and stating that its bank would not process the letter of credit without this information. On January 7, 1991, the defendant informed the plaintiff by fax that its U.S. supplier would not agree to let the propane gas be exported to Belgium, and therefore that the defendant could not deliver the propane. The next day the plaintiff notified the defendant that, because of the defendant's breach, the Dutch natural gas reseller had made a substitute purchase at a price above what the defendant had promised, and later the plaintiff forwarded the Dutch company's claim for $141,131 for the increased costs. The defendant rejected this claim, and the Dutch gas reseller and the plaintiff sued the defendant to cover their increased costs and the plaintiff's loss of profits of $15,000.

The trial court held in favor of the plaintiff, and the court of appeals affirmed its decision. The defendant then appealed to the Supreme Court.

DECISION OF THE COURT:

***

[The Breach]

[Following the making of the contract,] the plaintiff did not open a letter of credit and the plaintiff did not deliver the agreed goods (the natural gas).

The [United Nations Convention on Contracts for the International Sale of Goods (CISG),] Article 54, provides that "[t]he buyer's obligation to pay the price includes taking such steps and complying with such formalities as may be required under the contract or any laws and regulations to enable payment to be made." In light of this, a buyer in a sale of goods contract who has agreed to open a letter of credit must do so in a timely manner. In the case at hand, however, the plaintiff did not open the letter of credit because the defendant failed to notify it of the place where the natural gas would be loaded. And this was so, even though the defendant had expressly promised to do so in its fax of December 19, 1990. . . . The defendant cannot complain that the plaintiff did not fulfill its obligation [to open a letter of credit,] as the defendant's own obligation to notify the plaintiff as to the place where the goods were to be loaded had to happen first. The defendant knew that the plaintiff had to know the place of loading in order to open the letter, and it was the defendant's failure to notify the plaintiff of the place of loading that led to the plaintiff's failure to open the letter of credit. . . . In other words, the failure of the plaintiff to open the letter of credit was caused by the defendant's own failure to act. And, as stated in CISG, Article 80, "[a] party may not rely on a failure of the other party to perform, to the extent that such failure was caused by the first party's act or omission."

More significantly, the failure of the plaintiff to open a letter of credit was not the reason for the breach of this contract. As the lower courts have held, it was the defendant's failure to obtain the appropriate clearances . . . needed to export the propane gas to Belgium that was the cause of the breach. According to CISG, Article 30, "[t]he seller must deliver the goods, hand over any documents relating to them and transfer the property in the goods, as required by the contract. . . ." The defendant's argument (first made in this appeal) that it was the buyer that was obliged to obtain the appropriate authorization for the goods to be imported into Belgium is without merit. . . . A buyer is not obliged to ask a seller if there are any unusual restrictions that may keep the seller from performing. If the seller does not inform the buyer of such restrictions, the seller may reasonably assume that such circumstances do not exist. CISG, Article 41 says that "[t]he seller must deliver goods which are free from any right or claim of a third party" unless the buyer had agreed to accept such goods. If the seller's supplier will not allow the goods to be exported, then the goods are subject to a restriction. The buyer, of course, may agree to accept the goods anyway, but it doesn't have to. And, if the buyer doesn't agree to accept the goods, and the seller is then unable to deliver them because of the restriction, it is the seller that has breached the contract.

[Indemnification]

Because the seller breached the contract, the buyer is entitled to be fully indemnified for its losses. In other words, the non-breaching party is to be put in the position that it would have been had the breaching party performed as promised. The breaching party, moreover, does not have to be at fault or to have acted illegally to be liable in such a case.

[The parties sought to apply CISG, Articles 75 and 76 in ascertaining the damages due the plaintiff.]

The provisions in the CISG, Articles 75 and 76, deal with the awarding of damages when one party avoids the contract because of a breach by the other party. However, because there has been a breach, does not necessarily mean that there will be an avoidance. The CISG does not provide for avoidance as a matter of law, even if the non-breaching party is deprived of what it expected to receive.[124] Avoidance, under the CISG, can only come about by a unilateral declaration of the non-breaching party. Such a declaration, however, does not have to be in any particular form, nor (with the exception of certain cases set out in CISG, Article 49(2) which are inapplicable here) is it subject to any time limit.

The parties to this case argued over whether the declaration of avoidance described in CISG, Article 49(1), had to be made expressly or whether it could be implied from the non-breaching party's conduct. This argument, however, is irrelevant, because it is not the mere giving of notice that constitutes avoidance, but the non-breaching party's intention not to adhere to the contract that is important. This intention, moreover, must be clear to the breach party.

The findings of fact in the lower courts suggest that the plaintiff never actually notified the defendant that it was avoiding the contract. Indeed, the plaintiff never

MAP 10-5 Austria, Belgium, Germany, and the Netherlands (1991)

claimed that it had given such notice. Nor can one imply that such notice was given merely from the fact that the plaintiff gave the defendant a list of the losses suffered by its customer [the Dutch natural gas reseller].

Because the contract was not avoided, the damages [are not to be determined in accordance with CISG, Articles 75 and 76, but rather] are to be determined in accordance with CISG, Article 74. Article 74 applies to those cases when the damages come about because of delay in delivery or because of some defect in the goods.

[Loss of Profits]

When, as the case here, the non-breaching party is claiming a loss of profits from an expected resale of the goods to a third party, the loss of profits will only be considered if the breaching party had reason to know of this expected resale. Of course, when merchantable goods are sold to a merchant, the expected resale can be presumed. The defendant does not challenge this. Indeed, it has conceded that it knew that the plaintiff intended to resell the goods. [The plaintiff, accordingly, is entitled to the $15,000 claimed in lost profits.]

---

[124]Articles 25 and 49.

[Duty to Mitigate]

A non-breaching party may not claim damages, including a loss of profits, if it fails to make reasonable efforts to mitigate its losses. Such efforts are reasonable if a reasonable person in the position of the non-breaching party would have undertaken them in good faith.[125]

The defendant argues that the plaintiff breached this obligation. However, the burden of proving such a breach is on the defendant, and the defendant has failed to meet its burden. . . . It has not shown what the plaintiff did to breach this obligation, it has not shown that the plaintiff had other alternatives to what it did, nor has it shown how much the damages would have been lessened if the plaintiff had engaged in some alternative conduct. [In addition to lost profits, therefore, the plaintiff is entitled to recoup the $141,131 due the Dutch natural gas reseller.]

* * *

The decision of the Court of Appeals is affirmed. ■

CASEPOINT: In this case, the court considered whether a seller of propane gas had breached its contractual duties by failing to deliver the gas as promised, and if so, what damages were appropriate. First, the court looked at each party's duties under the CISG and found that the buyer was supposed to open a letter of credit. But here, the buyer could not do so because the seller never supplied the necessary information for the letter. Also, the breach was really due to the seller's failure to make proper arrangements to ship the gas, not because of the letter of credit. So, the court concluded that the seller had breached the contract and the buyer was entitled to damages.

TAKING DELIVERY

In connection with the taking of delivery, a buyer is obligated to cooperate with the seller to facilitate the transfer and to actually "take over the goods."[126] A buyer who fails to cooperate will be responsible for any resulting costs, and one who fails to take delivery assumes the risk for any damage to the goods after that time.[127]

J. THE PASSING OF RISK

passage of risk: The point in time when the buyer becomes responsible for losses to the goods.

The loss of goods through fire, theft, or other means can occur at any time: prior to delivery, during transit or inspection, or after delivery. The legal concept of **passage of risk** determines who is responsible for the loss. In most cases, the loss will be covered by insurance. Even so, it is important to determine whether the buyer or seller is responsible for obtaining the insurance.

To begin with, *passage of risk* is defined as the shifting of responsibility for loss or damage from the seller to the buyer. This means that once the risk passes, the buyer must pay the agreed-upon price for the goods involved. The buyer must then absorb the cost of the loss or lodge a claim against his insurer. Only if he can show that the loss or damage was due to an act or omission of the seller is he excused from paying the price.[128]

Like most domestic sales codes, CISG allocates risks by considering the agreement of the parties and the means of delivery. Unlike some domestic laws, however, CISG's risk allocation is not affected by breach of contract.

AGREEMENT OF THE PARTIES

CISG allows parties to allocate risk among themselves and to specify when the risk will pass between them.[129] The parties most commonly do so through the use of trade terms, such as *Free on Board (FOB)* or *Cost, Insurance, and Freight (CIF)*. Unlike most domestic sales

---

[125]United Nations Convention on Contracts for the International Sale of Goods, Article 77, [which provides: "A party who relies on a breach of contract must take such measures as are reasonable in the circumstances to mitigate the loss, including loss of profit, resulting from the breach. If he fails to take such measures, the party in breach may claim a reduction in the damages in the amount by which the loss should have been mitigated."]
[126]UN Convention on Contracts for the International Sale of Goods, Article 60 (1980).
[127]See *id.*, Articles 66–70.
[128]*Id.*, Article 66. This rule is common to virtually all domestic sale-of-goods laws: e.g., United Kingdom, Sale of Goods Act, § 20(2) (1893); Federal Republic of Germany, Civil Code, § 447(2); United States, Uniform Commercial Code, § 2-501.
[129]UN Convention on Contracts for the International Sale of Goods, Article 6 (1980).

laws,[130] CISG does not define any trade terms. The parties may use domestic trade terms or (in what is the most common practice) they may use the terms defined by the International Chamber of Commerce and known as *Incoterms*. Incoterms, which are described in more detail in Chapter 11, are well known, and their use in international sales is encouraged by trade councils, courts, and international lawyers.

MEANS OF DELIVERY

Goods may be transported by a carrier or delivered by the seller without being transported by a carrier.

Goods Transported by Carrier

CISG distinguishes between shipment, transshipment, in-transit, and destination contracts. No matter which of these contracts is used, however, the risk of loss will not pass until the goods are clearly "identified" to the contract by markings on the goods, shipping documents, notice given to the buyer, or otherwise.[131]

Shipment Contracts When a contract requires the seller to deliver the goods to a carrier for shipment and does not require the seller to deliver them to a particular place, the risk of loss passes when the goods are "handed over" to the first carrier.[132] For example, if the delivery term in a contract between a seller in Paris, France, and a buyer in Denver, Colorado, is "Free Carrier (FCA) Paris," the risk of loss will pass to the buyer when the seller delivers the goods to the trucking company in Paris that will transport them to the international carrier in Le Havre, France.

Transshipment Contracts If a contract requires the seller to deliver the goods to a carrier at a named place, who will then carry the goods to the buyer, the risk of loss passes to the buyer when the goods are handed over to the carrier at that place.[133] Thus, if the contract contains a "Free Alongside Ship (FAS) M/V *Ocean Trader*, Vancouver, British Columbia" delivery term, the seller in Calgary will bear the risk of loss until the goods are delivered alongside the M/V *Ocean Trader* at the port of Vancouver.

In-Transit Contracts Sometimes goods are sold after they are already aboard a carrier. In such a case, the risk of loss passes to the buyer at the time the contract is concluded. However, if, at the time the contract was made, the seller knew or ought to have known that goods had been lost or damaged and he did not disclose this to the buyer, the risk will remain with the seller.[134] For example, if the owner of crude oil being transported on a tanker from the Middle East to Houston, Texas, contracts to sell the oil to a buyer, the risk of loss will pass to the buyer at the time the contract is made. If, however, the seller knew that the oil had been contaminated and did not tell the buyer, the risk of loss will not pass.

Destination Contracts When a contract requires the seller to arrange transportation to a named place of destination, the risk of loss passes to the buyer when the goods are handed over or placed at his disposal at that place.[135] A contract containing a "Delivered Duty Paid (DDP) Seattle, Washington" trade term, for example, would require a seller in Tokyo to bear the risk of transporting the goods to Seattle.

---

[130]Most, but not all, countries use trade terms. Japan, for example, has no established set of domestic trade terms.
[131]UN Convention on Contracts for the International Sale of Goods, Article 67(2) (1980).
  The CISG rule for assigning risk when goods are shipped is the same rule found in many domestic codes: e.g., United States, Uniform Commercial Code, § 2–509; Federal Republic of Germany, Civil Code, §§ 446(1) and 447(1); Israel, Sales Law, § 22(b); Sweden, Sales Act, § 10; United Kingdom, Sale of Goods Acts, § 20 (1893 and 1979).
[132]UN Convention on Contracts for the International Sale of Goods, Article 67(1) (1980).
[133]*Id.*, Article 67(1).
[134]*Id.*, Article 68.
[135]*Id.*, Article 69(2).

Goods Delivered without Being Transported

When goods are not shipped to the buyer, the risk of loss passes when the goods are handed over by the seller or otherwise put at the buyer's disposal.[136] The goods are not considered to be put at the buyer's disposal, however, until they are clearly identified to the contract.[137] An example of such a contract is one containing an "Ex Works (EXW) Seller's City" trade term.

BREACH OF CONTRACT

Unlike the U.S. Uniform Commercial Code and some other domestic sales laws, the CISG rules on risk of loss are not concerned with breach of contract. That is, with the exception of in-transit contracts (in which risk passes at the time of contracting unless the seller knows or to ought to know that the goods are lost or damaged), the risk of loss passes to the buyer at the agreed-upon time and place of delivery.

K. REMEDIES

CISG provides for remedies that are (1) unique to the buyer, (2) unique to the seller, and (3) available to either party. Although the buyer's and seller's remedies relate to their specific needs, they are also interrelated, and anyone studying CISG's remedies must keep this in mind.

BUYER'S REMEDIES

cumulative: Able to be joined or taken together.

The buyer's remedies are **cumulative**. That is to say, the right to recover damages is not lost if a buyer exercises any other available remedy.[138] They are also immediate. In other words, unlike the rules in some civil law countries, CISG forbids a court or arbitral tribunal from granting the seller a period of grace (*délai de grâce*) in which to comply with a buyer's demand for a remedy.[139]

The remedies that are unique to the buyer are (1) to compel specific performance, (2) to avoid the contract for fundamental breach or nondelivery, (3) to reduce the price, (4) to refuse early delivery, and (5) to refuse excess quantities. Most of these remedies are common to virtually every legal system, but two—the right to set an additional time in which to perform and the right to reduce the price—are not. All are applicable whether the seller's breach affects the whole contract or only a part.

Specific Performance

As we have already seen, the availability of a decree of specific performance depends on the domestic rules applicable to the court hearing the suit. Assuming it is available, a buyer can ask that a seller either (1) deliver substitute goods or (2) make repairs. In either case, the buyer must first notify the seller that the goods are nonconforming, and, if he is asking for substitute goods, the nonconformity must amount to a fundamental breach. Also, the buyer cannot have avoided the contract or resorted to some other inconsistent remedy.[140]

Avoidance

Nachfrist notice: The fixing by the buyer of an additional reasonable period of time in which the seller may perform.

CISG's provisions for avoidance by a buyer are patterned after German law, especially in the convention's adoption of the German *Nachfrist*[141] notice. A comparative analysis of several different approaches to avoidance is given in Reading 10-1.

---

[136]*Id.*, Article 69(1).
[137]*Id.*, Article 69(3).
[138]*Id.*, Article 45(2). Until the 1940s, U.S. case law and the U.S. Uniform Sales Act (1906) required buyers to make an election. The idea was to make it difficult for buyers to rescind contracts for trivial purposes. The election-of-remedies rule was overturned with the adoption of § 2–711(1) of the Uniform Commercial Code.
[139]UN Convention on Contracts for the International Sale of Goods, Article 45(3) (1980). See G H. Treitel, "Remedies for Breach of Contract," in *International Encyclopedia of Comparative Law*, vol. 7, chap. 16, §§ 147–148 (1976), for a discussion of the French *délai de grâce*.
[140]UN Convention on Contracts for the International Sale of Goods, Article 46 (1980).
[141]German: "to fix an appointed time."

———— ✐✐✐ ————

Reading 10-1   THE BUYER'S RIGHT TO AVOID THE CONTRACT

John Honnold,
Uniform Law for International Sales under the 1980 United Nations Convention, pp. 307, 315–316 (1982).

THE PROBLEM OF AVOIDANCE IN DOMESTIC LAW

When does a breach of contract by one party release the other party from his contractual obligations? Attempts to answer this question have produced rules of domestic law of unusual technicality and uncertainty.

The common law initially found it difficult to release a party (Party A) from his promise because of breach by the other party (B), unless the promises of the two parties were linked by some verbal formula such as "A promises, in exchange for B's delivery of first-quality hemp, to pay. . . ." Late in the eighteenth century this technical approach was relaxed by the judicial creation of rules that performance by B could be a "condition" of A's duty of performance; under some of the case law, whether B's breach released A depended on questions of degree such as the seriousness of the breach.[142]

However, some of the more technical case law was frozen into statutory form in the (U.K.) Sale of Goods Act (1893). The buyer's right to reject (avoid the contract) could turn on various factors—whether the contract involved "specific goods, the property in which has passed to the buyer," whether the sale was "by description," or whether the buyer had "accepted" all, or even part, of the goods. . . .

The (U.S.) Uniform Commercial Code created a somewhat different set of distinctions. A buyer may reject

goods if the "goods or the tender of delivery fail in any respect to conform to the contract" (UCC, § 2-601). However, if the buyer has "accepted" the goods (even without an opportunity to ascertain the defect) he may refuse to keep the goods only if a "nonconformity substantially impairs its value" (UCC, § 2-608). The Code also applies this test of "substantial" impairment of value to contracts calling for delivery in separate lots or installments, even with respect to rejection of those goods that were defective (UCC, § 2-612). In an earlier study, this writer found these provisions to be casuistic and unresponsive to commercial practice and the significant interests of the parties.[143]

In France, the Code does not define the grounds for avoidance of a contract for breach, but erects procedural barriers by a general rule (pitted by exceptions) that a party must apply to the court for termination of his obligation to perform. Professor Treitel reports that in determining whether to grant this remedy the court will consider "various factors such as the defendant's degree of fault and the seriousness of the defect in performance."[144]

***

The notice avoidance approach of Articles 47 and 49(1)(b) of the Convention was inspired by a provision of German law that, on default by one party:

the other party may give him a reasonable period within which to perform his part with a declaration that he will refuse to accept the performance after the expiration of the period.

---

[142]An important contribution to this development was made by Lord Mansfield in Kingston v. Preston, *English Reports*, vol. 99, p. 437 (King's Bench, 1773). See William Searle Holdsworth, *History of English Law*, vol. 8, pp. 70–88 (2d ed., 1937); Arthur L. Corbin, "Conditions in the Law of Contract," *Yale Law Journal*, vol. 28, p. 739 (1919), reprinted in *Selected Essays in the Law of Contracts,* p. 871 (1939); Edwin W. Patterson, "Constructive Conditions in Contracts," *Columbia Law Review*, vol. 42, p. 903 (1942).
[143]John Honnold, "Buyer's Right of Rejection—A Study in the Impact of Codification on a Commercial Problem," *University of Pennsylvania Law Review*, vol. 97, p. 457 (1949). See also George L. Priest, "Breach and Remedy for the Tender of Nonconforming Goods under the UCC: An Economic Approach," *Harvard Law Review*, vol. 91, p. 960 (1978) (includes economic analysis of the UCC decisions).
[144]G. H. Treitel, "Remedies for Breach of Contract," *International Encyclopedia of Comparative Law*, vol. 7, chap. 16, § 147 (1976). This helpful study includes references to developments under other systems, such as those of Quebec and Louisiana, that have been influenced by French law. See also Konrad Zweigert and Hein Kötz, *An Introduction to Comparative Law*, vol. 2, pp. 168–170 (trans. Tony Weir, 1977) (means of overcoming practical difficulties of French rule requiring court action).

If performance is not made in due time, the person who gave the above notice (often termed a *Nachfrist*) may "withdraw from the contract."[145]

Other aspects of the German *Nachfrist* were not employed in the Convention. [For example,] . . . under the Convention when the seller commits a breach that is fundamental, the buyer may declare the contract avoided (Article 49(1)(b)) without giving the seller an "additional period of time of reasonable length." However, the opportunity by advance notice to clarify the situation for both parties has received widespread international approval; the basic utility of this legal tool was never seriously questioned in the UNCITRAL proceeding or at the Diplomatic Conference. ■

[145]German (F.R.G.) Civil Code, § 326. G. H. Treitel, "Remedies for Breach of Contract," *International Encyclopedia of Comparative Law*, vol. 7, chap. 16, §§ 149–151 (1976), on which the present discussion relies, helpfully discusses the above provision and similar provisions in other legal systems—e.g., Austrian Civil Code, § 918, Swiss Code of Obligations, § 107. Konrad Zweigert and Hein Kötz, *An Introduction to Comparative Law*, vol. 2, pp. 170, 178 (trans. Tony Weir, 1977) discusses comparable rules in England and Italy. The (U.S.) UCC does not explicitly establish an additional time notice comparable to *Nachfrist,* but the official Comments to UCC, § 2–309 commend the use of such notices to add certainty to the relationship between the parties (Comments 3 and 5).

Under CISG, a buyer may avoid a contract if either (1) the seller commits a fundamental breach or (2) the buyer gives the seller a *Nachfrist* notice and the seller rejects it or does not perform within the period it specifies.[146] A buyer's *Nachfrist* notice is the fixing of "an additional period of time of reasonable length for performance by the seller of his obligations."[147] The period must be definite, and the obligation to perform within that period must be clear. Once the *Nachfrist* period has run, or once the fundamental breach becomes clear, the buyer has a reasonable time in which to avoid the contract.[148]

During the *Nachfrist* period, the seller is entitled to correct (i.e., cure) the nonconformity at his own expense. Even if there has been a breach, the seller is entitled to make a cure, unless the circumstances—including the circumstance of the offer to make the cure—indicate that the breach is fundamental and the buyer chooses to avoid the contract.[149]

When a buyer's avoidance remedy may be applied is considered in Case 10-6.

[146]UN Convention on Contracts for the International Sale of Goods, Article 49(1) (1980).
[147]*Id.*, Article 47(1).
[148]*Id.*, Article 49(2): "[I]n cases where the seller has delivered the goods, the buyer loses the right to declare the contract avoided unless he does so: (a) in respect of late delivery, within a reasonable time after he has become aware that delivery has been made; (b) in respect of any breach other than late delivery, within a reasonable time: (i) after he knew or ought to have known of the breach; [or] (ii) after the expiration of any additional period of time fixed by the buyer . . . or after the seller has declared that he will not perform his obligations within such an additional period. . . ."
[149]*Id.*, Article 48.

Case 10-6   THE SHOE SELLER'S CASE

Germany, Court of Appeals, Frankfurt am Main, 1994. Case 5 U 15/93.
Journal of Law & Commerce, vol. 14, p. 201 (1995).

The plaintiff, an Italian business, contracted in January 1991 to sell women's shoes to the defendant, a German businesswoman. The plaintiff-seller was late in making its delivery, and the shoes did not completely conform to the original sample that had been shown to the defendant-buyer. Although the defendant accepted delivery, she refused to pay on two of the plaintiff's invoices. The plaintiff then brought suit in a German court to recover the amounts it had billed the defendant on its invoices. In the defendant's answer to the plaintiff's complaint, the defendant relied on the remedy of avoidance, maintaining that she was entitled to avoid the contract and be excused from any liability on the unpaid invoices because of (1) the plaintiff's late delivery and (2) the nonconformity of the goods. The court found in favor of the plaintiff and the defendant appealed.

JUDGMENT

***

The sales contract entered into by the parties in January 1991 is governed by the *United Nations Convention on Contracts for the International Sale of Goods* (Convention or CISG) pursuant to Articles 1 and 100(2) of that Convention. Both Italy and Germany were then, and are now, parties to the CISG, the CISG having come into force in Germany on January 1, 1991, and in Italy on January 1, 1988.

The plaintiff's claim in this case is based upon two unpaid invoices . . . relating to the sale of women's shoes. The plaintiff seeks to recover from the defendant . . . the unpaid balance due on those invoices. The defendant does not contest the making of the contract, her acceptance of delivery of the shoes, or the amount of the purchase price.

A buyer is excused from paying the purchase price for goods if the buyer can avoid the contract[150] and, except for the obligation to pay any damages that may be due, the avoidance of a contract releases both parties from their contractual obligations.[151]

The defendant's contention that she may avoid the contract because the plaintiff was late in delivering the goods is not by itself a sufficient basis for her to avoid the contract. Avoidance in such a case is only allowed after a buyer [gives a seller a *Nachfrist* notice and] defines an additional fixed period of time in which the seller may make delivery.[152] Because the defendant did not do so, she may not avoid the contract on this basis.

The defendant's contention that she may avoid the contract because the goods were predominantly nonconforming is also lacking in merit. According to the Convention, the tender of nonconforming goods does not amount to a failure to make delivery; it is only a breach of contract. Such a breach, moreover, may or may not be fundamental, and only in those cases in which the seller

FIGURE 10-6 West Germany and Italy (1991)

commits a fundamental breach of contract is the buyer entitled to use the remedy of avoidance.[153]

Germany's national sales law allows a buyer (with minor exceptions) to avoid a contract if the goods the seller delivers are defective. This is not so under the CISG. The CISG expects a buyer to accept deliveries of nonconforming goods [unless they are fundamentally nonconforming] and to invoke remedies other than avoidance (such as reduction of the price and damages) as compensation for the defects. For example, there would be no fundamental breach of contract [and no right to avoid the contract] in cases where the buyer is able to use some of the goods.[154]

---

[150]United Nations Convention on Contracts for the International Sale of Goods (1980), Article 49.
[151]*Id.*, Article 81(1).
[152]*Id.*, Articles 49(1)(b) and 47(1).
[153]*Id.*, Article 49(1)(a).
[154]Ernst von Caemmerer and Peter Schlechtriem, eds., *Commentary on the Uniform UN Law of Sales—CISG*, Article 46, n. 64, Article 49, n. 27 (1990); Piltz, *International Sales Law*, § 5, n. 247 (1993).

Thus, if a buyer contends that there is a fundamental breach of contract because the goods delivered do not conform to the original sample the parties relied on in making their contract, the buyer must introduce evidence that (1) describes the exact nature of the defects and (2) shows that the goods cannot be used in any way. If a buyer does not do this, the court will be unable to determine if there was a fundamental breach.

In this case, the defendant only testified that . . . "[the shoes] were defectively made." She said that the materials had "defects," that the manufacture was "not uniform," that some of the shoes were "stitched together" while others were merely "folded," and overall that the shoes did not correspond to the original sample she had been shown. From this testimony it is not possible to determine the precise nature of the defects. More importantly, the defendant's evidence about how the shoes were different from the sample does not help us ascertain whether or not she could reasonably be expected to use the shoes.

In her allegations, the defendant . . . also complained that the shoes were made from a material called "S. Oro" rather than "Metallic Gold Leather" and that this caused the shoes to have heavy wrinkles rather than a smooth finish. Again, however, these allegations do not allow us to determine if the shoes—apart from their being made of different material and having a different appearance—were defective or unfit for use.

***

The Court of Appeals affirmed the decision in favor of the plaintiff. ∎

CASEPOINT: Here the parties had a contract for a delivery of shoes from an Italian seller to a German buyer. Claiming that some of the shoes were defective, the buyer did not pay for two invoices, and the seller sued. The legal question was whether, under the CISG, the buyer had grounds to avoid the contract. The court stated that in order to use the CISG avoidance remedy, either (1) the buyer must have sent a *Nachfrist* notice giving the seller more time to perform or (2) the seller must have committed a fundamental breach of contract. Since neither of these tests were met here, the court ruled in favor of the plaintiff.

Reduction in Price

reduction in price: Remedy that allows a buyer to pay less for nonconforming goods in those cases where the buyer is not entitled to damages.

If a buyer is not entitled to damages when a seller delivers nonconforming goods, the buyer will be entitled to a **reduction in price**.[155] This remedy has its origins in the Roman law remedy of *actio quanti minoris*,[156] a remedy commonplace in civil law countries but generally unknown in the common law world. At the proceedings leading up to the adoption of CISG, many delegates argued that the price reduction remedy is little different from damages and therefore served no real purpose. Nevertheless, most representatives from the civil law countries felt that it was different, and eventually it was incorporated in the convention.

The price reduction remedy is different from damages because it applies to a very special situation. First, the buyer must have accepted goods that are nonconforming. Second, the seller must not be responsible for the nonconformity. An example of such a case is one where the goods were damaged by *force majeure*[157] or an act of nature. Consider the following situation. A seller in New Orleans agrees to deliver grade No. 1 corn to a buyer at the buyer's mill in Karachi for a price of $80,000. While the corn is in transit on the SS *Skipper*, a war breaks out and the ship is detained by one of the warring countries for three months. When the SS *Skipper* arrives in Karachi, the corn is moldy and graded only as No. 3. The buyer is happy to have the corn, even though it is moldy, because the war has interrupted all of its orders. Under the damage provisions of CISG, the buyer is not entitled to damages.[158] The buyer is, however, entitled to a price reduction.

The amount of the reduction is determined by a formula that considers the relative price of conforming and nonconforming goods at the time of delivery. That is, "the buyer may reduce the price in the same proportion as the value that the goods actually delivered had at

---

[155]UN Convention on Contracts for the International Sale of Goods, Article 50 (1980).
[156]Latin: "action to determine the extent of a reduction."
[157]French: "superior force." An event or effect that cannot be reasonably anticipated or controlled.
[158]UN Convention on Contracts for the International Sale of Goods, Article 79 (1980).

the time of delivery bears to the value that conforming goods would have had at that time."[159] In other words,

$$\text{Price Reduction} = [\text{Price}] - \left[\frac{\text{Price} \times \text{Value of goods as delivered}}{\text{Value of conforming goods at the time of delivery}} \right]$$

In our example, let us assume that the price for 25,000 bushels of No. 3 corn in Karachi at the time of delivery is $75,000 and the price for the same amount of No. 1 corn is $100,000. The original price ($80,000) will therefore be reduced by the ratio of the price of the No. 3 to the price of the No. 1 corn. Accordingly, the reduction will be $20,000 and the buyer will pay only $60,000.

Refusing Early Delivery and Excess Quantity

If the seller delivers early, the buyer is under no obligation to take delivery.[160] If the seller delivers more than the amount agreed upon, the buyer may also accept or reject the excess part. However, if the buyer does accept, he must pay for the excess goods at the contract rate.[161]

The Effect of Nonconformity in a Part of the Goods

Assume the following facts: A seller agrees to sell a buyer 1,000 bags of flour. At the time of delivery, 100 bags are vermin infested and totally unusable. May the buyer reject the 100 bags and accept the balance? May the buyer reject the entire contract?

As to the defective part, CISG provides that the buyer may seek specific performance, obtain a price reduction, or avoid that part of the contract. In doing so, however, he must comply with CISG's rules for those particular remedies.[162] As for avoiding the whole contract, a buyer may do so only if the partial delivery amounts to a fundamental breach of the whole.[163]

SELLER'S REMEDIES

The seller's remedies in CISG mirror those of the buyer. Like the buyer's remedies, the seller's remedies are both cumulative and immediate. That is, the right to recover damages is not lost if a seller exercises any other available remedy, and courts will not grant the buyer a grace period in which to perform.[164]

The remedies that are unique to the seller are (1) to compel specific performance, (2) to avoid the contract for a fundamental breach or failure to cure a defect, and (3) to obtain missing specifications. Again, each of these remedies is meant to mirror the buyer's remedies.

Specific Performance

Assuming that a decree of specific performance is available under local law, a seller may require a buyer to (1) take delivery and pay the contract price or (2) perform any other obligation required by the contract.[165]

This rather unusual remedy is included in the convention primarily for symmetry, as a balance to the buyer's specific performance remedy. Its inclusion stresses the fact that CISG requires both parties to perform their obligations. However, because Article 28 of the convention limits the availability of specific performance decrees to cases where the domestic court has powers to grant a similar decree, the likelihood that it will be used very often is small.

---

[159]*Id.*, Article 50.
[160]*Id.*, Article 52(1). The buyer, however, may have an obligation under Article 86 to take possession of the goods on behalf of the seller to prevent the seller from suffering injury.
[161]*Id.*, Article 52(2).
[162]*Id.*, Article 51(1).
[163]*Id.*, Article 51(2).
[164]*Id.*, Article 61.
[165]*Id.*, Article 62.

In common law countries, a suit to recover the full price from the buyer is not a form of specific performance. Historically, specific performance was a decree issued by a court of equity. A suit to recover the price, normally called an action in *debt*, was obtained from a different court, a court of law. An action in debt, moreover, was available only on a *quid pro quo*[166] basis. The seller could recover the price only for the things actually received by the buyer, and the buyer (at least in a court of law) could not be compelled to take delivery of the goods. This tradition survives in both the U.K. Sale of Goods Act of 1893 (§ 49) and the U.S. Uniform Commercial Code (§ 2-709), as well as in the statutes of other common law countries. The seller may recover the price, but only after "the property in the goods has passed to the buyer."[167]

Unlike the common law countries, the sales codes in civil law countries do have provisions that can require the buyer to take delivery and pay the full price. As a practical matter, however, they are seldom used.[168] Rather, when a buyer refuses to take delivery, the seller commonly resells the goods on the buyer's account and brings an action to recover any deficiency. Such a remedy for damages is also allowed under the convention.[169]

Avoidance

The seller's avoidance remedy truly is the mirror image of the buyer's remedy. Like the buyer, the seller may avoid the contract only if there has been a fundamental breach or, following a *Nachfrist* notice, the buyer refuses to cure any defect in his performance.[170] The rules applying to fundamental breach and the *Nachfrist* notice, discussed earlier, apply here as well.

Missing Specifications

missing specifications:
Remedy that allows a seller to ascertain specifications himself when the buyer fails to supply them as required by the contract or within a reasonable time after the seller requests them.

The **missing specifications** remedy applies to a special problem that can face sellers: obtaining specifications for goods that the buyer fails to supply. If the buyer does not produce the measurements that the seller needs by the date specified in the contract or within a reasonable time after the seller asks for them, CISG allows the seller to ascertain them himself "in accordance with the requirements of the buyer that may be known to him."[171] The seller must then inform the buyer of what he has done and set a reasonable time period for the buyer to supply different specifications. However, if the buyer does not respond, the seller's specifications become "binding."[172]

REMEDIES AVAILABLE TO BOTH BUYERS AND SELLERS

The remedies available to both buyers and sellers are (1) suspension of performance, (2) avoidance in anticipation of a fundamental breach, (3) avoidance of an installment contract, and (4) damages.

Suspension of Performance

suspension of performance:
Remedy available to either party when it becomes clear that the other party will not perform a substantial part of his obligation because of a serious deficiency in his ability to perform, his creditworthiness, his preparations for performing, or his performance.

CISG, Article 71, describes the remedy of **suspension of performance** as follows:

1. A party may suspend the performance of his obligations if, after the conclusion of the contract, it becomes apparent that the other party will not perform a substantial part of his obligations as a result of: (a) a serious deficiency in his ability to perform or his creditworthiness; or (b) his conduct in preparing to perform or in performing the contract.

---

[166]Latin: "something for something." One thing in return for another. In the traditional English common law, the giving of one valuable thing for another—called *mutual consideration*—was a necessary requirement for a contract to be valid.
[167]United Kingdom, Sale of Goods Act, § 49 (1893).
[168]See John Philip Dawson, "Specific Performance in France and Germany," *Michigan Law Review*, vol. 57, p. 495 (1959); and G. H. Treitel, "Remedies for Breach of Contract," in *International Encyclopedia of Comparative Law*, vol. 7, chap. 16, §§ 10–29, (1976).
[169]UN Convention on Contracts for the International Sale of Goods, Article 75 (1980).
[170]*Id.*, Article 64.
[171]*Id.*, Article 65(1).
[172]*Id.*, Article 65(2).

2. If the seller has already dispatched the goods before the grounds described in the preceding paragraph become evident, he may prevent the handing over of the goods to the buyer even though the buyer holds a document which entitles him to obtain them. The present paragraph relates only to the rights in the goods as between the buyer and the seller.

3. A party suspending performance, whether before or after dispatch of the goods, must immediately give notice of the suspension to the other party and must continue with performance if the other party provides adequate assurance of his performance.

Paragraph (1) applies to threats of nonperformance, paragraph (2) applies to threats of nonpayment discovered after the goods are in transit, and paragraph (3) requires a suspending party to give notice and to resume his obligations under the contract if the other party provides adequate assurances of his capability to perform.

Paragraph (2) applies to a special set of circumstances. The threat that the buyer will not pay must be discovered after the goods are shipped but before they are handed over by the carrier, and the seller must not have retained control over the goods (e.g., he may have turned over a negotiable bill of lading to the buyer).[173] In this situation, the seller can prevent the carrier from delivering the goods to the buyer. This right, however, "relates only to the rights in the goods as between the buyer and the seller." Should a third person acquire legal rights in the goods (e.g., as the holder in due course of a negotiable bill of lading), CISG will not apply.[174] Instead, the matter is left to domestic law; and, in most cases, the third party's right will prevail.

Anticipatory Avoidance

anticipatory avoidance:
Remedy available to either party when it becomes clear that the other party will commit a fundamental breach.

Anticipatory avoidance is different from the avoidance remedies that apply specifically to buyers and sellers. Those remedies apply only after an offending party has committed a fundamental breach. The remedy provided in Article 72 arises as soon as "it is clear" that the other party "will commit a fundamental breach."

There seem to be only a few cases where this remedy can be invoked. These include (1) the specific goods promised to the buyer are wrongfully sold to a third party; (2) the seller's only employee capable of producing the goods dies or is fired; and (3) the seller's manufacturing plant is sold.[175] In most other cases the breach will already have occurred, or the circumstances will be such that a suspension of performance is the appropriate remedy.

If a party opts to anticipatorily avoid, CISG requires him, "if time allows," to notify the other party so that the latter can "provide adequate assurance of his performance."[176] In practice, this is worth doing, both to comply with the convention's general requirement of "good faith" and to minimize any challenges to the use of the remedy.[177]

Avoidance of Installment Contracts

CISG's rule for avoiding installment contracts uses the same logic found in its other avoidance provisions. First, as to a particular installment, if there was a "fundamental breach with respect to that installment," then "the other party may declare the contract avoided with respect to that installment."[178] Second, if the breach of one installment gives a party "good grounds" to believe that a fundamental breach of later installments "will occur," then those later installments may be anticipatorily avoided.[179] Finally, if the installments are interdependent, a fundamental breach of one installment will allow a party to avoid the entire contract (past and future installments included).[180]

---

[173]Similar provisions can be found in many domestic codes: e.g., United States, Uniform Commercial Code, § 2–704; Sweden, Sales Act, § 39; and United Kingdom, Sale of Goods Act, §§ 44–46 (1893 as amended in 1979).
[174]UN Convention on Contracts for the International Sale of Goods, Article 4(b) (1980).
[175]See James C. Gulotta Jr., "Anticipatory Breach—A Comparative Analysis," *Tulane Law Review*, vol. 50, p. 932 (1976).
[176]UN Convention on Contracts for the International Sale of Goods, Article 72(2) (1980).
[177]See John Honnold, Uniform Law for International Sales under the 1980 United Nations Convention, p. 402, n. 2 (1982).
[178]UN Convention on Contracts for the International Sale of Goods, Article 73(1) (1980).
[179]*Id.*, Article 73(2).
[180]*Id.*, Article 73(3).

Damages

The basic rule on damages in CISG is common to both the civil law and common law worlds. Article 74 states:

> Damages for breach of contract by one party consist of a sum equal to the loss, including loss of profit, suffered by the other party as a consequence of the breach. Such damages may not exceed the loss which the party in breach foresaw or ought to have foreseen at the time of the conclusion of the contract, in the light of the facts and matters of which he then knew or ought to have known, as possible consequence of the breach of contract.

This rule, that a breaching party is liable for any foreseeable damages, is derived from Section 1150 of the French Civil Code, which limits damages to those "which were foreseen or which could have been foreseen at the time of the contract." In England, the French law was referred to with favor in the landmark 1854 case of *Hadley v. Baxendale*, which established the **foreseeability or improbability** test as a common law rule.[181] A similar but slightly different test is followed in Germany and the Scandinavian countries.[182]

foreseeability test: A breaching party is liable only for those damages that he foresaw or ought to have foreseen.

To calculate the damages, the convention uses two different rules. First, if an avoiding party has entered into a good-faith substitute transaction—the buyer obtaining substitute goods or the seller reselling the goods to another party—then damages are measured by the difference between the contract price and the price received in the substitute transaction.[183]

Alternatively, if the avoiding party did not enter into a substitute transaction, then the damages are calculated by taking the difference between the contract price and the current price at the time of avoidance.[184] The current price is defined as "the price prevailing at the place where delivery of the goods should have been made or, if there is not current price at that place, the price at such other places as serves as a reasonable substitute."[185]

mitigation: Obligation of a party claiming damages to keep the damages to a minimum.

No matter which of the two CISG damage rules applies, the party claiming damages is under an obligation to take reasonable measures "to **mitigate** the loss." If the claiming party fails to take such action, the other may seek a proportionate reduction in the damages.[186]

L. EXCUSES FOR NONPERFORMANCE

Two excuses are provided in CISG for a party's failure to perform. One is *force majeure*; the other is *dirty hands*.

FORCE MAJEURE

A party is not liable for any damages resulting from his failure to perform if he can show (1) that his failure was "due to an impediment beyond his control," (2) that the impediment was not something he could have reasonably taken into account at the time of contracting, and (3) that he remains unable to overcome the impediment or its consequences.[187]

---

[181]*English Reports*, vol. 156, p. 145. The English rule was codified in the Sale of Goods Act, §§ 50(2), 51(2), and 53(2) (1893); however, the phrase "loss directly and naturally resulting in the ordinary course of events" is used rather than the word *foreseeable*. The U.S. Uniform Commercial Code, § 2-715(2), speaks of "any loss resulting from general or particular requirements and needs of which the seller at the time of contracting had reason to know."

[182]G. H. Treitel, "Remedies for Breach of Contract," *International Encyclopedia of Comparative Law*, vol. 7, chap. 16, §§ 91–93 (1976), examines the extent to which the German concept of *adequate causation* approximates the *foreseeability* test. The Scandinavian countries' adoption of the German rule is discussed in Kurt Heller, "The Limits of Contractual Damages in the Scandinavian Law of Sales," *Scandinavian Studies*, vol. 10, pp. 40–79 (1978).

[183]UN Convention on Contracts for the International Sale of Goods, Article 75 (1980).

[184]*Id.*, Article 76(1).

[185]*Id.*, Article 76(2).

[186]*Id.*, Article 77. Related to the requirement of mitigation of damages is the requirement to preserve goods. Thus, a seller must preserve goods in his possession if the buyer is late taking delivery (Article 85), and a buyer must preserve goods in his possession if he intends to reject them (Article 86). In doing so, the goods can either be deposited in a warehouse at the expense of the other party (Article 87) or sold when the other party has unreasonably delayed in reclaiming them (Article 88).

[187]UN Convention on Contracts for the International Sale of Goods, Article 79(1) (1980).

force majeure: (French: "superior force.") An event or effect that cannot be reasonably anticipated or controlled.

This excuse, commonly known as *force majeure*, is not only narrowly defined, it is also limited in its application.[188] It applies to situations—such as natural disasters, war, embargoes, strikes, breakdowns, and the bankruptcy of a supplier—that frustrate both the party attempting to perform and the party expecting performance. Because neither party is really at fault, the breaching party is excused from paying damages. He is not, however, exempted from the application of any other appropriate remedy (such as suspension of performance or avoidance).

A party seeking to use CISG's excuse of *force majeure* is under some additional limitations. First, he has a duty to promptly notify the other party of "the impediment and its effect on his ability to perform."[189] Second, if his claim is based on the failure of a third person to perform (such as a supplier), the third person must himself be able to claim the excuse.[190] Finally, the excuse may be used only as long as the underlying impediment continues in existence.[191]

In Case 10-7, the court was asked to determine if the CISG applied to the dispute and whether the seller was excused from performing because of "an impediment beyond his control or because of "commercial impracticability."

---

[188]The CISG rule, based on civil law practice, is much broader, however, than the rule followed in common law countries. For example, in the United States, the Uniform Commercial Code, § 2-615, applies only to a seller and only in respect to two aspects of his performance: delay in delivery and nondelivery. For a comparison of the CISG provision with various domestic rules, see John Honnold, *Uniform Law for International Sales under the 1980 United Nations Convention*, pp. 425–427 (1982).
[189]UN Convention on Contracts for the International Sale of Goods, Article 79(4) (1980).
[190]*Id.*, Article 79(2).
[191]*Id.*, Article 79(3).

❧❧❧

Case 10-7 NUOVA FUCINATI, SPA v. FONDMETALL INTERNATIONAL, AB

Italy, Civil Court of Monza, 1993.
Il Foro italiano, vol. 1994, part 1, pp. 916–923 (1994)
Giurisprudenza italiana, vol. 1994, part 1, pp. 146–154.[192]

On February 3, 1988, the plaintiff, Nuova Fucinati, SpA, of Monza, Italy, agreed to deliver 1,000 metric tons of chromite (a brownish-black mineral ore consisting of an oxide of iron and chromium—used by the metalcasting industry as a specialty sand to produce high-quality castings) to the defendant, Fondmetall International, A.B., of Goteborg, Sweden, between March 20, 1988, and April 10, 1998. When the plaintiff failed to make delivery, the defendant petitioned the Civil Court in Monza, Italy, for a decree of specific performance. On July 20, 1988, the chief judge of that court issued the requested decree.

On September 29, 1988, the plaintiff initiated this proceeding to have the original contract set aside on grounds of commercial impracticability. According to the plaintiff,

the price of chromite had risen dramatically between the time of the contract and the time of delivery, beyond what could reasonably be anticipated, such that it was too costly for the plaintiff to perform without a price adjustment, which the defendant refused to accept.

The defendant argued that the United Nations Convention on Contracts for the International Sale of Goods (CISG) governed this contractual relationship and that CISG did not provide for the excuse of commercial impracticability.

OPINION

***

The defendant argues that the contract should not be dissolved both as a matter of law [because CISG does not provide for the excuse of commercial impracticability] and because the plaintiff has not alleged facts sufficient to

---

[192]A summary of this case in Italian is posted on the Internet at http://soi.cnr.it/-crdes/crdcs/it140193f.htm. Another English translation is posted at cisgw3.law.pace.edu/cases/930329i3.html.

meet the requirements of Article 1467 of the Italian *Civil Code* [which defines commercial impracticability]. . . .

This is an international sale of goods contract, between an Italian corporation (the seller) and a Swedish corporation (the buyer). The first question we must resolve, therefore, is whether it is governed by [the] *United Nations Convention on Contracts for the International Sale of Goods.*[193] This is not an insignificant question. If the Convention applies, the excuse that a seller may set aside an onerous contract on the grounds of commercial impracticability does not seem to be available. If the Convention does not apply, then the Article 1467 of the [Italian] *Civil Code* will apply, and this article does allow a seller to set aside an onerous contract on the basis of commercial impracticability. . . .

[THE EXCUSE OF COMMERCIAL IMPRACTICABILITY]

Article 79 of [the] CISG [which the defendant relies upon] provides:

> A party is not liable for a failure to perform any of his obligations if he proves that the failure was due to an impediment beyond his control and that he could not reasonably be expected to have taken the impediment into account at the time of the conclusion of the contract. . . .

This article, however, is not concerned with the excuse of commercial impracticability. Rather, it deals with an intervening change in circumstances beyond the control of the breaching party, similar to the excuse of impossibility of performance that is set out in Article 1463 of the *Civil Code*. The breaching party invokes it after breaching a contract as an excuse for not performing as required.

Indeed, the main remedy that the CISG grants to a non-breaching party[194] is the remedy of avoidance (or "dissolution" as it is called in the *Civil Code*), and this remedy can only be invoked after a contract has been breached. By comparison, the excuse of commercial impracticability is unrelated to a breach. [It is invoked by a seller before there has been a breach to avoid a contract that the seller can perform, but at great cost.] Thus, commercial impracticability does not fit within the general scheme of remedies or excuses set out in the CISG.

. . . This conclusion is confirmed by Article 4 of [the] CISG, which states:

> This Convention governs only the formation of the contract of sale and the rights and obligations of the seller and the buyer arising from such a contract. In particular, except as otherwise expressly provided in this Convention, it is not concerned with:
>
> a. the validity of the contract or of any of its provisions or of any usage; [or]
> b. the effect which the contract may have on the property in the goods sold.

Avoidance of a contract because of commercial impracticability would affect neither the validity of the contract nor the property in the goods (except indirectly, by avoiding the seller's obligation to deliver the goods and thereby keeping the goods from being identified to the contract).

[EFFECT OF THE CISG'S APPLICATION]

The CISG is a "special law." [That is, it governs a specific subject matter.] As a consequence, if it does apply in this case, it will preempt the more general provision set out Article 1467 *et seq.* of the *Civil Code*.

[APPLICATION OF THE CISG]

The United Nations Convention came into force in Italy on January 1, 1988. This was before the contract was concluded on February 3, 1988. . . . However, the Convention did not come into force in Sweden until January 1, 1989 [after the contract was concluded]. . . .

Because of an express statement that the buyer added to its acceptance (that is, "law: Italian law shall apply"), the law governing this contract is Italian law. At the time of the contract, of course, the CISG was in effect in Italy and it therefore must be applied like any other law.

***

Article 1(1) of the CISG states:

> This Convention applies to contracts of sale of goods between parties whose places of business are in different States:
>
> a. when the States are Contracting States; or
> b. when the rules of private international law lead to the application of the law of a Contracting State.

[The first of these possibilities, option (a), does not lead us to apply the CISG because Sweden was not a Contracting State at the time that the contract was concluded.]

The second possibility, option (b), which directs us to apply the Italian rules of private international law, does not lead us to apply the CISG [either]. The rules of private international law set out in Article 25 of the Introductory Provisions of the [Italian] *Civil Code* direct us to apply Swedish law. That is because the contract was concluded in Sweden.[195] However, the CISG was not in

---

[193]Italy ratified the convention on December 11, 1985, by Law No. 765 and it came into force on January 1, 1988.

[194]Article 61 *et seq.* defines seller's remedies and Article 45 *et seq.* defines a buyer's remedies.

[195]Article 1326(1) of the *Civil Code* provides that the law of the state where a contract is made shall govern the interpretation and enforcement of the contract.

force in Sweden when the contract was made. So, again, the CISG cannot apply.

Therefore, because the "special law" (the CISG) does not apply, the "general law" (Article 1467 *et seq.* of the *Civil Code*) is not preempted, and it must be applied as the parties directed that it should. As a consequence, the seller can invoke the excuse of commercial impracticability. . . .

[THE PLAINTIFF'S CLAIM]

The plaintiff asserted that it was entitled to invoke the excuse of commercial impracticability on the fact that, between February 3, 1988 (the date when the contract was concluded) and April (when the plaintiff asserts that the goods were to be delivered), the fair market price of chromite had increased by 43.71 percent. That is from 1,496 lira per kilogram to 2,150 lira per kilogram. This increase, even though proven by the plaintiff, is simply not enough to show that the plaintiff is excused from performing as a matter of commercial impracticability. [Such an excuse is allowed only when performance is so economically burdensome that the seller would not have the resources to perform.]

The plaintiff's case was dismissed. Because it was obvious that the buyer had breached the contract, the chief judge's order for specific performance was rescinded and the case was remanded to the examining magistrate for further inquiry into the defendant's claim for compensatory damages. ■

CASEPOINT: The parties entered into a contract for the sale and delivery of chromite from a company in Italy to a company in Sweden. The court pointed out the differences between CISG Article 79, dealing with the excuse for a party's nonperformance based on "an impediment beyond his control," and the doctrine of "commercial impracticability." The court analyzed whether

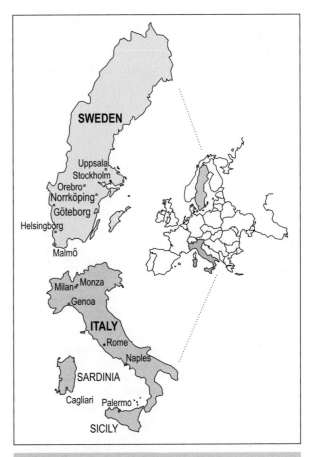

MAP 10-7 Italy and Sweden (1993)

the CISG applied to the dispute and found that it did not, since Sweden had not ratified the treaty when the contract was concluded. Thus, the theory of commercial impracticability was applied here, but the 43 percent increase in price was not enough for the plaintiff to use this theory as an excuse for non-performance.

DIRTY HANDS

dirty hands: Maxim that a party whose actions cause the other party to breach may not complain.

The **dirty hands** excuse is based on a very simple premise, succinctly stated in CISG, Article 80:

> A party may not rely on a failure of the other party to perform, to the extent that such failure was caused by the first party's act or omission.

For example, if a seller agrees to deliver goods to a buyer at the buyer's warehouse, but the buyer's warehouse is locked and inaccessible at the time that the seller is supposed to make delivery, the buyer cannot complain that the seller failed to deliver on time.

Chapter Questions

Application of the CISG

1. Seller, whose place of business is in State A, and Buyer, whose place of business is in State B, enter into a contract that stipulates that the CISG applies. Neither State A nor State B is a contracting state. Does the convention apply?

Various Provisions of the CISG

2. Retailer in State A decides to go into the catalog sales business in State B. Both countries are parties to the CISG. Retailer purchases a mailing list from Ace Credit Card Company. The list has the names and addresses of 500,000 persons owning Ace credit cards in State B, and Retailer uses this to prepare mailing labels. John Q. Public receives a catalog addressed to him personally from Retailer. The catalog describes various types of widgets and gives prices for each one. Has the retailer made an offer to sell the widgets? If John accepts, will there be a binding contract under the CISG?

3. On January 1, Seller sent a letter to Buyer offering to sell to Buyer 5,000 widgets for $25 apiece. The letter also stated: "This offer is binding and irrevocable until February 1." On January 5, prior to Buyer's receipt of the letter, Seller called Buyer on the telephone and left the following message on the answering machine at Buyer's place of business: "Ignore my letter of January 1. I have decided to withdraw the offer contained in it." On January 7, after listening to her answering machine and reading the letter that arrived that same day, Buyer sent Seller the following telegram: "I accept your offer of January 1." Is there a contract under the CISG?

Rejection Under the CISG

4. On December 1, Seller sent Buyer an offer to sell 5,000 widgets to Buyer for $25 apiece. The offer stated: "The offer will remain open until December 31." On December 10, Buyer answered: "The price is too high; I don't accept your offer." Then, on December 15, Buyer changed his mind and sent a telegram stating: "I accept your December 1 offer after all." Seller replied: "Your acceptance is too late, since you already rejected the offer." In turn, Buyer answered: "The acceptance is good, since you promised to keep your offer open until December 31." Is there a contract under the CISG?

Is Silence Acceptance Under the CISG?

5. Buyer received a letter in her mail on January 1 offering to sell Buyer 5,000 widgets for $20 apiece. Seller's letter closed with the following statement: "I know that this offer is so attractive that I will assume that you accept it unless I hear otherwise by January 31." Buyer did not reply. Seller shipped the widgets on February 1. What are Buyer's responsibilities under the CISG?

Modification of Contract and Reliance Under the CISG

6. Seller and Buyer entered into a written contract for the manufacture by Seller of 10,000 widgets of a design specified by Buyer and set out in the contract. The contract also provided: "This contract may only be modified in a writing signed by both parties." Before Seller began work on the widgets, Buyer and Seller agreed by telephone to a change in the specifications for 2,500 of the widgets. Seller then produced and delivered the 2,500 widgets as specified. Buyer refused to accept them because they did not conform to the specifications in the original contract. Assuming the CISG applies, who breached?

What Are the Requirements of a *Nachfrist* Notice?

7. Buyer and Seller entered into a contract governed by the CISG for Seller to deliver a sophisticated computer to Buyer by January 1. Seller was late in delivering the machine, so Buyer wired Seller on January 2: "Anxious to take delivery of the computer. Hope that it arrives by February 1." Seller delivers the computer on February 5, but Buyer refuses to accept it and declares that the contract is avoided because Seller failed to hand over the computer before the February 1 date specified in the January 2 telegram. Both Buyer and Seller agree that there has not been a fundamental breach. Is Buyer able to avoid the contract under these circumstances?

Risk of Loss Under the CISG

8. Dealer in the United States owned a cargo of 10,000 barrels of oil that had been shipped from Mexico on January 1 for arrival in the United States on February 1. On January 15, Dealer informed Buyer that the oil was en route and they concluded a contract. On arrival, inspection showed that the oil had been contaminated by seawater at some indeterminate time during the voyage. Assuming the CISG applies, who bears the risk?

Avoidance of Installment Contracts Under the CISG

9. Seller agreed to deliver three software programs to Buyer that are specially designed for Buyer's business. The first was to be delivered in January, the second in February, and the third in March. The program delivered in January worked fine, but the one delivered in February was defective. It not only failed to function properly, it also made the other two programs effectively worthless. Seller was unable to correct the defect, and no suitable replacement could be found from another supplier. What CISG remedies are available to Buyer?

Damages for Breach of Contract Under the CISG

10. Seller contracted to deliver 1,000 barrels of oil to Buyer for $14,000. When the oil arrived, 975 barrels complied fully with the contract description. Twenty-five were contaminated and unacceptable. Oil in comparable barrels was available in the local market for a price of $18 a barrel in 25-barrel lots. Seller offered not to charge Buyer for the barrels. Is there a contract under the CISG? If so, what payment is due to the Seller?

CHAPTER 11
TRANSPORTATION
——⟋⟍——

A. TRADE TERMS

Sales contracts involving transportation customarily contain abbreviated terms describing the time and place where the buyer is to take delivery. These **trade terms**, such as *free on board* (*FOB*) and *cost, insurance, and freight* (*CIF*), may also define a variety of other matters, including the time and place of payment, the price, the time when the risk of loss shifts from the seller to the buyer, and the costs of freight and insurance.

    The same trade abbreviations are widely used in both domestic and international transactions. Unfortunately, they have different meanings, depending on the governing

trade terms: Standardized terms used in sales contracts that describe the time, place, and manner for the transfer of goods from the seller to the buyer.

Incoterms: Trade terms published by the International Chamber of Commerce.

law.[1] In the United States, for example, the Uniform Commercial Code defines trade terms for domestic and export sales. In the United Kingdom, the terms are defined by reference to case law.[2] Virtually all domestic laws, however, allow the parties to define the terms themselves, or to incorporate definitions from foreign legislation or from a specific set of private rules. The United Nations Convention on Contracts for the International Sale of Goods similarly allows parties to incorporate trade terms of their choosing.[3]

The most widely used private trade terms are those published by the International Chamber of Commerce (ICC). Called **Incoterms**, they are well known throughout the world, and their use in international sales is encouraged by trade councils, courts, and international lawyers.[4] First published in 1936, the current version is *Incoterms 2000*.[5] Parties who adopt the Incoterms, or any other trade terms, should make sure they express their desire clearly. For example, a contract might refer to "FOB (Incoterms 2000)" or "CIF (U.S. Uniform Commercial Code)." Courts will otherwise apply the definitions used in their own jurisdictions.[6] Parties should also refrain from casually adopting any particular set of terms. The ICC's Incoterms, which are possibly the most complete of all such rules, are lengthy and deserve careful study. Finally, parties should be wary about making additions or varying the meaning of any particular term, except to the extent that it is allowed by the rules they adopt or by judicial decision. Courts are as apt to ignore a variation, or hold that the entire term is ineffective, as they are to apply it.[7]

> The Incoterms Web site is
>
> http://www.iccwbo.org/incoterms/id3042/index.html.

The parties' failure to use any trade term at all can also produce unexpected results. Courts are then left to divine the parties' intent and to decide the case based on local commercial practice. Such a problem arose in Case 11-1.

---

[1]See *Trade Terms*, an International Chamber of Commerce publication (Document No. 16, issued in 1955), which describes how 10 major trade terms are defined in 18 countries. Not all countries use trade terms, however. Japan, for example, has no established set of domestic trade terms. Hisashi Tanikawa, "Risk of Loss in Japanese Sales Transactions," *Washington Law Review*, vol. 42, p. 475 (1967).

[2]See D. Michael Day, *The Law of International Trade*, pp. 40–80 (1981).

[3]UN Convention on the International Sale of Goods, Article 6 (1980), provides: "The parties may exclude the application of this Convention, or . . . derogate from or vary the effect of any of its provisions."

[4]The National Foreign Trade Council in New York, which issued its own definitions, the *Revised American Foreign Trade Definitions*, in 1941, has since 1980 encouraged traders to use the Incoterms instead. See Paul H. Vishny, *Guide to International Commerce Law*, § 2–36 (1998).

[5]International Chamber of Commerce, Incoterms 2000 (Pub. No. 560, 2000). The Incoterms are currently revised every ten years.

[6]Frederic Eisemann, "Incoterms and the British Export Trade," *Journal of Business Law*, vol. 1965, p. 119 (1965), doubts that Incoterms have become sufficiently accepted to constitute trade usage or custom.

[7]Paul H. Vishny, *Guide to International Commerce Law*, § 2–37 (1998).

Case 11-1 ST. PAUL GUARDIAN INSURANCE COMPANY v. NEUROMED MEDICAL SYSTEMS & SUPPORT, GmbH

United States District Court for the Southern District of New York
LEXIS United States District Court Cases, no. 5096 (2002).

DISTRICT JUDGE SIDNEY H. STEIN:

Plaintiffs St. Paul Guardian Insurance Company and Travelers Property Casualty Insurance Company have brought this action as subrogees[8] of Shared Imaging,

---

[8]Subrogees are persons who have been subrogated to the legal claim of another; that is, persons who have assumed the legal right to collect another's debt or damages.

Inc., to recover $285,000 they paid to Shared Imaging for damage to a mobile magnetic resonance imaging system ("MRI") purchased by Shared Imaging from defendant Neuromed Medical Systems & Support GmbH ("Neuromed"). Neuromed has moved to dismiss the complaint . . . . [It contends that] the complaint fails to state a claim for relief. . . .

The crux of Neuromed's argument is that it had no further obligations regarding the risk of loss once it delivered the MRI to the vessel at the port of shipment due to a "CIF" clause included in the underlying contract. Plaintiffs respond that . . . the generally understood definition of the "CIF" term as defined by the International Chamber of Commerce's publication, INCOTERMS 1990, is inapplicable here. . . .

Pursuant to the applicable German law—the U.N. Convention on Contracts for the International Sale of Goods (CISG)—the "CIF" term in the contract operated to pass the risk of loss to Shared Imaging at the port of shipment, at which time, the parties agree, the MRI was undamaged and in good working order. Accordingly, Neuromed's motion to dismiss the complaint should be granted and the complaint dismissed.

BACKGROUND

Shared Imaging, an American corporation, and Neuromed, a German corporation, entered into a contract of sale for a Siemens Harmony 1.0 Tesla mobile MRI. Thereafter, both parties engaged various entities to transport, insure, and provide customs entry service for the MRI. Plaintiffs originally named those entities as defendants, but the action has been discontinued against them by agreement of the parties. Neuromed is the sole remaining defendant.

According to the complaint, the MRI was loaded aboard the vessel "Atlantic Carrier" undamaged and in good working order. When it reached its destination of Calmut City, Illinois, it had been damaged and was in need of extensive repair, which led plaintiffs to conclude that the MRI had been damaged in transit.

The one page contract of sale contains nine headings, including: "Product," "Delivery Terms," "Payment Terms," "Disclaimer," and "Applicable Law." Under "Product" the contract provides, the "system will be delivered cold and fully functional." Under "Delivery Terms" it provides, "CIF New York Seaport, the buyer will arrange and pay for customs clearance as well as transport to Calmut City."

Under "Payment Terms" it states, "By money transfer to one of our accounts, with following payment terms: U.S. $93,000—downpayment to secure the system;

U.S. $744,000—prior to shipping; U.S. $93,000—upon acceptance by Siemens of the MRI system within three business days after arrival in Calmut City." In addition, under "Disclaimer" it states, "system including all accessories and options remain the property of Neuromed till complete payment has been received." Preceding this clause is a handwritten note, allegedly initialed by Raymond Stachowiak of Shared Imaging, stating, "Acceptance subject to Inspection."

Discussion

Neuromed contends that because the delivery terms were "CIF New York Seaport," its contractual obligation, with regard to risk of loss or damage, ended when it delivered the MRI to the vessel at the port of shipment and therefore the action must be dismissed because plaintiffs have failed to state a claim for which relief can be granted. Plaintiffs respond that the generally accepted definition of the "CIF" term as defined in INCOTERMS 1990, is inapplicable. Moreover, plaintiffs suggest that other provisions of the contract are inconsistent with the "CIF" term because Neuromed, pursuant to the contract, retained title subsequent to delivery to the vessel at the port of shipment and thus, Neuromed manifestly retained the risk of loss.

***

B. Applicable Law

***

The parties have each submitted relevant opinions of German legal experts and the Court has independently researched the applicable foreign law. On the basis of those submissions and analysis, the Court finds the expert opinion of Karl-Ulrich Werkmeister for the defendants to be an accurate statement of German law.

2. Applicable German Law The parties concede that pursuant to German law, the UN Convention on Contracts for the International Sale of Goods ("CISG") governs this transaction because (1) both the U.S. and Germany are Contracting States to that Convention, and (2) neither party chose, by express provision in the contract, to opt out of the application of the CISG.[9]

The CISG aims to bring uniformity to international business transactions, using simple, non-nation specific language. To that end, it is comprised of rules applicable to the conclusion of contracts of sale of international goods. In its application regard is to be paid to comity and interpretations grounded in its underlying principles rather than in specific national conventions.[10]

---

[9]See CISG, Article 1(1)(a). . . .

[10]See CISG Article 7(1), (2). . . .

Germany has been a Contracting State since 1991, and the CISG is an integral part of German law. Where parties, as here, designate a choice of law clause in their contract—selecting the law of a Contracting State without expressly excluding application of the CISG—German courts uphold application of the Convention as the law of the designated Contracting state. To hold otherwise would undermine the objectives of the Convention which Germany has agreed to uphold.

C. CISG, INCOTERMS and "CIF"

"CIF," which stands for "cost, insurance and freight," is a commercial trade term that is defined in INCOTERMS 1990, published by the International Chamber of Commerce ("ICC"). The aim of INCOTERMS, which stands for international commercial terms, is "to provide a set of international rules for the interpretation of the most commonly used trade terms in foreign trade." These "trade terms are used to allocate the costs of freight and insurance" in addition to designating the point in time when the risk of loss passes to the purchaser. INCOTERMS are incorporated into the CISG through Article 9(2) which provides that,

> The parties are considered, unless otherwise agreed, to have impliedly made applicable to their contract or its formation a usage of which the parties knew or ought to have known and which in international trade is widely known to, and regularly observed by, parties to contracts of the type involved in the particular trade concerned.

At the time the contract was entered into, INCOTERMS 1990 was applicable. INCOTERMS define "CIF" (named port of destination) to mean [that] the seller delivers when the goods pass "the ship's rail in the port of shipment." The seller is responsible for paying the cost, freight, and insurance coverage necessary to bring the goods to the named port of destination, but the risk of loss or damage to the goods passes from seller to buyer upon delivery to the port of shipment. Further, "CIF" requires the seller to obtain insurance only on minimum cover.

Plaintiffs' legal expert contends that INCOTERMS are inapplicable here because the contract fails to specifically incorporate them. Nonetheless, he cites and acknowledges that the German Supreme Court—the court of last resort in the Federal Republic of Germany for civil matters—concluded that a clause "fob" without specific reference to INCOTERMS was to be interpreted according to INCOTERMS "simply because the [INCOTERMS] include a clause 'fob.'"

Conceding that commercial practice attains the force of law under section 346 of the German Commercial Code, plaintiffs' expert concludes that the opinion of the BGH "amounts to saying that the [INCOTERMS] definitions in Germany have the force of law as trade custom." As encapsulated by defendant's legal expert, "It is accepted under German law that in case a contract refers to CIF-delivery, the parties refer to the INCOTERMS rules. . . ."

The use of the "CIF" term in the contract demonstrates that the parties "agreed to the detailed oriented [INCOTERMS] in order to enhance the Convention."[11] Thus, pursuant to CISG art. 9(2), INCOTERMS definitions should be applied to the contract despite the lack of an explicit INCOTERMS reference in the contract.

D. INCOTERMS, the CISG, and the Passage of Risk of Loss and Title

Plaintiffs argue that Neuromed's explicit retention of title in the contract to the MRI machine modified the "CIF" term, such that Neuromed retained title and assumed the risk of loss. INCOTERMS, however, only address passage of risk, not transfer of title. Under the CISG, the passage of risk is likewise independent of the transfer of title.[12] Plaintiffs' legal expert mistakenly asserts that the moment of "passing of risk" has not been defined in the CISG. Chapter IV of that Convention, entitled "Passing of Risk," explicitly defines the time at which risk passes from seller to buyer pursuant to Article 67(1),

> If the contract of sale involves carriage of the goods and seller is not bound to hand them over at a particular place, the risk passes to the buyer when the goods are handed over to the first carrier for transmission to the buyer in accordance with the contract of sale. If the seller is bound to hand the goods over to a carrier at a particular place, the risk does not pass to the buyer until the goods are handed over to the carrier at that place.

Pursuant to the CISG, "the risk passes without taking into account who owns the goods. The passing of ownership is not regulated by the CISG according to art. 4(b)."[13] Article 4(b) provides that the Convention is not concerned with "the effect which the contract may have on the property in the goods sold."[14] Moreover, according to Article 67(1), the passage of risk and transfer of

---

[11] Neil Gary Oberman, "Transfer of Risk from Seller to Buyer in International Commercial Contracts: A Comparative Analysis of Risk Allocation Under CISG, UCC and INCOTERMS," at http:www.cisg.law.pace.edu/cisg/thesis/Oberman.html.

[12] See CISG Article 67(1).

[13] Annemieke Romein, "The Passing of Risk: A Comparison Between the Passing of Risk under the CISG and German Law" (Heidelberg, June 1999), at http://www.cisg.law.pace.edu/cisg/biblio/romein.html.

[14] CISG Article 4(b).

title need not occur at the same time, as the seller's retention of "documents controlling the disposition of the goods does not affect the passage of risk."

Had the CISG been silent, as plaintiffs' expert claimed, the Court would have been required to turn to German law as a "gap filler." There again, plaintiffs' assertions falter. German law also recognizes passage of risk and transfer of title as two independent legal acts. In fact, it is standard "practice under German law to agree that the transfer of title will only occur upon payment of the entire purchase price, well after the date of passing of risk and after receipt of the goods by the buyer."[15] Support for this proposition of German law is cited by both experts. They each refer to section 447 of the German Civil Code, a provision dealing with long distance sales, providing in part—as translated by plaintiff's expert—that "the risk of loss passes to the buyer at the moment when the seller has handed the matter to the forwarder, the carrier or to the otherwise determined person or institution for the transport."[16]

Accordingly, pursuant to INCOTERMS, the CISG, and specific German law, Neuromed's retention of title did not thereby implicate retention of the risk of loss or damage.

***

Conclusion

For the foregoing reasons, Neuromed's motion to dismiss for failure to state a claim is granted and the complaint is dismissed. ■

[15]Werkmeister's Reply Opinion at p. 7.
[16]Strube's Opinion at p. 5.

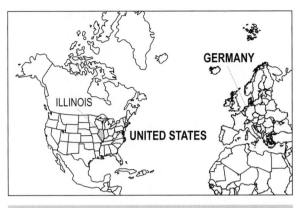

MAP 11-1   Germany and United States (2002)

CASEPOINT: This case involves the sale of an expensive piece of medical equipment (an MRI scanner) by a seller in Germany to a buyer in the United States. The scanner was damaged when it arrived at the buyer's place of business. It was thus important to determine when the risk of loss passed. The contract shipping terms were "CIF, New York seaport." The court stated that the CISG incorporated the relevent Incoterms, unless the parties had specified otherwise, and found that the term "CIF, New York" meant that the risk of loss effectively moved from seller to buyer when the goods were loaded onto the carrier in Germany for the trip to New York. The Incoterms regarding risk of loss are not tied to the passage of title, as the buyer claimed, so here the loss must fall upon the buyer.

A NOTE ON THE INCOTERMS

Because the ICC's Incoterms are the most commonly used trade terms, most of this discussion of trade terms will focus on them.

The 2000 revision makes few changes from the previous revision, *Incoterms 1990.*[17] The 1990 revision made several significant modifications to the earlier terms, reflecting changes both in technology and in shipping practices that occurred during the 1980s. According to the ICC, "The main reason for the 1990 revision of *Incoterms* was the desire to adapt terms to the increasing use of electronic data interchange (EDI)." The terms, accordingly, allow parties to transmit documents electronically, including negotiable bills of lading, so long as their contract specifically allows them to do so. The second major reason for the revision stemmed "from transportation techniques, particularly the unitization of cargo in containers, multimodal transport, and roll-on roll-off traffic with road vehicles and railway wagons in 'short sea' maritime transport." Older terms that applied to peculiar modes of land and air

[17]International Chamber of Commerce, Pub. No. 460.

transport—such as *free on rail* (*FOR*), *free on truck* (*FOT*), and *FOB airport*—were eliminated and the *free carrier* term was expanded.

The Incoterms are classified into four groups arranged according to the parties' obligations. The "E" Group (i.e., ex works [EXW]) requires the buyer to take delivery of the goods at the buyer's premises. The "F" Group (i.e., free carrier [FCA], free alongside ship [FAS], and free on board) requires the seller to deliver goods to a carrier. The "C" Group (i.e., cost and freight [CFR]; cost, insurance, and freight [CIF]; carriage paid to [CPT]; and carriage and insurance paid to [CIP]) requires the seller to arrange and pay for carriage, but he does not assume the risk for loss or damage once the goods are delivered to the carrier(as we saw in Case 11-1). The "D" Group (i.e., delivered at frontier [DAF], delivered ex ship [DES], delivered ex quay [DEQ], delivered duty unpaid [DDU], and delivered duty paid [DDP]) requires the seller to bear all costs and risks of bringing the goods to the buyer's country.

Certain Incoterms apply only to particular forms of transport. FAS, FOB, CFR, CIF, DES, and DEQ apply only to sea and inland waterway transport. The other terms—EXW, FCA, CPT, CIP, DAF, DDU, and DDP—apply to any form of transport. These last are especially important when several different forms of transport (i.e., *multimodal* transport) are used to get goods to their destination. The most important Incoterms are discussed in the text.

"FREE" TERMS

free: When used in a trade term, it means that the seller has an obligation to deliver goods to a named place for transfer to a carrier.

Several of the common trade terms begin with the word **free** (e.g., *free on board, free alongside, free carrier*). *Free* means that the seller has an obligation to deliver the goods to a named place for transfer to a carrier. National laws sometimes treat the "free" terms as interchangeable, so it is important for contracting parties to identify not only the term but also the set of rules that applies to their particular transaction.[18]

FOB—FREE ON BOARD

free on board: Seller fulfills his obligations to deliver when the goods have passed over the ship's rail at the named port of shipment.

Historically, **free on board**, as its name suggests, is a maritime trade term, and in most of the world its use remains limited to seaborne commerce. The ICC's *Incoterms 2000*, accordingly, uses it only in connection with the carriage of goods by sea. In common law countries, however, it is also used for inland carriage aboard any "vessel, car or other vehicle."[19]

The FOB (port of shipment) contract requires a seller to deliver goods on board a vessel that is to be designated by the buyer in a manner customary at the particular port. For example, *FOB Singapore* requires the buyer to name the ship that will accept delivery in Singapore, and the seller must deliver the goods on board the ship as required by the port rules in Singapore.

The essence of an FOB contract is the notion that a seller is responsible for getting goods on board a ship designated by a buyer. What is meant by *on board* has been the issue in many cases and is described in detail in the Incoterms. Traditionally (and according to the Incoterms), goods are on board a ship the moment they cross its rail. A seller's responsibility, however, does not end at that point unless the goods are also "appropriated to the contract"—that is, they are "clearly set aside or otherwise identified as the contract goods." Thus, the seller continues to be responsible for the goods even after the buyer's chosen ship takes control of the goods at the end of its cargo boom and begins to hoist the goods off the dock. Moreover, the seller may remain responsible for the goods even after they are loaded onto the ship if they remain unidentified to the buyer's contract.

---

[18]In France, for example, the distinction between FOB and FAS is sometimes blurred. Frederic Eisemann, *Usages de la Vente Commerciale Internationale*, p. 83 (1972).

[19]United States, Uniform Commercial Code, § 2–319(1)(c). For the practice in the United Kingdom, see D. Michael Day, *The Law of International Trade*, p. 42 (1981).

FAS—FREE ALONGSIDE

free alongside ship: The seller fulfills his obligations to deliver when the goods have been placed alongside the vessel on the quay or in lighters at the named port of shipment.

The term **free alongside** or **free alongside ship** requires the seller to deliver goods to a named port alongside a vessel to be designated by the buyer and in a manner customary to the particular port.[20] *Alongside* has traditionally meant that the goods must be within reach of a ship's lifting tackle. This may, as a consequence, require that the seller hire lighters to take the goods out to a ship in ports where this is the practice. In other respects, the requirements of an FAS term are the same as those of an FOB contract. The seller's responsibilities end upon delivery of the goods alongside.

CIF—COST, INSURANCE, AND FREIGHT

cost, insurance, and freight: The seller must pay the costs and freight necessary to bring the goods to a named port of destination and must procure marine insurance against the buyer's risk of loss to the goods during the carriage.

The most important and most commonly used shipping term is **cost, insurance, and freight**. The CIF term is preferred by buyers because it means that they have little to do with the goods until the goods arrive at a port of destination in their country. A CIF price quote also allows buyers to compare prices from suppliers around the world without having to take into consideration differing freight rates, since the seller pays the freight and insurance. Export-sellers are often under pressure from their governments to use domestic carriers and insurers, so they too like the term. On the other hand, sellers may not be able to find domestic carriers or insurers; and buyers, under pressure from governments that are also concerned about employing national carriers and insurers, may settle for an FOB contract.

In short, a CIF contract requires the seller to arrange for the carriage of goods by sea to a port of destination and to turn over to the buyer the documents necessary to obtain the goods from the carrier or to assert a claim against an insurer if the goods are lost or damaged. The three documents that the seller (as a minimum) has to provide—the invoice, the insurance policy, and the bill of lading—represent the three elements of the contract: cost, insurance, and freight. The seller's obligations are complete when the documents are tendered to the buyer. At that time, the buyer is obliged to pay the agreed-upon price.

CFR—COST AND FREIGHT

cost and freight (port of destination): The seller must pay the cost and freight necessary to bring the goods to the named port of destination.

The **cost and freight (port of destination)** term is the same as the CIF term except that the seller does not have to procure marine insurance against the risk of loss or damage to the goods during transit. Because the insurance required under a CIF contract only has to cover minimum conditions (the so-called FPA or *free from particular average* conditions), buyers wishing to purchase more extensive policies will want to use a CFR contract. The buyer's responsibilities under a CFR contract (known also as a *C & F contract*) are considered in Case 11-2.

---

[20]*Incoterms 2000*, p. 41 (International Chamber of Commerce, Pub. No. 560).

—◆◆◆—

Case 11-2 PHILLIPS PUERTO RICO CORE, INC. v. TRADAX PETROLEUM, LTD.

United States, Court of Appeals, Second Circuit, 1985.
Federal Reporter, Second Series, vol. 782, p. 314 (1985).

CIRCUIT JUDGE MANSFIELD: . . .

This convoluted maritime controversy had its origins in early September 1981 when Phillips, a corporation orga-

nized under Delaware law with its principal place of business in Puerto Rico, agreed to buy 25–30,000 metric tons of naphtha from Tradax, a corporation organized under Bermuda law, with its principal place of business in Switzerland. Tradax had just purchased the naphtha from another firm, Schlubach & Co., and the naphtha was located in Skikda, Algeria. The Tradax-Phillips contract, which was made by telephone and then confirmed by telex on September 3, 1981, specified that the sale was to be "C & F" (cost and freight) Guayama, Puerto Rico and that shipment was to be made between September 20–28, 1981. No dates for delivery were specified. The agreement incorporated the International Chamber of Commerce 1980 *Incoterms*, a set of standardized terms for international commercial contracts, which define a "C & F" contract as one in which the seller arranges and pays for the transport of the goods, but the buyer assumes title and risk of loss at the time of shipment. The contract was also to include Tradax's standard contract provisions "subject to [Phillips'] review and acceptance." These standard terms, including a *force majeure*[21] clause and an arbitration clause, were not recited in the telex but were subsequently mailed by Tradax to Phillips with a confirming letter and arrived several weeks later.

Soon after the original contract was entered into on September 8, 1981, a telex from Phillips to Tradax provided documentation and delivery instructions giving the destination in Puerto Rico and listing Phillips as consignee. The telex confirmed that "title and risk of loss to products shall pass to buyer at the time product reaches the vessel[']s flange at the load port." On September 16, Tradax nominated the Oxy Trader, an integrated tug barge, as the vessel for the journey, and after determining that the Trader would fit in the Puerto Rico berth and was available at the correct times, Phillips accepted the nomination.

The Trader arrived at Skikda for loading on the afternoon of September 20, 1981, and loading commenced the following day. The naphtha was completely loaded by the early morning of September 24 and at 1030 hours that morning the ship embarked. . . .

The Trader's voyage was cut short . . . when the ship was detained by the Coast Guard at Gibraltar for an inspection. Tradax relayed word of the delay to Phillips, which telexed back on October 1 that October 15 was the last acceptable delivery date. . . .

On October 7, Tradax received word that the Trader might have a latent defect . . . that the authorities were not letting the Trader proceed, and that the naphtha cargo would have to be transshipped. Tradax relayed this message to Phillips.

On October 9, Phillips telexed Tradax stating that it was "declar[ing] *force majeure*," that it would "not make any payments under the contract until the event of *force majeure* abates," and that it was reserving the right to cancel the contract if delivery did not occur within 30 days. Tradax responded, reiterating its claim that its responsibility ended at the time of shipment and notify-

ing Phillips that it would present the shipping documents for payment of the contract price the following day. Phillips again instructed its Puerto Rico office not to make payment if Tradax tendered the documents.

On October 13, a Tradax representative presented the shipping documents for payment at Phillips' Puerto Rico office. A Phillips employee examined the documents briefly—about 30 seconds according to Tradax's witness—and stated that they seemed to be in order but that he had been instructed not to pay. A telex back to Tradax that day reaffirmed Phillips' unwillingness to pay until the abatement of the claimed force majeure.

. . . [O]n November 9, Phillips informed Tradax that it was terminating the contract due to the "unseaworthiness" of the Trader, "discrepancies in the documents," and an "unreasonable delay" in performance. Although Phillips and Tradax representatives tried to negotiate a new contract by which Phillips would buy the naphtha on "delivery" terms, negotiations fell through when Tradax's management refused to accept that deal. The transshipment then began on November 13, with a bill of lading which left open the destination port. On November 19, Tradax informed Phillips that it would try to sell the naphtha on the open market and would hold Phillips liable for any damages. Tradax then sold the naphtha to a third party for $.88 per gallon, after first offering it to Phillips on condition that Tradax retain its right to claim in arbitration the difference between that price and the contract price. Tradax's total loss on the naphtha, compared to the contract price, was $911,710.31, plus incidental damages.

. . . On August 1, 1984, Judge Carter filed his decision in the case, finding Phillips liable to Tradax for $1,039,330.99 plus prejudgment interest from October 13, 1981. The court held that Phillips had anticipatorily breached the contract by declaring its unwillingness to pay because of *force majeure*. . . .

From this judgment Phillips appeals.

DISCUSSION

The 1980 *Incoterms* define a "C & F" contract as one in which:

[t]he seller must pay the costs and freight necessary to bring the goods to the named destination but the risk of loss of or damage to the goods, as well as of any cost increases, is transferred from the seller to the buyer when the goods pass the ship's rail in the port of shipment.

. . . As a "C & F" seller Tradax had two duties that are relevant here: to deliver the naphtha to an appro-

---

[21]French: "superior force." An event or effect that cannot be reasonably anticipated or controlled.

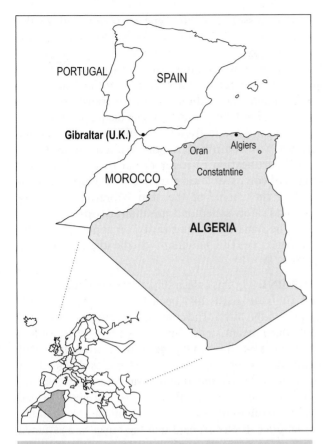

MAP 11-2 Algeria and Gibraltar (1981)

Force Majeure

Phillips first relies on the *force majeure* clause among Tradax's standard contract terms, which were to be included in the contract "subject to [Phillips'] review and acceptance;" the contract, however, did not actually arrive at Phillips' office for review until after the Oxy Trader left port. The standard *force majeure* clause reads:

> FORCE MAJEURE: In the event of any strike, fire or other event . . . preventing or delaying shipment or delivery of the goods by the seller . . . the unaffected party may cancel the unfulfilled balance of the contract. . . .

. . . We . . . look to the basic purpose of *force majeure* clauses, which is in general to relieve a party from its contractual duties when its performance has been prevented by a force beyond its control or when the purpose of the contract has been frustrated. . . . The burden of demonstrating *force majeure* is on the party seeking to have its performance excused, . . . and, as Judge Carter pointed out, the nonperforming party must demonstrate its efforts to perform its contractual duties despite the occurrence of the event that it claims constituted *force majeure*. . . .

With these principles in mind, we cannot agree that Phillips' performance was excused by its invocation of *force majeure*. Even if the detention of the ship by the Coast Guard constituted *force majeure*, and we are inclined to agree with Judge Carter that it did not, that detention did not frustrate the purpose of the contract or prevent Phillips from carrying out its obligation under the terms of the parties' contract to make payment. Indeed, to hold that the *force majeure* clause may be interpreted to excuse the buyer from that obligation, as Phillips urges, would be to wholly overturn the allocation of duties provided for in "C & F" sales. We do not find any evidence that the parties intended such a result.

. . . The *force majeure* clause thus did not alter the design of the "C & F" contract by requiring Tradax to assure delivery of the naphtha at the ultimate destination in Puerto Rico before it would be entitled to payment. The authorities Phillips cites in support of its contention that a "C & F" seller retains responsibility for events after the time of shipment are plainly distinguishable. The court in *Gatoil International Inc. v. Tradax Petroleum, Ltd.*[22] stated "tentative[ly]" that a "C & F" seller could be liable for having "wrongfully delay[ed] the actual delivery of the goods," in that case by instructing a ship to wait outside the harbor at the

priate carrier with which it had contracted for shipment and to tender proper documents to Phillips. Phillips in return was contractually obliged to pay for the naphtha when presented with the shipping documents by Tradax. It is undisputed that after Tradax loaded the naphtha on the Oxy Trader and presented Phillips with the shipping documents on October 13, 1981, Phillips refused to pay for the cargo. If Tradax had adequately performed its contractual duties, Phillips' refusal to pay for the naphtha constituted a breach of the contract as of October 13, unless it was somehow excused from performing.

Phillips asserts several grounds for its failure to pay Tradax on October 13: (1) the existence of a "*force majeure*," (2) unreasonable delay in Tradax's performance, (3) discrepancies in Tradax's shipping documents, and (4) unsuitability (unseaworthiness) of the Oxy Trader. On the undisputed circumstances of this case, however, none of these theories suffice to excuse Phillips' failure to pay on Tradax's presentation of the documents.

---

[22]Commercial Ct., Queen's Bench Division, Slip Opinion at p. 24 (July 31, 1984); *Lloyd's Law Reports*, Queen's Bench, vol. 1985, pt. 1, p. 350 (1985).

port of discharge. Here, in contrast, the absence of any such wrongful conduct on Tradax's part makes such deviation from the standard "C & F" division of responsibility inappropriate.

***

Defects in the Documents

There is equally little merit in Phillips' claim that it was excused from payment under the contract because Tradax tendered defective shipping documents. While it is true that in a sale by documents the seller's tender of the documents is judged very strictly, Phillips' objection to the documents here, as Judge Carter noted, "is an afterthought and must fail." Without having seen the shipping documents, Phillips twice instructed its agents that because of *force majeure*, they were not to pay Tradax when the latter presented the papers for payment. When Tradax presented the papers in Puerto Rico, a Phillips employee chose to give them only a cursory examination before stating that they seemed "okay," but that he had been instructed not to pay.

***

The Suitability of the Oxy Trader

Phillips was not relieved of its contractual obligation because of Tradax's selection of the Oxy Trader. The relevant provision in the 1980 *Incoterms* requires that a "C & F" seller contract for the carriage of the goods "in a seagoing vessel . . . of the type normally used for the transport of goods of the contract description." Although the Oxy Trader, an integrated tug barge, was of novel design in that the tug and the barge were married together, this feature did not disqualify the Trader as a ship that might "normally" be used for transport. A new design would not carry with it such a disqualification. Indeed, the status of the Trader as a ship normally used for transport was confirmed by the United States Coast Guard's certification of it for ocean transport and for carriage of comparable cargoes and by Phillips' own approval of the choice of the ship. Moreover, the Oxy Trader had safely sailed on transatlantic trips.

. . . The remaining claims raised on appeal need little discussion. . . . The judgment of the district court is affirmed. ■

CASEPOINT: In this case, a shipment of naphtha was delayed after the goods had been loaded onto a ship for transport to the buyer. The contract shipping terms were C and F, which meant, under Incoterms, that the risk of loss passed to the buyer when the goods were properly loaded aboard the carrier ship. After the ship was detained for some time, the buyer stated that it was refusing to take delivery and refused to pay the price of the goods, which were eventually sold by the seller for much less than the contract price. The court held that the buyer had assumed the risk of loss when the goods "passed the rail" under the Incoterms and, when the shipping documents were properly presented, was responsible to pay the contract price.

DES—DELIVERED EX SHIP

delivered ex ship: The seller fulfills his obligations to deliver when the goods are made available to the buyer on board the ship, uncleared for import, at the named port of destination.

A **delivered ex ship**, or arrival, contract requires the seller to deliver goods to a buyer at an agreed-upon port of arrival. Lord Sumner, in *Yangtsze Insurance Association, Ltd. v. Lukmanjee*, described the seller's obligations under such a contract as follows:[23]

> In the case of a sale "ex ship," the seller has to cause delivery to be made to the buyer from a ship which has arrived at the port of delivery and has reached a place therein which is usual for the delivery of goods of the kind in question. The seller has therefore to pay the freight, or otherwise release the shipowner's lien and to furnish the buyer with an effectual direction to the ship to deliver. Until this is done, the buyer is not bound to pay for the goods.

This is very different from a CIF contract. Under the DES contract, the seller is not required to deliver documents to the buyer, but to deliver the goods. In practice, however, he will probably provide the buyer with a delivery order or some other document that will enable the buyer to take possession from the ship rather than appear in person to make delivery.

Also, the seller remains responsible for the goods until they are delivered. Thus, unlike the CIF term, the seller is not obliged to obtain insurance for the buyer's benefit. In the

---

[23]*Law Reports, Appeal Cases*, vol. 1918, p. 585 at 589 (1918).

Yangtsze Insurance case, just quoted, timber to be delivered ex ship was off-loaded into the sea next to the carrier and consolidated into rafts for transfer ashore. However, before the transfer and delivery could be made, the timber was destroyed by bad weather. The English Court of Appeal observed that the risk for the loss of goods in an ex ship contract does not shift to the buyer until delivery is made. It consequently refused to hold that the insurance policy purchased by the seller for his own benefit could inure to the benefit of the buyer, because the buyer had yet to take delivery and therefore had no rights in the property.

FCA—FREE CARRIER

free carrier: The seller fulfills his obligations to deliver by handing over the goods, cleared for export, to a carrier named by the buyer.

The FCA term, which applies to any form of transport—maritime, inland waterways, air, rail, or truck—requires the seller to deliver goods to a particular carrier at a named terminal, depot, airport, or other place where the carrier operates. The costs of transportation and the risks for loss shift to the buyer at that time.[24]

EXW—EX WORKS

ex works: The seller fulfills his obligations to deliver by making the goods available at his premises.

Under an **ex works** contract, a seller is obliged only to deliver the goods at his own place of business. All the costs connected with transportation are the responsibility of the buyer.

B. TRANSPORTATION

The following is a typical example of how goods are transported by sea from a seller in Country A to a buyer in Country B. Goods are picked up at the seller's place of business by an inland carrier and transported to a seaport for carriage abroad. The inland carrier will deposit the goods in a warehouse or port depository for examination by customs officials and for consolidation with other goods if the load is not large enough to occupy a ship by itself. A stevedore company or the ship's crew will load the goods. The crew will then stow the goods aboard ship, mark the goods with *leading* marks, and issue a bill of lading to the shipper. At a seaport in Country B, the ship will be directed by port authorities to tie up at a pier or to anchor at a moorage in the harbor. When the buyer produces the bill of lading, the ship's crew will unload the goods onto the dock or, if the ship is anchored out, into a lighter for transfer ashore. The crew or a stevedoring company will then deliver the goods to a customhouse or a bonded warehouse for inspection. Once customs has inspected the goods and their related documents, and collected any import taxes or duties, the goods will be released for entry into Country B. A local inland carrier will then transport the goods to the buyer's place of business.

When goods are transported by air, rail, or truck, much the same procedure is followed, except that the carrier will issue an air waybill or similar nonnegotiable receipt instead of a bill of lading, and the transfer of goods will more commonly be done by the carriers without the assistance of stevedores or other intermediaries.

freight forwarder: A firm that makes or assists in the making of shipping arrangements.

In making arrangements for the transportation of goods, the buyer and seller will deal with a variety of intermediaries, such as **freight forwarders**, warehousemen, port authorities, stevedores, and customhouse brokers. The most important of these agents for most shippers is the freight forwarder, or confirming house.[25] Unless a merchant has a large staff dedicated

---

[24]The 1990 revision of *Incoterms* expanded the coverage of the free carrier term, eliminating older terms, such as *FOB airport, free on rail (FOR)*, and *free on truck (FOT)*. FOR contracts required a seller to deliver goods to a railway carrier and pay all expenses up to that time, including the cost of packaging the goods for rail carriage. FOT contracts were the same as FOR contracts, except that the seller also had to pay for loading the goods on the railway's cars (or "trucks").

[25]The term *freight forwarder* is used in North America, while the terms *confirming house* or *export house* are used in the United Kingdom.

to making shipping arrangements, the use of a freight forwarder will save time and expense. Freight forwarders, for example, arrange three out of every four shipments moved across the New York docks.[26]

Freight forwarders are companies with specialized knowledge of international markets, finance, transport, customs, sales law, and other related matters. In most countries they are licensed by the government. In the United States, for example, export freight forwarders are licensed by the International Air Transport Association (IATA) to handle air freight and the Federal Maritime Commission to handle ocean freight.[27] Unlicensed brokers and agents also are commonly available who perform much more limited services (such as the booking of ocean freight or the handling of air cargo). A full-service freight forwarder can help with or perform the following:

- Obtaining quotations on CIF and C & F contracts
- Determining the availability of ships and port facilities
- Estimating costs based on gross weight, cubic feet, value, description of the goods, and the port of destination
- Booking space
- Procuring export licenses
- Reviewing letter of credit terms
- Tracing inland shipments
- Preparing shipping documents, including export declarations
- Preparing and authenticating consular invoices
- Procuring certificates of origin from local Chambers of Commerce
- Purchasing insurance
- Presenting banking drafts and collecting payment

C. INLAND CARRIAGE

The first stage of transporting goods overseas almost always involves an inland carrier, either a trucking or rail company, which moves the seller's goods from the seller's place of business to a seaport or airport. Except for *ex works* contracts, it is common for the seller to arrange for inland carriage, with the inland carrier transferring the goods to a freight forwarder at a seaport or airport for the latter to arrange and oversee the shipment of the goods abroad.

In the absence of universal conventions, several regional agreements regulate transport by road and rail. In Europe, road transport is regulated by the 1956 Convention on the Contract for the International Carriage of Goods by Road (*Convention relative au contrat de transport international de merchandises par route* or *CMR*)[28] and rail transport is governed by the 1980 Convention Concerning International Carriage by Rail (*Convention relative aux*

---

[26]Gerald H. Ullman, *The Ocean Freight Forwarder, the Exporter and the Law*, p. 2 (1967).

[27]See "What Is a Freight Forwarder?" at the federal government's Web site. "An international freight forwarder is an agent for the exporter in moving cargo to an overseas destination. These agents are familiar with the import rules and regulations of foreign countries, the export regulations of the U.S. government, the methods of shipping, and the documents related to foreign trade." http://www.export.gov/logistics/exp_whatis_freight_forwarder.asp.

[28]The text of the *CMR* is posted on the Internet at http://www.unece.org/trans/conventn/cmr_e.pdf. The *CMR*'s member states as of June 2007 are Albania, Andorra, Armenia, Austria, Azerbaijan, Belarus, Belgium, Bosnia and Herzegovina, Bulgaria, Canada, Croatia, Cyprus, the Czech Republic, Denmark, Estonia, Finland, France, Georgia, Germany, Greece, Hungary, Iceland, Ireland, Israel, Italy, Kazakhstan, Kyrgyzstan, Latvia, Liechtenstein, Lithuania, Luxembourg, Malta, Moldova, Monaco, Montenegro, the Netherlands, Norway, Poland, Portugal, Romania, the Russian Federation, San Marino, Serbia, Slovakia, Slovenia, Spain, Sweden, Switzerland, Tajikistan, the Former Yugoslav Republic of Macedonia, Turkey, Turkmenistan, Ukraine, the United Kingdom, the United States, and Uzbekistan. Posted on the Internet at http://www.unece.org/oes/member_countries/member_countries.htm. Multilateral Treaties Deposited with the Secretary-General, Status as at June 2007, posted on the Internet at http://untreaty.un.org/English/Past_Events.asp.

transports international ferroviares or *COTIF*).[29] Similar agreements exist in other parts of the world, with the significant exception of North America.[30]

The *CMR* is representative of the conventions governing road transport. It applies whenever goods are shipped between two countries, at least one of which is a signatory of the convention. The convention requires a carrier to issue a consignment note. Unlike a bill of lading (including the bill of lading issued by inland carriers in the United States), the *CMR* consignment note is not a negotiable instrument. It is, nonetheless, *prima facie* evidence of the making of a transport contract and of the receipt and the condition of the goods. The convention also grants the consignee the right to demand delivery of the goods in exchange for a receipt and to sue the carrier in his own name for any loss, damage, or delay for which the carrier is responsible. However, up to the time that the goods are turned over to the consignee, the shipper (consignor) has the right to order the carrier to stop them in transit, to change the place for delivery, or to order them delivered to a different consignee.

If a road carriage contract involves the use of multiple carriers, each carrier is treated as a party to the contract, and each is responsible for the entire transaction. Suits can be brought against the first or last carrier or the carrier in possession at the time of the loss.

Carriers are liable for loss, damage, or delay up to the liability limit set by the convention, so long as the consignment note states that carriage is governed by the *CMR*. The liability limit is 8.33 Special Drawing Rights (SDRs) per kilogram unless the consignor declares a higher value and pays a surcharge. If the consignment note fails to include a reference to the *CMR*, the carrier will be liable for any resulting injury. In either case, the burden of proof rests on the carrier, which will be liable unless it can show that the loss, damage, or delay was caused by the consignor or the consignee, by an inherent defect in the goods, or "through circumstances which the carrier could not avoid and the consequences of which he was unable to prevent."[31] A consignee has to notify the carrier within seven days of delivery to assert a claim for loss or damages, and within 21 days to make a claim for losses resulting from delay.

The *COTIF*, which governs rail transport, contains in most respects the same provisions as the *CMR*. The carrier's liability for losses, however, is 17 SDRs per kilogram.[32]

D. CARRIAGE OF GOODS BY SEA

Most goods are transported by a common carrier, that is, a carrier holding itself to carry goods for more than one party. Only a few shipments are large enough to require the shipper to hire an entire vessel. The contract to employ an entire vessel is known as a *charterparty*. We will return to charterparties after discussing common carriage.

COMMON CARRIAGE

common carrier: A ship that carries goods for all persons who choose to employ it so long as there is room.

Where the owner or operator of a vessel is willing to carry goods for more than one person, the vessel is known as a *general ship* or *common carrier*.[33] Unlike private carriers, common carriers are the subject of extensive municipal legislation and international conventions.

---

[29]The text of the *COTIF* is posted on the Internet at http://www.unece.org/trade/cotif/Welcome.html. The member states as of June 2007 were Albania, Algeria, Austria, Belgium, Bulgaria, Croatia, the Czech Republic, Denmark, Finland, France, Germany, Greece, Hungary, Iran, Iraq, Ireland, Italy, Lebanon, Liechtenstein, Lithuania, Luxembourg, the Former Yugoslav Republic of Macedonia, Monaco, Morocco, the Netherlands, Norway, Poland, Portugal, Romania, the Slovak Republic, Slovenia, Spain, Sweden, Switzerland, Syria, Tunisia, Turkey, and the United Kingdom. See InforMare at http://www.informare.it/dbase/convuk.htm.
[30]Paul H. Vishny, *Guide to International Commerce Law*, § 2–34 (1998).
[31]CMR, Article 17.2.
[32]The liability limit for personal injury to a passenger is 70,000 SDRs.
[33]The definition of *common carrier* has been the subject of much litigation. See Yung F. Chiang, "The Characterization of a Vessel as a Common or Private Carrier," *Tulane Law Review,* vol. 48, p. 299 (1974).

Merchants who employ common carriers will find that there are three sorts. A **conference line** is an association of seagoing carriers that have joined together to offer common freight rates. **Independent lines** have their own rate schedules. **Tramp vessels** also have their own rate schedules, but unlike conference and independent lines, they do not operate on established schedules.

Exporters who agree to ship all or a large share of their cargoes with a conference line receive a discounted rate.[34] Independent lines, however, generally offer lower rates than a conference line's nondiscounted rates. In most countries, the tariffs of ocean carriers are not regulated, and both conference and independent lines commonly offer regular shippers substantial rebates. In the United States, however, ocean carriers have to file their tariffs with the Federal Maritime Commission, and American law forbids rebates.[35]

THE BILL OF LADING

A **bill of lading** is an instrument issued by an ocean carrier to a shipper with whom the carrier has entered into a contract for the carriage of goods.[36] The multilateral treaty governing bills of lading is the International Convention for the Unification of Certain Rules of Law Relating to Bills of Lading.[37] This treaty is known both as the 1921 Hague Rules—because they were originally proposed by the International Law Association at a meeting at The Hague in 1921—and the Brussels Convention of 1924—because they were recommended for adoption at a diplomatic conference held in Brussels in 1924. The Hague Rules were extensively revised in 1968 by a Brussels Protocol, and the amended 1968 version is known as the Hague-Visby Rules.[38] Most countries, including the United States, are parties to the 1921 Hague Rules.[39] A few, including France and the United Kingdom, have adopted the Hague-Visby amendments.[40] The domestic laws implementing these conventions are

[34]Conference lines offer their regular customer rebates in two ways: (1) by a contract system in which the shipper signs a contract to use only conference ships and (2) by a system of deferred rebates of varying amounts that require the shipper to not use nonconference ships to send goods to the area in question for a period of time (commonly three or six months). Under the first of these arrangements the shipper is entitled to an immediate discount; under the second, the rebate is retained by the *Schmitthoff's Export Trade: The Law & Practice of International Trade* carrier until the shipper has met the condition of not using nonconference ships. Clive M. Schmitthoff, p. 548 (8th ed., 1990).
[35]*United States Code*, Title 46, Appendix, § 1709, paras. (b)(1) and (b)(2).
[36]In the United States, a bill of lading is also issued by inland carriers. See Uniform Commercial Code, §§ 2–319 and 2–320.
[37]The text of the Hague Rules is posted on the Internet at http://www.austlii.edu.au/au/other/dfat/treaties/19560002.html.
[38]The text of the Hague Rules as modified by the Brussels Protocol (the Hague-Visby Rules) is posted on the Internet at http://www.jus.uio.no/lm/sea.carriage.hague.visby.rules.1968/doc.html and at http://www.admiraltylaw.com/statutes/ hague.html. The Brussels Protocol itself is posted at http://www.austlii.edu.au/au/other/dfat/treaties/1993/23.html.

A United Nations Convention on the Carriage of Goods by Sea, drafted and signed in 1978 (the Hamburg Rules), came into force among 20 developing states in November 1992. As to those states, it modifies the Hague-Visby rules by establishing a single basis of liability for a carrier's breach of duty and it also governs "through transport," that is, shipments from the point of departure ashore through their final delivery inland via truck, rail, or plane. Because these rules also increase the liability of carriers, they have been ignored by all of the major maritime states. The text of the Hamburg Rules is posted at http://www.uncitral.org/english/texts/transport/hamburg.htm. As of June 2007, there were 26 states parties to the Hamburg Rules. Multilateral Treaties Deposited with the Secretary-General, Status as at June 2007, http://www.icao.int/cgi/ goto_leb.pl?icao/en/leb/treaty.htm.
[39]The member states of the Hague Rules as of June 2007 were Algeria, Angola, Anguilla, Antigua and Barbuda, Argentina, Australia, Norfolk, the Bahamas, Barbados, Belgium, Belize, Bolivia, Cameroon, Cape Verde, Cyprus, Croatia, Cuba, the Dominican Republic, Ecuador, Egypt, Fiji, France, Gambia, Germany, Ghana, Goa, Greece, Grenada, Guyana, Guinea-Bissau, Hungary, Iran, Ireland, Israel, Ivory Coast, Jamaica, Kenya, Kiribati, Kuwait, Lebanon, Macao, Madagascar, Malaysia, Mauritius, Monaco, Mozambique, Nauru, Nigeria, Papua New Guinea, Paraguay, Peru, Poland, Portugal, Romania, the Russian Federation , Sao Tomé and Principe, Sarawak, Senegal, Seychelles, Sierra-Leone, Singapore, Slovenia, the Solomon Islands, Somalia, Spain, Sri-Lanka, St. Kitts and Nevis, St. Lucia, St. Vincent and the Grenadines, Switzerland, the Syrian Arab Republic, Tanzania , Timor, Tonga, Trinidad and Tobago, Turkey, Tuvalu, the United States, and Zaire. Comite Maritime International, Status of Ratifications to Maritime Conventions posted at http://www.comitemaritime. org/ratific/brus/bru05.html.
[40]The member states of the Hague-Visby Rules as of June 2007 were Belgium, Denmark, Ecuador, Egypt, Finland, France, Greece, Italy, Lebanon, the Netherlands, Norway, Poland, Russia, Singapore, Sri-Lanka, Sweden, Switzerland, Syria, Tonga, and the United Kingdom. See *id.* at http://www.comitemaritime.org/ratific/brus/bru06.html.

typically called Carriage of Goods by Sea acts.[41] In addition, many states have supplementary legislation that also governs bills of lading in both municipal and international settings.[42]

A bill of lading serves three purposes: First, it is a carrier's receipt for goods. Second, it is evidence of a contract of carriage. Finally, it is a document of title; that is, the person rightfully in possession of the bill is entitled to possess, use, and dispose of the goods that the bill represents.[43] A bill of lading and samples of the documents that a carrier collects in order to prepare a bill of lading are shown in Exhibits 11-1 through 11-4 on pages 586–589.

Receipt for Goods

A bill of lading describes the goods put on board a carrier, states the quantity, and describes their condition. The form itself is normally filled out in advance by the shipper; then, as the goods are loaded aboard the ship, the carrier's tally clerk will check to see that the goods loaded comply with the goods listed. The carrier, however, is responsible only to check for outward compliance—that is, that the labels comply and that the packages are not damaged. If all appears proper, the appropriate agent of the carrier will sign the bill and return it to the shipper.[44] Bills certifying that the goods have been properly loaded on board are known as *on board bills of lading* or **clean bills of lading**.

clean bill of lading: A bill of lading indicating that the goods have been properly loaded on board the carrier's ship.

Should there be a discrepancy between the goods loaded and the goods listed, the statement on the bill is considered *prima facie* evidence that the goods were received in the condition shown in any dispute between the shipper and the carrier.[45] Nevertheless, the carrier can, if it is able, introduce evidence to rebut this evidence. However, once the bill is endorsed and negotiated to a third party, this is no longer the case. An endorsee's knowledge of the goods is limited to what is on the bill of lading. For this reason, the Hague and Hague-Visby Rules hold that the bill is conclusive evidence as to the goods loaded once the bill has been negotiated in good faith to a third party. The carrier is then barred from introducing evidence to contradict the bill of lading.

claused bill of lading: A bill of lading indicating that some discrepancy exists between the goods loaded and the goods listed on the bill.

If, at the time the goods are being loaded, the carrier's tally clerk notes a discrepancy, a notation to this effect may be added to the bill of lading. Called a **claused bill of lading**, such bills are normally unacceptable to third parties, including a buyer of the goods under a CIF contract or a bank that has agreed to pay the seller under a documentary credit on receipt of the bill of lading and other documents. Such a notation, however, may be made on the bill only at the time the goods are loaded. Later notations will have no effect, and the bill will be treated as if it were "clean." The significance of clean and claused bills of lading is discussed in Case 11-3.

---

[41]The United Kingdom's statute is the Carriage of Goods by Sea Act (1971) in *Statutes*, vol. 41, chap. 1312. The United States Carriage of Goods by Sea Act is codified in the *United States Code*, Title 46, § 1300 *et seq.*

[42]In the United States, the two other important acts are the Bill of Lading Act (Interstate and Foreign Commerce), in *United States Code*, Title 46, § 14306, and the Harter Act, in *United States Code*, Title 46, §§ 190–196. In the United Kingdom, the Bill of Lading Act (1855) in *Statutes*, vol. 31, Chap. 44 also applies.

[43]In re Marine Sulphur Queen, *Federal Reporter, Second Series*, vol. 460, p. 89 at p. 103 (Second Circuit Ct. of Appeals, 1972).

[44]The United States Carriage of Goods by Sea Act, *United States Code*, Title 46, § 1303(3), provides: After receiving the goods into his charge the carrier, or the master or agent of the carrier, shall, on demand of the shipper, issue to the shipper a bill of lading showing among other things—

(a) The leading marks necessary for identification of the goods as the same are furnished in writing by the shipper before the loading of such goods starts, provided such marks are stamped or otherwise shown clearly upon the goods if uncovered, or on the cases or coverings in which such goods are contained, in such manner as should ordinarily remain legible until the end of the voyage.

(b) Either the number of packages or pieces, or the quantity or weight, as the case may be, as furnished in writing by the shipper.

(c) The apparent order and condition of the goods: Provided, that no carrier, master, or agent of the carrier, shall be bound to state or show in the bill of lading any marks, number, quantity, or weight which he has reasonable grounds for suspecting not accurately to represent the goods actually received, or which he has had no reasonable means of checking.

[45]*Id.*, § 1303(4), provides: "Such a bill of lading shall be prima facie evidence of the receipt by the carrier of the goods as described in accordance with paragraphs (3)(a), (b) and (c), of [§ 1303]...."

International Sales Company
1234 Main Street
Pullman, Washington 99163
U.S.A.

INVOICE

Date:	**August 1, 2008**	Invoice No.	030701

		Order No.	080202

To: **Compañía Mundial, S.A.**
567 Avenida de Mayo
Buenos Aires
1103 Argentina

Shipped: **via M/V La Plata**
from Seattle, WA to
Buenos Aires, Arg. on
August 1, 2008

Payment: **L/C #099762**
dated August 1, 2008
Banco del Sur,
Buenos Aires, Arg.

Identifying Marks & Numbers	Quantity	Description	Unit Price	Amount
			US $	US $
Cía Mundial	432 ea	**Type "A" Widgets**	1.23	531.36
	288 ea	**Type "B" Widgets**	4.56	1313.28
Buenos	144 ea	**Type "C" Widgets**	7.89	<u>1136.16</u>
Aires ARGENTINA Made in USA		**TOTAL FOB PORT OF SEATTLE**		2980.80

International Sales Company

Jane Doe

Jane Doe, Pres.

EXHIBIT 11-1   A Commercial Invoice

International Sales Company 1234 Main Street Pullman, Washington 99163 U.S.A.	**PACKING LIST**

Date:	**August 1, 2008**	Invoice No.	**030701**

To:	**Compañía Mundial, S.A.** **567 Avenida de Mayo** **Buenos Aires** **1103 Argentina** **Notify:** **Agencia Rosas** **987 Calle de los Marineros** **Buenos Aires** **1117 Argentina**

Order No.	**080202**
Shipped:	**via M/V La Plata** **from Seattle, WA to** **Buenos Aires, Arg. on** **August 1, 2008**
Payment:	**L/C #099762** **dated August 1, 2008** **Banco del Sur,** **Buenos Aires, Arg.**

Identifying Marks & Numbers	Quantity	Description	Net Weight	Gross Weight	Measurement Cu. Meters
Cía. Mundial Buenos Aires ARGENTINA Made in USA					
No. 1-3	**432 ea**	**Type "A" Widgets**	**32 kg**	**42 kg**	**.006m³**
Ditto No. 4-5	**288 ea**	**Type "B" Widgets**	**24 kg**	**28 kg**	**.004m³**
Ditto No. 6	**144 ea**	**Type "C" Widgets**	**12 kg**	**14 kg**	**.002m³**
6 ctns			**72 kg**	**84 kg**	**.012m³**

International Sales Company

Jane Doe

Jane Doe, Pres.

EXHIBIT 11-2 A Packing List

Seagoing Carrier Company 665 Dockside Drive Seattle, Washington 98203 U.S.A.	**D O C K** **R E C E I P T** NOT NEGOTIABLE

Shipper: **International Sales Co. 1234 Main St, Pullman, WA 99163**

Vessel	Voyage Number	Flag	Port of Loading	Pier
La Plata	**03 W**	**Panama**	**Seattle**	**18**

PORT OF DISCHARGE (Where goods are to be delivered to consignee or on carrier)

Buenos Aires

For TRANSSHIPMENT (If goods are to be transshipped or forwarded at port of discharge)

PARTICULARS FURNISHED BY SHIPPER OF GOODS

Identifying Marks & Numbers	Number of Packages	Description	Gross Weight	Measurement Cu. Meters
Cía. Mundial **Buenos Aires** **ARGENTINA** **Made in USA**				
	6	**Widgets - Type "A", "B"** **and "C"** **ATTN: RECEIVING CLERK** **ONLY CLEAN DOCK RECEIPT ACCEPTED**	**84 kg**	**0.12m^3**

DIMENSIONS AND WEIGHT OF PACKAGES TO BE SHOWN ON REVERSE SIDE

RECEIVED THE ABOVE-DESCRIBED MERCHANDISE FOR SHIPMENT AS INDICATED HEREON, SUBJECT TO ALL CONDITIONS OF THE UNDERSIGNED'S USUAL FORM OF DOCK RECEIPT AND BILL OF LADING. COPIES OF THE UNDERSIGNED'S USUAL FORM OF DOCK RECEIPT AND BILL OF LADING MAY BE OBTAINED FROM THE MASTER OF THE VESSEL OR THE VESSEL'S AGENT.

LIGHTER TRUCK ————————————

ARRIVED Date ——————— Time ————

UNLOADED Date ——————— Time ————

CHECKED BY ———————————

PLACED [ ] IN SHIP [ ] ON DOCK

LOCATION ——————————

Agent for Master

BY _____
Receiving Clerk

Date _____

EXHIBIT 11-3 A Dock Receipt

Seagoing Carrier Company
665 Dockside Drive
Seattle, Washington 98203
U.S.A.

BILL OF LADING
NOT NEGOTIABLE UNLESS
CONSIGNED TO ORDER

Shipper: **International Sales Co. 1234 Main St, Pullman, WA 99163**

Consignee: **To Order Banco del Sur, 17 Ave. Evita, Buenos Aires**

Address Arrival Notice to:	Also Notify:
Agencia Rosas **987 Calle Marineros** **Buenos Aires** **1117 Argentina**	**Compañia Mundial, S.A.** **567 Avenida de Mayo** **Buenos Avenida** **1103 Argentina**

Vessel **La Plata**	Voyage No. **03 W**	Flag **Panama**	Port of Loading **Seattle**

PARTICULARS FURNISHED BY SHIPPER OF GOODS

Identifying Marks & Numbers	Number of Packages	Description	Gross Weight	Measurement Cu. Meters
Cía. Mundial **Buenos Aires** **ARGENTINA** **Made in USA**		FINAL DESTINATION OF GOODS **BUENOS AIRES**		
	6	**Widgets – Type "A", "B"** **and "C"** **FREIGHT COLLECT** **LADEN ABOARD**	**84 kg**	**0.12m^3**

THESE COMMODITIES LICENSED BY U.S. FOR ULTIMATE DESTINATION. DIVERSION CONTRARY TO U.S. LAW PROHIBITED.

Freight Payable at: **Buenos Aires**

Gross Weight	Measurements Cu. Meters	Rate	Ocean Freight	Receiving Charge	Delivery Charge	Total Charge	Total Prepaid	Total Collect
84 Kg	**0.12m^3**	**2.70**	**226.80**	**15.87**	**27.22**	**$269.89**		**$269.89**

Bill of Lading No. **582 63409**	Issued at **Seattle**	Date **Aug. 1, 2008**

WHEN VALIDATED, CARGO LADEN ON BOARD
ON THE DATE APPEARING HEREON

DATED AT PORT OF LOADING SHOWN ABOVE
Seagoing Carrier Company

Validation:

By _____
Agent - For the Master

EXHIBIT 11-4   A Bill of Lading

Case 11-3 M. GOLODETZ & CO., INC. v. CZARNIKOW-RIONDA CO., INC. (THE GALITIA)

England, Queen Bench's Division (1978).
All England Law Reports, vol. 1979, pt. 2, p. 726 (1979).[46]

The sellers contracted to sell to the buyers between 12,000 and 13,200 tons of sugar, C & F Bandarshapur, Iran. The contract provided, among other things, that payment was to be made against a complete set of clean "on board" bills of lading evidencing that freight had been paid. After part of the consignment of sugar had been loaded, a fire broke out on the ship, as a result of which 200 tons of sugar were damaged and had to be discharged. The remainder of the consignment was loaded and carried to its destination. The sellers tendered two bills of lading to the buyers. The first was in respect to the 200 tons of sugar that had been lost and the second was in respect to the balance of the consignment. The first bill in its printed clauses acknowledged shipment of the goods in apparent good order and condition. In addition, however, it bore a typewritten note stating that the cargo covered by the bill had been discharged because it had been damaged by fire and/or water. The second bill was taken up and paid for by the buyers, but the first bill was rejected by them on the ground that it was not a clean bill of lading. The sellers claimed that the typewritten note did not prevent it from being a clean bill of lading and that they were entitled to be paid the price of the 200 tons of sugar that had been lost.

JUDGE DONALDSON

***

THE DISPUTE

The parties to this dispute are household names in the world trade in sugar. Both are based in New York. The sugar concerned was to be shipped from Kandla in India to Iran. The reason why the matter comes to the English Commercial Court is that the contract incorporated the rule of the Refined Sugar Association and provided for arbitration in London.

...The question at issue is, of course, who is to stand the loss in respect of the 200 tons of sugar which was destroyed by or as a consequence of the fire? The board of appeal of the Refined Sugar Association has held that the loss must fall on the sellers. The sellers now appeal.

***

The Sellers' Claim to the Price

Under the terms of the contract, the sellers are entitled to be paid the price on tender of "clean 'On Board' bills of lading evidencing freight having been paid." Counsel for the sellers submitted that this bill of lading qualified for this description, notwithstanding the notation recording that the sugar had been discharged fire damaged. . . . In his submission, the sellers, having tendered this bill of lading, were entitled to be paid the price. Alternatively, the sugar was at the risk of the buyers when it was destroyed and, that being so, the sellers were entitled to be paid the price whether or not they tendered this or any other bill of lading.

Counsel for the buyers challenged these submissions root and branch. In his submission, there were no less than eight reasons why the sellers were not entitled to be paid the price. It is, of course, for the sellers to make out their case, but in all the circumstances, it is convenient to consider whether they have done so in the context of counsel's objections.

(a) That the Bill of Lading Was Not "Clean"

(i) The Practical Test Counsel for the buyers submits that there are two possible tests to be applied, the practical and the legal. The practical test is whether a bill of lading in this form is acceptable to banks generally as being a "clean" bill of lading. Since 1962, virtually all banks have accepted the international rules set out in a document issued by the International Chamber of Commerce entitled *Uniform Customs and Practices for Documentary Credits* ("UCP Rules"). Rule 16 provides as follows:

> A clean shipping document is one which bears no superimposed clause or notation which expressly declares a defective condition of the goods and/or the packaging. Banks will refuse documents bearing such clauses or notations unless the credit expressly states clauses or notations which may be accepted.

---

[46]Affirmed by the Court of Appeal, Civil Division, *All England Law Reports*, vol. 1980, pt. 1, p. 501 (1980). The statement of facts is from the appellate report.

This definition fails to specify the time with respect to which the notation speaks. The bill of lading and any notation speak at the date of issue, but they may speak about a state of affairs which then exist or about an earlier state of affairs or both. If the rule refers to notations about the state of affairs at the time of the issue of the bill of lading or, indeed, at any time after shipment of the 200 tons was completed, the bill of lading is not "clean" within the meaning of that word in the rule, for the notation clearly draws attention to the cargo being damaged. If, however, it refers to notations about the state of affairs on completion of shipment, the bill of lading is equally clearly clean for it shows that the goods were in apparent good order and condition on shipment and suggests only that they were damaged after shipment.

Counsel for the buyers draws attention to the fact that this bill of lading was rejected by two different banks. The first rejection was by the sellers' own bank when the bill of lading was tendered by the shippers under the FOB supply contract. The second rejection was by the buyers' subpurchasers bank when it was tendered to them by the buyers without prejudice to the rights of the parties as between sellers and buyers. On these facts, counsel for the buyers invites me to hold that this bill of lading is not a "clean" bill in commercial or practical terms.

Let me consider this "practical" test. The information as to what prompted the banks' action is somewhat sparse....

... There is no contemporary note of why the banks refused to accept the documents, but there is a letter dated March 24, 1976, reading:

> Your draft and documents valued $183,732.00, payment for which was not effected because Bills of Lading showing the following clause Quote "Cargo covered by this Bill of Lading has been discharged at Kandla View damaged by fire and/or water used to extinguish fire for which general average declared" Unquote, whereas credit class of clean (unclaused) Bills of Lading.

It is not uninteresting that it was not the buyers' bank which rejected the documents, but the buyers themselves (by a letter of April 22nd, 1975, referred to in the [arbitration] award). Furthermore, although they gave as a reason the fact that the clause prejudiced their ability to negotiate the documents with their buyers, the letter of 24th March 1976 set out above suggests that the documents were only rejected by the subbuyers' bank some weeks later on May 13th, 1975. However, there may have been more than one rejection.

It is clear that the subbuyers' bank thought that a letter of credit incorporating the UCP rules and calling

for "clean" bills of lading was only satisfied if the bills were wholly unclaused. This goes further than the UCP rules justify since they appear to take exception only to a "superimposed clause or notation which expressly declares a defective condition of the goods and/or the packaging," whatever that may mean.

There is, I think, more than one answer to this "practical test" objection. First, the contract ... does not provide that the documents shall be such as to satisfy the UCP rules as to "clean" bills of lading.... Furthermore, if there is ambiguity as to the meaning of those rules, that ambiguity should, if possible, be resolved in a way which will result in the rules reflecting the position under general maritime and commercial law. So construed they add nothing to the legal test which I consider hereafter.

Second, the evidence does not disclose that banks generally would reject such a bill of lading as that relating to the 200 tons as not being a "clean" bill of lading or that, if they would do so, it would be for any better reason than that they were applying what they though the UCP rules required.

Third, I am not satisfied that it is right to apply a practical test.... What is really being said here is that the very fact that the buyers and two banks rejected these documents proves that they are not "clean." This is a proposition which I decline to accept.

(ii) The Legal Test I, therefore, proceed to apply the legal test. As Judge Salmon remarked in *British Imex Industries, Ltd., v. Midland Bank, Ltd.,*[47] a "clean bill of lading" has never been exhaustively defined. I have been referred to a number of textbooks and authorities which support the proposition that a "clean" bill of lading is one in which there is nothing to qualify the admission that the goods were in apparent good order and condition and that the seller has no claim against the goods except in relation to freight. Some clearly regard the relevant time as being that of shipment. Some are silent as to what is the relevant time. None refers expressly to any time subsequent to shipment.

As between the shipowner and the shipper (including those claiming through the shippers as holders of the bill of lading) the crucial time is shipment. The shipowner's prime obligation is to deliver the goods at the contractual destination in the like good order and condition as when shipped. The cleanliness of the bill of lading may give rise to an estoppel and the terms of the bill of lading contract may exempt the shipowner from a breach of this obligation, but everything stems from the state of the goods as shipped. As between seller and CIF or C&F buyer, the property and risk normally pass on the negotiation of the bill of lading, but do so as from

---

[47]*All England Law Reports,* vol. 1958, pt. 1, p. 264 (Queen's Bench, 1958).

shipment. Thus, the fact that the ship and goods have been lost after shipment or that a liability to contribute in general average or salvage has arisen is no reason for refusing to take up and pay for the documents.

In these circumstances, it is not surprising that there appears to be no case in which the courts or the textbook writers have had to consider a bill of lading which records the fate of the goods subsequent to shipment and, indeed, I have never seen or heard of a bill of lading like that in the present case. Nor is it surprising that some of the judgments and textbooks do not in terms say that when reference is made to the condition of the goods what is meant is their condition on shipment.

However, I have no doubt that this is the position. The bill of lading with which I am concerned casts no doubt whatsoever on the condition of the goods at that time and does not assert that at that time the shipowner had any claim whatsoever against the goods. It follows that in my judgment this bill of lading, unusual though it is, passes the legal test of cleanliness.

(b) The Bill of Lading Was Rightly Rejected as Being Unmerchantable   Counsel for the buyers submits that documents tendered under a C & F contract must be merchantable and that, in the context of a bill of lading, this may be a factor of cleanliness or an independent quality which is required. He seeks to support this proposition by reference to *Hansson v. Hamel & Horley, Ltd.*[48] in which Lord Sumner said:

> When documents are to be taken up the buyer is entitled to documents which substantially confer protective rights throughout. He is not buying a litigation, as Lord Trevethin (then Judge A. T. Lawrence) says in the *General Trade Co.'s Case*.[49] These documents have to be handled by banks, they have to be taken up or rejected promptly and without any opportunity for prolonged inquiry, they have to be such as can be re-tendered to sub-purchasers, and it is essential that they should so conform to the accustomed shipping documents as to be reasonable and readily fit to pass current in commerce.

I need hardly say that I accept this proposition unreservedly. A tender of documents which, properly read and understood, calls for further enquiry or are such as to invite litigation is clearly a bad tender. But the operative words are "properly read and understood." I fully accept that the clause on this bill of lading makes it unusual, but properly read and understood it calls for no inquiry and it casts no doubt at all on the fact that the goods were shipped in apparent good order and condition or on the protection which

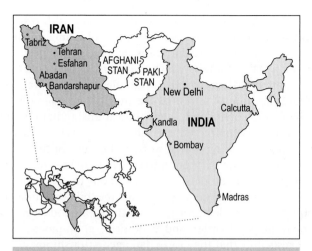

MAP 11-3   Iran and India (1978)

anyone is entitled to expect when taking up such a document whether as a purchaser or as a lender on the security of the bill....

The only ground for holding that the bill of lading was not "reasonably and readily fit to pass current in commerce" is that the form is unusual and that two banks and the buyers rejected it. If the buyers wanted bills of lading which were not only "clean," but also in "usual form," they should have contracted accordingly. They did not do so and I am not prepared to hold that the bill was unmerchantable....

CONCLUSION

For the reasons which I have sought to express, I consider that this was a "clean" bill of lading and that the buyers should have accepted it and paid the price. In reaching this conclusion, I have, regretfully, to disagree with the decision of the board of appeal [of the Refined Sugar Association]. That decision seems to me to have been based solely on considerations of law. Had it been a conclusion based on trade practice and included, for example, a finding that a bill in this form was not acceptable in the trade, my decision would, of course, have been different.

. . . Accordingly, for the reasons which I have expressed, I answer the questions of law in favor of the sellers.

Order accordingly. Leave to appeal to the Court of Appeal. ■

CASEPOINT: The decision turned on whether the bill of lading here was clean and merchantable. The goods were apparently delivered to the ship in good condition, and

---

[48]*All England Law Reports*, vol. 1922, p. 237 at p. 241 (Ct. of Appeal, 1922).
[49]Re General Trading Co. & Van Stolk's Commissiehandel, *Commercial Cases*, vol. 16, p. 95 (1911).

then 200 tons of the sugar were destroyed by fire and water. Two bills of lading were then issued, one covering the 200 tons, which noted that this portion of the goods was destroyed, and a second bill of lading covering the balance of the shipment. The second bill of lading was paid without problem, but the buyers refused to pay the first.

The court thoroughly examined both a "practical test" and a "legal test" and concluded that the key point of time was when the goods were "shipped" by the seller (loaded on the ship). Since the bill of lading did not note any problems with the goods "when shipped," the document was therefore clean under applicable law, despite the notation.

Contract of Carriage

Between the shipper and the carrier, the bill of lading is evidence of their contract of carriage. Either may rebut this by producing evidence of other terms. However, as is the case where the bill functions as a receipt, the bill becomes conclusive evidence of the terms of the contract of carriage once it is negotiated to a good-faith third party. Again, this is because the endorsee's knowledge of the terms of the contract of carriage is limited to what appears on the bill of lading.[50]

Document of Title

straight bill of lading: A bill of lading issued to a named consignee that is not negotiable.

order bill of lading: A bill of lading that is negotiable.

Two kinds of bills of lading need to be distinguished: the straight bill and the order bill. A straight bill is issued to a named consignee and is nonnegotiable. The transfer of a **straight bill** gives the transferee no greater rights than those of his transferor. An **order bill**, on the other hand, is negotiable and conveys greater rights. The holder of an order bill of lading, provided he has received it in good faith through due negotiation, has a claim to title and, by surrendering the bill, to delivery of the goods. In 1883, Lord Justice Bowen wrote what has become the time-honored definition of the order bill of lading:[51]

> A cargo at sea while in the hands of the carrier is necessarily incapable of physical delivery. During this period of transit and voyage, the bill of lading by the law merchant is universally recognized as its symbol, and the endorsement and delivery of the bill of lading operates as a symbolical delivery of the cargo. Property in the goods passes by such endorsement and delivery of the bill of lading, whenever it is the intention of the parties that the property should pass, just as under similar circumstances the property would pass by an actual delivery of the goods. And for the purpose of passing such property in the goods and completing the title of the endorsee to full possession thereof, the bill of lading, until complete delivery of the cargo has been made on shore to someone rightfully claiming under it, remains in force as a symbol, and carries with it not only the full ownership of the goods, but also all rights created by the contract of carriage between the shipper and the shipowner. It is a key which in the hands of the rightful owner is intended to unlock the door of the warehouse, floating or fixed, in which the goods may chance to be.

Order bills, although they are negotiable instruments, should not be confused with bills of exchange (such as checks or trade acceptances). Maritime commercial practice is less developed than the law of commercial paper, and though both classes of instruments are related, they are also distinct.

Like bills of exchange, order bills of lading may be made out *to bearer* or *to the order* of a named party. Bearer instruments are transferred by delivery; order instruments by negotiation, that is, by endorsement and delivery. In practice, bills of lading are seldom made out to bearer, as they are documents of title that serve as the symbol or token of the goods described in the bill.

The negotiation of an order bill transfers title in the goods. This is what makes the bill valuable. Because the bill is *negotiable*, so too are the goods. This enables the person named on the bill to transfer the goods while a ship is in transit. In other words, possession of the order bill is in most respects the same as possession of the goods.

---

[50]In the Emilien Marie Case, *Law Journal Reports, Admiralty*, vol. 44, p. 9 (1875), the carrier issued three bills of lading to the shipper with the understanding that the last would apply only if there was enough of the perishable cargo left at the port of destination. The shipper nonetheless negotiated the bill to a third party who was unaware of the understanding. The court held that the endorsee was entitled to demand the full quantity.

[51]Sanders v. Maclean & Co., *Law Reports, Queen's Bench Division*, vol. 11, p. 327 at p. 341 (1883).

Unlike transferees of bills of exchange (as discussed in Chapter 12), a transferee who obtains an order bill of lading in good faith and for value paid is not a holder in due course who is entitled to claim the goods from the carrier *free of equities* or *free of personal defenses*.[52] This is a significant difference. In practice, it means that should an order bill of lading be obtained by fraud and endorsed to a bona fide purchaser for value, the recipient will not acquire title to the goods described in the bill. On the other hand, if the same thing were to happen with a bill of exchange (such as a draft, check, or note) that was neither overdue nor dishonored, the recipient (who would be a holder in due course) would be entitled to the money or property described in that bill. Because of this difference, an order bill of lading is sometimes described as only a *quasi-negotiable* instrument.[53]

The definitional basis for this difference between bills of exchange and order bills of lading can be found in Lord Justice Bowen's description, quoted earlier. Even when a bill of lading is properly endorsed and delivered, title to the goods will pass only when the bill of lading is negotiated with the intention of transferring the goods. For example, a seller may endorse a bill of lading to his agent in the port where the goods are to be discharged so that the agent can deal directly with a particular buyer. Because the seller did not intend to pass title to the agent by his endorsement, title would not pass. If the agent were to fraudulently sell the bill to a third party, the third party would also not have title. In such a circumstance, the seller could order the carrier to deliver the goods only to the intended buyer, or if delivery had already been made to the third party, the seller could sue that person for conversion. This is so because the transferee of an order bill of lading acquires both the rights and the liabilities of his transferor.[54]

Bills of lading are also distinct from bills of exchange because they additionally represent a contract for carriage. Negotiation of an order bill of lading produces the unique result of a transfer of the right to enforce the underlying transportation agreement. For example, in the case of *The Albazero*, cargo was lost due to the alleged negligence of the carrier. The holders of the bill of lading were unable to sue because the statute of limitation set by the Hague Rules had run. Accordingly, the charterers, who were business affiliates of the holders, attempted to sue under the charterparty, which was not subject to the same statutory time limits. The British House of Lords held that the charterers could not sue. By endorsing the bill of lading, which also represented the contract of carriage, they had transferred all of their contractual rights to the transferee.[55]

CARRIER'S DUTIES UNDER A BILL OF LADING

A carrier transporting goods under a bill of lading is required by the Hague and Hague-Visby Rules to exercise "due diligence" in:[56]

(a) Making the ship seaworthy.
(b) Properly manning, equipping, and supplying the ship.
(c) Making the holds, refrigerating, and cool chambers, and all other parts of the ship in which goods are carried, fit and safe for their reception, carriage, and preservation.
(d) Properly and carefully loading, handling, stowing, carrying, keeping, caring for, and discharging the goods carried.

Most courts strictly enforce this obligation. For example, in *Riverstone Meat Co. Pty., Ltd. v. Lancashire Shipping Co., Ltd.*, cargo was damaged by water due to the negligent work

---

[52]British practice uses the phrase *free of equities*; American practice uses *free of personal defenses*. Both refer to a class of adverse claims that the person obliged to perform may assert against a holder, but not a holder in due course. Such equities or personal defenses include breach of contract, lack or failure of consideration, fraud in the inducement, some forms of illegality, mental incapacity, ordinary duress, discharge by payment or cancellation, and nondelivery.
[53]Leo D'Arcy, *Schmitthoff's Export Trade: The Law and Practice of International Trade*, p. 276 (10th ed., 2000).
[54]The rule was applied in a more roundabout way in Sewell v. Burdick, *Law Reports, Appeal Cases*, vol. 10, p. 74 (1884). There, a bank that was the holder of the bill of lading argued that it was not obligated to pay the cost for storing the goods after they were discharged from the carrier because the shipper had not intended to transfer title to it. The court agreed, noting that the shipper had given the bill of lading to the bank only as a pledge for a loan.
[55]*All England Law Reports*, vol. 1976, pt. 3, p. 129 (House of Lords, 1976).
[56]International Convention for the Unification of Certain Rules of Law Relating to Bills of Lading, Article 3 (1924) (the 1921 Hague Rules); Brussels Protocol, Article 3 (1968) (the Hague-Visby Rules).

of a shipfitter employed by a ship repair company. The court held that the carrier had failed to use due diligence in making the ship seaworthy.[57]

CARRIER'S IMMUNITIES

Both the Hague and Hague-Visby Rules exempt carriers from liability from damages that arise from any[58]

   (a) Act, neglect, or default of the master, mariner, pilot, or the servants of the carrier in the navigation or in the management of the ship;
   (b) Fire, unless caused by the actual fault or privity of the carrier;
   (c) Perils, dangers, and accidents of the sea or other navigable water;
   (d) Act of God;
   (e) Act of war;
   (f) Act of public enemies;
   (g) Arrest or restraint of princes, rulers, or people, or seizure under legal process;
   (h) Quarantine restrictions;
   (i) Act or omission of the shipper or owner of the goods, or his agent or representative;
   (j) Strikes or lockouts or stoppage or restraint of labor from whatever cause, whether partial or general; provided that nothing herein contained shall be construed to relieve a carrier from responsibility for the carrier's own acts;
   (k) Riots and civil commotions;
   (l) Saving or attempting to save life or property at sea;
   (m) Wastage in bulk or weight or any other loss or damage arising from inherent defect, quality, or vice of the goods;
   (n) Insufficiency of packing;
   (o) Insufficiency or inadequacy of marks;
   (p) Latent defects not discoverable by due diligence; and
   (q) Any other cause arising without the actual fault and privity of the carrier and without the fault or negligence of the agents or servants of the carrier, but the burden of proof shall be on the person claiming the benefit of this exception to show that neither the actual fault or privity of the carrier nor the fault or neglect of the agents or servants of the carrier contributed to the loss or damage.

These immunities are narrowly construed. If cargo is injured and the injury falls within one of the exemptions, the carrier will nonetheless be responsible if the underlying cause was the result of the carrier's failure to exercise due diligence in carrying out its fundamental duties. This point is illustrated in Case 11-4.

---

[57]*All England Law Reports*, vol. 1961, pt. 1, p. 495 (1961).
[58]International Convention for the Unification of Certain Rules of Law Relating to Bills of Lading, Article 4, (1924) (the 1921 Hague Rules); Brussels Protocol, Article 4, (1968) (the Hague-Visby Rules).

Case 11-4 GREAT CHINA METAL INDUSTRIES CO. LTD. v. MALAYSIAN INTERNATIONAL SHIPPING CORP.

High Court of Australia.
High Court of Australia Reports, vol. 1998, no. 65 (1998).

JUSTICES GAUDRON, GUMMOW AND HAYNE:

In 1989, 40 cases of aluminum can body stock in coils were consigned from Sydney to Keelung, Taiwan. The respondent issued a bill of lading dated 5 October 1989, acknowledging receipt of the goods in apparent good order and condition. The vessel named in the bill as the intended vessel was the MV *Bunga Seroja*.

The shipper named in the bill was Strang International Pty. Ltd. ("Strang") as agent for Comalco Aluminium Ltd. Strang packed the containers in which the cargo was shipped. The appellant was named in the bill as "the notify party" and property in the goods duly passed to it.

The bill provided that it should have effect subject to legislation giving effect to the Hague Rules. By the *Sea-Carriage of Goods Act 1924* (Commonwealth),[59] the Hague Rules applied to the carriage of the goods. The parties to the bill of lading were deemed by §§ 4(1) and 9(1) of that statute to have intended to contract according to the Hague Rules.

In the course of its passage across the Great Australian Bight, the vessel encountered heavy weather. That weather had been forecast before the vessel left port. Some of the goods were damaged.

Although, as will appear, it is not determinative of the outcome of the appeal, the question to which submissions primarily were directed is the meaning and effect of Art. IV rule 2(c) of the Hague Rules that:

"Neither the carrier nor the ship shall be responsible for loss or damage arising or resulting from—

***

(c) perils, dangers, and accidents of the sea or other navigable waters ... "

The appellant contended that:

- this exception (the "perils of the sea" exception) does not apply if damage to cargo results from sea and weather conditions which could reasonably be foreseen and guarded against;
- the weather encountered by the Bunga Seroja was foreseen; and
- the statement of Judges Mason and Wilson in *Shipping Corporation of India Ltd. v Gamlen Chemical Co (A/Asia) Pty Ltd.*[60] that "sea and weather conditions which may reasonably be foreseen and guarded against may constitute a peril of the sea" is wrong and should not be followed.

The appellant pleaded that the respondent had failed to meet its responsibility under Art. III rule 1 of the Hague Rules to exercise, before and at the beginning of the voyage, due diligence to make the ship seaworthy; to properly man, equip, and supply the ship; and to make the holds and all other parts of the ship in which the goods were carried fit and safe for their reception, carriage, and preservation. It also pleaded failure by the respondent to properly and carefully load, handle, stow, carry, keep, care for, and discharge the goods carried (Art. III rule 2). By its defense, the respondent relied upon various immunities specified in Art. IV rule 2. In particular, the respondent pleaded that it was not re-

sponsible for any loss or damage to the goods arising or resulting from perils of the sea and that any damage to the goods resulted or occurred by reason of that matter.

The trial judge (Judge Carruthers) entered judgment for the respondent. His Honor concluded:

"In my view, the [respondent] has established to the requisite degree that the damage to the subject cargo was occasioned by perils of the sea. . . . In summary, the evidence satisfies me that, bearing in mind the anticipated weather conditions: (i) when the *Bunga Seroja* sailed from Burnie she was fit in all respects for the voyage; (ii) the [respondent] properly and carefully loaded, handled, stowed, carried, kept, and cared for the subject cargo; and (iii) there was no neglect or default of the master or other servants of the [respondent] in the management of the ship or cargo.

I am satisfied that the damage to the subject cargo was occasioned by perils of the sea, in that, the pounding of the ship by reason of the heavy weather caused the coils within the container to be dislodged and thereby sustain damage."

The New South Wales Court of Appeal dismissed an appeal. The appeal to this Court also should be dismissed.

***

In understanding the operation of the Hague Rules, there are three important considerations. The rules must be read as a whole, they must be read in the light of the history behind them, and they must be read as a set of rules devised by international agreement for use in contracts that could be governed by any of several different, sometimes radically different, legal systems. It is convenient to begin by touching upon some matters of history.

UNIFORM CONSTRUCTION

Because the Hague Rules are intended to apply widely in international trade, it is self-evidently desirable to strive for uniform construction of them. As has been said earlier, the rules seek to allocate risks between cargo and carrier interests and it follows that the allocation of those risks that is made when the rules are construed by national courts should, as far as possible, be uniform. Only then can insurance markets set premiums efficiently and the cost of double insurance be avoided.

In *Gamlen*, Judges Mason and Wilson note that:[61]

[t]here is a difference between the Anglo-Australian conception of "perils of the sea" and the United States-Canadian conception. According to the latter,

---

[59]Section 4(1). This has now been replaced by the Carriage of Goods by Sea Act 1991 (Commonwealth), which incorporates the Hague-Visby Rules.
[60]*Commonwealth Law Reports*, vol. 147, p. 142 at p. 166 (1980).
[61]*Id.,* at pp. 165–166.

"perils of the sea" include losses to goods on board which are peculiar to the sea and "are of an extraordinary nature or arise from irresistible force or overwhelming power, and which cannot be guarded against by the ordinary exertions of human skill and prudence."[62] In the United Kingdom and Australia it is not necessary that the losses or the cause of the losses should be "extraordinary."[63] Consequently sea and weather conditions which may reasonably be foreseen and guarded against may constitute a peril of the sea.

When reference is made to occurrences identified as "extraordinary," the question arises as to the nature of the relativity which is contemplated. Thus it has been said that the events which occurred "may be considered extraordinary as compared with an even voyage upon a placid sea; and yet [they] may be an entirely ordinary occurrence as compared with transportation by sea generally."[64]

It may be that the difference between Anglo-Australian and American-Canadian construction of the "perils of the sea" exception is less than might appear from reference to cases such as *The Giulia*[65] or *The Rosalia*[66]—both decisions of the [United States] Second Circuit Court of Appeals. In *The Rosalia* a peril of the sea was described as "something so catastrophic as to triumph over those safeguards by which skillful and vigilant seamen usually bring ship and cargo to port in safety." More recent authority in the United States has, perhaps, placed less emphasis on whether what happened was extraordinary and catastrophic. But whether or not that is an accurate reflection of more recent developments, there is great force in what Judge Learned Hand said in *Philippine Sugar Centrals Agency v. Kokusai Kisen Kabushiki Kaisha*:[67]

> The phrase, "perils of the sea," has at times been treated as though its meaning were esoteric: Judge Hough's vivid language in *The Rosalia* . . . has perhaps given currency to the notion. That meant nothing more, however, than that the weather encountered must be too much for a well-found vessel to withstand. . . . The standard of seaworthiness, like so many other legal standards, must always be uncertain, for the law cannot fix in advance those precautions in hull and gear which will be necessary to meet the manifold dangers of the sea. That Judge Hough meant no more

than this in *The Rosalia* . . . is shown by his reference to the definition in *The Warren Adams*[68] . . . as the equivalent of what he said. That definition was as follows: "That term may be defined as denoting 'all marine casualties resulting from the violent action of the elements, as distinguished from their natural, silent influence.'" It would be too much to hope that *The Rosalia* . . . will not continue to be cited for more than this, but it would be gratifying if it were not.

***

Thus there are statements to be found in the United States authorities that a "perils of the sea" exception may apply even if the weather encountered was no more than expected.

Nor should statements made in the many English cases dealing with perils of the sea be read divorced from their context. Some can, we think, be seen as no more than decisions about particular facts. Others examine questions of onus of proof and concurrent causation, which do not arise in this case. [For example in the *"Xantho"*[69] Lord Herschell drew a distinction] between perils of the sea and other losses of which the sea is the immediate cause. He said:

> I think it clear that the term "perils of the sea" does not cover every accident or casualty which may happen to the subject-matter of the insurance on the sea. It must be a peril "of" the sea. Again, it is well settled that it is not every loss or damage of which the sea is the immediate cause that is covered by these words. They do not protect, for example, against that natural and inevitable action of the winds and waves, which results in what may be described as wear and tear. There must be some casualty, something which could not be foreseen as one of the necessary incidents of the adventure.

The distinction drawn by his Lordship is important and must be borne in mind when considering the operation of the "perils of the sea" exception. . . .

Many other cases were mentioned in argument or can be found in the books. We think it desirable to touch briefly on only three other streams of authority. First, it seems that in German law, a peril of the sea need not be an extraordinary event and that a storm of a certain force is regarded as a peril of the sea.[70] Similarly, in French law

---

[62]The Giulia, *Federal Reporter*, vol. 218, p. 744 (U.S. 2nd Circuit Ct. of Appeals, 1914), adopting Joseph Story, *Commentaries on the Law of Bailments: with Illustrations from the Civil and the Foreign Law*, § 512(a) (9th ed. 1878).

[63]Thomas G. Carver, *Carriage by Sea*, vol. 1, § 161, (12th ed., 1971); Skandia Insurance Co. Ltd. v. Skoljarev, *Commonwealth Law Reports*, vol. 142, p. 375 at pp. 386–387 (1979)....

[64]Clinchfield Fuel Co. v. Aetna Insurance Co., *South Eastern Reporter*, vol. 114, p. 543 at p. 546 (Supreme Ct. of South Carolina, 1922).

[65]*Federal Reporter*, vol. 218, p. 744 (U.S. 2nd Circuit Ct. of Appeals, 1914).

[66]*Id.*, vol. 264, p. 285 (U.S. 2nd Circuit Ct. of Appeals, 1920).

[67]*Id.*, vol. 106, p. 32 at pp. 34–35 (U.S. 2nd Circuit Ct. of Appeals, 1939).

[68]*Id.*, vol. 74, p. 413 at p. 415 (U.S. 2nd Circuit Ct. of Appeals, 1896).

[69]*Law Reports, Appellate Cases*, vol. 12, p. 503 (1887).

[70]General Motors Overseas Operation v SS Goettingen, *Federal Supplement*, vol. 225, p. 902 at pp. 904–905 (U.S. Dist. Ct. S. Dist. of N.Y., 1964).

a peril of the sea need not be "unforeseeable and insurmountable."[71] Finally, the Supreme Court of Canada held in *Goodfellow Lumber Sales v. Verreault*[72] that:

> . . . even if the loss is occasioned by Perils of the sea, the ship owner is nevertheless liable if he failed to exercise due diligence to make the ship seaworthy at the beginning of the voyage and that unseaworthiness was a decisive cause of the loss.

How then are these disparate streams of authority to be brought together? In our view one must begin by recognizing that the inquiry is, in large part, a factual inquiry—is the carrier immune in respect of what otherwise would be its failure to discharge its responsibilities under Art. III because the loss or damage to the goods arose or resulted from a cause which brings the carrier within the immunity conferred by Art. IV, rule 2?

If cargo has been lost or damaged and if the vessel was seaworthy, properly manned, equipped, and supplied, what led to the loss or damage? Did it arise or result from want of proper stowing (Art. III rule 2)? Did it arise from the "act, neglect or default of the master . . . or the servants of the carrier in the navigation, or in the management of the ship" (Art. IV rule 2(a))? Or, did it result from some other cause peculiar to the sea? The last is a peril of the sea.

In *Gamlen,* Judges Mason and Wilson said that "sea and weather conditions which may reasonably be foreseen and guarded against may constitute a peril of the sea." The fact that the sea and weather conditions that were encountered could reasonably be foreseen, or were actually forecast, may be important in deciding issues like an issue of alleged want of seaworthiness of the vessel, an alleged default of the master in navigation or management, or an alleged want of proper stowage. . . . But if it is necessary to consider the "perils of the sea" exception, the fact that the conditions that were encountered could reasonably be expected or were forecast should not be taken to conclude that question. . . . Such an approach, even if it is different from the American and Canadian approach, better reflects the history of the rules, their international origins, and is the better construction of the rules as a whole.

THE PRESENT APPEAL

In the present case, the trial judge held that there was no breach of Art. III, rule 1 or rule 2. That is, the trial judge rejected the contentions that due diligence had not been exercised to make the ship seaworthy, to properly man, equip, and supply the ship and to "make the holds . . . and all other parts of the ship in which goods are carried, fit and safe for their reception, carriage and preservation." Indeed the trial judge found that in fact the vessel was fit

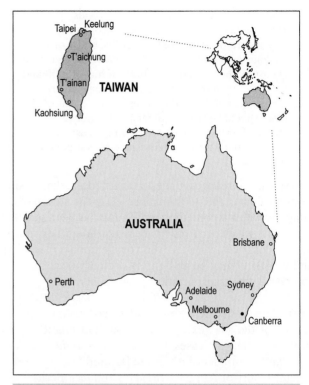

MAP 11-4 Australia and Taiwan (1998)

in all respects for the voyage when it left port, [and that the goods had been properly stowed. . . .]

It was submitted by the appellant that the master should not have left port or should have diverted so as to avoid the weather which was forecast. The former contention appears not to have been made at trial. The latter was, but was rejected. The trial judge, having heard the evidence of experts called by both parties, said that he was "unable to conclude that any deficiencies in the conduct of the ship and her cargo by [the ship's master] have been demonstrated." There is no basis for departing from that finding. Once it was made, the trial judge's conclusion that there was no neglect or default of the master or other servants of the carrier in the management of the ship or cargo was inevitable. To the extent that the appellant now seeks to expand its contention to include the proposition that the vessel should not have left port, it is enough to say that, if the judge's finding does not meet the contention, it is a contention that could be made only with evidence to support it and there was none.

***

The failure of the submissions by the appellant makes it unnecessary to consider grounds urged in

---

[71]William Tetley, *Marine Cargo Claims*, p. 441 (3rd ed., 1988).
[72]*Supreme Court Reports*, vol. 1971 p. 522 at p. 528 (1971).

support of the decision of the Court of Appeal by the respondent in its Notice of Contention.

The appeal should be dismissed with costs. ∎

CASEPOINT: This case turned on the interpretation of the phrase *perils of the sea*. This term is one of the exceptions mentioned in the Hague Rules, which protect the carrier from liability when goods are damaged because of *perils of the sea*. The court noted that there was some difference in interpretation of this phrase in England and Australia compared to interpretations in the United States and Canada (which appear to require that the peril be something *extraordinary*). However, the court found that the differences were not as large as some had argued, that Germany and France had viewed the phrase in the same way as England and Australia, and that the need to interpret the phrase in a uniform way was important. In conclusion, the court ruled that where there was no negligence on the part of the carrier and the goods had been properly loaded and stowed, that the damage caused by the rough voyage was one of the perils of the sea.

LIABILITY LIMITS

Carriers have long attempted to set monetary limits on their liability in the event that they are found liable for loss of or damage to a cargo. The permissible limits are now established by convention. The Hague Rules of 1921 limit a carrier's liability to (1) UK £100 per package or (2) UK £100 per unit when shipped in "customary freight units."[73]

One reason many nations had a strong interest in amending the Hague Rules in the 1960s was the belief that its monetary limits were inadequate. The limits were dramatically raised in the Hague-Visby Rules. Those rules set the limits at "10,000 gold francs per package or unit, or thirty gold francs per kilo of the gross weight of the goods lost or damaged, whichever is the higher."[74] This gold or *Poincaré* franc is not a unit of currency but rather an amount of gold. At current conversion rates, it is equivalent to approximately U.S. $1 or U.K. £0.60.

The limits do not apply if the parties agree to higher amounts. They also do not apply if the carrier acted either (1) "with intent to cause damage" or (2) "recklessly and with knowledge that damage would probably result."[75]

The low limits set in the Hague Rules—which remain in effect in the United States—have forced shippers suing in American courts to suggest creative definitions for the terms *package* and *customary freight unit* as a way to obtain a respectable recovery. Courts, not unsympathetic to their plight, have sometimes adopted these suggestions. One such court produced the opinion in Case 11-5.

---

[73]International Convention for the Unification of Certain Rules of Law Relating to Bills of Lading, Article 4, § 5 (1924) (the 1921 Hague Rules). Article 9 provides: "Those contracting states in which the pound sterling is not a monetary unit reserve to themselves the right of translating the sums indicated in this convention in terms of pounds sterling into terms of their own monetary system in round figures."
[74]*Id.*, Article 4, § 5.
[75]*Id.* and Brussels Protocol, Article 4, § 5 (1968) (the Hague-Visby Rules).

Case 11-5 CROFT & SCULLY CO. v. M/V SKULPTOR VUCHETICH ET AL.

United States, Court of Appeals, Fifth Circuit, 1982.
Federal Reporter, Second Series, vol. 664, p. 1277 (1982).

CIRCUIT JUDGE JOHN R. BROWN:

Appellant Croft & Scully Co. appeals from a decision by the District Court limiting to $500 its recovery in an incident where the parties stipulated negligence. . . .

Things Go Better with Coke

Croft & Scully contracted to ship 1755 cases of soft drink from Houston, Texas, to the middle eastern country of Kuwait. Apparently, Kuwaitis would like to be Peppers, too. Croft & Scully arranged to ship the soft drinks on board M/V *Skulptor Vuchetich*, which arrived in Houston December 8, 1977. Baltic Shipping Co., owner of *Skulptor*, dispatched a 20-foot steel container to Croft & Scully's warehouse in Wharton, Texas. Employees of the supplier loaded the 1755 cases, each containing 4 "6-packs" or 24 cartons, into the container, closed, and sealed it—a real Teem effort. The supplier then trucked the container to Goodpasture's yard, near the Houston Ship Channel, which Baltic had selected as convenient storage facility pending arrival of *Skulptor*.

During the Refreshing Pause between arrival of the container and arrival of *Skulptor*, the vessel's agent prepared a Bill of Lading, and hired Shippers Stevedoring, Inc., to load the soft drink container on board *Skulptor*.

Pepsi Cola Hits the Spot—On the Pavement

As one of the Stevedore's employees was lifting the container, with the use of a forklift, he negligently dropped it. By our calculations, 42,120 cans of soft drinks crashed to the ground, never a thirst to quench. In the Crush, the cans were damaged. The stevedore, no doubt, was in no mood to have a Coke and a smile.

Dr. Pepper at 10, 2, and § 1304

Croft & Scully sued Goodpasture, Shippers Stevedoring, and *Skulptor* and her owners to pick up the Tab for its damages. The District Court dismissed the suit as to Goodpasture because it had no agency relationship with Shippers Stevedoring. Relying upon a so-called Himalaya Clause in the Bill of Lading, it granted the remaining defendants' motion for summary judgment and, finding that the container constituted a "package" within the meaning of § 4(5) of [the *Carriage of Goods by Sea Act* (COGSA), which implements the Hague Rules in the United States,] limited Shippers Stevedoring's liability to $500. Croft & Scully appeals. Things Go Better on appeal, and we reverse and remand.

A Peek at the Himalaya Clause

Croft & Scully asserts that the Himalaya Clause limiting recovery to $500 violates public policy. That claim fails to make the grade, given our decision in *Brown & Root v. M/V Peisander*[76] upholding such a clause. Indeed, the conflict which we surmounted there does not even arise in this case. Clause 17 of the Bill of Lading makes clear provision for an increased valuation at a higher freight rate. A more unequivocal declaration, in fact, one could not find. As Croft & Scully could have availed itself of extra loss or damage protection, but chose not to, the District Court ruled that the Himalaya Clause applied.

Don't Judge the Package by Its Appearance

Even if liability is limited to $500 per package, Croft & Scully argues, the cardboard cases of soft drinks rather than the 20-foot container should constitute the relevant "package." Shippers Stevedoring responds with equal fervor that the container is the "package." Their argument, we think, given the recent decision in *Allstate Insurance Co. v. Inversiones Navieras Imparca*,[77] holds no water, carbonated or otherwise.

We begin by pointing out that COGSA does not apply by its own force and effect, since the incident occurred in the yard and not on the vessel. Rather the Bill of Lading incorporates COGSA. Thus, its provisions are merely terms of the contract of carriage which, like any other contractual terms, call out for judicial interpretation in case of dispute....

The District Court further observed that the Fifth Circuit had not established a test to determine what constitutes a "package" under COGSA. Since the date of its order, this Court has formulated such a test in whose good hands the parties—and the District Court—must rest.

Allstate involved the loss of 341 cartons of stereo equipment. The shipper loaded the cartons inside a container, sealed it, and had its agent deliver it to the carrier. The carrier issued a Bill of Lading which described the contents both in number and in kind. When the container arrived in Venezuela, it was as empty as a can of soda on a hot summer day. The shipper sought recovery for its full damages, but the carrier relying on COGSA, sought shelter in the $500 limitation. Although the District Court concluded that the container was the COGSA package, the winds of judicial change Schwepped away the $500 shelter and exposed the carrier to full liability.

Judge Anderson, writing for the Court, after reviewing the history of COGSA and decisions in other Circuits, found that each stereo carton was a discrete "package." He based his decision on a case in the Second Circuit, *Mitsui & Co. v. American Export Lines*.[78] There Judge Friendly expressly rejected as unworkable and unsound the old "functional economics" test.[79] . . . Instead, relying on dicta in *Leather's Best, Inc. v. S.S. Mormaclynx*[80] he looked to see whether the carrier had clear, unequivocal notice of the container's contents:

Clearly the goal of international uniformity is better served by the approach in *Leather's Best* that generally a container supplied by the carrier is not a

[76]*Federal Reporter, Second Series*, vol. 648, p. 415 (Fifth Circuit Ct. of Appeals, 1981).
[77]Id., vol. 646, p. 169 (Fifth Circuit Ct. of Appeals, 1981).
[78]Id., vol. 636, p. 807 (Second Circuit Ct. of Appeals, 1981).
[79]That test, which lingered beyond its time as a Sprite disrupting the admiralty for some years, looks to see whether the goods as packaged prior to shipping were "functional," i.e., fit for shipping and transport individually as packed. It necessitated much judicial guessing work, and we are well rid of it.
[80]*Federal Reporter, Second Series*, vol. 800, p. 815 (Second Circuit Ct. of Appeals, 1971).

COGSA package if its contents and the number of packages or units are disclosed....

We find nothing in the Bill of Lading to indicate that the contracting parties intended some special meaning of the term "package." Since Croft & Scully included information about the contents of the container and their number, *Allstate* governs. Therefore, the District Court erred in granting summary judgment on the "package" issue.

Customary Freight Unit

Even if the container was not a COGSA "package," Shippers Stevedoring contends, the Court should uphold the $500 award because the container was a "customary freight unit" within the ambit of § 4(5) of COGSA, and thus the Himalaya Clause still applies....

Caterpillar Americas Co. v. S/S Sea Roads[81] held that the "customary freight unit" was a tractor and its parts rather than hundredweight units, "regardless of the harshness or seemingly illogic of such result":

> With respect to the words "customary freight unit," the authorities are conclusive that this phrase refers to the *unit upon which the charge for freight is computed* and not to the physical shipping unit. As thus construed, the statute gives the court the task of determining what unit was actually used by the carrier for computing the freight charge on the shipment in question. Under the statute the freight unit, if one exists, will control the question of limitation of liability, unless the freight unit employed was a mere sham, and, therefore not a "customary" unit within the meaning of the statute....

From these cases, we deduce that "customary freight unit" is a question of fact that will vary from contract to contract. Of particular importance in this as in any contractual dispute, then, is the parties' intent, as expressed in the Bill of Lading, applicable tariff, and perhaps elsewhere....

Although Croft & Scully admitted that the freight charge was $2200, calculated on a "flat container rate," we do not know how the parties arrived at that rate. Does it depend upon the contents, weight, value, custom of the trade, applicable tariffs, if any, or other factors? The District Court must consider these questions on remand. If it finds that the container was a "customary freight unit," then the Court should reinstate the $500 limitation of liability. If not, then it should hold further proceedings to determine the amount of damages. We, of course, express no opinion concerning the outcome.

Recap

We affirm the District Court's dismissal of Goodpasture and its conclusion that the Himalaya Clause applies. We

MAP 11-5   Texas (1982)

reverse its grant of summary judgment for Shippers Stevedoring and its finding that the steel container was a COGSA package. As the District Judge never reached the important factual question whether the container of soft drink cartons was a "customary freight unit," we remand for further inquiry into the facts and for consideration of the parties' intent, factors that will guide the trial Court in determining the meaning of that COGSA clause.

Affirmed in part, reversed in part and remanded. ■

CASEPOINT: In this humorous opinion, Judge Brown of the U.S. Fifth Circuit Court of Appeals discusses what is a *customary freight unit* in connection with the loss of 42,120 cans of soft drinks during loading onto a ship. A so-called Himalaya Clause in the bill of lading, allowed by the Hague Rules, limited the liability of the carrier and that of the stevedore to $500 per customary freight unit (CFU). So, the question was whether the CFU was the 20-foot steel container holding the 1,755 cases of soft drinks or the 1,755 cases (each containing four six-packs of drinks). The district court had held that there was only one package and limited the liability to $500. But on appeal, the court held that additional inquiry into this factual issue was necessary, specifically as to the type of packing unit upon which the shipping charges are based. This case was sent back to the lower court for further hearings on that issue.

---

[81]*Federal Supplement*, vol. 231, p. 647 (Dist. Ct. S. Dist. of Florida, 1964), affirmed, *Federal Reporter, Second Series*, vol. 364, p. 829 (Fifth Circuit Ct. of Appeals, 1966).

TIME LIMITATIONS

A claim for loss or damages must be instituted within one year after the goods were or should have been delivered.[82] The claim may be initiated by filing suit or commencing an arbitration proceeding.[83]

THIRD-PARTY RIGHTS (HIMALAYA CLAUSE)

The Hague and Hague-Visby Rules apply only to the carrier and the party or parties shipping goods under a bill of lading. Third parties who help in the transport of the goods but who are not parties to the carriage-of-goods contract contained in the bill of lading have no contractual right to claim the liability limits established by the conventions. Thus, officers, crew members, agents, and brokers who work for a carrier, as well as stevedores who commonly work for a unit of a shipping line, can be sued under local laws of tort or delict without the convention-imposed cap.

Himalaya Clause: A term in a bill of lading that purports to extend to third parties the carrier's liability limits established by the Hague and Hague-Visby Rules.

To extend the liability limits of the conventions to their employees, agents, and even independent contractors (such as stevedores), carriers have added a clause to their bills of lading, known as a **Himalaya Clause**, which entitles them to claim the protection of the Hague or the Hague-Visby Rules. These clauses are valid in the United States but are generally unenforceable in the United Kingdom. Most U.K. courts refuse to enforce the Himalaya Clause because of a doctrine known as *privity of contract*, which says that only persons party to a contract may enforce its provisions.[84]

In the United States, on the other hand, the doctrine of privity is, at best, haphazardly enforced. As a consequence, most American courts allow the persons named in a Himalaya Clause to claim the rights it grants as third-party beneficiaries, as the previous case (*Croft & Scully*) demonstrated.[85]

---

[82]International Convention for the Unification of Certain Rules of Law Relating to Bills of Lading, Article 3, § 6 (1924) (the 1921 Hague Rules); Brussels Protocol, Article 3, § 6 (1968) (the Hague-Visby Rules).
[83]The Merak, *All England Law Reports*, vol. 1965, pt. 1, p. 230 (1965).
[84]In 1962, the Court of Appeal refused to enforce a Himalaya Clause in Scruttons, Ltd. v. Midland Silicones, Ltd., *All England Law Reports*, vol. 1962, pt. 1, p. 1 (1962). In 1975, the House of Lords in the case of New Zealand Shipping Co., Ltd. v. Satterthwaite, *All England Law Reports*, vol. 1974, pt. 1, p. 1015 (1974), said that there might be circumstances where stevedores could be treated as parties to a contract containing a Himalaya Clause. However, in 1980 the Privy Council reapplied the doctrine of privity and found the Himalaya Clause unenforceable in Port Jackson Stevedoring, Pty. Ltd. v. Salmond and Spraggon (Australia) Pty., *All England Law Reports*, vol. 1980, pt. 3, p. 257 (1980).
[85]Brown & Root v. M/V Peisander, *Federal Reporter, Second Series*, vol. 648, p. 415 (Fifth Circuit Ct. of Appeals, 1981).

Reading 11-1   CARGO THEFT AND TERRORISM

Source: Robert F. Caton, "The Other Cargo Security Threat" *Journal of Commerce*, New York, January 23, 2006, p. 1.

Robert F. Caton, president of a cargo shipping firm in New York, stated in an article published in January 2006 that terrorism continued to be the major transportation security concern. Even prior to Sept. 11, 2001, cargo theft was low on law enforcement's list of priorities. Mr. Caton wondered whether theft is getting any attention today at all, even though statistics indicate that cargo theft is rising annually—perhaps as $40 billion of merchandise is stolen per year in North America alone.

Cargo theft can be complicated and difficult to investigate, because of the supply chain involved. An average air-cargo shipment is handled 16 to 32 times from the shipper to the consignee. Suppose that a shipment starts in Toronto, is trucked through New York to JFK Airport and ultimately is delivered in London. If, upon arrival at the consignee's warehouse, the cargo is found to be pilfered, where does the investigation begin? Which law-enforcement agency will investigate? In this example, the freight has traveled through the following jurisdictions: Toronto Police, Canadian Customs, U.S. Customs, New York State Police, New York City Police, JFK Airport Police, FBI, British Customs and finally Scotland Yard.

The main security concern in the United States is focused on terrorism and possible criminal activity that impacts human life, leaving little room for attention to cargo theft, which might be a serious flaw, considering a ship-

ment's vulnerability to terrorism. Law-enforcement agencies and prosecutors are hard-pressed for time to investigate and prosecute reported thefts and many shippers believe carriers and warehouse operators are reporting only a fraction of the volume of thefts actually occurring. Mr. Caton argued that a simple database and a structured reporting method along with a group of knowledgeable and experienced cargo-theft investigators are needed. He stated that shippers can no longer sit idly by knowing that cargo theft could lead to more significant security risks.

E. CHARTERPARTIES

charterparty: A contract to hire an entire ship for a particular voyage or for a particular period of time.

A **charterparty** is a contract for the hire of an entire ship for a particular voyage or a set period of time. Oil, sugar, grain, ores, coal, and other bulk commodities are almost always shipped under such contracts.

The Hague and Hague-Visby Rules do not apply to charterparties unless a bill of lading issued by the shipowner comes into the hands of a third party. The charterer and the owner are free to set the terms of their contract, and commonly they use standardized contracts drafted at various conferences and known by such code names as Baltime and Gencon. Interpretations and legal obligations vary from country to country, so a forum selection clause and a choice-of-law clause are common, and important, provisions.[86]

VOYAGE CHARTERPARTIES

voyage charterparty: A contract to hire an entire ship for a particular voyage.

dead freight: A charge imposed on a charterer when a chartered ship has less than a full load.

When a charterer employs a ship and its crew for the carriage of goods from one place to another, the charterer and shipowner have entered into a **voyage charterparty**. Under the terms most commonly used in such a contract, the owner agrees to provide the ship at a named port at a specified time and to carry the goods to the contract destination. The charterer agrees to provide a full cargo and to arrange for its loading at an agreed-upon time. If less than a full load is provided, the shipowner is entitled to charge **dead freight** for the amount of the deficiency. This dead-freight charge will be noted on the bill of lading issued by the shipowner, and a holder who acquires the bill will be obliged to pay the charge before the ship will turn over the cargo.

lay days: The number of days that a charterer may keep a chartered ship idle for the loading of goods.

demurrage: A charge made by a shipowner when a charterer keeps a ship idle for more than the agreed-upon number of lay days.

If the shipowner fails to arrive at the original port for loading at the specified time, the charterer will commonly be able to terminate the contract by virtue of a cancellation clause. The charterparty will also describe the number of **lay days** that the ship may be idle while goods are loaded or discharged. Because modern cargo ships are expensive and have a short working life, the charterparty will additionally describe damages, known as **demurrage**, that the shipowner can charge for every idle day that exceeds the agreed-upon number of lay days. The obligation to pay the demurrage will be secured by a lien on the cargo, which any holder of the corresponding bill of lading will have to pay off before taking delivery.

TIME CHARTERPARTIES

time charterparty: A contract to hire an entire ship for a particular period of time.

Under a **time charterparty** the charterer engages the use of a vessel for a stated period of time. The charterer normally pays *hire* monthly, and the shipowner is entitled to withdraw

---

[86]The law of charterparties is vast and its terminology peculiar. Reference to one of the standard texts on the subject is vital for a complete understanding. See, for example, J. Bes, *Chartering and Shipping Terms* (10th ed., 1977); Michael Wilford, Terrance Coghlin, and Nicholas Healy, *Time Charters* (2nd ed., 1982); Wharton Poor, *American Law of Charter Parties and Ocean Bills of Lading* (5th ed. supp. by R. Bauer, 1974); and Stewart C. Boyd, Andrew S. Burrows, and David Foxton, *Scrutton on Charterparties and Bills of Lading* (20th ed., 1996).

the ship from the charterer's use if a monthly installment is not paid promptly. Questions of demurrage and dead freight do not arise because the shipowner receives hire while the ship is loading and unloading and whether or not it is carrying a cargo.

The charterer has the right to direct the ship to proceed to wherever it is needed. Ordinarily, the only limitation on this right is the charterer's promise to engage only in lawful trades, to carry only lawful goods, and to direct the vessel only to safe ports. If the shipowner attempts to interfere with the charterer's use of the vessel, he will be in breach of the charterparty.

CHARTERPARTIES AND BILLS OF LADING

The contract of carriage between a charterer and a shipowner is the charterparty. The shipowner will commonly issue the charterer a bill of lading when goods are loaded on board; however, between the two of them, the bill will be only a receipt for goods and a document of title. Should the charterer transfer the bill, the position of the third-party endorsee will be different. The Hague or Hague-Visby Rules will apply, and the contract between the shipowner and the endorsee will be governed by the bill of lading. Of course, the bill of lading may incorporate the terms of the charterparty. In that case, the endorsee will be governed by its terms. To incorporate the terms of the charterparty, the bill of lading must do so clearly and unambiguously, and the terms of the charterparty must not conflict with any express terms of the bill of lading or (if they apply) the Hague or Hague-Visby Rules.

F. MARITIME LIENS

maritime lien: A charge or claim against a vessel or its cargo.

A lien is a charge or claim against property that exists to satisfy some debt or obligation. A **maritime lien** is a charge or claim against a vessel, its freight, or its cargo.[87] The main purpose of maritime liens is to ensure that a vessel can adequately obtain credit to properly outfit itself for a voyage.

In common law countries, a vessel is regarded as a juridical person separate and apart from its owner. Thus, a ship itself may be liable for the shipowner's breach of contract or for the crew's negligence, or even for damages caused without the shipowner's or crew's fault, as when port regulations require the ship to use a pilot and the pilot causes the injury. In sum, the owner is not essential to the existence of a lien against a ship. In civil law countries, on the other hand, a maritime lien (or *privilege*) is a right in property, but the property is not independent of the owner. The lien, in essence, exists against the owner as a debtor.

res: (Latin: "a thing.") The vessel or cargo to which a maritime lien attaches.

The distinctive characteristic of maritime liens, whether defined by the common or the civil law, is that they do not require possession. They attach to the *res* (i.e., the vessel, freight, or cargo) and travel with it. They are also secret.[88] If a vessel is sold, the lien "goes with the ship," even if the new owner is unaware of its existence. In common law countries, the foreclosure of a maritime lien follows a peculiar procedure. The *res* is seized (if it is a vessel, it is *arrested*) without prior notice to the owner. An admiralty court takes custody, and a suit proceeds against the thing. If the lien-holder's claim succeeds, the *res* is sold, the proceeds are distributed among the various lien-holders, and the title to the property is transferred to the purchaser of the *res* free of all claims. In civil law countries, by comparison, the *res* is not regarded as something distinct from its owner. A foreclosure suit is initiated against the owner,

---

[87]A *vessel* is practically any floating object capable of being propelled for the purpose of carrying goods, including any equipment or appurtenances on board. *Cargo* is the goods carried aboard a vessel. *Freight* is the sum of money paid for the carriage of cargo. Geoffrey H. Longnecker, "Development of the Law of Maritime Liens," *Tulane Law Review*, vol. 45, p. 574 (1971).

[88]In some civil law countries, however, shipbuilding liens (known as *maritime mortgages*) must be recorded with a government agency. Ivon d'Almeida Pires-Filho, "Priority of Maritime Liens in the Western Hemisphere: How Secure Is Your Claim?" *University of Miami Inter-American Law Review*, vol. 16, p. 507 (1985). The same is technically true in common law countries, because shipbuilding liens are not considered to be maritime transactions. See North Pacific S.S. Co. v. Hall Bros. Co., *United States Reports,* vol. 249, p. 119 (Supreme Ct., 1919).

and the *res* is then seized as a way to compel the owner to appear and furnish security before the *res* can be released.

When there are multiple lien-holders, the various claims must be ranked. A multilateral treaty, the 1926 International Convention for the Unification of Certain Rules Relating to Maritime Liens and Mortgages (known as the Brussels Convention), establishes a hierarchy among lien claims.[89] Although the convention has not been widely adopted, its ranking of liens is representative of most municipal schemes.[90] Under the convention, claims are ranked as follows:

1. Judicial costs and other expenses
2. Seaman's wages
3. Salvage and general average
4. Tort claims
5. Repairs, supplies, and necessaries
6. Ship mortgages

Case 11-6 illustrates how courts go about applying this ranking.

---

[89]*League of Nations Treaty Series*, vol. 120, p. 187. The 1926 convention was revised and updated in 1967. The text of the 1967 convention is posted at http://www.admiraltylawguide.com/conven/liens1967.html.
[90]For a comparison of the 1926 Brussels Convention with the maritime lien laws of North and South America, see Ivon d'Almeida Pires-Filho, "Priority of Maritime Liens in the Western Hemisphere: How Secure Is Your Claim?" *University of Miami Inter-American Law Review*, vol. 16, p. 507 (1985).

Case 11-6 THE CHINESE SEAMEN'S FOREIGN TECHNICAL SERVICES CO. v. SOTO GRANDE SHIPPING CORP., SA

People's Republic of China, Shanghai Maritime Court, 1987.
Journal of Maritime Law and Commerce, vol. 20, p. 217 (1989).[91]

THE FACTS

The plaintiff in this action was engaged in the provision of crewing services for vessels in maritime commerce. The defendant was the owner of the Panamanian M/V *Pomona*. The plaintiff and the defendant shipowner executed a crewing services contract on December 17, 1984, in Shanghai. The contract required the plaintiff to provide 25 seamen, including a master, officers, and crew, to serve for one year aboard the *Pomona*. The defendant was to pay monthly wages of $20,833 to the plaintiff. On January 14, 1985, the plaintiff dispatched the 25 seamen

to the vessel. By September 16, 1985, the plaintiff had received only two payments, totaling $21,455 for wages and $840.80 for ship's stores. The plaintiff claimed $225,283.05 in wage payments from the defendant shipowner.

THE SEIZURE AND SALE

On September 16, 1985, the plaintiff submitted to the Shanghai Maritime Court a petition for the seizure of the *Pomona*. The petition prayed for an order directing the shipowner to post security in the amount of U.S. $200,000, or alternatively, for an order directing the sale of the vessel. The court found that the petition was procedurally correct, that it alleged a claim for which seizure of foreign flag vessels is allowed under Chinese law, and that it set forth a reasonable basis for seizure.

---

[91]This decision was reported in the *Bulletin of the Supreme People's Court (Zhonghua Renmin Gongheguo Zuigao Renmin Fayuan Gongbao)*, vol. 13, published March 20, 1988. The actual decision of the Shanghai Maritime Court is not available for public reference. Case files in Chinese courts are generally available for review only by court personnel and the attorneys for the parties. This summary was prepared by Todd L. Platek, Esq., Kirlin, Campbell & Keating, New York.

On September 28, the court therefore ordered the vessel's seizure.

Due to the failure of the shipowner to furnish security, the court ordered the sale of the *Pomona* in accordance with Article 93, clause 3 of the Law of Civil Procedure (For Trial Implementation) of the People's Republic of China.

Clause 3 . . . provides that if the property under legal custody cannot be held and maintained for a long period, the People's Court may compel a sale and deposit the proceeds in the court's registry. The *Pomona* was sold at public auction on October 18, 1985, and sales proceeds of $430,000 were generated and deposited in the court's registry. Simultaneously, the court published an official announcement that all creditors of the vessel should apply to register their claims within 30 days.

THE SUIT

On October 3, 1985, the plaintiff commenced suit in the Shanghai Maritime Court and sought, in addition to the above-mentioned back wages of the seamen, the fuel expenses which it had covered for the vessel, the cost of the vessel arrest, its legal fees, liquidated damages for breach of contract, and interest. The total amount of plaintiff's claim was $259,636.03.

The shipowner failed to file answering papers within the time limit prescribed by law. Although twice formally summoned by the court, the shipowner consistently failed to submit any legitimate reasons for its refusal to enter a formal appearance in the action. Having given the defendant the requisite opportunity to be heard, the court conducted a trial of the action in the shipowner's absence.

THE RULINGS

The court ruled that the shipowner had breached the terms of the contract and should bear full responsibility for the consequences of its unfulfilled obligations. Following international custom and practice as well as Chinese law, the court ruled as follows:

1. The shipowner was required to compensate the plaintiff for crew wages in the amount of $190,149.24;

2. The shipowner was required to compensate the plaintiff for fuel expenses in the amount of $3,500.00;

3. The plaintiff's claims for other expenses were denied;

4. The shipowner was required to bear certain costs of litigation, including the filing fee ($1,176.87), the application fee for seizure of the vessel ($625), and miscellaneous litigation expenses ($139.90), totaling $1,941.77. Those expenses were to be deducted from the sales proceeds after the effective date of the ruling.

THE PRELIMINARY DISTRIBUTION OF THE SALES PROCEEDS

The order took effect after it was served upon the parties and the time for appeal had expired. In accordance with a recent Supreme People's Court directive entitled "Special Rules on the Payment of Claims Against Vessels Sold by Court Order," the court directed the convening of a meeting of creditors to engage in the liquidation of the debts arising out of this case. It publicly verified the sum of money available for distribution, the priority of claims, the nature and extent of each creditor's claim, and the methods of negotiating the creditors' claims. After marshalling the creditors' evidence and examining the value of the claims, the court certified four creditors' claims in addition to the plaintiff's judgment for crew wages. The additional claims certified by the court were the following:

1. A claim for seamen's wages in the sum of $171,840.26 put forward by the Chinese Seamen's Foreign Technical Services Company (CSFTSC) of the Shanghai Maritime Transport Bureau;

2. Claims totaling $23,292.18 for harbor usage, ship's stores and other items put forward by the Ningpo Branch of the China Ocean Shipping Agency (COSA);

3. A ship mortgage in the amount of $1,931,530.34 held by the National Westminster Bank, USA.

4. A claim asserted by the Repair Center of the Shanghai Shipbuilding Industry Corporation (SSIC) for repairs totaling $39,000.

The *Pomona* sales proceeds were applied first to litigation costs and certain . . . *custodia legis*[92] expenses. The costs and expenses paid in this manner consisted of the $1,941.77 in costs awarded to the plaintiff, $25,185.88 in claims and expenses arising from the sale of the vessel, and $3,500 for the diesel oil and lighterage expenses incurred by the plaintiff during the period of seizure. The remaining amount of U.S. $399,372.35 was augmented by $17,921.67 in interest earned while the sales proceeds were held in legal custody at the Bank of China. The fund available to creditors was thereby raised to U.S. $417,294.02.

The priority rules established by the aforementioned directive rank seamen's wages in the first priority class. The plaintiff's judgment for seamen's wages and the wage claim of the Shanghai CSFTSC, which together amounted to $361,989.50, were therefore paid first out of the remaining sales proceeds.

The second priority class established by the directive includes national taxes, harbor usage fees and other port expenses. The claim of the Ningpo COSA included

---

[92]Latin: "in the custody of the law." Refers to property held in the custody of a court.

items totalling $9,574.29, which fell within the second class. Those items were accordingly paid next.

There were no other claims in the first three priority classes established by the directive. The next highest claim was the mortgage held by the National Westminster Bank, which was listed between the fourth and fifth priority classes. The remaining claims of the Ningpo COSA, including claims for fuel and water supplied to the vessel, and the repair costs claimed by the Repair Center of SSIC, were deemed "other registered claims" within the meaning of the directive. They fell within the fifth priority class, below the mortgage. The balance of the sales proceeds, totalling $45,730.23 was therefore distributed to the mortgagee, and the remaining claims were left unpaid.

THE FINAL DISTRIBUTION OF SALES PROCEEDS

After another step in the deliberations, the Shanghai CS-FTSC "reconsidered" the effect of the plaintiff's lead in this case and agreed to transfer $12,400.26 to the plaintiff from its own portion of the preliminary distribution. The Shanghai CSFTSC and the National Westminster Bank then "reconsidered" the actual losses of the Repair Center of SSIC Corporation and the Ningpo Branch of COSA, and agreed to allow them, from their portions of the preliminary distribution, "suitable amounts" to remedy their losses. In this way, the five claimants arrived at the following final distribution of payments:

- The plaintiff received $202,549.50;
- The Shanghai CSFTSC received $150,000;
- The Ningpo Branch of COSA received $15,274.29;
- The National Westminster Bank USA received $44,970.23;

- The Repair Center for SSIC Corporation received $4,500.00. ■

CASEPOINT: In this case, a shipowner had contracted for a crew of 25 seamen for a one- year period, but nine months after the crew started work, only a small portion of the wages had been paid. Thus, the law in China (as elsewhere) allowed the seizure and sale of the ship to satisfy the wage and other claims. The owner was notified but did not answer the court petition, so judgment was entered for the plaintiff and the ship was sold at auction. The court then decided how to distribute the proceeds of the sale.

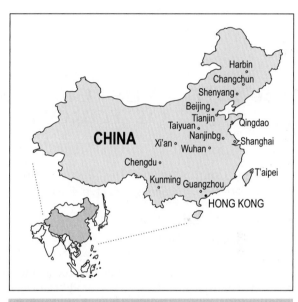

MAP 11-6   China (1987)

G. MARITIME INSURANCE

The trade terms the parties choose in their sales contract determine who is responsible for purchasing maritime insurance and who benefits from it. However, even when the risk of loss shifts from the seller to the buyer, the seller continues to have an interest in seeing that the goods are insured. If the goods are lost and the buyer is either bankrupt or unwilling to pay, insurance may be the only basis for recovery available to the seller.

Should a party who is required to purchase insurance be involved in an isolated sale, he can purchase a special cargo policy covering the single sale. It is more common, however, for cargo to be covered by an open cargo policy. Such a policy is an open-ended contract that insures all the cargo of an exporter during a particular time period. All of the exporter's shipments, whether by truck, rail, air, or vessel, are covered. Parties involved in an isolated sale often arrange to have their goods covered by the open cargo policy of a freight forwarder or customhouse broker.

PERILS

The perils covered by special and open cargo policies commonly include the following:

1. Loss or damage from the sea (e.g., weather, collision, stranding, sinking)
2. Fire
3. Jettison (i.e., the dumping of cargo in order to protect other property)
4. Forcible taking of the ship
5. Barratry (i.e., the fraudulent, criminal, or wrongful conduct of the captain or crew)
6. Explosion
7. Fumigation damage
8. Damage from loading, discharging, or transshipping cargo

The coverage of maritime insurance policies is examined in Case 11-7.

Case 11-7   WESTERN ASSURANCE CO. OF TORONTO v. SHAW

United States, Court of Appeals, Third Circuit, 1926.
Federal Reporter, Second Series, vol. 11, p. 495 (1926).

CIRCUIT JUDGE DAVIS:

This was an action to recover on a contract of maritime insurance against the Western Assurance Company for the total loss of the barge *Holly*, while moored at a wharf in Chester, Pennsylvania. She was insured "against the adventures and perils of the harbors, bays, sounds, seas, rivers," etc. She was loaded with three large boilers, weighing 60 tons each, which she was to take to Norfolk, Virginia. They were lying in the middle of the barge, lengthwise and end to end. On the night of December 18, 1919, she listed to the starboard and sank early the next morning. When she listed, the boilers rolled to starboard and caused or hastened her sinking.

The learned trial judge found that "the final plunge was due to the swell of a steamer breaking over the part of the deck, which served as a washboard and filling her," that this was a peril against which she was insured, and so decreed that the respondent pay for the loss sustained. The case is here on appeal.

The insurance company urged, as a defense in the District Court and here, that the libelant did not establish a loss by "perils of the seas" against which the company insured, and that the proximate cause of the loss was the unseaworthiness of the boat.

In order to recover, it is necessary for the libelant to bring his claim for loss within the provisions of the policy and establish that the loss was caused by one of the perils against which the barge was insured. . . .

It is difficult to give a definition which will neither be too narrow nor too broad, of the phrase, "perils of the sea." In defining it, courts have used various expressions which cannot be easily reconciled. The learned trial judge defined a "peril of the sea" as "any threatening danger from the sea," the "operative cause," "the efficient cause," "the *causa causans*."[93] In an enlarged sense all losses from maritime adventures arise from perils of the sea, but such losses do not come under this phrase within the meaning of maritime insurance policies. "Perils of the sea" against which underwriters insure are confined to extraordinary occurrences, such as stress of weather, winds and waves, lightning, tempests, rocks, etc. . . .

If a loss arises from the ordinary circumstances or wear and tear of a voyage, the insurer is not liable because a seaworthy vessel is supposed to endure usual and customary occurrences. The words are therefore used to describe abnormal causes and extraordinary circumstances. . . .

---

[93]Latin: "the immediate cause."

The testimony by which libelant sought to establish that a steamer in fact passed which might have produced a swell is very unsatisfactory. By leading questions, Nicholein A. Delegeorgen, captain of the barge, was led to say that waves from a passing steamer caused the barge to roll. But, on the contrary, he said again and again that he did not see any boat or anything on the river at that time.

Assuming, however, that the swell from a passing steamer did cause the barge to roll, the further question arises: Was it a "peril of the sea," within the meaning of the policy? Was it an extraordinary, abnormal occurrence against which the insured could not protect himself with ordinary precaution? Or was it a normal, customary circumstance that may occur at Chester every day? The passing of steamers along the Delaware between the port of Philadelphia and the sea is a normal occurrence that may be expected at any time. It was not extraordinary or unusual. It does not seem to us that waves from a passing steamer washing against the shores of the Delaware are a "peril of the sea" against which the barge was insured. The following statement from the opinion of the learned trial judge indicated that he was inclined to this view, or at least had misgivings about the contrary conclusion:

> It is difficult for any one to believe that a barge of a size and in condition to navigate the waters of the Delaware and Chesapeake Bays, in the lower reaches of which heavy weather and a nasty sea are often encountered, would be swamped by the swell from a passing steamer. If the latter fact was all which appeared, the mind would draw and would cling to the inference of unseaworthiness.

The respondent says that the barge was unseaworthy in respect to its loading and that this was the proximate cause of the loss. While the boilers rested on cradles or saddles, it is admitted that they had not been, as yet, shored or chocked at the sides, so as to keep them steady and from rolling. If they had been, the testimony tends to show, and we think does show, that they would have remained stationary when the barge rolled. If they had so remained, the barge would not have sunk.

The testimony conclusively establishes that to leave round boilers, such as the three loaded on the *Holly* were, unchocked and not shored over night is unsafe and improper stowage or loading. The boilers were loaded by the Sun Ship Building Company, and the captain of the barge asked the riggers, entrusted with the loading, to chock the boilers. They could not do so. The failure, therefore, to shore or chock the boilers, as safe and proper loading required, set in motion

a train of consequences—the opening of seams, consequent leaking, the fastening of wire rope or cables to the boilers and wharf—that caused the sinking and occasioned the loss. It seems to us that there is no escape from the conclusion that there was "want of ordinary care and skill in loading" and that this resulted in an unseaworthy condition of the barge with respect thereto. . . .

The policy excepted from the risks insured against all claims arising "from the want of ordinary care and skill in loading and stowing the cargo." The proofs not only show that the claim does not come within the risks against which the barge was insured, but they clearly show that it arises from the want of ordinary care and skill in loading, and comes within the above exception.

Therefore the decree is reversed, with directions to the District Court to dismiss the libel, with costs. ■

CASEPOINT: In this case, a barge loaded with three heavy boilers had sunk during the night while tied to a wharf. The key question was whether the sinking was due to a peril of the sea, for which the cargo was insured, or to lack of ordinary care and skill in loading and stowing the cargo, which was not covered by the maritime insurance policy. After reviewing the facts, the court determined that the boilers had not been properly stowed to keep them from rolling, and when some waves from a passing steamer caused the ship to roll, the boilers shifted, thus resulting in the ship's sinking. Such an occurrence was not within the definition of a peril of the sea but rather was due to lack of ordinary care in loading and stowing the cargo.

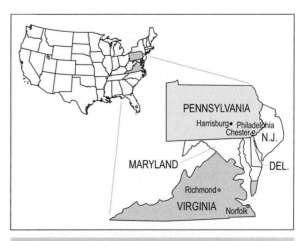

MAP 11-7 Pennsylvania and Virginia (1926)

AVERAGE CLAUSES

The loss of cargo can be either total or partial. Total loss is ordinarily governed by a *constructive loss* clause in a maritime insurance policy. This usually includes (1) losses exceeding one-half the value of the cargo or (2) losses where the cost of recovery exceeds the cargo's value.[94]

particular average: A loss to a ship or its cargo that is not to be shared in by contributions from all those interested, but is to be borne by the owner of the injured thing.

A partial loss is known in the marine insurance industry as a **particular average**. A *free from particular average* (FPA) policy provides the most limited recovery for partial losses. Such a policy ordinarily covers only losses from fire, stranding, sinking, or collision of the vessel. A *with average* (WA) policy provides more protection; however, it ordinarily contains a *franchise* clause that provides for payment only if the loss exceeds a specified minimum amount (the franchise amount). WA policies can also be purchased without a franchise clause.[95]

general average: A contribution by those jointly involved in a maritime venture to make good the loss by one of them for his voluntary sacrifice of a part of the ship or cargo to save the residue of the property and the lives on board, or for the extraordinary expenses necessarily incurred for the benefit and safety of all.

General average comes about in the carriage of goods at sea when, in order to avoid some threat to the whole venture, some expense has to be incurred, or some loss or damage is deliberately inflicted, in order to save the ship and its cargo. For example, a ship may run aground. In order to get it afloat, some of the cargo or some of the ship's supplies may have to be jettisoned, or salvage tugs may have to be hired. When this happens, everyone having an interest in the ship and its various cargoes will have benefited. Each must then contribute, in proportion to the value of his interest, to restoring the party who suffered the loss or damage or who incurred the expense. This is called a *general average* contribution.

Normally, marine insurance will cover each shipper's contribution. However, if insurance is not purchased or if a policy does not cover general average, then the shipper must pay the contribution before the ship's crew will release the goods. Similarly, if a buyer has already paid for the goods and received a bill of lading, then the buyer (because the bill of lading will transfer the risk of loss to the buyer at that point) must come up with the contribution before the ship's crew will turn over the goods. In either case, the ship will have a lien claim against the goods, and if the contribution is not paid, it may foreclose on the goods, sell them, and retain that portion of the sale price it receives to cover the cost of the contribution.

A person seeking to claim a general average contribution from other parties must show (1) that the loss was incurred to benefit everyone and (2) that the person making the claim was not responsible for causing the danger. For example, a shipping company cannot claim general average when it has hired tugs to refloat a ship that ran aground because of the captain's faulty navigation.

H. CARRIAGE OF GOODS BY AIR

The carriage of goods on aircraft is regulated by the 1929 Warsaw Convention (formally known as the Convention for the Unification of Certain Rules Relating to International Carriage by Air).[96] Four amendments to the convention have been adopted and are now in

---

[94]Leslie J. Buglass, *Marine Insurance Claims; American Law and Practice*, p. 16 (2nd ed., 1972).

[95]W. Grunde, *Servicing World Markets: Administrative Procedures,* p. 61 (1979).

[96]The text of the Warsaw Convention is in *United Nations Treaty Series*, vol. 261, p. 421, and vol. 266, p. 444. A copy is posted at http://www.iasl.mcgill.ca/private.htm and at http://www.jus.uio.no/lm/air.carriage.warsaw.convention.1929/doc.html.

The 150 states parties to the Warsaw Convention as of June 2007 were Afghanistan, Algeria, Angola, Argentina, Armenia, Australia, Austria, Azerbaijan, the Bahamas, Bahrain, Bangladesh, Barbados, Belarus, Belgium, Benin, Bolivia, Bosnia and Herzegovina, Botswana, Brazil, Brunei Darussalam, Bulgaria, Burkina Faso, Cambodia, Cameroon, Canada, Cape Verde, Chile, China, Colombia, Comoros, Congo, Costa Rica, Croatia, Cuba, Cyprus, the Czech Republic, Democratic Republic of the Congo, Denmark, the Dominican Republic, Ecuador, Egypt, Equatorial Guinea, Estonia, Ethiopia, Fiji, Finland, France, Gabon, Germany, Ghana, Greece, Guatemala, Guinea, Honduras, Hungary, Iceland, India, Indonesia, Iran, Iraq, Ireland, Israel, Italy, Ivory Coast, Japan, Jordan, Kenya, Kuwait, Kyrgyzstan, Laos, Latvia, Lebanon, Lesotho, Liberia, Libya, Liechtenstein, Luxembourg, Macedonia, Madagascar, Malawi, Malaysia, Maldives, Mali, Malta, Mauritania, Mauritius, Mexico, Moldova, Mongolia, Morocco, Myanmar, Nauru, Nepal, the Netherlands, New Zealand, Niger, Nigeria, North Korea, Norway, Oman, Pakistan, Panama, Papua New Guinea, Paraguay, Peru, the Philippines, Poland, Portugal, Qatar, Romania, Russia, Rwanda, Saint Vincent and the Grenadines, Samoa, Saudi Arabia, Senegal, the Seychelles, Sierra Leone, Singapore, Slovakia, Slovenia, the Solomon Islands, South Africa, Spain, Sri Lanka, Sudan, Sweden, Switzerland, Syria, Togo, Tonga, Trinidad and Tobago, Tunisia, Turkey, Turkmenistan, Uganda, Ukraine, the United Arab Emirates, the United Kingdom, the United Republic of Tanzania, the United States, Uruguay, Uzbekistan, Vanuatu, Venezuela, Vietnam, Yemen, Yugoslavia , Zambia, and Zimbabwe. International Civil Aviation Organization Treaty Collection at http://www.icao.int/cgi/goto_leb.pl?icao/en/leb/treaty.htm.

force:[97] the Hague Protocol of 1955,[98] Montreal Protocol No. 1,[99] Montreal Protocol No. 2,[100] and Montreal Protocol No. 4 of 1975.[101] As with inland carriage, the documents used in air carriage—the air waybills and consignment notes—are not documents of title.[102] This reflects the practical difference between air flight and ship transport. The bills and notes used in air transportation arrive with the goods rather than being sent separately.

air waybill: An instrument issued by an air carrier to a shipper that serves as a receipt for goods and as evidence of the contract of carriage but is not a document of title for the goods

At the heart of the Warsaw Convention is a definition of the **air waybill**. In states that are parties to the convention—but not to Montreal Protocol No. 4—the bill must describe (1) the nature of the goods being shipped; (2) the method of packing and any marks or numbers; (3) the weight, quantity, volume, or dimensions of the goods; (4) the apparent condition of the goods and their packaging; and (5) a statement that the carriage is subject to the convention's rules.[103] Montreal Protocol No. 4, which encourages carriers to use electronic records, requires only three things to appear on the paper waybill that accompanies a consignment of goods: (1) the places of departure and destination, (2) an intermediate stopping

---

[97]Montreal Protocol No. 3 of 1975 was also adopted but it is not yet in force. The text of Protocol No. 3 is posted at http://www.mcgill.ca/files/iasl/montreal1975c.pdf.

[98]The text of the Hague Protocol is in *United Nations Treaty Series*, vol. 1963, p. 373, and is posted at *id.* The Hague Protocol increased the liability limits for injuries to passengers and their baggage to 250,000 francs from the 20,000 francs set in the 1929 convention. Warsaw Convention (as amended by the Hague Protocol), Article 22. States parties to the Hague Protocol as of June 2007 were Afghanistan, Algeria, Angola, Argentina, Australia, Austria, Azerbaijan, the Bahamas, Bahrain, Bangladesh, Belarus, Belgium, Benin, Bosnia and Herzegovina, Brazil, Bulgaria, Cambodia, Cameroon, Canada, Cape Verde, Chile, China, Colombia, Congo, Costa Rica, Côte d'Ivoire, Croatia, Cuba, Cyprus, the Czech Republic, Denmark, the Dominican Republic, Ecuador, Egypt, El Salvador, Estonia, Fiji(18), Finland, France, Gabon, Germany, Ghana, Greece, Grenada, Guatemala, Guinea, Hungary, Iceland, India, Iran , Iraq, Ireland, Israel, Italy, Japan, Jordan, Kenya, Kuwait, Kyrgyzstan, Laos , Latvia, Lebanon, Lesotho, Libya, Liechtenstein, Lithuania, Luxembourg, Macedonia, Madagascar, Malawi, Malaysia, the Maldives, Mali, Mauritius, Mexico, Monaco, Morocco, Nauru, Nepal, the Netherlands, New Zealand, Niger, Nigeria, North Korea, Norway, Oman, Pakistan, Panama, Papua New Guinea, Paraguay, Peru, the Philippines, Poland, Portugal, Qatar, the Republic of Korea, the Republic of Moldova, Romania, the Russian Federation, Rwanda, Saint Vincent and the Grenadines, Samoa, Saudi Arabia, Senegal, the Seychelles, Singapore, Slovakia, Slovenia, the Solomon Islands, South Africa, Spain, Sri Lanka, Sudan, Swaziland, Sweden, Switzerland, Syria, Togo, Tonga, Trinidad and Tobago, Tunisia, Turkey, Ukraine, the United Arab Emirates, the United Kingdom, Uzbekistan, Vanuatu, Venezuela, Vietnam, Yemen, Yugoslavia, Zambia, and Zimbabwe. See the International Civil Aviation Organization Treaty Collection at http://www.icao.int/cgi/goto_leb.pl?icao/en/leb/treaty.htm.

[99]The text of Protocol No. 1 posted is at http://www.mcgill.ca/files/iasl/montreal1975a.pdf.
Protocol No. 1 limits a carrier's damages to 8,300 Special Drawing Rights (SDRs) for liability to passengers, to 17 SDRs per kilogram for loss of baggage and cargo, and to 332 SDRs for carry-on items.
States parties to Protocol No. 1 as of June 2007 were Argentina, Azerbaijan, Bahrain, Bosnia and Herzegovina, Brazil, Canada, Chile, Colombia, Croatia, Cuba, Cyprus, Denmark, Egypt, Estonia, Ethiopia, Finland, France, Ghana, Greece, Guatemala, Guinea, Honduras, Ireland, Israel, Italy, Jordan, Kenya, Kuwait, Lebanon, Macedonia, Mexico, the Netherlands, New Zealand, Niger, Norway, Peru, Portugal, Slovenia, Spain, Sweden, Switzerland, Togo, Tunisia, the United Kingdom, Uzbekistan, Venezuela, and Yugoslavia. See the International Civil Aviation Organization Treaty Collection at http://www.icao.int/cgi/goto_leb.pl?icao/en/leb/treaty.htm.

[100]The text of Protocol No. 2 is posted at http://www.iasl.mcgill.ca/private.htm.
Protocol No. 2 limits a carrier's damages to 16,600 SDRs for liability to passengers, to 17 SDRs per kilogram for loss of baggage and cargo, and to 332 SDRs for carry-on items.
States parties to Protocol No. 2 as of June 2007 were Argentina, Azerbaijan, Bahrain, Bosnia and Herzegovina, Brazil, Canada, Chile, Colombia, Croatia, Cuba, Cyprus, Denmark, Egypt, Estonia, Ethiopia, Finland, France, Ghana, Greece, Guatemala, Guinea, Honduras, Ireland, Israel, Italy, Jordan, Kenya, Kuwait, Lebanon, Macedonia, Mexico, the Netherlands, New Zealand, Niger, Norway, Oman, Peru, Portugal, Slovenia, Spain, Sweden, Switzerland, Togo, Tunisia, the United Kingdom, Uzbekistan, Venezuela, and Yugoslavia. See the International Civil Aviation Organization Treaty Collection at http://www.icao.int/cgi/goto_leb.pl?icao/en/leb/treaty.htm.

[101]The text of Protocol No. 4 is posted at http://www.mcgill.ca/files/iasl/montreal1975b.pdf.
States parties to Protocol No. 4 as of June 2007 were Argentina, Australia, Azerbaijan, Bahrain, Bosnia and Herzegovina, Brazil, Canada, Colombia, Croatia, Cyprus, Denmark, Ecuador, Egypt, Estonia, Ethiopia, Finland, Ghana, Greece, Guatemala, Guinea, Honduras, Hungary, Ireland, Israel, Italy, Japan, Jordan, Kenya, Kuwait, Lebanon, Macedonia, Mauritius, Nauru, the Netherlands, New Zealand, Niger, Norway, Oman, Portugal, Singapore, Slovenia, Spain, Sweden, Switzerland, Togo, Turkey, the United Arab Emirates, the United Kingdom, the United States, Uzbekistan, and Yugoslavia. See the International Civil Aviation Organization Treaty Collection at http://www.icao.int/cgi/goto_leb.pl?icao/en/leb/ treaty.htm.
Note: the states parties to the Montreal Protocol are automatically states parties to the Warsaw Convention as amended by the Hague Protocol. Montreal Protocol No. 4, Article XVII(2).

[102]Article 15(3) of the convention as amended by the Hague Protocol, however, provides that "Nothing in this Convention prohibits the issue of a negotiable waybill."

[103]Warsaw Convention of 1929, Article 8.

place in a different state (if the places of departure and destination are in the same state), and (3) the weight of the consignment.[104]

The incentive the convention offers carriers for including these required elements on a waybill is a limitation on liability. This is set at 17 Special Drawing Rights (SDRs) per kilogram.[105] This means that any provision in the waybill establishing a lower amount is void. Of course, a shipper may declare a higher value and pay the cost for insuring the excess.

The benefit to the shipper in using a Warsaw Convention air waybill is that the shipper does not have to prove that the carrier caused the injury to any lost, damaged, or delayed goods. The shipper has to make a claim within seven days when the bills are governed by the Warsaw Convention and 14 days if they are covered by the Amended Convention, but the burden is then on the carrier to prove that it did not take "all necessary measures" to avoid the loss, damage, or delay.[106]

In addition to regulating the carriage of goods, the two Warsaw Conventions regulate the carriage of passengers. Again, the liability of the carrier is limited so long as the airline ticket contains a notice of the applicability of one of the conventions.

---

[104]Warsaw Convention as amended by Montreal Protocol No. 4, Article 8.

[105]The Warsaw Convention of 1929 specifies a liability limit of 250 gold or *Poincaré* francs per kilogram (or approximately 200 SDRs per kilogram at current exchange rates).

[106]Lord Justice Greer in Grein v. Imperial Airways, Ltd., *Law Reports, King's Bench*, vol. 1937, pt. 1, p. 50 at p. 57 (1937), observed: "The effect of [the phrase 'all necessary measures'] is to put upon [the air carriers] the obligation of disproving negligence, leaving them liable for damages for negligence if they fail to disprove it." Under the Warsaw Convention of 1929, and as amended in 1955 by the Hague Protocol, a carrier may avoid all liability if it can show that the consignor was partly at fault. Montreal Protocol No. 4 changes this, establishing a system of comparative fault. If a percentage of loss or damage is attributable to both the consignor and the carrier, the air carrier will then be liable for its percentage share. Warsaw Convention as amended by Montreal Protocol No. 4, Article 21.

Chapter Questions

Shipping Terms—FOB, FAS and DES

1. Seller agreed to ship 10,000 tons of potatoes FOB Tacoma, Washington, to Buyer in Japan. Buyer designated the SS *Russet* to take delivery at pier 7 in Tacoma. On the agreed-upon date for delivery, Seller delivered the potatoes to pier 7, but the ship was not at the pier. Because another ship using the pier was slow in loading, the *Russet* had to anchor at a mooring buoy in the harbor and Seller had to arrange for a lighter to transport the potatoes in containers to the ship. The lighter tied up alongside the *Russet,* and a cable from the ship's boom was attached to the first container. As the container began to cross the ship's rail, the cable snapped. The container then fell on the rail, teetered back and forth for a while, and finally crashed down the side of the ship, causing the lighter to capsize. All of the potatoes were dumped into the sea. Buyer now sues Seller for failure to make delivery. Is Seller liable?

2. Suppose, in Question 1, the contract had been FAS Tacoma. Would Seller be liable?

3. Seller agreed to deliver 1,000 air conditioners to Buyer DES Port Moresby. The air conditioners were transported by ship to Port Moresby, where they were off-loaded to the customs shed for inspection. The ship then sent a cable to Buyer stating that the air conditioners were in the customs shed and that the ship was proceeding on its way. Before Buyer could arrive to pay the customs duties and collect the air conditioners, the customs shed burned down, destroying all the air conditioners. Buyer sues Seller for failing to make delivery. Is Seller liable?

Shipping Terms—DEQ and CIF

4. Suppose, in Question 3, the contract had been DEQ Port Moresby. Would Seller be liable?

5. Seller in Sydney, Australia, agreed to ship goods on or before December 31 under a CIF Sydney contract to Buyer in Honolulu. The seller was unable to assemble the goods for delivery in time to reach the ship in Sydney and had to transship the goods by rail to Melbourne, where the ship was taking on goods on January 3. Seller did load the goods aboard railway cars in Sydney on December 29 and received a bill of lading from the railway company on that date. Seller later obtained a bill of lading from the ship, and together with an invoice and a marine insurance policy,

tendered both bills of lading to Buyer. Buyer refused to accept the documents or to pay Seller. Seller sues to enforce the contract. Will Seller win?

6. Seller in San Francisco agreed to ship goods to Buyer in London under a CIF San Francisco contract. After the goods were loaded aboard the ship, but before it departed from San Francisco, Seller tendered the documents required by the contract to Buyer and asked to be paid. Buyer refused, asserting that it had a right to inspect the goods upon their arrival in London, and that it did not have to pay until it did so and was satisfied that the goods were in compliance with the contract. Seller sues for immediate payment. Will Seller win?

Effect of the Bill of Lading

7. Seller in Bombay sells 5,000 bales of cotton to Buyer, C & F (*Incoterms 1990*) Liverpool. Seller transports the cotton to the Bombay harbor and to the ship designated by Buyer, the SS *Allthumbs*. Due to an error in counting, only 4,987 bales were loaded. The ship's bill of lading, however, shows a quantity of 5,000 bales. Seller then signs over the bill of lading to Buyer in exchange for payment in full for the cotton. When the *Allthumbs* arrives in Liverpool, the quantity error is discovered, and Buyer sues the ship for the lost value of the missing bales. Is the ship liable? Would it matter if Seller admitted that the error was not the ship's fault, but that of Seller?

The Hague and Hague-Visby Rules

8. The SS *Anxious* was transporting goods to several ports on the east coast of Africa, including Beira in Mozambique. While still several hundred miles at sea, the *Anxious* learned that rebel forces opposing the Mozambique government were attacking Beira. The ship, nonetheless, pulled into Beira and tied up at a pier. Immediately thereafter, it was struck by a mortar round. The goods in the ship's main cargo hold were destroyed. Is the ship liable for the loss?

Maritime Liens

9. Mr. Ess, the owner of the SS *Skimpy* and an American citizen, borrows money from MultiBank in London to outfit his ship, giving the bank a maritime lien. Mr. Ess sells the *Skimpy* to Mr. Tee, a Canadian. Mr. Tee is unaware of the lien and unaware that Mr. Ess has defaulted on the loan. When the ship pulls into a British port, the bank arranges for it to be arrested and sold to pay off the balance due on the loan. Can the bank do this?

CHAPTER 12
FINANCING

INTRODUCTION

International financing encompasses the financing of foreign trade and the underwriting of investments in foreign countries. Foreign trade financing is primarily concerned with how goods and services are paid for across international borders. Long-standing mechanisms for expediting international trade include bills of lading, bills of exchange, and letters of credit. The rights and responsibilities of buyers and sellers in using these documents to expedite international trade are explored in depth in this chapter. The final section of the chapter discusses how a company can finance the establishment or expansion of its overseas operations.

A. FINANCING FOREIGN TRADE

International traders must know the kinds of documents, trade terms, and financing arrangements used in international sales.

The documents used in international sales are also used in domestic sales, but their domestic use is much less common. Most domestic sales are financed through open-account credit arrangements. That is, the buyer does not sign a formal debt instrument. Formalities are not needed because the seller enters into sales only after investigating the buyer's creditworthiness. In international sales, by comparison, buyers and sellers are separated both by distance and by the differing financial practices of their home countries. This means that it is difficult for the seller to determine the credit standing of a foreign buyer and equally difficult for the buyer to establish reliably the foreign seller's integrity and reputation. To compensate for this, foreign traders use formal documents that assure the parties that their sale will go forward as agreed. The most important of these documents are (1) the bill of lading, which is the transportation document and document of title described in Chapter 11; (2) bills of exchange and promissory notes, which are, respectively, orders to pay money and promises to pay money; and (3) the letter of credit, which is a third party's guarantee of a buyer's creditworthiness.

B. BILLS OF LADING

bill of lading: An instrument issued by a warehouseman or carrier to a shipper that serves as a receipt for goods shipped, as evidence of the contract of carriage, and as a document of title for the goods.

The essential document for all international sales is the **bill of lading**. As described in Chapter 11, the bill of lading is a document of title. That is, it represents the goods.

In international trade, goods shipped from one country to another might be in the possession of a carrier or warehouseman for several weeks: from the time they are shipped to the time they are delivered. The bill of lading is important, therefore, because it lets the buyer and the seller (or their banks) exchange control over the goods while the goods are in the possession of the warehouseman or carrier. As one British judge once described it, the bill of lading is the "key" that permits its holder "to unlock the door of the warehouse, fixed or floating, in which the goods may chance to be."[1]

This ability to transfer title by the transfer of a bill of lading is central to the use of bills of exchange and letters of credit, the two basic financing and payment instruments used in international trade.

C. BILLS OF EXCHANGE

bill of exchange: A written, dated, and signed three-party instrument containing an unconditional order by a drawer that directs a drawee to pay a definite sum of money to a payee on demand or at a specified future date.

A **bill of exchange** (or *draft*, as it is sometimes called) is a written, dated, and signed instrument that contains an unconditional order from the drawer that directs the drawee to pay a definite sum of money to a payee on demand or at a specified future date. It is a useful instrument because it allows one party (the drawer) to direct another (the drawee) to pay money either to himself, to his agent, or to a third party. Of course, the order is valid only if the drawee has an underlying obligation to pay money to the drawer. This can arise in situations where the drawee is holding money on account for the drawer (i.e., the drawee is a bank), where the drawer lent money to a drawee (i.e., the drawee is a borrower), or where the drawer has sold goods to the drawee and the drawee owes the sale price to the drawer (i.e., the drawee is a buyer).

---

[1]Saunders v. Maclean, *Law Reports, Queen's Bench Division*, vol. 11, p. 341 (1883).

In the first of these situations (where the drawee is a bank), the bill involved is known as a *check*. In the second situation (where the drawee is a borrower), the bill is called a *note*. The bills referred to in the third situation (where the drawee is a buyer) are called *trade acceptances*.

Bills of exchange are important devices for facilitating international trade because they are negotiable instruments. A person properly holding a negotiable instrument takes it free of most claims or defenses that the drawer might have that the underlying contract was improperly performed or that the instrument was improperly made. This freedom from the so-called *equities* or *personal defenses* of the drawer makes bills of exchange more readily salable, and therefore useful financial tools for raising money.

THE LAW GOVERNING BILLS OF EXCHANGE

Until the middle of the seventeenth century, bills of exchange were governed by a single international law, the *lex mercatoria*.[2] This law defined the bill of exchange as an instrument that allowed a *permutatio pecuniae presentis cum absenti* (an exchange of money by one who is present with one who is absent). Because the bill applied specifically to an exchange between *loci distantia* (distant places), it was exempt from the medieval Christian Church's prohibition against interest on loans. Because of this exemption, it rapidly became the key instrument of medieval banking.

In the seventeenth century, however, the rise of national laws brought about differences in the rules governing bills of exchange. The French bill of exchange came to be governed by the *Savary Code* of 1673, the *Perfect Tradesman*, and the works of Jousse. In Germany, the applicable law was the *Wechselrecht*. In England, the courts created a case law that reflected the practice in English banks.

Bills of Exchange Act (BEA): English act of 1882 regulating bills of exchange.

At the end of the nineteenth century, the *lex mercatoria* was codified in England in the **Bills of Exchange Act (BEA)** of 1882. Today, the BEA continues in force in the United Kingdom and in virtually all of Britain's former colonies.

Uniform Commercial Code (UCC): Model U.S. act. Article 3 regulates negotiable instruments.

In 1896, in the United States, the National Conference on Commissioners of Uniform Laws drafted a Uniform Negotiable Instruments Law (UNIL), which was largely based on the BEA. By 1920, all of the American states had adopted the UNIL. Then, in the 1940s, the UNIL was modernized and integrated into the more comprehensive **Uniform Commercial Code (UCC)**, which by 1950 had been adopted in all states except Louisiana.[3]

Geneva Conventions on the Unification of the Law Relating to Bills of Exchange (ULB): League of Nations–sponsored conventions signed at Geneva in 1930 that regulate negotiable instruments.

On the European continent, there were calls throughout the latter half of the nineteenth century for the creation of an international negotiable instruments law. Finally, in 1907, a conference convened at The Hague to draw up a convention. A draft was agreed to in 1912, but World War I interrupted ratification. The League of Nations then organized a series of conferences to update the 1912 draft. In 1930, three **Geneva Conventions on the Unification of the Law Relating to Bills of Exchange (ULB)** were signed.[4] The following year, two additional Geneva Conventions on Unification of the Law Relating to Checks (ULC) were also signed.[5] Within fifteen years, the ULB and ULC had been ratified by most continental European countries, and today they are the standard laws governing bills of exchange and

---

[2]Latin: "law merchant." Common commercial rules and procedures used throughout Europe during the Renaissance.

[3]The text of the UCC is posted on the Legal Information Institute's Web site at http://www.law.cornell.edu/ucc/ucc.table.html.

[4]The three are the Convention Providing a Uniform Law for Bills of Exchange and Promissory Notes, the Convention for the Settlement of Certain Conflicts with Bills of Exchange and Promissory Notes, and the Convention on the Stamp Laws in Connection with Bills of Exchange and Promissory Notes.

[5]They are the Convention Providing a Uniform Law for Checks and the Convention for the Settlement of Certain Conflicts of Laws in Connection with Checks.

checks in virtually every nation,[6] with the exception of the Anglo-American common law countries.[7]

Although there are currently no uniform worldwide rules governing bills of exchange and promissory notes, there is a widely followed set of international rules governing the collection of checks[8]: the International Chamber of Commerce's (ICC) Uniform Rules for Collections.[9] Most domestic laws allow banks to incorporate the ICC's Rules into their collection instructions, and this is the common practice for international collections worldwide.[10]

TYPES OF BILLS OF EXCHANGE

A bill of exchange is an unconditional written order. The party creating the bill (the drawer) orders another party (the drawee) to pay money, usually to a third party (a payee).

The form that a bill of exchange must take depends on the governing law. The common law requires only that a bill (or draft) be in writing and be payable either to order or to bearer.[11] The ULB adds to this the requirements that a bill (1) contain the term *bill of exchange* in the body and language of the check,[12] (2) state the place where the bill is drawn, (3) state the place where payment is to be made, and (4) be dated. These requirements are summarized in Exhibit 12-1.

Common Law	ULB
1. In writing	1. In writing
2. Payable to order or to bearer	2. Payable to order or to bearer
	3. Contain the term Bill of Exchange or Promissory Note
	4. State the place where drawn
	5. State the place where payable
	6. Be dated

EXHIBIT 12-1   Form Requirements for Bills of Exchange and Promissory Notes

---

[6]For a brief history of negotiable instrument law in Europe, as well as the text of the ULB, see Frederick Wallace, *Introduction to European Commercial Law*, pp. 92–123 (1953).

[7]The differences between the Anglo-American rules and the Geneva conventions (which are fairly substantial) led to calls in the 1950s for the drafting of a new international convention with true international appeal. The call was taken up belatedly by the UN Commission on International Trade Law (UNCITRAL), which produced a final text in May 1988. In December 1988, the UN General Assembly approved a resolution adopting the text and opened the convention—called the Convention on International Bills of Exchange and International Promissory Notes (CIBN)—for ratification. Although only 10 states must ratify the convention before it will come into effect, as of 2005 only Gabon, Guinea, Honduras, and Mexico had ratified the CIBN. Canada, Russia, and the United States have signed but not ratified the convention. It seems unlikely that it will come into effect anytime soon. See Multilateral Treaties Deposited with the Secretary-General: Status listed as of November 2005, accessed June 26, 2007, posted on the Internet at http://www.jus.uio.no/lm/un.bills.of.exchange.and.promissory.notes.convention. 1988/doc.html.

For a brief history and description of the CIBN, as well as the text, see "United Nations Convention on International Bills of Exchange and International Promissory Notes," *International Legal Materials*, vol. 28, pp. 170–211 (1989), with John Spagnole's "Introductory Note."

[8]Both the common law countries and the countries that follow the continental European practice have distinct rules governing bank deposits and the collection of checks. See, e.g., Article 4 of the UCC, entitled "Bank Deposits and Collections," along with the ULC.

[9]ICC Publication No. 522 (1996). The Uniform Rules for Collection was first published in 1956. The 1996 edition was the second revision. See the ICC Web site at http://www.iccbooks.com/ Product/ProductInfo.aspx?id=484 for information on this and other ICC publications.

[10]For example, UCC, § 4-102(3), states that the provisions in Article 4 (Bank Deposits and Collections) of the UCC may be varied by agreement, except that "no agreement can disclaim a bank's responsibility for its own lack of good faith or failure to exercise ordinary care."

[11]UCC, § 3-104(2), provides: "A writing . . . is (a) a 'draft' ('bill of exchange') if it is an order; (b) a 'check' if it is drawn on a bank and payable on demand; (c) a 'certificate of deposit' if it is an acknowledgement by a bank of receipt of money with an engagement to repay it; (d) a 'note' if it is a promise other than a certificate of deposit."

[12]In the case of a promissory note, the term would be *promissory note* and, according to the ULC, a check requires the term *check*.

November 22, 2008 $ 10,000.00
New York, NY

      Ninety days after above date   PAY TO THE ORDER OF
              Bank of the River
              100 Hudson Ave.
              New York, NY 02167
      ------ Ten Thousand and 00/00 -------   Dollars
        for value received and charge the same to the account of

To: _____

_____   _____

_____   _____
Drawer/Buyer   Drawee/Seller

EXHIBIT 12-2   Time Bill

Time and Sight Bills

time bill: Bill of exchange that is payable at a definite future time.

Bills may be either time bills or sight bills. A **time bill** is payable at a definite future time. A **sight bill** (or demand bill) is payable when the holder presents it for payment or at a stated time after presentment. Exhibit 12-2 shows an example of a time bill.

sight bill: Bill of exchange that is payable at the time it is presented or at a stated time after presentment.

Trade Acceptances

trade acceptance: Bill of exchange on which the drawer and the payee are the same person.

A **trade acceptance** is the bill of exchange most commonly used in the sale of goods. On this bill, the seller of the goods is both the drawer and the payee. The bill orders the buyer—the drawee—to pay a specified sum of money.

The use of a trade acceptance is best illustrated with an example. SunnySales, Inc., in California has traditionally sold raisins to GuttenTag, GmbH, in Germany on terms that require GuttenTag to make payment in 90 days. This year, however, SunnySales needs cash. To get cash, it draws a trade acceptance that orders GuttenTag to pay $100,000 to the order of SunnySales ninety days later. SunnySales then presents the bill to GuttenTag. GuttenTag accepts by signing the bill on its face and returning the bill to SunnySales. GuttenTag's acceptance creates an enforceable promise to pay the bill when it comes due in 90 days.

The advantage to SunnySales of having a trade acceptance is that it can sell the bill of exchange in the money market more easily than it can assign a $100,000 account receivable. A trade acceptance is shown in Exhibit 12-3.

Checks

check: Bill of exchange on which the drawee is a bank.

When the drawee of a bill of exchange is a bank, the bill is known as a **check**. Unlike other bills of exchange, checks are always payable on demand.[13] See Exhibit 12-4.

D. PROMISSORY NOTES

promissory note: A written, dated, and signed two-party instrument containing an unconditional promise by a maker to pay a definite sum of money to a payee on demand or at a specified future date.

A written promise to pay a determinate sum of money made between two parties is a **promissory note**, or simply a *note*. The party who promises to pay is called the *maker*; the

---

[13]ULC, Article 28; UCC, § 3-104(2)(b).

101 Embarcadero   **December 31, 2007**
San Francisco, California

To: __GuttenTag GmBH_____
On ____**Mar. 31, 2008**_____ PAY TO THE ORDER OF _____**SunnySales, Inc.**_____
_____**One Hundred Thousand and 00/100**_____ DOLLARS **100,000.00**
The obligations of the drawee/acceptor of this bill arise out of the purchase of goods from the drawer. The drawee/acceptor may accept this bill payable at any bank or trust company in the United States which the drawee/acceptor may designate.

Accepted at _____**Essen,Germany**_____ on _____**December 31,2007**
Payable at _____**Bank of the River**_____ _____**SunnySales, Inc.**_____
_____**100 Hudson Ave**_____
_____**New York, NY 02167**_____
Buyer's Signature ____**GuttenTag, GmBH**_____
By Agent or Officer _____ by _____

EXHIBIT 12-3 Trade Acceptance

party who is to be paid is the *payee*. Exhibit 12-5 defines the different parties to bills of exchange and promissory notes.

The only difference between a promissory note and a bill of exchange is that the maker of a note promises to personally pay the payee rather than ordering a third party to do so. Exhibit 12-6 shows examples of typical promissory notes.

                                                    Nov. 22, 2008   11-95/980

PAY TO THE ORDER OF _____**Sandra Smith**_____ $ __**100.00**__
_____**One Hundred and 00/100**_____ DOLLARS

BANK OF THE RIVER
100 Hudson Ave.
New York, NY 02167
123456789-09876543 _____

Check
                                    2 November, 2008 at Paris, France

THIS CHECK IS TO BE
PAID TO THE ORDER OF _____**Sandra Smith**_____ € __**500.00**__
_____**Five Hundred and 00/100**_____ EUROS

by the EX-PATRIOT BANK
at 100 Cours Albert 1er
75008 Paris, France
123456789-09876543 _____

EXHIBIT 12-4 American Check/French Check

Maker	The issuer of a promissory note
Drawer	The issuer of a bill of exchange
Drawee	The person ordered to pay a bill of exchange
Payee	The person to whom a bill or note is to be paid
Endorser	A payee who has signed (endorsed) and delivered a bill or note to an endorsee
Endorsee	A person who receives an endorsed bill or note from an endorser
Bearer	A person who has physical possession of a bill or note that is payable to anyone ("to bearer") or that has been endorsed without naming an endorsee (endorsed "in blank")
Holder	A person who has physical possession of a bill or note that was drawn, issued, or endorsed to him or her, or to his or her order, or to the bearer, or in blank
Holder in due course	Under common law (but not civil law), a person who acquires a bill or note for value, in good faith, and without notice that it is defective, overdue, or that any person has a claim to or defense against it
Acceptor	A drawee of a bill who, by signing the bill on its face, agrees to pay the bill when it is due
Accommodation party	A person who signs a bill or note to lend his or her credit to another party
Accommodation maker or aval	A person who signs a bill or note as a surety and comaker
Accommodation endorser	A person who endorses a bill or note as a guarantor of an endorsee

EXHIBIT 12-5 Parties to Negotiable Instruments

Nov. 22, 2008 $ ___10,000.00___
New York, New York

_____**Ninety days after above date**_____ for value received, the undersigned jointly and severally
promise(s) to pay to the order of: BANK OF THE RIVER, at its offices at 100 Hudson Ave., New York, New York 02167,

_____ **Ten Thousand and 00/100** _____ _____DOLLARS

with interest thereon from the date above at the rate of **-11-** percent per annum (computed on the basis of actual days and a year of 360 days) payable at maturity.

Officer: _____**Jones**_____   _____
No.   _____**990-11-9999**_____   _____
                                                                     Makers

22 Nov. 2008   PROMISSORY NOTE   € ___10,000.00___
Paris, France

_____**Ninety days after above date**_____ for value received, the undersigned jointly and severally
promise(s) to pay in French Francs this Promissory Note to the order of the EX-PATRIOT BANK at its offices at 100 Cours Albert 1er, 75008 Paris, France, at the official exchange rate on the date of maturity, the equivalent of

_____ **Ten Thousand and 00/100** _____ _____EUROS

with interest thereon from the date above at the rate of **-11-** percent per annum (computed on the basis of actual days and a year of 360 days) payable at maturity.

Officer: _____**Mitterand**_____   _____
No.   _____**1118-1-7932**_____   _____
                                                                     Makers

EXHIBIT 12-6 American Promissory Note/French Promissory Note

```
SMALLTOWN BANK                         88-11/980              Number:        99053
901 Main St.                                                  Jan. 1, 2008
Pullman, Washington 99163    NEGOTIABLE CERTIFICATE OF DEPOSIT
```

THIS CERTIFIES to the deposit in this Bank the sum of

Ten Thousand and 00/100 _____ DOLLARS

which is payable to the order of ____ **Apples-R-Us, Inc.** ____ on the **1st** day of

January, 2009 ____ against presentation and surrender of this certificate, and bears interest at the rate of

6-3/4 percent per annum, computed (on the basis of actual days elapsed and a year of 360 days) to, and payable at, maturity. No payment may be made prior to, and no interest accrues after, that date. Payable at maturity in federal funds, and if desired, at the Major National Trust Company, New York.

THE SMALLTOWN BANK OF PULLMAN, WASHINGTON

By: _____

Signature

EXHIBIT 12-7   Certificate of Deposit

The rules governing bills of exchange apply to promissory notes as well. The forms of both instruments are also alike. Thus, whereas the common law does not require that a note contain the words *promissory note*, the ULB does.

Notes are used in a variety of credit transactions and are commonly given the name of the transaction involved. For example, a *collateral note* is one secured by personal property; a *mortgage note* is secured by real property; an *installment note* is payable in installments.

certificate of deposit (CD):
A promissory note on which the maker is a bank.

When a bank is the maker promising to repay money it has received, plus interest, the promissory note is called a **certificate of deposit (CD)**. CDs in amounts up to $100,000 are customarily called *small CDs*; those for $100,000 or more, *large CDs*. Most large CDs and some small CDs are negotiable. Exhibit 12-7 shows a negotiable CD.

E. NEGOTIABILITY OF BILLS AND NOTES

Bills of exchange and promissory notes may be either negotiable or nonnegotiable. For trade to run smoothly, especially international trade, these instruments need to be negotiable—that is (generally speaking), as freely exchangeable as money. Indeed, so long as the form and content of the instruments are proper, the law guarantees the full transferability of the right to receive payment. If there is any limitation on this right, an instrument is said to be nonnegotiable.

To be negotiable, a bill or note must (1) be in the proper form and (2) contain a promise by the maker or drawer to make payment. The requirements for form were discussed earlier (see Exhibit 12-1). To meet the promissory requirements, a bill or note must do the following:

1. State an unconditional promise or order to pay
2. State a definite sum of money or a monetary unit of account
3. Be payable on demand or at a definite time
4. Be signed by the maker or drawer

UNCONDITIONAL PROMISE OR ORDER TO PAY

A bill or note must contain a promise or an order to pay that is unconditional.

Promise or Order

A bill or note must contain an affirmative promise by the maker, or an order to a drawee, to be negotiable. The promise is inadequate if it is only implied.

For example, an *I.O.U.* only acknowledges an obligation of indebtedness. Although it may imply an obligation to pay, it does not contain an affirmative undertaking to do so. It is not, therefore, a negotiable instrument.

The promissory notes shown in Exhibit 12-6 are different because they clearly state that the makers promise to pay the payees. Similarly, the bills of exchange shown in Exhibits 12-2, 12-3, and 12-4 each order a drawee to pay a payee.

Unconditionality

The promise or order to pay made in a bill or note cannot be conditioned upon the performance of some other obligation. The reason for this is basic to the concept of negotiability. If the holder of a bill or note had to determine whether a collateral promise had or had not been fulfilled, the utility of these instruments would be greatly reduced.

To illustrate, if Ivan promises to pay Pierre only if Pierre delivers goods to Ivan before July 4, anyone who might be interested in purchasing this promissory note would have to determine whether delivery was actually made. This would be both expensive and, if an error were made, risky. Thus, both the law and the pragmatic requirements of trade dictate that a bill or note containing a promise or order to pay that is conditioned on the performance of a collateral obligation is nonnegotiable.

Mere reference to some other agreement, however, does not make a bill or note nonnegotiable. It is common practice, in fact, to mention the underlying contract that caused the drawer or maker to issue the bill or note, either for record keeping or for informational purposes. Thus, statements that the bill or note arises out of a separate agreement, or that it is drawn under a letter of credit, or that the ability of the drawer or maker to perform is secured by a mortgage or a security interest do not affect negotiability. [14]

DEFINITE SUM OF MONEY OR MONETARY UNIT OF ACCOUNT

A bill or note must be payable in money, which must be for a definite sum.

Money

money: A medium of exchange authorized or adopted by a domestic or foreign government; it includes a monetary unit of account established by an intergovernmental organization or by agreement between two or more nations.

Both the common law and the ULB specify that the sum paid must be money.[15] The common law defines **money** as "a medium of exchange authorized or adopted by a domestic or foreign government and includes a monetary unit of account established by an intergovernmental organization or by agreement between two or more nations."[16] The ULB provides that the "usages of the place of payment" determine the meaning and the value of money.[17]

In international practice or usage, the parties to international bills and notes routinely define their monetary obligations by referring to monetary units of account (such as the International Monetary Fund's Special Drawing Right or the EU's euro) or to an *ad hoc* basket of several foreign currencies (see Chapter 6). Both the common law and the ULB, accordingly, allow bills and notes to be payable in the currency of one country, of several countries, or a monetary unit of account defined by an intergovernmental organization (IGO).

Definite Sum

The sum to be paid must be *certain* or *determinate*.[18] In other words, the amount to be paid must be ascertainable from the bill or note itself without reference to an outside source. For example, a promissory note that provides for the payment of £1,000 plus interest of 10 percent per annum until the time it is cashed states a definite sum because the parties can figure out the amount that is due from the information provided on the face of the note.

Both of the principal negotiable instruments laws set out exceptions to this basic rule. Both allow the parties to define the sum to be paid in one currency (the money of account) while requiring payment to be made in another (the money of payment), even though this

---

[14]See UCC, § 3-105(1).
[15]UCC, § 3-104(a); ULB, Article 1. Article 1 of the ULC contains the same provision for checks.
[16]UCC, § 1-201(24).
[17]ULB, Article 41.
[18]UCC, § 3-106(1), uses the phrase *sum certain*; ULB, Article 1(1), uses *determinate sum*.

requires the parties to refer to exchange rates that are not embodied in the bill or note.[19] In addition, the common law allows for payments to be made in installments (the ULB does not).[20] Neither, however, permits the use of variable interest rates.[21]

PAYABLE ON DEMAND OR AT A DEFINITE TIME

For a bill or note to function reliably in commerce, the time when it is payable has to be ascertainable from its face.[22] The time requirement actually serves several functions. It tells the maker, drawee, accommodation maker, or acceptor when he is required to pay. It allows secondary parties, such as drawers, endorsers, and accommodation endorsers, to determine the date when their obligations arise. It establishes when the statute of limitations will run. And finally, with interest-bearing bills or notes, it defines the period for calculating the present value of the instrument.

SIGNED BY THE MAKER OR DRAWER

signature: (From Latin: *signare*, "to mark.") The name of a person, written by that person, or any distinctive mark meant to authenticate a writing.

Bills of exchange must be signed by the drawer and promissory notes by their maker. For this purpose, a **signature** can be "any symbol executed or adopted by a party with present intention to authenticate a writing."[23] Signatures do not have to be put on bills or notes at any particular time. Bills and notes lacking a drawer's or maker's signature are simply incomplete, as Case 12-1 illustrates.

---

[19]UCC, § 3-107(2); ULB, Article 41.
[20]UCC, § 3-106(1)(a); ULB, Article 5.
[21]UCC, § 3-106(1)(a); ULB, Article 5.
[22]So long as a final definite date for payment can be ascertained from the face of the instrument, this requirement is satisfied. The common law makes exceptions to this rule for acceleration clauses (which push forward the date when an instrument is payable in the event that an installment payment is missed), and the common law also allows for extension clauses (which let a maker or drawer postpone payment for a fixed time period). UCC, § 3-109(1)(c).
[23]UCC, § 1-201(39). No definition is given in the ULB, but commercial practice in Europe follows the common law usage.

Case 12-1 CONSTANTARAS v. ANAGNOSTOPOULOS

South Africa, Witwatersrand Local Division, 1987.
South African Law Reports, vol. 1988, pt. 3, p. 769 (1988).

The defendant, Mr. Anagnostopoulos, signed several checks as an accommodation maker, or aval (i.e., as a surety and coprincipal). A Mr. Evangelous Souloutas had drawn the checks, but Mr. Souloutas had not signed them at the time that the defendant put his signature on them. When the bank on which the checks were drawn refused to pay on two of the checks, each in the amount of 4,200 rand, the holder, Mr. Constantaras, sought to obtain payment from Mr. Anagnostopoulos. When Mr. Anagnostopoulos refused to pay, Mr. Constantaras brought this suit.

JUDGE KRIEGLER:

***

I turn then to consider the . . . defense which was . . . that no liability *qua* aval arose because of the alleged sequence in which the defendant and Souloutas put their respective signatures on the check. Souloutas had allegedly not yet signed the checks as drawer when defendant, by his signature over the appropriate stamp, signified to the world at large, and in particular to subsequent holders of the check, that he bound himself as surety and co-principal debtor for the obligations reflected on the face thereof. Therefore, so it was contended, defendant's signature was legally ineffectual.

Of course the argument was not as bluntly put as that. Its steps were the following. First, a contract of aval is unique in that it is a real undertaking of suretyship signified on and in respect of the obligation evidenced by a bill of exchange. That then entails, secondly, that the document on which it is recorded must be a bill of exchange. Thirdly, one then goes to the definition in the *Bills of Exchange Act*, § 34 of 1964 to ascertain what a bill of exchange is. Reference is then made to the definitions in § 1 of the Act of the terms "bill" and "check," which in turn direct one to § 2. Subsections (1) and (2) of § 2 of the Act read as follows:

1. A bill of exchange is an unconditional order in writing, addressed by one person to another, signed by the person giving it, requiring the person to whom it is addressed to pay on demand, or at a fixed or at a determinable future time, a sum certain in money to a specified person or his order, or to bearer.
2. An instrument which does not comply with the requirements specified in subsection (1) or which orders any act to be done in addition to the payment of money, is not a bill.

The argument then focuses on the fifth characteristic of the bill as defined, namely that it is to be signed by the person giving it and, drawing support from subsection (2), [the defendant] argues that an unsigned check is not a bill. Therefore, so the argument concludes, the signature of an aval put on a check before the drawer has signed it is a nullity.

In my view the argument is fallacious. In the first instance it . . . [gives too much importance to] the heading to § 2, which reads "Definition of and requirements for a bill of exchange."[24] It is clear to me that the Legislature, in one and the same breath, defined a bill and listed the prerequisites for its validity. [It does not follow] . . . that an instrument, complete and regular in every other respect but lacking a signature, is some innominate[25] piece of paper, as Mr. Roos, for the defendant, would have it. It is simply a bill which, for lack of a signature, is inchoate,[26] e.g., an unsigned check.

The use of the term "an unsigned check" is common, not only in laymen's language but in a legal context. There are many examples, of which this case is but

one. The defendant admitted in paragraph 2 of his opposing affidavit that he signed "the checks, annexes A and B to the summons" and in paragraph 3.3 alleged that "not one of the checks . . . had been signed." To my mind there is nothing anomalous in that choice of language.

They were, indeed, unsigned checks. If one looks at the *Bills of Exchange Act* itself, there are several examples of similar use of language. Thus § 16(1) provides:

> A bill may be accepted—(a) before it has been signed by the drawer. . . .

Clearly the notional lawgiver (in fact, the draftsman of § 18 of the United Kingdom progenitor of our § 16, namely in the *Bills of Exchange Act* 1882)[27] realized that a bill, before it has been signed by the drawer, is a bill capable of being accepted. So, too, the opening words of § 24(1) ("If a person signs a bill as drawer . . .") indicate that before the drawer has signed the instrument, it is a bill. The subtlety necessarily involved in regarding the document as something unknown and unnamed until the moment the drawer has put the last dot of his signature on it, is unrealistic, not consonant with commercial or legal parlance, and inconsistent with the very language of the Act.

***

Furthermore, the defendant unequivocally undertook specific obligations in the knowledge that the checks were as yet unsigned and, obviously, before they had been delivered he knew they had to be signed by the drawer and would be signed by him before they were delivered. Until delivery they would be inchoate (see § 88 of the Act), but once delivered the contract of the drawer would be concluded. *See* Denis V. Cowen, *The Law of Negotiable Instruments in South Africa*.[28] The learned author . . . points out that:

> [t]here is no authority on the question whether the contract of aval is incomplete and revocable until delivery.

That question does not arise in the present case. Here the checks were delivered, as defendant intended them to be. In my opinion the defendant's obligations *qua* aval arose at the latest when the checks were delivered. They were delivered, bearing his signature,

---

[24]"Omskrywing van en vereistes vir'n wissel" in the Afrikaans text. As to the propriety of referring to the heading of a section as an aid in interpretation, see L. C. Steyn, Uitleg van Wette, pp. 147, 148 (5th ed. 1974).
[25]From Latin *innominatus*: "unnamed" or "anonymous."
[26]From Latin *inchoatus*: "has begun." It means "in its early stages of development" or "incipient."
[27]Victoria, Anno 45–46, Chap. 16.
[28]At p. 175 (4th ed. 1966).

recording an obligation which he undertook to secure through his personal suretyship. The checks were delivered precisely as the defendant intended them to be. They signify to the payee and to any further holders of the checks that defendant stood surety for the obligations of the drawer. In my view, he is bound by that indication. It matters not that the drawer's signature had not yet been affixed when the aval signed on the reverse of the checks.

The defendant was ordered to pay the plaintiff 8,400 rand, plus interest. ■

CASEPOINT: The case involves a check (one type of bill of exchange) that was signed by a person as surety before the drawer had signed the instrument. The legal question was whether the man who signed the check as a surety was liable when the bank refused to pay—was the check a "nullity" prior to the drawer's signature, or was it a legal bill of exchange? The court held that it was a bill when properly prepared, and when the defendant signed as surety, he became bound on the instrument.

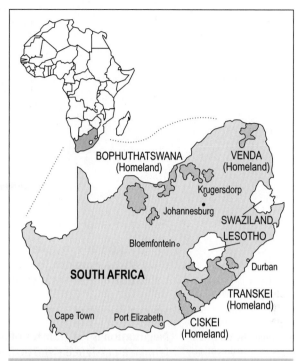

MAP 12-1   South Africa (1987)

F. THE NEGOTIATION AND TRANSFER OF BILLS AND NOTES

To satisfy commercial needs, bills and notes have to be freely transferable. Contract law governs the relationships between the original parties to a bill or note. Once a negotiable instrument circulates beyond the original parties, however, the laws governing negotiation come into play.

ASSIGNMENT

assignment: The transfer of all or part of an assignor's contractual rights to an assignee.

The transfer of rights under a contract is called an **assignment**. When an assignment is made, the assignee acquires only those rights that the assignor possessed. Moreover, any objections to honoring the assigned obligations that could be raised against the assignor can also be raised against the assignee.

For example, Anna promises to deliver 10 widgets to Chekhov and Chekhov gives her an I.O.U. for $100. Anna promptly assigns the I.O.U. to Vanya, who several days later presents the I.O.U. to Chekhov, asking him to pay it. Anna, however, failed to deliver the promised widgets, so Chekhov refuses to pay the I.O.U. Because an I.O.U. is a nonnegotiable instrument (as mentioned earlier), Vanya can only be an assignee. He has no more rights in the I.O.U. than Anna had. As a consequence, Chekhov can use Anna's failure to make delivery of the widgets as an excuse (or *defense*) for not paying Vanya. Vanya's only recourse is to return to Anna—if Anna can be found—and get back whatever money he may have paid for the I.O.U.

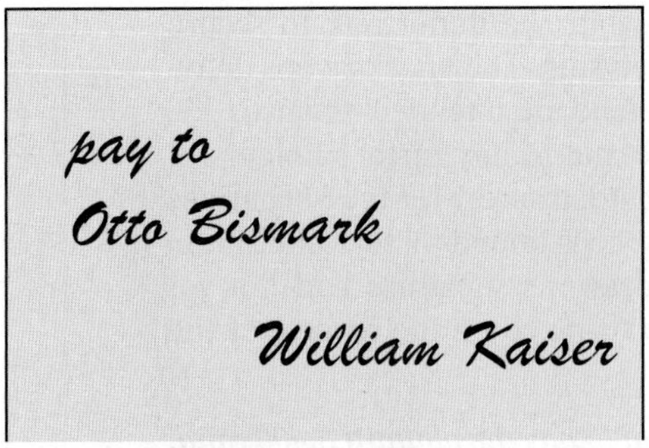

pay to
Otto Bismark

William Kaiser

EXHIBIT 12-8 Special Endorsement

Bankers and merchants, who are well aware of the problems that arise in taking instruments by assignment, are not anxious to do so. They prefer to be paid in cash or by a negotiable instrument—that is, by an instrument that is, for most purposes, the same as cash.

NEGOTIATION

negotiation: The transfer of rights in an instrument, either by endorsement and delivery or merely by delivery, that entitles the holder to sue in his own name and to take the instrument free of some of the claims that persons obliged to pay on the instrument have against the transferor.

Negotiation is the transfer of a bill or note in such a way that the recipient becomes a holder. Unlike an assignee (who acquires only the rights of the assignor), a holder can acquire more rights from the transferor than the transferor possessed. The rights that a holder acquires depend on the manner in which the instrument was negotiated and the governing law.

Negotiating Order Paper

order paper: A bill of exchange or promissory note that is payable to a named payee.

Order paper is a bill or note that either (1) contains the name of a payee capable of endorsing it, such as "pay to the order of Francisco Madero," or (2) contains as its last endorsement a so-called *special endorsement*—that is, for example, "pay to Otto Bismarck." (See Exhibit 12-8.) Order paper is negotiated by delivery and endorsement. That is, a bill payable to the order of Giulio Romano would be negotiated when Giulio signed the back and delivered it to a holder.

Negotiating Bearer Paper

bearer paper: A bill of exchange or promissory note that is payable to the bearer or to cash.

Bearer paper is an instrument that either (1) contains on its face an order to pay the bearer or to pay in cash or (2) contains as its last endorsement a so-called *blank endorsement*, that is, the signature of the payee or the signature of the last endorsee named in a special endorsement. (See Exhibit 12-9.) Bearer paper is negotiated by delivery alone.

The use of bearer paper is riskier than the use of order paper. If it is lost or stolen it must still be paid, a rule that has existed for more than 200 years, as Case 12-2 points out.

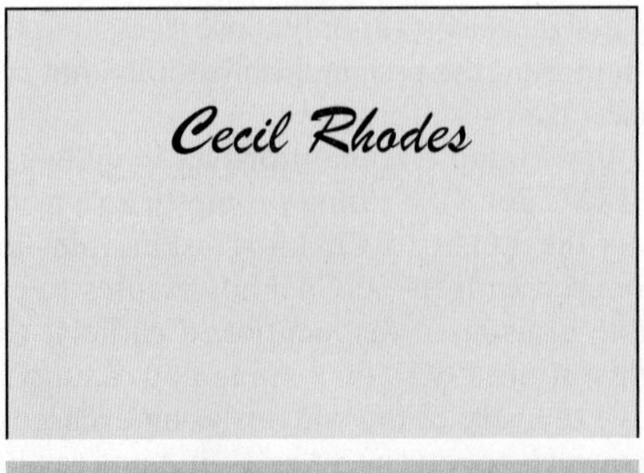

Cecil Rhodes

EXHIBIT 12-9 Blank Endorsement

=⧸⧹⧸⧹⧸=

Case 12-2   MILLER v. RACE

England, Court of King's Bench, 1758.
English Reports, vol. 97, p. 398.

William Finney owed 21 pounds and 10 shillings to Bernard Odenharty. Finney purchased a note in that amount from the Bank of England that was drawn upon the bank itself and that was made payable to bearer. Finney then sent the bank's note to Odenharty in the mail on December 11, 1756. That night the mail was robbed, and the note in question and several other notes were carried off by the robber. On December 12, the note came into the possession of an innkeeper by the name of Miller.

On December 13, having learned of the robbery, Finney applied to the Bank of England to stop payment on the note. The bank agreed to do so.

Shortly thereafter, Miller presented the note to the Bank of England for payment. The bank's clerk, who was named Race, refused either to pay the note or return it to Miller. Miller thereupon brought suit against Race to compel him to make payment.

At issue was the following question: "Whether, under the circumstances of this case, the plaintiff had a sufficient

MAP 12-2   England (1758)

property in this bank note, to entitle him to recover in the present action."

LORD MANSFIELD

***

[This case] has been very ingeniously argued by Sir Richard Lloyd for the defendant. But the whole fallacy of the argument turns upon comparing bank notes to what they do not resemble, *viz.* to goods, or to securities, or documents for debts.

Now they are not goods, not securities, nor documents for debts, nor are they so esteemed—but are treated as money, as cash, in the ordinary course and transaction of business, by the general consent of mankind; which gives them the credit and currency of money, to all intents and purposes. They are as much money as guineas themselves are; or any other current coin, that is used in common payments, as money or cash.

. . . Here, an innkeeper took it, bona fide, in his business from a person who made an appearance of a gentleman. Here is no pretense or suspicion of collusion with the robber—for this matter was strictly inquired and examined into at the trial—and it is so stated in the case, "that he took it for full and valuable consideration, in the usual course of business." Indeed, if there had been any collusion, or any circumstances of unfair dealing, the case had been much otherwise. If it had been a note for 1,000£ it might have been suspicious, but this was a small note for 21£ 10s only, and money was given in exchange for it.

. . . A bank note is constantly and universally, both at home and abroad, treated as money, as cash; and paid and received, as cash; and it is necessary, for the purposes of commerce, that their currency should be established and secured.

. . . No dispute ought to be made with the bearer of a cash note—in regard to commerce, and for the sake of credit—though it may be both reasonable and customary, to stay the payment, till inquiry can be made, whether the bearer of the note came by it fairly, or not.

Judgment for the plaintiff. ■

CASEPOINT: The court considered whether a note payable to bearer was more like cash or like goods. The judge looked at the purpose of bearer instruments and stated that they were used as a substitute for cash, and in the absence of any obvious irregularities could be negotiated as cash. Where, as here, the innkeeper gave consideration and took the note in payment "in the ordinary course of business," it was to be treated as cash and the bank had to honor its payment obligation.

Converting Order to Bearer Paper and Bearer to Order Paper

Order paper can be converted to bearer paper by an endorsement in blank or by an endorsement to pay to the bearer. Bearer paper can be converted to order paper through the use of a special endorsement, such as "Pay to John Adams."

The manner in which a bill or note must be negotiated depends on its character at the time of negotiation. If it is order paper, it must be negotiated by delivery and endorsement; if it is bearer paper, by delivery alone. To illustrate: A note is made payable to Mustafa Kemal, who endorses it by signing his name on the back. The note can now be negotiated by delivery alone, and whoever receives it from Kemal can also negotiate by delivery alone. Any subsequent holder can, of course, add a special endorsement to convert the note back to order paper. For example, the note may come into the possession of Ali Jinnah, who could add the statement "pay Ahmad Khan," sign the note himself, and deliver it to Khan. Khan would then have to endorse it himself before he could negotiate the note.

Endorsements

endorsement: The act of a payee, drawee, accommodation party, or holder of a negotiable instrument in signing the back of the instrument, with or without qualifying words, to transfer rights in the instrument to another.

An **endorsement** is required to negotiate a bill or note that is in the form of order paper, and it may optionally be added to bearer paper. Endorsements are signatures, with or without additional statements, that are commonly written on the back of the instrument. There are four basic kinds: (1) special endorsements, (2) blank endorsements, (3) qualified endorsements, and (4) restrictive endorsements. The first two have already been described.

qualified endorsement: An endorsement in which the endorser does not guarantee that an instrument will be accepted and paid by the drawer or maker.

Qualified Endorsements   Normally, an endorser guarantees that the instrument will be accepted and paid by the drawee or maker. The endorser can avoid this guarantee, however, by making a **qualified endorsement**. Commonly, this is done by adding the words *without recourse*.[29] Qualified endorsements are commonly used by persons acting in a representative capacity. For example, a lawyer may receive a check that is payable to him, which is really meant to be paid to a client. Because the lawyer is only endorsing the check to make it possible for the client to cash it, he should not have to make good on the check if it is later dishonored. By adding a qualified endorsement, he will not have to do so. (See Exhibit 12-10.)

restrictive endorsement: An endorsement that restricts the rights of subsequent holders.

Restrictive Endorsements   **Restrictive endorsements** limit the rights of subsequent holders. There are several types, including conditional endorsements, endorsements for

without recourse
Edgar A. Poe

EXHIBIT 12-10   Qualified Endorsement

---

[29]The words *without recourse* are required in the common law countries. UCC, § 3-417(3). No particular words are required in Europe. ULB, Article 15.

pay to Muhammad Ali on condition he deliver 1 pair of boxing gloves to me in 1 week
Joe Frazier

EXHIBIT 12-11 Conditional Endorsement

collection, endorsements prohibiting further endorsements, and agency endorsements. None of these, however, prevents the further transfer or negotiation of a bill or note.[30]

conditional endorsement: An endorsement that conditions payment on the occurrence of some event.

A **conditional endorsement** contains a statement that conditions payment on the occurrence of a specified event. (See Exhibit 12-11.) The effect of this endorsement is to make the bill or note a nonnegotiable instrument as to the endorser only. No subsequent holder has the right to enforce the payment against a conditional endorser until the condition is met.

endorsement for collection: An endorsement that makes the endorsee a collection agent for the endorser.

An **endorsement for collection** makes an endorsee (usually a bank) a collecting agent for the endorser. In common law countries, such an endorsement is usually written as *for deposit only*, *for collection only*, or *pay any bank*. In civil law countries, the phrases *value in collection* and *by procuration* are also commonly used.

The effect of an endorsement for collection is to put the instrument into the bank collection process. In common law countries, only a bank can become a holder once this endorsement has been added to a bill or note, unless the instrument is specially endorsed by a bank to a person who is not a bank.[31] Under the ULB, anyone can become a holder, but he can only endorse the instrument for the purpose of making collection.[32]

endorsement prohibiting further endorsements: An endorsement that states that the instrument may be paid only to a particular person.

An **endorsement prohibiting further endorsements** states that the instrument may be paid only to a particular person. An example is "Pay to Harry Potter only." This endorsement is treated differently by the two main commercial law systems.

In common law countries, an endorsement prohibiting further endorsements is treated as if it were a special endorsement—that is, as though the example said, "Pay to Harry Potter."[33] The ULB treats such an endorsement as if it were a qualified endorsement (e.g., "Pay to Harry Potter, without recourse"); in other words, the endorser does not guarantee acceptance or payment.[34]

agency endorsement: An endorsement that requires the endorsee to pay the proceeds from the negotiation of the instrument to the endorser or a designated third party.

An **agency endorsement** requires the endorsee to pay the proceeds from the negotiation of a bill or note to the endorser or to some third party. In common law countries, such an endorsement is phrased as "Pay to Alexander Leslie, agent for Oliver Cromwell [signed] Oliver Cromwell" or "Pay to Alexander Leslie in Trust for Charles Tudor [signed] Oliver Cromwell." In civil law countries, the wording is "Pay to Maximilien Robespierre, for value in security [signed] Napoleon Bonaparte" or "Pay Maximilien Robespierre, for value in pledge to Louis Bourbon [signed] Napoleon Bonaparte."

Under the common law and the ULB, an agency endorsee may properly negotiate the instrument only as directed. This restriction on rights, however, applies only to the immediate endorsee and not to any subsequent holder.[35]

[30]UCC, § 3-206(1); ULB, Article 15.
[31]UCC, § 4-201(2).
[32]ULB, Article 18.
[33]UCC, § 3-206(1).
[34]ULB, Article 15.
[35]UCC, § 3-206(1); ULB, Article 19.

Type of Endorsement	Example	Endorsee's Status	
		Common Law	**ULB**
Blank	[*signed*] Cecil Rhodes	Holder	Holder
Special	Pay to Otto Bismark, [*signed*] William Kaiser	Holder	Holder
Qualified	Pay to Jane Austen, without recourse, [*signed*] Edgar Poe	No rights against endorser	No rights against endorser
Conditional	Pay to Muhammad Ali on condition he deliver 1 pair of boxing gloves to me in 1 week, [*signed*] Joe Frazier	No rights against endorser until condition is met	No rights against endorser until condition is met
For collection	For collection only, [*signed*] Tom Dewey	Collecting agent for endorser	Collecting agent for endorser
Prohibiting further endorsements	Pay to Harry Potter only, [*signed*] J.K. Rowling	Holder	No rights against endorser
Agency	Pay to Alexander Leslie, agent for Oliver Cromwell [*signed*] Oliver Cromwell	Collecting agent for endorser	Collecting agent for endorser

EXHIBIT 12-12 Effect of Different Endorsements under the Common Low and the ULB

FORGED ENDORSEMENTS

forgery: The false making or altering of a writing with the intent to defraud.

When an endorsement is **forged**, the question arises as to who should have to sue the forger or, if the forger cannot be found, who has to assume the loss. There are several possible ways to answer this question. The one that makes most sense commercially (i.e., the one that is most likely to encourage the free transfer and exchange of bills and notes) is to make the drawer or maker liable. This is the rule adopted by the ULB. The ULB makes a forged endorsement fully effective, and both the person taking an instrument with such an endorsement and all subsequent holders are entitled to payment.[36]

Another possibility is to impose liability on the person who was best able to prevent the forgery from happening. This is possibly the fairest rule, but it also encourages excessive and expensive litigation. It is the rule followed in most common law countries. As a general rule, the common law makes a forged endorsement ineffective, placing the burden for determining the validity of an endorsement on the endorsee taking an instrument from a forger. Case 12-3 illustrates this rule.

---

[36]ULB, Article 7.

Case 12-3 MAIR v. BANK OF NOVA SCOTIA

Court of Appeal of Eastern Caribbean States, Civil Division, 1983.
West Indian Reports, vol. 31, p. 186 (1983).

APPELLATE JUDGE BERRIDGE

This is an appeal from a decision of Judge Robotham dated June 18, 1980, in which judgment was given for the respondent bank in respect of a claim by the appellant alleging negligence and breach of duty in the sum of $6,000 and interest, together with costs.

The brief facts of the case are that sometime in 1974 the appellant, an architect by profession, engaged one Barbara Hill of Barbados, herself an architect, to assist him in Antigua by doing specific architectural work. Hill took

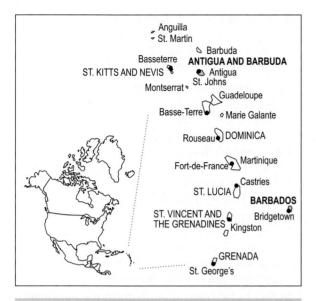

MAP 12-3 Antigua and Barbados (1983)

up her assignment with the appellant who gave her an advance of $6,000 payable by check drawn on the St John's, Antigua, branch of the Bank of Nova Scotia for work already done and to be done in the future. Shortly thereafter Hill returned to Barbados following differences which arose between her and the appellant and in respect of which there is litigation which is not before the court.

The check was dated January 16, 1974, and made payable to "Barbara Hill"; but it was altered on the face of it by the addition of the word "Associates" as payee, endorsed "Barbara Hill" and deposited at the branch of the respondent bank at Worthing, Christchurch, Barbados, on January 23, 1974, to the credit of "Barbara Hill Associates".

On January 29, 1974, the check was returned to the Antigua branch of the bank who deducted $6,000 from the appellant's account and in due course the canceled check was forwarded to the appellant who, by letter dated May 7, 1974, drew the bank's attention to the alteration and demanded reimbursement on the grounds that (i) it was negligent in not observing the alteration in which event it should not have paid, and (ii) it had not carried out his instructions. The bank refused to reimburse the appellant and as a consequence proceedings were instituted by the appellant.

***

In arguing the . . . appeal, counsel submitted that the alteration was a material alteration on the face of the in-

strument which [made it void] under Section 64 of the *Bills of Exchange Act* [of Antigua and Barbuda] the provisions of which are similar to, if not identical with, comparable legislation throughout the Commonwealth. Counsel further contended that (i) the mandate of the drawer of the check was not substantially carried out, (ii) the alteration was apparent, (iii) the bank was not a holder in due course, and (iv) the damage suffered was the debiting of the appellant's account with a payment to someone other than the payee stated by the appellant.

It is pertinent at this stage to set out the provisions of Section 64 of the Bills of Exchange Act, which reads as follows:

1. Where a bill or acceptance is materially altered without the assent of all parties liable on the bill, the bill is avoided except as against a party who has himself made, authorized, or assented to the alteration, and subsequent endorsers. Provided that, where a bill has been materially altered, but the alteration is not apparent and the bill is in the hands of a holder in due course, such holder may avail himself of the bill as if it had not been altered, and may enforce payment of it according to its original tenor.
2. In particular the following alterations are material, namely, any alteration of the date, the sum payable, the time of payment, the place of payment, and where a bill has been accepted generally, the addition of a place of payment without the acceptor's assent.

In *Vance v. Lowther*,[37] where an alteration related to the date of the check, it was held that it was material and invalidated the check; and that the circumstance that the plaintiff had not been guilty of negligence in taking it was immaterial. Baron[38] Pollock said:[39]

> Any material alteration of a bill or note invalidates it, and the question is, what is the true principle on which the materiality must be determined. The county court judge seems to have thought that it was necessary to consider the surrounding circumstances in each case. In that I think he was wrong, and that we ought to look at the question of materiality with reference to the contract itself, and not with reference to the surrounding circumstances.

But it would be unreasonable if the alteration to an earlier date debarred the banker form debiting the customer, if paid after the original date.

Similar in a number of respects to the facts in the instant case are those in *Slingsby v. District Bank, Ltd.*[40] where words were inserted between the payee's name and the words "or order" and endorsed to conform with

---

[37]Law Reports, Exchequer's Division, vol. 1, p. 176 (1876).
[38]"Baron" is the title for the judges of the English Court of Exchequer.
[39]*Id.*, at p. 178.
[40]*All England Law Reports,* vol. 1931, p. 143 (King's Bench, 1931).

the designation of the payee as altered. It was held that the check had been materially altered within the body of Section 64 (1) of the *Bills of Exchange Act* and therefore the check had been avoided.

The materiality of the alteration being dependent upon its character and effect, it necessarily follows that if the mandate of the customer has been substantially complied with then the banker can charge the customer, the alteration notwithstanding. Authority for the foregoing is to be found in *Halsbury's Laws of England*.[41]

I am of the opinion that the check was materially altered without the assent of the appellant.

To constitute an apparent alteration within the meaning of the *Bills of Exchange Act* it should be apparent upon inspection of the bill that its text has undergone a change. The document itself must show that some revision of the text has taken place and its appearance must be consistent with the revision having occurred after completion or issue, although it may also be consistent with the revision having occurred before completion.[42]

An inspection of the check reveals that the alteration is obviously in a different handwriting from that in which the rest of the document was drawn and it should have been observed that it had undergone a change.

In regard to the difference between the rights of a "holder in due course" and a "holder" I can do no better than quote from the words of Lord Justice Denning in *Arab Bank, Ltd. v. Ross*:[43]

> The difference between the rights of a "holder in due course" and those of a "holder" is that a holder in due course may get a better title than the person from whom he took, whereas a holder gets no better title. In this regard a person who takes a bill, which is irregular on the face of it, is in the same position as a person who takes a bill which is overdue. He is a holder, but not a holder in due course. He does not receive

the bill on its own intrinsic credit. He takes it on the credit of the person who gives it to him. He can sue in his own name but he takes it subject to the defects of title of prior parties: see Section 38 of the Act of 1882.

In the instant case the bank took the check which was irregular on the face of it. The bank was not a holder in due course and cannot [therefore] avail itself of the proviso to Section 64(1) of the *Bills of Exchange Act.*

On the question of damages, the appellant's claim is in contract. It is a well-established principle that whenever a party proves a breach of contract but no actual damage (as was contended by learned counsel for the bank) he recovers as a rule nominal damages only.

In the instant case the appellant claims that the damage suffered by him is the debiting of his bank account with an amount payable by check drawn by him to "Barbara Hill" and not "Barbara Hill Associates"; but, I am unable to perceive what damage the appellant has suffered on account of the alteration of the check.

. . . In the circumstances, I would allow the appeal and vary the order of the trial judge by entering judgment for the appellant in the sum of $5 nominal damages. . . . ■

CASEPOINT: This case concerns the effect of a forgery of part of the payee's name on a check. Someone (probably the payee) added the word *Associates* to the name of the payee and then negotiated the check. Later, when the drawer of the check noticed the change, he asked the bank to recredit his account. The court held that this was indeed an alteration, which made the bank a *holder* but not a *holder in due course* (who takes the instrument free of underlying defenses). But since the drawer could not show that he had suffered any actual damages due to the alteration, he was awarded only a nominal sum by the court.

---

[41]Vol. 2, p. 205, para. 380 (3rd ed.).

[42]Automobile Finance Co. of Australia, Ltd. v. Law, *Commonwealth Law Reports*, vol. 49, p. 1 (Australia, High Court, 1933) refers.

[43]*All England Law Reports*, vol. 1952, pt. 1, p. 709 at p. 717 (Court of Appeal, 1952).

common law imposter rule:
A person who pretends to be another so as to have a negotiable instrument drawn, made, or endorsed to that person may effectively endorse the pretended person's signature on the instrument.

There are two major exceptions to the general common law rule that a forged endorsement is ineffective. One is the **imposter rule**. This says that when a drawer, maker, or endorser draws, makes, or endorses an instrument to an imposter, the imposter's subsequent endorsement is effective. For example, a man walks into a shop, says that he is John Lender, a creditor of the shop owner, Pete Gullible, and asks to be paid. Gullible, believing the man to be his creditor, writes a check made out in favor of John Lender. The man then cashes the check at a nearby supermarket and disappears. Because the man was an imposter, the forged signature he put on the check is effective. Gullible cannot stop payment, and his bank must negotiate the check when the supermarket presents it.

Situation	Common Law	ULB
A stolen instrument is forged.	Immediate endorsee	Drawer
The forger is an imposter.	Drawer	Drawer
The forger endorses for a fictitious payee.	Drawer	Drawer

EXHIBIT 12-13 Liability When a Negotiable Instrument Is Forged

common law fictitious payee rule: A person who solicits and obtains a negotiable instrument drawn or made to a fictitious person may effectively endorse the fictitious person's signature on the instrument.

The second common law exception to the rule that a forged signature is ineffective is the **fictitious payee rule**. This says that when the instrument is issued in the name of a fictitious payee, the person purporting to be that payee can make an effective endorsement. To illustrate: A disgruntled employee, Ann Sly, tells her employer that he needs to sign a check that she has made out so that she can pay a supplier. He does so. Ann then forges the supplier's endorsement and cashes the check herself. In reality, the supplier (whether or not it really exists or was a fiction) has no claim against Sly's employer. The supplier's forged endorsement, however, is effective, and the employer must honor the check when an innocent holder presents it for payment.

The difficulty with the general common law rule is that the determination of whether one or the other of the two exceptions applies has to be made after the fact. In the meantime, the maker, drawer, or drawee can refuse to make payment, and the last holder will have to initiate suit against the dishonoring party to determine who is responsible for pressing the claim against the forger. The loser of that suit will, assuming the forger can be located, have to initiate a second suit to recoup the lost funds. This rule may assure employment for lawyers, but it does not promote the free transferability of negotiable instruments.

The liabilities of endorsers and drawers for forged instruments under the common law and the ULB are compared in Exhibit 12-13.

LIMITATIONS ON THE EXCUSES THAT DRAWERS AND MAKERS CAN USE TO AVOID PAYING OFF A BILL OR NOTE

The major disadvantage of taking a bill, note, or other contractual obligation by assignment is that the maker or drawer can make a wide range of excuses for not having to pay off the instrument. The advantage of taking an instrument by negotiation is that many of these excuses are limited.[44]

ULB holder: A person who acquires an instrument by negotiation.

The most extensive limitations imposed on the excuses of makers and drawers are those contained in the ULB. Anyone who acquires a bill or note by negotiation is a **holder** who is entitled to payment from the maker or drawer. There are only three excuses available to these parties. One is that the possessor is not a holder because he did not acquire title through an uninterrupted series of endorsements. For example, someone possessing an instrument that is payable on its face to one person but endorsed on the back by another cannot be a holder.

ULB bad faith: Acquiring an instrument knowing that it was not properly negotiated to you.

The second excuse is that the holder acquired the instrument in bad faith. **Bad faith** includes such things as the actual theft of the instrument; having actual knowledge that the instrument is stolen, lost, or misplaced; or having actual knowledge that the payee, or some prior holder, is not properly entitled to payment.

ULB gross negligence: Acquiring an instrument in such a careless or reckless manner that one should have known that it was not properly negotiated.

The third excuse is that the holder acquired the instrument through **gross negligence**. This is essentially the same as bad faith, except that the holder does not have to have actual knowledge. He must, however, have acted in a truly careless manner in failing to detect some defect in the instrument or in the rights of the maker, drawer, or a prior holder.[45] These excuses are summarized in Exhibit 12-14.

---

[44]In the United States, the courts and statutory materials refer to *defenses* rather than excuses. In the United Kingdom, the phrase is *failure of equities*. In the civil law countries, the terms *defenses, justifications,* and *excuses* are all used. *Excuses* will generally be used in this book.
[45]ULB, Article 16.

Person in Possession	Excuse
Not a holder	1. Not a holder
Holder	1. Acquired instrument in bad faith
	2. Acquired instrument through gross negligence

EXHIBIT 12-14 ULB Excuses That Drawers and Makers Can Use to Avoid Paying Bills of Exchange and Promissory Notes

In contrast to the ULB, the common law imposes very few limitations on the excuses that makers and drawers can use to get out of their obligation to pay off a bill or note. To cut short these excuses, a possessor must first (as is the case in the ULB) be a **holder**—that is, someone who acquired the bill or note through an uninterrupted series of endorsements. A person who is not a holder is not entitled to the instrument and must give it up.

When the possessor of a bill or note is an ordinary holder, a maker or drawer can draw upon a lengthy list of excuses for not paying. (See Exhibit 12-15.) The list is narrowed, however, if the holder can prove that he is entitled to the additional status of a **holder in due course (HDC)**.[46] An HDC is a holder who acquires an instrument (1) for value, (2) in good faith, and (3) without notice that it is overdue, that it has been dishonored, or that the maker, drawer, or a prior endorser has a valid excuse for not paying it off.[47] The requirement that an HDC has to give value for an instrument means that someone who receives an instrument as a gift or by inheritance can only be an ordinary holder. Good faith means that the holder cannot have known—or have reasonably suspected—that the instrument was defective.

common law holder: A person who acquires an instrument by negotiation.

common law holder in due course: A holder who acquires a negotiable instrument for value, in good faith, and without notice that it is overdue, that it has been dishonored, or that persons required to pay on it have a valid excuse for not doing so.

LIABILITIES OF MAKERS, DRAWERS, DRAWEES, ENDORSERS, AND ACCOMMODATION PARTIES

Two kinds of liability are imposed on makers, drawers, and endorsers of bills and notes. One is liability *on the instrument*—that is, liability arising out of a signature. The other is *warranty*

Person in Possession	Excuse
Not a holder	Not a holder
Holder	Breach of contract (including breach of contract warranties)
	Lack or failure of consideration
	Fraud in the inducement
	Illegality, incapacity (other than minority), or duress, if the contract is voidable
	Previous payment of the instrument
	Unauthorized completion of an incomplete instrument
	Nondelivery of the instrument
Holder or holder in due course	Forgery
	Fraud in the execution
	Material alteration
	Discharge in bankruptcy
	Minority, if the contract is voidable
	Illegality, incapacity, or duress, if the contract is void

EXHIBIT 12-15 Common Law Excuses That Drawers and Makers Can Use to Avoid Paying Bills of Exchange and Promissory

[46]A holder has the burden of proving that he is a holder in due course. UCC, § 3-307(3).
[47]*Id.*, § 3-303.

liability—that is, responsibility arising out of the implied guarantees a person makes at the time he transfers or presents a negotiable instrument. In neither case, it is important to note, is liability based on the underlying contract.

Liability on the Instrument

presentment: A production of an instrument to a party liable to pay on it for that party's acceptance (i.e., commitment to pay) or payment.

A person who signs an instrument has a contractual obligation to make payment. For makers, drawees, and accommodation parties, this obligation is *primary*; that is, they must make payment on **presentment** of the instrument. If it is other than a demand instrument, it must be presented on the day it is due. If it is a demand instrument, it must be presented within a reasonable time after it was signed.

Sometimes the failure to present a check for payment within a reasonable time will prevent the holder from collecting on the instrument, as the following case demonstrates.

Case 12-4　FAR EAST REALTY INVESTMENT, INC. v. COURT OF APPEALS ET AL.

The Philippines, Supreme Court, Second Division, 1988. *Supreme Court Reports Annotated, Second Series*, vol. 166, p. 256 (1988).

On September 13, 1960, Dy Hian Tat, Siy Chee, and Gaw Suy An went to the Manila office of Far East Realty Investment, Inc. (Far East) and obtained a loan in the sum of P4,500.00 (Philippine currency), which they needed in their business and which they promised to pay, jointly and severally, in one month's time together with interest at the rate of 14 percent per annum. To assure Far East that it would be repaid, Dy Hian Tat drew a check on his account with China Banking Corporation (the bank), dated September 13, 1960, for P4,500.00, and Siy Chee and Gaw Suy An signed the check on its back as accommodation parties. The three men were to redeem the check in one month's time by paying cash to Far East in the sum of P4,500.00; otherwise, Far East was to present the check for payment at the bank.

Almost four years later, on March 5, 1964, Far East presented the check to the bank for payment. The bank refused to pay, as the account of Dy Hian Tat had been closed for some time. Far East then made a demand on Dy Hian Tat, Siy Chee, and Gaw Suy An for repayment of their loan. When they refused to pay, Far East brought suit. The City Court of Manila ruled in favor of Far East, so Dy Hian Tat, Siy Chee, and Gaw Suy An appealed. The Court of First Instance of Manila also ruled in favor of Far East but the Court of Appeals reversed, holding that Far East had not presented the check for payment within a reasonable time. Far East (the petitioner) then appealed to the Philippine Supreme Court.

MAP 12-4　Philippines (1988)

JUSTICE PARAS

***

The main issue in this case is whether or not presentment for payment and notice of dishonor of the questioned check were made within reasonable time.

. . . Where the instrument is not payable on demand, presentment must be made on the day it falls due. Where it is payable on demand, presentment must be made within a reasonable time after issue, except that in the case of a bill of exchange, presentment for payment will be sufficient if made within a reasonable time after the last negotiation thereof.[48]

Notice may be given as soon as the instrument is dishonored, and, unless delay is excused, must be given within the time fixed by the law.[49]

No hard and fast demarcation line can be drawn between what may be considered as a reasonable or an unreasonable time, because "reasonable time" depends upon the peculiar facts and circumstances in each case.[50]

It is obvious in this case that presentment and notice of dishonor were not made within a reasonable time.

"Reasonable time" has been defined as so much time as is necessary under the circumstances for a reasonable, prudent and diligent man to do, conveniently, what the contract or duty requires should be done, having a regard for the rights and possibility of loss, if any, to the other party.[51]

In the instant case, the check in question was issued on September 13, 1960, but was presented to the drawee bank only on March 5, 1964, and dishonored on the same date. After dishonor by the drawee bank, a formal notice of dishonor was made by the petitioner through a letter dated April 27, 1968. Under these circumstances, the petitioner undoubtedly failed to exercise prudence and diligence on what he ought to do as required by law. The petitioner likewise failed to show any justification for the unreasonable delay.

PREMISES CONSIDERED, the petition is DENIED and the decision of the Court of Appeals is AFFIRMED.

So Ordered. ■

CASEPOINT: This case concerned whether the check (a demand instrument) was presented for payment within a reasonable time. The Philippines Supreme Court found that the payee's delay of almost four years in presenting the check for payment was not within a reasonable time, and thus the bank did not have to honor the check.

---

[48]Negotiable Instruments Law, § 71.
[49]*Id.*, § 102.
[50]Arturo M. Tolentino, *Commentaries and Jurisprudence on the Commercial Laws of the Philippines*, vol. 1, p. 327 (8th ed., 1986–1988).
[51]Citizens' Bank Bldg. v. L. & E. Wertheirmer, *South Western Reporter*, vol. 189, p. 361, at 362 (Arkansas Supreme Ct., 1917).

Liability on the instrument for drawers, endorsers, and accommodation endorsers is *secondary*; that is, they have to pay only if the maker, drawee, or accommodation maker fails to do so.

When a holder or transferee is unable to obtain payment from the maker, drawee, or accommodation maker, she must take three preliminary steps before she can seek recourse from the parties with secondary liability. First, the instrument has to be properly presented. That is, it must contain all necessary endorsements, and it must be timely presented at the place required. Second, if the instrument is a bill of exchange, it must be **protested**. In other words, a formal certification of dishonor must be issued by "a person authorized to certify dishonor by the law of the place where the dishonor occurs."[52] In the United States, such a person is a notary public.[53] The certification has to show (1) who presented the instrument for payment, (2) the place where this was done, and (3) the reason given by the maker or drawee for refusing to make payment.[54]

The third requirement is to give notice to the parties with secondary liability. This is done, initially, by notifying the drawer (if the instrument is a bill) and the last endorser. At the same time, any other endorser whose address the holder is aware of must also be notified. In turn,

protest: Formal certification that a negotiable instrument was dishonored by a party liable for its payment.

---

[52]UCC, § 3-509(1).
[53]UCC, § 3-509(1). In the United States, protest is required only in connection with a bill of exchange (draft) "which appears to be drawn or payable outside of . . . the United States." UCC, § 3-501(3).
[54]UCC, § 3-509(2). If the maker or drawee could not be found, this fact can be substituted for the statement of the reason for refusal.

any endorser who receives such a notice must—to maintain his rights against his immediate endorser—notify that person. In the United States, notice has to be given within three business days[55]; in Europe, the requirement is two business days.[56] Any form of notice is sufficient so long as it identifies the instrument and states that the instrument has been dishonored.[57]

Warranty Liability

The most dramatic difference between negotiable instrument law in the United States and in Europe (including the United Kingdom) shows up in connection with warranty liability. In Europe, liability can arise only on the instrument. That is, unless someone signs an instrument, he will have no liability for its payment. In sum, there is no warranty liability.

In the United States, by comparison, any person who transfers an instrument in exchange for consideration—which includes a transferor of bearer paper who does not endorse the instrument—makes five warranties, or implied guarantees, to his immediate transferee and to every subsequent holder who takes the instrument in good faith. These are as follows:

1. The transferor has good title to the instrument or is otherwise authorized to obtain payment or acceptance on behalf of one who does have good title.
2. All signatures are genuine or authorized.
3. The instrument has not been materially altered.
4. No defense of any party is good against the transferor.
5. The transferor has no knowledge of any insolvency proceedings against the maker, the acceptor, or the drawer of an unaccepted instrument.

THE ROLE OF BANKS IN COLLECTING AND PAYING NEGOTIABLE INSTRUMENTS

Banks perform at least four functions in connection with the negotiation of bills and notes. First, they may issue instruments themselves, such as certified checks or certificates of deposit. Second, they may function as the drawee on a bill of exchange or as the acceptor of a bill or promissory note, assuming primary liability for payment. Third, they can act as an agent for a holder or transferee to make collection. Fourth, they can take an instrument as an endorsee, paying the endorser and presenting the instrument for payment in their own right.

The significance of acting as an endorser rather than as an agent for collection—especially in connection with international transactions—is considered in Case 12-5.

---

[55]Banks must give notice within one day. UCC, § 3-508(2).
[56]ULB, Article 44.
[57]UCC, § 3-508(3).

⟞✐⟝

Case 12-5   CHARLES R. ALLEN, INC. v. ISLAND COOPERATIVE SERVICES COOPERATIVE ASSOCIATION

United States, Supreme Court of South Carolina, 1959. *South Carolina Reports*, vol. 234, p. 537 (1959).

Island Cooperative Services Cooperative Association, Ltd. ("Island Coop"), a Canadian corporation, sold some seed potatoes to the Charleston County Wholesale Vegetable Market, Inc. ("Vegetable Market"), of Charleston, South Carolina, for a purchase price of $19,620. After the pota- *toes had been put aboard a ship in Charlottetown, Prince Edward Island, Canada, for shipment to Charleston, South Carolina, Island Coop prepared a draft (or bill of exchange) in the amount of $19,620 on February 7, 1955. Island Coop was the drawer, the Vegetable Market was the drawee, and the Bank of Nova Scotia's branch office at Charlottetown, Prince Edward Island, was the payee.*

Island Coop offered this and several other drafts to the Bank of Nova Scotia at a discount, and the bank agreed to take them. Island Coop delivered the drafts to the Bank of Nova Scotia on February 7, 1955, accompanied by the following agreement:

1. *The above bills, which represent amounts due to us for goods sold and delivered, are offered for discount. Our claims against Drawee are hereby transferred to you in the event of nonacceptance of any draft. The relative goods have already been shipped.*

2. *Credit Proceeds to Current A/C Savings A/C No..*

The Bank of Nova Scotia endorsed the draft drawn on the Vegetable Market and forwarded it through its correspondent, the Bank of New York, to the South Carolina National Bank of Charleston for collection. The Vegetable Market paid the South Carolina Bank the full $19,620 on February 14, 1955.

At the same time that this transaction was going on between Island Coop, the Vegetable Market, and the three banks, Charles R. Allen, Inc. ("Allen"), a South Carolina corporation, brought suit for breach of contract against Island Coop, and won. The judgment Allen received entitled it to attach Island Coop's assets in South Carolina. Allen thereupon attached the $19,620 held in the South Carolina National Bank, claiming it was an asset of Island Coop. The Bank of Nova Scotia disagreed, and it promptly served a claim on Allen, stating that the proceeds of the draft belonged to it.

The trial court held that the Bank of Nova Scotia had taken the draft as an agent for collection and not as a purchaser, and therefore Island Coop had been the owner of the proceeds of the draft. Accordingly, the trial court held that Allen's attachment was proper. The Bank of Nova Scotia appealed.

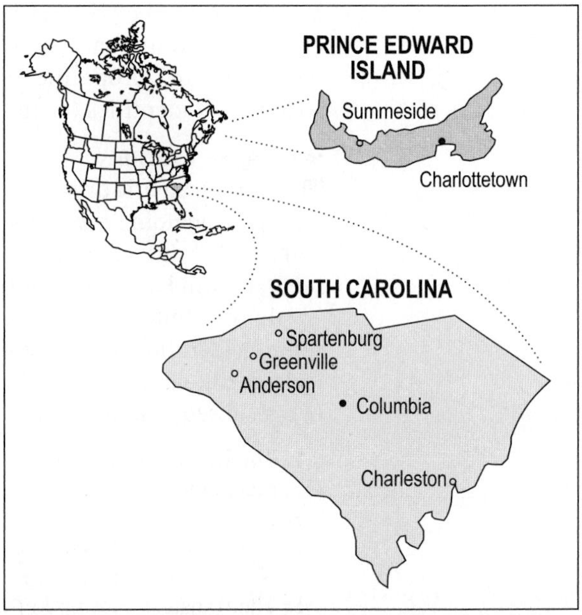

JUSTICE MOSS

***

The basic question for determination in this case is whether the appellant, Bank of Nova Scotia, was the absolute owner of the proceeds of the draft at the time of the attachment of the funds by the respondent. If the appellant was the owner thereof, and Island Coop had no interest therein, then this action must fail. . . .

The appellant, in its claim to the proceeds of the draft here involved, asserted that under the laws of Canada that it had full and complete ownership and title to the draft and the proceeds thereof at the time of the attachment. The law of Canada has been proved to the effect that under the facts of this case surrounding the discount transaction as it took place in Canada, the Bank of Nova Scotia acquired under Canadian law an

MAP 12-5   South Carolina and Prince Edward Island (1959)

absolute title to and ownership of the draft in Canada at the time the draft was discounted on February 7, 1955. A consideration of the law of Canada and of the law of South Carolina, as applicable to factual situation here, leads us to the conclusion that the laws of Canada and South Carolina are in accord. The application of the laws of Canada or South Carolina requires us to reach the same conclusion. We will, therefore, as is contended for by the respondent, apply the law of South Carolina in this case.

It is the contention of the respondent that because the appellant had the right, in the event of nonpayment of the draft in question, to charge the dishonored draft back to the account of the depositor, that such showed that the appellant was a collecting agent and not the owner of the draft in question. This contention is contrary to the rule in this State. Likewise, the collection of interest upon the draft in question did not prevent the bank from becoming the sole owner thereof.

In the case of *Campbell v. Noble-Trotter Rice Milling Co., Inc. (Ex parte Calcasieu-Marine National Bank)* this Court completely answered these contentions when it said[58]:

> According to the prevailing view, the rule as to the passing of title to commercial paper, deposited and credited as cash, applies, although the bank has the right to charge dishonored paper back to the depositor instead of proceeding against the maker.

---

[58]*South Carolina Reports*, vol. 188, p. 212.

And it has been held that an interest arrangement will not prevent a bank from becoming the sole owner of a draft. Thus, where the bank advances the full amount of a draft, it becomes the unconditional owner, though it is understood it will collect interest on the amount advanced, depending upon the time it takes for collection.

***

In the case of *Lawton v. Lower Main Street Bank*, it is said:[59]

... where an item is endorsed without restriction by a depositor, nothing appearing to indicate that it was received for collection, and it is at once passed to his credit by the bank, and he is permitted to check upon the account, he becomes the creditor of the bank, which, as the owner of the paper, is not the agent of the depositor in collecting it but collects on its own behalf. ...

We think that under the authority of the case of *Campbell v. Noble-Trotter Rice Milling Co., Inc.* . . . the lower court must be reversed. The only factual difference between the present case and the *Campbell* case is that in the latter case the bank discounted a draft with a bill of lading attached, while here it discounted the draft only. This factual difference does not make the case inapplicable to the present situation.

In the *Campbell* case it appears that Noble-Trotter Rice Milling Co., Inc., a Louisiana corporation, drew a draft on Allen Bros. Milling Co., Columbia, South Carolina, which represented the purchase price of a shipment of rice. Attached to the draft was a bill of lading covering the shipment, an invoice thereof, and a certificate of insurance. This draft was made payable directly to the Calcasieu-Marine National Bank, located at Lake Charles, Louisiana, and was deposited . . . by the Rice Milling Company in that bank, where it maintained a regular account, and where it had been transacting business for years. The draft, according to the contention of the bank, was not entered for collection, but was treated as cash and was immediately and unconditionally placed to the credit of Rice Milling Co. and made subject to its check.

In due course, the draft, together with attached papers, was forwarded by the bank for collection to the First National Bank, Columbia, South Carolina, where it was paid by the drawee, Allen Bros. Milling Co. The day the draft was paid to the First National Bank of Columbia, South Carolina, the proceeds were attached by one M. P. Campbell for the satisfaction of an unliquidated demand against Noble-Trotter Rice Milling Co. The Louisiana bank intervened, claiming the proceeds of the draft by reason of its ownership thereof. Judgment was

rendered in favor of Campbell and the case was appealed to this Court. The question for decision was whether the bank took the draft as owner thereof or as a mere collecting agent for the customer. This court held that the Louisiana bank was entitled to the proceeds of the draft in question. It was said that the determination of the question of title to commercial paper transferred to a bank, which credits it to the depositor's account, involves a question of intention. The Court then discussed how it may be shown that the bank became the owner of the commercial paper rather than a mere agent for collection, and it was expressly stated that the right accorded to a depositor to draw upon funds is especially material as showing an intention that title should pass to the bank. It was stated that another means of ascertaining the intention is a consideration of course of conduct or the ordinary course of business as disclosed by the evidence. It was also held that where there was a deposit of a draft in the ordinary course of banking business, whereby the depositor received from the bank an unconditional credit of the amount as cash against which the depositor had a right to draw, with nothing to qualify the effect of such act, such operated *prima facie* to transfer title of the draft to the bank.

Applying the rule set forth in *Campbell v. Noble-Trotter Rice Milling Co.* to the evidence in this case, and keeping in mind that the burden of proof was upon the respondent [who was the plaintiff in this case] to show ownership of the draft by Island Coop rather than by the Bank of Nova Scotia, we think that under the evidence the only conclusion that can be reached is that the respondent failed to carry the burden of proof. The evidence in behalf of the appellant is conclusive that it was the owner of the draft in question. Island Coop had been a customer of the appellant for a number of years, and over this period of time the bills of Island Coop had been discounted. The draft in question was handled by the discount department rather than by the collection department of said bank. The bank, upon discounting the draft in question, placed it without restriction and unconditionally to the checking account of Island Coop and accorded to it the right to draw upon the funds, which said right was exercised. There is no evidence contradictory of these facts.

. . . We conclude, after a consideration of all the facts in this case, that under the applicable law thereto, that the title to the draft in question passed to the Bank of Nova Scotia, and that it is entitled to the proceeds now held in the custody of the South Carolina National Bank in Charleston, South Carolina.

***

Judgment reversed. ■

[59]*South Carolina Reports*, vol. 170, p. 334.

CASEPOINT: In this case, the legal question was whether a bank holding a draft was the owner of the instrument or had taken it as an agent for collection. The court held that (1) where there was a deposit of a draft in the ordinary course of banking business such that the depositor got from the bank an unconditional credit of that amount as cash against which the depositor had a right to draw and (2) there was nothing to qualify the effect of such act, the bank had acquired the title of the draft and was the owner and therefore entitled to the proceeds.

G. LETTERS OF CREDIT

Assume that a buyer purchases goods overseas. When must the buyer make payment? The seller, undoubtedly, would prefer to be paid in advance. The buyer, on the other hand, would like to make sure, before paying, that (1) the goods are actually shipped and that (2) the goods shipped meet his contractual specifications; and, in actuality, he would prefer (3) to take delivery before paying.

Depending on the relative bargaining power of the buyer and seller, any of these possible arrangements can be included as a term in the sales contract. If the seller is unable to determine the buyer's creditworthiness, he may insist upon *cash in advance*. If the buyer wants to confirm that the goods have been shipped, the term **documents against payment** can be used. In such a case, the seller agrees to deliver a bill of lading to a bank in the buyer's country so that the buyer can confirm that the goods have been shipped. The bank is then to deliver the bill of lading (which is also title to the goods) to the buyer after the buyer delivers a receipt from the seller acknowledging that the seller has received payment. If the buyer insists upon taking delivery before making payment, a **documents against acceptance** term can be used. In this event, the buyer will instruct a bank in the seller's country to release payment only on the bank's receipt of an acknowledgment of delivery issued by the buyer.

None of these terms are used very often. In part, this is so because they imply that both sides distrust each other. To avoid this, contracting parties use a *letter of credit* (or *documentary credit* or *banker's credit* or, simply, a *credit*).[60]

A **letter of credit** is an instrument issued by a bank, or another person, at the request of a customer (called an **account party**). It is a conditional agreement between the issuer and the account party that is intended to benefit a third party. In accordance with this agreement, the issuer is obliged to pay a bill of exchange drawn by the account party, up to a certain sum of money, within a stated time period, and upon presentation by the **beneficiary** of documents designated by the account party.[61]

The function of the letter of credit in international sales transactions is to substitute the credit of a recognized international bank for that of the buyer. In such an undertaking, the buyer is the account party, the buyer's bank is the issuing bank, and the seller is the beneficiary. Exhibit 12-16 sets out the chronology of a typical letter-of-credit transaction. The mechanics and the reasons for using a letter of credit are described in the following oft-quoted passage of Lord Justice Scrutton from the case of *Guaranty Trust Co. of New York v. Hannay & Co.*[62]

> The enormous volume of sales of produce by a vendor in one country to a purchaser in another has led to the creation of an equally great financial system intervening between vendor and

documents against payment: Term in a sales contract that provides for the seller to deliver shipping documents and title to a bank for release to the buyer after the buyer delivers to the bank a receipt from the seller verifying that the seller has received payment.

documents against acceptance: Term in a sales contract that provides for the buyer to deliver payment to a bank for release to the seller after the seller delivers to the bank a receipt acknowledging that the buyer has accepted the goods.

letter of credit: An instrument issued by a bank or another person at the request of an account party that obliges the issuer to pay to a beneficiary a sum of money within a certain period of time upon the beneficiary's presentation of documents specified by the account party.

account party: The person who requests a bank or some other person to issue a letter of credit.

beneficiary: A person who is not a party to a contract who is designated by a party to receive the benefits of the contract.

---

[60]*Letter of credit* is the term most often used in English-speaking countries. *Documentary credit*, which is a literal translation of the French *crédit documentaire*, and similar terms in other languages, is widely used in the rest of the world. It is the term preferred by the Paris-based ICC.
[61]The ICC's Uniform Customs and Practices for Documentary Credits defines a documentary credit or letter of credit as "any arrangement, however named or described, whereby a bank (the issuing bank) acting at the request and in accordance with the instructions of a customer (the applicant for the credit) (i) is to make a payment to or to the order of a third party (the beneficiary) or is to pay or accept bills of exchange (drafts) drawn by the beneficiary, or (ii) authorizes another bank to effect such payment, or to pay, accept or negotiate such bills of exchange (drafts) against stipulated documents, provided that the terms and conditions of the credit are complied with."
[62]*Law Reports, King's Bench*, vol. 1918, pt. 2, p. 659 (1918).

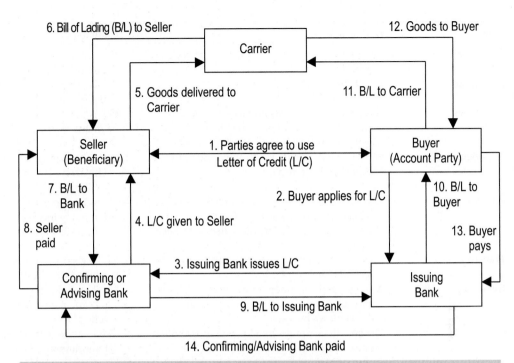

EXHIBIT 12-16   A Typical Letter of Credit Transaction

purchaser, and designed to enable commercial transactions to be carried out with the greatest money convenience to both parties. The vendor, to help the finance of his business, desires to get his purchase price as soon as possible after he has dispatched the goods to his purchaser; with this object he draws a bill of exchange for the price, attaches to the draft the documents of carriage and insurance of the goods sold and sometimes an invoice for the price, and discounts the bill—that is, sells the bill with documents attached to an exchange house.

The vendor thus gets his money before the purchaser would, in the ordinary course, pay; the exchange house duly presents the bill for acceptance, and has, until the bill is accepted, the security of a pledge of the documents attached and the goods they represent. The buyer on the other hand may not desire to pay the price till he has resold the goods. If the draft is drawn on him, the vendor or exchange house may not wish to part with the documents of title until the acceptance given by the purchaser is met at maturity. But if the purchaser can arrange that a bank of high standing shall accept the draft, the exchange house may be willing to part with the documents on receiving the acceptance of the bank. The exchange house will then have the promise of the bank to pay, which, if in the form of a bill of exchange, is negotiable and can be discounted at once. The bank will have the documents of title as security for its liability on the acceptance, and the purchaser can make arrangements to sell and deliver the goods.

Letters of credit exist in a wide variety of forms. The different types of credits are named and defined in Exhibit 12-17. Although they are defined separately, they are not necessarily mutually exclusive. Thus, for example, a letter of credit can be both clean and irrevocable (but not, of course, both revocable and irrevocable).

GOVERNING LAW

Uniform Customs and Practices for Documentary Credit (UCP): Model rules issued by the International Chamber of Commerce for regulating letters of credit.

Virtually all letters of credit are governed by the ICC's **Uniform Customs and Practices for Documentary Credits (UCP).**[63] Although it is neither a treaty nor a legislative enactment, most banks incorporate the UCP in the terms of the credits they issue.

---

[63]1993 Revision, ICC Pub. No. 500 (effective January 1, 1994).

Name	Description	Comments
Irrevocable	Cannot be altered without the beneficiary's express consent.	Preferred by beneficiaries because it provides the most security.
Revocable	Revocable by the issuing bank.	Disliked by beneficiaries because it provides the least security.
Confirmed	A second bank adds its endorsement to the credit, indicating that it too will make payment against the specified documents.	Gives the beneficiary additional assurance that payment will be made.
Negotiable	Permits the designated bills of exchange to be negotiated at any bank.	Only the issuing bank is obliged to pay. However, if another bank pays, it is assured by the issuing bank that it will be reimbursed.
Back to back	The buyer arranges for two credits: one to finance the purchase from the seller; a second, to be used by the seller, to finance a purchase from the seller's supplier.	Helps an exporter who may have difficulty obtaining local financing to make an export sale by facilitating the acquisition of supplies.
Transferable	Permits a beneficiary to transfer the credit to a second beneficiary.	Has the same advantages as a back-to-back credit, but only one credit has to be issued.
Revolving	A standing arrangement in which the buyer is allowed to replenish the credit after it is drawn down by a seller.	Used by large importers with a good credit record who import regularly from the same seller.
Clean	The beneficiary may obtain payment without presenting any documentation.	Used only where the buyer and issuer have a longstanding relationship with the seller.
Standby	A credit obtained by a seller naming the buyer as the beneficiary.	Used as a guarantee that the goods the seller delivers will perform as promised. If they do not, the buyer may return the goods and obtain reimbursement of the purchase price from the bank issuing this credit.
Sight bill	The buyer's bills of exchange will be paid when presented.	The default arrangement.
Time bill	The buyer's bills of exchange will be paid at a specified date or after a specified time.	Gives the buyer time in which to resell the goods before paying the seller.
Deferred payment	The seller agrees not to present a sight bill of exchange until after a specified period after the documents are presented.	Same as a time bill credit, except that the underlying bill is a sight bill.
Red clause	Advances are made to the seller before the seller presents the required documents.	A way to provide the seller with funds prior to shipment. It is beneficial to middlemen and dealers who require prefinancing.

EXHIBIT 12-17 Types of Letters of Credit

Source: Uniform Customs and Practices for Documentary Credits: Model rules issued by the ICC for regulating letters of credit. See information on the new UCP 600, effective July 1, 2007, at: http://www.iccwbo.org/policy/banking.

A few countries do have legislation governing letters of credit. In the United States, for example, Article 5 of the UCC has been adopted in all 50 states. However, even where there is a statute, the UCP can still be made to apply by agreement of the parties. The UCC, again as an example, allows the parties to an agreement, including an agreement creating a letter of credit, to vary the statutory terms.[64]

The UCP gets revised about once every ten years by the ICC. The rules were first published in 1933. Revised versions were issued in 1951, 1962, 1974, 1983, and 1993. A new version, UCP 600, took effect July 1, 2007, replacing UCP 500, which had been in force since 1994. The rules are extremely important, since approximately $1 trillion worth of world

---

[64]UCC, § 1-102(3). Moreover, the legislatures of Alabama, Arizona, Missouri, and New York, have adopted an amendment to the UCC that makes the code ineffective whenever a letter of credit is subject, by its terms (even in part), to the UCP. See, e.g., NY UCC, § 5-102(4).

trade (14 percent of the world's total) changed hands using letters of credit in 2006. UCP 600 went through 15 drafts and involved 9 key members, with a consulting group of 41 members from 26 countries. The new UCP 600 reduces the number of articles from 49 (UCP 500) to 39.

One of the goals of the new revisions is to reduce the *discrepancy rate* of letters of credit—in which there is a difference between the documents mentioned in the letter of credit and those presented to the bank. Although few discrepancies result in nonpayment, there are often delays. One change in the rules is reducing the number of days a bank has to examine the documents from seven banking days to five. Another change in the new UCP rules makes it more difficult to issue a *revocable letter of credit*. This type of letter of credit was used occasionally in the past when the price of the underlying goods sold fluctuated greatly. The new rules require that a *revocable* letter of credit be very clearly specified as such. There are also new articles on *definitions* and *interpretations* providing more clarity in the rules.

Other modifications of the UCP rules include: (1) the word *clean* is not required to appear on a transport document; (2) the addresses of the beneficiary and applicant on the letter of credit do not need to match those on the invoices, since a company may have multiple addresses; (3) inclusion of the 12 articles of the eUCP, the ICC supplement governing the presentation of documents electronically in letter-of-credit transactions; and (4) a definitive description of the negotiation as *purchase* of drafts of documents.[65]

APPLYING FOR A LETTER OF CREDIT

In most cases, a person who needs a letter of credit must apply to a bank with which he has an existing relationship. In all cases, a Letter of Credit Application must be completed (see Exhibit 12-18). The application is not an application for credit, but rather a set of instructions telling the bank—which will be the issuing bank—what needs to be included in the letter of credit.[66] Of course, if the bank has not already extended a line of credit to the applicant, or if the applicant does not have sufficient funds on deposit in the bank to cover the face value of the credit, the bank may refuse to issue the letter.

The instructions the buyer needs to provide on the application include the following:

- The amount of the credit
- Whether the credit is revocable or irrevocable
- Whether the credit is transferable
- Whether the credit is to be made available by payment, deferred payment, acceptance, or negotiation
- How the credit is to be advised
- If there are bills of exchange involved, the party on whom they are drawn
- Details of the documents required as a prerequisite to making payment
- When the documents need to be delivered
- Whether partial shipments are prohibited
- Whether transshipment is prohibited
- The date and place at which the credit will expire

The Consequences of Not Obtaining a Letter of Credit

When a buyer and seller enter into a contract and the buyer agrees to obtain a letter of credit (or a seller agrees to obtain a standby letter of credit), the consequences of failure to do so depend on whether the letter was (1) a condition precedent to the formation of the contract or (2) a condition for the performance of the contract. In the first case, there will be no contract and consequently no breach. In the second, because the contract already exists, the

---

[65]*New Rules Ahead for Letters of Credit,* Business Credit, March 2007, p. 56; for further information on the new UCP 600, see also the ICC site at http://www.iccwbo.org/policy/banking/iccjjdi/index.html.
[66]Although the account party and the issuing bank will be parties to a contract, the applicant is not required to pay any consideration for the issuance, or even the modification, of a letter of credit. See UCC, § 5-105.

Applicant	Issuing Bank
The Importer, Ltd. **76 Fleet Street** **London, England**	**IMPORTERS BANK, PLC** **Lnd Branch, 13 Trenton** **Mews** **London, England**

Date of Application: **1 June 2008**	Date and place of expiration of the credit: **14 July 2008** **Buenos Aires, Argentina**
[X] Issue by (air) mail [ ] Issue by air mail with brief advice by telegram or other written communication [ ] Issue by telegram or other written communication (which shall be the operative credit instrument) [ ] Transferable credit	Beneficiary **Compañía de Exportes, S.A.** **203 Avenida de las** **Americas** **Buenos Aires, Argentina**
Confirmation of the credit to the beneficiary [X] Not requested [ ] Requested	Amount **£18,500 (eighteen thousand** **five hundred pounds** **sterling)**
[ ] Insurance will be covered by the applicant	
Partial Shipment [ ] Allowed [X] Not Allowed Transshipments [ ] Allowed [X] Not Allowed	Credit available with
Shipment/Dispatch/Delivery to **Buenos Aires** not later than **7 July 2008 for** **transportation to London**	by [ ] sight payment [X] acceptance [ ] negotiation [ ] deferred payment at against the documents detailed here [X] and beneficiary's draft at **sight** on **yourselves**
Goods (brief description without excessive detail) **10,000 pairs of woolen** **mittens @ £ 1.85/pair**	[ ] FOB [X] CIF **London** [ ] C&F [ ] Other terms

Commercial invoice and three (3) copies.
Full set of clean on board bills of lading to order and blank endorsed, marked Freight Paid and Notify The Importer, Ltd., 76 Fleet Street, London, England.
Insurance and certificate for invoice value plus 10% covering marine and war risks and including all risks.
Certificates of Origin issued by a Chamber of Commerce in three (3) copies evidencing that the goods are of Argentine origin.
Packing lists in three (3) copies.

Documents to be presented within **7** days after date of issuance of the transport documents but within the validity of the credit.

Additional conditions

We request you to issue your IRREVOCABLE letter of credit for our account in accordance with the above instructions (marked with an X where appropriate). The credit shall be subject to the Uniform Customs and Practices for Documentary Credit (1993 Revision, Publication No. 500 of the International Chamber of Commerce, Paris, France), insofar as they are applicable. We authorize you to debit our account.

for The Importer, Ltd.

No. 994578-213

Treasurer
Name stamp and authorized signature of the applicant

EXHIBIT 12-18 Letter of Credit Application

failure to obtain a letter of credit will be a breach that will entitle the injured party to sue for damages.

Lord Justice Denning examined the legal consequences that can flow from an ill-defined agreement to obtain a letter of credit in Case 12-6.

═══════

Case 12-6 TRANS TRUST SPRL v. DANUBIAN TRADING CO., LTD.

United Kingdom, England, Court of Appeal, 1952.
All England Law Reports, vol. 1952, pt. 1, p. 970 (1952).

In September 1950, a British seller agreed to sell 1,000 tons of rolled steel sheets to a Belgian buyer for a price of 8,025 Belgian francs per 1,000 kilos and to deliver them FOB Antwerp in December 1950. To be able to carry out the contract, the British seller had arranged to buy the steel from an American company, S.A. Azur, which was a wholesaler for the manufacturer, S.A. Metallurgique d'Esperance Londoz.

The seller understood that the buyer was to arrange for a confirmed letter of credit with the Krediet Bank in Brussels, made out in favor of S.A. Azur, which would require the bank to pay cash upon the presentation of shipping documents. The buyer, however, did not arrange for the letter of credit and, when prompted to do so by the seller, sent the seller a letter on October 16, 1950, refusing to do so. The seller then sued the buyer, alleging that the contract it had with the buyer required the buyer to arrange for a letter to be opened and confirmed immediately, and that the buyer's failure to do so constituted a breach of contract. The buyer answered that the contract was conditional on a letter of credit being provided and that, if no such letter was provided, no obligation was to be assumed by the buyer.

The trial judge held that there had been a binding agreement between the parties, that a term of that agreement was that the buyer would see that a credit was opened immediately, and that the buyer was in breach of that agreement. The judge awarded the seller £3,214 5s. 8d. damages, which was the loss of profit suffered by the seller based on the difference between the price at which the seller had agreed to buy from S.A. Azur and the price it would have received had the contract been performed.

LORD JUSTICE DENNING

This is another case concerned with the modern practice whereby a buyer agrees to provide a banker's confirmed credit in favor of the seller. This credit is an irrevocable promise by a banker to pay money to the seller in return for the shipping documents. One reason for this practice is because the seller wishes to be assured in advance, not only that the buyer is in earnest, but also that he, the seller, will get his money when he delivers the goods. Another reason is because the seller often has expenses to pay in connection with the goods and he wishes to use the credit to pay those expenses. He may, for instance, be himself a merchant, who is buying the goods from the growers or the manufacturers and has to pay for them before he can get delivery, and his own bank may only grant him facilities for the purpose if he has the backing of a letter of credit. The ability of the seller to carry out the transaction is, therefore, dependent on the buyer providing the letter

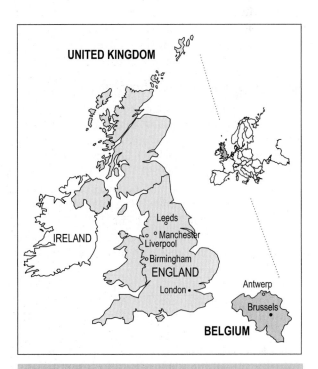

MAP 12-6 United Kingdom and Belgium (1950)

of credit, and for this reason the seller stipulates that the credit should be provided at a specified time well in advance of the time for delivery of the goods.

What is the legal position of such a stipulation? (1) Sometimes it is a condition precedent to the formation of a contract, that is, it is a condition which must be fulfilled before any contract is concluded at all. In those cases the stipulation "subject to the opening of a letter of credit" is rather like a stipulation "subject to contract." If no credit is provided, there is no contract between the parties. (2) In other cases a contract is concluded and the stipulation for a credit is a condition which is an essential term of the contract. In those cases the provision of the credit is a condition precedent, not to the formation of a contract, but to the obligation of the seller to deliver the goods. If the buyer fails to provide the credit, the seller can treat himself as discharged from any further performance of the contract and can sue the buyer for damages for not providing the credit.

The first question is: What was the nature of the stipulation in this case? When the buyers sent their order, they stated in writing on Sept. 25, 1950, that "a credit will be opened forthwith." It was suggested that the buyers were not making any firm promise on their own account, but were only passing on information which had been given to them by their American buyers. The judge did not accept that suggestion and I agree with him. The statement was a firm promise by the buyers by which they gave their personal assurance that a credit would be opened forthwith. At that time there were some discrepancies about gauges and dates of delivery which had to be cleared up, but these were all resolved at the meetings in Brussels, and there was then, as the judge found, a concluded contract by the sellers to sell, and the buyers to buy, the steel for December/January delivery, and it was a part of that contract that the buyers would be personally responsible for seeing that a credit should be opened forthwith. On those findings it is clear that the stipulation for a credit was not a condition precedent to the formation of any contract at all. It was a condition which was an essential term of a contract actually made. That condition was not fulfilled. The sellers extended the time for the credit, but it never came, not even after reasonable notice. The sellers were, therefore, discharged from any further performance on their side, and are entitled to claim damages.

But what is the measure of damages? That is the important question in the case. The price of the goods had steadily risen from the date of the contract onwards and the buyers say that the sellers could at any time have resold the goods for more than the contract price, and are, therefore, only entitled to nominal damages. If the claim of the sellers had been for damages for nonacceptance of goods or for repudiation of the obligation to take delivery, then the damages would, no doubt, be nominal. But it is none of those things. It is a claim for damages for not providing a letter of credit. The buyers say that, even so, the credit is only a way of paying the price, and that the damages recoverable on that score are only nominal because the seller could resell the goods at a profit. This argument . . . treats the obligation to provide a credit as the same thing as the obligation to pay the price. That is, I think, a mistake. A banker's confirmed credit is a different thing from payment. It is an assurance in advance that the seller will get paid. It is even more than that. It is a chose in action[67] which is of immediate benefit to the seller. It is irrevocably by the banker, and it is often expressly made transferable by the seller. The seller may be relying on it to get the goods himself. If it is not provided, the seller may be prevented from getting the goods at all. The damages he will then suffer will not, in fact, be nominal. Even if the market price of the goods has risen, he will not be able to take advantage of the rise because he will not have any goods to re-sell. His loss will be the profit which he would have made if the credit had been provided. Is he entitled to recover that loss? I think he is, if he can show that such a loss was at the time of the contract foreseeable by the buyer as the probable consequence of a breach. That was clearly the case here. The buyers knew that the sellers could not get the goods at all unless the credit was provided. The foreseeable loss was the loss of profit, no matter whether the market price of the goods went up or down. It is, therefore, the proper measure of damages. ■

CASEPOINT: The parties had a contract for the sale of goods, which included a promise by the buyer to furnish a letter of credit forthwith. The buyer never did arrange for a letter of credit, and the goods were never delivered. Now the seller has sued for damages for loss of profits. The court stated that some letters of credit were part of the contract, while others were "precedent" to the making of the contract. Here, clearly the seller was depending on the letter of credit as an essential part of the agreed-upon contract, and thus the breach of this obligation will require payment of damages by the buyer.

---

[67]*Chose* is French for "a thing." A *chose in action* is a "thing in action." It is the right to bring an action, or suit, in a court of law to procure the return of a thing or the payment of a sum of money.

DOCUMENTARY FORMALITIES

Although a letter of credit does not have to be in any particular form, it does need to be (1) in writing, (2) signed by the issuer, and (3) complete and precise.[68] A credit must also clearly indicate if it is irrevocable. Should there be any doubt, the credit will be interpreted as being revocable.[69] An example of an irrevocable letter of credit is shown in Exhibit 12-19.

Letters of credit must additionally indicate clearly when and how they are to be paid. That is, they must "clearly indicate whether they are available by sight payment, by deferred payment, by acceptance, or by negotiation."[70] Finally, they must name the bank that is authorized to pay the credit, or to accept bills of exchange drawn in accordance with the letter, or to negotiate the credit.[71]

ADVISING AND CONFIRMING LETTERS OF CREDIT

advising bank: A bank engaged by the issuer of a letter of credit to advise the beneficiary that it has a credit for delivery and to deliver the credit upon verification of the beneficiary's signature.

confirming bank: A bank that makes an independent promise to pay, accept, or negotiate a letter of credit issued by another bank when the documents named in the credit are delivered to it.

Once a bank issues a letter of credit, it will commonly deliver the credit to a correspondent bank located in the beneficiary's county, which will in turn deliver the credit to the beneficiary. The correspondent, formally known as an **advising bank**, assumes no liability for paying the letter of credit. Its only obligation is to the issuing bank, to ensure that the beneficiary is advised and the credit delivered, and to take "reasonable care to check the apparent authenticity of the credit."[72] It does this by comparing the signature on the credit with the authorized signatures it maintains on file.

An issuing bank may also request another bank to confirm an irrevocable letter of credit. A confirmation is an independent promise by a **confirming bank** that it will pay, accept, or negotiate a credit, as appropriate, when the documents specified in the credit are presented to it and the other terms and conditions of the credit have been complied with.[73] An example of a confirmation is shown in Exhibit 12-20.

A confirming bank is entitled to reimbursement from the issuing bank if the documents it receives are in order. If they are not, the confirming bank will be left with title to the goods in its own name, and it will have to assume the risk of liquidating them as best it can. A confirming bank also assumes the risk that the issuing bank or the account party may be unable to reimburse it. Again, it would retain title to the goods, so its losses may be partly offset by whatever price it gets from the sale of the goods.

THE OBLIGATIONS OF BANKS

An issuing bank, or any bank that pays, accepts, or negotiates a letter of credit, is obliged to "examine all documents with reasonable care to ascertain that they appear on their face in accordance with the terms and conditions of the credit."[74] If a paying, accepting, or negotiating bank believes the documents are irregular, it is required to pass them along to the issuing bank for the latter to determine whether it will honor or refuse them. The issuing bank must do so "on the basis of the documents alone."[75]

---

[68]UCC, § 5-104 provides:

"(1) Except as otherwise required in subsection (1)(c) of Section 5-102 on scope, no particular form of phrasing is required for a credit. A credit must be in writing and signed by the issuer and a confirmation must be in writing and signed by the confirming bank. A modification of the terms of a credit or confirmation must be signed by the issuer or confirming bank.

(2) A telegram may be a sufficient signed writing if it identifies its sender by an authorized authentication. The authentication may be in code and the authorized naming of the issuer in an advice of credit is a sufficient signing."
[69]UCP, Article 7 states: (a) Credits may be either [i] revocable, or [ii] irrevocable. (b) All credits, therefore, should clearly indicate whether they are revocable or irrevocable. (c) In the absence of such indication the credit shall be deemed to be revocable.
[70]*Id.*, Article 11(a).
[71]*Id.*, Article 11(b).
[72]*Id.*, Article 8.
[73]*Id.*
[74]*Id.*, Article 15.
[75]*Id.*, Article 16(b).

IRREVOCABLE LETTER OF CREDIT Number 07889	Issuing Bank IMPORTERS BANK PLC London Branch, 13 Trenton Mews London WC1, England
Place and date of issue **London, 15 June 2008**	Beneficiary **Compañía de Exportes, S.A. 203 Avenida de las Americas Buenos Aires, 1109 Argentina**
Date and place of expiration of the credit **London, 14 July 2008, at the counters of the advising bank**	
Applicant **The Importer, Ltd. 76 Fleet Street London, England**	Amount **£18,500 (eighteen thousand five hundred pounds sterling)** [ ] Insurance will be covered by applicant
Advising Bank **Banco del Sur 47 Calle Corto Buenos Aires 1117 Argentina**	Credit available with by [ ] sight payment [X] acceptance [ ] negotiation [ ] deferred payment at against the documents detailed here
Partial Shipment [ ] Allowed [X] Not Allowed Transshipments [ ] Allowed [X] Not Allowed	

Shipment/Dispatch/Taking in charge from/at
Buenos Aires
for transportation to:
London
	[X] and beneficiary's draft at **sight**
	on **Banco del Sur
	        47 Calle Corto, Buenos
	        Aires, 1117 Argentina**

SIGNED INVOICE IN THREE (3) COPIES certifying that the goods are in accordance with The Importer, Ltd.'s Order No. 0791 of 22 May 2008.

FULL SET OF CLEAN ON BOARD BILLS OF LADING to order and blank endorsed, marked Freight Paid and Notify The Importer, Ltd., 76 Fleet Street, London, England.

INSURANCE AND CERTIFICATE for invoice value plus 10% covering marine and war risks and including all risks.

CERTIFICATES OF ORIGIN issued by a Chamber of Commerce in three (3) copies evidencing that the goods are of Argentine origin.

Packing lists in TRIPLICATE.
covering woolen mittens, CIF, London.

Documents to be presented within   **7**   days after date of issuance of the transport documents but within the validity of the credit.

Additional conditions

We hereby issue this IRREVOCABLE letter of credit in your favor. It is subject to the Uniform Customs and Practices for Documentary Credit (1993 Revision, Publication No. 500 of the International Chamber of Commerce, Paris, France), insofar as they are applicable. The number and state of the credit and the name of our bank must be quoted in all drafts requested if the credit is available by negotiation, each presentation must be noted on the reverse of this advice by the bank where the credit is available.

IMPORTERS BANK PLC
London Branch

This document consist of **1** signed page(s)

EXHIBIT 12-19 An Irrevocable Letter of Credit

Notification of IRREVOCABLE LETTER OF CREDIT	Advising Bank Number **07889** **BANCO DEL SUR** 47 Calle Corto Buenos Aires, 1117 Argentina
Issuing Bank **Importers Bank, Plc.** **London Branch** **13 Trenton Mews** **London, England**	Reference Number of Advising Bank **1534**
	Place and date of notification **Buenos Aires, 17 June 2008**
Reference Number of Issuing Bank **07889**	Amount **£18,500 (eighteen** **thousand five hundred pounds** **sterling)**
Applicant **The Importer, Ltd.** **76 Fleet Street** **London, England**	Beneficiary **Compañía de Exportes, S.A.** **203 Avenida de las Americas** **Buenos Aires, Argentina**

We have been informed by our correspondent (the issuing bank above) that the letter of credit described above has been issued in your favor. Please find enclosed the advice intended for you.

PLEASE CHECK THE CREDIT TERMS CAREFULLY. If you do not agree with the terms and conditions or if you feel that you are unable to comply with any of the terms and conditions, please ARRANGE AN AMENDMENT OF THE CREDIT THROUGH YOUR CONTRACTING PARTY (the applicant for the credit).

[ ] This notification and the enclosed advice are sent to you without engagement on our part.
[**X**] As requested by our correspondent, we hereby confirm the credit described above.

BANCO DEL SUR

EXHIBIT 12-20   Confirmation of an Irrevocable Letter of Credit

One should note that the issuing bank's obligations only relate to the appearance of the documents. So long as the documents appear regular on their face, the bank must pay. A bank is not to concern itself with matters "off the document," such as the condition of the goods or even their existence.[76] This was emphasized in *Maurice O'Meara Co. v. National Park Bank of New York.* In that case, the issuing bank refused to pay on a letter of credit because it said that it had a reasonable doubt about the quality of the goods (newspaper print) involved. The seller, who was forced to sell the goods at a loss, sued the bank. In its decision in favor of the seller, the court said:[77]

> [The letter of credit] . . . was in no way involved in or connected with, other than the presentation of the documents, the contract for the purchase and sale of the paper mentioned. That was a contract between buyer and seller, which in no way concerned the bank. The bank's obligation was to pay sight drafts when presented if accompanied by genuine documents specified in the letter of credit. If the paper when delivered did not correspond to what had been purchased, either in weight, kind, or quality, then the purchaser had his remedy against the seller for damages. . . . The bank was concerned only in the drafts and the documents accompanying them. This was the extent of its interest. If the drafts, when presented, were accompanied by the proper documents, then it was absolutely bound to make the payment under the letter of credit, irrespective of whether it knew, or had reason to believe, that the paper was not of the tensile strength contracted for. . . . It has never been held, so far as I am able to discover, that a bank has the right or is under an obligation to see that the description of the merchandise contained in the documents presented is correct.

The Rule of Strict Compliance

rule of strict compliance:
A bank may reject a document submitted by a beneficiary seeking to obtain payment on a letter of credit when the document does not exactly comply with the description stated in the credit.

In determining whether the documents submitted by the beneficiary are in order, a bank is entitled to apply the so-called **rule of strict compliance**. In other words, a bank may reject documents that do not exactly comply with the terms specified in the letter of credit. For example, in the case of *Moralice (London), Ltd. v. E. D. and F. Man*, an English court held that an issuing bank had properly refused to pay on a letter of credit involving the shipment of 5,000 bags when the bill of lading the seller presented indicated that only 4,997 bags had been shipped.[78] Similarly, an American court, in the case of *Beyene v. Irving Trust Co.,* held that the misspelled name ("Soran" instead of "Sofan") of the person entitled to notice of the arrival of the goods being shipped was a material discrepancy that relieved a confirming bank from its duty to honor a letter of credit.[79]

Amendments

Discrepancies can come about in documents in a wide variety of ways, including typographical errors and simple mistakes. In cases where only a minor discrepancy exists, banks will commonly obtain a written waiver from the account party. The new UCP 600 rules (2007) issued by the ICC attempt to prevent minor discrepancies from causing major problems with letters of credit. If there is a major discrepancy or if the seller is unable to perform as originally agreed, the letter of credit can be amended. Amendments, however, require the approval of the issuing bank, the confirming bank (if there is one), and the beneficiary.[80]

---

[76]*Id.*, Article 17 provides: "Banks assume no liability or responsibility for the form, sufficiency, accuracy, genuineness, falsification, or legal effect of any documents, or for the general and/or particular conditions stipulated in the documents or superimposed thereon; nor do they assume any liability or responsibility for the description, quantity, condition, packing, delivery, value, or existence of the goods represented by any documents, or for the good faith or acts and/or omissions, solvency, performance, or standing of the consignor, the carriers, or the insurers of the goods, or any other person whomsoever."

[77]*New York Reports*, vol. 239, p. 386 (1925).

[78]*Lloyd's Reports*, vol. 2, p. 533 (1954).

[79]*Federal Reporter, Second Series*, vol. 762, p. 4 (2nd Circuit Ct. of Appeals, 1985).

[80]UCP, Article 10(d).

Waiver

Should an issuing bank be notified of a discrepancy, it has "a reasonable time in which to examine the documents and to determine . . . whether to take up or to refuse the documents."[81] The new UCP 600 rules provide that if the bank fails to act in a timely fashion or if it fails to return the documents to the person who presented them, "it is precluded from claiming that the documents are not in accordance with the terms and conditions of the credit."[82] In other words, failure to act is tantamount to an implied waiver.

Fraud

fraud: A knowing misrepresentation made with intent of causing another to rely upon it to the latter's detriment.

Suppose that a bank is aware that the seller has perpetrated a **fraud** on the buyer. For example, suppose that a seller delivers mislabeled goods to a carrier to obtain the documents it needs to collect against a letter of credit. The documents themselves are obviously genuine. May the issuing bank pay the seller if it knows of this fraud? The answer is yes. The UCP states that "banks assume no liability or responsibility for the form, sufficiency, accuracy, genuineness, falsification or legal effect of any documents."[83]

The harder question is: May the bank refuse to pay on the credit when the underlying transaction is fraudulent? If the letter of credit is revocable, the answer is obviously yes. If the credit is irrevocable, the answer seems to be no. The UCP states that the obligation to pay on an irrevocable letter of credit "constitutes a definite undertaking of the issuing bank, provided that the stipulated documents are presented and the terms and conditions of the credit are complied with."[84] The UCP also states that "credits, by their nature, are separate transactions from the sales or other contracts on which they may be based and banks are in no way concerned with or bound by such contracts."[85] Read together, these two provisions suggest that the issuing bank must pay, regardless of any underlying fraud.

The suggestion in the UCP is supported by case law. In the case of *Discount Records, Ltd. v. Barclays Bank, Ltd.*, an English court was asked to enjoin payment of an irrevocable credit on an allegation of fraud. Judge Megarry refused, observing: "I would be slow to interfere with bankers' irrevocable credits, and not least in the sphere of international banking, unless a sufficiently good cause is shown; for interventions by the court that are too ready or too frequent might gravely impair the reliance which, quite properly, is placed on such credits."[86]

Nonetheless, Judge Megarry's decision and the UCP leave open the possibility that a court may intervene in exceptionally grievous circumstances. Case 12-7 is a famous example of just such a case.[87]

---

[81]*Id.*, Article 16(c).

[82]*Id.*, Article 16(e).

[83]*Id.*, Article 17.

[84]*Id.*, Article 10(a). The UCC takes a slightly different stand. UCC, § 5-114(2), provides: "Unless otherwise agreed when documents appear on their face to comply with the terms of a credit but a required document does not in fact conform to the warranties made on negotiation or transfer of a document of title (Section 7-507) or of a certificated security (Section 8-306) or is forged or fraudulent or there is fraud in the transaction:

(a) the issuer must honor the draft or demand for payment if honor is demanded by a negotiating bank or other holder of the draft or demand which has taken the draft or demand under the credit and under circumstances which would make it a holder in due course (Section 3-302) and in an appropriate case would make it a person to whom a document of title has been duly negotiated (Section 7-502) or a bona fide purchaser of a certificated security (Section 8-302); and (b) in all other cases as against its customer, an issuer acting in good faith may honor the draft or demand for payment despite notification from the customer of fraud, forgery, or other defect not apparent on the face of the documents but a court of appropriate jurisdiction may enjoin such honor."

It should be noted, however, that courts have hardly ever actually enjoined honor using this provision.[85] UCP, Article 3. Similarly, Article 4 provides: "In credit operations all parties concerned deal in documents, and not in goods, services and/or other performances to which the documents relate.

[85]UCP, Article 3. Similarly, Article 4 provides: "In credit operations all parties concerned deal in documents, and not in goods, services and/or other performances to which the documents relate."

[86]*All England Law Reports*, vol. 1975, pt. 1, p. 1075 (Chancery Division, 1974).

[87]A case examining the spread of the rule suggested in Discount Records, Ltd. v. Barclays Bank, Ltd. and set out in Sztejn v. J. Henry Schroeder Banking Corp. to most English-speaking jurisdiction is The Inflatable Toy Co. Pty Ltd. v. State Bank of New South Wales, *New South Wales Unreported Judgments* (1998), BC9405157 (Supreme Ct. of New South Wales, Equity Division, 1994).

Case 12-7 SZTEJN v. J. HENRY SCHROEDER BANKING CORP.

United States, New York County Supreme Court, Special Term, 1941.

New York Supplement, Second Series, vol. 31, p. 631 (1941).

Transea Traders in India contracted to sell hog bristles to Sztejn, the plaintiff. At the request of Sztejn, the J. Henry Schroeder Banking Corp. (Schroeder), the defendant, issued an irrevocable letter of credit in favor of Transea covering the shipment of the hog bristles and payable upon presentation of certain documents, including a maritime bill of lading. Transea allegedly filled 50 cases with cow hair and other rubbish and delivered these to the carrier in order to obtain the required bill of lading. This bill, along with the other required documents, and a draft payable to Transea, were presented to Schroeder by the Chartered Bank of India, acting as an agent for Transea. Before Schroeder could pay on the credit, Sztejn brought this action against Schroeder to enjoin it from doing so. Schroeder asked the court to dismiss the case.

JUSTICE SHIENTAG

One of the chief purposes of the letter of credit is to furnish the seller with a ready means of obtaining prompt payment for his merchandise. It would be most unfortunate interference with business transactions if a bank before honoring drafts drawn upon it was obliged or even allowed to go behind the documents, at the request of the buyer, and enter into controversies between the buyer and the seller regarding the quality of the merchandise shipped.... Of course, the application of this doctrine presupposes that the documents accompanying the draft are genuine and conform in terms to the requirements of the letter of credit.

However, I believe that a different situation is presented in the instant action. This is not a controversy between the buyer and seller concerning a mere breach of warranty regarding the quality of the merchandise; on the present motion, it must be assumed that the seller has intentionally failed to ship any goods ordered by the buyer. In such a situation, where the seller's fraud has been called to the bank's attention before the drafts and documents have been presented for payment, the principle of independence of the bank's obligations under the letter of credit should not be extended to protect the unscrupulous seller. It is true that even though the docu-

ments are forged or fraudulent, if the issuing bank has already paid the draft before receiving notice of the seller's fraud, it will be protected if it exercised reasonable diligence before making such payment. However, in the instant action Schroeder has received notice of Transea's active fraud before it accepted or paid the draft....

Although our courts have used broad language to the effect that a letter of credit is independent of the primary contract between the seller and buyer, that language was used in cases concerning alleged breaches of warranty; no case has been brought to my attention on this point involving an intentional fraud on the part of the seller which was brought to the bank's notice with the request that it withhold payment of the draft on this account. The distinction between a breach of warranty and active fraud on the part of the seller is supported by authority and reason. As one court has stated: "Obviously, when the issuer of a letter of credit knows that a document, although correct in form, is, in point of fact, false or illegal, he cannot be called upon to recognize

MAP 12-7 India (1941)

such a document as complying with the terms of a letter of credit.". . .

While the primary factor in the issuance of the letter of credit is the credit standing of the buyer, the security afforded by the merchandise is also taken into account. In fact, the letter of credit requires a bill of lading made out to the order of the bank and not the buyer. Although the bank is not interested in the exact detailed performance of the sales contract, it is vitally interested in assuring itself that there are some goods represented by the documents.

Accordingly, the defendant's motion to dismiss . . . is denied. ■

CASEPOINT: As has been explained in the previous section of this chapter, letters of credit are designed to facilitate payment in sales of goods transactions without requiring the bank to determine if the correct goods were delivered on time and at the right place. Normally, if the documents are prepared and delivered in correct form, the letter of credit must be honored and paid by all. However, in the extremely rare case such as this one–where the bank knows before it has accepted or paid the draft that the seller has engaged in deliberate fraud—the bank might be enjoined from honoring the letter of credit.

Fraud in the Collection Process

In addition to the buyer, a collecting bank may also perpetrate fraud. To illustrate: X Company agrees to sell a large number of widgets to Y Corp., and Y Corp. arranges for Bank I to issue a letter of credit that requires X Company to present a bill of lading as a prerequisite to being paid. X Company is not able to deliver all of the widgets ordered, and it has to alter the bill of lading in order for the bill to comply with the requirements of the letter of credit. X Company takes the letter of credit and the bill of lading to Bank C. X Company is a longtime customer of Bank C, and X Company owes Bank C substantial sums. Bank C realizes that if X Company does not collect on the letter of credit, X will be bankrupt and unable to pay any of its obligations. Bank C agrees to pay the letter of credit, even though it knows that X altered the bill of lading. But it does so only if X will agree to use the money to first pay off the loans it has from Bank C. X Company agrees. Bank C pays, and X turns over the letter of credit and the bill of lading. Bank C, in turn, forwards the credit and the bill to Bank I, demanding to be reimbursed. In the case of *Pubali Bank v. City National Bank*, which involved a similar (but more complex) set of facts, the court held that the issuing bank did not have to pay. The court said that because the paying bank had participated in the fraud, it could "not hide behind the cloak" of a neutral collecting bank. The paying bank was therefore liable for the money it had paid out.[88]

RIGHTS AND RESPONSIBILITIES OF THE ACCOUNT PARTY

The account party's rights and obligations are based on two contracts: the underlying contract with the beneficiary (usually the seller) and the contract with the issuing bank relating to the letter of credit. Ordinary contract law determines the account party's rights under the first contract. International practice limits the account party's rights under the second contract.

The main limitation on an account party's rights under the contract with the issuing bank is the doctrine of privity. That is, because the account party is in privity (i.e., in a contractual relationship) only with the issuing bank, it can look only to the issuing bank for performance. In other words, it has no right to bring an action against the advising or confirming banks based on their contract with the issuing bank.

To illustrate, in the case of *Auto Servicio San Ignacio v. Compañía Anonima Venezolana de Navigación*, an account party sued a confirming bank for its negligence in failing to verify the authenticity of a bill of lading containing misleading information and in honoring the related letter of credit. Judge Schwarz dismissed the complaint, observing that the confirming bank owed a duty only to its customer, the issuing bank, and not to the issuing bank's customer, the account party, even though that party was involved in the underlying contract.[89]

---

[88] *Federal Reporter, Second Series*, vol. 676, p. 1326 (Ninth Circuit Ct. of Appeals, 1982).

RIGHTS AND RESPONSIBILITIES OF BENEFICIARIES

The right of beneficiaries to collect on letters of credit is based not on contract, but on commercial practice. This is important, because it means that the beneficiary has no subsidiary contractual rights with respect to the letter-of-credit transaction. UCP, Article 6, puts it plainly: "A beneficiary can in no case avail himself of the contractual relationships existing between the banks or between the applicant for credit and the issuing bank."

Before a beneficiary is entitled to collect on a letter of credit, he must comply with the terms and conditions of the credit and present to the issuer (or the issuer's agent) the documents designated in the credit.[90] Commonly, these include

* a certificate of origin—to comply with customs requirements;
* an export license and/or a health inspection certificate—to show that the goods are approved for export;
* a certificate of inspection—to show that all of the goods have been shipped;
* a commercial invoice—to identify the shipment;
* a bill of lading—to show title to the goods; and
* a marine insurance policy.

As soon as a letter of credit is delivered to a beneficiary for advisement, he needs to examine it carefully to make sure that it reflects the underlying agreement he has with the account party. Changes can be made by amendment, but they need to be made promptly.[91]

Standby Letters of Credit

standby letter of credit: A letter of credit obtained by a buyer naming the seller as a beneficiary.

To ensure that a seller will perform, a buyer can insist that the seller procure a **standby letter of credit**. Standby credits are most commonly used in situations where the seller is delivering a product that the buyer needs time to evaluate, such as a stand-alone factory or a computer installation. If the goods delivered do not perform as promised, the buyer may be left in the awkward position of absorbing the loss or suing the seller. To avoid this, the buyer may insist that the seller arrange for an irrevocable credit, one that will reimburse the buyer in the event that the goods do not perform.

H. FINANCING FOREIGN OPERATIONS

Multinational enterprises cannot always generate internally all of the funds they need for capital investment and operating expenses. To expand, to avoid cash flow problems, and for a variety of other reasons, they have to turn to the world's capital markets, and to governmental and intergovernmental investment and development programs.

PRIVATE SOURCES OF CAPITAL

equity funding: Investments in the capital of a company.

debt funding: Loans to a person or company.

As we discussed in Chapter 6, both equity and debt funding are available from the private sector to finance the operations of multinational ventures. **Equity funding** is generally available from stock exchanges, although it is not uncommon, especially for smaller firms, to raise funds privately. **Debt funding** is available in the multinational enterprise's home country, in its host countries, and now, more commonly, in a large number of so-called *capital-exporting* countries.[92]

GOVERNMENTAL SOURCES OF CAPITAL

Both host and home governments provide capital for foreign investors.

---

[89] *Federal Supplement*, vol. 586, p. 259 (Dist. Ct. for E. Dist. of Louisiana, 1984).
[90] UCP, Article 10(a).
[91] *Id.*, Article 10(d).
[92] WorldHot.com maintains links to 100 international capital venturers at
http://www.worldhot.com/business/venturecapital.

Host Country Development Banks and Government Agencies

As discussed in Chapter 5, virtually every country—including less developed and developing nations—has an established bureaucracy that promotes local investment. Many have development banks that provide low-interest-rate, long-term loans to foreign investors. Morocco's Banque Nationale pour le Development Economique and Greece's National Investment Bank for Industrial Development are just two examples.

Information about investment opportunities in host countries is available from their embassies and consulates. A current list of embassies and consulates can be found in the *Europa Encyclopedia*. Most embassies and consulates also have Web sites.[93]

Home Country Import and Export Financing Agencies

Virtually every developed country has a variety of agencies that finance imports and exports. In the United States, for example, the U.S. Agency for International Development (AID) lends money directly to foreign governments to finance purchases from American exporters. As discussed in Chapter 2, the U.S. Overseas Private Investment Corporation (OPIC) provides loans, loan guarantees, and insurance to American firms to underwrite activities in developing countries. The U.S. Export-Import Bank promotes international trade by making loans to both American importers and foreign exporters.[94] And the U.S. Small Business Administration provides loans to American exporters.[95]

U.S. Export-Import Bank Website
http://www.exim.gov.

U.S. Small Business Administration Web site
http://www.sba.gov.

REGIONAL AND INTERNATIONAL DEVELOPMENT AGENCIES

A number of regional development agencies promote investment within their regions. The African Development Bank,[96] the Asian Development Bank,[97] the Central American Bank for Economic Integration,[98] the European Bank for Reconstruction and Development,[99] the European Investment Bank,[100] and the Inter-American Development Bank[101] are the principal examples.

African Development Bank Web site
http://www.afdb.org.

European Bank for Reconstruction and Development Web site
http://www.ebrd.com.

Inter-American Development Bank Website
http://www.iadb.org.

---

[93]For a list of embassy and consulate Web sites see http://www.embassyworld.com/embassy/directory.htm.
[94]Information about sources of export financing in the United States is available from the U.S. Department of Commerce's Commercial Service on the Internet at http://www.ita.doc.gov/uscs.The United Nations also publishes Business Development Online on the Internet. It provides information on projects financed by the leading development banks, including the African, Asian, Caribbean, Inter-American, and North American development banks; the European Bank for Reconstruction and Development; and the World Bank. See http://www.devbusiness.com.
[95]The Small Business Administration's international trade loans are described at http://www.sba.gov/financing/frinternational.html.
[96]The African Development Bank's Web site is at http://www.afdb.org.
[97]The Asian Development Bank's Web site is at http://www.adb.org.
[98]The Central American Bank for Economic Integration's Web site (in English) is at http://www.bcie.org/english/index.php.
[99]The European Bank for Reconstruction and Development's Web site is at http://www.ebrd.com.
[100]The European Investment Bank's Web site is at http://www.eib.org.
[101]The Inter-American Development Bank's Web site is at http://www.iadb.org.

The world's development bank is the International Bank for Reconstruction and Development (IBRD), commonly called the World Bank.[102] The World Bank, together with its two subsidiary agencies, the International Development Association (IDA) and the International Finance Corporation (IFC), have a combined capital of more than $107 billion for investment, primarily in the less developed and developing countries.[103]

The World Bank and the IDA provide funds directly to governments. The IFC, on the other hand, provides funds to private companies.

> The World Bank Web site is
> http//www.worldbank.org.

I. COUNTERTRADE

countertrade: Any transaction linking exports and imports of goods or services in addition to, or in place of, a financial settlement.

Not all international trade involves the sale of goods or services for a monetary price. Often what is exchanged is not money, but goods or services. Such an exchange, when it is made in addition to, or in place of, a financial settlement is known as a **countertrade**.

Contracting parties agree to countertrade for a number of reasons: when the buyer lacks commercial credit or a convertible currency; when the buyer wants to exploit a favorable market position to obtain better terms; or when a government purchaser seeks to protect or stimulate the output of domestic industries or to maintain the balance of its overseas trade. A number of transactions fit the definition of a countertrade, including:

- *Barter:* The exchange of a seller's goods or services for a buyer's goods or services.
- *Buyback:* An arrangement in which an exporter provides equipment or technology and the buyer uses it to produces goods that are used to pay for the equipment or technology.
- *Counter purchase:* A business deal in which the parties enter into two separate contracts specifying the goods or services to be delivered under the first contract and then the goods or services to be delivered under the second contract at a later date. Such an arrangement allows performance of the first contract to go ahead when the performance of the second needs to be delayed. An example of a counter purchase is the delivery of goods in exchange for agricultural produce that is to be harvested at a later date.
- *Offset:* An agreement between a seller of high-priced items (such as military aircraft) and a government procurement agency in which the seller agrees to buy goods from the purchasing country to "offset" the negative effects of the large foreign purchase on the country's balance-of-payments account.
- *Production sharing:* A transaction, similar to a buyback, but used in mining and energy projects where the developer is paid out of a share of a mine or well's production.
- *Swap:* An agreement used when both parties (usually one of which is a government) face large debt burdens. It involves the exchange of a monetary debt for another form of debt, such as an equity share or an obligation to deliver products goods or services.
- *Tolling:* A foreign supplier employs a processor to process raw materials that the processor cannot afford to purchase. The supplier then sells the processed goods to a third party to pay for the processing.

A countertrade is agreed to by negotiation and contracting. The basic terms of a countertrade contract are the same as those for any other contract. They include a description of the goods or services, the time and place for performance, the price (if money is to be exchanged), guarantees and warranties, remedies in the event of a breach, the governing law, and agreement as to the settlement of disputes. The United Nations Commission on International

---

[102]The World Bank Group's Web site is at http://www.worldbank.org.
[103]See "Frequently Asked Questions about the World Bank" at http://web.worldbank.org/WBSITE/EXTERNAL/EXTSITETOOLS/0~contentMDK:20062181pagePK:98400piPK:98424theSitePK:95474,00.html.

Trade Law's (UNCITRAL's) *Legal Guide on International Countertrade Transactions* provides detailed guidance for entering into a countertrade contract.[104]

Reading 12-1 examines the benefits and shortcomings of countertrades.

---

[104]The guide is available in Arabic, Chinese, English, French, Russian, and Spanish. To order this document and for a wide variety of other resources related to countertrade, see the UNCITRAL Countertrade Web site at http://www.uncitral.org/uncitral/en/uncitral_texts/ procurement_online/countertrade.html. Additional information is available from the Global Offset and Countrade Organization at http://www.globaloffset.org.

Reading 12-1   THE PROS AND CONS OF COUNTERTRADE

Ross Davis, "A Deal with Strings Attached."
Financial Times, p. 8 (July 18, 2002).

When governments do international trade deals, what they buy is not always the chief consideration. As a recent U.S. Department of Commerce report to Congress explained: "Some governments readily admit that they are no longer concerned with the price or quality of the defense systems purchased but rather with the scope of the offset package offered.

"Recently, the Czech Republic announced that in competition for its jet fighter procurement, offset would be the deciding factor as opposed to technical and performance criteria and price." Such nuggets help explain why interest is taking off in offset—or countertrade, as this form of finance through reciprocal trade is also known.

According to Trade Partners U.K., a U.K. government agency that promotes British companies abroad, between 5 percent and 40 percent of world trade is countertrade-related, an indication of how substantial a part it now plays in international political and commercial transactions.

Countertrade is also growing. For example, it is spreading from arms and aerospace purchases to civil infrastructure projects. In a move likely to be followed by other Gulf states, the Kuwaiti Finance Ministry has begun requiring countertrade commitments from "all foreign companies, or national companies acting as agents for foreign companies" on civil-sector contracts of more than KD10 million (U.S. $33 million) with the Kuwaiti government.

There are five main strands of countertrade: barter; buyback; counter purchase; tolling; and offset, the biggest of the lot, which in turn divides into direct and indirect offsets. Two or more of the five may be stitched together to create a countertrade and if that is not complicated enough, the terms are sometimes used interchangeably.

In direct offset, the supplier agrees to incorporate materials, components, or sub-assemblies procured from the importer country. It is a way of promoting import substitution and local manufacture of defense or other equipment.

With indirect offset, suppliers enter into long-term cooperation and undertake to stimulate inward investment unconnected to the supply contract—again to support, increase, or diversify the local industrial base. These investments need not be made by the company winning the original contract and may be totally different in nature from the first sale.

Countertrade investments, the Kuwaitis say, promote and stimulate the private sector, attract modern technology, open up investment channels, help in training, and create jobs.

Poor countries also like countertrade, which casts them as "trade partners" of technologically and economically richer countries, rather than aid recipients. Countertrade contracts are also more reliable than pledges of aid.

Countertrade can also help to stifle domestic dissent, especially since South Africa raised its countertrade demands for military deals and is now asking—and getting—not Kuwaiti's 35 percent but 300 percent of the contract price in countertrade investments.

In late 1999, Mosiuoa Lekota, South Africa's Defense Minister, announced that the country was to spend R21.3 billion (then U.S. $3.5 billion—equivalent to half the education budget) on European-made helicopters, jets, Corvettes, and submarines—a move that raised eyebrows even within the ruling ANC. The deal was cut back by a third and the pill sweetened by screwing down the contracts—at a bad time for the arms industry—to a much bigger countertrade commitment than South Africa's normal requirement, which is 30 percent of any state arms purchase of more than U.S. $16 million. For example, a deal with Saab of Sweden and BAE of the U.K., for U.S. $2.5 billion of Hawk trainer jets and Gripen fighter jets, requires a total offset commitment, direct and indirect, of U.S. $8.7 billion, much of it in civil investment.

But countertrade is not universally loved. Some economists argue that, given half a chance, weapons contractors factor the cost of countertrade into the price of the contracts. South Africa's deal may be unique, since few companies could sell arms to South Africa during apartheid. As the first big arms deal in 30 years, it gives manufacturers the change to get a foot in the door—such as equity stakes in Denel, the state-owned arms conglomerate.

Opponents of countertrade say it is a restraint of free trade that costs jobs in the supplier nation. If the U.S. Department of Commerce and Congress are taking an interest in the offset game, it may be because U.S. companies have to comply with offset demands when selling arms abroad, while there is no similar requirement for foreign companies selling into the U.S., other than needing a U.S. presence.

BAE Systems, for example, is interested in acquiring TRW to build up its U.S. base. TRW had to sign up for an "industrial participation" deal with the British Ministry of Defense [MOD] when it won a contract to supply an ocean surveillance information system. Britain requires U.S. and other offshore arms suppliers to place defense and defense-related work in the U.K. on any deal of U.K. £10 million or more.

Indeed, although the U.K. has yet to go as far as the Czech Republic, the "industrial participation" element in a contract bid "contributes to the selection process," according to the MOD. Brinley Salzmann, of the British Defense Manufacturers Offset Group, which represents 62 companies doing business in 92 countries, says: "Our members have between £12 billion and £15 billion in offset obligations outstanding around the world, which equates to the total annual production turnover of the U.K. defense industry."

Expansion of countertrade to the civil sector, thinks John Burge, former head of countertrade at Dresdner

Trading is heavy today. ***Source***: © The New Yorker Collection from cartoonbank.com. All rights reserved.

Kleinwort Wasserstein, will be a problem for exporters that lack experience in this type of reciprocal trade.

"Other Gulf countries, to begin with, could follow the Kuwaitis; and that's going to be painful for a great number of civil-sector companies around the world who've long thought they don't have to worry about countertrade," says Mr. Burge. "Everybody will be in the same boat—the French, the Germans, the Italians, the Japanese, and the South Koreans—it's not easy finding solutions to countertrade requirements."

How complex some countertrade contracts can get is shown in one current Middle Eastern arms deal that requires the contractor to generate inward investments worth only 30 percent of the contract price within eight years. That may sound simple enough, but the investment has to be in an oil economy where investment in oil is not allowed—and where there is more money chasing permitted investments than the other way around.

As countertrade grows in importance, the British government is putting £250,000 into a new unit to advise novice companies. Baroness Symons, Minister for International Trade and Development, says it is "essential" for U.K. exporters to get to grips with countertrade.

"Many developing countries find it hard to buy much-needed goods or equipment due to a lack of foreign exchange," she says; in some countries, countertrade may be the only effective mechanism for doing business.

Chapter Questions

Types of Instruments

1. Identify the following instruments:
   a. A written promise by a bank to repay money received from a depositor.
   b. A written promise to pay another a certain sum of money.
   c. An instrument drawn by one person ordering another to pay a third at a definite future time.

    d.   An instrument drawn by one person ordering another to pay a third at presentment or at a stated time after presentment.

    e.   An instrument drawn by person A ordering person B to pay person A.

    f.   An instrument drawn by one person ordering a bank to pay a third person on demand.

    g.   A written promise to pay another a certain sum of money that is secured by personal property.

    h.   A written promise to pay another a certain sum of money that is secured by real property.

    i.   A written promise to pay another a certain sum of money that is due in installments.

    j.   An instrument that serves as a carrier's receipt for goods, as evidence of a contract of carriage, and as a document of title.

Negotiability Issues

2. The following instrument was written on a luncheonette napkin: "I, the undersigned, do acknowledge that I owe Vladimir Lenin ten thousand rubles, with interest, payable at Moscow out of the proceeds from the sale next month of my dacha in St. Petersburg. Payment is due on or before six months from this date. Signed at Berlin. Otto von Bismarck." Is this instrument negotiable or nonnegotiable?

3. Muhammad Mussadegh purchased a store in Abadan from Reza Khan for 100,000 pounds sterling. To pay for the store, Mussadegh signed a promissory note that contained the following two clauses: (a) "On or before January 1, 1992, I promise to pay Reza Khan or bearer 100,000 pounds sterling in cash or deliver title to my house in Tehran, at the holder's option" and (b) "The maker of this promissory note hereby reserves the right to extend the time of payment for six months; and the holder reserves the right to extend the time of payment indefinitely." What are the effects of these clauses on the negotiability of the note?

Liability of the Drawer Where the Payee Is Fictitious

4. Ben Arnold has been an employee of Tom Jefferson for several years. During that time, Jefferson has relied on Arnold to prepare payroll checks, checks to pay suppliers, etc. Unknown to Jefferson, Arnold is a compulsive gambler who owes large sums of money to various underworld figures. Arnold, who has been threatened with death if he fails to pay on his debts, prepares a check payable to a nonexistent supplier. Jefferson innocently signs the check. Arnold then endorses the check with "Pay to Ben Arnold" and the supplier's name. Later, Arnold takes the check to his bank, endorses it in blank, deposits it in his personal checking account, and then, later still, withdraws the money and flees the country. Meanwhile, Arnold's bank sends the check through the collection process and Jefferson's bank pays the check. When Jefferson discovers that Arnold has abandoned his job and defrauded him of a large sum of money, he demands that Arnold's bank credit his account at his bank. Must Arnold's bank do so? Under the BEA or UCC? Under the ULB?

Rights of the Holder

5. Ms. V, a wealthy art collector in Country W, is interested in buying a rare painting from Mr. Y in Country Z. Both parties agree that the price is to be determined by an independent appraiser. V informs Y that she will send her agent, X, with a check to collect the painting. V draws a check payable to Y but leaves the amount blank. She gives the check to X and instructs him to deliver it to Y. Without authority, X fills in the amount for $1 million and presents it to Y, who has, in the meantime, received the appraisal. The appraised price is $750,000. X tells Y that Ms. V had made the check out for $1 million to ensure that it will exceed the appraisal price, and that V has instructed X to return with the painting and the difference in cash. Y gives X the painting and $250,000. X delivers the painting but then disappears with the $250,000 in cash. When V discovers what has happened, she stops payment on her check and offers to pay Y $750,000 for the painting. Y insists that V must pay the check's full face value of $1 million. Is Y correct?

Effect of Alteration of the Instrument

6. Doug Drawer makes out a check for $9 to Phil Payee. Phil cleverly alters the number 9 to 90 and the written nine to ninety and then cashes the check at a local convenience store. Must Doug (or Doug's bank) pay $90 to the store? Under the BEA or UCC? Under the ULB?

Fraud in the Execution

7. John Johnson, who works for a well-known parcel delivery service, delivered a large package to Pete Peterson and had Pete sign what Pete believed was an acknowledgment of delivery.

The package contained component stereo parts that Pete had ordered from a foreign supplier, and Pete was delighted to receive them. Pete did not give the matter a second thought until several months later, when Donna Doe demanded payment of $5,000. Pete discovered that he had signed a three-month negotiable promissory note, rather than the acknowledgment of a delivery, and that Donna had innocently purchased the note from John. Must Pete pay the note? Under the BEA or UCC? Under the ULB?

Letter-of-Credit Requirements

8. Cee Company in Canada agreed to sell 10,000 gallons of maple syrup to Dee Company in Denmark. Dee Company arranged for a letter of credit with its bank in Copenhagen. The credit required payment on the presentation of a bill of lading and an inspection certificate issued by a quality control company, Vigilance, Inc., of Toronto. Cee Company produced both the bill and the inspection certificate. The Copenhagen bank refused to pay because the inspection certificate stated that "based on a sample taken from 5 gallons, the maple syrup is not of the kind ordered." The bank argued that the certificate, on its face, did not certify the regularity of the entire order. Was the bank correct in refusing payment?

Duty of a Bank Under a Letter of Credit

9. Rousseau et Fils has signed a contract to buy 10,000 "new coffee percolators in the manufacturer's original packaging, with standard manufacturer's warranty," from Schwartz, GmBH. Schwartz agrees to ship the percolators CIF, and Rousseau agrees to make payment by means of an irrevocable letter of credit. Rousseau contacts Thermidor Bank, which issues a letter of credit promising to honor a promissory note payable to Schwartz when it is accompanied by an invoice and a clean, on board bill of lading for "10,000 new coffee percolators in the manufacturer's original packaging, with standard manufacturer's warranty." Rousseau learns from Weiss, a competitor of Schwartz, that even though Schwartz had obtained actual bills identifying the goods as "10,000 new coffee percolators in the manufacturer's original packaging, with standard manufacturer's warranty," the percolators were actually used and inoperable. Is there anything that Rousseau can do?
10. In Question 9, would it make any difference if Rousseau had positive proof that a fraud had been perpetrated?
11. In Question 9, would it make any difference if Schwartz's bank had confirmed the letter of credit and paid the promissory note before Rousseau learned of the supposedly defective shipment?

CHAPTER 13
TAXATION

An individual or business entity active internationally can expect to pay different kinds and amounts of taxes to two (or more) states, and also to find that two states seek to impose a tax on the same income or activity. The basis for sovereign states' "right" to tax under international law will be discussed in this chapter, along with the typical forms of business organizations operating globally and how they are taxed. The nature and categorization of income, tax rates, and relief for taxpayers from double taxation through treaties will also be discussed. Finally, concerns about tax evasion and the role of offshore tax havens are highlighted in this chapter.

Sovereign states impose taxes for diverse purposes: to raise revenue for government, to encourage or restrict certain kinds of investments, to protect consumers, to protect local producers, to conserve resources, or to better align human action with economic theory. But the most common rationale for adopting or changing a particular tax is to improve revenues, and the most common method is by imposing income taxes.

A. INCOME TAXES

income tax: Compulsory governmental levy on a person's income and profits.

schedular tax model: Imposes different flat taxes on different kinds of income.

Worldwide, taxes on the income of individuals and the profits of companies are the most widely used basic taxes and the principal source of revenue for most countries. Two models may be used to describe (in abstract terms) how governments collect **income taxes**. The **schedular tax model** imposes taxes at flat rates on different sources of income. That is, a different flat rate will be imposed on different kinds of income, such as manufacturing, retail sales, agriculture, or employment income. The advantages of a schedular model include its simplicity in calculating taxes and its ability to encourage, or discourage, development of particular economic sectors within a country. The model has substantial shortcomings, however. It is regressive—that is, it imposes the same tax on the rich (those most able to afford the tax) as it does on the poor (those least able to afford it). It is also anti-entrepreneurial— that is, only the established and well-to-do are encouraged to expand and take risks.

global tax model: Imposes uniform (usually progressive) taxes on all types of income.

progressive tax: A tax in which the rate of taxation increases as income increases.

The **global tax model** imposes uniform rates on all sources of income. In other words, a taxpayer will pay taxes on the total of all income from all sources. Commonly, this is done on a progressive basis, a **progressive tax** being one that increases as income increases.[1] For example, in Indonesia, individuals pay taxes as follows:

- On the first 25,000,000 rupiahs   5%
- On the next 25,000,000 rupiahs   10%
- On the next 50,000,000 rupiahs   15%
- On the next 105,000,000 rupiahs   25%
- On income above 200,000,000 rupiahs 35%

The global model, especially one with progressive income rates, has the advantages of not being regressive and not being anti-entrepreneurial. On the other hand, uniform rates do not encourage development in particular economic sectors. The schedular model is seldom adopted in its pure form. In contrast to the schedular model, the global model is often adopted in a relatively pure form, while about one-third of sovereign states impose a relatively straightforward global income tax on resident companies, and most (approximately 90 percent) impose a similar tax on resident individuals. Argentina, for example, imposes a flat rate of 35 percent on the net income of companies and a progressive rate, varying from 9 to 35 percent, on the net graduated income of individuals. Readers seeking current information on individual and corporate tax rates worldwide are advised to consult the various Web sites of the global accounting firms.[2]

B. TAXPAYERS

taxpayer: A person who must pay a tax.

Countries treat both individuals and juridical entities as **taxpayers**—that is, as separate legal entities that must pay taxes. Individuals, of course, are natural persons. Juridical entities—as discussed in Chapter 4—are legal fictions created by states.

---

[1]Normally, with a progressive tax, the higher rates apply only to each higher segment of income, as is the case for Indonesia in the example. However, if the entire amount of income is taxed at the highest rate, the progressive tax is being applied according to the so-called *slab* principle. Kuwait, for example, applies income taxes on nonresidents companies at rates that vary from 5 to 55 percent on the total amount of their income. Thus, a nonresident company that earns 10,000 Kuwaiti dinars pays 5 percent or 500 dinars, while a nonresident company that earns 1,000,000 dinars pays 550,000 dinars in taxes.

[2]See, for example, KPMG's Corporate and Indirect Tax Rate Survey at http://www.kpmg.com/Services/Tax/Business/IntCorp/CTR/CTR2007.htm. PriceWaterhouseCoopers also has a useful site at http://www.pwc.com.

COMPANY TAXPAYERS

The juridical entity most commonly subject to taxation is the company. Companies take many forms and a variety of names, but the most common are joint stock companies (or corporations), limited liability companies (or closely held corporations), limited liability partnerships, and general partnerships.

The form that a company takes is important for determining its tax liability. Particular companies may be taxed either at (1) general company rates, (2) special company rates, or (3) individual rates. For example, in the United States, domestic corporations (both publicly traded and privately held) are taxed at general company rates, whereas partners in a partnership (whether a general or a limited partnership) are taxed as individuals. In Thailand, however, publicly traded corporations are taxed at the general company rate, and privately held corporations and limited liability partnerships are taxed at a higher special company rate.

When a company organized in one country is obliged to pay taxes in another country, the taxing country will categorize the company according to its own rules. In many countries, this is done by a central registrar (which is independent of the taxing agency) at the time the company begins doing business within the country. In the United Kingdom, the Registrar of Companies performs this task; in India and Korea it is done by the Central Bank; and in Portugal it is done by both the Commercial Registrar and the Portuguese Foreign Trade Institute. In other countries, the taxing agency will determine the appropriate tax category at the time a company submits its tax return.

The categorization of companies is uniformly done by analogy: The central registrar or taxing agency looks for the domestic company that is most like the company to be categorized. In many countries this is done on an *ad hoc* basis—especially in less developed countries and in countries where all juridical entities (stock companies, limited liability companies, partnerships, trusts, etc.) are taxed as entities—but in other countries there are administrative guidelines for making this determination. The U.S. Internal Revenue Service, for example, uses the following factors to determine if a foreign company is equivalent to an American corporation: (1) Are there associates? (2) Is the business carried on for profit? (3) Does the company have continuity of life? (4) Is there centralized management? (5) Do the owners have limited liability? and (6) Are ownership interests freely transferable?[3]

SUBORDINATE BUSINESS STRUCTURES

In addition to choosing a business form, an international company must choose the subordinate business structure it will use to carry out its overseas operations. There are four possibilities: representative offices, agencies, branches, and subsidiaries.

representative office: A contact point where interested parties can obtain information about a company. It does not conduct business for the company.

A **representative office** is set up to promote imported products and to provide technical assistance to local importers and distributors. Such an office, however, may not engage directly in commercial activities, such as taking orders, making sales, or collecting debts.[4]

agent: An independent person or company with authority to act on behalf of another.

An **agent** is an individual or a local company that acts on behalf of, and under the supervision of, a foreign firm. Unlike a representative office, an agent conducts business on behalf of the foreign firm (or principal), taking orders, making sales, and collecting debts.

branch: Unit or part of a company. It is not separately incorporated.

A **branch** is a unit of a foreign parent company that is normally set up to offer some expertise or service that is unavailable locally. It involves not only the placement of individuals in a particular locale but also the establishment of a facility, such as an assembly plant, mining operation, or service office. In essence, it is a large agency.

subsidiary: Company owned by a parent or a parent's holding company. Unlike a branch, it is separately incorporated.

A **subsidiary** is a locally established or incorporated company that is owned by a foreign parent but is legally independent of it. Most countries allow foreign parents to maintain 100 percent ownership of a subsidiary, although many require that it be organized as a joint venture, with local citizens or domestic companies sharing in its control.

---

[3]U.S. Treasury Regulations, § 301.7701-1(a).
[4]Representative offices may be established in most countries, with Thailand being the only exception known to the author.

For tax purposes, the representative office is the most advantageous of the subordinate business structures. Because it does not engage in any commercial activities within the host country, it is not subject to taxation. Such an entity, however, is frequently inadequate to meet other business requirements.

Agencies and branches are treated the same way from a tax perspective. Because they are under the direct control of a foreign firm, they generally are subjected to less favorable administrative and tax treatment than either domestic companies or subsidiaries. Their principal advantage is the ease and low cost of obtaining local registration. Their disadvantages vary from country to country but can include (1) higher tax rates; (2) the requirement to disclose the accounts of the entire company, either at the time of registration, during an audit, or as part of a civil or criminal suit (see the *In Re Sealed* case in Chapter 6)[5]; (3) ineligibility for deductions, exemptions, incentives, or grants; (4) ineligibility to participate in some business activities;[6] (5) liability of the parent for the tax, contractual, and tortious obligations of the agency or branch; and (6) the attribution of funds earned by the parent from sales outside the country—or from sales facilitated by the presence of an independent representative office—to the local branch.

The tax laws of many countries encourage foreign investors to establish subsidiaries—especially joint ventures. Some of the advantages of setting up a subsidiary may include (1) lower tax rates ; (2) limited liability for the foreign parent; (3) the possibility of attracting local participation in the equity capital of the subsidiary company; (4) eligibility for the same deductions, exemptions, incentives, and grants offered to domestic companies; (5) the right to participate in the same activities as domestic companies; and (6) insulation of the parent company from audits by local authorities. The disadvantages may include (1) the higher costs of incorporation and operation, (2) the mandatory participation of local joint venturers, (3) the mandatory appointment of local citizens to hold some percentage of the seats on the board of directors, (4) more extensive audits than those imposed on branches, and (5) the filing of more detailed returns with the registrar of companies or the tax agency.

The distinguishing characteristic of a subsidiary is its separate legal status from the parent company. This insulates the parent from the tax, contract, and tort liabilities of the subsidiary. It also—as Case 13-1 shows—insulates the subsidiary from the obligations of the parent.

---

[5]Kenya, while permitting foreign parent companies to negotiate with its Tax Department as to the scope of a particular audit, can require the parent to disclose its entire accounts to the Registrar of Companies at the time it registers a branch. Coopers & Lybrand International Tax Network, *1998 International Tax Summaries: A Guide for Planning and Decisions*, p. K-19 (George J. Yost III, ed., 1998).
[6]For example, prior to Taiwan's accession to the World Trade Organization, an agency or branch of a foreign company could not engage in the following businesses: restaurants, consigned processing, investment, travel agencies, shipping agencies, leasing, container terminals, and construction and related activities. *Id.*, p. T-10.

Case 13-1 REISS AND COMPANY (NIGERIA), LTD. v. FEDERAL BOARD OF INLAND REVENUE

Nigeria, Federal Revenue Court, 1977.
African Law Reports, Commercial Law Series, vol. 1977, pt. 2, p. 209 (1977).

Reiss & Co. (Nigeria), Ltd., was a joint stock company incorporated in Nigeria. Handelsvereeniging v/h Reiss &

Co. (Amsterdam) was a private limited liability company incorporated in the Netherlands and a holder of 55 percent of the shares in Reiss & Co. (Nigeria), Ltd.

The Nigerian subsidiary served as an agent for the Dutch parent company, introducing Nigerian customers and forwarding orders for goods to be purchased by those customers from the parent. Once having introduced the customers and placed their orders, the Nigerian company took no further part in the subsequent transactions. The Dutch company accepted or rejected the orders in Amsterdam, communicating that decision directly to the customers. Invoices for the price of the goods sold were sent directly to customers. Profits on these sales were 14 percent of the invoice price.

By an unwritten agreement, the Nigerian subsidiary was entitled to half of the profits (i.e., 7 percent of the sale price) on the transactions accepted by the parent as payment for its services. Upon receipt of payments from customers, the parent paid this amount to the Nigerian company.

The Nigerian company submitted tax returns in Nigeria for the years 1971–72 through 1974–75, showing income for half of the profits it was sharing with the Dutch parent. Nigeria's Federal Board of Inland Revenue made an additional assessment on a best judgment basis, assessing the Nigerian company for taxes on the entire amount of the profits paid to the Dutch company by its Nigerian customers.

After losing an appeal before the Board of Appeal Commissioners (which held that it was impossible to disentangle the accounts of the Nigerian subsidiary from those of its Dutch parent), Reiss & Co. (Nigeria), Ltd., appealed to Nigeria's Federal Revenue Court. The Nigerian company contended, among other things, that although the Dutch company owned a majority of its shares, the Dutch parent did not control the subsidiary's affairs and that the two companies should have been treated entirely separately for tax purposes.

JUDGE KARIBI-WHYTE

***

Whilst not disputing that the appellants are assessable to tax, counsel for the appellants contended that they are only assessable in respect of earned income and no more. Chief Williams [the appellants' counsel] pointed out that the circumstances in which Nigerian and overseas companies are assessable to tax are clearly stated in § 18 of the *Companies Income Tax Act* (1961). He argued that the appellants share the profits with Reiss & Co. (Amsterdam) and cannot be assessed to tax in respect of the whole.

In order to understand the situation, it is necessary to state the relationship between Reiss & Co. (Nigeria) and Reiss & Co. (Amsterdam) apart from the agency arrangement. In his evidence, the managing director of Reiss & Co. (Nigeria) stated on oath that the company's

founder and principal shareholder is Reiss & Co. (Amsterdam). He said that the appellant company was incorporated on September 23rd, 1960. Mr. Jacob Dirk Moraal, assistant managing director of Reiss & Co. (Amsterdam) in his evidence on oath stated that Reiss & Co. (Amsterdam) owns 55 percent of the shares in Reiss & Co. (Nigeria). Notwithstanding this controlling shareholding, both witnesses stated in their evidence that Reiss & Co. (Amsterdam) does not control the affairs or management of the appellant company in any way. The services rendered under the agency agreement are paid out on the basis of a "gentlemen's agreement." There is no formal contract embodying the percentage due the appellants, although there is an understanding that 50 percent is due to the appellants.

It is vital in the circumstances to determine from where the source of income tax has accrued and to whom. Section 17(a) of the *Companies Income Tax Act* (1961) provides:

> The tax shall, subject to the provisions of this Act, be payable at the rate hereinafter specified for each year of assessment upon the profits of any company accruing in, derived from, brought into, or received in, Nigeria in respect of—
>
> a. any trade or business for whatever period of time such trade or business may be carried on.

This enables profits of Nigerian companies to be assessed to tax wherever they have been made, if they are derived from, brought into or received in Nigeria. The profit must be made in a trade or business carried on by such company. Wherever such profits have arisen and whether or not they have been brought into or received in Nigeria they shall be deemed to accrue in Nigeria.[7]

On the other hand, the situation with respect to a non-Nigerian company is different. Section 18(2) of the *Companies Income Tax Act* (1961) provides:

> The profits of a company other than a Nigeria company from any trade or business shall be deemed to be derived from Nigeria to the extent to which such profits are not attributable to any part of the operations of the company carried on outside Nigeria.

The evidence that the appellant company is an intermediary of Reiss & Co. (Amsterdam) for the purposes of introducing Nigerian customers has not been controverted. There is no evidence that the appellant company does anything more with respect to such customers. This was clearly brought out by the evidence in chief and answers to cross-examination of the appellants' managing director. The assistant director of Reiss & Co. (Amsterdam) in his evidence gave a full description of the duties

---

[7]Section 18(1).

of the appellants and Reiss & Co. (Amsterdam) in respect of orders of customers. All the appellant company does is to take a pro forma invoice from the customer and send this to Reiss & Co. (Amsterdam). The deposit received by the appellants is refunded to the customer if Reiss & Co. (Amsterdam) rejects the order. Every other activity in respect of the transaction, and the financial obligations thereon, are carried on in Amsterdam by Reiss & Co. (Amsterdam). Simply put, all operations relating to the transaction are carried on outside Nigeria by Reiss & Co. (Amsterdam). It therefore follows that it is not a trade or business carried on in Nigeria by a Nigerian company in accordance with § 18. Rather it is a trade or business carried on by a company other than a Nigerian company in Nigeria in accordance with § 18(2) of the *Companies Income Tax Act* (1961).

Considerable importance has been attached to and emphasis laid on the relationship between the appellants and Reiss & Co. (Amsterdam). It is in evidence that the appellant company was before September 23rd, 1960, only an overseas branch of Reiss & Co. (Amsterdam). Following the promulgation of the *Companies Decree* (1968), the Nigerian branch became incorporated as a separate legal entity with its own managing director and board of directors. There is, however, evidence before me that Reiss & Co. (Amsterdam) still has a controlling shareholding of 55 percent of the shares of the appellant company. There is no evidence before me of any actual control of affairs of the appellant company by Reiss & Co. (Amsterdam). The only evidence before me, which has remained uncontroverted, is the oral evidence of a sharing agreement in respect of commissions payable to the appellant company on the profits of business introduced to Reiss & Co. (Amsterdam). Although there is a considerable dark cloud of suspicion regarding the genuineness of this transaction, especially because the two companies were the same before the legal separation, the natural philosophical variety in the arrangement is more indicative of the arrangement generally understood of companies within the same group. The separate legal identity of the appellants and Reiss & Co. (Amsterdam), cannot be denied. . . . The respondent cannot impugn the legal situation successfully without adducing sufficient evidence to the contrary. It is not sufficient to allege that the profits in the transaction accrue to the appellants. It must be shown how they so accrue, notwithstanding the clear words of § 18(1) of the *Companies Income Tax Act* (1961).

In *F. L. Smidth & Co. v. Greenwood*[8] the facts were similar to [those in] this case. The appellants carried on business at Copenhagen in Denmark, as manufacturers of and dealers in cement-making and other allied machinery. All the partners were resident in Copenhagen where they had their head office. They had an employee in London, who was paid a salary and a bonus based on the profits of the entire turnover of the business. The appellants rented an office in London where the employee, whose duty was to ascertain the requirements of intending purchasers, inspect the proposed site of any proposed installation of machinery, and take samples of earth, used to report to the appellants in Copenhagen. Otherwise, the employee had no responsibility for the negotiation of contracts which were made directly with the appellants in Copenhagen. All machinery was sent FOB from Copenhagen. During the war, the appellants purchased parts of the machinery in the United Kingdom in order to complete installation or to carry out repairs. It was admitted that the appellants were liable to tax in respect of the profits arising from resale of the goods so purchased. It was held that, apart from the goods locally purchased and resold in the United Kingdom, the evidence before the Commission did not justify the conclusion of fact that the firm exercised a trade within the United Kingdom.

In the High Court, Judge Rowlatt gave a definition of where the trade or business is exercised, which is acceptable to me and was indeed accepted by the Court of Appeal and the House of Lords. He said. . . . :

> . . . [T]he real place where the trade is exercised is the place where the transactions forming the alleged business are closed, in the case of the selling business, by the sale of the commodity and profit thereby realized. It seems to me that is a clear and definite principle. Until the sale is effected, the trade is incomplete. Trading is buying or making and selling, and if I am right in supporting that one single place has to be treated as the place where the trade is exercised it seems to me that it must be where the profit-bearing transactions are closed.

. . . [This description] largely support[s] the agreed facts of the case before me, which is that the appellants' company's only duty is to introduce customers to Reiss & Co. (Amsterdam). This function has been aptly described by Lord Herschell in *Grainger & Son v. Gough*[9] . . . as: ". . . only ancillary to the exercise of his trade in the country where he buys or makes stores, and sells his goods."

On examination of the facts, the appellant company in *F. L. Smidth & Co. v. Greenwood* was more involved in the transactions than were the appellants in this case.

---

[8]*Law Reports, King's Bench*, vol. 1920, pt. 3, p. 275 (1920); on appeal *Law Reports, King's Bench*, vol. 1921, pt. 3, p. 583 (1921); on further appeal, *Law Reports, Appeal Cases*, vol. 1922, pt. 1, p. 417 (Court of Appeal, 1922).
[9]*Id.*, vol. 1896, p. 325 at p. 336 (Court of Appeal, 1896).

It would seem from the cases referred to above as if the place of the conclusion of the contract of sale is of itself decisive of the test of the place where business is carried on. This is not so. As was said by Lord Justice Atkin in *Smidth's case,* there is no exhaustive test as to what constitutes trading within or outside a place by a nonresident. Regard must be had to the whole circumstances of the case in order to see from the operations taking place where the profits in substance arise.

... The facts of *Mitchell v. Egyptian Hotels, Ltd.,*[10] a divided decision of the House of Lords, are very similar to the facts of the case before me if all the evidence necessary to establish the relationship between the appellants and Reiss & Co. (Amsterdam) has been adduced. ... The facts of *Mitchell's case* are that the appellant company incorporated in England owned and carried on a hotel business in Egypt. In 1908, the company altered its articles of association by providing for a local board in Egypt to manage its Egyptian business including the hotel to the exclusion of any board of directors of the company itself. The local board was to exercise all the powers of the company in regard to the hotel. They were to retain all the profits made by the hotel and remit to England to the company only so much as was necessary to pay dividends to shareholders resident in England and for expenses incurred by the London board. The accounts of the company were kept in London, which recommended dividends and controlled the capital. The company was assessed tax upon the full amount of its profits, on the basis that the controlling power of the company remained with the London board. The assessment was upheld on appeal by the Revenue Commissioners, and Judge Horridge dismissed the appeal of the company to the High Court. His decision was reversed by the Court of Appeal. On a further appeal to the House of Lords, the decision of the Court of Appeal was affirmed by the House being equally divided.

It was clear from the evidence that a considerable part of the essential management of the income-producing capital was in London. In affirming the decision of the Court of Appeal, Lord Parker of Weddington reviewed the facts and came to the conclusion that:

> Under these circumstances it appears to me indisputable that no single act has been done in or directed from this country by way of participation in or furtherance of the trade or business of the company from which the profits or gains said to be chargeable to income tax since August 28, 1908, have arisen.[11]

On this reasoning his lordship came to the conclusion as follows:

> In the absence of any act done or directed by any person resident here in participation or furtherance of the business operations in Egypt from which the profits and gains in question arose, I think your Lordships are bound to come to the conclusion that this trade or business was carried on wholly outside the United Kingdom.[12]

Lord Sumner agreed with this, but Earl Loreburn and Lord Parmoor held the contrary. The decision of the Court of Appeal was therefore affirmed.

I think the view of the Court of Appeal affirmed by this decision ought to be followed. I apply that decision as consistent with judicial authority and more in consonance with the express provisions of the enabling statutes. There is no doubt that the participation of the appellants in the profit earning business in Amsterdam is not significant. The appellant company can conveniently be regarded as a sleeping partner. ... Again, from the evidence before me, there is nothing to show that any part of the transaction was carried on in this country. Apart from introducing customers who thereafter dealt directly with the principal, the appellant company has not featured again in any other important aspect of the transaction.

In *Grainger & Sons v. Gough,* one of the champagne cases, whose essential facts are fairly similar to [those in] the case before me, it was held that a foreign merchant who canvasses through agents in the United Kingdom for orders for the sale of his merchandise to customers in the United Kingdom does not exercise a trade in the United Kingdom within the meaning of the Income Tax Acts, so long as all contracts for the sale and all deliveries of merchandise are made in a foreign country.

So in this case all the appellants did was to canvass for customers in Nigeria, as Grainger & Sons did to Louis Roederer, the French wine merchant in that case, who was held not to have exercised any trade in the United Kingdom. On my findings of fact on the evidence no trade or business was carried on in Nigeria either by the appellants or by Reiss & Co. (Amsterdam). This is because the acceptance of the orders is by Reiss & Co. (Amsterdam). The purchase of the goods is made outside Nigeria and the invoice is prepared outside Nigeria, and from there sent directly to the customer in Nigeria. Payment is made to Reiss & Co. (Amsterdam) in Amsterdam. That they are paid in Nigeria through Nigerian banks is a matter of convenience in accordance with

[10]*Id.,* vol. 1915, p. 1022 (Court of Appeal, 1915).
[11]*Id.,* at p. 1038.
[12]*Id.,* at p. 1039.

modern commercial practice. The delivery is also made in Amsterdam, outside this country.

I am of the opinion that whenever profitable contracts are habitually made in this country, by or for foreigners, with persons in this country because they are to do something for or to supply something to those persons, such persons are exercising a profitable trade in the country even though everything to be done by them to fulfill the contract is done abroad. It is otherwise when the same result is achieved through an agent without coming into this country. It has been held in *Colquhoun v. Brooks*[13] that where there is resident in a country a sleeping partner with respect to a business carried on abroad, in the management of which he does not take part, such partner is only liable to be assessed on such parts of the profits as are remitted to him from abroad.

This accentuates the two different situations of trading in a country and carrying on a trade within the country. It would seem to me that Reiss & Co. (Amsterdam) in exporting goods to Nigerians or persons in Nigeria, through the appellant company, who only introduces customers to it, does not thereby carry on business in Nigeria. If, as I have held, Reiss & Co. (Amsterdam) does not carry on business in this country, I do not see how the activities of the appellant company, whose only association and participation on the transaction is to introduce customers, will amount to carrying on business. This is because the appellant company cannot be credited with what its principal cannot and does not do.

It follows, therefore, that all the profits shown in the invoices complained of were profits which were due to Reiss & Co. (Amsterdam) and not to the appellants. Counsel for the respondent contended that, the source of this income being Nigeria, the income was taxable. I cannot subscribe to that proposition. . . .

In *Mitchell v. Egyptian Hotels, Ltd.*, it was held that where the business of a company was wholly carried on abroad, it was not assessable to income tax. The facts of the case before me themselves exclude, by virtue of § 18(2) of the *Companies Income Tax* (1961), the possibility of imposing taxes on a foreign company not carrying on any trade or business within this country. Counsel for respondent has contended that the provisions of § 18(1) can be construed by virtue of the meaning of the word "deemed" used therein to include the profits of the foreign company. . . . I do not accept this view. The provisions of the two subsections of § 18 of the *Companies Income Tax* (1961) are intended to achieve similar objectives but with different subject matters and circumstances in contemplation. Where a Nigerian company is contemplated it is not allowable to transpose the situa-

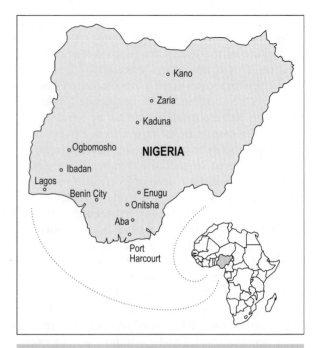

MAP 13-1 Nigeria (1977)

tion and include a non-Nigerian company. If it was intended to apply the same standard it would have been necessary to place them in two different subsections. It could be observed that the expression "deemed" was also used in § 18(2) but in different circumstances. I am of the opinion that the construction contended for cannot be enlarged to bring foreign income earned by foreign companies operating entirely outside this country within the scope of § 18(1), as this is entirely within the provisions of § 18(2). . . .

***

The appeal of the appellants against the judgment of the Board of Appeal Commissioners is allowed. . . . The appellants are entitled to a refund of any tax assessed and paid on the agency commission in excess of the 7 percent commission due to the appellants by the agreement. . . . ■

CASEPOINT: (1) In order to disregard the separate legal entity status of a subsidiary, it must be proven that the parent controls the subsidiary. (2) The real place where trade takes place is where the transaction closes. (3) The Nigerian tax code (Sec. 18(2)) provides that income earned by Nigerian companies can be deemed to have been brought into Nigeria, but it does not provide for the same thing for non-Nigerian companies. Here, there is no proof that

---

[13]*All England Law Reports*, vol. 1886–1890, p. 1063 (Court of Appeal, 1889).

the Dutch parent controlled the Nigerian subsidiary, and the underlying transaction took place outside of Nigeria since the sales were closed in the Netherlands. Only the agreement to pay the Nigerian subsidiary 7 percent of the sales price is connected to Nigeria, so the subsidiary is only obligated to pay taxes on the 7 percent.

C. BASES OF INCOME TAXATION

National tax systems are based on (1) the nationality of the taxpayer, (2) the residence of the taxpayer, (3) the source of the taxpayer's income, or (4) some combination of these variables.

NATIONALITY PRINCIPLE

nationality principle: A state may tax the world-wide income of its nationals.

Countries that use the **nationality principle** tax their citizens or nationals on their worldwide income no matter where they may reside.[14] A citizen is an individual who is a member of a state or nation (usually a republic), who owes allegiance to it, and who is entitled to full civil rights. A national is an individual who owes allegiance and fealty to a sovereign. Domestic companies are sometimes treated as citizens or nationals of their home country.

In Case 13-2, the U.S. Supreme Court was asked whether the U.S. Constitution or international law is violated by a U.S. tax of the worldwide income of a citizen who resides and is

[14]J. D. R. Adams and John Whaley, *The International Taxation of Multinational Enterprises in Developed Countries*, pp. 10–11 (1977).

Case 13-2   COOK v. TAIT, UNITED STATES COLLECTOR OF INTERNAL REVENUE FOR THE DISTRICT OF MARYLAND

United States, Supreme Court, 1924.
United States Reports, vol. 265, p. 47 (1924).

MR. JUSTICE MCKENNA delivered the opinion of the Court:

Action by plaintiff . . . to recover the sum of $298.34 as the first installment of an income tax paid, it is charged, under the threats and demands of Tait.

***

Plaintiff is a native citizen of the United States and was such when he took up his residence and became domiciled in the city of Mexico. A demand was made upon him by defendant . . . to make a return of his income for the purpose of taxation under the Revenue Laws of the United States. Plaintiff complied with the demand, but under protest, the income having been derived from property situated in the city of Mexico. . . .

The question in the case . . . is . . . whether Congress has power to impose a tax upon income received by a native citizen of the United States, who, at the time the income was received, was permanently resident and domiciled in the city of Mexico, the income being derived from real and personal property located in Mexico.

Plaintiff assigns against the power not only his rights under the Constitution of the United States, but under international law; and, in support of the assignments, cites many cases. It will be observed that the foundation of the assignments is the fact that the citizen receiving the income, and the property of which it is the product, are outside the territorial limits of the United States. These two facts, the contention is, exclude the existence of the power to tax. . . . The contention is not justified, and that it is not justified is the necessary deduction of recent cases. In *United States v. Bennett*[15] the power of

[15]*United States Reports*, vol. 232, p. 299.

the United States to tax a foreign-built yacht owned and used during the taxing period outside of the United States, by a citizen domiciled in the United States, was sustained. The tax passed on was imposed by a tariff act, but necessarily the power does not depend upon the form by which it is exerted.

It will be observed that the case contained only one of the conditions of the present case, the *property* taxed was outside of the United States. In *United States v. Goelet*[16] the yacht taxed was outside of the United States, but owned by a citizen of the United States who was "permanently resident and domiciled in a foreign country." It was decided that the yacht was not subject to the tax, but this as a matter of construction. Pains were taken to say that the question of power was determined "wholly irrespective" of the owner's "permanent domicile in a foreign country." And the court put out of view the *situs*[17] of the yacht. That the court had no doubt of the power to tax was illustrated by reference of the income tax laws of prior years and the express extension to those domiciled abroad. The illustration has pertinence to the case at bar, for the case at bar is concerned with an income tax, and the power to impose it.

We may make further exposition of the national power, as the case depends upon it. It was illustrated at once in *United States v. Bennett* by a contrast with the power of a state. It was pointed out that there were limitations upon the latter that were not on the national power. The taxing power of a state, it was decided, encountered at its borders the taxing power of other states and was limited by them. There was no such limitation, it was pointed out, upon the national power, and that the limitation upon the states affords, it was said, no ground for constructing a barrier around the United States, "shutting that government off from the exertion of powers which inherently belong to it by virtue of its sovereignty."

The contention was rejected that a citizen's property without the limit of the United States derives no benefit from the United States. The contention, it was said, came from the confusion of thought in "mistaking the scope and extent of the sovereign power of the United States as a nation, and its relations to its citizens and their relation to it." And that power, in its scope and extent, it was decided, is based on the presumption that government, by its very nature, benefits the citizen and his property wherever found, and that opposition to it holds on to

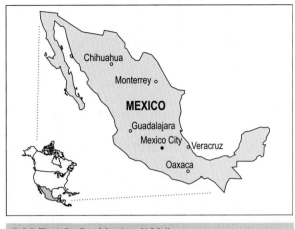

MAP 13-2 Mexico (1924)

citizenship while it "belittles and destroys its advantages and blessings by denying the possession by government of an essential power required to make citizenship completely beneficial." In other words, the principle was declared that the government, by its very nature, benefits the citizen and his property, wherever found, and therefore has the power to make the benefit complete. Or, to express it another way, the basis of the power to tax was not and cannot be made dependent upon the *situs* of the property in all cases, it being in or out of the United States, nor was not and cannot be made dependent upon the domicile of the citizen, that being out of the United States, but upon the relation as citizen to the United States, and the relation of the latter to him as citizen. The consequence of the relations is that the native citizen who is taxed may have domicile, and the property from which his income is derived may have *situs*, in a foreign country, and the tax be legal—the government has power to impose the tax.

The judgment of the trial court was affirmed. ■

CASEPOINT: A national government may impose taxes on the worldwide income of a citizen regardless of that person's residency. Unlike a U.S. state, whose taxing authority may not overlap with the taxing authority of other U.S. states, there is no such limitation on the national government. The existence of the U.S. government benefits all U.S. citizens no matter where they are, and thus the U.S. government may insist upon their paying the taxes that maintain that government.

---

[16]*Id.,* at p. 293.
[17]Latin: The place where something is located.

permanently domiciled abroad, and who receives all of his income from outside the United States. The Court held that neither was violated.

RESIDENCY PRINCIPLE

residency principle: A state may tax the worldwide income of persons residing within its territory.

According to the **residency principle**, a country taxes the worldwide income of persons legally resident within its territorial jurisdiction.[18]

Residence of Individuals

Generally, the residence of natural persons is determined by one of three tests. One test is objective: the length of time a person resides within the borders of a particular state; the second is subjective: the intent of the individual to make a place his or her permanent domicile or household; and the third is declarative: the individual obtains admission to a country as a resident.

India, Indonesia, Japan, Panama, Singapore, Taiwan, and Venezuela have all adopted a simple objective test (e.g., a stay within the country for an arbitrary period of time, most commonly at least six months).[19] Belgium uses a subjective test: It looks for a person's domicile or a principal home. Brazil uses a declarative test: Individuals with permanent visas are residents; individuals with temporary visas are nonresidents (unless they stay in the country for more than one year).

Many countries, however, use two or more of these tests in combination. Luxembourg, for example, treats an individual as a resident if he has a permanent home in the country or has been living in the country continuously for six months. Poland uses the same test. Mexico regards an individual who has established a home in Mexico as a resident unless the person has been outside the country for at least 183 days and can demonstrate residency in another country. Brazil, as already noted, treats both permanent and temporary visa holders who have been in the country for more than one year as residents.

Residence of Companies

The residence of companies is determined by two tests: (1) where the company was organized or (2) where the company is managed and controlled. In the United States, only the first is used. That is, corporations formed under the laws of any of the states or the federal government are regarded as residents. In the United Kingdom, its colonies, and former colonies, residence is determined solely by the place where the "central management and control" of the trade or business is exercised—the second test. In Germany, France, and most other civil law countries, both tests are applied. That is, a company is a resident if either its statutory seat or its center of management is within the country. Companies in civil law countries may, as a consequence, have dual residency.

The residency of a Bahamian company was the principal issue in Case 13-3.

---

[18]J. D. R. Adams and John Whaley, *The International Taxation of Multinational Enterprises in Developed Countries*, pp. 10–11 (1977).

[19]India: 182 days; Indonesia: 183 days; Japan: one year; Panama: 60 days; Singapore: 183 days; Taiwan: any 183 days in a calendar year; Venezuela: any 180 days, or, having been classified as a resident the previous year, any one day in the current year.

Note: There are two categories of nonresidents in Taiwan. One who resides in the country for less than 90 days is liable for taxes only on income actually paid to the nonresident in Taiwan. One who resides in the country for more than 90 days but less than 183 days in a calendar year must pay taxes on income received from sources both within and without Taiwan so long as the services being reimbursed were rendered within Taiwan.

─◆◈◆─

IN BRIEF: Case 13-3   CROWN FOREST INDUSTRIES LTD. v. CANADA

Canada, Supreme Court
Supreme Court Reports, vol. 1995, part 2, p. 802 (1995).

FACTS

In the 1987, 1988, and 1989 taxation years, Crown Forest paid rent to Norsk for the use of certain barges. These barges were used to transport wood chips to pulp mills, and goods from those mills to markets in Canada and the United States. Norsk was incorporated in the Bahamas in 1962 but its only office and place of business has been in the United States, in the San Francisco area. At this office it employed approximately 19 people with a monthly payroll of about U.S. $75,000. Both Norsk and Crown Forest are owned by the same New Zealand corporation, Fletcher Challenge Limited.

For each of the years under review, the only income tax returns filed by Norsk with the United States Internal Revenue Service were entitled "Income Tax Return of a Foreign Corporation" (Form 1120F); however, Norsk has never filed income tax returns in Canada, the Bahamas, or any country other than the United States. To this end, Norsk is a foreign corporation for U.S. income tax purposes. Its primary source of income arises from the transportation of newsprint internationally.

In the relevant taxation years, Norsk paid no U.S. tax on the barge rental payments, claiming an exemption to which it was entitled as an international shipping company under § 883 of the *U.S. Internal Revenue Code, 1986*. This exemption accrued to Norsk owing to the fact that it had been incorporated in the Bahamas; given that the Bahamas has, in its income tax legislation, accorded a similar tax exemption to companies incorporated in the United States, these dual exemptions are reciprocal.

Crown Forest withheld 10 percent tax on the rental payments, using the argument that Norsk was a "resident of a Contracting State" for the purposes of the *Canada-United States Income Tax Convention* (1980). For residents, the usual 25 percent rate of withholding tax paid by non-residents[20] is reduced to 10 percent by virtue of Article XII of the 1980 Convention. Within the meaning of Article IV of the Convention, the term "resident of a Contracting State" means any person who, under the laws of that State, is liable to tax therein by reason of his domicile, residence, place of management, place of incorporation, or any other criterion of a similar nature."

Although the Minister of National Revenue ("Minister") re-assessed Crown Forest at 25 percent, this finding was quashed by Judge Muldoon of the Federal Court Trial Division who found Norsk to be a resident of a contracting party (the United States). Judge Muldoon's decision was upheld by the Federal Court of Appeal, Judge Décary dissenting. The Minister appeals to this Court and is supported by the intervener, the Government of the United States of America, neither of which wishes Norsk to be considered a "resident" under the Convention.

ISSUE

Was Norsk a U.S. resident and eligible for the reduced withholding tax rate provided for by the Canada-U.S. Income Tax Convention?

HOLDING

No.

LAW

"The tax convention defines a resident as a person who is liable in one of the contracting states to pay tax therein by reason of domicile, residence, place of management, place of incorporation, or any other criterion of a similar nature."

EXPLANATION BY JUSTICE IACOBUCCI

"... [I]t is important to take a step backwards and isolate exactly whom the Convention was intended to benefit. The target groups are Canadians working in the United States (or *vice versa*) and Canadian companies operating in the United States (again, or *vice versa*). It was deemed important, in order to promote international trade between Canada and the U.S., to spare such individuals and corporations double taxation (consequently promoting the equitable allocation of profits of enterprises doing business in both countries).[21] An ancillary goal would

---

[20]Pursuaant to §. 212(1) of the Income Tax Act, Statues of Canada, 1970–71–72, chap. 63, as amended.

[21]*See* Preamble to the Convention; *see also* Utah Mines Ltd. v. The Queen, *Dominion Tax Cases*, vol. 92, p. 6194 (Federal Ct. of Appeals), and U.S. Senate (Foreign Relations Committee), *Tax Convention and Proposed Protocols with Canada*, at p. 2: "The principal purposes of the proposed income tax treaty between the United States and Canada are to reduce or eliminate double taxation of income earned by citizens and residents of either country from sources within the other country, and to prevent avoidance or evasion of income taxes of the two countries."

also be to mitigate the administrative complexities occasioned by having to file simultaneously income tax returns in two uncoordinated taxation systems.

***

In the case at bar, I underscore that there is no need to prevent double taxation because the U.S. has declined to tax Norsk's revenue. Although this does not affect Norsk's tax liability, the effect is still that Norsk is not required to pay any tax in the United States by virtue of the § 883(a) exemption, this exemption arising by virtue of a reciprocal arrangement between the U.S. and the Bahamas, where Norsk is incorporated. Further, it is unclear whether the specific rental income at issue is even, independent of the exemption, subject to taxation in the U.S. because, pursuant to § 864(c)(4) of the *Internal Revenue Code*, it might not be considered to be effectively connected with the conduct of Norsk's American trade or business. Allowing Norsk to benefit from the Convention in this case would actually lead to the avoidance of tax on the rental income because the liability for tax asserted by the Canadian authorities would be reduced notwithstanding that the United States chooses not to impose any tax thereon or does not even have the jurisdiction therefore.

***

Under the prevailing practice, a country entering into an income tax treaty extends the benefits of the treaty to a person or entity that is a "resident of (the other) Contracting State." "Residence," in turn, is defined in terms of taxing jurisdiction. A person or entity is considered resident in a country if that country asserts an unlimited right to tax his or its income—that is, a right based upon the taxpayer's personal connection with the country (as opposed to the source of the income or other income- or asset-related factors). The test of residence requires that the person or entity claiming treaty benefits be "fully taxable" in the residence country, in the sense of being fully subject to its plenary taxing jurisdiction.

Full tax liability is not satisfied in a case where an entity is liable to tax in a jurisdiction only on a part of its income.

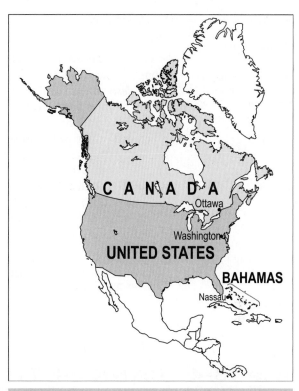

MAP 13-3 U.S., Canada, and Bahamas (1995)

ORDER

Crown Forest is liable for the 25 percent withholding tax. ∎

CASEPOINT: The tax convention defines a resident as a person who is liable in one of the contracting states to pay tax therein by reason of domicile, residence, place of management, place of incorporation, or any other criterion of a similar nature. It is not enough for Norsk to be a resident; it also must be liable to taxes in the United States as a consequence of its residence status. As it does not pay taxes, it is not a resident for the purposes of the tax convention.

SOURCE PRINCIPLE

source principle: A state may tax income derived from sources within its territory.

Countries applying the **source principle** tax all income from sources within their territorial jurisdiction and generally exempt from taxation income accruing abroad. [22]

Countries that impose taxes on the worldwide income of domestic and resident taxpayers typically impose taxes on the domestic income of nonresident taxpayers as well.

---

[22]J. D. R. Adams and John Whaley, *The International Taxation of Multinational Enterprises in Developed Countries,* pp. 10–11 (1977).

worldwide income: Income derived from all sources and from all parts of the world.

domestic income: Income derived from sources within a particular state.

Worldwide income, of course, is income derived from any source from any part of the world. **Domestic income** is income originating within a particular country.

Rules for Determining Domestic Income Sources

Domestic income is often described as income *accruing* or *deemed to be accruing*, or, alternatively, *derived* or *deemed to be derived* from *sources* within a country.

Sometimes these terms are interpreted in the tax laws; at other times, administrative agencies are given discretion (often "wide" discretion) to interpret them.[23] Commonly, income that is accrued or derived from sources within a country will include three kinds: (1) income derived from property located within the country (including interest, dividends, fees, royalties, etc.), (2) income derived from any trade or profession carried on through any agency or branch within the country (with agriculture, mining, and manufacturing often being mentioned as examples), and (3) income derived from employment carried on within the country.

In Case 13-4, a court was asked to determine if interest income earned abroad was a source of domestic income.

---

[23]Coopers & Lybrand International Tax Network, *1998 International Tax Summaries: A Guide for Planning and Decisions,* p. S-22 (George J. Yost III, ed., 1998).

Case 13-4   BANK OF THE FEDERATED STATES OF MICRONESIA v. GOVERNMENT OF THE FEDERATED STATES OF MICRONESIA

Federated States of Micronesia, Supreme Court, Trial Division, 1992.
Civil Action No. 1991-016.

DESIGNATED JUSTICE EDWARD C. KING

This action has been filed by the Bank of the Federated States of Micronesia to challenge the assertion of the national government of the Federated States of Micronesia that the bank must pay FSM income taxes on income realized by the bank from funds invested in banks in Chicago and Honolulu in the United States.

The case is now before the Court on the bank's motion for summary judgment. The bank seeks a ruling that the bank's investments in Chicago and Honolulu are not business activities within the Federated States of Micronesia and therefore are not taxable under *Federated States of Micronesia Code*, title 54, § 141.

I. BACKGROUND

The parties have stipulated to the material facts in this case. The bank is a banking corporation organized and operating under the banking laws of the Federated States of Micronesia. Since the bank has full service branches in each state of the Federated States of Micronesia and does

not engage in general banking activities elsewhere, there is no dispute that most revenues generated by the bank are subject to the national tax on gross revenues.

The dispute here concerns only the income realized from the bank's investment of excess funds in overnight loans or "fed funds" in accounts maintained by the bank with First Hawaiian Bank in Honolulu and with Boulevard Bank in Chicago.

Although interest from these investments in Chicago and Honolulu is reflected in the books and records of the bank, the bank has excluded that investment revenue for FSM income tax purposes on the theory that the revenue was derived from business outside the Federated States of Micronesia.

The government rejected the bank's interpretation and assessed taxes upon the bank's unreported investment income for the years 1987 through 1989. The bank has tendered the disputed amount to the Court for safekeeping and has filed this lawsuit to obtain a court ruling.

II. LEGAL ANALYSIS

The national income tax law does not seem to represent an effort to tax all income realized from all business activities of a business entity operating within the Federated

States of Micronesia. The law does not contemplate taxation of business income generated outside of the Federated States of Micronesia.

"Business" under the FSM income tax law means "a . . . undertaking carried on for a pecuniary profit and include all activities . . . *carried on within the Federated States of Micronesia* for economic benefit either direct or indirect. . . ."[24] Limitation of this definition to activities carried on within the Federated States of Micronesia strongly implies that activities carried on elsewhere by a business functioning within the Federated States of Micronesia are not subject to FSM income tax.

The implication of section 112(1) is confirmed by *Federated States of Micronesia Code*, title 54, § 142, which provides a method of apportionment for the earnings of a business which "derives its gross revenue from business activities or undertakings both within and without the Federated States of Micronesia during the taxable year. . . ."[25]

Section 142(1) creates a presumption that all of the revenue of such a business was "derived from sources within the Federated States of Micronesia." However, the section goes on to provide a method for rebutting the presumption. "The business may file for an apportionment of the tax on a form prescribed by the Secretary and the tax shall be levied only on that portion which is earned in or derived from sources or transactions within the Federated States of Micronesia."[26]

The government has not questioned the procedures employed by the bank in seeking apportionment. The only question then is whether the investment income generated by the deposits of funds in Honolulu and Chicago is derived from "sources or transactions or parts of transactions" within the Federated States of Micronesia.

In rejecting the bank's request for apportionment, the government pointed out that the funds invested by the bank in Honolulu and Chicago have been obtained from depositors in the FSM. The government therefore asserted that the funds are derived from "sources of transactions" within the Federated States of Micronesia.

This approach, focusing on the source of funds used to generate the additional revenue, ignores the statutory scheme, which emphasizes the location of the business activity which generates the revenue in question. The fact that the funds invested flowed from sources and transactions within the Federated States of Micronesia

MAP 13-4 Micronesia (1992)

does not alter the fact that the investment transactions themselves, which actually generated the new revenue sought to be taxed, took place outside of the Federated States of Micronesia. Those investments in Chicago and Honolulu were the source of this new revenue. Thus, the revenue is not subject to FSM income tax under the existing statute.

This result makes it unnecessary for the court to reach the other questions, relating to assessment of penalties, raised in the bank's motion for summary judgment.

III. CONCLUSION

The motion of plaintiff Bank of the Federated States of Micronesia for summary judgment is granted and declaratory judgment is granted in favor of the plaintiff. The funds tendered to the Court by the bank to be held while this case remains pending may be returned to the bank. ∎

CASEPOINT: Under the Micronesian income tax law, a business is a for-profit undertaking carried on within Micronesia. The government argues that the funds being invested in Honolulu and Chicago are obtained from investors in Micronesia. It therefore asserts that the funds are derived from *sources or transactions* in Micronesia. However, the fact that the funds invested flow from sources and transactions within Micronesia does not alter the fact that the investment transactions themselves (which actually generated the revenue sought to be taxed) took place outside of Micronesia. The bank's request for summary judgment was granted.

---

[24]*Federated States of Micronesia Code*, title 54, § 112(1) (emphasis added).
[25]*Id.*, § 142(1).
[26]*Id.*, § 142(2).

To determine if a trade or profession is *carried on* within a country, several countries' laws or regulatory rules provide a checklist of factors to be considered. These include (1) a fixed place of trade or business, (2) the manufacturing or assembly of a product, (3) the regular and continuous presence of employees, (4) the regular and continuous presence of after-sale support personnel, and (5) the active management of locally situated real estate.

To determine if particular income is *derived* from a trade or profession carried on within a country, the following factors are also commonly considered: (1) whether the gain was derived from assets used in the conduct of the trade or profession and (2) whether the activities of the trade or profession were a material factor in realizing the gain.

deemed income: Income is deemed to have come from a particular place depending upon the activity involved.

Deemed Income

Special rules often apply to deem where certain kinds of activities take place for tax purposes. The most important of these relates to sales transactions. Thus, a sale is usually *deemed to happen* where the buyer takes control or possession of the property. For example, the sale by a Costa Rican seller of 1,000 tons of bananas FOB London to a buyer in Poland would be deemed to have taken place in London. Similarly, the sale by an Egyptian of real property located in Uruguay to a Taiwanese would be deemed to have taken place in Uruguay. However, in some countries, a sale of personal property that is not in the ordinary course of business is deemed to have taken place in the taxpayer's country of residence.[27] Therefore, an American resident who speculates in stock sold on the Sidney Stock Exchange would have U.S.-source income on the sale of the stock.

INTERRELATIONSHIP OF TAXATION BASES

For countries that use more than one basis for determining taxation, one will be used as the ordinary, or default, rule and the other, or others, will be used as special or supplementary rules. The most common of the ordinary, or default, rules is the source principle. In such a case, nationality and residency are considered supplemental and subordinate rules that will either include or exclude the income of particular taxpayers, depending on the goals of the particular tax system.

PERSONS IMMUNE FROM TAXATION

The only foreign persons commonly able to escape taxes are foreign governments, diplomats, and international organizations. Governments can claim sovereign immunity. However, as we discussed in Chapter 3, sovereign, or state, immunity applies only to noncommercial transactions (i.e., transactions that do not involve the exercise of sovereign authority). Transactions of a commercial nature—such as the purchase or sale of goods or services, loans, guarantees, and employment contracts—are all potentially subject to taxation. Nevertheless, many countries choose not to tax foreign governments or to exempt them from certain types of taxation. For example, the U.S. Internal Revenue Code exempts "foreign governments," including "the integral parts [and] controlled entities of a foreign sovereign," from taxation on interest income, dividend income, and gains on sales of securities, and from branch profits taxes and withholding.[28] Income earned by foreign central banks from U.S. government obligations and from bank deposits is similarly exempt.[29]

Foreign diplomats are exempt from tax liability by the provisions of the Vienna Convention on Diplomatic Relations.[30] Embassy technical and support staff and consular

---

[27]United States, Internal Revenue Code, § 865.

[28]*Id.*, § 892. United States, Internal Revenue Service Regulations, § 1.892T(a) defines foreign governments, foreign agencies and instrumentalities, and controlled entities. The latter must (a) be wholly owned and controlled by the government, either directly or through other controlled entities, (b) be organized under the laws of that government, (c) have no part of its earnings inure to any private person, and (d) turn over all of their assets to the government upon liquidation.

[29]United States, Internal Revenue Code, § 895.

[30]Vienna Convention on Diplomatic Relations (1961), Articles 34 and 36.

officials are exempt only with respect to their employment in the embassy or consulate[31] (See Chapter 3.)

The immunity of an international organization and its personnel from taxation does not exist as a matter of course in international law. Exemptions depend on (1) the instrument creating the organization, (2) agreements between the organization and the particular state, (3) the applicability of multilateral tax conventions, (4) local tax law,[32] and (5) the applicability of general principles of international private law.

D. INCOME

INCOME CATEGORIES

personal income: The earnings or profits made by individuals.

business income: The earnings or profits made by companies.

capital gains: Increases in the value of capital or other long-term investments.

Taxable income may be categorized as personal or business income or capital gains income. **Personal income** and **business income** are the earnings or profits made by individuals and businesses. **Capital gains** are the increases in value of the underlying capital owned or invested in by individuals and businesses.

Many countries distinguish between personal or business income and capital gains income. In some countries, capital gains—which are commonly calculated only at the time of the sale of capital assets—are taxed at a different (usually lower) rate; in other countries, taxpayers are given tax breaks on their capital gains, depending on how long the assets are held or to what purpose the proceeds are put.[33] The main criticism of a capital gains tax is its implicit penalty on savings. Advocates look upon it as a social welfare measure. (The converse of these arguments is used when tax breaks are applied to capital gains.)

In contrast to those countries that impose taxes on capital gains at special rates, the great majority regard all sales of proceeds from a company as taxable at ordinary rates. In other words, all income derived from corporate assets is business income. In these countries, both capital gains and ordinary profits are treated as business income.

COMPUTATION OF INCOME

profit-and-loss statement method of computing income: Income is determined after offsetting allowable losses and deductions from all income received during an accounting period.

balance sheet method of computing income: Income is determined by calculating the difference in net worth at the beginning and end of an accounting period.

The income of employed persons is based on their salaries and wages. Income for self-employed persons and companies is calculated by one of two methods. The **profit-and-loss statement method** (where gross business income is offset by allowable losses and deductions) is used in the United States, the United Kingdom, Canada, Mexico, and the Philippines. Most of the rest of the world—including France, Germany, Italy, and the Netherlands—uses the **balance sheet method** (in which income is calculated as the difference between net worth at the beginning and the end of the accounting period). Countries using either of these methods make various adjustments to reflect local definitions of income. These typically include personal exemptions, deductions for expenses, and credits for double taxation.

INCOME TAX RATES

Only a few nations (Bolivia, Estonia, Jamaica, Latvia, Lithuania, and Sweden) impose flat rates on personal income. While some nations impose no personal income taxes, those that do generally use a graduated scale of rates, some with a large number of gradations. Flat rates are more commonly applied to company income; nearly two-thirds of all taxing jurisdicitons impose them. About half of these countries have different flat rates for companies that are involved in particular industries or activities, or that have a particular form of ownership, or both. Papua New Guinea, for example, imposes a flat rate of 25 percent but

---

[31]*Id.*, Article 37; Vienna Convention of Consular Relations (1963), Article 31.
[32]United States, Internal Revenue Code, § 892 grants a blanket exemption to international organizations. Section 893 exempts the income of employees of international institutions, unless they are U.S. citizens.
[33]Y. Neeman, "General Report," *Cahiers de Droit Fiscal International*, vol. 61b, pp. 20–22 (National report on "The definition of capital gains in various countries," 1976).

increases it to 30 percent for companies involved in natural gas and other mining operations, and to 50 percent for companies engaged in petroleum mining operations.[34]

Countries imposing graduated rates on companies are more likely to use fewer gradations (two or three rates being the most common) when compared to the graduated rates they impose on individuals. Also, in comparison to individual rates, the lowest company rate is likely to be higher than the lowest individual rate, while the highest rate is likely to be lower than this highest individual rate. Company tax rates are also sometimes different for foreign branches. The vast majority impose the same tax rates on domestic companies and foreign branches.

Many developing countries also make other special adjustments. Countries suffering from high inflation rates adjust their taxes using various mechanisms, including inflation indexes, accounting adjustments, and secondary currencies.[35] Peru, for example, uses an official index (known as the Applicable Taxable Unit) to calculate individual liability to income tax.[36]

In several developing countries, income rates may also be adjusted if the country decides that an investor or company has failed to report a reasonable profit. In Case 13-5, Mobil Oil (Nigeria), Ltd., reported diminished income following the loss of its facilities in eastern Nigeria to Biafran rebel attacks. Nigeria's Federal Board of Inland Revenue felt that Mobil's reported income was too low, and it imposed a higher adjusted tax rate. Mobil appealed the case to Nigeria's Supreme Court.

---

[34]PriceWaterhouseCoopers, *Corporate Taxes 2001–2002: Worldwide Summaries*, p. 633 (2001).
[35]Paul H. Vishny, *Guide to International Commerce Law*, vol. 2, § 2.06, pp. 9–12 (1998).
[36]Coopers & Lybrand International Tax Network, *1998 International Tax Summaries: A Guide for Planning and Decisions*, p. P-53 (George J. Yost III, ed., 1998) and PriceWaterhouseCoopers, *Corporate Taxes 2001–2002: Worldwide Summaries*, p. 646 (2001).

=✺=

Case 13-5 MOBIL OIL (NIGERIA), LTD. v. FEDERAL BOARD OF INLAND REVENUE

Nigeria, Supreme Court, 1977.
African Law Reports, Commercial Law Series, vol. 1977, pt. 1, p. 1 (1977).

Mobil Oil (Nigeria), Ltd., submitted audited tax returns to Nigeria's Federal Board of Inland Revenue for the tax years 1968 and 1969. Based on that return the Inland Revenue assessed, and Mobil paid, the amount of tax due.

In 1970, the Inland Revenue reexamined the company's accounts and informed Mobil that since its rate of profit for the years in question was lower than might have been expected, additional assessments were being made under Section 30A of Nigeria's Companies Income Tax Act (1961) on a percentage (15 percent) of Mobil's turnover for those years.

Mobil objected to this assessment, arguing that it had suffered losses in the Eastern Provinces of Nigeria that had

been part of the secessionist Republic of Biafra. (Biafran leaders had declared it independent in July 1967. After a prolonged civil war, its leaders surrendered in January 1970.) The Federal Board then agreed to assess Mobil on a lower percentage of its turnover (10 percent).

Mobil, nevertheless, appealed to the Appeal Commissioners. It asserted that its audited accounts were accurate; that its profits, as revealed in those accounts, were in line with the prevailing conditions of the market; and that the Inland Revenue was not entitled to make any additional assessments under Section 30A of Nigeria's Companies Income Tax Act (1961). Mobil also asserted that the Inland Revenue, having first accepted the company's audited return and having assessed the company on its assessable profits under Section 49(2)(a), was forbidden, by Section 60 of the Act, from imposing any additional assessments.

The Appeal Commissioners dismissed the appeal, holding that the assessed profits were less than what might have been reasonably expected. They also held that the original assessment under Section 49(2)(a) was not conclusive and that the Inland Revenue could collect additional taxes under Section 30A.

Mobil appealed to the Federal Revenue Court, which affirmed the decision of the Appeal Commissioners, and then to the Supreme Court. Mobil contended, among other things, that Section 60 of the Companies Income Tax Act (1961) permitted an additional assessment only if that did not "involve reopening any issue, on the same facts" and, since no new facts had been discovered, that Section 40 made the original assessment final and conclusive. The Inland Revenue answered this by arguing that under a proper interpretation of Section 60 an assessment could be reopened on the same facts if new issues—such as whether the company's profits for the years in question were lower than might have reasonably been expected—were discovered.

JUSTICE BELLO

***

There still remains the question as to whether the provisions of proviso (*b*) to Section 60 which authorizes the reopening of an assessment that has become final and conclusive under the main section are dependent upon the discovery of a new fact. The relevant part of the section is in these terms:

> Where no valid objection or appeal has been lodged within the time limited by Sections 53, 56, or 59 of this Act, as the case may be, against an assessment as regards the amount of the total profits assessed thereby, or where the amount of the total profits has been agreed to under subsection (3) of Section 53 of this Act, or where the amount of such total profits has been determined on objection, revision under the proviso to Subsection (3) of Section 53 of this Act, or on appeal, the assessments as made, agreed to, revised, or determined on appeal, as the case may be, shall be final and conclusive for all purposes of this Act as regards the amounts of such total profits. . . .
>   Provided that: . . .

(b) nothing in Section 53 or in Part XI of this Act shall prevent the Board from making any assessment or additional assessment for any year of assessment which does not involve reopening any issue, on the same facts, which has been determined for that year of assessment under Subsection (3) of 53 of this Act by agreement or otherwise or on appeal.

Chief Williams [counsel for Mobil Oil (Nigeria), Ltd.] conceded that notwithstanding the finality and conclusiveness of an assessment under the main section, the proviso permits the Board to make an additional as-

sessment "which does not involve reopening any issue, on the same facts, which has been determined for that year of assessment under Subsection (3) of 53 of this Act by agreement or otherwise or on appeal." He contended that as the first assessment on the assessable profits of the company had been determined by agreement, that assessment has therefore become final and conclusive and can only be reopened by virtue of the provisions of the proviso if there is a new fact. He concluded that since there is no new fact the finality and conclusiveness of the first assessment is absolute. In answer to this submission, Dr. Akintan [counsel for the Federal Board of Inland Revenue] contended that no new fact is needed to reopen an assessment.

It is pertinent to paraphrase the relevant provisions of Section 60 in order to highlight what is intended to be "final and conclusive" within the purview of the section. It may be read as follows:

> Where no valid objection or appeal has been lodged . . . against an assessment as regards *the amount of the total profits assessed* thereby, or where the *amount of the total profits* has been agreed to . . . or where the *amount of such total profits* has been determined on objection, revision . . . or on appeal . . . *shall be final and conclusive* for all purposes of this Act as regards *the amounts of such total profits.* . . . [Emphasis added.]

It is clear from the words of the section that the finality and conclusiveness of an assessment is restricted to the *amount of total profits* which has been agreed to or which has been determined on objection, revision or on appeal. It follows therefore that the *issue* in reaching such agreement or such determination is simply: What is the total profit of the company? The Act provides the means of resolving that *issue* which is the deduction from the turnover of the company of all its expenses, reliefs, and other matters in accordance with the provisions of Sections 27 to 38 inclusive of the Act. The amount arrived at from that exercise is *the total profit* of the company which will be final and conclusive if agreed to or determined.

Now to reiterate the facts of the case in hand: upon the returns submitted by the appellant company, the Board computed *the total profits* for the two years in question and assessed accordingly. The company agreed and paid. In the terms of Section 60 that assessment had become final and conclusive as regard *the total profits* made by the company for the years in question. Moreover, in terms of provision (*b*) to the section, *the issue* relating to that assessment, to wit: what were *the total profits* of the company for the two years, has been determined by agreement and cannot thereafter be reopened on the same facts.

It is not in dispute that the additional assessment under Section 30A was made on the same facts as the first assessment. The questions then are: What were *the issues* in making the assessment under Section 30A? Since *those issues* arose from the same facts, did they involve reopening the issue in the first assessment, which was: what were *the profits* of the company? If the answer to second question is in the affirmative, then the Board is prevented by the proviso from reopening it.

It seems that *the issues* in making the assessment under Section 30A are: Firstly, what were the total profits of the company? Secondly, were those total profits lower than might be expected? Thirdly, what fair and reasonable percentage of the turnover would the Board charge? The answer to first question has been agreed to in the first assessment and cannot therefore be reopened by virtue of the provisions of proviso. However, the second and third questions were *new issues* which did not arise at the time of making the first assessment and were not determined by agreement or otherwise at that time. Those two new issues subsequently arose after the Chief Inspector had made his discovery that the total profits of the company were lower than might be expected. Furthermore, neither of the *new issues* involved reopening the issue that had been determined in the first assessment. As a matter of fact, far from reopening the issue as to what were the total profits of the company, the Board partly relied on those total profits to make the additional assessment.

In our view the interpretation to be given to the provisions of proviso (*b*) to Section 60 of the Act is this: that the Board is prevented from making an assessment or additional assessment which may involve reopening any issue, on the same facts, which has been determined for that year of assessment; but the Board is not prevented from making an assessment or additional assessment not only on the discovery of new facts but also on the discovery of new issues which, though founded on the same facts, have not previously been determined. It seems to us that to construe the provisions so that it means that discovery of new facts is necessary in order to raise new issues for determination before making an additional assessment would defeat and frustrate the power of the Board under Section 50 of the Act, which power is expressly preserved by the proviso. A simple arithmetic error or error of law in making an assessment might never be corrected if such a construction were put on the proviso.

Accordingly, all the grounds of appeal argued relating to the liability of the appellant company for the additional assessment under Section 30A have failed.

The appeal was dismissed. ■

CASEPOINT: Should the original assessment be deemed final and conclusive, so that no new tax could be imposed by the Nigerian government? There were three issues involved: (1) What were the total profits of the company? (2) Were those profits lower than might have been expected? (3) What fair and reasonable percentage of the turnover should the Inland Revenue charge? Only the first had been decided at the time of the original assessment. The tax code does not prohibit the opening of new issues even if they are based on old facts. The company's appeal was dismissed.

INTEGRATION OF COMPANY AND PERSONAL INCOME TAXES

Countries differ in the ways they attempt to integrate company taxes and personal income taxes through the device of company dividends. Various systems have been devised, but all impose taxes based on the following three factors: (1) who the taxpayer is (i.e., the company or the shareholder), (2) whether the dividends have been distributed or not, and (3) whether income from dividends is treated as ordinary income or as a separate class of income. Here are the most important of these systems.

classical system for integrating company and personal taxes: Company taxes are imposed on a company's earnings and personal taxes are imposed on distributed dividends.

shareholder imputation system for integrating company and personal taxes: Shareholders are given credits for taxes paid by the company on distributed dividends.

The **classical system** of company taxation—which is used in most countries—imposes a tax on company earnings at the time they are received and on company dividends when they are distributed. That is, taxes are first imposed at ordinary company tax rates on the profits of a company. Later, when dividends are distributed, the recipients are taxed at ordinary personal income rates. The distributions are not deductible from the profits of the company, nor are the recipients entitled to a credit for the taxes already paid by the company. In other words, distributed profits are subject to both ordinary personal and ordinary company taxation, whereas undistributed profits are subject only to ordinary company taxes.

The **shareholder imputation system** is similar to the classical system: Ordinary company taxes are imposed on all profits, and shareholders must pay ordinary personal income taxes on distributed dividends. Shareholders, however, are given a credit for the taxes paid by the

company deduction system for integrating company and personal taxes: Companies are allowed to deduct distributed dividends as business expenses.

company two-rate system for integrating company and personal taxes: Companies pay higher rates on retained profits and lower rates on distributed profits.

shareholder two-rate system for integrating company and personal taxes: Shareholders pay lower tax rates on income from dividends.

shareholder exempt system for integrating company and personal taxes: Shareholders pay no tax on income from dividends.

full-integration system for integrating company and personal taxes: Shareholders pay taxes on all profits earned by a company, whether they are distributed or not. The company pays no taxes.

company on distributed dividends, which they may use to offset their personal income tax obligation. The company tax is *imputed* to the shareholder.[37]

The **company deduction system** is the converse of the shareholder imputation system. Companies are allowed to deduct distributed dividends as an operating expense before determining their company income (which they then pay at ordinary rates). Shareholders pay ordinary income taxes on the dividends they receive.

The **company two-rate system** applies two rates of company taxes: a higher rate for undistributed profits and a lower rate for distributed profits. Distributed profits are taxed at a lower rate to compensate for the personal income tax to be paid by the shareholder (at the ordinary rate).[38]

The **shareholder two-rate system** imposes a lower personal tax rate for income received as dividends. Companies are taxed at the ordinary company rate.

The **shareholder exempt system** imposes no taxes on dividend income received by shareholders. Companies pay ordinary income taxes.

Other systems are generally variations on these. Fiji, for example, uses the imputation system, except that it allows shareholders to deduct from their income the taxes paid by the company, rather than giving them a credit against their tax obligation. Peru uses a company two-rate system, except that it charges companies a higher (rather than a lower) rate on profits distributed as income.

One unique system is the **full-integration system**. This system imposes no company taxes; rather, all company profits, whether they are distributed or not, are deemed to be distributed to shareholders, and shareholders pay personal income taxes accordingly. This system, however, is not adopted as a general approach to taxation in any country. It has been adopted for smaller companies in a few countries, notably in the United States for S Companies and in Spain for small limited liability companies.

Two other factors that affect the amount of taxes collected by countries are (1) the nationality or residency of the shareholder and (2) the shareholder's personality (whether a natural or a juridical person). Thus, foreign shareholders may be subject to higher or lower personal income taxes on dividend income than nationals or residents. Similarly, many countries provide substantial tax breaks when the shareholder is a juridical person (i.e., a company). To illustrate, Portugal allows a holding company that owns more than 25 percent of a subsidiary to deduct 95 percent of the dividends it receives as a business expense. Sweden, on the other hand, exempts the subsidiary from paying taxes on any income distributed to a 25 percent holding company.

OTHER TAX-GENERATING TRANSACTIONS

merger: The absorption of one firm by another.

When one company **merges** into another, countries vary in the way they tax both the surviving company and the former shareholders of the merged company. The surviving company is commonly taxed only on the increase in book value of the transferred assets.[39] In Germany, for example, a taxable gain arises if the value of the transferred assets exceeds book value.[40] In Japan, a taxable gain exists when the value of the assets entered on the books of the surviving company exceeds the total amount paid to the merged company's shareholders in cash, shares, and swapped property.[41]

Similarly, the shareholders of the merged company are usually taxed only if they make a capital gain at a later sale of the shares they receive from the surviving company. To illustrate: Shareholder A buys one share in Company X for $10 in 2001. In 2002, Company X

---

[37]The shareholder imputation system is currently used in Canada, France, New Zealand, and Norway, among other countries.

[38]The company two-rate system is currently used in Germany, Japan, and Panama, among other countries.

[39]J. Van Hoorn Jr., "Taxation of Business Organizations," *International Encyclopedia of Comparative Law*, vol. 13, pp. 87–98 (1974).

[40]Paul H. Vishny, *Guide to International Commerce Law*, vol. 2, § 9.16, pp. 9-27 to 9-28 (2001).

[41]*Id.*, at p. 9-28.

merges into Company Y, and Shareholder A receives one share of Company Y in exchange for the Company X share. Shareholder A would have no tax obligation at this time. However, upon selling the share in 2003 for $12, Shareholder A would have a $2 capital gain and would be taxed accordingly. This is the rule in Belgium, France, Germany, Italy, the Netherlands, the United Kingdom, and the United States.[42] In countries that have no capital gains taxes, either the subsequent sale will be tax exempt (e.g., Costa Rica, Hong Kong, Hungary, Jamaica, Kenya, Malta, New Zealand, Poland, Portugal, South Africa, and Uganda) or shareholders of certain kinds of businesses will be subject to a special tax (e.g., Chile).[43]

consolidation: When two companies join to become parts of a new company.

Consolidations (or *enterprise mergers*), where two companies merge to form a new company, are generally tax-exempt transactions. As with mergers, the shareholders will be subject to capital gains only on a later sale of shares; and the new company will generally have no tax obligations as long as the assets of the merged companies are carried over at their book value.[44]

Shareholders of companies that are liquidated (i.e., closed down) may incur tax liabilities. In most countries, the liquidating firm will be taxed on profits made from the sale of assets but otherwise will incur no further tax liability. Shareholders will normally be taxed at ordinary rates on the distribution of assets. A few countries impose no taxes on shareholders at the time of liquidation.[45]

Companies that retain income are sometimes subject to a levy on the accumulation that is not distributed. Australia, for example, imposes a tax when a company has an *insufficient distribution* of dividend income and other related income. Brazil imposes a tax on reserves or retained earnings until they are distributed or converted to capital. Japan imposes a tax on close or family-owned companies that do not distribute earnings. Venezuela imposes a tax surcharge on stock companies that fail to distribute at least 50 percent of their income.[46]

E. DOUBLE TAXATION

Taxpayers who earn income in two or more countries face the problem of dual taxation. That is, income earned in one country may be (and often is) taxed a second time in another country.

SYSTEMS FOR RELIEF FROM DOUBLE TAXATION

double taxation: The payment of taxes on one source of income to two different states.

exemption system for relieving dual taxation: Income is taxed in one state and exempted from taxation in another.

It is now the practice in virtually all countries to provide relief from **double taxation** either unilaterally or through a bilateral or multilateral treaty. Relief may take the form of an exemption, a credit, or a deduction.

The **exemption system** provides for income that is subject to taxation in two or more states to be taxed in only one and exempted from tax in the others. Income may be exempted in either the host state (the state that is the source of income) or the home state (the state where the taxpayer resides). Commonly, an exemption system exempts income that has been taxed in a host state from further taxation in the home state. To illustrate, assume that the Transnational Nickel Co. (TNC) is a resident company in the state of Alpha. TNC establishes a subsidiary in the state of Sigma. The subsidiary earns $1,000,000 in Sigma and pays a 30 percent tax on those earnings. The balance of the earnings is then paid to TNC. TNC, under an exemption system, would have no tax liability on that income in Alpha. This would be so even if the income tax rate it would normally pay in Alpha is 40 percent or 20 percent.

---

[42]J. Van Hoorn Jr., "Taxation of Business Organizations," *International Encyclopedia of Comparative Law*, vol. 13, pp. 93–94 (1974).
[43]PriceWaterhouseCoopers, Corporate Taxes 2001–2002: Worldwide Summaries, passim (2001).
[44]J. Van Hoorn Jr., "Taxation of Business Organizations," *International Encyclopedia of Comparative Law*, vol. 13, pp. 90–94 (1974).
[45]*Id.*, pp. 84–87.
[46]Paul H. Vishny, *Guide to International Commerce Law*, vol. 2, § 9.17, pp. 9-28 to 9-29 (2001).

credit system for relieving dual taxation: Tax paid in one state may be used as credit for tax due in another state.

The **credit system** allows the tax paid in one state to be used as a credit against a taxpayer's liability in another state. The credit will be in the form of either a direct credit for an overseas branch or an indirect credit for a foreign subsidiary.

First, an example of a direct credit. Suppose that the International Business Co. (IBC) is a resident of the state of Beta, with a branch in the state of Omega. IBC has income in Beta of $1,000,000 and the subsidiary has income of $100,000 in Omega. Assume that Beta has an income tax rate of 50 percent on the worldwide income of its residents' companies, while Omega has an income tax rate of 30 percent on foreign branch income. Omega will collect $30,000 from the subsidiary, which IBC may then use as a tax credit. IBC's taxes in Beta (before the credit is taken) will be 50 percent of $1,100,000 (the $1,000,000 of income earned in Beta plus the $100,000 earned in Omega), or $550,000. The tax credit of $30,000 will then be applied, bringing IBC's tax bill in Beta down to $520,000.

Note, in the preceding example, the total tax bill paid by IBC amounts to $550,000, which is 50 percent of IBC's total worldwide income. The 50 percent rate is the same as the higher rate paid in the two countries.

Now, an example of an indirect credit. Assume that the Multinational Sales Co. (MSC), a company in the state of Gamma, has a subsidiary in the state of Lambda. The subsidiary earns $100,000, which is subject to a 30 percent tax in Lambda, or $30,000. To determine the amount of taxes due on the $70,000 dividend paid by the subsidiary to MSC in Gamma, a four-step *grossing-up* procedure will be followed.

First, the *deemed* amount of foreign taxes paid by the subsidiary to Lambda will be determined. This is the amount of foreign taxes paid multiplied by the ratio of dividends paid out to the after-tax earnings of the subsidiary.

Second, the dividend is grossed up by adding to it the amount of *taxes deemed paid* that were just calculated.

Third, Gamma's taxes are determined before the credit is applied. Assume that Gamma has a 50 percent tax rate.

Fourth, the taxes deemed paid to Lambda are credited to the amount of the grossed-up tax to determine the actual taxes due to Gamma.

Note that, as with the direct credit example, the total taxes paid on the $100,000 of income earned by the subsidiary amount to $50,000, or 50 percent: the higher rate of the two countries.

deduction system for relieving dual taxation: Tax paid in one state may be deducted as an expense from the tax due in another state.

The **deduction system** allows a taxpayer to deduct the tax paid to one state from the profits liable to taxation in another state. To illustrate, assume that the Global Commerce Co. (GCC), located in the state of Theta, has a branch in the state of Kappa. The branch earns $100,000 and Kappa subjects it to a 40 percent foreign branch tax on the remission of profits to GCC, or $40,000. Theta allows GCC to deduct the tax paid by the branch to Kappa from the income earned overseas. Thus, GCC subtracts $40,000 from $100,000, leaving taxable income of $60,000. This is then subject to Theta's tax. Assuming that the rate is 50 percent, GCC must pay Theta $30,000 in taxes. Note that the total tax bill in this example is $40,000 paid to Kappa and $30,000 paid to Theta, or $70,000.

COMPARISON OF THE DOUBLE TAXATION RELIEF SYSTEMS

From the perspective of the taxpayer, the most advantageous system of double taxation is the exemption system. By being exempt from tax liabilities in one state, the taxpayer is (generally speaking) subject to a lower overall tax bill. The least advantageous system is the deduction system. Because it only allows the tax paid in one state to be deducted from gross income in the other state, the overall tax bill tends to be higher. The principal adverse feature of the credit system is that the taxpayer ends up paying the higher rate of the two taxing countries. In sum, for most taxpayers, the tax relief systems can be ranked as follows: exemption system—best, credit system—intermediate, deduction system—worst.

From the perspective of states concerned with raising tax revenues, the ranking would be the reverse of that for taxpayers. The exemption system raises the least revenue, the credit system an intermediate amount, and the deduction system the most. Taking in the most tax revenues, however, is not always the principal concern of countries. Host countries often want to entice foreign businesses to establish branch offices or local subsidiaries, and home countries want to encourage businesses and employees to repatriate profits and incomes earned abroad. As a consequence, the least used of all the double taxation relief systems is the deduction system. The most popular—and almost universally applied system—is the credit system.

When asked to interpret double taxation treaties, a municipal court will take into consideration its state's objectives in granting this type of tax relief. Because home states are seeking to maximize the monies their nationals repatriate, and therefore maximize the tax revenues they can collect, courts in such states construe the relevant provisions in a tax treaty so as to favor the governmental tax-collecting agency. Host states, on the other hand, are looking to encourage foreign investment. Courts in host states, accordingly, generally interpret double taxation treaties in favor of the taxpayer. Case 13-6 provides an example of this.

━━◦◦◦◦◦━━

Case 13-6 DIRECTOR GENERAL OF INLAND REVENUE v. ROTHMANS OF PALL MALL (MALAYSIA) BHD.

Malaysia, Supreme Court (Kuala Lumpur), 1988.
Malayan Law Journal, vol. 1989, pt. 1, p. 32 (1989).

JUSTICE WAN HAMZAH

The question for determination by the Supreme Court in this appeal is whether Rothmans of Pall Mall (Malaysia) Bhd (the respondent company) is entitled, under the *Double Taxation Agreement* (1968) between Malaysia and Singapore, to double taxation relief in Malaysia for the Malaysian year of assessment [of] 1969 in respect of the Singapore income tax of $531,770.20 paid by the respondent company in Singapore on the profit for the period January 1, 1968 to June 30, 1968.

The following are the facts of the case. The respondent company was incorporated in Malaysia in 1961 and has a place of business at Petaling Jaya, Selangor. It had branch in Singapore which ceased business permanently on 30 June 1968. When the branch ceased business, the Singapore authorities assessed income tax on the respon-dent company for the Singapore year of assessment 1968 on the income of the branch for the period from January 1, 1968 to June 30, 1968 pursuant to the *Singapore Income Tax Act*. The income amounted to $1,329,433 and the income tax assessed thereon was $531,770.20. The respondent company paid it. There was no assessment of income tax on the respondent company for the Singapore year of assessment 1969. In Malaysia the income of the respondent company total-

ing $3,436,029 was charged to income tax of $1,546,214.40 for the Malaysian year of assessment 1969. This income included the same income of $1,329,433 of the branch in respect of which the respondent company paid in Singapore the income tax of $531,770.20 for the Singapore year of assessment 1968. The respondent company claimed from the Director General of Inland Revenue of Malaysia (the appellant) double taxation relief in the sum of $531,770.20 in respect of the income tax which it paid in Singapore, but the appellant disallowed it. The Special Commissioners dismissed the respondent company's appeal and affirmed that the respondent company was not entitled to the relief. The Special Commissioners stated as follows:

> It has to be noted that the 1968 Agreement only provides the double taxation relief on the basis of the year of assessment, which is very clear and explicit and effect should be given to it. In the instant case, the Malaysia tax was for the year of assessment 1969, whereas there was no corresponding assessment raised by the Singapore tax authorities for the year of assessment 1969. As such, there was no way possible to apply the double taxation relief as advocated under the 1968 Agreement.

The respondent company's further appeal to the High Court was allowed, and the appellant now asks the Supreme Court to restore the order of the Special Commissioners.

The provisions of the *Double Taxation Agreement* (1968) which are relevant in this case are those contained in Article XVIII, paragraph 2(i), which reads as follows:

> Subject to the provisions of the laws of Malaysia regarding the allowance as a credit against Malaysian tax of tax payable in any country other than Malaysia, Singapore tax payable whether directly or by deduction, in respect of income derived from Singapore, shall be allowed as a credit against Malaysian tax chargeable in respect of that income.

It should be noted that in paragraph 2(i) of Article XVIII, no reference is made to any year of assessment, so that it is immaterial and irrelevant which year of assessment the tax mentioned in that paragraph is in respect of. It is important to note the words "that income" at the end of that paragraph. These words specifically and expressly refer to the same "income derived from Singapore" referred to earlier in that paragraph. Thus, that paragraph means that Singapore tax payable in respect of certain income derived from Singapore shall be allowed as a credit against Malaysian tax assessed on that same income derived from Singapore, irrespective of which year of assessment that Singapore tax was assessed for and irrespective of which year of assessment that Malaysian tax was assessed for. In the present case, the Singapore income tax of $531,770.20 referred to above was assessed on the income of the respondent company's Singapore branch of $1,329,433. The Malaysian income tax of $1,546,214.40 referred to above includes income tax assessed on that same income of $1,329,433 of the branch. Therefore a credit of $531,770.20 representing the amount of that Singapore income tax should be given against that Malaysian income tax of $1,546,214.40 although that Singapore income tax was not in respect of the same year of assessment as that Malaysian income tax.

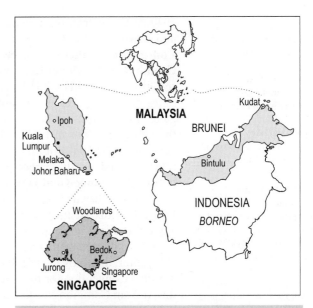

MAP 13-5 Malaysia and Singapore (1988)

Therefore the decision of the High Court is correct. We dismiss this appeal with costs.

The appeal was dismissed. ■

CASEPOINT: The Malaysia-Singapore *Double Taxation Agreement* provides that "Singapore tax . . . shall be allowed as a credit against Malaysian tax chargeable in respect of *that income.*" It is important to note the words *that income*. These words mean that Singapore tax payable in respect of *certain income* derived from Singapore shall be allowed as a credit against Malaysian tax assessed on that *same income* derived from Singapore, irrespective of which year the Singapore tax was assessed and irrespective of which year the Malaysian tax was assessed.

F. TAX TREATIES

The problems presented by double taxation—as well as other problems that arise from tax incentives, tax avoidance, and tax evasion—can be dealt with unilaterally (i.e., exclusively by one state) or through the use of reciprocal tax treaties. Although a few commentators have suggested that these problems can best be dealt with unilaterally,[47] most authorities hold that they can be better handled in treaties.[48]

Among the earliest advocates for the adoption of bilateral tax treaties was the League of Nations, which sponsored a group of experts who drafted several model tax treaties in the

---

[47]Robert Hellawell, "The Home-Country Tax Credit," *Negotiating Foreign Investments: A Manual for the Third World*, vol. 1, para. 3.2C1 (Robert Hellawell and Don Wallace, Jr., eds., 1982); Elizabeth A. Owens, "United States Income Tax Treaties: Their Role in Relieving Double Taxation," *Rutgers Law Review*, vol. 17, p. 428 (1963).

[48]T. Modibo Ocram, "Double Taxation and Transnational Investment: A Comparative Study," *The Transnational Lawyer*, vol. 2, p. 142 (1989); Klaus Vogel, "Double Tax Treaties and Their Interpretation," *International Tax and Business Law*, vol. 4, p. 10 (1986).

OECD Model Convention for the Avoidance of Double Taxation with Respect to Taxes on Income and Capital (OECD Model Tax Treaty): Model tax treaty promulgated by the Organization for Economic Cooperation and Development.

UN Model Double Taxation Convention between Developed and Developing Countries (UN Model Tax Treaty): Model tax convention promulgated by the United Nations for use between developed and developing nations.

1920s.[49] These draft treaties were later used by the Organization for Economic Cooperation and Development (OECD) in drafting its influential model treaty.[50] The OECD's **Model Convention for the Avoidance of Double Taxation with Respect to Taxes on Income and Capital (OECD Model Tax Treaty)** was issued first in 1963; it was revised and reissued most recently in 1998.[51] Possibly because the OECD model is aimed primarily at resolving tax disputes between developed countries, the United Nations focused its efforts on formulating guidelines for treaties between developed and developing countries. Committees set up by the United Nations in 1968 and 1974 both advocated the drafting of a model bilateral convention that would contain as many standardized clauses as possible.[52] In 1980, the UN Secretariat acted on these recommendations, issuing a **Model Double Taxation Convention between Developed and Developing Countries (UN Model Tax Treaty)**.[53]

Most tax treaties are bilateral agreements. Indeed, the United Nations' *ad hoc* Group of Experts on Tax Treaties between Developed and Developing Countries doubted in 1968 that any effort should be expended on developing multilateral agreements. Nevertheless, several multilateral agreements have been concluded, including the Double Taxation Agreement of 1966, entered into by the member states of the African and Malagasy Common Organization; the 1966 Convention for the Avoidance of Double Taxation, adopted by the member states of the Andean Common Market; and the 1972 Nordic Convention Regarding Mutual Assistance in Matters Relating to Tax, signed by Denmark, Finland, Iceland, Norway, and Sweden.

Some of the principal topics addressed in tax treaties—whether bilateral or multilateral—are (1) the persons and taxes covered by the treaty, (2) the basis (i.e., nationality, residence, or source) for imposing tax liability, (3) provisions for avoiding double taxation, and (4) provisions against tax avoidance and tax evasion.

COVERAGE OF TAX TREATIES

Most tax treaties mirror the coverage provisions of the OECD and UN model treaties (which themselves contain identical provisions). The taxes covered are income taxes, capital gains taxes, and taxes on net wealth. The persons covered are both natural persons and companies.[54]

BASIS FOR TAXATION

Both the OECD and the UN model tax treaties base taxation on the residency of persons within the contracting states. This was not always so. Some older treaties—including some League of Nations model treaties—based tax liability on citizenship. Today, with one notable exception, states do not insist upon taxing their nonresident citizens. The exception is the United States. In every tax treaty to which the United States is a party, without exception, the United States has refused to yield its right to tax the income of its citizens. The U.S. position is set out in Article 1 of the United States Model Income Tax Treaty, which provides:

> Notwithstanding any provision of the Convention . . . a Contracting State may tax . . . its citizens, as if this Convention had not come into effect. For this purpose the term "citizen" shall

---

[49]*Report by the Government Experts on Double Taxation and Evasion of Taxation*, Annex I (League of Nations Doc. F.50.1923.II, 1923).

[50]The U.S. Model Income Tax Treaty, published by the U.S. Treasury Department in 1976, revised and reissued in 1981, withdrawn in 1991, and revised and reissued in 1996, is based on the 1995 revision of the OECD Model Convention. The U.S. Model Tax Treaty is posted on the Internet at http://www.ustreas.gov/taxpolicy/t0txmod2.html. The 2005 update to the OECD Convention can be purchased on the Internet from the OECD online bookshop at http://www.oecdbookshop.org/oecd/display.asp?lang=EN&sf1= identifiers&st1=232005051p1.

[51]The OECD Model Tax Treaty is posted at http://www.lemaitre.de/dba-e/OECDE2000.html and at http://www. intltaxlaw.com/TREATIES/OECD%20Model.pdf.

[52]United Nations, *Guidelines for Tax Treaties between Developed and Developing Countries* (UN Doc. ST/ESA/14, 1974).

[53]UN Doc. ST/ESA/102 (1980). The UN Model Tax Treaty is posted at http://www.law.wayne.edu/mcintyre/text/UN_Model-color.pdf and at http://www.law.nyu.edu/vannr/spring00/1980.pdf.

[54]OECD, Model Tax Treaty, Articles 2–3; UN, Model Tax Treaty, Articles 2–3.

include a former citizen whose loss of citizenship had as one of its principal purposes the avoidance of income tax, but only for a period of 10 years following such loss.

The United States has said that its reason for retaining the right to tax citizens is based on the importance accorded citizenship in the United States. Economic factors, however, seem to be the predominant concern of the U.S. government. By retaining the right to tax citizens, the United States can discourage wealthy Americans from setting up a permanent residence in a low-tax country and obtaining substantial tax relief because of a tax treaty provision. [55]

Aside from this one exception, residency is the key factor in determining the coverage of most tax treaties. It is typically established by domestic law—that is, by domicile, residence, place of management, or some similar rule. If individuals have dual residency, their tax status will then be determined by a series of tie-breaking rules set out in the treaty. The following are the rules from both the OECD and the UN model treaties:

1. An individual is normally a resident of the country in which he has *a permanent home available to him.*
2. If an individual has a permanent home in both or neither of the counties, then his residence is in the country *with which his personal and economic relations are closest (center of vital interests).*
3. If a center of vital interest cannot be ascertained, residence is in the country of the individual's *habitual abode.*
4. If an individual has a habitual abode in both or neither of the countries, then his residence is in the country of which he is a citizen or national.
5. If all of the foregoing fail to determine residence, then "the competent authorities of the contracting states shall settle the question by mutual agreement."[56]

Both treaties also have a tie-breaking rule for companies with dual residency. Treaty residence in such a case is determined by the place of *effective management* of the company.

DOUBLE TAXATION PROVISIONS

The provisions in most treaties—including the OECD and UN model treaties—for eliminating double taxation depend on three factors: (1) residency, (2) personality, and (3) type of income.

The general rule for avoiding double taxation relates to residency. That is, persons may be taxed only by the states of which they are residents.

The exceptions to this general rule relate to the taxpayer's personality and the types of income involved. The first of these exceptions pertains to the following persons: (1) persons providing independent or professional services, (2) employed persons, (3) companies, and (4) certain special persons.

Persons providing independent or professional services include individuals who carry on "independent scientific, literary, artistic, educational, or teaching activities," as well as self-employed "physicians, lawyers, engineers, architects, dentists, and accountants." Such persons may be taxed by a contracting state where they are not residents if they maintain a fixed base within that state. However, only the income attributable to the fixed base may be taxed.[57]

Nonresident employed persons may be taxed in a contracting state to the extent of the earnings they receive in that state. They are not to be taxed, however, if (1) they are present in that state for less than 183 days, (2) they are paid by a nonresident employer, and (3) the

---

[55]See Donald R. Whittaker, "An Examination of the OECD and UN Model Tax Treaties: History, Provisions and Application to U.S. Foreign Policy," *North Carolina Journal of International Law and Commercial Regulation,* vol. 8, p. 39 at p. 47 (1982–1983).
[56]OECD, Model Tax Treaty, Article 4; UN, Model Tax Treaty, Article 4.
[57]OECD, Model Tax Treaty, Article 14; UN, Model Tax Treaty, Article 14. United Nations, Guidelines for Tax Treaties between Developed and Developing Countries (UN Doc. ST/ESA/14, 1974).The text of the Convention is posted at http://unpan1.un.org/intradoc/groups/public/documents/UN/UNPAN004554.pdf.

nonresident employer does not have a fixed base or permanent establishment within that state.[58] Case 13-7 illustrates how this works.

---

[58]OECD, Model Tax Treaty, Article 14; UN, Model Tax Treaty, Article 14. UN Doc. ST/ESA/102 (1980). The UN Model Tax Treaty is posted at http://www.law.wayne.edu/mcintyre/text/Treaty_Class/UN_Model-color.pdf. A comparison of the OECD and UN Model Tax Treaties is posted at http://www.law.wayne.edu/tad/Documents/Teaching_Materials/model_treaties.pdf.

—⟨⟨⟨⟩⟩⟩—

Case 13-7   JOHANSSON v. UNITED STATES

United States, Court of Appeals, Fifth Circuit, 1964.
Federal Reporter, Second Series, vol. 336, p. 809 (1964).

Ingemar Johansson, a Swedish citizen, fought Floyd Patterson three times for the heavyweight boxing championship of the world, winning the title in 1959 but losing it back to Patterson in 1960. Each of their matches was held in the United States. The U.S. government assessed Johansson taxes of approximately $1,000,000 on the resulting income. The government brought suit to collect the taxes, arguing that it was authorized by the Internal Revenue Code and not disallowed by a U.S. tax convention with Switzerland, which Johansson claimed exempted him from taxation.

CIRCUIT JUDGE RIVE

***

. . . However, Johansson claims an exemption under the Income Tax Convention with Switzerland [of] May 24, 1951 . . . (effective September 27, 1951). Particular reliance is placed upon Article X(1), which provides:

1. An individual resident of Switzerland shall be exempt from United States Tax upon compensation for labor or personal services performed in the United States . . . if he is temporarily present in the United States for a period or periods not exceeding a total of 183 days during the taxable year, and

   a. his compensation is received for such labor or personal services performed as an employee of, or under contract, with a resident or corporation or other entity of Switzerland. . . .

It is undisputed that Johansson was not present in the United States for more than 183 days in either of the tax years in question. But to bring himself within the purview of the treaty, Johansson had to establish (1) that he was a resident of Switzerland and (2) that he received the income in question as an employee of, or under contract with, a Swiss entity.

The term "resident" is nowhere defined in the Swiss treaty, but under article II(2) each country is authorized to apply its own definition to terms not expressly defined "unless the context otherwise requires." Johansson contends that, because of its position within the phrase "an individual resident of Switzerland," the term "resident" must be defined according to Swiss law. As conclusive proof that he comes within the Swiss definition of "resident" for tax purposes, he relies upon a determination by the Swiss tax authorities that he became a resident of Switzerland on December 1, 1959. Although the evidence on this point is ambiguous, the determination by the Swiss tax authorities may well have been based primarily upon Johansson's own declaration as to his residence in that country. . . . Be this as it may, we are not bound by the determination of the Swiss tax authorities. Article II(2) does no more than to provide the standard for defining the terms used in the rest of the treaty; application of that standard to particular facts remains, in this case, the job of the courts. There is no reason to decide whether the applicable standard for defining "resident" as used in the Swiss treaty is to be found in Swiss or American law, for under both laws the criteria are the same.[59]

Applying this standard to the facts of the present case, the district court concluded that Johansson was not a resident of Switzerland during the period in question. This conclusion is fully supported by the evidence. In the year and a half between the date Johansson claims to have moved to Switzerland and March 13, 1961, the record shows that he spent only 79 days in that country as compared with 120 days in Sweden and 218 days in

---

[59]*Compare* Locher, statement of Dec. 29, 1962, in Commerce Clearing House, *Standard Federal Taxation Reports*, para. 6407, p. 71286 (1963) ("sojourn . . . with the intention to remain"), with *Treasury Regulations* § 1.871-2(b) ("intentions with regard to the length and nature of his stay").

the United States. Except for his activities in the United States during this period, his social and economic ties remained predominantly with Sweden. Indeed, the summary of Johansson's ties with Switzerland presented in his brief to this Court cites only his maintenance of an apartment and bank account there, his self-declaration of residence, and two acts by the Swiss government that may well have been predicated upon his self-declaration of residence. . . .

Even if we were to find that the district court erred in determining that Johansson was not a resident of Switzerland, the tax exemption in the Swiss treaty does not apply unless Johansson received the income in question as an employee of or under contract with a Swiss entity. A contract of employment was entered into by Johansson in December 1959 with Scanart, SA, a Swiss corporation formed that very month. Scanart's sole employee and sole source of income is Johansson, who is entitled under the terms of the contract to seventy percent of Scanart's gross income, plus a pension fund. All expenses are to be paid by Scanart. During the period in question, Johansson conducted his affairs largely independent of Scanart's sole director or its stockholders. The circumstances surrounding the formation of Scanart, the terms of the contract, and the conduct of the parties under the contract led the district court to find that:

> Scanart, SA, had no legitimate business purpose, but was a device which was used by Ingemar Johansson as a controlled depository and conduit by which he attempted to divert temporarily, his personal income, earned in the United States, so as to escape taxation thereon by the United States. . . .

As with the question of Johansson's residence, the record amply supports this finding.

Of course, the fact that Johansson was motivated in his actions by the desire to minimize his tax burden can in no way be taken to deprive him of an exemption to which an applicable treaty entitled him. . . . And in determining the applicability of a treaty, we recognize the necessity for liberal construction. . . . But "To say that we should give a broad and efficacious scope to a treaty does not mean that we must sweep with the Convention what are legally and traditionally recognized to be . . . taxpayers not clearly within its protections."[60] . . .

The primary objective of our treaty with Switzerland, as well as of those with more than twenty other countries, is the elimination of impediments to international commerce resulting from the double taxation of

international transactions. The basic mechanism of these treaty arrangements is the establishment of standards for determining the single most appropriate locus for the taxation of any given transaction. Although some treaty provisions are inevitably the results of political compromise, the dominant criterion for determining the appropriate taxing locus is economic impact. Thus, as a general rule, the income from services is taxable where the services are rendered. Where, as here, services are performed in the United States and the compensation for them is drawn from the wealth of the United States, this is the country of primary economic impact and, consequently, the appropriate taxing locus.

There are, however, a number of prudential exceptions to the general "economic impact" rule. Among these is the view that a business enterprise engaged in international commerce ought not to be subject to taxation in every country in which it may transact some business. Although such an enterprise does draw upon the wealth of all the various countries with which it comes into contact, the overall objective of encouraging international commerce, as well as the practical necessities of business planning, are better satisfied by a centralized regime of taxation at the enterprise's "business seat" or "permanent establishment." The "business seat" exception is found in Article III of the Swiss treaty.

Elements of this exception are also found in Article X. Typical of what have become known as "commercial

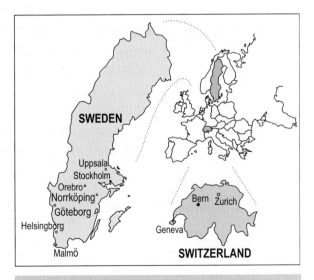

MAP 13-6 Sweden and Switzerland (1964)

traveler provisions" in international tax conventions, the article is designed to assure business establishments in each of the contracting states that they may freely send their agents and employees into the other contracting state without thereby subjecting those employees to the latter's taxes. Like Article III, it is an exception to the "economic impact" rule carved out in the interest of facilitating international trade. Where the practical reasons for the exception do not obtain, however, the general rule must apply. Thus, while Johansson may have brought himself within the words of the Swiss treaty by his "residence" in Switzerland and his "employment" by a "Swiss corporation," he has failed to establish any substantial reasons for deviating from the treaty's basic rule that income from services is taxable where the services were rendered. International trade will not be seriously encumbered by our refusal to grant special tax treatment to one only marginally, if at all, a Swiss resident and only technically, if at all, employed by a paper Swiss corporation. Therefore we affirm the district court's judgment that Johansson is liable for the taxes assessed against him in 1960 and 1961.... ■

CASEPOINT: The treaty grants an exemption from U.S. income taxes to Swiss residents who did not reside within the United States for more than 183 days and who derived their income from a Swiss employer. (1) The treaty does not define individual residency, but both Swiss and U.S. law define a resident as someone who *intends to stay* within a country. (2) The treaty defines the residency of a Swiss company as being the place of its *business seat* or *permanent establishment*. Between December 1, 1959 (when he claimed to have become a Swiss resident) and March 13, 1961, Johansson had resided in Switzerland only 79 days, as compared with 120 days in Sweden and 218 days in the United States. He clearly did not intend to stay in Switzerland. (2) Scanart was set up by Johansson as a conduit to allow him to escape taxation in the United States. Johansson, however, ignored the company and its stockholders and conducted his business on his own in the United States. Scanart was only a "paper" company, and what business it did was done within the United States. At best, Johansson was only technically a Swiss resident employed by a firm that was only technically a Swiss company. This was not enough to allow him to claim the treaty's exemption.

═══❦═══

permanent establishment: A fixed place of business wherein a nonresident carries on commercial activity.

Nonresident companies may be taxed by a contracting state if they maintain a **permanent establishment** within that state. However, as is the case for income earned by professionals from a fixed base, only the income attributable to a company's permanent establishment may be taxed.[61]

Because of its importance for avoiding double taxation for companies, the phrase *permanent establishment* is defined at some length in most treaties. The OECD and the UN model treaties use the term to refer to a fixed place of business at which a nonresident carries on any commercial activity, either wholly or partly. This includes, but is not limited to the following:[62]

1. Branch offices, factories, and workshops
2. Mines, oil and gas wells, quarries, and other places for extracting natural resources
3. Building sites, construction projects, and assembly projects that last for more than 12 months[63]

A permanent establishment does not, however, include any of the following:

1. The use of facilities to store, display, or deliver goods
2. The maintenance of a stock of goods or merchandise for the purpose of storage, display, delivery, or processing by another
3. The maintenance of a facility for purchasing goods or merchandise, for scientific research, or for collecting or disseminating information

---

[61]OECD, Model Tax Treaty, Article 5; UN, Model Tax Treaty, Article 5.
[62]In 1984, the United Nations conducted a survey of member countries asking them to identify the differences between the UN Model Tax Treaty and the bilateral tax treaties they had entered into between 1977 and 1983. As to the definition of a permanent establishment, most respondents indicated few differences. It was not uncommon, however, for the following to also be included: storehouses, warehouses used for the storage of goods for other sales outlets, plantations and other establishments for the exploration of natural resources, and service establishments. *International Cooperation in Tax Matters: Report of the Ad Hoc Group of Experts on International Cooperation in Tax Matters,* p. 26 (UN Doc. ST/ESA/185, 1987).
[63]The 12-month period is the time set by the OECD Model Tax Treaty. The UN Model Tax Treaty shortens this to 6 months.

4. The maintenance of a facility for advertising, marketing, or any other activity of a preparatory or auxiliary nature

5. The maintenance of a building site, construction project, or assembly project that lasts for twelve or fewer months

6. The carrying on of business through a broker, general commission agent, or any other agent of independent status acting in the ordinary course of business

The OECD and the UN model treaties differ in their approach to determining the income that may be attributed to a permanent establishment. The UN model allows profits to be attributed from a wider range of sources than does the OECD model by following what is known as the **force-of-attraction rule**. This rule says that if a company in Country A has a permanent establishment in Country B, then Country B may tax not only the profits generated by the company through the permanent establishment but also any profits that come to the company from trade or business that is carried on in Country B independent of the permanent establishment.

force-of-attraction rule: Because a firm has a permanent establishment within a state, that state may tax all of the firm's income, whether earned by the permanent establishment or not.

There are also certain special persons, such as the estates of deceased individuals and personal trusts, who are subject to taxation by a contracting state. Although these persons are juridical entities similar to companies, they are not business entities. Because they exist to manage the assets of an individual (e.g., a deceased, or the beneficiary of a trust), the OECD and UN model treaties look to the residency of that individual in determining their residency.[64]

In addition to the exceptions relating to a taxpayer's personality, the general rule that states may tax only their residents is also limited by special rules relating to different types of property. These special rules pertain to (1) immovable property, (2) dividends, (3) royalties, and (4) capital gains.

Immovable property is treated in virtually all tax treaties by a long-standing rule: "Income from real property shall be taxable only in the State in which the property is situated."[65]

The taxation of company dividends varies among tax treaties. Older treaties allowed only the contracting state where the capital was invested (i.e., the *source* state) to tax the resulting dividends.[66] The OECD Model Tax Treaty takes a different approach. If a parent company in Country A owns more than a 25 percent share of a subsidiary in Country B, Country B may impose no greater than a 15 percent withholding tax on dividends remitted to the parent; and Country A may tax the dividends received by the parent.[67] The UN Model Tax Treaty approaches dividends in a fashion similar to that of the OECD treaty, except that it leaves open for negotiation between the contracting states the percentage ownership of the subsidiary and the percentage of withholding tax that a source country may impose.[68]

The UN Model Tax Treaty treats the taxation of interest the same way that it treats dividends.[69] The OECD treaty takes a different (and more traditional) approach. It allows the state where the recipient of the interest is a resident to impose taxes. Additionally, the source state may tax the same interest by imposing a withholding tax, but that tax is limited to a rate of 10 percent.[70] However, if the recipient carries on a business or trade in the source state through a permanent establishment or a fixed base, then these interest rules do not apply. Instead, the interest is treated as ordinary income attributable to a company or to a person providing independent or professional services.[71]

---

[64]OECD, Model Tax Treaty, Article 14; UN, Model Tax Treaty, Article 14.

[65]Model Bilateral Convention for the Prevention of the Double Taxation of Income (Mexico Draft), Article 2 (League of Nations Doc. C.88.M.88.1946.II.A, 1946); Model Bilateral Convention for the Prevention of the Double Taxation of Income and Property (London Draft), Article 2 (League of Nations Doc. C.88.M.88.1946.II.A, 1946); OECD, Model Tax Treaty, Article 11; UN, Model Tax Treaty, Article 11.

[66]E.g., Model Bilateral Convention for the Prevention of the Double Taxation of Income and Property (London Draft), Article 2 (League of Nations Doc. C.88.M.88.1946.II.A, 1946).

[67]OECD, Model Tax Treaty, Article 10.

[68]UN, Model Tax Treaty, Article 10.

[69]*Id.*, Article 11.

[70]OECD, Model Tax Treaty, Article 11. Compare Model Bilateral Convention for the Prevention of the Double Taxation of Income and Property (London Draft), Article 9 (League of Nations Doc. C.88.M.88.1946.II.A, 1946).

[71]OECD, Model Tax Treaty, Article 4.

Royalties are also treated differently by the OECD and UN model treaties. Under the OECD treaty, they are to be taxed only in the state where the recipient is a resident (i.e., the home state).[72] Under the UN treaty, both the source state and the home state may tax royalties, but the contracting parties are to set a limit on the withholding rate that the source state may impose.[73]

The taxation of capital gains is treated similarly in both the OECD and UN treaties. Article 13 of the OECD Model Tax Treaty provides:

1. Gains derived by a resident of a contracting state from the alienation of immovable property . . . situated in the other contracting state may be taxed in that other state.
2. Gains from the alienation of movable property forming part of the business property of a permanent establishment which an enterprise of a contracting state has in the other contracting state or a movable property pertaining to a fixed base available to a resident of a contracting state in the other contracting state . . . may be taxed in that other state.
3. Gains from the alienation of ships or aircraft operated in international traffic, boats engaged in inland waterways transport, or movable property pertaining to the operation of such ships, aircraft, or boats, shall be taxable only in the Contracting State in which the place of effective management of the enterprise is situated.
4. Gains from the alienation of any property other than that referred to in paragraphs 1, 2, and 3, shall be taxed only in the contracting state of which the alienator is a resident.

Finally, it should be noted that while tax treaties are designed to avoid double taxation, there may well be loopholes that result in little or no tax collected from economic activity in the signatory state. In Reading 13-1, the government of South Korea learned that a four-billion-dollar (U.S.$) capital gain earned in Seoul might not be taxable. That, at least, was the claim of the U.S. hedge fund that made the investment.

---

[72]*Id.*, Article 12.
[73]UN, Model Tax Treaty, Article 12.

❦

Reading 13-1 TAX AND TRADE ENTWINED: SOUTH KOREA AND THE LONE STAR FUND

Foreign funds entered South Korea in the aftermath of the 1997–98 Asian financial crisis, buying distressed assets and selling them later for large profits when Korea's economy rebounded.[74] While this seems to be the fair fruits of entrepreneurial risk-taking, Korean press and politicians are concerned that tax treaties have made it possible for foreign companies to profit handsomely from investments in Korea without paying significant taxes. The story of Lone Star Fund provides an interesting example.

The Asian financial crisis spawned an era of relative deregulation in South Korea, creating a vibrant economy that is the 10th largest, according to the International Monetary Fund.[75] Opening South Korea's protected economy after the crisis made South Korea a popular destination for direct foreign investment. According to

---

[74]Carlyle Group (Delaware, PPB Washington DC), Newbridge Capital (based in California), Steel Partners II (hedge fund based in New York) and Lone Star Funds (a hedge fund based in Dallas Texas) have all found profit opportunities in South Korea in the aftermath of the 1997–98 Asian financial crisis.
[75]Martin Fackler, "U.S. Firm Has Korea Up in Arms," *New York Times*, July 6, 2006.

the Korea Trade-Investment Promotion Agency, South Korea attracted $9.6 billion in FDI, or 1.2 percent of its entire $800 billion GDP.

In 2003, the Lone Star Fund, a Dallas-based hedge fund, bought a 50.5 percent stake in the Korea Exchange Bank for 1.38 trillion won (approximately $US 1.5 billion). Either before or after Lone Star announced its plan in March of 2006 to sell its stake to Kookmin Bank (Korea's largest) for $6.6 billion, allegations surfaced that the original purchase price was artificially low because bank management and government regulators had falsified KEB's financial books. In November of 2006, Korean officials arrested the head of KEB during the bank's acquisition by Lone Star, for allegedly selling the bank at less than fair value. This allegedly cost shareholders US $24 million through breach of trust.[76] In December of 2006, South Korean prosecutors said that the fund's original purchase was illegal. The Seoul Central District Court has sought since then to extradite Lone Star executives for questioning.

As of May of 2007, a Seoul court was still looking into whether Lone Star conspired with local officials to drive down the price of KEB when Lone Star bought the stake in 2003, and whether Lone Star officials and others manipulated the share price of KEB's credit card unit to acquire it cheaply.

In March of 2006, when Lone Star announced its plan to sell the bank, a profit of $4.4 billion was projected. This provoked disapproving commentary in Korea, especially as Lone Star claimed the benefits of a Korea–Belgium double taxation treaty that would effectively shelter most of the gain from Korean tax. Legislative plans to amend the tax treaty were quickly afoot (Fackler, Mar. 2006). The Lone Star tax disputes with South Korea are said to include whether Lone Star bought KEB for less than its true value and whether bank officials and government bureaucrats accepted bribes in return for approving the deal.

At an April 19, 2006 news conference in Seoul, Lone Star Funds founder John Grayken repeated an earlier promise by Lone Star in an April 14, 2006, letter to the South Korean finance minister to set aside approximately $760 million in a South Korean bank account to cover any taxes owed on the proposed KEB transaction. The $760 million would cover the normal 11 percent withholding tax that would be imposed on the deal's proceeds in the absence of a treaty.

Throughout 2006 and early 2007, Korean prosecutors' investigations were preventing the Lone Star–Kookmin deal (valued at more than US $7 billion) from closing. While the investigation of Lone Star has fueled public resentment of Lone Star's use of tax treaties to avoid capital gains on the potential U.S. $4 billion profit.

Lone Star is not the only U.S.-based entity that faces inquiries from Korea. In April of 2006, prosecutors indicted the local head of the United States private equity firm Warburg Pincus on insider trading charges stemming from the 2003 purchase of LG Card, a credit card company. Newbridge Capital, another American investment fund, was investigated in 2006 by tax authorities after avoiding taxes on its $1.2 billion in profit from the sale of Korea First Bank. The American private equity firm Carlyle Group was criticized for not paying taxes on its $740 million profit from the sale of KorAm Bank two years ago.

Lone Star says it does not owe Korean taxes because Korea Exchange Bank was purchased by the fund's subsidiary in Belgium, a country with which South Korea has a treaty that alleviates its tax burden to Seoul. Lone Star said it would pay taxes on the sale in Belgium, where the rates are lower than those in South Korea. Carlyle did something similar with its sale of KorAm Bank, using a subsidiary in Malaysia, another treaty country.

Lone Star's battle with Korean prosecutors follows similar nationalistic reactions in the region. Some foreign investors believe that the investigation points to political uncertainties of investing in South Korea. A *New York Times* article by Choe Sang-Hun noted in February of 2007 that Lone Star's legal troubles follow "similar nationalistic reactions in the region" and have become a "test of the ability of South Korean authorities to balance protectionist local politics with the free-market behavior that outside investors expect from one of the world's largest economies."[77]

But it is not evident that all of Lone Star's moves in Korea were transparent, ethical, and legal, and Korea's right to close loopholes in its double taxation treaties with U.S. and European nations is not in doubt. Whether Korean politicians will deem it prudent to do so is another matter.

Ironically, Lone Star may be recouping significant portions of its gain even as the sale of its interest in KEB is held up by prosecutors. KEB officials announced in

---

[76]On November 16, 2006, a Seoul court issued warrants for the arrest of Ellis Short, Lone Star's global vice-chairman, and Mike Thomson, the company's legal adviser. Prosecutors wanted to question the two in connection with alleged manipulation of the price of shares in KEB's credit card unit prior to Lone Star's US $$1.2 billion acquisition of 50.5 percent of KEB in 2003. Short and Thomson face up to 10 years in prison and fines if convicted of charges that they misled minority shareholders by disseminating false information about a capital reduction plan at the KEB unit. But it appeared when the warrants were issued that the Korean government did not have the necessary evidence against either man to successfully pursue their extradition from the United States.

[77]Choe Sang-Hun, "Lone Star Gets Big Dividend in Korean Deal," *New York Times*, Feb. 3, 2007, at C9.

February of 2007 that shareholders would receive 1,000 won per share as a dividend (its first in a decade), despite a 48 percent plunge in its net profits in 2006. In June of 2007, Lone Star sold a 13.6 percent stake in KEB in a block sale for 1.19 trillion won (US $1.28 billion). It also said it was looking for a strategic investor which will take over the remaining stake.

South Korea's attempts to revise double taxation treaties with three European countries created some uncertainty for investors in Korea, according to European Union officials in May of 2007.[78] The EU had foreign direct investment inflows of €3.9bn ($5.3bn, £2.7bn) in 2006, making it the largest single investor in Korea. Trade talks in 2007 between the E.U. and Korea were set in the context of Seoul's concern that treaty shoppers were abusing its double taxation treaties, and Seoul was seeking to revise the agreements and impose tax on Korea-sourced income derived by foreign investors through tax shelters, especially those using tax arrangements between Korea and Belgium, Ireland, and the Netherlands.

The E.U. was eager to conclude a bilateral trade agreement with Korea, as the U.S. and Korea had concluded a bilateral trade treaty in July of 2007. Yet approval "KORUS FTA" may not be quick or easy. Labor interests in the U.S. were opposed, and South Korean auto workers went on strike in protest. Any agreements between the U.S. and Korea would only take effect when legislatures in both countries approve it. Democratic leaders in the U.S. Congress were not promising quick approval, and increased wariness over bilateral tax and trade treaties in Korea signals that balance and fairness are difficult to obtain, and that the actions of investors exploiting legal opportunities in double taxation loopholes may create frictions that slow the free exchange of products, services, and capital in a global economy.

---

[78]Anna Fifield, "Tax Treaty Threat to Trade Talks," *Financial Times*, May 3, 2007.

G. TAX INCENTIVES

Host and home states both attempt to encourage international trade with their taxation schemes. Host states primarily encourage trade through local tax incentives; home states generally concentrate on relief from double taxation.

There are many forms of tax incentives. Some of the most important are

1. Income tax holidays for foreign investors.
2. Capital allowances, such as accelerated depreciation.
3. The carrying forward of allowances for income tax deductions.
4. Exemptions, deductions, or credits for
   a. property taxes, including exemptions from mining taxes, forestry fees, and land levies.
   b. indirect taxes, including capital gains taxes, value added taxes, sales taxes, excise taxes, purchase taxes, etc.
   c. taxes paid on dividends to shareholders.
   d. social security and employment taxes.
   e. research and development costs.
   f. loans.
5. Import incentives, such as waivers or deductions from import duties on equipment, spare parts, and raw materials.
6. Export incentives, such as export subsidies, waivers of export tariffs, and the waiver of import duties for intermediate goods used in the manufacture of export goods.
7. The deferment of corporation registration fees and duties.
8. Tax exemptions for expatriate employees.

Tax incentives are generally meant to assist new industries during their first years, when they are subject to many start-up costs and to competition from existing competitors. Sometimes, host states are overly anxious to grant incentives. This can result in situations where a multinational enterprise plays one potential host state off against another as the multinational enterprise looks for a profitable place to site a branch office or subsidiary.[79] It can also result in situations where the multinational enterprise does not benefit from the tax incentives. This happens where the home state does not recognize tax sparing.

TAX SPARING

Tax sparing entails the recognition by the home state of tax incentives granted by the host state as being equivalent to the payment of a tax. To illustrate the consequences of the absence of a tax-sparing provision in a home state, consider the following example. Transworld Co., a resident of the state of Sigma, has a branch office in the state of Omicron. The branch was set up in Omicron because Omicron (a developing country anxious for new industry) granted Transworld a 10-year holiday from the payment of its income taxes. Sigma, on the other hand, taxes Transworld on its worldwide income, and its double taxation relief provisions grant a credit only for taxes actually paid abroad. Because Transworld does not pay any taxes in Omicron, there is no creditable foreign tax. In effect, Transworld receives no benefit from Omicron's tax holiday. Instead, Sigma's taxing authority gets a windfall.

So that companies can benefit from host state tax incentives, home states must recognize tax sparing. Tax-sparing provisions commonly appear in tax treaties, especially in treaties between the United Kingdom and less developed countries and between continental European countries and less developed countries. The United States does not recognize tax sparing.[80]

THE INTERACTION OF TAX SYSTEMS

For legislators writing national tax laws and business managers developing an international development strategy for their companies, it is vital to understand that double taxation, double taxation relief, tax incentives, and tax sparing, as well as the tax laws of home and host countries, all interact to form a matrix of international tax law. For every goal that may be achievable by tax legislation, there are always potentially adverse consequences, depending on the mechanism chosen. Exhibit 13-1 shows some examples.

Goal	Mechanism	Consequences
Encourage investment	Lower taxes	Decreased tax revenue
Raise tax revenues	Raise taxes	Discourages investment
Encourage foreign investment	Allow foreign direct investment	Foreign ownership of local business
Encourage local ownership of business	Discourages foreign investment	Limit foreign direct investment
Restrict access to local markets	Tax foreign-owned subsidiaries	Discourages foreign investment
Encourages access to foreign markets	Reciprocal access to home markets	Loss of local jobs
Protect local jobs	Tax foreigners with access to local markets	Retaliatory loss of foreign markets

EXHIBIT 13-1   Adverse Consequences of Some Tax Mechanisms

[79]T. Modibo Ocran, "Double Taxation Treaties and Transnational Investment: A Comparative Study," *Transnational Lawyer*, vol. 2, p. 141 (1989).
[80]Robert Hellawell, "The Home-Country Tax Credit," *Negotiating Foreign Investments: A Manual for the Third World*, vol. 1, paras. 3.2D16 and 3.2D17 (Robert Hellawell and Don Wallace Jr., eds., 1982).

H. TAX AVOIDANCE AND EVASION

Tax avoidance involves efforts by individuals and companies to take advantage of loopholes in the tax laws or, where some doubt exists as to the interpretation of a tax law, to benefit from that doubt. Tax evasion, by comparison, is the deliberate and illegal nonpayment of taxes. The former is legal, if sometimes only technically legal; the latter is illegal. The dividing line between the two, however, is seldom clear. Tax avoidance can easily become tax evasion, or vice versa.

In 1984, an *ad hoc* United Nations Group of Experts on International Cooperation in Tax Matters devised a list of examples of tax avoidance and tax evasion. That list is summarized in Exhibit 13-2.

Tax Avoidance Devices

Transformation of Income
Transformation of ordinary income into capital gains
Transformation of capital gains into ordinary income
Transformation of payments for goods or services into interest-free or indefinite loans

Thin Capitalization
Use of high ratio of loans to equity to achieve a tax advantage
Use of investments in exchange for royalties or fees to achieve a tax advantage
Transfer of legal ownership while retaining beneficial ownership
Transfer of income or assets to a controlled company that is tax exempt
Transfer of income or assets to a controlled company subject to lower tax rates

Transfer Pricing
Transfer income to a branch or subsidiary in a low-tax country
Transfer income to a branch or subsidiary in a country with a double-tax treaty
Transfer income to a branch or subsidiary in a country with incentives or reliefs
Allocate expenses to a branch or subsidiary in a high-tax country

Tax Evasion Devices

Failure to Provide Tax-Related Information
Failure to file a return
Failure to report all income or assets subject to tax

Misrepresentation of Items of Income
Improper characterization of a gift of property as a sale
Improper characterization of a gift of money as a loan
Improper characterization of fees, interest, or royalties as dividends
Improper characterization of the lease of equipment as a purchase

Misrepresentation of Items of Expense
Allocation of inflated head-office expenses to branches
Allocation of inflated parent-company expenses to subsidiaries
Charging inflated fees for technical assistance and special services
Overstatement of costs incurred in the implementation of turnkey projects

Material Concealment
Concealment of imported or exported goods
Concealment of wealth
Concealment of transfer of money

Concealment through Falsification of Accounts
Preparation of separate accounts
False invoicing
Inclusion of personal expenditure in company accounts under overhead

---

EXHIBIT 13-2 Tax Avoidance and Tax Evasion Devices

Sales without invoicing
Invoicing without sales
Claiming false deductions

Flight of Taxpayer to Another Country
Remuneration splitting
Misrepresentation that services were performed abroad

Disguising Remuneration
Disguising remuneration as reimbursement of expenses
Disguising perquisites

EXHIBIT 13-2   *(continued)*

Source: International Cooperation on Tax Matters: Guidelines for International Cooperation Against the Evasion and Avoidance of Taxes (with Special Reference to Taxes on Income, Profits, Capital and Capital Gains) (UN Doc. ST/ESA/142, 1984).

TAX AVOIDANCE

tax avoidance: Taking advantage of legal or arguably legal tax loopholes.

Tax avoidance provides some of the most difficult problems for tax authorities to counteract. Multinational enterprises frequently have armies of accountants ready to evaluate every possible loophole for its tax-saving potential and hordes of lawyers prepared to advocate the legitimacy of those that have maximum economic value to the company. Revenue agencies, on the other hand, especially in less developed and developing countries, often lack the manpower necessary to respond to the tax avoidance schemes devised by foreign multinationals. Moreover, a revenue agency in one country is frequently forbidden (by domestic constitutional and legal constraints) or limited (by jealousy, bureaucratic inertia, or the absence of an international accord) in sharing information with a sister agency in another country. Despite these constraints, some countries (most notably the members of the OECD) have taken both individual and cooperative action to counter the most tax-costly forms of tax avoidance. These are generally grouped under the names *tax havens*, *transfer pricing*, *treaty shopping*, and *thin capitalization*.

Tax Havens

tax haven: A state that imposes taxes that are substantially lower than those in other states.

Countries or territories that provide a refuge from taxes for (1) taxpayers themselves, (2) the taxpayers' income, or (3) the taxpayers' capital and other assets are known as **tax havens**. Commonly, tax havens not only impose few if any taxes, they also have secrecy laws that forbid foreign governments from obtaining information about the ownership of particular assets, as well as rules that allow for the full and complete transfer and exchange of currencies. The idea of offering either partial or complete exemption from taxation to foreigners is not a modern idea. In the Middle Ages, the city of London exempted merchants of the Hanseatic League from all its taxes. Flanders, in the fifteenth century, eliminated duties on most of its overseas trade. This (along with the absence of exchange restrictions on the repatriation of profits) attracted foreign merchants, especially English merchants who preferred to sell their wool in Flanders rather than pay England's high duties. The Netherlands, in the sixteenth, seventeenth, and eighteenth centuries, also imposed low duties and few restrictions. Each of these places became international commercial centers and thriving ports of trade. Today, many countries and territories—some that are commercial centers and others that aspire to be—continue to function as tax havens.

In the past several decades, the scale on which individuals and companies have moved their operating bases to tax havens to obtain relief or refuge from political interference with their assets has grown dramatically. At the same time, this growth has been paralleled by an increase in the number of attempts to define and to curtail tax havens.

The term *tax haven*, although in widespread use, has no internationally accepted definition. In part, this is because the concept is a relative one. One country with substantially lower tax rates on some (or all) taxable income may be considered a tax haven by a second country with substantially higher rates. It is also because the term has often been used pejoratively, so that countries with lower tax rates are unwilling to accept the *tax haven* label.

Several approaches to defining tax havens are used in national legislation. One is to make a list of countries that are regarded as tax havens. Germany, Australia, and Japan, for example, have compiled such lists. A second approach is to define tax havens quantitatively. Article 238A of the French General Tax Code, for example, describes a tax haven as a foreign state or territory that imposes "taxes on profits or income that are substantially lower than in France." What is meant by *substantially lower* is stated—albeit indirectly—in Article 81A:

> Salaries and wages received as remuneration for activities undertaken abroad by French nationals having their fiscal domicile in France who are sent abroad by an employer established in France are not subject to income tax when the taxpayer can prove that the remuneration concerned was in fact subject to income tax in the State where the activities are undertaken and that the foreign tax is equal to at least two-thirds of the tax he would have had to pay in France on the same tax basis.

The United Kingdom has taken a similar approach, defining a tax haven as one that imposes taxes on a company controlled by U.K. residents that are less than one-half of what the company would pay in the United Kingdom.

Other approaches involve neither making a list of nor defining tax havens. Canada, for example, has adopted a *functional* approach. Instead of enacting legislation directed particularly or exclusively at tax havens, it has adopted general legislation that effectively limits the usefulness of tax havens to Canadian taxpayers. The United States has taken a *transactional* approach, imposing restrictions on certain types of income (generally income from foreign holding companies controlled by Americans) and certain types of transactions (typically transactions with related persons) that commonly involve the use of tax havens.

Because individuals and companies do business in tax havens, this does not necessarily mean that they do so to escape high taxes. Some of the nontax reasons why individuals and firms may do business in a tax haven are the following: (1) to cater to the needs of the tax haven country itself; (2) to remain anonymous for reasons other than avoiding taxes (such as concealing one's identity for personal safety, or to avoid possible boycotts of one's products, or to conceal one's activities from competitors); (3) to protect a company or corporate group from nationalization, political unrest, revolution, or war; and (4) to avoid rules and regulations in a home country (such as national banking laws that dictate interest rate ceilings and set reserve requirements, company laws that prescribe particular management structures, or regulations that restrict foreign exchange).

Of course, many operations carried out in tax havens are tax motivated, at least in part. Many of these are legitimate forms of tax avoidance (as compared to tax evasion), conforming to the laws both in the tax haven country and in the investor's home state. In such instances, of course, the possibility of minimizing one's taxes will depend not only on the tax relief offered by the tax haven country but also on the anti–tax haven laws in force in the home country. Some of the legitimate tax-motivated uses of tax havens are the following: (1) overall reduction of a person's tax burden; (2) deferral of tax payments on income from foreign sources until after it is repatriated to the home country so that profits can be accumulated without being depleted by tax payments; (3) minimizing taxes on certain types of income (such as investment income, income from shipping, etc.) that are covered by exceptions to the home country's anti-tax haven legislation; and (4) centralizing income in a tax haven country and repatriating it to the home country in a nontaxable form.

What might best be described as a model worldwide anti-tax haven law is the so-called Subpart F of the U.S. Internal Revenue Code.[81] Other countries with similar laws—including Canada, France, Germany, Japan, and the United Kingdom—have modeled their legislation on the American provisions. Several of these (France, Germany, Japan, and the United Kingdom) have, however, restricted the application of their laws to income derived from

---

[81]Sections 951–964, which constitute Subpart F of Part III of Subchapter N of Chapter 1 of Subtitle A of the Internal Revenue Code. These sections of the Internal Revenue Code are posted on the Internet at http://www4.law.cornell.edu/uscode/26/951.html.

countries listed or defined as tax havens. As mentioned earlier, the U.S. rules are not limited to income derived from any particular country.[82]

The U.S. Subpart F rules apply to certain U.S. shareholders of controlled foreign corporations (CFCs). A CFC is a foreign business entity equivalent to an American corporation that on any day of the entity's taxable year has more than 50 percent of all of its voting stock owned or controlled by U.S. shareholders. U.S. shareholders are "United States persons" (i.e., citizens, residents, domestic partnerships, corporations, estates, or trusts) who own more than 10 percent of the voting stock of the foreign business entity. Such shareholders are taxed on certain deemed income of the CFC whether or not it has been distributed. The deemed income includes (1) income from investments in the United States and (2) Subpart F income. Subpart F income is (1) income derived from the insurance of risks in the United States; (2) income earned by a foreign holding company[83]; (3) income earned from sales to a related company (i.e., one that controls the CFC, is controlled by the CFC, or is controlled by the persons who control the CFC); (4) income from services provided to a related company; (5) income derived from the use of an aircraft or vessel in foreign commerce; (6) income accrued from processing, transporting, or distributing oil or gas when these activities are located in a foreign country other than the country in which the oil or gas is extracted; (7) income produced from participation in an international boycott; and (8) the amounts of any illegal bribes, kickbacks, or other payments made to any official, employee, or agent of a government.[84]

Although the U.S. Subpart F Rules are intended to discourage U.S. corporations from re-incorporating outside the United States to take advantage of lower corporate tax rates, a number of U.S. companies have done so anyway. Among the companies who have become U.S. "tax dodgers" are Accenture, Foster Wheeler, Global Crossing, Ingersoll-Rand, Stanley Works, and Tyco.[85]

---

[82]For a comparison of the anti-tax haven laws of Canada, France, Germany, Japan, the United Kingdom, and the United States, see Organization for Economic Cooperation and Development, *International Tax Avoidance and Evasion,* pp. 55–57 (1987).

As of November 2000, the following countries had adopted legislation (in the years indicated) similar to the U.S. CFC legislation: Germany (1972); Canada (1972); Japan (1978); France (1980); United Kingdom (1984); New Zealand (1988); Sweden (1990); Australia (1990); Norway (1992); Finland (1995); Spain (1995); Indonesia (1995); Portugal (1995); Denmark (1995); Korea (1996); Hungary (1997); Mexico (1997); South Africa (1997); Estonia (2000); Italy (2000). Department of the Treasury, The Deferral of Income Earned Through U.S. Controlled Foreign Corporations, p. 58, n. 10 (2000) at http://www.treas.gov/offices/tax-policy/library/subpartf.pdf.

[83]The United States also has rules that impose taxes directly on the shareholders of foreign personal holding companies (FPHCs). United States, Internal Revenue Code, §§ 551–556. These rules are similar to those that govern CFCs. Indeed, there is substantial overlap; and, to the extent there is overlap, the rules governing CFCs are applied. Id., § 951(d).

[84]The Taxpayer Relief Act of 1997, United States Statues, title 111, § 788 (1997) exempted from deemed income that income received from the active conduct of a banking, financing, or similar business.

[85]Daniel Gross, "Dodging the Costs of Corporate Citizenship." Business 2.0 (March 27, 2002) at http://money.cnn.com/2002/03/27/technology/techinvestor/tech_investor/index.htm.

Reading 13-2 HOW DIRTY MONEY THWARTS CAPITALISM'S TRUE COURSE

RAYMOND BAKER AND JENNIFER NORDIN, *Financial Times*, October 10, 2005.

If smuggling drugs across borders is bad, is smuggling profits across borders through abusive transfer pricing also bad? If tax evasion out of one country is harmful, is the inflow of tax-evading money into another also harmful? If money laundering by terrorists is dangerous, is the use of similar techniques by companies dangerous?

More than at any time in capitalism's history, our

economic system is beset by the tension between what is legal, what is ethical and what serves the common good. This tension points to a fundamental question: which should come first for the global capitalist–maximising profits or pursuing lawful and just business transactions?

Over the past four decades or so, a structure has been perfected that facilitates illegal cross–border financial transactions. This "dirty money" structure consists of tax havens, secrecy jurisdictions, abusive transfer pricing, dummy companies, anonymous trusts, hidden accounts, solicitation of ill-gotten gains, kickbacks and loopholes left in the laws of western countries that encourage incoming criminal and tax–evading funds.

Only the bare outlines of this dirty money structure were available in, say, 1960. Today, perhaps half of cross-border commerce involves parts of this system, often used to generate, shift and hide illicit proceeds. Many multinational companies and international banks regularly use this structure, which functions by ignoring or skirting customs, tax, financial and money laundering laws. The result is nothing less than the legitimization of illegality.

If tax evasion was the only consequence of this dirty money structure, some might argue that it serves a useful purpose by maximizing profits and shareholder values. But the ugly truth is that this same system aids drug lords, mafia dons and terrorist groups. By our estimate, it moves some $500bn a year illegally out of developing and transitional economies into western coffers. The Tax Justice Network (UK) estimates that $11,000bn is stashed away in tax havens and secrecy jurisdictions. The missing trillions further weaken poor countries, contributing to crime, terrorism, destabilization, and deprivation for billions of people.

Why has so much unethical behaviour become business as usual? One explanation is greed, pure and simple. But this does not adequately explain the phenomenon and demeans many in business who believe they are operating in an ethical manner. An overriding commitment to maximizing gains, taking priority over other principles, comes closer.

How did we get here? We trace our capitalist roots to the revolutionary concepts of Adam Smith. He articulated the ideas that free and open trade benefits nations, taxation should be fair and predictable and competition should be unfettered by monopolies. Drawing on his primary interest in moral philosophy, his vision for this new economic order anticipated leaders of integrity, prudence, modesty and grace who would operate the free-market system with a sense of justice and fair play.

Unfortunately, Smith's moral sentiments got separated from his economics. The greatest good for the greatest number–maximizing–became the foundation of utilitarianism, a competing school of thought much more compatible with budding capitalists. A key concern for capitalism in the 21st century is the question of priorities.

Will it be maximizing before justice or justice before maximizing? This is an issue of everyday importance for business people operating globally.

It is fairly easy to do business in foreign countries without breaking laws or perpetrating injustices. It is virtually impossible to do business using tax havens, secrecy jurisdictions, abusive transfer pricing, anonymous entities and secret accounts without breaking laws and perpetrating injustices in many countries.

The free-market system has enormous advantages over any other. Yet the great amount of good that capitalism has wrought disguises the fact that it could accomplish so much more. Making just business transactions a top priority is necessary if capitalism is to achieve its fullest potential and spread prosperity to all. Dismantling the dirty money structure is a crucial first step.

━━━◈━━━

Transfer Pricing

transfer pricing: A device used by affiliated companies to take advantage of differing tax rates in different countries. On transfers between the affiliates, a high price is charged to the affiliate in the high-tax state, so that it will have a small profit, and a low price is charged to the affiliate in the low-tax state so that it will have a large profit. The result for the worldwide operation is a net savings.

Consider two associated business establishments that are residents of different states. They may be loosely linked affiliates or close-knit elements of a multinational enterprise. In either case, they are under common ownership, and in both cases they **transfer** goods or merchandise back and forth between themselves. The price they set on the transfer of goods and services from one establishment to another is arbitrary. If the same taxing authority were taxing both establishments, the price would also be irrelevant, because the profit made by the overall enterprise would always be the same, and so would the taxes. However, if one enterprise is located in a low-tax country and the other in a high-tax country, this would not be the case. By charging the enterprise in the high-tax state a high price on transfers from the enterprise in the low-tax state, the first enterprise will have a lower profit and therefore less taxable income that is subject to taxation at high rates, whereas the second enterprise will have a higher profit and more taxable income to be taxed at low rates. The effect for the overall enterprise, of course, is a substantial tax saving.[86]

---

[86]A thorough discussion on transfer pricing can be found in Organization for Economic Cooperation and Development, *Transfer Pricing and Multinational Enterprises* (1979).

arm's length principle:
Transactions between affiliated firms must be carried on as if they were unrelated companies dealing at arm's length.

Tax authorities commonly approach this problem by assessing the profits earned by affiliated enterprises from international transactions between themselves on the basis of the **arm's length principle**. This principle has been widely accepted in domestic legislation, in model treaties (including the OECD and UN model treaties), and in most bilateral treaties for the avoidance of double taxation. The arm's length principle attributes to an affiliated establishment those profits that it would earn if it were a completely independent entity dealing with another affiliate as if the latter were a distinct and separate enterprise and both were operating under conditions and selling at prices prevailing in the regular market.

The arm's length principle lets tax authorities in the countries where affiliates are located determine the earnings of each affiliate as if it were an independent enterprise dealing with its associates at arm's length. This is true whether the affiliate is a branch, a subsidiary, or the head office.

Three methods for calculating an arm's length price are in common use. (1) The *comparable uncontrolled market price* method uses prices charged in comparable transactions between independent enterprises or between the concerned multinational enterprise and unrelated parties. This is often difficult to ascertain, either because comparable uncontrolled market prices are unavailable or because adjustments have to be made for a variety of factors, such as shipping costs or differences in quantity or quality. When a comparable uncontrolled market price cannot be ascertained, taxing authorities use the cost plus or resale minus methods. (2) The *cost plus* method begins with the actual cost of goods, services, and the like, and then adds appropriate cost and profit markups. (3) The *resale minus* method starts with the final selling price and then deducts the appropriate markups for cost and profit. Of course, the complexities of business in the real world make it difficult to apply any of these three methods in its pure form. In practice, as a consequence, taxing authorities use a mixture of these and other methods.[87]

unitary business rule: A state may tax a multinational enterprise on a share of its total worldwide income.

Another approach to countering transfer pricing is used in California (the taxing entity that originated the approach) and some 10 other states of the United States. It is known as the **unitary business rule**, and it taxes multinational enterprises on a percentage of their worldwide income, regardless of where it is earned or by whom.

Instead of beginning with the local affiliated enterprise and adjusting its income so that it is treated as an independent arm's length entity, the unitary business rule begins with the worldwide enterprise and determines the share of income that it has earned locally. Because transfer pricing can distort the amount of profits earned locally, the unitary business rule does not compare local profits to worldwide profits. Instead, it uses three other factors to determine the share of income earned locally: property, payroll, and sales. The ratio between the local and worldwide figures for each of these factors is then used to adjust the total consolidated income of all the affiliates of the worldwide enterprise. The equation for this is as follows:

$$\frac{\left[\dfrac{\substack{\text{Taxpayer's}\\\text{property}\\\text{in state}}}{\substack{\text{Taxpayer's and}\\\text{taxpayer's affiliates'}\\\text{worldwide property}}} + \dfrac{\substack{\text{Payroll of}\\\text{taxpayer}\\\text{in state}}}{\substack{\text{Taxpayer's and}\\\text{taxpayer's affiliates'}\\\text{worldwide payroll}}} + \dfrac{\substack{\text{Sales of}\\\text{taxpayer}\\\text{in states}}}{\substack{\text{Taxpayer's and}\\\text{taxpayer's affiliates'}\\\text{worldwide sales}}}\right]}{3} \times \substack{\text{Consolidated}\\\text{worldwide}\\\text{taxable income}\\\text{of taxpayer}\\\text{and taxpayer's}\\\text{affiliated}} = \substack{\text{Income}\\\text{deemed to}\\\text{be taxable}\\\text{by state}}$$

The argument in favor of using this rule is the same as that for the arm's length rule: to give the local taxing authority a fairer (and purportedly larger) share of the income earned by multinational enterprises doing business within its territory. The arguments against the unitary business rule are (1) that it imposes a heavy accounting burden on the worldwide

---

[87]*International Cooperation in Tax Matters: Guidelines for International Cooperation against the Evasion and Avoidance of Taxes (with Special Reference to Taxes on Income, Profits, Capital and Capital Gains)*, p. 28 (UN Doc. ST/ESA/142, 1984).

enterprise, which must determine figures for property, payroll, sales, and profits for every one of its worldwide affiliates by American accounting standards in addition to the accounting systems used in other countries; (2) that income is based on worldwide book value rather than taxable income determined after deductions, exemptions, and credits have been taken; and (3) that although it does not violate bilateral U.S. tax treaties (because U.S. tax treaties apply only to U.S. federal taxes), it does violate the Treaties of Friendship, Commerce and Navigation that the United States has entered into with many countries.[88]

Many major U.S. trading partners oppose the unitary business rule, which they consider to be contrary to the international tax system.[89] In 1985, the Reagan administration proposed legislation to prevent unitary taxation by the American states, but the legislation was never adopted.[90] As a consequence, the individual states are free to impose their own taxes on enterprises operating within their boundaries—a freedom reaffirmed in several recent U.S. Supreme Court decisions, including Case 13-8.

---

[88]David R. Milton, "Worldwide Unitary Taxation: A Kaleidoscope of Inconsistencies and Double Taxation," *Journal of State Taxation*, vol. 3, pp. 17–18 (1984).
[89]*Id.*, p. 15.
[90]*International Legal Materials*, vol. 25, p. 750 (1986).

Case 13-8   BARCLAYS BANK, PLC v. FRANCHISE TAX BOARD OF CALIFORNIA

United States, Supreme Court, 1994.
United States Reports, vol. 512, p. 298 (1994); *International Legal Materials,* vol. 33, p. 909 (1994).[91]
JUSTICE GINSBURG Delivered the Opinion of the Court.

Eleven years ago, in *Container Corp. of America v. Franchise Tax Bd.*,[92] this Court upheld California's income-based corporate franchise tax, as applied to a multinational enterprise, against a comprehensive challenge made under the Due Process and Commerce Clause of the [United States] Federal *Constitution. Container Corp.* involved a corporate taxpayer domiciled and head-quartered in the United States; in addition to its stateside components, the taxpayer had a number of overseas subsidiaries incorporated in the countries in which they operated. The Court's decision in *Container Corp.* did not address the constitutionality of California's taxing scheme as applied to "domestic corporations with foreign parents or [to] foreign corporations with either foreign parents or foreign subsidiaries."[93] In the consolidated cases before us,[94] we return to the taxing scheme earlier consid-

ered in *Container Corp.* and resolve matters left open in that case. The petitioner in [the first case], Barclays Bank, PLC (Barclays), is a United Kingdom corporation in the Barclays Group, a multinational banking enterprise. The petitioner in [the second case], Colgate-Palmolive Co. (Colgate), is the United States–based parent of a multinational manufacturing and sales enterprise. Each enterprise has operations in California. During the years here at issue, California determined the state corporate franchise tax due for these operations under a method known as "worldwide combined reporting." California's scheme first looked to the worldwide income of the multinational enterprise, and then attributed a portion of that income (equal to the average of the proportions of worldwide payroll, property, and sales located in California) to the California operations. The state imposed its tax on the income thus attributed to Barclays and Colgate's California business.

Barclays urges that California's tax system distinctively burdens foreign-based multinationals and results in double international taxation, in violation of the Commerce and Due Process Clauses [of the United States Federal *Constitution*]. . . . We reject [this and other] argu-

---

[91]This case is posted on the Internet at http://laws.findlaw.com/U.S./000/U10358.html.
[92]*United States Reports*, vol. 463, p. 159 (Supreme Ct., 1983).
[93]*Id.*, at p. 189, n. 26.
[94][Barclays Bank, PLC v. Franchise Tax Board of California was consolidated with Colgate-Palmolive Company v. Franchise Tax Board of California.]

ments, and hold that the *Constitution* does not impede application of California's corporate franchise tax to Barclays and Colgate. Accordingly, we affirm the judgments of the California Court of Appeals [from which judgments this appeal was made].

I

A

The Due Process and Commerce Clauses of the *Constitution*, this Court has held, prevent states that impose an income-based tax on nonresidents from "tax[ing] value earned outside [the taxing state's] borders."[95] But when a business enterprise operates in more than one taxing jurisdiction, arriving at "precise territorial allocations of 'value' is often an elusive goal, both in theory and in practice."[96] Every method of allocation devised involves some degree of arbitrariness.[97]

One means of deriving locally taxable income, generally used by states that collect corporate income-based taxes, is the "unitary business" method. As explained in *Container Corp.*, unitary taxation "rejects geographical or transactional accounting," which is "subject to manipulation" and does not fully capture "the many subtle and largely unquantifiable transfers of value that take place among the components of a single enterprise."[98] The "unitary business/formula apportionment" method

> calculates the local tax base by first defining the scope of the "unitary business" of which the taxed enterprise's activities in the taxing jurisdiction form one part, and then apportioning the total income of that "unitary business" between the taxing jurisdiction and the rest of the world on the basis of a formula taking into account objective measures of the corporation's activities within and without the jurisdiction.[99]

During the income years at issue in these cases—1977 for Barclays, 1970–1973 for Colgate—California assessed its corporate franchise tax by employing a "worldwide combined reporting" method. California's scheme required the taxpayer to aggregate the income of all corporate entities composing the unitary business enterprise, including in the aggregation both affiliates

operating abroad and those operating within the United States. Having defined the scope of the "unitary business" thus broadly, California used a long-accepted method of apportionment, commonly called the "three-factor" formula, to arrive at the amount of income attributable to the operations of the enterprise in California. Under the three-factor formula, California taxed a percentage of worldwide income equal to the arithmetic average of the proportions of worldwide payroll, property, and sales located inside the state.[100] Thus, if a unitary business had 8 percent of its payroll, 3 percent of its property, and 4 percent of its sales in California, the state took the average—5 percent—and imposed its tax on that percentage of the business' total income.[101]

B

The corporate income tax imposed by the United States [federal government] employs a "separate accounting" method, a means of apportioning income among taxing sovereigns used by all major developed nations. In contrast to combined reporting, separate accounting treats each corporate entity discretely for the purpose of determining income tax liability.[102]

Separating accounting poses the risk that a conglomerate will manipulate transfers of value among its components to minimize its total tax liability. To guard against such manipulation, transactions between affiliated corporations must be scrutinized to ensure that they are reported on an "arm's length" basis, i.e., at a price reflecting their true market value.[103] Assuming that all transactions are assigned their arm's length values in the corporate accounts, a jurisdiction using separate accounting taxes corporations that operate within its borders only on the income those corporations recognize on their own books.[104]

At one time, a number of states [within the United States] used worldwide combined reporting, as California did during the years at issue. In recent years, such states, including California, have modified their systems at least to allow corporate election of some variant of an approach that confines combined reporting to the United States' "water's edge."[105] California's 1986 modifi-

[95]ASARCO Inc. v. Idaho State Tax Comm'n, *United States Reports*, vol. 458, p. 307 at p. 315 (Supreme Ct., 1982).
[96]Container Corp. of America v. Franchise Tax Bd., *id.*, vol. 463, p. 159 at p. 164 (Supreme Ct., 1983).
[97]*Id.*, at p. 182.
[98]*Id.*, at pp. 164–165.
[99]*Id.*, at p. 165.
[100]California Revenue and Tax Code Annotated, § 25128 (1992).
[101]In 1993, California modified the formula to double the weight of the sales factor. *Id.*, § 25128 (1994); California Statutes, Chap. 946, § 1 (1993).
[102]An affiliated group of domestic corporations may, however, elect to file a consolidated federal tax return in lieu of separate returns. *United States Code*, Title 26, § 1501.
[103]*See id.*, § 482.
[104]*See* Container Corp. of America v. Franchise Tax Bd., *United States Reports*, vol. 463, p. 159 at p. 185 (Supreme Ct., 1983).
[105]*See* Jerome R. Hellerstein and Walter Hellerstein, *State Taxation: Corporate Income and Franchise Taxes*, vol. 1, para. 8.16, pp. 8–187 (2nd ed., 1993).

cation of its corporate franchise tax, effective in 1988,[106] made it nearly the last state to give way.[107]

California corporate taxpayers, under the state's water's edge alternative, may elect to limit their combined reporting group to corporations in the unitary business whose individual presence in the United States surpasses a certain threshold.[108] The 1986 amendment conditioned a corporate group's water's edge election on payment of a substantial fee, and allowed the California Franchise Tax Board (Tax Board) to disregard a water's edge election under certain circumstances. In 1993, California again modified its corporate franchise tax statute, this time to allow domestic and foreign enterprises to elect water's edge treatment without payment of a fee and without the threat of disregard.[109] The new amendments became effective in January 1994.

C

The first of these consolidated cases . . . is a tax refund suit brought by two members of the Barclays Group, a multinational banking enterprise. Based in the United Kingdom, the Barclays Group includes more than 220 corporations doing business in some 60 nations. The two refund-seeking members of the Barclays corporate family did business in California and were therefore subject to California's franchise tax. Barclays Bank of California (Barcal), one of the two taxpayers, was a California banking corporation wholly owned by Barclays Bank International, Limited (BBI), the second taxpayer. BBI, a United Kingdom corporation, did business in the United Kingdom and in more than 33 other nations and territories.

In computing its California franchise tax based on 1997 income, Barcal reported only the income from its own operations. BBI reported income on the assumption that it participated in a unitary business composed of itself and its subsidiaries, but not its parent corporation and the parent's other subsidiaries. After auditing BBI's and Barcal's 1977 income year franchise tax returns, the Tax Board, respondent here, determined that both were part of a worldwide unitary business, the Barclays Group. Ultimately, the Board assessed additional tax liability of $1,678 for BBI and $152,420 for Barcal.

Barcal and BBI paid the assessments and sued for refunds. . . .

The petitioner [in the second case], Colgate-Palmolive Co., is a Delaware corporation headquartered in New York. Colgate and its subsidiaries doing business in the United States engaged principally in the manufacture and distribution of household and personal hygiene products. In addition, Colgate owned some 75 corporations that operated entirely outside the United States; these foreign subsidiaries also engaged primarily in the manufacture and distribution of household and personal hygiene products. When Colgate filed California franchise tax returns based on 1970–1973 income, it reported the income earned from its foreign corporations on a separate accounting basis. Essentially, Colgate maintained that the [United States federal] *Constitution* compelled California to limit the reach of its unitary principle to the United States' water's edge. The Tax Board determined that Colgate's taxes should be computed on the basis of worldwide combined reporting, and assessed a four-year deficiency of $604,756. Colgate paid the tax and sued for a refund.

[Because the California courts ultimately upheld the unitary business tax method, the petitioners appealed to the United States Supreme Court.]

***

II

The Commerce Clause expressly gives Congress power "[t]o regulate Commerce with foreign Nations and among the several States."[110] It has long been understood, as well, to provide "protection from state legislation inimical to the national commerce [even] where Congress has not acted. . . ."[111] The Clause does not shield interstate (or foreign) commerce from its "fair share of the state tax burden."[112] Absent congressional approval, however, a state tax on such commerce will not survive Commerce Clause scrutiny if the taxpayer demonstrates that the tax either (1) applies to an activity lacking a substantial nexus to the taxing state; (2) is not fairly apportioned; (3) discriminates against interstate commerce; or (4) is not fairly related to the services provided by the state. [These factors were set out in, and are known as, the] *Complete Auto Transit, Inc. v. Brady*[113] [criteria].

In "the unique context of foreign commerce," a state's power is further constrained because of "the special need

---

[106]California Statutes, Chap. 660, § 6 (1986).

[107]Jerome R. Hellerstein and Walter Hellerstein, *State Taxation: Corporate Income and Franchise Taxes*, vol. 1, para. 8.16, pp. 8–187 (2nd ed., 1993).

[108]California Revenue and Tax Code Annotated, § 25110 (1992).

[109]California Statutes, Chap. 31, § 53; Chap. 881, § 22 (1993). See California Revenue and Tax Code, § 25110 (1994).

[110]United States, *Constitution*, Article I, § 8, Clause 3.

[111]Southern Pacific Co. v. Arizona ex rel. Sullivan, *United States Reports*, vol. 325, p. 761 at p. 769 (Supreme Ct., 1945).

[112]Department of Revenue of Washington v. Association of Washington Stevedoring Cos., *id.*, vol. 435, p. 734 at p. 750 (Supreme Ct., 1978).

[113]*Id.*, vol. 430, p. 274 at p. 279 (Supreme Ct., 1977).

for federal uniformity."[114] "In international relations and with respect to foreign intercourse and trade the people of the United States act through a single government with unified and adequate national power."[115] A tax affecting foreign commerce therefore raises two concerns in addition to the four delineated in *Complete Auto*. The first is prompted by "the enhanced risk of multiple taxation."[116] The second relates to the Federal government's capacity to "speak with one voice when regulating commercial regulations with foreign governments."[117]

California's worldwide combined reporting system easily meets three of the four *Complete Auto* criteria. The nexus requirement is met by the business all three taxpayers—Barcal, BBI, and Colgate—did in California during the years in question.[118] The "fair apportionment" standard is also satisfied. Neither Barclays nor Colgate has demonstrated the lack of a "rational relationship between the income attributed to the state and the intrastate values of the enterprise";[119] nor have the petitioners shown that the income attributed to California is "out of all appropriate proportion to the business transacted by the [taxpayers] in that state."[120] We note in this regard that, "if applied by every jurisdiction," California's method "would result in no more than all of unitary business' income being taxed."[121] And surely California has afforded Colgate and the Barclays taxpayers "protection, opportunities, and benefits" for which the state can exact a return.[122]

Barclays (but not Colgate) vigorously contends, however, that California's worldwide combined reporting scheme violates the antidiscrimination component of the *Complete Auto* test. Barclays maintains that a foreign-owner of a taxpayer filing a California tax return "is forced to convert its diverse financial and accounting records from around the world into the language, currency, and accounting principles of the United States" at "prohibitive" expense.[123] Domestic-owned taxpayers, by contrast, need not incur such expense because they "already keep most of their records in English, in United States currency, and in accord with United States accounting principles."[124] Barclays urges that imposing this "prohibitive administrative burden"[125] on foreign-owned enterprises gives a competitive advantage to their U.S.-owned counterparts and constitutes "economic protectionism" of the kind that this Court has often condemned.[126]

Compliance burdens, if disproportinately imposed on out-of-jurisdiction enterprises, may indeed be inconsonant with the Commerce Clause. . . . The factual predicate of Barclays' discrimination claim, however, is infirm.

Barclays points to provisions of California's implementing regulations setting out three discrete means for a taxpayer to fulfill its franchise tax reporting requirements. Each of these modes of compliance would require Barclays to gather and present much information not maintained by the unitary group in the ordinary course of business. California's regulations, however, also provide that the Tax Board "shall consider the effort and expense required to obtain the necessary information" and, in "appropriate cases, such as when the necessary data cannot be developed from financial records maintained in the regular course of business," may accept "reasonable approximations."[127] As the [California] Court of Appeal comprehended, in determining Barclays' 1977 worldwide income, Barclays and the Tax Board "used these [latter] provisions and [made] computations based on reasonable approximations,"[128] thus allowing Barclays to avoid the large compliance costs of which it complains. Barclays has not shown that California's provision for "reasonable approximations" systematically "overtaxes" foreign corporations generally or BBI or Barcal in particular.

In sum, Barclays has not demonstrated that California's tax system in fact operates to impose inordinate compliance burdens on foreign enterprises. Barclays' claim of unconstitutional discrimination against foreign commerce therefore fails.

---

[114]Wardair Canada, Inc. v. Florida Dept. of Revenue, *id.*, vol. 477, p. 1 at p. 8 (Supreme Ct., 1986).

[115]Japan Line, Ltd. v. County of Los Angeles, *id.*, vol. 441, p. 434 at p. 448 (Supreme Court, 1979) quoting Board of Trustees v. United States, *id.*, vol. 289, p. 59 (Supreme Ct., 1933).

[116]Container Corp. of America v. Franchise Tax Bd., *id.*, vol. 463, p. 159 at p. 185 (1983).

[117]Japan Line, Ltd. v. County of Los Angeles, *id.*, vol. 441, p. 434 at p. 449 (Supreme Court, 1979) quoting Michelin Tire Corp. v. Wages, *id.*, vol. 423, p. 276 at p. 285 (Supreme Ct., 1976).

[118]See Mobil Oil Corp. v. Commissioner of Taxes of Vt., *id.*, vol. 445, p. 425 at pp. 436–437 (Supreme Ct., 1980).

[119]Container Corp. of America v. Franchise Tax Bd., *id.*, vol. 463, p. 159 at pp. 180–181 (1983).

[120]*Id.*, at p. 181.

[121]*Id.*, at p. 169.

[122]Wisconsin v. J. C. Penney Co., *id.*, vol. 311, p. 435 at p. 444 (1940).

[123]Brief for Petitioner in [Barclays case] at p. 44.

[124]*Id.*, at p. 45.

[125]5*Id.*, at p. 43.

[126]*Id.*, at pp. 43–46.

[127]California Code of Regulations, Title 18, § 25137–6(e)(1) (1985).

[128]*California Appellate Reports, Fourth Series*, vol. 10, p. 1742 at p. 1756 (3rd Dist. Ct. of Appeal, 1992).

III

***

B

We turn, finally, to the question ultimately and most energetically presented: Did California's worldwide combined reporting requirement, as applied to Barcal, BBI, and Colgate, "impair federal uniformity in an area where federal uniformity is essential,"[129] in particular, did the state's taxing scheme "preven[t] the Federal government from 'speaking with one voice' in international trade"?[130]

***

As in *Container Corp* . . . we discern no "specific indications of congressional intent" to bar the state action here challenged. Our decision upholding California's franchise tax in *Container Corp.* left the ball in Congress' court; had Congress, the branch responsible for the regulation of foreign commerce,[131] considered nationally uniform use of separate accounting "essential,"[132] it could have enacted legislation prohibiting the states from taxing corporate income based on the worldwide combined reporting method. In the 11 years that have elapsed since our decision in *Container Corp.*, Congress has failed to enact such legislation.

***

Given . . . Congress' willingness to tolerate states' worldwide combined reporting mandates . . . we cannot conclude that "the foreign policy of the United States—whose nuances . . . are much more the province of the Executive Branch and Congress than of this Court—is [so] seriously threatened"[133] by California's practice as to warrant our intervention. This Court has no constitutional authority to make the policy judgments essential to regulating foreign commerce and conducting foreign affairs. Matters relating "to the conduct of foreign relations . . . are so exclusively entrusted to the political branches of government as to be largely immune from judicial inquiry or interference."[134] For this reason, Barclays' . . . argument that California's worldwide combined reporting requirement is unconstitutional . . . is directed to the wrong forum.

***

MAP 13-7   California (1994)

Affirmed. ■

CASEPOINT: (1) While U.S. states are forbidden by the federal Constitution from imposing taxes on earnings from outside the borders of the United States, arriving at a precise territorial allocation is an elusive goal and inherently involves some arbitrariness. (2) Although the U.S. Constitution forbids the states from enacting legislation that discriminates against (burdens) interstate or international commerce, California's requirement that a multinational enterprise report its worldwide income was not burdensome as the plaintiffs were allowed to make approximations and avoid the large cost of making a precise report. (3) Since the Supreme Court first approved the unitary method in 1983, the U.S. Congress has failed to take action to forbid the states from using the unitary business method. Presumably, therefore, it is not opposed to the use of the method.

---

[129]Japan Line, Ltd. v. County of Los Angeles, *id.*, vol. 441, p. 434 at p. 448 (Supreme Court, 1979).
[130]*Id.*, at p. 453.
[131]See United States, *Constitution*, Article I, § 8, Clause 3.
[132]Japan Line, Ltd. v. County of Los Angeles, *United States Reports*, vol. 441, p. 434 at p. 448 (Supreme Court, 1979).
[133]Container Corp. of America v. Franchise Tax Bd., *id.*, vol. 463, p. 159 at p. 196 (1983).
[134]Harisiades v. Shaughnessy, *id.*, vol. 342, p. 580 at p. 589 (Supreme Ct., 1952).

Treaty Shopping

Treaty shopping means that a taxpayer "shops" for countries with beneficial tax treaty provisions, then sets up subsidiary enterprises in those countries to take advantage of their treaties.

The expression *treaty shopping* was first used in congressional hearings on offshore tax havens held in the United States in April 1971.[135] The tax problem it describes, however, has been around for quite some time. A 1945 tax treaty between the United States and the United Kingdom, for example, contains an *abuse* clause.[136] The OECD has been studying the problem since 1961; and it is discussed in the commentary to Article 1 of the OECD's 1977 Model Treaty.[137] A 1983 OECD Working Paper entitled "The Improper Use of Tax Conventions through Conduit Companies by Persons Not Entitled to Their Benefits" examines treaty shopping in depth, as does a 1987 United Nations report by the *ad hoc* Group of Experts on International Cooperation in Tax Matters.[138]

Treaty shopping involves two basic situations: the use of *direct conduit companies* and the use of *stepping-stone conduit companies*. Both involve taxpayers who take advantage of tax treaties that were not meant to apply to them.

Direct Conduit Companies   Company A in State A has a subsidiary, Company B, in State B. When Company B remits dividends, interest, or royalties to Company A, State B withholds substantial taxes. To avoid these taxes, Company A shops around for a country, State C, that has a beneficial tax treaty with State A (i.e., a treaty that reduces or eliminates withholding taxes charged by State C when dividends, interest, or royalties are remitted to a company in State A) and State B (i.e., a treaty that reduces or eliminates withholding taxes charged by State B when dividends, interest, or royalties are remitted to a company in State A).

Having "shopped" and found State C, Company A will set up a subsidiary, Company C, in State C and make it the parent of Company B. Company B will then remit its dividends, interest, or royalties to Company C (Company C serving as a **direct conduit company**.) (See Exhibit 13-3.)

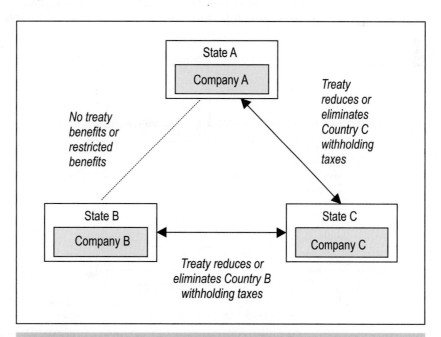

EXHIBIT 13-3   Treaty Shopping: Direct Conduit Companies

---

[135]David Rosenbloom, "Tax Treaty Abuse: Policies and Issues," *Law & Policy in International Business*, vol. 16, p. 783 (1983).
[136]Commerce Clearing House, *Tax Treaties*, vol. 2, § 8111.
[137]OECD, Model Tax Treaty, Article 1, note 9, commentary (1977).
[138]The OECD paper is reproduced in *International Tax Avoidance and Evasion*, pp. 87–106 (1987); the UN report is in *Contributions to International Cooperation in Tax Matters* (UN Doc. ST/ESA/203, 1988).

The major tax consequence of this arrangement is the elimination or reduction of the tax collected by State B. Indeed, neither State A nor State C has to be a tax haven for Company A to have a tax advantage. The principal savings for Company A will be the difference between the tax imposed by State B on remittances to State A and the lower tax (or absence of tax) imposed on remittance to State C.

stepping-stone conduit companies: Holding companies organized in states that have a mutually beneficial tax treaty—one of which also has a beneficial tax treaty with a state where a parent company is located, while the other also has a beneficial tax treaty with a state where the subsidiary is located.

tax sink: A state that imposes no income taxes.

Stepping-stone Conduit Companies   A **stepping-stone conduit companies** arrangement is similar to the direct conduit situation, except that a second intermediary country (State D) and company (Company D) has to be used to move profits from the source company (Company B) back to the parent (Company A). In this situation there is no tax treaty between State A and State C, and State C does impose taxes on profits earned by Company C. To remedy this, Company A shops for a second country, State D, to serve as a **tax sink**. To qualify as a tax sink, State D must impose no income taxes. In addition, State C must (because of a tax treaty or local legislation) allow its companies to deduct from their earnings any expenses paid to companies in State D.

Again, having "shopped" and found a tax sink in State D, Company A will set up a second subsidiary, Company D, in State D. Company D will be made an affiliate of Company C. Company D will grant Company C the technology licenses, the franchises, the loans, and so forth it needs to carry on its business. Company C will then pay Company D high fees, commissions, interest, and so forth, all of which Company C may deduct in State C from its income. Company C will, as a consequence, pay little or no income tax to State C. The income, having been transferred to Company D in State D, will then be remitted to Company A, free from the taxes of both State B and State C. (See Exhibit 13-4.)

Abuse   Most tax authorities consider treaty shopping to be improper. Three reasons are most commonly given for this: One, the states that signed a tax treaty meant for it to benefit only their residents and their states. Each gave up something in exchange for some benefit. If a person from a third state is allowed to take advantage of this, the principle of reciprocity is violated. Two, in granting benefits to residents of the other treaty state, the first state is

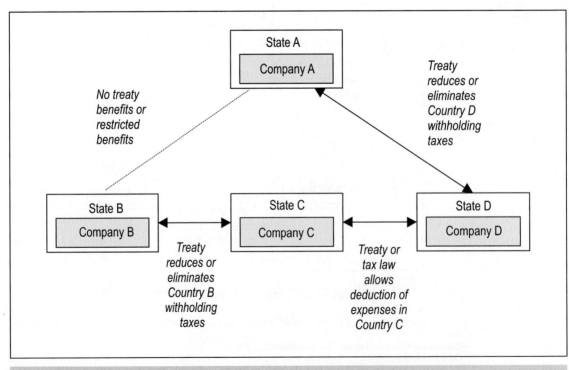

EXHIBIT 13-4   Treaty Shopping: Stepping-Stone Conduit Companies

assuming that those residents will be subject to the normal tax regime of the other state. Three, third states have little incentive to enter into tax treaties if their residents can take advantage of existing tax treaties.

Countermeasures   The tax authorities opposed to treaty shopping have found solutions to the problem both in national legislation and through the use of specific anti-abuse provisions in tax treaties.

Only two countries have anti-abuse legislation: Switzerland and the United States. Switzerland enacted an anti-abuse ordinance in 1962 that suspends treaty benefits whenever a Swiss company makes a claim for a tax reduction that is abusive.[139] A claim is abusive (1) if a substantial part of a Swiss company's income is given to persons not entitled to treaty benefits, (2) if a substantial share of the Swiss company is held by nonresidents, (3) if the Swiss company is an agent of a nonresident, or (4) if the income is given to a Swiss family foundation or Swiss partnership of which nonresidents own a substantial portion.

The U.S. Tax Reform Act of 1986 introduced a national treaty abuse provision that limited treaty benefits to companies that are "qualified" residents of either the United States or the foreign country that was a signatory of the particular treaty.[140] Unqualified corporations are those with more than 50 percent of their stock in the hands of residents of third-party states or that disburse more than 50 percent of their income to third-party residents.[141]

In countries that do not have specific anti-abuse legislation, the problem of treaty shopping is attacked using general principles of equity. Common law countries (including Australia, Canada, and the United Kingdom) use a *substance over form* approach. That is, their tax authorities attempt to determine if the movement of income between foreign affiliated companies is based on legitimate commercial reasons or if it is merely a sham set up in order to obtain treaty benefits. Civil law countries (including France and Germany) use an *abuse* approach. In other words, their tax authorities ask whether a particular arrangement of companies constitutes an abuse, a misuse, or an improper use of a tax treaty.[142]

Tax Treaty Provisions   Anti-abuse provisions are becoming more common in bilateral tax treaties.[143] Several approaches are possible. Those that have appeared so far include

look-through approach: A company is entitled to tax treaty benefits only if it is owned completely by residents of the state in which it was organized.

exclusion approach: Holding companies and domestic companies that pay low taxes are not entitled to tax treaty benefits.

subject-to-tax approach: Tax treaty benefits are available only if income is subject to taxation in one or the other of the signatory states.

channel approach: Tax treaty benefits are denied if a share of a company's income is paid to a nonresident holding company.

1. The **look-through approach**. Treaty benefits are granted to a company only if it is owned completely or substantially by residents of the state in which it is organized. This is the most common approach and the one taken by the UN Model Tax Treaty and the 1981 United States Model Treaty.[144]
2. The **exclusion approach**. Low-taxed holding and domiciliary companies are excluded from treaty benefits.[145]
3. The **subject-to-tax approach**. Treaty benefits are based on the condition that income derived in one state must actually be subject to taxation in the other state. In other words, company income may not be exempt from taxation in both states.
4. The **channel approach**. This provision is primarily meant to address the stepping-stone arrangement. Treaty benefits are denied to a company if a certain percentage of its

---

[139]*Bundesratbesscluss betr. die ungerechtfertigte Inanspruchnahme von Doppelbesteuerungs abkommen* (December 14, 1962), *Eidgenössische Gesetzesammlung*, vol. 1962, p. 1622, amended by *Kreisschreiben der Eidgenössischen Steuerverwaltung* (December 31, 1962).

[140]United States, Internal Revenue Code, § 884.

[141]*Id.*, § 884(e)(B). Special provisions are made for publicly traded corporations. Regardless of the stock ownership of the corporation, they will be treated as qualified residents if their stock is traded regularly and primarily on an established securities market in the signatory foreign state.

[142]Deloitte, Haskins & Sells International, *Treaty Shopping: An Emerging Tax Issue andIts Present States in Various Countries*, p. 7 (1988).

[143]For a current survey of anti-abuse provisions in the bilateral treaties of 19 countries, see Deloitte, Haskins & Sells International, *Treaty Shopping: An Emerging Tax Issue and Its Present States in Various Countries* (1988).

[144]UN, Model Tax Treaty, Article 16 (Alternative Draft published December 23, 1981); United States, Model Tax Treaty, Article 16 (1981 Draft).

[145]The treatment of holding and domiciliary companies in seven European countries is examined by Ned Shelton and Freddy de Petter in "Holding Companies: A Review of the New Luxembourg Rules and Six Other Countries," *European Taxation*, vol. 31, p. 63 (March/April 1991).

bona fide approach: To be entitled to tax treaty benefits, a company must show that its structure and transactions are motivated by sound business reasons.

abstinence approach: Refusal by a state to enter into a tax treaty with a tax haven state.

thin capitalization: The intentional financing of a company with debt funding rather than equity funding.

tax evasion: The intentional misrepresentation or concealment of a person's tax obligations.

income is used to pay for charges made by individuals or companies who are not residents of one of the contracting states.

5. The **bona fide approach**. Affiliated companies are not entitled to treaty benefits unless they can demonstrate that the structure and the transactions of their business arrangements are motivated by sound commercial reasons. To qualify, they must meet certain standards. These standards may address the motives for setting up the affiliated structure, the amount of business activity in an affiliate's state of residence, the amount of taxes paid in the state of residence, and whether or not the affiliate's shares are traded on an approved stock exchange.

6. The **abstinence approach**. Because tax haven countries often encourage treaty abuse, states opposed to it have simply abstained from entering into tax treaties with those countries. Liechtenstein, the Channel Islands, Monaco, and Panama, as a consequence, have no or only a few tax treaties.

Thin Capitalization **Thin capitalization** is a term used to describe the situation where a company is purposely financed by loans rather than by equity capital. For example, a parent company may contribute money to a subsidiary in the form of loans, or it may contribute physical assets or technology, also in the form of loans. The result is a company with a high debt to equity (debt/equity) ratio.

The reason for thinly capitalizing a company relates to the fact that the tax treatment of interest differs from the treatment of dividends and other profit distributions. Interest is almost always deductible in determining taxable income, whereas dividends and other profit distributions—being part of that income—are not deductible. To illustrate: The Amalgamated Company has income of $100,000. If it pays out $25,000 in interest to creditors, it will have net taxable income of $75,000. On the other hand, if it pays out that same $25,000 as dividends to shareholders, its net taxable income will remain $100,000.

Thin capitalization is most commonly countered by national legislation rather than in tax treaties. The usual mechanism is to disallow the deduction of interest payments when the debt/equity ratio exceeds a particular norm. In some countries, this is modified by allowing a company to show that its debt/equity ratio is an arm's length ratio or that it is otherwise commercially reasonable.[146]

TAX EVASION

The distinguishing feature of **tax evasion**, as compared to tax avoidance, is that it involves the willful and conscious misrepresentation or concealment of one's tax obligations or (rarely) the flight of a taxpayer to another country. Also, unlike tax avoidance, it is universally regarded as illegal.

Tax authorities are faced with several significant problems in trying to combat tax evasion internationally. First are the constitutional and political difficulties that many states face in helping a foreign tax authority collect taxes. Taxation is closely tied up with sovereignty, and to some extent a state abrogates its sovereignty by cooperating with a foreign tax authority. In addition, helping a foreign tax authority examine local records runs contrary to the right of privacy guaranteed by an ever-growing body of human rights legislation in many developed countries. The examination of local records is also at odds with the bank secrecy laws that are valued so highly in tax haven countries as tools for attracting foreign investment.

Second, the enforcement of foreign tax judgments puts burdens on local tax authorities and tax courts that they are often unprepared or unwilling to assume. Because the tax authorities in one state know little about the tax and legal system in a second state, they are commonly unable to reassure themselves that foreign taxes are equitable and that a taxpayer is being adequately protected from arbitrary treatment. Courts, similarly, are not

---

[146]*Contributions to International Cooperation in Tax Matters: Treaty Shopping, Thin Capitalization, Cooperation between Tax Authorities, Resolving International Tax Disputes*, pp. 24–27 (UN Doc. ST/ESA/203, 1988).

always equipped to reach a just decision in enforcing a foreign tax judgment or to fairly determine that the documents provided by an applicant state are not flawed. By long tradition, both the local tax authorities and local courts have been quick to use the rule of *forum non conveniens*[147] as an excuse for ignoring foreign requests for tax information or for assistance in enforcing foreign tax judgments.

A third reason that local tax authorities have difficulty in helping their foreign colleagues combat tax evasion has to do with purely practical problems. These include the lack of an adequate local library of foreign statutory and case materials, the problem of dealing with documents in foreign languages, and the difficulty of examining audits or other bookkeeping records maintained by an unfamiliar accounting system.

Despite these difficulties, taxing authorities are frequently successful in tracking down and prosecuting tax evaders. Case 13-9 is a case in point.

---

[147]See Chapter 3 for a discussion of the doctrine of *forum non conveniens*.

Case 13-9   KALO v. COMMISSIONER OF INTERNAL REVENUE

United States, Sixth Circuit Court of Appeals, 1998. *United States Tax Cases* (CCH), vol. 98, pt. 2, para. 50,514; 81 (1998).

CIRCUIT JUDGE RONALD LEE GILMAN:

Circuit Judge. Jacob Kalo ("taxpayer") appeals the Tax Court's decision upholding the assessment by the Commissioner of Internal Revenue ("Commissioner") of penalties and interest for fraudulently failing to report income derived from interest-bearing foreign bank accounts. Since we find no error in the Tax Court's decision in this case, we AFFIRM.

I. Background

Taxpayer and his wife . . . (collectively "Kalos"), live in West Bloomfield, Michigan. He is an obstetrician and gynecologist whose patients often pay in cash for his medical services. Although a practicing physician, taxpayer does not carry medical malpractice insurance coverage. During the years 1986 through 1989, taxpayer was both a partner and an employee of Jacob Kalo, M.D. P.C. ("Kalo P.C."). Kalo P.C. operated five medical clinics in Michigan, including a clinic at 15650 E. Eight Mile Road in Detroit, Michigan ("East GYN Office"). Kalo P.C.'s business operations were in turmoil during the years 1986 through 1989 because of a legal dispute between taxpayer and his two former business partners. Taxpayer's business problems and his lack of malpractice insurance prompted him to hide a significant amount of money in foreign bank accounts.

To help him in making decisions concerning foreign investments, taxpayer consulted with an accountant and a financial advisor. The financial advisor provided financial services for taxpayer specifically tailored to foreign investment for nearly twelve years, including discussions concerning foreign interest rates and foreign investments. From these extensive dealings, the financial advisor formed the opinion that taxpayer had a better than average knowledge about foreign investments.

The Kalos filed joint income tax returns for the years 1986 through 1989. They held a number of overseas bank accounts during this period of time, particularly in Canada. For the years 1985 through 1988, taxpayer made numerous cash deposits into Canadian bank accounts, seven of which exceeded $10,000. Taxpayer, for example, deposited more than $230,000 in cash into a bank account at the Royal Bank of Canada during this three-year period. By 1989, the Kalos had deposited approximately $1 million with the Royal Bank of Canada and more than $3 million in all of their Canadian bank accounts combined.

The couple, however, neither disclosed the existence of these foreign bank accounts nor reported how much interest income they received from them when they filed their original income tax returns. In fact, when answering Question 10 on Schedule B of their income tax returns, the couple specifically denied having any foreign bank accounts until the 1988 tax year. The total amount of interest income the Kalos failed to report for the years 1986 through 1989 was $309,322.

Beginning in 1990 and continuing into 1991, the Internal Revenue Service's Criminal Investigation Division ("CID") investigated the Kalos for possible income tax violations. Prodded by the efforts of the CID's investigation, the Kalos belatedly filed amended tax returns for the years 1986 through 1989. In these amended tax returns, the Kalos reported the previously undisclosed interest income from their foreign bank accounts and paid the additional taxes due.

As part of the investigation, CID special agents interviewed taxpayer on April 18, 1990. During the interview, the special agents asked taxpayer whether he had any money in foreign bank accounts. Taxpayer responded by telling the agents of a bank account in Israel that he first reported on his 1988 tax return, and that he might also have a bank account in Europe. When specifically questioned about Canadian bank accounts, taxpayer stated that the only bank account he held in Canada was a joint bank account shared with his father. At the time, this joint bank account held only $37. Taxpayer claimed that all the money in the joint bank account belonged to his father. In fact, taxpayer specifically told the special agents that he had nothing to do with this account because his father handled all of the banking transactions.

When questioned about business records for the East GYN Office, the special agents were informed by taxpayer that the state of Michigan had seized the business records during a Medicaid audit and had never returned them. In truth, the state of Michigan had never audited the business records, much less taken them. Instead, it was taxpayer who removed business records from the East GYN Office after the CID began its criminal investigation. In a further attempt to cover his tracks, taxpayer told one of his employees at the East GYN Office that if anyone asked about the records to say that the state of Michigan took the records during a Medicaid audit. In a subsequent interview with CID special agents, taxpayer indicated that the state of Michigan had returned the business records. The CID subpoenaed these records, along with records from the other Kalo P.C. clinics. Taxpayer, however, never produced the records subpoenaed.

In an interview with special agents on August 23, 1990, taxpayer stated that the East GYN Office never had a day where the cash receipts were more than $2,000. This statement was also false. On the following day, taxpayer asked two of his employees ... to write letters to the CID stating that the daily cash flow at the clinic ranged from $40 to $800. Both employees refused, stating that those dollar amounts were false. Taxpayer nevertheless adhered to this dollar amount in subsequent discussions with the CID. Also during the August 23, 1990 interview, taxpayer informed the special agents that he believed that interest income was not taxable until withdrawn from a foreign bank because his accountant led him to believe this. When asked for his accountant's name, taxpayer's attorney interrupted and stated that it was not the accountant who gave this advice, but that his client heard or knew of it from someone else.

Taxpayer's accountant later testified that he never told taxpayer that the interest earned from foreign bank accounts was not taxable until withdrawn. In fact, when preparing the Kalos' tax returns for the years 1986 through 1989, the accountant specifically asked whether the couple had any foreign bank accounts. Taxpayer, however, never informed the accountant that the couple had any foreign bank accounts until the 1988 taxable year, when he told the accountant about the bank account in Israel. The accountant promptly reported the interest from the Israeli account on the Kalos' 1988 and 1989 income tax returns. Similarly, taxpayer never informed his financial advisor that he was receiving interest income from foreign bank accounts.

In light of the accountant's testimony, taxpayer refined his story and told the CID special agents that an unnamed bank official at an unnamed Canadian bank informed him that he did not have to pay taxes on the interest income. Proof was presented, however, that the policy of the Royal Bank of Canada is not to give advice to foreigners about the taxability of interest generated in their bank accounts.

On September 9, 1992, the United States Attorney filed an information charging taxpayer with four counts of willfully failing to disclose information on his income tax returns, a violation of 26 U.S.C. § 7203. On January 29, 1993, taxpayer pled guilty to one count of violating § 7203 for the 1987 tax year. The court sentenced taxpayer to 180 days of home confinement, one year of probation, and fined him $51,318.

On October 7, 1994, the Commissioner issued a notice of tax deficiencies against the Kalos for the 1986 tax year. The notice also assessed additions to and penalties on tax against the Kalos due to fraud for the tax years 1986 through 1989. The Commissioner later withdrew the deficiency assessment after the Kalos amended their income tax return for the 1986 tax year to reflect the underpayment in tax. On November 7, 1994, the Kalos filed a petition in Tax Court seeking a redetermination of the Commissioner's additions to and penalties on tax.

... During trial, counsel for the Kalos objected to the introduction of evidence related to the operation of the East GYN Office. Counsel asserted that the evidence was not relevant to a determination of fraud concerning foreign bank accounts. ... The Commissioner responded by noting that "one of the indications of fraud [in this case] is that the monies that were in the foreign accounts were skimmed income [from the clinics]." The Tax Court overruled the objection and allowed the Commissioner to introduce evidence concerning taxpayer's management of the East GYN Office.

After the trial, the Tax Court issued its decision upholding the Commissioner's determinations of additions to and penalties on taxes due from taxpayer. Specifically, the Tax Court held that the Commissioner had proven by clear and convincing evidence that taxpayer underpaid his taxes for each year in question due to fraud. The Tax Court, however, disallowed the Commissioner's determinations against [taxpayer's spouse.]. The Tax Court's judgment was entered January 7, 1997. This appeal followed.

II. Analysis

***

... [T]axpayer contends that the Tax Court erred in finding that his failure to report interest income was due to fraud. The Tax Court's finding of fraud is a question of fact and will only be reversed if shown to be clearly erroneous. . . .

For the relevant period in question, former § 6653(B) [of the United States *Internal Revenue Code*] provided that "if any part of any underpayment . . . of tax . . . is due to fraud, there shall be added to the tax an amount equal to . . . 50 percent . . . of the underpayment." The Commissioner has the burden of proving by clear and convincing evidence that there was an underpayment of taxes and that some part of that underpayment was due to fraud. In the present case, it is uncontested that an underpayment of taxes occurred. The only remaining issue concerns taxpayer's alleged fraudulent intent.

A court may infer fraudulent intent by looking to various kinds of circumstantial evidence. Such "badges of fraud" include: (1) failure to file tax returns; (2) an understatement of income over an extended period; (3) failure to furnish the government with access to records; (4) failure to keep adequate books and records; (5) the sophistication of the taxpayer; (6) concealment of bank accounts; (7) giving implausible or inconsistent explanations of behavior; and (8) willingness to defraud another in a business transaction. While no single factor is necessarily conclusive, the combination of a number of these badges of fraud constitutes persuasive evidence of fraud.

The Tax Court found that taxpayer: (1) understated his income over a period of four years; (2) was relatively sophisticated with respect to issues concerning foreign investments; (3) attempted to conceal his activities with respect to his foreign bank accounts by giving false statements on his tax returns; (4) pled guilty to willfully failing to disclose information concerning his foreign bank accounts; and (5) misled authorities through evasion and

MAP 13-8 Michigan (1998)

obfuscation concerning the existence of the bank accounts and of business records pertinent to the CID's investigation. Since many badges of fraud were present, the Tax Court held that taxpayer's underpayment of interest income was due to fraud.

Taxpayer now claims that the Tax Court's findings of fact were clearly erroneous. Specifically, taxpayer claims that: (1) the Commissioner introduced no evidence that taxpayer was familiar with the tax laws; (2) his accountant lied when he testified that taxpayer failed to tell him about the foreign bank accounts; (3) the Tax Court failed to take into account that he reported interest income from his Israeli bank account for the years 1988 and 1989; (4) the Tax Court misconstrued his statements to the CID special agents concerning the Canadian bank accounts; and (5) the Tax Court failed to consider the fact that his true purpose in hiding the money in the foreign bank accounts was not to avoid paying taxes, but to hide his assets from potential malpractice claimants and former business partners.

Taxpayer's arguments are unpersuasive. First, and foremost, taxpayer's contention regarding his true purpose in opening the foreign bank accounts only serves to implicate another badge of fraud, i.e., taxpayer's willingness to defraud others in business transactions. We also find taxpayer's arguments regarding his accountant's testimony and the "true" nature of his statements to the CID agents equally unavailing. When presented with conflicting testimony, the Tax Court is free to resolve the conflict by judging the witnesses' credibility. The fact that the Tax Court believed the testimony of the accountant and the CID agents over that of taxpayer does not make the Tax Court's decision clearly erroneous.[148] Furthermore, taxpayer's contention that the Tax Court did not adequately

---

[148]Conti v. Commissioner, *Federal Reporter, Third Series*, vol. 39, p. 658 at p. 664 (6th Circuit Ct. of Appeals 1994).

take into account his disclosure of the Israeli bank account is simply not supported by the record. The Tax Court explicitly acknowledged in its opinion that taxpayer had disclosed the existence of the Israeli bank account in his original income tax returns for 1988 and 1989. We cannot say that the Tax Court's refusal to give much weight to this "disclosure" was unjustified. Acknowledging the existence of this small bank account could just as easily be viewed as an attempt, albeit an unsuccessful one, to divert the Commissioner from investigating whether taxpayer had other foreign bank accounts with much larger balances.

Simply put, taxpayer's arguments go to the weight of the evidence presented and to the credibility of the witnesses who testified. "The Tax Court, like any other court, may disregard uncontradicted testimony by a taxpayer where it finds that testimony lacking in credibility, . . . or finds the testimony to be improbable, unreasonable or questionable."[149] Given taxpayer's inconsistent and implausible statements, his large understatement of income, his guilty plea for willfully failing to disclose information on his income tax returns, and his relative sophistication, the Tax Court did not err in finding that the Commissioner had established fraud.

III. Conclusion

For the foregoing reasons, we AFFIRM the Tax Court's decision in all respects. ■

CASEPOINT: Indications of fraud include (1) failure to file tax returns, (2) understatement of income, (3) failure to furnish records, (4) failure to keep books and records, (5) sophistication of the taxpayer, (6) concealment of bank accounts, (7) giving inconsistent and implausible explanations, and (8) willingness to defraud others in business transactions. Given taxpayer's inconsistent and implausible statements, his large understatement of income, his guilty plea for willfully failing to disclose information, and his relative sophistication, the Tax Court did not err in finding that taxpayer committed fraud.

---

[149]*Id.*, at p. 664.

International Cooperation

The key to overcoming tax evasion in the international arena is cooperation. Although formal arrangements are still few, they are becoming more commonplace.

A few multilateral arrangements for the international exchange of information have been adopted. The 1972 Nordic Convention Regarding Mutual Assistance in Matters Relating to Tax is the most prominent. It provides for (1) exchanges of information automatically, on request, and spontaneously; (2) the presence of a tax official from one country at a tax investigation in another country when the investigation is of interest to both countries; and (3) one country to carry out a tax investigation or audit at the request of another.

The European Community adopted a tax collaboration directive in 1977 that is similar to the Nordic Convention.[150] Unlike the Nordic Convention, however, the EC directive places several restrictions on the exchange of information between member states. First, a state does not have to provide the requested information if, under its own laws, it is not allowed to obtain that information for its own purposes. Second, a state may refuse to provide information that would disclose a commercial, industrial, or technical secret or that would be contrary to the state's public policy. Third, a state does not have to provide information if the requesting state is unable to reciprocate (whether for practical or legal reasons) with equivalent information. Finally, a state receiving confidential information must treat it according to the stricter of the secrecy provisions of the states involved.

The Council of Europe and the OECD drafted a Convention on Mutual Administrative Assistance in Tax Matters in 1972, which came into force in 1995.[151] This convention mirrors the provisions of the EC directive in most respects but adds a significant provision requiring

---

[150]Council Directive 77/799/EEC of December 19, 1977. It has subsequently been amended by Directive 79/1070/EEC of December 6, 1979, and Council Directive 92/12/EEC of February 25, 1992. These directives are available on the Eur-Lex Web site at http://europa.eu.int/eur-lex/en/search/index.html.

[151]The convention is posted on the Council of Europe's Web site at http://www.oecd.org/document/14/0,3343, en _2649_201185_2489998_1_1_1_1,00.html.

As of May 24, 2007, the parties to the convention are Azerbaijan, Belgium, Denmark, Finland, France, Iceland, Italy, the Netherlands, Norway, Poland, Sweden and the United States. Canada, Ukraine, and the United Kingdom have signed the convention and are still in the process of ratification.

contracting states to "take the necessary steps to recover tax claims of [a requesting] state as if they were its own tax claims."[152]

Bilateral tax cooperation agreements are much more common than multilateral agreements. Both the UN Model Tax Treaty and the OECD Model Tax Treaty have articles requiring the tax authorities of the contracting states to exchange information.[153] Both articles are similar to the EC directive provisions, except that the tax information received by a state may be used only in connection with "taxes covered by the Convention." The EC directive, by comparison, allows information a state receives to be used for any "taxation purpose."

National Schemes for Combating Tax Evasion

Countries vary greatly in their ability to combat tax evasion. Developed countries with large tax bureaucracies are often able to deploy a large number of investigators to undertake audits and other tax investigations, but not always. Less developed countries often have very small tax bureaucracies and consequently have greater difficulties in identifying and pursuing tax evaders.

tax amnesty: One-time authorization for taxpayers to pay delinquent taxes and thereby avoid possible prosecution.

Frequently, both rich and poor countries have to turn to other devices. One of the most common is the **tax amnesty**. A tax amnesty allows delinquent taxpayers to pay all or part of their overdue taxes and thereby avoid possible prosecution. The goal of such amnesties is an increase in tax revenues, either through an immediate increase in funds collected or through a broadening of the tax base. The tax base is broadened when either new taxpayers or previously unreported sources of income are identified.

I. OTHER FORMS OF TAXATION

From an international perspective, income taxes are the most important form of taxation. In most countries they are the principal source of government revenue. Also, unlike most other forms of taxation, many countries impose income taxes on worldwide income. Income taxes are not, however, the only source of government revenue, and in a few countries, other kinds of taxes are far more important.

TURNOVER TAXES

turnover tax: A tax paid when a good or a service is transferred from one person to another.

Next to income taxes, **turnover taxes** are the most important source of government revenue. The term *turnover tax*—which is not of English origin—is a translation of phrases such as the German *Umsatzsteuer*, the French *taxe sur le chiffre d'affaires*, and the Dutch *omzetbelasting*. The term applies both to these taxes and to such levies as the *sales taxes* used in the United States, the *impuestos a las ventas* of Latin America, and the *value-added taxes* now commonly adopted around the world.

All these forms of turnover taxes are similar in that they are collected from persons other than those who are meant to bear the economic burden—that is, they are collected from manufacturers, wholesalers, retailers, etc., and not from consumers. For this reason, they are generally referred to as *indirect* taxes. Because they increase the cost of goods and services, they are also sometimes known as *cost price increasing* or *cost* taxes.

Categories of Turnover Taxes

Turnover taxes may be either special or general. Special turnover taxes apply only to goods and services specifically listed in the tax law. Examples include taxes on gasoline sales and hotel rooms. General turnover taxes apply to all goods and services except for stated exclusions.

Turnover taxes may also be cumulative or noncumulative. Cumulative taxes are imposed on the total consideration paid, or the total value of goods sold or services provided at all or at several stages of the production or distribution process, without any credits or deductions for taxes paid at previous stages. To illustrate: A mining company extracts iron ore from the

---

[152]Convention on Mutual Administrative Assistance in Tax Matters, Article 11.
[153]OECD, Model Tax Treaty, Article 26; UN, Model Tax Treaty, Article 26.

ground and sells it to a mill. The mining company must charge the mill a turnover tax. The mill then converts the ore into steel sheets and sells it to a manufacturing company. Again, the mill must charge a turnover tax. So, too, must the manufacturing company when it sells its finished products to a wholesaler. This process is repeated when the wholesaler sells it to the retailer and when the retailer sells it to the consumer. Except for the original extractor of raw materials, every entity in the chain is charged a turnover tax. Indeed, at each level the purchase price includes an increasing amount of tax—because tax is being paid on tax.

Noncumulative taxes take a variety of forms. The simplest is a single-stage tax—that is, a tax paid at only one point in the production or distribution process, with the preceding and subsequent transactions being tax free. Special turnover taxes are examples of a single-stage tax.

fractionalized production tax: Taxpayers pay taxes on goods they sell after deducting the taxes they paid on the materials and supplies.

Another kind of noncumulative tax is a **fractionalized production tax**. This tax system requires taxpayers to pay taxes on their sales of goods or services, but it allows them to deduct the tax they paid when purchasing raw materials or supplies. As a consequence, the taxpayer pays only a fraction of the total tax.

value-added tax (VAT): Taxes paid by a taxpayer only on the value added to a good.

A sophisticated example of a fractionalized production tax is the **value-added tax (VAT)**. The VAT "is a tax on turnover whose payment is split between all the economic stages that it covers, in the sense that at each of the stages that a product passes through, the tax is only levied on the value added to the product at that stage."[154]

Reading 13-3 attempts to provide a succinct definition of the VAT.

[154]Report of Subgroup C, *The EEC Reports on Tax Harmonization*, p. 54 (H. Thurston, trans., 1963).

Reading 13-3   DEFINING THE VALUE-ADDED TAX

Liam Ebrill, Michael Keem, Jean-Paul Bodin, and Victoria Summers, "*The Modern VAT*", pp. 1–4 (2001).

Value-Added Tax or VAT, first introduced less than 50 years ago, remained confined to a handful of countries until the late 1960s. Today, however, most countries [about 123] have a VAT, which raises, on average, 25 percent of their tax revenue....

WHAT IS A VAT?

Despite its name, the VAT is not generally intended to be a tax on value added as such: rather it is usually intended as a tax on consumption. Its essence is that it is charged at all stages of production, but with the provision of some mechanism enabling firms to offset the tax they have paid on their own purchase of goods and services against the tax they charge on their sales of goods and services.

Although this characteristic feature is very clear-cut, the VATs observed in practice show considerable diversity as regards, among other things, the range of inputs for which tax offsetting is available and the range of economic activity to which the tax applies (that is, the base of the tax). Some major countries (such as China) currently do not grant credits for taxes on capital goods purchases; moreover, of those that allow credits in respect of such purchases, some do not refund excess credits (any excess of tax paid on inputs over tax chargeable on outputs). Most countries exclude exports from the VAT, in the sense that tax is not charged on sales for export but tax paid on inputs is recoverable, although some (in the BRO[155] region, at least until recently) have systematically levied VAT on some exports. Some countries extend the VAT only to the manufacturing stage; others do not levy it on services.[156] Practice also varies in how tax offsetting is implemented: by far the most common method is through the use of invoices, but the same effect can be achieved on the basis of books of account....

As a result of the diversity of practice, there can be disagreement as to whether a given tax is properly called

[155]The Baltic countries, Russia, and other countries of the former Soviet Union.
[156]Bangladesh affords an example of the former, Pakistan an example of the latter.

a VAT or not.[157] For definiteness, though at the risk of creating the impression of an overly sharp dichotomy, we take a VAT to be:

> *A broad-based tax levied on commodity sales up to and including, at least, the manufacturing stage, with systematic offsetting of tax charged on commodities purchased as inputs—except perhaps on capital goods—against that due on outputs.*

This leaves scope for dispute, but does highlight what is taken here to be the key feature of the VAT: the tax is charged and collected throughout the production process, with provision for tax payable to be reduced by the tax paid in respect of purchases.

This definition is broad enough, for example, to encompass not only the dominant "invoice-credit" form of VAT (under which tax paid on inputs is offset by a means of a credit against tax due on output, tax paid being recorded by invoices issued by seller to buyer) but also the subtraction method (under which the offsetting is achieved implicitly, by charging tax on the difference between the values of output and inputs). . . .

The definition excludes, on the other hand, any scheme that allows crediting only in particular sectors of the economy, as well as sales taxes that grant credits only for inputs deemed to be physically incorporated into the output. "Ring" systems—under which tax that would otherwise be charged by one firm on sales to another is suspended for sales to a subset of firms with

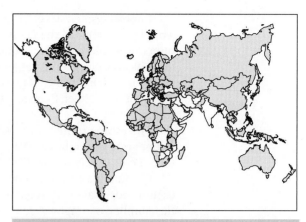

MAP 13-9   Countries with VATs (2000)

the "ring"—are also excluded, on the ground that it is an intrinsic feature of a VAT that tax is actually collected at intermediate stages of production. There is of course an issue of judgment as to when the exclusion from tax becomes so widespread that the tax ceases to be a VAT: the exclusion of services in some countries, for instance, is not taken to prevent a tax being labeled a VAT; the former Indian MODVAT, on the other hand, which offered crediting only of central excise taxes (rather than a broad-based output tax) is not regarded [by us] as being a VAT. More generally, it is immediately clear that VATs come in many different shapes and forms.

---

[157]Malawi is a striking example. It was deemed by the Fiscal Affairs Department (FAD) of the IMF [International Monetary Fund] to have a VAT by 1999, though the tax did not extend to the retail stage. The adoption of a VAT—meaning extension to the retail stage—was then part of IMF program conditionality in 1996. In addition, many countries choose to call by some other name—a general sales tax, a goods and services tax—what is clearly a VAT. The label chosen is of no importance to this report.

The Impact of Turnover Taxes

Turnover taxes will always have an impact on national economies because they increase the price of goods and services to the consumer. Several effects may flow from this, one being a lower level of consumption. This may be beneficial if production has exceeded demand; it can be adverse, however, if it leads to demands for higher wages or if production has to be curtailed because the purchasing power of the ultimate consumer has been diminished. The possibility that a turnover tax will have adverse effects on production is increased if the tax has a differentiated rate structure, with exemptions and low, intermediate, and "luxury" tax rates. In this case, consumer demand can easily shift from one kind of product to another.

Other consequences of imposing turnover taxes depend on the kind of tax imposed. Single-level taxes imposed at the retail level are, as many tax administrators have found, difficult to apply. If they are imposed at the retail level (i.e., upon the delivery of goods to the final consumer), the tax must be collected from a large number of retailers, including many small entrepreneurs. Tax evasion—whether done negligently or intentionally—is prevalent and often impossible to combat.

Imposing single-level taxes at a stage earlier than the retail level produces other problems. For example, if the tax is imposed on the retailer who purchases goods from manufacturers or wholesalers, the retailer is faced with the potential problem of recovering the tax from its consumers. The retailer's profit margin will be reduced unless it can sell all of the goods on which it has paid taxes. Furthermore, unless the retailer can resell the goods immediately, it is, in effect, financing the state treasury on an interest-free basis until the goods are resold.

The escape route for the retailer in the previous example is vertical integration. That is, to integrate into a larger enterprise that can more easily absorb the tax cost. The result of this, of course, can be the distortion of free competition.

Cumulative turnover taxes have a similar impact. If the tax burden is increased with each turnover at every stage of production and distribution, there is a tendency to decrease the number of stages. Again, vertical integration is encouraged, along with its attendant diminution of competition.

To avoid the impetus toward vertical integration that is inherent in cumulative turnover taxes, several countries have devised schemes to make their tax systems neutral. These schemes generally follow two methods. The first is to grant the benefits stemming from vertical integration to nonintegrated business. The second (which is the reverse of the first) is to take away the benefits of the vertically integrated business. This is done by treating internal transfers within the vertically integrated business as taxable transactions.

Since the 1950s, the most important development in improving turnover taxes has been the evolution of the VAT. As noted earlier, the VAT is a multistage tax that is imposed at all (or several) stages in the process of manufacturing and distributing goods or in the process of delivering services. However, tax paid at one stage is creditable against taxes payable at a subsequent stage. Only the final consumer is not entitled to a credit.

As originally adopted in France in 1954, the tax was not completely neutral.[158] This was because the VAT did not provide a full credit against the VAT paid at prior stages for certain transactions. Also, it did not apply to retail sales, which were subject to a local tax that could not be credited against the VAT. By the 1970s, however, these exceptions had been eliminated and a reasonably "pure" VAT exists not only in France but in the large number of other countries that have adopted it. (See Exhibit 13-5.)

"In its pure form the VAT is both completely noncumulative and entirely neutral in impact."[159] It avoids the main drawbacks of the cumulative turnover taxes because (assuming that one disregards the effect of profit) the total tax payable is the same no matter how many stages the goods or services pass through prior to reaching the consumer. To illustrate, assume that a product will be sold to the final consumer for $100. Regardless of whether the product goes directly from the manufacturer to the consumer or through several intermediary stages, so long as the final price is $100, a 10 percent "tax on the value added" will result in the same tax in either case.

MISCELLANEOUS TAXES

In addition to income and value-added taxes, all countries impose a variety of other taxes. Some of the most common are (1) taxes on contributions to the capital stock of companies, (2) documentary stamp taxes for transfers of real estate, (3) documentary stamp taxes for transfers of securities, (4) net worth taxes, (5) import duties, (6) export duties, (7) excise taxes on certain products, and (8) payroll taxes.

---

[158]Law No. 54-404 *portant réforme fiscale* (April 10, 1954), *Journal Officiel de la République Française*, p. 3482 (April 11, 1954).
[159]J. Van Hoorn Jr., "Taxation of Business Organizations," *International Encyclopedia of Comparative Law*, vol. 13, chap. 11, p. 22 (1974).

Country	Type of Tax			Special Rates		No Tax on Exports
	VAT	Sales or Other	Basic Rate	Luxury	Low	
1. Antigua and Barbuda	•		2.5–7.5%			
2. Argentina	•		21%			•
3. Australia	•		10%			•
4. Austria	•		20%		10%	•
5. Azerbaijan	•		18%			•
6. Bahamas			None			•
7. Bahrain			None			•
8. Barbados	•		15%		7.5%	•
9. Belgium	•		21%		1%/6%/12%	•
10. Bermuda			None			•
11. Bolivia	•		13%			•
12. Botswana		•	10%			•
13. Brazil	•		11%	17%	9%	•
14. Brunei			None			•
15. Bulgaria	•		20%			•
16. Cambodia	•		10%			•
17. Cameroon	•		17%		8%	•
18. Canada	•		7%			•
19. Cayman Islands			None			•
20. Chile	•		18%			•
21. China	•		17%		13%	•
22. Colombia		•	16%	20%/35%/45%/60%		•
23. Congo (Zaire)		•	13%	15%/18%/25%	3%/6%	
24. Costa Rica		•	13%	10%–75%		
25. Croatia	•		22%			•
26. Cyprus	•		10%			•
27. Czech Republic	•		5%	22%		•
28. Denmark	•		25%			•
29. Dominican Republic	•		8%			•
30. Ecuador	•		12%			•
31. Egypt		•	10%		5%	•
32. Estonia	•		18%			•
33. Fiji	•		10%			•
34. Finland	•		22%		8%/17%	•
35. France	•		19.6%		2.1%/5.5%	•
36. Germany	•		16%		7%	•
37. Ghana	•		12.5%			•
38. Greece	•		18%		4%/8%	•
39. Guatemala	•		10%			•
40. Guyana			None			•
41. Hong Kong			None			•
42. Hungary	•		25%		12%	•
43. India		•	Local			
44. Indonesia	•		10%	15%	5%	•
45. Iran			None			•
46. Ireland	•		20%		4.3%/12.5%	•
47. Israel	•		17%		8.5%	•
48. Italy	•		20%		4%/10%	•
49. Ivory Coast	•		20%			•
50. Jamaica	•		15%			•
51. Japan	•		5%			•
52. Kazakhstan	•		20%			•
53. Kenya	•		18%		16%	•
54. Korea	•		10%			•

(continued)

EXHIBIT 13-5   Turnover Taxes in 115 Countries (2001)

Country	Type of Tax			Special Rates		No Tax on Exports
	VAT	Sales or Other	Basic Rate	Luxury	Low	
55. Kuwait			None			●
56. Laos		●	5%/10%			
57. Latvia	●		18%			●
58. Liechtenstein	●		7.6%		2.4%	●
59. Lithuania	●		18%			●
60. Luxembourg	●		15%		3%/6%/12%	●
61. Malawi			None			●
62. Malaysia		●	5–25%			●
63. Malta	●		15%		5%	●
64. Mauritius	●		10%			●
65. Mexico	●		15%		10%	●
66. Monaco	●		20.6%		5%	●
67. Morocco	●		20%		7%	●
68. Mozambique	●		17%			●
69. Myanmar			None			●
70. Namibia	●		15%	30%		●
71. Netherlands	●		19%		6%	●
72. New Zealand	●		12.5%			●
73. Nigeria	●		5%			●
74. Norway	●		24%			●
75. Oman			None			●
76. Pakistan	●		15%			●
77. Panama	●		5%	10%		●
78. Papua New Guinea	●		10%			●
79. Paraguay	●		10%			●
80. Peru	●		8%			●
81. Philippines	●		10%			●
82. Poland	●		22%		7%	●
83. Portugal	●		17%		5%/12%	●
84. Qatar			None			●
85. Romania	●		19%			●
86. Russia	●		20%		10%	●
87. St. Lucia			None			●
88. Saudi Arabia			None			●
89. Senegal	●		20%		10%	●
90. Singapore	●		3%			●
91. Slovakia	●		23%		10%	●
92. Slovenia		●	20%	32%	3%/5%/10%	
93. Solomon Islands	●		10%			●
94. South Africa	●		14%			●
95. Spain	●		16%		4%/7%	●
96. Sri Lanka	●		12.5%			●
97. Swaziland		●	12%	25%		●
98. Sweden	●		25%		12%/21%	●
99. Switzerland	●		7.6%		2.4%/3.6%	●
100. Tahiti	●		6%		2%/4%	●
101. Taiwan	●		5%		1%/2%	●
102. Tanzania	●		20%			●
103. Thailand	●		7%			●
104. Trinidad and Tobago	●		15%			●
105. Turkey	●		17%	25%/40%	1%/8%	●
106. Uganda	●		17%			●
107. Ukraine	●		20%			●

EXHIBIT 13-5 (Continued)

Country	Type of Tax		Basic Rate	Special Rates		No Tax on Exports
	VAT	Sales or Other		Luxury	Low	
108. United Kingdom	•		17.5%		5%	•
109. United States		Local	0%–9.8%			
110. Uruguay	•		23%		14%	•
111. Uzbekistan	•		20%			•
112. Venezuela	•		14.5%			•
113. Vietnam		•	10%	20%	2%/3%/5%	•
114. Zambia	•		17.5%			•
115. Zimbabwe		•	15%	25%	5%	

EXHIBIT 13-5 *(Continued)*

Source: PriceWaterhouseCoopers, *Corporate Taxes: Worldwide Summaries 2001–2002* (2001) and online resources.

Chapter Questions

Income Taxes

1. You were a resident of Indonesia and earned 60,000,000 rupiahs during tax year 1990. Income from rents on an office building that you own was 30,000,000 rupiahs. Professional income from your work as an international tax lawyer was 30,000,000 rupiahs. Using the tax schedule for Indonesia from the text, determine the income tax you would have paid that year. Assume that you were entitled to no deductions, exemptions, or credits.

Legal Status of a Subsidiary

2. Padre Co. is a multinational enterprise involved in selling cement mixers worldwide. It has established several subsidiaries in countries in Latin America. One subsidiary, Hijo Co., is located in Country X. Hijo is responsible for locating customers for Padre. Once the customer is put in touch with Padre, Hijo does nothing more. If the customer buys mixers, Padre pays Hijo 5 percent of the sales price as a finding fee. Payments by the customer are made directly to Padre at its home office in Topeka, Kansas, U.S.A. Padre itself does no business whatsoever in Country X, other than to pay Hijo its finding fees.

   During the current tax year, Padre sold U.S. $10,000,000 worth of cement mixers in Country X. It earned for itself (after paying Hijo $500,000) $1,500,000.

   Country X's Internal Revenue Agency (IRA) has assessed taxes on Hijo of $400,000, which is 20 percent (the appropriate tax rate) of $2,000,000. The IRA contends that Padre and Hijo are in reality one company and that Hijo's taxes are assessable on the total income of both Padre and Hijo. Is the IRA correct? Explain.

Residence of the Taxable Entity

3. The Schizophrenic Co. was organized in the state of Delaware in the United States. All of its business is done in France. Its managerial offices are located in Luxembourg. Its board of directors holds its regular meeting in Luxembourg. The shareholders are all Swiss, and they hold their annual meeting in Innsbruck, Austria. Of which country (countries) is Schizophrenic a resident for tax purposes? Explain.

The Rule of Attraction

4. The Amalgamated Manufacturing Company (AMC), a resident of State A, has a subsidiary, Bambino Retailing Co. (BRC), which is a resident of State B.

   In the current tax year, BRC earned $125,000 and remitted $100,000 in dividends (before paying withholding taxes) to AMC, retaining the $25,000 balance for itself.

   State B law imposes a tax of 10 percent on earned and undistributed income. According to the double taxation treaty between State A and State B, State B is to charge a 25 percent withholding tax on dividends remitted from a subsidiary in State B to a parent in State A.

   State A has a flat company income tax rate of 50 percent. State A's law also provides an indirect credit to companies in State A that receive income from subsidiaries in State B.

Assuming no other exemptions, credits, or deductions, how much tax does BRC owe State B on its earnings? How much tax does AMC owe State A on the income remitted by BRC to it?

Treaty Shopping

5. The Mother Construction Co. (MCC), a resident of State X, has a branch office in the western part of State Y. During the current tax year the branch earned £100,000. Also, during the current year, MCC undertook to build a highway in the eastern part of State Y. Because of the distance between the branch office and the construction site, the branch office was not involved in this project. The road was built in four months, and the construction site was abandoned after five months. MCC earned £250,000 from building the road.

   State X and State Y have entered into a double taxation treaty based on the UN Model Tax Treaty. On what income may State Y impose taxes? Explain.

6. Invento Co., a resident of State I, has just developed a new patent it wishes to license in State J. State I and State J have no tax treaties, however, and Invento would have to pay high taxes in both states if it remitted its royalty earnings directly from State J to State I.

   Invento has discovered that State K has double taxation treaties with both State J and State I. Royalties remitted to State K from State J are subject to no withholding taxes, nor are dividends remitted from State K to State I.

   Invento sets up a subsidiary in State K, and it assigns its patents to the subsidiary. Royalties remitted by the licenses in State J are not taxed by State J. Dividends remitted by the subsidiary in State K are not taxed.

   State K is delighted to have Invento doing business in its territory through a subsidiary. State I is not affected one way or another. State J, however, is displeased at not being able to collect its taxes. Can State J do anything about this? If so, what?

Multinational Enterprises and the Unitary Method

7. Big Company, a multinational manufacturer of automotive parts, has 33 percent of its employees in California, pays 27 percent of its payroll in California, and sells 30 percent of its goods in California. On its books worldwide the Big Company earns a before-tax profit of $180 million. In California it actually loses about $3 million. Can California collect any income taxes from Big? Explain.

CASE INDEX

‌Principal cases are indicated by boldface page numbers.

Key:
Arb.—Arbitration Tribunal
EFTA—European Free Trade Area
ICJ—International Court of Justice
ICSID—International Center for the Settlement of Investment Disputes
ILO—International Labor Organization Administrative Tribunal
ITLOS—International Tribunal for the Law of the Sea
PCA—Permanent Court of Arbitration
PCIJ—Permanent Court of International Justice
UAE—United Arab Emirates
UK—United Kingdom
US—United States
WTO—World Trade Organization

STATUTORY INDEX

TOPICAL INDEX